Praise for Anne Bishop
and *The Black Jewels Trilogy*

"Vividly painted . . . dramatic, erotic, hope-filled."
—Lynn Flewelling, author of *Stalking Darkness*

"Intense . . . erotic, violent, and imaginative. This one is white-hot."
—Nancy Kress

"[Anne Bishop's] poignant storytelling skills are surpassed only by her flair for the dramatic and her deft characterization. . . . A talented author."
—*Affaire de Coeur*

"Daemon, Lucivar, and Saetan ooze more sex appeal than any three fictional characters created in a very long time. . . . A fascinating world."
—*The Romance Reader*

ANNE BISHOP

THE BLACK JEWELS TRILOGY

DAUGHTER OF THE BLOOD

HEIR TO THE SHADOWS

QUEEN OF THE DARKNESS

A ROC BOOK

ROC
Published by New American Library, a division of
Penguin Group (USA) Inc., 375 Hudson Street,
New York, New York 10014, USA
Penguin Group (Canada), 90 Eglinton Avenue East, Suite 700, Toronto,
Ontario M4P 2Y3, Canada (a division of Pearson Penguin Canada Inc.)
Penguin Books Ltd., 80 Strand, London WC2R 0RL, England
Penguin Ireland, 25 St. Stephen's Green, Dublin 2,
Ireland (a division of Penguin Books Ltd.)
Penguin Group (Australia), 250 Camberwell Road, Camberwell, Victoria 3124,
Australia (a division of Pearson Australia Group Pty. Ltd.)
Penguin Books India Pvt. Ltd., 11 Community Centre, Panchsheel Park,
New Delhi - 110 017, India
Penguin Group (NZ), 67 Apollo Drive, Rosedale, North Shore 0632,
New Zealand (a division of Pearson New Zealand Ltd.)
Penguin Books (South Africa) (Pty.) Ltd., 24 Sturdee Avenue,
Rosebank, Johannesburg 2196, South Africa

Penguin Books Ltd., Registered Offices:
80 Strand, London WC2R 0RL, England

Published by Roc, an imprint of New American Library, a division of Penguin Group (USA) Inc.
Previously published in separate Roc trade paperback and mass market editions.

First Roc Printing (Omnibus Edition), December 2003
20   19   18   17   16   15   14   13   12   11   10

Introduction copyright © Anne Bishop, 2003
Daughter of the Blood copyright © Anne Bishop, 1998
Heir to the Shadows copyright © Anne Bishop, 1999
Queen of the Darkness copyright © Anne Bishop, 2000
All rights reserved

 REGISTERED TRADEMARK—MARCA REGISTRADA

LIBRARY OF CONGRESS CATALOGING-IN-PUBLICATION DATA:

Bishop, Anne.
The black jewels trilogy / Anne Bishop.
p. cm.
Contents: Daughter of the blood—Heir to the shadows—Queen of the darkness.
ISBN 978-0-451-52901-5
1. Witches—Fiction. 2. Fantasy fiction, American. I. Title.

PS3552.I7594B57 2003
823'.92—dc21   2003046616

Set in Bembo
Cover design by Ray Lundgren
Dragon art by Patrick Jones

Printed in the United States of America

For all the readers
who have made this journey with me
to share in the wonder of Story
and
For all the friends whose
encouragement and enthusiasm kept me going
while I wrote this story about the Blood.
I couldn't have done it without you.

CONTENTS

INTRODUCTION

What can I say about a story that has been a part of my life for more than a decade? What can I say about characters who became people I cared about—and still do? Perhaps the best thing is to answer the question I'm most often asked: "How did you come up with this story and these characters?"

The answer is both complex and simple. I asked, *what if?*

What if a culture was based on the dark side of fantasy? What kind of morality would it have? What kind of code of honor? What protocols would develop to protect the weaker from the stronger? What if it was a culture that was elegant in its darkness and had tenderness as well as temper, passion as well as violence? What if the males were aggressive, intelligent, passionate, sensual—warriors with a veneer of the civilized? What if the female was the dominant gender and males served, so that the Nurturer controlled the Warrior? What if some of the social and sexual mores that had applied to females in our world were applied to the males in this world? How would they act? How would they live? Who would they be?

From these wonderings, among others, a three-layered place called the Realms and a people called the Blood slowly emerged. For a while, I was content with making up scenarios and playing them out in my head to see how the characters that were taking shape reacted to different situations. I had fun developing the different races—the unicorns and the rest of the kindred, the Dea al Mon, the Eyriens and others. I had fun with the characters—Daemon, with his cold elegance and his passion for Jaenelle; Lucivar, with his earthy approach to life and those glorious wings; Ladvarian, who was the first of the kindred to appear; and Jaenelle, with her immense power and emotional scars.

Then, one day, came another *what if?*: If the survival of the Blood's culture depends on dancing on the knife edge of trust, what happens if it goes wrong?

I didn't have an answer, so I continued to play with the puzzle pieces of this world—until the High Lord showed up one day, a man with power that was feared, a past that held regrets, and the hard-won wisdom that comes from experience. Suddenly all the pieces clicked into place. I had a father and two estranged sons whose lives were tangled with two greedy, ambitious High Priestesses. I had a world gone wrong and a culture spiraling toward destruction. And I had a dream that, when made flesh, changed the lives of those three men and, by doing so, changed everything.

I had a story about love and betrayal, magic and mystery, honor and passion . . . and the price that is paid for a dream. I had the story you now hold in your hands.

Enter the world of the Blood.

Welcome to *The Black Jewels Trilogy.*

Jewels

White
Yellow
Tiger Eye
Rose
Summer-sky
Purple Dusk
Opal★
Green
Sapphire
Red
Gray
Ebon-gray
Black

★Opal is the dividing line between lighter and darker Jewels because it can be either.

When making the Offering to the Darkness, a person can descend a maximum of three ranks from his/her Birthright Jewel.

Example: Birthright White could descend to Rose.

AUTHOR'S NOTE

The "Sc" in the names Scelt, Sceval, and Sceron is pronounced "Sh."

Blood Hierarchy/Castes

MALES:

landen—non-Blood of any race

Blood male—a general term for all males of the Blood; also
refers to any Blood male who doesn't wear Jewels

Warlord—a Jeweled male equal in status to a witch

Prince—a Jeweled male equal in status to a Priestess or a
Healer

Warlord Prince—a dangerous, extremely aggressive Jeweled
male; in status, slightly lower than a Queen

FEMALES:

landen—non-Blood of any race

Blood female—a general term for all females of the Blood;
mostly refers to any Blood female who doesn't wear
Jewels

witch—a Blood female who wears Jewels but isn't one of the
other hierarchical levels; also refers to any Jeweled female.

Healer—a witch who heals physical wounds and illnesses;
equal in status to a Priestess and a Prince

Priestess—a witch who cares for altars, Sanctuaries, and Dark
Altars; witnesses handfasts and marriages; performs offerings; equal in status to a Healer and a Prince

Black Widow—a witch who heals the mind; weaves the tangled webs of dreams and visions; is trained in illusions and
poisons

Queen—a witch who rules the Blood; is considered to be the
land's heart and the Blood's moral center; as such, she is
the focal point of their society

DAUGHTER
OF THE
BLOOD

BOOK I

PROLOGUE

Terreille

I am Tersa the Weaver, Tersa the Liar, Tersa the Fool.

When the Blood-Jeweled Lords and Ladies hold a banquet, I'm the entertainment that comes after the musicians have played and the lithesome girls and boys have danced and the Lords have drunk too much wine and demand to have their fortunes told. "Tell us a story, Weaver," they yell as their hands pass over the serving girls' rumps and their Ladies eye the young men and decide who will have the painful pleasure of serving in the bed that night.

I was one of them once, Blood as they are Blood.

No, that's not true. I *wasn't* Blood as they are Blood. That's why I was broken on a Warlord's spear and became shattered glass that only reflects what might have been.

It's hard to break a Blood-Jeweled male, but a witch's life hangs by the hymenal thread, and what happens on her Virgin Night determines whether she is whole to practice the Craft or becomes a broken vessel, forever aching for the part of her that's lost. Oh, some magic always remains, enough for day-to-day living and parlor tricks, but not the Craft, not the lifeblood of our kind.

But the Craft can be reclaimed—if one is willing to pay the price.

When I was younger, I fought against that final slide into the Twisted Kingdom. Better to be broken and sane than broken and mad. Better to see the world and know a tree for a tree, a flower for a flower rather than to look through gauze at gray and ghostly shapes and see clearly only the shards of one's self.

So I thought then.

As I shuffle to the low stool, I struggle to stay at the edge of the Twisted Kingdom and see the physical world clearly one last time. I carefully place the wooden frame that holds my tangled web, the web of dreams and visions, on the small table near the stool.

The Lords and Ladies expect me to tell their fortunes, and I always have, not by magic but by keeping my eyes and ears open and then telling them what they want to hear.

Simple. No magic to it.

But not tonight.

For days now I have heard a strange kind of thunder, a distant calling. Last night I surrendered to madness in order to reclaim my Craft as a Black Widow, a witch of the Hourglass covens. Last night I wove a tangled web to see the dreams and visions.

Tonight there will be no fortunes. I have the strength to say this only once. I must be sure that those who must hear it are in the room before I speak.

I wait. They don't notice. Glasses are filled and refilled as I fight to stay on the edge of the Twisted Kingdom.

Ah, there he is. Daemon Sadi, from the Territory called Hayll. He's beautiful, bitter, cruel. He has a seducer's smile and a body women want to touch and be caressed by, but he's filled with a cold, unquenchable rage. When the Ladies talk about his bedroom skills, the words they whisper are "excruciating pleasure." I don't doubt he's enough of a sadist to mix pain and pleasure in equal portions, but he's always been kind to me, and it's a small bone of hope that I throw out to him tonight. Still, it's more than anyone else has given him.

The Lords and Ladies grow restless. I usually don't take this long to begin my pronouncements. Agitation and annoyance build, but I wait. After tonight, it will make no difference.

There's the other one, in the opposite corner of the room. Lucivar Yaslana, the Eyrien half-breed from the Territory called Askavi.

Hayll has no love for Askavi, nor Askavi for Hayll, but Daemon and Lucivar are drawn to one another without understanding why, so wound into each other's lives they cannot separate. Uneasy friends, they have fought legendary battles, have destroyed so many courts the Blood are afraid to have them together for any length of time.

I raise my hands, let them fall into my lap. Daemon watches me. Nothing about him has changed, but I know he's waiting, listening. And because he's listening, Lucivar listens too.

"She is coming."

At first they don't realize I've spoken. Then the angry murmurs begin when the words are understood.

"Stupid bitch," someone yells. "Tell me who I'll love tonight."

"What does it matter?" I answer. "She is coming. The Realm of Terreille will be torn apart by its own foolish greed. Those who survive will serve, but few will survive."

I'm slipping farther from the edge. Tears of frustration spill down my cheeks. Not yet. Sweet Darkness, not yet. I must say this.

Daemon kneels beside me, his hands covering mine. I speak to him, only to him, and through him, to Lucivar.

"The Blood in Terreille whore the old ways and make a mockery of everything we are." I wave my hand to indicate the ones who now rule. "They twist things to suit themselves. They dress up and pretend. They wear Blood Jewels but don't understand what it means to be Blood. They talk of honoring the Darkness, but it's a lie. They honor nothing but their own ambitions. The Blood were created to be the caretakers of the Realms. That's why we were given our power. That's why we come from, yet are apart from, the people in every Territory. The perversion of what we are can't go on. The day is coming when the debt will be called in, and the Blood will have to answer for what they've become."

"They're the Blood who rule, Tersa," Daemon says sadly. "Who is left to call in this debt? Bastard slaves like me?"

I'm slipping fast. My nails dig into his hands, drawing blood, but he doesn't pull away. I lower my voice. He strains to hear me. "The Darkness has had a Prince for a long, long time. Now the Queen is coming. It may take decades, even centuries, but she is coming." I point with my chin at the Lords and Ladies sitting at the tables. "They will be dust by then, but you and the Eyrien will be here to serve."

Frustration fills his golden eyes. "What Queen? Who is coming?"

"The living myth," I whisper. "Dreams made flesh."

His shock is replaced instantly by a fierce hunger. "You're sure?"

The room is a swirling mist. He's the only thing still in sharp focus. He's the only thing I need. "I saw her in the tangled web, Daemon. I saw her."

I'm too tired to hang on to the real world, but I stubbornly cling to his hands to tell him one last thing. "The Eyrien, Daemon."

He glances at Lucivar. "What about him?"

"He's your brother. You are your father's sons."

I can't hold on anymore and plunge into the madness that's called the Twisted Kingdom. I fall and fall among the shards of myself. The world spins and shatters. In its fragments, I see my once-Sisters pouring around the tables, frightened and intent, and Daemon's hand casually reaching out, as if by accident, destroying the fragile spidersilk of my tangled web.

It's impossible to reconstruct a tangled web. Terreille's Black Widows may spend year upon frightened year trying, but in the end it will be in vain. It will not be the same web, and they will not see what I saw.

In the gray world above, I hear myself howling with laughter. Far below me, in the psychic abyss that is part of the Darkness, I hear another howling, one full of joy and pain, rage and celebration.

Not just another witch coming, my foolish Sisters, but Witch.

PART 1

CHAPTER ONE

1 / Terreille

Lucivar Yaslana, the Eyrien half-breed, watched the guards drag the sobbing man to the boat. He felt no sympathy for the condemned man who had led the aborted slave revolt. In the Territory called Pruul, sympathy was a luxury no slave could afford.

He had refused to participate in the revolt. The ringleaders were good men, but they didn't have the strength, the backbone, or the balls to do what was needed. They didn't enjoy seeing blood run.

He had not participated. Zuultah, the Queen of Pruul, had punished him anyway.

The heavy shackles around his neck and wrists had already rubbed his skin raw, and his back was a throbbing ache from the lash. He spread his dark, membranous wings, trying to ease the ache in his back.

A guard immediately prodded him with a club, then retreated, skittish, at his soft hiss of anger.

Unlike the other slaves who couldn't contain their misery or fear, there was no expression in Lucivar's gold eyes, no psychic scent of emotions for the guards to play with as they put the sobbing man into the old, one-man boat. No longer seaworthy, the boat showed gaping holes in its rotten wood, holes that only added to its value now.

The condemned man was small and half-starved. It still took six guards to put him into the boat. Five guards held the man's head, arms, and legs. The last guard smeared bacon grease on the man's genitals before sliding a wooden cover into place. It fit snugly over the boat, with holes cut out for the head and hands. Once the man's hands were tied to iron rings on the outside of the boat, the cover was locked into place so that no one but the guards could remove it.

One guard studied the imprisoned man and shook his head in mock dismay. Turning to the others, he said, "He should have a last meal before being put to sea."

The guards laughed. The man cried for help.

One by one, the guards carefully shoved food into the man's mouth before herding the other slaves to the stables where they were quartered.

"You'll be entertained tonight, boys," a guard yelled, laughing. "Remember it the next time you decide to leave Lady Zuultah's service."

Lucivar looked over his shoulder, then looked away.

Drawn by the smell of food, the rats slipped into the gaping holes in the boat.

The man in the boat screamed.

Clouds scudded across the moon, gray shrouds hiding its light. The man in the boat didn't move. His knees were open sores, bloody from kicking the top of the boat in his effort to keep the rats away. His vocal cords were destroyed from screaming.

Lucivar knelt behind the boat, moving carefully to muffle the sound of the chains.

"I didn't tell them, Yasi," the man said hoarsely. "They tried to make me tell, but I didn't. I had that much honor left."

Lucivar held a cup to the man's lips. "Drink this," he said, his voice a deep murmur, a part of the night.

"No," the man moaned. "No." He began to cry, a harsh, guttural sound pulled from his ruined throat.

"Hush, now. Hush. It will help." Supporting the man's head, Lucivar eased the cup between the swollen lips. After two swallows, Lucivar put the cup aside and stroked the man's head with gentle fingertips. "It will help," he crooned.

"I'm a Warlord of the Blood." When Lucivar offered the cup again, the man took another sip. As his voice got stronger, the words began to slur. "You're a Warlord Prince. Why do they do this to us, Yasi?"

"Because they have no honor. Because they don't remember what it means to be Blood. The High Priestess of Hayll's influence is a plague that has been spreading across the Realm for centuries, slowly consuming every Territory it touches."

"Maybe the landens are right, then. Maybe the Blood are evil."

Lucivar continued stroking the man's forehead and temples. "No. We are what we are. Nothing more, nothing less. There is good and evil among every kind of people. It's the evil among us who rule now."

"And where are the good among us?" the man asked sleepily.

Lucivar kissed the top of the man's head. "They've been destroyed or enslaved." He offered the cup. "Finish it, little Brother, and it will be finished."

After the man took the last swallow, Lucivar used Craft to vanish the cup.

The man in the boat laughed. "I feel very brave, Yasi."

"You are very brave."

"The rats . . . My balls are gone."

"I know."

"I cried, Yasi. Before all of them, I cried."

"It doesn't matter."

"I'm a Warlord. I shouldn't have cried."

"You didn't tell. You had courage when you needed it."

"Zuultah killed the others anyway."

"She'll pay for it, little Brother. Someday she and the others like her will pay for it all." Lucivar gently massaged the man's neck.

"Yasi, I—"

The movement was sudden, the sound sharp.

Lucivar carefully let the lolling head fall backward and slowly rose to his feet. He could have told them the plan wouldn't work, that the Ring of Obedience could be fine-tuned sufficiently to alert its owner to an inner drawing of strength and purpose. He could have told them the malignant tendrils that kept them enslaved had spread too far, and it would take a sweeter savagery than a man was capable of to free them. He could have told them there were crueler weapons than the Ring to keep a man obedient, that their concern for each other would destroy them, that the only way to escape, for even a little while, was to care for no one, to be alone.

He could have told them.

And yet, when they had approached him, timidly, cautiously, eager to ask a man who had broken free again and again over the centuries but was still enslaved, all he had said was, "Sacrifice everything." They had gone away, disappointed, unable to understand he had meant what he'd said. Sacrifice everything. And there was one thing he couldn't—wouldn't—sacrifice.

How many times after he'd surrendered and been tethered again by that cruel ring of gold around his organ had Daemon found him and pinned him against a wall, snarling with rage, calling him a fool and a coward to give in?

Liar. Silky, court-trained liar.

Once, Dorothea SaDiablo had searched desperately for Daemon Sadi after he'd vanished from a court without a trace. It had taken a hundred years to find him, and two thousand Warlords had died trying to recapture him. He could have used that small, savage Territory he had held and conquered half the Realm of Terreille, could have become a tangible threat to Hayll's encroachment and absorption of every people it touched. Instead, he had read a letter Dorothea sent through a messenger. Read it and surrendered.

The letter had simply said: "Surrender by the new moon. Every day you are gone thereafter, I will take a piece of your brother's body in payment for your arrogance."

Lucivar shook himself, trying to dislodge the unwelcome thoughts. In some ways, memories were worse than the lash, for they led to thoughts of Askavi, with its mountains rising to cut the sky and its valleys filled with towns, farms, and forests. Not that Askavi was that fertile anymore, having been raped for too many centuries by those who took but never gave anything back. Still, it was home, and centuries of enslaved exile had left him aching for the smell of clean mountain air, the taste of a sweet, cold stream, the silence of the woods, and, most of all, the mountains where the Eyrien race soared.

But he was in Pruul, that hot, scrubby desert wasteland, serving that bitch Zuultah because he couldn't hide his disgust for Prythian, Askavi's High Priestess, couldn't leash his temper enough to serve witches he despised.

Among the Blood, males were meant to serve, not to rule. He had never challenged that, despite the number of witches he'd killed over the centuries. He had killed them because it was an insult to serve them, because he was an Eyrien Warlord Prince who wore Ebon-gray Jewels and refused to believe that serving and groveling meant the same thing. Because he was a half-breed bastard, he had no hope of attaining a position of authority within a court, despite the rank of his Jewels. Because he was a trained Eyrien warrior and had a temper that was explosive even for a Warlord Prince, he had even less hope of being allowed to live outside the social chains of a court.

And he was caught, as all Blood males were caught. There was something bred into them that made them crave service, that compelled them to bond in some way with a Blood-Jeweled female.

Lucivar twitched his shoulder and sucked air through his teeth as a lash wound reopened. When he gingerly touched the wound, his hand came away wet with fresh blood.

He bared his teeth in a bitter smile. What was that old saying? A wish, offered with blood, is a prayer to the Darkness.

He closed his eyes, raised his hand toward the night sky, and turned inward, descending into the psychic abyss to the depth of his Ebon-gray Jewels so that this wish would remain private, so that no one in Zuultah's court could hear the sending of this thought.

Just once, I'd like to serve a Queen I could respect, someone I could truly believe in. A strong Queen who wouldn't fear my strength. A Queen I could also call a friend.

Dryly amused by his own foolishness, Lucivar wiped his hand on his baggy cotton pants and sighed. It was a shame that the pronouncement Tersa had made seven hundred years ago had been nothing more than a mad delusion. For a while, it had given him hope. It had taken him a long time to realize that hope was a bitter thing.

Hello?

Lucivar looked toward the stables where the slaves were quartered. The guards would make their nightly check soon. He'd take another minute to savor the night air, even if it smelled hot and dusty, before returning to the filthy cell with its bed of dirty, bug-infested straw, before returning to the stink of fear, unwashed bodies, and human waste.

Hello?

Lucivar turned in a slow circle, his physical senses alert, his mind probing for the source of that thought. Psychic communication could be broadcast to everyone in an area—like shouting in a crowded room—or narrowed to a single Jewel rank or gender, or narrowed even further to a single mind. That thought seemed aimed directly at him.

There was nothing out there except the expected. Whatever it was, it was gone.

Lucivar shook his head. He was getting as skittish as the landens, the non-Blood of each race, with their superstitions about evil stalking in the night.

"Hello?"

Lucivar spun around, his dark wings flaring for balance as he set his feet in a fighting stance.

He felt like a fool when he saw the girl staring at him, wide-eyed.

She was a scrawny little thing, about seven years old. Calling her plain would have been kind. But, even in the moonlight, she had the most extraordinary eyes. They reminded him of a twilight sky or a deep mountain lake. Her clothes were of good quality, certainly better than a beggar child would wear. Her gold hair was done up in sausage curls that indicated care even if they looked ridiculous around her pointed little face.

"What are you doing here?" he asked roughly.

She laced her fingers and hunched her shoulders. "I-I heard you. Y-you wanted a friend."

"You *heard* me?" Lucivar stared at her. How in the name of Hell had she heard him? True, he had sent that wish out, but on an Ebon-gray thread. He was the only Ebon-gray in the Realm of Terreille. The only Jewel darker than his was the Black, and the only person who wore *that* was Daemon Sadi. Unless . . .

No. She couldn't be.

At that moment, the girl's eyes flicked from him to the dead man in the boat, then back to him.

"I have to go," she whispered, backing away from him.

"No, you don't." He came toward her, soft-footed, a hunter stalking his prey.

She bolted.

He caught her within seconds, heedless of the noise the chains made. Looping a chain over her, he wrapped an arm around her waist and lifted her off her feet, grunting when her heel banged his knee. He ignored her attempts to scratch, and her kicks, while bruising, weren't the same kind of deterrent one good kick in the right place would have been. When she started shrieking, he clamped a hand over her mouth.

She promptly sank her teeth into his finger.

Lucivar bit back a howl and swore under his breath. He dropped to his knees, pulling her with him. "Hush," he whispered fiercely. "Do you want to bring the guards down on us?" She probably did, and he expected her to struggle even harder, knowing there was help nearby.

Instead, she froze.

Lucivar laid his cheek against her head and sucked air. "You're a spitting little cat," he said quietly, fighting to keep the laughter out of his voice.

"Why did you kill him?"

Did he imagine it, or did her voice change? She still sounded like a young girl, but thunder, caverns, and midnight skies were in that voice. "He was suffering."

"Couldn't you take him to a Healer?"

"Healers don't bother with slaves," he snapped. "Besides, the rats didn't leave enough of him to heal." He pulled her tighter against his chest, hoping physical warmth would make her stop shuddering. She looked so pale against his light-brown skin, and he knew it wasn't simply because she was fair-skinned. "I'm sorry. That was cruel."

When she started struggling against his hold, he raised his arms so that she could slip under the chain between his wrists. She scrambled out of reach, spun around, and dropped to her knees.

They studied each other.

"What's your name?" she finally asked.

"I'm called Yasi." He laughed when she wrinkled her nose. "Don't blame me. I didn't choose it."

"It's a silly word for someone like you. What's your real name?"

Lucivar hesitated. Eyriens were one of the long-lived races. He'd had 1,700 years to gain a reputation for being vicious and violent. If she'd heard any of the stories about him . . .

He took a deep breath and released it slowly. "Lucivar Yaslana."

No reaction except a shy smile of approval.

"What's your name, Cat?"

"Jaenelle."

He grinned. "Nice name, but I think Cat suits you just as well."

She snarled.

"See?" He hesitated, but he had to ask. Zuultah's guessing he'd killed that slave and knowing for sure would make a difference when he was stretched between the whipping posts. "Is your family visiting Lady Zuultah?"

Jaenelle frowned. "Who?"

Really, she did look like a kitten trying to figure out how to pounce on a large, hoppy bug. "Zuultah. The Queen of Pruul."

"What's Pruul?"

"This is Pruul." Lucivar waved a hand to indicate the land around them and then swore in Eyrien when the chains rattled. He swallowed the last curse when he noticed the intense, interested look on her face. "Since you're not from Pruul and your family isn't visiting, where are you from?" When she hesitated, he tipped his head toward the boat. "I can keep a secret."

"I'm from Chaillot."

"Chai—" Lucivar bit back another curse. "Do you understand Eyrien?"

"No." Jaenelle grinned at him. "But now I know some Eyrien words."

Should he laugh or strangle her? "How did you get here?"

She fluffed her hair and frowned at the rocky ground between them. Finally she shrugged. "Same way I get to other places."

"You ride the Winds?" he yelped.

She raised a finger to test the air.

"Not breezes or puffs of air." Lucivar ground his teeth. "The Winds. The Webs. The psychic roads in the Darkness."

Jaenelle perked up. "Is that what they are?"

He managed to stop in mid-curse.

Jaenelle leaned forward. "Are you always this prickly?"

"Most people think I'm a prick, yes."

"What's that mean?"

"Never mind." He chose a sharp stone and drew a circle on the ground between them. "This is the Realm of Terreille." He placed a round stone in the circle. "This is the Black Mountain, Ebon Askavi, where the Winds meet." He drew straight lines from the round stone to the circumference of the circle. "These are tether lines." He drew smaller circles within the circle. "These are radial lines. The Winds are like a spider web. You can travel on the tether or the radial lines, changing direction where they intersect. There's a Web for each rank of the Blood Jewels. The darker the Web, the more tether and radial lines there are and the faster the Wind is. You can ride a Web that's your rank or lighter. You can't ride a Web darker than your Jewel rank unless you're traveling inside a Coach being driven by someone strong enough to ride that Web or you're being shielded by someone who can ride that Web. If you try, you probably won't survive. Understand?"

Jaenelle chewed on her lower lip and pointed to a space between the strands. "What if I want to go there?"

Lucivar shook his head. "You'd have to drop from the Web back into the Realm at the nearest point and travel some other way."

"That's not how I got here," she protested.

Lucivar shuddered. There wasn't a strand of any Web around Zuultah's compound. Her court was deliberately in one of those blank spaces. The only way to get here directly from the Winds was by leaving the Web and gliding blind through the Darkness, which, even for the strongest and the best, was a chancy thing to do. Unless . . .

"Come here, Cat," he said gently. When she dropped in front of him, he rested his hands on her thin shoulders. "Do you often go wandering?"

Jaenelle nodded slowly. "People call me. Like you did."

Like he did. Mother Night! "Cat, listen to me. Children are vulnerable to many dangers."

There was a strange expression in her eyes. "Yes, I know."

"Sometimes an enemy can wear the mask of a friend until it's too late to escape."

"Yes," she whispered.

Lucivar shook her gently, forcing her to look at him. "Terreille is a dangerous place for little cats. Please, go home and don't go wandering anymore. Don't . . . don't answer the people who call you."

"But then I won't see you anymore."

Lucivar closed his gold eyes. A knife in the heart would hurt less. "I know. But we'll always be friends. And it's not forever. When you're grown up, I'll come find you or you'll come find me."

Jaenelle nibbled her lip. "How old is grown up?"

Yesterday. Tomorrow. "Let's say seventeen. It sounds like forever, I know, but it's really not that long." Even Sadi couldn't have spun a better lie than that. "Will you promise not to go wandering?"

Jaenelle sighed. "I promise not to go wandering in Terreille."

Lucivar hauled her to her feet and spun her around. "There's one thing I want to teach you before you go. This will work if a man ever tries to grab you from behind."

When they'd gone through the demonstration enough times that he was sure she knew what to do, Lucivar kissed her forehead and stepped back. "Get out of here. The guards will be making the rounds any minute now. And remember—a Queen never breaks a promise made to a Warlord Prince."

"I'll remember." She hesitated. "Lucivar? I won't look the same when I'm grown up. How will you know me?"

Lucivar smiled. Ten years or a hundred, it would make no difference. He'd always recognize those extraordinary sapphire eyes. "I'll know. Good-bye, Cat. May the Darkness embrace you."

She smiled at him and vanished.

Lucivar stared at that empty space. Was that a foolish thing to say to her? Probably.

A gate rattling caught his attention. He swiftly rubbed out the drawing of the Winds and slipped from shadow to shadow until he reached the stables. He passed through the outside wall and had just settled into his cell when the guard opened the barred window in the door.

Zuultah was arrogant enough to believe her holding spells kept her slaves from using Craft to pass through the cell walls. It was uncomfortable to pass through a spelled wall but not impossible for him.

Let the bitch wonder. When the guards found the slave in the boat, she'd suspect him of breaking the man's neck. She suspected him when *anything* went wrong in her court—with good reason.

Maybe he would offer a little resistance when the guards tried to tie him to the whipping posts. A vicious brawl would keep Zuultah distracted, and the violent emotions would cover up any lingering psychic scent from the girl.

Oh, yes, he could keep Lady Zuultah so distracted, she would *never* realize that Witch now walked the Realm.

2 / Terreille

Lady Maris turned her head toward the large, freestanding mirror. "You may go now."

Daemon Sadi slipped out of bed and began dressing slowly, tauntingly, fully aware that she watched him in the mirror. She always watched the mirror when he serviced her. A bit of self-voyeurism perhaps? Did she pretend the man in the mirror actually cared about her, that her climax aroused him?

Stupid bitch.

Maris stretched and sighed with pleasure. "You remind me of a wild cat, all silky skin and rippling muscles."

Daemon slipped into the white silk shirt. A savage predator? That was a fair enough description. If she ever annoyed him beyond his limited tolerance for the distaff gender, he would be happy to show her his claws. One little one in particular.

Maris sighed again. "You're so beautiful."

Yes, he was. His face was a gift of his mysterious heritage, aristocratic and too beautifully shaped to be called merely handsome. He was tall and broad-shouldered. He kept his body well toned and muscular enough to please. His voice was deep and cultured, with a husky, seductive edge to it that made women go all misty-eyed. His gold eyes and thick black hair were typical of all three of Terreille's long-lived races, but his warm, golden-brown skin was a little lighter than the Hayllian aristos—more like the Dhemlan race.

His body was a weapon, and he kept his weapons well honed.

Daemon shrugged into his black jacket. The clothes, too, were weapons, from the skimpy underwear to the perfectly tailored suits. Nectar to seduce the unwary to their doom.

Fanning herself with her hand, Maris looked directly at him. "Even in this weather, you didn't work up a sweat."

It sounded like the complaint it was.

Daemon smiled mockingly. "Why should I?"

Maris sat up, pulling at the sheet to cover herself. "You're a cruel, unfeeling bastard."

Daemon raised one finely shaped eyebrow. "You think I'm cruel? You're quite right, of course. I'm a connoisseur of cruelty."

"And you're proud of it, aren't you?" Maris blinked back tears. Her face tightened, showing all the petulant age lines. "Everything they said about you is true. Even that." She waved a hand toward his groin.

"That?" he asked, knowing perfectly well what she meant. She, and every woman like her, would forgive every vicious thing he did if she could coax him into an erection.

"You're not a true man. You never were."

"Ah. In that, too, you're quite right." Daemon slipped his hands into his trouser pockets. "Personally, I've always thought it's the discomfort of the Ring of Obedience that's caused the problem." The cold, mocking smile returned. "Perhaps if you removed it . . ."

Maris became so pale he wondered if she was going to faint. He doubted Maris wanted to test his theory badly enough that she would actually remove that gold circle around his organ. Just as well. She wouldn't survive one minute after he was free.

Most of the witches he'd served hadn't survived anyway.

Daemon smiled that cold, familiar, brutal smile and settled next to her on the bed. "So you think I'm cruel." Her eyes were already glazing from the psychic seduction tendrils he was weaving around her.

"Yes," Maris whispered, watching his lips.

Daemon leaned forward, amused at how quickly she opened her mouth for a kiss. Her tongue flirted hungrily with his, and when he finally raised his head, she tried to pull him down on top of her. "Do you really want to know why I don't work up a sweat?" he asked too gently.

She hesitated, lust warring with curiosity. "Why?"

Daemon smiled. "Because, my darling Lady Maris, your so-called intelligence bores me to tears and that body you think so fine and flaunt whenever and wherever possible isn't fit to be crowbait."

Maris's lower lip quivered. "Y-you're a sadistic brute."

Daemon slipped off the bed. "How do you know?" he asked pleasantly. "The game hasn't even begun."

"Get out. GET OUT!"

He quickly left the bedroom, but waited a moment outside the door. Her wail of anguish was perfect counterpoint to his mocking laughter.

A light breeze ruffled Daemon's hair as he followed a gravel path through the back gardens. Unbuttoning his shirt, he smiled with pleasure as the breeze caressed his bare skin. He pulled a thin black cigarette from its gold case, lit it, and sighed as the smoke drifted slowly out of his mouth and nostrils, burning away Maris's stench.

The light in Maris's bedroom went out.

Stupid bitch. She didn't understand the game she played. No—she didn't understand the game *he* played. He was 1,700 years old and just coming into his prime. He'd worn a Ring of Obedience controlled by

Dorothea SaDiablo, Hayll's High Priestess, for as long as he could remember. He had been raised in her court as her cousin's bastard son, had been educated and trained to serve Hayll's Black Widows. That is, taught enough of the Craft to serve those witch-bitches as they wanted to be served. He'd been whoring in courts long turned to dust while Maris's people were just beginning to build cities. He'd destroyed better witches than her, and he could destroy her, too. He'd brought down courts, laid waste to cities, brought about minor wars as vengeance for bedroom games.

Dorothea punished him, hurt him, sold him into service in court after court, but in the end, Maris and her kind were expendable. He was not. It had cost Dorothea and Hayll's other Black Widows dearly to create him, and whatever they had done, they couldn't do again.

Hayll's Blood was failing. In his generation, there were very few who wore the darker Jewels—not surprising since Dorothea had been so thorough about purging the stronger witches who might have challenged her rule after she became High Priestess, leaving her followers within Hayll's Hundred Families, lighter-Jeweled witches who had no social standing, and Blood females who had little power as the only ones capable of mating with a Blood male and producing healthy Blood children.

Now she needed a dark bloodline to mate with her Black Widow Sisters. So while she gladly humiliated and tortured him, she wouldn't destroy him because, if there was any possibility at all, she wanted his willing seed in her Sisters' bodies, and she would use fools like Maris to wear him down until he was ready to submit.

He would never submit.

Seven hundred years ago, Tersa had told him the living myth was coming. Seven hundred years of waiting, watching, searching, hoping. Seven hundred heartbreaking, exhausting years. He refused to give up, refused to wonder if she'd been mistaken, refused because his heart yearned too much for that strange, wonderful, terrifying creature called Witch.

In his soul, he knew her. In his dreams, he saw her. He never envisioned a face. It always blurred if he tried to focus on it. But he could see her dressed in a robe made of dark, transparent spidersilk, a robe that slid from her shoulders as she moved, a robe that opened and closed as she walked, revealing bare, night-cool skin. And there would be a scent in the room that was her, a scent he would wake to, burying his face in her pillow after she was up and attending her own concerns.

It wasn't lust—the body's fire paled in comparison to the embrace of mind to mind—although physical pleasure was part of it. He wanted to touch her, feel the texture of her skin, taste the warmth of her. He wanted to caress her until they both burned. He wanted to weave his life into hers until there was no telling where one began and the other ended. He wanted to put his arms around her, strong and protecting, and find himself protected; possess her and be possessed; dominate her and be dominated. He wanted that Other, that shadow across his life, who made him ache with every breath while he stumbled among these feeble women who meant nothing to him and never could.

Simply, he believed that he had been born to be her lover.

Daemon lit another cigarette and flexed the ring finger of his right hand. The snake tooth slid smoothly out of its channel and rested on the underside of his long, black-tinted fingernail. He smiled. Maris wondered if he had claws? Well, this little darling would impress her. Not for very long, though, since the venom in the sac beneath his fingernail was extremely potent.

He was lucky that he'd reached sexual maturity a little later than most Hayllians. The snake tooth had come along with the rest of the physical changes, a shocking surprise, for he'd thought it was impossible for a male to be a natural Black Widow. During that time, he'd been serving in a court where it was fashionable for men to wear their nails long and tint them, so no one had thought it strange when he assumed the fashion, and no one had ever questioned why he continued to wear them that way.

Not even Dorothea. Since the witches of the Hourglass covens specialized in poisons and the darker aspects of the Craft, as well as dreams and visions, he'd always thought it strange that Dorothea had never guessed what he was. If she had, no doubt she would have tried to maim him beyond recognition. She might have succeeded before he had made the Offering to the Darkness to determine his mature strength, when he had still worn the Red Jewel that had come to him at his Birthright Ceremony. If she tried now, even with her coven backing her, it would cost her dearly. Even Ringed, a Black-Jeweled Warlord Prince would be a formidable enemy for a Red-Jeweled Priestess.

Which is why their paths seldom crossed anymore, why she kept him away from Hayll and her own court. She had one trump card to keep him submissive, and they both knew it. Without Lucivar's life in the balance, even the pain inflicted by the Ring of Obedience wouldn't hold him anymore. Lucivar . . . and the wild card that Tersa had added to the game of submission and control. The wild card Dorothea didn't know about. The wild card that would end her domination of Terreille.

Once, the Blood had ruled honorably and well. The Blood villages within a District would look after, and treat fairly, the landen villages that were bound to them. The District Queens would serve in the Province Queen's court. The Province Queens, in their turn, would serve the Territory Queen, who was chosen by the majority of the darker-Jeweled Blood, both male and female, because she was the strongest and the best.

Back then, there was no need for slavery to control the strong males. They followed their hearts to the Queen who was right for them. They handed over their lives willingly. They served freely.

Back then, the Blood's complicated triangle of status hadn't leaned so heavily on social rank. Jewel rank and caste had weighed just as heavily in the balance, if not more. That meant control of their society was a fluid dance, with the lead constantly changing depending on the dancers. But in the center of that dance, always, was a Queen.

That had been the genius and the flaw in Dorothea's purges. Without any strong Queens to challenge her rise to power, she had expected the males to surrender to her, a Priestess, the same way they surrendered to a Queen. They didn't. So a different kind of purge began, and by the time it was done, Dorothea had the sharpest weapons of all—frightened males who stripped any weaker female of her power in order to feel strong and frightened females who Ringed potentially strong males before they could become a threat.

The result was a spiraling perversion of their society, with Dorothea at its center as both the instrument of destruction and the only safe haven.

And then it spread outward, into the other Territories. He had seen those other lands and people slowly crumble, crushed beneath Hayll's relentless, whispered perversion of the ways of the Blood. He had seen the strong Queens, bedded much too young, rise from their Virgin Night broken and useless.

He had seen it and grieved over it, furious and frustrated that he could do so little to stop it. A bastard had no social standing. A slave had even less, no matter what caste he was born to or what Jewels he wore. So while Dorothea played out her game of power, he played out his. She destroyed the Blood who opposed her. He destroyed the Blood who followed her.

In the end, she would win. He knew that. There were very few Territories that didn't live in Hayll's shadow now. Askavi had spread its legs for Hayll centuries ago. Dhemlan was the only Territory in the eastern part of the Realm that was still fighting with its last breaths to stay free of Dorothea's influence. And there were a handful of small Territories in the far west that weren't completely ensnared yet.

In another century, two at the most, Dorothea would achieve her ambition. Hayll's shadow would cover the entire Realm and she would be *the* High Priestess, the absolute ruler of Terreille, which had once been called the Realm of Light.

Daemon vanished the cigarette and buttoned his shirt. He still had to attend to Marissa, Maris's daughter, before he could get some sleep.

He'd only gone a few steps when a mind brushed against his, demanding his attention. He turned away from the house and followed the mental tug. There was no mistaking that psychic sent, those tangled thoughts and disjointed images.

What was she doing here?

The tugging stopped when he reached the small woods at the far end of the gardens.

"Tersa?" he called softly.

The bushes beside him rustled and a bony hand closed on his wrist. "This way," Tersa said, tugging him down a path. "The web is fragile."

"Tersa—" Daemon half-dodged a low-hanging branch that slapped him in the face and got his arm yanked for the effort. "Tersa—"

"Hush, boy," she said fiercely, dragging him along.

He concentrated on dodging branches and avoiding roots that tried to trip him. Gritting his teeth, he forced himself to ignore the tattered dress that clothed her half-starved body. As a child of the Twisted Kingdom, Tersa was half wild, seeing the world as ghostly grays through the shards of what she had been. Experience had taught him that when Tersa was intent upon her visions, it was useless talking to her about mundane things like food and clothes and safe, warm beds.

They reached an opening in the woods where a flat slab of stone rested above two others. Daemon wondered if it was natural, or if Tersa had built it as a miniature altar.

The slab was empty except for a wooden frame that held a Black Widow's tangled web.

Uneasy, Daemon rubbed his wrist and waited.

"Watch," Tersa commanded. She snapped the thumbnail of her left hand against the forefinger nail. The forefinger nail changed to a sharp point. She pricked the middle finger of her right hand, and let one drop of blood fall on each of the four tether lines that held the web to the frame. The blood ran down the top lines and up the bottom ones. When they met in the middle, the web's spidersilk threads glowed.

A swirling mist appeared in front of the frame and changed into a crystal chalice.

The chalice was simple. Most men would have called it plain. Daemon thought it was elegant and beautiful. But it was what the chalice held that pulled him toward the makeshift altar.

The lightning-streaked black mist in the chalice contained power that slithered along his nerves, snaked around his spine, and sought its release in the sudden fire in his loins. It was a molten force, catastrophic in intensity, savage beyond a man's comprehension . . . and he wanted it with all his being.

"Look," Tersa said, pointing to the chalice's lip.

A hairline crack ran from a chip in the chalice's lip to the base. As Daemon watched, a deeper crack appeared.

The mist swirled inside the chalice. A tendril passed through the glass at the bottom into the stem.

Too fragile, he thought as more and more cracks appeared. The chalice was too fragile to hold that kind of power.

Then he looked closer.

The cracks were starting from the outside and going in, not starting from the inside and going out. So it was threatened by something beyond itself.

He shivered as he watched more of the mist flow into the stem. It was a vision. There was nothing he could do to change a vision. But everything he was screamed at him to *do* something, to wrap his strength around it and cherish it, protect it, keep it safe.

Knowing it would change nothing that happened here and now, he still reached for the chalice.

It shattered before he touched it, spraying crystal shards over the makeshift altar.

Tersa held up what was left of the shattered chalice. A little of mist still swirled inside the jagged-edged bottom of the cup. Most of it was trapped inside the stem.

She looked at him sadly. "The inner web can be broken without shattering the chalice. The chalice can be shattered without breaking the inner web. They cannot reach the inner web, but the chalice . . ."

Daemon licked his lips. He couldn't stop shivering. "I know the inner web is another name for our core, the Self that can tap the power within us. But I don't know what the chalice stands for."

Her hand shook a little. "Tersa is a shattered chalice."

Daemon closed his eyes. A shattered chalice. A shattered mind. She was talking about madness.

"Give me your hand," Tersa said.

Too unnerved to question her, Daemon held out his left hand.

Tersa grabbed it, pulled it forward, and slashed his wrist with the chalice's jagged edge.

Daemon clamped his hand over his wrist and stared at her, stunned.

"So that you never forget this night," Tersa said, her voice trembling. "That scar will never leave you."

Daemon knotted his handkerchief around his wrist. "Why is a scar important?"

"I told you. So you won't forget." Tersa cut the strands of the tangled web with the shattered chalice. When the last thread broke, the chalice and web vanished. "I don't know if this will be or if it may be. Many strands in the web weren't visible to me. May the Darkness give you courage if you need it, when you need it."

"The courage for what?"

Tersa walked away.

"Tersa!"

Tersa looked back at him, said three words, and vanished.

Daemon's legs buckled. He huddled on the ground, gasping for air, shuddering from the fear that clawed at his belly.

What had the one to do with the other? Nothing. *Nothing!* He would be there, a protector, a shield. He *would!*

But where?

Daemon forced himself to breathe evenly. That was the question. Where.

Certainly not in Maris's court.

It was late morning before he returned to the house, aching and dirty. His wrist throbbed and his head pounded mercilessly. He had just reached the terrace when Maris's daughter, Marissa, flounced out of the garden room and planted herself in front of him, hands on her hips, her expression a mixture of irritation and hunger.

"You were supposed to come to my room last night and you didn't. Where have you been? You're filthy." She rolled her shoulder, looking at him from beneath her lashes. "You've been naughty. You'll have to come up to my room and explain."

Daemon pushed past her. "I'm tired. I'm going to bed."

"You'll do as I say!" Marissa thrust her hand between his legs.

Daemon's hand tightened on Marissa's wrist so fast and so hard that she was on her knees whimpering in pain before she realized what happened. He continued squeezing her wrist until the bones threatened to shatter. Daemon smiled at her then, that cold, familiar, brutal smile.

"I'm not 'naughty.' Little boys are naughty." He pushed her away from him, stepping over her where she lay sprawled on the flagstones. "And if you ever touch me like that again, I'll rip your hand off."

He walked through the corridors to his room, aware that the servants skittered away from him, that an aftertaste of violence hung in the air around him.

He didn't care. He went to his room, stripped off his clothes, lay down on his bed, and stared at the ceiling, terrified to close his eyes because every time he did he saw a shattered crystal chalice.

Three words.

She has come.

3 / Hell

Once, he'd been the Seducer, the Executioner, the High Priest of the Hourglass, the Prince of the Darkness, the High Lord of Hell.

Once, he'd been Consort to Cassandra, the great Black-Jeweled, Black Widow Queen, the last Witch to walk the Realms.

Once, he'd been the only Black-Jeweled Warlord Prince in the history of the Blood, feared for his temper and the power he wielded.

Once, he'd been the only male who was a Black Widow.

Once, he'd ruled the Dhemlan Territory in the Realm of Terreille and her sister Territory in Kaeleer, the Shadow Realm. He'd been the only male ever to rule without answering to a Queen and, except for Witch, the only member of the Blood to rule Territories in two Realms.

Once, he'd been married to Hekatah, an aristo Black Widow Priestess from one of Hayll's Hundred Families.

Once, he'd raised two sons, Mephis and Peyton. He'd played games with them, told them stories, read to them, healed their skinned knees and broken hearts, taught them Craft and Blood Law, showered them with his love of the land as well as music, art, and literature, encouraged them to look with eager eyes upon all that the Realms had to offer—not to conquer but to learn. He'd taught them to dance for a social occasion and to dance for the glory of Witch. He'd taught them how to be Blood.

But that was a long, long time ago.

Saetan, the High Lord of Hell, sat quietly by the fire, a hearth rug wrapped around his legs, turning the pages of a book he had no interest in reading. He sipped a glass of yarbarah, the blood wine, taking no pleasure in its taste or warmth.

For the past decade, he'd been a quiet invalid who never left his private study deep beneath the Hall. For more than 50,000 years before that, he'd been the ruler and caretaker of the Dark Realm, the undisputed High Lord.

He no longer cared about Hell. He no longer cared about the demon-dead family and friends who were still with him, or the other demon-dead and ghostly citizens of this Realm, the Blood who were still too strong to return to the Darkness even after their bodies had died.

He was tired and old, and the loneliness he'd carried inside him all his life had become too heavy to bear. He no longer wanted to be a Guardian, one of the living dead. He no longer wanted the half-life a handful of the Blood had chosen in order to extend their lifetimes into years beyond imagining. He wanted peace, wanted to quietly fade back into the Darkness.

The only thing that kept him from actively seeking that release was his promise to Cassandra.

Saetan steepled his long, black-tinted nails and rested his golden eyes on the portrait hanging on the far wall between two bookcases.

She'd made him promise to become a Guardian so that the extended half-life would allow him to walk among the living when his daughter was born. Not the daughter of his loins, but the daughter of his soul. The daughter she'd seen in a tangled web.

He'd promised because what she'd said had made his nerves twang like tether lines in a storm, because that was her price for training him to be a Black Widow, because, even then, the Darkness sang to him in a way it didn't sing to other Blood males.

He had kept his promise. But the daughter never came.

The insistent knocking on the door of his private study finally pulled him from his thoughts.

"Come," he said, his deep voice a tired whisper, a ghost of what it once had been.

Mephis SaDiablo entered and stood beside the chair, silent.

"What do you want, Mephis?" Saetan asked his eldest son, demon-dead since that long ago war between Terreille and Kaeleer.

Mephis hesitated. "Something strange is going on."

Saetan's gaze drifted back to the fire. "Someone else can look into it, if anyone so desires. Your mother can look into it. Hekatah always wanted power without my interference."

"No," Mephis said uneasily.

Saetan studied his son's face and found that he had a hard time swallowing. "Your . . . brothers?" he finally asked, unable to hide the pain that the question caused him. He'd been a flattered fool to cast the spell that temporarily gave him back the seed of life. He couldn't regret Daemon's and Lucivar's existence, but he'd tortured himself for centuries with reports of what had been done to them.

Mephis shook his head and stared at the dark-red marble mantle. "On the *cildru dyathe*'s island."

Saetan shuddered. He'd never feared anything in Hell, but he'd always felt an aching despair for the *cildru dyathe*, the demon-dead children. In Hell, the dead retained the form of their last living hour. This cold, blasted Realm had never been a kind place, but to look upon those children, to see what had been done to them by another's hand, for there to be no escape from those blatant wounds. . . . It was too much to bear. They kept to their island, unwilling to have any contact with adults. He never intruded on them, having Char, their chosen leader, come to him once in a while to bring back the books, games, and whatever else he could find that might engage their young minds and help wile away the unrelenting years.

"The *cildru dyathe* take care of themselves," Saetan said, fussing with the hearth rug. "You know that."

"But . . . every so often, for the past few weeks, there's another presence there. Never for very long, but I've felt it. So has Prothvar when he's flown over the island."

"Leave them alone," Saetan snapped, his temper returning some strength to his voice. "Perhaps they've found an orphaned Hound pup."

Mephis took a deep breath. "Hekatah has already had an altercation with Char over this. The children are hiding from everyone who approaches because of it. If she had any authority to—"

Before Saetan could respond to the sharp rap on the study door, it swung open. Andulvar Yaslana, once the Eyrien Warlord Prince of Askavi, strode into the room. His grandson, Prothvar, followed him, carrying a large globe covered with a black cloth.

"SaDiablo, there's something you should see," Andulvar said. "Prothvar brought this from the *cildru dyathe*'s island."

Saetan assumed an expression of polite interest. As young men, he and Andulvar had become unlikely friends and had served together in a number of courts. Even Hekatah hadn't severed that friendship when she'd strutted around, gleefully carrying a child that wasn't his—Andulvar's child. It didn't turn him against the only man he'd ever called a friend—who could blame a man for getting tangled up in one of Hekatah's schemes?—but it had ended his stormy marriage.

Saetan looked at each man in turn and saw the same uneasiness in three pairs of gold eyes. Mephis was a Gray-Jeweled Warlord Prince and almost unshakable. Prothvar was a Red-Jeweled Eyrien Warlord, a warrior bred and trained. Andulvar was an Eyrien Warlord Prince who wore the Ebon-gray, the second darkest Jewel. They were all strong men who didn't frighten easily—but now they *were* frightened.

Saetan leaned forward, their fear pricking the bubble of indifference he'd sealed himself in a decade ago. His body was weak and he needed a cane to walk, but his mind was still sharp, the Black Jewels still vibrant, his skill in the Craft still honed.

Suddenly, he knew he would need all that strength and skill to deal with whatever was happening on the *cildru dyathe*'s island.

Andulvar pulled the cloth off the globe. Saetan just stared, his face full of wonder and disbelief.

A butterfly. No, not just a butterfly. This was a huge fantasy creature that gently beat its wings within the confines of the globe. But it was the colors that stunned Saetan. Hell was a Realm of forever-twilight, a Realm that muted colors until there was almost no color at all. There was nothing muted about the creature in the globe. Its body was pumpkin orange, its wings an unlikely blend of sky blue, sun yellow, and spring-grass green. As he stared, the butterfly lost its shape, and the colors bled together like a chalk painting in the rain.

Someone on the *cildru dyathe*'s island had created that glorious piece of magic, had been able to hold the colors of the living Realms in a place that bleached away the vitality, the vibrancy of life.

"Prothvar threw a shielded globe around this one," Andulvar said.

"They dissolve almost immediately," Prothvar said apologetically, pulling his dark, membranous wings tight to his body.

Saetan straightened in his chair. "Bring Char to me, Lord Yaslana." His voice was soft thunder, caressing, commanding.

"He won't come willingly," Prothvar said.

Saetan stared at the demon-dead Warlord. "Bring Char to me."

"Yes, High Lord."

The High Lord of Hell sat quietly by the fire, his slender fingers loosely steepled, the long nails a glistening black. The Black-Jeweled ring on his right hand glittered with an inner fire.

The boy sat opposite him, staring at the floor, trying hard not to be frightened.

Saetan watched him through half-closed eyes. For a thousand years now, Char had been the leader of the *cildru dyathe*. He'd been twelve, maybe thirteen, when someone had staked him and set him on fire. The will to survive had been stronger than the body, and he'd tumbled through one of the Gates to end up in the Dark Realm. His body was so burned it was impossible to tell what race he had come from. Yet this young demon boy had gathered the other maimed children and created a haven for them, the *cildru dyathe*'s island.

He would have been a good Warlord if he'd been allowed to come of age, Saetan thought idly.

Andulvar, Mephis, and Prothvar stood behind Char's chair in a half circle, effectively cutting off any means of escape.

"Who makes the butterflies, Char?" Saetan asked too quietly.

There were winds that came down from the north screaming over miles of ice, picking up moisture as they tore over the cooling sea until, when they finally touched a man, the cold, knife-sharp damp seeped into his bones and chilled him in places the hottest fire couldn't warm. Saetan, when he was this calm, this still, was like those winds.

"Who makes the butterflies?" he asked again.

Char stared at the floor, his hands clenched, his face twisted with the emotions raging within him. "She's ours." The words burst from him. "She belongs to us."

Saetan sat very still, cold with the fury rising in him. Until he had an answer, he had no time for gentleness.

Char stared back, frightened but willing to fight.

All of Hell's citizens knew the subtle nuances of death, that there was dead and there was *dead*. All of Hell's citizens knew the one person capable of obliterating them with a thought was their High Lord. Still, Char openly challenged him, and waited.

Suddenly, something else was in the room. A soft touch. A question running on a psychic thread. Char hung his head, defeated. "She wants to meet you."

"Then bring her here, Char."

Char squared his shoulders. "Tomorrow. I'll bring her tomorrow."

Saetan studied the trembling pride in the boy's eyes. "Very well, Warlord, you may escort her here . . . tomorrow."

4 / Hell

Saetan stood at the reading lectern, the candle-lights spilling a soft glow around him as he leafed through an old Craft text. He didn't turn at the quiet knock on his study door. A swift psychic probe told him who was there.

"Come." He continued to leaf through the book, trying to rein in his temper before dealing with that impudent little demon. Finally, he closed the book and turned.

Char stood near the doorway, his shoulders proudly pulled back.

"Language is a curious thing, Warlord," Saetan said with deceptive mildness. "When you said 'tomorrow,' I didn't expect five days to pass."

Fear crept into Char's eyes. His shoulders wilted. He turned toward the doorway, and a strange blend of tenderness, irritation, and resignation swept over his face.

The girl slipped through the doorway, her attention immediately caught by the stark Dujae painting, *Descent into Hell,* hanging over the fireplace. Her summer-sky blue eyes flitted over the large blackwood desk, politely skipped over him, lit up when she saw the floor-to-ceiling bookcases that covered most of one wall, and lingered on Cassandra's portrait.

Saetan gripped his silver-headed cane, fighting to keep his balance while impressions crashed over him like heavy surf. He'd expected a gifted *cildru dyathe.* This girl was *alive!* Because of the skill needed to make those butterflies, he'd expected her to be closer to adolescence. She couldn't be more than seven years old. He'd expected intelligence. The expression in her eyes was sweet and disappointingly dull-witted. And what was a living child doing in Hell?

Then she turned and looked at him. As he watched the summer-sky blue eyes change to sapphire, the surf swept him away.

Ancient eyes. Maelstrom eyes. Haunted, knowing, *seeing* eyes.

An icy finger whispered down his spine at the same moment he was filled with an intense, unsettling hunger. Instinct told him what she was. It took a little longer for him to find the courage to accept it.

Not the daughter of his loins, but the daughter of his soul. Not just a gifted witch, but Witch.

She lowered her eyes and fluffed her sausage-curled golden hair, apparently no longer sure of her welcome.

He stomped down the desire to brush out those ridiculous curls.

"Are you the Priest?" she asked shyly, lacing her fingers. "The High Priest of the Hourglass?"

One black eyebrow lifted slightly, and a faint, dry smile touched his lips. "No one's called me that in a long time, but, yes, I'm the Priest. I am Saetan Daemon SaDiablo, the High Lord of Hell."

"Saetan," she said, as if trying out the name. "Saetan." It was a warm caress, a sensuous, lovely caress. "It suits you."

Saetan bit back a laugh. There had been many reactions to his name in the past, but never this. No, never this. "And you are?"

"Jaenelle."

He waited for the rest, but she offered no family name. As the silence lengthened, a sudden wariness tinged the room, as if she expected some kind of trap. With a smile and a dismissive shrug to indicate it was of no importance, Saetan gestured toward the chairs by the fire. "Will you sit and talk with me, witch-child? My leg can't tolerate standing for very long."

Jaenelle went to the chair nearest the door, with Char in close, possessive attendance.

Saetan's gold eyes flashed with annoyance. Hell's fire! He'd forgotten about the boy. "Thank you, Warlord. You may go."

Char sputtered a protest. Before Saetan could respond, Jaenelle touched Char's arm. No words were spoken, and he couldn't feel a psychic thread. Whatever passed between the two children was very subtle, and there was no question who ruled. Char bowed politely and left the study, closing the door behind him.

As soon as they were settled by the fire, Jaenelle pinned Saetan to his chair with those intense sapphire eyes. "Can you teach me Craft? Cassandra said you might if I asked."

Saetan's world was destroyed and rebuilt in the space of a heartbeat. He allowed nothing to show on his face. There would be time for that later. "Teach you Craft? I don't see why not. Where is Cassandra staying now? We've lost touch over the years."

"At her Altar. In Terreille."

"I see. Come here, witch-child."

Jaenelle rose obediently and stood by his chair.

Saetan raised one hand, fingers curled inward, and gently stroked her cheek. Anger instantly skimmed her eyes, and there was a sudden pulse in the Black, within him. He held her eyes, letting his fingers travel slowly along her jaw and brush against her lips, all the way around and back. He didn't try to hide his curiosity, interest, or the tenderness he felt for most females.

When he was done, he steepled his fingers and waited. A moment later, the pulse was gone, and his thoughts were his own again. Just as well, because he couldn't stop wondering why being touched made her so angry. "I'll make you two promises," he said. "I want one in return."

Jaenelle eyed him warily. "What promise?"

"I promise, by the Jewels that I wear and all that I am, that I'll teach you whatever you ask to the best of my ability. And I promise I'll never lie to you."

Jaenelle thought this over. "What do I have to promise?"

"That you'll keep me informed of any Craft lessons you learn from others. Craft requires dedication to learn it well and discipline to handle the responsibilities that come with that kind of power. I want the assurance that anything you learn has been taught correctly. Do you understand, witch-child?"

"Then you'll teach me?"

"Everything I know." Saetan let her think this over. "Agreed?"

"Yes."

"Very well. Give me your hands." He took the small, fair hands in his light-brown ones. "I'm going to touch your mind." The anger again. "I won't hurt you, witch-child."

Saetan carefully reached with his mind until he stood before her inner barriers. They were the shields that protected the Blood from their own kind. Like rings within rings, the more barriers that were passed, the more personal the mental link. The first barrier protected everyday thoughts. The last barrier protected the core of the Self, the essence of a being, the inner web.

Saetan waited. As much as he wanted answers, he wouldn't open her by force. Too much now depended on trust.

The barriers opened, and he went in.

He didn't rummage through her thoughts or descend deeper than was necessary, despite his curiosity. That would have been a shocking betrayal of the Blood's code of honor. And there was a strange, deep blankness to her mind that troubled him, a soft neutrality that he was sure hid something very different. He quickly found what he was looking for—the psychic thread that would vibrate in sympathy with a plucked, same-rank thread and would tell him what Jewels she wore, or would wear after her Birthright Ceremony. He began with the White, the lightest rank, and worked his way down, listening for the answering hum.

Hell's fire! Nothing. He hadn't expected anything until he'd reached the Red, but he'd expected a response at that depth. She had to wear Birthright Red in order to wear the Black after she made the Offering to the Darkness. Witch always wore the Black.

Without thinking, Saetan plucked the Black thread.

The hum came from below him.

Saetan released her hands, amazed that his own weren't shaking. He swallowed to get his heart out of his throat. "Have you had the Birthright Ceremony yet?"

Jaenelle drooped.

He gently lifted her chin. "Witch-child?"

Misery filled her sapphire eyes. A tear rolled down her cheek. "I f-failed the t-test. Does that mean I have to give the Jewels back?"

"Failed the— What Jewels?"

Jaenelle slipped her hand into the folds of her blue dress and pulled out a velvet bag. She upended it on the low table beside his chair with a proud but watery smile.

Saetan closed his eyes, leaned his head against the back of the chair, and sincerely hoped the room would stop spinning. He didn't need to look at them to know what they were: twelve uncut Jewels. White, Yellow, Tiger Eye, Rose, Summer-sky, Purple Dusk, Blood Opal, Green, Sapphire, Red, Gray, and Ebon-gray.

No one knew where the Jewels had come from. If one was destined to wear a Jewel, it simply appeared on the Altar after the Birthright Ceremony or the Offering to the Darkness. Even when he was young, receiving an uncut Jewel—a Jewel that had never been worn by another of the Blood—was rare. His Birthright Red Jewel had been uncut. When he'd been gifted with the Black, it, too, had been uncut. But to receive an entire set of uncut Jewels . . .

Saetan leaned over and tapped the Yellow Jewel with the tip of his nail. It flared, the fire in the center warning him off. He frowned, puzzled. The Jewel already identified itself as female, as being bonded to a witch and not a Blood male, but there was the faintest hint of maleness in it too.

Jaenelle wiped the tears from her cheeks and sniffed. "The lighter Jewels are for practice and everyday stuff until I'm ready to set these." She upended another velvet bag.

The room spun in every direction. Saetan's nails pierced the leather arms of his chair.

Hell's fire, Mother Night, and may the Darkness be merciful!

Thirteen uncut Black Jewels, Jewels that already glittered with the inner fire of a psychic bond. Having a child bond with one Black Jewel without having her mind pulled into its depths was disturbing enough, but the inner strength required to bond and hold *thirteen* of them . . .

Fear skittered up his spine, raced through his veins.

Too much power. Too much. Even the Blood weren't meant to wield this much power. Even Witch had never controlled this much power.

This one did. This young Queen. This daughter of his soul.

With effort, Saetan steadied his breathing. He could accept her. He could love her. Or he could fear her. The decision was his, and whatever he decided here, now, he would have to live with.

The Black Jewels glowed. The Black Jewel in his ring glowed in answer. His blood throbbed in his veins, making his head ache. The power in those Jewels pulled at him, demanding recognition.

And he discovered the decision was an easy one after all—he had actually made it a long, long time ago.

"Where did you get these, witch-child?" he asked hoarsely.

Jaenelle hunched her shoulders. "From Lorn."

"L-Lorn?" *Lorn?* That was a name from the Blood's most ancient legends. Lorn was the last Prince of the Dragons, the founding race who had created the Blood. "How . . . where did you meet Lorn?"

Jaenelle withdrew further into herself.

Saetan stifled the urge to shake the answer out of her and let out a theatrical sigh. "A secret between friends, yes?"

Jaenelle nodded.

He sighed again. "In that case, pretend I never asked." He gently rapped her nose with his finger. "But that means you can't go telling him *our* secrets."

Jaenelle looked at him, wide-eyed. "Do we have any?"

"Not yet," he grumped, "but I'll make one up just so we do."

She let out a silvery, velvet-coated laugh, an extraordinary sound that hinted at the voice she'd have in a few years. Rather like her face, which was too exotic and awkward for her now, but, sweet Darkness, when she grew into that face!

"All right, witch-child, down to business. Put those away. You won't need them for this."

"Business?" she asked, scooping up the Jewels and tucking the bags into the folds of her dress.

"Your first lesson in basic Craft."

Jaenelle drooped and perked up at the same time.

Saetan twitched a finger. A rectangular paperweight rose off the black-wood desk and glided through the air until it settled on the low table. The paperweight was a polished stone taken from the same quarry as the stones he'd used to build the Hall in this Realm.

Saetan positioned Jaenelle in front of the table. "I want you to point one finger at the paperweight . . . like this . . . and move it as far across the table as you can."

Jaenelle hesitated, licked her lips, and pointed her finger.

Saetan felt the surge of raw power through his Black Jewel.

The paperweight didn't move.

"Try again, witch-child. In the other direction."

Again there was that surge, but the paperweight didn't move.

Saetan rubbed his chin, confused. This was simple Craft, something she shouldn't have any trouble with whatsoever.

Jaenelle wilted. "I try," she said in a broken voice. "I try and try, but I never get it right."

Saetan hugged her, feeling a bittersweet ache in his heart when her arms wrapped around his neck. "Never mind, witch-child. It takes time to learn Craft."

"Why can't I do it? All my friends can do it."

Reluctant to let her go, Saetan forced himself to hold her at arm's length. "Perhaps we should start with something personal. That's usually easier. Is there anything you have trouble with?"

Jaenelle fluffed her hair and frowned. "I always have trouble finding my shoes."

"Good enough." Saetan reached for his cane. "Put one shoe in front of the desk and then stand over there."

He limped to the far side of the room and stood with his back to Cassandra's portrait, grimly amused at giving his new Queen her first Craft lesson under the watchful but unknowing eyes of his last Queen.

When Jaenelle joined him, he said, "A lot of Craftwork requires translating physical action into mental action. I want you to imagine—by the way, how *is* your imagination?" Saetan faltered. Why did she look so bruised? He'd only meant to tease a little since he'd already seen that butterfly. "I want you to imagine picking up the shoe and bringing it over here. Reach forward, grasp, and bring it in."

Jaenelle stretched her arm as far as it would go, clenched her hand, and yanked.

Everything happened at once.

The leather chairs by the fire zipped toward him. He countered Craft with Craft and had a moment to feel shocked when nothing happened before one of the chairs knocked him off his feet. He fell into the other one and had just enough time to curl into a ball before the chair behind the blackwood desk slammed into the back of the chair he was in and came down on top of it, caging him. He heard leather-bound books whiz around the room like crazed birds before hitting the floor with a thump. His shoes pattered frantically, trying to escape his feet. And over all of it was Jaenelle wailing, "Stop stop stop!"

Seconds later, there was silence.

Jaenelle peered into the space between the chair arms. "Saetan?" she said in a small, quivery voice. "Saetan, are you all right?"

Using Craft, Saetan sent the top chair back to the blackwood desk. "I'm fine, witch-child." He stuffed his feet into his shoes and gingerly stood up. "That's the most excitement I've had in centuries."

"Really?"

He straightened his black tunic-jacket and smoothed back his hair. "Yes, really." And Guardian or not, a man his age shouldn't *have* his heart gallop around his rib cage like this.

Saetan looked around the study and stifled a groan. The book that had been on the lectern hung in the air, upside down. The rest of the books formed drifts on the study floor. In fact, the only leather object that hadn't answered that summons was Jaenelle's shoe.

"I'm sorry, Saetan."

Saetan clenched his teeth. "It takes time, witch-child." He sank into the chair. So much raw power but still so vulnerable until she learned how to use it. A thought shivered across his mind. "Does anyone else know about the Jewels Lorn gave you?"

"No." Her voice was a midnight whisper. Fear and pain filled her sapphire eyes, and something else, too, that was stronger than those surface feelings. Something that chilled him to the core.

But he was chilled even more by the fear and pain in her eyes.

Even a strong child, a powerful child, would be dependent on the adults around her. If her strength could unnerve *him,* how would her people, her family, react if they ever discovered what was contained inside that small husk? Would they accept the child who already was the strongest Queen in the history of the Blood, or would they fear the power? And if they feared the power, would they try to cut her off from it by breaking her?

A Virgin Night performed with malevolent skill could strip her of her power while leaving the rest intact. But, since her inner web was so deep in the abyss, she might be able to withdraw far enough to withstand the physical violation—unless the male was able to descend deep enough into the abyss to threaten her even there.

Was there a male strong enough, dark enough, vicious enough?

There was . . . one.

Saetan closed his eyes. He could send for Marjong, let the Executioner do what was needed. No, not yet. Not to that one. Not until there was a reason.

"Saetan?"

He reluctantly opened his eyes and watched, at first stupidly and then with a growing sense of shock, as she pushed up her sleeve and offered her wrist to him.

"There's no need for a blood price," he snapped.

She didn't drop her wrist. "It will make you better."

Those ancient eyes seared him, stripped him of his flesh until he shivered, naked before her. He tried to refuse, but the words wouldn't come. He could smell the fresh blood in her, the life force pumping through her veins in counter-rhythm to his own pounding heart.

"Not that way," he said huskily, drawing her to him. "Not with me." With a lover's gentleness, he unbuttoned her dress and nicked the silky skin of her throat with his nail. The blood flowed, hot and sweet. He closed his mouth over the wound.

Her power rose beneath him, a slow, black tidal wave skillfully controlled, a tidal wave that washed over him, cleansed him, healed him even as his mind shuddered to find itself engulfed by a mind so powerful and yet so gentle.

He counted her heartbeats. When he reached five, he raised his head. She didn't look shocked or frightened, the usual emotions the living felt when required to give blood directly from the vein.

She brushed a trembling finger against his lips. "If you had more, would it make you completely well?"

Saetan called in a bowl of warm water and washed the blood off her throat with a square of clean linen. He wasn't about to explain to a child what those two mouthfuls of blood were already doing to him. He ignored the question, hoping she wouldn't press for an answer, and concentrated on the Craft needed to heal the wound.

"Would it?" she asked as soon as he vanished the linen and bowl.

Saetan hesitated. He'd given his word he wouldn't lie. "It would be better for the healing to take place a little at a time." That, at least, was true enough. "Another lesson tomorrow?"

Jaenelle quickly looked away.

Saetan tensed. *Had* she been frightened by what he'd done?

"I . . . I already promised Morghann I'd see her tomorrow and Gabrielle the day after that."

Relief made him giddy. "In three days, then?"

She studied his face. "You don't mind? You're not angry?"

Yes, he minded, but that was a Warlord Prince's instinctive possessiveness talking. Besides, he had a lot to do before he saw her next. "I don't think your friends would care much for your new mentor if he took up all your time, do you?"

She grinned. "Probably not." The grin vanished. The bruised look was back in her eyes. "I have to go."

Yes, he had a great deal to do before he saw her next.

She opened the door and stopped. "Do you believe in unicorns?"

Saetan smiled. "I knew them once, a long time ago."

The smile she gave him before disappearing down the corridor lit the room, lit the darkest corners of his heart.

"Hell's fire! What happened, SaDiablo?"

Saetan waggled Jaenelle's abandoned shoe at Andulvar and smiled dryly. "A Craft lesson."

"What?"

"I met the butterfly maker."

Andulvar stared at the mess. "She did this? Why?"

"It wasn't intentional, just uncontrolled. She isn't *cildru dyathe* either. She's a living child, a Queen, and she's Witch."

Andulvar's jaw dropped. "Witch? Like Cassandra was Witch?"

Saetan choked back a snarl. "Not like Cassandra but, yes, Witch."

"Hell's fire! Witch." Andulvar shook his head and smiled.

Saetan stared at the shoe. "Andulvar, my friend, I hope you've still got all that brass under your belt that you used to brag about because we're in deep trouble."

"Why?" Andulvar asked suspiciously.

"Because you're going to help me train a seven-year-old Witch who's got the raw power right now to turn us both into dust and yet"—he dropped the shoe onto the chair—"is abysmal at basic Craft."

Mephis knocked briskly and entered the study, tripping on a pile of books. "A demon just told me the strangest thing."

Saetan adjusted the folds of his cape and reached for his cane. "Be brief, Mephis. I'm going to an appointment that's long overdue."

"He said he saw the Hall shift a couple of inches. The whole thing. And a moment later, it shifted back."

Saetan stood very still. "Did anyone else see this?"

"I don't think so, but—"

"Then tell him to hold his tongue if he doesn't want to lose it."

Saetan swept past Mephis, leaving the study that had been his home for the past decade, leaving his worried demon-dead son behind.

CHAPTER TWO

1 / Terreille

In the autumn twilight, Saetan studied the Sanctuary, a forgotten place of crumbling stone, alive with small vermin and memories. Yet within this broken place was a Dark Altar, one of the thirteen Gates that linked the Realms of Terreille, Kaeleer, and Hell.

Cassandra's Altar.

Cloaked in a sight shield and a Black psychic shield, Saetan limped through the barren outer rooms, skirting pools of water left by an afternoon storm. A mouse, searching for food among the fallen stones, never sensed his presence as he passed by. The Witch living in this labyrinth of rooms wouldn't sense him either. Even though they both wore the Black Jewels, his strength was just a little darker, just a little deeper than hers.

Saetan paused at a bedroom door. The covers on the bed looked fairly new. So did the heavy curtains pulled across the window. She would need those when she rested during the daylight hours.

At the beginning of the half-life, Guardians' bodies retained most of the abilities of the living. They ate food like the living, drank blood like the demon-dead, and could walk in the daylight, though they preferred the twilight and the night. As centuries passed, the need for sustenance diminished until only yarbarah, the blood wine, was required. Preference for darkness became necessity as daylight produced strength-draining, physical pain.

He found her in the kitchen, humming off-key as she took a wineglass out of the cupboard. Her shapeless, mud-colored gown was streaked with dirt. Her long braided hair, faded now to a dusty red, was veiled with cobwebs. When she turned toward the door, still unaware of his presence, the firelight smoothed most of the lines from her face, lines he knew were there because they were in the portrait that hung in his private study, the portrait he knew so well. She had aged since the death that wasn't a death.

But so had he.

He dropped the sight shield and psychic shield.

The wineglass shattered on the floor.

"Practicing hearth-Craft, Cassandra?" he asked mildly, struggling to tamp down an overwhelming sense of betrayal.

She backed away from him. "I should have realized she'd tell you."

"Yes, you should have. You also should have known I'd come." He tossed his cape over a wooden chair, grimly amused at the way her emerald eyes widened when she noticed how heavily he leaned on the cane. "I'm old, Lady. Quite harmless."

"You were never harmless," she said tartly.

"True, but you never minded that when you had a use for me." He looked away when she didn't answer. "Did you hate me so much?"

Cassandra reached toward him. "I never hated you, Saetan. I—"

—was afraid of you.

The words hung between them, unspoken.

Cassandra vanished the broken wineglass. "Would you like some wine? There's no yarbarah, but I've got some decent red."

Saetan settled into a chair beside the pine table. "Why aren't you drinking yarbarah?"

Cassandra brought a bottle and two wineglasses to the table. "It's hard to come by here."

"I'll send some to you."

They drank the first glass of wine in silence.

"Why?" he finally asked.

Cassandra toyed with her wineglass. "Black-Jeweled Queens are few and far between. There was no one to help me when I became Witch, no one to talk to, no one to help me prepare for the drastic changes in my life after I made the Offering." She laughed without humor. "I had no idea what being Witch would mean. I didn't want the next one to go through the same thing."

"You could have told me you intended to become a Guardian instead of faking the final death."

"And have you stay around as the loyal, faithful Consort to a Queen who no longer needed one?"

Saetan refilled the glasses. "I could have been a friend. Or you could have dismissed me from your court if that's what you wanted."

"Dismiss you? *You?* You were ... are ... Saetan, the Prince of the Darkness, High Lord of Hell. No one dismisses you. Not even Witch."

Saetan stared at her. "Damn you," he said bitterly.

Cassandra wearily brushed a stray hair from her face. "It's done, Saetan. It was lifetimes ago. There's the child to think about now."

Saetan watched the fire burning in the hearth. She was entitled to her own life, and certainly wasn't responsible for his, but she didn't understand—or didn't want to understand—what that friendship might have meant to him. Even if he'd never seen her again, knowing she still existed would have eased some of the emptiness. Would he have married Hekatah if he hadn't been so desperately lonely?

Cassandra laced her fingers around her glass. "You've seen her?"

Saetan thought of his study and snorted. "Yes, I've seen her."

"She's going to be Witch. I'm sure of it."

"Going to be?" Saetan's golden eyes narrowed. "What do you mean, 'going to be'? Are we talking about the same child? Jaenelle?"

"Of course we're talking about Jaenelle," she snapped.

"She isn't 'going to be' Witch, Cassandra. She already *is* Witch."

Cassandra shook her head vigorously. "Not possible. Witch always wear the Black Jewels."

"So does the daughter of my soul," Saetan replied too quietly.

It took her a moment to understand him. When she did, she lifted the wineglass with shaking hands and drained it. "H-how do you ..."

"She showed me the Jewels she was gifted with. A full uncut set of the 'lighter' Jewels—and that was the first time I'd ever heard *anyone* refer to the Ebon-gray as a lighter Jewel—and thirteen uncut Blacks."

Cassandra's face turned gray. Saetan gently chafed her ice-cold hands, concerned by the shock in her eyes. She was the one who'd first seen the child in her tangled web. She was the one who'd told him about it. Had she only seen Witch but not understood what was coming?

Saetan put a warming spell on his cape and wrapped it around her, then warmed another glass of wine over a little tongue of witchfire. When her teeth stopped chattering, he returned to his own chair.

Her emerald eyes asked the question she couldn't put into words.

"Lorn," he said quietly. "She got the Jewels from Lorn."

Cassandra shuddered. "Mother Night." She shook her head. "It's not supposed to be like this, Saetan. How will we control her?"

His hand jerked as he refilled his glass. Wine splashed on the table. "We don't control her. We don't even try."

Cassandra smacked her palm on the table. "She's a child! Too young to understand that much power and not emotionally ready to accept the responsibilities that come with it. At her age, she's too open to influence."

He almost asked her whose influence she feared, but Hekatah's face popped into his mind. Pretty, charming, scheming, vicious Hekatah, who had married him because she'd thought he would make her the High Priestess of Terreille at least or, possibly, the dominant female influence in all three Realms. When he'd refused to bend to her wishes, she'd tried on her own and had caused the war between Terreille and Kaeleer, a war that had left Terreille devastated for centuries and had been the reason why many of Kaeleer's races had closed their lands to outsiders and were never seen or heard from again.

If Hekatah got her claws into Jaenelle and molded the girl into her own greedy, ambitious image . . .

"You have to control her, Saetan," Cassandra said, watching him.

Saetan shook his head. "Even if I were willing, I don't think I could. There's a soft fog around her, a sweet, cold, black mist. I'm not sure, even young as she is, that I'd like to find out what lies beneath it without her invitation." Annoyed by the way Cassandra kept glaring at him, Saetan looked around the kitchen and noticed a primitive drawing tacked on the wall. "Where did you get that?"

"What? Oh, Jaenelle dropped it off a few days ago and asked me to keep it. Seems she was playing at a friend's house and didn't want to take the picture home." Cassandra tucked stray hairs back into her braid. "Saetan, you said there's a soft fog around her. There's a mist around Beldon Mor, too."

Saetan frowned at her. What did he care about some city's weather? That picture held an answer if he could just figure it out.

"A psychic mist," Cassandra said, rapping her knuckles on the table, "that keeps demons and Guardians out."

Saetan snapped to attention. "Where's Beldon Mor?"

"On Chaillot. That's an island just west of here. You can see it from the hill behind the Sanctuary. Beldon Mor is the capital. I think Jaenelle lives there. I tried to find a way into—"

Now she had his full attention. "Are you mad?" He combed his fingers through his thick black hair. "If she went to that much effort to retain her privacy, why are you trying to invade it?"

"Because of what she is," Cassandra said through clenched teeth. "I thought that would be obvious."

"Don't invade her privacy, Cassandra. Don't give her a reason to distrust you. And the reason for *that* should be obvious, too."

Minutes passed in tense silence.

Saetan's attention drifted back to the picture. A creative use of vivid colors, even if he couldn't quite figure out what it was supposed to be. How could a child capable of creating butterflies, moving a structure the size of the Hall, and constructing a psychic shield that only kept specific kinds of beings out be so hopeless at basic Craft?

"It's clumsy," Saetan whispered as his eyes widened.

Cassandra looked up wearily. "She's a child, Saetan. You can't expect her to have the training or the motor control—"

She squeaked when he grabbed her arm. "But that's just it! For Jaenelle, doing things that require tremendous expenditures of psychic energy is like giving her a large piece of paper and color-sticks she can wrap her fist around. Small things, the basic things we usually start with because they don't require a lot of strength, are like asking her to use a single-haired brush. She doesn't have the physical or mental control yet to do them." He sprawled in the chair, exultant.

"Wonderful," Cassandra said sarcastically. "So she can't move furniture around a room, but she can destroy an entire continent."

"She'll never do that. It's not in her temperament."

"How can you be sure? How will you control her?"

They were back to that.

He took his cape back and settled it over his shoulders. "I'm not going to control her, Cassandra. She's Witch. No male has the right to control Witch."

Cassandra studied him. "Then what are you going to do?"

Saetan picked up his cane. "Love her. That will have to be enough."

"And if it's not?"

"It will have to be." He paused at the kitchen door. "May I see you from time to time?"

Her smile didn't quite reach her eyes. "Friends do."

He left the Sanctuary feeling exhilarated and bruised. He'd loved Cassandra dearly once, but he had no right to ask anything of her except what Protocol dictated a Warlord Prince could ask of a Queen.

Besides, Cassandra was his past. Jaenelle, may the Darkness help him, was his future.

2 / Hell

Dropping from the Black Wind, Saetan appeared in an outer courtyard that held one of the Keep's official landing webs, which was etched in the stone with a clear Jewel at its center. The clear Jewels acted as beacons for those who rode the Winds—a kind of welcoming candle in the window—and every landing web had a piece of one. It was the only use that had ever been found for them.

Leaning heavily on his cane, Saetan limped across the empty courtyard to the huge, open-metal doors embedded into the mountain itself, rang the bell, and waited to enter the Keep, the Black Mountain, Ebon Askavi, where the Winds meet. It was the repository for the Blood's history as well as a sanctuary for the darkest-Jeweled Blood. It was also the private lair of Witch.

The doors opened silently. Geoffrey, the Keep's historian/librarian, waited for him on the other side. "High Lord." Geoffrey bowed slightly in greeting.

Saetan returned the bow. "Geoffrey."

"It's been a while since you've visited the Keep. Your absence has been noted."

Saetan snorted softly, his lips curving into a faint, dry smile. "In other words, I haven't been useful lately."

"In other words," Geoffrey agreed, smiling. As he walked beside Saetan, his black eyes glanced once at the cane. "So you're here."

"I need your help." Saetan looked at the Guardian's pale face, a stark, unsettling white when combined with the black eyes, feathery black eyebrows, black hair with a pronounced widow's peak, the black tunic and trousers, and the most sensuous blood-red lips Saetan had ever seen on anyone, man or woman. Geoffrey was the last of his race, a race gone to dust so long ago that no one remembered who they were. He was ancient when Saetan first came to the Keep as Cassandra's Consort. Then, as now, he was the Keep's historian and librarian. "I need to look up some of the ancient legends."

"Lorn, for example?"

Saetan jerked to a stop.

Geoffrey turned, his black eyes carefully neutral.

"You've seen her," Saetan said, a hint of jealousy in his voice.

"We've seen her."

"Draca, too?" Saetan's chest tightened at the thought of Jaenelle confronting the Keep's Seneschal. Draca had been caretaker and overseer of Ebon Askavi long, long before Geoffrey had ever come. She still served the Keep itself, looking after the comfort of the scholars who came to study, of the Queens who needed a dark place to rest. She was reserved to the point of coldness, using it as a defense against those who shuddered to look upon a human figure with unmistakably reptilian ancestry. Coldness as a defense for the heart was something Saetan understood all too well.

"They're great friends," Geoffrey said as they walked through the twisting corridors. "Draca's given her a guest room until the Queen's apartment is finished." He opened the library door. "Saetan, you are going to train her, aren't you?"

Hearing something odd in Geoffrey's voice, Saetan turned with much of his old grace. "Do you object?" He immediately choked back the snarl in his voice when he saw the uneasiness in Geoffrey's eyes.

"No," Geoffrey whispered, "I don't object. I'm . . . relieved." He pointed to the books neatly stacked at one end of the blackwood table. "I pulled those out anticipating your visit, but there are some other volumes, some very ancient texts, that I'll pull out for you next time. I think you'll need them."

Saetan settled into a leather chair beside the large blackwood table and gratefully accepted the glass of yarbarah Geoffrey offered. His leg ached. He wasn't up to this much walking.

He pulled the top book off the stack and opened it at the first marker. Lorn. "You did anticipate."

Geoffrey sat at the other end of the table, checking other books. "Some. Certainly not all." They exchanged a look. "Anything else I can check for you?"

Saetan quickly swallowed the yarbarah. "Yes. I need information about two witches named Morghann and Gabrielle." He started reading the entry about Lorn.

"If they wear Jewels, they'll be in the Keep's registry."

"It's a safe bet you'll find them in the darker ranks," Saetan said, not looking up.

Geoffrey pushed his chair back. "What Territories?"

"Hmm? I've no idea. Jaenelle's from Chaillot, so start with Territories around there where those names are common."

"Saetan," Geoffrey said with annoyed humor, "sometimes you're as useful as a bucket with a hole in the bottom. Can you give me a little more of a starting point?"

Pulled away from his third attempt to read the same paragraph, Saetan snapped, "Between the ages of six and eight. Now will you let me read?"

Geoffrey replied in a language Saetan didn't understand, but translation wasn't required. "I'll have to check the registry at Terreille's Keep, so this may take a while even if any of your information is remotely accurate. Help yourself to more yarbarah."

The hours melted away. Saetan read the last entry Geoffrey had marked, carefully closed the book, and rubbed his eyes. When he finally looked up, he found Geoffrey studying him. A strange look was in the librarian's black eyes. Two registers lay on the table.

Saetan rested his steepled fingers on his chin. "So?"

"You got the names and the age range right," Geoffrey said softly.

That icy finger whispered down Saetan's spine. "Meaning?"

Geoffrey slowly, almost reluctantly, opened the first book at the page marker. "Morghann. A Queen who wears Birthright Purple Dusk. Almost seven years old. Lives in the village of Maghre on the Isle of Scelt in the Realm of Kaeleer."

"Kaeleer!" Saetan tried to jump up. His leg buckled immediately. "How in the name of Hell did she get into the Shadow Realm?"

"Probably the same way she got into the Dark Realm." Geoffrey opened the second register and hesitated. "Saetan, you will train her well, won't you?" He didn't wait for an answer. "Gabrielle. A Queen who wears Birthright Opal. Seven years old. Strong possibility she's a natural Black Widow. Lives in the Realm of Kaeleer in the Territory of the Dea al Mon."

Saetan pillowed his head in his arms and moaned. The Children of the Wood. She'd seen the Children of the Wood, the fiercest, most private race ever spawned in Kaeleer. "It's not possible," he said, bracing his arms on the table. "You've made a mistake."

"I've made no mistake, Saetan."

"She lives in Terreille, not Kaeleer. You've made a mistake."

"I've made no mistake."

Ice whispered down his spine, freezing nerves, turning into a cold dagger in his belly. "It's not possible," Saetan said, spacing out the words. "The Dea al Mon have never allowed anyone into their Territory."

"It appears they've made an exception."

Saetan shook his head. "It's not possible."

"Neither is finding Lorn," Geoffrey replied sharply. "Neither is walking with impunity through the length and breadth of Hell. Yes, we know about that. The last time she visited here, Char came with her."

"The little bastard," Saetan muttered.

"You asked me to find Morghann and Gabrielle. I found them. Now what are you going to do?"

Saetan stared at the high ceiling. "What would you have me do, Geoffrey? Shall we take her away from her home? Confine her in the Keep until she comes of age?" He let out a strained laugh. "As if we could. The only way to confine her would be to convince her she couldn't get out, to brutalize her instincts until she wasn't sure of anything anymore. Do you want to be the bastard responsible for that emotional butchering? Because I won't do it. By the Darkness, Geoffrey, the living myth has come, and this is the price required to have her walk among us."

Geoffrey carefully closed the registers. "You're right, of course, but . . . is there nothing you can do?"

Saetan closed his eyes. "I will teach her. I will serve her. I will love her. That will have to be enough."

3 / Terreille

Surreal swung through the front door of Deje's Red Moon house in Beldon Mor, flashed a smile at the brawny red-coated doorman, and continued through the plant-strewn, marble-floored entryway until she reached the reception desk. Once there, she smacked the little brass bell on the desk enough times to annoy the most docile temper.

A door marked "Private" snapped open, and a voluptuous middle-aged woman hurried out. When she saw Surreal, her scowl vanished and her eyes widened with delighted surprise.

"So, you've come again at last." Deje reached under the desk, pulled out a thick stack of small papers, and waved them at Surreal. "Requests. All willing to pay your asking price—and everyone knows what a thief you are—and all wanting a full night."

Without taking them, Surreal riffled the stack with her fingertip. "If I accommodated them all, I could end up being here for months."

Deje tilted her head. "Would that be so bad?"

Surreal grinned, but there was something sharp and predatory in her gold-green eyes. "I'd never get my asking price if my"—she twiddled her fingers at the papers—"friends thought I'd always be around. That would cut into your profit margin, too."

"Too true," Deje said, laughing.

"Besides," Surreal continued, hooking her black hair behind her delicately pointed ears, "I'll only be here for a few weeks, and I'm not looking for a heavy schedule. I'll work enough days to pay for room and board and spend the rest of the time sightseeing."

"How many ceilings do you want to see? That's all you'll look at in this business."

"Why, Deje!" Surreal fanned herself. "That's not at all true. Sometimes I get to see the patterns in the silk sheets."

"You could always take up horseback riding." Deje stuffed the papers under the desk. "I hear there are some pretty trails just outside the city proper."

"No thanks. When the work's done, I'm not interested in mounting anything else. You want me to start tonight?"

Deje patted her dark, richly dressed hair. "I'm sure there's someone who made a reservation tonight who'll rise to the occasion."

They grinned at each other.

Deje called in a slim leather folder and removed a piece of expensive parchment. "Hmm. A full house. And there's always one or two who'll show up sure that they're too important to need a reservation."

Surreal propped her elbows on the desk, her face in her hands. "You've got an excellent chef. Maybe they're just here for dinner."

Deje smiled wickedly. "I try to accommodate all kinds of hunger."

"And if the special's taken, the main entrées are still delicious."

Deje laughed, her shaking bosom threatening to shimmy out of her low-cut gown. "Well put. Here." She pointed to a name on the list. "I remember you saying you don't mind him. He'll probably be half-starved, but he appreciates appetizers as well as the main course."

Surreal nodded. "Yes, he'll do nicely. One of the garden rooms?"

"Of course. I've done a little redecorating since you were last here. I think you'll like it. You have a true appreciation for such things." Deje reached into one of the little cubbyholes in the wall behind the desk and pulled out a key. "This one will suit."

Surreal palmed the key. "Dinner in the room, I think. Is there a menu there? Good. I'll order ahead."

"How do you remember all their likes and dislikes, particularly from so many places, so many different customs?"

Surreal looked mockingly offended. "Deje. You used to play the rooms before you got ambitious. You know perfectly well that's what little black books are for."

Deje shooed Surreal from the desk. "Away with you. I have work to do, and so do you."

Surreal walked down the wide corridor, her sharp eyes taking in the rooms on either side. It was true. Deje was ambitious. Starting out with a packet of gifts from satisfied clients, she had bought a mansion and converted it into the best Red Moon house in the district. And unlike the other houses, at Deje's a man could find more than just a warm body in a bed. There was a small private dining room that served excellent food all night; a reception room, where those with an artistic temperament made a habit of gathering to debate each other while they ate the tidbits and drank good wine; a billiards room, where the politically ambitious met to plan their next move; a library filled with good books and thick leather chairs; private rooms, where a man could get away from his everyday life and be catered to, receiving nothing more than a good dinner, an expert massage, and peace; and, finally, the rooms and the women who would satisfy the carnal appetites.

Surreal found her room, locked the door, and took a long look around, nodding in approval. Soft, thick rugs; white walls with tasteful watercolor paintings; dark furniture; an oversized, gauze-enveloped poster bed; music spheres and the ornate brass stand to hold them; sliding glass doors that led out into a walled private garden with a small fountain and petite willow trees as well as a variety of night-blooming flowers; and a bathroom with a shower and a large walk-up sunken tub that was positioned in front of the glass window overlooking the garden.

"Very good, Deje," Surreal said quietly. "Very, very good."

She quickly settled into the room, calling in her work clothes and carefully hanging them in the wardrobe. She never carried much, just enough variety to satisfy the different appetites in whatever Territory she was in. Most of her things were scattered in a dozen hideaways throughout Terreille.

Surreal suppressed a shudder. It was better not to think of those hideaways. Certainly better not to wonder about *him*.

Opening the glass doors so she could listen to the fountain, Surreal settled into a chair, her legs tucked beneath her. Two black leather books appeared, floating before her. She took one, leafed through to the last written page, called in a pen, and made a notation.

That contract was finished. It hadn't taken the fool as long to die as she would have liked, but the pain had been exquisite. And the money had been very, very good.

She vanished the book and opened the other one, checked the entry she needed, wrote out her menu, and with a flick of her wrist sent it to the kitchen. Vanishing the second book, she got up and stretched. Another flick of her wrist and there was the familiar weight of the knife's handle, its stiletto blade a shining comfort. Turning her wrist the other way, she vanished the knife and smacked her hands together. One was all she'd need tonight. He never gave her any trouble. Besides—she smiled at the memory—she was the one who had taught him, how long ago? Twelve, fourteen years?

She took a quick shower, dressed her long black hair so it could be easily unpinned, made up her face, and slipped into a sheer gold-green dress that hid as much as it revealed. Finally, clenching her teeth against the inevitable, she walked over to the freestanding mirror and looked at the face, at the body, she had hated all her life.

It was a finely sculpted face with high cheekbones, a thin nose, and slightly oversized gold-green eyes that saw everything and revealed nothing. Her slender, well-shaped body looked deceptively delicate but had strong muscles that she had hardened over the years to ensure she was always in peak condition for her chosen profession. But it was the sun-kissed, light-brown skin that made her snarl. Hayllian skin. Her father's skin. She could easily pass for Hayllian if she wore her hair down and wore tinted glasses to hide the color of her eyes. The eyes would mark her as a half-breed. The ears with the tips curving to a delicate point . . . those were Titian's ears.

Titian, who came from no race Surreal had met in all her travels through Terreille. Titian, who had been broken on Kartane SaDiablo's spear. Titian, who had escaped and whored for her keep so Kartane couldn't find her and destroy the child she carried. Titian, who was found one day with her throat slit and was buried in an unmarked grave.

All the assassinations, all those men going to their planned deaths, were dress rehearsals for patricide. Someday she would find Kartane in the right place at the right time, and she would pay him back for Titian.

Surreal turned away from the mirror and forced the memories aside. When she heard the quiet knock on the door, she positioned herself in the center of the room so her guest would see her when he first walked in. And she would see him and plan the evening accordingly.

Using Craft, she opened the door before he turned the handle, and let the seduction tendrils flow from her like some exotic perfume. She opened her arms and smiled as the door locked behind him.

He came at her in a rush, need flowing out of him, the Gray Jewel around his neck blazing with his fire. She put her hands on his chest, stopping him and caressing him with one smooth stroke. Breathing hard, he clenched and unclenched his hands, but he didn't touch her.

Satisfied, Surreal glided to the small dining table near the glass doors and sent a thought to the kitchen. A moment later, two chilled glasses and a bottle of wine appeared. She poured the wine, gave him a glass, and raised hers in a salute. "Philip."

"Surreal." His voice was husky, aching.

She sipped her wine. "Doesn't the wine please you?"

Philip consumed half the glass in a swallow.

Surreal hid her smile. Who did he really hunger for that he couldn't have? Who did he pretend she was when he closed the curtains and turned off all the lights so he could satisfy his lust while clinging to his illusions?

She kept the meal to a leisurely pace, letting him consume her with his eyes as he drank the wine and ate the delicacies. As he always did, he talked to her in a meandering, obscure fashion, telling her more than he realized or intended.

Philip Alexander. Gray-Jeweled Prince. A handsome man with sandy hair and honest, troubled gray eyes. Half brother to Robert Benedict, a premiere political player since he had tied himself to Hayll, to . . . Kartane. Robert only wore the Yellow, and barely that, but he was the legitimate son, entitled to his father's estate and wealth. Philip, a couple of years younger and never formally acknowledged, was raised as his brother's accessory. Tired of playing the grateful bastard, he broke with his family and became an escort/consort for Alexandra Angelline, the Queen of Chaillot.

Subtle cultural poisoning over a couple of generations had allowed Chaillot's Blood males to twist matriarchal rule into something unnatural and wrest control of the Territory from the Queens, so Alexandra was nothing more than a figurehead, but she was still the Queen of Chaillot and wore an Opal Jewel. A little strange, too. Well, unusual. It was rumored that she still had dealings with the Hourglass covens even though Black Widows had been outlawed by the Blood males in power. She had one daughter, Leland, who was Robert Benedict's wife.

And they all lived together at the Angelline estate in Beldon Mor.

She played dinner as long as she could before beginning to play the bed. A Gray-Jeweled Prince who had gone without pleasure for a long time could be an unintentionally rough companion, but he didn't worry her. She, too, wore the Gray, but never for this job. She always wore her Birthright Green, or no Jewel at all, allowing her clients to feel in control. Still, tonight he wouldn't mind a little rough handling, and he was one of the few men she knew in her second profession who actually wanted to give as well as receive pleasure.

Yes, Philip was a good way to begin this stay.

Surreal dimmed the candle-lights, turning the room to smoke, to dusk. He didn't rush now. He touched, tasted, savored. And she, subtly guiding, let him do what he had come here to do.

★　★　★

It was dawn before Philip dressed and kissed her good-bye.

Surreal stared at the gauze canopy. He'd gotten his money's worth and more. And he'd been a pleasant distraction from the memories that had been crowding her lately, that were the reason she'd come to Chaillot. Memories of Titian, of Tersa . . . of the Sadist.

Surreal was ten years old when Titian brought Tersa home one afternoon and tucked the bedraggled witch into her own bed. During the few days the mad Black Widow stayed with them, Titian spent hours listening to Tersa's gibberish interspersed with strange jokes and cryptic sayings.

A week after Tersa left them, she returned with the coldest, handsomest man Surreal had ever seen. The first Warlord Prince she had ever seen. He said nothing, letting Tersa babble while he watched Titian, while his gaze burned the child trembling beside her mother.

Finally Tersa stopped talking and tugged at the man's sleeve. "The child is Blood and should be trained in the Craft. She has the right to wear the Jewels if she's strong enough. Daemon, please."

His golden eyes narrowed as he came to a decision. Reaching into the inner pocket of his jacket, he removed several gold hundred-mark notes from a billfold and laid them carefully on the table. He called in a piece of paper and a pen, wrote a few words, and left the paper and a key on top of the notes.

"The place isn't elegant, but it's warm and clean." His deep, seductive voice sent a delightful shiver through Surreal. "It's a few blocks from here, in a neighborhood where no one asks questions. There are the names of a couple of potential tutors for the girl. They're good men who got on the wrong side of the ones who have power. You're welcome to use the flat as long as you want."

"And the price?" Titian's soft voice was full of ice.

"That you don't deny Tersa access to the place whenever she's in this part of the Realm. I won't make use of it while you're there, but Tersa must be able to use the refuge I originally acquired for her."

So it was agreed, and a few days later Surreal and Titian were in the first decent place the girl had ever known. The landlord, with a little tremor of fear in his voice, told them the rent was paid. The hundred-mark notes went for decent food and warm clothes, and Titian gratefully no longer had to allow any man to step over her threshold.

The next spring, after Surreal had begun making some progress with her tutors, Tersa returned and took Surreal to the nearest Sanctuary for her Birthright Ceremony. Surreal returned, proudly holding an uncut Green. With tears in her eyes, Titian carefully wrapped the Jewel in soft cloth and stored it in a strangely carved wooden box.

"An uncut Jewel is a rare thing, little Sister," Titian said, removing something from the box. "Wait until you know who you are before you have it set. Then it will be more than a receptacle for the power your body can't hold; it will be a statement of what you are. In the meantime"—she slipped a silver chain over Surreal's head—"this will help you begin. It was mine, once. You're not a moon child; gold would suit you better. But it's the first step down a long road."

Surreal looked at the Green Jewel. The silver mounting was carved into two stags curved around the Jewel, their antlers interlocking at the top, hiding the ring where the chain was fastened. As she studied it, her blood sang in her veins, a faint summoning she couldn't trace.

Titian watched her. "If ever you meet my people, they will know you by that Jewel."

"Why can't we go to see them?"

Titian shook her head and turned away.

Those two years were good ones for Surreal. She spent her days with her tutors, one teaching her Craft, the other all the basic subjects for a general education. At night, Titian taught her other things. Even broken, Titian was expert with a knife, and there was a growing uneasiness in her, as if she were waiting for something that made her relentless in the drills and exercises.

One day, when Surreal was twelve, she returned home to find the apartment door half open and Titian lying in the front room with her throat slit, her horn-handle dagger nearby. The walls pulsed with violence and rage . . . and the warning to run, run, run.

Surreal hesitated a moment before racing into Titian's bedroom and removing the carved box with her Jewel from its hiding place. At a stumbling run, she swept the dagger up from the floor and vanished it and the box as she'd been taught to do. Then she ran in earnest, leaving Titian and whoever had been hunting them behind.

Titian had just turned twenty-five.

Less than a week after her mother's death, Surreal was speared for the first time. As she fought without hope, she saw herself falling down a long, dark tunnel, her thread in the abyss. At the level of the Green was a shimmering web that stretched across the tunnel. As she fell toward it, out of control, as the pain of being broken into washed the walls with red, Surreal remembered Tersa, remembered Titian. If she hit her inner web while out of control, she would break it and return to the real world as a shadow of her self, forever aware and grieving the loss of her Craft and what she might have been.

Remembering Titian gave her the inner strength to fight the pounding that seemed to go on forever, each thrust driving her closer to her inner web. She hung on, fighting with all her heart. When the thrusts stopped . . . when it was finally over . . . she was barely a hand's span away from destruction.

Her mind cowered there, exhausted. When the man left, she forced herself to ascend. The physical pain was staggering, and the sheets were soaked with her blood, but she was still intact in the most important way. She still wore the Jewels. She was still a witch.

Within a month, she made her first kill.

He was like all the others, taking her to a seedy room, using her body and paying her with a copper mark that would barely buy her enough food to stagger through the next day. Her hatred for the men who used her, and Titian before her, turned to ice. So when his thrusts became stronger, when he arched his back and his chest rose above her, she called in the horn-handle dagger and stabbed him in the heart. His life force pumped into her while his life's blood spilled out.

Using Craft, Surreal pushed his heavy body off hers. This one wouldn't hit her or refuse to pay. It was exhilarating.

For three years she roamed the streets, her child's body and unusual looks a beacon to the most sordid. But her skill with a knife was not unknown, and it became common knowledge in the streets that a wise man paid Surreal in advance.

Three years. Then one day as she was slipping down an alley she'd already probed to be sure it was empty, she felt someone behind her. Whirling around, dagger in hand, she could only stare at Daemon Sadi as he leaned against the wall, watching her. Without thinking, she ran up the alley to get away from him, and hit a psychic shield that held her captive until his hand locked on her wrist. He said nothing. He simply caught the

Winds and pulled her with him. Never having ridden one of those psychic Webs, Surreal clung to him, disoriented.

An hour later, she was sitting at a kitchen table in a furnished loft in another part of the Realm. Tersa hovered over her, encouraging her to eat, while Daemon watched her as he drank his wine.

Too nervous to eat, Surreal threw the words at him. "I'm a whore."

"Not a very good one," Daemon replied calmly.

Incensed, Surreal hurled every gutter word she knew at him.

"Do you see my point?" he asked, laughing, when she finally sputtered into silence.

"I'll be what I am."

"You're a child of mixed blood. Part Hayllian blood." He toyed with his glass. "Your mother's people live—what—a hundred, two hundred years? You may see two thousand or more. Do you want to spend those years eating scraps dumped in alleys and sleeping in filthy rooms? There are other ways of doing what you do—for better rooms, better food, better pay. You'd have to start as an apprentice, of course, but I know a place where they'd take you and train you well."

Daemon spent several minutes making out a list. When he was done, he pushed it in front of Surreal. "A woman with an education may be able to spend more time sitting in a chair instead of lying on her back. A sound advantage, I should think."

Surreal stared at the list, uneasy. There were the expected subjects—literature, languages, history—and then, at the bottom of the page, a list of skills more suited to the knife than to paid sex.

As Tersa cleared the table, Daemon rose from his chair and leaned over Surreal, his chest brushing her back, his warm breath tickling her pointed ear. "Subtlety, Surreal," he whispered. "Subtlety is a great weapon. There are other ways to slit a man's throat than to wash the walls with his blood. If you continue down that road, they'll find you, sooner or later. There are so many ways for a man to die." He chuckled, but there was an underlying viciousness in the sound. "Some men die for lack of love . . . some die because of it. Think about it."

Surreal went to the Red Moon house. The matron and the other women taught her the bedroom arts. The rest she learned quietly on her own. Within ten years, she was the highest-paid whore in the house—and men began to bargain for her other skills as well.

She traveled throughout Terreille, offering her skills to the best Red Moon house in whatever city she was in and carefully accepting contracts for her other profession, the one she found more challenging—and more pleasurable. She carried a set of keys to town houses, suites, lofts—some in the most expensive parts of town, others in quiet, backwater streets where people asked no questions. Sometimes she met Tersa and gave her whatever care she could.

And sometimes she found herself sharing a place with Sadi when he slipped away from whatever court he was serving in for a quiet evening. Those were good times for Surreal. Daemon's knowledge was expansive when he felt like talking, and when she chattered, his golden eyes always held the controlled amusement of an older brother.

For almost three hundred years they came and went comfortably with each other. Until the night when, already a little drunk, she consumed a bottle of wine while watching him read a book. He was comfortably slouched in a chair, shirt half unbuttoned, bare feet on a hassock, his black hair uncharacteristically tousled.

"I was wondering," Surreal said, giving him a tipsy smile.

Daemon looked up from his book, one eyebrow rising as a smile began to tweak the corners of his mouth. "You were wondering?"

"Professional curiosity, you understand. They talk about you in the Red Moon houses, you know."

"Do they?"

She didn't notice the chill in the room or the golden eyes glazing to a hard yellow. She didn't recognize the dangerous softness in his voice. She just smiled at him. "Come on, Sadi, it would be a real feather in my cap, career-wise. There isn't a whore in the Realm who knows firsthand what it's like to be pleasured by Hayll's—"

"Be careful what you ask for. You may get it."

She laughed and arched her back, her nipples showing through the thin fabric of her blouse. It wasn't until he uncoiled from his chair with predatory speed and had her pressed against him with her hands locked behind her back that she realized the danger of taunting him. Pulling her hair hard enough to bring tears to her eyes, he forced her head up. His hand tightened on her wrists until she whimpered from the pain. Then he kissed her.

She expected a brutal kiss, so the tenderness, the softness of his lips nuzzling hers frightened her far more. She didn't know what to think, what to feel with his hands deliberately hurting her while his mouth was so giving, so persuasive. When he finally coaxed her mouth open, each easy stroke of his tongue produced a fiery tug between her legs. When she could no longer stand, he took her to the bedroom.

He undressed her with maddening slowness, his long nails whispering over her shivering skin as he kissed and licked and peeled the fabric away. It was sweet torture.

When she was finally naked, he coaxed her to the bed. Psychic ropes tightened around her wrists and pulled her arms over her head. Ropes around her ankles held her legs apart. As he stood by the bed, Surreal became aware of the cold, unrelenting anger coiling around her . . . and a soft, controlled breeze, a spring wind still edged with winter, running over her body, caressing her breasts, her belly, riffling the black hair between her legs before splitting to run along the inside of her thighs, circling her feet, traveling up the outside of her thighs, past her ribs to circle around her neck and begin again.

It went on and on until she couldn't stand the teasing, until she was desperate for some kind of touch that would give her release.

"Please," she moaned, trying to shake off the relentless caress.

"Please what?" He slowly stripped off his clothes.

She watched him hungrily, her eyes glazing as she waited to see the proof of his pleasure. The shock of seeing the Ring of Obedience on a totally flaccid organ made her realize the anger swirling around her had changed. His smile had changed.

As he stretched out beside her, his warm body cool compared to the heat inside her, as his living hand began to play the same game the phantom one had, she finally understood what was in the air, in his smile, in his eyes.

Contempt.

He played with deadly seriousness. Each time his hands or his tongue gave her some release, the gauze veils of sensuality were ripped from her mind and she was forced to drink cup after cup of his contempt. When he brought her up the final time, she thrust her hips toward him while pleading for him to stop. His cold, biting laughter tightened around her ribs until she couldn't breathe. Just as she started sliding into a sweet, unfeeling release, it stopped.

Everything stopped.

As her head cleared, she heard water running in the bathroom. A few minutes later, Daemon reappeared, fully dressed, wiping his face with a towel. There was a throbbing need between her legs to be filled, just once. She begged him for some small comfort.

Daemon smiled that cold, cruel smile. "Now you know what it's like to get into bed with Hayll's Whore."

She began to cry.

Daemon tossed the towel onto a chair. "I wouldn't try using a dildo if I were you," he said pleasantly. "Not for a couple of days anyway. It won't help, and it might even make things much, much worse." He smiled at her again and walked out of the apartment.

She didn't know how long he'd been gone when the ropes around her wrists and ankles finally disappeared and she was able to roll over, her knees tucked tight to her chest, and cry out her shame and rage.

She became afraid of him, dreaded to feel his presence when she opened a door. When they met, he was coldly civil and seldom spoke— and never again looked at her with any warmth.

Surreal stared at the gauze canopy. That was fifty years ago, and he had never forgiven her. Now . . . She shuddered. Now, if the rumors were true, there was something terribly wrong with him. There hadn't been a court anywhere that could keep him for more than a few weeks. And too many of the Blood disappeared and were never heard from again whenever his temper frayed.

He had been right. There were many, many ways for a man to die. Even as good as she was, she still had to make some effort to dispose of a body. The Sadist, however, never left the smallest trace.

Surreal stumbled into the shower and sighed as her tight muscles relaxed under the pounding hot water. At least there didn't seem to be any danger of stumbling upon him while she stayed in Beldon Mor.

4 / Hell

Even the fierce pounding on his study door couldn't compete with Prothvar's unrestrained cursing and Jaenelle's shrieks of outrage.

Saetan closed the book on the lectern. There was a time, and not that long ago, when no one wanted to open that door, let alone pummel it into kindling. Easing himself onto a corner of the blackwood desk, he crossed his arms and waited.

Andulvar burst into the room, his expression an unsettling blend of fear and fury. Prothvar came in right behind him, dragging Jaenelle by the back of her dress. When she tried to break his grip, he grabbed her from behind and lifted her off her feet.

"Put me down, Prothvar!" Jaenelle cocked her knee and pistoned her leg back into Prothvar's groin.

Prothvar howled and dropped her.

Instead of falling, Jaenelle executed a neat roll in the air before springing to her feet, still a foot above the floor, and unleashing a string of profanities in more languages than Saetan could identify.

Saetan forced himself to look authoritatively neutral and decided, reluctantly, that this wasn't the best time to discuss Language Appropriate for Young Ladies. "Witch-child, kicking a man in the balls may be an effective way to get his attention, but it's not something a child should do." He winced when she turned all her attention on him.

"Why not?" she demanded. "A friend told me that's what I should do if a male ever grabbed me from behind. He made me promise."

Saetan raised an eyebrow. "This friend is male?" How interesting.

Before he could pursue it further, Andulvar rumbled ominously, "That's not the problem, SaDiablo."

"Then what is the problem?" Not that he really wanted to know.

Prothvar pointed at Jaenelle. "That little . . . she . . . tell him!"

Jaenelle clenched her hands and glared at Prothvar. "It was your fault. You laughed and wouldn't teach me. *You* knocked me down."

Saetan raised one hand. "Slow down. Teach you what?"

"He wouldn't teach me to fly," Jaenelle said accusingly.

"You don't have wings!" Prothvar snapped.

"I can fly as well as you can!"

"You haven't got the training!"

"Because you wouldn't teach me!"

"And I'm damn well not going to!"

Jaenelle flung out an Eyrien curse that made Prothvar's eyes pop.

Andulvar's face turned an alarming shade of purple before he pointed to the door and roared, "OUT!"

Jaenelle flounced out of the study with Prothvar limping after her.

Saetan clamped a hand over his mouth. He wanted to laugh. Sweet Darkness, how he wanted to laugh, but the look in Andulvar's eyes warned him that if he so much as chuckled, they were going to engage in a no-holds-barred brawl.

"You find this amusing," Andulvar rumbled, rustling his wings.

Saetan cleared his throat several times. "I suppose it's difficult for Prothvar to find himself on the losing end of a scrap with a seven-year-old girl. I didn't realize a warrior's ego bruises so easily."

Andulvar's grim expression didn't change.

Saetan became annoyed. "Be reasonable, Andulvar. So she wants to learn to fly. You saw how well she balances on air."

"I saw a lot more than that," Andulvar snapped.

Saetan ground his teeth and counted to ten. Twice. "So tell me."

Andulvar crossed his muscular arms and stared at the ceiling. "The waif's friend Katrine is showing her how to fly, but Katrine flies like a butterfly and Jaenelle wants to fly like a hawk, like an Eyrien. So she asked Prothvar to teach her. And he laughed, which, I admit, wasn't a wise thing to do, and she—"

"Got her back up."

"—jumped off the high tower of the Hall."

There was a moment of silence before Saetan exploded. *"What?"*

"You know the high tower, SaDiablo. You built this damned place. She climbed onto the top of the wall and jumped off. Do you still find it amusing?"

Saetan clamped his hands on the desk. His whole body shook. "So Prothvar caught her when she fell."

Andulvar snorted. "He almost killed her. When she jumped off, he dove over the side after her. Unfortunately, she was standing, *on the air,* less than ten feet below the ledge. When he went over the side, he barreled into her and took them both down almost three quarters of the way before he came out of the dive."

"Mother Night," Saetan muttered.

"And may the Darkness be merciful. So what are you going to *do?*"

"Talk to her," Saetan replied grimly as he flicked a thought at the door and watched it open smoothly and swiftly. "Witch-child."

Jaenelle approached him, her anger now cooled to the unyielding determination he'd come to recognize all too well.

Fighting to control his temper, Saetan studied her for a moment. "Andulvar told me what happened. Have you anything to say?"

"Prothvar didn't have to laugh at me. I don't laugh at him."

"Flying usually requires wings, witch-child."

"You don't need wings to ride the Winds. It's not that different. And even Eyriens need a little Craft to fly. Prothvar said so."

He didn't know which was worse: Jaenelle doing something outrageous or Jaenelle being reasonable.

Sighing, Saetan closed his hands over her small, frail-looking ones. "You frightened him. How was he to know you wouldn't just plummet to the ground?"

"I would have told him," she replied, somewhat chastened.

Saetan closed his eyes for a moment, thinking furiously. "All right. Andulvar and Prothvar will teach you the Eyrien way of flying. You, in turn, most promise to follow their instructions and *take the training in the proper order.* No diving off the tower, no surprising leaps from cliffs . . ." Her guilty look made his heart pound in a very peculiar rhythm. He finished in a strangled voice, ". . . no testing on the Blood Run . . . or any other Run until they feel you're ready."

Andulvar turned away, muttering a string of curses.

"Agreed?" Saetan asked, holding his breath.

Jaenelle nodded, unhappy but resigned.

Like the Gates, the Runs existed in all three Realms. Unlike the Gates, they only existed in the Territory of Askavi. In Terreille, they were the Eyrien warriors' testing grounds, canyons where winds and Winds collided in a dangerous, grueling test of mental and physical strength. The Blood Run held the threads of the lighter Winds, from White to Opal. The other . . .

Saetan swallowed hard. "Have you tried the Blood Run?"

Jaenelle's face lit up. "Oh, yes. Saetan, it's such fun." Her enthusiasm wavered as he stared at her.

Remember how to breathe, SaDiablo. "And the Khaldharon?"

Jaenelle stared at the floor.

Andulvar spun her around and shook her. "Only a handful of the best Eyrien warriors each year dare try the Khaldharon Run. It's the absolute test of strength and skill, not a playground for girls who want to flit from place to place."

"I don't flit!"

"Witch-child," Saetan warned.

"I only tried it a little," she muttered. "And only in Hell."

Andulvar's jaw dropped.

Saetan closed his eyes, wishing the sudden stabbing pain in his temples would go away. It would have been bad enough if she'd tried the Khald-haron Run in Terreille, the Realm furthest from the Darkness and the full strength of the Winds, but to make the Run in Hell . . . "You will not make the Runs until Andulvar says you're ready!"

Startled by his vehemence, Jaenelle studied him. "I scared you."

Saetan circled the room, looking for something he could safely shred. "You're damn right you scared me."

She fluffed her hair and watched him. When he returned to the desk, she performed a respectful, feminine curtsy. "My apologies, High Lord. My apologies, Prince Yaslana."

Andulvar grunted. "If I'm going to teach you to fly, I might as well teach you how to use the sticks, bow, and knife."

Jaenelle's eyes sparkled. "Sceron is teaching me the crossbow, and Chaosti is showing me how to use a knife," she volunteered.

"All the more reason you should learn Eyrien weapons as well," Andulvar said, smiling grimly.

When she was gone, Saetan looked at Andulvar with concern. "I trust you'll take into account her age and gender."

"I'm going to work her ass off, SaDiablo. If I'm going to train her, and it seems I have no choice, I'll train her as an Eyrien warrior should be trained." He grinned maliciously. "Besides, Prothvar will love being her opponent when she learns the sticks."

Once Andulvar was gone, Saetan settled into his chair behind the blackwood desk, unlocked one of the drawers, and pulled out a sheet of expensive white parchment half filled with his elegant script. He added three names to the growing list: Katrine, Sceron, Chaosti.

With the parchment safely locked away again, Saetan leaned back in his chair and rubbed his temples. That list disturbed him because he didn't know what it meant. Children, yes. Friends, certainly. But all from Kaeleer. She must be gone for hours at a time in order to travel those distances, even on the Black Wind. What did her family think about her disappearances? What did they say? She never talked about Chaillot, her home, her family. She evaded every question he asked, no matter how he phrased it. What was she afraid of?

Saetan stared at nothing for a long time. Then he sent a thought on an Ebon-gray spear thread, male to male. *Teach her well, Andulvar. Teach her well.*

5 / Hell

Saetan left the small apartment adjoining his private study, vigorously toweling his hair. His nostrils immediately flared and the line between his eyebrows deepened as he stared at the study door.

Harpies had a distinctive psychic scent, and this one, patiently waiting for him to acknowledge her presence, made him uneasy.

Returning to the bedroom, he dressed swiftly but carefully. When he was seated behind the blackwood desk, he released the physical and psychic locks on the door and waited.

Her silent, gliding walk brought her swiftly to the desk. She was a slender woman with fair skin, oversized blue eyes, delicately pointed ears, and long, fine, silver-blond hair. She was dressed in a forest-green tunic and pants with a brown leather belt and soft, calf-high boots. Attached to the belt was an empty sheath. She wore no Jewels, and the wound across her throat was testimony to how she had died. She studied him, as he studied her.

The tension built in the room.

Harpies were witches who had died by a male's hand. No matter what race they originally came from, they were more volatile and more cunning than other demon-dead witches, and seldom left their territory, a territory that even demon-dead males didn't dare venture into. Yet she was here, by her own choice. A Dea al Mon Black Widow and Queen.

"Please be seated, Lady," Saetan said, nodding to the chair before the desk. Without taking her eyes off him, she sank gracefully into the chair. "How may I help you?"

When she spoke, her voice was a sighing wind across a glade. But there was lightning in that voice, too. "Do you serve her?"

Saetan tried to suppress the shiver her words produced, but she sensed it and smiled. That smile brought his anger boiling to the surface. "I'm the High Lord, witch. I serve no one."

Her face didn't change, but her eyes became icy. "Hell's High Priestess is asking questions. That isn't good. So I ask you again, *High Lord,* do you serve her?"

"Hell has no High Priestess."

She laughed grimly. "Then no one has informed Hekatah of that small detail. If you don't serve, are you friend or enemy?"

Saetan's lip curled into a snarl. "I don't serve Hekatah, and while we were married once, I doubt she considers me a friend."

The Harpy looked at him in disgust. "She's important only because she threatens to interfere. The child, High Lord. Do you serve the child? Are you friend or enemy?"

"What child?" An icy dagger pricked his stomach.

The Harpy exploded from the chair and took a swift turn around the room. When she returned to the desk, her right hand kept rubbing the sheath as if searching for the knife that wasn't there.

"Sit down." When she didn't move, the thunder rolled in his voice. "Sit down." Hekatah was suspicious of recent activities, and rumors of a strange witch appearing and disappearing from the Dark Realm had sharpened her interest. But he had no control of where Jaenelle went or who she saw. If the Harpies knew of her, then who else knew? How long would it be before Jaenelle followed a psychic thread that would lead her straight into Hekatah's waiting arms? And was this Harpy a friend or an enemy? "The child is known to the Dea al Mon," he said carefully.

The Harpy nodded. "She is friends with my kinswoman Gabrielle."

"And Chaosti."

A cruel, pleased smile brushed her lips. "And Chaosti. He, too, is a kinsman."

"And you are?"

The smile faded. Cold hatred burned in her eyes. "Titian." She swept her eyes over his body and then leaned back in the chair. "The one who broke me . . . he carries your family name but not your bloodline. I was barely twelve when I was betrayed and taken from Kaeleer. He took me for his amusement and broke me on his spear. But everything has a price. I left him a legacy, the only seed of his that will ever come to flower. In the end, he'll pay the debt to her. And when the time comes, she'll serve the young Queen."

Saetan exhaled slowly. "How many others know about the child?"

"Too many . . . or not enough. It depends upon the game."

"This isn't a game!" He became very still. "Let me in."

Loathing twisted Titian's face.

Saetan leaned forward. "I understand why being touched by a male disgusts you. I don't ask this lightly . . . or for myself."

Titian bit her lip. Her hands dug into the chair. "Very well."

Focusing his eyes on the fire, Saetan made the psychic reach, touched the first inner barrier, and felt her recoil. He patiently waited until she felt ready to open the barriers for him. Once inside, he drifted gently, a well-mannered guest. It didn't take long to find what he was looking for, and he broke the link, relieved.

They didn't know. Titian wondered, guessed too close. But no one outside his confidence knew for sure. A strange child. An eccentric child. A mysterious, puzzling child. That would do. His wise, cautious child. But he couldn't help wondering what experience had made her so cautious so young.

He turned back to Titian. "I'm teaching her Craft. And I serve."

Titian looked around the room. "From here?"

Saetan smiled dryly. "Your point's well taken. I've grown tired of this room. Perhaps it's time to remind Hell who rules."

"You mean who rules in proxy," Titian said with a predatory smile. She let the words linger for a moment. "It's good you're concerned, High Lord," she acknowledged reluctantly. "It's good she has so strong a protector. She's fearless, our Sister. It's wise to teach her caution. But don't be deceived. The children know what she is. She's as much their secret as their friend. Blood sings to Blood, and all of Kaeleer is slowly turning to embrace a single dark star."

"How do you know about the children?" Saetan asked suspiciously.

"I told you. I'm Gabrielle's kinswoman."

"You're dead, Titian. The demon-dead don't mingle with the living. They don't interfere with the concerns of the living Realms."

"Don't they, High Lord? You and your family still rule Dhemlan in Kaeleer." She shrugged. "Besides, the Dea al Mon aren't squeamish about dealing with those who live in the forever-twilight of the Dark Realm." Hesitating, she added, "And our young Sister doesn't seem to understand the difference between the living and the dead."

Saetan stiffened. "You think knowing me has confused her?"

Titian shook her head. "No, the confusion was there before she ever knew of Hell or met a Guardian. She walks a strange road, High Lord. How long before she begins to walk the borders of the Twisted Kingdom?"

"There's no reason to assume she will," Saetan replied tightly.

"No? She will follow that strange road wherever it leads her. What makes you think a child who sees no difference between the living and the dead will see a difference between sanity and the Twisted Kingdom?"

"NO!" Saetan leaped out of his chair and went to stand before the fire. He tried to suppress the thought of Jaenelle sliding into madness, unable to cope with what she was, but the anxiety rolled from him in waves. No one else in the history of the Blood had worn the Black as a Birthright Jewel. No one else had had to shoulder the responsibility—and the isolation—that was part of the price of wearing so dark a Jewel at so young an age.

And he knew she had already seen things a child shouldn't see. He had seen the secrets and shadows in her eyes.

"Is there no one in Terreille you can trust to watch over her?"

Saetan let out a pained laugh. "Who would you trust, Titian?"

Titian rubbed her hands nervously on her trousers.

She was barely a woman when she died, he thought with tender sadness. So frail beneath all that strength. As they all are.

Titian licked her lips. "I know a Black-Jeweled Warlord Prince who sometimes looks after those who need help. If approached, he might—"

"No," he said harshly, pride warring with fear. How ironic that Titian considered Daemon a suitable protector. "He's owned by Hekatah's puppet, Dorothea. He can be made to comply."

"I don't believe he'd harm a child."

Saetan returned to his desk. "Perhaps not willingly, but pain can make a man do things he wouldn't willingly do."

Titian's eyes widened with understanding. "You don't trust him." She thought it over and shook her head. "You're wrong. He's—"

"A mirror." Saetan smiled as she drew in a hissing breath. "Yes, Titian. He's blood of my blood, seed of my loins. I know him well . . . and not at all. He's a double-edged sword capable of cutting the hand that holds him as easily as he cuts the enemy." He led her to the door. "I thank you for your counsel and your concern. If you hear any news, I would appreciate being informed."

She turned at the doorway and studied him. "What if she sings to his blood as strongly as she sings to yours?"

"Lady." Saetan quietly closed the door on her and locked it. Returning to his desk, he poured a glass of yarbarah and watched the small tongue of fire dance above the desktop, warming the blood wine.

Daemon was a good Warlord Prince, which meant he was a dangerous Warlord Prince.

Saetan drained the glass. He and Daemon were a matched pair. Did he really believe his namesake was a threat to Jaenelle or was it jealousy over having to yield to a potential lover, especially when that lover was also his son? Because he honestly couldn't answer that question, he hesitated to give the order for Daemon's execution.

As yet there was no reason to send for Marjong the Executioner. Daemon was nowhere near Chaillot and, for some reason, Jaenelle didn't wander around Terreille as she did Kaeleer. Perhaps Titian was right about Daemon, but he couldn't take the chance. His namesake had the cunning to ensnare a child and the strength to destroy her.

But if Daemon had to be executed to protect Jaenelle, it wouldn't be a stranger's hand that put him in his grave.

He owed his son that much.

PART II

CHAPTER THREE

1 / Kaeleer

Saetan smiled dryly at his reflection. His full head of black hair was more silvered at the temples than it had been five years ago, but the lines left in his face by illness and despair had softened while the laugh lines had deepened.

Turning from the mirror, he strolled the length of the second-floor gallery. His bad leg still stiffened if he walked too long, but he no longer needed that damned cane. He laughed softly. Jaenelle was a bracing tonic in more ways than one.

As he descended the staircase that ended in the informal reception room, he noticed the tall, slim woman watching him through narrowed eyes. He also noticed the ring of keys attached to her belt and felt relieved that finding the current housekeeper had been so easy.

"Good afternoon," he said pleasantly. "Are you Helene?"

"And what if I am?" She crossed her arms and tapped her foot.

Well, he hadn't expected an open-armed welcome, but still . . . He smiled at her. "For a staff who's had no one to serve for so long and so little incentive, you've kept the place quite well."

Helene's shoulders snapped back and her eyes glinted with anger. "We care for the Hall because it's the Hall." Her eyes narrowed even further. "And who are you?" she demanded.

He raised an eyebrow. "Who do you think I am?"

"An interloper, that's what I think," Helene snapped, placing her hands on her hips. "One of those who sneaks in here from time to time to gawk and 'soak up the atmosphere.' "

Saetan laughed. "They'd do well not to soak up too much of the atmosphere of this place. Although it was always calmer than its Terreille counterpart. I suppose after so many years away, I am an interloper of sorts, but . . ." He raised his right hand. As the Black Jewel in the ring flashed, there was an answering rumble from the stones of SaDiablo Hall.

Helene paled and stared at him.

He smiled. "You see, my dear, it still answers my call. And I'm afraid I'm about to wreak havoc with your routine."

Helen fumbled a low curtsy. "High Lord?" she stammered.

He bowed. "I'm opening the Hall."

"But . . ."

Saetan stiffened. "There's a problem with that?"

There was a gleam in Helene's gold eyes as she briskly wiped her hands on her large white apron. "A thorough cleaning will help, to be sure, but"—she looked pointedly at the drapes—"some refurbishing would help even more."

The tension drained out of him. "And give you something to be proud of instead of having to make do with an empty title?"

Helene blushed and chewed her lip.

Hiding a smile, Saetan vanished the drop cloths and studied the room. "New drapes and sheers definitely. With a good polishing, the wood pieces will still do, providing the preservation spells have held and they're structurally sound. New sofas and chairs. Plants by the windows. A few new paintings for the walls as well. New wallpaper or paint? What do you think?"

It took Helene a moment to find her voice. "How many rooms are you thinking of restoring?"

"This one, the formal receiving room across the hall, the dining room, my public study, my suite, a handful of guest rooms—and a special suite for my Lady."

"Then perhaps your Lady would like to oversee the redecorating."

Saetan looked at her with horrified amusement. "No doubt she would. However, my Lady will be twelve in four months, and I'd much prefer that she live in a suite I've decorated on her behalf than that I live in a Hall decorated with her somewhat . . . eclectic . . . tastes."

Helene stared at him for a moment but refrained from asking the question he saw in her eyes. "I could have some swatch books brought up to the Hall for you to choose from."

"An excellent idea, my dear. Do you think you can have this place presentable in four months?"

"The staff is rather small, High Lord," Helene said hesitantly.

"Then hire the help you need." Saetan strolled to the door that opened onto the great hall. "I'll meet you again at the end of the week. Is that sufficient time?"

"Yes, High Lord." She curtsied again.

Having been born in the slums of Draega, Hayll's capital, as the son of an indifferent whore, he'd never expected or wanted servants to grovel in his presence. He didn't mention this to Helene because, if he read her right, that was the last curtsy he would ever receive.

At the end of the great hall, he hesitated before opening the door of his public study. He walked around the room, lightly touching the covered furniture, grimacing slightly at his dusty fingertips.

He'd once ruled Dhemlan Kaeleer from this room. Still ruled, he reminded himself. He'd given Dhemlan Terreille to Mephis when he became a Guardian, but not her sister land in the Shadow Realm.

Ah, Kaeleer. It had always been a sweet wine for him, with its deeper magic and its mysteries. Now those mysteries were coming out of the mist once more, and the magic was still strong. Strand by strand, Jaenelle was rebuilding the web, calling them all to the dance.

He hoped she'd be pleased to have the use of this place. He hoped he'd be invited when she established her own court. He wanted to see who she selected for her First Circle, wanted to see the faces attached to that list of names. Did they know about each other? Or him?

Saetan shook his head and smiled.

Whether she'd intended to or not, his fair-haired daughter of the soul had certainly thrown him back among the living.

2 / Terreille

Surreal switched the basket of groceries from one hand to the other and fished her keys out of her trouser pocket as she climbed the stairs to her third-floor apartment. When she reached the landing and saw the dark shape curled up against her door, the keys vanished, replaced by her favorite stiletto.

The woman pushed the matted black hair from her face and staggered to her feet.

"Tersa," Surreal whispered, vanishing the stiletto as she leaped toward the swaying woman.

"You must tell him," Tersa muttered.

Surreal dropped the basket and wrapped her arm around Tersa's waist. After calling in her keys and unlocking the door, she half-carried the muttering woman to the sofa, swearing under her breath at the condition Tersa was in.

She retrieved the basket and locked the door before returning to the sofa with a small glass of brandy.

"You must tell him," Tersa muttered, weakly batting at the glass.

"Drink this. You'll feel better," Surreal said sternly. "I haven't seen him in months. He doesn't have much use for me anymore."

Tersa grabbed Surreal's wrist and said fiercely, "Tell him to beware of the High Priest of the Hourglass. He's not a forgiving man when someone threatens what is his. Tell him to beware of the Priest."

Sighing, Surreal pulled Tersa to her feet and helped the older woman shuffle to the bathroom.

Tell him? She didn't want to get anywhere *near* him.

And what was she going to do with Tersa? There were only two beds in the place. She knew better than to give up her own, so Tersa would have to use Sadi's. But Hell's fire, he'd become so sensitive about having a woman in his room, he could tell if there had been a different cleaning woman, even if she came only once. Shit. He wasn't likely to show up—sweet Darkness, please don't let him show up—but if he did and he objected to Tersa's using his bed, *he* could throw her out.

Surreal stripped off Tersa's tattered clothing. "Come on, Tersa. You need a hot bath, a decent meal, and a good night's sleep."

"You must tell him."

Surreal closed her eyes. She owed him. She never forgot that she owed him. "I'll tell him. Somehow, I'll tell him."

3 / Terreille

After several minutes of uncomfortable silence, Philip Alexander shifted on the couch and faced his niece. He reached for her limp hand. She pulled away from his touch.

Frustrated, Philip raked his fingers through his hair and tried, once more, to be reasonable.

"Jaenelle, we're not doing this to be cruel. You're a sick little girl, and we want to help you get better."

"I'm not sick," Jaenelle said softly, staring straight ahead.

"Yes, you are." Philip kept his voice firm but gentle. "You can't tell the difference between make-believe and the real world."

"I know the difference."

"No, you don't," Philip insisted. He rubbed his forehead. "These friends, these places you visit . . . they aren't real. They were *never* real. The only reason you see them is because you're not well."

Pain, confusion, and doubt filled her summer-sky blue eyes. "But they feel so real," she whispered.

Philip pulled her close to him, grateful that she didn't push him away. He hugged her as if that would cure what years of treatment hadn't. "I know they feel real to you, sweetheart. That's the problem, don't you see? Dr. Carvay is the leading healer for—"

Jaenelle twisted out of his arms. "Carvay is *not* a healer, he's—"

"Jaenelle!" Philip took a deep breath. "That's exactly what we're talking about. Making up vicious stories about Dr. Carvay isn't going to help you. Making up stories about magical creatures—"

"I don't talk about them anymore."

Philip sighed, frustrated. That was true. She'd been cured or had outgrown those fantasies, but the stories she made up now were a different coat cut from the same cloth. A much more dangerous coat.

Philip rose and straightened his jacket. "Maybe . . . maybe if you work hard and let Dr. Carvay help you, you'll be cured this time and will be able to come home for good. In time for your birthday."

Jaenelle gave him a look he couldn't decipher.

Philip guided her to the door. "The carriage is outside. Your father and grandmother will go with you, help you get settled."

As he watched the carriage disappear down the long drive, Philip sincerely hoped that this time would be the last time.

4 / Kaeleer

Saetan sat behind the blackwood desk in his public study, a half-empty wineglass in his hand, and looked around the refurbished room.

Helene had worked her hearth-Craft well. Not only were the rooms he had requested to be refurbished done, but most of the public rooms and an entire wing of the living quarters as well. That she'd hired practically the whole village of Halaway to accomplish it . . . Well, they all needed a purpose. Even him. Especially him.

A sharp rapping on the door finally drew his attention. "Come," he said, draining the wineglass.

Helene gave the room a satisfied look before approaching the desk and squaring her shoulders. "Mrs. Beale wants to know how much longer she should hold dinner."

"An excellent meal such as Mrs. Beale has prepared shouldn't be wasted. Why don't you and the others enjoy her efforts?"

"Then your guest isn't coming?"

"Apparently not."

Helene put her hands on her hips. "A hoyden, that's what she is, not to have the manners at least to send her regrets when—"

"You forget yourself, madam," Saetan snarled softly. There was no mistaking the anger in his words, or the threat.

Helene shrank from the desk. "I . . . I beg your pardon, High Lord."

Somewhat mollified, Saetan took a deep breath and exhaled slowly. "If she couldn't come, she had her reasons. Don't judge her, Helene. If she's here and you have some complaint about serving her, then come to me and I'll do what I can to alleviate the problem. But don't judge." He slowly walked to the door. "Keep sufficient staff on hand to serve any guests who may arrive. And keep a record of who comes and goes—especially anyone who inquires about the Lady. No one enters here without identifying themselves beforehand. Is that clear?"

"Yes, High Lord," Helene answered.

"Enjoy your dinner, my dear." Then he was gone.

* * *

Saetan walked the long stone corridor toward his private study deep beneath the Hall in the Dark Realm. He had abandoned the small apartment adjoining it, having returned to his suite several floors above, but as the days and weeks had passed, he found himself returning, and staying. Just in case.

A slight figure stepped away from the shadows near the study door. Anxiety rolled out of the boy in waves as Saetan unhurriedly unlocked the door and beckoned him in. A glance at the candle-lights produced a soft glow, blurring the room's edges and relieving the feeling of immense power that filled the room he'd occupied for so long.

"Would you join me in a glass of yarbarah, Char?" Without waiting for an answer, Saetan poured a glass from the decanter on his desk and warmed it with a little tongue of fire. He handed the glass to Char.

The boy's hand shook as he took the glass, and his eyes were filled with fear.

Uneasy, Saetan warmed a glass for himself before settling into the other chair by the fire.

Char drank quickly, a momentary smile on his lips as he savored the last mouthful. He glanced at the High Lord, at the face that seldom betrayed any flicker of emotion, and looked away. He tried to speak, but no sound came out. Clearing his throat, he tried again. "Have you seen her?" he asked in a cracked whisper.

Saetan sipped the blood wine before answering. "No, Char, I haven't seen her in three months. And you?".

Char shook his head. "No, but . . . something's been happening on the island. Others have come."

Saetan leaned forward. "Others? Not children?"

"Children, yes, but . . . something happens when they come. They don't come through the Gates, or find the island by riding the Winds. They come . . ." Char shook his head, stumbling for the words.

Saetan dropped his voice into a deep, soothing croon. "Will you let me in, Char? Will you let me see?" Char's relief was so intense, it made Saetan more uneasy. Leaning back in his chair, he reached for the boy's mind, found the barriers already opened, and followed Char to the memory of what he had seen that had troubled him so much.

Saetan expelled his breath in a hiss of recognition and severed the link as quickly as he could without harming the boy.

When had Jaenelle learned to do *that*?

"What is it?" Char asked.

"A bridge," Saetan answered. He drained his glass and poured another, surprised that his hand was steady, since his insides were shaking apart. "It's called a bridge."

"It's very powerful."

"No, the bridge itself has no power." He met Char's troubled look and allowed the boy to see the turmoil he felt. "However, the one who made the bridge *is* very powerful." He put the glass down and leaned forward, elbows resting on his knees, his steepled fingers brushing his chin. "Where do these children come from? Do they say?"

Char licked his lips. "From a place called Briarwood. They won't say if it's a village or a town or a Territory. They say a friend told them about the island, showed them the road." He hesitated, suddenly shy. "Would you come and see? Maybe . . . you'd understand."

"Shall we go now?" Saetan rose, tugging on his jacket's sleeves.

Char stared at the floor. "It must be an awful place, this Briarwood." He looked up at Saetan, his troubled eyes pleading for some comfort. "Why would she go to such an awful place?"

Pulling Char to his feet, Saetan put an arm around the boy's thin shoulders, more troubled than he wanted to admit when Char leaned into him, needing the caress. Locking the study door, he kept his pace slow and steady as he fed the boy drop after psychic drop of strength and the feeling of safety. When Char's shoulders began to straighten again, Saetan let his arm casually drop away.

Three months. There had been no word from her for three months. Now children were traveling over a bridge to the *cildru dyathe*'s island.

Jaenelle's new skill would have intrigued him more if Char's question hadn't been pounding in his blood, throbbing in his temples.

Why would she go to such an awful place? Why, why, why?

And where?

5 / Terreille

"Briarwood?" Cassandra warmed two glasses of yarbarah. "No, I've never heard of Briarwood. Where is it?" She handed a glass to Saetan.

"In Terreille, so it's probably on Chaillot somewhere." He sipped the blood wine. "Maybe a small town or village near Beldon Mor. You wouldn't have a map of that damned island, would you?"

Cassandra blushed. "Well, yes. I went to Chaillot. Not to Beldon Mor," she added hurriedly. "Saetan, I had to go because . . . well, something strange has been happening. Every once in a while, there's a sensation on the Webs, almost as if . . ." She made a frustrated sound.

"Someone was plucking them and then braiding the vibrations," Saetan finished dryly. He and Geoffrey had spent hours poring over Craft books in the Keep's library in order to figure out that much, but they still couldn't figure out *how* Jaenelle had done it.

"Exactly," Cassandra said.

Saetan watched her call in a map and spread it on the kitchen table. "What you've been sensing is a bridge that Jaenelle built." He deftly caught the glass of yarbarah as it fell from her hand. Setting both glasses on the table, he led her to a bench by the hearth and held her, stroking her hair and crooning singsong words. After a while, she stopped shaking and found her voice.

"That's not how a bridge is built," she said tightly.

"Not how you or I would—or could—build one, no."

"Only Blood at the peak of their Craft can build a bridge that spans any distance worth the effort. I doubt there's anyone left in Terreille who has the training to do it." She pushed at him, then snarled when he didn't let her go. "You'll have to talk to her about this, Saetan. You really will. She's too young for this kind of Craft. And why is she building a bridge when she can ride the Winds?"

Saetan continued to stroke her hair, holding her head against his shoulder. Five years of knowing Jaenelle and she still didn't understand what they were dealing with, still didn't understand that Jaenelle wasn't a young Queen who would become Witch but already *was* Witch. But, right now, he wasn't sure he understood either. "She's not traveling on the bridge, Cassandra," he said carefully. "She's sending others over. Those who wouldn't be able to come otherwise."

Would the truth frighten her as much as it had frightened him? Probably not. She hadn't seen those children.

"Where are they coming from?" she asked uneasily.

"From Briarwood, wherever that is."

"And going to?"

Saetan took a deep breath. "The *cildru dyathe*'s island."

Cassandra pushed him away and stumbled to the table. She grabbed the edge to hold herself upright.

Saetan watched her, relieved to see that, although she was frightened, she wasn't beyond reason. He waited until she'd regained her composure, saw the moment when she stopped to consider, and appreciate, the Craft required.

"She's building a bridge from here *into Hell*?"

"Yes."

Cassandra pushed a stray lock of hair from her face, the vertical line between her eyebrows deepening as she thought. She shook her head. "The Realms can't be spanned that way."

Saetan retrieved his glass of yarbarah and drained it. "Obviously, with that kind of bridge, they *can*." He studied the map, beginning at the south end of the island and working north toward Beldon Mor, section by section. He rapped the table with his long nails. "Not listed. If it's a small village near Beldon Mor, it might not be deemed significant enough to identify."

"If it's a village at all," Cassandra murmured.

Saetan froze. "What did you say?"

"What if it's just a place? There are a lot of places that are named, Saetan."

"Yes," he crooned, a faraway look in his eyes. But what kind of place would do that to children? He snarled in frustration. "She's hiding something behind that damned mist. That's why she doesn't want anyone from the Dark Realm in that city. Who is she protecting?"

"Saetan." Cassandra tentatively placed a hand on his arm. "Perhaps she's trying to protect herself."

Saetan's golden eyes instantly turned hard yellow. He pulled his arm from beneath her hand and paced around the room. "I'd never harm her. She knows me well enough to know that."

"I believe she knows you wouldn't deliberately harm her."

Saetan spun on the balls of his feet, a graceful dancer's move. "Say what you're going to say, Cassandra, and be done with it." His voice, although quiet, was full of thunder and a rising fury.

Cassandra moved around the room, gradually putting the table between them. Not that it would stop him. "It's not just you, Saetan. Don't you understand?" She opened her arms, pleading. "It's me and Andulvar and Prothvar and Mephis, too."

"They wouldn't harm her," he said coldly. "I won't speak for you."

"You're insulting," she snapped, and then took a deep breath to regain control. "All right. Say you show up on her family's doorstep tonight. Then what? It's unlikely they know about you, about any of us. Have you considered what kind of shock it will be to them to find out about your association with her? What if they desert her?"

"She can live with me," he snarled.

"Saetan, be reasonable! Do you want her to grow up in Hell, playing with dead children until she forgets what it feels like to walk among the living? Why would you inflict that on her?"

"We could live in Kaeleer."

"For how long? Remember who you are, Saetan. How eager will those little friends be to come to the house of the High Lord of Hell?"

"Bitch," he whispered, his voice shaking with pain. He splashed yarbarah into his glass, drank it cold, and grimaced at the taste.

Cassandra dropped into a chair by the table, too weary to stand. "Bitch I may be, but your love is a luxury she may not be able to afford. She has deliberately kept all of us out, and she doesn't come around anymore. Doesn't that tell you something? You haven't seen her, no one's seen her for the past three months." She gave him a wavering smile. "Maybe we were just a phase she was going through."

A muscle twitched in Saetan's jaw. There was a queer, sleepy look in his eyes. When he finally spoke, his words were soft and venomous. "I'm not a phase, Lady. I'm her anchor, her sword, and her shield."

"You sound as though you serve her."

"I *do* serve her, Cassandra. I served you once, and I served you well, but no longer. I'm a Warlord Prince. I understand the Blood Laws that apply when my kind serve, and the first law is not to serve, it's to protect."

"And if she doesn't want your protection?"

Saetan sat down opposite her, his hands tightly clasped. "When she forms her own court, she can toss me out on my ass if that's what she wants. Until then . . ." The words trailed away.

"There may be another reason to let her go." Cassandra took a deep breath. "Hekatah came to see me a few days ago." She flinched at Saetan's hiss of anger but continued in a sassy voice, "On the surface, she came to see your newest amusement."

Saetan stared at her. She was inviting him to make light of it, to dismiss Hekatah's appearance as if it meant nothing! No, she understood the danger. She just didn't want to deal with his rage.

"Go on," he said too softly. That blend of fear and wariness in her eyes was too familiar. He'd seen that look in every woman he'd ever bedded after he began wearing the Black. Even Hekatah, although she had hidden it well for her own purposes. But Cassandra was Witch. She wore the Black. At that moment he hated her for being afraid of him. "Go on," he said again.

"I don't think she was very impressed," Cassandra said hurriedly, "and I doubt she knew who I was. But she was disconcerted when she realized I was a Guardian. Anyway, she seemed more interested in finding out if I knew of a child that might be of interest to you, a 'young feast,' as she put it."

Saetan swore viciously.

Cassandra flinched. "She went out of her way to tell me about your interest in young flesh, hoping, I suppose, to create sufficient jealousy to make me an ally."

"And what did you tell her?"

"That your interest here was the restoration of the Dark Altar that was named in honor of the Queen you once served, and while I was flattered that she thought you might find me amusing, it was, unfortunately, not true."

"Perhaps I should rectify that impression."

Cassandra gave him a saucy smile, but there was panic in her eyes. "I don't tumble with just anyone, Prince. What are your credentials?"

Out of spite, Saetan walked around the table, drew Cassandra to her feet, and gave her a gentle, lingering kiss. "My credentials are the best, Lady," he whispered when he finally lifted his lips from hers. He released her, stepped away, and settled his cape over his shoulders. "Unfortunately, I'm required elsewhere."

"How long are you going to wait for her?"

How long? Dark witches, strong witches, powerful witches. Always willing to take what he offered, in bed and out, but they had never liked him, never trusted him, always feared him. And then there was Jaenelle. How long would he wait?

"Until she returns."

6 / Hell

It tingled his nerves, persistent and grating.

Growling in his sleep, Saetan rolled over and pulled the bedcovers up around his shoulders.

The tingling continued. A calling. A summons.

Along the Black.

Saetan opened his eyes to the night-dark room, listening with inner as well as outer senses.

A shrill cry of fury and despair flooded his mind.

"Jaenelle," he whispered, shivering as his bare feet touched the cold floor. Pulling on a dressing robe, he hurried into the corridor, then stopped, unsure where to go. Gathering himself, he sent one thunderous summons along the Black. *Jaenelle!*

No answer. Just that tingling laced with fear, despair, and fury.

She was still in Terreille. The thought spun through his head as he raced through the twisting corridors of the Hall. No time to wonder how she'd sent that thought-burst between the Realms. No time for anything. His Lady was in trouble and out of easy reach.

He ran into the great hall, ignoring the burning pain in his bad leg. A thought ripped the double front doors off the Hall. He raced down the broad steps and around the side of the Hall to the separate building where the Dark Altar stood.

Gasping, he tore the iron gate off its hinges and entered the large room. His hands shook as he centered the four-branched silver candelabra on the smooth black stone. Taking a deep breath to steady himself, he lit the three black candles that represented the Realms in the proper order to open a Gate between Hell and Terreille. He lit the candle in the center of the triangle made by the other three, the candle that represented the Self, and summoned the power of the Gate, waiting impatiently as the wall behind the Altar slowly changed from stone to mist and became a Gate between the Realms.

Saetan walked into the mist. His fourth step took him out of the mist and into the ruin that housed this Dark Altar in Terreille. As he passed the Altar, he noticed the black candle stubs in the tarnished candelabra and wondered why this Altar was getting so much use. Then he was outside the building, and there was no more time to wonder.

He gathered the strength of the Black Jewels and set a thought along a tight psychic thread. *Jaenelle!* He waited for a response, fighting the urge to catch the Black Web and fly to Chaillot. If he was on the Winds, he'd be out of reach for several hours. By then it might be too late. *Jaenelle!*

Saetan? Saetan! From the other side of the Realm, her voice came to him as a broken whisper.

Witch-child! He poured his strength into that tenuous link.

Saetan, please, I have to . . . I need . . .

Fight, witch-child, fight! You have the strength!

I need . . . don't know how to . . . Saetan, please.

Even the Black had limits. Grinding his teeth, Saetan swore as his long nails cut his palms and drew blood. If he lost her now . . . No. He *wouldn't* lose her! No matter what he had to do, he'd find a way to send her what she needed.

But this link between them was spun out so fine that anything might snap it, and most of her attention was focused elsewhere. If the link broke, he wouldn't be able to span the Realm and find her again. Holding his end of it was draining the Black Jewel at a tremendous rate. He didn't want to think about what it had cost her to reach him in Hell. If he could use someone as a transfer point, if he could braid his strength with another's for a minute . . . Cassandra? Too far. If he diverted any of his strength to search, he might lose Jaenelle altogether.

But he needed another's strength!

And it was there. Wary, angry, intent. Another mind on the Black psychic thread, turned toward the west, toward Chaillot.

Another male.

Saetan froze. Only one other male wore the Black Jewels.

Who are you? It was a deep, rich, cultured voice with a rough, seductive edge to it. A dangerous voice.

What could he say? What did he *dare* say to this son he'd loved for a few short years before he'd been forced to walk away from him? There was no time to settle things between them. Not now. So he chose the title that hadn't been used in Terreille in 1,700 years. *I'm the High Priest of the Hourglass.*

A quiver passed between them. A kind of wary recognition that wasn't quite recognition. Which meant Daemon had heard the title somewhere but couldn't name the man who held it.

Saetan took a deep breath. *I need your strength to hold this link.*

A long silence. *Why?*

Saetan ground his teeth, not daring to let his thoughts stray. *I can't give her the knowledge she needs without amplifying the link, and if she doesn't get the knowledge, she may be destroyed.* Even without a full link between them, he felt Daemon weighing his words.

Suddenly a stream of raw, barely controlled Black power rushed toward him as Daemon said, *Take what you need.*

Saetan tapped into Daemon's strength, ruthlessly draining it as he sent a knife-sharp thought toward Chaillot. *Lady!*

Help . . . Such desperation in that word.

Take what you need. Words of Protocol, of service, of surrender.

Saetan threw open his inner barriers, giving her access to everything he knew, everything he was. He sank to his knees and grabbed his head, sure his skull would shatter from the pain as Jaenelle slammed into him and rummaged through his mind as if she were opening cupboards and flinging their contents onto the floor until she found what she wanted. It only took a moment. It felt like forever. Then she withdrew, and the link with her faded.

Thank you. A faint whisper, almost gone. *Thank you.*

The second "thank you" wasn't directed at him.

It seemed like hours, not minutes, before his hands dropped to his thighs and he tilted his head back to look at the false-dawn sky. It took a minute more to realize he wasn't alone, that another mind still lightly touched his with something more than wariness.

Saetan swiftly closed his inner barriers. *You did well, Prince. I thank you . . . for her sake.* He cautiously began to back away from the link between them, not sure he could win a confrontation with Daemon.

But Daemon, too, backed away, exhausted.

As the link faded, just before Saetan was once more alone within himself, Daemon's voice came to him faintly, the words a silky threat.

Don't get in my way, Priest.

Grabbing one of the posts of the four-poster bed, Daemon hauled himself to his feet just as the door burst open and six guards cautiously entered the room.

Normally they had good reason to fear him, but not tonight. Even if he hadn't drained his strength to the point of exhaustion, he wouldn't have fought them. Tonight, whatever happened to him, he was buying time because she, wherever she was, needed a chance to recover.

The guards circled him and led him to the brightly lit outer courtyard. When he saw the two posts with the leather straps secured at the base and top, he hesitated for the briefest moment.

Lady Cornelia, the latest pet Queen who had bought his services from Dorothea SaDiablo, stood near the posts. Her eyes sparkled. Her voice dripped with excitement. "Strip him."

Daemon angrily shrugged off the guards' hands and began undressing when a bolt of pain from the Ring of Obedience made him catch his breath. He looked at Cornelia and lowered his hands to his sides.

"Strip him," she said.

Rough hands pulled his clothes off and dragged him to the posts. The guards lashed his ankles and wrists to the posts, tightening the leather straps until he was stretched taut.

Cornelia smiled at him. "A slave is forbidden to use the Jewels. A slave is forbidden to do anything but basic Craft, as you well know."

Yes, he knew. Just as he'd known that Cornelia would sense the unleashing of that much dark power and punish him for it. For most males, the threat of pain—especially the pain that could be produced by the Ring of Obedience—was enough to keep them submissive. But he'd learned to embrace agony like a sweet lover and used it to fuel his hatred for Dorothea and everything and everyone connected with her.

"The punishment for this kind of disobedience is fifty strokes," Cornelia said. "*You* will do the counting. If you miss a stroke, it will be repeated until you give the count. If you lose your place, the counting will begin again."

Daemon forced his voice to remain neutral. "What will Lady SaDiablo say about your treatment of her property?"

"Under the circumstances, I don't think Lady SaDiablo will mind," Cornelia replied sweetly. Then her voice became a whip crack. "Begin!"

Daemon heard the lash whistle before it struck. For a brief moment, a strange shiver of pleasure ran through him before his body recognized the pain. He drew in a ragged breath. "One."

Everything has a price. "Two." A Blood Law, or part of a code of honor? "Three." He'd never heard of the High Priest of the Hourglass until he'd found one of Surreal's warnings, but there was something vaguely familiar about that other mind. "Four." Who *was* the Priest? "Five." A Warlord Prince . . . "Six." . . . like himself . . . "Seven." . . . who wore the Black Jewels. "Eight." Everything has a price. "Nine." Who had taught him that? "Ten." Older. More experienced. "Eleven." To the east of him. "Twelve." And she was to the west. "Thirteen." He didn't know who she was, but he *did* know *what* she was. "Fourteen. Fifteen."

Everything has a price.

The guards dragged him back to his room and locked the door.

Daemon fell heavily onto his hands and knees. Pressing his forehead to the floor, he tried to dull the burning pain in his back, buttocks, and legs long enough to get to his feet. Fifty strokes, each one slicing through his flesh. Fifty strokes. But no more. He hadn't missed the count once, despite the bursts of pain that Cornelia had sent through the Ring of Obedience to distract him.

Slowly gathering his feet under him, he pushed himself to an almost upright position and shuffled to the bathroom, unable to stifle the moaning sob that accompanied each step.

When he finally reached the bathroom, he braced one trembling hand against the wall and turned the water taps to fill the bath with warm water. His vision kept blurring, and his body shook with pain and exhaustion. It took three tries to call in the small leather case that held his stash of healing supplies. Once he had it open, it took a minute for his vision to clear sufficiently to find the jar he wanted.

When combined with water, the powdered herbs cleansed wounds, numbed pain, and allowed the healing process to begin—*if* he could keep his mind fixed enough, and *if* he could withdraw far enough into himself to gather the power, the Craft he would need to heal the torn flesh.

Daemon's lips twisted in a grim smile as he turned off the water. If he sent a summons along the Black, if he asked the Priest for help, would he get it? Unlikely. Not an enemy. Not yet. But Surreal had done well to leave those notes warning him about the Priest.

Daemon let out a cry as the jar slipped from his hands and shattered on the bathroom floor. He sank to his knees, hissing as a piece of glass sliced him, and stared at the powder, tears of pain and frustration welling in his eyes. Without the powder to help heal the wounds, he might still

be able to heal them to some extent, still be able to stop the bleeding . . .
but he would scar. And he didn't need a mirror to know what he would
look like.

No! He wasn't aware of sending. He was only trying to relieve the
frustration.

A minute later, as he knelt on the bathroom floor, shaking, trying not
to vent the sobs building in him, a hand touched his shoulder.

Daemon twisted around, his teeth bared, his eyes wild.

There was no one in the room. The touch was gone. But there was a
presence in the bathroom. Alien . . . and not.

Daemon probed the room and found nothing. But it was still there,
like something seen out of the corner of the eye that vanishes when you
turn to look at it. Breathing hard, Daemon waited.

The touch, when it came again, was hesitant, cautious. He shivered as
it gently probed his back. Shivered because along with exhaustion and
dismay, that gentle touch was filled with a cold, cold anger.

The powdered herbs and broken glass vanished. A moment later a brass
ball, perforated like a tea ball, appeared above the bath and sank into the
water. Small phantom hands, gentle yet strong, helped him into the bath.

Daemon gasped when the open wounds touched the water, but the
hands pushed him down, down, down until he was stretched out on his
back, the water covering him. After a moment he couldn't feel the hands.
Dismayed that the link might be broken, he struggled to rise to a sitting
position only to find himself held down. He relaxed and slowly realized
that his skin felt numb from his chin down, that he no longer felt the pain.
Sighing with gratitude, Daemon leaned his head against the bath and
closed his eyes.

A sweet, strange darkness rolled through him. He moaned, but it was
a moan of pleasure.

Strange how the mind could wander. He could almost smell the sea,
feel the power of the surf. Then there was the rich smell of fresh-turned
earth after a warm spring rain. And the luscious warmth of sunlight on a
soft summer afternoon. The sensual pleasure of slipping naked between
clean sheets.

When he reluctantly opened his eyes, her psychic scent still lingered,
but he knew she was gone. He moved his foot through the now-cold
water. The brass ball was gone too.

Daemon carefully got out of the bath, opened the drain, and swayed on his feet, unsure what to do. Reaching for a towel, he patted the front of his body to absorb most of the water, but he was reluctant to touch the back. Gritting his teeth, he turned his back to the mirror and looked over his shoulder. Best to know how bad the damage was.

Daemon stared.

There were fifty white lines, like chalk lines on his golden-brown skin. The lines looked fragile, and it would take days of being careful before the wounds were truly, strongly knit, but he was healed. If he didn't reopen the wounds, those lines would fade. No scars.

Daemon carefully walked to the bed and lay face down, inching his arms upward until they were under the pillow, supporting his head. It was hard to stay awake, hard not to think about how a meadow looks so silvery in the moonlight. Hard . . .

Someone had been touching his back for some time before he was aware of it. Daemon resisted the urge to open his eyes. There would be nothing to see, and if she knew he was awake, she might pull away.

Her touch was firm, gentle, knowing. It traveled in slow, circular lines down his back. Cool, soothing, comforting.

Where was she? Not nearby, so how was she able to make the reach? He didn't know. He didn't care. He surrendered to the pleasure of that phantom touch, a hand that someday he would hold in the flesh.

When she was gone again, Daemon slowly eased one arm around and gingerly touched his back. He stared at the thick salve on his fingers and then wiped them on the sheet. His eyes closed. There was no point in fighting the sleep he so desperately needed.

But just before he surrendered to need, he thought once more about the kind of witch who would come to a stranger's aid, already exhausted from her own ordeal, and heal his wounds. "Don't get in my way, Priest," he muttered, and fell asleep.

CHAPTER FOUR

1 / Hell

Saetan slammed the book down on the desk and shook with rage. A month since that plea for knowledge. A month of waiting for some word, *some* indication that she was all right. He'd tried to enter Beldon Mor, but Cassandra had been right. The psychic mist surrounding the city was a barrier that only the dead could feel, a barrier that kept them all out. Jaenelle was taking no chances with whatever secret lay behind the mist, and her lack of trust was a blade between his ribs.

Embroiled in his own thoughts, he didn't realize someone else was in the study until he heard his name called a second time.

"Saetan?" Such pain and pleading in that small, weary voice. "Please don't be angry with me."

His vision blurred. His nails dug into the blackwood desk, gouging its stone-hard wood. He wanted to vent all the fear and anger that had been growing in him since he'd last seen her, months ago. He wanted to shake her for daring to ask him to swallow his anger. Instead he took a deep breath, smoothed his face into as neutral a mask as he could create, and turned toward her.

The sight of her made him ill.

She was a skeleton with skin. Her sapphire eyes were sunk into her skull, almost lost in the dark circles beneath them. The golden hair he loved to touch hung limp and dull around her bruised face. There were rope burns and dried blood on her ankles and wrists.

"Come here," he said, all emotion drained from his voice. When she didn't move, he took a step toward her. She flinched and stepped back. His voice became soft thunder. "Jaenelle, come here."

One step. Two. Three. She stared at his feet, shaking.

He didn't touch her. He didn't trust himself to control the jealousy and spite that seared him as he looked at her. She preferred staying with her family and being treated like this over being with him, who loved her with all his being but wasn't entrusted with her care because he was a Guardian, because he was the High Lord of Hell.

Better that she play with the dead than become one of them, he thought bitterly. She wasn't strong enough right now to fight him. He would keep her here for a few days and let her heal. Then he would bring that bastard of a father to his knees and force him to relinquish all paternal rights. He would—

"I can't leave them, Saetan." Jaenelle looked up at him.

The tears sliding down her bruised face twisted his heart, but his face was stone-carved, and he waited in silence.

"There's no one else. Don't you see?"

"No, I don't see." His voice, although controlled and quiet, rumbled through the room. "Or perhaps I do." His cold glance raked her shaking body. "You prefer enduring this and remaining with your family to living with me and what I have to offer."

Jaenelle blinked in surprise. Her eyes lost some of their haunted look, and she became thoughtful. "Live with you? Do you mean it?"

Saetan watched her, puzzled.

Slowly, regretfully, she shook her head. "I can't. I'd like to, but I can't. Not yet. Rose can't do it by herself."

Saetan dropped to one knee and took her frail, almost transparent hands in his. She flinched at his touch but didn't pull away. "It wouldn't have to be in Hell, witch-child," he said soothingly. "I've opened the Hall in Kaeleer. You could live there, maybe attend the same school as your friends."

Jaenelle giggled, her eyes momentarily dancing with amusement. "Schools, High Lord. They live in many places."

He smiled tenderly and bowed his head. "Schools, then. Or private tutors. Anything you wish. I *can* arrange it, witch-child."

Jaenelle's eyes filled with tears as she shook her head. "It would be lovely, it truly would, but . . . not yet. I can't leave them yet."

Saetan bit back the arguments and sighed. She had come to him for comfort, not a fight. And since he couldn't officially serve her until she established a court, he had no right to stand between her and her family, no matter what he felt. "All right. But please remember, you have a place to come to. You don't have to stay with them. But . . . I'd be willing to make the appropriate arrangements for your family to visit or live with you, under my supervision, if that's what you wish."

Jaenelle's eyes widened. "Under your supervision?" she said weakly. She let out a gurgle of laughter and then tried to look stern. "You wouldn't make my sister learn sticks with Prothvar, would you?"

Saetan's voice shook with amusement and unshed tears. "No, I wouldn't make her learn sticks with Prothvar." He carefully drew her into his arms and hugged her frail body. Tears spilled from his closed eyes when her arms circled his neck and tightened. He held her, warmed her, comforted her. When she finally pulled away from him, he stood quickly, wiping the tears from his face.

Jaenelle looked away. "I'll come back as soon as I can."

Nodding, Saetan turned toward the desk, unable to speak. He never heard her move, never heard the door open, but when he turned back to say good-bye, she was already gone.

2 / Terreille

Surreal lay beneath the sweating, grunting man, thrusting her hips in the proper rhythm and moaning sensuously whenever a fat hand squeezed her breasts. She stared at the ceiling while her hands roamed up and down the sweaty back in not-quite-feigned urgency.

Stupid pig, she thought as a slobbering kiss wet her neck. She should have charged more for the contract—and would have if she'd known how unpleasant he would be in bed. But he only had the one shot, and he was almost at his peak.

The spell now. Ah, to weave the spell.

She turned her mind inward, slipped from the calm depths of the Green to the stiller, deeper, more silent Gray, and quickly wove her death spell around him, tying it to the rhythms of the bed, to the quickened heartbeat and raspy breathing.

Practice had made her adept at her Craft.

The last link of the spell was a delay. Not tomorrow, but the day after, or the one after that. Then, whether it was anger or lust that made the heart pound, the spell would burst a vessel in his heart, sear his brain with the strength of the Gray, shatter his Jewel, and leave nothing but carrion behind.

It was an offhand remark Sadi had made once that convinced Surreal to be thorough in her kills. Daemon entertained the possibility that the Blood, being more than flesh, could continue to wear the Jewels after the body's death—and remember who had helped them down the misty road to Hell. He'd said, "No matter what you do with the flesh, finish the kill. After all, who wants to turn a corner one day and meet up with one of the demon-dead who would like to return the favor?"

So she always finished the kill. There would be nothing traceable, nothing that could lead them to her. The Healers that practiced in Terreille now, such as they were, would assume he had burned out his mind and his Jewels trying to save his body from the physical death.

Surreal came out of her reverie as the grunts and thrusts increased for a moment. Then he sagged. She turned her head, trying not to breathe the enhanced odor of his unwashed body.

When he finally lay on his back, snoring, Surreal slipped out of bed, pulled on a silk robe, and wrinkled her nose. The robe would have to be cleaned before she could wear it again. Hooking her hair behind her ears, she went to the window and pulled the curtain aside.

She had to decide where to go now that this contract was done. She should have made the decision days ago, but she'd kept hesitating because of the recurring dreams that washed over her mind like surf over a beach. Dreams about Titian and Titian's Jewel. Dreams about needing to be someplace, about being *needed* someplace.

Except Titian couldn't tell her where.

Maybe there were just too many lights in this old, decrepit city. Maybe she couldn't decide because she couldn't see the stars.

Stars. And the sea. Someplace clean, where she could take a light schedule and spend her days reading or walking by the sea.

Surreal smiled. It had been three years since she'd last spent time with Dejé. Chaillot had some beautiful, quiet beaches on the east side. On a clear day, you could even see Tacea Island. And there was a Sanctuary

nearby, wasn't there? Or some kind of ancient ruin. Picnic lunches, long
solitary walks. Deje would be happy to see her, wouldn't push to fill every
night.

Yes. Chaillot.

Surreal turned from the window when the man grunted and thrashed
onto his side. The Sadist was right. There were so many ways to efficiently
kill a man other than splattering his blood over the walls.

It was too bad they didn't give her as much pleasure.

3 / Terreille

Lucivar Yaslana listened to the embroidered half-truths Zuultah was
spewing about him to a circle of nervous, wide-eyed witches and wondered if snapping a few female necks would add color to the stories. Reluctantly putting aside that pleasant fantasy, he scanned the crowded room
for some diversion.

Daemon Sadi glided past him.

Lucivar sucked in his breath, suppressed a grin, and turned back to Zuultah's circle. The last time the Queens had gotten careless about keeping
them separated, he and Daemon had destroyed a court during a fight that
escalated from a disagreement over whether the wine being served was
just mediocre or was really colored horse piss.

Forty years ago. Enough time among the short-lived races for the
randy young Queens to convince themselves that they could control him
and Daemon or, even better, that they were the Queens strong-willed
enough and wonderful enough to tame two dark-Jeweled Warlord
Princes. Well, this Eyrien Warlord Prince wasn't tameable—at least, not for
another five years. As for the Sadist . . . Any man who referred to his bedroom skills as poisoned honey wasn't likely to be tamed or controlled unless he chose to be.

It was late in the evening before Lucivar got the chance to slip out to
the back garden. Daemon had gone out a few minutes before, after an
abrupt, snarling disagreement with Lady Cornelia.

Moving with a hunter's caution, Lucivar followed the ribbon of
chilled air left by Daemon's passing. He turned a corner and stopped.

Daemon stood in the middle of the gravel path, his face raised to the night sky while the delicate breeze riffled his black hair.

The gravel under Lucivar's feet shifted slightly.

Daemon turned toward the sound.

Lucivar hesitated. He knew what that sleepy, glazed look in Daemon's eyes meant, remembered only too well what had happened in courts when that tender, murderous smile had lasted for more than a brief second. Nothing, and no one, was safe when Daemon was in this mood. But, Hell's fire, that's what made dancing with the Sadist fun.

Smiling his own lazy, arrogant smile, Lucivar stepped forward and slowly stretched his dark wings their full span before tucking them tight to his body. "Hello, Bastard."

Daemon's smile thawed. "Hello, Prick. It's been a long time."

"So it has. Drunk any good wines lately?"

"None that you'd appreciate." Daemon studied Lucivar's clothes and raised an eyebrow. "You've decided to be a good boy?"

Lucivar snorted. "I decided I wanted decent food and a decent bed for a change and a few days out of Pruul, and all I have to do is lick the bottom of Zuultah's boots when she returns from the stable."

"Maybe that's your trouble, Prick. You're not supposed to lick her boots, you're supposed to kiss her ass." He turned and glided down the path.

Remembering why he'd wanted to talk to Daemon, Lucivar followed reluctantly until they reached a gazebo tucked in one corner of the garden where they couldn't be seen from the mansion. Daemon smiled that cold, sweet smile and stepped aside to let him enter first.

Never let a predator smell fear.

Annoyed by his own uneasiness, Lucivar turned to study the luminescent leaves of the firebush nearby. He stiffened when Daemon came up behind him, when the long nails whispered over his shoulders, teasing his skin in a loverlike fashion.

"Do you want me?" Daemon whispered, brushing his lips against Lucivar's neck.

Lucivar snorted and tried to pull away, but the caressing hand instantly became a vice. "No," he said flatly. "I endured enough of that in Eyrien hunting camps." With a teeth-baring grin, he turned around. "Do you really think your touch makes my pulse race?"

"Doesn't it?" Daemon whispered, a strange look in his eyes.

Lucivar stared. Daemon's voice was too crooning, too silky, too dangerously sleepy. Hell's fire, Lucivar thought desperately as Daemon's lips brushed his, what was *wrong* with him? This wasn't his kind of game.

Lucivar jerked back. Daemon's nails dug into the back of his neck. The sharp thumbnails pricked his throat. Keeping his fists pressed against his thighs, Lucivar closed his eyes and submitted to the kiss.

No reason to feel humiliation and shame. His body was responding to stimulation the same way it would to cold or hunger. Physical response had nothing to do with feelings or desire. Nothing.

But, Mother Night, Daemon could set a stone on fire!

"Why are you doing this?" Lucivar gasped. "At least tell me why."

"Why not?" Daemon replied bitterly. "I have to whore for everyone else, why not you?"

"Because I don't want you to. Because you don't want to. Daemon, this is madness! Why are you doing this?"

Daemon pressed his forehead against Lucivar's. "Since you already know the answer, why ask me?" He kneaded Lucivar's shoulders. "I can't stand being touched by them anymore. Ever since . . . I can't stand the feel of them, the smell of them, the taste of them. They've raped everything I am until there's nothing clean left to offer."

Lucivar wrapped his hands around Daemon's wrists. The shame and bitterness saturating Daemon's psychic scent scraped a nerve he had refused to probe over the past five years. Once she was old enough to understand what it meant, *would* that sapphire-eyed little cat despise them for the way they'd been forced to serve? It wouldn't matter. He would fight with everything in him for the chance to serve her. And so would Daemon. "Daemon." He took a deep breath. "Daemon, she's come."

Daemon pulled away. "I know. I've felt her." He stuffed his shaking hands into his trouser pockets. "There's trouble around her—"

"What trouble?" Lucivar asked sharply.

"—and I keep wondering if he can—if he *will*—protect her."

"Who? *Daemon!*"

Daemon dropped to the floor, clutching his groin and moaning.

Swearing under his breath, Lucivar wrapped his arms around Daemon and waited. Nothing else could be done for a man enduring a bolt of pain sent through the Ring of Obedience.

By the time it was over and Daemon got to his feet, his beautiful, aristocratic face had hardened into a cold, pain-glazed mask and his voice was empty of emotion. "It seems Lady Cornelia requires my presence." He flicked a twig off his jacket sleeve. "You'd think she would know better by now." He hesitated before he left the gazebo. "Take care, Prick."

Lucivar leaned against the gazebo long after Daemon's footsteps had faded away. What had happened between Daemon and the girl? And what did "Take care, Prick" mean? A warm farewell . . . or a warning?

"Daemon?" Lucivar whispered, remembering another place and another court. "Daemon, no." He ran toward the mansion. *"Daemon!"*

Lucivar charged through the open glass doors and shoved his way through gossiping knots of women, briefly aware of Zuultah's angry face in front of him. He was halfway up the stairs leading to the guest rooms when a bolt of pain from the Ring of Obedience brought him to his knees. Zuultah stood beside him, her face twisted with fury. Lucivar tried to get to his feet, but another surge from the Ring bent him over so far his forehead pressed against the stairs.

"Let me go, Zuultah." His voice cracked from the pain.

"I'll teach you some manners, you arrogant—"

Lucivar twisted around to face her. "Let me go, you stupid bitch," he hissed. "Let me go before it's too late."

It took her a long minute to understand she wasn't what he feared, and another long minute before he could get to his feet.

With one hand pressed to his groin, Lucivar hauled himself up the stairs and pushed himself into a stumbling run toward the guest wing. There was no time to think about the crowd growing behind him, no time to think about anything except reaching Cornelia's room before . . .

Daemon opened Cornelia's door, closed it behind him, calmly tugged his shirt cuffs into place, and then smashed his fist into the wall.

Lucivar felt the mansion shudder as the power of the Black Jewel surged into the wall.

Cracks appeared in the wall, running in every direction, opening wider and wider.

"Daemon?"

Daemon tugged his shirt cuffs down once more. When he finally looked at Lucivar, his eyes were as cold and glazed as a murky gemstone—and no more human.

Daemon smiled.

Lucivar shivered.

"Run," Daemon crooned. Seeing the crowd filling the hall behind Lucivar, he calmly turned and walked the other way.

The mansion continued to shudder. Something crashed nearby.

Licking his lips, Lucivar opened Cornelia's door. He stared at the bed, at what was on the bed, and fought to control his heaving guts. He turned away from the open door and stood there, too numb to move.

He smelled smoke, heard the roar of flames consuming a room. People screamed. The mansion walls rumbled as they split farther and farther. He looked around, confused, until part of the ceiling crashed a few feet away from him.

Fear cleared his head, and he did the only sensible thing.

He ran.

4 / Terreille

Dorothea SaDiablo, the High Priestess of Hayll, paced the length of her sitting room, the floor-length cocoon she wore over a simple dark dress billowing out behind her. She tapped her fingertips together, over and over, absently noting that her cousin Hepsabah grew more agitated as the silence and pacing continued.

Hepsabah squirmed in her chair. "You're not really bringing him back *here*?" Her voice squeaked with her growing panic. She tried to keep her hands still because Dorothea found her nervous gestures annoying, but the hands were like wing-clipped birds fluttering hopelessly in her lap.

Dorothea shot a dagger glance in Hepsabah's direction and continued pacing. "Where else can I send him?" she snapped. "It may be *years* before anyone is willing to sign a contract for him. And with the stories flying, I may not be able to even make a present of the bastard. With so much of that place burned beyond recognition . . . and Cornelia's room untouched. Too many people saw what was in that bed. There's been too much talk."

"But . . . he's not there, and he's not here. Where is he?"

"Hell's fire, how should I know. Nearby. Skulking somewhere. Maybe twisting a few other witches into shattered bones and pulped flesh."

"You could summon him with the Ring."

Dorothea stopped pacing and stared at her cousin through narrowed eyes. Their mothers had been sisters. The bloodline was good on that side. And the consort who'd sired Hepsabah had shown potential. How could two of Hayll's Hundred Families have produced such a simpering idiot? Unless her dear aunt had seeded herself with a piece of gutter trash. To think Hepsabah was the best she had to work with to try to keep some rein on him. That had been a mistake. Maybe she should have let that mad Dhemlan bitch keep him. No. There were other problems with that. The Dark Priestess had warned her. As much good as it did.

Dorothea smiled at Hepsabah, pleased to see her cousin shrink farther into the chair. "So you think I should summon him? Use the Ring when the debris in that place is barely cooled? Are *you* willing to be the one to welcome him home if I bring him back that way?"

Hepsabah's smooth, carefully painted face crumpled with fear. "Me?" she wailed. "You wouldn't make me do that. You *can't* make me do that. He doesn't *like* me."

"But you're his *mother*, dear," Dorothea purred.

"But you know . . . you know . . ."

"Yes, I know." Dorothea continued pacing, but slower. "So. He's in Hayll. He signed in this morning at one of the posting stations. He'll be here soon enough. Let him have a day or two to vent his rage on someone else. In the meantime, I'll have to arrange a bit of educational entertainment. And I'll have to think about what to do with him. The Hayllian trash and the landens don't understand what he is. They *like* him. They think that pittance generosity he shows them is the way he is. I should have preserved the image of Cornelia's bedroom in a spelled crystal and shown them what he's really like. No matter. He won't stay long. I'll find *someone* foolish enough to take him."

Hepsabah got to her feet, smoothed her gold dress over her padded, well-curved body, and patted her coiled black hair. "Well. I should go and see that his room is ready." She let out a tittering laugh behind her hand. "That's a mother's duty."

"Don't rub against his bedpost too much, dear. You know how he hates the scent of a woman's musk."

Hepsabah blinked, swallowed hard. "I never," she sputtered indignantly, and instantly began to pout. "It's just not fair."

Dorothea tucked a stray hair back into Hepsabah's elegant coils. "When you start getting thoughts like that, dear, remember Cornelia."

Hepsabah's brown skin turned gray. "Yes," she murmured as Dorothea led her to the door. "Yes, I'll remember."

5 / Terreille

Daemon glided down the crowded sidewalk, his ground-eating stride never breaking as people around him skittered out of his way, filling back in as he passed. He didn't see them, didn't hear the murmuring voices. With his hands in his trouser pockets, he glided through the crowds and the noise, unaware and uncaring.

He was in Draega, Hayll's capital city.

He was home.

He'd never liked Draega, never liked the tall stone buildings that shouldered against one another, blocking out the sun, never liked the concrete roads and the concrete sidewalks with the stunted, dusty trees growing out of circular patches of earth cut out of the concrete. Oh, there were a thousand things to do here: theaters, music halls, museums, places to dine. All the things a long-lived, arrogant, useless people needed to fill the empty hours. But Draega . . . If he could be sure that two particular witches would lie crushed and buried in the rubble, he would tear the city apart without a second thought.

He swung into the street, weaving his way between the carriages that came to a stuttering halt, oblivious of their irate drivers. One or two passengers thrust their heads through a side window to shout at him, but when they saw his face and realized who he was, they hastily pulled their heads back in, hoping he hadn't noticed them.

Since he'd arrived that morning, he'd been following a psychic thread that tugged him toward an unknown destination. He wasn't troubled by the pull. Its chaotic meandering told him who was at the other end. He didn't know why she was in Draega of all places, but her need to see him was strong enough to pull him toward her.

Daemon entered the large park in the center of the city, veered to the footpath leading to the southern end, and slowed his pace. Here among the trees and grass, with the street sounds muted, he breathed a little easier. He crossed a footbridge that spanned a trickling creek, hesitated for a moment, then took the right-hand fork in the path that led farther into the park.

Finally he came to a small oval of grass. A lacy iron bench filled the back of the oval. A half-circle of lady's tears formed a backdrop, the small, white-throated blue flowers filling the bushes. Two old, tall trees stood at either end of the oval, their branches intertwining high above, letting a dappling of sunlight reach the ground.

The tugging stopped.

Daemon stood in the oval of grass, slowly turning full circle. He started to turn away when a low giggle came from the bushes.

"How many sides does a triangle have?" a woman's husky voice asked.

Daemon sighed and shook his head. It was going to be riddles.

"How many sides does a triangle have?" the voice asked again.

"Three," Daemon answered.

The bushes parted. Tersa shook the leaves from her tattered coat and pushed her tangled black hair from her face. "Foolish boy, did they teach you nothing?"

Daemon's smile was gentle and amused. "Apparently not."

"Give Tersa a kiss."

Resting his hands on her thin shoulders, Daemon lightly kissed her cheek. He wondered when she'd eaten last but decided not to ask. She seldom knew or cared, and asking would only make her unhappy.

"How many sides does a triangle have?"

Daemon sighed, resigned. "Darling, a triangle has three sides."

Tersa scowled. "Stupid boy. Give me your hand."

Daemon obediently held out his right hand. Tersa grasped the long, slender fingers with her own frail-looking sticks and turned his hand palm up. With the forefinger nail of her right hand, she began tracing three connecting lines on his palm, over and over again. "A Blood triangle has four sides, foolish boy. Like the candelabra on a Dark Altar. Remember that." Over and over until the lines began to glow white on his golden-brown palm. "Father, brother, lover. Father, brother, lover. The father came first."

"He usually does," Daemon said dryly.

She ignored him. "Father, brother, lover. The lover is the father's mirror. The brother stands between." She stopped tracing and looked up at him. It was one of those times when Tersa's eyes were clear and focused, yet she was looking at some place other than where her body stood. "How many sides does a triangle have?"

Daemon studied the three white lines on his palm. "Three."

Tersa drew in her breath, exasperated.

"Where's the fourth side?" he asked quickly, hoping to avoid hearing the question again.

Tersa snapped her thumb and forefinger nail together, then pressed the knife-sharp forefinger nail into the center of the triangle in Daemon's palm. Daemon hissed when her nail cut his skin. He jerked his hand back, but her fingers held him in a grip that hurt.

Daemon watched the blood well in the hollow of his palm. Still holding his fingers in an iron grip, Tersa slowly raised his hand toward his face. The world became fuzzy, unfocused, mist-shrouded. The only painfully clear thing Daemon could see was his hand, a white triangle, and the bright, glistening blood.

Tersa's voice was a singsong croon. "Father, brother, lover. And the center, the fourth side, the one who rules all three."

Daemon closed his eyes as Tersa raised his hand to his lips. The air was too hot, too close. Daemon's lips parted. He licked the blood from his palm.

It sizzled on his tongue, red lightning. It seared his nerves, crackled through him and gathered in his belly, gathered into a white-hot ember waiting for a breath, a single touch that would turn his kindled maleness into an inferno. His hand closed in a fist and he swayed, clenching his teeth to keep from begging for that touch.

When he opened his eyes, the oval of grass was empty. He slowly opened his hand. The lines were already fading, the small cut healed.

"Tersa?"

Her voice came back to him, distant and fading. "The lover is the father's mirror. The Priest . . . He will be your best ally or your worst enemy. But the choice will be yours."

"Tersa!"

Almost gone. "The chalice is cracking."

"*Tersa!*"

A surge of rage honed by terror rushed through him. Closing his hand, he swung his arm straight and shoulder-high. The shock of his fist connecting with one of the trees jarred him to his heels. Daemon leaned against the tree, eyes closed, forehead pressed to the trunk.

When he opened his eyes, his black coat was covered with gray-green ashes. Frowning, Daemon looked up. A denial caught in his throat, strangling him. He stepped back from the tree and sat down on the bench, his face hidden in his hands.

Several minutes later, he forced himself to look at the tree.

It was dead, burned from within by his fury. Standing among the green living things, its gray skeletal branches still reached for its partner. Daemon walked over to the tree and pressed his palm against the trunk. He didn't know if there was a way to probe it to see if sap still ran at its core, or if it had all been crystallized by the heat of his rage.

"I'm sorry," he whispered. Gray-green dust continued to fall from the upper branches. A few minutes ago, that dust had been living green leaves. "I'm sorry."

Taking a deep breath, Daemon followed the path back the way he'd come, hands in his pockets, head down, shoulders slumped. Just before leaving the park, he turned around and looked back. He couldn't see the tree, but he could feel it. He shook his head slowly, a grim smile on his lips. He'd buried more of the Blood than they would ever guess, and he mourned a tree.

Daemon brushed the ash from his coat. He'd have to report to Dorothea soon, tomorrow at the latest. There were two more stops he wanted to make before presenting himself at court.

6 / Terreille

"Honey, what've you been doing to yourself? You're nothing but skin and bones."

Surreal slumped against the reception desk, grimaced, and sucked in her breath. "Nothing, Deje. I'm just worn out."

"You been letting those men make a meal out of you?" Deje looked at her shrewdly. "Or is it your other business that's run you down?"

Surreal's gold-green eyes were dangerously blank. "What business is that, Deje?"

"I'm not a fool, honey," Deje said slowly. "I've always known you don't really like this business. But you're still the best there is."

"The best female," Surreal replied, wearily hooking her long black hair behind her pointed ears.

Deje put her hands on the counter and leaned toward Surreal, worried. "Nobody paid you to dance with . . . Well, you know how fast gossip can fly, and there was talk of some trouble."

"I wasn't part of it, thank the Darkness."

Deje sighed. "I'm glad. That one's demon-born for sure."

"If he isn't, he should be."

"You know the Sadist?" Deje asked, her eyes sharp.

"We're acquainted," Surreal said reluctantly.

Deje hesitated. "Is he as good as they say?"

Surreal shuddered. "Don't ask."

Deje looked startled but quickly regained her professional manner. "No matter. None of my business anyway." Coming around the desk, she put an arm around Surreal's shoulders and led her down the hall. "A garden room, I think. You can sit out quietly in the evening, eat your meals in your room if you choose. If anyone notices you're here and makes a request for your company, I'll tell them it's your moontime and you need your rest. Most of them wouldn't know the difference."

Surreal gave Deje a shaky grin. "Well, it's the truth."

Deje shook her head and clucked her tongue in annoyance as she opened the door and led Surreal into the room. "Sometimes you've no more sense than a first-year chit, pushing yourself at a time when the Jewels will squeeze you dry if you try to tap into them." She muttered to herself as she pulled down the bedcovers and plumped the pillows. "Get into a nice comfy nightie—not one of those sleek things—and get into bed. We've got a hearty soup tonight. You'll have that. And I've got some new novels in the library, nice fluff reading. I'll bring a few of them; you can take your pick. And—"

"Deje, you should've been someone's mother," Surreal laughed.

Deje put her hands on her ample hips and tried to look offended. "A fine thing to say to someone in my business." She made a shooing motion with her hands. "Into bed and not another word from you. Honey? Honey, what's wrong?"

Surreal sank onto the bed, tears rolling silently down her cheeks. "I can't sleep, Deje. I have dreams that I'm supposed to be somewhere, do something. But I don't know where or what it is."

Deje sat on the bed and wiped the tears from Surreal's face. "They're only dreams, honey. Yes, they are. You're just worn out."

"I'm scared, Deje," Surreal whispered. "There's something really wrong with him. I can feel it. Once I started running, hoping I was going in the opposite direction, that whole damn continent wasn't big enough. I need a clean place for a while." Surreal looked at Deje, her large eyes full of ghosts. "I need time."

Deje stroked Surreal's hair. "Sure, honey, sure. You take all the time you need. Nobody's going to push you in my house. Come on now, get into bed. I'll bring you something to eat and a little something to help you sleep." She gave Surreal a quick kiss on the forehead and hurried out of the room.

Surreal put on an old, soft nightgown and climbed into bed. It was good to be back at Deje's house, good to be back in Chaillot. Now if only the Sadist would stay away, maybe she could get some sleep.

7 / Terreille

Daemon knocked on the kitchen door.

Inside, the spright little tune someone was singing stopped.

Waiting for the door to open, Daemon looked around, pleased to see that the snug little cottage was in good repair. The lawn and flower beds were neatly tended. The summer crop in the vegetable garden was almost done, but the healthy vines at one end promised a good crop of pumpkins and winter squash.

Still too early for pumpkins. Daemon sighed with regret while his mouth watered at the memory of Manny's pumpkin tarts.

At the back of the yard were two sheds. The smaller one probably contained gardening tools. The larger one was Jo's woodshop. The old man was probably tucked away in there coaxing an elegant little table out of pieces of wood, oblivious to everything except his work.

The kitchen door remained closed. The silence continued.

Concerned, Daemon opened the door enough to slip his head and shoulders inside and look around.

Manny stood by her worktable, one floury hand pressed to her bosom.

Damn. He should have realized a Warlord Prince's appearance would frighten her. He'd changed enough since he'd last seen her that she might not recognize his psychic scent.

Putting on his best smile, he said, "Darling, if you're going to pretend you're not home, the least you can do is close the windows. The smell of those nutcakes will draw the most unsavory characters."

Manny gave a cry of relief and joy, hustled around the worktable, and shuffle-ran toward the door, her floury hands waving cheerfully in front of her. "Daemon!"

Daemon stepped into the kitchen, slid one arm around the woman's thick waist, and twirled her around.

Manny laughed and flapped her arms. "Put me down. I'm getting flour all over your nice coat."

"I don't care about the coat." He kissed her cheek and set her carefully on her feet. With a bow and a flourish of his wrist, he presented her with a bouquet of flowers. "For my favorite lady."

Misty-eyed, Manny bent her head to smell the flowers. "I'll put these in some water." She bustled around the kitchen, filled a vase, and spent several minutes arranging the flowers. "You go into the parlor and I'll bring out some nutcakes and tea."

Manny and Jo had been servants in the SaDiablo court when he was growing up. Manny had taken care of him, practically raised him. And the darling was still trying.

Hiding a smile, Daemon stuffed his hands in his pockets and scuffed his gleaming black shoe against the kitchen floor. He looked at her through his long black lashes. "What'd I do?" he said in a sad, slightly pouty, little-boy voice. "What'd I do not to deserve a chair in the kitchen anymore?"

Trying to sound exasperated, Manny only laughed. "No use trying to raise you proper. Sit down, then, and behave yourself."

Daemon laughed, lighthearted and boyish, and plunked himself gracelessly into one of the kitchen chairs. Manny pulled out plates and cups. "Although why you want to stay in the kitchen is beyond me."

"The kitchen is where the food is."

"Guess there's some things boys never grow out of. Here." Manny set a glass in front of him.

Daemon looked at the glass, then looked at her.

"It's milk," she added.

"I did recognize it," he said dryly.

"Good. Then drink it." She folded her arms and tapped her foot. "No milk, no nutcakes."

"You always were a martinet," Daemon muttered. He picked up the glass, grimaced, and drank it down. He handed her the glass, giving her his best boyish smile. "Now may I have a nutcake?"

Manny laughed, shaking her head. "You're impossible." She put the kettle on for tea and began transferring the nutcakes to a platter. "What brings you here?"

"I came to see you." Daemon crossed his legs and steepled his fingers, resting them lightly on his chin.

She glanced up, gasped, and then busily rearranged the cakes.

Puzzled by the stunned look on her face, Daemon watched her rearrange everything twice. Searching for a neutral topic, he said, "The place looks good. Keeping it up isn't too much work for you?"

"The young people in the village help out," Manny said mildly.

Daemon frowned. "Aren't there sufficient funds for a handyman and cleaning woman?"

"Sure there are, but why would I want some other grown woman clumping about my house, telling me how to polish my furniture?" She grinned slyly. "Besides, the girls are willing to help with the heavy work in exchange for pocket money, a few of my special recipes, and a chance to flirt with the boys without their parents standing around watching them. And the boys are willing to help with the outside work in exchange for pocket money, food, and an excuse to strip off their shirts and show their muscles to the girls."

Daemon's laughter filled the kitchen. "Manny, you've become the village matchmaker."

Manny smiled smugly. "Jo's working on a cradle right now for one of the young couples."

"I hope there was a wedding beforehand."

"Of course," Manny said indignantly. She thumped the platter of nutcakes in front of him. "Shame on you, teasing an old woman."

"Do I still get nutcakes?" he asked contritely.

She ruffled his hair in answer and took the kettle off the stove.

Daemon stared into space. So many questions, and no answers.

"You're troubled," Manny said, filling the tea ball.

Daemon shook himself. "I'm looking for information that may be hard to find. A friend told me to beware of the Priest."

Manny slipped the tea ball into the pot to steep. "Huh. Anyone with a lick of sense takes care around the Priest."

Daemon stared at her. She knew the Priest. Were the answers really this close? "Manny, sit down for a moment."

Manny ignored him and hurriedly slid the cups onto the table, keeping out of his reach. "The tea's ready now. I'll call Jo—"

"Who is the Priest?"

"—he'll be glad to see you."

Daemon uncoiled from the chair, clamped one hand around her wrist, and pulled her into the other chair. Manny stared at his hand, at the ring finger that wore no Jeweled ring, at the long, black-tinted nails.

"Who is the Priest?"

"You mustn't talk about him. You must never talk about him."

"Who is the Priest?" His voice became dangerously soft.

"The tea," she said weakly.

Daemon poured two cups of tea. Returning to the table, he crossed his legs and steepled his fingers. "Now."

Manny lifted the cup to her lips but found the tea too hot to drink. She set the cup down again, fussing with its handle until it was exactly parallel to the edge of the table. Finally she dropped her hands in her lap and sighed.

"They never should have taken you away from him," she said quietly, looking at memories. "They never should have broken the contract. The Hourglass coven in Hayll has been failing since then, just like he said it would. No one breaks a contract with the Priest and survives.

"You were supposed to go to him for good that day, the day you got your Birthright Jewel. You were so proud that he was going to be there, even though the Birthright Ceremony was in the afternoon instead of evening like it usually is. They planned it that way, planned to make him come in the harshest light of day, when his strength would be at its lowest.

"After you had your Birthright Red Jewel and were standing with your mother and Dorothea and all of Dorothea's escorts, waiting for the okay to walk out of the ceremonial circle to where he was waiting and kneel to him in service . . . that's when that woman, that cruel, scheming woman said you belonged to the Hourglass, that paternity was denied, that he couldn't have sired you, that she'd had her guards service the Dhemlan witch afterward to ensure she was seeded. It was a warm afternoon, but it got so cold, so awfully cold. Dorothea had all the Hourglass covens there, dozens and dozens of Black Widows, watching him, waiting for him to walk into the circle and break honor with them.

"But he didn't. He turned away.

"You almost broke free. Almost reached him. You were crying, screaming for him to wait for you, fighting the two guards who were holding your arms, your fingers clenched around that Jewel. There was a flash of Red light, and the guards were flung backward. You hurled yourself forward, trying to reach the edge of the circle. He turned, waiting. One of the guards tackled you. You were only a handspan away from the edge. I think if so much as a finger had crossed that circle, he would have swept you away with him, wouldn't have worried anymore if it was good for you to live with him, or to live without your people.

"You didn't make it. You were too young, and they were too strong.

"So he left. Went to that house you keep visiting, the house you and your mother lived in, and destroyed the study. Tore the books apart, shredded the curtains, broke every piece of furniture in the room. He couldn't get the rage out. When I finally dared open the door, he was kneeling in the middle of the room, his chest heaving, trying to get some air, a crazy look in his eyes.

"He finally got up and made me promise to look after you and your mother, to do the best I could. And I promised because I cared about you and her, and because he'd always been kind to me and Jo.

"After that, he disappeared. They took your Red Jewel and put the Ring of Obedience on you that night. You wouldn't eat. They told me I had to make you eat. They had plans for you and you weren't going to waste away. They locked Jo up in a metal box, put him out where there wasn't any shade and said he'd get food and water when I got you to eat. When I got you to eat two days in a row, they'd let him out.

"For three days you wouldn't eat, no matter how I begged. I don't think you heard me at all during those days. I was desperate. At night, when I'd go out and stand as close to the box as I was allowed, I'd hear Jo whimpering, his skin all blistered from touching that hot metal. So I did something bad to you. I dragged you out one morning and made you look at that box. I told you you were killing my man out of spite, that he was being punished because you were a bad boy and wouldn't eat, and if he died I would hate you forever and ever.

"I didn't know Dorothea had run your mother off. I didn't know I was all you had left. But you knew. You felt her go.

"You did what I said. You ate when I told you, slept when I told you. You were more a ghost than a child. But they let Jo out."

Manny wiped the tears from her face with the edge of her apron. She took a sip of cold tea.

Daemon closed his eyes. Before coming here, he'd gone to that crumbling, abandoned house he'd once lived in, searching for answers as he did every time he was in this part of the Realm. Memories, so elusive and traitorous, always teased him when he walked through the rooms. But it was the wrecked study that really drew him back, the room where he could almost hear a deep, powerful voice like soft thunder, where he could almost smell a sharp, spicy, masculine scent, where he could almost feel strong arms around him, where he could almost believe he had once been safe, protected, and loved.

And now he finally knew why.

Daemon slipped his hand over Manny's and squeezed gently. "You've told me this much, tell me the rest."

Manny shook her head. "They did something so you would forget him. They said if you ever found out about him, they'd kill you." She looked at him, pleading. "I couldn't let them kill you. You were the boy Jo and I couldn't have."

A door in his mind that he'd never known existed began to open.

"I'm not a boy anymore, Manny," Daemon said quietly, "and I won't be killed that easily." He made another pot of tea, put a fresh cup in front of her, and settled back in his chair. "What was . . . is his name?"

"He has many names," Manny whispered, staring at her cup.

"Manny." Daemon fought for patience.

"They call him the Seducer. The Executioner."

He shook his head, still not understanding. But the door opened a little wider.

"He's the High Priest of the Hourglass."

A little wider.

"You're stalling," Daemon snapped, clattering the cup against the saucer. "What's my father's name? You owe me that. You know what it's been like for me being a bastard. Did he ever sign the register?"

"Oh, yes," she said hurriedly. "But they changed that page. He was so proud of you and the Eyrien boy. He didn't know, you know, about the girl being Eyrien. Luthvian, that was her name. She didn't have wings or scars where wings were removed. He didn't know until the boy was born. She wanted to cut the wings off, raise the boy as Dhemlan maybe. But he said no, in his soul the boy was Eyrien, and it would be kinder to kill him in the cradle than to cut his wings. She cried at that, scared that he really would kill the babe. I think he would have if she'd ever done anything that might have damaged the wings. He built her a snug little cottage in Askavi, took care of her and the boy. He would bring him to visit sometimes. You'd play together . . . or fight together. It was hard to tell which. Then she got scared. She told me Prythian, Askavi's High Priestess, told her he only wanted the boy for fodder, wanted a supply of fresh blood to sup on. So she gave the boy to Prythian to hide, and ran away. When she went back for him, Prythian wouldn't tell her where he was, just laughed at her, and—"

"Manny," Daemon said in a soft, cold voice. "For the last time, who is my father?"

"The Prince of the Darkness."

A little wider.

"Manny."

"The Priest is the High Lord, don't you understand?" Manny cried.

"His name."

"No."

"His name, Manny."

"To whisper the name is to summon the man."

The door blew open and the memories poured out.

Daemon stared at his hands, stared at the long, black-tinted nails.

Mother Night.

He swallowed hard and shook his head. It wasn't possible. As much as he would like to believe it, it wasn't possible. "Saetan," he said quietly. "You're telling me my father is Saetan?"

"Hush, Daemon, hush."

Daemon leaped up, knocking the chair over. "No, I will not hush. He's dead, Manny. A legend. An ancestor far removed."

"Your father."

"He's *dead.*"

Manny licked her lips and closed her eyes. "One of the living dead. One of the ones called Guardians."

Daemon righted the chair and sat down. He felt ill. No wonder Dorothea used to beat him when he would nurse the hurt of being excluded by pretending that Saetan was his father. It hadn't been pretend after all. "Are you sure?" he asked finally.

"I'm sure."

Daemon laughed harshly. "You're mistaken, Manny. You must be. I can't imagine the High Lord of Hell bedding that bitch Hepsabah."

Manny squirmed.

Memories kept pouring over him, puzzle pieces floating into place.

"Not Hepsabah," he said slowly, feeling crushed by the magnitude of the lies that had made up his life. No, not Hepsabah. A Dhemlan witch . . . who'd been driven out of the court. "Tersa." He braced his head in his hands. "Who else could it be but Tersa."

Manny reached toward him but didn't touch him. "Now you know."

Daemon's hands shook as he lit a black cigarette. He watched the smoke curl and rise, too weary to do anything else. "Now I know." He closed his eyes and whispered, "My best ally or my worst enemy. And the choice will be mine. Sweet Darkness, why did it have to be him?"

"Daemon?"

He shook his head and tried to smile reassuringly.

He spent another hour with Manny and Jo, who had finally come in from the woodshop. He entertained them with slightly risqué stories about the Blood aristos he'd served in various courts and told them nothing about his life. It would hurt him beyond healing if Manny ever thought of him as Hayll's Whore.

When he finally left, he walked for hours. He couldn't stop shaking. The pain of a lifetime of lies grew with each step until his rage threatened to tear apart what was left of his self-restraint.

It was dawn when he caught the Red Wind and rode to Draega.

For the first time in his life, he wanted to see Dorothea.

CHAPTER FIVE

1 / Terreille

As Kartane SaDiablo walked from his suite to the audience rooms, he wondered if he'd fortified himself with one glass of brandy too many before appearing before his mother and making a formal return to her court. If not, the whole damn court was acting queer. The Blood aristos scurried through the halls, eyes darting ahead and behind them as they traveled in tight little clusters. The males in the court usually acted like that, jostling and shoving until one of them was pushed to the front and offered as the sacrifice. Being the object of Dorothea's attention, whether she was pleased with a man or angry, was always an unpleasant experience. But for the women to act that way as well . . .

When he saw a servant actually smile, he finally understood.

By then it was too late.

He felt the cold as he swung around a corner and skidded to a stop in front of Daemon. He'd stopped trying long ago to understand his feelings whenever he saw Daemon—relief, fear, anger, envy, shame. Now he simply wondered if Daemon was finally going to kill him.

Kartane retreated to the one emotional gambit he had left. He pulled his lips into a sneering smile and said, "Hello, *cousin*."

"Kartane." Daemon's toneless court voice, laced with boredom.

"So you've been called back to court. Was Aunt Hepsabah getting lonely?" That's it. Remind him of what he is.

"Was Dorothea?"

Kartane tried to keep the insolence in his voice, tried to keep the sneer, tried not to remember all the things he couldn't forget.

"I was about to report to Dorothea," Daemon said mildly, "but I can delay it for a few more minutes. If you have to see her, why don't you go ahead. She's never in the best of moods after she's seen me."

Kartane felt as if he'd been slapped. Daemon hated him, had hated him for centuries for what he'd said, for the things he'd done. But Daemon remembered, too, and because he remembered, he would still extend this much courtesy and compassion toward his younger cousin.

Not daring to speak, Kartane nodded and hurried down the hall.

He didn't go directly to the audience room where Dorothea waited. Instead, he flung himself into the first empty room he could find. Leaning against the locked door, he felt tears burn his eyes and trickle down his cheeks as he whispered, "Daemon."

Daemon was the cousin whose position within the family had never quite been explained to the child Kartane except that it was tenuous and different from his own. Kartane had been Dorothea's spoiled, privileged only child, with a handful of servants, tutors, and governesses jumping to obey his slightest whim. He had also been just another jewel for his mother, property that she preened herself with, showed off, displayed.

It wasn't Dorothea or the tutors or governesses that Kartane ran to as a child when he scraped his knee and wanted comforting, or felt lonely, or wanted to brag about his latest small adventure. Not to them. He had always run to Daemon.

Daemon, who always had time to talk and, more important, to listen. Daemon, who taught him to ride, to fence, to swim, to dance. Daemon, who patiently read the same book to him, over and over and over, because it was his favorite. Daemon, who took long, rambling walks with him. Daemon, who never once showed any displeasure at having a small boy attached to his heels. Daemon, who held him, rocked him, soothed him when he cried. Daemon, who plundered the kitchen late at night, even though it was forbidden, to bring Kartane fruit, rolls, cold joints of meat—anything to appease the insatiable hunger he always felt because he could never eat his fill under his mother's watchful eye. Daemon, who had been caught one night and beaten for it, but never told anyone the food wasn't for himself.

Daemon, whose trust he had betrayed, whose love he lost with a single word.

★   ★   ★

Kartane was still a gangly boy when Daemon was first contracted out to another court. It had hurt to lose the one person in the whole court who truly cared about him as a living, thinking being. But he also knew there was trouble in the court, trouble that swirled around Daemon, around Daemon's position in the court hierarchy. He knew Daemon served Dorothea and Hepsabah and Dorothea's coven of Black Widows, although not in the same way the consorts and other men serviced them when summoned. He knew about the Ring of Obedience and how it could control a man even if he were stronger and wore darker Jewels. He puzzled over Daemon's aversion to being touched by a woman. He puzzled over the fights between Daemon and Dorothea, shouting matches that made stone walls seem paper-thin and grew more and more vicious. More often than not, those arguments ended with Dorothea using the Ring, punishing with agonizing pain until Daemon begged for forgiveness.

Then one day Daemon refused to service one of Dorothea's coven.

Dorothea summoned the First, Second, and Third Circles of the court. With her husband, Lanzo SaDiablo, by her side—Lanzo, the drunken womanizer whose only value was in providing Dorothea with the SaDiablo name—she began the punishment.

Kartane had hidden behind a curtain, chilled with fear, as he watched Daemon fight the Ring, fight the pain, fight the guards who held him so he couldn't attack Dorothea. It took an hour of agony to bring him to his knees, sobbing from the pain. It took another half hour to make him crawl to Dorothea and beg forgiveness. When she finally stopped sending pain through the Ring, Dorothea didn't allow him to go to his room, where Manny would give him a sedative and wash his sweat-chilled body so he could sleep while the pain slowly subsided. Instead, she had him tied hand and foot to one of the pillars, had him gagged so his moans of pain would be muffled, and left him there to humiliate him and warn others by the example while she leisurely conducted the other business of the court.

The lesson was not lost on Kartane. To be Ringed was the severest form of control. If Daemon couldn't stand the pain, how could he? It became very important not to give Dorothea a reason to Ring him.

That night, after Daemon had been allowed to rest a little, he was ordered to serve the witch he'd earlier refused.

That night was the first time Daemon went cold.

Among the Blood, there were two kinds of anger. Hot anger was the anger of emotion, superficial even in its fury—the anger between friends, lovers, family, the anger of everyday life. Cold anger was the Jewel's anger—deep, untouchable, icy rage that began at a person's core. Implacable, almost always unstoppable until the fury was spent, cold anger wasn't blunted by pain or hunger or weariness. Rising from so deep within, it made the body that housed it insignificant.

That first night, no one recognized the subtle change in the air when Daemon walked by on his way to the witch's chamber.

It wasn't until the maid came in the next morning and found the windows and mirrors glazed with ice, discovered the obscenity left in the bed, that Dorothea realized she had broken something in Daemon during that punishment, had stripped away a layer of humanity.

Hekatah, the self-proclaimed High Priestess of Hell, would have recognized the look in Daemon's eyes if she had seen it, would have understood how true the bloodline ran. It took Dorothea a little longer. When she finally understood that what Daemon had inherited from his father was far darker and far more dangerous than she'd imagined, she gifted him to a pet Queen who ruled a Province in southern Hayll.

Dorothea said nothing about the killing. Among the Blood, there was no law against murder. She said little about Daemon's reaction to kneeling in service, commending his training as a pleasure slave and only adding that he could be somewhat temperamental if used too often.

Before the week ended, Daemon was gone.

Not long after, Kartane learned what Daemon's presence had spared him. Dorothea's appetite for a variety of pretty faces was no less demanding than Lanzo's, the only difference in their taste being gender, and she kept a stable of young Warlords at the court to do the pretty for her and her coven. Until then, Kartane had been nothing more than Dorothea's handsome, spoiled son.

One night she summoned Kartane to her chamber. He went to her nervously, mentally ticking off the things he'd done that day and wondering what might have displeased her. But she soothed and stroked and petted. Those caresses, which always made him uneasy, now frightened him. As she leaned toward him, she told him his father had been loyal to her and she expected him to be loyal too. Kartane was too busy trying to figure out how Lanzo's spearing a different serving girl every night could be considered loyalty to recognize the intent. It wasn't until he felt

Dorothea's tongue slide into his mouth that he understood. He pushed her away, threw himself off the couch, and crawled backward toward the door, not daring to take his eyes off her.

She was furious with his refusal. It earned him his first beating.

The welts were still sore when she summoned him again. This time he sat quietly as she stroked his arms and thighs and explained in her purring voice that a Ring could help him be more responsive. But she didn't really think that would be necessary. Did he?

No, he didn't think it would be necessary. He submitted. He did what he was told.

Lying in his own bed later that night, Kartane thought of Daemon, of how night after night, year after year Daemon had done what Kartane had been forced to do. He began to understand Daemon's aversion to touching a female unless he was forced to. And he wondered how old Daemon had been the first time Dorothea had taken him into her bed.

It didn't end with that first time. It didn't end until years later when Dorothea sent him away to a private school because he was spearing the serving girls so viciously that Lanzo and his companions complained that the girls weren't usable for days afterward.

The private school he attended, where the boys all came from the best Hayllian families, put the final polish on Kartane's taste for cruelty. He found Red Moon houses disgusting and could satisfy himself with an experienced woman only if he hurt her. After being barred from a couple of houses, he discovered that it was easy to dominate younger girls, frighten them, make them do whatever he wanted.

He began to appreciate Dorothea's pleasure in having power over someone else.

But even the youngest whore was still a witch with her Virgin Night behind her, and she was protected by the rules of the house. He didn't have, as his mother had, absolute power over whoever he mounted.

He began to look elsewhere for his pleasure, and found, quite accidentally, what he craved.

Kartane and his friends went to an inn one night to drink, to gamble, to get the nectar free. They came from the best families, families no mere innkeeper would dare approach. The others had their sport with the young women who served ale and supper, using the small private dining room, like most inns had for important guests. But Kartane had been intrigued by the innkeeper's young daughter. She had the beginning blush of womanhood, the merest hint of curves. When he dragged her toward the door of the private room, the innkeeper rushed him, bellowing with rage. Kartane raised his hand, sent a surge of power through the Jeweled ring on his finger, and knocked the man senseless. Then he dragged the girl into the room and closed the door.

Her trembling, paralyzing fear felt delicious. She had no musky smell of woman, no psychic scent of a witch come to power. He reveled in her pain, stunned by the intoxication and pleasure it gave him to drive her beyond the web of herself and break her.

When he finally left the room, feeling in control of his life for the first time in oh-so-many years, he threw a couple of gold mark notes on the bar, gathered his friends, and disappeared.

That was the beginning.

Dorothea never disapproved of his chosen game as long as he satisfied her whenever he returned to court and as long as he didn't spoil any of the witches she wanted for her court. For two hundred years Kartane played his game with non-aristo Blood. Sometimes he kept the same girl for several weeks or months, playing with her, honing her fear, becoming more depraved in his requirements, until he seeded her. Many times even a broken witch was still capable of spontaneous abortion and would choose it rather than bear the seed of a man she hated, even though she would never bear any other child. Sometimes, if the girl hadn't gone completely numb and was still amusing, he got a Healer corrupted by hunger and hard times to provide the cleansing brew. Most times he simply turned them out, let them return to their families or a Red Moon house or the gutter. It was all the same to him.

Kartane played his game for two hundred years. Then, on one of his required returns to court, he found Daemon waiting for him.

By then Kartane understood why Daemon was Sadi not SaDiablo, why that was as much of a compromise as the family was willing to make. But seeing the anger in Daemon's eyes, he knew that, unlike Dorothea, Daemon would never approve of what Kartane had done. As he listened to a blistering lecture about honor, Kartane struck out at Daemon's weak spot. He told Daemon that he, Kartane, the High Priestess's son, didn't have to listen to a bastard.

A bastard.

A bastard.

A bastard.

He never forgot the shock and pain in Daemon's eyes. Never forgot how it felt when the one person he'd loved and who had loved him gathered himself into that aloof court demeanor and apologized for speaking out of turn. Would always know that if he'd run after Daemon right then and apologized, begged to be forgiven, explained about the pain and the fear, asked for help . . . he would have had it. Daemon would have found a way to help him.

But he didn't. He let the word stand. He drove it in again and again until the wedge became a chasm and the only thing they had in common was their fury with each other.

In the end, Dorothea sent Daemon away and lost him for one hundred years. By the time he returned, he'd made the Offering to the Darkness. The rumors were that Daemon had come away from the ceremony wearing a Black Jewel, but no one knew for sure because no one had seen it.

It didn't matter to Kartane what Jewels Daemon wore. He was frightened enough by what Daemon had become. Since then, they'd done their best to avoid each other.

Kartane wiped the tears from his face and straightened his jacket. He would see Dorothea and make his escape as quickly as possible. Escape from her, from the court . . . and from Daemon.

2 / Terreille

Daemon glided through the corridors of the SaDiablo mansion until he reached his suite of rooms. Presenting himself to Dorothea had been as unpleasant as usual, but at least it had been brief. Seeing her had frayed his temper to the breaking point, and right now his self-control was tenuous at best. He needed a quiet hour before dressing for dinner and spending the evening doing the pretty for Dorothea and her coven.

He walked into his sitting room and choked back the snarl when he noticed the visitor waiting for him.

Hepsabah turned toward him, a smile flickering on her lips, her flitting hands performing an intricate dance with each other. He loathed the hunger in her eyes and the muskiness of her psychic scent, but knowing he was required to play the game, he smiled at her and closed the door.

"Mother," he said with barely disguised irony. He bent his head to kiss her cheek. As always, she turned her head at the last minute so his lips brushed against hers. Her arms wound around his neck, her tongue greedily thrusting into his mouth as she pressed herself against him. Usually he pushed her away, disgusted that his mother could want such intimacy. Now he stood passively, neither giving nor taking, simply analyzing the lies that had made up his life.

Hepsabah stepped away from him, pouting. "You're not pleased to see me," she accused.

Daemon wiped his mouth with the back of his hand. "As pleased as I usually am." There she was, dressed in an expensive silk dress while Tersa, his real mother, wore a tattered coat and slept who knew where. Despite Dorothea's and Hepsabah's efforts, Tersa had given him what love she could, in her own shattered way. Somehow he was going to make it up to her, just as he was going to repay them. "What do you want?"

"It would be *nice* if you could be a little more respectful to your mother." She smoothed her dress, running her hands over her breasts and belly, looking at him from beneath her eyelashes.

"I have a great deal of respect for my mother," he replied blandly.

Looking uneasy, she patted the air near his sleeve and said with brittle cheerfulness, "I've got your room all ready for you. Nice and comfy. Maybe after dinner we can sit and have a nice little coze, hmm?" She turned toward the door, swinging her hips provocatively.

Daemon's temper snapped. "You mean I should be more amenable to putting my face between your legs." He ignored her shocked gasp. "I won't be more amenable, *Mother*. Not tonight. Not any night. Not to you or anyone else in this court. If I'm commanded to kneel while I'm here, I promise you that what happened to Cornelia will be nothing compared to what I'll do here. If you think the Ring can stop me, you'd better think again. I'm not a boy anymore, Hepsabah, and I want you *dead*."

Hepsabah backed away from him, her eyes wide with terror. She snatched at the door handle and flung herself into the corridor.

Daemon opened a bottle of brandy, paused only long enough to probe it to be sure there were no sedatives or other nasty surprises added to the liquor, put the bottle to his mouth, and tipped his head back. It burned his throat and caught fire in his stomach, but he continued to swallow until he needed to breathe. The room swam a little but steadied quickly as his metabolism consumed the liquor as it consumed food. That was a drawback to wearing darker Jewels—it took a massive amount of alcohol to get pleasantly drunk. Daemon didn't want to get pleasantly drunk. He wanted to numb the anger and the memories. He couldn't afford a full confrontation with Dorothea now. He could break the Ring, and Dorothea with it. Over the past few years he'd become sure of that. What he wasn't sure of was how much damage she might do to him before he destroyed her, wasn't sure if he'd be permanently maimed by the time he got the Ring off, wasn't sure what other damage he might do to himself that might prevent him from ever wearing the Black again. And there was a Lady out there, somewhere, that he wanted to be whole for. Once he found her . . .

Daemon smiled coldly. The Priest owed him a favor, and two Black Jewels, even if one was Ringed, should be quite sufficient to take care of an arrogant Red-Jeweled High Priestess.

Laughing, Daemon went into his bedroom and dressed for dinner.

3 / Terreille

Chewing his lower lip, Kartane walked up to Daemon, who was studying a closed door. They hadn't been seated near each other at dinner last night, and Daemon had retired early—to everyone's relief—so this was the first time since their abrupt meeting yesterday afternoon that they were together without dozens of people to act as a buffer.

Kartane wasn't a small man, and even with his excesses he remained trim and well toned, but standing next to Daemon made him feel like he was still in a boy's body. It was more the breadth of Daemon's shoulders than the couple of inches in height, the face matured by pain rather than age that made Kartane feel slight next to him. It was also the difference between a long-lived youth and a male in his prime.

"Do you know what this is about?" Daemon asked quietly.

Kartane shook his head. "She just said our presence is required for an entertainment."

Daemon took a deep breath. "Damn." He opened the door, then stood aside for Kartane to enter.

Kartane took a couple of steps into the room and felt the air behind him chill as the door closed. He glanced at Daemon's face, at the narrowed eyes suddenly turned hard yellow, and wondered, as he surveyed the room, what had provoked Daemon's temper.

It was an austere room, furnished with several rows of chairs arranged in a semicircle in front of two posts attached to the floor. Beside the posts was a long table with a white cloth pulled over it. Under and around the posts was a thick pile of white sheets.

Daemon swore viciously under his breath. "At least as the privileged son you can rest easy that you won't be part of the entertainment. You'll only have to endure watching it."

Kartane stared at the posts. "I don't understand. What is it?"

Pity flashed in Daemon's eyes before his face became impassive and his voice took on that toneless, bored quality he always used in court. "You've never seen this?"

"It seems a bit overdone if she's going to have someone whipped," he said, trying to put a sneer into his voice to hide his growing fear.

"Not whipped," Daemon said bitterly. "Shaved."

The look in Daemon's eyes turned Kartane's guts to water.

Daemon didn't speak again until they reached the first row of chairs. "Listen, Kartane, and listen well. What happens to the poor fool Dorothea's going to tie between those posts is going to depend on how much you squirm. If you stay disinterested, she won't do any less than she's already planned but at least it will be done quicker, and you'll have to endure watching for less time. Understand?"

"Shaved?" Kartane said in a strangled voice.

"Didn't anyone ever tell you how they make eunuchs?" Daemon slipped his hands in his pockets and turned away.

"But . . ." Kartane tensed when Dorothea and her coven walked through the door. "Why this?" he whispered. "Why all these chairs?"

Daemon's eyes had a worried, faraway look in them. "Because they find it amusing, Lord Kartane. This *is* the afternoon's entertainment. And if we're both lucky, we'll only be the guests of honor."

Kartane looked quickly at Daemon and then at the posts. Dorothea wouldn't. She *couldn't*. Was that why Daemon warned him, because he wasn't sure if . . . No. Not to Daemon. Not to *Daemon*.

Kartane kicked a chair before dropping into another with his arms crossed and his legs sprawled forward, looking like a sulky child. "I have better ways to spend my afternoon," he snarled.

Daemon turned, one eyebrow raised in question. Dorothea walked toward them, her eyes flashing with annoyance at Kartane's behavior.

"Well, darling," she purred, "we'll do our best to amuse you." She settled into the chair next to Kartane's, and with a gracious gesture of her hand, indicated to Daemon that he should sit on her left.

Kartane sat up straighter, but kept a sulky look on his face. He flinched as the chairs behind him filled and female voices murmured as if they were in a theater waiting for the play to begin.

Dorothea clapped her hands, and the room became silent. Two massive, raw-looking guards bowed to Dorothea and left the room. They returned a moment later leading a slightly built man.

Daemon flicked a bored glance at the man being led to the posts, leaned away from Dorothea, and propped his chin in his hand.

Dorothea hissed quietly.

Daemon straightened in his chair, crossed his legs, and steepled his fingers. "Not that it matters," he drawled, "but what did he do?"

Dorothea put her hand on his thigh. "Curious?" she purred.

Daemon shrugged, ignoring the fingers sliding up his thigh.

Dorothea removed her hand, annoyed by the bored expression on Daemon's face. "He didn't do anything. I just felt like having him shaved." She smiled maliciously, nodded to the guards, and watched with great interest as they fastened their victim spread-eagle to the posts. "He's a Warlord but a valet by profession. Comes from a family who specializes in personal service to darker-Jeweled Blood. But after today, I doubt there'll be a male in all of Hayll who'll want him around. What do you think?"

Daemon shrugged and once more propped his chin on his hand.

When the man was securely fastened to the posts, one of the guards pulled the cloth off the table. There were appreciative murmurs from the audience as whips, nutcrushers, and various other instruments of torture were presented for view. The last things the guard picked up were the shaving knives.

Kartane felt ill and yet hopeful. If all of those things were being presented, maybe . . .

No, Daemon said on a spear thread, male to male. *She'll shave him.*

You don't know for sure.

You can't have the entertainment end too quickly.

Kartane swallowed hard. *You don't know for sure.*

You'll see.

Dorothea raised one hand. The guard went to the far end of the table and raised the first whip. "What shall it be today, Sisters?" Dorothea called out gaily. "Shall we whip him?"

"Yes, yes, yes," a number of female voices yelled.

"Or . . ."

There was applause and laughter as the guard, looking more nervous, raised the nutcrusher for their viewing.

"Or . . ." Dorothea pointed, and the guard lifted the shaving knives.

Kartane studied the floor, trying not to shake, trying not to bolt for the door. He knew he wouldn't be allowed to leave, and he wondered with a touch of bitterness how Daemon could sit there looking so bored. Maybe because Sadi didn't have any use for those organs anyway.

"Shave him, shave him, shave him!" The room thundered with the coven's voices.

Kartane had been to dogfights, cockfights, any number of spectacles where dumb animals were pitted against each other. He'd heard the roar of male voices urging their favorite to victory. But he'd never heard, in all those places, the glee he heard now as the coven urged their decision.

He jumped when Dorothea's hand squeezed his knee, her cold smile letting him know she was pleased by his fear.

Dorothea raised her hand for silence. When the room was absolutely still, she said in her most melodious purr, "Shave him." She paused a long moment, then smiled sweetly. "A full shave."

Kartane's head snapped around in disbelief, but before he could say anything, Daemon turned his head just enough to look at him. The look in Daemon's eyes was more frightening than Dorothea could ever be, so Kartane swallowed the words and slumped a little farther in his chair.

The Healer and the barber entered the room and walked slowly to the table. The barber, a cadaverous man wearing a tightly cuffed black robe, had a receding hairline, pencil-line lips, and dirty yellow eyes. He bowed to Dorothea and then bowed to the coven.

The Healer, a drab woman retained to handle the servants' ills since she wasn't well versed enough in her Craft to attend to the Blood aristos, called in a bowl of warm water and soap. She held the bowl while the barber washed his hands.

Then the barber leisurely soaped his victim's testicles.

Why? Kartane sent on a spear thread.

Makes them slippery, Daemon replied. *Harder to get a clean cut the first time.*

The barber picked up a small curved knife and held it up for them to see. He positioned himself behind the man.

So everyone can see, Daemon explained.

Kartane clenched his fists and stared at the floor.

"Watch, my dear," Dorothea purred, "or we'll have to do it again."

Kartane fixed his eyes on one of the posts just as the barber pulled the knife back. A moment later, a small dark lump lay on the swiftly reddening sheets.

The Warlord tied to the posts let out a howl of agony and then clenched his teeth to stifle the sound.

Kartane's stomach churned as a disappointed murmur swept through the room. Mother Night! They'd been hoping for a second cut!

The barber set the bloody knife on a tray and washed his hands while the Healer sealed the blood vessels. When she stepped aside, he took a straight knife and positioned himself in front of a post. He pulled the man's organ to its full length, turned to his audience, shook his head sadly, and said, "There's so little here, it will hardly make a difference."

The coven laughed and applauded. Dorothea smiled.

Kartane expected a swift severing. But when the barber laid the knife on the Warlord's organ and leisurely sawed through the flesh, each stroke of the knife accompanied by a scream, Kartane found himself mesmerized, unable to look away.

They deserved what he did. They were foul things only fit for breeding and a man's pleasure. It was right to break them young, *good* to break them young before they became things like the ones sitting here. Break them all. Destroy them all. Blood males should rule, must rule. If only he could kill her. Would Daemon help him rid Hayll of that plague carrier? All of them would have to be killed, of course. Then break all the young ones and train them to serve. It was the only way. The only way.

The silence made him blink.

Dorothea rose from her chair, furiously pointing a finger at the Healer.

"I told you to give him something to make sure he wouldn't faint on us. Look at him!" Her finger swung to the man hanging limply from the posts, his head dropped to his chest.

"I did as you asked, Priestess," the Healer stammered, wringing her hands. "I swear by the Jewels I did."

Was it his imagination, or was Daemon pleased about something?

"We'll have no more sport today because of your incompetence," Dorothea screamed. She made an impatient gesture. "Take it away." Then she swept from the room, her coven trailing behind her.

"I really did give him the potion," the Healer wailed, trailing after the barber as he left the room.

Kartane sat in his chair, too numb to move, until the guards bundled the man into the bloody sheets along with the discarded organs. Then he bolted for the nearest bathroom and was violently ill.

4 / Terreille

Dorothea slowly paced her sitting room. Her flowing gown swished with the sway of her hips, and the low-cut bodice displayed to advantage the small breasts that still rode high. She picked up a feather quill from a table as she passed. Most men's backbones turned to jelly when she picked up a quill. Daemon, however, just watched her, his cold, bored expression never changing.

She brushed her chin with the quill as she passed his chair. "You've been a naughty boy again. Perhaps I should have you whipped."

"Yes," Daemon replied amiably, "why don't you? Cornelia could tell you how effective that is in making me come around."

Dorothea staggered but continued walking. "Perhaps I should have you shaved." She waved the feather at him. "Would you enjoy being one of the brotherhood of the quill?"

"No."

She feigned surprise. "No?"

"No. I prefer being neat when I piss."

Dorothea's face twisted with anger. "You've gotten crude, Daemon."

"Must be the company I keep."

Dorothea paced rapidly, slowly down only when she noticed the cold amusement in Daemon's eyes. *Damn him,* she thought as she tapped the quill against her lips. He knew how much he upset her, and he enjoyed it. She didn't trust him, couldn't trust being able to control him anymore. Even the Ring didn't stop him when he went cold. And he just sat there, so sure of himself, so uncaring.

"Perhaps I *should* have you shaved." Her usual purr turned into a growl. She twitched the quill in the direction of his groin. "After all, it's not as if you have any use for it."

"Hardly good for business, though," Daemon said calmly. "The Queens won't pay you for my service if there's nothing to buy."

"A worthless piece of meat since you can't use it anyway!"

"Ah, but they do so enjoy looking at it."

Dorothea threw the feather down and stamped on it. "Bastard!"

"So you've told me time and time again." Daemon waved one hand in irritation. "Enough theatrics. You won't shave me, now or ever."

"Give me one reason why I shouldn't!"

In one fluid move Daemon was out of the chair, pinning her against the table. His hands tightened on her upper arms, hurting her, while his mouth clamped down on hers, bruising her lips with his teeth. He thrust his tongue into her mouth with such controlled savagery that she couldn't think of anything but the feel of him and the sudden liquid heat between her legs.

It was always like this with him. Always. It was more than just his body. Not quite the Jewels, not quite a link. She could never touch his thoughts or feelings, never reach him. Yet there was such a sense of savage, controlled power, of maleness, that flowed from him, swirled around him. His hands, his tongue . . . just channels for that flow. Sensory conductors.

When she thought she couldn't stand any more, when she thought she had to push him away or drown in the sensation, he thrust his hips forward and swayed against her. Moaning, Dorothea pushed herself against him, wanting to feel him harden, needing him to want her.

Just as she raised her arms to wrap them around his neck, Daemon stepped back, smiling, his golden eyes hot with anger, not desire.

"That's why you won't shave me, Dorothea." His silky voice roughened with disgust. "There's always a chance, isn't there, that someday I'll catch fire, that the hunger will become unbearable and I'll come crawling to you for whatever release you'll grant me."

"I'd never let you go hungry," Dorothea cried, one hand reaching for him. "By the Jewels, I swear—" Shaking with anger, Dorothea forced herself to stand up straight. Once again she'd humiliated herself by begging him.

Daemon smiled that cold, cruel smile he wore whenever he had twisted the love game to hurt the woman he was serving. It's so easy, his smile said. You're all so foolish. You can punish the body all you want, all you dare, but you can never touch *me*.

"Bastard," Dorothea whispered.

"You could always kill me," Daemon said softly. "That would solve both our problems, wouldn't it?" He took a step toward her. She immediately pushed back against the table, frightened. "Why don't you want me dead, Dorothea? What will happen on the day when I no longer walk among the living?"

"Get out," she snapped, trying not to sound as weak as she suddenly felt. Why was he saying this? What did he know? She had to get him away from Hayll, away from that *place*, and quickly. Furious, she threw herself at him, but he glided away, and she fell heavily to the floor. "Get out!" she screamed, beating the floor with her fists.

Daemon left the room, whistling a tuneless little song. As a butterball Warlord puffed his way down the hall toward Dorothea's room, Daemon turned halfway to face him. "I wouldn't go in there until she's a little calmer," he said cheerfully. Then he winked at the startled man and continued down the hall, laughing.

"Damn your soul to the bowels of Hell, hurry up with that!" Kartane screamed at the manservant assigned to him when he was at court. He threw his shirts into one trunk and fastened the straps.

When the trunks were packed, Kartane's eyes swept the room for anything he might have missed.

"Lord Kartane," the manservant panted.

"I'll take care of this. You're dismissed. Get out. Get out!"

The manservant scurried out of the room.

Kartane wrapped his arms around the bedpost. He desperately wanted to rest, but every time he closed his eyes, he saw the bloody sheets, heard the screams.

Away from here. And quickly. Before Dorothea summoned him, before he was trapped. Someplace where the witches were already being silenced. A place that stood in Hayll's shadow, where they would fawn over the Priestess's son, but not yet completely tainted with the ancient land's decay. Not quite virgin territory, but still a maid learning Hayll's desecrations.

"Chaillot," Kartane whispered, and he smiled. The other side of the Realm. Hayll had an embassy there, so no one would question his appearance. Robert Benedict was an astute protégé. And there was that wonderful place he'd helped them build in Beldon Mor, that "hospital" for young, high-strung girls from aristo Blood families, where men like Lord Benedict could partake of delicacies that no respectable Red Moon house would offer. It could take weeks for Dorothea to track him down, particularly if he impressed on the embassy staff that he was there doing research for the Priestess. They'd be too frightened of what he might say about them to report his presence.

Kartane vanished the trunks and slipped from his room to the landing web. He caught the Red Web and rode hard toward the west, toward Chaillot.

5 / Hell

Hekatah flowed into the parlor, the spidersilk gown swirling around her small body, the diamonds sewn into the high neckline glittering like stars against a bloodred sky. She'd dressed with care for this well-thought-out "chance" meeting. Despite the plebeian gallantry that made him courteous to any woman, whether she was pretty or not, Saetan did appreciate a woman who displayed herself to advantage, and even past her prime, Hekatah had never wanted for men.

But he, gutter-child bastard that he was, glanced at her over the half-moon glasses he'd begun wearing, marked the page in his book, and vanished the glasses before, finally, giving her his full attention.

"Hekatah," he said with pleasant wariness.

Biting back her fury, she strolled around the room. "It's wonderful to see the Hall refurbished," she said, her girlish voice full of the cooing warmth that had once made him cautiously open to her.

"It was time to have it done."

"Any special reason?"

"I thought of giving a demon ball," he replied dryly.

She tipped her chin down and looked up at him through her lashes, not realizing it was a parody of the sulky, sensuous young witch she'd been long centuries ago. "You didn't redo the south tower."

"There was no need. It's been emptied and cleaned. That's all."

"But the south tower has always been my apartment," she protested.

"As I said, there was no need."

She stared at the sheer ivory curtains beneath the tied-back red velvet drapes. "Well," she said, as if giving the matter slow consideration, "I suppose I could take a room in your wing."

"No."

"But, Saetan—"

"My dear, you've forgotten. You've never had an apartment in the Hall in this Realm. You haven't lived in any house I own since I divorced you, and you never will again."

Hekatah knelt beside his chair, pleased by the way the gown pooled around her, one shimmering wing of her sleeve draped across his legs. "I know we've had our differences in the past, but, Saetan, you need a woman here now." She could have shouted with triumph as his eyebrow rose in question and a definite spark of interest showed in his eyes.

He raised one hand and stroked her still-black hair, flowing long and loose down her back. "Why do I need a woman now, Hekatah?" he asked in a gentle, husky voice.

His lover's voice. The voice that always enraged her because it sounded so caring and weak. Not a man's voice. Not her father's voice. Her father would never have coaxed. *He* would never have allowed her to refuse him. But *he* had been a Hayllian Prince, one of the Hundred Families, as proud and arrogant as any Blood male, and not this . . .

Hekatah lowered her eyes, hoping Saetan hadn't seen, again, what she thought of him. All that power. They could have ruled all of Terreille, and Kaeleer too, if he'd been the least bit ambitious. Even if he'd been too lazy, *she* could have done it. Who would have *dared* challenge her with the Black backing her? He wouldn't even do that. Wouldn't even support her in Dhemlan, his own Territory. Kept her leashed to Hayll, where her family had enough influence to make her the High Priestess. All that power wasted in a *thing* that had to give himself a name because his sire didn't think the seed fit enough to claim. But Terreille would be hers yet, even if she had to use a weak little puppet like Dorothea to get it.

"Why do I need a woman now?" Saetan's voice, less gentle now, called her back.

"For the child, of course," she replied, turning her head to press a kiss into his palm.

"The child?" Saetan lifted his hand and steepled his fingers. "One of our sons has been demon-dead for 50,000 years, and you, my dear, probably know better than anyone where the other one lies."

Hekatah drew in her breath with a hiss and exhaled with a smile. "The girl child, High Lord. Your little pet."

"I have no pets, Priestess."

Hekatah hid her clenched fists in her lap. "Everyone knows you're training a girl child to serve you. All I'm trying to point out is she needs a woman's guidance in order to fulfill your needs."

"What needs are those?"

Hekatah smacked the arm of the chair. "Don't play word games with me. If the girl has any talent, she should be trained in the Craft by her Sisters. What you do with her afterward is your concern, but at least let me train her so she won't be an embarrassment."

Saetan eased out of the chair, went to the long windows, and pulled the sheer curtains aside for a clear view of Hell's ever-twilight landscape. "This doesn't concern you, Hekatah," he said slowly, his voice whispering thunder. "It's true I've accepted a contract to tutor a young witch. I'm bored. It amuses me. If she's an embarrassment to someone, it's no concern of mine." He turned from the window to look at her. "And no concern of yours. Leave it that way. Because if you persist in making her your concern, a great many things I've overlooked in the past are going to become mine."

Saetan dropped the edge of the curtain, flicked the folds back into place, and left the room.

Using the chair for support, Hekatah got to her feet, drifted to the windows, and studied the sheer curtains. She reached up slowly.

Selfish bastard. There were ways around him. Did he think after all this time she didn't know his weak spot? It had been such good sport to watch him squirm, the great High Lord chained by his honor, as those two sons she'd helped Dorothea create were battered year after year, century after century. *They hate you now, High Lord. What bastard doesn't hate the sire who won't claim him?*

The half-breed had been a bonus. Who could have anticipated Saetan having so much fire and need left? Fine, strapping boys, and neither one capable of being a man. At least the half-breed could get it up, which was a great deal more than anyone could say for the other.

With her help, Dorothea had gotten the strong, dark SaDiablo bloodline returned to Hayll. Waiting until Daemon's Birthright Ceremony to break the contract with Saetan had been a risk, but that was the time when paternity was formally acknowledged or denied. Up to that point, a male could claim a child as his, could do everything a father might do for his offspring. But until he was formally acknowledged, he had no rights to the child. Once the acknowledgment was made, however, a male child belonged to his father.

Which had been the problem. They had wanted the bloodline, but not the man. Having watched him raise two sons, Hekatah had known from the beginning that any child who grew up under Saetan's hand could never be reshaped into a male who would give his strength for her ambitions. She had thought that, since he visited each boy for only a few hours a week, his influence would be diluted, that the mark he would leave on them wouldn't begin until they were his and he began their training in earnest.

She'd been wrong. Saetan had already planted his code of honor deep in the boys' minds, and by the time she had realized that, it was too late to lead them down another path. Without knowing why, they had fought against anything that didn't fit that code of honor until the fighting, and the pain and the punishment, had shaped them, too.

And now there was this girl child.

Five years ago, she'd sensed a strange, dark power on the *cildru dyathe*'s island. Ever since then, she'd been following whispered snippets of talk, leads that faded to nothing. The tangled webs she'd created had only shown her dark power in a female body, the kind of power that, if it were molded and channeled the right way, could easily control a Realm.

It had taken five years to discover that Saetan was training the child, which infuriated her. That girl should have been hers from the start, should have been an emotionally dependent tool that would have fulfilled all of her dreams and ambitions. With that kind of power at her disposal, nothing—and no one—could have stopped her.

But, again, she was too late.

If Saetan had been willing to share the girl, she might have reconsidered. Since he wasn't willing, and she wasn't going to let that child mature to become a threat to her plans, she was going to use the most brutal weapon she had at her disposal: Daemon Sadi.

He would have no love for his father. He could be offered ten years of controlled freedom—still held by the Ring, of course, but not required to serve in a court. Ten years—no, a hundred—not to kneel for any witch. What would eliminating one child be, a stranger fawned over by the very man who had abandoned him, compared with not having to serve? And if the half-breed were thrown in for good measure? Sadi had the strength to defy even the High Lord. He had the cunning and the cruelty to ensnare a child and destroy her. But how to get him close enough for an easy strike? She'd have to think about that. Somewhere to the far west of Hayll. She had tracked the girl as far as that, and then nothing . . . except that strange, impenetrable mist on that island.

Oh, how Saetan would twist, screaming, on the hook of his honor when Sadi destroyed his little pet.

Hekatah lowered her arms and smiled at the curtains hanging in shreds from the rod. She made a moue as she pulled a bit of fabric from a snag in one of her nails and hurried out of the parlor, eager to get away from the Hall and begin her little plan.

Saetan Black-locked his sitting room door before going to the corner table that held glasses and a decanter of yarbarah. A mocking smile twisted his lips when he noticed how badly his hands shook. Ignoring the yarbarah, he pulled a bottle of brandy out of the cupboard below, filled a glass, and drank deep, gasping at the unfamiliar burn. It had been centuries since he'd drunk straight alcohol. He settled into a chair, the brandy glass cradled in his trembling hands.

Hekatah would be elated if she knew how badly she'd frightened him. If Jaenelle became twisted by Hekatah's ambition and greedy hunger to crush and rule . . . No, not Jaenelle. She must be gently, lightly chained to the Blood, must accept the leash of Protocol and Blood Law, the only things that kept them all from being constantly at each others' throats. Because soon, too soon, she would begin walking roads none of them had ever walked before, and she would become as far removed from the Blood as they were from the landens. And the power. Mother Night! Who could stop her?

Who *would* stop her?

Saetan refilled his glass and closed his eyes. He couldn't deny what his heart knew too well. He would serve his fair-haired Lady. No matter what, he would serve.

When he had ruled Dhemlan in Kaeleer and Dhemlan in Terreille, he had never hesitated to curb Hekatah's ambition. He'd believed then, and still believed, that it was wrong to use force to rule another race. But if Jaenelle wanted to rule . . . It would cost him his honor, to say nothing of his soul, but he would drive Terreille to its knees for her pleasure.

The only way to protect the Realms was to protect Jaenelle from Hekatah and her human tools.

Whatever the price.

6 / Terreille

Daemon reached his bedroom very late that evening. The wine and brandy he'd drunk throughout the night had numbed him enough for him to hold his temper despite the onslaught of innuendoes and coy chatter he'd listened to at the dinner table, despite the bodies that "accidentally" brushed against him all evening.

But he wasn't numb enough not to sense the woman's presence in his room. Her psychic scent struck him the moment he opened his bedroom door. Snarling silently at the intrusion, Daemon lifted his hand. The candle-lights beside the bed immediately produced a dim glow.

The young Hayllian witch lay in the center of his bed, her long black hair draped seductively over the pillows, the sheet tucked demurely beneath her pointed chin. She was new to Dorothea's court, an apprentice to the Hourglass coven. She had watched him throughout the evening but hadn't approached.

She smiled at him, then opened her small, pouty mouth and ran the tip of her tongue over her upper lip. Slowly peeling off the sheet, she stretched her naked body and lazily spread her legs.

Daemon smiled.

He smiled as he picked up the clothes she'd strewn across the floor and tossed them out the open door into the hall. He smiled as he teased the sheet and bedcovers off the bed and tossed them after the clothes. He was still smiling when he lifted her off the bed and pitched her out the door with enough force that she hit the opposite wall with a bone-breaking thud. The mattress followed, missing her only because she'd slumped over on her side as she began to scream.

Following the sound of running feet, Dorothea rushed through the corridors while the mansion walls shook with barely restrained violence. She pushed her way through the pack of growling guards until she reached the abigails and other witches of the coven whose concerned twittering was drowned by screams increasing in pitch and volume.

"What in the name of Hell is going on here?" she shouted, her usual melodious purr sounding more like a cat in heat.

Daemon stepped out of his bedroom, calmly tugging his shirt cuffs into place. The hallway walls instantly glazed with ice.

Dorothea studied Daemon's face. She'd never actually seen him when he was deep in the cold rage, had seen him only when he was coming back from it, but she sensed he was in the eye of the storm and something as insignificant as the wrong inflection on a single word would be enough to set off a violent explosion that would tear the court apart.

She narrowed her eyes and tried not to shiver.

It was more than the cold rage this time. Much more.

His face looked so lifeless it could have been carved from a fine piece of wood, and yet it was so filled with *something*. He appeared unnaturally calm, but those golden eyes, as glazed as the walls, looked at her with a predator's intensity.

Something had been pushing him toward the emotional breaking point, and he had finally snapped.

Among the short-lived races, pleasure slaves became emotionally unstable after a few years. It took decades among the long-lived races, but eventually the combination of aphrodisiacs and constant arousal without being allowed any release twisted something inside the males. After that, with careful handling, they still had their uses, but not as pleasure slaves.

Daemon had been a pleasure slave for most of his life. He'd come close to this point several times in the past, but he'd always managed to step back from the edge. This time, there was no stepping back.

Finally Daemon spoke. His voice came out flat, but there was a hint of thunder in it. "When you've gotten the stench completely out of my room, I'll be back. Don't call me until then." He glided down the hall and out of sight.

Dorothea waited, counting the seconds. Several minutes passed before the front door was slammed with such force that the mansion shook and windows shattered throughout the building.

Dorothea turned to the witch, a promising, vicious little creature now modestly covered with the sheet and bravely whimpering about her cruel treatment. She wanted to rake her nails over that pretty face.

There was no way to control Sadi, not after tonight. Pain or punishment would only enrage him further. She had to get him away from Hayll, send him somewhere expendable. The Dark Priestess had been full of suggestions when he'd been conceived and when they broke the contract in order to keep the boy for the Hayllian Hourglass. Well, the bitch could come up with a suggestion now when he was cold and possibly sliding into the Twisted Kingdom.

Straightening the collar of her dressing gown, Dorothea gave the young witch a last look. "That bitch is expelled from the Hourglass and dismissed from my court. I want her and everything to do with her out of my house within the hour."

Taking the arm of the young Warlord who'd been warming her bed before the screams began, she returned to her wing of the mansion, smiling at the wail of despair that filled the hall behind her.

7 / Terreille

Dorothea hurried up the broad path to the Sanctuary, clutching at her cloak as the wind tried to whip it from her body. The old Priestess, bent and somewhat feeble-minded, opened the heavy door for her and then fought with the wind to close it.

Dorothea gave the old woman the barest nod of acknowledgment as she rushed past her, desperate to reach the meeting place.

The inner chamber was empty except for two worn chairs and a low table placed before a blazing fire. Throwing off her cloak with one hand, she carefully placed the bottle she had held tight against her body on the table and sank into one of the chairs with a moan.

Two short days ago, she had felt insolent about asking for help from the Dark Priestess, had chafed at the offerings she had to provide from her court or Hayll's Hourglass. Now she was ready to beg.

For two days, Sadi had stalked through Draega, restlessly and relentlessly trying to blunt his rage. In that time, he'd killed a young Warlord from one of the Hundred Families—an exuberant youth who was only trying to have his pleasure with a tavern owner's daughter. The man had dared protest because his daughter was virgin and wore a Jewel. The Warlord had dealt with the father—not fatally—and was dragging the girl to a comfortable room when Sadi appeared, took exception to the girl's frightened cries, and savaged the young Warlord, shattering his Jewels and turning his brain into gray dust.

The grateful tavern owner gave Sadi a good meal and an ever-full glass. By morning the story was all over Draega, and then there were no tavern owners or innkeepers, Blood or landen, who didn't have a hot meal, a full glass, or a bed waiting for him if he walked down their street.

She wasn't sure the Ring would stop him this time, wasn't sure he wouldn't turn his fury on her if she tried to control him. And if he outlasted the pain . . .

Dorothea put her hands over her face and moaned again. She didn't hear the door open and close.

"You're troubled, Sister," said the crooning girlish voice.

Dorothea looked up, trembling with relief. She sank to her knees and bowed her head. "I need your help, Dark Priestess."

Hekatah smiled and hungrily eyed the contents of the bottle. Keeping her cloak's hood pulled well forward to hide her face, she sat in the other chair and, with a graceful turn of her hand, drew the bottle toward her. "A gift?" she asked, feigning surprised delight. "How generous of you, Sister, to remember me." With another turn of her hand, she called in a ravenglass goblet, filled it from the bottle, and drank deeply. She sighed with pleasure. "How sweet the blood. A young, strong witch. But only one voice to give so much."

Dorothea crawled back into her chair and straightened her gown. Her lips curved in a sly smile. "She insisted on being the only one, Priestess, wanting you to have her best." It was the least the little bitch could do, having caused the trouble in the first place.

"You sent for me," Hekatah said impatiently, then dropped her voice back into the soothing croon. "How can I help you, Sister?"

Dorothea jumped out of the chair and began to pace. "Sadi has gone mad. I can't control him anymore. If he stays in Hayll much longer, he'll tear us all apart."

"Can you use the half-breed to curb him?" Hekatah refilled her glass and sipped the warm blood.

Dorothea laughed bitterly. "I don't think anything will curb him."

"Hmm. Then you must send him away."

Dorothea spun around, hands clenched at her sides, lips bared to show her gritted teeth. "Where? No one will have him. Any Queen I send him to will die."

"The farther away the better," Hekatah murmured. "Pruul?"

"Zuultah has the half-breed, and you know those two can't be in the same court. Besides, Zuultah's actually been able to keep that one on a tight leash, and Prythian doesn't want to move him."

"Since when have you been concerned about what that winged sow wants?" Hekatah snapped. "Pruul is west, far west of Hayll, and mostly desert. An ideal place."

Dorothea shook her head. "Zuultah's too valuable to our plans."

"Ah."

"We're still cultivating the western Territories and don't have a strong enough influence yet."

"But you have some. Surely Hayll must have made overtures *someplace* where not *all* the Queens are so valued. Is there nowhere, Sister, where a Queen has been an impediment? Nowhere a gift like Sadi might be useful to *you?*"

Dorothea settled into her chair, her long forefinger nail tapping against her teeth. "One place," she said quietly. "That bitch Queen has opposed me at every turn. It's taken three of their generations to soften their culture enough to create an independent male counsel strong enough to remake the laws. The males we've helped rise to power will gut their own society in order to have dominance, and once they do that, the Territory will be ripe for the picking. But she keeps trying to fight them, and she's always trying to close my embassy and dilute my influence." Dorothea sat up straight, her eyes glittering. "Sadi would be a perfect gift for her."

"And if his temper gets out of control . . ." Hekatah laughed.

Dorothea laughed with her. "But how to get him there."

"Make a gift of him."

"She wouldn't accept it." She paused. "But her son-in-law is Kartane's companion and a strong leader in the counsel—through Hayll's graces. If the gesture was made to *him,* how could he refuse?"

Hekatah toyed with her glass. "This place. It's to the west?"

Dorothea smiled. "Yes. Even farther than Pruul. And backward enough to make him chafe." Dorothea reached for her cloak. "If you'll excuse me, Priestess. There are things I must attend to. The sooner we're rid of him, the better."

"Of course, Sister," Hekatah replied sweetly. "May the Darkness speed your journey."

Hekatah stared dreamily at the fire for several minutes. Emptying the bottle, she admired the dark liquid in the smoky black glass, then raised the goblet in a small salute. "The sooner you're rid of him, the better. The sooner he's in the west, the better still."

8 / Hell

"SaDiablo, there's something you should know."

Silence. "Have you seen her?"

"No." A long pause. "Saetan, Dorothea just sent Daemon Sadi to Chaillot."

PART III

CHAPTER SIX

1 / Terreille

Instantly awake, Surreal probed the dark room and the corridors beyond for whatever had disturbed her sleep.

Men's voices, women's voices, muted laughter.

No danger she could feel. Still . . .

A dark, cold ripple, coming from the east, rolled over Chaillot.

Surreal snuggled deeper into the bed, tucking the covers around her. The night was cool, the bed warm, and the sleeping draught Deje had given her gently pulled her back into the dreamless sleep she'd enjoyed for the past few nights.

Whatever it was, it wasn't looking for her.

Kartane slammed the door of his suite and locked it with a vicious snap of his hand. For an hour he paced his rooms, cursing softly.

It had been a delightful night, spent with a frightened, porcelain-faced girl who had been gratifyingly revolted by everything she'd had to do for him—and everything he had done to her. He had left that private playground relaxed and sated until Robert Benedict had stopped him at the door and told him how delighted, how *honored* his family was to receive such a gift from Lady SaDiablo. Of course, his bastard brother, Philip, performed consort duties for Lady Angelline, and she probably wouldn't put him *completely* aside for a pleasure slave, no matter how celebrated, but they were *honored*.

Kartane cursed. He'd woven his web of lies to Hayll's embassy tight enough to ensure that Dorothea, even if she found him quickly, wouldn't be able to call him back without embarrassment to herself. It also meant he couldn't bolt now without answering some difficult, and very unwanted, questions. Besides, this had become his favorite playground, and he had planned to stay a while.

He undressed and fell wearily into bed.

There was time. There was time. Daemon wasn't here.

Yet.

Cassandra stood in the Sanctuary doorway and watched the sun rise, unable to pinpoint the cause of her nervousness. Whatever it was, it was coming over the horizon with the sun.

Closing her eyes and taking a slow, deep breath, she descended to the depth of the Black, took that one mental step to the side that Black Widows were trained to take, and then she stood at the edge of the Twisted Kingdom. With eyes gauzed by the dreamscape of visions, she looked at the sun climbing above the horizon.

She stared for a long moment, then shook her head violently to clear her sight and pressed her body hard against the stone doorway, hoping for support. When she was sure she was truly out of the dreamscape, she went into the Sanctuary, keeping her back to the sun.

She stumbled to the kitchen, hurriedly pulled the curtains across the windows, and sat on the bench by the banked fire, grateful for the dark.

A Black Widow who stood on the edge of the Twisted Kingdom could see the true face behind whatever mask a person wore; she could draw memories from wood and stone to know what happened in a place; she could see warnings about things to come.

The sun, when Cassandra had looked at it through the dreamscape of visions, had been a torn, bloody orb.

Alexandra Angelline studied the room with a critical eye. The wood floor gleamed, the throw rugs were freshly washed, the windows sparkled, the bed linen was crisp and new, and the wardrobe was filled with freshly washed and pressed clothes that hung in a straight row above the polished shoes. She breathed deeply and smelled autumn air and lemon polish.

And something else.

With an angry sigh, she shook her head and turned to her housekeeper. "It's still there. Faint, but there. Clean it again."

* * *

Lucivar studied the cloudless sky. Heat waves already shimmered up from the Arava Desert in Pruul, but Lucivar shivered, chilled to the bone. His outer senses told him nothing, so he turned inward and instantly felt the cold, dark fury. Nervously licking his lips, he sent a thought on an Ebon-gray spear thread narrowed toward a single mind.

Bastard?

Whatever rode the Winds over Pruul passed him and continued west.

Bastard?

Cold silence was his only answer.

In Hell, Saetan sat behind the blackwood desk in his private study deep beneath the Hall and stared at the portrait across the room, a portrait he could barely see in the dim light. He'd been sitting there for hours, staring at Cassandra's likeness, trying to feel something—love, rage—anything that would ease the pain in his heart.

He felt nothing but bitterness and regret.

He watched Mephis open the study door and close it behind him. For a long moment he stared at his eldest son as if he were a stranger, and then turned back to the portrait.

"Prince SaDiablo," Saetan said, his voice full of soft thunder.

"High Lord?"

Saetan stared at the portrait for several minutes more. He sighed bitterly. "Send Marjong the Executioner to me."

In a private compartment on a Yellow Web Coach, Daemon Sadi sat across from two nervous Hayllian ambassadors. Behind a face that looked like a cold, beautiful, unnatural mask, his rage was contained but undiminished. He'd said nothing to his escorts throughout the journey. In fact, he'd barely moved since they left Hayll.

Now he stared at a blank wall, deaf to the men's lowered voices. His right hand continued to seek his left wrist, the fingers gently rubbing back and forth, back and forth, as if needing reassurance that the scar Tersa had gifted him with was still there.

2 / Terreille

Daemon stared out the window as the carriage rolled along the smooth road leading to the Angelline estate, aware that his escort, Prince Philip Alexander, covertly watched him. He'd been relieved when Philip had stopped defensively pointing out things of interest as they rode through Beldon Mor. He understood the man's defensiveness—Hayllian ambassadors prided themselves on their ability to subtly sneer at the cultural heritage of their host cities—but he was too intrigued by the elusive puzzle that had brushed his mind shortly after arriving in Beldon Mor to give Philip more than terse, civil replies.

A few decades ago, Beldon Mor had probably been a beautiful city. It was still lovely, but he recognized the taint of Hayll's influence. In a couple more generations, Beldon Mor would be nothing more than a smaller, younger Draega.

But there was an undercurrent beneath the familiar taint, a subtle *something* that eluded recognition. It had crept up on him during the hours he'd spent at the Hayllian embassy, like a mist one could almost feel but couldn't see. He'd never experienced anything like it and yet it felt familiar somehow.

"This is all part of the Angelline estate," Philip said, breaking the silence. "The house will be visible around the next bend."

Pushing the puzzle aside, Daemon forced himself to show some interest in the place where he would be living.

It was a large, well-proportioned manor house that gracefully fit into its natural surroundings. He hoped the interior decor was as quietly elegant as the exterior. It would be a relief to live in a place that didn't set his teeth on edge.

"It's lovely," Daemon said when they reached the house.

Philip smiled warily. "Yes, it is."

As he climbed out of the carriage and followed Philip up the steps to the door, Daemon's nerves tingled. His inner senses stretched. The moment he crossed the threshold, he slid to a stop, stunned.

The psychic scent was almost gone, but he recognized it. A dark scent. A powerful, terrifying, wonderful scent.

He breathed deeply, and the lifetime hunger in him became intense. She was here. She was *here!*

He wanted to shout in triumph, but the puzzled, wary expression in Philip's gray eyes sharpened Daemon's predatory instincts. By the time he reached Philip's side, he had thought of half a dozen ways a Gray-Jeweled Prince could quietly disappear.

Daemon smiled, pleased to see Philip's involuntary shiver.

"This way," Philip said tersely as he turned and walked toward the back of the house. "Lady Angelline is waiting."

Daemon slipped his hands into his pockets, settled his face into his bored court expression, and fell into step beside Philip with graceful indifference. As impatient as he was to meet the witches in this family and find the one he sought, it wouldn't do to make Philip too uneasy, too defensive.

They'd almost reached the door when a man came out of the room. He was fat, florid, and generally unattractive, but there were enough similarities between him and Philip to mark them as brothers.

"So," Robert Benedict said with a hearty sneer. "This is Daemon Sadi. The girls are most excited to have you here. Most excited." His eyes folded up into the fat as he gave Philip a nasty smile before turning back to Daemon. "Leland spent the whole morning dressing for the occasion. Philip's more of a steward now, so he doesn't have the time to see to the girls' comfort the way you will." He rubbed his hands together in malicious glee. "If you'll excuse me, duty calls."

Stepping aside to let Robert pass, they stood in silence until the front door closed. Philip was white beneath his summer tan, his breath whistled through his clenched teeth, and he shook with the effort of controlling some strong emotion.

"They're waiting," Daemon said quietly.

Philip's eyes were full of naked hatred. Daemon calmly returned the look. A Black-Jeweled Warlord Prince had nothing to fear from a Gray-Jeweled Prince. Philip at his worst temper wasn't equal to Daemon at his best, and they both knew it.

"In here," Philip snapped, leading Daemon into the room.

Trying not to act too eager, Daemon stepped into the sunny room that overlooked an expanse of green lawn and formal gardens, certain that he would know her the moment he saw her.

Seconds later, he swallowed a scream of rage.

There were two women and a girl about fourteen, but the one he sought wasn't there.

Alexandra Angelline, the matriarch of the Angelline family and the Queen of Chaillot, was a handsome woman with long dark hair just beginning to silver, a fine-boned oval face, and eyes the color of Purple Dusk Jewels. Her clothes were simply cut but expensive. The Blood Opal that hung from her neck was set in a simple gold design. Sitting in a high-backed chair, she held her slender body straight and proud as she studied him.

Daemon studied her in turn. Not a natural Black Widow, but there was a feel about her that suggested she had spent some time in an Hourglass coven. Though why she would begin an apprenticeship and not continue . . . Unless Dorothea had already begun her purge of Chaillot's Hourglass covens by then. Eliminating potential rivals was one of the first things Dorothea did to soften a Territory, and other Black Widows were far more dangerous rivals than the Queens because they practiced the same kind of Craft. It didn't take that many stories whispered in the dark to change a wariness of Black Widows into an active fear, and once the fear set in, the killing began. Once the killing began, the Black Widows would go into hiding, and the only ones who would be trained in their Craft were the daughters born to the Hourglass.

Since she was the sole heir to one of the largest fortunes on Chaillot and the strongest Queen the island had, her continued presence in an Hourglass coven would have been a dangerous risk for them all.

Leland Benedict, Alexandra's only daughter and Robert's wife, was a paler, frivolous version of her mother. The frothy neckline and frothy sleeves of her gown didn't suit her figure, and the hair done too elaborately for the hour of the day made her look more matronly than her mother. Daemon found her air of shy curiosity particularly irritating. The ones who began shyly curious tended to become the cruelest and most vindictive once they discovered what kind of pleasure he could provide. Still, he felt sorry for her. He could almost feel the core of her still molten, still wanting something cleaner, richer, more fulfilling than this caged freedom she had. Then she fluttered her eyelashes at him, and he wanted to strike her.

Last was the girl, Wilhelmina, the only child from Robert's first marriage. Unlike her father, who had a ruddy complexion and sandy-red hair, she was raven-haired and very fair, with a startling blush in her cheeks and blue-gray eyes. She was a beautiful girl and would become even more so when her body began to fill out and curve. In fact, that was the only flaw Daemon could see in her appearance—she was thin to the point of looking unhealthy. He wondered—as he had wondered in so many other places—if these people, Blood as he was Blood, had any idea of what they were, had any understanding of what wearing the Jewels entailed—not just the pleasures or the power that could be had but the physical and emotional hardships that were part of it too. If the girl wore Jewels darker than the other women in her family, perhaps they didn't recognize what was so apparent to him.

Anyone who wore the Jewels, especially a child, had a higher metabolism. It was possible, more for a witch because of the physical demands of her moontime than for her male counterparts, to burn up her own body in a matter of days if enough food wasn't available.

Setting the small chip of Red Jewel that was hidden beneath the rubies in his cuff links to auditory retention, Daemon let his mind drift as Alexandra told him about the household and his "duties." The Jewel chip would retain the conversation until he was ready to retrieve it. Right now, he had something more important to think about.

Where was she? *Who* was she? A relation who only visited? A guest who had stayed a few days and recently left? He couldn't ask anyone. If they didn't suspect that Witch had been in their presence, his questions, no matter how innocuous, might endanger her. Dorothea already had her cancerous tentacles embedded in Chaillot. If she became aware that this Other had touched the island . . . No. He couldn't ask. Until she returned, he would do whatever was required to keep these women satisfied and unsuspecting. But after she returned . . .

Finally he was shown to his room. It was directly below Alexandra's apartment and next to a back stairway, since he was mostly here for her pleasure, Leland needing nothing more than an escort when Robert wasn't available, and Wilhelmina being too young. It was a simple room with a chair, lamp, and writing desk as well as a single bed, a dresser with a mirror hanging above it, a wardrobe—and, Daemon noted gratefully, an adjoining modern bathroom.

As he had anticipated, the conversation at dinner was strained. Alexandra talked about the cultural activities that could be explored in Beldon Mor, and Daemon asked the polite questions expected of him. While Alexandra's conversation was painstakingly impersonal, Leland was fluttery, nervous, and far too prone to ask leading questions that made her blush no matter how delicately Daemon phrased his answers—if he answered at all. Robert, who had returned unexpectedly for dinner, looked too pleased with the arrangement, made sly comments throughout the meal, and took pains to touch Leland at every opportunity to stress his claim to her. Daemon ignored him, finding Philip's distress and growing rage at Robert far more interesting.

As dinner wore on, Daemon wished Wilhelmina were there, since she was the one he was most curious about, the one he could most easily tap for information. But she was considered too young to have late dinner and sit with the adults.

Finally free to retire but too restless to sleep, Daemon paced his room. Tomorrow he would begin searching the house. A room where she had slept would still be strong with her psychic scent, even if it had been cleaned. There wasn't time to waste, but he couldn't afford to be found prowling around in the early morning hours his first night there, not now, not when he might finally see, hear, touch what his soul had been aching for his whole life. Blood Law was nothing to him. The Blood were nothing to him. She would be Blood and yet Other, something alien and yet kindred. She would be terrifyingly magnificent.

As he paced his room, undressing in a slow striptease for no one, Daemon tried to imagine her. Chaillot born? Quite probable. Living in Beldon Mor? That would explain the subtle *something* he'd felt. And if she never physically strayed from the island, that explained why he hadn't felt her presence anywhere else in the past few years. Wise, certainly cautious to have escaped notice for so long.

He slid into bed, turned off the light . . . and groaned as an image of a wise, skinny old crone filled his mind.

No, he begged the still night. *Sweet Darkness, heed the prayer of one of your sons. Now that she's so close, let her be young enough to want me. Let her be young enough to need me.*

The night gave him no answer, and the sky was a pre-dawn gray before he finally slept.

3 / Terreille

For two days Daemon played the polite, considerate escort as the fluttery Leland made an endless round of calls showing off Lady SaDiablo's gift. For two nights he prowled the house, his control on his temper fraying from lack of sleep and frustration. He had toured every public room, probed every guest room, flattered and cajoled his way through the servants' quarters—and had found nothing.

Not quite nothing. He had found the library tucked away on the second floor of the nursery wing. It wasn't the library visitors saw, or the one the family used. This was the small room that contained volumes on the Craft and, like so many others he had seen in the past few decades, it had the feel of a room that was almost never used.

Almost never.

Silently closing the door, Daemon moved unerringly through the dark, cluttered room to a table in the far corner that held a shaded candle-light. He touched it, stroking downward on the crystal to dim the glow, leaned against the built-in bookcases, and tilted his head back to rest on a shelf.

The scent was strong in this room.

Daemon closed his eyes, breathed deeply, and frowned. Even though it was clean, the room had the dusty, musty smell of old books, but a physical scent wouldn't obscure a psychic one. That dark scent . . . Like the body that housed it, a witch's psychic scent had a muskiness that a Blood male could find as arousing as the body—if not more so. This dark, sweet scent was chillingly clean of that muskiness, and as he continued to breathe deeply, to open himself to that which was stronger than the body, he felt distressed to find it so.

Pushing away from the bookshelves, Daemon extinguished the candle-light and waited for his eyes to adjust to the darkness before leaving the room. So, she'd spent much of her time in that room, but she must have *stayed* somewhere. His eyes flicked toward the ceiling as he slipped among the shadows and silently climbed the stairs. The only place left to look was the nursery, the third floor rooms where Wilhelmina and her governess, Lady Graff, spent most of their days. It was also the only place Philip had vehemently told him to stay away from, since his services weren't required there.

Daemon glided down the corridor, his probing mind identifying the rooms as he passed: classroom, music room, playroom, Lady Graff's sitting room and adjoining bedroom (which Daemon immediately turned away from, his lips curling in a snarl, as he caught the wispy scent of erotic dreaming), bathrooms, a couple of guest rooms, Wilhelmina's bedroom. And the corner room that overlooked the back gardens.

Daemon hesitated, suddenly unwilling to further invade the privacy of children. As was his custom, he had gleaned basic facts about the family before entering service. The Hayllian ambassador, annoyed at being questioned, became quite garrulous once he noticed the cold look in Daemon's eyes, saying nothing of much interest except that there were two daughters. Daemon had met Wilhelmina.

There was only one room left.

His hand shook as he turned the doorknob and slipped into the room.

The sweet darkness washed over him, but even here it was faint, as though someone had been trying to scrub it away. Daemon pressed his back against the door and silently asked forgiveness for what he was about to do. He was male, he was intruding, and, like her, it would only take a few minutes for his own dark psychic scent to be impressed on the room for anyone to read.

Cautiously lifting one hand, he engaged a candle-light by the bed, keeping it bright enough to see by but dim enough that, he hoped, the light wouldn't be noticed beneath the bedroom door if someone walked past. Then he looked around, his brow wrinkling in puzzlement.

It was a young girl's room: white dresser and wardrobe, white canopy and counterpane decorated with little pink flowers covering the four-poster bed, gleaming wood floors with cute throw rugs scattered around.

It was totally wrong.

He opened every drawer of the dresser and found clothing suitable for a young girl, but when he touched it it was like touching a tiny spark of lightning. The bed, too, when he ran his hand lightly over the counterpane, sent a spark along his nerves. But the dolls and stuffed animals—the scent was on them only because they were in this room. If any of them had been rich with her puzzling darkness, he would have taken it back to his room to hold throughout the night. Finally he turned to the wardrobe and opened the doors.

The clothes were a child's clothes, the shoes were meant for small feet. It had been a while since they'd been worn, and the scent was faint in them, too. The wardrobe itself, however . . .

Daemon went through it piece by piece, touching everything, growing more hopeful and more frantic with each discarded item. When there was nothing left to check, his trembling fingers slid along the inside walls, his tactile sense becoming a conductor for the inner senses.

Kneeling on the floor, exhausted by disappointment, he leaned forward until his hand touched the far back corner of the wardrobe.

Lightning pulsed through him until he thought his blood would boil.

Puzzled, he cupped his hands and created a small ball of witchlight. He studied the corner, vanished the witchlight, and leaned back on his heels, even more puzzled.

There was nothing there . . . and yet there was. Nothing his physical senses could engage, but his inner senses insisted something was there.

Daemon reached forward again and shivered.

The room was suddenly, intensely cold.

His thinking was slowed by fatigue, and it took him a full minute to understand what the cold meant.

"Forgive me," he whispered as he carefully withdrew his hand. "I didn't mean to invade your private place. I swear by the Jewels it won't happen again."

With trembling hands, Daemon replaced the clothes and shoes exactly the way he'd found them, extinguished the candle-light, and silently glided back to his room. Once there, he dug out the bottle of brandy hidden in his own wardrobe and took a long swallow.

It didn't make sense. He could understand finding her psychic scent in the library. But in the child's room? Not on the toys, but on the clothes, on the bed-things an adult might handle daily if she took care of the child. When he had made an innocuous comment about there being another daughter, he'd been told, snappishly, that she wasn't at home, that she was ill.

Was his Lady assuming a Healer's duties? Had she slept in a cot in the girl's room in order to be nearby? Where was she now?

Daemon put the brandy away, undressed, and slid into bed. Tersa's warning about the chalice cracking frayed his nerves, but there was nothing he could do. He couldn't hunt for her as he had in other courts. She was nearby, and he couldn't risk being sent away.

Daemon punched his pillow and sighed. When the child returned, his Lady would return.

And he would be waiting.

4 / Terreille

Surreal tilted her head back, smiling at the sun's warmth on her face and the smell of clean sea air. Her moontime had passed; tonight she would begin working for her keep to pay Deje back for her kindness. But the day was hers, and as she meandered up the path that led to Cassandra's Altar, she enjoyed the rough landscape, the sun on her back, the crisp autumn wind teasing her long black hair.

When she rounded a bend and saw the Sanctuary, Surreal wrinkled her nose and sighed. She'd trekked all this way to see a ruin. Even though she was just beginning what might be a long, long life, she had already lived enough years to see that places where she had stayed sometimes had become crumbled piles of stone by the time she next returned. What was ancient history for so many was actual memory for her. She found the thought depressing.

Pushing her hair off her face, she stepped through an open doorway and looked around, noting the gaps in the stone walls and the holes in the roof. Sitting in the autumn sun was more appealing than wandering through chilly, barren rooms, so she turned to leave, but when she reached the doorway, she heard footsteps behind her.

The woman who stepped out from the inner chambers wore a tunic and trousers made of a shimmery, dusty black material. Her red hair, which flowed over her shoulders, was held in place by a silver circlet that fit snugly around her head. A Red Jewel hung just above her breasts. Her smile of greeting was warm but not effusive.

"How may I serve you, Sister?" she asked quietly.

The hair, faded of its vibrant color by time, and the lines on the woman's face spoke of long years, but the emerald eyes and the proud carriage said this was not a witch to trifle with.

"My apologies, Lady." Surreal met the other's steady gaze. "I came to see the Altar. I didn't know someone lived here."

"To see or to ask?"

Surreal shook her head, puzzled.

"When one seeks a Dark Altar, it's usually for help that can't be given elsewhere, or for answers to questions of the heart."

Surreal shrugged. She hadn't felt this awkward since her first client at her first Red Moon house, when she realized how little she had learned in all those dirty little back rooms. "I came to . . ." The woman's words finally penetrated. Questions of the heart. "I'd like to know who my mother's people were."

Surreal suddenly felt a whisper of something that had been there all along, a darkness, a strength she hadn't been attuned to. As she looked at the Sanctuary again, she realized that the things built around this place were insignificant. The place itself held the power.

The woman's gaze never wavered. "Everything has a price," she said quietly. "Are you willing to pay for what you ask?"

Surreal dug into her pocket and extended a handful of gold coins.

The woman shook her head. "Those who are what I am are not paid in that kind of coin." She turned back toward the doorway she'd come through. "Come. I'll make some tea and we'll talk. Perhaps we can help each other." She went down the passage, letting Surreal leave or follow, as she chose.

Surreal hesitated for a moment before dropping the coins into her pocket and following the woman. It was partly the sudden feeling of awe she had for the place, partly curiosity about what sort of price this witch would require for information, partly hope that she might finally have an answer to a question that had haunted her ever since she'd fully understood how different Titian was from everyone else. Besides, she was good with a knife and she wore the Gray. The place might hold her in awe, but the witch didn't.

The kitchen was cozy and well ordered. Surreal smiled at the contrast between the feel of this room and the rest of the Sanctuary. The woman, too, seemed more like a gentle hearth-witch than a Sanctuary Priestess as she hummed a cheery little tune while the water heated. Surreal sat in a chair, propped her elbows on the pine table, and watched in amused silence as a plate of nutcakes, a small bowl of fresh butter, and a mug for the tea were placed before her.

When the tea was ready, the woman joined her at the table, a glass of wine in her hand. Suddenly suspicious, Surreal looked pointedly at the tea, the nutcakes, and the butter.

The woman laughed. "At my age, my dietary requirements preclude such things, unfortunately. But test them if it troubles you. I won't be offended. Better you should know I mean you no ill. Else, how can we talk honestly?"

Surreal probed the food and found nothing but what should be there. Picking up a nutcake, she broke it neatly in half, buttered it, and began to eat. While she ate, the woman spoke of general things, telling her about the Dark Altars, how there were thirteen of these great dark places of power scattered throughout the Realm.

The wineglass was empty and Surreal sipped her second cup of tea before the woman said, "Now. You want to know about your mother's people. True?" She stood up and leaned toward Surreal, her hands outstretched to touch Surreal's face.

Surreal pulled back, long years of caution making her wary.

"Shh," the woman murmured soothingly, "I just want to look."

Surreal forced herself to sit quietly as the woman's hands followed the curves of her face, neck, and shoulders, lifted her long hair, and traced the curve of her ear to its delicate point. When she was done, the woman refilled her wineglass and said nothing for a while, her expression thoughtful, her eyes focused on some other place.

"I can't be certain, but I could tell you what I think."

Surreal leaned forward, trying not to appear too eager and yet holding her breath in anticipation.

The woman's gaze was disconcertingly steady. "There is, however, the matter of the price." She toyed with her wineglass. "It's customary that the price be named and agreed upon before help is given. Contracts such as these are never broken because, if they are, the price is then usually paid in blood. Do you understand, Sister?"

Surreal took a slow, steadying breath. "What's your price?"

"First, I want you to understand that I'm not asking you to endanger yourself. I'm not asking you to take any risks."

"All right."

The woman placed the stem of the wineglass between her palms and slowly rolled the glass back and forth. "A Warlord Prince has recently come to Chaillot, either into Beldon Mor or an immediate outlying village. I need to know his precise whereabouts, who he's serving."

Surreal itched to call in the stiletto, but she kept her face carefully blank. "Does this Prince have a name?"

"Daemon Sadi."

"No!" Surreal jumped up and paced the room. "Are you mad? No one toys with the Sadist if they want to stay this side of the grave." She stopped pacing and gripped the back of the chair so hard it shook from the tension. "I won't do a contract on Sadi. Forget it."

"I'm not asking you to do anything but locate him."

"So you can send someone else to do the job? Forget it. Why don't you find him yourself?"

"For reasons that are my own, I can't go into Beldon Mor."

"And you've just given me a good reason to get out."

The woman stood up and faced Surreal. "This is very important."

"Why?"

The silence grew between them, straining, draining them both. Finally the woman sighed. "Because he may have been sent here to destroy a very special child."

"You got anything to drink around here besides tea and that wine?"

The woman looked pained and amused. "Will brandy do?"

"Fine," Surreal snapped, dropping back into her chair. "Bring the bottle and a clean mug." When the bottle and mug were placed before her, she filled the mug and slugged back a third of the brandy. "Listen up, sugar," she said tartly. "Sadi may be many things, and the Darkness only knows all that he's done, but he has never, *ever* hurt a child. To suggest that—"

"What if he's forced to?" the woman said urgently.

"Forced to?" Surreal squeaked. "*Forced to?* Hell's fire, who is going to be dumb enough to force the Sadist? Do you know what he does to people who push him?" Surreal drained the mug and filled it again. "Besides, who would want to destroy this kid?"

"Dorothea SaDiablo."

Surreal swore until she could feel the words swirling around the room like smoke. She finally stopped when she noticed the woman's expression of amazed amusement. She took another drink and swore again because her anger burned up the brandy so fast she couldn't feel even a little bit mellow. Thumping the mug down on the table, she ran her hands through her hair. "Lady, you really know how to knife someone in the guts, don't you?" She glared at the woman. If the witch had returned her gaze calmly, Surreal would have knifed her, but when she saw the tears and the pain—and the fear—in those emerald eyes . . .

Titian lying on the floor with her throat slit and the walls thundering the order to run, run, run.

"Look. I owe him. He took care of my mother, and he took care of me. He didn't have to, he just did. But I'll find him. After that, we'll see." Surreal stood up. "Thanks for the tea."

The woman looked troubled. "What about your mother's people?"

Surreal met her gaze. "If I come back, we'll exchange information. But I'll give you a bit of advice for free. Don't play with the Sadist. He's got a very long memory and a wicked temper. If you give him a reason to, he'll turn you to dust. I'll see myself out."

Surreal left the Sanctuary, caught a Wind, and rode past Chaillot, chasing the setting sun far out into the ocean until she felt weary enough to return to Deje's and be civil to whomever she was supposed to bed that night.

5 / Hell

Saetan toyed with the silver-handled letter opener, keeping his back to the man who stood just inside his study door. "Is it done?"

"Forgive me, High Lord," came the ragged, whispery answer. "I could not do it."

For a flickering second before he turned to face Marjong the Executioner, Saetan wasn't sure if he felt annoyed or relieved. He leaned against his blackwood desk and studied the giant man. It was impossible to read Marjong's expressions because his head and shoulders were always covered with a black hood.

"He is in that misted city, High Lord," Marjong apologized, shifting the huge, double-headed ax from one hand to the other. "I could not reach him to carry out your request."

So. Daemon was in Beldon Mor.

"I can wait, High Lord. If he travels out of the misted city, I—"

"No." Saetan took a slow, steadying breath. "No. Do nothing more unless I specifically request it. Understood?"

Marjong bowed and left the study.

With a weary sigh, Saetan sank into his chair and slowly spun the letter opener around and around. He picked it up and studied the thin ravenglass blade and the beautifully sculpted silver handle. "An effective tool," he said quietly, balancing it on his fingertips. "Elegant, efficient. But if one isn't careful . . ." He pressed one finger against the point and watched a drop of blood well up on the finger pad. "Like you, namesake. Like you. The dance is ours now. Just between us."

6 / Terreille

Daemon's days settled into a routine. Every morning he rose early, exercised, showered, and shared breakfast with Cook in the kitchen. He liked the Angellines' cook, a brisk, warm woman who reminded him of Manny—and who had been as appalled as Manny would have been when he'd asked her consent to have the first meal of the day in the kitchen instead of in the breakfast room with the family. She'd relented when she realized he was going hungry while dancing attendance to Leland's endless stream of nervous requests. Since he joined the family for breakfast anyway, Daemon wryly noted that his breakfast in the kitchen was usually better fare than what was served in the breakfast room.

After breakfast, he met with Philip in the steward's office, where he was grudgingly handed the list of activities for the day. After that was a half hour walk through the gardens with Wilhelmina.

Alexandra had decided that Wilhelmina needed some light exercise before beginning her Craft lessons with Lady Graff, an unspeakably harsh woman whom Daemon had taken an instant dislike to—as she had to him, more because he had ignored her coquettish suggestions than for any other reason. Leland then suggested that Daemon accompany the girl, since Wilhelmina had an unreasonable fear of men and exposure to a Ringed male who couldn't be a threat to her might help relieve her fear. So when the weather permitted, he escorted Wilhelmina around the grounds.

The first few days he attempted conversation, tried to find out her interests, but she skittered away from his attempts while still trying to be a polite young lady. It struck him one morning, when a silence had stretched beyond expected comfort, that this was probably one of the rare times in the day when she had the luxury of her own thoughts. Since she spent most of her time in Graff's steely presence, she wasn't allowed to "moon about"—a phrase he'd heard Graff use one day in a tone that implied it was a usual scold. So he stopped trying to talk to her, letting her have her solitary half hour while he walked respectfully on her left, hands in his pockets, enjoying the same luxury of having time for his own thoughts.

She always had a destination, although she never seemed to reach it. No matter what paths they took through the gardens, they always ended up at a narrow path that led into a heavily overgrown alcove. Her steps would falter when she reached the place, and then she would rush past it, breathing hard, as if she'd been running for a long time. He wondered if something had happened to her there, something that frightened her, re-pelled her, and yet drew her back.

One morning when he was lost in thought, thoroughly absorbed with the puzzle his Lady had left him, he realized they'd stopped walking and Wilhelmina had been watching him for some time. They were standing by the narrow path.

"I want to go in there," she said defiantly, her hands clenched at her sides.

Daemon bit the inside of his lip to keep his face neutral. It was the first spark of life she'd shown, and he didn't want it squelched by a smile that might be misunderstood as condescension. "All right."

She looked surprised, obviously expecting an argument. With a timid smile, she led him down the path and through a trellis arch.

The small garden within the garden was completely surrounded by large yews that looked as if they hadn't been trimmed on this side in sev-eral years. A maple tree dominated one end, girdled by a circular iron bench that had been white once, but the paint was now peeling badly. In front of the yews were the remains of flower beds, tangled, weedy, uncared for. But the thing that made his breath catch, made his heart pound too fast, too hard, was the bed of witchblood in the far corner.

Flower or weed, witchblood was beautiful, deadly, and—so legend said—indestructible. The blood-red flowers, with their black throats and black-tipped petals, were in full bloom, as they always were from the first breath of spring to the last dying sigh of autumn.

Wilhelmina stood by the bed, hugging herself and shivering.

Daemon walked over to the bed, trying to understand the pain and hope in Wilhelmina's face. Witchblood supposedly grew only where a witch's blood had been spilled violently or where a witch who had met a violent death was buried.

Daemon stepped back, reeling.

Even with the fresh air and the other garden smells, the dark psychic scent was strong there. Sweet Darkness, it was strong there.

"My sister planted these," Wilhelmina said abruptly, her voice quivering. "One for each. As remembrance." She bit her lip, her blue eyes wide and frightened as she studied the flowers.

"It's all right," Daemon said soothingly, trying to calm the panic rising in her while fighting his own. "I know what witchblood is and what it stands for." He searched for words that might comfort them both. "This is a special place because of it."

"The gardeners won't come here. They say it's haunted. Do you think it's haunted? I hope it is."

Daemon considered his next words carefully. "Where's your sister?"

Wilhelmina began to cry. "Briarwood. They put her in Briarwood." The sobs became a brokenhearted keening.

Daemon held her gently while he stroked her hair, murmuring the "words of gentle sorrow" in the Old Tongue, the language of Witch.

After a minute, Wilhelmina pushed him away, sniffling. He handed her his handkerchief and, smiling, took it back when she stared at it, uncertain what to do with it after using it.

"She talks like that sometimes," Wilhelmina said. "We'd better get back." She left the alcove and hurried down the path.

Dazed, Daemon followed her back to the house.

Daemon stepped into the kitchen and gave Cook his best smile. "Any chance of a cup of coffee?"

Cook snapped a sharp, angry look in his direction. "If you like."

Confused by this sudden display of temper, Daemon shrugged out of his topcoat and sat at the kitchen table. As he puzzled over what he'd done to upset her, she thumped a mug of coffee on the table and said, "Miss Wilhelmina was crying when she came in from the garden."

Daemon ignored the coffee, more interested in Cook's reaction. "There was an alcove in the garden she wanted to visit."

The stern look in Cook's eyes instantly softened, saddened. "Ah, well." She cut two thick slabs of fresh bread, piled cold beef between them, and set it before him, an unspoken apology.

Daemon took a deep breath. "Cook, what is Briarwood?"

"A foul place, if you ask me, but no one here does," she snapped, then immediately gave him a small smile.

"What is it?"

With a sigh, Cook brought her own mug of coffee over to the table and sat down across from Daemon. "You're not eating," she said absently as she sipped her coffee.

Daemon obediently took a bite out of the sandwich and waited.

"It's a hospital for emotionally disturbed children," Cook said. "Seems a lot of young witches from good families become high-strung of a sudden when they start leaving childhood behind, if you understand me. But Miss Jaenelle's been in and out of that place since she was five years old for no better reason that I could ever see except that she used to make up fanciful stories about unicorns and dragons and such." She cocked her head toward the front of the house. "*They* say she's unbalanced because she's the only one in the family who doesn't wear the Jewels, that she tries to make up for not being able to do the Craft lessons by making up stories to get attention. If you ask me, the last thing Miss Jaenelle wants is attention. It's just that she's . . . different. It's a funny thing about her. Even when she says wild things, things you know can't be true, somehow . . . you start to wonder, you know?"

Daemon finished his sandwich and drained his mug. "How long has she been gone?"

"Since early spring. She put a flea in *all* their ears this last time. That's why they've left her there so long."

Daemon's lip curled in disgust. "What could a child possibly say that would make them want to lock her up like that?"

"She said . . ." Cook looked nervous and upset. "She said Lord Benedict wasn't her father. She said Prince Philip . . ."

Daemon let out an explosive sigh. Yes, from what he'd observed of the dynamics of this family, a statement like that *would* throw them all into a fury. Still . . .

Cook gave him a long, slow look and refilled the mugs. "Let me tell you about Miss Jaenelle.

"Two years ago, the Warlord my daughter was serving decided he wanted a prettier wench and turned my daughter out, along with the child she'd borne him. They came here to me, not having any other place to go, and Lady Alexandra let them stay. My girl, being poorly at the time, did some light parlor work and helped me in the kitchen. My grand-daughter, Lucy—the cutest little button you ever saw—stayed in the kitchen with me mostly, although Miss Jaenelle always included her in the games whenever the girls were outside. Lucy didn't like being out on her own. She was afraid of Lord Benedict's hunting dogs, and the dog boys, knowing she was scared, teased her, getting the dogs all riled up and then slipping them off the leash so they'd chase her.

"One day it went too far. The dogs had been given short rations be-cause they were going to be taken out and they were meaner than usual, and the boys got them too riled up. The pack leader slipped his leash, took off after Lucy, and chased her into the tackroom. She tripped, and he was on her, tearing at her arm. When we heard the screams, my daughter and I came running from the kitchen, and Andrew, one of the stable lads, a real good boy, came running too.

"Lucy was on the floor, screaming and screaming with that dog tear-ing at her arm, and all of a sudden, there was Miss Jaenelle. She said some strange words to the dog, and he let go of Lucy right away and slunk out of the tackroom, his tail between his legs.

"Lucy was a mess, her arm all torn up, the bone sticking up where the dog had snapped it. Miss Jaenelle told Andrew to get a bucket of water quick, and she knelt down beside Lucy and started talking to her, quiet-like, and Lucy stopped screaming. Andrew came back with the water, and Miss Jaenelle pulled out this big oval basin from somewhere, I never did notice where it came from. Andrew poured the water in the basin, and Miss Jaenelle held it for a minute, just held it, and the water started steam-ing like it was over a fire. Then she put Lucy's arm in the basin and took some leaves and powders out of her pocket and poured them in the water. She held Lucy's arm down, singing all the while, quiet. We just stood and watched. No point taking the girl to a Healer, even if we could have scraped up the coin to pay a good one. I knew that. That arm was too mangled. The best even a good Healer could have done was cut it off. So we watched, my daughter, Andrew, and me. Couldn't see much, the water all bloody like it was.

"After a while, Miss Jaenelle leaned back and lifted Lucy's arm out of the basin. There was a long, deep cut from her elbow to her wrist . . . and that was all. Miss Jaenelle looked each of us in the eye. She didn't have to say anything. We weren't about to tell on her. Then she handed me a jar of ointment, my daughter being too upset to do much. 'Put this ointment on three times a day, and keep it loosely bandaged for a week. If you do, there'll be no scar.'

"Then she turned to Lucy and said, 'Don't worry. I'll talk to them. They won't bother you again.'

"Prince Philip, when he found out Lucy'd gotten hurt because the dogs were chasing her, gave the dog boys a fierce tongue-lashing; but that afternoon I saw Lord Benedict pressing coins into the dog boys' hands, laughing and telling them how pleased he was they were keeping his dogs in such fine form.

"Anyway, by the next summer, my daughter married a young man from a fine, solid family. They live in a little village about thirty miles from here, and I visit whenever I can get a couple of days' leave."

Daemon looked into his empty mug. "Do you think Miss Jaenelle talked to them?"

"She must have," Cook replied absently.

"So the boys stopped teasing Lucy," Daemon pressed.

"Oh, no. They went right on with it. They weren't punished for it, were they? But the dogs . . . After that day, there was nothing those boys could do to make the dogs chase Lucy."

Late that night, unable to sleep, Daemon returned to the alcove. He lit a black cigarette and stared at the witchblood through the smoke.

She has come.

He'd spent the evening reviewing the facts he had, turning them over and over again as if that would change them. It hadn't, and he didn't like the conclusion he had reached.

My sister planted these. As remembrance.

A child. Witch was still a child.

No. He was misinterpreting something. He *had* to be. Witch wore the Black Jewels.

Maybe he'd gotten the information mixed up. Maybe Wilhelmina was the younger sister. He'd still been fighting to regain his emotional control when he'd arrived at the Hayllian embassy in Beldon Mor. It would make more sense if Jaenelle was almost old enough to make the Offering to the Darkness. She'd be on the cusp of opening herself to her mature strength, which would be the Black Jewels.

But the bedroom, the clothes. How could he reconcile those things with the power he'd felt when she'd healed his back after Cornelia tied him to the whipping posts?

She talks like that sometimes.

He could count on both hands the people still able to speak a few phrases of the Blood's true language. Who could have taught her?

He shied away from the answer to that.

It's a hospital for emotionally disturbed children.

Could a child wear a Jewel as dark as the Black without becoming mentally and emotionally unbalanced? He'd never heard of anyone being gifted with a Birthright Jewel that was darker than the Red.

The chalice is cracking.

He stopped thinking, let his mind quiet. The facts fell into place, forming the inevitable conclusion.

But it still took him a few more days before he could accept it.

7 / Terreille

After parting with Wilhelmina, Daemon changed into his riding clothes and headed for the stables. He had a free morning, the first since he'd arrived at the Angelline estate, and Alexandra had given him permission to take one of the horses out.

As he reached the stableyard, Guinness, the stable master, gave him a curt wave and continued his instructions to one of the stable lads.

"Going to hack out this morning?" Guinness said when Daemon approached, his gruff manner softened by a faint smile.

"If it's convenient," Daemon replied, smiling. Here, like most places where he'd served, he got along well with the staff. It was the witches he was supposed to serve that he couldn't tolerate.

"Ayah." Guinness's eyes slowly rode up Daemon's body, starting with his boots. "Good, straight, solid legs. Strong shoulders."

Daemon wondered if Guinness was going to check his teeth.

"How's your seat?" Guinness asked.

"I ride fairly well," Daemon replied cautiously, not certain he cared for the faint gleam in Guinness's eye.

Guinness sucked on his cheek. "Stallion hasn't been out for a few days.

Andrew's the only one who can ride him, and he's got a bruised thigh. Can't let the boy go out with a weak leg. You willing to try?"

Daemon took a deep breath, still suspicious. "All right."

"Andrew! Saddle up Demon."

Daemon's eyebrows shot up practically to his hairline. "Demon?"

Guinness sucked on his cheek again, refusing to notice Daemon's outraged expression. "Name's Dark Dancer, but in the stableyard, when we're out of hearing"—he shot a look at the house—"we call him what he is."

"Hell's fire," Daemon muttered as he crossed the yard to where Andrew was saddling the big bay stallion. "Anything I should know?" he asked the young man.

Andrew looked a bit worried. Finally he shrugged. "He's got a soft mouth and a hard head. He's too smart for most riders. He'll run you into the trees if you let him. Keep to the big open field, that's best. But watch the drainage ditch at the far end. It's too wide for most horses, but he'll take it, and he doesn't care if he lands on the other side without his rider."

"Thanks," Daemon growled.

Andrew grinned crookedly and handed the reins to Daemon. "I'll hold his head while you mount."

Daemon settled into the saddle. "Let him go."

Demon left the stableyard quietly enough, mouthing the bit, considering his rider. Except for showing some irritation at being held to a walk, Demon behaved quite well—until they reached a small rise and the path curved left toward the open field.

Demon pricked his ears and lunged to the right toward a lone old oak tree, almost throwing Daemon from the saddle.

The battle began.

For some perverse reason of his own, Demon was determined to reach the oak tree. Daemon was equally determined to turn him toward the field. The horse lunged, bucked, twisted, circled, fought the reins and bit. Daemon held him in check enough not to be thrown, but, circle by hard-fought circle, the stallion made his way toward the tree.

Fifteen minutes later, the horse gave up and stood with his shaking legs spread, his head down, and his lathered sides heaving. Daemon was sweat-soaked and shivering from exhaustion, and slightly amazed that his arms were still in their sockets.

When Daemon gathered the reins once more, Demon laid back his ears, prepared for the next round. Curious about what would happen, Daemon turned them toward the tree and urged the horse onward.

Demon's ears immediately pricked forward, his neck arched, and his step became high-spirited sassy.

Daemon didn't offer any aids, letting the horse do whatever he wanted. Demon circled the tree over and over, sniffing the air, alert and listening . . . and growing more and more upset. Finally the stallion bugled angrily and launched himself toward the path and the field.

Daemon didn't try to control him until they headed for the ditch. He won that battle—barely—and when Demon finally slowed down, too tired to fight anymore, Daemon turned him toward the stable.

The stable lads stared openmouthed as Daemon rode into the yard. Andrew quickly limped up and took the reins. Guinness shook his head and strode across the yard, grasped Daemon's arm as he slid wearily from the saddle, and led him to the small office beside the tackroom.

Pulling glasses and a bottle from his desk, Guinness poured out a two-finger shot and handed it to Daemon. "Here," he said gruffly, pouring a glass for himself. "It'll put some bone back in your legs."

Daemon gratefully sipped the whiskey while rubbing the knotted muscles in his shoulder.

Guinness looked at Daemon's sweat-soaked shirt and rubbed his bristly chin with his knuckles. "Gave you a bit of a time, did he?"

"It was mutual."

"Well, at least he'll still respect you in the morning."

Daemon choked. When he could breathe again, he almost asked about the tree but thought better of it. Andrew was the one who rode Demon.

After Guinness left to check on the feed, Daemon walked across the yard to where Andrew was grooming the horse.

Andrew looked up with a respectful smile. "You stayed on him."

"I stayed on him." Daemon watched the boy's smooth, easy motions. "But I had some trouble with him by a certain tree."

Andrew looked flustered. The hand brushing the stallion stuttered a little before picking up the rhythm again.

Daemon's eyes narrowed, and his voice turned dangerously silky. "What's special about that tree, Andrew?"

"Just a tree." Andrew glanced at Daemon's eyes and flinched. He shifted his feet, uneasy. "It's on the other side of the rise, you see. The first place out of sight of the house."

"So?"

"Well . . ." Andrew looked at Daemon, pleading. "You won't tell, will you?" He jerked his head toward the house. "It could cause a whole lot of trouble up there if they found out."

Daemon fought to keep his temper reined in. "Found out what?"

"About Miss Jaenelle."

Daemon shifted position, the motion so fluid and predatory that Andrew instantly stepped back, staying close to the horse as if for protection. "What about Miss Jaenelle?" he crooned.

Andrew gnawed on his lip. "At the tree . . . we . . ."

Daemon hissed.

Andrew paled, then flushed crimson. His eyes flashed with anger, and his fists clenched. "You . . . you think I'd . . ."

"Then what *do* you do at that tree?"

Andrew took a deep breath. "We change places."

Daemon frowned. "Change places?"

"Change horses. I've got a slight build. The pony can carry me."

"And she rides . . . ?"

Andrew put a tentative hand on the stallion's neck.

Daemon exploded. "You little son of a whoring bitch, you put a young girl up on *that*?"

The stallion snorted his displeasure at this display of temper.

Common sense and dancing hooves won out over Daemon's desire to throttle the stable lad.

Caught between the stallion and the angry Warlord Prince, Andrew's lips twitched with a wry smile. "You should see her up on *that*. And he takes care of her, too."

Daemon turned away, his anger spent. "Mother Night," he muttered, shaking his head as he walked toward the house and a welcome hot shower. "Mother Night."

CHAPTER SEVEN

1 / Terreille

"I just told you," Philip snapped. "You won't be needed today."

"I heard what you—"

A muscle in Philip's jaw twitched. "You have a free day. I realize Hayllians think we're a backward people, but we have museums and art galleries and theaters. There must be *something* you could do for a day that wouldn't be beneath you."

Daemon's eyes narrowed. At breakfast Leland had been skittish and unnaturally quiet, Alexandra had been unaccountably tense, Robert had been nowhere in sight, and now Philip was displaying this erratic anger and trying to force him out of the house for the day. "Very well."

Accepting a curt dismissal, he requested a carriage to take him into the shop district of Beldon Mor and went to the kitchen to see if Cook knew what was going on. But that lady, too, was in a fine fit of temper, and he retreated before she saw him, wincing as she slammed a heavy roasting pan onto her worktable.

He spent the morning wandering in and out of bookshops, gathering a variety of novels by Chaillot authors and puzzling over what could have put everyone in the household into such a state. Whatever it was, the answers weren't in the city.

He returned to the Angelline estate by lunchtime, only to find out that the entire family had left on an errand.

Annoyed at being thwarted, Daemon stacked the books on the writing desk, changed his clothes, and went to the stables.

There, too, everyone was on edge. Guinness snapped at the stable lads while they struggled to control overwrought horses.

"I'll take the stallion out if you want," Daemon offered.

"You tired of living?" Guinness snapped. He took a deep breath and relented. "It would help to get that one out of the yard for a while."

"Things are a bit tense around here."

"Ayah."

When Guinness offered nothing more, Daemon went to the stallion's box stall and waited for Andrew to saddle him. The boy's hands shook while he checked the girth. Tired of evasiveness, Daemon took the horse out of the yard and headed for the field.

Once they were out of the yard, Demon was eager, responsive, and excited. Whatever was setting the humans on edge, the stallion felt it too, but it made that simpler mind happy.

Not interested in a fight, Daemon turned them toward the tree.

Demon stopped at the tree and watched the rise they'd just come over, patiently waiting. The horse stood that way for ten minutes before eagerness gave way to dejection. When Daemon turned the horse toward the path, there was no resistance, and the gallop was halfhearted at best.

An hour later, Daemon handed the reins to Andrew and entered the house by a back door. He felt it as soon as he stepped through the doorway, and a rush of blazing anger crested and broke over him.

Striding through the corridors, Daemon slammed into his room, hurriedly showered and dressed. If he had encountered Philip during that brief walk to his room, he would have killed him.

How dare that Gray-Jeweled fool try to keep him away? How *dare* he?

Daemon knew his eyes were glazed with fury, but he didn't care. He tore out of his room and went hunting for the family.

He spun around a corner and skidded to a halt.

Wilhelmina looked pale but relieved. Graff scowled. Leland and Alexandra stared at him, startled and tense. Philip's shoulders straightened in obvious challenge.

Daemon saw it all in an instant and ignored it. The other girl commanded his full attention.

She looked emaciated, her arms and legs little more than sticks. Her head hung down, and lank strands of gold hair hid most of her face.

"Have you forgotten your manners?" Graff's bony fingers poked the girl's shoulder.

The girl's head snapped up at Graff's sharp prod, and her eyes, those *eyes,* locked onto his for a brief moment before she lowered her gaze, made a wobbly curtsy, and murmured, "Prince."

Daemon's heart pounded and his mouth watered.

Knowing he was out of control, he bowed curtly and harshly replied, "Lady." He nodded to Philip and the others, turned on his heel, and once out of sight, bolted for the library and locked the door.

His breath came in ragged sobs, his hands shook, and may the Darkness help him, he was on fire.

No, he thought fiercely as he stormed around the room looking for some explanation, some kind of escape. NO! He was not like Kartane. He had *never* hungered for a child's flesh. He was *not* like Kartane!

Collapsing against a bookcase, Daemon forced one shaking hand to slide to the mound between his trembling legs . . . and sobbed with relief to find those inches of flesh still flaccid . . . unlike the rest of him, which was seared by a fierce hunger.

Pushing away from the bookcase, Daemon went to the window and pressed his forehead against the cold glass. *Think, damn you, think.*

He closed his eyes and pictured the girl, piece by piece. As he concentrated on remembering her body, the fire eased. Until he remembered those sapphire eyes locking onto his.

Daemon laughed hysterically as tears rolled down his face.

He had accepted that Witch was a child, but he hadn't been prepared for his reaction when he finally saw her. He could take some comfort that he didn't want the child's body, but the hunger he felt for what lived inside that body scared him. The thought of being sent to another court where he couldn't see her at all scared him even more.

But it had been decades since he'd served in a court for more than a year. How was he going to keep this dance going until she was old enough to accept his surrender?

And how was he going to survive if he didn't stay?

2 / Terreille

Early the next morning Daemon staggered to the kitchen, his eyes hot and gritty from a sleepless night, his stomach aching from hunger. After leaving the library yesterday afternoon, he'd stayed in his room, unwilling to have dinner with the family and unwilling to meet anyone if he slipped down to the kitchen for something to eat.

As he reached the kitchen, the muffled giggles immediately stopped as two very different pairs of blue eyes watched him approach. Cook, looking happier than he'd ever seen her, gave him a warm greeting and told him the coffee was almost ready.

Moving cautiously, as though approaching something young and wild, Daemon sat down at one end of the kitchen table, on Jaenelle's left. With a pang of regret, he looked at the remains of a formidable breakfast and the one nutcake left on a plate.

There was an awkward moment of silence before Jaenelle leaned over and whispered something to Wilhelmina, Wilhelmina whispered something back, and the giggling started again.

Daemon reached for the nutcake, but, without looking, Jaenelle took it. She was just about to bite into it when Cook put the mug of coffee on the table and gasped.

"Now what's the Prince going to do for a breakfast, I ask you?" she demanded, but her eyes glowed with pride at the empty plates.

Jaenelle looked at the nutcake, reluctantly put it back on the plate, and edged the plate toward Daemon.

"It's all right," Daemon said mildly, looking directly at Cook. "I'm really not hungry."

Cook opened her mouth in astonishment, closed it again with a click of her teeth, and went back to her worktable, shaking her head.

He felt a warmth in his cheeks for telling so benign a white lie while those sapphire eyes studied him, so he concentrated on his coffee, avoiding her gaze.

Jaenelle broke the nutcake in half, handing him one half in a gesture that was no less a command for being unspoken, and began to eat the other half.

"You don't want to get yourself too stuffed during the day, you know," Cook said pleasantly as she puttered at her worktable. "We're having leg for dinner."

Daemon looked up, startled, as the nutcake Jaenelle was holding dropped to the table. He had never seen anyone go so deathly pale. Her eyes, enormous unblinking pools, stared straight ahead. Her throat worked convulsively.

Daemon pushed his chair back, ready to grab her and get her to the sink if she was going to be sick. "Don't you like lamb, Lady?" he asked softly.

She slowly turned her head toward him. He wanted to scream as his insides twisted at the pain and horror in her eyes. She blinked, fought for control. "L-lamb?"

Daemon gently closed one hand over hers. Her grip was painfully, surprisingly strong. Her eyes didn't waver from his, and he sensed that, with the physical link between them, he was completely vulnerable. There could be no dissembling, no white lies. "Lamb," he said reassuringly.

Jaenelle released his hand and looked away, and Daemon breathed a quiet sigh of relief.

Jaenelle turned to Wilhelmina. "Do you have time for a walk in the garden before you go to Graff?"

Wilhelmina's eyes flicked toward Daemon. "Yes. I take a walk most mornings."

Jaenelle was out of her chair, into her coat, and out the door before Wilhelmina got her chair pushed back.

"I'll be along in a minute," Daemon said quietly.

Wilhelmina slipped into her coat and hurried after her sister.

Cook shook her head. "I don't understand it. Miss Jaenelle has always liked lamb."

But you didn't say lamb, you said leg, Daemon thought as he shrugged into his topcoat. What other kind of leg would they serve in that hospital that would horrify a young girl so?

"Here." Cook handed him another mug of coffee and three apples. "At least this will get you started. Put the apples in your pocket—and mind you keep one for yourself."

Daemon slipped the apples into his pocket. "You're a darling," he said as he gave Cook a quick kiss on the cheek. He turned away to hide his smile and also so she could tell herself—and believe it—that he hadn't seen how flustered and pleased he'd made her.

The girls were nowhere in sight. Unconcerned, he strolled along the garden paths, sipping his coffee. He knew where to find them.

They were in the alcove, sitting on the iron bench.

Wilhelmina was chattering as though the words couldn't tumble out fast enough and gesturing with an animation startlingly at odds with the quiet, sedate girl he was accustomed to. When he approached, the chattering stopped and two pairs of eyes studied him.

Daemon polished two apples on his coat sleeve and solemnly gave one to each of them. Then he walked to the other end of the alcove. He couldn't make himself turn his back on them, couldn't give up looking at her altogether, but he settled his face into a bland expression and began to eat the apple. After a moment, the girls began to eat too.

Two pairs of eyes. Wilhelmina's eyes held a look of uncertainty, caution, hesitation. But Jaenelle's . . . When he came into the alcove, those eyes had told him she'd already come to some decision about him. He found it unnerving that he didn't know what it was.

And her voice. He was far enough away not to catch the quiet words, but the cadence of her voice was lovely, lilting, murmuring surf on a beach at sunset. He frowned, puzzled. Then, too, there was her accent. There was a common language among the Blood, even though the Old Tongue was almost forgotten, as well as a native language among each race. So every people, even speaking the same language, had a distinctive accent—and hers was different from the general Chaillot accent. It was a swirling kind of thing, as if she'd learned various words in various places and had melded them together into a voice distinctly her own. A lovely voice. A voice that could wash over a man and heal deep wounds of the heart.

The sudden silence caught him unaware, and he turned toward them, one eyebrow raised in question. Wilhelmina was looking at Jaenelle. Jaenelle was looking intently in the direction of the house.

"Graff's looking for you," Jaenelle said. "You'd better hurry."

Wilhelmina jumped up from the bench and ran lightly down the path.

Jaenelle shifted position on the seat and studied the bed of witchblood. "Did you know that if you sing to them correctly, they'll tell you the names of the ones who are gone?" Her eyes slid from the bed to study his face.

Daemon walked up to her slowly. "No, I didn't know."

"Well, they can." A bitter smile flickered on her lips, and for a brief moment there was a savage look in her eyes. "As long as Chaillot stands above the sea, the ones they were planted for won't be forgotten. And someday the blood debt will be paid in full."

Then she was a young girl again, and Daemon told himself, insisted, that the midnight, sepulchral voice he'd just heard was the result of his own light-headedness from lack of sleep and food.

"Come," Jaenelle said, waiting for him to fall into step. They strolled up the garden paths toward the house.

"Don't you have lessons with Lady Graff too?"

Anguish and grim resignation washed the air around her. "No," she said in a carefully neutral voice. "Graff says I have no ability in the Craft and there's no point holding Wilhelmina back, since I can't seem to learn even the simpler lessons."

Daemon slid a narrow-eyed look toward her and said nothing for a moment. "Then what do you do while Wilhelmina is having lessons?"

"Oh, I . . . do other things." She stopped quickly, head cocked, listening. "Leland wants you."

Daemon made a rude noise and was rewarded with an astonished giggle. Her pale, frail-looking hand gripped his arm and pulled him forward. His heart thumped crazily as she tugged him up the path, laughing. They continued playing all the way to the house. She tugged, he protested. Finally she tugged him into the kitchen, through the kitchen, ignoring Cook's astonished gasp, and toward the doorway leading into the corridor.

Two feet from the doorway, Daemon dug in his heels. Leland could go to Hell for all he cared. He wanted to stay with Jaenelle.

She pressed her hands against his back and propelled him through the doorway.

Landing on the other side, Daemon spun around and stared at a closed door. There hadn't been time for her to close a door. Come to think of it, he didn't remember there *being* an actual door there.

Daemon stared a moment longer, his eyes molten gold, his lips fighting to break into a grin. He made another rude noise for the benefit of whoever might be listening on the other side of the door, shrugged out of his coat, and went to see what Leland wanted.

3 / Terreille

Daemon undid the silk tie and loosened his collar. After the morning walk, he'd gone shopping with Leland. Until now he hadn't cared what she wore, except to acknowledge to himself that the frilliness of her clothes and the frothiness of her personality irritated him. Today he saw her as Jaenelle's mother, and he'd coaxed and cajoled her into a blue silk dress with simple lines that suited her trim body. She'd been different after that, more at ease. Even her voice didn't scrape his nerves as it usually did.

When Leland's shopping was done, he'd had the afternoon to himself. In any other court, he would have put the time to good use reviewing the papers his man of business sent to a post box in the city.

They would be amazed, he thought with a chilly smile, if they knew how much of their little island he owned.

Gambling at business was a mental game he excelled in. With the annual income he drew in from all corners of the Realm, he could have owned every plank of wood and every nail in Beldon Mor—and that didn't count the half dozen accounts in Hayll that Dorothea knew about and plundered occasionally when her lifestyle exceeded her own income. He always kept enough in those accounts to convince her that they were his total investments. For himself . . . Without the freedom to live as he chose, his personal indulgences were clothes and books, the books being the more personal acquisition since the clothes, like his body, were used to manipulate whomever he served.

In any other court, he would have put a free afternoon to good use. Today he'd been bored, bored, bored, chafing because he was forbidden the nursery wing and whatever was going on there.

The evening had been taken up with dinner and the theater. On the spur of the moment, Robert had decided to go with them, and Daemon had found the jockeying for seats in their private box and the tension between Philip and Robert more interesting than the play.

So here he was at the end of the day, unable to stop his restless wandering. He walked past the Craft library and stopped, his attention caught by the faint light coming from beneath the door.

The moment he opened the door, the light went out.

Daemon slipped into the room and raised his hand. The candle-light in the far corner glowed dimly, but the light was sufficient.

His golden eyes shone with pleasure as he wound his way through the cluttered room until he was standing by the bookcases, looking at a golden-haired head studiously looking at the floor. Her bare feet peeked out from beneath her nightgown.

"It's late, little one." He chided himself for the purring, seductive throb in his voice, but there was nothing he could do about it. "Shouldn't you be in bed?"

Jaenelle looked up. The distrust in her eyes was a cold slap in the face. That morning he'd been her playmate. Why was he suddenly a stranger and suspect?

Trying to think of something to say, Daemon noticed a book on the top shelf that was pulled halfway out. Taking a hopeful guess about the reason for her sudden distrust, he pulled the book off the shelf and read the title, one eyebrow rising in surprise. If this was her idea of bedtime reading, it was no wonder she had no use for Graff's Craft lessons. Without a word, he gave her the book and reached up to brush the others on the top shelf. When he was done, the space where the book had been was no longer there, and anyone quickly glancing at the shelves wouldn't notice its absence.

Well? He didn't say it. He didn't send it. Still, he was asking the question and waiting for an answer.

Jaenelle's lips twitched. Beneath the wariness was amusement. Beneath that . . . perhaps the faintest glimmer of trust?

"Thank you, Prince," Jaenelle said with laughter in her voice.

"You're very welcome." He hesitated. "My name is Daemon."

"It would be impolite to call you that. You are my elder."

He snarled, frustrated.

Laughing, she gave him an impudent curtsy and left the room.

"Irritating chit," he growled as he left the library and returned to his room. But the gentle, hopeful smile wouldn't stop tugging at his lips.

Alexandra sat on her bed, her arms wrapped around her knees. A bell cord hung on either side of her bed. The one on the left would summon her maid. The one on the right—she looked at it for the sixth time in fifteen minutes—would ring in the bedroom below hers.

She rested her head on her arms and sighed.

He had looked so damned elegant in those evening clothes so perfectly cut to show off that magnificent body and beautiful face. When he'd spoken to her, his voice had been such a sensual caress it had caused a fluttering in her stomach—a feeling no other man had ever produced. That voice and body were maddening because he seemed completely unaware of the effect he had. At the theater, there'd been more opera glasses focused on him than on the stage.

There was his reputation to consider. However, outside of his being coolly civil, she had found nothing to fault him on. He answered when summoned, performed his duties as an escort with intuition and grace, was always courteous if never flattering—and produced so much sexual heat that every woman who had been in the theater was going to be looking for a consort or a lover tonight.

And that was the problem, wasn't it?

She hadn't had a steady lover since she'd asked Philip to take care of Leland's Virgin Night. She'd always known about Philip's passionate love for her daughter. It wouldn't have been fair to any of them to demand his presence in her bed after that night.

While a part of her objected to keeping males solely for sexual purposes, her body hadn't given up craving a man's touch. Most of the time, she satisfied that craving whenever she was a guest at a lower Queen's court—or when she sneaked away to spend a night or two with a couple of Black Widow friends and feasted on and with the males who served that coven.

Now, in the room below hers, there was a Warlord Prince who made her pulse race, a Warlord Prince who had centuries of training in providing sexual pleasure, a Warlord Prince who was hers to command.

If she dared.

Alexandra pulled the bell cord on the right side. She waited a minute and pulled it again. How did one act with a pleasure slave? They weren't considered in the same category as consorts or lovers, that much she knew. But what should she do? What should she say?

Alexandra combed her hair with her fingers. She would figure it out. She had to. If she didn't get some relief tonight, she would go mad.

Despite her frustration, she almost gave up and turned off her light, almost felt relieved that he hadn't obeyed, when there was a quiet tap on her door.

"Come in." She sat up, trying for a measure of dignity. Her palms were wet with nervous sweat. She flushed when he entered the room and leaned back against the door. He was still in evening dress, but his hair was slightly disheveled, and the half-unbuttoned shirt gave her a glimpse of his smooth, muscular chest.

Her body reacted to his physical presence, leaving her unable to think, unable to speak. She had resisted this since he arrived, but now she wanted to know what it felt like to have him in her bed.

For a long time, he said nothing. He did nothing. He leaned against the door and stared at her.

And something dangerous flickered in his golden eyes.

She waited, unwilling to dismiss him, too frightened to demand.

In the end, he came to the bed and showed her what a pleasure slave could do.

4 / Hell

Saetan ignored the light tap on his study door, as he had ignored everything these past few weeks. He watched the doorknob turn, but the door was Black-locked, and whoever was on the other side would stay on the other side.

The knob turned again and the door opened.

His lips curling in a snarl at this blatant intrusion, he limped around the desk and froze as Jaenelle slipped through the door and closed it behind her. She stood there, shy and uncertain.

"Jaenelle," he whispered. "Jaenelle!"

He opened his arms. She ran across the room and leaped into them, her thin arms gripping his neck in a stranglehold.

Saetan staggered as his weak leg started to give, but he got them to a chair by the fire. He buried his face in the crook of her neck, his arms tight around her. "Jaenelle," he whispered over and over as he kissed her forehead, kissed her cheeks. "Where have you been?"

After a while, Jaenelle braced her hands on his shoulders and pushed back. She studied his face and frowned. "You're limping again," she said in an aggrieved voice.

"The leg's weak," he replied curtly, dismissing it.

She unbuttoned the top of her blouse and pushed back the collar.

"No," he said firmly.

"You need the blood. You're limping again."

"No. You've been ill."

"No, I haven't," she protested sharply and then quickly looked away.

Saetan's eyes turned hard yellow, and he drew in a hissing breath. *If you haven't been ill, witch-child, then what was done to your body was done deliberately. I haven't forgotten the last time I saw you. That family of yours has much to explain.*

"Not really ill," Jaenelle amended.

It almost sounded like she was pleading with him to agree. But, Hell's fire, how could he look at her and agree?

"The blood's strong, Saetan." She definitely was pleading now. "And you need the blood."

"Not while you need every drop for yourself," Saetan snarled. He tried to shift position, but with Jaenelle straddling him, he was effectively tethered. He sighed. He knew that determined look too well. She wasn't about to let him go until he'd taken the blood.

And it occurred to him that she had her own reasons for wanting to give it beyond it being beneficial to him. She seemed more fragile—and not just physically. It was as if rejecting the blood would confirm some deep-seated fear she was trying desperately to control.

That decided him. He gently closed his mouth on her neck.

He took a long time to take very little, savoring the contact, hoping she would be fooled. When he finally lifted his head and pressed his finger against the wound to heal it, he read doubt in her eyes. Well, two could play that game.

"Where have you been, witch-child?" he asked so gently that it was a whip-crack demand.

The question effectively silenced her protest. She gave him a bland, innocent look. "Saetan, is there anything to eat?"

Stalemate, as he'd known it would be.

"Yes," he said dryly, "I think we can come up with something."

Jaenelle edged backward out of the chair and watched him struggle to his feet. Without a word, she fetched the cane leaning against the blackwood desk and handed it to him.

Saetan grimaced but took the cane. With one arm resting lightly around her shoulders, they left the study and the lower, rough-hewn corridors, traveled the upstairs labyrinth of hallways, and finally reached the double front doors. He led her around the side of the Hall to the Sanctuary that held the Dark Altar.

"There's a Dark Altar next to the Hall?" Jaenelle asked as she looked around with interest.

Saetan chuckled softly as he lit the four black candles in proper order. "Actually, witch-child, the Hall is built next to the Altar."

Her eyes widened as the stone wall behind the Altar turned to mist. "Ooohh," she whispered in a voice as close to awe as he'd ever heard from her. "Why's it doing that?"

"It's a Gate," Saetan replied, puzzled.

"A Gate?"

He pushed the words out. "A Gate between the Realms."

"Ooohh."

His mind stumbled. Since she'd been traveling between the Realms for years now, he'd always assumed she knew how to open the Gates. If she didn't even know there *were* Gates, how in the name of Hell had she been getting into Kaeleer and Hell all this time?

He couldn't ask. He wouldn't ask. If he asked, she'd tell him and then he'd have to strangle her.

He held out his hand. "Walk forward through the mist. By the time you count slowly to four, we'll be through the Gate."

Once they were on the other side, he led her back around the side of the Hall and through the front doors.

"Where are we?" Jaenelle asked as she studied the prisms made by the arched, leaded-glass window above the doors.

"SaDiablo Hall," he replied mildly.

Jaenelle turned slowly and shook her head. "This isn't the Hall."

"Oh, but it is, witch-child. We just went through a Gate, remember? This is the Hall in the Shadow Realm. We're in Kaeleer."

"So there really is a Shadow Realm," she murmured as she opened a door and peered into the room.

Certain she hadn't meant for him to hear that, he didn't answer. He simply filed it with the other troubling, unanswered questions that shrouded his fair-haired Lady. But it made him doubly relieved that he'd decided to introduce her to the Hall in Kaeleer.

Even before her long disappearance, he'd wanted to wean her away from Hell. He knew she would still visit Char and the rest of the *cildru dyathe,* would visit Titian, but Hekatah was too much in evidence lately, stirring up mischief with the small group of demon witches she called her coven, mischief designed to distract him, draw his attention, while her smug smiles and overly contrite apologies filled him with a dread that was slowly crystallizing into icy rage. Every day he kept Jaenelle away from Hekatah was one more day of safety for them all.

Jaenelle finished her peek at the rooms off the great hall and skipped back to him, her eyes sparkling. "It's wonderful, Saetan."

He slipped his arm around her shoulders and kissed the top of her head. "And somewhere among all these corridors is a kitchen and an excellent cook named Mrs. Beale."

They both looked up at the *click-click* of shoes coming purposefully toward them from the service corridor at the end of the great hall. Saetan smiled, recognizing that distinctive *click-click*. Helene, coming to see exactly who was in "her" house. He started to tell Jaenelle who was coming, but he was too stunned to speak.

Her face was the coldest, smoothest, most malevolent mask he had ever seen. Her sapphire eyes were maelstroms. The power in her didn't spill out in an ever-widening ring as it would have with any other witch whose temper was up, acting as a warning to whoever approached. No, it was pulling inward, spiraling downward to her core, where she would then turn it outward, with devastating results. She was turning cold, cold, cold, and he was helpless to stop her, helpless to bridge the distance that was suddenly, inexplicably, between them. She twitched her shoulders from beneath his arm, and with a grace that would have made any predator envious, began to glide in front of him.

Saetan glanced up. Helene would enter the great hall at any moment—and die. He summoned the power in his Jewels, summoned all his strength. Everything was going to ride on one word.

He thrust out his right hand, the Black Jewel ablaze, stopping Jaenelle's movement. "Lady," he said in a commanding voice.

Jaenelle looked at him. He shivered but kept his hand steady. "When Protocol is being observed and a Warlord Prince makes a request of his Queen, she graciously yields to his request unless she's no longer willing to have him serve. I ask that you trust my judgment in choosing who serves us at the Hall. I ask permission to introduce you to the housekeeper, who will do her utmost to serve you well. I ask that you accompany me to the dining room for something to eat."

He had never taught her about Protocol, about the subtle checks and balances of power among the Blood. He had assumed she'd picked up the basics through day-to-day living and observation. He'd thought he would have time to teach her the fine points of interaction between Queens and dark-Jeweled males. Now it was the only leash he had. If she failed to answer . . . "Please, witch-child," he whispered just as Helene entered the great hall and stopped.

The Darkness swirled around him. Mother Night! He'd never felt anything like this!

Jaenelle studied his right hand for a long time before slowly placing her hand over it. He shuddered, unable to control it, seeing the truth for just a moment before she kindly shut him out.

"This is my housekeeper, Helene," Saetan said, never taking his eyes off Jaenelle. "Helene, this is Lady——" He hesitated, at a loss. To say "Lady Jaenelle" was too familiar.

Jaenelle turned her maelstrom eyes on Helene, who cringed but, with the instinct of a small hunted creature, didn't move. "Angelline." The word rolled out of her in a midnight whisper.

"Angelline." Saetan looked at Helene, willing her to remain calm. "My dear, would you see what Mrs. Beale might have for us today?"

Helene remembered her station and curtsied. "Of course, High Lord," she replied with dignity. Turning around, she left the great hall with a steady, measured step that Saetan silently applauded.

Jaenelle moved away from him, her head down, her shoulders slumped.

"Witch-child?" Saetan asked gently.

The eyes that met his were pained and haunted, full of a grieving that twisted his heart because he didn't know what caused it—or, perhaps, because he did.

He hadn't shuddered because, with her touch, he had found himself looking at power as far beneath him as he was to the White. He hadn't turned away from *her*. It was what he had seen there that horrified him—during those months when she'd been gone, she'd learned the one lesson he had never wanted her to learn.

She had learned to hate.

Now he had to find a way to convince her that he hadn't turned away from her because of what she was, had to bridge the distance between them, had to find a way to bring her back. He had to understand.

"Witch-child," he said in a carefully neutral voice, "why were you going to strike Helene?"

"She's a stranger."

Rocked by her cold response, Saetan's weak leg buckled. Her arms immediately wrapped around his waist, and he didn't feel the floor at all. Somewhat bemused, he looked down and tapped the floor with his shoe. He stood on air, a quarter inch above the floor. If he walked normally, it would take a keen eye to realize he wasn't walking on the floor itself. That and the lack of sound.

"It will help you," Jaenelle explained, her voice so full of apology and concern that the arm he'd been sliding around her shoulders pulled her to him in a fierce hug.

As they walked toward the dining room, Saetan used the excuse of his weak leg to move slowly, to give himself time to think. He had to understand what had brought out that ferocity in her.

Helene was a stranger, true. But he had a score of names on a sheet of paper locked in his desk drawer, and all of them had been strangers once. Because Helene was an adult? No. Cassandra was an adult. So was Titian, so was Prothvar, Andulvar, and Mephis. So was he. Because Helene was living? No, that wasn't the answer either.

In frustration, he replayed the last few minutes, forcing himself to view it from a distance. The sound of footsteps, the sudden change in Jaenelle, her predatory glide . . . in front of him.

He stopped suddenly, shocked, but got tugged along for a few more steps before Jaenelle realized he wasn't trying to walk.

He'd wondered what her reaction would be to being with him in Kaeleer, being with him outside the Realm he ruled, and now he knew. She cared for him. She was ready to protect him because, to her anyway, a weak leg might make him vulnerable against an adversary.

Saetan smiled, squeezed her shoulder, and began walking again.

Geoffrey had been right. He had a more potent leash than Protocol to keep her in check. Unfortunately, that leash worked two ways, so from now on, he was going to have to be very, very careful.

Saetan looked with growing dismay at the amount of food on the table. Along with a bowl of stew and sticks of cornbread, there were fruit, cheese, nutcakes, cold ham, cold beef, a whole roasted chicken, a platter of vegetables, fresh bread, honeybutter, and a pitcher of milk. It ended there only because he'd refused to allow the footman to bring in the last heavily laden tray. The volume would have daunted a hungry full-grown male, let alone a young girl.

Jaenelle stared at the dishes arranged in a half-circle around her place at the table.

"Eat your stew while it's hot," Saetan suggested mildly, sipping a glass of yarbarah.

Jaenelle picked up her spoon and began to eat, but after one bite she put the spoon down, once more shy and uncertain.

Saetan began to talk in a leisurely manner. Since he talked as if he had nothing else to do and nowhere else to go and was going to sit at the table for quite some time, Jaenelle picked up the spoon again. He noticed that every time he stopped talking she put the spoon down, as if she didn't want her eating to detain him. So he gossiped, telling her about Mephis, Prothvar, Andulvar, Geoffrey, and Draca, but he ran out very quickly. *The dead don't do much,* he thought dryly as he launched into a long discourse about the book he'd been reading, completely unconcerned with whether or not it was over her head.

He started feeling a bit desperate about what to say next when she finally leaned back, her hands folded over a bulging tummy, and gave him the sweet, sleepy smile of a well-fed, content child. He put his glass up to his lips to hide his smile and briefly glanced at the carnage in front of him. Perhaps he'd been too hasty in sending that last tray back to the kitchen.

"I have a surprise for you," he said, biting his cheek as she wrestled herself into a sitting position.

He led her to the second floor of his wing. The doors along the right side led into his suite of rooms. He opened a door on the left.

He had put a lot of thought into these rooms. The bedroom had the feel of a seascape with its soft, shell-colored walls, plush sandy carpets, deep sea-blue counterpane on the huge bed, warm brown furniture, and throw pillows the color of dune grass. The adjoining sitting room belonged to the earth. The rooms still required personal touches that he'd deliberately kept absent to make them feminine.

Jaenelle admired, examined, exclaimed, and shouted back to him when she saw the bathroom, "You could swim in this bathtub!"

When she finally returned to him, he asked, "Do you like them?"

She smiled at him and nodded.

"I'm glad, because they're your rooms." He ignored her delighted gasp and continued. "Of course, they'll need your personal touches and lady's paraphernalia to give them character, and I didn't put any paintings on the walls. Those are for you to choose."

"My rooms?"

"Whenever you want to use them, whether I'm here or not. A quiet place, all your own."

He watched with pleasure as she explored the rooms again, a territorial gleam in her eyes. His smile didn't fade until she tried the door on the opposite side of the bedroom. Finding it locked, she turned away, not interested enough to question it.

When Jaenelle returned to the bathroom to ponder the possibilities of the bathtub, Saetan studied the locked door.

He loved her dearly, but he was no fool. On the other side of that locked door was another suite of rooms, somewhat smaller but no less carefully decorated. Someday a consort would reside in those rooms whenever she came to visit. For now, or at least until she asked, there was no reason to tell her what was on the other side of that door or what its occupant would be for.

"Saetan?"

He came out of his dark reverie to find her beside him again, her happiness putting a little color back into her cheeks. "Do you think we could begin my lessons again?"

"Of course." He thought for a moment. "Do you know how to create witchlight?"

Jaenelle shook her head.

"Then that's a good place to begin." He paused and added casually, "How about having your lessons here?"

"Here?"

"Yes, here. That way—"

"But then I wouldn't see Andulvar and Prothvar and Mephis," Jaenelle protested.

For the briefest moment, he was honest enough to acknowledge the jealousy he felt at her wanting to see them, at her not being exclusively his. "Of course you can see them," he said mildly, trying not to grind his teeth. "There's no reason they can't come here."

"I thought demons didn't leave Hell."

"Most of the time it's more comfortable for the dead to remain among the dead, just as it's more comfortable for the living for the dead to remain among the dead. But we all lived so long ago . . ." He shrugged. "Besides, even if it's been a long time, Mephis has been here and still handles a number of my business arrangements in this Realm. I think he would enjoy an excuse to get out of the Dark Realm—as would Andulvar and Prothvar." He hoped he wasn't going to botch this by being too sly. "And when your lessons are over, you could stop in and see your friends in Kaeleer more easily."

"That's true," Jaenelle said slowly, considering. "That way, most of the time I'd only have to jump the Webs once instead of twice." Her eyes lit up and she snapped her fingers. "Or I can even use the Gates if you show me how to open them."

His mind didn't stumble. It went head over mental heels and landed in a heap. He tried to swallow, but his mouth was desert dry. "Quite so," he finally choked out. He definitely had to strangle her. Otherwise, he'd do himself an injury with the mental acrobatics required to translate the impossible into something reasonably probable. "Your lessons," he croaked, hoping, a bit hysterically, that this would be a safe subject.

Jaenelle beamed at him, and he sighed, defeated.

"When would you like to begin?"

Jaenelle thought about this. "It's getting late today. I'll be missed if I don't come to lunch." She wrinkled her nose. "I should see Lorn tomorrow. I haven't seen him in a while and he'll be worried."

He'll be worried! Saetan bit back a growl.

"The day after tomorrow? Wilhelmina has her lessons in the morning, so no one would really miss me before lunchtime."

"Done." He kissed the top of her head, led her to the front door of the Hall, and watched her vanish as she waved good-bye. He stayed long enough to make sure Helene was over any shock she might have had, left explicit instructions about conduct when Jaenelle arrived—particularly if she arrived without him—and made his way back to his private study in the Dark Realm.

Andulvar found him there a little later, pouring a very large brandy. The Eyrien's eyes narrowed when he noticed Saetan's shaking hands. "What are you doing?"

"I'm going to get very drunk," Saetan replied calmly, taking a large swallow of brandy. "Care to join me?"

"Demons don't drink straight alcohol, and for that matter, neither should Guardians. Besides," Andulvar persisted as Saetan knocked back a second glass, "why do you want to get drunk?"

"Because I'll strangle her if I don't get drunk."

"The waif's back and you didn't tell us?" Andulvar braced his fists on his hips and growled, "Why do you want to strangle her?"

Saetan carefully poured his third large brandy. Why had he given up drinking brandy? Such a delightful drink. Like pouring water on a blazing mental fire. Or was it like pouring oil? No matter. "Did you know she jumps the Webs?"

Andulvar shrugged, unimpressed. "At least half the Jeweled Blood can jump between the ranks of the Winds."

"She doesn't jump between the ranks, my darling Andulvar, she jumps between the Realms."

Andulvar gulped. "That isn't possible," he gasped, grateful that Saetan was pouring brandy into a second glass.

"That's what I always thought. And I'm not even going to think about the danger of doing it while I can still think. That's how she's been coming and going all these years, by the way. Until today, she didn't know there were Gates."

Andulvar eyed the bottle of brandy. "That's not enough to get us both drunk—assuming, of course, it's still *possible* to get drunk."

"There's more."

"Ah, well, then."

They settled in the chairs by the fire, intent upon their task.

5 / Hell

"Guardians shouldn't drink, you know," Geoffrey said, too amused to be sympathetic.

Saetan gave the other Guardian a baleful look, then closed his eyes, hoping they would just fall out so at least some part of his head didn't hurt. He cringed when Geoffrey scraped his chair along the library floor and sat down.

"Names again?" Geoffrey asked, keeping his voice low.

"A surname, Angelline, probably from Chaillot, and Wilhelmina."

"A surname and a place to start. You're too kind, Saetan."

"I wish you dead." Saetan winced at the sound of his own voice.

"Wish granted," Geoffrey replied cheerfully as he left to get the appropriate register.

The library door opened. Draca, the Keep's Seneschal, glided to the table and placed a cup in front of Saetan. "Thiss will help," she said as she turned away. "Although you don't desserve it."

Saetan sipped the steaming brew, grimaced at the taste, but got down half of it. He leaned back in the chair, his hands loosely clasped around the cup, and listened to Geoffrey considerately turn the register's pages with the least possible amount of noise. By the time he finished the brew Draca had made, the pages had stopped turning.

Geoffrey's black eyebrows formed a V below his prominent widow's peak. He pressed his sensuous blood-red lips together. "Well," he said finally, "there's a Chaillot witch named Alexandra Angelline, who is the Queen of the Territory. She wears the Blood Opal. Her daughter, Leland, wears the Rose and is married to a Yellow-Jeweled Warlord named Robert Benedict. There's no witch named Wilhelmina Angelline, but there *is* a Wilhelmina Benedict who is fourteen years old, Chaillot-born, and wears the Purple Dusk."

Saetan sat very still. "Any other family connections?" he asked too quietly.

Geoffrey glanced up sharply. "Only one of interest. A Gray-Jeweled Prince named Philip Alexander shares a paternal bloodline with Robert Benedict and serves Alexandra Angelline. If the bloodline wasn't formally acknowledged, it's not unusual for a bastard to take a surname that reflects the Queen he serves."

"I'm aware of that. What about Jaenelle?"

Geoffrey shook his head. "Not listed."

Saetan steepled his fingers. "She said her name was Angelline, which would indicate that she, at least, is continuing the old tradition of the distaff gender following the matriarchal bloodline. She said she could come in the mornings when Wilhelmina had her lessons. Same family?"

Geoffrey closed the book. "Probably. Terreille has become lax about registering Blood family lines. But if they registered one child, why not the other?"

"Because one child wears Purple Dusk," Saetan replied with a cold smile. "They don't realize the other child wears the Jewels at all."

"Considering the fair-haired Lady, it would be hard to miss."

Saetan shook his head. "No, it wouldn't. She's never worn the Jewels she was gifted with, and she's lousy at basic Craft. If she never mentioned the more creative ways she uses Craft, they would have no way of knowing she could do anything at all." A cold fist settled between his shoulder blades. "Unless they didn't believe her," he finished softly, remembering what Jaenelle had said about the Shadow Realm. He filed that thought for later consideration and looked at the empty cup. "This stuff tastes vile, but it is helping my head. Any chance of another cup?"

"Always a chance," Geoffrey said with a hint of laughter in his voice as he pulled the bell cord. "Especially if it tastes vile."

Saetan brushed his fingers against his chin. "Geoffrey, you've been the Keep's librarian for a long, long time and probably know more about the Blood than the rest of us put together. Have you ever heard of anyone spiraling down to reach the depth of her Jewels?"

"Spiraling?" Geoffrey thought for a moment and shook his head. "No, but that doesn't mean it can't happen. Ask Draca. Compared to her, you're still in the nursery and I'm just a stripling." He pursed his lips and frowned. "There's something I read once, a long time ago, part of a poem, I think, about the great dragons of legend. How did it go? 'They spiral down into ebony—' "

" '—catching the sstars with their tailss.' " The cup in front of Saetan vanished as Draca placed the fresh one before him.

"That's it," Geoffrey said. "Saetan was asking if it was possible for the Blood to spiral down to the core."

Draca turned her head, her slow, careful movement a testimony more to great age than to grace, and fixed her reptilian eyes on Saetan. "You wish to undersstand thiss?"

Saetan looked into those ancient eyes and reluctantly nodded.

"Remove the book," Draca said to Geoffrey. She waited until she had their complete attention. "Not the Blood."

A square tank filled with water appeared on the table, each side as long as Saetan's arm and just as high. Slowly withdrawing her hands from the long sleeves of her robe, Draca opened one loosely clenched fist over the tank. Little bangles, the kind that women sew on clothing to shimmer in the light, fell into the water and floated on the surface. The bangles were the same colors as the Jewels.

In her other hand, Draca held a smooth egg-shaped stone attached to a thin silk cord. "I will demonsstrate the wayss the Blood reach the inner web, the Sself'ss core." Slowly and smoothly she lowered the stone into the water until it was suspended an inch above the bottom of the tank. She had broken the water with such ease that there was no disturbance. The bangles floated on the still surface.

"When desscent into the abysss or asscent out of the abysss iss made sslowly," she said, pulling the stone toward the surface, "it iss a private matter, a communion with onesself. It doess not dissturb thosse around. When anger, fear, or great need requiress a fasst desscent to the core to gather the power and asscend . . ." She dropped the stone into the tank. It plunged to the full length of the cord, stopping an inch above the bottom.

Saetan and Geoffrey silently watched the ripples on the surface spread out toward the edge of the tank, watched the bangles dance on the ever-widening rings.

Draca quickly jerked her hand. The stone shot straight up out of the tank, a little jet of water coming with it. Tossed back and forth in the waves, some of the light-colored bangles sank.

Draca waited for them to absorb this. "A sspiral."

The stone moved in a circular motion above the tank. As it touched the surface, the water moved with it, circling, circling, circling as the stone leisurely made its descent. The bangles, caught in the motion, followed the stone. The spiraling descent continued until the stone was an inch from the bottom. By then all the water was in motion, all the bangles caught.

"A whirlpool," Geoffrey whispered. He glanced uneasily at Saetan, who was watching the tank, his lips pressed tight, his long nails digging into the table.

"No." Draca pulled the stone straight up. The water rose with the stone, well above the tank, and splashed down on the table. The bangles, pulled out of the tank with the water, lay on the table like tiny dead fish. "A maelsstrom."

Saetan turned away. "You said the Blood don't spiral."

Draca put her hand on his arm, forcing him to turn and look at her. "Sshe iss more than Blood. Sshe iss Witch."

"It doesn't matter if she's Witch. She's still Blood."

"Sshe iss Blood and sshe iss Other."

"No." Saetan backed away from Draca. "She's still Blood. She's still one of us. She has to be." And she was still his gentle, inquisitive Jaenelle, the daughter of his soul. Nothing anyone could say would change that.

But someone had taught her to hate.

"Sshe iss Witch," Draca said with more gentleness than he'd ever heard from her. "Sshe will almosst alwayss sspiral, High Lord. You cannot alter her nature. You cannot prevent the ssmall sspiralss, the flashess of anger. You cannot prevent her from sspiraling down to her core. All the Blood needss to desscend from time to time. But the maelsstrom . . ." Draca slipped her hands into the sleeves of her robe. "Sshield her, Ssaetan. Sshield her with your sstrength and your love and perhapss it will never happen."

"And if it does?" Saetan asked hoarsely.

"It will be the end of the Blood."

CHAPTER EIGHT

1 / Terreille

Daemon shuffled the deck of cards as Leland glanced at the clock—again. They'd been playing cards for almost two hours, and if she followed the routine, she would let him go in ten minutes or one more hand, whichever came first.

It was the third night that week that Leland had requested his company when she retired. Daemon didn't mind playing cards, but it annoyed him that she insisted on playing in her sitting room instead of the drawing room downstairs. And her coquettish remarks at breakfast about how well he'd entertained her annoyed him even more.

The first morning after they'd played cards, Robert had flushed burgundy and blustered as he listened to Leland's chatter until he noticed Philip's silent rage. After that, since a pleasure slave wasn't considered a "real" man and, therefore, wasn't a rival, Robert had gleefully patted Leland's hand and told her he was pleased that she found Sadi such good company since he had to work so many evenings.

Philip, on the other hand, became brutally terse, tossing the day's itinerary at Daemon and spitting out verbal orders. He also joined Daemon and the girls for their morning walk, putting Jaenelle and Wilhelmina on either side of him, forcing Daemon to follow behind.

Neither man's reaction pleased Daemon, and Leland's pretending to be oblivious to the mounting tension pleased him even less. She wasn't as frothy or feather-headed as he'd first thought. When they played cards alone and she concentrated on the game, he saw the quiet cunning in her, the skill at dissembling so that, superficially at least, she fit into Robert's circle of society.

None of that explained why she was using him as a tease. Philip was jealous enough of his brother's right to stretch out in Leland's bed. She didn't have to flaunt another male at him.

Daemon curbed his impatience and concentrated on the cards. Leland's reason for watching the clock was no concern of his. He had his own reasons for wanting the evening to end.

Finally dismissed, Daemon headed for the Craft library. Finding it empty, he throttled the desire to destroy the room out of frustration.

That was the most irritating part about Leland's sudden attention. Jaenelle always took a nocturnal ramble around midnight, ending in the library, where he usually found her poring over some of the old Craft books. He kept his intrusions brief, never asked why she was roaming the house at that hour, and was rewarded with equally brief, although sometimes startling, snippets of conversation.

Those snippets fascinated him. They were an unsettling blend of innocence and dark perception, ignorance and knowledge. If, during their conversation, he managed to note the book and the section she was reading, he could sometimes, if he worked at it, untangle a little of what she'd said. Other times he felt as if he were holding a handful of pieces to a jigsaw puzzle the size of Chaillot itself. It was infuriating—and it was wonderful.

Daemon had almost given up waiting when the door suddenly opened and Jaenelle popped into the room. Twitching his hips out of the way so she wouldn't brush against him below the waist—something he'd taken great care to avoid since he wasn't sure what his physical reaction would be—he put his hand on her shoulder to steady her and keep her from bolting when she realized someone was in the room.

He felt a giddy pleasure when she wasn't surprised to see him. As he closed the door and lit the shaded candle-light, her right hand fluffed her hair, something she did when thinking.

"Do you like to play cards?" she asked when they'd settled on the dark brown leather couch, a discreet distance between them.

"Yes, I do," Daemon replied cautiously. Did nothing go on in this house that she didn't know about? That idea didn't please him. If she knew about his playing cards with Leland, what did she know, or understand, about his required visits to Alexandra's room?

Jaenelle fluffed her hair. "If it rains some morning and we can't take a walk, maybe you could play a card game with Wilhelmina and me."

Daemon relaxed a little. "I'd like that very much."

"Why doesn't Leland say you were playing cards? Why does she make it sound so secrety? Does she always lose?"

"No, she doesn't always lose." Daemon tried not to squirm. Why did she ask so damn many uncomfortable questions? "I think ladies like to seem mysterious."

"Or they may know things that need to stay hidden."

For a moment, Daemon forgot how to breathe. His right hand clenched the top of the couch and he winced. Damn. He'd let it slip up on him. The snake tooth had to be milked, and he hadn't taken the time to find an easily obtainable poison that wouldn't make him ill.

Jaenelle looked intently at his hand.

Suddenly uneasy, Daemon shifted position, casually dropping that hand in his lap. He'd guarded the secret of the snake tooth for centuries, and he wasn't about to tell a twelve-year-old girl about it.

He hadn't counted on her tenacity or her strength. Her hand closed on his wrist and pulled upward. He made a fist to hide his nails and pulled back, trying to break her hold. When he couldn't, he snarled in anger. It was a sound that had made strong men back away and Queens think twice about what they had ordered him to do.

Jaenelle simply looked him in the eyes. Daemon looked away first, shaking slightly as he opened his hand for her examination.

Her touch was feather-light, gentle, and knowing. She studied each finger in turn, finding the length of his nails of particular interest, and finally focused on the ring finger for a long time.

"This one's warmer than the others," she said, half to herself. "And there's something beneath it."

Daemon jumped up, pulling her halfway to the floor before she let go of his wrist. "Leave it alone, Lady," he said tightly, carefully putting his hands in his pockets.

Out of the corner of his eye, Daemon watched her resettle on the couch and study her own hands. It seemed as if she were struggling to say something, and it struck him that she, too, was considering what might inadvertently be revealed.

Finally she said shyly, "I know some healing Craft."

"I'm not ill," Daemon replied, staring straight ahead.

"But not well." Suddenly her voice sounded years older.

"There's nothing wrong, Lady," Daemon said firmly. "I thank you for your concern, but there's nothing wrong."

"It seems ladies aren't the only ones who like to seem mysterious," Jaenelle said dryly as she headed for the door. "But there is something wrong with your finger, Prince. There is pain there."

He felt cornered. If anyone else had found out about the snake tooth, he would have been creating a quiet grave right now. But Jaenelle . . . Daemon sighed and turned to look at her. From a distance, particularly in dim light, she seemed like such a frail, plain child, friendly enough but not terribly intelligent. From a distance. When you got close enough to see those eyes change from summer-sky blue to sapphire, it was hard to remember you were talking to a child, hard not to feel a shiver of apprehension at the sharp, slightly feral intelligence just beneath the surface that was drawing its own conclusions about the world.

"I helped you once," she said quietly, daring him to deny it.

Too startled to respond, Daemon stared at her. How long had she known he was the one who had given his strength to the Priest the night she had asked for help, the night Cornelia had whipped him? When he realized the answer, he could have kicked himself for being such a fool. How long? Since the first morning in the alcove when she'd made her decision about him.

"I know," he said respectfully. "I was, and am, grateful for the healing. But this isn't a wound or an illness. It's part of what I am. There's nothing you can do."

He shivered under her intense scrutiny.

Finally she shrugged and slipped out the door.

Daemon extinguished the candle-light and stood in the musty, comforting dark for a few minutes before going to his room. His secret was in her hands now. He wouldn't protect himself against anything she might say or do.

A few minutes later, Alexandra's bell began to ring.

2 / Kaeleer

Saetan looked up from the book he was reading aloud and suppressed a shiver. Jaenelle had been intently studying the book's cover for the past half hour, with that vague look in her eyes that meant she was absorbing the lesson as he intended but was also considering the information in an entirely different way. He continued to read aloud, but his mind was no longer on the words.

A few minutes later, he gave up and put the book and his half-moon glasses on the table. Jaenelle's eyes didn't follow the book as he'd expected. She focused on his right hand, her forehead puckered in concentration while she fluffed her hair.

Ah. While it was difficult to be certain until a witch reached puberty, Jaenelle showed a strong inclination to being a natural Black Widow. It would be a few years yet before the physical evidence was apparent, but her interest demanded that the training begin now.

With one eyebrow rising in amusement, Saetan held out his right hand. "Would you care to examine it more closely, Lady?"

Jaenelle gave him a distracted smile and took his hand.

He watched her explore his hand, turning it this way and that, until her fingers finally came to rest on his ring-finger nail.

"Why do you wear your nails long?" she asked in a soft voice as she studied the black-tinted nails.

"Preference," he replied easily and waited to see how much she could detect.

Jaenelle gave him a long look. "There's something beneath this one." She lightly brushed the ring-finger nail.

"I'm a Black Widow." He turned his hand so she could see beneath the nail, flexed his finger, and watched her eyes widen as the snake tooth slid out of its sheath. "That's a snake tooth. The small venom sac it's attached to lies beneath the nail. Careful," he warned as her finger moved to touch it. "My venom may not be as strong as it used to be, but it's still potent enough."

Jaenelle considered the snake tooth for a while. "Your finger isn't hot. What does it mean if your finger gets hot?"

Saetan's amusement fled. So this wasn't idle curiosity after all. "It means trouble, witch-child. If the venom isn't used, the snake tooth has to be milked every few weeks. Otherwise the venom thickens. It can even crystallize. If it can still be forced through the snake tooth, it will be a painful procedure at best." He shrugged his shoulders unhappily. "If it can't, removal of the tooth and the sac would be the only way to stop the pain."

"Why would someone wait to milk it?"

Again Saetan shrugged. "Venom needs venom. After the venom sac fills, a Black Widow's body craves poison of some kind. But what's taken into the body must be taken with care. The wrong poison can be as deadly to a Black Widow as poison generally is to the rest of the Blood. The best poison is your own. Usually Black Widows milk the sac right before their moontime so that during those days when they must rest, their bodies, stimulated by a few drops of their own venom, will slowly refill the sac with no discomfort."

"And if it's thick?"

"No good. The body will reject it." Saetan reclaimed his hand and steepled his fingers. "Witch-child—"

"If you can't use your own venom, is there a safe poison?"

"There are some poisons that can be used," he said cautiously.

"Could I have some?"

"Why?"

"Because I know someone who needs it." Jaenelle stepped away from him, suddenly hesitant.

Saetan's rib cage clamped around his heart and lungs. He fought against a desire to sink his nails into flesh and tear it. "Male or female?" he asked silkily.

"Does it make a difference?"

"Indeed it does, witch-child. If the distillation of poisons isn't blended to take gender into account, the effects could be unpleasant."

Jaenelle studied him, her eyes troubled. "Male."

Saetan sat still for a long time. "I have something I can give you. Why don't you see what sort of snack Mrs. Beale has for you? This will take a few minutes."

As soon as Jaenelle was distracted by taste-testing Mrs. Beale's offerings, Saetan returned to his private study in the Dark Realm. He locked the door and checked the adjoining rooms before going to the secret door in the paneling beside the fireplace. His workshop was Gray-locked, a sensible precaution that kept Hekatah out but still allowed Mephis and Andulvar to reach him. He flicked a thought at the candle-lights at the end of the narrow corridor, locked the door behind him, and went into his Widow's den.

This was the place where he brewed his poisons and wove his tangled webs of dreamscapes and visions. Going to the worktable that ran the entire length of one wall, he called in a small key and opened the solid wood doors of one of the large cupboards that hung above it.

The poisons sat in neat rows, their glass containers precisely labeled in the Old Tongue. Another precaution, since Hekatah had never mastered the Blood's true language.

He removed a small stoppered jar and held the glass up to the candle-light. He opened the jar and sniffed, then dipped his finger into it and tasted. It was the distillation he used for himself. Since he wasn't born a Black Widow, his body couldn't produce the venom on its own. He replaced the stopper on the jar, looked in the cupboard again, and took out a jar of tiny, blood-red flakes.

Just a flake or two of dried witchblood added to the distillation and the pain Daemon felt now would be a sweet caress compared to the agony that would be his last experience among the living. Men had actually opened themselves with a knife and pulled their own guts out trying to relieve the pain. Or this one. A softer death but just as sure. Because he was sure now that Daemon was too close. Jaenelle was reaching out to help him, but how would Daemon repay that kindness?

Saetan hesitated. And yet . . .

When he'd walked among the living and raised his sons, Mephis and Peyton, he was one note and they were two others, harmonious but different. Lucivar, too, was a different note, more often than not a sharp. Saetan had known from the first time Lucivar hauled himself to his feet, his little wings stirring the air to help him keep his balance, that this son would be a father's plague as he threw himself at the world with that arrogant Eyrien respect for all things that belong to sky and earth.

But Daemon. From the first moment Saetan had held him, he had sensed on some deep, instinctive level that the Darkness would sing to this son in the same way it sang to him, that this son would be the father's mirror. So he'd given Daemon a legacy and a burden he'd never intended to give any of his children.

His name.

He had intended to teach Daemon about honor and the responsibility that came with wearing Jewels as devastating as the Black. But because of honor, he hadn't been there. Because he believed in the Blood Laws and Protocol, he had accepted the lie when Dorothea denied him paternity. And because he had accepted the lie, Daemon had been raised as a bastard and a slave, an outcast who had no place in Blood society.

So how could he condemn Daemon to death when it was his failure to protect the child that had helped shape the man? And how could he not make that choice when Jaenelle's life might be at risk?

Saetan replaced the dried witchblood and locked the cupboard door.

There had been many times in his long, long life when he'd been required to make hard choices, bitter choices. He used the same measuring stick to make this one.

Daemon had given his strength to help Jaenelle when she needed it.

He couldn't repay that debt with a bottle full of death.

Honor forbade it.

He returned to the Kaeleer Hall, gave the distillation to Jaenelle, and went over and over the instructions with her until he was sure she had them exactly right.

3 / Terreille

Daemon sat on the edge of his bed, his right hand cradled in his lap. His shirt clung to him, sweat-soaked from the fever and the pain.

He had tried to milk the snake tooth that morning, but the venom had thickened more quickly than he'd expected, and except for inflaming already tender flesh, he'd accomplished nothing. He'd managed to get through the day, and after dinner he had asked to be excused, claiming, truthfully, that he was unwell. Since Philip had gone to dinner elsewhere and hadn't returned and Robert was going about his usual nightly business, Alexandra and Leland had been sympathetic enough not to demand anything further from him.

Now, as midnight approached and the pain was a sharp, thin line that ran from his finger up to his elbow and slowly climbed toward his shoulder, Daemon vaguely wondered what Leland and Alexandra would do when they found him. He might lose the finger or the hand, possibly even the arm at this point. Given a choice, he would rather die within his own pain. That would be preferable to what Dorothea would do to him after learning about the snake tooth, particularly since he doubted he would be capable of protecting himself.

His bedroom door opened and closed.

Jaenelle stood in front of him, solemn and still.

"Let me see your hand," she said, holding out her own.

Daemon shook his head and closed his eyes.

Jaenelle touched his shoulder. Her fingers unerringly followed the line of pain from shoulder to elbow, elbow to wrist, wrist to finger.

Daemon slowly opened his eyes. Jaenelle held his hand, but he couldn't feel it, couldn't feel his arm at all. He tried to speak but was silenced by the dark look she gave him. Positioning the small bowl he used to milk the snake tooth beneath his hand, she slowly stroked the finger from knuckle to nail tip. He felt no pain, only a growing pressure at his fingertip.

Then a faint sound, as if a grain of salt had been dropped into the bowl. Then another, and another, and one more before she squeezed a thin, white, steady thread of thickened venom out of the tooth.

"May I recite the lesson I learned today?" Jaenelle asked quietly as she continued to stroke his finger. "It will help me remember."

"If you like," Daemon replied slowly. It was hard to think, hard to concentrate as he stared at the little coil of venom at the bottom of the bowl, at the crystallized grains that had caused so much pain.

When Jaenelle began to speak, Daemon's head cleared enough to listen and understand. She told him about the snake tooth and about venom, about how a Black Widow uses four drops of her own venom mixed with a warm drink to restore the balance of poison her body needs after milking the snake tooth, about the dangers of letting venom thicken, and on and on. In the time it took her to completely milk the thick venom from the tooth, she had told him more than he'd been able to glean from centuries of effort. The fact that what she told him contradicted most of what he'd learned didn't surprise him. Dorothea and her coven made an effort to educate their Sisters in other Territories, an education Daemon knew they themselves didn't ascribe to. It explained why so many potential rivals died in such agony.

Finally it was done.

"There," Jaenelle said with satisfaction. She plumped the pillows. "You should lie back and rest now." She frowned at his shirt.

His mind felt fuzzy. She had him half out of the shirt before he realized what she was doing and made a fumbling effort to help her. Holding the drenched material by her fingertips, she wrinkled her nose and vanished it. She disappeared into the bathroom with the bowl, returned with a towel, rubbed him dry, and pushed him back onto the pillows.

Daemon closed his eyes. He felt light, dizzy, and empty to the marrow of his bones. He also felt a craving for poison that was so fierce he almost would have welcomed the pain back.

He heard water running in the bathroom, heard it stop. He opened his eyes to find Jaenelle standing by the bed holding one of Cook's mugs. "Drink this."

Daemon clumsily took the cup in his left hand and obediently sipped. His body tingled. He drank gratefully, relieved when the craving started to disappear. "What is this?" he finally asked.

"A distillation of poisons that are safe for you to drink."

"Where did—"

"Drink." She darted back into the bathroom.

He finished the drink before she returned. She placed the clean bowl on the bedside table, took the empty cup, and vanished it. "You need to sleep now." She pulled off his shoes and reached for his belt.

"I can undress myself," he growled, ashamed of how harsh his voice sounded after she'd done so much to help him.

Jaenelle stepped back. "You're embarrassed."

Daemon studied her. She wasn't being coy. "I don't undress in front of young girls."

She gave him a strange, thoughtful look. "Very well. The snake tooth hasn't drawn back into its sheath yet, so be careful not to snag it." She turned and went to the door.

It hurt to have her use that neutral, formal voice. "Lady," he called softly. When she returned to the bed, Daemon raised her hand to his lips for a light kiss. "Thank you. If you ever want to recite another lesson to help you remember it, I'd be very pleased to listen."

She smiled at him. He was asleep before she slipped out the door.

4 / Terreille

Surreal tried to shift her hips to a more comfortable position, but the arm around her tightened and the hand resting on her arm gripped with bruising force.

Philip Alexander had arranged for this evening with her early that morning. That was the only predictable thing he'd done. There was no leisurely dinner, no conversation, no turning out the lights, no light love-making before he covered her. He took her, hard, with the candle-lights glaring at full intensity so there could be no illusion about who was under him. When he was through, he rolled off her, ate the cold dinner, drank most of the wine, and took her again. Now he stared at the canopy above the bed, grinding his fingers into her bruised arm.

She could have stopped him, Gray against Gray. Her Green Jewel had shielded her a little, but not enough to keep her from getting hurt. The Gray was her surprise weapon, and she didn't want to give up that edge until she absolutely had to. After the second time, he'd done nothing but hold her tight against him, but she felt the anger in him, watched his Jew-els flash as they absorbed the energy.

"I'd kill that bastard if I could," Philip said through clenched teeth. "He acts as if nothing's happening while she . . ."

"Who?" Surreal tried to lift her head. "Who's a bastard?" If she had *some* idea what had made him act this way, she might be able to get through the rest of the night.

"That 'gift' Dorothea SaDiablo sent to Alexandra. There's more warmth in a glacier than there is in him, and yet Leland . . ."

Surreal smelled blood. She turned her head just a little. Philip, in his rage, had bitten his lip.

She'd already guessed that Philip's attachment to the Angelline court had more to do with the daughter than the mother. Wasn't that what the completely dark room was all about, being able to pretend he was leisurely making love to Leland? Were there hurried couplings when Robert Benedict wasn't there, couplings so tainted with the fear of being found out that there was no pleasure in them? Now Sadi was there, and Leland could be physically gratified by another male under Robert's watchful and approving eye.

Surreal shivered, remembering all too well what it felt like to be grat-ified by the Sadist.

"Cold?" Philip asked, his voice a little gentler.

Surreal let him tuck the quilt up around them. Now that she knew where to look, it wouldn't be difficult to reach Sadi—if she wanted to. Still, there was that red-haired witch at Cassandra's Altar who was asking about him, and she did owe him.

Surreal pushed herself up on one elbow, fighting Philip's restraining hand. She smoothed her hair away from her face, letting it fall in a long black curtain across her back and shoulder. "Philip, why do you believe Sadi is serving Lady Benedict?"

"She publicly summons him to her room so that the whole family and most of the staff knows he's with her," Philip snarled. His anger made his gray eyes look flat and cold. "And at the breakfast table, she chatters on about how entertaining he was."

"She actually says he was entertaining?" Surreal flung herself backward and laughed. Damn. Leland was smarter than she'd thought.

Philip threw himself on her, pinning her to the bed. "You find this amusing?" he spat at her. "You think this is funny?"

"Ah, sugar," Surreal said, gulping back her laughter. "From what I know about Sadi, he can be *very* entertaining out of bed, but he's seldom entertaining *in* bed."

Philip's grip eased a little. He frowned, puzzled.

"She's not the first, you know," Surreal said with a smile.

"First what?"

"The first woman to so blatantly call attention to the use of a pleasure slave." She stifled her laughter. He still didn't get it.

"Why—"

"So that after people come to expect it and the maids aren't going to gossip about rumpled linen because the story's already stale, the slave can be dismissed quietly and the lady's lover can spend a couple of leisurely hours with her without anyone suspecting." Surreal looked him in the eye. "And Lady Benedict does have a lover, doesn't she?"

Philip stared at her for a moment. He started to smile and winced when it pulled his cut lip.

Surreal playfully pushed him away, rolled off the bed, and casually walked into the bathroom. She turned on the light and studied her reflection. There were bruises on her arms and shoulders from his hands, bruises on her neck from his teeth. She winced at the raw ache between her legs. Deje was going to lose her for a few days.

By the time she returned to the bedroom, Philip had straightened the bed and was lying back comfortably, his hands under his head. The Gray Jewel glowed softly as he pulled the covers back to let her in. He studied the bruises, brushing them gently with his fingers.

"I hurt you. I'm sorry."

"Professional hazard," Surreal replied with sweet venom. He deserved a short knife in the ribs.

Philip settled her head on his shoulder and tucked the covers around them once again. She knew he was looking for a way to get back on familiar ground, to take back the pain he'd caused. She let the silence stretch and strain, making no effort to help him. She was a whore now because it was the easiest way to get close to males, learn their habits, and make a kill. Since Philip was in only one of her two books, and unlikely to be in the other, she didn't care if he ever came back.

Sadi was a different problem. She had to find a way to meet him that wouldn't arouse suspicion. That, however, was something she would consider after some sleep.

"You didn't get anything to eat," Philip said quietly.

Surreal waited for a couple of heartbeats before accepting the peace offering. "True, and I'm ravenous." She sent an order to the kitchen for two prime ribs with the works and another bottle of wine. The hefty tab Deje was going to hand him would disconcert him, but it would also alleviate some of his guilt for hurting her.

"I wouldn't worry about Sadi," Surreal said as she slipped out of bed and wrapped a dressing gown around her slim body. "Although"—how nice to see that immediate flicker of worry in his eyes—"a lover who requires his silent participation and discretion would do well to understand that Sadi remembers courtesies just as he remembers slights."

She smiled as the obelisk on the table chimed and the two meals appeared on the table. *Let him chew on that,* she thought, as she cut into the prime rib.

5 / Terreille

Daemon glided into the breakfast room but stopped just inside the door when he saw Leland and Philip engrossed in quiet conversation. Philip's back was to the door, and as he talked, his hand moved gently up and down Leland's arm. Leland's eyes, as she listened to him, were lit with the fire of a woman in love.

She was dressed in riding clothes, her hair pulled back from her face in a simple, becoming style. Yes, underneath the frills and fripperies she wore for the society ladies beat the heart of a witch.

As Leland smiled at something Philip said, she looked over his shoulder and saw Daemon. Her eyes became chilly. Stepping away from Philip, she went to the buffet table and began to fill her plate.

Philip's eyes became hard when he noticed Daemon, but he managed a smile and a courteous greeting.

Well, well, well, Daemon thought as he filled his own plate. Something was in the wind. He was supposed to go riding with Leland that morning, but he noticed Philip was also dressed to ride.

Breakfast was over and Leland had left for the stables before Philip spoke directly to Daemon. He sounded like a polite host dealing with a not-quite-welcome guest. "There's no reason for you to go out, unless you want to, of course. Since I'd planned to ride this morning, Lady Benedict doesn't require another escort."

Or a chaperon, Daemon thought as he sipped his coffee. Overnight Philip's attitude had changed from terse and jealous to this attempt at courtesy. Why? Not that it mattered. He knew exactly what he would do with a free morning—and it would be free with Leland and Philip out of the house. Alexandra was visiting a friend and wouldn't be back until after lunch, and Robert, always so occupied with his all-consuming "business," spent as little time as possible at the estate.

In fact, as that delicious dark scent once again permeated the walls of the Angelline mansion, Robert seemed more and more uncomfortable about staying there. It had reached the point that Daemon always knew when Robert came back even if he didn't see him because, in the front hallway and on the stairs leading up to the family's living quarters, there was always the slight stink of fear.

Daemon poured another cup of coffee and shrugged in response to Philip's suggestion. "I don't mind not riding this morning," he said in his bored court voice. "Most likely you're a more enthusiastic rider and would therefore be a more suitable companion."

Philip's eyes narrowed, but there was nothing in Daemon's silky, bored voice that gave any indication of an intended double meaning.

Daemon smiled and reached for another piece of toast. "You shouldn't keep the lady waiting, Prince Alexander."

Philip hesitated at the doorway. Daemon buttered his toast with slow, sensuous strokes, knowing that Philip was watching him and uneasily imagining something other than toast beneath his hand. Well, if Philip actually believed someone like Leland could make a Black-Jeweled Warlord Prince pant, the fool deserved to sweat.

The moment Philip was gone, Daemon went to his room and swiftly changed his clothes. Wilhelmina was with Graff having her lessons; Cook was in the kitchen, sipping a cup of tea and starting to plan the lunch menu; and the servants were bustling about doing their various chores. There was only one person left.

Daemon whistled a cheery little tune as he headed for the private alcove to spend a pleasant morning with his Lady.

He had prowled the gardens, prowled the house, slipped in and out of the stableyard, checked the Craft library, and finally stood in the nursery wing feeling frustrated and concerned. He simply couldn't find her. He had even checked her room, tapping quietly on the door in case she was resting or wanted some privacy. When there'd been no answer, he had slipped into the room for a cursory look.

Daemon caught his lower lip between his teeth and listened to Graff scolding Wilhelmina. He'd wondered why that harsh and not terribly educated woman was teaching Craft to a young witch from such a powerful family until he'd learned that Robert Benedict had hired her. Since Wilhelmina wasn't directly related to Leland and Alexandra, Robert's preference had overruled their objections. Daemon conceded that Graff was a good choice if a man's intention was to have a girl's sensibilities about what she was and the power she contained mangled to such an extent that she would never find any joy in the Craft or in herself. Yes, Graff was an excellent choice to bruise a young girl's ego and make her susceptible to more intimate brutality when she got a little older.

Daemon approached the classroom to see if Jaenelle might possibly be there at the same time Graff yelled, "You're worthless this morning. Absolutely worthless. You call that Craft? Go on. The lesson's over. Go do something useless. *That* you can manage. GO!"

Wilhelmina flew out the door and barreled into him. Daemon caught her by the shoulders, planting his feet to keep them both upright. She gave him a shaky smile of thanks.

"So, you're free," Daemon said, smiling in return. "Where's—"

"Oh, good, you're here," Wilhelmina said in a loud, commanding voice. "Help me practice my duet." She turned toward the music room.

"First tell me where—"

Wilhelmina stepped back and planted her heel squarely on Daemon's toes. Hard. He grunted from the pain but said nothing because Graff was now standing in the doorway, watching them closely.

Wilhelmina stepped aside. "Oh, I'm sorry. Did I hurt you?" Without waiting for an answer, she hauled him toward the music room. "Come on, I want to practice."

Once they reached the music room, she went to the piano and started digging through the music for the duet she was learning. "You can play the bass part," she said as she placed her hands on the keys.

Daemon limped to the bench and sat down. "Miss Wil—"

Wilhelmina hit the keys, drowning him out. She continued for a few bars and then turned to him and said accusingly, "You're not playing."

It was such a perfect imitation of Graff's scolding voice that Daemon's lips curled in a snarl as he twisted around to face her, but the look on her face was a plea for understanding and her eyes were glazed with fear. Grinding his teeth, he placed his hands on the keys. "One, two, three, four." They began to play.

She was badly frightened, and it had something to do with him. As they stumbled through the duet, he noticed Graff standing in the music room doorway, listening, observing, spying. They finished the duet and started again. The longer they played and the longer Graff watched them the more Wilhelmina mangled the music until Daemon wondered if they were playing the same piece. Certainly the sheet music he was reading had nothing to do with what he was hearing, and he winced more than once at the sounds being produced.

When Wilhelmina doggedly began the duet for the third time, Graff turned away with a grimace, and Daemon felt sourly envious of her ability to leave. As soon as she left, however, Wilhelmina began to play more smoothly, more quietly.

"You must never ask about Jaenelle," she said so quietly Daemon had to lean toward her to hear. 'If you can't find her, you must never ask anyone where she is."

"Why?"

Wilhelmina stared straight ahead. Her throat worked convulsively as if she were choking on the words. "Because if they find out, she might get into trouble, and I don't want her to get into trouble. I don't want her to go back to Briarwood." She stopped playing and turned toward him, her eyes misty. "Do you?"

He smoothed her hair away from her face and lightly caressed her cheek. "No, I don't want her to go back. Wilhelmina . . . Where is she?"

Wilhelmina started playing again, but quietly. "She goes for lessons in the mornings now. Sometimes she goes and sees friends."

Daemon frowned, puzzled. "If she goes for lessons, surely your father or Alexandra or Leland had arranged—"

"No."

"But a maid must accompany her and would—"

"No."

As Daemon considered this, his hands slowly closed into fists. "She goes alone?" he finally said, keeping his voice carefully neutral.

"Yes."

"And your family doesn't know she goes at all?"

"No, they mustn't know."

"And you don't know where she goes or who gives her these lessons?"

"No."

"But if your family found out about the lessons or who's giving her lessons, they might put her back in the hospital?"

Wilhelmina's chin quivered. "Yes."

"I see." Oh, yes, he did see. Beware of the Priest. She belongs to the Priest. It was careless of him to forget so formidable a rival. But she did have an innocent way of dazzling a man. He'd forgotten about the Priest. Was she with him now? What could Saetan, one of the living dead, have to offer that was preferable to what he, a living man, could offer her? But then, she wasn't ready for what a man could offer. Would Saetan try to keep her away from him? If her family ever found out about the High Lord . . .

There were too many undercurrents in this family, too many secrets. Alexandra balanced on a political knife's edge, trying to remain the ruling power of Chaillot while Robert's position in the male council that opposed her constantly undermined the trust she needed from the other Chaillot Queens. The rivalry between Robert and Philip was an open secret among the aristo Blood in Beldon Mor, and Alexandra's inability to control her own family was causing doubts about her ability to rule the Territory. Add to that the social embarrassment of having a granddaughter who had been going in and out of a hospital for emotionally disturbed children since she was five years old.

And add to that having that same child admit that the High Lord of Hell, the Prince of the Darkness, the most powerful and dangerous Warlord Prince in the history of the Blood, was teaching her Craft.

Even if they thought it was just another story, they would lock her away for good to keep her from telling anyone who might listen. But if, for once, they did believe her, what else might they do to her to end the High Lord's interest in her and keep themselves safe? And Daemon felt sure that there were things going on in Beldon Mor that Saetan wouldn't be willing to overlook or forgive.

Daemon looked up and breathed a sigh of relief.

Jaenelle stood in the doorway wearing riding clothes. Her golden hair was braided and a riding hat perched on top of her head at a rakish angle. "I'm going riding. Want to come?"

"Oh, yes!" Wilhelmina said happily. "I'm done practicing."

As he watched Wilhelmina dash out of the room, there was a bitter taste in Daemon's mouth. The ashes of dreams. After all, he was Hayll's Whore, a pleasure slave, an amusement for the ladies no matter what their age, a way to pass the time. He closed the music and made a pretense of straightening the stack. Why should he hope Jaenelle felt anything for him? Why should he hurt now like a child who's not picked for a game?

Daemon turned. Jaenelle stood by the piano, studying him, a puzzled frown wrinkling her forehead.

"Don't you ride, Prince?"

"Yes, I ride."

"Oh." She considered this. "Don't you want to come?"

Daemon blinked. He looked at her beautiful, clear sapphire eyes. It had never occurred to her to exclude him. He smiled at her and gave her braid a gentle, playful tug. "Yes, I would like to come."

She studied him again. "Don't you have any other clothes?"

Daemon choked. "I beg your pardon?"

"You're always dressed like that."

Daemon looked at his perfectly tailored black suit and white silk shirt, completely taken aback. "What's wrong with the way I dress?"

"Nothing. But if you wear those clothes, you're going to get wrinkled."

Daemon started coughing and thumped his chest to give himself time to swallow the laughter. "I have some riding clothes," he wheezed.

"Oh, good." Her eyes sparkled with amusement.

Little imp. You know why I'm choking, don't you? You're a merciless little creature to mock a man's vanity.

Jaenelle trotted to the door. "Hurry up, Prince. We'll meet you at the stable."

"My name is Daemon," he growled softly.

Jaenelle spun around, gave him an impudent curtsy and grinned before running down the hall.

Daemon walked to his room as quickly as his still-sore toes allowed. His name was Daemon, not Prince, he growled to himself as he changed clothes. It always sounded like she was calling a damn dog even if it *was* his proper Protocol title. It wouldn't hurt to call him by name, but she wouldn't because he was her elder.

Daemon paused as he pulled on his boots. He started to laugh. If *he* was her elder, then what did she think about the Priest?

When Daemon got to the stableyard, there were two ponies saddled as well as a gray mare and Dark Dancer. Not sure which horse was intended for him, he approached Andrew. The stable lad gave Daemon a wobbly smile before ducking his head and rechecking Dancer's saddle.

"Be careful," Andrew said quietly. "He's jumpy today."

"Compared to what?" Daemon asked dryly.

Andrew hunched his shoulders.

Daemon's eyes narrowed. "Is there a reason for this jumpiness?"

The shoulders hunched a bit more.

Feeling the tension running through the yard, Daemon looked around.

Jaenelle was talking quietly to one of the ponies. Wilhelmina stood nearby, waiting for someone to help her mount. Her cheeks were prettily flushed from the crisp autumn air and the excitement of riding, but she kept glancing nervously in his direction and refused to acknowledge him. "Mother Night," he muttered and went over to Wilhelmina to give her a leg up.

After helping Wilhelmina mount, Daemon turned to give Jaenelle a hand, but she was already on her pony, grinning at him.

"We'd best be off if we're going," Andrew said nervously.

As Daemon turned to answer him, he glanced around the yard. All the stable lads stood absolutely still, watching him. They all know, he thought as he mounted Dark Dancer. She was their precious secret.

Guinness came out of his office and headed toward them, his head down and shoulders hunched as if he were walking into a heavy wind. When he reached them, he sucked his cheek for a minute, cleared his throat a couple of times, and looked in their direction without looking at any of them. He cleared his throat again. "Now, you ladies haven't been out for a while, so I want you to take a nice easy hack. No rough riding, none of them big jumps. Nothing faster than a canter. And De—Dark Dancer there hasn't been out much either"—he glanced guiltily at Daemon—"so I don't want you to let him have his head and hurt himself. Understand?"

"We understand, Guinness," Jaenelle said quietly. Her voice was serious, but her lips twitched and her eyes sparkled.

"Lady Benedict and Prince Alexander are still out riding, so you watch for them, you hear?" Guinness sucked on his cheek. He waved a hand at them and said gruffly, "Go on now."

The girls took the lead, walking their ponies sedately through the yard and down the path while Daemon and Andrew followed.

"I don't remember Guinness ever calling this horse by name before," Daemon said.

Andrew shrugged his shoulders and smiled. "Miss Jaenelle doesn't like us calling him Demon. She says it makes him unhappy."

"You know, Andrew," Daemon said in a quiet, silky voice, "if this horse breaks her neck, I'm going to break yours."

Andrew chuckled. Daemon raised one eyebrow at the response.

"Wait until you see them together. It's worth watching," Andrew said. "When we get to the tree, you can have the mare. I don't think the pony can carry you."

"Very considerate of you," Daemon said dryly.

They kept to a walk all the way to the tree. When Andrew and Daemon got there, Jaenelle was already dismounted and waiting. Daemon's heart thumped crazily at the soft, shining look in her eyes, and then felt squeezed by a taloned hand when he realized she wasn't looking at him.

The stallion nickered softly and thrust his head forward. "Hello, Dancer," Jaenelle said in a voice that was a sweet, sensuous caress.

Sweet Darkness, he would give his soul if her voice sounded like that when she talked to him, Daemon thought as he dismounted. He adjusted the stirrups for her. "Give you a leg up?"

Andrew's head whipped around as if the suggestion was totally inappropriate. Perhaps it was. Daemon had the feeling she didn't need the help, but what he wouldn't have admitted to anyone for anything was that he wanted—he needed—to be able to touch her in some innocent way, even if it was just to feel her small booted foot in his cupped hands.

Jaenelle's eyes met his and held them. He fell into those sapphire pools, and he knew she saw what he didn't want to admit.

"Thank you . . . Daemon." Her voice was a feathery caress down his spine that set him on fire and soothed him.

A little giddy, Daemon cupped his hands and bent over. For the briefest moment, she pressed her foot into his hands. Then she lifted it just slightly and propelled herself into the saddle.

Daemon stared at his empty hands and slowly straightened up. The eyes looking at him were amused, but they didn't belong to a child.

"Shall we go?" Jaenelle said quietly.

As Daemon mounted the mare, Jaenelle vanished her hat and undid her braid, letting her hair float behind her in a golden wave. They set out for the field, Jaenelle riding ahead of them, her murmuring voice floating back on the breeze.

Relieved that Philip and Leland weren't in the field, it took Daemon a moment to realize that Dark Dancer was cantering far ahead of them and stretching into a ground-eating gallop.

"They're heading for the ditch!" Just as Daemon started to urge the mare forward to cut across the field and head the stallion off, Andrew grabbed his arm.

"Watch," Andrew said.

Daemon gritted his teeth and held the mare still.

Dark Dancer came up to the ditch fast, his black tail and Jaenelle's golden hair streaming behind them like flags of glory. As they approached the ditch, he checked his speed and made a wide, easy turn back toward the center of the field where the small jumps were placed. He took the little wooden jumps as if they were brick walls, high and showy, and as he cantered toward them, Daemon heard Jaenelle's silvery, velvet-coated laugh of delight.

She turned the stallion to circle the field again. Daemon urged the mare forward and they circled at an easy pace, side by side, with Wilhelmina and Andrew following.

As they reached the beginning of the circle, Jaenelle slowed Dancer to a walk. "Isn't he wonderful?" She stroked his sweaty neck.

"He's been a little more ambitious when I've ridden him," Daemon said dryly.

Jaenelle's forehead wrinkled. "Ambitious?"

"Mm. He's wanted to teach me to fly."

She laughed. The sound sang in his blood. She turned toward him then. Beneath the high spirits her eyes were haunted and sad. "Perhaps he'd like you more if you talked to him—and listened."

Daemon wanted to say something light and cheerful to take away the look in her eyes, but there was something about the way the stallion suddenly twitched his ears and seemed to be listening to them that pricked his nerves. "People talk to him all the time. He probably knows more of the stable lads' secrets than any other living thing."

"Yes, but they don't listen to him, do they?"

Daemon kept quiet, trying to steady his breathing.

"He's Blood, Daemon, but just a little. Not enough to be kindred, but too much to be . . ." Jaenelle made a small gesture with her hand that took in the mare and the ponies.

Daemon licked his lips, but his mouth was too dry. He remembered Cook's story about the dogs. "What do you mean, kindred?"

"Blood, but not the same. Blood, but not human. Kindred is . . . like but not like."

Daemon looked up. A few fluffy clouds floated in the deep blue autumn sky, and the sun shone down with its last warmth. No, the physical day hadn't changed. That's not what made him shiver. "He's half-Blood," he finally said, reluctant to know the truth. "Half Blood, half landen, forever caught in between."

"Yes."

"But you can understand him, talk to him?"

"I listen to him." Jaenelle urged Dancer into a trot.

Daemon held the mare back and watched the girl and horse circle the field. "Damn." It hurt. Dark Dancer was a Brother, and knowing that hurt worse than knowing about the human half-Bloods Daemon had seen over the years who were too strong, too driven, and too aching with an unanswered need to fit into the life of a landen village yet were still left standing on the other side of a great psychic ravine from where the weakest of the Blood stood because they weren't strong enough to cross over. But humans could at least talk to other humans. Who did this four-footed Brother have? No wonder he took such care with her.

Suddenly Jaenelle and Dancer hurtled toward Andrew as he flung himself off the pony and frantically adjusted the stirrups. Daemon put his heels into the mare and galloped over to join them.

"Andrew—"

"Hurry! Get Dancer's stirrups down!"

Daemon dropped the mare's reins and hurried over to the stallion. "Easy, Dancer," he said, stroking the horse's neck before reaching for the stirrups.

"Miss Jaenelle." Andrew grabbed her by the waist and tossed her up onto the pony. He turned in a circle, his eyes sweeping the ground. "Your hat. Damn it, your hat."

"Here." Jaenelle held the hat up and put it on her head. Her hair still flowed down her back, tangled by her ride.

Wilhelmina glanced at Jaenelle, all the color gone from her face. "Graff's going to be mad when she sees your hair."

"Graff is a bitch," Jaenelle snapped, her eyes on the path where it took a bend through some trees.

The ponies must be mares, Daemon thought as he adjusted the stirrups. All the males had flinched at the knife-edge in her voice.

"That's it," Andrew said, sliding under Dancer's neck. "Stay on the mare. There's no time to do more." He mounted, gathered the reins, and started walking forward. The stallion was furious, and showed it, but kept moving toward the path. Wilhelmina followed behind Andrew, trying to calm the nervous pony and only upsetting it more.

Daemon mounted, started forward, and then stopped. Jaenelle sat perfectly still, her eyes fixed on the bend in the path. Pain and anger filled those eyes, a hurt that went so deep he knew he had no magic to help her. Beneath the childish features was an ancient face that seared him, froze him, wrapped silk chains around his heart.

He blinked away tears, and there was Miss Jaenelle with her childish face and her not-too-intelligent summer-sky blue eyes. She gave him a little-girl smile and urged her pony to a trot just as Philip and Leland rounded the bend and stopped.

Across the field, Philip stared first at Daemon, then at Jaenelle. He said nothing when they reached the group, but he maneuvered his horse so that Jaenelle was riding beside him all the way back to the stable.

Daemon fastened the ruby cuff links onto his shirt and reached for his dinner jacket. He hadn't had a moment to himself since leaving the stable that morning. First Leland had needed an escort for an extended shopping trip on which she'd bought nothing, then Alexandra suddenly decided to visit an art gallery, and finally Philip insisted they needed to go over invitation by boring invitation all the possible social functions Daemon might have to escort Leland or Alexandra to.

Something in the field this morning had made them all nervous, something that had swirled and crackled like mist and lightning. They wanted to blame him, wanted to believe he'd done something to upset the girls, wanted to believe that the scent of the restrained violence was male and not female in origin. More than that, they wanted to believe they weren't the cause of it, and that was possible only if he was the source.

Ladies like to seem mysterious.

Not Lady Jaenelle Benedict. She didn't try to be mysterious, she simply was. She walked in full sunlight shrouded in a midnight mist that swirled around her, hiding, revealing, tantalizing, frightening. Her honesty had been blunted by punishment. Perhaps that was for the best. She was good at dissembling, had some understanding about her family's reaction if they learned some of the truths about her, and yet she couldn't dissemble enough because she cared.

How many people knew about her? Daemon wondered as he brushed his hair. How many people looked upon her as their secret?

All the stable lads as well as Guinness knew she rode Dark Dancer.

But Philip, Alexandra, Leland, Robert, and Graff didn't know.

Cook knew about her ability to heal. So did Andrew. So did a young parlor maid who'd had her lip split by the senior footman when she refused his amorous advances. Daemon had seen her that particular morning with her lip still leaking blood. An hour later she had passed him in the hallway, her lip slightly swollen but otherwise undamaged, a stunned, awed expression in her eyes. So did one of the old gardeners, who now had a salve for his aching knees. So did he.

But Philip, Alexandra, Leland, Robert, and Graff didn't know.

Wilhelmina knew her sister disappeared for hours at a time to visit unnamed friends and an unknown mentor, knew how the witchblood had come to grow in that alcove.

He knew about her midnight wandering and her secret reading of the ancient Craft texts, knew there was something terrifying and beautiful within the child cocoon that, when it came of age and finally emerged, would no longer be able to live with these people.

But Philip, Alexandra, Leland, Robert, and Graff didn't know. They saw a child who couldn't learn simple Craft, a child they considered eccentric, strange, and fanciful, a child willing to speak brutal truths that adults would never speak and didn't want to know, a child they couldn't love enough to accept, a child who was like a pin hidden in a garment that constantly scratched the skin and yet could never be found.

How many beyond Chaillot knew what she was?

But not Philip or Alexandra or Leland or Robert or Graff. Not the people who should protect her, keep her safe. They were the ones she wasn't safe from. They were the ones who had the power to harm her, to lock her away, to destroy her. They, the ones who should have kept her safe, were her enemies.

And, therefore, they were his.

Daemon studied his cold reflection one last time to make sure nothing was out of place, then joined the family for dinner.

6 / Terreille

Leland smiled nervously and glanced at the clock in her brightly lit sitting room. Instead of cards, the table held a bottle of chilled wine and two glasses. The bedroom door stood partially open, and soft light spilled out.

Daemon's stomach tightened, and he welcomed the familiar chill that began to ice his veins. "You requested my presence, Lady Benedict."

Leland's smile slipped. "Um . . . yes . . . well . . . you look tired. I mean, we've all kept you so busy these last few days and, well . . . maybe you should go to your room now and get a good night's sleep. Yes. You do look tired. Why don't you just go to your room? You *will* just go to your room, won't you? I mean . . ."

Daemon smiled.

Leland glanced at the bedroom door and blanched. "It's just . . . I'm feeling a bit off tonight. I really don't want to play cards."

"Nor do I." Daemon reached for the wine bottle and corkscrew.

"You don't have to do that!"

Daemon narrowed his eyes, studying her.

Leland scurried behind a chair.

He set the bottle and corkscrew down and slipped his hands into his pockets. "You're quite right, Lady. I am tired. With your kind permission, I'll retire now." But not to his room. Not yet.

Leland smiled weakly but stayed behind the chair.

Daemon left the room, walked down the corridor, turned the corner, and stopped. He counted to ten and then took two steps backward.

Philip stood outside Leland's door, frozen by Daemon's appearance at the end of the corridor. They stared at each other for the space of eight heartbeats before Daemon nodded in courteous greeting and stepped out of sight. He stopped and listened. After a long pause, Leland's door quietly opened, closed, and locked.

Daemon smiled. So that was their game. A pity they hadn't come to it sooner. It would have spared him all those interminable hours of playing cards with Leland. Still, he'd never been adverse to using the knowledge he gathered about the people he served, and this was just the kind of quiet leverage he needed to keep Philip out of his way. Oh, he would be a splendid silent partner in their game. He had always been a splendid partner, sympathetic and ever so helpful—unless someone crossed him. Then . . . Well, he wasn't called the Sadist for nothing.

He found it strangely flattering that she didn't look up when he slipped into the library and locked the door. She sat cross-legged on the couch, absorbed in the book tucked in her lap, her right hand fluffing her hair as she read.

He glided around the furniture, his smile becoming warmer with each step. When he reached the couch, he bowed formally. "Lady Benedict."

"Angelline," Jaenelle replied absently.

Daemon said nothing. He had discovered that if he kept his voice quiet and neutral when she was distracted with something else, she usually spoke without considering her words, responding with a simple, brutal honesty that always left him feeling as though the ground was cracking beneath his feet.

"Witch follows the matriarchal bloodline," Jaenelle said, turning a page. "Besides, Uncle Bobby isn't my father."

"Then who is your father?"

"Philip. But he won't acknowledge me." Jaenelle turned another page. "He's Wilhelmina's father too, but he was in a dream web when he sired her so he doesn't know that."

Daemon sat on the couch, so close that her arm brushed his side. "How do you know he's Wilhelmina's father?"

"Adria told me." She turned another page.

"Who's Adria?"

"Wilhelmina's mother. She told me."

Daemon considered his next words very carefully. "I had understood Wilhelmina's mother died when your sister was just an infant."

"Yes, she did."

Which meant Adria was demon-dead.

"She was a Black Widow but was broken just before she had completed her training," Jaenelle continued. "But she already knew how to weave a dream web, and she didn't want to be seeded by Bobby."

Daemon took a deep breath. When he tried to exhale, it shuddered out of him. With an effort, he dismissed what she'd just said. He wasn't here to talk about Adria. "How was your lesson this morning?"

Jaenelle became very still.

Daemon closed his eyes for a moment. He was afraid of what she might say if she answered, but he was more afraid of what might happen if she didn't. If she shut him out now . . .

"All right," she said hesitantly.

"Did you learn anything interesting?" Daemon rested his arm on the back of the couch and tried to look relaxed and lazy. Inside, he felt as if he'd swallowed shards of glass. "My own education was regrettably spotty. I envy you having such a learned mentor."

Jaenelle closed the book and stared straight ahead.

Daemon swallowed hard but pushed on. "Why don't you have your lessons here? It's customary for the tutor to come to the pupil, not the other way around." She wasn't fooled, and he knew it.

"He can't come here," she said slowly. "He mustn't come here. He mustn't find out about . . ." Jaenelle pressed her lips together.

"Why can't he come here?" Keep her talking, keep her talking. If she shut him out now, she might shut him out forever.

"His soul is of the night."

It took all of Daemon's self-control to sit still, to look relaxed and only mildly interested.

Jaenelle paused. "And I don't think he'd approve."

"You mean Philip wouldn't approve of his teaching you?"

"No. *He* wouldn't approve of Philip." She shook her head. "He wouldn't approve at all."

Nor do I, my Lady. Nor do I. As Daemon thought about the little he knew about Guardians and the stories he'd heard or read about the High Lord of Hell, he saw Jaenelle swallow, and his own throat tightened. Guardians. The living dead. They drank . . . "He doesn't hurt you, does he?" he asked harshly, instantly regretting the words.

Jaenelle twisted to face him, her eyes skimmed with icy anger.

Daemon immediately retreated, trying to find a way to soften what he'd just said. "I mean . . . does he scold you if you don't get a lesson right? The way Graff does?"

The anger left her eyes, but she was still wary. "No, he doesn't scold." She repositioned herself until she was sitting back on her heels. "Well, most of the time he doesn't. Only once, really, but that was because I scared them and it was really Prothvar's fault because I asked him to teach me and he wouldn't teach me he just laughed and said I couldn't but I knew I could so I did to show him I could but he didn't know I could and then he got scared and they got angry and that's when I got scolded. But it was really Prothvar's fault." Her eyes were full of an appeal for him to be on her side.

Daemon felt dizzied by the explanation and grasped the one thing he could pull out. "Who's Prothvar?"

"Andulvar's grandson."

Daemon was getting a headache. He'd spent too many nights getting into heated but friendly arguments with Lucivar over who was the most powerful Warlord Prince in the history of the Blood not to know who Andulvar was. Mother Night, he thought as he surreptitiously rubbed his aching temple, how many of the dead did she know? "I agree," he said decisively. "I think Prothvar was at fault."

Jaenelle blinked. She grinned. "That's what I think too." She wrinkled her nose. "Prothvar didn't think so. He still doesn't."

Daemon shrugged. "He's Eyrien. Eyriens are stubborn."

Jaenelle giggled and snuggled up next to him. Daemon slowly lowered his arm until his hand lightly caressed her shoulder, and sighed, content.

He would have to make peace with the Priest. He wouldn't step aside, but he didn't want her trapped in the middle of that kind of rivalry. Besides, the High Lord was just a rival, not an enemy. She might need him too.

"Your mentor is called the Priest, is he not?" Daemon asked in a sleepy, silky voice.

Jaenelle tensed but didn't pull away. Finally she nodded.

"When you next see him, would you tell him I send my regards?"

Jaenelle's head shot up so fast that Daemon's teeth snapped together, just missing his tongue. "You know the Priest?"

"We were briefly acquainted . . . a long time ago," Daemon said as his fingers became entangled in her hair.

Jaenelle snuggled closer, hiding a huge yawn with both hands. "I'll remember," she promised sleepily.

Daemon kissed the top of her head, reluctantly drew her to her feet, put the book back on the shelf, and led her out of the library. He pointed her toward the stairs that would take her up to her bedroom on the floor above. "Go to bed—and sleep." He tried to sound stern, but even to his own ears it came out lovingly exasperated.

"You sound like him sometimes," Jaenelle grumbled. She climbed the stairs and disappeared.

Daemon closed his eyes. Liar. Silky, court-trained liar. He didn't want to smooth away a rivalry. That wasn't why he sent the message. He wanted—secondhand and only for an instant—he wanted to force Saetan to acknowledge his son.

But what kind of message would the Priest send in return, if he cared to send any at all?

7 / Terreille

Greer stood before the two women seated by the fire, his hands clasped loosely behind his back. He was the High Priestess of Hayll's most trusted servant, her favorite assassin, her caretaker of meddlesome, messy details. This assignment was an exquisite reward for his loyalty.

"You understand what you're to do?"

Greer turned slightly toward the one called the Dark Priestess. Until tonight he had never understood why his powerful Priestess should feel so compelled to make accommodations for this mysterious "adviser." Now he understood. She had the scent of the graveyard about her, and her keen malevolence frightened and excited him. He was also aware that the "wine" she drank came from a different kind of vineyard.

"I understand and am honored that you have chosen me for this assignment." While Dorothea may have chosen who would take on the task, it quickly became apparent that the assignment had come from the other. It was something he would keep in mind for the future.

"He won't balk because you're the one explaining the terms of the agreement?" Dorothea said, glancing at his right arm. "His dislike for you is intense."

Greer gave Dorothea an oily smile and turned his attention fully on the Dark Priestess. So. Even the choice of who hadn't been made by Hayll's High Priestess. "All the more reason for him to listen—particularly if I'm not pleased to be offering such generous terms. Besides, if he chooses to lie about what he knows, I may be able to detect it far better than one of the ambassadors who"—he put his left hand over his breast in an expression of sincerity—"although most highly qualified for their usual assignments are, regrettably, reluctant to deal with Sadi except in the most perfunctory ways."

"You're not afraid of Sadi?" the Dark Priestess asked.

Her girlish voice annoyed Greer because it was at odds with her deliberately concealed face and her attitude of being a dark, powerful force. No matter. Tonight he finally understood who really controlled Hayll. "I'm not afraid of Sadi," he said with a smile, "and it will give me great pleasure to see him dirty his hands with a child's blood." Great pleasure.

"Very well. When can you leave?"

"Tomorrow. I'll allow my journey to seem casual so that it will go unremarked. While I'm there, I'll take the opportunity of looking around their quaint little city. Who knows what I might find that would be of value to you Ladies."

"Kartane's in Beldon Mor," Dorothea said as she refilled her wineglass.

"No doubt he can save you a great deal of preliminary work. Contact him while you're there."

Greer gave her another oily smile, bowed to them both, and left.

"You don't seem pleased with the choice, Sister," Hekatah said as she drained her glass and stood to leave.

Dorothea shrugged. "He was your choice. Remember that if it goes wrong." She didn't look up when Hekatah raised her hands and pulled the hood away from her face.

"Look at me," Hekatah hissed. "Remember what I am."

It always amazed Dorothea that the demon-dead didn't look any different from the living. The only distinction was the faint odor of meat beginning to spoil. "I never forget what you are," Dorothea said with a smile. Hekatah's eyes blazed with anger, but Dorothea didn't look away. "And you should remember who owns Sadi, and that it's my generosity and my influence over Prythian that's making your little game of vengeance possible."

Hekatah flipped the hood back over her face and flung out one hand. The door opened with a crash, its brass knob embedded in the stone wall. With another hiss of anger, she was gone.

Dorothea refilled her wineglass. She'd seen the slight sneer, the change in Greer's eyes after he'd met the Dark Priestess. But what was she anyway? A bag of bones that didn't know enough to fall to dust. A leech. A scheming little harpy who was still trying to get back at a man who cared for nothing in Terreille. Nothing at all. She wasn't sure she believed this story about a child the Priest was besotted with, wasn't sure what difference it made if he was. Let him have his toy. She'd thrown enough youths into the Dark Priestess's lair. Now the walking carrion wanted her to give up the use of Sadi for a hundred years, and as gratitude for Dorothea's willingness to make such an accommodation, was trying to sway her best servant, to make him untrustworthy.

Very well. Let Greer fawn. The day would come when he would realize his error—and pay for it.

Greer sat in a dark corner booth, sipping his second tankard of ale and watching the worn, weary faces of the men at the other tables. He could have gone to a tavern where he would have had a better dinner and the ale wouldn't have left an aftertaste of wash water in his mouth, but he would have had to smile and fawn over the Blood aristos that crowded a place like that. Here, because they were afraid of him, he had the table of his choice, the best cut of meat, and privacy.

He drained the tankard and raised a finger at the barmaid who hurried to refill it for him, fending off roaming hands as she passed between the tables. Greer smiled. That, too, in this place, he could have for the asking.

When he was sure everyone else was preoccupied, he lifted his right hand and laid it on the table.

He still didn't know why Sadi had done that to him, what had provoked the Sadist to such calculated destruction. He'd been sitting quietly in a tavern not unlike this one, exploring a wench's luxuries, when Sadi had walked up to his table and held out his right hand. Since Sadi had said nothing, since there was only that blank, bored face looking down at him, Greer had extended his own right hand, thinking Sadi had come to grovel for some favor. The moment Sadi's hand had closed around his, everything changed. One moment there was only the firm pressure of a handshake, the next he felt his bones being crushed, his fingers snapping, felt himself held in a mental vice so he didn't even have the luxury of fainting to escape. When the vice finally did allow him to escape . . .

His first thought when he came to was to get to a Healer right away, get to someone who could reshape the pulp that used to be a valuable tool. But someone had already done a healing. Someone had tenderly shaped his hand into a twisted claw and healed the bones sufficiently so that a Healer would have to crush them all over again in order to straighten the hand, and even Greer knew the best a second healing could do was make the shape a little better. It could never make that twisted claw into a usable hand.

Sadi had done the healing, knowing what the result would be. Sadi, who had never failed thereafter to greet him courteously, mockingly, hatefully, whenever they were both in attendance at Dorothea's court. Sadi, who now was going to butcher a child for the illusion of freedom.

Greer drained the tankard for the last time and threw a few coins on the table. There was a Web Coach heading west in an hour's time. He had wanted to wait, wanted to seem casual, but in truth, he couldn't wait to make this offer.

CHAPTER NINE

1 / Kaeleer

Saetan sat in a comfortable chair in what had become known as the "family" room at the Kaeleer Hall, his legs crossed at the knee, his fingers steepled and resting on his chin. He watched Jaenelle happily weave bright-colored ribbons through a thin sheet of wood.

Her lessons were no longer private, and he resented having so little time alone with her, but she was a living ball of witchlight who drew the males of his family to her; and he, who understood so well what drew them, couldn't find it in himself to shut them out.

Today Prothvar and Mephis haphazardly played chess while Andulvar relaxed in a chair with his eyes half-closed. Jaenelle sat on the floor in front of Saetan's chair, brightly colored sticks, playing cards, and ribbons scattered around her.

The lessons were getting better, Saetan thought dryly as he watched Jaenelle weave another ribbon through the wood. All he had to remember was to start at the end and work back to the beginning.

The lesson was supposed to be on how to pass one physical object through another. The idea was that once a witch knew how to pass one object through another, she could eventually learn how to pass living matter through non-living matter, thus being able to pass through a door or a wall. That was the idea anyway.

He had explained it in every way he could think of, had demonstrated it over and over again. She simply didn't get it. Finally, after an hour of frustration, he'd said brusquely, "If you wanted to pass your arm through that wood, what would you do?"

Jaenelle paused for the briefest moment, thrust her arm through the wood, and wiggled her fingers on the other side. "Like this?"

Andulvar had muttered something that sounded like "Mother Night." Mephis and Prothvar had upset the game table, spilling all the chess pieces on the floor. Saetan's eyes had glazed as he studied the wiggling fingers. "Like that," he'd finally said, choking.

Working backward from what she already knew made him queasy— he had never forgotten the young Warlord who had been too cocky about the lessons and then had panicked halfway through the pass—but it had only taken a few minutes to translate from flesh and wood to ribbons and wood, and it had been so pleasing to see that spark in her eyes, to almost hear the click when she put the pieces together and understood.

So now she was happily weaving ribbons through a piece of solid wood with an ease that women at a loom would envy.

"Oh, I almost forgot," Jaenelle said as she picked up another ribbon. "The Prince asked me to send his regards."

Andulvar's eyes flew open and immediately closed again. Mephis's hand froze above the piece he was about to move. Prothvar's head whipped around and immediately whipped back. Only Saetan, who was sitting in front of her, didn't react.

"The Prince?" he asked lazily.

"Mm. We have a Hayllian Warlord Prince living with us now. He's sort of a playmate for Leland and Alexandra." She paused in her weaving, her brow puckered. "I don't think he likes it much. He doesn't seem happy when he's with them. But he doesn't mind playing with Wilhelmina and me."

"And what does he play with you and Wilhelmina?" Saetan asked softly. He noticed Andulvar's sharp look, but he ignored it. Daemon wasn't just in Beldon Mor, he was in the damn house!

Jaenelle brightened. "Lots of things. We take walks, and he rides well, and he knows lots of stories, and he plays the piano with Wilhelmina, and he reads to us, and he's not like lots of grown-ups who think our games are silly." She picked up two ribbons and braided them through the wood. "He's like you in lots of ways." She tilted her head and studied his face. "He looks like you in some ways."

Saetan's blood roared in his ears. He lowered his hands and pressed one against his stomach. "And what way is that, witch-child?"

"Oh, the way your eyes get that funny look sometimes, like you've got a tummy ache and you want to laugh but you know it would hurt." She looked at the hand, now curled into a fist, that was pressing into his stomach. "Is there something wrong with your tummy?"

"Not yet."

Andulvar suddenly found the ceiling intensely interesting. Prothvar and Mephis just stared at her back. Saetan ground his teeth.

"He's really very nice, Saetan," Jaenelle said, puzzled by the strange emotional currents. "One day when it was raining, he played cradle with Wilhelmina and me for hours and hours."

"Cradle?" he said in a strangled voice.

Jaenelle embedded the Queen of Hearts into the wood. "It's a card game. The rules are pretty tricky, and the Prince kept forgetting some of them and then he'd lose."

"Did he?" Saetan bit his cheek. Hard to believe that Daemon would find the rules to any game "tricky."

"Mm. I didn't want him to feel bad, so . . . well, I was dealing, and I helped him win a game."

The ceiling above Andulvar was *intensely* interesting. Mephis started to cough. Prothvar found the texture of the curtains riveting.

Saetan cleared his throat and pushed his fist deeper into his stomach. "Did . . . did the Prince say anything?"

Jaenelle wrinkled her nose. "He said he'd be happy to teach me poker if he didn't have to bet against me. What did he mean, Saetan?"

Mephis and Prothvar leaped toward the game board and smacked their heads together. Andulvar started to shake and held the arms of the chair as if they were the only things keeping him close to the ground.

Saetan felt sure that if he didn't laugh soon his insides were going to be pulverized by the strain. "I think . . . he meant . . . that he would have liked . . . to have won by himself."

Jaenelle considered this and shook her head. "No, I don't think that's what he meant."

There was a muffled *ack ack ack* as Prothvar desperately tried to hold in the laughter, but the sound acted like a trigger and all four of them helplessly exploded.

Saetan's body felt like jelly. He slid out of the chair, landed with a thump on the floor, pitched over on his side, and howled.

Jaenelle looked at them and smiled as if willing to join in if someone would explain the joke. After a minute, she got to her feet, smoothed down her dress with the quiet pride and dignity of a young Queen, stepped over Saetan's legs, and headed for the door.

Saetan instantly sobered. Pushing himself up on one elbow, he said, "Witch-child? Where are you going?" The other three men stayed silent, waiting for an answer.

Jaenelle turned and looked down at Saetan. "I'm going to the bathroom and then I'm going to see if Mrs. Beale has anything to eat." She walked to the door, stiff-legged. The last thing they heard her mutter before she closed the door on them was, "Males."

There was a moment's more silence before the laughter sputtered to life again, continuing until none of them could stand anymore.

"I'm glad I'm dead," Andulvar said as he wiped at his eyes.

Saetan, lying on his back, tilted his head to look at his friend. "Why?"

"Because she'd be the death of me otherwise."

"Ah, but Andulvar, what a glorious way to die."

Andulvar sobered. "What are you going to do now? He went out of his way to tell you where he is. A challenge?"

Saetan slowly got to his feet, straightened his clothes, and smoothed back his hair. "Do you think he's that careless?"

"Maybe that arrogant."

Saetan thought it over and shook his head. "No, I don't think it's arrogance, but it is a challenge." He turned to face Andulvar. "To me. He may trust my intentions as little as I trust his. Perhaps we both need to trust . . . a little."

"So what will you do?"

Saetan sighed. "Send my regards in return."

2 / Terreille

As Greer looked out the embassy windows at the city called Beldon Mor, he heard the door quietly open and close. He probed the room behind him, expecting that some hand-wringing ambassador was waiting to tell him the meeting would be delayed. Instead he felt nothing but a slight chill. The fools who served here had a decent expense account. The least they could do was heat the rooms. Perhaps the little sniveler had entered, seen him, and scurried out without speaking.

Sneering, Greer turned from the windows and took one involuntary step backward.

Daemon Sadi stood by the closed door, his hands in his trouser pockets, his face that familiar, cool, bored mask. "Lord Greer," he said in a silky croon.

"Sadi," Greer replied contemptuously. "The High Priestess sent me with an offer for you."

"Oh?" Daemon said, raising one eyebrow. "Since when does Dorothea have her favorite act as a messenger boy?"

"This wasn't my idea," Greer snapped and immediately changed tack. "I do as I'm told, the same as you. Please." He gestured with his left hand toward two chairs. "Let's at least be comfortable."

Greer stiffened as Sadi glided over to the chairs and gracefully settled into one of them. The way the man moved pricked at him. There was something feline, something not altogether human in that movement. Greer sat in the other chair, the sunlight to his back, so that he could easily observe Sadi's face.

"I have an offer for you," Greer repeated. "It doesn't please me to be the one to bring it."

"So you've said."

Greer pressed his lips together. There wasn't even a spark of interest in the bastard's face. "The offer is this: one hundred years without having to serve in a court, to live where you choose and do what you choose, to spend your time in whatever society amuses you." Greer paused for dramatic effect. "And the offer includes the same terms for the Eyrien half-breed. Excuse me—your brother."

"The Eyrien is Ringed by the High Priestess of Askavi. Dorothea has no say as to what is done with him."

That was a lie, as Sadi well knew, but it annoyed Greer that there were no questions, no subtle changes in voice or expression. Could things have changed? Did he no longer have any interest in Yaslana?

"It's a generous offer," Greer said, fighting to control his desire to lash out, to force Sadi to react.

"Beyond words."

Greer's left hand clutched the chair. He took a deep breath. *He* had wanted to do the goading.

"And what's the string attached to this generous offer?" Sadi said with a feral smile.

234 THE BLACK JEWELS TRILOGY

Greer shivered. Damn those little idiots. When he was done with them, they'd know how to heat a room! He had to make this offer just right, and it was hard to think with the room so cold. "A good friend of the High Priestess has discovered that her consort has been dallying with a young witch, is besotted with her, in fact. She would like to do something to end that activity, but because of political sensitivities is unable to do anything herself."

"Mm. I would think that if she wants her consort quietly buried, you'd be more skilled to handle it than I."

"It's not the consort she wants buried." Hell's fire, it was cold!

"Ah. I see." Sadi crossed his legs at the knee and steepled his fingers, resting his long nails on his chin. "However, as you must know, my ability to travel is severely limited by the desires of the Queen I'm serving. An unexplained jaunt would be difficult."

"And not necessary. That's why the offer is being made to you."

"Oh?"

"The High Priestess's friend has reason to believe that her nemesis is in this very city." Greer's feet were numb. He wanted to rub his hands together to warm them, but Sadi didn't seem to notice the cold, and he wasn't about to show any sign of weakness.

Sadi frowned, the first change in his face since the interview began. "And how old is this nemesis? What does she look like?"

"Hard to tell exactly. You know how hard it can be to judge these flash-in-a-day races. Young, though, at least in looks. Golden hair. That's the only definite feature. Probably has a strange aura—"

Sadi laughed, an unnerving sound. He looked highly amused, but there was something queer about the glitter in his eyes. "My dear Lord Greer, you're talking about half the females living on this clump of rock. Strange aura? Compared to what? High-strung eccentricity is a prepubescent epidemic here. You won't find an aristo family on the whole damn island that doesn't have at least one daughter with a 'strange aura.' What do you expect me to do? Approach each one while her chaperon looks on and ask her if she's screwing a Hayllian from one of the Hundred Families?" He laughed again.

Greer ground his teeth. "Then you're refusing the offer?"

"No, Greer, I'm simply telling you that without more information, the friend's consort is going to be playing with his toy for a very long time.

So unless you can tell me more than that, it isn't worth the effort." Sadi stood up and tugged his jacket sleeves down over his cuffs. "The offer is intriguing, however, and if I stumble across a golden-haired girl with a taste for Hayllians, I'll give her a very good look. Now if you'll excuse me, I'm overdue at a dressmaker's shop where my tasteful opinions are required." He bowed mockingly and left.

Greer counted to ten before leaping out of the chair and stumbling to the door on his numb feet. He clawed at the door, the knob so cold it almost stuck to his skin. He finally pulled the door open, stepped into the hallway—and sagged against the wall.

The hallway felt like an oven.

Daemon stared at the bed of witchblood in the alcove. Unable to sleep, he'd gone for a walk and had ended up here. The night air was cold and he'd forgotten his topcoat, but it felt good to be numbed by a cold that wasn't coming from within.

Dorothea was looking for Jaenelle. It didn't matter if she was looking for her own reasons or at someone else's behest. Dorothea always tried to destroy strong young witches who might one day rival her power. Once she found out who and what Jaenelle was, she would use every weapon at her disposal to destroy the girl.

Greer was sniffing around for information, which meant Dorothea wasn't certain that Jaenelle lived in Beldon Mor. But there was no reason to think that Greer's visit would be brief, and if he stayed around long enough, sooner or later he would overhear someone talking about Leland Benedict's eccentric, golden-haired daughter. And then?

Have you taught her how to kill, Priest? Can you teach her such a thing? She's so wise in her innocence, so innocent in her wisdom.

He should have killed Greer instead of just crippling the hand that had slit Titian's throat. But the timing had been wrong, and even if she had had no proof, Dorothea would have suspected him. An oversight he still couldn't correct without drawing too much attention to this house. There was no place he could hide Jaenelle that would be safe enough, not with her propensity to wander, and he wasn't willing to give her to the Priest yet, even if she would go and stay away. Not yet.

Daemon shook his head. The night was fleeing, and since he'd reached the alcove, he'd known what he had to do. If the offer had been made for him alone, there would have been no question about his answer. But it hadn't been made for him alone. He took a deep breath and sent a spear thread along the Ebon-gray.

Prick? Prick, can you hear me?

There was the sudden awareness of someone waking instantly from a light sleep. *Bastard?* A stirring, a focusing. *Bastard, what—*

Listen. There's not much time. Greer made me an offer today.

Greer? Icy wariness. *Why?*

A friend of Dorothea's wants a favor. Daemon swallowed hard and shut his eyes tight. *One hundred years out of court service . . . for both of us . . . if I kill a child.*

The next words floated into Daemon's mind, venomously sweet. *Any child? Or one in particular?*

Daemon looked down. His right hand was rubbing the scar on his left wrist. *A very special child. An extraordinary child.*

And your answer was?

I told you. The offer wasn't for me al—

Where are you?

Chaillot.

A hiss of fury. *Listen to me, you son of a whoring bitch. If you accept that offer for my sake, the first thing I'll do is kill you.*

The first thing I'd do is let you. Daemon sank to his knees, shaking with relief. *Thank you.*

What? The waves of fury rolling through the thread stopped.

Thank you. I . . . had hoped . . . that would be your answer, but I had to ask. Daemon took a deep breath. *There's something else you should—*

The bitch is up. There's no time. Take care of her, Bastard. If you have to bleed everyone else dry, do it, but take care of her.

Lucivar was gone.

Daemon slowly got to his feet. He'd taken a tremendous risk contacting Lucivar. If they were caught communicating, a whipping would be the least of the punishments. He wasn't worried for himself. He was too far away from Hayll for Dorothea to detect it through her primary controlling ring, and he was confident of his ability to slide around Alexandra, who wore the secondary controlling ring. But Zuultah wasn't Alexandra, and Lucivar didn't always walk cautiously.

Be careful, Prick, Daemon thought as he slowly walked back to the house. *Be careful.* In a few more years, Jaenelle would be of age. And then they would serve the kind of Queen they'd always dreamed of.

He could have followed the Ebon-gray spear thread back to Lucivar to find out if Zuultah had detected their communication, but he didn't because he didn't want to know for certain that Zuultah was using the Ring. He didn't want to know that Lucivar was in pain.

Daemon glanced up at the windows of the nursery wing. Not a glimmer of light. He wanted to slip up the stairs, slide into that small bed, and curl himself around her, warmed by the knowledge that she was alive and safe. Because if Lucivar was in pain . . .

Daemon let himself into the house and went to his room. He undressed quickly and got into bed. His room was crowded with shadows, and as the sky lightened with the coming dawn, he kept wondering what the sun was witnessing in Pruul.

3 / Terreille

Surreal unbuttoned her coat as she meandered down a path in the Angelline public gardens, a part of the estate that Alexandra Angelline had opened for the city's use. The gardens were one of the few places left in Beldon Mor where people could walk on grass or sit under a tree, and it seemed like all of the Blood aristos were there, enjoying one of the last warm days of autumn.

Twenty years ago, when Surreal had come to the city to lend her reputation to Deje for the opening of the Red Moon house, there had been grass and trees aplenty. Now Beldon Mor was just a newer, cleaner version of Draega, thanks to the Hayllian ambassadors' skill at prostituting the council and leeching away the strength of the Blood.

More than the landens of each race, the Blood needed to stay in touch with the land. Without that contact, it was too easy to forget that, according to their most ancient legends, they were created to be the caretakers. It was too easy to become embroiled in their own egos.

Surreal walked along the garden paths, amused by the reactions to her presence. Young men on the strut watched her with calculated interest; young men walking with the Ladies they were courting glanced at her and blushed while their companions hastily tugged them in a different direction; men who were making an obligatory public appearance with their wives stared straight ahead, while their wives looked from Surreal to their husbands' pale, tight-lipped faces and back to Surreal again. She ignored all of them, to the intense relief of her clients. Well, almost all. She did smile intimately at one Warlord who had treated a young whore very harshly a few nights ago and waggled her fingers at him in greeting before hurrying away, laughing quietly and wishing she could hear his blustering explanation.

But that was enough fun. Time for business.

Surreal continued her meandering, moving closer and closer to the wrought-iron fence that separated the private gardens from the public ones. Beneath her shirt she wore the Gray Jewel mounted in a gold setting that was an exact replica of Titian's Green Jewel. She'd been probing with the Gray since she entered the gardens, hoping she wouldn't get a flickering answer because that would mean Philip was nearby—and it wasn't Philip she was looking for.

As she neared the fence, she sent the private signal Daemon had taught her so many years ago, the signal that told him she needed him. Then she turned away and continued exploring the smaller paths nearby.

Maybe he wasn't at the house. Maybe he was but couldn't get away. Maybe he wouldn't answer the signal. She hadn't dared use it since the night she pushed him into showing her Hayll's Whore.

She felt him before she saw him, coming up a path behind her. Turning, she headed toward him, pausing now and then to admire a late-blooming flower. The path was an offshoot, with less chance of someone seeing them, but even so, Surreal didn't want anyone asking questions. As she passed him, she pretended to stumble and turn her foot.

"Damn," she said as Daemon held her arm to steady her. "Hold still a minute, would you, sugar?" She put a hand on his shoulder, leaned against him, and fiddled with her shoe. "There's someone looking for you." She felt him tense, saw the small ring of frost around his feet.

"Oh? Why?"

Still fiddling with her shoe, Surreal couldn't see his face, but she knew there would be nothing but a bored, slightly put-upon expression despite the silky chill in his voice.

"She thinks you're interested in a child here, one, apparently, of great interest to her, one that Dorothea wants out of the way. If I were you, I'd watch my back. She didn't hire me for a contract, but that doesn't mean she hasn't been interviewing others who would be willing to have a try at you." She put her foot down and wobbled her ankle as if testing it.

"Do you know who she is?"

Surreal frowned and shook her head, still studying her shoe. "A witch staying at Cassandra's Altar. No way to tell how long she's been there. There are a couple of rooms fixed up. That's about it. I've stayed in worse places."

Daemon kept his head turned away from her. "Thank you for the warning. Now if you'll ex—."

"Prince? Prince, you must come and see."

Surreal turned toward the sound of the girl's voice. It sounded like silk feels, she thought as the thin, golden-haired girl skipped around the bend and stopped in front of them, her smile warm, her eyes—eyes that seemed to shift color depending on the way the sunlight found its way through the leaves—full of high spirits and curiosity.

"Hello," the girl said as she studied Surreal's face.

"Lady," Surreal replied, trying to sound respectful and dignified, but she'd heard Sadi's exasperated sigh and wanted to laugh.

"We should be getting back," Daemon said, moving to the girl's side and trying to turn her toward the private gardens.

Surreal was about to slip away when she heard Daemon say, "Lady." The coaxing, pleading note in his voice rooted her to the path. She'd never heard him sound like that. She looked at the girl, who had planted her feet and refused to be turned.

"Jaenelle," he said a bit desperately.

Jaenelle ignored him as she studied Surreal's face and chest.

That was when Surreal realized that the Gray Jewel had slipped out from under her shirt when she bent over to examine her shoe. She looked at Daemon, silently asking what she should do.

As Daemon gently squeezed Jaenelle's shoulder to get her attention, Jaenelle said, "Are you Surreal?" When Surreal didn't answer, Jaenelle tipped her head back to look at Daemon. "Is she Surreal?"

Daemon's face had a guarded, trapped look. He took a deep breath and released it, slowly. "Yes, she's Surreal."

Jaenelle clasped her hands in front of her and smiled happily at Surreal. "I have a message for you."

Surreal blinked, totally at a loss. "A message?"

"Lady, just give her the message. We have to go," Daemon said, trying to put some strength into his words.

Jaenelle frowned at him, obviously puzzled by his lack of courtesy, but she obeyed. "Titian sends her love."

Surreal's legs buckled at the same time Daemon grabbed her. "Is this your idea of a joke?" she whispered savagely, hiding her face against his chest.

"May the Darkness help me, Surreal, this is no joke."

Surreal looked up at him. Fear, too, was something she'd never heard in his voice. She braced herself and stepped away from him. "Titian is dead," she said tightly.

Jaenelle looked even more puzzled. "Yes, I know."

"How do you know Titian?" Daemon asked quietly, but his voice vibrated with tension. He shivered, and Surreal knew it had nothing to do with the fresh little breeze that had sprung up.

"She's Queen of the Harpies. She told me her daughter's name is Surreal, and she told me what she looked like, and she told me her Jewel's setting might look like the family crest. The Dea al Mon usually wear it in silver, but the gold looks right on you." Jaenelle looked at them. She was still pleased that she'd been able to deliver the message, but their reactions made no sense.

Surreal wanted to run, wanted to escape, wanted to hold on to this child who didn't think it strange to be a bridge between the living and the dead. She tried to say something, anything, but only an inarticulate sound came out, so she looked to Daemon for help and realized he wasn't standing on solid ground either.

Finally he shook himself, slipped an arm around Jaenelle's shoulders, and led her toward the private gardens.

"Wait," Surreal called. She swayed but stayed on her feet. Tears filled her eyes, filled her voice. "If you should see Titian again, send my love in return."

The smile she saw through the blur of tears was gentle and understanding. "I will, Surreal. I won't forget."

Then they were gone.

Surreal stumbled to a tree and wrapped her arms around it, tears streaming down her cheeks. Dea al Mon. The family name? The people Titian had come from? She didn't know, but it was more than she'd ever had before. She felt torn apart inside, and yet, for the first time since she'd stumbled into that room and saw Titian lying dead, she didn't feel alone.

4 / Terreille

As Cassandra opened the cupboard where she kept the wineglasses, she felt the dark male presence at the kitchen door, that unmistakable scent of the Black. Without turning, she reached for a wineglass and said, "I didn't expect you until later."

"I'm surprised you expected me at all."

She missed the glass. Only one male's psychic scent could be mistaken for Saetan's. Buying time while she vanished the Red Jewel and called in her Black, she took two glasses from the cupboard and set them on the counter before turning around.

He leaned against the door frame, his hands in his trouser pockets.

Ah, Saetan, look what you've sired. Cassandra's heart beat in an odd little rhythm as she admired his body and the almost too beautiful face. If there had been the merest hint of seduction in the air, her ancient pulse would have been racing. But there was only a bone-chilling cold and a look in his eyes that she couldn't meet.

Think, woman, think. She was a Guardian, one of the living dead, but he didn't know that. If he damaged her body, she could instantly make the transition to demon and keep fighting. She doubted he had the knowledge or skill to destroy her completely. Black against Black. She could hold her own against him.

She glanced at his eyes and knew, with shocking certainty, that it wasn't true. He had come for the kill, and he knew exactly who and what she was.

"You disappoint me, Cassandra. Your legends paint you differently," Daemon said softly, his voice thick with malevolence.

"I'm a Priestess serving at this Altar," she said, working to keep her voice steady. "You're mistaken if you think—"

He laughed softly. She stepped back from the sound and found herself pressed against the counter.

"Do you think I can't tell the difference between a Priestess and a Queen? And the Jewels, my dear, name you for what you are."

She bent her head slightly in acknowledgment. "So I'm Cassandra. What do you want, Prince?"

He eased away from the door and stepped toward her. "More to the point, Lady"—he put a nasty edge on the word—"what do *you* want?"

"I don't understand." Training demanded she stand her ground. Instinct screamed at her to run.

He kept moving toward her, smiling as she edged around the table to keep it between them. It was a seducer's smile, soft and almost gentle, except it was carved from ice. "Who are you waiting for?" He withdrew his hands from his pockets.

Cassandra glanced at his hands. The momentary relief of not seeing a ring on his right hand was stripped away by the realization of how long he wore his nails. Mother Night, he was his father's son! She kept easing around the table. If she could get to the door . . .

Daemon changed directions, blocking her escape. "Who?"

"A friend."

He shook his head in mocking sadness.

Cassandra stopped moving. "Would you like some wine?" He was dangerous, dangerous, dangerous.

"No." He paused and studied the nails on his right hand. "You don't think I can create a grave deep enough to hold you, do you?" His voice was silky, crooning, almost sleepy. Terrifying. And familiar. Another deep voice with a slightly different cadence, but the crooning rage was the same. "For your information, just in case you've been considering it, I *know* you can't create one deep enough to hold *me.*"

Cassandra lifted her chin and looked him in the eye. She'd used that pause to put a strengthening spell on her nails, making them as strong and sharp as daggers. "Maybe not, but I'm going to try."

Daemon lifted one eyebrow. "Why?" he asked too gently.

Cassandra's temper flared. "Because you're dangerous and cruel. You're Hekatah's puppet and Dorothea's pet sent here to destroy an extraordinary witch. I won't let you. I won't. You may put me in the grave for good, but I'll give you a taste of it, too."

She flung herself at him, her hand curved and ready, the Black Jewel blazing. He caught her wrists, holding her off with an ease that made her scream. He hit the Black shields on her inner barriers hard enough to make her work to keep them intact, but they wouldn't keep him out for long. She was draining her Jewels and he hadn't tapped his yet. When her Black were drained, there would be no way to stop him from shattering her mind.

She tried to twist away from him, tried to eliminate the immediate physical danger so she could concentrate on protecting her mind. Then she froze as his snake tooth pressed into her wrist. She didn't think his venom would be deadly to a Guardian, but if he pumped his full shot into her, it would paralyze her long enough for him to pick her apart at his leisure.

She looked up at him defiantly, her teeth bared, ready to fight to the end. It was the look on his face, the change in his eyes that arrested her. There was wariness there. And hope?

"You don't like Dorothea," he said slowly, as if puzzling out a difficult problem.

"I like Hekatah even less," she snapped.

"Hekatah." Daemon released her, swearing softly as he paced the room. "Hekatah still exists? Like you?"

Cassandra sniffed. "Not like me. I'm a Guardian. She's a demon."

"I beg your pardon," he said dryly as he prowled the room.

"Are you saying you weren't sent here to kill the girl?" Cassandra rubbed her sore wrists.

Daemon stopped pacing. "I'll take some wine, if you're still offering it."

Cassandra got the glasses, a bottle of red wine, and the decanter of yarbarah. Pouring a glass of each, she handed him the wine.

Daemon tested it, sniffed it, and took a sip. One eyebrow rose. "You have excellent taste in wine, Lady."

Cassandra shrugged. "Not my taste. It was a gift." When he didn't say anything else, she prodded, "Is that why you're here?"

"Perhaps," he said slowly, thinking it over. Then he smiled wryly. "I was of the opinion that I was sent here because I had been a bit too troublesome of late and there wasn't another court that would have me, or another Queen that Dorothea was willing to sacrifice in order to blunt my temper." He sipped the wine appreciatively. "However, if what you believe is true—and recent events do seem to support that belief—it was a grave error on her part." He laughed softly, but there was a brutality to the sound that made Cassandra shiver.

"Why is it an error? If she offered you something of value to—"

"Like my freedom?" The wariness was back in his eyes. "Like a century of not having to kneel and serve?"

Cassandra pressed her lips together. This was going wrong, and if he turned against her again, he wouldn't relent a second time. "The girl means everything to us, Prince, and she means nothing to you."

"Nothing?" He smiled bitterly. "Do you think that someone like me, having lived as I've lived, being what I am, would destroy the one person he's been looking for his whole life? Do you think me such a fool I don't recognize what she is, what she'll become? She's magic, Cassandra. A single flower blooming in an endless desert."

Cassandra stared at him. "You're in love with her." Sudden anger washed over her at the next thought. "She's just a child."

"That fact hasn't eluded me," he said dryly as he refilled his wineglass. "Who is 'us'?"

"What?"

"You said 'the girl means everything to us.' Who?"

"Me . . ." Cassandra hesitated, took a deep breath. "And the Priest."

Daemon's expression was a mixture of relief and pain. He licked his lips. "Does he . . . Does he think I mean her harm?" He shook his head. "No matter. I've wondered the same about him."

Cassandra gasped, incensed. "How could—" She stopped herself. If they had presumed that about him, why would he not presume the same about them? She sat at the kitchen table. He hesitated and then sat across from her. "Listen to me," she said earnestly. "I can understand why you feel bitter toward him, but you don't feel half as bitter as he does. He never wanted to walk away from you, but he had no other choice. No matter what you think of him because of the way you've had to live, one thing is true: he adores her. With every breath, with every drop of his blood, he adores her."

Daemon toyed with the wineglass. "Isn't he a little old for her?"

"I'd say he was experienced," Cassandra replied tartly. "She'll be a powerful Queen and should have an older, experienced Steward."

Daemon glanced at her, amused. "Steward?"

"Of course." She studied him. "Do you have ambitions to wear the Steward's ring?"

Daemon shook his head. His lips twitched. "No, I don't have any ambitions to wear the *Steward's* ring."

"Well, then." Cassandra's eyes widened. Now that the chill was gone, now that he was a little more relaxed . . . "You really are your father's son," she said dryly and was startled by his immediate, warm laughter. Her eyes narrowed. "You thought—that's wicked!"

"Is it?" His golden eyes caressed her with disturbing warmth. "Perhaps it is."

Cassandra smiled. When the anger and cold were gone, he really was a delightful man. "What does she think of you?"

"How in the name of Hell should I know?" he growled. His eyes narrowed as she laughed at him.

"Does she try your patience to the breaking point? Exasperate you until you want to scream? Make you feel as if you can't tell from one step to the next if you're going to touch solid ground or fall into a bottomless pit?"

He looked at her with interest. "Do you feel that way?"

"Oh, no," Cassandra said lightly. "But then, I'm not male."

Daemon growled.

"That's a familiar sound." It was fun teasing him because, despite his strength, he didn't frighten her the way Saetan did. "You and the Priest might have more in common than you think where she's concerned."

He laughed, and she knew it was the idea of Saetan being as bewildered as he that amused him, consoled him, linked him to them.

Daemon finished his wine and stood up. "I'm . . . glad . . . to have met you, Cassandra. I hope it won't be the last time."

She linked her arm through his and walked with him to the outer door of the Sanctuary. "You're welcome anytime, Prince."

Daemon raised her hand to his lips and kissed it lightly.

She watched him until he was out of sight before returning to the kitchen and washing the glasses.

Now there was just the delicate little matter of explaining this meeting to his father.

5 / Terreille

There are some things the body never forgets, Saetan thought wryly as Cassandra snuggled closer to him, her hand tracing anxious little circles up and down his chest. Before tonight he'd politely refused to stay with her, wary that she might want more from him than he was willing—or able—to give. But she, too, was a Guardian, and that kind of love was no longer part of her life. There were, after all, some penalties to the half-life. Still, it pleased him to feel skin against skin, to caress the curves of a feminine body. If only she'd get to the point and stop making those damn little circles, because he remembered only too well what they meant.

He captured her hand and held it against his chest. "So?" As he turned his head and kissed her hair, he felt her frown. He pressed his lips together, annoyed. Had she forgotten how easy it was for him to read a woman's body, to pick up her subtlest moods? Was she going to deny what had screamed at him the moment he stepped into the kitchen?

"So?" She lightly, teasingly, kissed his chest.

Saetan took a deep breath. His patience frayed. "So when are you going to get around to telling me what happened this afternoon?"

She tensed. "What happened this afternoon?"

He clenched his teeth. "The walls remember, Cassandra. I'm a Black Widow, too. Do you want me to pull it out of the walls and replay it, or are you going to tell me yourself?"

"There's really not much—"

"Not much!" Saetan swore as he rolled away from her and leaned against the headboard. "Have the centuries addled your mind, woman?"

"Don't . . ."

Saetan looked into her eyes. "I frighten you," he said bitterly. "I've never harmed you, never touched you in anger, seldom even raised my voice at you. I loved you, served you well, and used my strength to keep a vow to you through all those desolate years. And I frighten you. Since the day I returned with the Black, I've frightened you." He leaned his head back and stared at the ceiling. "You're frightened of me, and yet you have the audacity to provoke *my son* into a murderous rage and try to dismiss it as if nothing happened. What I don't understand is why this place is standing at all, why I'm not trying to locate your remains, or why he wasn't standing on the threshold waiting for me. Did you tell him about me? Was I your trick card to make him hesitate long enough for you to try to smooth it over?"

"It wasn't like that!" Cassandra pulled the sheet around her.

"Then what was it like?" His voice sounded flat with the effort to keep his temper in check.

"He came here because he thought I—we—wanted to harm Jaenelle."

Saetan shook his head. "You, perhaps. Not me. He already knew about me." He looked away. He didn't want to see her confusion, didn't want to consider what might happen if that tenuous link between Daemon and himself shattered.

"Saetan . . . listen to me." Cassandra reached out to him.

He hesitated a moment before holding out his arm and letting her settle on his shoulder. He listened, without interrupting, while she told him about her meeting with Daemon, suspecting that she had blunted far too many edges, had given him the bone without any of the meat.

"You were very lucky," he said when she finally stopped talking.

"Well, I realize he wears the Black."

Saetan snorted and shook his head. "There is a range of strength within every Jewel. You know that as well as I."

"He's not really trained."

"Don't mistake ability for polish. He may not do everything he wants to with finesse, but that doesn't mean he can't do it."

She fidgeted, annoyed because he wasn't soothed by her rendition of the meeting. But there was still all that meat he hadn't gotten.

"You sound as if you're afraid of him," she said crossly.

"I am."

She gasped.

Saetan suddenly felt weary. Weary of Cassandra, weary of Hekatah, weary of all the witches he'd known who, no matter what they did or didn't feel for him as a man, all looked at his Jewels and saw the potential to achieve their own ends. Only the one with sapphire eyes saw him as Saetan. Just Saetan.

"Why?" Cassandra asked, watching his face intently.

Saetan closed his eyes. So weary. And there was another man, a far more desperate man, who had seen only seventeen centuries and was just as weary. "Because he's stronger than me, Cassandra. And not just because he's living. He's stronger than I was in my prime, and he's . . . more ruthless."

Cassandra bit her lip. "He knows about Jaenelle. I had the impression he knows where to find her."

Saetan let out a sharp laugh. "Oh, I imagine he does. It's probably not that far a walk from his room to hers."

"What?"

"He's serving her family, Cassandra. He's living in the same house." He leaned toward her, taking her chin between his fingers. "Now do you begin to understand? He knows about me because Jaenelle told him, completely ignorant, I'm sure, that it would make him climb the walls. And I know about him because he sent a message to me, through Jaenelle. A polite message, basically warning me off his territory."

"He doesn't want to be Steward of the court."

Saetan laughed, genuinely amused. "No, I wouldn't think he would. He's in his prime, virile, living, and well trained in seduction. That twelve-year-old body must be driving him out of his skin."

Cassandra hesitated. "He thought you wanted to be her Consort."

Saetan gave her a sidelong look. "What did you tell him?"

"That she needed an older, experienced Steward."

"Very kind of you."

Cassandra sighed. "You're still angry about my talking to him."

"No, I'm not. I just wish . . ." *That I could have seen him, talked to him, felt the strength of his grip, heard the sound of his voice. That we could have judged each other honestly. We're forced to trust each other because Jaenelle is asking us to, because she trusts.*

He caressed Cassandra's hair. "Promise me you'll be careful. Hekatah's searching for Jaenelle. If Dorothea is supporting the effort, he'll know best where to look for danger from that quarter. Whether or not he'll ask us for help will depend on whether or not he trusts us. I want that trust, Cassandra, and not just for Jaenelle's sake. You owe me that much."

CHAPTER TEN

1 / Terreille

Why does she ask so damn many uncomfortable questions? Daemon thought, clenching his teeth and staring straight ahead as they walked through the garden. He almost missed Wilhelmina, who was in bed with a cold. At least when her sister was present, Jaenelle didn't ask questions that made him blush.

"You're not going to answer, are you?" Jaenelle asked after a minute of teeth-grinding silence.

"No."

"Don't you know the answer?"

"Whether I know the answer or not is beside the point. It's not something a man discusses with a young girl."

"But you know the answer."

Daemon growled.

"If I were older, would you tell me?" Jaenelle persisted.

There might be a way out of this yet. "Yes, if you were older."

"How old?"

"What?"

"How old would I have to be?"

"Nineteen," he said quickly, beginning to relax. Who knew what sort of questions she might have in seven years, but at least he wouldn't have to answer this one.

"Nineteen?"

Daemon's stomach fluttered. He walked a little faster. The pleased way she said that made him distinctly uncomfortable.

"The Priest said he wouldn't tell me until I was twenty-five," Jaenelle said happily, "but you'll tell me six years sooner."

Daemon skidded to a stop. His eyes narrowed as he regarded the happy, upturned face and clear sapphire eyes. "You asked the Priest?"

Jaenelle looked a little uncomfortable, which made him feel a little better. "Well . . . yes."

Daemon imagined Saetan trying to deal with the same question and fought the urge to laugh. He cleared his throat and tried to look stern. "Do you always ask me the same questions you ask him?"

"It depends on whether or not I get an answer."

Daemon clamped his teeth together in order to keep a wonderfully pithy response from escaping. "I see," he said in a strangled voice. He started walking again.

Jaenelle skipped ahead to examine some leaves. "Sometimes I ask lots of people the same question."

His head hurt. "What do you do if you don't get the same answer?"

"Think about it."

"Mother Night," he muttered.

Jaenelle gathered some of the leaves and then frowned. "There are some questions I'm not allowed to ask again until I'm a hundred. I don't think that's fair, do you?"

Yes!

"I mean," she continued, "how am I supposed to learn anything if people won't tell me?"

"There are some questions that shouldn't be asked until a person is mature enough to appreciate the answers."

Jaenelle stuck her tongue out at him. He responded in kind.

"Just because you're a little older than me doesn't mean you have to be so bossy," she complained.

Daemon looked over his shoulder to see if anyone else was around. There wasn't, so that meant she was referring to him. When did he change from being an elder to being just a *little* older . . . and bossy?

Impertinent chit. Maddening, impossible . . . how did the Priest stand it? How . . .

Daemon put on his best smile, which was difficult since his teeth were still clenched. "Are you seeing the Priest today?"

Jaenelle frowned at him, suspicious. "Yes."

"Would you give him a message?"

Her eyes narrowed. "All right," she said cautiously.

"Come on, I've got some paper in my room."

As Jaenelle waited outside his room, Daemon penned his question and sealed the envelope. She eyed it, shrugged, and slipped it into the pocket of her coat. They parted then, he to escort Alexandra on her morning visits, and she to her lessons.

Saetan looked up from his book. "Aren't you supposed to be with Andulvar?" he asked as Jaenelle bounced into his public study. He and Andulvar had decided that, under the guise of studying Eyrien weapons, Andulvar would teach her physical self-defense while he concentrated on Craft weaponry.

"Yes, but I wanted to give you this first." She handed him a plain white envelope. "Is Prothvar going to be helping with the lesson?"

"I imagine so," Saetan replied, studying the envelope.

Jaenelle wrinkled her nose. "Boys play rough, don't they?"

He's pushing because he's afraid for you, witch-child. "Yes, I guess they do. Go on now."

She gave him a choke-hold hug. "Will I see you after?"

He kissed her cheek. "Just try to leave without seeing me."

She grinned and bounced out of the room.

Saetan turned the envelope over and over in his hands before finally, carefully, opening the flap. He took out the single sheet of paper, read it, read it again . . . and began to laugh.

When she returned and had plundered her way through the sandwich and nutcakes that were waiting for her, Saetan handed her the envelope, resealed with black wax. She stuffed it into her pocket, tactfully showing no curiosity about this exchange between himself and Daemon.

After she left, he sat in his chair, a smile tugging at his lips, and wondered what his fine young Prince would do with his answer.

Daemon was helping Alexandra into her cloak when Jaenelle popped into the hallway. He'd spent the day teetering between curiosity and apprehension, regretting his impulsiveness at sending that message. Now he and Alexandra were on their way to the theater, and it wasn't the right time or place to ask Jaenelle about the message.

"You look wonderful, Alexandra," Jaenelle said as she admired the elegant dress.

Alexandra smiled, but her brow puckered in a little frown. It always annoyed her that Jaenelle persisted in addressing everyone on a first-name basis. Except him. "Thank you, dear," she said a bit stiffly. "Shouldn't you be in bed by now?"

"I just wanted to say good night," Jaenelle said politely, but Daemon noticed the slight shift in her expression, the sadness beneath the child mask. He also noticed that she said nothing to him.

They were on their way out the door when he suddenly felt something in his jacket pocket. Slipping his fingers inside, he felt the edge of the envelope, and his throat tightened.

He spent the whole evening surreptitiously touching the envelope, wanting to find an excuse to be alone for a minute so he could pull it out. Years of self-control and discipline asserted themselves, and it wasn't until he left Alexandra drifting into a satisfied sleep and was in his own room that he allowed himself to look at it.

He stared at the black wax. The Priest had read it, then. He licked his lips, took a deep breath, and broke the seal.

The writing was strong, neat, and masculine with an archaic flourish. He read the reply, read it again . . . and began to laugh.

Daemon had written: "What do you do when she asks a question no man would give a child an answer to?"

Saetan had replied: "Hope you're obliging enough to answer it for me. However, if you're backed into a corner, refer her to me. I've become accustomed to being shocked."

Daemon grinned, shook his head, and hid the note among his private papers. That night, and for several nights after, he fell asleep smiling.

2 / Terreille

Frowning, Daemon stood beneath the maple tree in the alcove. He had seen Jaenelle come in here a few minutes ago, could sense that she was very nearby, but he couldn't find her. Where . . .

A branch shook above his head. Daemon looked up and swallowed hard to keep his heart from leaping past his teeth. He swallowed again—

hard—to keep down the tongue-lashing that was blistering his throat in its effort to escape. All that swallowing made his head hurt. As his nostrils flared in an effort to breathe and his breath puffed white in the cold air, Jaenelle let out her silvery velvet-coated laugh.

"Dragons can do that even if it isn't cold," she said gaily as she looked down at him from the lowest branch, a good eight feet above his head. She squatted on the branch with her arms around her knees and no discernible way to save herself if she overbalanced.

Daemon wasn't interested in dragons, and his heart was no longer trying to leap out—it was trying to crawl into his stomach and hide.

"Would you mind coming down from there, Lady?" he said, astounded that his voice sounded so casual. "Heights make me a bit queasy."

"Really?" Jaenelle's eyebrows lifted in surprise. She shrugged, stood up, and leaped.

Daemon jumped forward to catch her, pulled himself back in time, and was rewarded by having a muscle in his back spasm in protest. He watched, wide-eyed, as she drifted down as gracefully as the leaves dancing around her, finally settling on the grass a few feet from him.

Daemon straightened up, winced as the muscle spasmed again, and looked at the tree. *Stay calm. If you yell at her, she won't answer any questions.*

He took a deep breath, puffed it out. "How did you get up there?"

She gave him an unsure-but-game smile. "The same way I got down."

Daemon sighed and sat down on the iron bench that circled the tree. "Mother Night," he muttered as he leaned his head against the tree and closed his eyes.

There was a long silence. He knew she was watching him, fluffing her hair as she tried to puzzle out his seemingly strange behavior.

"Don't you know how to stand on air, Prince?" Jaenelle asked hesitantly, as though she was trying not to offend him.

Daemon opened his eyes a crack. He could see his knees—and her feet. He sat up slowly and studied the feet planted firmly on nothing. "It would seem I missed that lesson," he said dryly. "Could you show me?"

Jaenelle hesitated, suddenly turning shy.

"Please?" He hated the wistfulness in his voice. He hated feeling so vulnerable. She'd begun to make some excuse, but that note in his voice stopped her, made her look at him closely. He had no idea what she saw in his face. He only knew he felt raw and naked and helpless under the steady gaze of those sapphire eyes.

Jaenelle smiled shyly. "I could try." She hesitated. "I've never tried to teach a grown-up before."

"Grown-ups are just like children, only bigger," Daemon said brightly, snapping to his feet.

She sighed, her expression one of harried amusement. "Up here," she said as she stood on the iron bench.

Daemon stepped up beside her.

"Can you feel the bench under your feet?"

Indeed he could. It was a cold day that promised snow by morning, and he could feel the cold from the iron bench seeping up through his shoes. "Yes."

"You have to really *feel* the bench."

"Lady," Daemon said dryly, "I really *feel* the bench."

Jaenelle wrinkled her nose at him. "Well, all you have to do is extend the bench all the way across the alcove. You step"—she placed one foot forward and it looked as if she was stepping on something solid—"and you continue to feel the bench. Like this." She brought the other foot forward so that she was standing on the air at exactly the same height as the bench. She looked at him over her shoulder.

Daemon took a deep breath, puffed it out. "Right." He imagined the bench extending before him, put one foot out, placed it on the air, and pitched forward since there was nothing beneath him. His foot squarely hit the hard ground, jarring him from his ankle to his ears.

He brought his other foot to the ground and gingerly tested his ankle. It would be a little sore, but it was still sound. He kept his back half turned from her as he ground his teeth, waiting for the insolent giggle he'd heard in so many other courts when he'd been maneuvered into looking foolish. He was furious for failing, furious because of the sudden despair he felt that she would think him an inadequate companion.

He had forgotten that Jaenelle was Jaenelle.

"I'm sorry, Daemon," said a wavering, whispery voice behind him. "I'm sorry. Are you hurt?"

"Only my pride," Daemon said as he turned around, his lips set in a rueful smile. "Lady?" Then, alarmed. "Lady! Jaenelle, no, darling, don't cry." He gathered her into his arms while her shoulders shuddered with the effort not to make a sound. "Don't cry," Daemon crooned as he stroked her hair. "Please don't cry. I'm not hurt. Honestly I'm not." Since her face was buried against his chest, he allowed himself a pained smile as he kissed her hair. "I guess I'm too much of a grown-up to learn magic."

"No, you're not," Jaenelle said, pushing away from him and scrubbing the tears off her face with the backs of her hands. "I've just never tried to explain it to anyone before."

"Well, there you are," he said too brightly. "If you've never shown any-one—"

"Oh, I've *shown* lots of my other friends," Jaenelle said brusquely. "I've just never tried to explain it."

Daemon was puzzled. "How did you show them?"

Instantly he felt her pull away from him. Not physically—she hadn't moved—but within.

Jaenelle glanced at him nervously before ducking behind her veil of hair. "I . . . touched . . . them so they could understand."

The ember in his loins that had been warming him ever since the first time he saw her flared briefly and subsided. To touch her, mind to mind, to get beneath the shadows . . . He would never have dared suggest it, would never have dared make the first overture until she was much, much older. But now. Even to connect with her, just briefly, inside the first inner barrier—ah, to touch Jaenelle.

Daemon's mouth watered.

There was the risk, of course. Even if she initiated the touch, it might be too soon. He was what he was, and even at the first barrier there was the swirl of anger and predatory cunning that was the Warlord Prince called Daemon Sadi. And he was male, full grown. That, too, would be ev-ident.

Daemon took a deep breath. "If you're afraid of hurting me by the touch, I—"

"No," she said quickly. She closed her eyes, and he could sense her hurting. "It's just that I'm . . . different . . . and some people, when I've touched them . . ." Her voice trailed away, and he understood.

Wilhelmina. Wilhelmina, who loved her sister and was glad to have her back, had, for some reason, rejected that oh-so-personal touch.

"Just because some people think you're different—"

"No, Daemon," Jaenelle said gently, looking up at him with her ancient, wistful, haunted eyes. "*Everyone* knows I'm different. It just doesn't matter to some—and it matters a lot to others." A tear slipped down her cheek. "Why am I different?"

Daemon looked away. Oh, child. How could he explain that she was dreams made flesh? That for some of them, she made the blood in their veins sing? That she was a kind of magic the Blood hadn't seen in so very, very long? "What does the Priest say?"

Jaenelle sniffed. "He says growing up is hard work."

Daemon smiled sympathetically. "It is that."

"He says every living thing struggles to emerge from its cocoon or shell in order to be what it was meant to be. He says to dance for the glory of Witch is to celebrate life. He says it's a good thing we're *all* different or Hell would be a dreadfully boring place."

Daemon laughed, but he wasn't about to be sidetracked. "Teach me." It was an arrogant command softened only by the gentle way he said it.

She was there. Instantly. But in a way he'd never experienced before. He felt her sense his confusion, felt her cry of despair at his reaction.

"Wait," Daemon said sharply, raising one hand. "Wait."

Jaenelle was still linked to him. He felt the quick beating of her heart, the nervous breathing. Cautiously, he explored.

She wasn't inside the first barrier, where thoughts and feelings were open for perusal, and yet this was more than the simple inner communication link the Blood used. And it was more than the physical monitoring he usually did in bed. This was sharing physical experience. He felt her hair brushing against her cheek as if it were his own, felt the texture of her dress against her skin.

Oh, the possibilities of this kind of link during . . .

"Okay," he said after a while, "I think I've got the feel of it. Now what?" His face burned as she watched him warily.

At last she said, "Now we walk on air."

It was queer to feel that his legs were both long and short, and it took him a couple of tries to stand on the bench again. Amused, he just shook his head at her puzzled expression. Naturally, if all the other friends had been children, they were probably all close to the same age and the same size. And the same gender? He pushed that thought away before he had time to feel jealous.

After that, it was amazingly simple, and he reveled in it. He learned by experiencing her movements. It was similar to floating an object on air, except you did it to yourself. They practiced straight walking parading around the alcove. Next came straight up and down. Pretending to climb stairs took longer to get the hang of, since he wanted a distance more compatible with his own legs and kept tripping on nothing.

Then the link was gone, and he was standing on air, alone, with Jaenelle watching him, her eyes shining with pride and pleasure. When he lowered himself to the ground with a graceful flourish, she clapped her hands in delight.

Daemon opened his arms. Jaenelle skated to him and wrapped her arms around his neck. He held her tightly, his face buried in her hair. "Thank you," he said hoarsely. "Thank you."

"You're welcome, Daemon." Her voice was a lovely, sensuous caress.

Holding her so close, with his lips so near her neck, he didn't want to let her go, but caution finally won over desire.

He didn't push her away. Rather, he gently held her shoulders and stepped back. "We'd better get back before someone comes looking."

Jaenelle's happy glow dimmed. She carelessly dropped to the ground. "Yes." She looked at the bed of witchblood. "Yes." She walked out of the alcove, not waiting for him.

Daemon stayed for another minute. Better not to come in together. Better not to make it obvious. To keep her safe, he had to be careful.

He glanced at the witchblood and bolted from the alcove. As he glided along the garden paths, his face settled into its familiar cold mask, the happiness he'd felt a few minutes before honing the blade of his temper so sharp he could have made the air bleed.

If you sing to them correctly, they'll tell you the names of the ones who are gone.

Everything has a price.

Whatever the price, whatever he had to do, he would make sure one of those plants wasn't for her.

3 / Terreille

Daemon pulled the bright, deep-red sweater over his head and adjusted the collar of the gold-and-white-checked shirt. Satisfied, he studied his reflection. His eyes were butter melted by humor and good spirits, his face subtly altered by the relaxed, boyish grin. The change in his appearance startled him, but after a moment he just shook his head and brushed his hair.

The difference was Jaenelle and the incalculable ways she worried, intrigued, fascinated, incensed, and delighted him. More than that, now, when he was so long past it, she was giving him—the bored, jaded Sadist—a childhood. She colored the days with magic and wonder, and all the things he'd ceased to pay attention to he saw again new.

He grinned at his reflection. He felt like a twelve-year-old. No, not twelve. He was at least a sophisticated fourteen. Still young enough to play with a girl as a friend, yet old enough to contemplate the day he might sneak his first kiss.

Daemon shrugged into his coat, went into the kitchen, pinched a couple of apples from the basket, sent Cook a broad wink, and gave himself up to a morning with Jaenelle.

The garden was buried under several inches of dry snow that puffed around his legs like flour. He followed the smaller footprints that walked, hopped, skipped, and leaped along the path. When he reached the small bend that mostly took him out of sight of anyone looking out the upper windows of the house, the footprints disappeared.

Daemon immediately checked all the surrounding trees and let out a gusty sigh of relief when she wasn't in any of them. Had she backed up in her own tracks waiting for him to pass her?

Grinning, he gathered some snow in his gloved hands, but it was too fluffy and wouldn't pack. As he straightened up, something soft hit his neck. He yowled when the clump of snow went down his back.

Daemon pivoted, his eyes narrowing even as his lips twitched. Jaenelle stood a few feet from him, her face glowing with mischief and good fun, her arm cocked to throw the second snowball. He put his fists on his hips. She lowered her arm and looked at him from beneath her lashes, trying to look solemn as she waited for the tongue-lashing.

He gave her one. "It is totally unfair," he said in his most severe voice, "to engage in a snowball fight when only one combatant can make snowballs." He waited, loving the way her eyes sparkled. "Well?"

Even without reading the thoughts beneath it, he could tell her touch was filled with laughter. Daemon bent down, gathered some snow, and learned how to make a snowball from snow too fluffy to pack. This, too, was similar to a basic lesson in Craft—creating a ball of witchlight—yet it required a subtler, more intrinsic knowledge of Craft than he'd ever known anyone to have.

"Did the Priest teach you how to do this?" he asked as he straightened up, delighted with the perfect snowball in his hand.

Jaenelle stared at him, aghast. Then she laughed. "Noooo." She quickly cocked her arm and hit him in the chest with her snowball.

The next few minutes were all-out war, each of them pelting the other as fast as they could make snowballs.

When it was over, Daemon was peppered with clumps of white. He leaned over, resting his hands on his knees. "I leave the field to you, Lady," he panted.

"As well you should," she replied tartly.

Daemon looked up, one eyebrow rising.

Jaenelle wrinkled her nose at him and ran for the alcove.

Daemon leaped forward to follow her, ran a few steps, stopped, and looked behind him. His were the only footprints. He squatted, examining the snow. Well, not quite. There *were* the merest indentations in the snow leading toward the alcove path. Daemon laughed and stood up. "Clever little witch." He raised one foot, placed it on top of the snow, and concentrated until he had the sensation of standing on solid ground. He positioned his other foot. Step, step, step. He looked back and grinned at the lack of footprints. Then he ran to the alcove.

Jaenelle was struggling to push the bottom of a snowman into the center of the alcove. Still grinning, Daemon helped her push. Then he started on the middle ball while she made the one for the head. They worked in companionable silence, he filling in the spaces while she stood on air and fashioned the head.

Jaenelle stepped back, looked at what they had fashioned, and began to laugh. Daemon stepped back, looked at it, and started to cough and groan and laugh. Even though it was crudely shaped, there was no mistaking the face above the grossly rotund body.

"You know," he choked, "if any of the groundskeepers see that and word gets back to Graff . . . we're going to be in deep trouble."

Jaenelle gave him a slant-eyed look sparking with mischief, and he didn't care how much trouble they got into.

He took the apples from his pocket and handed her one. Jaenelle took a bite, chewed thoughtfully, and sighed. "It won't last, you know," she said regretfully.

Daemon looked at her quizzically. "They never do." He looked at the sun beginning to peek out from behind the clouds. "I don't think this snow's going to last. Feels like it's warming up."

Jaenelle shook her head and took another bite. "No," she said, swallowing. "It'll go before it melts. I can't hold it very long." She frowned and fluffed her hair as she studied the snow-Graff. "Something's missing. Something I don't know about yet that would be able to hold it longer—"

That you can do it at all is beyond what most achieve, Lady.

"—would be able to weave it—"

Daemon shivered. He tossed the apple core toward the bushes for the birds to find. "Don't think of it," he said, not caring that his voice sounded harsh.

She looked at him, surprised.

"Don't think about experimenting with dream weaving without being instructed by someone who can do it well." He put his hands on her shoulders and squeezed gently. "Weaving a dream web can be very dangerous. Black Widows don't learn how to do it until the second stage of their training because it's so easy to become ensnared in the web." He held her at arm's length, searching her face. "Promise me, please, that you won't try to do this by yourself. That you'll get the very best there is to train you." *Because I couldn't bear it if there was only a blank-eyed, empty shell to love and I knew you were lost somewhere beyond reach, beyond return.*

Daemon's hands tightened on her shoulders. Her thoughtful expression frightened him.

"Yes," she said at last. "You're right, of course. If I'm going to learn, I should ask the ones who were born to it to teach me." She studied the snow-Graff. "See? Already it goes."

The snow was starting to lose its shape, to sift into a fluffy pile in the center of the alcove.

Together they air-walked to the main garden path. Dropping into the snow, Jaenelle trudged away from the house for a few feet, turned, and trudged back, kicking up the snow, leaving a very clear trail. Daemon looked back at the unmarked path, considered what the consequences would be if the others found out that Jaenelle could move about without leaving a trace, lowered himself to the ground, and trudged behind her, back to the house.

4 / Terreille

Daemon stormed into his room, slammed the door, stripped off his clothes, showered, and stormed back into the bedroom.

Bitch. Stupid, mewling *bitch*! How dare she? How *dare* she?

Leland's words burned through him. *We're having a gathering this evening, just a few of my friends. You'll be serving us, of course, so I expect you to dress appropriately.*

The cold swept over him, crusting him with glacial calm. He took a deep breath and smiled.

If the bitch wanted a whore tonight, he'd give her a whore.

Lifting one hand, Daemon called in two private trunks. Wherever he traveled, the trunks that contained his clothes and "personal" effects were always openly displayed and the contents could be examined by any Queen or Steward who chose to rummage through his things. Those were the only ones he ever acknowledged. The private trunks contained the items that were, in some way, of value to him.

One of those trunks was half empty and held personal mementos, a testimony to the paucity of his life. It also contained the locked, velvet-lined cases that held his Jewels—the Birthright Red and the cold, glorious Black. The other trunk contained several outfits that he sneeringly referred to as "whore's clothes"—costumes from a dozen different cultures, designed to titillate the female senses.

He opened the costume trunk and examined the contents. Yes, that outfit would do very nicely.

He removed a pair of black leather pants, the leather so soft and cut so well they fit like a second skin. He pulled them on, adjusting the bulge in the front to best advantage. Next came black, ankle-high leather boots with a high stacked heel. The perfectly tailored white silk shirt formed a slashing *V* from his neck to his waist, where two pearl buttons held it closed, and had billowing, tight-cuffed sleeves. Next he took out the paint pots, and with cold, cruel deliberation, applied subtle color to his cheeks, eyes, and lips. It was done with such skill that it made him look androgynous and yet more savagely male, an unsettling blend. Returning the paint pots to the trunks, he took a small gold hoop from its box and slipped it into his ear. He brushed his hair and used Craft to set it in a rakishly disheveled style. Last was a black felt hat with a black leather band and a large white plume. Standing before the full-length mirror, he carefully set the hat in place and inspected his reflection.

As Daemon smiled in anticipation of Leland's reaction to his dress, someone quickly tapped on his door before it opened and closed.

He saw her in the mirror. For just a moment, shame threatened to splinter the cold crust of rage, but he held on to it. She was, after all, female. His cruel, sensuous smile bloomed as he turned around.

Jaenelle stared at him, her eyes huge, her mouth dropping open. Daemon did nothing, said nothing. He simply waited for the inspection, waited for the damning words.

She started at this feet, her eyes slowly traveling up his body. His breath hitched when she reached his hips. He waited for the all-too-familiar speculation of what hung between his legs or the quick, flushed glance back down after hurrying past. Jaenelle didn't seem to notice. Her inspection never changed speed as she studied the shirt, the earring, the face, and finally the hat. Then she started from the hat and went back down.

Daemon waited.

Jaenelle opened her mouth, closed it, and finally said timidly, "Do you think, when I'm grown up, I could wear an outfit like that?"

Daemon bit his cheek. He didn't know whether to laugh or cry. Buying time, he looked down at himself. "Well," he said, giving it slow consideration, "the shirt would have to be altered somewhat to accommodate a female figure, but I don't see why not."

Jaenelle beamed. "Daemon, it's a wonderful hat."

It took him a moment to admit it to himself, but he was miffed. He stood in front of her, on display as it were, and the thing that fascinated her most was his *hat*.

You do know how to bruise a man's ego don't you, little one? he thought dryly as he said, "Would you like to try it on?"

Jaenelle bounced to the mirror, brushing against him as she passed.

The sudden heat, the jolt of pleasure, the intense desire to hold her against him shocked him sufficiently to make him jump out of her way.

His hands shook as he placed the hat on her head, but a moment later he was laughing as the hat rested on the tip of her nose and the only part of her face he could see was her chin.

"You'll have to grow into it, Lady," he said warmly. Using Craft, he positioned the hat above her head and locked it on the air.

He instantly regretted it.

She was going to be devastating, he realized as he stared at the face looking at his reflection, his nails biting into his palms.

In that moment he saw the face she would wear in a few years when the pointed features were finally balanced out. The eyebrows and eyelashes. Were they a soot-darkened gold or a gold-dusted black? The eyes, no longer hiding behind childish pretenses, summoned him down a darker road than he had ever known existed, one he felt desperate to follow.

For the first time in his life, Daemon felt a hungry stirring between his legs. He closed his eyes, gritted his teeth, and dug his nails deeper into his palms.

No, he pleaded silently. Not now. Not yet. He couldn't, mustn't respond yet. No one must know he *could* respond. They were lost, both of them, if anyone felt that physical response through the Ring. Please, please, please.

"Daemon?"

Daemon opened his eyes. Jaenelle the child watched him, her forehead puckered in concern. He smiled shakily as he slowly unclenched his hands and took the hat.

"Leland's guests will be arriving anytime now and I still have to dress, so scat."

There was something strange about the way she looked at him, but he couldn't figure it out. Then she was gone, and he slumped on the bed, staring at the open trunk. After a minute, he took off the shirt, pants, and boots and returned them and the hat to the trunk. He vanished both private trunks, taking the time to make sure they were safely stored, before dressing in formal evening attire.

The painted face and the earring would have to do for Leland. The clothes in that trunk would be worn for only one woman's pleasure.

5 / Terreille

Daemon woke instantly. Something was wrong, something that made his nerves quiver. He lay on his back, listening to the hard, cold rain beat against the windows. Shivering, he tossed back the covers, pulled on his robe, and pushed open the curtains to look outside.

Only the rain. And yet . . .

Taking a deep, steadying breath, he began a slow descent into the abyss, testing each rank of the Jewels, waiting for the answering quiver along his nerves.

Above the Red, nothing. The Red, nothing. The Gray, the Ebon-gray. Nothing. He reached the level of the Black and pain flooded his nerves as an eerie keening filled his mind, a dirge full of anger, pain, and sorrow. The voice that sang it was pure and strong—and familiar.

Daemon closed his eyes and leaned his head against the glass as he ascended to the Red. No one else here would be able to hear it. No one else would know.

He'd known since he met her that she was Witch—and Witch wore the Black Jewels. He'd known, but he'd been able to deceive himself into believing she'd wear the Black at maturity, not *now*. In all the Blood's long history, only a handful of witches had worn the Black, and they had been gifted with it after the Offering to the Darkness. *No one* had ever worn the Black as their Birthright.

It had been a foolish deceit, especially when the evidence was right in front of him. She could do things the rest of the Blood had never dreamed of. She had sought out the High Lord of Hell to be her mentor. There were facets of her that were breathtaking and terrifying.

Birthright Black. She wore Birthright Black. Sweet Darkness, what would become of her when she made the Offering?

Daemon opened his eyes and saw a small white figure moving slowly along the garden path. He opened his window and was instantly soaked by the cold rain, but he didn't notice. He whistled once, softly, sharply, sending it on an auditory thread directed toward the figure.

It turned toward him, resigned, and made its way to his window.

Daemon leaned over as Jaenelle floated up to him, grasped her beneath the arms, and pulled her in. He set her on the floor, closed and locked the window, pulled the curtains together. Then he looked at her, and his heart squeezed with pain.

She stood there, shivering, dripping on the rug, her eyes glazed and pain-filled. Her nightgown, bare feet, and hands were muddy.

Daemon picked her up, took her into the bathroom, and filled the tub with hot water. She'd been unnaturally quiet all day, and he'd feared she was becoming ill. Now he feared she was in shock. There were dark smudges beneath her eyes, and she didn't seem to know where she was.

She struggled when he tried to lift the nightgown over her head. "No," she said feebly as she attempted to hold the garment down.

"I know what girls look like," Daemon snapped as he pulled off the nightgown and lifted her into the tub. "Sit there." He pointed a finger at her. She stopped trying to get out of the tub.

Daemon went into the bedroom and got the brandy and glass he kept tucked in the bottom drawer of the nightstand. Returning to the bathroom, he sat on the edge of the tub, poured a healthy dose into the glass, and handed it to her.

"Drink this." He watched her take a small taste and grimace before he put the bottle to his own lips and took a long swallow. "Drink it," he said angrily when she tried to hand him the glass.

"I don't like it." It was the first time he'd ever heard her sound so young and vulnerable. He wanted to scream.

"What—" He knew. Suddenly, all too clearly, he knew. The mud, the dirge, her hands cut up from digging in the hard ground, the dirt beneath her fingernails. He knew.

Daemon took another long swallow of brandy. "Who?"

"Rose," Jaenelle replied in a hollow voice. "He killed my friend Rose." Then a savage light burned in her eyes and her lips curled in a small, bitter smile. "He slit her throat because she wouldn't lick the lollipop." Her eyes slid to his groin before drifting up to his face. "Is that what you call it, Prince?"

Daemon's throat closed. His blood pounded in him, pounded him, angry surf against rock. It was so very, very hard to breathe.

The sepulchral voice. The midnight, cavernous, ancient, raging voice that held a whisper of madness. He hadn't imagined it, that other time. Hadn't imagined it.

Birthright Black.

Witch.

She wanted to kill him because he was male. Accepting that made it easier to be calm.

"It's called a penis, Lady. I have no use for euphemisms." He paused. "Who killed her?"

Jaenelle sipped the brandy. "Uncle Bobby," she whispered. She rocked back and forth as tears slid down her cheeks. "Uncle Bobby."

Daemon took the glass from her and set it aside. It didn't matter if she killed him, didn't matter if she hated him for touching her. He lifted her out of the tub and cradled her in his arms, letting her cry until there were no tears left.

When he felt her breathing even out and knew she was falling into exhausted sleep, he wrapped her in a towel, carried her to her room, found a clean nightgown, and tucked her into bed. He watched her for a few minutes to be sure she was asleep before returning to his room.

He paced, gulping brandy, feeling the walls close in on him.

Uncle Bobby. Rose. Lollipop. How did she know? All day she must have known, must have waited for the night so she could plant her living memento mori. All day, while Robert Benedict had been so conspicuously at home.

If you sing to them correctly, they'll tell you the names of the ones who are gone.

He snarled quietly. His pacing slowed as cold rage filled him.

There was something wrong with this place. Something evil in this place. Chaillot had too many secrets. Added to that, Dorothea and Hekatah were hunting for Jaenelle, and Greer was still in Beldon Mor sniffing around.

Tersa had said the Priest would be his best ally or his worst enemy.

He would have to decide soon, before it was too late.

Finally, exhausted, he stripped off the robe and fell into bed. And dreamed of shattered crystal chalices.

CHAPTER ELEVEN

1 / Terreille

The only thing in the cell besides the overflowing slop bucket was a small table that held a plate of food and a metal pitcher of water.

Lucivar stared at the pitcher, clenching and unclenching his fists. The chains that tethered his ankles and wrists to the wall were long enough to reach one end of the table and the food, but not long enough to reach over and tear out the throat of the guard who brought it.

He needed food. He was desperate for water. These little ovens that Zuultah laughingly referred to as her "enlightenment" chambers were located in the Arava Desert, where the sun was voracious. The heat was sufficient by midday to make his own waste steam.

The first three days he'd been locked up, the guards had brought food and water and emptied the slop bucket. During the first two, he'd eaten what he was given. The third day, the food and water were laced with *safframate,* a vicious aphrodisiac that would keep a man hard and needy enough to satisfy an entire coven at one of their gatherings. It would also drive a man to the point of madness because, while it made it possible for him to be an enduring participant, it also prohibited him from physical release.

He'd sensed it before he consumed anything. A less vigilant man wouldn't have noticed, but Lucivar had experienced *safframate* before and wasn't about to experience it again for Zuultah's entertainment.

Lucivar licked his cracked lips as he stared at the pitcher of water, his tongue prodding the cracks, wetting itself with his blood.

His answer, that third day, had been to throw the plate and pitcher against the wall. The viper rats—large, venomous rodents that were able to live anywhere—scurried out of the shadowy corners and fell upon the food. He'd spent the rest of the day watching them tear each other apart in frenzied mating.

For the next two days no one came. There was no food, no water. The slop bucket filled. There was nothing but the rats and the heat.

An hour ago, a guard had come in with the food and water. Lucivar had snarled at him, his dark wings unfurling until the tips touched the walls. The guard scurried out with less dignity than the rats.

Lucivar approached the table, his legs shaking. He picked up the pitcher and licked the condensation off the outside.

It wasn't nearly enough.

He looked at the plate. The stench of the slop bucket warred with the smell of food, but his stomach twisted with hunger, and over all of it was the need for the water that was so close. So very close.

Holding the pitcher in both hands so that he wouldn't drop it, he took a mouthful of water.

The *safframate* ran through him, a fiery ice.

Lucivar's mouth twisted into a teeth-baring grin. His lips cracked wider and bled.

There was only one reason to eat, to submit to what would come, and it wasn't to stay alive. He fiercely loved life, but he was Eyrien, a hunter, a warrior. Growing up with death had dulled his fear of it, and a part of him rather relished the idea of being a demon.

There was only one reason. One sapphire-eyed reason.

Lucivar lifted the pitcher again and drank.

2 / Terreille

Lucivar clenched his teeth and squeezed his eyes shut. He hated being on his back. All Eyrien males hated being on their backs, unable to use their wings. It was the ultimate gesture of submission. But tied as he was to the "game bed," there was nothing he could do but endure.

As one of Zuultah's witches moved on him, intent on her pleasure, he silently swore the most vicious curses he could think of. His hands clenched the brass rails of the headboard, had been clenching them throughout the night with such pressure that the shape of his fingers was embedded in them.

Again and again and again, one after another. With each the pain grew worse. He hated them for the pain, for their pleasure, for their laughter, for the food and water they taunted him with, trying to make him beg.

He was Lucivar Yaslana, an Eyrien Warlord Prince. He wouldn't beg. Wouldn't beg. Wouldn't.

Lucivar opened his eyes to silence. The bed curtains were closed at the bottom of the bed and along one side, cutting off his view of the room. He tried to shift position and ease his stiff muscles, but he'd been stretched out when they tied him, and there wasn't any slack.

He licked his lips. He was so thirsty, so tired. So easy to slip away from the pain, from memories.

Male voices murmured in the hallway. Movement in the room, hidden by the closed curtains. At last, Zuultah saying, "Bring him."

The room was gray, a sweet, misty gray where the light danced through shards of glass and voices were heard under water.

The guards untied his hands and feet, retied his hands behind his back. Lucivar snarled at them, but it was a faraway sound of no importance, no importance at all.

For a moment, when he saw the marble lady, his vision cleared, and the pain made his legs buckle. The guards dragged him to the leather leg straps, forced him to his knees, and strapped him to the floor behind his knees and at his ankles. They rolled the marble cylinder, with its smoothly carved orifices, into position. When he was fitted into an orifice, they held him in place with a leather strap beneath his buttocks. There was enough slack for him to thrust but not enough for him to withdraw.

The gray. The sweet, twisting gray.

"That will be all," Zuultah said arrogantly, waving the guards out of the room with her switch and locking the door.

The floor hurt his knees. Pain. Sweet pain.

The switch hit his buttocks. Blood trickled over the leather strap. Scented silk brushed against his shoulder and face.

"Are you thirsty, Yasi?" Zuultah cooed as she swung herself up on the flat top of the marble lady. "Want some cream?" She opened her robe and spread her thighs, revealing the dark triangle of hair.

The switch hit his shoulder. "This is your reward, Yasi. This is your pleasure."

Red streaks in the gray. Red streaks and a dark triangle.

"Thrust, you bastard." The switch hitting, cutting where one wing joined his back.

Thrust, thrust, thrust into the gray. Lips against the wet. Tongue obedient. Thrust, thrust. Deeper into the pain, the wet, the dark, the dark, the dark, the pain twisting to a sweetness, shards of glass, twisting, the wet, the dark, the dark streaked with red, the hunger, the pain, the red fire boiling, rising, the Ebon-gray boiling, rising, the hunger, the hunger, teeth, pleasure, pain, moaning, moaning, teeth, pleasure, rising, boiling, pain, pleasure, moaning, hunger, teeth, moaning, teeth, screaming, screaming, screaming, red, red, hot sweet red, boiling, rushing, free.

Lucivar swayed, confused. Zuultah rolled on the floor, screaming, screaming. He tried to lick the moisture from his lips but something was in the way. He turned his head and spat.

For a long time, while guards pounded on the locked door and Zuultah screamed, he stared at the small thing his teeth had found to ease the hunger. At first he didn't understand what it was. When his flaccid organ finally slipped out of the orifice and he recognized the red for what it was, Lucivar lifted his head and let out a howling, savage laugh.

3 / Terreille

"You have a visitor," Philip said tersely as he tapped piles of papers into neat stacks, something he did when annoyed.

Daemon raised an eyebrow. "Oh?"

Philip glanced toward him but refused to look at him. "In the gold salon. Keep it brief, if possible. You have a full schedule today."

Daemon glided to the gold salon. The psychic scent hit him before he touched the door. He settled his face into its cold mask, locked away his heart, and opened the door.

"Lord Kartane," he said in a bored voice as he closed the door and leaned against it, his hands in his trouser pockets.

"Sadi." Kartane's eyes were filled with malicious glee. Still, he took a nervous step backward.

Daemon waited, watching Kartane pace one side of the room.

"Probably no one's thought to tell you, so I took it upon myself to bring the news," Kartane said.

"About what?"

"Yasi."

The anticipation in Kartane's eyes made Daemon's heart pound and his mouth go dry. He shrugged. "The last time I heard anything about him, he was serving the Queen of Pruul. Zuultah, isn't it?"

"Apparently he's served her better than he's ever served anyone," Kartane said maliciously.

Get to the point, you little bastard.

Kartane paced. "The story's a bit muddled, you understand, but it appears that, while under the influence of a substantial dose of *safframate,* Yasi went berserk and bit Zuultah." Kartane let out a high-pitched, nervous laugh.

Daemon sighed. Lucivar's temper in the bedroom was legendary. At the best of times, he was unpredictable and violent. Under the influence of *safframate* . . . "So he bit her. She's not the first."

Kartane laughed again. It was almost a hysterical giggle. "Well, actually, *shaved* might be a better way to describe it. Anything she mounts now won't be for *her* pleasure."

No, Lucivar, no. By the Darkness, no. "They killed him," Daemon said flatly.

"He wasn't that lucky. Zuultah wanted to, when she finally came to her senses and realized what he'd done. He also killed ten of her best guards while they were trying to subdue him." Kartane wiped nervous sweat from his forehead. "Prythian intervened as soon as she found out. For some insane reason, she still thinks she can eventually tame him and breed him. However, Zuultah wasn't going to let him get away without *some* kind of punishment." Kartane waited, but Daemon didn't rise to the bait. "She put him in the salt mines."

"Then she's killed him." Daemon opened the door. "You were right," he said too gently, turning to look at Kartane, "no one else would have dared tell me that."

He closed the door with a silence that made the whole house shake.

All the tears were gone now, and Daemon felt as dry and empty as the Arava Desert.

Lucivar was Eyrien. He would never survive in the salt mines of Pruul. In those tunnels with all the salt and the heat, no room for him to stretch his wings, no air to dry the sweat. There were a dozen different molds that could infect that membranous skin and eat it away. And without wings . . . An Eyrien warrior was nothing without his wings. Lucivar had once said he'd rather lose his balls than his wings, and he'd meant it.

Oh, Lucivar, Lucivar, his brave, arrogant, foolish brother. If he'd accepted that offer, Lucivar would be hunting in Askavi right now, gliding through the dusk, searching for prey. But they had known it might come to this. The wisest thing for Lucivar to do would be to end it quickly while his strength was intact. He would be welcome in the Dark Realm. Daemon was sure he would be.

She won't go unpunished, I promise you that. No matter how long it takes to do it properly, I'll see the debt paid in full.

"Lucivar," Daemon whispered. "Lucivar."

"They've all been looking for you."

He hadn't heard her come in, which wasn't surprising. It wasn't surprising she was there even though he'd locked the library door.

Daemon shifted on the couch. He held out one hand, watching her small fingers curl around his own. That gentle touch, so full of understanding, was agony.

"What happened to him?"

"Who?" Daemon said, fighting the grief.

"Lucivar," Jaenelle said with steely patience.

Daemon recognized that strange, unnerving something in her face and voice—Witch focusing her attention. He hesitated a moment, then took her in his arms. He needed to hold her, feel her warmth against him, needed reassurance that the sacrifice was worth it. He didn't know how or when the tears began falling again.

"He's my friend, my brother," he whispered into her shoulder. "He's dying."

"Daemon." Jaenelle gently stroked his hair. "Daemon, we have to help him. I could—"

"No!" *Don't tempt me with hope. Don't tempt me to take that kind of risk.* "You can't help him. Nothing can help him now."

Jaenelle tried to push back to look at him, but he wouldn't let her. "I know I promised him I wouldn't wander around Terreille, but—"

Daemon licked a tear. "You met him? He saw you once?"

"Once." She paused. "Daemon, I might be able to—"

"*No*," Daemon moaned into her neck. "He wouldn't want you there, and if something happened to you, he'd never forgive me. Never."

Witch asked, "Are you sure, Prince?"

The Warlord Prince replied, "I am sure, Lady."

After a moment, Jaenelle began to sing a death song in the Old Tongue, not the angry dirge she'd sung for Rose, but a gentle witchsong of grief and love. Her voice wove through him, celebrating and acknowledging his pain and grief, tapping the deep wells he would have kept locked.

When her voice finally faded, Daemon wiped the tears from his face. He blindly allowed Jaenelle to lead him to his room, stand over him while he washed his face, and coax a glass of brandy into him. She said nothing. There was nothing she needed to say. The generous silence and the understanding in her eyes were enough.

Lucivar would have been proud to serve her, Daemon thought as he brushed his hair, preparing to face Alexandra and Philip. He would have been proud of her.

Daemon took a shuddering breath and went to find Alexandra.

Everything has a price.

CHAPTER TWELVE

1 / Terreille

Winsol approached rapidly. The most important holiday in the Blood calendar, it was held when the winter days were shortest, and it was a celebration of the Darkness, a celebration of Witch.

Daemon wandered through the empty hallways. The servants had been given a half-day off and had deserted the house to shop or begin their holiday preparations. Alexandra, Leland, and Philip were off on their own excursions. Robert, as usual, was not at home. Even Graff had gone out, leaving the girls in Cook's care. And he . . . Well, it wasn't kindness that had made them leave him behind. His temper had been too sharp, his tongue too cutting the last time he'd escorted Alexandra to a party. They'd left hastily after he'd told a simpering young aristo witch that the cut of her dress would make any woman in a Red Moon house envious, even if what she was displaying didn't.

Daemon climbed the stairs to the nursery wing. The only thing that eased the ache he'd felt since Kartane had told him about Lucivar was being with Jaenelle.

The music room door stood open. "No, Wilhelmina, not like that," Jaenelle said in that harried, amused tone.

Daemon smiled as he looked into the room. At least he wasn't the only one who made her sound like that.

The girls stood in the center of the room. Wilhelmina looked a bit grumpy while Jaenelle looked patiently exasperated. She glanced toward the door and her eyes lit up.

Daemon suppressed a sigh. He knew that look, too. He was about to get into trouble.

Jaenelle rushed over to him, grabbed his wrist, and hauled him into the room. "We're going to attend one of the Winsol balls and I've been trying to teach Wilhelmina how to waltz but I'm not explaining it well because I don't really know how to lead but you'd know how to lead because boys—"

Boys?

"—lead in dancing so you could show Wilhelmina, couldn't you?"

As though he had a choice. Daemon looked at Wilhelmina. Jaenelle stood to one side, her hands loosely clasped, smiling expectantly.

"Yes, men," he said dryly, putting a slight emphasis on that word, "do lead when dancing."

Wilhelmina blushed, instantly understanding his distinction.

Jaenelle looked baffled. She shrugged. "Men. Boys. What's the difference? They're all males."

Daemon gave her a calculating look. In a few more years, he'd be able to show her the difference. He smiled at Wilhelmina and patiently explained the steps. "Some music, Lady?" he said to Jaenelle.

She raised her hand. The crystal music sphere sparkled in the brass holder, and stately music filled the room.

As Daemon waltzed with Wilhelmina, he watched her expression change from concentration to relaxation to pleasure. The exertion brought a glow to her cheeks and a sparkle to her blue eyes. He smiled at her warmly. Dancing was the only activity he enjoyed with a woman, and he regretted that court dancing was no longer in vogue.

If you want to bed a woman, do it in the bedroom. If you want to seduce her, do it in the dance.

It was hard to imagine the Priest saying that to a small boy, but it was like so many other things that had come to him over the years in those moments between sleep and waking, and he no longer questioned whose voice seemed to whisper up from somewhere deep within him, a voice he'd always known wasn't his own.

When the music faded, Daemon released Wilhelmina and made an elegant, formal bow. He turned to Jaenelle. Her strange expression made his heart jump. The crust of civility he lived behind, all the rules and regulations, cracked beneath her gaze. Her psychic scent distracted him. His mind sharpened, turned inward, and he reveled in the keen awareness of his body, the smooth feline way he moved.

The music began again. Jaenelle raised one hand. He raised the opposite hand. Stepping toward each other, their fingertips touched, and the court dance began.

He didn't need to think about the steps. They were natural, sensual, seductive. The music caressed him, narrowing his senses to the young body that moved with him. Fingertips touched fingertips, hands touched hands, nothing more. The Black sang in him, wanting more, wanting much, much more, and yet it pleased him to have his senses teased this way, to feel so alive, so male.

When the music faded again, Jaenelle stepped back, breaking the spell. She skipped to the brass holder, changed the music sphere, and began a lively folk dance, hands on her hips, feet flying.

Daemon and Wilhelmina were applauding when Cook came in carrying a tray. "I thought you'd like some sandwiches . . ." Her words faded as Daemon, with a dazzling smile, took the tray from her, placed it on a table, and led her to the center of the room. He bowed; with a pleased smile, she curtsied. He swept her into his arms and they waltzed to a Chaillot tune he'd heard at a number of balls. As they whirled about the room, he grinned at the girls, who were whirling around with them.

Then Cook stumbled and moaned, her eyes fixed on the doorway.

"What's the meaning of this?" Graff said nastily as she stepped into the room. She nailed Cook with an icy stare. "You were entrusted to look after the girls for a few short hours, and here I return to find you engaged in questionable entertainment." Her eyes snapped to Daemon's arm, which was still around Cook's waist. She sniffed, maliciously pleased. "Perhaps, when this is reported, Lady Angelline will find someone with culinary talent."

"Nothing happened, Graff."

Daemon shivered at the chilling fury in Jaenelle's too calm voice.

Graff turned. "Well, we'll just see, missy."

"Graff." It was a thunderous, malevolent whisper.

Daemon shook. Every instinct for self-preservation screamed at him to call in the Black and shield himself.

There had been a strange swirling when Graff first appeared that had made him think he was being pulled into a spiral. He'd never felt anything like that before and hadn't realized that Jaenelle was gliding down into the abyss. Now something rose from far below him, something very angry and so very, very cold.

Graff turned slowly, her eyes staring wide and empty.

"Nothing happened, Graff," Jaenelle said in that cold whisper that shrieked through Daemon's nerves. "Wilhelmina and I were in the music room practicing some dance steps. Cook had brought some sandwiches for us and was just leaving when you arrived. You didn't see the Prince because he was in his room. Do you understand?"

Graff's eyebrows drew together. "No, I—"

"Look down, Graff. Look down. Do you see it?"

Graff whimpered.

"If you don't remember what I've told you, that's what you'll see . . . forever. Do you understand?"

"Understand," Graff whispered as spittle dribbled down her chin.

"You're dismissed, Graff. Go to your room."

When they heard a door close farther down the corridor, Daemon led Cook to a chair and eased her into it. Jaenelle said nothing more, but there was pain and sadness in her eyes as she looked at them before going to her room. Wilhelmina had wet herself. Daemon cleaned her up, cleaned up the floor, took the tray of sandwiches back to the kitchen, and dosed Cook with a liberal glass of brandy.

"She's a strange child," Cook said carefully after her second glass of brandy, "but there's more good than harm in her."

Daemon gave her calm, expected responses, allowing her to find her own way to justify what she'd felt in that room. Wilhelmina, too, although embarrassed that he'd witnessed her accident, had altered the confrontation into something she could accept. Only he, as he sat in his room staring at nothing, was unwilling to let go of the fear and the awe. Only he appreciated the terrible beauty of being able to touch without restraint. Only he felt knife-sharp desire.

2 / Terreille

Daemon sat on the edge of his bed, a pained, gentle smile tugging his lips. Even with preservation spells, the picture's colors were beginning to fade, and it was worn around the edges. Still, nothing could fade the hint of a brash smile and the ready-for-trouble gleam in Lucivar's eyes. It was the only picture Daemon had of him, taken centuries ago when Lucivar still had an aura of youthful hope, before the years and court after court had turned a handsome, youthful face into one so like the Askavi mountains he loved—beautifully brutal, holding a trace of shadow even in the brightest sunlight.

There was a shy tap on his door before Jaenelle slipped into the room. "Hello," she said, uncertain of her welcome.

Daemon slipped an arm around her waist when she got close enough. Jaenelle rested both hands on his shoulder and leaned into him. The skin beneath her eyes looked bruised, and she trembled a little.

Daemon frowned. "Are you cold?" When she shook her head, he pulled her closer. There wasn't any kind of outside heat that could thaw what chilled her, but after he'd been holding her for a while, the trembling stopped.

He wondered if she'd told Saetan about the music room incident. He looked at her again and knew the answer. She hadn't told the Priest. She hadn't gone roaming for three days. She'd been locked in her cold misery, alone, wondering if there was any living thing that wouldn't fear her. He had come to the Black as a young man, but mature and ready, and even then living that far into the Darkness had been unsettling. For a child who had never known anything else, who had been traveling strange, lonely roads since her first conscious thought, who tried so hard to reach toward other people while suppressing what she was . . . But she couldn't suppress it. She would always shatter the illusion when challenged, would always reveal what lay beneath.

Daemon intently studied the face that, in turn, studied the picture he still held. He sucked in his breath when he finally understood. He wore the Black; Jaenelle *was* the Black. But with her, the Black was not only dark, savage power, it was laughter and mischief and compassion and healing . . . and snowballs.

Daemon kissed her hair and looked at the picture. "You would have gotten along well with him. He was always ready to get into trouble." He was rewarded with a ghost of a smile.

She studied the picture. "Now he looks more like what he is." Her eyes narrowed, and then she shot an accusing look at him. "Wait a minute. You said he was your brother."

"He was." Is. Would always be.

"But he's Eyrien."

"We had different mothers."

There was a strange light in her eyes. "But the same father."

He watched her juggling the mental puzzle pieces, saw the moment when they all clicked.

"That explains a lot," she murmured, fluffing her hair. "He isn't dead, you know. The Ebon-gray is still in Terreille."

Daemon blinked. "How—" He sputtered. "How do you know that?"

"I looked. I didn't go anywhere," she added hurriedly. "I didn't break my promise."

"Then how—" Daemon shook his head. "Forget I said that."

"It's not like trying to sort through Opals or Red from a distance to find a particular person." Jaenelle had that harried, amused look. "Daemon, the only other Ebon-gray is Andulvar, and he doesn't live in Terreille anymore. Who else can it be?"

Daemon sighed. He didn't understand, but he was relieved to know.

"May I have a copy of that picture?"

"Why?" Jaenelle gave him a look that made him wince. "All right."

"And one of you, too?"

"I don't have one of me."

"We could get one."

"Why—never mind. Is there a reason for this?"

"Of course."

"I don't suppose you'd tell me what it is?"

Jaenelle raised one eyebrow. It was such a perfect imitation, Daemon choked back a laugh. *Serves me right,* he thought wryly. "All right," he said, ruefully shaking his head.

"Soon?"

"Yes, Lady, soon."

Jaenelle skipped away, turned, gave him a feather-light kiss on the cheek, and was gone.

Raising one eyebrow, Daemon looked at the closed door. He looked at the picture. "You stupid Prick," he said fondly. "Ah, Lucivar, you would have had such fun with her."

3 / Hell

Saetan leaned back in his chair, steepling his fingers. "Why?"

"Because I'd like one."

"You said that before. Why?"

Jaenelle loosely clasped her hands, looked at the ceiling, and said in a prim, authoritative voice, " 'Tis not the season for questions."

Saetan choked. When he could breathe again, he said, "Very well, witch-child. You'll have a picture."

"Two?"

Saetan gave her a long, hard look. She gave him her unsure-but-game smile. He sighed. There was one unshakable truth about Jaenelle: Sometimes it was better not to know. "Two."

She pulled a chair up to the blackwood desk. Resting her elbows on the gleaming surface, her chin propped in her hands, she said solemnly, "I want to buy two frames, but I don't know where to buy them."

"What kind do you want?"

Jaenelle perked up. "Nice ones, the kind that open like a book."

"Swivel frames?"

She shrugged. "Something that will hold two pictures."

"I'll get them for you. Anything else?"

She was solemn again. "I want to buy them myself, but I don't know how much they cost."

"Witch-child, that's not a problem—"

Jaenelle reached into her pocket and pulled something out. Resting her loosely closed fist on the desk, she opened her hand. "Do you think if you sold this, it would buy the frames?"

Saetan gulped, but his hand was steady when he picked up the stone and held it up to the light. "Where did you get this, witch-child?" he asked calmly, almost absently.

Jaenelle put her hands in her lap, her eyes focused on the desk. "Well . . . you see . . . I was with a friend and we were going through this village and some rocks had fallen by the road and a little girl had her foot caught under one of the rocks." She scrunched her shoulders. "It was hurt, the foot I mean, because of the rock, and I . . . . healed it, and her father gave me that to say thank you." She added hurriedly, "But he didn't say I had to keep it." She hesitated. "Do you think it would buy two frames?"

Saetan held the stone between thumb and forefinger. "Oh, yes," he said dryly. "I think it will be more than adequate for what you want."

Jaenelle smiled at him, puzzled.

Saetan struggled to keep his voice calm. "Tell me, witch-child, have you received other such gifts from grateful parents?"

"Uh-huh. Draca's keeping them for me because I didn't know what to do with them." She brightened. "She's given me a room at the Keep, just like you gave me one at the Hall."

"Yes, she told me she was going to." He smiled at her obvious relief that he wasn't offended. "I'll have the pictures and frames for you by the end of the week. Will that be satisfactory?"

Jaenelle bounced around the desk, strangled him, and kissed his cheek. "Thank you, Saetan."

"You're welcome, witch-child. Off with you."

Jaenelle bumped into Mephis on her way out. "Hello, Mephis," she said as she headed wherever she was headed.

Even Mephis. Saetan smiled at the bemused, tender expression on his staid, ever-so-formal eldest son's face.

"Come look at this," Saetan said, "and tell me what you think."

Mephis held the diamond up to the light and whistled softly. "Where did you get this?"

"It was a gift, to Jaenelle, from a grateful parent."

Mephis groped for the chair. He stared at the diamond in disbelief. "You're joking."

Saetan retrieved the diamond, holding it between thumb and forefinger. "No, Mephis, I'm not joking. Apparently, a little girl got her foot caught under a rock and hurt it. Jaenelle healed it, and the grateful father presented her with this. And, apparently, this is not the first such gift that's been bestowed upon her for such service." He studied the large, flawless gem.

"But . . . how?" Mephis sputtered.

"She's a natural Healer. It's instinctive."

"Yes, but—"

"But the real question is, what really happened?" Saetan's golden eyes narrowed.

"What do you mean?" Mephis said, puzzled.

"I mean," Saetan said slowly, "the way Jaenelle told the story, it didn't sound like much. But how severe an injury by how large a rock, when healed, would make a father grateful enough to give up this?"

4 / Kaeleer

"Witch-child, since a list of your friends would be as long as you are tall, you can't possibly give each of them a Winsol gift. It's not expected. You don't expect gifts from all of them, do you?"

"Of course not," Jaenelle replied hotly. She slumped in the chair. "But they're my friends, Saetan."

And you are the best gift they could have in a hundred lifetimes.

"Winsol is the celebration of Witch, the Blood's remembrance of what we are. Gifts are condiments for the meat, and that's all."

Jaenelle eyed him skeptically—and well she should. How many times over the past few days had he caught himself daydreaming of what it would be like to celebrate Winsol with her? To be with her at sunset when the gifts were opened? To share a tiny cup of hot blooded rum with her? To dance, as the Blood danced at no other time of the year, for the glory of Witch? The daydreams were bittersweet. As he walked through the corridors of the Kaeleer Hall watching the staff decorate the rooms, laughing and whispering secrets; as he and Mephis prepared the benefaction list for the staff and all the villagers whose work directly or indirectly served the Hall; as he did all the things a good Prince did for the people who served him, a thought rubbed at him, rubbed and rubbed: She would be spending that special day with her family in Terreille, away from those who were truly her own.

The one small drop of comfort was that she would also be with Daemon.

"What should I do?"

Jaenelle's question brought him back to the present. He lightly rubbed his steepled fingers against his lips. "I think you should select one or two of your friends who, for whatever reason, might be left out of the celebrations and festivities and give gifts to them. A small gesture to one who otherwise will have nothing will be worth a great deal more than another gift among many."

Jaenelle fluffed her hair and then smiled. "Yes," she said softly, "I know exactly the ones who need it most."

"It's settled, then." A paper-wrapped parcel lifted from the corner of his desk and came to rest in front of Jaenelle. "As you requested."

Jaenelle's smile widened as she took the parcel and carefully unwrapped it. The soft glow in her eyes melted century upon century of loneliness. "You look splendid, Saetan."

He smiled tenderly. "I do my best to serve, Lady." He shifted in his chair. "By the way, the stone you gave me to sell—"

"Was it enough?" Jaenelle asked anxiously. "If it wasn't—"

"More than enough, witch-child." Remembering the expression on the jeweler's face when he brought it in, it was hard not to laugh at her concern. "There were, in fact, a good number of gold marks left over. I took the liberty of opening an account in your name with the remainder. So anytime you want to purchase something in Kaeleer, you need only sign for it, have the store's proprietor send the bill to me at the Hall, and I'll deduct it from your account. Fair enough?"

Jaenelle's grin made Saetan wish he'd bitten his tongue. The Darkness only knew what she might think to purchase. Ah, well. It was going to be just as much of a headache for the merchants as it was going to be for him—and he found the idea too amusing to really mind.

"I suppose if you *did* want to get an unusual gift, you could always get a couple of salt licks for the unicorns," he teased.

He was stunned by the instant, haunted look in her eyes.

"No," Jaenelle whispered, all the color draining from her face. "No, not salt."

He sat for a long time after she left him, staring at nothing, wondering what it was about salt that could distress her so much.

5 / Kaeleer

Draca stepped aside to let Saetan enter. "What do you think?"

Saetan whistled softly. Like all the rooms in the Keep, the huge bedroom was cut out of the living mountain. But unlike the other rooms, including the suite Cassandra had once had, the walls of this room had been worked and smoothed to shine like ravenglass. A wood floor peeked out from beneath immense, thick, red-and-cream patterned rugs that could only have come from Dharo, the Kaeleer Territory renowned for its cloth and weaving. The four-poster blackwood bed could comfortably sleep four people. The rest of the furniture—tables, nightstands, bookcases, storage cupboard—was also blackwood. There was a dressing room with wardrobes and storage cupboards of cedar, and a private bath with a sunken marble tub—black veined with red—a large shower stall, double sinks, and a commode enclosed in its own little room. On the other side of the bedroom was a door leading into a sitting room.

"It's magnificent, Draca," Saetan said as his eyes drank in the odds and ends scattered on the tables—a young girl's treasures. Fingering the lid of a box that had an intricate design created from a number of rare woods, he opened it and shook his head, partly amused and partly stunned. One finger idly stirred the contents of the box, stirred the little seashells that had obviously come from widely distant beaches, stirred the diamonds, rubies, emeralds, and sapphires that were no more than pretty stones to a child. He closed the box and turned, one eyebrow rising in amusement.

Draca lifted her shoulders in the merest hint of a shrug. "Would you have it otherwisse?"

"No." He looked around. "This room will please her. It's truly a dark sanctuary, something she'll need more and more as the years pass."

"Not all ssanctuariess are dark, High Lord. The room you gave her pleasess her, too." For the first time in all the years he'd known her, Draca smiled. "Sshall I desscribe it to you? I have heard about it often enough."

Saetan looked away, not wanting her to see how pleased he was.

"I wanted to sshow you the Winssol gift I have for her." Draca retreated into the dressing room and returned holding a wisp of black. She spread it out on the bed's satin coverlet. "What do you think?"

Saetan stared at the full-length dress. There was a lump in his throat he couldn't swallow around, and the room was suddenly misty. He fingered the black spidersilk. "Her first Widow's weeds," he said huskily. "This is what she should wear for Winsol." He let the silk slip through his fingers as he turned away. "She should be with us."

"Yess, sshe sshould be with her family."

"She will be with her family," Saetan said bitterly. He laughed, but that was bitter, too. "She'll be with her grandmother and mother . . . and her father."

"No," Draca said gently. "Not with her father. Now, finally, doess sshe have a father."

Saetan took a deep breath. "I used to be the coldest bastard to ever have walked the Realms. What happened?"

"You fell in love . . . with the daughter of your ssoul." Draca made a little sound that might have been a laugh. "And you were never sso cold, Ssaetan, never sso cold ass you pretended to be."

"You might spare my pride by allowing me my illusions."

"For what purposse? Doess sshe allow you to be cold?"

"At least she allows me my illusions," Saetan said, warming to the gentle argument. "However," he added wryly, "she doesn't let me get away with much else." He sighed, his expression one of pained amusement. "I must go. I have to talk to some distressed merchants."

Draca escorted him out. "It hass been a long time ssince you celebrated Winssol. Thiss year, when the black candless are lit, you will drink the blooded rum and dance for the glory of Witch."

"Yes," he said softly, thinking of the spidersilk dress, "this year I will dance."

6 / Hell

Saetan settled his cape around his shoulders. On the floor of his private study were six boxes filled with the many brightly wrapped gifts he had purchased for the *cildru dyathe*. Since the children were so skittish of adults, it was impossible to know how many were on the island. The best he could do was fill a box for each age group and leave it to Char to distribute the gifts. There were books and toys, games and puzzles, from as many Kaeleer Territories as he had access to. If he had been overly indulgent this year, it was to fill the hole in his heart, to make up for the gifts he wanted to give Jaenelle and couldn't. There could be no trace of him in Beldon Mor, no gift that might provoke questions. Knowledge was the only thing he could give her that she could take back to Terreille.

He vanished the boxes one by one, left his study, and caught the Black Wind to the *cildru dyathe's* island.

Even for Hell, it was a bleak place made of rocks, sand, and barren fields. A place where even Hell's native flora and fauna couldn't thrive. He'd always wondered why Char had chosen that place instead of one of the many others that wouldn't have been so stark. And then Jaenelle had unthinkingly given him the answer: The island, in its starkness, in its unyielding bleakness, held no deceptions, no illusions. Poisons weren't sugar-coated, brutality wasn't masked by silk and lace. There was nowhere for cruelty to hide.

He took his time reaching that rocky place that was as close to a shelter as the children would condone. As he reached the final bend in the twisting path and mentally prepared himself to watch them flee from him, he heard laughter—innocent, delighted laughter. He wrapped his cape tightly around him, hoping to blend into the rocks and remain unnoticed for a moment. To hear them laugh that way . . .

Saetan eased around the last rock and gasped.

In the center of their open "council" area stood a magnificent evergreen, its color undimmed by Hell's forever-twilight. Throughout the branches, little points of color winked in and out like a rainbow of fireflies performing a merry dance. Char and the other children were hanging icicles—real icicles—from the branches. Little silver and gold bells tinkled as they brushed against the branches. There was laughter and purpose, an animation and sparkle in their young faces that he'd never seen before.

Then they saw him and froze, small animals caught in the light. In another moment, they would have run, but Char turned at that instant, his eyes bright. He stepped toward Saetan, holding out his hands in an ancient gesture of welcome.

"High Lord." Char's voice rang with pride. "Come see our tree."

Saetan came forward slowly and placed his hands over Char's. He studied the tree. A single tear slipped down his cheek, and his lips trembled. "Ah, children," he said huskily, "it's truly a magnificent tree. And your decorations are *wonderful*."

They smiled at him, shyly, tentatively.

Without thinking, Saetan put his arm around Char's shoulders and hugged him close. The boy jerked back, caught himself, and then hesitantly put his arms around Saetan and hugged him in return.

"You know who gave us the tree, don't you?" Char whispered.

"Yes, I know."

"I've never . . . most of us have never . . ."

"I know, Char." Saetan squeezed Char's shoulder once more. He cleared his throat. "They seem a bit . . . dull . . . compared with this, but there are gifts for you to put beneath the tree."

Char rubbed his hand across his face. "She said it would only last the thirteen days of Winsol, but that's all they ever last, isn't it?"

"Yes, that's all they ever last."

"High Lord." Char hesitated. "How?"

Saetan smiled tenderly at the boy. "I don't know. She's magic. I'm only a Warlord Prince. You can't expect me to explain magic."

Char smiled in return, a smile from one man to another.

Saetan called in the six boxes. "I'll leave these in your keeping." One finger gently stroked Char's burned, blackened cheek. "Happy Winsol, Warlord." He turned and glided quickly toward the path. As he passed the first bend, a sound came from a smattering of voices. When it was repeated, it was a full chorus.

"Happy Winsol, High Lord."

Saetan choked back a sob and hurried back to the Hall.

7 / Hell

"You did tell me to give a Winsol gift to someone who might not get one, so . . . well . . ." Jaenelle nervously brushed her fingers along the edge of Saetan's blackwood desk.

"Come here, witch-child." Saetan gently hugged her. Putting his lips close to her ear, he whispered, "That was the finest piece of magic I've ever seen. I'm so very proud of you."

"Truly?" Jaenelle whispered back.

"Truly." He held her at arm's length so he could see her face. "Would you share the secret?" he asked, keeping his voice lightly teasing. "Would you tell an old Warlord Prince how you did it?"

Jaenelle's eyes focused on his Red Birthright Jewel hanging from its gold chain. "I promised the Prince, you see."

"See what?" he asked calmly as his stomach flip-flopped.

"I promised that if I was going to do any dream weaving I'd learn from the best who could teach me."

And you didn't come to me? "So who taught you, witch-child?"

She licked her lips. "The Arachnians," she said in a small voice.

The room blurred and spun. When it stopped revolving, Saetan gratefully realized he was still sitting in his chair. "Arachna is a closed Terri-tory," he said through clenched teeth.

Jaenelle frowned. "I know. But so are a lot of places where I have friends. They don't mind, Saetan. Truly."

Saetan released her and locked his hands together. Arachna. She'd gone to Arachna. Beware the golden spider that spins a tangled web. There wasn't a Black Widow in all the history of the Blood who could spin dream webs like the Arachnians. The whole shore of their island was lit-tered with tangled webs that could pull in unsuspecting—and even well-trained—minds, leaving the flesh shell to be devoured. For her to blithely walk through their defenses . . .

"The Arachnian Queen," Saetan said, fighting the urge to yell at her. "Whom did she assign to teach you?"

Jaenelle gave him a worried little smile. "She taught me. We started with the straight, simple webs, everyday weaving. After that . . ." Jaenelle shrugged.

Saetan cleared his throat. "Just out of curiosity, how large is the Arachnian Queen?"

"Um . . . her body's about like that." Jaenelle pointed at his fist.

The room tilted. Very little was known about Arachna—with good reason, since very few who had ever ventured there had returned intact—but one thing was known: the larger the spider, the more powerful and deadly were the webs.

"Did the Prince suggest you go to Arachna?" Saetan asked, desperately trying to keep the snarl out of his voice.

Jaenelle blinked and had the grace to blush. "No. I don't think he'd be too happy if I told him."

Saetan closed his eyes. What was done was done. "You will remember courtesy and Protocol when you visit them, won't you?"

"Yes, High Lord," Jaenelle said, her voice suspiciously submissive.

Saetan opened his eyes to a narrow slit. Jaenelle's sapphire eyes sparkled back at him. He snarled, defeated. Hell's fire, if he was so outmaneuvered by a twelve-year-old girl, what in the name of Darkness was he going to do when she was full grown?

"Saetan?"

"Jaenelle."

She held out a brightly though clumsily wrapped package with a slightly mangled bow. "Happy Winsol, Saetan."

His hand shook a little as he took the package and laid it gently on the desk. "Witch-child, I—"

Jaenelle threw her arms around his neck and squeezed. "Draca said it was all right to open your gift before Winsol because I should only wear it at the Keep. Oh, thank you, Saetan. Thank you. It's the most wonderful dress. And it's *black*." She studied his face. "Wasn't I supposed to tell you I already opened it?"

Saetan hugged her fiercely. *You, too, Draca. You, too, are not as cold as you pretend to be.* "I'm glad it pleases you, witch-child. Now." He turned to her package.

"No," Jaenelle said nervously. "You should wait for Winsol."

"You didn't," he gently teased. "Besides, you won't be here for Winsol, so . . ."

"No, Saetan. Please?"

It piqued his curiosity that she would give him something and not want to be there when he opened it. However, tomorrow was Winsol, and he didn't want her leaving him feeling heartsore. Adeptly turning the conversation to the mounds of food being prepared at the Kaeleer Hall and broadly hinting that Helene and Mrs. Beale just might be willing to parcel some out before the next day, he sent her on her way and leaned back in his chair with a sigh.

The package beckoned.

Saetan Black-locked the study door before carefully unwrapping the package. His heart did a queer little jig as he stared at the back of one of the swivel frames he had purchased for her. Taking a deep breath, he opened the frame.

In the left side was a copy of an old picture of a young man with a hint of a brash smile and a ready-for-trouble gleam in his eyes. The face would have changed by now, hardened, matured. Even so.

"Lucivar," he whispered, blinking away tears and shaking his head. "You had that look in your eyes when you were five years old. It would seem there are some things the years can't change. Where are you now, my Eyrien Prince."

He turned to the picture on the right, immediately set the frame on the desk, leaned back in his chair and covered his eyes. "No wonder," he whispered. "By all the Jewels and the Darkness, no wonder." If Lucivar was a summer afternoon, Daemon was winter's coldest night. Sliding his hands from his face, Saetan forced himself to study the picture of his namesake, his true heir.

It was a formal picture taken in front of a red-velvet background. On the surface, this son of his was not a mirror—he far exceeded his father's chiseled, handsome features—but beneath the surface was the recognizable, chilling darkness, and a ruthlessness Saetan instinctively knew had been honed by years of cruelty.

"Dorothea, you have re-created me at my worst."

And yet . . .

Saetan leaned forward and studied the golden eyes so like his own, eyes that seemed to look straight at him. He smiled in thanks and relief. Nothing would ever undo what Dorothea had done to Daemon, what she had turned him into, but in those golden eyes was a swirling expression of resignation, amusement, irritation, and delight—a cacophony of emotions he was all too familiar with. It could only mean one thing: Jaenelle had maneuvered Daemon into this and had gone with him to make sure it was done to her satisfaction.

"Well, namesake," Saetan said quietly as he positioned the frame on the corner of his desk, "if you've accepted the leash she's holding, there's hope for you yet."

8 / Terreille

For Daemon, Winsol was the bitterest day of the year, a cruel reminder of what it had been like to grow up in Dorothea's court, of what had been required of him after the dancing had fired Dorothea's and Hepsabah's blood.

His stomach tightened. The stone he sharpened his already honed temper on was the knowledge that the one witch he wanted to dance with, the only one he would gladly surrender to and indulge was too young for him—for any man.

He celebrated Winsol because it was expected of him. Each year he sent a basket of delicacies to Surreal. Each year he sent gifts to Manny and Jo—and to Tersa whenever he could find her. Each year there were the expected, expensive gifts for the witches he served. Each year he got nothing in return, not even the words "thank you."

But this year was different. This year he'd been caught up in a whirl-wind called Jaenelle Angelline—as impossible to deflect as she was to stop—and he had become an accomplice in all sorts of schemes that, even in their innocence, had been thrilling. When he had dug in his heels and balked at one of her adventures, he'd been dragged along like a toy so well loved it didn't have much of its stuffing left. With his defenses breached, with his temper dulled and battered by love and his coldness trampled by mischief, he had briefly thought to appeal to the Priest for help until, with amused dismay, he realized the High Lord of Hell was probably faring no better than he.

Now, however, as he thought of the kinds of adventures Alexandra and Leland and their friends would require of him, the cold once more whispered through his veins and his temper cut with every breath.

After a light meal that would hold off hunger until the night's huge feast, they gathered in the drawing room to unwrap the Winsol gifts. Flushed from her dizzying work in the kitchen, Cook carried in the tray with the silver bowl filled with the traditional hot blooded rum. The small silver cups were filled to be shared.

Robert shared his cup with Leland, who tried not to look at Philip. Philip shared his with Wilhelmina. Graff sneeringly shared hers with Cook. And he, because he had no choice, shared his with Alexandra.

Jaenelle stood alone, with no one to share her cup.

Daemon's heart twisted. He remembered too many Winsols when he had been the one standing alone, the outcast, the unwanted. He would have damned the tradition that said only one cup was shared, but he saw that strange, unnerving light flicker in her eyes for just a moment before she lifted her cup in a salute and drank.

There was a moment of nervous silence before Wilhelmina jumped in with a brittle smile and asked, "Can we open the gifts now?"

As the cups were put back on the tray, Daemon maneuvered to Jaenelle's side. "Lady—"

"It's fitting, don't you think, that I should drink alone?" she said in a midnight whisper. Her eyes were full of awful pain. "After all, I am kin-dred but not kind."

You're my Queen, he thought fiercely. His body ached. She was his Queen. But with her family surrounding them, watching, there was noth-ing he could say or do to help her.

During the next hour, Jaenelle played her expected role of the slightly befuddled child, fawning over gifts so at odds with what she was that it made Daemon want to paint the walls in blood. No one else noticed she was fighting harder and harder to draw breath with each gift she unwrapped until it seemed the bright paper and bows were fists pounding her small body. When he opened her gift of handkerchiefs, she flinched and went deathly pale. With a gasp, she leaped to her feet and ran from the room while Alexandra and Leland sternly called for her to come back.

Not caring what they thought, Daemon left the room, cold fury rolling off him, and went to the library. Jaenelle was there, gasping for breath, feebly trying to open a window. Daemon locked the door, strode across the room, viciously twisted the lock on the sash, and snapped the window open with wall-shaking force.

Jaenelle leaned over the narrow window seat, gulping in the winter air. "It hurts so much to live here, Daemon," she whimpered as he cradled her in his arms. "Sometimes it hurts so much."

"Shh." He stroked her hair. "Shh."

As soon as her breathing slowed to normal, Daemon closed and locked the window. He leaned against the wall, one leg stretched out along the window seat, and drew her forward until she was pressed against him. Then he hooked his other foot under his leg, effectively capturing her in a tight triangle.

It was insane to have her pushed up against him that way. Insane to take such pleasure in her hands resting on his thighs. Insane not to stop the slow uncurling of those psychic tendrils of seduction.

"I'm sorry I couldn't share the cup with you."

"It doesn't matter," Jaenelle whispered.

"It does to me," he replied sharply, his deep, silky voice having more of a husky edge than usual.

Jaenelle's eyes were getting confused and smoky. He pulled the tendrils back a little.

"Daemon," Jaenelle said hesitantly. "Your gift . . ."

There was a rumbling in Daemon's throat—his bedroom laugh, except there was fire in it instead of ice, and his eyes were molten gold. "That was no more your choice than the paint set was truly mine." He raised one eyebrow. "I had considered getting you a saddle that would fit both you and Dark Dancer—"

Jaenelle's eyes widened and she laughed.

"—but that wouldn't have been practical." One long-nailed finger idly stroked her arm. He knew he should walk away from this—now—when he had amused her, but her pain had twisted something inside him, and he wasn't going to let her believe she was alone here. It made him wonder about something else. "Jaenelle," he said cautiously as he watched his finger, "did the Priest . . ." If Saetan hadn't given her a Winsol gift, would his asking hurt her more?

"Oh, Daemon, it's so wonderful. I can't wear it here, of course."

He started to untwist. "Wear what?"

"My dress." She squirmed in his tight triangle and almost sent him through the wall. "It's floor-length and it's made of spidersilk and it's black, Daemon, *black*."

Daemon concentrated on breathing. When he was sure his heart remembered its proper rhythm, he reached into his inner jacket pocket and took out a small square box. "Then this, I think, would be a proper accessory."

"What is it?" Jaenelle asked, hesitantly taking the box.

"Your Winsol gift. Your *real* Winsol gift."

Smiling shyly, Jaenelle unwrapped the box, opened it, and gasped.

Daemon's throat tightened. It was an inappropriate gift for a man like him to give a young girl, but he didn't care about that, didn't care about anything except whether or not it pleased her.

"Oh, Daemon," Jaenelle whispered. She took the hammered silver cuff bracelet from the box and placed it on her left wrist. "It will be perfect with my dress." She reached up to hug him and froze.

He watched her emotions swirl in her eyes, too fast for him to identify. Instead of hugging him, she lowered her hands to his shoulders, leaned forward, and kissed him lightly on the mouth, a girl child testing the waters of womanhood. His hands closed on her arms with just enough pressure to keep her close to him. When she pulled back, he saw in her eyes a whisper of the woman she would become.

Seeing that, he couldn't let it finish there.

Gently cupping her face in his hands, Daemon leaned forward and returned her kiss. His kiss was as light and close-lipped as hers had been, but it wasn't innocent and it wasn't chaste. When he finally raised his head, he knew he was playing a dangerous game.

Jaenelle swayed, bracing her hands on his thighs for support. She licked her lips and looked at him with slightly glazed eyes. "Do . . . do all boys kiss like that?"

"Boys don't kiss like that at all, Lady," he said quietly, seriously. "Neither do most men. But I'm not like most men." He slowly pulled in his seduction tendrils. He had done more than he should have already tonight; anything else would harm her. Tomorrow he would be the companion he'd been yesterday, and the day before that. But she would remember that kiss and compare every kiss from every weak-willed Chaillot boy against it.

He didn't care how many boys kissed her. They were, after all, boys. But the bed . . . When the time came, the bed would be *his.*

He removed the bracelet from her wrist and put it back in its box. "Vanish that," he said quietly while he disposed of the ribbon and paper. When the box was gone, he unwound his legs and led her back to the drawing room, where Graff immediately hurried the girls off to bed.

Philip glared at him. Robert smirked. Leland was fluttery and pale. It was Alexandra's jealous, accusing look that unsheathed his temper. She rose to confront him, but at that moment the guests began arriving for the night-long festivities.

That night Daemon didn't wait for Alexandra to "ask" him to accommodate a female guest. He seduced every woman in the house—beginning with Leland—teasing them into climaxes while he danced with them, watching them shudder while they bit their lips until they bled, trying not to cry out with so many people crowded around them. Or slipping away with one of the women to a little alcove, and after the first ice-fire kiss, standing primly against the wall, his hands in his trouser pockets, while his phantom touch played mercilessly with her body until she was sprawled on the floor, pleading for the caress of a real hand—and then his merest touch, the tickling slide of his nails along her inner thigh, the briefest touch to the undergarments in the right place, and she would be glutted—and starved.

Still, Daemon wasn't done.

He had deliberately avoided Alexandra, taunting her with his open seduction of all the other women, frustrating her beyond endurance. Before the door shut on the last guest, he swept her into his arms, climbed the stairs, and locked them into her bedroom. He made up for everything. He showed her the kind of pleasure he could give a woman when inspired. He showed her why he was called the Sadist.

When he stumbled into his own room long after dawn, the first thing he noticed was that his bed had been fussed with. One swift, angry probe located the package beneath his pillow. Cautiously pulling back the covers and tossing the pillow aside, Daemon looked at the clumsily wrapped package and the folded note tucked under the ribbon. He smiled tenderly, sinking gratefully onto the bed.

She must have put it there as soon as he'd left the room.

The note said: "I couldn't give you the gift I wanted to because the others wouldn't understand. Happy Winsol, Daemon. Love, Jaenelle."

Daemon unwrapped the package and opened the swivel frame. The left side was empty, waiting for Lucivar's picture. On the right . . .

"It's funny," Daemon said quietly to the picture. "I'd always thought you'd look more formal, more . . . distant. But for all your splendor, all your Craft and power, you really wouldn't mind putting your feet up and downing a tankard of ale, would you? I'd never guessed how much of you is in Lucivar. Or how much of you is in me. Ah, Priest." Daemon gently closed the frame. "Happy Winsol, Father."

CHAPTER THIRTEEN

1 / Terreille

"We should have brought the others," Cassandra said as she clenched Saetan's arm.

He laid his hand over hers and gave it a gentle squeeze. "He didn't ask to see the others. He asked to see me."

"He didn't ask," Cassandra snapped. She glanced nervously at the Sanctuary and lowered her voice. "He didn't ask, High Lord, he *demanded* to see you."

"And I'm here."

"Yes," she said with an undercurrent of anger, "you're here."

Sometimes you make it hard for me to remember why I loved you so much for so long. "He's my son, Cassandra." He smiled grimly. "Are you offended by his manners on my behalf or because your vanity's pricked that he wasn't sufficiently obsequious?"

Cassandra snatched her hand from his arm. "He's charming when he wants to be," she said nastily. "And I've no doubt his bedroom manners are flawless, since he's had so much practice perfecting . . ." Her words faded when she noticed Saetan's glacial stare.

"If his manners leave something to be desired, Lady, I'll thank you to remember whose court trained him."

Cassandra lifted her chin. "You blame me, don't you?"

"No," Saetan said softly, bitterly. "I knew the price for what I became. The responsibility for him rests solely with me. But I'll allow no one, *no one,* to condemn him for what he's become because of it." Saetan breathed deeply, trying to gather his frayed temper. "Why don't you go to your room? It's better that I meet him alone."

"No," Cassandra said quickly. "We both wear the Black. Together we can—"

"I didn't come here to fight him."

"But he's come to fight you!"

"You don't know that."

"You weren't the one he pinned to the wall while he made his demands!"

"I'll give him a slap. Will that appease you?" Saetan snarled as he marched into the ruins of the Sanctuary, heading toward the kitchen and another confrontation.

Halfway to the kitchen, Saetan slowed down. He'd kept his promise to Draca. On Winsol he had danced for the glory of Witch. Thanks to the blood Jaenelle insisted on giving him, he no longer needed a cane or walked with a limp, but the dancing had stiffened his bad leg, had shortened his fluid stride. He regretted that he might appear old or infirm for this first meeting with Daemon after so many, many years.

Fury poured out the kitchen doorway as Saetan approached. So. Cassandra hadn't exaggerated about that. At least the rage was hot. They might still be able to talk.

Daemon prowled the kitchen with panther grace, his hands in his trouser pockets, his body coiled with barely restrained rage. When he sent a dagger glance toward the doorway and noticed Saetan, he didn't alter his stride; he simply pivoted on the ball of his foot and came straight toward the High Lord.

That picture told only half the truth, Saetan thought as he watched Daemon's swift approach and waited to see if blood would be drawn.

Daemon stopped an arm's length away, nostrils flaring, eyes stabbing, silent.

"Prince," Saetan said calmly. He watched Daemon fight for control, fight the searing rage in order to return the greeting.

"High Lord," Daemon said through clenched teeth.

Slowly approaching the table, aware of Daemon watching his every move, Saetan took off his cape, laying it across a chair. "Let's have a glass of wine, and then we'll talk."

"I don't want any wine."

"I do." Saetan got the wine and glasses. Settling into a chair, he opened the wine, poured two glasses, and waited.

Daemon stepped forward, carefully placing his hands on the table.

Dorothea was blind not to know what Daemon was, Saetan thought as he sipped the wine. Having expected to see them, Saetan found Daemon's long nails less disconcerting than his ringless fingers. If he could be this formidable without wearing a Jewel to help focus his strength . . .

No wonder Cassandra had been terrified. Black Jewels or no, she was no match for this son of his.

"Do you know where she is?" Daemon asked, obviously straining not to scream.

Saetan's eyes narrowed. Fear. All that fury was covering an avalanche of fear. "Who?"

Daemon sprang away from the table, swearing.

When the torrent of expletives showed no sign of abating, Saetan said dryly, "Namesake, do you realize you're making this room quite uninhabitable?"

"What?" Daemon pivoted and sprang back to the table.

"Leash your rage, Prince," Saetan said quietly. "You sent for me, and I'm here." He looked over his shoulder toward the window. "However, the dawn is a few short hours away, and you can't afford to be here beyond that, can you?"

As Daemon dropped into the chair across from him, Saetan handed him a glass of wine. Daemon drained it. Saetan refilled it. After refilling it for the third time, he said dryly, "From experience I can tell you that getting drunk doesn't lessen the fear. However, the agony of the hangover can do wonders for a man's perception."

There was dismayed amusement in Daemon's eyes.

"Bluntly put, my fine young Prince, this is obviously the first time our fair-haired Lady has scared the shit out of you."

Daemon frowned at the empty wine bottle, found a full one in the cupboard, and refilled both glasses. "Not the first time," he growled.

Saetan chuckled. "But it is a matter of degree, yes?"

There was a hint of warmth in Daemon's reluctant smile. "Yes."

"And this time is bad."

Daemon closed his eyes. "Yes."

Saetan sighed. "Start at the beginning and let's see if we can untangle this."

"She's not at her family's estate."

"It *is* the Winsol season. Could her . . . family"—Saetan choked on the word—"have left her with friends to visit?"

Daemon shook his head. "*Something's* there, but it isn't Jaenelle. It looks like her, talks like her, plays the obedient daughter." Daemon looked at Saetan, his eyes haunted. "But what makes Jaenelle Jaenelle isn't there." He laughed scornfully. "Her family has been most gratified that she's been behaving so well and not embarrassing them when the girls are presented to guests." He played with his wineglass. "I'm afraid something has happened to her."

"Unlikely." Fascinated, Saetan watched the anger melt from Daemon's face. He liked the man he saw beneath it.

"How can you be sure?" Daemon asked hopefully. "Have you seen something like that before?"

"Not quite like that, no."

"Then how—"

"Because, namesake, what you're describing is called a shadow, but there's no one in any of the Realms, including me, who has the Craft to create a shadow that's so lifelike—except Jaenelle."

Daemon sipped his wine and brooded for a minute. "What, exactly, is a shadow?"

"Basically, a shadow is an illusion, a re-creation of an object's physical form." Saetan looked pointedly at Daemon, who shrank in his chair just a little. "Some children have been known to create a shadow in order to appear to be asleep in their beds while they are really off having adventures that, if discovered, would prevent them from comfortably sitting down for a week." He saw the briefest flicker of memory in Daemon's eyes and the beginning of a wry smile. "That's a first-stage shadow and is stationary. A second-stage shadow can move around, but it has to be manipulated like a puppet. That kind of shadow looks solid but can't be felt, doesn't have tactile capabilities. The third-stage shadow, which is the strongest I've ever heard of being achieved, has one-way tactile ability. It can touch but can't be touched. However, it, too, must be manipulated."

Daemon thought this over and shook his head. "This is more."

"Yes, this is much, much more. This is a shadow so skillfully created that it can act independently through expected routines. I don't imagine the conversation's stimulating"—that made Daemon snort—"but it does mean the originator can be doing something entirely different."

"Such as?"

"Ah," Saetan said as he refilled their glasses, "*that* is the interesting question."

Daemon's eyes flashed with relieved anger. "Why would she create one?"

"As I said, *that* is the interesting question."

"Is that it? We just wait?"

"For now. But whoever gets to her first gets to go up one side of her and down the other. Twice."

A slow smile curled Daemon's lips. "You're worried."

"You're damn right I'm worried," Saetan snapped. Now that he didn't have to rein in Daemon's temper, he felt free to unleash his own. "Who in the name of Hell knows what she's up to this time?" He slumped in his chair, snarling.

Daemon leaned back in his chair and laughed.

"Don't be so amused, boy. *You* deserve a good kick in the ass."

Daemon blinked. *"Me?"*

Saetan leaned forward. "You. The next time you suggest she get proper instruction before trying something, you'd damn well better remember to add that I'm the one to give the proper instruction."

"What—"

"Dream weaving. Do you remember dream weaving, namesake?"

Daemon paled. "I remember. But I—"

"Told her to be instructed by the best. Which she did."

"Then what—"

"Have you ever heard of Arachna?"

Daemon got paler. "That's a legend," he whispered.

"Most of Kaeleer's a legend, boy," Saetan roared. "That hasn't stopped her from meeting some *very* interesting individuals."

They glared at one another. Finally Daemon said with menacing quiet, "Like you?"

Damn, this boy was fun! Saetan took a deep breath and sighed dramatically. "I used to be interesting," he said mournfully. "I used to be respected, even feared. My study was a private sanctuary no one willingly entered. But I've gotten long in the tooth"—Daemon flicked a startled glance at his mouth—"and now I have demons pounding on my door, some upset because she hasn't visited with them, some upset because she has. My cook backs me into corners, wanting to know if the Lady will be coming today so her favorite meat pie can be prepared. And I have merchants cluttering up my doorstep, cringingly seeking an audience, actually relieved to be in my presence while they wring their hands and pour out their tales of woe."

Daemon, who had become more and more amused, frowned slightly. "The demons and the cook I understand. Why the merchants?"

Saetan let out another dramatic sigh, but his eyes glowed with dark amusement. "I opened a blanket account for her in Kaeleer."

Daemon sucked in his breath. "You mean . . ."

"Yes."

"Mother Night."

"That's the kindest thing that's been said to me on that score." Enjoying the drama, Saetan continued, "And it's going to get worse. You do realize that?"

"Worse?" Daemon said suspiciously. "Why will it get worse?"

"She's only twelve, namesake."

"I know," Daemon almost moaned.

"Just consider what sort of mischief she'll have the capacity to get into when she's seventeen and has her own court."

Daemon groaned, but there was a sharp, hopeful look in his eyes. "She can have her own court at seventeen? And fill it?"

Ah, namesake. Saetan sat quietly for a moment, thinking of a politic way to explain. "Most positions can be filled then." Daemon's instant bitterness stunned him.

"Of course you'll want better for her than a whore who's serviced almost every Queen in Terreille," Daemon said, refilling his wineglass.

"That isn't what I meant," Saetan said, despairing that any explanation now might seem a poor bone.

"Then what did you mean?" Daemon snapped.

"What if, at seventeen, she isn't ready for a consort?" Saetan countered softly. "What if it takes a few more years before she's ready for the bed? Will you hold an empty office, becoming comfortable and familiar while lesser men intrigue her because they're strangers? Time has great magic, namesake, if you know how to play the game."

"You talk as though it's decided," Daemon said quietly, with only an aftertaste of bitterness.

"It is . . . as far as I'm concerned."

Daemon's naked, grateful look was agony.

They sat quietly, companionably, for a few minutes. Then Daemon said, "Why do you keep calling me namesake?"

"Because you are." Saetan looked away, uncomfortable. "I never intended to give any of my sons that name. I knew what I was. It was difficult enough for them to have me as a father. But the first time I held you, I knew no other name would suit you. So I named you Saetan Daemon SaDiablo."

Daemon's eyes were tear bright. "Then you really did acknowledge paternity? Manny said the Blood register in Hayll had been changed, but I had wondered."

"I'm not responsible for Dorothea's lies, Prince," Saetan said bitterly. "Or for what the Hayllian register does or doesn't say. But in the register kept at Ebon Askavi, you—and Lucivar—are named and acknowledged."

"So you called me Daemon?"

Saetan knew there was much, much more Daemon would have liked to ask, but he was grateful his son chose to step back, to try for lighter conversation in the short time left to them.

"No," Saetan said dryly, "*I* never called you anything but Saetan. It was Manny and Tersa"—he hesitated, wondering if Daemon knew about Tersa, but there was no surprise—"who called you Daemon. Manny informed me one day, when I pointed out her error, that if I thought she was going to stand at the back door bellowing that name to get a boy to come in for supper I had better think again."

Daemon laughed. "Come now, Manny's a sweetheart."

"To *you*." Saetan chuckled. "Personally I always thought she just wanted to avoid having both of us answer that summons."

"Would you have?" Daemon asked warmly.

"Considering the tone of voice used, I wouldn't have dared not to."

They both laughed.

The parting was awkward. Saetan wanted to embrace him, but Daemon became tense, almost skittish. Saetan wondered if, after all those years in Dorothea's court, Daemon had an aversion to being touched.

And there was Lucivar. He had wanted to ask about Lucivar, but Daemon's haunted expression at the mention of his brother's name eliminated that possibility. Since he wanted to know his sons, he would have to have the patience to let them approach when they were ready.

2 / Terreille

Jaenelle returned a teeth-grinding day and a half later.

After a hectic afternoon of social calls with Alexandra, Daemon was prowling the corridors, too restless to lie down and get some badly needed rest, when he saw the girls come in from a walk in the garden.

"But you must remember how funny it was," Wilhelmina said as he approached. She looked bewildered. "It only happened yesterday."

"Did it?" Jaenelle replied absently. "Oh, yes, I remember now."

Daemon gave them an exaggerated bow. "Ladies."

Wilhelmina giggled. Jaenelle raised her eyes to meet his.

He didn't like the weariness in her face, didn't like how ancient her eyes looked even though they were the dissembling summer-sky blue, but he met her steady gaze. "Lady, may I have a word with you?"

"As you wish," Jaenelle said, barely suppressing a sigh.

They waited until Wilhelmina climbed the stairs to the nursery before going to the library. Daemon locked the door. Before he could decide what to say, Jaenelle grumbled, "Don't be scoldy, Prince."

Hackles rising, Daemon slipped his hands into his pockets and leisurely walked toward her. "I haven't said a word."

Jaenelle removed her coat and hat, dropping them on the couch. She slumped beside them. "I've already had one scolding today."

So the Priest had gotten to her first. Just as well. All Daemon wanted to do was hug her. He settled beside her, perversely wanting to take the sting out of the very scolding he had wanted to administer. "Was the scolding very bad?" he asked gently.

Jaenelle scowled at him. "He wouldn't have scolded at all if you hadn't told him. Why'd you tell him?"

"I was scared. I thought something had happened to you."

"Oh," Jaenelle said, immediately chastened. "But I worked so hard to create that shadow so no one would worry, so there wouldn't be any difference. No one else noticed the difference."

They noticed, my Lady. They were grateful for the difference. It amused him—a little—that she was more concerned that her Craft hadn't been as effective as she'd thought than she was about the worry she'd caused. "It took the Black to notice the difference, and even I wasn't sure until a whole day had gone by."

"Really?" Jaenelle perked up.

"Really." Daemon tried to smile but couldn't quite do it. "Don't you think I'm entitled to an explanation?"

Jaenelle ducked her face behind her golden veil of hair. "I was going to tell you. I promised I'd tell you. And I had to tell the Priest because he has to arrange some things."

Daemon frowned. "Promised who?"

"Tersa."

Daemon counted to ten. "How do you know Tersa?"

"It was time, Daemon," Jaenelle said, ignoring his question.

Daemon counted to ten again. "Tersa's very special to me."

"I know," Jaenelle said quietly. "But you're grown up now, Daemon. You don't really need her anymore. And it was time for her to leave the Twisted Kingdom . . . but she'd been there so long, she couldn't find her way back by herself."

The room was so cold—not the cold of anger, the cold of fear. Daemon held Jaenelle's hands between his own, taking small comfort from their warmth. He didn't want to understand. He truly did not want to understand. But he did. "You went into the Twisted Kingdom, didn't you?" he said, trying desperately to keep his voice calm. "You walked the roads of madness to find her and led her back to sanity—at least as far as she can come."

"Yes."

"Didn't you think—" His voice broke from the strain. "Didn't it occur to you it might be dangerous?"

Jaenelle looked puzzled. "Dangerous?" She shook her head. "No. It's just a different way of seeing, Daemon."

Daemon closed his eyes. Did she fear nothing? Not even madness?

"Besides, I've traveled that far before, so I knew the way back."

Daemon tasted blood where his teeth had nicked his tongue.

"But it took a while to find her, and it took a while to convince her it was time to go, that she didn't need to stay inside the visions all the time." Jaenelle gave his hands a little squeeze. "The Priest is going to buy a cottage for her in a little village near the Hall in Kaeleer. She'll have people there who will look after her, and a garden to work in, and Black Widow Sisters to talk to."

Daemon pulled her into his arms and held her tight. "You convinced her to live there?" he whispered into her hair. "She'll really be in a decent house with decent clothes and good food and people who will understand?" Her head moved up and down. He sighed. "Then it was worth the worry. A hundred times that would have been worth it."

"That's what the Priest said—after the scolding."

Daemon smiled against her hair. "Did he say anything else?"

"Lots of things," Jaenelle grumbled. "Something about sitting down comfortably, but I didn't understand him and he wouldn't repeat it."

Daemon coughed. Jaenelle raised her head, eyeing him suspiciously. He tried for a bland expression. She looked more suspicious.

Passing footsteps in the corridor made him turn, his body tensed, his eyes fixed on the door.

"You'd better join your sister." He handed her the coat and hat. Before he opened the door, Daemon paused. "Thank you." It was far from adequate, but it was all he could think of to say.

Jaenelle nodded and slipped out the door.

3 / Terreille

Daemon had just finished brushing his hair, ready for another day of Winsol activity, when Jaenelle tapped lightly on his door and bounced into the room. He wasn't sure when his room had become mutual territory, but he was much less casual about the way he dressed—and undressed—than he had been.

Jaenelle bounced up beside him, her eyes fixed on his face. Daemon smiled. "Do I meet with your approval?"

She reached up, brushed her fingers against his cheek, and frowned. "Your face is smooth."

One eyebrow rising, Daemon turned back to the mirror to check his collar. "Hayllian men don't have facial hair." He paused. "Neither do Dhemlans or Eyriens, for that matter."

Jaenelle still frowned. "I don't understand."

Daemon shrugged. "Differences in race is all."

"No." Jaenelle shook her head. "If you don't have to take the hair off the way Philip does, why did Graff say you might serve better if you were shaved? Philip does it hims—"

Daemon's fist hit the top of the dresser, splitting the wood from end to end. He gripped the edges while he fought for control. The bitch. The *bitch*, to make such a suggestion!

"It means something else, doesn't it?" Jaenelle said in her midnight voice.

"It's nothing," Daemon growled through clenched teeth.

"What does it mean, Daemon?"

"Leave it alone, Jaenelle."

"Prince."

Daemon's fist smashed the dresser again. "If you're so curious, ask your damn mentor!" He turned away, struggling to regain control. After a moment, he turned again, saying, "Jaenelle, I'm sorry."

She was already gone.

4 / Hell

Saetan and Andulvar sat around the blackwood desk, drinking yarbarah while waiting for Jaenelle. Saetan had returned to the private study beneath the Hall in order to have some private, concentrated time with Jaenelle for her lessons after discovering that *all* of the Kaeleer staff seemed to make their way into his public study on some pretense or other just to say hello to her.

"What's the lesson to be today?" Andulvar asked.

"How should I know?" Saetan replied dryly.

"You're the one in charge."

"I'm delighted that someone thinks so."

"Ah." Andulvar refilled his glass and warmed the blood wine. "You're still annoyed about Tersa?"

Saetan studied his silver goblet. "Annoyed? No." He rested his head against the back of his chair. "But Hell's fire, Andulvar, trying to keep up with these leaps she makes . . . the enormity of the raw strength it must take to do some of these things. I want her to have a childhood. I want her to do all the silly things young girls do, whatever they are. I want her to be young and carefree."

"She'll never have a normal childhood, SaDiablo. She knows us, the *cildru dyathe*, Geoffrey and Draca—and Lorn, whatever and wherever he may be. She's seen more of Kaeleer than anyone else in thousands of years. How can you hope for a normal childhood?"

"Those things *are* normal, Andulvar," Saetan said wearily, ignoring Andulvar's grunt of denial. "Do you wish you'd never met her? Don't scowl at me that way; I know the answer." He leaned forward, resting his folded hands on the desk. "The point is, a child plays with the unicorns in Sceval. A child visits friends in Scelt and Philan and Glacia and Dharo and Narkhava and Dea al Mon—and in Hell—and who knows how many other places. I've listened to her stories, the innocent, albeit nerve-racking, adventures of young, strong witches growing up and learning their Craft. No matter where she is when she's doing those things, she's a child."

"Then what's the problem?"

"The only place she never mentions, the only place that doesn't figure into these adventures of hers, is Beldon Mor. She says nothing about her family."

Andulvar thought about this. "SaDiablo, you're jealous enough as it is. Would you really want to know that the people who have more claim to her adore her as much as you? Would a child as sensitive to others' moods as she is be willing to tell you?"

"Jealous?" Saetan hissed. "You think it's jealousy that makes me want to tear them apart?"

Andulvar eyed his friend before saying cautiously, "Yes, I do."

Saetan snapped away from his desk, rose halfway out of his chair, then reconsidered. "Not jealousy," he said, closing his eyes. "Fear. I keep wondering what happens when she leaves here. I keep wondering about some of the things she's asked me to teach her, wondering why a child wants to know about some things, wondering why I sometimes hear desperation in her voice or, worse, a chilling anger." He looked at Andulvar. "We survived brutal childhoods and stayed true to the Blood because that's what we are. Blood. But she . . . Oh, Andulvar, in a few short years she'll make the Offering, and when she does, she'll be beyond reach. If she feels isolated from us . . . Do you really want to see Jaenelle in her full, dark glory ruling from the Twisted Kingdom?"

"No," Andulvar said quietly, a faint tremor in his voice. "No, I don't want to see our waif in the Twisted Kingdom."

"Then—" There was a quiet knock on the door. Saetan and Andulvar exchanged a look. Andulvar's face settled into a frown. Saetan's became neutral. "Come."

Both men tensed when Jaenelle walked into the room, the set of her shoulders all the warning they needed.

"High Lord," she said, giving him a regal nod. "Prince Yaslana."

"A bit formal, aren't you, waif?" Andulvar said with good-humored gruffness.

Saetan pressed his lips together, gratefully dismayed. Trust an Eyrien to push a battle into the open. What made him wary was Jaenelle's lack of response.

She turned to Saetan, her sapphire eyes pinning him to the chair. "High Lord, I want to ask a question, and I don't want to be told I'm too young for the answer."

Saetan could see Andulvar become very still, gathering his strength in case it was needed. "Your question, Lady?"

"What does being shaved mean?"

Andulvar stifled a gasp. Saetan felt as if he were falling down a bottomless chasm. He licked his lips and said quietly, "It means to remove a man's genitals."

For a brief moment the room felt the way a sky full of lightning looks. Saetan didn't dare take his eyes off Jaenelle's, didn't dare miss whatever he might read in them.

It made him ill.

After the flash of anger, he could see her considering, weighing, deciding something. Even though he knew what she was going to say, he dreaded hearing the words.

"Teach me."

"Wait a minute, waif!"

Jaenelle raised her hand. Not even the Demon Prince would challenge that imperious order for silence. "High Lord?"

This was how it must feel to be a dried-out husk. "There are two ways," Saetan said stiffly. "The easiest way requires skill with a knife. It also requires physical contact. The other way is subtler but requires knowledge of male anatomy to be effective. Which would you prefer to learn?"

"Both."

Saetan looked away. "May I have until tomorrow to prepare?"

Jaenelle nodded. "High Lord. Prince Yaslana."

They watched her leave. For a while they said nothing, neither willing to meet the other's eyes.

Finally Andulvar said tensely, "You're going to do it, aren't you?"

Saetan leaned back in his chair and closed his eyes, rubbing his temples to ease a searing headache. "Yes, I am."

"You're mad!" Andulvar roared, leaping from his chair. "She's only twelve, Saetan. How can she understand what it means to a man to be shaved?"

Saetan slowly opened his eyes. "You didn't see her eyes. She already appreciates the ramifications of shaving a man. That's why she wants to learn how to do it."

"And who is to be the first victim?" Andulvar snarled.

Saetan shook his head. "The question, my friend, is *why* is there going to be a victim? And where?"

5 / Terreille

When Surreal realized what sort of party this was going to be, she almost told her escort she wanted to leave, but she'd extracted his promise to take her to a Winsol party under the most distracting—and persuasive—circumstances and didn't want to give him an excuse to bolt. At another time, it would have been amusing to watch his flustered cockiness as he tried to seem nonchalant about the woman he'd brought, a woman whose name would never be mentioned in any family of good repute—at least not while the women were in hearing. But this . . . Surreal itched to call in the stiletto and slip it between a few ribs.

It was the children's party, the girls' party. And the uncles were there in force, almost drooling as they eyed the prospects.

Even worse, Sadi was present, looking bored as usual, but the sleepy look in his eyes and the lazy way he moved around the room made her uneasy. As she sipped sparkling wine and stroked her escort's arm in a way that made his ears burn, she watched Sadi, finally realizing that he, too, was keeping an unobtrusive, continuous watch over someone. Her eyes slid around the room, catching and holding men's glances for an uncomfortable heartbeat before passing by them, until they came back to the group of girls clustered in a corner, whispering and giggling.

Except one.

For a moment, Surreal was caught by those wary sapphire eyes. When she was allowed to look away, she found Sadi studying her.

"I need some air," Surreal said to her young Warlord, slipping away from him to find a terrace, an open window, anything.

The terrace was deserted. Surreal called in a heavy shawl and wrapped it around her shoulders. It was foolish to stand out here, but the lust stench in the crowded rooms was unbearable.

"Surreal."

Surreal tensed. She hadn't heard him come out, hadn't heard even the softest scrape of shoe on stone. She stared at the unlit garden, seeing nothing, waiting.

"Cigarette?" Daemon said, holding his gold case out to her.

Surreal took one and waited for him to create the little tongue of witchfire to light it. They smoked in silence for a while.

"Your escort doesn't quite know what to do with himself this evening," Daemon said with a touch of dry amusement.

"He's an ass." Surreal flicked the cigarette into the garden. "Besides, if I'd known what kind of party this was going to be, I wouldn't have come."

"And what kind is that?"

Surreal let out an unladylike snort. "With Briarwood's esteemed here? What kind of party do you think it's going to be?"

The night was still and cold. Now it was filled with something more still—and colder.

"What do you know about Briarwood, Surreal?" Daemon crooned.

Surreal flinched when he stepped toward her. "Nothing more than everyone who works in a Red Moon house knows," she said defensively.

"And what is that?"

"Why?" she said sharply, wishing for her knife and not daring to call it in. "Have you become an uncle, Sadi?"

Daemon's voice was too soft, too sleepy. "And what is an uncle?"

She'd been looking into his eyes, frozen by what she saw in them, and didn't feel his hand close around her wrist until it was too late.

Anger. Anger was the only defense.

"An uncle is a man who likes to play with little girls," she said with sweet venom.

Daemon's expression didn't change. "What does that have to do with Briarwood?"

"Kartane helped build the place," she snapped. "Does that answer your question?" She jerked her wrist out of his hand, half surprised that he didn't break it instead of letting go. "No respectable Red Moon house would sell a girl that young or allow her to be . . ." She rubbed her wrist. "The Chaillot whores call it the breaking ground. The 'emotionally unstable' girls from good families are eventually sent home, married off. The other ones . . . The lower-class Red Moon houses are filled with girls who got too old to be amusing."

"It explains so much," Daemon whispered, shaking. "It explains so very much."

Surreal put a tentative hand on his arm. "Sadi?"

He pulled her into his arms. She struggled, frightened to be this close to him with no way to gauge what he might do. His arms tightened around her. "Surreal," he whispered in her ear. "Let me hold you. Please. Just for a moment."

Surreal forced herself to relax. Once she did, his hold loosened a little, making it possible to breathe. Resting her head on his shoulder, she tried to think. Why was he so upset about Briarwood? It wasn't the first place Kartane had helped build for that purpose. Did he know someone who was in Briarwood? Or had been in . . .

"No." Surreal shook her head fiercely, wanting to deny what she'd seen but hadn't understood in those wary sapphire eyes. "No." She pushed far enough away from Daemon to wrap her hands in his jacket's lapels. "Not that one." She continued to shake her head. "Not her."

"In and out since she was five," Daemon said in a trembling voice.

"No," Surreal wailed, hiding her face against his chest, grateful for his arms around her. Suddenly she pushed away from him, brushing the tears off her cheeks, her eyes gold-green chips of stone. "You have to get her out of here. You have to keep her away from them."

"I know," Daemon said, straightening his jacket. "I know. Come on, I'll take you back in."

"Don't you realize what they'll do to her? What—" Surreal ran her hands through her hair, never noticing the combs that fell and broke on the stone terrace. "They can't have taken her all the way yet. She doesn't act like she's been broken yet." She grabbed Daemon's arms and tried to shake him. It was like trying to shake the building. "You've got to get her away from here. She's special, Sadi. She's—"

"Shh," Daemon said, brushing his fingers over her lips. His hands ran through her hair, coaxing it back into some semblance of the style she was wearing. "Calm yourself, Surreal."

"How—"

"Calm yourself."

She hadn't known him this long without knowing an order when she heard it. Calm. Yes. Outsiders weren't supposed to know about the extra little party that was going to take place.

Daemon led her back to the main hall, his hand lightly resting on her shoulder. "Tell your escort you have a headache. Too much heat, too much sparkling wine. Whatever."

"That won't be hard." From the doorway, Surreal scanned the crowd in the ballroom, searching for the young Warlord. Instead she saw a Hayllian Warlord standing with a group of men, quietly discussing something while they watched some of the girls having their first dance with selected partners. "Who's that?" she asked, tilting her chin in the Hayllian's direction. Daemon's hand tightened on her shoulder.

"That, my dear Surreal, is Kartane SaDiablo."

Her knife was in her hand before he'd finished speaking. Kartane! Finally to see Kartane.

Surreal tried to step forward, intending to slip through the crowd until she was close enough to be sure of the kill, but she couldn't shake off Daemon's vice grip.

"No, Surreal," Daemon said quietly.

"He owes me for Titian," she hissed through clenched teeth.

"Not here. Not in Beldon Mor."

"He owes me, Sadi."

The pain in her shoulder got worse.

"If you kill him now, Dorothea will start asking questions. I don't want anyone asking any more questions. Do you understand?"

Surreal vanished the knife. It didn't please her, but she understood. However, that didn't mean she couldn't study her quarry.

"Go now, Surreal."

"I think I'll—"

"Go." Once again, it was an order.

Surreal left, aware that Daemon watched her. She didn't see her Warlord escort. No matter. He was probably too drunk by now to know what he fell into bed with.

Chaillot had too many secrets, Daemon thought as he watched the party. And this particular secret was a twisted, vicious one.

Why hadn't Saetan done something about Briarwood? Why had he left Jaenelle in such danger?

Daemon froze. Jaenelle's words, the first time he'd mentioned the Priest, spun through his mind. *He mustn't come here. He mustn't find out about . . .*

Saetan didn't know about Briarwood.

Which also explained why Cassandra had never come to Beldon Mor. Jaenelle had done something to keep them out, to keep Saetan from learning about Briarwood.

Why? *Why?* Did she think Saetan would shun her for *that*? Or did she fear his vengeance on her family if he found out they had knowingly put a child in such a place?

No. Alexandra couldn't know about Briarwood. Nor Philip or Leland. Robert?

Rose. Lollipop. *Uncle* Bobby.

Yes, Robert Benedict knew about Briarwood and, knowing, put his daughter into that place.

He had to talk to Alexandra. If she knew the truth about Jaenelle, and Briarwood, she would help protect her granddaughter. She was struggling to keep her people out of Hayll's snare. She would understand and value a Queen who could stand against Dorothea.

Daemon saw Alexandra near a curtained archway, talking with several women. He slipped past them, doubled back and was just about to step out from behind the curtain when he heard Alexandra say, "Witch is only a symbol of the Blood, an ideal we celebrate, a myth."

"But Witch did rule the Realms once, a long time ago," said another voice, one Daemon didn't recognize. "I remember hearing stories about Cassandra, who was a Black-Jeweled Queen. They called her Witch."

"I remember hearing stories, too," Alexandra said. "But that's all they are: stories that have been dimmed by time and softened by romantic notions about a woman who probably didn't live at all. But if she did, do you really believe that, with that much power, she was a generous and benevolent Queen? Not likely. She would have been more of a monster than Dorothea SaDiablo."

"Brrr," said another woman as she indulged in a theatrical shudder.

"But what if Witch really did appear?" the first woman persisted.

Alexandra's next words cut him. Cut him again and again and again. "Then I would hope, for all our sakes, that someone would have the courage to strangle it in the cradle."

Daemon went back to the terrace, grateful for the cold air he gulped to keep down the scream of rage and despair. Why had he tried to fool himself into thinking she would help?

Because there was no one else. He was Ringed and could be incapacitated. It would take time, but not that long. Even if he did slip the Ring he would be declared rogue, and there would be no place fit for a young girl to live where they'd be safe. The only way was to get Jaenelle to Saetan and then convince her not to come back.

First he had to get her away from here.

His chance came when Jaenelle left the ballroom and headed down the hall toward a bathroom. Wrapping himself in a sight shield, he followed close behind her, waiting impatiently outside the door while she took care of her private needs. When she opened the door to leave, he pushed her back inside, locked the door, and dropped the shield.

Jaenelle lifted one eyebrow, striving for amusement.

Daemon knelt in front of her, holding her hands. "Listen to me, Jaenelle. You're in danger here, great danger."

"I've always been in danger here, Daemon," Jaenelle said quietly in her Witch voice.

"More so now. You don't understand what's going to happen here."

"Don't I?" Her voice was whispery thunder.

"Jaenelle . . ." Daemon closed his eyes and leaned forward until his head rested against her small, too thin, fragile chest. He felt her heart beating. It made him desperate. He would do anything now to keep that heart beating. "Jaenelle, please. The Priest . . . The Priest would let you stay with him, wouldn't he? I mean, you wouldn't have to live in the Dark Realm. He'd find another place, like he found for Tersa, wouldn't he? Jaenelle . . . sweetheart . . . you can't stay here anymore."

"I have to, Daemon," Jaenelle said gently. Her fingers stroked his head, tangling in his hair.

"Why?" Daemon cried. He raised his head, his eyes pleading. "I know you care for your family—"

"Family?" Jaenelle let out a small, bitter laugh. "My family lives in Hell, Prince."

"Then why won't you go? If you don't think the Priest will take you, at least go to Cassandra. A Sanctuary offers some protection."

"No."

"Why?"

Jaenelle backed away from him, troubled. "Saetan asked me to live with him, and I promised him I would, but I can't yet."

Daemon leaned back on his heels. This was brutal, and it was blackmail, but she wasn't leaving him any choice. "I know about Briarwood."

Jaenelle shuddered. "Then you know why I can't go yet."

Daemon grabbed her with bruising force and shook her. "No, I don't know why. If I tell him—"

Jaenelle looked at him, her eyes huge and horrified. "Please don't tell him, Daemon," she whispered. "Please."

"Why?" he snapped. "He won't turn on you because of what's been done. Do you really think he'll stop caring for you if he finds out?"

"He might."

Daemon leaned back, stunned. Since it made no difference to him, except that it made him want to protect her more, he'd assumed Saetan would feel the same. *Would* it make a difference?

"Daemon," Jaenelle pleaded, "if he finds out I've been . . . sick . . . if he thinks I'm not good enough to teach the Craft to . . ."

"What do you mean, 'sick'?" But he knew. A hospital for "emotionally disturbed" children. A child who told stories about unicorns and dragons, who visited friends no one else saw because, wherever they existed, it wasn't in Terreille. A child whose sense of reality had been twisted in Briarwood for so many years she didn't know what to believe or whom she could trust.

Daemon held her close, stroking her hair. He felt her tears on his neck and his heart bled. She was only twelve. For all her Craft, for all her magic, for all her strength, she was still only twelve. She believed all the lies they'd told her. Even though she struggled against them, even though she tried to doubt the words they'd pounded into her for so many years, she believed their lies. And because she believed, she was more afraid of losing her mentor and friend than she was of losing her life.

He kissed her cheek. "If I promise not to tell, will you promise to go—and not come back?"

"I can't," Jaenelle whispered.

"Why?" Daemon said angrily. He was losing patience. They were losing precious time.

Jaenelle leaned back and looked at him with her ancient, haunted eyes. "Wilhelmina," she said in a flat voice. "Wilhelmina's strong, Daemon, stronger than she knows, strong enough to wear the Sapphire if she isn't broken. I have to help her until she makes the Offering. Then she'll be stronger than most of the males here, and they won't be able to break her. Then I'll go live with the Priest."

Daemon looked away. It would be at least four years before Wilhelmina could make the Offering. Jaenelle, if she stayed in Beldon Mor, would be long dead by then.

A sharp rap on the door startled them. A woman called out, "You all right in there, missy? Hurry up, now. The girls are selecting partners for the dance."

Daemon slowly got to his feet. He felt old, beaten. But if he could keep her safe until tomorrow, Saetan might have more persuasive weapons at his disposal. Wrapping the sight shield around himself, he opened the door and slipped out behind Jaenelle. The woman, impatiently waiting outside, took a firm hold of Jaenelle's arm and steered her back into the ballroom.

Daemon slipped along the edge of the room silently, invisibly. It was such a small thing to stop a heart, to reach in and nick an artery. Was there any man here who wasn't expendable, including himself? No, not when the ice whispered in his veins, not when the double-edged sword was unsheathed. He slipped up behind his cousin and heard Kartane say, "That one? She's a whey-faced little bitch. The sister's prettier."

Daemon smiled. Still wrapped in the sight shield, his right hand reached out toward Kartane's shoulder. For a moment, before his hand tightened in a malevolent grip, he felt Kartane lean against him, enjoying the sensuous, shivery caress of the long nails. Daemon enjoyed feeling the sensuous shiver change to shivery fear as his nails pierced Kartane's jacket and shirt.

"Cousin," Daemon whispered in his ear. "Come out to the terrace with me, cousin."

"Get away from me," Kartane growled out of the corner of his mouth as he tried to shrug off Daemon's hand. "I've business here."

Daemon continued to smile. Foolish of the boy to try to bluff when he could smell the fear. "You've business with me first." He pivoted slowly, pulling Kartane with him.

"Bastard," Kartane said softly, walking toward the terrace to keep from being dragged there.

"By birth and by temperament," Daemon agreed with amiable coldness.

When they were out on the terrace, Daemon dropped the sight shield. Compared to the fiery cold he felt inside himself, the air seemed balmy. While he waited for Kartane to stop looking at the garden and face him, he absently brushed the branches of a small potted bush. He smiled as ice instantly coated them. He kept stroking the bush until the whole thing was coated. Then, with a shrug, he took his gold case from his pocket, lit a cigarette, and waited. He was between Kartane and the door. His cousin wasn't going to leave before he was ready to let him.

Shivering violently, Kartane turned.

"The whey-faced little bitch," Daemon crooned while the cigarette smoke ringed his head.

"What about her?" Kartane asked nervously.

"Stay away from her."

"Why?" Kartane said sneeringly. "Do you want her?"

"Yes."

Daemon watched Kartane stagger back and grip the terrace railing for support. Finally, the truth. He wanted her. Already, in ways Kartane and his kind would never understand, he was her lover.

"There are prettier ones if you want a taste," Kartane coaxed.

"Flesh is irrelevant," Daemon replied. "My hunger goes deeper." He pitched the cigarette, watching it sail past Kartane's cheek before falling into the garden. "But, cousin, if you should ever mention my . . . lapse . . . or my choice . . ."

The unspoken threat hung in the air.

"You'd kill me?" Kartane laughed in disbelief. "Kill *me*? Dorothea's son?"

Daemon smiled. "Killing your body is the least of what I'd do to you. Remember Cornelia? When the time came, she was actually grateful for

what I did to the flesh." It took only a moment for Daemon to slip beneath Kartane's inner barriers and, with the delicacy of a snowflake, drop
into his mind the memory of what Cornelia's room had looked like just
before Daemon left. He waited patiently for Kartane to finish heaving.
"Now—"

A shriek of rage and the sound of breaking glass in one of the rooms
above the ballroom cut him off.

Daemon swayed. Why was the ground—not the ground—why was *he*
spinning this way, spiraling toward something that made him shiver?

Spiraling.

The last time he'd felt something like that was when . . .

Daemon ran through the ballroom, through the hallway, and raced up
the stairs. He hesitated when he saw Alexandra, Philip, Leland, and Robert
standing with a group of people outside one of the doors, but another
crash and a scream pulled him forward. He hit the door running and exploded into the room.

The only light in the room came from the open door. The lamps were
shattered. A small brass bed, conspicuous because it didn't belong in a sitting room, was twisted almost beyond recognition. Broken vases crunched
under him. A group of men, pressed together in the center of the room,
stared, deathly pale, at something in the corner.

Daemon turned toward that corner of the room.

Wilhelmina huddled in the corner, shaking, whimpering. Her dress,
partially undone, had slipped down, revealing one round young shoulder.

Jaenelle stood in front of her sister, holding the neck of a broken wine
bottle with an ease that spoke of long familiarity with a knife. Her blazing sapphire eyes were fixed on the group of men.

Daemon moved toward her slowly, careful not to break her line of vision. He stopped an arm's length from her. If she lunged, she could gut
him. It didn't occur to him to be frightened of her. That shadowy voice
he could finally put a name to whispered up from the depths of his own
being: Protocol. Protocol. Protocol.

Jaenelle spoke.

Daemon glanced at the men, at Philip and Alexandra and the others
who were creeping in through the doorway. They looked shocked by the
wreckage. He wondered how many of them would have been shocked by
what was supposed to have happened here. Philip and Alexandra stared at

Jaenelle, and he knew they were hearing unintelligible nonsense. Even he didn't know the Old Tongue well enough to translate all of her beautiful, deadly words.

"Dr. Carvay?" Philip said, his eyes still on Jaenelle.

Dr. Carvay, the head of Briarwood, stepped away from the group of men, glanced at Jaenelle, and shook his head. "I'm afraid the child has become unstrung by all the excitement," he said solicitously.

Lady. Daemon sent his thoughts along a Black thread. Protocol. *Lady, they can't understand you.*

Jaenelle stopped speaking. As Philip and Alexandra conferred with Dr. Carvay, she struggled to find the common language.

Dr. Carvay walked toward Jaenelle. "Jaenelle," he said in a too smooth voice that made Daemon turn squarely to face him, "come with Dr. Carvay now, dear. You're upset. You need some of your medicine."

"Stay aware from her," Daemon growled. An instant later he felt a tightening pain between his legs. He stared at Alexandra, who looked frightened but determined. She was using the Ring against him. Now, when Jaenelle needed him, she was threatening to bring him to his knees. He clenched his teeth against the pain and waited.

"Come, Jaenelle," Dr. Carvay said again.

"You can't have my sister," Jaenelle finally said, her voice husky with rage. "Not ever."

Every man in the room shuddered at the sound of her voice.

"We don't want your sister. We want to make you bet—"

"I'll send you into the bowels of Hell," Jaenelle said, her voice rising with her rage. "I'll feed you to the Harpies you helped create. I'll shave you if you ever touch my sister. I'll shave you all!"

"JAENELLE!" Alexandra stepped forward, eyes flashing. "You disgrace your family with this behavior. Put that down." She pointed at the broken bottle.

Daemon watched, heartsick, as Jaenelle, rage and confusion warring in her eyes, lowered her arm and dropped the bottle.

Alexandra grabbed Jaenelle by the shoulder to lead her from the room. When Daemon moved to follow, Alexandra swung around and pointed a finger at him. "You," she said venomously, "stay with Prince Alexander and see to Leland and Wilhelmina."

Bitch, Daemon thought. She was doing this out of jealousy. He started to argue with her to take both girls home now, but another surge of pain through the Ring made him suck in his breath. Arguing now would only make things worse.

Daemon watched Jaenelle leave the room, escorted by Alexandra, Dr. Carvay, and Robert Benedict. She looked so frail, so vulnerable. He would talk to her again once Wilhelmina was home, take her by force to Cassandra's Altar if that's what he had to do. Saetan had to have enough influence over her to keep her away from Chaillot.

Saetan. Once he got her away from Beldon Mor, at least he would have some help protecting her.

By the time the pain from the Ring subsided enough for Daemon to move, Philip had already gotten Wilhelmina to her feet and was tugging ineffectually at her dress. With a low snarl, Daemon turned her around, settled the dress back over her shoulders, and deftly buttoned up the back. Her eyes had a glazed, drugged look, and she was shaking, more from fear than cold.

"Wilhelmina," Philip said, taking hold of her arm.

Wilhelmina screamed, flailing her arms at him as she stumbled back into the corner.

Pushing Philip aside, Daemon stood in front of Wilhelmina and snapped his fingers twice in quick succession. Once her eyes focused on his hand, he raised it slowly until it was level with his face. Then he lowered his hand and held it out to her. "Come, Lady Benedict," he said in a respectful, formal voice. "Prince Alexander and I will escort you home." He held his hand steady, giving her time to decide whether or not to accept it. When she finally did, she threw herself against him, locking her other arm around his waist.

In the end, despite Philip's glaring at him, he untangled himself from her grasp and carried her downstairs to the waiting carriage and home, where, he fervently hoped, there would be someone who would take care of her.

CHAPTER FOURTEEN

1 / Terreille

As she paced around her bedroom, Alexandra nervously twisted the secondary controlling ring she wore on her right hand. She had done what she had to do. The girl was obviously out of control. Dr. Carvay said Jaenelle had probably been under undue strain for a while, but this last episode—threatening members of Chaillot's council with a broken bottle and speaking gibberish!

Alexandra knew where to place the blame. She hadn't wanted to believe Robert's hints, hadn't wanted to believe Sadi's interest in the girls was less than innocent, hadn't wanted to believe he might actually have . . . with Jaenelle! With all the perverse things Sadi was capable of doing, was it any wonder that Jaenelle had mistaken the intent of the men who had taken Wilhelmina upstairs so she could rest a bit after overindulging in her first taste of sparkling wine? But to threaten the council, to put them all at risk while Lord Kartane was there and would no doubt send this tale winging back to Hayll! Of course Hayll's High Priestess would be only too happy to send additional assistance, until Chaillot became a mere puppet dancing while Dorothea held the strings.

Sadi. She would have to send him back to—

Alexandra's bedroom door clicked as the lock slipped back into place. She whirled, her right hand raised, but before she could use the controlling ring she lay sprawled on the floor, one side of her face ablaze from the blow of a phantom hand.

Pushing herself into a sitting position, Alexandra stared at Daemon, leaning so casually against the door.

"My dear," he said in a gentle voice so full of murderous rage it terrified her worse than the most violent shout, "if you ever use the Ring on me again, I'll decorate the walls with your brains."

"If I use the Ring—"

Daemon laughed. It was an eerie sound—hollow, malevolent, cold. "I can survive a great deal of pain. Can you?" He smiled a brutal smile. "Shall we put it to the test? Your strength against mine? Your ability to withstand what I'll do to your body—not to mention your mind—while you try to hold me off with that pathetic piece of metal?" He walked toward her. "The trust women have in the Ring is so misplaced. Haven't you learned that much from the stories you've heard about me?"

"What do you want?" Alexandra tried to scoot backward, but Daemon stepped on her dressing gown, pinning her to the floor.

"What I've wanted since I came here. What I've always wanted. And you're going to get her back for me. Tonight."

"I don't know what—"

"You put her back in that . . . place, didn't you, Alexandra? You put her back in that nightmare."

"She's ill!" Alexandra protested. "She's—"

"She isn't ill," Daemon snarled. "She was never ill. And you know it. Now you're going to get her out of there." He smiled. "If you don't get her back, I will. But if I have to do it, I'll flood the streets of Beldon Mor with blood before I'm through, and you, my dear, will be one of the corpses washed into the sewer. Get her out of Briarwood, Alexandra. After that, you won't have to trouble yourself with her. I'll take care of her."

"Take care of her?" Alexandra spat. "You mean twist her, use her for your own perverse needs. Is that why you walk with her in the farthest parts of the garden? So you can fondle . . ." Alexandra choked, but the words kept tumbling out. "No wonder you can't act like a man around a real woman. You need to force children—"

"Before you begin accusing me, look to your own house, Lady." Daemon pulled her to her feet, one hand holding her wrists behind her back while the other tangled in her hair, pulling her head up.

"Get her out, Alexandra," he said too softly. "Get her out before the sun rises."

"I can't!" Alexandra cried. "Dr. Carvay is the head of Briarwood. He'll have to sign the release papers. So will Robert."

"You put her in there."

"With Robert! Besides, she was so distraught, she was heavily sedated and shouldn't be moved."

"How long?" Daemon snapped, letting her fall to the floor.

"What?" She felt weak and helpless with him towering over her.

"How long before you can bring her back here?"

Time. She needed a little time. "Tomorrow afternoon."

When he was silent for so long, she dared to look up, but quickly looked away. She flinched when he squatted beside her.

"Listen to me, Alexandra, and listen well. If Jaenelle isn't back here, unharmed, by tomorrow afternoon, you, my dear, will live long enough to regret betraying me."

Alexandra sank full length on the floor, covering her head with her hands. She couldn't stop seeing that look in his eyes, and she would go mad if she couldn't stop seeing that look in his eyes. Even when she heard him cross the room, heard the door open and quietly click shut, she was still too frightened to move.

It was so dark.

Alexandra woke, slowly opening her eyes. She was lying on her back in a lumpy, chilly, damp bed.

Something tickled her forehead.

As Alexandra raised her arm to brush the hair from her face, her hand hit something solid a few inches above her head.

Dirt trickled down, hitting her neck and shoulders.

Her other hand pressed against the bed—and found dirt.

She flung her arms out with bruising force—and found dirt.

Her toes, when she stretched her legs a little, found dirt.

No, she thought, fighting the panic, this was a dream. A bad dream. She couldn't be . . . buried. Couldn't be.

Shutting her eyes to keep the dirt out, she blindly explored.

It was a neatly cut rectangle. A well-made grave. If it was a grave, the earth above would be loose. Whoever did this would have had to dig down to put her there.

Half sobbing, half gasping, Alexandra clawed at the dirt above her face. When her hand hit tree roots, she stopped, stunned.

That wasn't right. Someone would have had to dig around the roots.

Scooting down a little, she began clawing at the dirt again. It was packed solid, frozen.

Think. *Think.* A witch could pass through solid objects. It was dangerous, yes, but she could do it if she didn't panic.

Alexandra forced herself to breathe slowly and steadily as she concentrated. Raising one hand, she slowly passed it through the dirt, moving upward, upward, slowly, slowly. She raised her other hand.

Her hands were moving through the dirt, moving upward to freedom. Alexandra let out a small laugh of relief.

Then her hands hit something more solid than the earth.

Her fingers poked, prodded. She felt nothing, and yet *something* was there.

Concentrating her energy on making the pass, she pushed against that nothingness while her Opal Jewel glowed with her effort, drawing on her reserves, focusing her strength. She sent the force of the Jewel into her hands and pushed.

A dark, crackling, overwhelming energy snaked down her fingers into her arms. Alexandra shot backward, hitting her head against a dirt wall.

Her strength was gone. The Jewel hung around her neck, dark and empty. If she'd pushed against that energy another moment longer, her Jewel would have broken, and her mind would probably have shattered with it.

"No," Alexandra moaned. She beat her hands against the floor of her dirt coffin. "No." She felt dizzy. The air. There was no more air. Gathering her legs beneath her as best she could, Alexandra sprang upward, trying to break free of the earth.

"NO!"

Alexandra's chin hit the end of her bed.

She lay on her stomach, gasping, shivering.

A dream. It was, after all, a dream.

A soft, icy laugh filled her mind. *Not a dream, my dear.* Daemon's voice rolled through her mind, sentient thunder. *A taste. I'm a *very* good, *very* discreet gravedigger. I've had centuries of practice. Just remember, Alexandra. If Jaenelle isn't back, unharmed, by tomorrow afternoon, you will feed the worms.*

He was gone.

Alexandra rolled onto her back. It was a trick, a dream. He *couldn't* have.

She raised a shaking hand, closing her eyes against the weak glow of the candle-light.

A dream. An evil dream.

Alexandra pushed herself up on one elbow—and stared at her hands.

Her nails were broken, her hands laced with scratches. Her nightgown was torn and dirt-smeared. A sudden, wet warmth flooded down her legs. She stared at the spreading dampness for a full minute before she understood she had wet herself.

It was almost an hour before she dragged herself off the bed, washed herself, and dressed in a clean nightgown. Then she huddled in a chair with a quilt wrapped around her, staring out the window, desperately waiting for the dawn.

2 / Terreille

Kartane inserted a key into a small, inset door hidden by a row of shrubs. The parents who came to Briarwood during visiting hours didn't know about that entrance—unless a parent was also a select member. They didn't know about these softly lit corridors, thickly carpeted to muffle sounds. They didn't know about the gaming room or the sitting room or the little soundproofed cubicles that were just big enough to hold a chair, a bed, and other amusing necessities. They didn't know about the tears and screams and pain. They didn't know about the special "medicines."

They didn't know about many things.

Kartane strolled through the corridors to the "playpen," hungry for some amusement. He was furious with Sadi and that little bitch for spoiling the game tonight. It was hard enough to bring girls in. Oh, they could buy lower-class Blood—the right kind of drink during the right kind of game and a pretty girl became a marker on the card table. But it was the aristos, the girls gently brought up with delicate sensibilities that were the most fun—and the hardest to procure. It usually took enticing the father in order to get the child . . . except during Winsol, when a little *safframate* could be slipped into the sparkling wine. Then the girl could be broken and cleaned up before being brought back to her naive parents. The day after, when the hysteria started, Dr. Carvay would just happen to call and explain to the distraught parents about this prepubescent hysteria that was claiming a number of aristo girls of the Blood. The girl would be tenderly led away for a stay at Briarwood, and in a month or two—or a year or two—she would be returned to the bosom of her family, and eventually married off to spend the rest of her life with that slightly glazed look in her eyes, never understanding her husband's disappointment in her, never remembering what a fine little playmate she'd once been.

Of course, a few genuinely disturbed girls were also admitted. That little tart Rose had been one. And Sadi's whey-faced bitch.

Kartane shivered as he stepped into the "playpen," that guarded room where the girls selected for that evening waited in their lacy nighties for the uncles. The girls didn't seem to notice the cold, but the attendant had his shoulders hunched and kept rubbing his hands to warm them. It was like this sometimes. Not always, but sometimes.

Kartane's perusal of the girls stopped when he met a glazed, unblinking sapphire stare.

The attendant followed Kartane's gaze, shivered, and looked away. "They topped that one up after bringing her in, but something went queer. She oughtta be panting and rubbing against anything that'll come near her, but she just got real quiet." He shrugged.

She was nothing to look at, Kartane thought. What was it about her that intrigued Sadi? What was so special about this one that he would risk Dorothea's vengeance?

Kartane lifted his chin in Jaenelle's direction. "Have her in my room in ten minutes."

The attendant flinched but nodded his head.

While he waited, Kartane fortified himself with brandy. He was curious, that was all. If Daemon had taught the girl bedplay, she must know a few amusing tricks. Not that he would actually play with her after Sadi had warned him off. People could disappear so mysteriously after being around the Sadist. And Cornelia's room . . .

The brandy churned in Kartane's stomach. No, he was just curious. He wanted a few minutes alone with her to see if he could understand Daemon's interest, and he wouldn't do anything that would provoke the Sadist's temper.

The finger locks on the cubicles were set high in the wall both in the corridor and in the room itself. That kept anxious little girls from escaping at inconvenient moments. Kartane let himself into the room. Once inside, however, he couldn't stop shivering.

She was sitting on the bed, staring at the wall like a stiff doll someone had tried to arrange in a realistic pose. Kartane sat on the chair. After studying her for several minutes, he said sharply, "Look at me."

Jaenelle's head turned slowly until her eyes locked onto his face.

Kartane licked his lips. "I understand Sadi is your friend."

No answer.

"Did he show you how to be a good girl?"

No answer.

Kartane frowned. Had they given her something besides *safframate*? He'd had the shyest, most distraught girls crawling all over him, whimpering and begging, doing anything he wanted when they were dosed with that aphrodisiac. She shouldn't be able to sit on the bed like that. She shouldn't be able to sit still.

Kartane's frown smoothed into a smile. He had decided not to touch her body, but that didn't mean he couldn't touch her at all. He wore a Red Jewel. She wore nothing.

He sent a probing link to her mind, intending to at least force open the first barrier and find out what it was Sadi found so intriguing. The first barrier opened almost before he touched it, and he found . . .

Nothing.

Nothing but a black mist filled with lightning. Kartane had the sensation of standing on the edge of a deep chasm, not sure if stepping forward or back would plunge him into the abyss. He hung there, uncertain, while the mist coiled around him, slithering along the psychic link toward his mind.

The mist wasn't empty.

Far, far below him, he sensed something dark, something terrifying and savage slowly turning toward him, drawn by his presence. He was caught in a beast's lair, blind and uncertain whether the attack would come from in front of him or behind. Whatever it was, it was slowly spiraling up out of the mist. If he actually saw it, he'd . . .

Kartane broke the link. His hands were in front of him, trying to hold an invisible something at bay. His shirt was soaked with sweat. Drawing in ragged breaths, he forced himself to lower his hands.

Jaenelle smiled.

Kartane leaped from the chair and pressed his back against the wall, too frightened to remember how to unlock the door.

"You're one of us," Jaenelle said in a hollow, pleased voice. "That's why you hate us so. You're one of us."

"I'm not!" He couldn't unlock the door without turning around, and he didn't dare turn around.

"You do to us what was done to you. She lets you be her tool. Even now, though you hate her as much as you fear her, you serve Dorothea."

"NO!"

"Her blood is the only blood that can pay that debt. But your debt is greater. You owe so many. In the end, you'll pay them all."

"What are you?" Kartane screamed.

Jaenelle stared at him for a long moment. "What I am," she said quietly in a voice that sang of the Darkness.

The locked door slid open.

Kartane bolted into the corridor.

The door slid shut.

Kartane leaned against the wall, shaking. Evil little bitch. Sadi's little whore. Whatever she was, if she joined with the Sadist . . .

Kartane straightened his clothes and smiled. *He* wouldn't soil himself with teaching that little bitch her rightful place. But Greer. Greer had found his visit to Briarwood most gratifying, and he had asked Kartane if he'd noticed any unusual girls.

This one should be unusual enough for his taste.

3 / Terreille

Surreal knelt beside a tree at the back edge of Briarwood's snow-covered lawn. She had watched Kartane disappear behind some bushes and not come out, so she felt sure there must be a private entrance there.

Surreal frowned. The wide expanse of lawn offered no cover, and if someone came around the building instead of through that door, she might be discovered too soon. To the right of the lawn were the remains of a very large vegetable garden, but that, too, offered no cover. She could use a sight shield, but she wasn't that adept at creating one and holding it while moving. Surreal shivered, pulling her coat tighter around her as the night wind gusted for a moment.

Something gently brushed her shoulder.

Twisting around, she probed the shrub garden behind her. Finding nothing, she glanced at the tree before focusing her attention once more on the hidden door.

The tree had a perfect branch. With all these girls locked away here, the uncles could at least put up a swing.

The wind died. In the still night air, Surreal heard the click of a door being closed, and tensed. There was enough moonlight to see Kartane leaning against the side of the building for a moment before hurrying away.

More than anything, she wanted to pursue him, find him in some shadowy corner, and watch the blood pump from his throat. Sadi was being unreasonable. He . . .

The air crackled. The lawn and building looked gauzy. Surreal felt a queer kind of spinning.

Something brushed her shoulder.

Surreal glanced up, stared, then clamped her hand over her mouth.

The girl swinging from the noose tied to the tree's perfect branch stared back from empty sockets. She and the rope were transparent, ghostly, yet Surreal didn't doubt she was there, didn't doubt the dark bloodstains that ran down the girl's cheeks, didn't doubt the dark stains on the dress.

"Hello, Surreal," said a whispery midnight voice. "That's Marjane. She told an uncle once she couldn't stand the sight of him, so they smeared honey on her eyes and hung her there. She wasn't supposed to die, but she struggled so much when the crows came and pecked out her eyes, the knot slipped and the noose killed her."

"Can't . . . can't you get her down?" Surreal whispered, still not willing to turn around and face whatever was behind her.

"Oh, her body's been gone years and years. Marjane's just a ghost now. Even so, when I'm here, she still has some strength. Girls are safe around this tree. Uncles don't like being kicked."

Surreal turned and stifled a scream.

"Hush," Jaenelle said with a savagely sweet smile. She was as transparent as Marjane, and the lacy nighty she wore didn't move when the wind gusted. Only the sapphire eyes seemed alive.

Surreal looked away. She felt drawn by those eyes, and she knew instinctively that anything drawn into those eyes now would never come back.

"The debt's not yours to pay, Surreal," Jaenelle said in her midnight whisper. "He doesn't owe his blood to you."

"But the ones he owes can't call in the debt!" Surreal hissed, keeping her voice low.

Jaenelle laughed. It was like hearing the winter wind laugh. "You think not? There is dead and there is dead, Surreal."

"He owes me for Titian," Surreal insisted.

"He owes Titian for Titian. When the time comes, he'll pay the debt to her."

"He killed her."

"No, he broke her, seeded her. A man named Greer, Dorothea's hound, killed her."

Surreal brushed at the tears spilling down her cheeks. "You're dead, aren't you?" she said wearily.

"No. My body's still there." Jaenelle pointed toward Briarwood and frowned. "They gave me some of their special 'medicine,' the one that's supposed to make girls behave, but something went wrong. I'm still connected to my body. I can't break the link and leave it, but this misty place is very nice. Do you see the mist, Surreal?"

Surreal shook her head.

"When I'm in the mist, I can see them all." Jaenelle smiled and held out a transparent hand. "Come, Surreal. Let me show you Briarwood."

Surreal stood up, brushing the snow from her knees. Jaenelle laughed softly. It was the most haunting, terrifying sound Surreal had ever heard.

"Briarwood is the pretty poison," Jaenelle said softly. "There is no cure for Briarwood. Beware the golden spider who spins a tangled web." Her hand touched Surreal's arm, drawing her toward the garden. "Rose said I should build a trap, something that will snap shut if my blood is spilled. So I did. If they spring the trap . . . dying is what they'll wish for, but their wish will be long in coming."

"You'll still be dead," Surreal said hoarsely. As she saw the shadows in the garden beginning to take shape, she tried to stop, tried to turn and run, but her legs wouldn't obey her.

Jaenelle shrugged. "I've walked among the *cildru dyathe*. Hell doesn't frighten me."

"She's too old to be one of us," said a voice Surreal knew had come, at one time, from a poorer section of Beldon Mor.

Surreal turned. A few minutes ago, seeing a girl walking toward her in a bloody dress with her throat slit would have been a shock. Now it was something her numbed mind cataloged as simply part of Briarwood.

"This is Rose," Jaenelle said to Surreal. "She's demon-dead."

"It's not so bad," Rose said, shrugging. "Except I can only cause trouble now after the sun goes down." She laughed. It was a ghastly sound. "And when I tickle a lollipop, it makes them feel *so* queer."

Jaenelle plucked at Surreal's sleeve. Her smile was sweetly vicious. "Come. Let me introduce you to some of my friends."

Surreal followed Jaenelle to the garden, grateful that Rose had disappeared.

Jaenelle's giggle held the echo of madness. "This is the carrot patch. This is where they bury the redheads."

Two redheaded girls sat side by side in blood-soaked dresses.

"They don't have any hands," Surreal said quietly. She felt feverish and slightly dizzy.

"Myrol wasn't behaving for an uncle and he hurt her. Rebecca hit him to make him stop hurting Myrol, and when he hit Rebecca, Myrol started hitting him, too." Jaenelle was silent for a moment. "No one even tried to stop the bleeding. They'd been bought from a poor family, you see. Their parents never expected them back, so it didn't make any difference." Jaenelle gestured toward the whole garden filled with misty shapes. "None of them were asked about. They 'ran away' or 'disappeared.' "

They walked to the end of the garden.

Surreal frowned. "Why are some of them easy to see and others so misty?"

"It depends on how long they've been here, how strong they were when they died. Rose was the only one strong enough to become *cildru dyathe* who wanted to stay. The other *cildru dyathe* have gone to the Dark Realm. Char will look after them. These girls have always been ghosts, too strong to slip into the ever-night but not strong enough to move away from where their bodies lay." Jaenelle nodded to the girl at the end of the garden. To Surreal's eyes, she looked more vivid, more "real" than Jaenelle. "This is Dannie." Jaenelle's voice quivered with pain. "They served her leg for dinner one night."

Surreal ran for the nearby bushes and retched. When she turned around, the garden was empty. A low wind swept over the snow, wiping away her footprints. When it was done, there was only the building, the empty lawn, and the garden with its secrets.

4 / Terreille

Daemon Sadi watched the sun rise.

All through the long, long night, he'd listened along the Black threads of a psychic web he'd created around Beldon Mor for any disturbance, any indication that Jaenelle might be in danger. Without using the Black Jewels to aid him, it was a strain to keep the web functioning, but like a determined spider, he stayed in the center, aware of the most minute vibration along every strand.

It had been a reluctant gamble to leave her in Briarwood. He didn't trust Alexandra, but if Jaenelle had been drugged, especially with something like *safframate,* it was safer for her to come out of it in the same surroundings. He'd seen too many young witches flee into the Twisted Kingdom when their minds couldn't understand the change in their surroundings, couldn't comprehend that they were safe. The thought of Jaenelle lost in madness was unbearable, so he could only hope the drugged sleep would make her uninteresting prey. If it didn't . . .

There was no reason for him to stay among the living without Jaenelle, but if he did go to the Dark Realm, he promised himself he wouldn't be the only new subject kneeling before the High Lord.

Daemon stripped off his clothes, showered, dressed in riding clothes, and quietly slipped down to the kitchen. He put a kettle on for coffee and made breakfast. When Jaenelle returned, they would have to leave quickly, not giving Philip or Alexandra any additional time to present obstacles. There would be no time for good-byes. He'd seldom had time for good-byes. Besides, there hadn't been that many people in his life who'd regretted seeing him go. But there was one here who deserved to know the Lady would be gone forever.

By the time he'd washed his breakfast dishes and was drinking his second cup of coffee, Cook stumbled into the kitchen, sinking heavily into one of the kitchen chairs. She looked at him sadly as Daemon set a cup of coffee in front of her.

"She's back in that hospital, isn't she?" Cook dabbed at her eyes.

Daemon sat beside her. "Yes," he said quietly. He held her hands and rubbed gently. "But not for long. She'll be out this afternoon."

"Do you think so?" She gave him a grateful, trembling smile. "In that case, I can—"

"No." Daemon squeezed her hands. "She'll be out of Briarwood, but she won't be coming back."

Cook withdrew her hands. Her lips quivered. "You're taking her away, aren't you?"

Daemon tried to be gentle. "There's a place she can live where she'll be cared for and she'll be safe."

"She's cared for here," Cook protested sharply.

It hurt to watch her eyes fill with tears. "But not safe. If this continues, she'll break under the strain or die." He wiped the tears from her cheeks. "I promise you, she'll be in a safe place, and no one will ever lock her away again."

Cook dabbed her eyes with her apron. "They're good people, these folk you found for her? They won't be . . . critical . . . of her odd ways?"

"They don't think her ways are odd." Daemon sipped his coffee. This, too, was a gamble. "However, I would appreciate your not mentioning any of this until we're gone. There are some here who want to harm her, who would use whatever means they could to stop us if they realized I'm going to take her out of their reach."

Cook thought about this, nodded, sniffed, and rose briskly from the table. "You'll be needing some breakfast, then."

"I've eaten, thanks." Daemon set his cup on the counter. Putting his hands on her shoulders, he turned her around, and kissed her lightly on the mouth. "You're a sweetheart," he said huskily. Then he was out the back door, heading for the stables.

Even this early in the morning, the stables were in an uproar. The stable lads scowled at him as he entered. Guinness stood in the center of the square, a bottle tucked in the crook of his arm, snarling orders and swearing under his breath. When he saw Daemon, his heavy eyebrows formed a fierce line over bleary eyes.

"And what would the high and mighty want at this hour of the morning?" Guinness snapped. He put the bottle to his lips and took a long swallow.

They knew, Daemon thought as he took the bottle from Guinness and helped himself. Whatever it was Jaenelle brought to this place was already fading, and they knew. Handing the bottle back to Guinness, he said quietly, "Saddle Dark Dancer."

"Have ya been kicked in the head recently?" Guinness shouted, glaring at Daemon. "That one kicked down half his stall last night and tried to turn Andrew into pulp. You won't get a brisk morning gallop out of him if that's what you're thinking."

Daemon looked over his shoulder. Andrew leaned against the door of Dark Dancer's stall, favoring one leg. "I'll saddle him." Daemon brushed past the stable lads, ignoring Guinness's dark muttering.

When Daemon pulled the latch to open the top half of the door, Andrew thrust out a shaking hand to stop him. "He wants to kill something," Andrew whispered.

Daemon looked at the sunken eyes in the pale, frightened face. "So do I." He opened the door.

The stallion lunged toward the opening.

"Hush, Brother, hush," Daemon said softly. "We must talk, you and I." Daemon opened the bottom half of the door. The horse trembled. Daemon ran his hand along Dancer's neck, regretting having washed Jaenelle's scent from his skin when the horse turned its head toward him, looking for reassurance. Daemon kept his movements slow. When Dancer was saddled, Daemon led him into the square and mounted.

They went to the tree.

Daemon dismounted and leaned against the tree, staring in the direction of the house. The stallion jiggled the bit, reminding him he wasn't alone.

"I wanted to say good-bye," Daemon said quietly. For the first time, he truly saw the intelligence—and loneliness—in the horse's eyes. After that, he couldn't keep his voice from breaking as he tried to explain why Jaenelle was never going to come to the tree again, why there would be no more rides, no more caresses, no more talks. For a moment, something rippled in his mind. He had the odd sensation he was the one being talked to, explained to, and his words, echoing back, lacerated his heart. To be alone again. To never again see those arms held out in welcome. To never hear that voice say his name. To . . .

Daemon gasped as Dark Dancer jerked the reins free and raced down the path toward the field. Tears of grief pricked Daemon's eyes. The horse might have a simpler mind, but the heart was just as big.

Daemon walked to the field, staring at its emptiness for a long moment before slowly making his way to the wide ditch at the far end.

Would it have been better not to have told him? To have left him waiting through the lonely days and weeks and months that would have followed? Or worse, to have promised to come back for him and not have been able to keep that promise?

No, Daemon thought as he reached the ditch. Jaenelle was Dancer's Queen. He deserved the truth. He deserved the right to make a choice.

Daemon slid down the side of the deep, wide ditch. Dancer lay at the bottom, twisted and dying. Daemon sat beside him, gently putting the horse's head in his lap. He stroked Dancer's neck, murmuring words of sorrow in the Old Tongue.

Finish the kill. Dancer's strength was ebbing. One narrow, searing probe into the horse's mind would finish it. Daemon took a deep breath . . . and couldn't do it.

If Hell was where the Blood's dead walked when the body died but the Self was still too powerful to fade into the ever-night, did the kindred Jaenelle spoke of go there too? Was there a herd of demon-dead horses racing over a desolate landscape?

"Ah, Dancer," Daemon murmured as he continued to stroke the horse's neck. A mind link now wouldn't help, but . . .

Daemon looked at his wrist. Blood. According to the legends, the demon-dead maintained their strength with blood from the living. That's why blood offerings were made when someone petitioned the Dark Realm for help.

Daemon shifted slightly. Pushing up his right sleeve, he positioned his wrist over Dancer's mouth. Gathering himself so that what he offered was the strongest he had to give, he nicked a vein with a long nail and watched his blood flow into Dancer's mouth. Daemon counted to four before pressing his thumb to the wound and healing it with Craft.

All he could do now was wait with his four-footed Brother.

For a long time, while Dancer's eyes glazed, nothing happened. Then something pricked at Daemon, made the land shift and shimmer. He no longer saw the ditch, no longer felt the cold and wet of the snow-covered ground. In front of him was a huge wrought-iron gate. Beyond it was lightning-filled mist. As he watched, the gate slowly opened with chilling silence. A faint sound came then, muffled, but drawing closer to the gate. Daemon watched Dancer race toward the gate, head high, mane and tail streaming out behind him. A moment later, the stallion was lost in the mist, and the gate swung shut.

Daemon looked down at the unblinking eyes. Gently setting the head on the ground, he climbed out of the ditch and wearily made his way back to the stable.

They all came running when he walked in alone. Daemon looked at Andrew, and only Andrew, when he finally got his voice under control enough to say, "He's in the ditch." Not trusting himself to say anything more, Daemon turned abruptly and went back to the house.

5 / Terreille

"I understand your difficulty, Lady Angelline, but you must realize that neither the ambassador nor I has the authority to remove Sadi from service without the High Priestess's consent." Greer leaned against the desk, trying to look sympathetic. "Perhaps if you exerted more effort to discipline him," he suggested.

"Haven't you been listening to me?" Alexandra said angrily. "He threatened to kill me last night. He's out of control."

"The controlling ring—"

"Doesn't work," Alexandra snapped.

Greer studied her face. She was pale, and there were dark smudges under her eyes. Sadi had frightened her badly. After so many months of quiet, when Sadi had been almost too accommodating, what had she done to provoke this explosion? "The controlling ring does work, Lady Angelline, if it's used forcefully enough and soon enough. Even he can't dismiss the pain of a Ring of Obedience."

"Is that why so many of the Queens he has served have died?" Alexandra said sharply. She rubbed her temples with her fingertips. "It's not just me. He's perverted, twisted."

Oh? "You shouldn't allow him to perform any service not to your liking, Lady," Greer said with sneering sternness.

Alexandra glared at him. "And how do I keep him from performing services on my granddaughters that are not to my liking?"

"But they're just children," Greer protested.

"Yes," Alexandra choked, "children." There was an edge in her voice that made Greer fight to hide a smile. "He's all right with the eldest one, but the other . . ."

Frowning as if this was a difficult decision, Greer said slowly, "I'll send a message to the High Priestess requesting permission to remove Sadi from Chaillot as soon as possible. It's the best I can do." He held up his good hand to cut off Alexandra's protest. "However, I realize how difficult it may be for you to keep him at your estate, especially if he should, by chance, discover you've been to see us. Therefore, I, with an armed escort, will collect him this afternoon and hold him at the embassy until we have the High Priestess's consent to return him to Hayll." He held out his hand, smiling. "I will, of course, need your controlling ring to disable him quickly and assure your safety."

Greer held his breath while Alexandra hesitated. Finally she pulled the secondary controlling ring off her finger and dropped it into his hand. Greer nodded to the ambassador who had been hovering near the door. The man hurried forward and escorted Alexandra out, muttering soothing lies.

Greer waited until the door closed behind them before fumbling to slip the ring over his little finger. He held his left hand out, admiring the gold circle.

Bastard, Greer thought gleefully. *I have you now, bastard.* First there was Kartane, almost frightened out of his skin, inviting Greer to partake in a "special party" at Briarwood, and now there was this Queen bleating about Sadi's interest in her granddaughters. And all the time Greer had been searching for the Dark Priestess's prey, the Sadist was playing with the little hussy while the half-breed sweated and bled in Pruul. *If we told him about the offer you sneeringly declined and then stretched you between two posts and handed him a whip, how much of your skin would be left before he became too tired to complete a stroke? And what part of your anatomy might be lacking when he was through?*

Greer mentally shook himself. Those tantalizing prospects would have to wait. Here was the chance he'd waited for, the chance to cut Sadi to the core and please the Dark Priestess in the bargain.

Alexandra was a fool to relinquish her only defense against the Sadist. If she'd used the controlling ring with the same brutality he intended to use, she could have brought Sadi to his knees, drained him sufficiently to reduce the threat. And the threat had to be reduced.

He didn't want Daemon Sadi in any condition to go anywhere tonight.

6 / Terreille

Daemon gave his room a cursory glance. His trunks were packed and vanished so they would travel with him. He'd even slipped into the nursery wing and packed a small suitcase for Jaenelle. It troubled him that he might have left behind something she valued. That cold corner in her wardrobe probably contained her most private possessions, but he didn't have the time or energy to spare to try to unravel whatever lock she might have on it. He hoped that, once she was safely out of Beldon Mor, he and Saetan could retrieve them for her.

Daemon opened his door, startling Cook, who stood with her hand raised as if she were about to knock.

"You're wanted in the front hall," she said worriedly.

Daemon's eyes narrowed. Why send Cook with the message? "Is Jaenelle back?"

"Don't know. Lady Angelline was gone for a while this morning, but after she came back, she and Lady Benedict stayed in the nursery with Miss Wilhelmina and Graff. I don't think Lord Benedict's home, and Prince Alexander has been in the steward's office all day."

Daemon opened his mind to the psychic scents around him. Worry. Fear. That was to be expected. Relief? His golden eyes hardened as he brushed past Cook and glided toward the front hallway. If Alexandra was playing some game . . .

He entered the main hallway and saw Greer with twenty armed Hayllian guards. A moment later, the pain from the Ring almost made his legs buckle. He fought to stay on his feet as he flicked a dagger glance at Alexandra, who stood to one side with Leland and Philip.

"No, Sadi," Greer said in his oily voice, "you answer to me now." He raised his good hand so that the gold controlling ring caught the light.

"Bitch," Daemon said softly, never taking his eyes off Greer. "I made you a promise, Lady Angelline, and I always keep my promises."

"Not this time," Greer said. He closed his hand and thrust it forward. The controlling ring flashed.

Daemon staggered backward, grabbing the wall for support as the pain from the Ring increased.

"Not this time," Greer said again, walking toward Daemon.

The cold. The sweet cold.

Daemon counted to three, thrust his right hand toward Greer, and unleashed a wide band of dark energy. Philip, wearing the Gray Jewel, thrust his hand forward at the same time. The two forces met, exploding the chandelier, snapping the furniture to kindling. Three of the guards fell to the floor, twitching. Greer shrieked with rage. Leland and Alexandra screamed. Philip continued to channel his strength through the Gray Jewel, trying to break Daemon's thrust, but the Black leached around the Gray, and where it did, the walls scorched and cracked.

Daemon braced himself against the wall. Greer continued channeling power into the Ring, intensifying the pain. Dying would be better than surrendering to Greer, but there was one chance—if he could get there intact enough to do what he had to do.

Unleashing a large ball of witchfire, Daemon made a last thrust against the Gray, counting on Philip to meet the attack. When the witchfire met the Gray shield, it exploded into a wall of fire.

Daemon pushed off from the wall and ran toward the back of the house. The pain got worse as he ran through the corridors to the kitchen. Too late he saw the young housemaid on her knees and the puddle of soapy water. He leaped, missing the girl, but his foot landed at the edge of the puddle, and he slip-skidded until his hips hit the kitchen table, pitching him forward.

The pain in his groin was agony.

Daemon clenched his teeth, drawing on his anger because he didn't dare draw on the Jewels. Not yet.

Two pairs of arms grabbed his shoulders and waist. Snarling, he tried to twist free, but Cook's "Hurry up, now" cleared his head sufficiently to realize she and Wilhelmina were trying to help him. The young housemaid, tight-lipped and pale, ran ahead of them and opened the door.

"I'm all right," Daemon gasped as he grabbed the doorway. "I'm all right. Get out of here. All of you."

"Hurry," Cook said. She gave him a shove that almost knocked his feet from under him. As he stumbled and half turned, the last thing he saw before the kitchen door closed was Cook grabbing the pail of soapy water and flinging it across the kitchen floor.

Another burst of pain from the Ring forced him to his knees. He stifled a scream, jerked himself to his feet, and stumbled forward until the momentum pushed him into a run toward the stables and the path that would lead to the field.

The pain. The pain.

Each step was a knife in Daemon's groin as Greer continued to channel his power through the controlling ring into the Ring of Obedience.

Daemon ran along the bridle path past the stables, vaguely aware of Guinness and the stable lads pouring out of the yard to form an angry, solid wall at his back. He ran down the snowy path until another burst of pain from the Ring pulled his legs out from under him. He flew through the air as his momentum carried him forward before hitting the ground with a bone-jarring thud.

Daemon sobbed as he tried to get to his knees. Behind him was a faint, muffled sound. He turned his head, trying to see through tears of pain. There was nothing there, but the sound kept coming toward him, finally stopped beside him. Daemon flung out an arm to get his balance.

His hand hit a leg.

He saw nothing, but he could feel . . .

"Dancer?" Daemon whispered as his hand traveled upward.

A moist warmth blew in his face.

Clenching his teeth, Daemon got to his feet. He was running out of time. His hands found the phantom back. Daemon propelled himself onto the demon stallion's back, gasping as he pulled his leg around. With his head bent low over Dancer's neck and his hands twisted in the mane for balance, Daemon tightened his knees, urging Dancer forward.

"To the tree, Brother," Daemon groaned. "As fast as you can fly, get me to the tree."

Daemon almost fell when Dancer surged forward, but he hung on, grimly determined to reach the one escape left to him.

When they reached their destination, Daemon slid from the horse's

back, remembering in time what Jaenelle had taught him about air walking. For a moment, he lay on his side in the air, his knees curled to his
chest, fighting the pain and gathering his strength.

Deep beneath this tree was a neatly cut rectangle already protected by
a Black shield that would keep the others out just as much as it had kept
Alexandra in.

Daemon looked back. Apparently demons didn't leave tracks. And he,
fortunately, hadn't left any telltale marks in the snow. All he needed was a
few uninterrupted moments to make the pass.

Fighting for patience, Daemon waited for the next burst of pain from
the Ring. Once it passed, he could slip down into the earth. Behind him
were shouts, sounds of fighting. He waited, feeling his strength seeping
out of him as the cold and pain seeped in.

Just as Daemon decided not to wait, the pain hit again. He twisted and
rolled, trying to escape it. This time, however, there was no letup. Greer
was sending a steady pulse through the controlling ring into the Ring of
Obedience.

Daemon crawled on air until he was over the proper place. There was
no more time. With his hands clenched so hard his nails broke his skin, he
took a deep, shuddering breath, closed his eyes, and plunged downward
into the earth.

The moment he felt emptiness instead of earth, he pulled his feet forward so they wouldn't be locked in the frozen ground and stop the pass.
He felt his pant legs catch in the earth above him, felt the skin on his
knees tear as they ripped through the last crust of earth. Landing squarely
on his back, it took him a moment to get his breath.

A moment was all he had. They might not be able to reach him physically, but the pain still pulsed through the Ring. Not even the Black
shield could protect him from that.

With shaking hands, Daemon undid his belt, unzipped his trousers,
and reached down to close his right hand on his organ and the Ring of
Obedience. He screamed when his fingers accidentally touched his balls.
Taking sobbing, gasping breaths, Daemon kept his hand steady and called
in the Black Jewels.

It had been so very long since he'd felt a Jewel around his neck or on
his finger. They pulsed with his heartbeat as he drew on their stored energy. It was a risk. He'd always known it was a risk. But there was some-

thing at stake now more important than his body. Taking a deep breath, Daemon turned inward and plunged toward the Black.

It was an oiled high dive speeding him into the Darkness, faster and faster as he hurtled toward the shimmering dark web that was himself, gaining speed as he unleashed his rage. He continued to plunge downward as his web seemed to rush upward to meet him. There was no time to check his descent. If he missed the turn and shattered the web, the least he would do was break himself, stripping himself of the ability to wear the Black or, possibly, even his Birthright Red. If he couldn't stop his descent and continued falling into the abyss, he would die or go mad.

Daemon pushed faster, watching for the moment when he could make the turn and draw the most from himself. A long way away, he could feel the tight agony in his heels and the corded muscles in his neck as they supported the arched, pain-racked body. Still he plunged downward. At the last moment he turned, tight to the web, drew all the reserve power out of his Black Jewels and hurtled upward, a tidal wave of cold black rage, a dark arrow speeding toward the center of a gold circle.

All the way up, Daemon kept his strength tight and rapier-thin, but the moment he pierced the center of the circle, he unleashed all of his Black strength. It exploded outward, forcing the circle to expand with him until it shattered under the strain.

Daemon slowly opened his eyes. He shook from exhaustion, shivered from cold. The smallest movement, even breathing, brought excruciating pain. Reaching down with his left hand, Daemon felt for the Ring of Obedience. When he drew his hands toward his chest, each hand held half a Ring.

He was free.

Since his Black Jewels were completely drained, he vanished them and called in his Birthright Red in order to do one last thing.

If Dorothea or Greer had escaped the shattering of the Ring, they could still use one of the controlling rings to trace the pieces to his hiding place.

Daemon closed his eyes, concentrated on a spot he knew well, and vanished the two pieces of the Ring of Obedience.

In a small alcove, the two halves of the Ring hovered in the air for a moment before dropping into the snowy bed of witchblood.

Daemon's last conscious thought was to call in a blanket, charge it with a warming spell, and wrap it around himself as best he could. The psychic web he'd created was gone. There was no way to tell if Jaenelle was still unharmed. There was nothing he could do for her right now. There was nothing more he could do for himself. Until his body had some rest, he didn't have the strength to get out of his grave.

7 / Terreille

Cassandra paced.

The mist around Beldon Mor kept Guardians and the demon-dead out. It didn't keep things in.

Thankfully, she'd been wearing the Black Jewel instead of her Birthright Red when the rippling aftershock of Sadi hurtling toward the Darkness hit her. Even with that much protection, her body had vibrated from the intensity of the dive.

As she'd picked herself up off the floor, she'd wondered how many of the Blood, not trained well enough to know that one must ride with those psychic waves instead of trying to shield against them, had been shattered, or at least broken back to their Birthright Jewel.

And what about Jaenelle? Had he turned against her? Was she fighting against him for her life?

Cassandra shook her head and continued pacing. No, he loved the girl. Then why the descent? She feared him now as much as she feared his father, but didn't he realize she would stand with him, fight with him to protect Jaenelle?

Descending slowly to the Black, she closed her eyes and opened her mind, sending a probing shaft westward on a Black thread. The probe hit the mist, penetrating just a little for just a moment before fading away.

It was enough.

She spent the next hour cleaning the Altar, polishing the four-branched candelabra, digging out the stubs of the old black candles and replacing them with new candles. When she was done, the Altar was once again ready to be what it was, what it had not been for centuries.

A Gate.

She bathed in hot scented water, washed and dressed her hair. She slipped on a simple gown of black spidersilk that molded itself to her body. Her Black Jewel in its ancient setting filled the dress's open neckline. The Black-Jeweled ring, in its deceptively feminine setting, slipped easily onto her finger. Two silver cuff bracelets with chips of her Red Jewel embedded in the center of an hourglass pattern fit over the tight sleeves of her dress. Last came the black slippers, made by forgotten craftsmen, which never betrayed a footfall.

She was ready. Whatever storm the night would bring, she was ready.

With a listening, thoughtful expression on her face and a faraway look in her emerald eyes, Cassandra settled down to wait.

8 / Terreille

As the slaves were brought up from the salt mines of Pruul, Lucivar turned toward the west. The salt sweat stung the new cuts on his back. The heavy chains that manacled his wrists to his waist pulled at his already aching arms. Still he stood quietly, breathing the clean evening air, watching the last sliver of sun sink beneath the horizon.

He'd ridden the dark aftershocks that hit Pruul with a lover's passion, using his Ebon-gray strength to fortify those waves and keep them rolling east a little longer. His only regret was not joining Sadi in the bloodletting. Not that the Sadist needed his help. Not that it would be safe to be in the same city with a man that deeply enraged.

As a frightened guard shook his whip at the slaves to begin leading them to their dark, stinking cells, Lucivar smiled and whispered, "Send them to Hell, Bastard. Send them *all* to Hell."

9 / Terreille

Philip Alexander sat at his desk, his head braced in his hands, staring at the shattered Gray Jewel.

It had taken—what—a minute? A bare minute to produce so much destruction? Some of the guards had felt it first, a shuddery feeling, like trying to stand against a strong wind that kept growing stronger. Then Leland. Then Alexandra. He'd been puzzled, in those moments, wondering why they had become so pale and still, why they all were straining to hear something. When it hurtled past the Gray, heading downward, he'd had a moment, just a moment, to realize what it was, a moment to throw his arms around Leland and Alexandra, pulling them to the floor, a moment to try to form a Gray shield around the three of them. A moment.

Then his world exploded.

He had held on for less than a minute before that titanic explosion of Black strength shattered the Gray and swept him along like driftwood caught in a wave before the wave smashes it into the sand. He'd felt Alexandra try to hold him before she, too, was swept away.

A minute.

When it was over, when his head finally cleared . . .

Of the Hayllian guards who had remained in the hall, all but two were dead or had their minds burned away. Leland and Alexandra, shielded from the first impact, were shaken but all right. He'd been broken back to the Green, his Birthright Jewel.

Still in shock, the three of them had staggered from the hall. They had found Graff in the nursery wing, staring empty-eyed at the ceiling, her body twisted and torn almost beyond recognition.

Most of the staff had come away from the psychic explosion frightened but intact. They'd found them huddled in the kitchen where Cook, with shaking hands, liberally filled cups with brandy.

Wilhelmina had frightened them. She had sat quietly in the kitchen chair, cheeks glowing with color, eyes flashing. When Philip had asked if she was all right, she had smiled at him and said, "She said to ride it, so I did. She said to ride it."

In that moment before the world exploded, he had heard a young, commanding female voice shouting "Ride it, ride it," but he hadn't understood—and still didn't. What was more frightening, Wilhelmina now wore a Sapphire Jewel. Somehow, in that chaos, she had made her Offering to the Darkness, too young. Now that inexperienced girl was stronger than any of them.

Worst of all was the betrayal of Guinness and the stable lads, particularly Andrew. They had fought against the Hayllian guards, holding them up. If they hadn't interfered, Sadi might have been caught and Beldon Mor . . . Well, he had dismissed Guinness and Andrew and the others who'd survived. There was no reason to keep traitors, especially traitors who said . . . who called him . . . That they would side with Sadi against her *family*!

Philip closed his eyes, rubbed his aching temples. Who would have thought one man could destroy so much in a minute? Half the Blood in Beldon Mor were dead, mad, or broken.

Philip let out a sighing sob. His body was almost too weak to wear the Green, but he would recover. That much he would recover.

Half the Blood. If Sadi had struck again . . .

But after the ripples had finally passed, there had been no sign of Daemon Sadi.

And no one knew what had become of Greer.

10 / Terreille

Surreal sat with her back against the headboard, sipping from the whiskey bottle she hugged to her chest.

She and Deje had spent the past few hours looking after the other girls, sedating those who needed it, letting the rest get blistering drunk. Deje, her face gray with the strain, had gratefully let Surreal take care of the bodies. Fortunately there weren't many, the day after the Winsol holidays always being a slow time for Red Moon houses. Even so, she'd had to bundle them up in blankets before even the brawniest of Deje's male staff would enter the rooms and lug the bodies out.

Everyone, including herself, stank of fear.

But he was, after all, the Sadist.

It would have been worse, she told herself as she continued to sip the whiskey. It would have been much, much worse, if Jaenelle hadn't shouted that warning to ride it out. Funny. Every witch in Deje's house who wore a Jewel heard that warning and knew on some instinctive level what it meant. The men . . . There wasn't time for Jaenelle to be selective. Some heard her, some didn't. That's all there was to it. Those who didn't were dead.

What had happened to send him into such a rage? What sort of danger could have provoked that kind of unleashing?

Maybe the question to ask was, *who* was in danger?

Calmed by her own rising anger, Surreal set the whiskey bottle on the nightstand and called in a small leather rectangle. As soon as she was done, she'd get a little sleep. It was unlikely that anything would happen before tonight. The Sadist had seen to that, whether he'd meant to or not.

With her lips curved in the slightest of smiles, Surreal hummed softly as she slipped the whetstone out of its leather pouch and began sharpening her knives.

11 / Terreille

Dorothea watched the flames in the fireplace dance. Any moment now, the Dark Priestess would arrive at the old Sanctuary. Then she could give the bitch the message and return home.

Who would have thought he could break a Ring of Obedience? Who would have thought, with him being on the other side of the Realm, shattering the Ring could . . .

How very fortunate that she'd started letting each of the young witches in her coven wear the primary controlling ring for a day, letting them "get the feel" of handling a powerful male, even if he was so far away they couldn't really feel anything at all. How very unfortunate her favorite witch, her little prize who had shown *so* much potential, had been the one wearing it today.

Since the body, although empty of the witch herself, still lived, she would have to keep it around for a little while so the others wouldn't realize how disposable they really were. A month or two would be enough. The witch would, of course, be buried with dignity, with full honors commensurate with her Jewels and social rank.

Dorothea shuddered. Sadi was out there, somewhere, with no leash to hold him. They could try to use the Eyrien half-breed as bait to draw him back, but Yasi was so nicely tucked into Pruul's salt mines, and it would be a shame to pull him out before he was sufficiently broken in body and spirit. Besides, she doubted that even the Eyrien would be sufficient bait this time.

The sitting room door opened for the hooded figure.

"You sent for me, Sister?" Hekatah said, making no attempt to keep her annoyance out of her voice. She looked pointedly at the small table, empty of her expected carafe of blood. "It must be important to have made you forget such a paltry thing as refreshment."

"Yes, it is." *You bag of bones. You parasite. All Hayll is in danger now. I am in danger now!* Careful not to let her thoughts become apparent, Dorothea held up a note, slipping it in and out of her fingers. "From Greer."

"Ah," Hekatah said with barely suppressed excitement. "He has some news?"

"Better than that," Dorothea answered slowly. "He says he has found a way to take care of your little problem."

12 / Terreille

Greer sat on the white-sheeted bed in one of Briarwood's private rooms, cradling what was left of his good hand.

It could have been worse. If that limping stable brat hadn't slashed at him with a knife, slicing through his little finger so it only hung by a thread of skin, he never would have gotten the secondary controlling ring off in time when Sadi broke the Ring of Obedience. In that moment when he'd felt the Black explode, he'd ripped the finger off and flung it away from him. A guard, seeing something hurled toward him, grabbed instinctively, his hand closing around the ring.

Foolish man. Foolish, foolish man.

With the Ring of Obedience broken and with no way to know if Sadi had been hurt by the effort, Greer had run to Briarwood, where the healing would be done without questions. It was also the only place the Sadist wouldn't strike at blindly. Here they had some leverage—at least for a few hours more. After that he would be gone, speeding back to Hayll to melt away among the many, encircled by Dorothea's court. Briarwood and its patrons would still be here to quench Sadi's thirst for vengeance.

Greer lay down on the bed, letting the painkillers lull him into much-needed rest. In a few short hours, the Dark Priestess's little problem would be no more, and Sadi . . .

Let the bastard scream.

13 / Hell

Saetan made another erratic circuit around his private study.

He stared at Cassandra's portrait.

He stared at the tangled web he'd finished a short time ago, at the warning that may have come too late.

He shook his head slowly, denying what the vision in the tangled web had shown him.

An inner web still intact. A shattered crystal chalice. And blood. So much blood.

He had never invaded Jaenelle's privacy. Against his better judgment, against all his instincts, he had never invaded her privacy. But now . . .

"No," he said with soft malevolence. "You will not take my Queen from me. You will not take my daughter."

There was only one place from which he could penetrate the mist. Only one place he could use to amplify his strength to reach across the Realm. Only one witch who had the knowledge to help him do it.

Throwing his cape over his shoulders, he flicked a glance at the door, tearing it off the hinges. Gliding through the deep corridors of the Hall, his rage glazing the rough stones with ice, he brushed past Mephis and Prothvar, seeing no one, seeing nothing but that web.

"Where are you going, SaDiablo?" Andulvar called, striding to intercept him.

Saetan snarled softly.

The Hall trembled.

Andulvar hesitated for only a moment before setting himself squarely in the path of the High Lord of Hell.

"Yaslana." The rage had become very quiet, very still.

This was what they feared in him.

"You can tell me where you're going, or you can go through me," Andulvar said calmly. Only a tiny muscle tic in his jaw betrayed him.

Saetan smiled, raising his right hand in a lover's caress. Remembering in time that this man was his friend and also loved Jaenelle, he sheathed the snake tooth, and the hand gently squeezed Andulvar's shoulder.

"To Ebon Askavi," he whispered as he caught the Black Wind and vanished.

CHAPTER FIFTEEN

1 / Terreille

S urreal dreamed.

She and Titian were walking through a woods. Titian was trying to warn her about something, but Surreal couldn't hear her. The woods, Titian, everything, was silenced by the loud, steady pounding of a drum.

As they reached the edge of the woods, Surreal noticed a tree with a perfect branch, a tree sweating dark red sap.

Titian walked past the tree across a lawn filled with tall, silvery flowers. As she picked a flower here and there, it turned into a knife, sharp and shining. Smiling, she offered the bouquet to Surreal.

The drum beat louder, harder.

Someone was screaming.

Titian continued walking toward a large, mist-filled rectangle, pointing here and there. Every time she pointed, the mist drew away. Two redheads. A girl with no eyes. A girl with a slit throat whose eyes blazed with impotent fury. A girl with one leg.

At the far end of the rectangle was a mound of freshly dug earth.

The drum beat faster.

Someone was shrieking, enraged and in pain.

Surreal approached the mound, drawn by something lying over the dirt. As she approached, witchblood began to sprout and bloom, forming a crown around a length of golden hair.

"No!" Surreal yelled, flinging herself out of the bed.

The heartbeat drum pounded against her ribs.

The screaming in her head didn't stop.

2 / Hell

"You're going to help me," Saetan said, turning to face Draca.

"To do what, High Lord?" Draca asked. Her unblinking reptilian eyes revealed nothing.

"Penetrate the mist around Beldon Mor." His golden eyes locked with Draca's, willing her to yield.

Draca studied him for a long time. "There iss danger?"

"I believe so."

"You break faith with her."

"I'd rather have her hate me than have her lost to all of us," Saetan replied sharply.

Draca considered this. "Even the Black iss not sso far-reaching. At leasst not the Black you wear, High Lord. The help I can offer will only let you know what iss beyond the misst, to ssee but not to act. To act, you would need to link with another, sspear to sspear."

Saetan licked his lips, took a deep breath. "There is one there who may help, who may let me use him."

"Come." Draca led him through the corridors of Ebon Askavi toward a large stairwell that descended into the heart of the mountain.

As they reached the stairwell, hurrying footsteps made Saetan swing around in challenge.

Geoffrey appeared around the corner, followed by Andulvar, Prothvar, and Mephis. Andulvar and Prothvar were dressed for battle. Mephis's anger blazed from his Gray Jewel.

Saetan flicked a dagger glance at each of them before his eyes and his anger settled on Andulvar. "Why are you here, Yaslana?" Saetan asked in his soft, dangerous croon.

Andulvar clenched his hands. "That web in your study."

"Ah, so now you possess the ability to read the Hourglass's webs."

"I could snap you like kindling!"

"You'd have to reach me first."

A slow grin bared Andulvar's teeth. Then the grin faded. "The waif's in trouble, isn't she? That's what the web warned you about."

"It's not your concern."

"She doesn't belong just to you, High Lord!" Andulvar roared.

Saetan closed his eyes. *Sweet Darkness, give me the strength.* "No," he agreed, letting Andulvar see his pain, "she doesn't belong just to me. But I'm the only one strong enough to do what has to be done, and"—he raised a hand to stop their protests, his eyes never leaving Andulvar's face—"if someone has to stand responsible for what's going to happen, if someone is going to earn her hatred, let it be only one of us so the others can still cherish her—and serve her."

"Saetan," Andulvar said, his voice husky. "Ah, Saetan. Is there nothing we can do?"

Saetan blinked rapidly. "Wish me well."

"Come," Draca said urgently. "The Darknesss . . . We musst hurry."

Saetan followed her down the stairwell to the locked door at the bottom. Pulling a large key from her sleeve, Draca unlocked the door and pushed it open.

Etched in the floor of the enormous cavern was a huge web lined with silver. In the center where all the tether lines met was an iridescent Jewel the size of Saetan's hand, a Jewel that blended the colors of all the other Jewels. At the end of each silver tether line was an iridescent Jewel chip the size of his thumbnail.

As Saetan and Draca walked along the edge of the web, the Jewels began to glow. A low hum rose from the web, rising up and up until the cavern throbbed with the sound.

"Draca, what is this place?" Saetan whispered.

"It iss nowhere and everywhere." Draca pointed at his feet. "Your feet must be bare. Flessh musst touch the web." When Saetan had stripped off his shoes and socks, Draca pointed to a tether line. "Begin here. Walk sslowly to the center, letting the web draw you into itsself. When you reach the center, possition yoursself behind the Jewel sso you are facing the tether line closesst to Beldon Mor."

"And then?"

Draca studied Saetan, her thoughts hidden. "And the Blood sshall ssing to the Blood. Your blood, darkened by your sstrength, will feed the web. You will direct the power from thiss offering sso it iss channeled to the one tether line you need. You musst not break contact with the web once you begin."

"And then?"

"And then you will ssee what you have come here to ssee."

Saetan tapped into the reserve strength in his Black Jewels and stepped on the tether line. The power in the web stabbed into his heel like a needle. He sucked in his breath and began walking.

Each step drove the power of the web upward. By the time he reached the center, his whole body vibrated with the hum. Keeping one foot in contact with the web, Saetan positioned himself behind the Jewel, his eyes and will focused on that one tether line.

He held out his right wrist and opened his vein.

His blood hissed when it hit the Jewel in the center of the web, formed a red mist. The mist twisted into a fine thread and began to inch its way along the tether line.

Drop by drop, the thread moved toward Chaillot, toward Beldon Mor.

For a moment it stopped, a finger-length away from the Jewel chip, blocked. Then it crept upward, a red vine climbing an invisible wall, until a handspan above the floor, it was over, flowing back along the tether line.

He had breached Jaenelle's mist. The moment the blood thread touched the Jewel chip, he would be able to probe Beldon Mor.

The thread touched the Jewel chip.

Saetan's eyes widened. "Hell's fire, what—"

"Don't move!" Draca's voice seemed so far away.

What had Daemon done? Saetan thought as he picked up the after-taste of rage. Sinking beneath the cacophony of the lesser Jewels, Saetan searched the Black, the too-still Black. There should have been three minds within his probing reach. There was only one, the one farthest out, the one at the Dark Altar.

Keeping his eyes locked on the Jewel chip, Saetan sent a thought along the thread, spear to spear. *Namesake?*

His answer was a brief, annoyed flicker.

Saetan tried again, spear to distaff. *Witch-child?*

For a moment, nothing.

Saetan heard Draca gasp as light flickered around him. Out of the corner of his eye, he saw all the Jewel chips begin to glow, all the silver strands of the web blaze with a fiery cold light.

Something sped toward him. Not a thought. More like a soap bubble cocooned in mist. Faster and faster it sped toward the web.

The sudden light from the Jewel at his feet blinded him. He threw his arm up over his eyes.

The bubble reached the Jewel chip and burst, and the cavern . . .

The cavern vibrated with the sound of a child screaming.

3 / Terreille

The screaming stopped.

Surreal raced across Briarwood's empty lawn toward the hidden door. The Gray Jewel around her neck blazed with her anger. Tonight there wasn't a lock anywhere in Beldon Mor strong enough to keep her out. Once inside, however, she had no idea how to find the one she sought.

A few strides away from the door, someone shouted at her, "Hurry! This way. Hurry!" Swinging to the right, she saw Rose gesturing frantically.

"They're too strong," Rose said, grabbing Surreal's arm. "Kartane and Uncle Bobby are letting him draw on their strength. He's got the room shielded so I can't get through."

"Where?" There was a stitch in Surreal's side from running, and the cold night air burned her lungs. It made her angrier.

Rose pointed at the wall. "Can you make the pass?"

Surreal stared at the wall, probing. Pain and confusion. Rage and despair. And courage. "Why isn't she fighting back?"

"Too many medicines. She's in the misty place and she can't get out." Rose tugged on Surreal's sleeve. "Please help her. We don't want her to die. We don't want her to be like us!"

Her lips pressed into a tight, angry line, Surreal reached for the knife sheathed against her right thigh, but her hand swung across her body and pulled out the knife from the left sheath.

Titian's knife.

A slow smile curled Surreal's lips. Never taking her eyes away from the wall, she held out her other hand to Rose. "Come with me," she said as she stepped forward and melted into the wall.

Briarwood's outer walls were thick. Surreal didn't notice.

This time . . . This time she would wash the walls in blood.

The shield was there, braided by the strength of two. Fools. Two Reds might have slowed her down if they were aware of her presence. But Kartane and Uncle Bobby? Never. *Never.*

Surreal unleashed one short blast of power from her Gray Jewel. The shield around the room shattered.

Surreal leaped. Landing in the small room, she whirled to face the man on the bed. Even as he thrust into the too-still body under him, he raised his head, his face twisted with hatred and lust.

Lunging forward, Surreal grabbed his hair with one hand and slashed Titian's knife across his throat.

The blood sang as the white walls turned red.

Still pushing forward and up, Surreal drove the knife into his heart, lifting him off the bed with the strength of her rage.

He fell to the floor, Titian's knife still in his heart while his maimed hands groped feebly for one heartbeat, two.

Finish the kill.

Squatting over the still body, Surreal pulled out her other knife to drive it through his brain, intending to use the steel as a channel for the Gray to break and destroy what the husk still contained. As she raised her arm for the final strike, Rose's low moan made her glance at the bed.

There was a pool of blood between Jaenelle's legs. Too much blood.

Surreal leaned over the bed. Her stomach rolled.

Jaenelle stared at the ceiling, her unblinking eyes never changing when Surreal passed her hand in front of them. Her body was a mass of bruises; a cut on her lip leaked blood.

Surreal glanced back at the Warlord and noticed scratches on his face and shoulders. So. She had fought for a while.

Surreal felt for a pulse and found one. Weak and growing weaker.

Something hit the locked door.

"Greer!" someone shouted. "Greer, what's going on?"

"Damn!" The word exploded out with her breath as she quickly Gray-locked the door. Pulling Titian's knife from Greer's heart, Surreal hesitated for just a moment, then shook her head. She didn't have the minute it would take. She cut the cords that bound Jaenelle's ankles and wrists to the bed, wrapped the girl in the bloody sheet, lifted the bundle against her, and, Gray shielding herself and her precious burden, made the pass through the walls.

Once outside, Surreal ran. When they finally broke the Gray lock and found Greer, they would be pouring out of the doors in pursuit. And following the blood scent, they would be able to trace her.

There was only one place to go, and once there, she would need help. Putting her heart into it, Surreal sent a summons along the Gray.

Sadi!

No answer.

Sadi!

4 / Hell

"NO!"

Saetan's roar thundered through the cavern, drowning out the sound of feet racing down the stairs.

"SaDiablo!" Andulvar yelled as he leaped into the cavern. "We heard a scream. What's—"

Saetan pivoted, teeth bared, spearing Draca with eyes filled with cold rage. "And now?" he said too softly.

"We'll ride the Winds," Prothvar said, pulling out his knife.

"No time," Mephis countered. "It'll be too late."

"Draca," Geoffrey said.

Draca never blinked, never flinched from Saetan's glazed stare.

"Saetan—" Andulvar began.

Draca closed her eyes.

A voice filled their minds, a rumble as if the Keep itself sighed.

A male voice.

Sspear to sspear, High Lord. That iss the only way now. Her blood runss. If sshe diess now—

"She'll walk among the *cildru dyathe.*"

So much sorrow in that voice. *Dreamss made flessh do not become *cildru dyathe,* High Lord. Sshe will be losst to uss.*

"Who are you to say this to me?" Saetan snarled.

Lorn.

Saetan's heart stopped for a beat.

You have the courage, High Lord, to do what you musst do. The other male will be your insstrument.

The sighing rumble faded.

The cavern was very still.

Turning carefully, Saetan once more faced the red-misted tether line.

And the Blood shall sing to the Blood.

Don't think. Be an instrument.

Everything has a price.

Locked in his cold, still rage, Saetan slowly drew on the power in the web, the power in his Jewels, and the power in himself until he had formed a three-edged psychic spear. With his eyes and will fixed on the Jewel chip, he sent a single, thundering summons.

SADI!

5 / Terreille

Sadi!

Sadi!

SADI!

Daemon jerked awake, head pounding, heart pounding, body throbbing. Groaning, he rubbed his fist back and forth across his forehead.

And remembered.

Sadi, please.

Daemon frowned. Even that movement hurt. *Surreal?*

A gasping sob. *Hurry. To the Altar.*

Surreal, what—

She's bleeding!

He didn't remember making the pass. One moment he was cramped in the underground rectangle, the next he was braced against the tree, eyes closed, waiting for the world to stop spinning. *Surreal, get to the Altar. Now.*

The uncles will be coming after us.

The Sadist bared his teeth in a vicious smile. *Let them come.*

The link broke. Surreal was already riding the Winds to Cassandra's Altar.

Daemon clung to the tree. His body could give him nothing. The Black Jewels were still drained and could give him nothing. Needing strength, he greedily drained the reserve power in his Birthright Red.

SADI!

The power behind that thundering voice hit his Red strength and absorbed it as easily as a lake absorbs a pail of water.

Daemon clamped his hands over his head and fell to his knees. That power was tightening like a band of iron inside his head, threatening to smash his inner barriers. Snarling, he lashed back with the little strength he had left.

Daemon.

Glacial rage waited for him just outside the first barrier, but now he recognized the voice.

Priest? Daemon let out a gasp of relief. *Father, pull back a little. I can't . . . It's too strong.*

The power pulled back—a little.

You are my instrument.

No.

The psychic band tightened.

I serve no one but Witch. Not even you, Priest, Daemon snarled.

The band loosened, became a caress. *I, too, serve her, Prince. That's why I need you. Her blood runs.*

Daemon fought to stand up, fought to breathe. *I know. She's being taken to Cassandra's Altar.* He hurt. Hell's fire, how he hurt.

Let me in, namesake. I won't harm you.

Daemon hesitated, then opened himself fully. He clenched his teeth to keep from screaming as the icy rage swept into his mind. His vision doubled. He felt the tree against his back. He also felt cold stone beneath bare feet.

The stone faded, but not completely. He slowly opened and closed his hand. It felt as though he were wearing a glove beneath his skin. Then that too faded, but not completely.

You're controlling my body, Daemon said with a trace of bitterness.

Not controlling. By joining this way, my strength will be a well for you to tap and, in turn, I will be able to see and understand what we must do to help her.

Daemon pushed himself away from the tree. He swayed, but another pair of legs held firm. Taking a deep breath, he caught the Black Wind and hurled himself toward Cassandra's Altar.

Daemon hurried through the ruins of the Sanctuary's outer rooms. The footsteps he'd heard a moment ago stopped. Now an angry Gray wall blocked the corridor that led into the labyrinth of inner rooms.

"Surreal?" Daemon called softly.

A sob answered him. The Gray wall dropped.

Daemon ran toward her. Surreal waited for him, tears streaming down her face.

"I wasn't in time," she sobbed as Daemon took the sheet-wrapped bundle from her shaking arms and held it close to his chest. "I wasn't in time."

Daemon turned back the way he'd come. "Cassandra must have a room here somewh—"

Go to the Altar, namesake.

She needs—

The Altar.

Daemon turned again, racing toward the Altar that lay in the center of the Sanctuary. Surreal ran ahead to push open the Altar room's stiff wrought-iron gate. Daemon rushed in and carefully laid Jaenelle on the Altar.

"We need some light," he said, desperation making his voice harsh.

Witchlight bloomed overhead.

Cassandra stood behind the Altar. Her Black Jewels glowed. Her emerald eyes stabbed at him.

Daemon looked down and saw the blood on his shirt.

Courage, namesake.

"So," Cassandra said quietly, her eyes never leaving Daemon's face, "you're both here."

Daemon nodded as he swiftly unwrapped the sheet.

Cassandra clamped a hand over her mouth, stifling a scream.

Blood gushed between Jaenelle's legs. Daemon's hands were slick with it as his fingers rested at the junction of her thighs and became a channel for a delicate tendril of power and the little healing Craft he knew. He searched, probed.

Witches bled more on their Virgin Night than other women, and dark-Jeweled witches most of all. They paid for their strength with moments of fragility, moments when the balance of power shifted to the male's advantage and left them vulnerable.

But even that didn't explain this much blood.

Searching, probing.

Icy shock ran through him when he found the answer. Glacial rage followed.

"They used something to tear her open. The bastards *tore her open.*" He slid his hands over her torso, over the cuts and bruises. *How much healing Craft do you know?* he snapped at Saetan.

I have a great deal of knowledge, but even less of the healing gift than you. It's not enough, Daemon.

*Then who *has* enough?*

Jaenelle's blank eyes stared at him.

Daemon reached to cup her face in his hands.

"No," Cassandra said, coming around the Altar. "Let me. A Sister won't be a threat."

Daemon hated her for saying it. Hated her even more because, right now, it was true.

Let her try, namesake, Saetan said, forcing Daemon to step back.

Cassandra pressed her fingers against Jaenelle's temples and stared into the unblinking eyes. After a minute, she stepped back and wrapped her arms around herself, as if needing comfort. Her lips quivered. "She's out of reach," she said in a hoarse, defeated whisper.

It didn't mean anything. Jaenelle was stronger than the rest of them. She could descend further. It didn't mean anything.

But Tersa's vision of the shattered crystal chalice mocked him. *You know,* it said. *You know why she doesn't answer.*

"No." Daemon wasn't sure if the denial was his or Saetan's.

Surreal stepped forward. Her face was ashen, but her gold-green eyes flashed with determination. "The girl Rose said they'd given her too much medicine and she couldn't get out of the misty place. Probably a vile mixture of *safframate* and a sedative."

Saetan's voice sounded tightly calm. *I can't sense a link between her body and her Self. It's either very faint or she's severed it completely. If we don't draw her back now, we'll lose her.*

You mean I'll lose her, Daemon snapped at him. *If her body dies, *you'll* still have her, won't you?*

He felt heart-tearing pain come through the link.

No, Saetan whispered. *I was told by one who would know that dreams made flesh don't become *cildru dyathe.**

Daemon closed his eyes and took a deep breath. *How deep is your well, Priest?*

I don't know.

Then let's find out. Daemon turned to Surreal. *Go out. Keep watch. Those sons of whoring bitches will be coming soon. Buy us some time, Surreal."

Surreal glanced at the Altar. "I'll keep them out until I hear from you." She slipped through the wrought-iron gate and disappeared into the labyrinth of dark corridors.

"Go with her," Daemon said to Cassandra. "This is private."

Before she could protest, Saetan said, *Go, Lady.*

Daemon waited until he was sure she was gone. Then he stretched out on the Altar and took Jaenelle in his arms.

The power from Saetan flowed into him, wrapped around him.

Keep the descent at a steady pace, Saetan warned.

So easy to slip into that abandoned body, so easy to glide down through all that emptiness until he reached the depth of his own inner web. He held there, trying to probe further down.

Far, far, far below him, a flash of lightning lit up a swirling black mist.

Jaenelle! Daemon shouted. *Jaenelle!*

No answer.

Spinning out the link to make it thinner and longer, Daemon eased past the depth of his inner web.

Daemon! Saetan's worry vibrated through the link.

A little deeper. A little deeper.

He felt the pressure now, but kept spinning out the link.

Down down down.

Like diving too deep in water, the abyss pressed against him, pressed against his mind. That inner core of Self could go only so deep. Any deeper and the very power that made the Blood the Blood would try to pour into a vessel too small to hold it, crushing the spirit, shattering the mind.

Down down down. Gliding through the emptiness, spinning out the link between him and Saetan thinner and thinner.

Daemon! Saetan's voice was a hoarse, distant thunder. *You're too deep. Pull up, Daemon. Pull up!*

A tiny psychic feather rose out of the mist that was still far below him, brushed against him and withdrew, startled and puzzled.

Jaenelle! Daemon shouted. When he got no answer, he sent on a spear thread. *I felt her, Priest! I felt her!*

He also felt agony through the link and realized he was being pulled upward.

No! he yelled, fighting the upward pull. *NO!*

The link snapped.

No longer tied to the power Saetan was channeling, he became an empty vessel that the power in the abyss rushed to fill. Too much. Too fast. Too strong.

He screamed as his mind ripped, tore, shattered.

Shattering and shattering, he fell, screaming, and disappeared into the lightning-streaked black mist.

Surreal put the finishing touches on the spell she was weaving across a corridor that led to the inner rooms and toyed with the idea of shoving Cassandra into it just to see what would happen. She didn't have anything against the woman personally, but that sulky temper and the dagger glances Cassandra kept throwing back toward the Altar room were fraying nerves already stretched a little too thin.

She stepped back and rubbed her hands against her trouser seat. Calling in a black cigarette, she lit it with a little tongue of witchfire, took a puff, and then offered it to Cassandra, who just shook her head and glared.

"What are they trying to do that it has to be private?" Cassandra said for the tenth time in the past few minutes.

"Back off, sugar," Surreal snapped. "That smart-ass remark about her trusting you more than him was enough reason for him to toss you out the door."

"It's true," Cassandra said angrily. "A Sister—"

"Sister, shit. And I don't hear you bitching about the other one I caught a whiff of."

"I trust the Priest."

Surreal puffed on the cigarette. So that was the Priest. Not a male she'd care to tangle with. Then again, Sadi wasn't a male she cared to tangle with either.

She snubbed out the cigarette and vanished it. "Come on, sugar. Let's create a few more surprises for Briarwood's darling uncles."

Cassandra eyed the corridor. "What is it?"

"A death spell." A vicious gleam filled Surreal's eyes. "First one who walks through that—it'll burst his heart, burst his balls, and finish the kill with a blast of the Gray. The spell gets sucked into the body so there's nothing anyone can trace. I usually add a timing spell to it, but we want to hit them fast and dirty."

Cassandra looked shocked. "Where did you learn to build something like that?"

Surreal shook her head and headed for another corridor to set another trap. This wasn't the time to tell Cassandra that Sadi had taught her that particular little spell. Especially when she kept wishing he'd taught it to Jaenelle.

Daemon slowly opened his eyes.

He knew he was lying on his back. He knew he couldn't move. He also knew he was naked. Why was he naked?

Mist swirled around him, teasing him, offering him no landmarks. Not that he expected to find anything familiar, but even the mind had landmarks. Except this was Jaenelle's mind, not his, in a place too deep for the rest of the Blood to reach.

He remembered feeling a hint of her as he probed the abyss, remembered diving, falling. Shattering.

Something moved in the mist. He heard a quiet *clink clink,* like glass tapping glass.

He turned his head toward the sound, feeling as if it took all of his strength to do so little.

Don't move, said a lilting, lyrical voice that also contained caverns and midnight skies.

The mist drew back enough for him to see her standing next to slabs of stone piled up to form a makeshift altar.

Shock rippled through him. The crystal shards on the altar rattled in response.

Don't move, she said, sounding testy as she carefully fitted another shard of the shattered chalice into place.

It was Jaenelle's voice, but . . .

She was medium height, slender, and fair-skinned. Her gold mane—not quite hair and not quite fur—was brushed up and back from her exotic face and didn't hide the delicately pointed ears. In the center of her forehead was a tiny, spiral horn. A narrow strip of gold fur traced her spine, ending in a small gold and white fawn tail that flicked over her bare buttocks. The legs were human and shapely but changed below the calf. Instead of feet, she had dainty horse's hooves. Her human hands had sheathed claws like a cat's. As she shifted position to slip another shard into place, he saw the small, round breasts, the feminine curve of waist and hips, the dark-gold triangle of hair between her legs.

Who . . . ?

But he knew. Even before she walked over and looked at him, even before he saw the feral intelligence in those ancient, haunted sapphire eyes, he knew.

Terrifying and beautiful. Human and Other. Gentle and violent. Innocent and wise.

I am Witch, she said, a small, defiant quiver in her voice.

I know. His voice had a seductive throb in it, a hunger he couldn't control or mask.

She looked at him curiously, then shrugged and returned to the altar. *You shattered the chalice. That's why you can't move yet.*

He tried to raise his head and blacked out. By the time he could focus again, she had enough of the chalice pieced together for him to realize it wasn't the same one Tersa had shown him.

That's not your chalice, he shouted happily, too relieved to care that he'd startled her until she bared her teeth and snarled at him.

*No, you silly stubborn male, it's *yours.**

That sobered him a little, but her response sounded so much like Jaenelle the child, he didn't care about that either.

Taking it slow, he propped himself up on one elbow. *Then your chalice didn't shatter.*

She selected another piece, fit it into place. Her eyes filled with desperation and her voice became too quiet. *It shattered.*

Daemon lay down and closed his eyes. It took him a long moment to gather the courage to ask, *Can you repair it?*

She didn't answer.

He drifted after that. Minutes, years, what did it matter? Images swirled behind his closed eyes. Bodies of flesh and bone and blood. Webs that marked the inner boundaries. Crystal chalices that held the mind. Jewels for power. The images swirled and shifted, over and over. When they finally came to rest, they formed the Blood's four-sided triangle. Three sides—body, chalice, and Jewels—surrounding the fourth side, the Self, the spirit that binds the other three.

The images swirled again, became mist. He felt something settle into place inside him as the mist reformed into a crystal chalice, its shattered pieces carefully fitted together. Black mist filled in the cracks between each piece, as well as the places where tiny pieces were missing.

He felt brittle, fragile.

A finger tapped his chest.

A thin skin of black mist coated the chalice, inside and out, forming a delicate shield around it.

The finger tapped again. Harder.

He ignored it.

The next tap had an unsheathed nail at the end of it.

Cursing, he shot up onto his elbows. He forgot what he'd intended to say because she was straddling his thighs and he could have sworn he saw little flashes of lightning deep in her sapphire eyes.

Snarly male, she said, tapping his chest again. *The chalice is back together, but it's very fragile. It will be strong again if you keep it protected long enough for it to mend. You must take your body to a safe place until the chalice heals.*

I'm not leaving without you.

She shook her head. *The misty place is too dark, too deep for you. You can't stay here.*

Daemon bared his teeth. *I'm not leaving without you.*

Stubborn snarly male!

I can be as stubborn and as snarly as you.

She stuck her tongue out at him.

He responded in kind.

She blinked, huffed, and then began to laugh.

That silvery, velvet-coated laugh made his heart ache and tremble.

Before, he'd seen Witch beneath the child Jaenelle. Now he saw Jaenelle beneath Witch. Now he saw the difference—and no difference.

She looked at him, her eyes full of gentle sadness. *You have to go back, Daemon.*

So do you, he said quietly.

She shook her head. *The body's dying.*

You could heal it.

She shook her head more violently. *Let it die. Let them have the body. I don't want the body. This is my place now. I can see them all when I stand in this place. All the dreams.*

★What dreams?★

★The dreams in the Light. The dreams in the Darkness and the Shadow. All the dreams.★ She hesitated, looked confused. ★You're one of the dreams in the Light. A good dream.★

Daemon swallowed hard. Was that how she saw them? As dreams? She was the living myth, dreams made flesh.

Made flesh.

★I'm not a dream, Lady. I'm real.★

Her eyes flashed. ★What is real?★ she demanded. ★I see beautiful things, I hear them, I touch them with the body's hand, and they say bad girl to make up stories, those things are not real. I see bad things, cruel things, a twisted darkness that taints the land, a darkness that isn't the Darkness, and they say bad girl to make up stories, bad girl to tell lies. The uncles say no one will believe a sick-mind girl and they laugh and hurt the body so I go away to the misty place to see the gentle ones, the beautiful ones and leave them ice that hurts them when they touch it.★ She hugged herself and rocked back and forth. ★They don't want me. They don't want *me*. They don't love *me*.★

Daemon wrapped his arms around her and held her close, rocking with her as words kept tumbling out. He listened to the loneliness and confusion. He listened to the horrors of Briarwood. He listened to bits of stories about friends who seemed real but weren't real. He listened and understood what she didn't, what she couldn't.

If she didn't repair her shattered mind, if she didn't link with the body again, if she didn't re-form the four-sided triangle, she would be trapped here, becoming lost and entangled in the shards of herself until she could never find a way to reach what she loved most.

★No,★ he said gently when her words finally stopped, ★they don't want you. They don't love you, can't love you. But I *do* love you. The Priest loves you. The beautiful ones, the gentle ones—*they* love you. We've waited so long for you to come. We need you with us. We need you to walk among us.★

★I don't want the body,★ she whimpered. ★It hurts.★

★Not always, sweetheart. Not always. Without the body, how will you hear a bird's song? How will you feel a warm summer rain on your skin? How will you taste nutcakes? How will you walk on a beach at sunset and feel the sand and surf under your . . . hooves?★

He felt her mood lighten before he heard the sniffled giggle. As she raised her head to look at him, her thighs shifted where they straddled him.

A fire sparked in his loins and he stirred.

She leaned back and watched him swell and rise.

He saw innocence in her face, a kitten's curiosity. He saw a female shape that, if not fully mature, was also not a child.

He clenched his teeth and swore silently when she began stroking him lightly.

Stroke. Observe the reaction as if she'd never seen a man become aroused. Stroke. Observe.

He wanted to push her away. He wanted to pull her down on top of him. It was killing him. It was wonderful.

As he reached for her hand to stop her, she said in a quiet, wondering voice, *Your maleness has no spines.*

Rage froze him. The shards of the chalice rattled as he leashed the fury that had no outlet here. For a moment he tried very, very hard to believe she was comparing him to another species of male, but he knew too much about the twisted males who enjoyed breaking a young, strong witch on her Virgin Night.

Mother Night! No wonder she didn't want to go back.

She studied him, puzzled. *Does the body's maleness have spines?*

Daemon swallowed the rage. The Sadist transformed it into deadly silk. *No,* he crooned. *My maleness has no spines.*

Soft, she said as she stroked and explored.

His hands whispered over her thighs, over her hips. *It could give you pleasure,* he crooned softly.

Pleasure? Her eyes lit up with curiosity and anticipation.

The childlike trust stabbed him in the heart.

She must have sensed some change in him. Before he could stop her, she exploded, kicking his thigh as she leaped away from him. Out of reach, she hugged herself and glared at him.

You want to mate with the body. Like the others. You want me to make her well so you can put your maleness inside her.

Rage washed through him. *Who is her?* he asked too softly.

Jaenelle.

You're Jaenelle.

I AM WITCH!

He trembled with the effort not to attack her. *Jaenelle is Witch and Witch is Jaenelle.*

They never want me. She thumped her chest with her fist. *Not me. They don't want me inside the body. They want to mate with Jaenelle, not Witch.*

He felt her fragment more and more.

This is Witch, she screamed at him. *This is who lived inside the body. Do you want to mate with Witch?*

Anger made him lash out. *No, I don't want to mate with you. I want to make love to you.*

Whatever she was about to say went unsaid. She stared at him as if he were something unknown. She took a hesitant step toward him.

She'll take the bait, the Sadist whispered inside him. She'll take the bait and step into the pretty trap.

Another step.

Deadly, deadly silk.

Another.

A sweet trap spun from love and lies . . . and truth.

I've waited seven hundred years for you, he crooned. *For you.* His lips curved in a seducer's smile. *I was born to be your lover.*

Lover?

Almost within reach.

Without his body, the seduction tendrils weren't as potent, but he saw the change in her eyes when they reached her.

Still, she hovered out of reach. *Then why do you want the body?*

Because that body can sheathe me so that I can give you pleasure. He watched her think about this. *Do you like my body?*

It's beautiful, she said reluctantly, and then added hurriedly, *but you look the same here. And Witch can sheathe your maleness.*

The Sadist held out his hand. *Why don't we find out?*

She took his hand and gracefully settled over him, straddling his thighs. Then she looked at him expectantly.

He smiled at her while his hands explored her, soothing and arousing. When his fingers tickled the underside of her fawn tail, she squeaked and jumped. He resettled her tighter against him, wrapped one arm around her hips to keep her still while his other hand slid through the gold mane and cupped her head. Then he kissed her. A soft kiss. A melting kiss. She sighed when he caressed her breasts. She trembled when he licked the tiny spiral horn.

When he was sure she'd taken the bait, he whispered, *Sweetheart, you're right. This place is too dark for me. The chalice is too fragile and I . . . I hurt.*

She looked at him regretfully but nodded.

Wait, he said when she tried to move away. *Can you come up with me? Up to my inner web?* He licked her ear. His voice became a throbbing purr. *We'd still be safe there.*

He leashed the urgency he felt and waited for her answer. There was no way to tell how much time had passed at the Altar, no way to know if their bodies were still there, no way to know if hers still lived, no way to know if those monsters from Briarwood had reached the Sanctuary. No way to know what his body was doing.

He pushed the thought away. He didn't have a link now; the Priest did. Whatever he was doing, it was Saetan's problem.

The rushing ascent caught him by surprise. He grabbed her at the same moment she wrapped her legs around him.

Lover, she said, smiling at him. Then she giggled.

He wondered if, with a lifetime of wandering in that strange blend of innocence and formidable knowledge, she knew what the word meant.

Doesn't matter, the Sadist whispered. *She took the bait.*

They rose until they were high in the Black, comfortably above his inner web.

Better? she asked shyly.

Much better, he answered, fitting his mouth to hers.

He kissed her until she relaxed, and then he sighed again.

Hurry, the Sadist whispered.

He leaned his forehead against hers and yelped when the tiny spiral horn jabbed him.

She giggled and kissed his forehead. *Kisses make it better?*

Revulsion swamped him for a moment. That was a child's voice. A *young* child's voice.

He looked over her shoulder, trying to reconcile the female shape wrapped around him with that voice, and saw fragments of shattered crystal floating through the Black.

Pieces of her. Pieces and pieces of her. Part of her was still intact. Had to be. The part that held the knowledge of the Craft. How could she have put him together otherwise? But if she kept slipping in and out of those fragments . . .

Like Tersa. Worse than Tersa.

Daemon?

The midnight voice, with a deadly edge to it.

Remember this side of her, the Sadist warned. *Ignore the rest.*

Daemon smiled at her. *Lover,* he said, nipping her lower lip. Then he used every trick he'd ever learned to sweeten the bait.

But he wouldn't let her raise her hips to sheathe him.

Still too dark, he gasped when she began to whimper and snarl. *Let's go to the Red. It's my Birthright.*

She tried to shake off the seduction tendrils he'd woven around her, but he'd spun his trap well.

We can have a bed there, he coaxed.

She shuddered. Whimpered. There was no pleasure in the sound.

An image appeared. A bed just big enough for the game. A bed with straps attached to the ends to tie down wrists and ankles.

He dismissed the image and replaced it with his own. A large room with deep, soft carpets. A huge bed, its canopy made of gauze and velvet. Silk sheets and downy covers. Mounds of pillows. The only light came from a slow-burning fire and dozens of scented candles.

Blinded by romance, she sighed and melted against him.

He held the image, teasing, tantalizing as they rose to the Red.

As they settled among the silk and pillows, he tried to reach for some link—his body, the Priest, anything—and choked on frustration. So close. So close and there was nothing for him to tap into to finish it—except the power Jaenelle had shaped around his chalice to hold the pieces together.

Caressing and soothing, loving and lying, he kept her focused on the pleasure while he cautiously sipped the power forming the skin inside the chalice.

The skin shrank. The top fragments wobbled but held.

Enough.

He reached for Saetan. Found exhaustion and a killing fury.

He struck first. *Hush, Priest.* He waited a moment, tapped a little more of the power holding the chalice together. *Use whatever you can now to form a tether. And prepare for a fight. I'm bringing her back.*

He reached for his body next. It was still stretched out on the Altar, next to Jaenelle. He strengthened the connection enough so that his body imitated his movements.

Smiling, Daemon slowly rolled on top of her. Gently pinned her hands on either side of her head.

He kissed her, nuzzled her as they rose and rose and rose.

She rubbed against him. *Lover,* she whimpered.

Soon, he lied. *Soon.*

Up and up.

He was moments away from slipping back into his body when her eyes widened and she felt the trap spring around her.

No! she screamed.

Baring his teeth, he slammed both of them back into their bodies.

Her screams filled the Altar room. Blood gushed between her legs.

"Heal the body, Jaenelle!" Daemon shouted, fighting to keep her connected to her body while she tried to throw him off. *"Heal it!"*

Her fear pounded against his mind.

You lied to me. You LIED!

I would have said anything, done anything to get you back, he roared, his nails digging in to hold her. *Heal it!*

Letmego letmego letmego.

Bodies fought. Selves fought. As they tangled furiously, he felt Saetan slip the tether around her leg.

One flick of the power within her would tear him apart, would set her free. Instead she begged, pleaded.

Daemon, please. You're my friend. Please.

It hurt to hear her beg.

Witch-child. Saetan's voice, cracked and trembling.

Jaenelle stopped fighting. *Saetan?*

We don't want to lose you, witch-child.

You won't lose me. I can see you all in the misty place.

Saetan's words came slowly, as if each one pained him. *No, Jaenelle. You won't see us in the misty place. If you don't heal your body, Daemon and I will be destroyed.*

Daemon's breath hissed through his teeth. The Sadist wasn't the only one who could spin a deadly trap.

Her wail filled their minds, filled his ears as the child body echoed the sound.

He felt a tidal wave of dark power rush up out of the abyss, felt it fill the young body he held in his arms, felt it mend torn flesh.

Her body relaxed, went limp.

Daemon raised a shaking hand to stroke her golden hair.

"I'm sick," Jaenelle said, her voice muffled against his chest.

"No, sweetheart," he corrected gently. "You're hurt. That's different. But we'll get you to a safe place and—"

The Sanctuary shook as someone unleashed a dark Jewel.

An angry male voice changed to a terrified shriek.

Jaenelle screamed.

Daemon dove into the abyss a second before she did, catching her at the Red as she tried to flee the body.

Sucking the power from the chalice, he held onto her.

Pieces wobbled.

No, Daemon, Jaenelle shrieked. *You can't. You *can't.** Suddenly she collapsed against his chest. *I healed the body. It's still hurt, but it will mend. Let me go. Please, let me go. You can have the body. You can use the body.*

Daemon pressed her back against his chest. He rested his cheek against her gold mane. *No, sweetheart. No one's going to use your body but you.* He closed his eyes and held her tight. *Listen, my Lady Witch. I lied to you, and I'm sorry. So very sorry. But I lied because I love you. I hope you'll understand that one day.*

She sagged against him, saying nothing.

Listen to me, he said softly. *We're going to take your body away from here. We'll keep it safe. Is there some landmark in the misty place that you can always find?*

She nodded wearily.

There's a tether around your leg. Take it off and tie it around that landmark. That way, when you're ready, it'll show you the way back. It took him a moment to say the rest. *Please, Jaenelle, please repair the chalice. Find the shards and put it back together. Return to the body when the Priest tells you it's safe. Grow up and have a rich life. We need you,

Lady. Come back and walk among those who love you, those who have longed for you.★

He let her go.

She hesitated a moment before leaping away from him. When there was enough distance between them, she turned around.

Daemon swallowed hard. ★Try to remember that I love you. And if you can, please forgive me.★

He felt her lightly touch his mind, felt her dark power reform the thin skin that held him together.

She closed her sapphire eyes.

He watched her shape change.

When she opened her eyes, Jaenelle stood before him, not quite a woman but no longer a child. ★Daemon,★ she said, her voice a soft, sighing caress.

Then she dove into the abyss, and his heart shattered.

He made the ascent for the last time and tumbled into his body.

He heard angry male voices coming from the outer rooms. He heard shrieks of pain. Heard stone exploding. Heard the sizzle of power meeting power.

He didn't move. Didn't try. He laid his head on Jaenelle's chest and wept silently, bitterly.

★Daemon.★ Saetan brushed against his mind and pulled back. ★Daemon, what have you done?★

★I let her go,★ Daemon cried. ★I told her you'd tell her when it was safe to come back. I told her about the tether. I let her go, Priest. Sweet Darkness, I let her go.★

★What have you done to yourself?★

★I shattered the chalice. I lied to her. I seduced her into trusting me and *I lied to her.*★

A brief touch, gentle and hesitant. ★She'll understand, namesake. In time, she'll understand.★ Saetan faded, came back. ★I can't hold the link anymore. Cassandra will open the Gate and take you—★

Saetan was gone.

Daemon wiped his face with his sleeve. A little longer. He had to hold on a little longer. But he felt so empty, so terribly alone.

The sounds of fighting got closer. Closer.

Cassandra burst into the room. "There's no time left."

Daemon slid from the Altar and collapsed.

Ignoring him, Cassandra rushed over to the Altar and brushed her hand over Jaenelle's head. "You didn't bring her back."

Her anger sliced through the thin skin of power holding the chalice together, leaving weak spots.

"The body is healing," Daemon said hoarsely. "If you keep it safe, it will mend. And—"

Cassandra made a sharp, dismissive gesture.

Daemon cringed. The Altar room blurred. Sounds became muffled. He struggled to focus. Struggled to stand up.

By the time he was braced against the Altar, the bloody sheet was lying on the floor, Jaenelle was wrapped in a clean blanket, the black candles were lit, and the wall behind the Altar was turning to mist.

"How much time do you need?" Daemon asked.

Cassandra cradled Jaenelle in her arms and glanced at the mist. "Aren't you coming through the Gate?"

He wanted to go with them. Sweet Darkness, how he needed to go with them. But there was Surreal, who would keep fighting until he gave her a signal or she was destroyed.

And there was Lucivar.

Daemon shook his head. "Go," he whispered as tears filled his eyes. "Go."

"Count to ten," Cassandra said. "Then get rid of the candles. They won't be able to open the Gate without them." Holding Jaenelle tightly, she stepped into the mist and disappeared.

A male voice shouted, "There's a light!"

Surreal rushed into the Altar room. "I threw up a couple of shields to slow them down, but nothing short of blowing this place apart is going to hold them."

. . . four, five, six . . .

The Sanctuary rocked as the combined power of several Jewels blasted through one of the shields.

"Sadi, where . . ."

Another blast of power.

"Damn," Surreal hissed, pulling her knife from its sheath.

The angry voices came closer.

. . . eight, nine, ten.

Daemon tried to vanish the black candles. Not even that much power left. "Vanish the candles, Surreal. Hurry."

Surreal vanished the candles, grabbed Daemon's wrist, and hauled him through the stone wall just as Briarwood's uncles reached the Altar room's wrought-iron gate.

He wasn't prepared for a long pass through stone walls, and Surreal's attempt to shield him wasn't quite enough. By the time they finally got through the outside wall, his clothes were shredded and most of his skin was scraped raw.

"Shit, Sadi," Surreal said, grabbing him when his legs buckled. Using Craft to keep him upright, she studied his face. "Is she safe?"

Safe? He desperately needed to believe she was safe, that she would come back.

He started to cry.

Surreal wrapped her arms around him. "Come on, Daemon. I'll take you to Deje's. They'll never think to look for you in a Chaillot Red Moon house."

Before he could say anything, she caught the Green Web, taking him with her, first heading toward Pruul, then doubling back on other Webs, and finally heading for Chaillot and Deje's Red Moon house.

Daemon clung to Surreal as she flew along the Winds, too weak to argue, too spent to care. His heart, however . . . His heart held on fiercely to Jaenelle's soft, sighing caress of his name.

Everything has a price.

HEIR
TO THE
SHADOWS

BOOK II

PROLOGUE

Kaeleer

The Dark Council reconvened.

Andulvar Yaslana, the demon-dead Eyrien Warlord Prince, folded his dark wings and assessed the other Council members, not liking what he saw. Except for the Tribunal, who had to attend, only two-thirds of the members were required at each session to listen to petitions or pass judgment when disputes occurred between the Blood in Kaeleer that couldn't be settled by the Territory Queens. Tonight every chair was filled, except the one beside Andulvar.

But the chair's occupant was also there, standing patiently in the petitioner's circle, waiting for the Council's answer. He was a brown-skinned, golden-eyed man, with thick black hair that was silvered at the temples. Seeing him leaning on the elegant, silver-headed cane, one might simply have said he was a handsome Blood male at the end of his prime. His long, black-tinted nails and the Black-Jeweled ring on his right hand said otherwise.

First Tribune quietly cleared his throat. "Prince Saetan Daemon SaDiablo, you stand before the Council requesting guardianship of the child Jaenelle Angelline. You did not, as is customary in a Blood dispute, provide us with the information needed to contact the girl's family so that they could come here and speak on their own behalf."

"They don't want the child," was the quiet reply. "I do."

"We have only your word on that, High Lord."

Fools, Andulvar thought, watching the barely perceptible rise and fall of Saetan's chest.

First Tribune continued. "The most troubling aspect of this petition is that you're a Guardian, one of the living dead, and yet you want us to place the welfare of a living child into your hands."

"Not just any child, Tribune. *This* child."

First Tribune shifted uneasily in his chair. His eyes swept over the tiered seats on both sides of the large room. "Because of the . . . unusual . . . circumstances, the decision will have to be unanimous. Do you understand?"

"I understand, Tribune. I understand very well."

First Tribune cleared his throat again. "A vote will now be taken on the petition of Saetan Daemon SaDiablo for the guardianship of the child Jaenelle Angelline. Those opposed?"

A number of hands went up, and Andulvar shuddered at the peculiar, glazed look in Saetan's eyes.

After the hands were counted, no one spoke, no one moved.

"Take the vote again," Saetan said too softly.

When First Tribune didn't respond, Second Tribune touched his arm. Within seconds, there was nothing in First Tribune's chair but a pile of ash and a black silk robe.

Mother Night, Andulvar thought as he watched body after opposing body crumble. *Mother Night.*

"Take the vote again," Saetan said too gently.

It was unanimous.

Second Tribune rubbed her hand over her heart. "Prince Saetan Daemon SaDiablo, the Council hereby grants you all paternal—"

"Parental. All *parental* rights."

"—all parental rights to the child Jaenelle Angelline, from this hour until she reaches her majority in her twentieth year."

As soon as Saetan bowed to the Tribunal and began the long walk down the room, Andulvar left his seat and opened the large double doors at the far end of the Council chamber. He sighed with relief when Saetan, leaning heavily on his silver-headed cane, slowly walked past him.

It wasn't over, Andulvar thought as he closed the doors and followed Saetan. The Council would be more subtle next time in opposing the High Lord, but there *would* be a next time.

When they finally stepped out into the fresh night air, Andulvar turned to his longtime friend. "Well, she's yours now."

Saetan lifted his face to the night sky and closed his golden eyes. "Yes, she's mine."

PART 1

CHAPTER ONE

1 / Terreille

Surrounded by guards, Lucivar Yaslana, the half-breed Eyrien Warlord Prince, walked into the courtyard, fully expecting to hear the order for his execution. There was no other reason for a salt mine slave to be brought to this courtyard, and Zuultah, the Queen of Pruul, had good reason to want him dead. Prythian, the High Priestess of Askavi, still wanted him alive, still hoped to turn him to stud. But Prythian wasn't standing in the courtyard with Zuultah.

Dorothea SaDiablo, the High Priestess of Hayll, was.

Lucivar spread his dark, membranous wings to their full span, taking advantage of Pruul's desert air to let them dry.

Lady Zuultah glanced at her Master of the Guard. A moment later, the Master's whip whistled through the air, and the lash cut deep into Lucivar's back.

Lucivar hissed through his clenched teeth and folded his wings.

"Any other acts of defiance will earn you fifty strokes," Zuultah snapped. Then she turned to confer with Dorothea SaDiablo.

What was the game? Lucivar wondered. What had brought Dorothea out of her lair in Hayll? And who was the angry Green-Jeweled Prince who stood apart from the women, clutching a folded square of cloth?

Cautiously sending out a psychic probe, Lucivar caught all the emotional scents. From Zuultah, there was excitement and the usual underlying viciousness. From Dorothea, a sense of urgency and fear. Beneath the unknown Prince's anger was grief and guilt.

Dorothea's fear was the most interesting because it meant that Daemon Sadi had not been recaptured yet.

A cruel, satisfied smile curled Lucivar's lips.

Seeing the smile, the Green-Jeweled Prince became hostile. "We're wasting time," he said sharply, taking a step toward Lucivar.

Dorothea spun around. "Prince Alexander, these things must be do—"

Philip Alexander opened the cloth, holding two corners as he spread his arms wide.

Lucivar stared at the stained sheet. So much blood. Too much blood. Blood was the living river—and the psychic thread. If he sent out a psychic probe and touched that stain . . .

Something deep within him stilled and became brittle.

Lucivar forced himself to meet Philip Alexander's hostile stare.

"A week ago, Daemon Sadi abducted my twelve-year-old niece and took her to Cassandra's Altar, where he raped and then butchered her." Philip flicked his wrists, causing the sheet to undulate.

Lucivar swallowed hard to keep his stomach down. He slowly shook his head. "He couldn't have raped her," he said, more to himself than to Philip. "He can't. . . . He's never been able to perform that way."

"Maybe it wasn't bloody enough for him before," Philip snapped. "This is Jaenelle's blood, and Sadi was recognized by the Warlords who tried to rescue her."

Lucivar turned reluctantly toward Dorothea. "Are you sure?"

"It came to my attention—unfortunately, too late—that Sadi had taken an unnatural interest in the child." Dorothea lifted her shoulders in an elegant little shrug. "Perhaps he took offense when she tried to fend off his attentions. You know as well as I do that he's capable of anything when enraged."

"You found the body?"

Dorothea hesitated. "No. That's all the Warlords found." She pointed at the sheet. "But don't take my word for it. See if even you can stomach what's locked in that blood."

Lucivar took a deep breath. The bitch was lying. She *had* to be lying. Because, sweet Darkness, if she wasn't . . .

Daemon *had* been offered his freedom in exchange for killing Jaenelle. He had refused the offer—or so he had said. But what if he *hadn't* refused?

A moment after he opened his mind and touched the bloodstained sheet, he was on his knees, spewing up the meager breakfast he'd had an hour before, shaking as something deep within him shattered.

Damn Sadi. Damn the bastard's soul to the bowels of Hell. She was a *child*! What could she have done to deserve this? She was Witch, the living myth. She was the Queen they'd dreamed of serving. She was his spitting little Cat. *Damn you, Sadi!*

The guards hauled Lucivar to his feet.

"Where is he?" Philip Alexander demanded.

Lucivar closed his gold eyes so that he wouldn't have to see that sheet. He had never felt this weary, this beaten. Not as a half-breed boy in the Eyrien hunting camps, not in the countless courts he'd served in over the centuries since, not even here in Pruul as one of Zuultah's slaves.

"Where is he?" Philip demanded again.

Lucivar opened his eyes. "How in the name of Hell should I know?"

"When the Warlords lost the trail, Sadi was heading southeast—toward Pruul. It's well-known—"

"He wouldn't come here." That shattered something deep within him began to burn. "He wouldn't dare come here."

Dorothea SaDiablo stepped toward him. "Why not? You've helped each other in the past. There's no reason—"

"There *is* a reason," Lucivar said savagely. "If I ever see that cold-blooded bastard again, I'll rip his heart out!"

Dorothea stepped back, shaken. Zuultah watched him warily.

Philip Alexander slowly lowered his arms. "He's been declared rogue. There's a price on his head. When he's found—"

"He'll be suitably punished," Dorothea broke in.

"He'll be executed!" Philip replied heatedly.

There was a moment of heavy silence.

"Prince Alexander," Dorothea purred, "even someone from Chaillot should know that, among the Blood, there is no law against murder. If you didn't have sense enough to prevent an emotionally disturbed child from toying with a Warlord Prince of Sadi's temperament . . ." She shrugged delicately. "Perhaps the child got what she deserved."

Philip paled. "She was a good girl," he said, but his voice trembled with a whisper of doubt.

"Yes," Dorothea purred. "A good girl. So good your family had to send her away every few months to be . . . reeducated."

Emotionally disturbed child. The words were a bellows, stoking the fire within Lucivar to ice-cold rage. Emotionally disturbed child. *Stay away from me, Bastard. You'd better stay away. Because if I have the chance, I'll carve you into pieces.*

At some point, Zuultah, Dorothea, and Philip had withdrawn to continue their discussion in the cooler recesses of Zuultah's house. Lucivar didn't notice. He was barely aware of being led into the salt mines, barely aware of the pick in his hands, barely aware of the pain as his sweat ran into the new lash wound on his back.

All he saw was the bloodstained sheet.

Lucivar swung the pick.

Liar.

He didn't see the wall, didn't see the salt. He saw Daemon's golden-brown chest, saw the heart beating beneath the skin.

Silky . . . court-trained . . . *liar!*

2 / Hell

Andulvar settled one hip on a corner of the large, blackwood desk.

Saetan glanced up from the letter he was composing. "I thought you were going back to your eyrie."

"Changed my mind." Andulvar's gaze wandered around the private study, finally stopping at the portrait of Cassandra, the Black-Jeweled Queen who had walked the Realms more than 50,000 years ago. Five years ago, Saetan had discovered that Cassandra had faked the final death and had become a Guardian in order to wait for the next Witch.

And look what had happened to the next Witch, Andulvar thought bleakly. Jaenelle Angelline was a powerful, extraordinary child, but still as vulnerable as any other child. All that power hadn't kept her from being overwhelmed by family secrets he and Saetan could only guess at, and by Dorothea's and Hekatah's vicious schemes to eliminate the one rival who could have ended their stranglehold on the Realm of Terreille. He was certain they had been behind the brutality that had made Jaenelle's spirit flee from her body.

Too late to prevent the violation, a friend had taken Jaenelle away from her destroyers and brought her to Cassandra's Altar. There, Daemon Sadi, with Saetan's help, had been able to bring the girl out of the psychic abyss long enough to convince her to heal the physical wounds. But when the Chaillot Warlords arrived to "rescue" her, she panicked and fled back into the abyss.

Her body was slowly healing, but only the Darkness knew where her spirit was—or if she would ever come back.

Pushing aside those thoughts, Andulvar looked at Saetan, took a deep breath, and puffed his cheeks as he let it out. "Your letter of resignation from the Dark Council?"

"I should have resigned a long time ago."

"You had always insisted that it was good to have a few of the demon-dead serving in the Council because they had experience but no personal interest in the decisions."

"Well, my interest in the Council's decisions is very personal now, isn't it?" After signing his name with his customary flourish, Saetan slipped the letter into an envelope and sealed it with black wax. "Deliver that for me, will you?"

Andulvar reluctantly took the envelope. "What if the Dark Council decides to search for her family?"

Saetan leaned back in his chair. "There hasn't been a Dark Council in Terreille since the last war between the Realms. There's no reason for Kaeleer's Council to look beyond the Shadow Realm."

"If they check the registers at Ebon Askavi, they'll find out she wasn't originally from Kaeleer."

"As the Keep's librarian, Geoffrey has already agreed not to find any useful entries that might lead anyone back to Chaillot. Besides, Jaenelle was never listed in the registers—and won't be until there's a reason to include an entry for her."

"You'll be staying at the Keep?"

"Yes."

"For how long?"

Saetan hesitated. "For as long as it takes." When Andulvar made no move to leave, he asked, "Is there something else?"

Andulvar stared at the neat masculine script on the front of the envelope. "There's a demon in the receiving room upstairs who has asked for an audience with you. He says it's important."

Saetan pushed his chair away from the desk and reached for his cane.

"They all say that—when they're brave enough to come at all. Who is he?"

"I've never seen him before," Andulvar said. Then he added reluctantly, "He's new to the Dark Realm, and he's from Hayll."

Saetan limped around the desk. "Then what does he want with me? I've had nothing to do with Hayll for seventeen hundred years."

"He wouldn't say why he wants to see you." Andulvar paused. "I don't like him."

"Naturally," Saetan replied dryly. "He's Hayllian."

Andulvar shook his head. "It's more than that. He feels tainted."

Saetan became very still. "In that case, let's talk to our Hayllian Brother," he said with malevolent gentleness.

Andulvar couldn't suppress the shudder that ran through him. Fortunately, Saetan had already turned toward the door and hadn't noticed. They'd been friends for thousands of years, had served together, laughed together, grieved together. He didn't want the man hurt because, at times, even a friend feared the High Lord of Hell.

But as Saetan opened the door and looked at him, Andulvar saw the flicker of anger in his eyes that acknowledged the shudder. Then the High Lord left the study to deal with the fool who was waiting for him.

The recently demon-dead Hayllian Warlord stood in the middle of the receiving room, his hands clasped behind his back. He was dressed all in black, including a black silk scarf wrapped around his throat.

"High Lord," he said, making a respectful bow.

"Don't you know even the basic courtesies when approaching an unknown Warlord Prince?" Saetan asked mildly.

"High Lord?" the man stammered.

"A man doesn't hide his hands unless he's concealing a weapon," Andulvar said, coming into the room. He spread his dark wings, completely blocking the door.

Fury flashed over the Warlord's face and was gone. He extended his arms out in front of him. "My hands are quite useless."

Saetan glanced at the black-gloved hands. The right one was curled into a claw. There was one finger missing on the left. "Your name?"

The Warlord hesitated a moment too long. "Greer, High Lord."

Even the man's name somehow fouled the air. No, not just the man, although it would take a few weeks for the rotting-meat stink to fade. Something else. Saetan's gaze drifted to the black silk scarf. His nostrils flared as he caught a scent he remembered too well. So. Hekatah still favored that particular perfume.

"What do you want, Lord Greer?" Saetan asked, already certain he knew why Hekatah would send someone to see him. With effort, he hid the icy rage that burned within him.

Greer stared at the floor. "I . . . I was wondering if you had any news about the young witch."

The room felt so deliciously cold, so sweetly dark. One thought, one flick of his mind, one brief touch of the Black Jewels' strength and there wouldn't be enough left of that Warlord to be even a whisper in the Darkness.

"I rule Hell, Greer," Saetan said too softly. "Why should I care about a Hayllian witch, young or otherwise?"

"She wasn't from Hayll." Greer hesitated. "I had understood you were a friend of hers."

Saetan raised one eyebrow. "I?"

Greer licked his lips. The words rushed out. "I was assigned to the Hayllian embassy in Beldon Mor, the capital of Chaillot, and had the privilege of meeting Jaenelle. When the trouble started, I betrayed the High Priestess of Hayll's trust by helping Daemon Sadi get the girl to safety." His left hand fumbled with the scarf around his neck and finally pulled it away. "This was my reward."

Lying bastard, Saetan thought. If he didn't have his own use for this walking piece of carrion, he would have ripped through Greer's mind and found out what part the man had *really* played in this.

"I knew the girl," Saetan snarled as he walked toward the door.

Greer took a step forward. "Knew her? Is she . . ."

Saetan spun around. "She walks among the *cildru dyathe*!"

Greer bowed his head. "May the Darkness be merciful."

"Get out." Saetan stepped aside, not wanting to be fouled by any contact with the man.

Andulvar folded his wings and escorted Greer from the Hall. He returned a few minutes later, looking worried. Saetan stared at him, no longer caring that the rage and hatred showed in his eyes.

Andulvar settled into an Eyrien fighting stance, his feet apart to balance his weight, his wings slightly spread. "You know that statement will spread through Hell faster than the scent of fresh blood."

Saetan gripped the cane with both hands. "I don't give a damn who else he tells as long as that bastard tells the bitch who sent him."

"He said that? He really said that?"

Slumped in the only chair in the room, Greer nodded wearily.

Hekatah, the self-proclaimed High Priestess of Hell, twirled around the room, her long black hair flying out behind her as she spun.

This was even better than simply destroying the child. Now, with her torn mind and torn, dead body, the girl would be an invisible knife in Saetan's ribs, always twisting and twisting, a constant reminder that he wasn't the only power to contend with.

Hekatah stopped spinning, tipped her head back, and flung her arms up in triumph. "She walks among the *cildru dyathe*!" Sinking gracefully to the floor, she leaned against an arm of Greer's chair and gently stroked his cheek. "And you, my sweet, were responsible for that. She's of no use to him now."

"The girl is no longer useful to you either, Priestess."

Hekatah pouted coquettishly, her gold eyes glittering with malice. "No longer useful for my original plans, but she'll be an excellent weapon against that gutter son of a whore."

Seeing Greer's blank expression, Hekatah rose to her feet, slapping the dust from her gown as she *tsked* in irritation. "Your body is dead, not your mind. Do try to think, Greer darling. Who else was interested in the child?"

Greer sat up and slowly smiled. "Daemon Sadi."

"Daemon Sadi," Hekatah agreed smugly. "How pleased do you think he'll be when he finds out his little darling is so very, very dead? And who, with a little help, do you think he'll blame for her departure from the living? Think of the fun pitting the son against the father. And if they destroy each other"—Hekatah opened her arms wide—"Hell will fragment once more, and the ones who were always too frightened to defy him will rally around me. With the strength of the demon-dead behind us, Terreille will finally kneel to me as *the* High Priestess, as it would have done all those many, many centuries ago if that bastard hadn't always thwarted my ambition."

She looked around the small, almost-empty room in distaste. "Once he's gone, I'll reside again in the splendor that's my due. And you, my faithful darling, will serve at my side."

"Come," she said, guiding him into another small room. "I realize the body's death is a shock . . ."

Greer stared at the boy and girl cowering in a pile of straw.

"We're demons, Greer," Hekatah said, stroking his arm. "We need fresh, hot blood. With it, we can keep our dead flesh strong. And although some pleasures of the flesh are no longer possible, there are compensations."

Hekatah leaned against him, her lips close to his ear. "Landen children. A Blood child is better but more difficult to come by. But dining on a landen child also has compensations."

Greer was breathing fast, as if he needed air.

"A pretty little girl, don't you think, Greer? At your first psychic touch, her mind will burn to hot ash, but primitive emotions will remain . . . long enough . . . and fear is a delicious dinner."

3 / Terreille

You are my instrument.

Daemon Sadi shifted restlessly on the small bed that had been set up in one of the storage rooms beneath Deje's Red Moon house.

. . . *you are my instrument* . . . riding the Winds to Cassandra's Altar . . . Surreal already there, crying . . . Cassandra there, angry . . . so much blood . . . his hands covered with Jaenelle's blood . . . descending into the abyss . . . falling, screaming . . . a child who wasn't a child . . . a narrow bed with straps to tie down hands and feet . . . a sumptuous bed with silk sheets . . . the Dark Altar's cold stone . . . black candles . . . scented candles . . . a child screaming . . . his tongue licking a tiny spiral horn . . . his body pinning hers to cold stone while she fought and screamed . . . begging her to forgive him . . . but what had he done? . . . a golden mane . . . his fingers tickling a fawn tail . . . a narrow bed with silk sheets . . . a sumptuous bed with straps . . . *forgive me, forgive me* . . . his body pinning her down . . . what had he done? . . . Cassandra's anger cutting him . . . was she safe? . . . was she well? . . . a sumptuous stone bed . . . silk sheets with straps . . . a child screaming . . . so much blood . . . *you are my instrument . . . forgive me, forgive me . . .* WHAT HAD HE DONE?

Surreal sagged against the wall and listened to Daemon's muffled sobs. Who would have suspected that the Sadist could be so vulnerable? She and Deje knew enough basic healing Craft to heal his body, but neither of them knew how to fix the mental and emotional wounds. Instead of becoming stronger, he was becoming more fragile, vulnerable.

For the first few days after she had brought him here, he had kept asking what had happened. But she could tell him only what she knew.

With the help of the demon-dead girl, Rose, she had entered Briarwood, killed the Warlord who had raped Jaenelle, and then had taken Jaenelle to the Sanctuary called Cassandra's Altar. Daemon had joined her at the Sanctuary. Cassandra was there, too. Daemon had ordered them out of the Altar room in order to have privacy to try to bring Jaenelle's Self back to her body. Surreal had used that time to set traps for Briarwood's "rescue party." When the males arrived, she had held them off for as long as she could. By the time she'd retreated to the Altar room, Cassandra and Jaenelle were gone and Daemon could barely stand. She and Daemon had ridden the Winds back to Beldon Mor and had spent the last three weeks hiding in Deje's Red Moon house.

That's all she could tell him. It wasn't what he needed to hear. She couldn't tell him he had saved Jaenelle. She couldn't tell him the girl was safe and well. And it seemed like the more he struggled to remember, the more fragmented the memories became. But he still had the strength of the Black Jewels, still had the ability to unleash all of that dark power. If he lost his tenuous hold on sanity . . .

Surreal turned at the sound of a stealthy footfall on the stairs at the end of the dim passageway. The sobs behind the closed door stopped.

Moving swiftly, silently, Surreal cornered the woman at the bottom of the stairs. "What do you want, Deje?"

The dishes on the tray Deje was carrying rattled as the woman's body shook. "I—I thought—" She lifted the tray in explanation. "Sandwiches. Some tea. I—"

Surreal frowned. Why was Deje staring at her breasts? It wasn't the look of an efficient matron sizing up one of the girls. And why was Deje shaking like that?

Surreal looked down. Her clenched hand was holding her favorite stiletto, its tip resting against the Gray Jewel that hung on its gold chain above the swell of her breasts. She hadn't been aware of calling in the stiletto or of calling in the Gray. She had been annoyed with the intrusion, but . . .

Surreal vanished the stiletto, pulled her shirt together to hide the Jewel, and took the tray from Deje. "Sorry. I'm a bit edgy."

"The Gray," Deje whispered. "You wear the Gray."

Surreal tensed. "Not when I'm working in a Red Moon house."

Deje didn't seem to hear. "I didn't know you were that strong."

Surreal shifted the tray's weight to her left hand and casually let her right hand drop to her side, her fingers curled around the stiletto's comforting weight. If it had to be done, it would be fast and clean. Deje deserved that much.

She watched Deje's face while the woman mentally rearranged the bits of information she knew about the whore named Surreal, who was also an assassin. When Deje finally looked at her, there was respect and dark satisfaction in the woman's eyes.

Then Deje looked at the tray and frowned. "Best use a warming spell on that tea or it won't be fit to drink."

"I'll take care of it," Surreal said.

Deje started back up the stairs.

"Deje," Surreal said quietly. "I do pay my debts."

Deje gave her a sharp smile and nodded at the tray. "You try to get some food into him. He's got to get his strength back."

Surreal waited until the door at the top of the stairs clicked shut before returning to the storage room that held, perhaps now more than ever, the most dangerous Warlord Prince in the Realm.

Late that evening, Surreal opened the storage room's door without knocking and pulled up short. "What in the name of Hell are you doing?"

Daemon glanced up at her before tying his other shoe. "I'm getting dressed." His deep, cultured voice had a rougher edge than usual.

"Are you mad?" Surreal bit her lip, regretting the word.

"Perhaps." Daemon fastened his ruby cuff links to his white silk shirt. "I have to find out what happened, Surreal. I have to find *her.*"

Exasperated, Surreal scraped her fingers through her hair. "You can't leave in the middle of the night. Besides, it's bitter cold out."

"The middle of the night is the best time, don't you think?" Daemon replied too calmly, shrugging into his black jacket.

"No, I don't. At least wait until dawn."

"I'm Hayllian. This is Chaillot. I'd be a bit too conspicuous in day-light." Daemon looked around the empty little room, lifted his shoulders in a dismissive shrug, took a comb from his coat pocket, and pulled it through his thick black hair. When he was done, he slipped his elegant, long-nailed hands into his trouser pockets and raised an eyebrow as if ask-ing, Well?

Surreal studied the tall, trim but muscular body in its perfectly tailored black suit. Sadi's golden-brown skin was gray-tinged from exhaustion, his face looked haggard, and the skin around his golden eyes was puffy. But even now he was still more beautiful than a man had a right to be.

"You look like shit," she snapped.

Daemon flinched, as if her anger had cut him. Then he tried to smile. "Don't try to turn my head with compliments, Surreal."

Surreal clenched her hands. The only thing to throw at him was the tray with the tea and sandwiches on it. Seeing the clean cup and the un-touched food ignited her temper. "You fool, you didn't eat anything!"

"Lower your voice unless you want everyone to know I'm here."

Surreal paced back and forth, snarling every curse she could remember. "Don't cry, Surreal."

His arms were around her, and beneath her cheek was cool silk.

"I'm not crying," she snapped, gulping back a sob.

She felt rather than heard his chuckle. "My mistake." His lips brushed her hair before he stepped away from her.

Surreal sniffed loudly, wiped her eyes on her sleeve, and pushed her hair from her face. "You're not strong enough yet, Daemon."

"I'm not going to get any better until I find her," Daemon said quietly.

"Do you know how to open the Gates?" she asked. Those thirteen places of power linked the Realms of Terreille, Kaeleer, and Hell.

"No. But I'll find someone who does know." Daemon took a deep breath. "Listen, Surreal, and listen well. There are very few people in the entire Realm of Terreille who can connect you in any way with me. I've made the effort to make sure of that. So unless you stand on the roof and announce it, no one in Beldon Mor will have a reason to look in your di-rection. Keep your head down. Keep a rein on that temper of yours.

You've done more than enough. Don't get yourself in any deeper—because I won't be around to help you out of it."

Surreal swallowed hard. "Daemon . . . you've been declared rogue. There's a price on your head."

"Not unexpected after I broke the Ring of Obedience."

Surreal hesitated. "Are you sure Cassandra took Jaenelle to one of the other Realms?"

"Yes, I'm sure of that much," he said softly, bleakly.

"So you're going to find a Priestess who knows how to open the Gates and follow them."

"Yes. But I have one stop to make first."

"This isn't a good time for social calls," Surreal said tartly.

"This isn't exactly a social call. Dorothea can't use you against me because she doesn't know about you. But she knows about him, and she's used him before. I'm not going to give her the chance. Besides, for all his arrogance and temper, he's a damn good Warlord Prince."

Weary, Surreal leaned against the wall. "What are you going to do?"

Daemon hesitated. "I'm going to get Lucivar out of Pruul."

4 / Kaeleer

Saetan appeared on the small landing web carved into the stone floor of one of the Keep's many outer courtyards. As he stepped off the web, he looked up.

Unless one knew what to look for, one only saw the black mountain called Ebon Askavi, only felt the weight of all that dark stone. But Ebon Askavi was also the Keep, the Sanctuary of Witch, the repository of the Blood's long, long history. A place well and fiercely guarded. The perfect place for a secret.

Damn Hekatah, he thought bitterly as he slowly crossed the courtyard, leaning heavily on his cane. *Damn her and her schemes for power. Greedy, malicious bitch*. He'd stayed his hand in the past because he felt he owed her something for bearing his first two sons. But that debt had been paid. More than paid. This time, he would sacrifice his honor, his self-respect, and anything else he had to if that was the price he had to pay to stop her.

"Saetan."

Geoffrey, the Keep's historian/librarian, stepped from the shadow of the doorway. As always, he was neatly dressed in a slim black tunic and trousers and bare of any ornamentation except his Red Jewel ring. As always, his black hair was carefully combed back, drawing a person's eyes to the prominent widow's peak. But his black eyes looked like small lumps of coal instead of highly polished stone.

As Saetan walked toward him, the vertical line between Geoffrey's black eyebrows deepened. "Come to the library and have a glass of yarbarah with me," Geoffrey said.

Saetan shook his head. "Later perhaps."

Geoffrey's eyebrows pulled down farther, echoing his widow's peak. "Anger has no place in a sickroom. Especially now. Especially yours."

The two Guardians studied each other. Saetan looked away first.

Once they were settled into comfortable chairs and Geoffrey had poured a warmed glass of the blood wine for each of them, Saetan forced himself to look at the large blackwood table that dominated the room. It was usually piled with history, Craft, and reference books Geoffrey had pulled from the stacks—books the two men had searched for touchstones to understand Jaenelle's casual but stunning remarks and her sometimes quirky but awesome abilities. Now it was empty. And the emptiness hurt.

"Have you no hope, Geoffrey?" Saetan asked quietly.

"What?" Geoffrey glanced at the table, then looked away. "I needed . . . occupation. Sitting there, each book was a reminder, and . . ."

"I understand." Saetan drained his glass and reached for his cane.

Geoffrey walked with him to the door. As Saetan went into the corridor, he felt a light, hesitant touch and turned back.

"Saetan . . . do you still hope?"

Saetan considered the question for a long moment before giving the only answer he could give. "I have to."

Cassandra closed her book, rolled her shoulders wearily, and scrubbed her face with her hands. "There's no change. She hasn't risen out of the abyss—or wherever it is she's fallen. And the longer she remains beyond the reach of another mind, the less chance we have of ever getting her back."

Saetan studied the woman with dusty-red hair and tired emerald eyes. Long, long ago when Cassandra had been Witch, the Black-Jeweled Queen, he had been her Consort and had loved her. And she, in her own way, had cared for him—until he made the Offering to the Darkness and walked away wearing Black Jewels. After that, it was more a trading of skills—his in the bed for hers in the Black Widow's Craft—until she faked her own death and became a Guardian. She had played her deathbed scene so well, and his faith in her as a Queen had been so solid, it had never occurred to him that she had done it to end her reign as Witch— and to get away from him.

Now they were united again.

But as he put his arms around her, offering her comfort, he felt that inner withdrawal, that suppressed shudder of fear. She never forgot he walked dark roads that even she dared not travel, never forgot that the Dark Realm had called him High Lord while he still had been fully alive.

Saetan kissed Cassandra's forehead and stepped away. "Get some rest," he said gently. "I'll sit with her."

Cassandra looked at him, glanced at the bed, and shook her head. "Not even you can make the reach, Saetan."

Saetan looked at the pale, fragile girl lying in a sea of black silk sheets. "I know."

As Cassandra closed the door behind her, he wondered if, despite the terrible cost, she derived some small satisfaction from that fact.

He shook his head to clear his mind, pulled the chair closer to the bed, and sighed. He wished the room weren't so impersonal. He wished there were paintings to break up the long walls of polished black stone. He wished there was a young girl's clutter scattered on the blackwood furniture. He wished for so much.

But these rooms had been finished shortly before that nightmare at Cassandra's Altar. Jaenelle hadn't had the chance to imprint them with her psychic scent and make them her own. Even the small treasures she'd left here hadn't been lived with enough, handled enough to make them truly hers. There was no familiar anchor here for her to reach for as she tried to climb out of the abyss that was part of the Darkness.

Except him.

Resting one arm on the bed, Saetan leaned over and gently brushed the lank golden hair away from the too-thin face. Her body *was* healing, but slowly, because there was no one inside to help it mend. Jaenelle, his young Queen, the daughter of his soul, was lost in the Darkness—or in the inner landscape called the Twisted Kingdom. Beyond his reach.

But not, he hoped, beyond his love.

With his hand resting on her head, Saetan closed his eyes and made the inner descent to the level of the Black Jewels. Slowly, carefully, he continued downward until he could go no farther. Then he released his words into the abyss, as he had done for the past three weeks.

You're safe, witch-child. Come back. You're safe.

5 / Terreille

A hand caressed his arm, gently squeezed his shoulder.

Lucivar's temper flared at being pulled from the little sleep his pain-filled body permitted him each night. The chains that tethered his wrists and ankles to the wall weren't long enough for him to lie down and stretch out, so he slept crouched, his buttocks braced against the wall to ease the strain in his legs, his head resting on his crossed forearms, his wings loosely folded around his body.

Long nails whispered over his skin. The hand squeezed his shoulder a little harder. "Lucivar," a deep voice whispered, husky with frustration and weariness. "Wake up, Prick."

Lucivar raised his head. The moonlight coming through the cell's window slit wasn't much to see by, but it was enough. He looked at the man bending over him and, for just a moment, was glad to see his half brother. Then he bared his teeth in a feral smile. "Hello, Bastard."

Daemon released Lucivar's shoulder and stepped back, wary. "I've come to get you out of here."

Lucivar slowly rose to his feet, snarling softly at the noise the chains made. "The Sadist showing consideration? I'm touched." He lunged at Daemon, but the leg irons hobbled his stride, and Daemon glided away, just out of reach.

"Not a very enthusiastic greeting, brother," Daemon said softly.

"Did you really expect a greeting at all, *brother?*" Lucivar spat.

Daemon ran his fingers through his hair and sighed. "You know why I couldn't do anything to help you before now."

"Yes, I know why," Lucivar replied, his deep voice changing to a lethal croon. "Just as I know why you came here now."

Daemon turned away, his face hidden in the shadows.

"Do you really think setting me free will make up for it, Bastard? Do you really think I'll ever forgive you?"

"You have to forgive me," Daemon whispered. Then he shuddered.

Lucivar narrowed his gold eyes. There was an unexpected fragility in Daemon's psychic scent. At another time, it would have worried him. Now he saw it as a weapon. "You shouldn't have come here, Bastard. I swore I'd kill you if you accepted that offer, and I will."

Daemon turned to face him. "What offer?"

"Maybe trade is a better word. Your freedom for Jaenelle's life."

"I didn't accept that offer!"

Lucivar's hands closed into fists. "Then you killed her for the fun of it? Or didn't you realize she was dying under you until it was too late?"

They stared at each other.

"What are you talking about?" Daemon asked quietly.

"Cassandra's Altar," Lucivar answered just as quietly while his rage swelled, threatening to break his self-control. "You got careless this time. You left the sheet—and all that blood."

Swaying, Daemon stared at his hands. "So much blood," he whispered. "My hands were covered with it."

Tears stung Lucivar's eyes. "Why, Daemon? What did she do to deserve being hurt like that?" His voice rose. He couldn't stop it. "She was the Queen we had dreamed of serving. We had waited for her for so long. *You butchering whore, why did you have to kill her?*"

Daemon's eyes filled with a dangerous warning. "She's not dead."

Lucivar held his breath, wanting to believe. "Then where is she?"

Daemon hesitated, looked confused. "I don't know. I'm not sure."

Pain tore through Lucivar as fiercely as it had after he had probed the dried blood on the sheet. "You're not sure," he sneered. "You. The Sadist. Not sure where you buried the kill? Try a better lie."

"She's not dead!" Daemon roared.

There was a shout nearby, followed by the sound of running feet.

Daemon raised his right hand. The Black Jewel flashed. Outside the stables where the slaves were quartered, someone let out an agonized shriek. And then there was silence.

Knowing it wouldn't take that long for the guards to find enough courage to enter the stables, Lucivar bared his teeth and pushed to find a crippling weak spot. "Did you just throw her down and take her? Or did you seduce her, lie to her, tell her you loved her?"

"I *do* love her." Daemon's eyes held a shadow of doubt, a hint of fear. "I had to lie. She wouldn't listen to me. I had to lie."

"And then you seduced her to get close enough for the kill."

Daemon exploded into motion. He paced the small cell, fiercely shaking his head. "No," he said through gritted teeth. "No, no, *no!*" He spun around, grabbed Lucivar's shoulders, and shoved him against the wall. "Who told you she was dead? WHO?"

Lucivar snapped his arms up, breaking Daemon's grip. "Dorothea."

Pain flashed over Daemon's face. He stepped back. "Since when do you listen to Dorothea?" he asked bitterly. "Since when do you believe that lying bitch?"

"I don't."

"Then why—"

"Words lie. Blood doesn't." Lucivar waited for Daemon to absorb the implication. "You left the sheet, Bastard," he said savagely. "All that blood. All that pain."

"Stop," Daemon whispered, his voice shaking. "Lucivar, please. You don't understand. She was already hurt, already in pain, and I—"

"Seduced her, lied to her, raped a twelve-year-old girl."

"No!"

"Did you enjoy it, Bastard?"

"I didn't—"

"Did you enjoy touching her?"

"Lucivar, please—"

"DID YOU?"

"YES!"

With a howl of rage, Lucivar threw himself at Daemon with enough force to snap the chains—but not fast enough. He crashed to the floor, scraping the skin from his palms and knees. It took a minute for him to get his breath back. It took another minute for him to understand why he was shivering. He stared at the thick layer of ice that covered the cell's stone walls. Then he slowly got to his feet, swaying on shaking legs, feeling a bitterness so deep it lacerated his soul.

Daemon stood nearby, his hands in his trouser pockets, his face an ex-pressionless mask, his golden eyes slightly glazed and sleepy.

"I hate you," Lucivar whispered hoarsely.

"At the moment, *brother*, the feeling is very mutual," Daemon said too calmly, too gently. "I'm going to find her, Lucivar. I'm going to find her just to prove she isn't dead. And after I find her, I'm going to come back and tear out your lying tongue."

Daemon disappeared. The front of the cell exploded.

Lucivar dropped to the floor, his wings tight to his body, his arms pro-tecting his head while pebbles and sand rained down on him.

There were more shouts now. More running feet.

Lucivar sprang to his feet as the guards poured through the opening. He bared his teeth and snarled, his gold eyes shining with rage. The guards took one look at him and backed out of the cell. For the rest of the night, they blocked the opening but didn't try to enter.

Lucivar watched them, his breath whistling through clenched teeth.

He could have fought his way past the guards and followed Daemon. If Zuultah had tried to stop him by sending a bolt of pain through the Ring of Obedience around his organ, Daemon would have unleashed his strength against her. No matter how bitterly they fought with each other, he and Daemon were always united against an outside enemy.

He could have followed and forced the battle that would have de-stroyed one or both of them. Instead he remained in the cell.

He had sworn that he would kill Daemon, and he would. But he couldn't quite bring himself to destroy his brother. Not yet.

CHAPTER TWO

1 / Terreille

The knocking sounded forceful, urgent.

Dorothea SaDiablo hid her shaking hands in the folds of her nightgown and positioned herself in the middle of her bedroom, her back to the single candle-light that dimly lit the room.

She had been searching for Daemon Sadi for seven months now. In the hard light of day, with her court all around her, she could almost convince herself that he wouldn't come to Hayll, that he would stay in whatever hole he'd found to hide in. But at night, she was certain she would open a door or turn a corner and find him waiting. He would spin out the pain beyond even her imagining, and then he would kill her. The insult underneath that violence was that he wouldn't destroy her for all the things she'd done to him, he would destroy her because of that child.

That damned child. Hekatah's obsession, the High Lord's reappearance, Greer's death, her son Kartane's mysterious illness, Daemon's fury, Lucivar's sudden hatred for his half brother—all of it came back to that girl.

The doorknob turned. The door opened an inch.

"Priestess?" a male voice called softly.

Giddy relief was swiftly replaced by anger. "Come in," she snapped.

Lord Valrik, Dorothea's Master of the Guard, entered the room and bowed. "Forgive the intrusion at this hour, Priestess, but I felt you should know about this immediately." He snapped his fingers, and two guards entered, holding a man roughly by the arms.

Dorothea stared at the young Hayllian Blood male cowering between the guards. Little more than a boy really. And pretty. Just the way she liked them. Too much the way she liked them.

She took a step toward the youth, pleased at the fear in his glazed eyes. "You don't serve in my court," she purred. "Why are you here?"

"I was sent, Priestess. I was t-told to please you."

Dorothea studied him. The words sounded flat, forced. Not his words at all. There were some kinds of compulsion spells that could force a person into performing a specific set of tasks, even against his will.

She took another step toward him. "Who sent you?"

"He didn't tell me his—"

Before he could finish, Dorothea called in a dagger and drove it into his chest. Her attack was so fast and so vicious, the guards were pulled down with the youth. Then she unleashed the strength of her Red Jewel against his pitifully inadequate inner barriers and burned out his mind, leaving no one, leaving nothing to come back and haunt her.

"Take that to the woodlands beyond the city for whatever wants the carrion," she said through clenched teeth.

The guards grabbed the body and hurried out, Valrik following them.

Dorothea paced, clenching and unclenching her hands. Damn, damn, damn! She should have probed the youth's mind before destroying him so completely, should have found out for certain who had sent him. But this had to be Sadi's work! That bastard was toying with her, trying to wear down her vigilance, trying to catch her off guard.

She hid her face in her shaking hands.

Sadi was out there. Somewhere. Until he was dead. . . . *No!* Not dead. There would be *no* hope of controlling him then, and once he was demon-dead, he would surely join forces with the High Lord. And she had never forgotten the threat Saetan had made, his voice rising out of a swirling nightmare: when Daemon Sadi died, Hayll would die.

Finally exhausted, Dorothea returned to her bed. She hesitated a moment, then extinguished the candle-light completely. There was more safety in full darkness—if there was any safety at all.

Dorothea threw back her cloak's hood and took a deep breath before entering the small sitting room in the old Sanctuary. Hekatah was already sitting before the unlit hearth, her hood pulled up to hide her face. An empty ravenglass goblet sat on the table in front of her.

Dorothea called in a silver flask and set it beside the goblet.

Hekatah let out an annoyed sniff at the size of the flask, but pointed one finger at it. The flask opened and lifted from the table. Its hot, red contents poured into the goblet, which then glided through the air to Hekatah's waiting hand. She drank deeply.

Dorothea clenched her hands and waited. Finally out of patience, she snapped, "Sadi is still on the loose."

"And each day will hone his temper a little more," Hekatah said in that girlish voice that always seemed at odds with her vicious nature.

"Exactly."

Hekatah sighed like a sated woman. "That's good."

"Good?" Dorothea exploded from the chair. "You don't know him!"

"But I do know his father."

Dorothea shuddered.

Hekatah set the empty goblet on the table. "Calm yourself, Sister. I'm weaving a delicious web for Daemon Sadi, a web he won't escape from because he won't want to escape."

Dorothea went back to her chair. "Then he can be Ringed again."

Hekatah laughed softly, maliciously. "Oh, no, he'd be useless to us Ringed. But don't worry. He'll be hunting bigger prey than you." She wagged a finger at Dorothea. "I've been very busy on your behalf."

Dorothea pressed her lips together, refusing to take the bait.

Hekatah waited a minute. "He'll be going after the High Lord."

Dorothea stared. "Why?"

"To avenge the girl."

"But Greer is the one who destroyed her!"

"Sadi doesn't know that," Hekatah said. "By the time I'm done telling him the sad tale of *why* this happened to the girl, the only thing he'll want to do is tear out Saetan's heart. Naturally the High Lord will protest such action."

Dorothea sat back. It had been months since she'd felt this good. "What do you need from me?"

"A troop of guards to help me spring a trap."

"Then I'd better choose males who are expendable."

"Don't concern yourself about the guards. Sadi won't be any threat to them." Hekatah stood up, an unspoken dismissal.

When they were outside, Hekatah said coolly, "You've said nothing about my gift, Sister."

"Your gift?"

"The boy. I'd thought to keep him for myself, but you were entitled to some compensation for losing Greer. He's a most attentive servant."

"You know what to do?" Hekatah said, handing two vials to Greer.

"Yes, Priestess. But are you sure he'll go there?"

Hekatah caressed Greer's cheek. "For whatever reason, Sadi has gone to every Dark Altar, working his way east. He'll go there. It's the only Gate left before the one located near the ruins of SaDiablo Hall." She tapped her fingers against her lips and frowned. "The old Priestess there may be a problem. However, her assistant is a practical girl—a trait one finds in abundance among the less-gifted Blood. You'll be able to deal with her."

"And the old Priestess?"

Hekatah shrugged delicately. "A meal shouldn't be wasted."

Greer smiled, bowed over the hand she held out to him, and left.

Humming, Hekatah performed the first movements of a court dance. For seven months Daemon Sadi had slipped through her traps, and his retaliation every time he was driven away from a Gate had made even her most loyal servants in the Dark Realm afraid to strike at him. For seven months she had failed. But so had he.

There were very few Priestesses left in Terreille who knew how to open the Gates. Those who hadn't gone into hiding after her first warning had been eliminated.

It had cost her some of her strongest demons, but she'd made sure Sadi never had time to figure out for himself how to light the black candles in the correct sequence to open a Gate. Of course, if he had gone straight to Ebon Askavi, his search would have ended months ago. But she had spent century upon century turning a natural awe of the place into a subtle terror—which wasn't difficult since the one time she had been inside the Keep the place had terrified *her*. Now, *no one* in Terreille would willingly go there to ask for help or sanctuary unless he was desperate enough to risk anything—and most of the time, not even then.

So Sadi, with no safe place to go and no one he could trust, would continue hiding, searching, running. When he finally got to the Gate where she would be waiting, the strain of the past months would make him all the more susceptible to what she'd planned.

"Rule Hell while you can, you gutter son of a whore," she said as she hugged herself. "This time I have the perfect weapon."

2 / Hell

Saetan opened the door of his private study and froze as the Harpy standing in the corridor drew back the bowstring and aimed her arrow at his heart.

"A rather blunt way of requesting an audience, isn't it, Titian?" he asked dryly.

"None of my weapons are blunt, High Lord," the Harpy snarled.

Saetan studied her for a moment before stepping back into the room. "Come in and say what you've come to say." Leaning heavily on his cane, he limped to the blackwood desk, settled himself on one corner, and waited.

Titian came in slowly, her anger swirling like a winter storm. She stood at the other end of the room, facing him, fearless in her fury, a demon-dead Black Widow Queen of the Dea al Mon. Once more the bowstring was drawn back, the arrow aimed at Saetan's heart.

His patience, already frayed from the unrelenting months, snapped. "Put that thing down before I do something we'll both regret."

Titian didn't waver. "Haven't you already done something you regret, High Lord? Or are you so filled with the pus of jealousy you have no room for regret?"

The walls of the Hall rumbled. "Titian," he said too softly, "I won't warn you again."

Reluctantly, Titian vanished the bow and arrow.

Saetan crossed his arms. "Actually, your forbearance surprises me, Lady. I expected to have this conversation long before now."

Titian hissed. "Then it's true? She walks among the *cildru dyathe*?"

Saetan watched the tension building in her. "And if it is?"

Titian looked at him for one awful moment, then threw back her head and keened.

Saetan stared at her, shaken. He had known the rumor would drift through Hell. He had expected that Titian, like Char, the leader of the *cildru dyathe*, would seek him out. He had expected their fury. Their fury he could face. Their hatred he could accept. But not this.

"Titian," he said, his voice unsteady. "Titian, come here."

Titian continued to keen.

Saetan limped over to her. She didn't seem to notice when he took her in his arms and held her tightly against him. He stroked her long silver hair, and murmured words of sorrow in the Old Tongue.

"Titian," he said gently when the keening faded to a whimper, "I'm truly sorry for the pain I've caused you, but it couldn't be helped."

Titian buried her fist in his belly and sent him sprawling.

"You're sorry," she snarled as she stormed around the room. "Well, so am I. I'm sorry it was only my fist and not a knife just then. You deserve to be gutted for this! Jealous old man. *Beast!* Couldn't you let her enjoy an innocent romance without tearing her apart out of spite?"

Finally able to catch his breath, Saetan propped himself up on one elbow. "Witch doesn't become *cildru dyathe*, Titian," he said coldly. "Witch doesn't become one of the demon-dead. So tell me which you prefer: that I say she walks among the *cildru dyathe*, or that I leave a vulnerable young girl open to further enemy attacks?"

Titian stopped, an arrested look in her large blue eyes. She leaned over Saetan, searching his face. "Witch can't become demon-dead?"

"No. But you and Char are the only others in Hell who know that."

"I suppose," she said slowly, "that the most convincing way to fool an enemy would be to fool a friend." She considered this for a moment more and offered him a hand up. She retrieved his cane and looked him in the eye. "A Harpy is a Harpy because of the way she died. That made it easy to believe the rumors."

That was more of an apology than he'd thought to get from Titian.

Saetan took the cane from her, grateful for the support. "I'll tell you the same thing I told Char," he said. "If you're still a friend and want to help, there is something you can do."

"What is that, High Lord?"

"Stay angry."

A fire kindled in Titian's eyes. A smile brushed her lips and was gone. "An arrow that just misses would be highly convincing."

Saetan raised one eyebrow and clucked his tongue. "A Dea al Mon witch missing a target?"

Titian shrugged. "Even the Dea al Mon don't always succeed."

"Just in case you miss missing, try not to aim for anything terribly vital," Saetan said dryly.

Titian blinked. The smile brushed her lips again. "There's only one part of a male's anatomy a Harpy aims for, High Lord. How terribly vital do you consider it?"

"Go," Saetan said.

Titian bowed and left.

Saetan stared at the study door for a moment before limping to a chair. He sank into it with a sigh, stretching out his legs. A minute later he left the study, making his way through the corridors to the upper rooms in the Hall, hoping Mephis or Andulvar would be around.

He wanted company. Male company.

Having Titian for a friend didn't make a man feel comfortable.

3 / Terreille

In the moonlight, the lawn was a ghostly silver rippled by the wind. Throughout the hot midsummer's day, storm clouds had been piling up on the horizon, and thunder had rumbled in the distance.

Surreal buttoned her jacket and hugged herself for warmth. The air had turned cold. An hour from now the storm would break over Beldon Mor. But she would be back at Deje's Red Moon house by then, the guest of honor at her quiet retirement dinner.

After that night at Cassandra's Altar, she had discovered that she no longer had the stomach for playing the bed, not even when it would have made a kill easier. She wouldn't starve if she gave up whoring. Lord Marcus, Sadi's man of business, also handled her investments and handled them well. Besides, she'd always preferred being an assassin to being a whore.

Surreal shook her head. She could think about that later.

Moving silently through the small shrub garden that backed the lawn, she reached the large tree with the branch that was perfect for a swing. Something hung from that branch, but it wasn't a child's toy.

Surreal looked up, trying to feel the ghostly presence, trying to see the transparent shape.

"You won't find her," a girl's voice said. "Marjane is gone."

Surreal spun around and stared at the girl with the slit throat and bloody dress. She'd met Rose seven months ago when Jaenelle had shown her Briarwood's awful secret. The next night, she and Rose had gotten Jaenelle out of Briarwood, but too late to stop the vicious rape.

"What happened to her?" Surreal said, glancing toward the tree. A silly thing to ask about a girl long dead.

Rose shrugged. "She faded. All the old ghosts have finally returned to the Darkness." She studied Surreal. "Why are you here?"

Surreal took a deep breath. "I came to say good-bye. I'm leaving Chaillot in the morning—and I'm not coming back."

Rose thought about this. "If you hold my hand, maybe you'll be able to see Dannie. I don't know how Jaenelle always saw the ghosts. Even after I became a demon, I couldn't see the oldest ones unless she was here. She said that was because this was one of the living Realms."

Surreal took Rose's hand. They walked toward the vegetable garden.

"Is Jaenelle all right?" Rose asked hesitantly.

Surreal pushed her windblown hair from her face. "I don't know. She was hurt very badly. A witch at Cassandra's Altar took her away to a safe place. She might have reached a Healer in time."

They stopped at the carrot patch where two redheaded sisters had been buried in secret, as all these children had been buried. But there were no shapes, no whispery voices. Surreal didn't feel the numb horror she had the first time she'd seen this garden. Now there was grief mingled with the hope that those young girls were finally beyond the memory of what had been done to them.

Dannie was the only one there. Surreal tried hard not to look at the ghostly stump where a leg should have been. Her stomach tightened as she tried even harder not to remember what had been done with that leg.

Burying her pity, Surreal sent out a psychic thread of warmth and friendship toward the ghost-girl.

Dannie smiled.

Even in death the Blood were cruel, Surreal thought as she squeezed Rose's cold hand. How empty, how lonely the years must have been for those who weren't strong enough to become demon-dead but were too strong to return to the Darkness. They remained, chained to their graves, unseen, unheard, uncared for—except by Jaenelle.

What *had* happened to her?

Surreal and Rose finally walked back to the shrub garden. "They should all be gutted," Surreal growled, releasing Rose's hand. She leaned against the tree and stared at the building. Most of the windows were dark, but there were a few dim lights. Calling in her favorite stiletto, she balanced it in her hand and smiled. "Maybe one or two can feed the garden before I go."

"No," Rose said sharply, placing herself in front of Surreal. "You can't touch any of Briarwood's uncles. No one can."

Surreal straightened, a feral expression in her gold-green eyes. "I'm very good at what I do, Rose."

"No," Rose insisted. "When Jaenelle's blood was spilled, it woke the tangled web she created. It's a trap for all the uncles."

Surreal looked at the building, then at Rose. There *had* been rumors of a mysterious illness that was affecting a number of Chaillot's high-ranking members of the council—like Robert Benedict—as well as a few special dignitaries—like Kartane SaDiablo. "This trap will kill them?"

"Eventually," Rose said.

A vicious light filled Surreal's eyes. "What about a cure?"

"Briarwood is the pretty poison. There is no cure for Briarwood."

"Is it painful?"

Rose grinned. " 'To each will come what he gave.' "

Surreal vanished her stiletto. "Then let the bastards scream."

4 / Terreille

In the light of two smoking torches, the young Priestess double-checked the tools she had placed on the Dark Altar. Everything was ready: the four-branched candelabra with its black candles, the small silver cup, and the two vials of dark liquid—one with a white stopper, the other with a red.

When the stranger with the maimed hands had given her the vials, he'd assured her that the antidote would keep her from being affected by the witch's brew that had been designed to subdue a Warlord Prince.

She paced behind the Dark Altar, chewing on her thumbnail. It had sounded so easy, and yet . . .

She froze, not even daring to breathe as she tried to see beyond the wrought-iron gate into the dark corridor. Was something there?

Nothing but a silence within the night's silence, a shadow within the shadows, gliding toward the Altar with a predator's grace.

The Priestess squatted behind the Altar, broke the seal on the white-stoppered vial, and gulped the contents. She vanished the vial and rose. When she looked toward the wrought-iron gate, she clutched her Yellow Jewel as if it might protect her.

He stood on the other side of the Altar, watching her. Despite the rumpled clothing and the disheveled hair, he exuded a cold, carnal power.

The Priestess licked her lips and rubbed her damp hands on her robe. His golden eyes looked sleepy, slightly glazed.

Then he smiled.

She shivered and took a deep breath. "Have you come for advice or assistance?"

"Assistance," he said in a deep, cultured voice. "Have you the training to open the Gate?"

How could a man be so beautiful? she thought as she nodded. "There is a price." Her voice seemed to be swallowed by the shadows.

With his left hand, he drew an envelope out of an inner pocket in his coat and laid it on the Altar. "Will that be sufficient?"

As she reached for it, she glanced at him, her hand frozen above the thick white envelope. There was something in the question, although courteously asked, that warned her it had better be enough.

She forced herself to pick up the envelope and look inside. Then she leaned against the Altar for support. Gold thousand marks. At least ten times what the stranger with the maimed hands had offered.

But she already had an agreement with the stranger, and there would be time to pocket the marks before the guards arrived.

The Priestess carefully placed the envelope on the far corner of the Altar. "Most generous," she said, hoping she sounded unimpressed.

Taking a deep breath, she lifted the silver cup high over her head, then placed it carefully in front of her. She broke the seal on the red-stoppered vial, poured the contents into the cup, and held it out to him. "The journey through a Gate is a difficult undertaking. This will assist you."

He didn't take the cup.

She made an impatient sound and took a sip, trying not to gag on the bitter taste, then held out the cup.

He held it in his left hand, his nostrils flaring at the smell, but didn't drink.

A minute passed. Two.

With an imperceptible shrug, he gulped the contents of the cup.

The Priestess held her breath. How soon before it worked? How soon before the guards came?

His eyes changed. He swayed. Then he leaned across the Altar and looked at her the way a lover looks at his lady. She couldn't take her eyes off his lips. Soft. Sensual. She leaned toward him. One kiss. One sweet kiss.

Just before her lips touched his, his right hand closed around her wrist. "Bitch," he snarled softly.

Startled, she tried to pull away.

As his hand tightened, she stared at the Black-Jeweled ring.

His long nails pierced her skin. Then she felt the sharp needle prick of the snake tooth beneath his ring-finger nail, felt the venom chill her blood.

She flailed at him with her other hand, trying to reach his face, trying to scream for help as her vision blurred and her lungs refused to fill with needed air.

He broke both her wrists, snapping the bones as he thrust her away from him.

"The venom in my snake tooth doesn't work as quickly as you may think," he said too quietly, too gently. "In the end, you'll be able to scream. You'll tear yourself apart doing it, but you'll scream."

Then he was gone, and there was nothing but a silence within the night's silence, a shadow within the shadows.

By the time the guards arrived, she was screaming.

5 / Terreille

The floor rolled beneath him, teasing legs that already shook from exhaustion and were cramped by the foul witch's brew.

Behind that door was a safe place. As he reached for it, the floor rolled again, knocking his feet out from under him. His shoulder hit the door, cracking the old, rotting wood, and he fell into the room, landing heavily on his side.

"Bitch," he snarled softly.

Gray mist. A shattered crystal chalice. Black candles. Golden hair. Blood. So much blood.

Words lie. Blood doesn't.

"Shut up, Prick," he rasped.

The floor kept rolling under him. He dug his long nails into the wood, trying to keep his balance, trying to think.

His fever was dangerously high, and he knew he needed food, water, and rest. Right now, he was prey to whoever might think to look for him in this abandoned house where he had spent his earliest years with Tersa, his real mother.

Everything has a price.

If he had given up outside that Sanctuary three days ago, if he had let the Hayllian guards find him, he might not have become so ill from the brew. But he had ruthlessly pushed his body to the point of collapse in order to reach the Gate near the ruins of SaDiablo Hall.

And every time exhaustion crept in, every time his strength of will slipped a little, a gray mist began to cloud his mind, a mist he knew held something very, very terrible. Something he didn't want to see.

You are my instrument.

Words, like flickering black lightning, came out of that mist, threatening to sear his soul.

Words lie. Blood doesn't.

He was less than a mile from the Gate.

"Lucivar," he whispered. But he didn't have the strength to feel angry at his brother's betrayal.

You are my instrument.

"No." He tried to stand up, but he couldn't do it. Still, something in him required defiance. "No. I am not your instrument. I . . . am . . . Daemon . . . Sadi."

He closed his eyes, and the gray mist engulfed him.

With a groan, Daemon rolled onto his back and slowly opened his eyes. Even that was almost too much effort. At first, he wondered if he had gone blind. Then he began to make out dim shapes in the darkness.

Night. It was night.

Breathing slowly, he began to assess the physical damage.

He felt as dry as touchwood, as inflexible as stone. His muscles burned. His belly ached from hunger, and the craving for water was fierce. The fever had broken at some point, but . . .

Something was *wrong*.

Words lie. Blood doesn't.

The words Lucivar had spoken swam round and round, growing larger, growing solid. They crashed against his mind, fragmenting it further.

Daemon screamed.

You are my instrument.

As Saetan's words thundered inside him, there was more pain—and there was fear. Fear that the mist filling his mind might part and show him something terrible.

Daemon.

Holding on fiercely to the memory of Jaenelle saying his name like a soft, sighing caress, Daemon got to his feet. As long as he could remember that, he could hold the other voices at bay.

His legs felt too heavy, but he managed to leave the house and follow the remnants of the drive that would take him to the Hall. Even though every movement was a fiery ache, by the time he reached the Hall, he was almost moving with his usual gliding stride.

But there was still something very wrong. It was hard to hold on to the Warlord Prince called Daemon Sadi, hard to hold on to his sense of self. But he had to hold on for a little while longer. He had to.

Gathering the last of his strength and will, Daemon cautiously approached the small building that held the Dark Altar.

Hekatah prowled the small building that stood in the shadow of the ruins of SaDiablo Hall. She shook her fists in the air, frustrated beyond endurance by the past three days. Even so, every time she circled the Altar, she glanced at the wall behind it, fearful it would turn to mist and Saetan would step through the Gate to challenge her.

But the High Lord was too preoccupied with his own concerns lately to pay attention to her.

Her main problem now was Daemon Sadi.

After drinking the brew she'd made, he *could not* have walked away from that Dark Altar, despite what those idiot guards swore. But if he was actually making his way to this Gate . . . By now the second part of her brew, the part that would make his mind receptive to her carefully rehearsed words, would be at its peak. She had planned to whisper all her poisoned words while she nursed him through the fever and the pain so that, when the fever broke, those words would solidify into a terrible truth he wouldn't be able to escape. Then all that strength, all that rage would become a dagger aimed right at Saetan's heart.

All her carefully made plans were being *ruined* because . . .

Hekatah jerked to a stop.

There was a silence within the night's silence.

She glanced at the unlit torches on the walls and decided against lighting them. There was enough moonlight to see by.

Not wanting to waste her strength on a sight shield, Hekatah slipped into a shadowy corner. Once he entered the Altar room, she would be behind him and could startle him with her presence.

She waited. Just when she was sure she'd been mistaken, he was there, without warning, standing just outside the wrought-iron gate, staring at the Altar. But he didn't enter the room.

Frowning, Hekatah turned her head slightly to look at the Altar. It was just as it should be. The candelabra was tarnished, and the wax from the black candles she'd burned so carefully so they wouldn't look new hung like stalactites from the silver arms.

Fearing that he might actually leave, Hekatah stepped up to the wrought-iron gate. "I've been waiting for you, Prince."

"Have you?" His voice sounded rusty, exhausted.

Perfect.

"Are you the one I should thank for the demons at the other Altars?" he asked.

How could he know she was a demon? Did he know who she was? Suddenly, she didn't feel confident about dealing with this son who was too much like his father, but she shook her head sadly. "No, Prince. There's only one power in Hell that commands demons. I'm here because I had a young friend who was very special to me. A friend, I think, we had in common. That's why I've been waiting for you."

Hell's fire! Couldn't there be *some* expression in his eyes to tell her if she was getting through to him?

"Young is a relative term, don't you think?"

He was *playing* with her! Hekatah gritted her teeth. "A child, Prince. A special child." She forced a pleading note into her voice. "I've waited here at great risk. If the High Lord finds out I've tried to tell her friends . . ." She glanced at the wall behind the Altar.

Still no reaction from the man on the other side of the gate.

"She walks among the *cildru dyathe*," Hekatah said.

A long silence. "That isn't possible," he finally said. His voice was flat, totally without emotion.

"It's *true*." Was she wrong about him? Was he only trying to escape Dorothea? No. He had cared for the girl. She sighed. "The High Lord is a jealous man, Prince. He doesn't share what he claims for himself—especially if what he claims is a female body. When he discovered the girl's affection for another male, he did nothing to prevent her from being raped. And he could have, Prince. He *could* have. The girl managed to escape afterward. In time, and with help, she would have healed. But the High Lord didn't want her to heal, so, under the pretense of helping her, he used another male to finish what was begun. It destroyed her completely. Her body died, and her mind was torn apart. Now she's a dead, blank-eyed pet he plays with."

Hekatah looked up and wanted to scream with frustration. Had he heard any of it? "He should pay for what he's done," she said shrilly. "If you've courage enough to face him, I can open the Gate for you. Someone who remembers what she could have been should demand payment for what he did."

He looked at her for a long time. Then he turned and walked away.

Swearing, Hekatah began to pace. Why did he say nothing? It was a plausible story. Oh, she knew he'd been accused of the rape, but she also knew it wasn't true. And she wasn't completely convinced that he *had* been at Cassandra's Altar that night. All the males who'd sworn they had seen him had come from Briarwood. They could have said that to keep the Chaillot Queens from looking too closely at *them*. Surely—

A scream shattered the night.

Hekatah jumped, shaken by the awful sound. Bestial, animal, human. None and all. Whatever could make a sound like that . . .

Hekatah quickly lit the black candles and waited impatiently for the wall to change to mist. Just before stepping through the Gate, she realized there was no one here to snuff out the candles and close the entrance to the other Realms. If that thing . . .

Hekatah raised her hand and Red-locked the wrought-iron gate.

Another scream tore the night.

Hekatah bolted through the Gate. She might be a demon, but she didn't want whatever that was to follow her into the Dark Realm.

Words swam round and round, slicing his mind, slicing his soul.

The gray mist parted, showing him a Dark Altar.

Blood. So much blood.

. . . he used another male . . .

The world shattered.

You are my instrument.

His mind shattered.

. . . destroyed her completely.

Screaming in agony, he fled through the mist, through a landscape washed in blood and filled with shattered crystal chalices.

Words lie. Blood doesn't.

He screamed again and tumbled into the shattered inner landscape landens called madness and the Blood called the Twisted Kingdom.

PART II

CHAPTER THREE

1 / Kaeleer

Karla, a fifteen-year-old Glacian Queen, jabbed her cousin Morton in the ribs. "Who's that?"

Morton glanced in the direction of Karla's slightly lifted chin, then went back to watching the young Warlords gathering at one end of the banquet hall. "That's Uncle Hobart's new mistress."

Karla studied the young witch through narrowed, ice-blue eyes. "She doesn't look much older than me."

"She isn't," Morton said grimly.

Karla linked arms with her cousin, finding comfort in his nearness.

Glacian society had started to change after the "accident" that had killed her parents and Morton's six years ago. A group of aristo males had immediately formed a male council "for the good of the Territory"—a council led by Hobart, a Yellow-Jeweled Warlord who was a distant relation of her father's.

Every Province Queen, after declining to become a figurehead for the council, had also refused to acknowledge the Queen of a small village that the council finally had chosen to rule the Territory. Their refusal had fractured Glacia, but it had also prevented the male council from becoming too powerful or too effective in carrying out their "adjustments" to Glacian society.

Even so, after six years there was an uneasy feel in the air, a sense of wrongness.

Karla didn't have many friends. She was a sharp-tongued, sharp-tempered Queen whose Birthright Jewel was the Sapphire. She was also a natural Black Widow and a Healer. But, since Lord Hobart was now the head of the family, she spent much of her social time with the daughters of other members of the male council—and what those girls were saying was obscene: respectable witches defer to wiser, more knowledgeable males; Blood males shouldn't have to serve or yield to Queens because they're the stronger gender; the only reason Queens and Black Widows want the power to control males is because they're sexually and emotionally incapable of being real women.

Obscene. And terrifying.

When she was younger, she had wondered why the Province Queens and the Black Widows had settled for a stalemate instead of fighting.

Glacia is locked in a cold, dark winter, the Black Widows had told her. *We must do what we can to remain strong until the spring returns.*

But would they be able to hold out for five more years until she came of age? Would *she*? Her mother's and her aunt's deaths had not been an accident. Someone had eliminated Glacia's strongest Queen and strongest Black Widow, leaving the Territory vulnerable to . . . what?

Jaenelle could have told her, but Jaenelle . . .

Karla clamped down on the bitter anger that had been simmering too close to the surface lately. Forcing her attention away from memories, she studied Hobart's mistress, then jabbed Morton in the ribs again.

"Stop that," he snapped.

Karla ignored him. "Why is she wearing a fur coat indoors?"

"It was Uncle Hobart's consummation prize."

She fingered her short, spiky, white-blond hair. "I've never seen fur like that. It's not white bear."

"I think it's Arcerian cat."

"Arcerian cat?" That couldn't be right. Most Glacians wouldn't hunt in Arceria because the cats were big, fierce predators, and the odds of a hunter not becoming the prey were less than fifty-fifty. Besides, there was something *wrong* with that fur. She could feel it even at this distance. "I'm going to pay my respects."

"Karla." There was no mistaking the warning in Morton's voice.

"Kiss kiss." She gave him a wicked smile and an affectionate squeeze before making her way to the group of women admiring the coat.

It was easy to slip in among them. Some of the women noticed her, but most were intent on the girl's—Karla couldn't bring herself to call her a Sister—hushed gossip.

"—hunters from a faraway place," the girl said.

"I've got a collar made from Arcerian fur, but it's not as luxurious as this," one of the women said enviously.

"These hunters have found a new way of harvesting the fur. Hobie told me after we'd—" She giggled.

"How?"

"It's a secret."

Coaxing murmurs.

Mesmerized by the fur, Karla touched it at the same moment the girl giggled again, and said, "They skin the cat *alive*."

She jerked her hand away, shocked numb. *Alive*.

And some of the power of the one who had lived in that fur was still there. That's what made it so luxurious.

A witch. One of the Blood Jaenelle had called kindred.

Karla swayed. They had butchered a witch.

She shoved her way out of the group of women and stumbled toward the door. A moment later, Morton was beside her, one arm around her waist. "Outside," she gasped. "I think I'm going to be sick."

As soon as they were outside, she gulped the sharp winter air and started to cry.

"Karla," Morton murmured, holding her close.

"She was a witch," Karla sobbed. "She was a witch and they skinned her alive so that little bitch could—"

She felt a shudder go through Morton. Then his arms tightened, as if he could protect her. And he *would* try to protect her, which is why she couldn't tell him about the danger she sensed every time Uncle Hobart looked at her. At sixteen, Morton had just begun his formal court training. He was the only real family she had left—and the only friend she had left.

The bitter anger boiled over without warning.

"It's been two years!" She pushed at Morton until he released her. "She's been in Kaeleer for two years, and she hasn't come to visit once!" She began pacing furiously.

"People change, Karla," Morton said cautiously. "Friends don't always remain friends."

"Not Jaenelle. Not with me. That malevolent bastard at SaDiablo Hall is keeping her chained somehow. I know it, Morton." She thumped her chest hard enough to make Morton wince. "In here, I know it."

"The Dark Council appointed him her legal guardian—"

Karla turned on him. "Don't talk to me about guardians, Lord Morton," she hissed. "I know all about 'guardians.' "

"Karla," Morton said weakly.

" 'Karla,' " she mimicked bitterly. "It's always 'Karla.' Karla's the one who's out of control. Karla's the one who's becoming emotionally unstable because of her apprenticeship in the Hourglass coven. Karla's the one who's become too excitable, too hostile, too intractable. Karla's the one who's cast aside all those delightful simpering manners that males find appealing."

"Males don't find that—"

"And Karla's the one who will gut the next son of a whoring bitch who tries to shove his hand or anything else between her legs!"

"*What?*"

Karla turned her back to Morton. Hell's fire, Mother Night, and may the Darkness be merciful. She hadn't meant to say that.

"Is that why you cut your hair like that after Uncle Hobart insisted that you come back to the family estate to live? Is that why you burned all your dresses and started wearing my old clothes?" Morton grabbed her arm and swung her around to face him. "Is it?"

Tears filled Karla's eyes. "A broken witch is a complacent witch," she said softly. "Isn't that true, Morton?"

Morton shook his head. "You wear Birthright Sapphire. There aren't any males in Glacia who wear a Jewel darker than the Green."

"A Blood male can get around a witch's strength if he waits for the right moment and has help."

Morton swore softly, viciously.

"What if that's the reason Jaenelle doesn't come to visit anymore? What if he's done to her what Uncle Hobart wants to do to me?"

Morton stepped away from her. "I'm surprised you even tolerate me being near you."

She could almost see the wounds the truth had left on his heart. There was nothing she could do now about the truth, but there *was* something she could do about the wounds. "You're family."

"I'm *male.*"

"You're Morton. The exception to the rule."

Morton hesitated, then opened his arms. "Want a hug?"

Stepping into his arms, Karla held him as fiercely as he held her.

"Listen," he said hoarsely. "Write a letter to the High Lord and ask him if Jaenelle could come for a visit. Ask for a return reply."

"The Old Fart will never let me send a courier to SaDiablo Hall," Karla muttered into his shoulder.

"Uncle Hobart isn't going to know." Morton took a deep breath. "I'll deliver the letter personally and wait for an answer."

Before Morton could offer his handkerchief, Karla stepped back, sniffed, and wiped her face on the shirt she'd taken from his wardrobe. She sniffed again and was done with paltry emotions.

"Karla," Morton said, eyeing her nervously. "You will write a *polite* letter, won't you?"

"I'll be a polite as I can be," Karla assured him.

Morton groaned.

Oh, yes. She would write to the High Lord. And, one way or another, she would get the answer she wanted.

Please. Sweet Darkness, please be my friend again. I miss you. I need you. Drawing on the strength of her Sapphire Jewels, Karla flung one word into the Darkness. *Jaenelle!*

"Karla?" Morton said, touching her arm. "The banquet is about to start. We need to put in an appearance, if only for a little while."

Karla froze, not even daring to breathe. *Jaenelle?*

Seconds passed.

"Karla?" Morton said.

Karla took a deep breath and exhaled her disappointment. She took the arm Morton offered and went back into the banquet hall.

He stayed close to her for the rest of the evening, and she was grateful for his company. But she would have traded his caring and protection in an instant if that faint but so very dark psychic touch she'd imagined had been real.

2 / Kaeleer

When Andulvar Yaslana settled in the chair in front of the blackwood desk in Saetan's public study, Saetan looked up from the letter he'd been staring at for the past half hour. "Read this," he said, handing it to Andulvar.

While Andulvar read the letter, Saetan looked wearily at the stacks of papers on his desk. It had been months since he'd set foot in the Hall, even longer since he'd granted audiences to the Queens who ruled the Provinces and Districts in his Territory. His eldest son, Mephis, had dealt with as much of the official business of Dhemlan as he could, as he had been doing for centuries, but the rest of it . . .

"Blood-sucking corpse?" Andulvar sputtered.

Saetan watched with a touch of amusement as Andulvar snarled through the rest of the letter. He hadn't been amused during his first reading, but the signature and the adolescent handwriting had soothed his temper—and added another layer to his sorrow.

Andulvar flung the letter onto the desk. "Who is Karla, and how does she dare write something like this to you?"

"Not only does she dare, but the courier is waiting for a reply."

Andulvar muttered something vicious.

"As for who she is . . ." Saetan called in the file he usually kept locked in his private study beneath the Hall. He leafed through the papers filled with his notes and handed one to Andulvar.

Andulvar's shoulders slumped as he read it. "Damn."

"Yes." Saetan put the paper back in the file and vanished it.

"What are you going to say?"

Saetan leaned back in his chair. "The truth. Or part of it. I've kept the Dark Council at bay for two years, denying their not unreasonable requests to see Jaenelle. I've given no explanation for that denial, letting them think what they chose—and I am aware of what they've chosen to think. But her friends? Until now they've been too young, or perhaps not bold enough, to ask what became of her. Now they're asking." He straightened in his chair and summoned Beale, the Red-Jeweled Warlord who worked as the Hall's butler.

"Bring the courier to me," Saetan said when Beale appeared.

"Shall I go?" Andulvar asked, making no move to leave.

Saetan shrugged, already preoccupied with how to word his reply. There hadn't been much contact between Dhemlan and Glacia in the past few years, but he'd heard enough about Lord Hobart and his ties to Little Terreille to decide on a verbal reply instead of a written one.

Long centuries ago, Little Terreille had been settled by Terreilleans who had been eager for a new life and a new land. Despite that eagerness, the people had never felt comfortable with the races who had been born to the Shadow Realm. So even though Little Terreille was a Territory in Kaeleer, it had looked for companionship and guidance from the Realm of Terreille—and still did, even though most Terreilleans no longer believed Kaeleer existed because access to this Realm had been so limited for so long. Which meant any companionship and guidance coming from Terreille now was coming from Dorothea, one way or another—and that was reason enough for him to feel wary.

Saetan and Andulvar exchanged a quick look when Beale showed the courier into the room.

Andulvar sent a thought on a Red spear thread. *He's a bit young for an official courier.*

Silently agreeing with Andulvar's assessment, Saetan lifted his right hand. A chair floated from its place by the wall and settled in front of the desk. "Please be seated, Warlord."

"Thank you, High Lord." The young man had the typical fair skin, blond hair, and blue eyes of the Glacian people. Despite his youth, he moved with the kind of assurance usually found in aristo families and responded with a confidence in Protocol that indicated court training.

Not your typical courier, Saetan thought as he watched the young man try to control the urge to fidget. *So why are you here, boyo?*

"My butler must be having a bad day to overlook introducing you when you entered," Saetan said mildly. He steepled his fingers, his long, black-tinted nails resting against his chin.

The youth paled a little when he saw the Black-Jeweled ring. He licked his lips. "My name is Morton, High Lord."

Now you're not quite so sure that Protocol will protect you, are you, boyo? Saetan didn't allow his amusement to show. If this boy was going to approach a dark-Jeweled Warlord Prince, it was better he learn the potential dangers. "And you serve?"

"I—I don't exactly serve in a court yet."

Saetan raised one eyebrow. "You serve Lord Hobart?" he asked, his voice a bit cooler.

"No. He's just the head of the family. Sort of an uncle."

Saetan picked up the letter and handed it to Morton. "Read this." He sent a thought to Andulvar. *What's the game? The boy's not experienced enough to—*

"Nooo," Morton moaned. The letter fluttered to the floor. "She promised me she'd be polite. I told her I'd be waiting for a reply, and she promised." He flushed, then paled. "I'll strangle her."

Using Craft, Saetan retrieved the letter. Whatever doubts he'd had about motive were gone, but he was curious about why the question was being asked now. "How well do you know Karla?"

"She's my cousin," Morton replied in the aggrieved tone of a ruffled male.

"You have my sympathy," Andulvar said, rustling his dark wings as he shifted in the chair.

"Thank you, sir. Having Karla like you is better than having her not like you, but . . ." Morton shrugged.

"Yes," Saetan said dryly. "I have a friend who has a similar effect on me." He chuckled softly at Morton's look of astonishment. "Boyo, even being me doesn't make a difficult witch any less difficult."

Especially a Dea al Mon Harpy, Andulvar sent, amused. *Have you recovered yet from her latest attempt to be helpful?*

If you're going to sit there, be useful, Saetan shot back.

Andulvar turned to Morton. "Did your cousin keep her promise?" When the boy gave him a blank look, he added, "Was she being polite?"

The tips of Morton's ears turned red. He shrugged helplessly. "For Karla . . . I guess so."

"Oh, Mother Night," Saetan muttered. Suddenly a thought swooped down on him, and he choked. He used the time needed to catch his breath to consider some rather nasty possibilities.

When he was finally in control again, he chose his words carefully. "Lord Morton, your uncle doesn't know you're here, does he?" Morton's nervous look was answer enough. "Where does he think you are?"

"Somewhere else."

Saetan studied Morton, fascinated by the subtle change in his posture. No longer a youth intimidated by his surroundings and the males he faced, but a Warlord protecting his young Queen. *You were wrong, boyo,* Saetan thought. *You've already chosen whom you serve.*

"Karla . . ." Morton gathered his thoughts. "It isn't easy for Karla. She wears Birthright Sapphire, and she's a Queen and a natural Black Widow as well as a Healer, and Uncle Hobart . . ."

Saetan tensed at the bitterness in Morton's blue eyes.

"She and Uncle Hobart don't get along," Morton finished lamely, looking away. When he looked back, he seemed so young and vulnerable. "I know Karla wants her to come visit like she used to, but couldn't Jaenelle just write a short note? Just to say hello?"

Saetan closed his golden eyes. *Everything has a price,* he thought. *Everything has a price.* He took a deep breath and opened his eyes. "I truly wish, with all of my being, that she could." He took another deep breath. "What I'm about to tell you must go no further than your cousin. I must have your pledge of silence."

Morton immediately nodded agreement.

"Jaenelle was seriously hurt two years ago. She can't write, she can't communicate in any way. She . . ." Saetan stopped, then resumed when he was sure he could keep his voice steady. "She doesn't know anyone."

Morton looked ill. "How?" he finally whispered.

Saetan groped for an answer. The change in Morton's expression told him he needn't have bothered. The boy had understood the silence.

"Then Karla was right," Morton said bitterly. "A male doesn't have to be that strong if he picks the right time."

Saetan snapped upright in his chair. "Is Karla being pressed to submit to a male? At *fifteen*?"

"No. I don't know. Maybe." Morton's hands clenched the arms of the chair. "She was safe enough when she lived with the Black Widows, but now that she's come back to the family estate . . ."

"Hell's fire, boy!" Saetan roared. "Even if they don't get along, why isn't your uncle protecting her?"

Morton bit his lip and said nothing.

Stunned, Saetan sank back in his chair. Not here, too. Not in Kaeleer. Didn't these fools realize what was lost when a Queen was destroyed that way?

"You have to go now," Saetan said gently.

Morton nodded and rose to leave.

"Tell Karla one other thing. If she needs it, I'll grant her sanctuary at the Hall and give her my protection. And you as well."

"Thank you," Morton said. Bowing to Saetan and Andulvar, he left.

Saetan grabbed his silver-headed cane and limped toward the door.

Andulvar got there first and pressed his hand against the door to keep it closed. "The Dark Council will be screaming for your blood if you give another girl your protection."

Saetan didn't speak for a long time. Then he gave Andulvar a purely malevolent smile. "If the Dark Council is so misguided they believe Hobart is a better guardian than I am, then they deserve to see some of Hell's more unusual landmarks, don't you think?"

3 / The Twisted Kingdom

There was no physical pain, but the agony was relentless.

Words lie. Blood doesn't.

You are my instrument.

Butchering whore.

He wandered through a mist-filled landscape full of shattered memories, shattered crystal chalices, shattered dreams.

Sometimes he heard a scream of despair.

Sometimes he even recognized his own voice.

Sometimes he caught a glimpse of a girl with long golden hair running away from him. He always followed, desperate to catch up with her, desperate to explain . . .

He couldn't remember what he needed to explain.

Don't be afraid, he called to her. Please, don't be afraid.

But she continued to run, and he continued to follow her through a landscape filled with twisting roads that ended nowhere and caverns that were strewn with bones and splashed with blood.

Down, always down.

He followed her, always begging her to wait, always pleading with her not to be afraid, always hoping to hear the sound of her voice, always yearning to hear her say his name.

If he could only remember what it was.

4 / Hell

Hekatah carefully arranged the folds of her full-length cloak while she waited for her demon guards to bring her the *cildru dyathe* boy. She sighed with satisfaction as her hands stroked the cloak's fur lining. Arcerian fur. A Warlord's fur. She could feel the rage and pain locked in his pelt.

The kindred. The four-footed Blood. Compared to humans, they had simple minds that couldn't conceive of greatness or ambition, but they were fiercely protective when they gave someone their loyalty—and equally fierce when they felt that loyalty was betrayed.

She had made a few little mistakes the last time she had tried to become the High Priestess of all the Realms, mistakes that had cost her the war between Terreille and Kaeleer 50,000 years ago. One mistake had been underestimating the strength of the Blood who lived in the Shadow Realm. The other mistake had been underestimating the kindred.

One of the first things she had done after she'd recovered from the shock of being demon-dead was to exterminate the kindred in Terreille. Some went into hiding and survived, but not enough of them. They would have had to breed with landen animals, and over time the interbreeding had probably produced a few creatures who were almost Blood, but never anything strong enough to wear a Jewel.

The wilder kindred in Kaeleer, however, had withdrawn to their own Territories after the war and had woven countless spells to protect their borders. By the time those fierce defenses had faded enough for anyone to survive passing through them, the kindred had become little more than myths.

Hekatah began to pace. Hell's fire! How long could it take for two grown males to catch a boy?

After a minute, she stopped pacing and once again arranged the folds of her cloak. She couldn't allow the boy to see any hint of her impatience. It might make him perversely stubborn. She stroked the cloak's fur lining, letting the feel of it soothe her.

During the centuries while she had waited for Terreille to ripen again into a worthy prize, she had helped the Territory of Little Terreille maintain a thread of contact with the Realm of Terreille. But it was only in the past few years that she'd established a foothold in Glacia via Lord Hobart's ambition.

She had chosen Glacia because it was a northern Territory whose people could be isolated more easily from the Blood in other Territories; it had Hobart, a male whose ambitions outstripped his abilities; and it had a Dark Altar. So for the first time in a very long time, she had a Gate at her disposal, and a way for carefully chosen males to slip into Kaeleer in order to hunt challenging prey.

That wasn't the only little game she was playing in Kaeleer, but the others required time and patience—and the assurance that nothing would interfere with her ambitions this time.

Which was why she was here on the *cildru dyathe's* island.

She was just about to question the loyalty of her demon guards when they returned, dragging a struggling boy between them. With a savage curse, they pinned the boy against a tall, flat-sided boulder.

"Don't hurt him," Hekatah snapped.

"Yes, Priestess," one of the guards replied sullenly.

Hekatah studied the boy, who glared back at her. Char, the young Warlord leader of the *cildru dyathe*. Easy enough to see how he had come by that name. How had he been able to save so much of his body from the fire? He must have had a great deal of Craft skill for one so young. She should have realized that seven years ago when she had tangled with him the first time. Well, she could easily fix that misjudgment.

Hekatah approached slowly, enjoying the wariness in the boy's eyes. "I mean you no harm, Warlord," she crooned. "I just need your help. I know Jaenelle walks among the *cildru dyathe*. I want to see her."

What was left of Char's lips curled in a vicious smile. "Not all *cildru dyathe* are on this island."

Hekatah's gold eyes snapped with fury. "You lie. Summon her. *Now!*"

"The High Lord is coming," Char said. "He'll be here any moment."

"Why?" Hekatah demanded.

"Because I sent for him."

"*Why?*"

A strange light filled Char's eyes. "I saw a butterfly yesterday."

Hekatah wanted to scream in frustration. Instead, she raised her hand, her fingers curved into a claw. "If you want your eyes, little Warlord, you'll summon Jaenelle *now*."

Char stared at her. "You truly wish to see her?"

"YES!"

Char tipped his head back and let out a strange, wild ululation.

Unnerved by the sound, Hekatah slapped him to make him stop.

"HEKATAH!"

Hekatah ran from the fury in Saetan's thundering voice. Then she glanced over her shoulder and stopped, shocked excitement making her nerves sizzle.

Saetan leaned heavily on a silver-headed cane, his golden eyes glittering with rage. There was more silver in the thick black hair, and his face was tight with exhaustion. He looked . . . worn-out.

And he was only wearing his Birthright Red Jewel.

She didn't even take the time for a fast descent to gather her full strength. She just raised her hand and unleashed the power in her Red-Jeweled ring at his weak leg.

His cry of pain as he fell was the most satisfying sound she'd heard in years.

"Seize him!" she screamed at her demons.

A cold, soft wind sighed across the island.

The guards hesitated for a moment, but when Saetan tried to get up and failed, they drew their knives and ran toward him.

The ground trembled slightly. Mist swirled around the rocks, around the barren earth.

Hekatah also ran toward Saetan, wanting to watch the knives cut deep, wanting to watch his blood run. A Guardian's blood! The richness, the strength in it! She would feast on him before dealing with that upstart little demon.

A howl rose from the abyss, a sound full of joy and pain, rage and celebration.

Then a tidal wave of dark power flooded the *cildru dyathe*'s island. Psychic lightning set Hell's twilight sky on fire. Thunder shook the land. The howling went on and on.

Hekatah fell to the ground and curled up as tight as she could.

Her demons screamed in nerve-shattering agony.

Go away, Hekatah pleaded silently. *Whatever you are, go away.*

Something icy and terrible brushed against her inner barriers, and Hekatah blanked her mind.

By the time it faded away, the witch storm had faded with it.

Hekatah pushed herself into a sitting position. Her throat worked convulsively when she saw what was left of her demons.

There was no sign of Saetan or Char.

Hekatah slowly got to her feet. Was that Jaenelle—or what was left of Jaenelle? Maybe she *wasn't cildru dyathe.* Maybe she had faded from demon to ghost and all that was left was that bodiless power.

It was just as well the girl was dead, Hekatah thought as she caught a

White Wind and rode back to the stone building she claimed as her own. It was just as well that whatever was left of Jaenelle would be confined to the Dark Realm. Trying to control that savage power. . . . It was just as well the girl was dead.

Pain surrounded him, filled him. His head felt like it was stuffed with blankets. He clawed his way through, desperate to reach the muffled voices he heard around him: Andulvar's angry rumble, Char's distress.

Hell's fire! Why were they just sitting there? For the first time in two years, Jaenelle had responded to someone's call. Why weren't they trying to keep her within reach?

Because Jaenelle was gliding through the abyss too deep for anyone but him to feel her presence. But he couldn't just descend to the level of the Black and summon her. He had to be near her physically, he had to be with her to coax her into remaining with her body.

"Why did the witch storm hit him so bad?" Char asked fearfully.

"Because he's an ass," Andulvar growled in reply.

He redoubled his efforts to break through the muffling layers just so he could snarl at Andulvar. Maybe he *had* been channeling too much of the Black strength without giving his body a chance to recover. Maybe he *had* been foolish when he'd refused to drink fresh blood to maintain his strength. But that didn't give an Eyrien warrior the right to act like a stubborn, nagging Healer.

Jaenelle would have cornered him until he'd given in.

Jaenelle. So close. He might never have another chance.

He struggled harder. *Help me. I have to reach her. Help—* "me."

"High Lord!"

"Hell's fire, SaDiablo!"

Saetan grabbed Andulvar's arm and tried to pull himself into a sitting position. "Help me. Before it's too late."

"You need rest," Andulvar said.

"There isn't time!" Saetan tried to yell. It came out an infuriating croak. "Jaenelle's still close enough to reach."

"*What?*"

The next thing he knew he was sitting up with Andulvar supporting him and Char kneeling in front of him. He focused on the boy. "How did you summon her?"

"I don't know," Char wailed. "I don't know. I was just trying to keep Hekatah busy until you came. She kept demanding to see Jaenelle, so I thought . . . Jaenelle and I used to play 'chase me, find me' and that was the sound we used to make. I didn't know she would answer, High Lord. I've called like that lots of times since she went away, and she's never answered."

"Until now," Saetan said quietly. Why now? He finally noticed he was in a familiar bedroom. "We're at the Keep in Kaeleer?"

"Draca insisted on bringing you here," Andulvar said.

The Keep's Seneschal had given him a bedroom near the Queen's suite. Which meant he wasn't more than a few yards away from Jaenelle's body. Just chance? Or could Draca also feel Jaenelle's presence?

"Help me," Saetan whispered.

Andulvar half carried him the few yards down the corridor to the door where Draca waited.

"You will drink a cup of fressh blood when you return," Draca said.

If I return, Saetan thought grimly, as Andulvar helped him to the bed that held Jaenelle's frail body. There might not be another chance. He would bring her back or destroy himself trying.

As soon as he was alone with her, he took Jaenelle's head between his hands, drew every drop of power he had left in his Jewels, and made a quick descent into the abyss until he reached the level of the Black.

Jaenelle!

She continued her slow spiral glide deeper into the abyss. He didn't know if she was ignoring him or just couldn't hear him.

Jaenelle! Witch-child!

His strength was draining too quickly. The abyss pushed against his mind, the pressure quickly turning to pain.

You're safe, witch-child! Come back! You're safe!

She slipped farther and farther away from him. But little eddies of power washed back up to him, and he could taste the rage in them.

Chase me, find me. A child's game. He had been sending a message of love and safety into the abyss for two years. Char had been sending an invitation to play during that same time.

Silence.

In another moment, he would have to ascend or he would shatter.

Stillness.

Chase me, find me. Hadn't he really been playing the same game?

He waited, fighting for each second. ★Witch-child.★

She slammed into him without warning. Caught in her spiraling fury, he didn't know if they were rising or descending.

He heard glass shatter in the physical world, heard someone scream. He felt something hit his chest, just below his heart, hard enough to take his breath away.

Not knowing what else to do, he opened his inner barriers fully, a gesture of complete surrender. He expected her to crash through him, rip him apart. Instead, he felt a startled curiosity and a feather-light touch that barely brushed against him.

Then she tossed him out of the abyss.

The abrupt return to the physical world left him dizzy, his senses scrambled. That had to be why he thought he saw a tiny spiral horn in the center of her forehead. That had to be why her ears looked delicately pointed, why she had a golden mane that looked like a cross between fur and human hair. That had to be why his heart felt as if it were beating frantically against someone's hand.

He closed his eyes, fighting the dizziness. When he opened them a moment later, all the changes in Jaenelle's appearance were gone, but there was still that odd feeling in his chest.

Gasping, he looked down as he felt fingers curl around his heart.

Jaenelle's hand was embedded in his chest. When she withdrew her hand, she would pull his heart out with it. No matter. It had been hers long before he'd ever met her. And it gave him an odd feeling of pride, remembering the frustration and delight he'd felt when he'd tried to teach her how to pass one solid object through another.

The fingers curled tighter.

Her eyes opened. They were fathomless sapphire pools that held no recognition, that held nothing but deep, inhuman rage.

Then she blinked. Her eyes clouded, hiding so many things. She blinked again and looked at him. "Saetan?" she said in a rusty voice.

His eyes filled with tears. "Witch-child," he whispered hoarsely.

He gasped when she moved her hand slightly.

She stared at his chest and frowned. "Oh." She slowly uncurled her fingers and withdrew her hand.

He expected her hand to be bloody, but it was clean. A quick internal check told him he would feel bruised for a few days, but she hadn't done any damage. He leaned forward until his forehead rested against hers.

"Witch-child," he whispered.

"Saetan? Are you crying?"

"Yes. No. I don't know."

"You should lie down. You feel kind of peaky."

Shifting his body until it was beside hers exhausted him. When she turned and snuggled against him, he wrapped his arms around her and held on. "I tried to reach you, witch-child," he murmured as he rested his cheek against her head.

"I know," she said sleepily. "I heard you sometimes, but I had to find all the pieces so I could put the crystal chalice back together."

"Did you put it back together?" he asked, hardly daring to breathe.

Jaenelle nodded. "Some of the pieces are cloudy and don't fit quite right yet." She paused. "Saetan? What happened?"

Dread filled him, and he didn't have the courage to answer that question honestly. What would she do if he told her what had happened? If she severed the link with her body and fled into the abyss again, he wasn't sure he would ever be able to convince her to return.

"You were hurt, sweetheart." His arms tightened around her. "But you're going to be fine. I'll help you. Nothing can hurt you, witch-child. You have to remember that. You're safe here."

Jaenelle frowned. "Where is here?"

"We're at the Keep. In Kaeleer."

"Oh." Her eyelids fluttered and closed.

Saetan squeezed her shoulder. Then he shook her. "Jaenelle? Jaenelle, no! Don't leave me. Please don't leave."

With effort, Jaenelle opened her eyes. "Leave? Oh, Saetan, I'm so tired. Do I really have to leave?"

He had to get control of himself. He had to stay calm so that she would feel safe. "You can stay here as long as you want."

"You'll stay, too?"

"I'll never leave you, witch-child. I swear it."

Jaenelle sighed. "You should get some sleep," she murmured.

Saetan listened to her deep, even breathing for a long time. He wanted to open his mind and reach for her, but he didn't need to. He could feel the difference in the body he still held.

So he reached out to Andulvar instead. *She's come back.*

A long silence. *Truly?*

Truly. And he would need his strength for the days ahead. *Tell the others. And tell Draca I'll take the cup of fresh blood now.*

5 / Kaeleer

Guided by instinct and a nagging uneasiness, Saetan entered Jaenelle's bedroom at the Keep without knocking.

She stood in front of a large, freestanding mirror, staring at the naked body reflected there.

Saetan closed the door and limped toward her. While she'd been away from her body, there had still been just enough of a link so that she could eat and could be led on gentle walks that had kept her muscles from atrophying. There had still been enough of a link for her body to slowly answer the rhythm of its own seasons.

Blood females tended to reach puberty later than landens, and witches' bodies required even more time to prepare for the physical changes that separated a girl from a woman. Inhibited by her absence, Jaenelle's body hadn't started changing until after her fourteenth birthday. But while her body was still in the early stages of transformation, it no longer looked like a twelve-year-old's.

Saetan stopped a few feet behind her. Her sapphire eyes met his in the mirror, and he had to work to keep his expression neutral.

Those eyes. Clear and feral and dangerous before she slipped on the mask of humanity. And it was a mask. It wasn't like the dissembling she used to do as a child to keep the fact that she was Witch a secret. This was a deliberate effort simply to be *human*. And that scared him.

"I should have told you," he said quietly. "I should have prepared you. But you've slept through most of the past four days, and I . . ." His voice trailed off.

"How long?" she asked in a voice full of caverns and midnight.

He had to clear his throat before he could answer. "Two years. Actually, a little more than that. You'll be fifteen in a few weeks."

She said nothing, and he didn't know how to fill the silence.

Then she turned around to face him. "Do you want to have sex with this body?"

Blood. So much blood.

His gorge rose. Her mask fell away. And no matter how hard he looked, he couldn't find Jaenelle in those sapphire eyes.

He had to give her an answer. He had to give her the *right* answer.

He took a deep breath and let it out slowly. "I'm your legal guardian now. Your adopted father, if you will. And fathers do not have sex with their daughters."

"Don't they?" she asked in a midnight whisper.

The floor disappeared under his feet. The room spun. He would have fallen if Jaenelle hadn't thrown her arms around his waist.

"Don't use Craft," he muttered through gritted teeth.

Too late. Jaenelle was already floating him to the couch. As he sank into it, she sat beside him and brushed her shoulder-length hair away from her neck. "You need fresh blood."

"No, I don't. I'm just a little dizzy." Besides, he'd been drinking a cup of fresh human blood twice a day for the past four days—almost as much as he usually consumed in a year.

"You need fresh blood." There was a definite edge in her voice.

What he needed was to find the bastard who had raped her and tear him apart inch by inch. "I don't need your blood, witch-child."

Her eyes flashed with anger. She bared her teeth. "There's nothing wrong with my blood, High Lord," she hissed. "It isn't tainted."

"Of course it isn't tainted," he snapped back.

"Then why won't you accept the gift? You never refused before."

There were clouds and shadows now in her sapphire eyes. It seemed that, for her, the price of humanity was vulnerability and insecurity.

Lifting her hand, he kissed her knuckles and wondered if he could delicately suggest that she put on a robe without her taking offense. *One thing at a time, SaDiablo.* "There are three reasons I don't want your blood right now. First, until you're stronger, you need every drop of it for yourself. Second, your body is changing from child to woman, and the potency of the blood changes, too. So let's test it before I find myself drinking liquid lightning."

That made her giggle.

"And third, Draca has also decided that I need fresh blood."

Jaenelle's eyes widened. "Oh, dear. Poor Papa." She bit her lip. "Is it all right if I call you that?" she asked in a small voice.

He put his arms around her and held her close. "I would be honored to be called 'Papa.' " He brushed his lips against her forehead. "The room is a little chilly, witch-child. Do you think you could put on a robe? And slippers?"

"You sound like a parent already," Jaenelle grumbled.

Saetan smiled. "I've waited a long time to fuss over a daughter. I intend to revel in it to the fullest."

"Oh, lucky me," Jaenelle growled.

He laughed. "No. Lucky *me*."

6 / Kaeleer

Saetan stared at the tonic in the small ravenglass cup and sighed. He had the cup halfway to his lips when someone knocked on the door.

"Come," he said too eagerly.

Andulvar entered, followed by his grandson, Prothvar, and Mephis, Saetan's eldest son. Prothvar and Mephis, like Andulvar, had become demon-dead during that long-ago war between Terreille and Kaeleer. Geoffrey, the Keep's historian/librarian, entered last.

"Try this," Saetan said, holding out the cup to Andulvar.

"Why?" Andulvar asked, eyeing the cup. "What's in it?"

Damn Eyrien wariness. "It's a tonic Jaenelle made for me. She says I'm still looking peaky."

"You are," Andulvar growled. "So drink it."

Saetan ground his teeth.

"It doesn't smell bad," Prothvar said, pulling his wings tighter to his body when Saetan glared at him.

"It doesn't taste bad either," Saetan said, trying to be fair.

"Then what's the problem?" Geoffrey asked, crossing his arms. He frowned at the cup, his black eyebrows echoing his widow's peak. "Are you concerned that she doesn't have the training to make that kind of tonic? Do you think she's done it incorrectly?"

Saetan raised one eyebrow. "We're talking about Jaenelle."

"Ah," Geoffrey said, eyeing the cup with some trepidation. "Yes."

Saetan held the cup out to him. "Tell me what you think."

Andulvar braced his fists on his hips. "Why are you so eager to share it? If there's nothing wrong with it, why won't *you* drink it?"

"I do. I have. Every day for the past two weeks," Saetan grumbled. "But it's just so damn . . . potent." The last word was almost a plea.

Geoffrey accepted the cup, took a small sip, rolled the liquid on his tongue, and swallowed. As he handed the cup to Andulvar, he started gasping and pressed his hands to his stomach.

"Geoffrey?" Alarmed, Saetan grabbed Geoffrey's arm as the older Guardian swayed.

"Is it supposed to feel like that?" Geoffrey wheezed.

"Like what?" Saetan asked cautiously.

"Like an avalanche hitting your stomach."

Saetan sighed with relief. "It doesn't last long, and the tonic *does* have some astonishing curative powers, but . . ."

"The initial sensation is a bit unsettling."

"Exactly," Saetan said dryly.

Andulvar studied the two Guardians and shrugged. He took a sip, passed the cup to Prothvar, who took a sip and passed it to Mephis.

When the cup reached Saetan, it was still two-thirds full. He sighed, took a sip, and set the cup on an empty curio table.

Why couldn't Draca fill a table with useless bric-a-brac like everyone else? he thought sourly. At least then there would be a way to hide the damn thing since Jaenelle had put some kind of neat little spell on the cup that prevented it from being vanished.

"Hell's fire," Andulvar finally said.

"What does she put in it?" Mephis said, rubbing his stomach.

Prothvar eyed Geoffrey. "You know, you've almost got some color."

Geoffrey glared at the Eyrien Warlord.

"What did you all want to see me about?" Saetan asked.

That stopped them cold. Then they began talking all at once.

"You see, SaDiablo, the waif—"

"—it's a difficult time for a young girl, I do understand that—"

"—doesn't want to see us—"

"—suddenly so shy—"

Saetan raised his hand to silence their explanations.

Everything has a price. As he looked at them, he knew he had to tell them what the past two weeks had forced him to see. *Everything has a price, but, sweet Darkness, haven't we paid enough?*

"Jaenelle didn't heal." When no one responded, he wondered if he'd actually said it out loud.

"Explain, SaDiablo," Andulvar rumbled. "Her body is alive, and now that she's returned to it, it will get stronger."

"Yes," Saetan replied softly. "Her body is alive."

"Since she's obviously capable of doing more than basic Craft, her inner web must be intact," Geoffrey said.

"Her inner web is intact," Saetan agreed. Hell's fire. Why was he prolonging this? Because once he actually said it, it would be real.

He watched the knowledge—and the anger—fill Andulvar's eyes.

"The bastard who raped her managed to shatter the crystal chalice, didn't he?" Andulvar said slowly. "He shattered her mind, and that pushed her into the Twisted Kingdom." Pausing, he studied Saetan. "Or did it push her somewhere else?"

"Who knows what lies deep in the abyss?" Saetan said bitterly. "I don't. Was she lost in madness or simply walking roads the rest of us can't possibly comprehend? I don't know. I *do* know she is more and less and different than she was, and there are some days when it's hard to find anything left of the child we knew. She told me that she'd put the crystal chalice back together, and from what I can tell, she has. But she doesn't remember what happened at Cassandra's Altar. She doesn't remember anything that took place during the few months before that night. And she's hiding something. That's part of the reason she's withdrawing from us. Shadows and secrets. She's afraid to trust any of us because of those damn shadows and secrets."

Mephis finally broke the long silence. "Perhaps," he said slowly, "if she could be persuaded to see us in one of the public rooms, just for a few minutes at a time, it might help rebuild her trust in us. Especially if we don't push or ask any difficult questions." He added sadly, "And is being locked within herself while she lives in her body really any different than being lost in the abyss?"

"No," Saetan said softly. "It's not." It was a risk. Mother Night, was it a risk! "I'll talk to her."

Andulvar, Prothvar, Mephis, and Geoffrey left after agreeing to meet him in one of the smaller parlors. Saetan waited for several minutes before walking the few yards that separated his room from the Queen's suite. Once Jaenelle established her court, no males but her Consort, Steward, and Master of the Guard would be permitted in this wing unless they were summoned. Not even her legal guardian.

Saetan knocked quietly on her bedroom door. When he got no answer, he peeked into the room. Empty. He checked the adjoining sitting room. That was empty, too.

Running his fingers through his hair, he wondered where his wayward child had gone. He could sense that she was nearby. But he'd also learned that Jaenelle left such a strong psychic scent, it was sometimes difficult to locate her. Perhaps it had always been that way, but they'd never spent more than an hour or two together at any given time. Now her presence filled the huge Keep, and her dark, delicious psychic scent was a pleasure and a torment. To feel her, to yearn with all one's heart to embrace and serve her, and to be locked out of her life . . .

There could be no greater torture.

And it wasn't just for Andulvar, Mephis, Prothvar, and Geoffrey that he was willing to risk her emotional stability by asking for contact. There was one other, lately never far from his thoughts. If she didn't heal emotionally, if she could never endure a man's touch . . .

He wasn't the key that could unlock that final door. There was much he could do, but not that. He wasn't the key.

Daemon Sadi was.

Daemon . . . Daemon, where are you? Why haven't you come?

Saetan was about to retrace his steps, intending to find Draca—she always knew where *everyone* was in the Keep—when a sound made him turn toward a half-open door at the end of the corridor.

As he walked toward it, he noticed how much better his leg felt since Jaenelle started dosing him with her tonic. If he could stomach it for a couple more weeks, he'd be able to put the cane away—and hopefully the tonic with it.

He had almost reached the door when someone inside the room let out a startled squawk. There was a loud *pop fizz boosh,* and then a lavender, gray, and rose cloud belched out of the room, followed by a feminine voice muttering, "Damn, damn, and double damn!"

The cloud began a slow descent to the floor.

Saetan held out his hand and stared at the chalky lavender, gray, and rose flecks that covered his skin and shirt cuff. Butterflies churned in his stomach, and they tickled, leaving him with an irrational desire to giggle and flee.

He swallowed the giggle, strapped a bit of mental steel to his backbone, and cautiously peered around the doorway.

Jacnelle stood by a large worktable, her arms crossed and her foot tapping as she frowned at the Craft book hovering above the table. The candle-lights on either side of the book gave off a pretty, stained-glass glow, softening the surrounding chaos. The entire room—and everything in it, including Jaenelle—was liberally dusted with lavender, gray, and rose. Only the book was clean. She must have put a shield around it before beginning . . . whatever it was.

"I really don't think I want to know about this," Saetan said dryly, wondering how Draca was going to react to the mess.

Jaenelle gave him an exasperated, amused look. "No, you really don't." Then she gave him her best unsure-but-game smile. "I don't suppose you'd like to help anyway?"

Hell's fire! During all the years when he'd been teaching her Craft and trying to unravel one of these quirky spells after the fact, he'd hoped for just this invitation.

"Unfortunately," he said, his voice full of wistful regret, "there's something else we have to discuss."

Jaenelle sat down, on air, hooking her heels on the nonexistent rung of a nonexistent stool, and gave him her full attention.

He remembered, too late, how unnerving it could be to have Jaenelle's undivided attention.

Saetan cleared his throat and glanced around the room, hoping for inspiration. Maybe her workroom, with the tools of her Craft around her, was the best place to talk after all.

He stepped into the room and leaned against the doorframe. A good neutral place, not invading her territory but acknowledging a right to be there. "I'm concerned, witch-child," he said quietly.

Jaenelle cocked her head. "About what?"

"About you. About the way you avoid all of us. About the way you're shutting yourself away from everyone."

Ice filled her eyes. "Everyone has boundaries and inner barriers."

"I'm not talking about boundaries and inner barriers," he said, not quite able to keep his voice calm. "Of course everyone has them. They protect the inner web and the Self. But you've put up a *wall* between yourself and everyone else, excluding them from even simple contact."

"Perhaps you should be grateful for the wall, Saetan," Jaenelle said in a midnight voice that sent a shiver of fear up his spine.

Saetan. Not Papa. Saetan. And not the way she usually said his name. This sounded like a Queen formally addressing a Warlord Prince.

He didn't know how to respond to her words or the warning.

She stepped off her invisible stool and turned away from him, resting her hands on the dusty table.

"Listen to me," he said, restraining the urgency he felt. "You can't lock yourself away like this. You can't spend the rest of your life in this room creating glorious spells that no one else will see. You're a Queen. You'll have to interact with your court."

"I'm not going to have a court."

Saetan stared at her, stunned. "Of course you'll have a court. You're a Queen."

Jaenelle flashed a look at him that made him cringe. "I'm not required to have a court. I checked. And I don't want to rule. I don't want to control anyone's life but my own."

"But you're Witch." The moment he said it, the room chilled.

"Yes," she said too softly. "I am." Then she turned around.

She dropped the mask of humanity—and the mask called flesh—and let him truly see her for the first time.

The tiny spiral horn in the center of her forehead. The golden mane that wasn't quite fur and wasn't quite hair. The delicately pointed ears. The hands that had sheathed claws. The legs that changed below the knee to accommodate the small hooves. The stripe of golden fur that ran down her spine and ended at the fawn tail that flicked over her buttocks. The exotic face and those sapphire eyes.

Having been Cassandra's Consort all those years ago, he thought he knew and understood Witch. Now he finally understood that Cassandra and the other Black-Jeweled Queens who had come before her had been *called* Witch. Jaenelle truly was the living myth, dreams made flesh.

How foolish he'd been to assume all the dreamers had been human.

"Exactly," Witch said softly, coldly.

"You're beautiful," he whispered. And so very, very dangerous.

She stared at him, puzzled, and he realized there would never be a better time to say what he had to say.

"We love you, Lady," he told her quietly. "We've always loved you, and it hurts more than words can express to be locked out of your life. You don't know how hard it was for us to wait for those few precious minutes that you could spend with us, to wonder and worry about you when you were gone, to feel jealous of people who didn't appreciate what you are. Now . . ." His voice broke. He pressed his lips together and took a deep breath. "We surrendered to you a long time ago. Not even you can change that. Do with us what you will." He hesitated, then added, "No, witch-child, we are *not* grateful for the wall."

He didn't wait for an answer. He left the room as swiftly as he could, tears shining in his eyes.

Behind him came a soft, anguished cry.

He couldn't stand their kindness. He couldn't stand their sympathy and understanding. Geoffrey had warmed a glass of yarbarah for him. Mephis had tucked a lap rug over his legs. Prothvar had stoked the fire to help take away the chill. Andulvar had stayed close to him, silent.

He'd started shaking the moment he had entered the safety of the parlor. He would have collapsed on the floor if Andulvar hadn't caught him and helped him to the chair. They had asked no questions, and except for a hoarsely whispered, "I don't know," he had told them nothing about what had happened—or about what he had seen.

And they had accepted it.

An hour later, feeling somewhat restored physically and emotionally, he still couldn't stand their kindness. What he couldn't stand even more was not knowing what was happening in that workroom.

The parlor door swung open.

Jaenelle stood on the threshold, holding a tray that contained two small carafes and five glasses. All her masks were back in place.

"Draca said you were all hiding in here," she said defensively.

"We're not exactly 'hiding,' witch-child," Saetan replied dryly. "And, if we are, there's room for one more. Want to join us?"

Her smile was shy and hesitant, but her coltish legs swiftly crossed the room until she stood beside Saetan's chair. Then she frowned and turned toward the door. "This room used to be larger."

"Your legs used to be shorter."

"That explains why the stairs feel so awkward," she muttered as she filled two glasses from one carafe and three from the other.

Saetan stared at the glass she gave him. His stomach cringed.

"Um," Prothvar said, as Jaenelle handed out the other glasses.

"Drink it," Jaenelle snapped. "You've all been looking peaky lately." When they hesitated, her voice became brittle. "It's just a tonic."

Andulvar took a sip.

Thank the Darkness for that Eyrien willingness to step onto any kind of battlefield, Saetan thought as he, too, took a sip.

"How much of this do you make at one time, waif?" Andulvar rumbled.

"Why?" Jaenelle said warily.

"Well, you're quite right about us all feeling peaky. Probably wouldn't hurt to have another glass later on."

Saetan started coughing to hide his own dismay and give the others time to school their expressions. It was one thing for Andulvar to step onto the battlefield. It was quite another to drag them all with him.

Jaenelle fluffed her hair. "It starts to lose its potency an hour after it's made, but it's no trouble to make another batch later on."

Andulvar nodded, his expression serious. "Thank you."

Jaenelle smiled shyly and slipped out of the room.

Saetan waited until he was sure she was out of earshot before turning on Andulvar. "You unconscionable prick," he snarled.

"That's a big word coming from a man who's going to have to drink two glasses of this a day," Andulvar replied smugly.

"We could always pour it into the plants," Prothvar said, looking around for some greenery.

"I already tried that," Saetan growled. "Draca's only comment was that if another plant should suffer a sudden demise, she'd ask Jaenelle to look into it."

Andulvar chuckled, giving the other four men a reason to snarl at him. "Everyone expects Hayllians to be devious, but Eyriens are known for their forthright dealings. So when one of *us* acts deviously . . ."

"You did it so she'd have a reason to check up on us," Mephis said, eyeing his glass. "I thank you for that, Andulvar, but couldn't—"

Saetan sprang to his feet. "It loses its potency after an hour."

Andulvar raised his glass in a salute. "Just so."

Saetan smiled. "If we hold back half of each dose so that it's lost most of its potency and then mix it with the fresh dose . . ."

"We'll have a restorative tonic that has a tolerable potency," Geoffrey finished, looking pleased.

"If she finds out, she'll kill us," Prothvar grumbled.

Saetan raised an eyebrow. "All things considered, my fine demon, it's a little late to be concerned about *that*, don't you think?"

Prothvar almost blushed.

Saetan narrowed his golden eyes at Andulvar. "But we didn't know it would lose its potency until *after* you asked for a second dose."

Andulvar shrugged. "Most healing brews have to be taken shortly after they're made. It was worth the gamble." He smiled at Saetan with all the arrogance only an Eyrien male was capable of. "However, if you're admitting your balls aren't as big—"

Saetan said something pithy and to the point.

"Then there's no problem, is there?" Andulvar replied.

They looked at each other, centuries of friendship, rivalry, and understanding reflected in two pairs of golden eyes. They raised their glasses and waited for the others to follow suit.

"To Jaenelle," Saetan said.

"To Jaenelle," the others replied.

Then they sighed in unison and swallowed half their tonic.

7 / Kaeleer

Not quite content, Saetan watched the lights of Riada, the largest Blood village in Ebon Rih and the closest one to the Keep, shine up from the valley's fertile darkness like captured pieces of starlight.

He had watched the sun rise today. No, more than that. He had stood in one of the small formal gardens and had actually felt the sun's warmth on his face. For the first time in more centuries than he cared to count, there had been no lancing pain in his temples, no brutal stomach-twisting headache to tell him just how far he had stepped from the living, no weakening in his strength.

He was as physically strong now as when he first became a Guardian, first began walking that fine line between living and dead.

Jaenelle and her tonic had done that. Had done more than that.

He'd forgotten how sensual food could be, and over the past few days had savored the taste of rare beef and new potatoes, of roasted chicken and fresh vegetables. He'd forgotten how good sleep could feel, instead of that semiawake rest Guardians usually indulged in during the daylight hours.

He'd also forgotten how hunger pangs felt or how fuzzy-brained a man could be when he was beyond tired.

Everything has a price.

He smiled cautiously at Cassandra when she joined him at the window. "You look lovely tonight," he said, making a small gesture that took in her long black gown, the open-weave emerald shawl, and the way she'd styled her dusty-red hair.

"Too bad the Harpy didn't bother to dress for the occasion," Cassandra replied tartly. She wrinkled her nose. "She could have at least worn something around her throat."

"And you could have refrained from offering to lend her a high-necked gown," Saetan snapped. Then he clenched his teeth to trap the rest of the words. Titian didn't need a defender, especially after her slur about the delicate sensibilities of prissy aristo witches.

He watched the lights of Riada wink out, one by one.

Cassandra took a deep breath, let it out in a sigh. "It wasn't supposed to be like this," she said quietly. "The Black were never meant to be Birthright Jewels. I became a Guardian because I thought the next Witch would need a friend, someone to help her understand what she would become after making the Offering to the Darkness. But what has happened to Jaenelle has changed her so much she'll never be normal."

"*Normal?* Just what do you call 'normal,' Lady?"

She looked pointedly at the corner of the room where Andulvar, Prothvar, Mephis, and Geoffrey were trying to include Titian in the conversation and keep a respectful distance at the same time.

"Jaenelle just celebrated her fifteenth birthday. Instead of a party and a roomful of young friends, she spent the evening with demons, Guardians—and a Harpy. Can you honestly call that normal?"

"I've had this conversation before," Saetan growled. "And my answer is still the same: for her, that *is* normal."

Cassandra studied him for a moment before saying quietly, "Yes, you would see it that way, wouldn't you?"

He saw the room through a red haze before he got his temper tightly leashed. "Meaning what?"

"You became the High Lord of Hell while you were still living. You wouldn't see anything wrong with her having the *cildru dyathe* for play-mates or having a Harpy teach her how to interact with males."

Saetan's breath whistled between his teeth. "When you foresaw her coming, you called her the daughter of my soul. But those were just words, weren't they? Just a way to ensure that I would become a Guardian so that my strength would be at your disposal for the protection of your apprentice, the young witch who would sit at your feet, awed by the at-tention of the Black-Jeweled Witch. Except it didn't work out that way. The one who came really *is* the daughter of my soul, and she is awed by no one and sits at no one's feet."

"She may be awed by no one," Cassandra said coldly, "but she also *has* no one." Then her voice softened. "And for that, I pity her."

She has me!

The quick, sharp look Cassandra gave him cut his heart.

Jaenelle had him. The Prince of the Darkness. The High Lord of Hell. More than any other reason, *that* was why Cassandra pitied her.

"We should join the others," Saetan said tightly, offering his arm. De-spite the anger he felt, he couldn't turn his back on her.

Cassandra started to refuse his gesture of courtesy until she noticed Andulvar's and Titian's cold stares.

"Draca wants to talk with all of us," Andulvar growled as soon as they approached. He immediately moved away from them, giving himself room to spread his wings. Giving himself room to fight.

Saetan watched him for a moment, then began reinforcing his own considerable defenses. They were different in many ways, but he'd always respected Andulvar's instincts.

Draca entered the room slowly, calmly. Her hands, as usual, were tucked into the long sleeves of her robe. She waited for them to be seated, waited until their attention was centered on her before pinning Saetan with her reptilian stare.

"The Lady iss fifteen today," Draca said.

"Yes," Saetan replied cautiously.

"Sshe wass pleassed with our ssmall offeringss."

It was sometimes difficult to perceive inflections in Draca's sibilant voice, but the words sounded more like a command than a question. "Yes," Saetan said, "I think she was."

A long silence. "It iss time for the Lady to leave the Keep. You are her legal guardian. You will make the arrangementss."

Saetan's throat tightened. The muscles in his chest constricted. "I had promised her that she could stay here."

"It iss time for the Lady to leave. Sshe will live with you at SsaDiablo Hall."

"I propose an alternative," Cassandra said quickly, pressing her fists into her lap. She didn't even glance at Saetan. "Jaenelle could live with me. Everyone knows who—and what—Saetan is, but I—"

Titian twisted around in her chair. "Do you really believe no one in the Shadow Realm knows you're a Guardian? Did you really think your masquerading as one of the living had fooled anyone?"

Anger flared in Cassandra's eyes. "I've always been careful—"

"You've always been a liar. At least the High Lord has been honest about what he is."

"But he *is* the High Lord—and that's the point."

"The *point* is you want to be the one who shapes Jaenelle just like Hekatah wants to shape Jaenelle, to mold her into an image of *your* choosing instead of letting her be what she is."

"How dare you speak to me like that? I'm a Black-Jeweled Queen!"

"You're not my Queen," Titian snarled.

"*Ladies.*" Saetan's voice rolled through the room like soft thunder. He took a moment to steady his temper before turning his attention back to Draca.

"Sshe will live at the Hall," Draca said firmly. "It iss decided."

"Since you haven't discussed this with any of us until now, *who* decided this?" Cassandra said sharply.

"Lorn hass decided."

Saetan forgot how to breathe.

Hell's fire, Mother Night, and may the Darkness be merciful.

No one argued. No one made so much as a sound.

Saetan realized his hands were shaking. "Could I talk to him? There are some things he may not understand about—"

"He undersstandss, High Lord."

Saetan looked up at the Seneschal of Ebon Askavi.

"The time hass not yet come for you to meet him," Draca said. "But it *will* come." She tipped her head slightly. It was as much deference as she ever showed to anyone. Except, perhaps, to Jaenelle.

They watched her leave, listening to her slow, careful footsteps until the sound faded away completely.

Andulvar let his breath out in an explosive *ffooooh*. "When she wants to cut someone off at the knees, she's got an impressive knife."

Saetan leaned his head against the chair and closed his eyes. "Doesn't she though?"

Cassandra carefully rearranged her shawl and stood up, not looking at any of them. "If you'll excuse me, I'll retire now."

They rose and bid her good night.

Titian also excused herself. But before she left, she gave Saetan a sly smile. "Living at the Hall with Jaenelle will probably be difficult, High Lord, but not for the reasons you think."

"Mother Night," Saetan muttered before turning to the other men.

Mephis cleared his throat. "Telling the waif she has to leave isn't going to be easy. You don't have to do it alone."

"Yes, I do, Mephis," Saetan replied wearily. "I made her a promise. I'm the one who has to tell her I'm going to break it."

He said good night and slowly made his way through the stone corridors until he reached the stairs that would take him to Jaenelle's suite. Instead of climbing them, he leaned against the wall, shivering.

He had promised her that she could stay. He had *promised*.

But Lorn had decided.

It was long after midnight before he joined her in the private garden connected to her suite. She gave him a sleepy, relaxed smile and held out her hand. Gratefully, he linked his fingers through hers.

"It was a lovely party," Jaenelle said as they strolled through the garden. "I'm glad you invited Char and Titian." She hesitated. "And I'm sorry it was so difficult for Cassandra."

Saetan gave her a considering look through narrowed eyes.

She acknowledged the look with a shrug.

"How much did you hear?"

"Eavesdropping is rude," she said primly.

"An answer that neatly sidesteps the question," he replied dryly.

"I didn't *hear* anything. But I *felt* you all grumbling."

Saetan drifted closer to her. She smelled of wildflowers and sun-drenched meadows and fern-shaded pools of water. It was a scent that was gently wild and elusive, that captivated a male because it didn't try to capture him.

It relaxed him—and slightly aroused him.

Even knowing it was a Warlord Prince's natural response to a Queen he felt emotionally bound to, even knowing he would never cross the distinct line that separated a father's affection from a lover's passion, he still felt ashamed of his reaction.

He looked at her, wanting the sharp reminder of who she was and how young she was. But it was Witch who looked back at him, Witch whose hand tightened on his so that he couldn't break the physical link.

"I suppose even a wise man can sometimes be a fool," she said in her midnight voice.

"I would never—" His voice broke. "You know I would never—"

He saw a flicker of amusement in her ancient, haunted eyes.

"Yes, *I* know. Do you? You adore women, Saetan. You always have. You like to be near them. You like to touch them." She held up their hands.

"This is different. You're my daughter."

"And so you will keep your distance from Witch?" she asked sadly.

He pulled her into his arms and held her so tightly she let out a breathless squeak. "Never," he said fiercely.

"Papa?" Jaenelle said faintly. "Papa, I can't breathe."

He immediately loosened his hold but didn't let go.

Soft night sounds filled the garden. The spring wind sighed.

"This mood of yours has something to do with Cassandra, doesn't it?" Jaenelle asked.

"A little." He rested his cheek against her head. "We have to leave the Keep."

Her body tensed so much his ached in response.

"Why?" she finally asked, leaning back far enough to see his face.

"Because Lorn has decided we should live at the Hall."

"Oh." Then she added, "No wonder you're moody."

Saetan laughed. "Yes. Well. He does have a way of limiting one's options." He gently brushed her hair away from her face. "I do want to live at the Hall with you. I want that very much. But if you want to live somewhere else or have any reservations about leaving the Keep right now, I'll fight him over it."

Her eyes widened until they were huge. "Oh, dear. That wouldn't be a good idea, Saetan. He's *much* bigger than you."

Saetan tried to swallow. "I'll still fight him."

"Oh, dear." She took a deep breath. "Let's try living at the Hall."

"Thank you, witch-child," he said weakly.

She wrapped an arm around his waist. "You look a bit wobbly."

"Then I look better than I feel," he said, draping an arm around her shoulders. "Come along, little witch. The next few days are going to be hectic, and we'll both need our rest."

8 / Kaeleer

Saetan opened the front door of SaDiablo Hall and stepped into orchestrated chaos.

Maids flitted in every direction. Footmen lugged pieces of furniture from one room to another for no reason he could fathom. Gardeners trotted in with armloads of freshly cut flowers.

Standing in the center of the great hall, holding a *long* list in one hand while conducting the various people and parcels to their rightful places with the other, was Beale, his Red-Jeweled butler.

Somewhat bemused, Saetan walked toward Beale, hoping for an explanation. By the time he'd taken half a dozen steps, he realized that a walking obstacle had not been taken into account in this frenzied dance. Maids bumped into him, their annoyed expressions barely changing upon recognizing their employer, and their "Excuse me, High Lord," just short of being rude.

When he finally reached Beale, he gave his butler a sharp poke in the shoulder.

Beale glanced back, noticed Saetan's stony expression, and lowered his arms. A thud immediately followed, and a maid began wailing, "Now look what you've done."

Beale cleared his throat, tugged his vest down over his girth, and waited, a slightly flushed but once more imperturbable butler.

"Tell me, Beale," Saetan crooned, "do you know who I am?"

Beale blinked. "You're the High Lord, High Lord."

"Ah, good. Since you recognize me, I must still be in human form."

"High Lord?"

"I don't look like a freestanding lamp, for example, so no one's going to try to tuck me into a corner and put a couple of candle-lights in my ears. And I won't be mistaken for an animated curio table that someone will leash to a chair so I don't wander off too far."

Beale's eyes bugged out a bit but he quickly recovered. "No, High Lord. You look exactly as you did yesterday."

Saetan crossed his arms and took his time considering this. "Do you suppose if I go into my study and stay there, I might escape being dusted, polished, or otherwise rearranged?"

"Oh, yes, High Lord. Your study was cleaned this morning."

"Will I recognize it?" Saetan murmured. He retreated to his study and sighed with relief. It was all the same furniture, and it was all arranged the same way.

Slipping out of the black tunic-styled jacket, he tossed it over the back of a chair, settled into the leather chair behind his desk, and rolled up the sleeves of his white silk shirt. Looking at the closed study door, he shook his head, but his eyes were a warm gold and his smile was an understanding one. After all, he had brought this on himself by telling them in advance.

Tomorrow, Jaenelle was coming home.

CHAPTER FOUR

1 / Hell

"That gutter son of a whore is up to something. I can feel it."

Deciding it was better to say nothing, Greer sat back in the patched chair and watched Hekatah pace.

"For two glorious years he's barely been felt, let alone seen in Hell or Kaeleer. His strength was waning. I *know* it was. Now he's back, residing at the Hall in Kaeleer. *Residing.* Do you know how long it's been since he's made his presence felt in one of the living Realms?"

"Seventeen hundred years?" Greer replied.

Hekatah stopped pacing and nodded. "Seventeen hundred years. Ever since Daemon Sadi and Lucivar Yaslana were taken away from him." She closed her gold eyes and smiled maliciously. "How he must have howled when Dorothea denied him paternity at Sadi's Birthright Ceremony, but there was nothing he could do without sacrificing his precious honor. So he slunk away like a whipped dog, consoling himself that he still had the child Hayll's Black Widows couldn't claim." She opened her eyes and hugged herself. "But Prythian had already gotten to the boy's mother and told her all those wonderful half-truths one can tell the ignorant about Guardians. It was one of the few things that winged sow has ever done right." Her pleasure faded. "So why is he back?"

"Could—" Greer considered, shook his head.

Hekatah tapped her fingertips against her chin. "Has he found another darling to replace his little pet? Or has he finally decided to turn Dhemlan into a feeding ground? Or is it something else?"

She walked toward him, her swaying hips and coquettish smile making him wish he'd known her when he could have done more than just appreciate what her movements implied.

"Greer," she crooned as she slipped her arms around his neck and pressed her breasts against him. "I want a little favor."

Greer waited, wary.

Hekatah's coquettish smile hardened. "Have your balls shriveled up so quickly, darling?"

Anger flashed in Greer's eyes. He hid it quickly. "You want me to go to the Hall in Kaeleer?"

"And risk losing you?" Hekatah pouted. "No, darling, there's no need for you to go to that nasty Hall. We have a loyal ally living in Halaway. He's wonderful at sifting out tidbits of information. Talk to him." Balancing on her toes, she lightly kissed Greer's lips. "I think you'll like him. You're two of a kind."

2 / Kaeleer

Beale opened the study door. "Lady Sylvia," he announced as he respectfully stepped aside for Halaway's Queen.

Meeting her in the middle of the room, Saetan offered both hands, palms down. "Lady."

"High Lord," she replied, placing her hands beneath his, palms up in formal greeting, leaving wrists vulnerable to nails.

Saetan kept his expression neutral, but he approved of the slight pressure pushing his hands upward, the subtle reminder of a Queen's strength. There were some Queens who deeply resented having to live with the bargain that the Dhemlan Queens in Terreille *and* Kaeleer had made with him thousands of years ago in order to protect the Dhemlan Territory in Terreille from Hayll's encroachment, who deeply resented being ruled by a male. There were some who had never understood that, in his own way, he had always served a Queen, that he had always served Witch.

Fortunately, Sylvia wasn't one of them.

She was the first Queen born in Halaway since her great-grandmother had ruled, and she was the pride of the village. The day after she had formed her court, she had come to the Hall and had informed him with forceful politeness that, while Halaway might exist to serve the Hall, it was her territory and they were her people, and if there was anything he wanted from her village she would do her utmost to honor his request—provided it was reasonable.

Saetan now offered her a warm but cautious smile as he led her to the half of his study that was furnished for less formal discussions.

After watching her perch on the edge of one of the overstuffed chairs, he took a seat on the black leather couch, putting the width of the low blackwood table between them. He picked up the decanter of yarbarah, filled one of the ravenglass goblets, and warmed it slowly over a tongue of witchfire before offering it to her.

As soon as she took the glass, he busily prepared one for himself so that he wouldn't insult her by laughing at her expression. She probably had the same look when one of her sons tried to hand her a large, ugly bug that only a small boy could find delightful.

"It's lamb's blood," he said mildly as he leaned back and crossed his legs at the knee.

"Oh." She smiled weakly. "Is that good?"

Her voice got husky when she was nervous, he noted with amusement.

"Yes, that's good. And probably far more to your liking than the human blood you feared was mixed with the wine."

She took a sip, trying hard not to gag.

"It's an acquired taste," Saetan said blandly. Had Jaenelle tasted the blood wine yet? If not, he'd have to correct that omission soon. "You've piqued my curiosity." He altered his deep voice so that it was coaxing, soothing. "Very few Queens would willingly have an audience with me at midnight, let alone request one."

Sylvia carefully set her goblet on the table before pressing her hands against her legs. "I wanted a private meeting, High Lord."

"Why?"

Sylvia licked her lips, took a deep breath, and looked him in the eye. "Something's wrong in Halaway. Something subtle. I feel . . ." She frowned and shook her head, deeply troubled.

Saetan wanted to reach out and smooth away the sharp vertical line that appeared between her eyebrows. "What do you feel?"

Sylvia closed her eyes. "Ice on the river in the middle of summer. Earth leeched of its richness. Crops withering in the fields. The wind brings a smell of fear, but I can't trace the source." She opened her eyes and smiled self-consciously. "I apologize, High Lord. My former Consort used to say I made no sense when I explained things."

"Really?" Saetan replied too softly. "Perhaps you had the wrong Consort, Lady. Because I understand you all too well." He drained his goblet and set it on the table with exaggerated care. "Who among your people is being harmed the most?"

Sylvia took a deep breath. "The children."

A vicious snarl filled the room. It was only when Sylvia nervously glanced toward the door that Saetan realized the sound was coming from him. He stopped it abruptly, but the cold, sweet rage was still there. Taking a shuddering breath, he backed away from the killing edge.

"Excuse me." Giving her no time to make excuses to leave, Saetan walked out of his study, ordered refreshments, and then spent several minutes pacing the great hall until he had repaired the frayed leash that kept his temper in check. By the time he rejoined her, Beale had brought the tea and a plate of small, thin sandwiches.

She politely refused the sandwiches and didn't touch the tea he poured for her. Her uneasiness scraped at his temper. Hell's fire, he hated seeing that look in a woman's eyes.

Sylvia licked her lips. Her voice was very husky. "I'm their Queen. It's my problem. I shouldn't have troubled you with it."

He slammed the cup and saucer down on the table so hard the saucer broke in half. Then he put some distance between them, giving himself room to pace but always staying close enough so that she couldn't reach the door before he did.

It shouldn't matter. He should be used to it. If she'd been afraid of him from the moment she stepped into the room, he could have handled it. But she hadn't been afraid. Damn her, she *hadn't* been afraid.

He spun around, keeping the couch and the table between them. "I have never harmed you or your people," he snarled. "I've used my strength, my Craft, my Jewels, and, yes, my temper to protect Dhemlan. Even when I wasn't visible, I still looked after you. There are many services—including highly personal services—that I could have required of you or any other Queen in this Territory, but I've never made those kinds of demands. I've accepted the responsibilities of ruling Dhemlan, and, damn you, I have *never* abused my position or my power."

Sylvia's brown skin was bleached of its warm, healthy color. Her hand shook when she lifted her cup to take a sip of tea. She set the cup down, lifted her chin, and squared her shoulders. "I met your daughter recently. I asked her if she found it difficult living with your temper. She looked genuinely baffled, and said, 'What temper?' "

Saetan stared at her for a moment, then the anger drained away. He rubbed the back of his neck, and said dryly, "Jaenelle has a unique way of looking at a great many things."

Before he could summon Beale, the teapot and used cups vanished. A moment later a fresh pot of tea appeared on the table, along with clean cups and saucers and a plate of pastries.

Saetan gave the door a speculative look before returning to the couch. He poured another cup of tea for Sylvia and one for himself.

"He didn't bring them in," Sylvia said quietly.

"I noticed," Saetan replied—and wondered just how close his butler was standing to the study door. He put an aural shield around the room.

"Maybe he felt intimidated."

Saetan snorted. "Any man who is happily married to Mrs. Beale isn't intimidated by anyone—including me."

"I see your point." Sylvia picked up a sandwich and took a bite.

Relieved that her color was back and she was no longer afraid, he picked up his tea and leaned back. "I'll find out what's happening in Halaway. And I'll stop it." He sipped his tea to cover his hesitation, but the question had to be asked. "When did it start?"

Sylvia looked at him sharply. "Your daughter isn't the cause, High Lord. I met her only briefly one afternoon when Mikal, my youngest son, and I were out walking; but I know she isn't the cause." She fiddled with her cup, nervous again. "But she may be the catalyst. Maybe it's fairer to say that it's her presence that has made me aware of it."

Saetan held his breath, waiting. Coaxing Jaenelle to try the Halaway school for the last few weeks before summer had been difficult. He'd hoped reconnecting with other children might stir her interest in contacting her old friends. Instead, she'd become more withdrawn, more elusive. And the politely phrased queries from Lord Menzar about her formal education—or lack of it—had dismayed him because, except for the Craft he had taught her, he had no idea how her education had been structured. But with each day since they'd come to the Hall, he had seen the threads he was trying to weave between himself and her unravel as fast as he could weave them, and he had had no idea, no clue as to why that was so. Until now.

"Why?"

Sylvia, lost in her own thoughts, stared at him, puzzled.

"Why is she the catalyst?" Saetan repeated.

"Oh." The vertical line between Sylvia's eyebrows reappeared as she concentrated. "She's . . . different."

Don't lash out at her, Saetan reminded himself. *Just listen.*

"Beron, my older son, has some classes with her, and we've talked. Not that your household is fodder for gossip, but she puzzles him so he asks me things."

"Why does she puzzle him?"

She nibbled on a sandwich, considering. "Beron says she's very shy, but if you can get her to talk, she says the most amazing things."

"I can believe that," Saetan said dryly.

"Sometimes when she's talking to someone or giving an answer in class, she'll stop in mid-sentence and cock her head, as if she's listening intensely to something no one else can hear. Sometimes when that happens, she'll pick up the sentence where she left off. Sometimes she'll withdraw into herself and won't speak for the rest of the day."

What voices did Jaenelle hear? Who—or what—called to her?

"Sometimes during a rest break, she'll walk away from the other children and not return until the next morning," Sylvia said.

She didn't return to the Hall, or he would have known about this before now. And she wasn't riding the Winds. He would have felt her absence if she had traveled beyond easy awareness. Mother Night, where did she go? Back into the abyss?

The possibility terrified him.

Sylvia took a deep breath. Took another. "Yesterday, the older students went on a trip to Marasten Gardens. Do you know it?"

"It's a large estate near the border of Dhemlan and Little Terreille. It has some of the finest gardens in Dhemlan."

"Yes." Sylvia had trouble swallowing the last bite of her sandwich. She carefully wiped her fingers on the linen napkin. "According to Beron, Jaenelle got separated from the others, although no one noticed until it was time to leave. He went back to look for her and . . . he found her kneeling beside a tree, weeping. She'd been digging, and her hands were scratched and bleeding." Sylvia stared at the teapot, breathing quickly. "Beron helped her up and reminded her that they weren't supposed to dig up the plants. And she said, 'I was planting it.' When he asked her why, she said, 'For remembrance.' "

The cold made Saetan's muscles ache, made his blood sluggish. This wasn't the searing, cleansing cold of rage. This was fear. "Did Beron recognize the plant?"

"Yes. I had shown it to him only last year and explained what it was. None of it, thank the Darkness, grows in Halaway." Sylvia looked at him, deeply troubled. "High Lord, she was planting witchblood."

Why hadn't Jaenelle told him? "If the witchblood blooms . . ."

Sylvia looked horrified. "It won't unless . . . It mustn't!"

Saetan spaced his words carefully, feeling too fragile to have even words collide. "I'll have that area investigated. Discreetly. And I'll take care of the problem in Halaway."

"Thank you." Sylvia fussed with the folds of her dress.

Saetan waited, forcing himself to be patient. He wanted to be alone, wanted time to think. But Sylvia obviously had something else on her mind. "What?"

"It's trivial in comparison."

"But?"

In one swift glance, Sylvia examined him from head to toe. "You have very good taste in clothes, High Lord."

Saetan rubbed his forehead, trying to find a connection. "Thank you." Hell's fire! How did women make these mental jumps so easily? *Why* did they make them?

"But you're probably not aware of what is considered fashionable for a young woman these days." It wasn't quite a question.

"If that's your way of telling me that Jaenelle looks like she got her wardrobe from an attic, then you're right. I think the Seneschal of the Keep opened every old trunk that was left there and let my wayward child pick and choose." It was a small subject, a safe subject. He became happily grumpy. "I wouldn't mind so much if any of them fit—that's not true, I *would* mind. She should have new clothes."

"Then why don't you take her shopping in Amdarh, or one of the nearby towns, or even Halaway?"

"Do you think I haven't tried?" he growled.

Sylvia made no comment for several moments. "I have two sons. They're very good boys—for boys—but they're not much fun to go shopping with." She gave him a twinkling little smile. "Perhaps if it was just two women having lunch and then looking around . . ."

Saetan called in a leather wallet and handed it to Sylvia. "Is that enough?"

Sylvia opened the wallet, riffled through the gold marks, and laughed. "I think we can get a decent wardrobe or three out of this."

He liked her laugh, liked the finely etched lines around her eyes. "You'll spend some of that on yourself, of course."

Sylvia gave him her best Queen stare. "I didn't suggest this with the expectation of being paid for helping a young Sister."

"I didn't offer it as payment, but if you feel uncomfortable about using some of it to please yourself, then do it to please me." He watched her expression change from anger to uneasiness, and he wondered who the fool had been who had made her unhappy. "Besides," he added gently, "you should set a proper example."

Sylvia vanished the wallet and stood up. "I will, naturally, provide you with receipts for all of the purchases."

"Naturally."

Saetan escorted her to the great hall. Taking her cape from Beale, he settled it carefully over her shoulders.

As they slowly walked to the door, Sylvia studied the carved wooden moldings that ran along the top of each wall. "I've only been here half a dozen times, if that. I never noticed the carvings before.

"Whoever carved these was very talented," she said. "Did he also make the sketches for all these creatures?"

"No." He heard the defensiveness in his voice and winced.

"You made the sketches." She studied the carvings with more interest, then muffled a laugh. "I think the woodcarver played a little with one of your sketches, High Lord. That little beasty has his eyes crossed and is sticking his tongue out—and he's placed just about where someone would stop after walking in. Apparently the beasty doesn't think much of your guests." She paused and studied him with as much interest as she'd just given the carving. "The woodcarver didn't play with your sketch, did he?"

Saetan felt his face heat. He bit back a growl. "No."

"I see," Sylvia said after a long moment. "It's been an interesting evening, High Lord."

Not sure how to interpret that remark, he escorted her into her carriage with a bit more haste than was proper.

When he could no longer hear the carriage wheels, he turned toward the open front door, wishing he could postpone the next conversation. But Jaenelle was more attuned to him during the dark hours, more revealing when hidden in shadows, more—

The sound snapped his thoughts. Holding his breath, Saetan looked toward the north woods that bordered the Hall's lawns and formal gardens. He waited, but the sound didn't come again.

"Did you hear it?" he asked Beale when he reached the door.

"Hear what, High Lord?"

Saetan shook his head. "Nothing. Probably a village dog strayed too far from home."

She was still awake, walking in the garden below her rooms.

Saetan drifted toward the waterfall and small pool in the center of the garden, letting her feel his presence without intruding on her silence. It was a good place to talk because the lights from her rooms on the second floor didn't quite reach the pool.

He settled comfortably on the edge of the pool and let the peace of a soft, early summer night and the murmur of water soothe him. While he waited for her, he idly stirred the water with his fingers and smiled.

He'd told her to landscape this inner garden for her own pleasure. The formal fountain had been the first thing to go. As he studied the water lilies, water celery, and dwarf cattails she'd planted in the pool and the ferns she'd planted around it, he wondered again if she had just wanted something that looked more natural or if she had been trying to re-create a place she had known.

"Do you think it's inappropriate?" Jaenelle asked, her voice drifting out of the shadows.

Saetan dipped his hand into the pool and raised the cupped palm, watching the water trickle through his fingers. "No, I was wishing I'd thought of it myself." He flicked drops of water from his fingers and finally looked at her.

The dark-colored dress she was wearing faded into the surrounding shadows, giving him the impression that her face, one bare shoulder, and the golden hair were rising up out of the night itself.

He looked away, focusing on a water lily but intensely aware of her.

"I like the sound of water singing over stone," Jaenelle said, coming a little closer. "It's restful."

But not restful enough. How many things haunt you, witch-child?

Saetan listened to the water. He pitched his voice to blend with it. "Have you planted witchblood before?"

She was silent so long he didn't think she would answer, but when she did, her voice had that midnight, sepulchral quality that always produced a shiver up his spine. "I've planted it before."

Sensing her brittleness, he knew he was getting too close to a soul-wound—and secrets. "Will it bloom in Marasten Gardens?" he asked quietly, once more moving his fingers slowly through the water.

Another long silence. "It will bloom."

Which meant a witch who had died violently was buried there.

Tread softly, he cautioned himself. This was dangerous ground. He looked at her, needing to see what those ancient, haunted eyes would tell him. "Will we have to plant it in Halaway?"

Jaenelle turned away. Her profile was all angles and shadows, an exotic face carved out of marble. "I don't know." She stood very still. "Do you trust your instincts, Saetan?"

"Yes. But I trust yours more."

She had the strangest expression, but it was gone so swiftly he didn't know what it meant. "Perhaps you shouldn't." She laced her fingers together, pressing and pressing until dark beads of blood dotted her hands where her nails pierced her skin. "When I lived in Beldon Mor, I was often . . . ill. Hospitalized for weeks, sometimes months at a time." Then she added, "I wasn't physically ill, High Lord."

Breathe, damn you, breathe. Don't freeze up now. "Why didn't you ever mention this?"

Jaenelle laughed softly. The bitterness in it tore him apart. "I was afraid to tell you, afraid you wouldn't be my friend anymore, afraid you wouldn't teach me Craft if you knew." Her voice was low and pained. "And I was afraid you were just another manifestation of the illness, like the unicorns and the dragons and . . . the others."

Saetan swallowed his pain, his fear, his rage. There was no outlet for those feelings on a soft night like this. "I'm not part of a dreamscape, witch-child. If you take my hand, flesh will touch flesh. The Shadow

Realm, and all who reside in it, are real." He saw her eyes fill with tears, but he couldn't tell if they were tears of pain or relief. While she had lived in Beldon Mor, her instincts had been brutalized until she no longer trusted them. She had recognized the danger in Halaway before Sylvia had, but she had doubted herself so much she hadn't been willing to admit it—just in case someone told her it wasn't real.

"Jaenelle," he said softly, "I won't act until I've verified what you tell me, but please, for the sake of those who are too young to protect themselves, tell me what you can."

Jaenelle walked away, her head down, her golden hair a veil around her face. Saetan turned around, giving her privacy without actually leaving. The stones he sat on felt cold and hard now. He gritted his teeth against the physical discomfort, knowing instinctively that if he moved she wouldn't be able to find the words he needed.

"Do you know a witch called the Dark Priestess?" Jaenelle whispered from the nearby shadows.

Saetan bared his teeth but kept his voice low and calm. "Yes."

"So does Lord Menzar."

Saetan stared at nothing, pressing his hands against the stones, relishing the pain of skin against rough edges. He didn't move, did nothing more than breathe until he heard Jaenelle climb the stairs that led to the balcony outside her rooms, heard the quiet click when she closed the glass door. He still didn't move except to raise his golden eyes and watch the candle-lights dim one by one.

The last light in Jaenelle's room went out.

He sat beneath the night sky and listened to water sing over stone. "Games and lies," he whispered. "Well, I, too, know how to play games. You shouldn't have forgotten that, Hekatah. I don't like them, but you've just made the stakes high enough." He smiled, but it was too soft, too gentle. "And I know how to be patient. But someday I'm going to have a talk with Jaenelle's foolish Chaillot relatives, and then it will be blood and not water that will be singing over stone in a very . . . private . . . garden."

"Lock it."

Mephis SaDiablo reluctantly turned the key in the door of Saetan's private study deep beneath the Hall, the High Lord's chosen place for very private conversations. He took a moment to remind himself that he had done nothing wrong, that the man who had summoned him was his father as well as the Warlord Prince he served.

"Prince SaDiablo."

The deep voice pulled him toward the man sitting behind the desk.

It was a terrible face that watched him cross the room, so still, so expressionless, so contained. The silver in Saetan's thick black hair formed two graceful triangles at the temples, drawing one's gaze to the golden eyes. Those eyes now burned with an emotion so intense words like "hate" and "rage" were inadequate. There was only one way to describe the High Lord of Hell: cold.

Centuries of training helped Mephis take the last few necessary steps. Centuries and memories. As a boy, he had feared provoking his father's temper, but he'd never feared the man. The man had sung to him, laughed with him, listened seriously to childhood troubles, respected him. It wasn't until he was grown that he understood why the High Lord should be feared—and it wasn't until he was much older that he came to appreciate *when* the High Lord should be feared.

Like now.

"Sit." Saetan's voice had that singsong croon that was usually the last thing a man ever heard—except his own screams.

Mephis tried to find a comfortable position in the chair. The large blackwood desk that separated them offered little comfort. Saetan didn't need to touch a man to destroy him.

A little flicker of irritation leaped into Saetan's eyes. "Have some yarbarah." The decanter lifted from the desk, neatly pouring the blood wine into two glasses. Two tongues of witchfire popped into existence. The glasses tilted, traveled upward, and began turning slowly above the fires. When the yarbarah was warmed, one glass floated to Mephis while the other cradled itself in Saetan's waiting hand. "Rest easy, Mephis. I require your skills, nothing more."

Mephis sipped the yarbarah. "My skills, High Lord?"

Saetan smiled. It made him look vicious. "You are meticulous, you are thorough, and, most of all, I trust you." He paused. "I want you to find out everything you can about Lord Menzar, the administrator of Halaway's school."

"Am I looking for something in particular?"

The cold in the room intensified. "Let your instincts guide you." Saetan bared his teeth in a snarl. "But this is just between you and me, Mephis. I want no one asking questions about what you're seeking."

Mephis almost asked who would dare question the High Lord, but he already knew the answer. Hekatah. This had to do with Hekatah.

Mephis drained his glass and set it carefully on the blackwood desk. "Then with your permission, I'd like to begin now."

3 / Kaeleer

Luthvian hunched her shoulders against the intrusion and vigorously pounded the pestle into the mortar, ignoring the girl hovering in the doorway. If they didn't stop pestering her with their inane questions, she'd never get these tonics made.

"Finished your Craft lesson so soon?" Luthvian asked without turning around.

"No, Lady, but—"

"Then why are you bothering me?" Luthvian snapped, flinging the pestle into the mortar before advancing on the girl.

The girl cowered in the doorway but looked confused rather than frightened. "There's a man to see you."

Hell's fire, you'd think the girl had never seen a man before. "Is he bleeding all over the floor?"

"No, Lady, but—"

"Then put him in the healing room while I finish this."

"He's not here for a healing, Lady."

Luthvian ground her teeth. She was an Eyrien Black Widow and Healer. It grated her pride to have to teach Craft to these Rihlan girls. If she still lived in Terreille, they would have been her servants, not her pupils. Of course, if she still lived in Terreille, she would still be bartering her healing skills for a stringy rabbit or a loaf of stale bread. "If he's not here for—"

She shuddered. If she hadn't closed her inner barriers so tightly in order to shut out the frustrated bleating of her students, she would have felt him the moment he walked into her house. His dark scent was unmistakable.

Luthvian fought to keep her voice steady and unconcerned. "Tell the High Lord I'll be with him shortly."

The girl's eyes widened. She bolted down the hallway, caught a friend by the arm, and began whispering excitedly.

Luthvian quietly closed the door of her workroom. She let out a whimpering laugh and thrust her shaking hands into her work apron's pockets. That little two-legged sheep was trembling with excitement at the prospect of mouthing practiced courtesies to the High Lord of Hell. She was trembling too, but for a very different reason.

Oh, Tersa, in your madness perhaps you didn't know or care what spear was slipped into your sheath. I was young and frightened, but I wasn't mad. He made my body sing, and I thought . . . I thought . . .

Even after so many centuries, the truth still left a bitter taste in her mouth.

Luthvian removed her apron and smoothed out the wrinkles in her old dress as best she could. A hearth-witch would have known some little spell to make it look crisply ironed. A witch in personal service would have known some little spell to smooth and rebraid her long black hair in seconds. She was neither, and it was beneath a Healer's dignity to learn such mundane Craft. It was beneath a Black Widow's dignity to care whether a man—any man—expressed approval of how she dressed.

After locking her workroom and vanishing the key, Luthvian squared her shoulders and lifted her chin. There was only one way to find out why he was here.

As she walked down the main hallway that divided the lower floor of her house, Luthvian kept her pace slow and dignified as befitted a Sister of the Hourglass. Her workroom, healing room, dining room, kitchen, and storerooms took up the back part of the lower floor. Student workroom, study room, Craft library, and the parlor took up the front. Baths and bedrooms for her boarders were on the second floor. Her suite of rooms and a smaller suite for special guests filled the third floor.

She didn't keep live-in servants. Doun was just around the bend in the road, so her hired help went home each night to their own families.

Luthvian paused, not yet willing to open the parlor door. She was an Eyrien exiled among Rihlanders—an Eyrien who had been born without the wings that would have been an unspoken reminder that *she* came from the warrior race who ruled the mountains. So she snapped and snarled, never allowing the Rihlanders to become overly familiar. But that didn't mean she wanted to leave, that she didn't take some satisfaction in her work. She enjoyed the deference paid to her because she was a good Healer and a Black Widow. She had influence in Doun.

But her house didn't belong to her, and the land, like all the land in Ebon Rih, belonged to the Keep. Oh, the house had been built for her, to her specifications, but that didn't mean the owner couldn't show her the front door and lock it behind him.

Was that why he was here, to call in the debt and pay her back?

Taking a deep breath, Luthvian opened the parlor door, not fully prepared to meet her former lover.

He was surrounded by her students, the whole giggling, flirting, lash-batting lot of them. He didn't look bored or desperate to be rid of them, nor was he preening as a young buck might when faced with so much undiluted feminine attention. He was as he'd always been, a courteous listener who wouldn't interrupt inane chatter unless it was absolutely necessary, a man who could skillfully phrase a refusal.

She knew so well how skillfully he could phrase a refusal.

He saw her then. There was no anger in his gold eyes. There was also no warm smile of greeting. That told her enough. Whatever business he had with her was personal but not *personal*.

It made her furious, and a Black Widow in a temper wasn't a woman to tamper with. He saw the shift in her mood, acknowledged it with a slight lift of one eyebrow, and finally interrupted the girls' chatter.

"Ladies," he said in that deep, caressing voice, "I thank you for making my wait so delightful, but I mustn't keep you from your studies any longer." Without raising his voice, he managed to silence their vigorous protests. "Besides, Lady Luthvian's time is valuable."

Luthvian stepped away from the door just enough for them to scurry past her. Roxie, her oldest student, stopped in the doorway, looked over her shoulder, and fluttered her eyelashes at the High Lord.

Luthvian slammed the door in her face.

She waited for him to approach her with the cautious respect a male who serves the Hourglass always displays when approaching a Black Widow. When he didn't move, she blushed at the silent reminder that he didn't serve the Hourglass. He was still the High Priest, a Black Widow who outranked her.

She moved with studied casualness, as if getting close to him had no importance, but stopped with half the length of the room between them. Close enough. "How could you stand listening to that drivel?"

"I found it interesting—and highly educational," he added dryly.

"Ah," Luthvian said. "Did Roxie give you her tasteful or her colorfully detailed version of her Virgin Night? She's the only one old enough to have gone through the ceremony, and she primps and preens and explains to the other girls that she's really too tired for morning lessons these days because her lover's soooo demanding."

"She's very young," Saetan said quietly, "and—"

"She's vulgar," Luthvian snapped.

"—young girls can be foolish."

Tears pricked Luthvian's eyes. She wouldn't cry in front of him. Not again. "Is that what you thought of me?"

"No," Saetan said gently. "You were a natural Black Widow, driven by your intense need to express your Craft, and driven even harder by your need to survive. You were far from foolish."

"I was foolish enough to trust you!"

There was no expression in his golden eyes. "I told you who, and what, I was before I got into bed with you. I was there as an experienced consort to see a young witch through her Virgin Night so that when she woke in the morning the only thing broken was a membrane—not her mind, not her Jewels, not her spirit. It was a role I'd played many times before when I ruled the Dhemlan Territory in both Realms. I understood and honored the rules of that ceremony."

Luthvian grabbed a vase from a side table and flung it at his head. "Was impregnating her part of the understood rules?" she screamed.

Saetan caught the vase easily, then opened his hand and let it smash on the bare wood floor. His eyes blazed, and his voice roughened. "I truly didn't think I was still fertile. I didn't expect the spell's effects to last that long. And if you'll excuse an old man's memory, I distinctly remember asking if you'd been drinking the witch's brew to prevent pregnancy and I distinctly remember you saying that you had."

"What was I supposed to say?" Luthvian cried. "Every hour put me at risk of ending up destroyed under one of Dorothea's butchers. You were my only chance of survival. I knew I was close to my fertile time, but I had to take that risk!"

Saetan didn't move, didn't speak for a long time. "You knew there was a risk, you knew you'd done nothing to prevent it, you deliberately lied to me when I asked you, and *you still dare to blame me?*"

"Not for that," she screamed at him, "but for what came after." There was no understanding in his eyes. "You only cared about the baby. You didn't w-want to b-be with me anymore."

Saetan sighed and wandered over to the picture window, fixing his gaze on the low stone wall that surrounded the property. "Luthvian," he said wearily, "the man who guides a witch through her Virgin Night isn't meant to become her lover. That only happens when there's a strong bond between them beforehand, when they're already lovers in all but the physical sense. Most of the time—"

"You don't have to recite the rules, High Lord," Luthvian snapped.

"—after he rises from the bed, he may become a valued friend or no more than a soft memory. He cares about her—he has to care in order to keep her safe—but there can be a very big difference between caring and loving." He looked over his shoulder. "I cared about you, Luthvian. I gave you what I could. It just wasn't enough."

Luthvian hugged herself and wondered if she'd ever stop feeling the bitterness and disappointment. "No, it wasn't enough."

"You could have chosen another man. You should have. I told you that, even encouraged it."

Luthvian stared at him. *Hurt, damn you, hurt as much as I have.* "And how eager do you think those men were once they realized my son had been sired by the High Lord of Hell?"

The thrust went home, but the hurt and sorrow she saw in his eyes didn't make her feel better.

"I would have taken him, raised him. You knew that, too."

The old rage, the old uncertainties exploded out of her. "Raised him for what? For fodder? To have a steady supply of strong fresh blood? When you found out he was half Eyrien, you wanted to kill him!"

Saetan's eyes glittered. "You wanted to cut off his wings."

"So he'd have a chance at a decent life! Without them he would have passed for Dhemlan. He could have managed one of your estates. He could have been respected."

"Do you really think that would have been a fair trade? Living a lie of respectability against his never knowing about his Eyrien bloodline, never understanding the hunger in his soul when he felt the wind in his face, always wondering about longings that made no sense—until the day he looked at his firstborn and saw the wings. Or were you intending to clip each generation?"

"The wings would have been a throwback, an aberration."

Saetan was very, very still. "I will tell you again what I told you at his birth. He is Eyrien in his soul and that had to be honored above all else. If you had cut off his wings, then yes, I would have slit his throat in the cradle. Not because I wasn't prepared for it, which I wasn't since you took such pains not to tell me, but because he would have suffered too much."

Luthvian honed her temper to a cutting edge. "And you think he hasn't suffered? You don't know much about Lucivar, Saetan."

"And why didn't he grow up under my care, Luthvian?" he said too softly. "Who was responsible for *that*?"

The tears were back. The memories, the anguish, the guilt. "You didn't love me, and you didn't love him."

"Half right, my dear."

Luthvian gulped back a sob. She stared at the ceiling.

Saetan shook his head and sighed. "Even after all these years, trying to talk to each other is pointless. I'd better leave."

Luthvian wiped away the single tear that had escaped her self-control. "You haven't said why you came here." For the first time, she looked at him without the past blurring the present. He looked older, weighed down by something.

"It would probably be too difficult for all of us."

She waited. His uneasiness, his unwillingness to broach the subject filled her with apprehension—and curiosity.

"I wanted to hire you as a Craft tutor for a young Queen who is also a natural Black Widow and Healer. She's very gifted, but her education has been quite . . . erratic. The lessons would have to be private and held at SaDiablo Hall."

"No," Luthvian said sharply. "Here. If I'm going to teach her, it will have to be here."

"If she came here, she would have to be escorted. Since you've always found Andulvar and Prothvar too Eyrien to tolerate, it would have to be me."

Luthvian tapped a finger against her lips. A Queen who was also a Healer *and* a Black Widow? What a potentially deadly combination of strengths. Truly a challenge worthy of her skills. "She would apprentice with me for the healing and Hourglass training?"

"No. She still has difficulty with much of the Craft we consider basic, and that's what I wanted her to work on with you. I'd be willing to extend her training with you to the healing Craft as well, if that's of interest to you, but I'll take care of the Hourglass's Craft."

Pride demanded a challenge. "Just who is this witch who requires a Black-Jeweled mentor?"

The Prince of the Darkness, the High Lord of Hell studied her, weighing, judging, and finally replied, "My daughter."

4 / Hell

Mephis dropped the file on the desk in Saetan's private study and began rubbing his hands as if to clean away some filth.

Saetan turned his hand in an opening gesture. The file opened, revealing several sheets of Mephis's tightly packed writing.

"We're going to do something about him, aren't we?" Mephis snarled.

Saetan called in his half-moon glasses, settled them carefully on the bridge of his nose, and picked up the first sheet. "Let me read."

Mephis slammed his hands on the desk. "He's an obscenity!"

Saetan looked over his glasses at his eldest son, betraying none of the anger beginning to bloom. "Let me read, Mephis."

Mephis sprang away from the desk with a snarl and started pacing.

Saetan read the report and then read it again. Finally, he closed the file, vanished the glasses, and waited for Mephis to settle down.

Obscene was an inadequate word for Lord Menzar, the administrator of Halaway's school. Unfortunate accidents or illnesses had allowed Menzar to step into a position of authority at schools in several Districts in Dhemlan—accidents he couldn't be linked to, that had no scent of him. He always showed just enough deference to please, just enough self-assurance to convince others of his ability. And there he would be, carefully undercutting the ancient code of honor and snipping away at the fragile web of trust that bound men and women of the Blood.

What would happen to the Blood once that trust was destroyed? All one had to do was look at Terreille to see the answer.

Mephis stood before the desk, his hands clenched. "What are we going to do?"

"I'll take care of it, Mephis," Saetan said too softly. "If Menzar has been free to spread his poison this long, it's because I wasn't vigilant enough to detect him."

"What about all the Queens and their First Circles who also weren't vigilant enough to detect him when he was in their territories? You didn't ignore a warning that had been sent, you *never got* any warning until Sylvia came to you."

"The responsibility is still mine, Mephis." When Mephis started to protest, Saetan cut him off. "What would you have me do? Give this information to the Queens now? Show them the evidence of how they'd been manipulated *by a man*? Do you want *them* to call in the debt?"

Mephis shuddered. "No, I don't want that. Their rage would burn for a long time over this."

"And would burn more than the man responsible for it." Saetan forced his voice to be gentle. "There are young witches—Queens, Black Widows, and Priestesses among them—coming of age in Dhemlan who bear the scars of what he's done. We'll have to tell some of the stronger males in those Districts what's happened so they'll be prepared and then do what we can to help them rebuild the trust Menzar destroyed." He shook his head sadly. "No, Mephis, if I'm not willing to accept the responsibilities then I should relinquish my claim to this land."

"His blood shouldn't be on your hands alone," Mephis said quietly.

Thank you, Mephis. I do thank you for that. "A formal execution never has more than one executioner." He paused, then asked, "Is there anyone dependent upon him?"

Mephis nodded. "He has a sister who looks after his house."

"A hearth-witch?"

Mephis's eyes were yellow stones. "Not by training or inclination from what I could determine. It seems he lets her live with him on sufferance—she, according to village gossip no doubt seeded by him, not having the wit or wisdom to be self-sufficient—and lets her pay for her room and board with all manner of domestic services." His voice left no doubt about what kind of services Menzar required.

"Do you think she has the wit and wisdom to be self-sufficient?"

Mephis shrugged. "I doubt she's ever had the chance to try. She doesn't wear Jewels. Whether she never had the potential or had it stripped from her . . . it's difficult to say at this point."

Hekatah, you train your servants well. "Use some of the family income to quietly provide her with an allowance equal to Menzar's wages. The house is leased? Pay the lease for a five-year period."

Mephis crossed his arms. "Without the rent to pay, it will be more money than she's ever had at her disposal."

"It'll give her the time and the means to rest. There's no reason she should pay for her brother's crimes. If her wits have been buried beneath Menzar's manipulation, they'll surface. If she's truly incapable of taking care of herself, we'll make other arrangements."

Mephis looked troubled. "About the execution . . ."

"I'll take care of it, Mephis." Saetan came around the desk and brushed his shoulder against his son's. "Besides, there's something else I want you to do." He waited until Mephis looked at him. "You still have the town house in Amdarh?"

"You know I do."

"And you still enjoy the theater?"

"Very much," Mephis said, puzzled. "I rent a box each season."

"Are there any plays that might intrigue a fifteen-year-old girl?"

Mephis smiled in understanding. "A couple of them next week."

Saetan's answering smile was chilling. "Well-timed, I think. An outing to Dhemlan's capital with her elder brother before her new tutors begin making demands on her time will suit our plans very well."

5 / Terreille

Lucivar's legs quivered from exhaustion and pain. Chained facing the back wall of his cell, he tried to rest his chest against it to lessen the strain on his legs, tried to ignore the tension in his shoulders and neck.

The tears came, slow and silent at first, then building into rib-squeezing, racking sobs of pent-up grief.

The surly guard had performed the beating. Not his back this time but his legs. Not a whip to cut, but a thick leather strap to pound against muscle stretched tight. Working to a slow drum rhythm, the guard had applied the strap with care, making each stroke overlap the one before so that no flesh was missed. Down and back, down and back. Except for the breath hissing between his teeth, Lucivar had made no sound. When it was finally done, he'd been hauled to his feet—feet too brutalized to take his weight—and fitted with Zuultah's latest toy: a metal chastity belt. It locked tight around his waist but the metal loop between his legs wasn't tight enough to cause discomfort. He'd puzzled over it for a moment before being forced to walk to his cell. There wasn't room for anything but the pain after that. And when he got to the cell, he understood only too well what was supposed to happen.

There was a new, thick-linked chain attached to the back wall. The bottom loop of the belt was pulled through a slot in the band around his waist, and the chain was locked to it. The chain wasn't long enough for him to do anything but stand, and if his legs buckled, it wouldn't be his waist absorbing his weight. No doubt Zuultah was being oiled and massaged while she waited for his scream of agony.

That wasn't reason enough to cry.

Slime mold had begun forming on his wings. Without a cleansing by a Healer, it would spread and spread until his wings were nothing more than greasy strings of membranous skin hanging from the frame. He couldn't spread his wings in the salt mine without being whipped, and now his hands were chained behind his back each night, locking his wings tight against a body coated with salt dust and dripping with sweat.

He'd told Daemon once he would rather lose his balls than his wings, and he had meant it.

But that wasn't reason enough to cry.

He hadn't seen the sun in over a year. Except for the few precious minutes each day when he was led from his cell to the salt mines and back again, he hadn't breathed clean air or felt a breeze against his skin. His world had become two dark, stinking holes—and a covered courtyard where he was stretched out on the stones and regularly beaten.

But that wasn't reason enough to cry.

He'd been punished before, beaten before, whipped before, locked in dark cells before. He'd been sold into service to cruel, twisted witches before. He'd always responded by fighting with all the savagery within him, becoming such a destructive force they'd send him back to Askavi in order to survive.

He hadn't once tried to escape from Pruul, hadn't once unleashed his volatile temper to rend and tear and destroy. Not that many years ago, Zuultah's and the guards' blood would have been splashed over the walls of this place and he would have stood in the rubble filling the night with an Eyrien battle cry of victory.

But that was when he'd still believed in the myth, the dream. That was when he'd still believed that one day he would meet the Queen who would accept him, understand him, value him. Meeting her had been his dream, a sweet, ever-blooming flower in his soul. The Lady of the Black Mountain. The Queen of Ebon Askavi. Witch.

Then the dream became flesh—and Daemon killed her.

That was reason to grieve. For the loss of the Lady he'd ached to serve, for the loss of the one man he thought he could trust.

Now there was only an emptiness, a despair so deep it covered his soul like the slime mold was covering his wings.

There was only one dream left.

The ache in his chest finally eased. Lucivar swallowed the last sob and opened his eyes.

He'd always known where he wanted to die and how he wanted to die. And it wasn't in the salt mines of Pruul.

Lucivar's legs vibrated from the strain. He sank his teeth into his lower lip until it bled. A couple more hours and the guards would release him to take him to the salt mines. More pain, more suffering.

He would whimper a little, cringe a little. Next week he would cringe a little more when a guard approached. Little by little they would forget what should never be forgotten about him. And then . . .

Lucivar smiled, his lips smeared with blood.

There was still a reason to live.

6 / Terreille

Dorothea SaDiablo stared at her Master of the Guard. "What do you mean you've called off the search?"

"He's not in Hayll, Priestess," Lord Valrik replied. "My men and I have searched every barn, every cottage, every Blood and landen village. We've been down every alley in every city. Daemon Sadi is not in Hayll, *has not been* in Hayll. I would stake my career on it."

Then you've lost. "You called off the search without my consent."

"Priestess, I'd give my life for you, but we've been chasing shadows. No one has seen him, Blood or landens. The men are weary. They need to be home with their families for a while."

"And ten months from now an army of mewling brats will be testimony to how weary your men are."

Valrik didn't answer.

Dorothea paced, tapping her fingertips against her chin. "So he isn't in Hayll. Start searching the neighboring Territories and—"

"We've no right to make such a search in another Territory."

"All those Territories stand in Hayll's shadow. The Queens wouldn't dare deny you access to their lands."

"The authority of the Queens ruling those Territories is weak as it is. We can't afford to undermine it."

Dorothea turned away from him. He was right, damn him. But she had to get him to do *something*. "Then you leave me at the mercy of the Sadist," she said with a tearful quiver in her voice.

"*No*, Priestess," Valrik said strenuously. "I've talked to the Masters of the Guard in all the neighboring Territories, made them aware of his bestial nature. They understand their own young are at risk. If they find him in their Territory, he won't get out alive."

Dorothea spun around. "I *never* gave you permission to kill him."

"He's a Warlord Prince. It's the only way we'll—"

"*You must not kill him.*"

Dorothea swayed, pleased when Valrik put his arms around her and guided her to a chair. Wrapping her arms around his neck, she pulled his head down until their foreheads touched. "His death would have repercussions for all of us. He must be brought back to Hayll alive. You must at least supervise the search in the other Territories."

Valrik hesitated, then sighed. "I can't. For your sake and the sake of Hayll . . . I can't."

A good man. Older, experienced, respected, honorable.

Dorothea slid her right hand down his neck in a sensuous caress before driving her nails into his flesh and pumping all of her venom through the snake tooth.

Valrik pulled back, shocked, his hand clamped against his neck. "Priestess . . ." His eyes glazed. He stumbled back a step.

Dorothea daintily licked the blood from her fingers and smiled at him. "You said you would give your life for me. Now you have." She studied her nails, ignoring Valrik as he staggered out of the room, dying. Calling in a nail file, she smoothed a rough edge.

A pity to lose such an excellent Master of the Guard and a bother to have to replace him. She vanished the nail file and smiled. But at least Valrik, by example, would teach his successor a very necessary lesson: too much honor could get a man killed.

7 / Kaeleer

Saetan balled the freshly ironed shirt in his hands, massaging it into a mass of wrinkles. He shook it out, grimly satisfied with the results, and slipped it on.

He hated this. He had always hated this.

His black trousers and tunic jacket received the same treatment as the shirt. As he buttoned the jacket, he smiled wryly. Just as well he'd insisted that Helene and the rest of the staff take the evening off. If his prim housekeeper saw him dressed like this, she'd consider it a personal insult.

A strange thing, feelings. He was preparing for an execution and all he felt was relief that his appearance wouldn't bruise his housekeeper's pride.

No, not all. There was anger at the necessity and a simmering anxiety that, because of what he was about to do, he might look into sapphire eyes and see condemnation and disgust instead of warmth and love.

But she was with Mephis in Amdarh. She'd never know about tonight.

Saetan called in the cane he had put aside a few weeks ago.

Of course Jaenelle would know. She was too astute not to understand the meaning behind Menzar's sudden disappearance. But what would she think of him? What would it mean to her?

He had hoped—such a bittersweet thing!—that he could live here quietly and not give people reason to remember too sharply who and what he was. He had hoped to be just a father raising a Queen daughter.

It had never been that simple. Not for him.

No one had ever asked him why he'd been willing to fight on Dhemlan Terreille's behalf when Hayll had threatened that quiet land all of those long centuries ago. Both sides had assumed that ambition had been the driving force within him. But what had driven him had been far more seductive and far simpler: he had wanted a place to call home.

He had wanted land to care for, people to care for, children—his own and others—to fill his house with their laughter and exuberance.

He had dreamed of a simple life where he would use his Craft to enrich, not destroy.

But a Black-Jeweled, Black Widow Warlord Prince who was already called the High Lord of Hell couldn't slip into the quiet life of a small village. So he'd named a price worthy of his strength, built SaDiablo Hall in all three Realms, ruled with an iron will and a compassionate heart, and yearned for the day when he would meet a woman whose love for him was stronger than her fear of him.

Instead, he had met and married Hekatah.

For a while, a very short while, he'd thought his dream had come true—until Mephis was born and she was sure he wouldn't walk away, wouldn't forsake his child. Even then, having pledged himself to her, he had tried to be a good husband, had tried even harder to be a good father. When she conceived a second time, he'd dared to hope again that she cared for him, wanted to build a life with him. But Hekatah had been in love only with her ambitions, and children were her payment for his support. It wasn't until she carried their third child that she finally understood he would never use his power to make her the undisputed High Priestess of all the Realms.

He never saw his third son. Only pieces.

Saetan closed his eyes, took a deep breath, and cast the small spell tied to a tangled web of illusions that he'd created earlier in the day. His leg muscles trembled. He opened his eyes and studied hands that now looked gnarled and had a slight but noticeable shake. "I hate this." He smiled slowly. He sounded like a querulous old man.

By the time he made his way to the public reception room, his back ached from being unnaturally hunched and his legs began to burn from the tension. But if Menzar was smart enough to suspect a trap, the physical discomfort would help hide the web's illusions.

Saetan stepped into the great hall and hissed softly at the man standing silently by the door. "I told you to take the evening off." There was no power in his voice, no soft thunder.

"It would not be appropriate for you to open the door when your guest arrives, High Lord," Beale replied.

"What guest? I'm not expecting anyone tonight."

"Mrs. Beale is visiting with her younger sister in Halaway. I will join them after your guest arrives, and we will dine out."

Saetan rested both hands on the cane and raised an eyebrow. "Mrs. Beale dines out?"

Beale's lips curved up a tiny bit. "On occasion. With reluctance."

Saetan's answering smile faded. "Join your lady, Lord Beale."

"After your guest has arrived."

"I'm not expect—"

"My nieces attend the Halaway school." The Red Jewel flared beneath Beale's white shirt.

Saetan sucked air through his teeth. This had to be done quietly. There was nothing the Dark Council could do to him directly, but if whispers of this reached them. . . . He stared at his Red-Jeweled Warlord butler. "How many know?"

"Know what, High Lord?" Beale replied gently.

Saetan continued to stare. Was he mistaken? No. For just a moment, there *had* been a wild, fierce satisfaction in Beale's eyes. The Beales would say nothing. Nothing at all. But they would celebrate.

"You'll be in your public study?" Beale asked.

Accepting his dismissal, Saetan retreated to his study. As he poured and warmed a glass of yarbarah, he noticed that his hands were shaking from more than the spell he'd cast.

Hayllian by birth, he had served in Terreillean courts, and had ruled, for the most part, in Terreille and then Hell. Despite his claim to the Dhemlan Territory in Kaeleer, he had been more like an absentee land-lord, a visitor who only saw what visitors were allowed to see.

He knew what Terreille had thought of the High Lord. But this was Kaeleer, the Shadow Realm, a fiercer, wilder land that embraced a magic darker and stronger than Terreille could ever know.

Thank you, Beale, for the warning, the reminder. I won't forget again what ground I stand on. I won't forget what you've just shown me lies beneath the thin cloak of Protocol and civilized behavior. I won't forget . . . because this is the Blood that is drawn to Jaenelle.

Lord Menzar reached for the knocker but snatched his hand away at the last second. The bronze dragon head tucked tight against a thick, curving neck stared down at him, its green glass eyes glittering eerily in the torchlight. The knocker directly beneath it was a detailed, taloned foot curved around a smooth ball.

The Dark Priestess should have warned me.

Grabbing the foot with a sweaty hand, he pounded on the door once, twice, thrice before stepping back and glancing around. The torches created ever-changing shape-filled shadows, and he wished, again, that this meeting could have been held in the daylight hours.

He waved his hand to erase the useless thought and reached for the knocker again just as the door suddenly swung open. He almost stepped back from the large man blocking the doorway until he recognized the black suit and waistcoat that was a butler's uniform.

"You may tell the High Lord I'm here."

The butler didn't move, didn't speak.

Menzar surreptitiously chewed on his lower lip. The man was alive, wasn't he? Since he knew that many of Halaway's people worked for the Hall in one way or another, it hadn't occurred to him that the staff might be very different once the sun went down. Surely not with that girl here—although that might explain her eccentricities.

The butler finally stepped aside. "The High Lord is expecting you."

Menzar's relief at coming inside was short-lived. As shadow-filled as the outer steps, the great hall held a silence that was pregnant with interrupted rustling. He followed the butler to the end of the hall, disturbed by the lack of people. Where were the servants? In another wing, perhaps, or taking their supper? A place this size . . . half the village could be here and their presence would be swallowed up.

The butler opened the last right-hand door and announced him.

It was an interior room with no windows and no other visible door. Shaped like a reversed **L**, the long side had large chairs, a low blackwood table, a black leather couch, a Dharo carpet, candle-lights held in variously shaped wrought-iron holders, and powerful, somewhat disturbing paintings. The short leg . . .

Menzar gasped when he finally noticed the golden eyes shining out of the dark. A candle-light in the far corner began to glow softly. The short leg held a large blackwood desk. Behind it were floor-to-ceiling bookshelves. The walls on either side were covered with dark-red velvet. It felt different from the rest of the room. It felt dangerous.

The candle-lights brightened, chasing the shadows into the corners.

"Come where I can see you," said a querulous voice.

Menzar slowly approached the desk and almost laughed with relief.

This was the High Lord? This shrunken, shaking, grizzled old man? This was the man whose name everyone feared to whisper?

Menzar bowed. "High Lord. It was kind of you to invite me to—"

"Kind? Bah! Didn't see any reason why I should torture my old bones when there's nothing wrong with your legs." Saetan waved a shaking hand toward the chair in front of the desk. "Sit down. Sit down. Tires me just to watch you stand there." While Menzar made himself comfortable, Saetan muttered and gestured to no one. Finally focusing on his guest, he snapped, "Well? What's she done now?"

Tamping down his jubilation, Menzar pretended to consider the question. "She hasn't been in school this week," he said politely. "I understand she'll be tutored from now on. I must point out that socializing with children her own age—"

"Tutors?" Saetan sputtered, thumping his cane on the floor. "Tutors?" Thump. Thump. "Why should I waste my coin on tutors? She's got all the teaching she needs to perform her duties."

"Duties?"

Saetan's mouth curved in a leering smile. "Her mind's a bit queered up and she's not much to look at, but in the dark she's sweet enough."

Menzar tried not to stare. The Dark Priestess's friend had hinted, but. . . . He'd seen no bite marks on the girl's neck. Well, there were other veins. What else might Saetan be doing—or what might she be required to do for him while he supped from a vein? Menzar could imagine several things. They all disgusted him. They all excited him.

Menzar clamped one hand over the other to keep them still. "What about the tutors?"

Saetan waved his hand, dismissing the words. "Had to say something when that bitch Sylvia came sniffing around asking about the girl." He narrowed his eyes. "You strike me as a very discerning man, Lord Menzar. Would you like to see my special room?"

Menzar's heart smashed against his chest. *If he invites you to his private study, make an excuse, any excuse to leave.* "Special room?"

"My special, special room. Where the girl and I . . . play."

Menzar was about to refuse, but the doubts and the warnings melted away. The High Lord was just a lecherous old man. But no doubt a connoisseur of things Menzar had only read about. "I'd like that."

The walk through the corridors was painfully slow. Saetan went down

flights of stairs crabwise, muttering and cursing. Every time Menzar became uneasy about their descent, a leering grin and a highly erotic tidbit
vanished the doubts again.

They finally arrived at a thick wooden door with a lock as big as a
man's fist. Menzar waited restlessly while Saetan's shaking hand fit the key
into the lock, and then he had to help the High Lord push the heavy door
open. Who helped the High Lord at other times? That butler? Did the girl
follow him into the room like a well-trained pet or was she restrained?
Did Saetan require assistance? Did that butler watch while he . . . Menzar
licked his lips. The bed must be like . . . he couldn't even begin to imagine what the bed in this playroom would be like.

"Come in, come in," Saetan said querulously.

The torchlight from the corridor didn't penetrate the room. Standing
at the doorway, once more uncertain, Menzar strained his eyes to see the
furnishings, but the room was filled with a thick, full darkness, a waiting
darkness, something more than the absence of light.

Menzar couldn't decide whether to step back or step forward. Then
he felt a phantom *something* whisper past him, leaving a mist so fine it almost wasn't there. But that mist was full of many things, and in his mind
he saw a bouquet of young faces, the faces of all the witches whose spirits he had so carefully pruned. He'd always considered himself a subtle gardener, but this room offered more. Much, much more.

He stepped inside, drawn toward the center of the room by small phantom hands. Some playfully tugged, some caressed. The last one pressed
firmly against his chest, stopping him from taking another step, before sliding down his belly and disappearing just before it reached his expectation.

His disappointment was as sharp as the sound of the lock snapping
into place.

Cold. Dark. Silent.

"H-High Lord?"

"Yes, Lord Menzar," said a deep voice that rolled through the room
like soft thunder. A seductive voice, caressing in the dark.

Menzar licked his lips. "I must be going now."

"That isn't possible."

"I have another appointment."

Slowly the darkness changed, lessened. A cold, silver light spread along
the stone walls, floor, and ceiling, following the radial and tether lines of

an immense web. On the back wall hung a huge, black metal spider, its hourglass made of faceted rubies. Attached to the silver web embedded in the stone were knives of every shape and size.

The only other thing in the room was a table.

Menzar's sphincter muscles tightened.

The table had a high lip and channels running to small holes in the corners. Glass tubing ran from the holes to glass jars.

Stop this. Stop it. He was letting his own fear beat him. He was letting this room intimidate him. That old man certainly wasn't intimidating. He could easily brush aside that doddering old fool.

Menzar turned around, ready to insist on leaving.

It took him a long moment to recognize the man leaning against the door, waiting.

"Everything has a price, Lord Menzar," Saetan crooned. "It's time to pay the debt."

The water swirling into the drain finally ran clear. Saetan twisted the dials to stop the hard spray that had been pounding him. He held on to the dials for balance, resting his head on his forearm.

It wasn't over. There were still the last details to attend to.

He toweled himself briskly, dropped the towel on the narrow bed as he passed through the small bedroom adjoining his private study deep beneath the Hall in the Dark Realm. A carafe of yarbarah waited for him on the large blackwood desk. He reached for it, hesitated, then called in a decanter of brandy. He filled a glass almost to the rim and drank it down. The brandy would give him a fierce headache, but it would also soften the edges, blur the memories and twisted fantasies that had burst from Menzar's mind like pus from a boil.

Brandy also didn't taste like blood, and the taste, the smell of blood wasn't something he could tolerate tonight.

He poured his second glass and stood naked in front of the unlit hearth, staring at Dujae's painting *Descent into Hell*. A gifted artist to have captured in ambiguous shapes that mixture of terror and joy the Blood felt when first entering the Dark Realm.

He poured his third glass. He had burned the clothes he'd worn. He had never been able to tolerate keeping the clothing worn for an execution. Some part of the fear and the pain always seemed to weave itself into the cloth. To be assaulted by it afterward . . .

The glass shattered in his hand. Snarling, he vanished the broken glass before returning to the small bedroom and hurriedly dressing in fresh clothes.

He had scrubbed Menzar off his body, but would he ever be able to cleanse Menzar's thoughts from his mind?

"You understand what to do?"

Two demons, once Halaway men, eyed the large, ornate wooden chest. "Yes, High Lord. It will been done precisely as you asked."

Saetan handed each of them a small bottle. "For your trouble."

"It's no trouble," one said. He pulled the cork from the bottle and sniffed. His eyes widened. "It's—"

"Payment."

The demon corked the bottle and smiled.

"The *cildru dyathe* don't want this."

Saetan set the small bottle on a flat rock that served as a table. He had distributed all the others. This was the last. "I'm not offering it to the rest of the *cildru dyathe*. Only you."

Char shifted his feet, uneasy. "We wait to fade into the Darkness," he said, but his blackened tongue licked what was left of his lips as he eyed the bottle.

"It's not the same for you," Saetan said. His stomach churned. Thin needles of pain speared his temples. "You care for the others, help them adjust and make the transitions. You fight to stay here, to give them a place. And I know when offerings are made in remembrance of a child who has gone, you don't refuse them." Saetan picked up the bottle and held it out to the boy. "It's appropriate for you to take this. More than you know."

Char slowly reached for the bottle, uncorked it, and sniffed. He took a tiny sip and gasped, delighted. "This is undiluted blood."

Saetan clamped his teeth tight against the nausea and pain. He stared at the bottle, hating it. "No. This is restitution."

8 / Hell

Hekatah stared at the large, ornate wooden chest and tapped the small piece of folded white paper against her chin.

Beautifully decorated with precious woods and gold inlay, the chest reeked of wealth, a sharp reminder of the way she'd once lived and the kind of luxury she believed was her due.

Using Craft, Hekatah probed the interior of the chest for the fifth time in an hour. Still nothing. Perhaps there *was* nothing more.

Opening the paper, she studied the elegant masculine script.

> Hekatah,
> Here is a token of my regard.
> Saetan

There *must* be something more. This was just the wrapping, no matter how expensive. Perhaps Saetan had finally realized how much he needed her. Perhaps he was tired of playing the beneficent patriarch and ready to claim what he—what they—should have claimed so long ago. Perhaps his damnable honor had been sufficiently tarnished by playing with the girl-pet he'd acquired in Kaeleer to take Jaenelle's place.

She'd savor those thoughts after she opened her present.

The brass key was still in the envelope. She shook it into her hand, knelt by the chest, and opened the brass lock.

Hekatah lifted the lid and frowned. Fragrant wood shavings filled the chest. She stared for a moment, then smiled indulgently. Packing, of course. With an excited little squeal, she plunged one hand into the shavings, rummaging for her gift.

The first thing she pulled out was a hand.

Dropping it, she scrambled away from the chest. Her throat worked convulsively as she stared at the hand now lying palm up, its fingers slightly curled. Finally curiosity overrode fear. On hands and knees, she inched forward.

Porcelain or marble would have shattered on the stone floor.

Flesh then.

For a moment, she was grateful it was a normal-looking hand, not maimed or misshaped.

Breathing harshly, Hekatah got to her feet and stared once more at the open chest. She waved her hand back and forth. Lifted by the Craft wind, the shavings spilled onto the floor.

Another hand. Forearms. Upper arms. Feet. Lower legs. Upper legs. Genitals. Torso. And in the corner, staring at her with empty eyes, was Lord Menzar's head.

Hekatah screamed, but even she couldn't say if it was from fear or rage. She stopped abruptly.

One warning. That was all he ever gave. But why?

Hekatah hugged herself and smiled. Through his work at the Halaway school, Menzar must have gotten a little too close to the High Lord's new choice little morsel.

Then she sighed. Saetan could be so possessive. Since Menzar had been careless enough to provoke him into an execution, it was doubtful the girl would be allowed outside SaDiablo Hall without a handpicked escort. And she knew from experience that anyone handpicked by Saetan for a particular duty wasn't amenable to bribes of any kind. So . . .

Hekatah sighed again. It would take a fair amount of persuasion to convince Greer to slip into the Hall to see the High Lord's new pet.

It was a good thing the girl whining in the next room was such a choice little tidbit.

9 / Terreille

Surreal strolled down the quiet, backwater street where no one asked questions. Men and women sat on front stoops, savoring the light breeze that made the sticky afternoon bearable. They didn't speak to her, and she, having spent two years of her childhood on a street like this, gave them the courtesy of walking by as if they weren't there.

As she reached the building where she had a top-floor flat, Surreal noticed the eyes that met hers for a brief moment. She casually shifted the heavy carry-basket from her right hand to her left while she watched one man cross the street and approach her cautiously.

Not the stiletto for this one, she decided. A slashing knife, if necessary. From the way he moved, he might still be healing from a deep wound on his left side. He'd try to protect it. But maybe not, if he was a Warlord experienced in fighting.

The man stopped a body length away. "Lady."

"Warlord."

She saw a tremor of fear in his eyes before he masked it. That she could identify his caste so easily, despite his efforts to hide it, told him that she was strong enough to win any dispute with him.

"That basket looks heavy," he said, still cautious.

"A couple of novels and tonight's dinner."

"I could carry it up for you . . . in a few minutes."

She understood the warning. Someone was waiting for her. If she survived the meeting, the Warlord would bring up the basket. If she didn't, he would divide the spoils among a select few in his building, thus buying a little help if he should need it in the future.

Surreal set the basket on the sidewalk and stepped back. "Ten minutes." When he nodded, she swiftly climbed the building's front steps. Then she paused long enough to put two Gray protective shields around herself and a Green shield over them. Hopefully whoever was waiting for her would respond to the lesser Green shield first. She also called in her largest hunting knife. If the attack was physical, the knife's blade would give her a little extra reach.

With her hand on the doorknob, she made a quick psychic probe of the entryway. No one. Nothing unusual.

A fast twist of the knob and she was inside, turning toward the back of the door. She kicked the door shut, keeping her back against a wall pocked with rusty letter boxes. Her large, gold-green eyes adjusted quickly to the gloomy entryway and equally dim stairwell. No sounds. And no obvious feel of danger.

Up the stairs quickly, keeping her mind open to eddies of mood or thought that might slip from an enemy's mind.

Up to the third floor, the fourth. Finally to the fifth.

Pressed in the opposite corner from her own door, Surreal probed once more—and finally felt it.

A dark psychic scent. Muted, altered somehow, but familiar.

Relieved—and a little annoyed—that there wouldn't be a fight, Surreal vanished the knife, unlocked her door, and went inside.

She hadn't seen him since he'd left Deje's Red Moon house more than two years ago. It didn't look like they'd been easy years. His black hair was long and raggedly cut. His clothes were dirty and torn. When he didn't respond to her briskly closing the door and just continued to stare at the sketch she'd recently purchased, she began to feel uneasy.

That lack of response was wrong. Very wrong. Reaching back, Surreal opened the door just enough not to have to fumble with locks.

"Sadi?"

He finally turned around. The golden eyes held no recognition, but they held something else that was familiar, if only she could remember where she'd seen that look before.

"Daemon?"

He continued to stare at her, as if he were struggling to remember. Then his expression cleared. "It's little Surreal." His voice—that beautiful, deep, seductive voice—was hoarse, rusty.

Little Surreal?

"You're not here alone, are you?" Daemon asked uneasily.

Starting across the room, she said sharply, "Of course I'm here alone. Who else would be here?"

"Where's your mother?"

Surreal froze. "My mother?"

"You're too young to be here alone."

Titian had been dead for centuries. He *knew* that. It was centuries ago that he and Tersa . . .

Tersa's eyes. Eyes that strained to make out the ghostly, gray shapes of reality through the mist of the Twisted Kingdom.

Mother Night, what had happened to him?

Keeping his distance, Daemon began edging toward the door. "I can't stay here. Not without your mother. I won't . . . I can't . . ."

"Daemon, wait." Surreal leaped between him and the door. Panic flashed in his eyes. "Mother had to go away for a few days with . . . with Tersa. I'd . . . I'd feel safer if you stayed."

Daemon tensed. "Has anyone tried to hurt you, Surreal?"

Hell's fire, not *that* tone of voice. Not with that Warlord coming up the stairs any minute with the basket.

"No," she said, hoping she sounded young but convincing. "But you and Tersa are as close as we have to family and I'm . . . lonely."

Daemon stared at the carpet.

"Besides," she added, wrinkling her nose, "you need a bath."

His head snapped up. He stared at her with such transparent hope and hunger it scared her. "Lady?" he whispered, reaching for her. "Lady?" He studied the hair entwined around his fingers and shook his head. "Black. It's not supposed to be black."

If she lied, would it help him? Would he know the difference? She closed her eyes, not sure she could stand the anguish she felt in him. "Daemon," she said gently, "I'm Surreal."

He stepped away from her, keening softly.

She led him to a chair, unable to think of anything else to do.

"So. You're a friend."

Surreal spun toward the door, feet braced in a fighting stance, the hunting knife back in her hand.

The Warlord stood in the doorway, the carry-basket at his feet.

"I'm a friend," Surreal said. "What are you?"

"Not an enemy." The Warlord eyed the knife. "Don't suppose you could put that away."

"Don't suppose I could."

He sighed. "He healed me and helped me get here."

"Are you going to complain about services rendered?"

"Hell's fire, no," the Warlord snapped. "He told me before he started that he wasn't sure he knew enough healing Craft to mend the damage. But I wasn't going to survive without help, and a Healer would have turned me in." He ran a hand through his short brown hair. "And even if he killed me, it would have been better than what my Lady would have done to me for leaving her service so abruptly." He gestured toward Daemon, who was curled in the chair, still keening softly. "I didn't realize he was . . ."

Surreal vanished the knife. The Warlord immediately picked up the basket, pressing his left hand to his side and grimacing.

"Asshole," Surreal snapped, hurrying to take the basket. "You shouldn't carry something this heavy while you're still healing."

She tugged. When he wouldn't let go of the basket, she snarled at him. "Idiot. Fool. At least use Craft to lighten the weight."

"Don't be a bitch." Clenching his teeth, the Warlord carried the basket to the table in the kitchen area. He turned to leave, then hesitated. "The story going around is that he killed a child."

Blood. So much blood. "He didn't."

"He thinks he did."

She couldn't see Daemon, but she could still hear him. "Damn."

"Do you think he'll ever come out of the Twisted Kingdom?"

Surreal stared at the basket. "No one ever has."

"Daemon." When she got no response, Surreal chewed her lower lip. Maybe she should let him sleep, if he was actually sleeping. No, the potatoes were baking, the steaks ready to broil, the salad made. He needed food as much as rest. Touch him? There was no telling what he might be seeing in the Twisted Kingdom, how he might interpret a gentle shake. She tried again, putting some snap in her voice. "Daemon."

Daemon opened his eyes. After a long minute, he reached for her. "Surreal," he said hoarsely.

She gripped his hand, wishing she knew some way to help him. When his grip loosened, she tightened hers and tugged. "Up. You need a shower before dinner."

He got to his feet with much of his fluid, feline grace, but when she led him into the bathroom, he stared at the fixtures as if he'd never seen them before. She lifted the toilet seat, hoping he remembered how to use that at least. When he still didn't move, she tugged him out of the jacket and shirt. It had never bothered her when Tersa displayed this childlike passivity. His lack of response frayed her temper. But when she reached for his belt, he snarled at her, his hand squeezing her wrist until she was sure the bones would break.

She snarled back. "Do it yourself then."

She saw the inward crumbling, the despair.

Loosening his hold on her wrist, he raised her hand and pressed his lips against it. "I'm sorry. I'm—" Releasing her, he looked beaten as he unbuckled the belt and began fumbling with his trousers.

Surreal fled.

A few minutes later the water pipes rattled and wheezed as he turned on the shower.

As she set the table, she wondered if he'd actually removed all his clothes. How long had he been like this? If this was what was left of a once-brilliant mind, how had he been able to heal that man?

Surreal paused, a plate half-resting on the table. Tersa had always had her islands of lucidity, usually around Craft. Once when the mad Black Widow had healed a deep gash in Surreal's leg, she'd responded to Titian's worry by saying, "One doesn't forget the basics." When the healing was done, however, Tersa couldn't even remember her own name.

A few minutes later, she was hovering in the hallway when she heard the muffled yelp that indicated the hot water had run out. The pipes rattled and wheezed as he shut off the water.

No other sound.

Swearing under her breath, Surreal pushed the bathroom door open. Daemon just stood in the tub, his head down.

"Dry yourself," Surreal said.

Flinching, he reached for a towel.

Struggling to keep her voice firm but quiet, she added, "I put out some clean clothes for you. When you've dried off, go put them on."

She retreated to the kitchen and busied herself with cooking the steaks while listening to the movements in the bedroom. She was putting the meat on their plates when Daemon appeared, properly dressed.

Surreal smiled her approval. "Now you look more like yourself."

"Jaenelle is dead," he said, his voice hard and flat.

She braced her hands on the table and absorbed the words that were worse than a physical blow. "How do you know?"

"Lucivar told me."

How could Lucivar, who was in Pruul, be sure of something she and Daemon couldn't be sure of? And who was there to ask? Cassandra had never returned to the Altar after that night, and Surreal didn't know who the Priest was, let alone where to start looking for him.

She cut the potatoes and fluffed them open. "I don't believe him." She looked up in time to see a lucid, arrested look in his eyes. Then it faded. He shook his head.

"She's dead."

"Maybe he was wrong." She took two servings of salad from the bowl and dressed them before sitting down and cutting into her steak. "Eat."

He took his place at the table. "He wouldn't lie to me."

Surreal plopped soured cream onto Daemon's baked potato and gritted her teeth. "I didn't say he lied. I said maybe he was wrong."

Daemon closed his eyes. After a couple of minutes, he opened them and stared at the meal before him. "You fixed dinner."

Gone. Turned down another path in that shattered inner landscape.

"Yes, Daemon," Surreal said quietly, willing herself not to cry. "I fixed dinner. So let's eat it while it's hot."

* * *

He helped her with the dishes.

As they worked, Surreal realized Daemon's madness was confined to emotions, to people, to that single tragedy he couldn't face. It was as if Titian had never died, as if Surreal hadn't spent three years whoring in back alleys before Daemon found her again and arranged for a proper education in a Red Moon house. He thought she was still a child, and he continued to fret about Titian's absence. But when she mentioned a book she was reading, he made a dry observation about her eclectic taste and proceeded to tell her about other books that might be of interest. It was the same with music, with art. They posed no threat to him, had no time frame, weren't part of the nightmare of Jaenelle bleeding on that Dark Altar.

Still, it was a strain to pretend to be a young girl, to pretend she didn't see the uncertainty and torment in his golden eyes. It was still early in the evening when she suggested they get some sleep.

She settled into bed with a sigh. Maybe Daemon was as relieved to be away from her as she was from him. On some level he knew she wasn't a child. Just as he knew she'd been with him at Cassandra's Altar.

Mist. Blood. So much blood. Shattered crystal chalices.
You are my instrument.
Words lie. Blood doesn't.
She walks among the cildru dyathe.
Maybe he was wrong.
He turned round and round.
Maybe he was wrong.
The mist opened, revealing a narrow path heading upward. He stared at it and shuddered. The path was lined with jagged rock that pointed sideways and down like great stone teeth. Anyone going down the path would brush against the smooth downward sides. Anyone going up . . .

He started to climb, leaving a little more of himself on each hungry point. A quarter of the way up, he finally noticed the sound, the roar of fast water. He looked up to see it burst over the high cliff above the path, come rushing toward him.

Not water. Blood. So much blood.

No room to turn. He scrambled backward, but the red flood caught him, smashed him against the stone words that had battered his mind for so long. Tumbling and lost, he caught a glimpse of calm land rising above the flood. He fought his way to that one small island of safety, grabbed at the long, sharp grass, and hauled himself up onto the crumbling ground. Shuddering, he held on to the island of *maybe*.

When the rush and roar finally stopped, he found himself lying on a tiny, phallic-shaped island in the middle of a vast sea of blood.

Even before she was fully awake, Surreal called in her stiletto.

A soft, stealthy sound.

She slipped out of bed and opened her door a crack, listening.

Nothing.

Maybe it was only Daemon groping in the bathroom.

Gray, predawn light filled the short hallway. Keeping close to the wall, Surreal inspected the other rooms.

The bathroom was empty. So was Daemon's bedroom.

Swearing softly, Surreal examined his room. The bed looked like it had been through a storm, but the rest of the room was untouched. The only clothes missing were the ones she'd given him last night.

Nothing missing from the living area. Nothing missing—damn it!— from the kitchen.

Surreal vanished the stiletto before putting the kettle on for tea.

Tersa used to vanish for days, months, sometimes years before showing up at one of these hideaways. Surreal had intended to move on soon, but what if Daemon returned in a few days and found her gone? Would he remember her as a child and worry? Would he try to find her?

She made the tea and some toast. Taking them into the front room, she curled up on the couch with one of the thick novels she'd bought.

She would wait a few weeks before deciding. There was no hurry. There were plenty of men like the ones who had used Briarwood that she could hunt in this part of Terreille.

10 / Kaeleer

Stubbornly ignoring the steady stream of servants flowing past his study door toward the front rooms, Saetan reached for the next report.

They were only halfway up the drive. It would be another quarter hour before the carriage pulled up to the steps. What had Mephis been thinking of when he'd decided to use the landing web at Halaway instead of the one a few yards from the Hall's front door?

Grinding his teeth, he flipped through the report, seeing nothing.

He was the Warlord Prince of Dhemlan, the High Lord of Hell. He should set an example, should act with dignity.

He dropped the report on his desk and left his study.

Screw dignity.

He crossed his arms and leaned against the wall at a point that was midway between his study and the front door. From there he could comfortably watch everything without being stepped on. Maybe.

Fighting to keep a straight face, Saetan listened to Beale accept one implausible excuse after another for why this footman or that maid just had to be in the great hall at that moment.

Intent on their busy chaos and excuses, no one noticed the front door open until a very rumpled Mephis said, "Beale, could you—Never mind, the footmen are already here. There are some packages—"

Mephis glared at the footmen scrambling out the door before he spotted Saetan. Weaving his way through the maids, Mephis walked over to Saetan, braced himself against the wall, and sighed wearily. "She'll be here in a minute. She pounced on Tarl as soon as the carriage stopped to consult him on the state of her garden."

"Lucky Tarl," Saetan murmured. When Mephis snorted, he studied his rumpled son. "A difficult trip?"

Mephis snorted again. "I never realized one young girl could turn an entire city upside down in just five days." He puffed his cheeks. "Fortunately, I'll only have to help with the paperwork. The negotiations will fall squarely into your lap . . . where they belong."

Saetan's eyebrow snapped up. "What negotiations? Mephis, what—"

A few footmen returned, carrying Jaenelle's luggage. The others . . .

Saetan watched with growing interest as smiling footmen brought in armloads of brown-paper packages and headed for the labyrinth of corridors that would eventually take them to Jaenelle's suite.

"They aren't what you think," Mephis grumbled.

Since Mephis knew he'd been hoping Jaenelle would buy more clothes, Saetan growled in disappointment. Sylvia's idea of appropriate girl clothes hadn't included a single dress, and the only concession she and Jaenelle had made to his insistence that everyone at the Hall dress for dinner was *one* long black skirt and two blouses. When he had pointed out—and very reasonably, too—that trousers, shirts, and long sweaters weren't exactly feminine, Sylvia had given him a scalding lecture, the gist of it being that whatever a woman enjoyed wearing was feminine and anything she didn't enjoy wearing wasn't, and if he was too stubborn and old-fashioned to understand that, he could go soak his head in a bucket of cold water. He hadn't quite forgiven her yet for saying they would have to look hard to find a bucket big enough to fit his head into, but he admired the sass behind the remark.

Then Jaenelle bounded through the open door, dazzling Beale and the rest of the staff with a smile before politely asking Helene if she could have a sandwich and a glass of fruit juice sent to her suite.

She looks happy, Saetan thought, forgetting about everything else.

After Helene hurried off to the kitchen and Beale herded the remaining staff back to their duties, Saetan pushed away from the wall, opened his arms . . . and fought the sudden nausea as Menzar's fantasies and memories flooded his mind. He cringed at the thought of touching Jaenelle, of somehow dirtying the warmth and high spirits that flowed from her. He started to lower his arms, but she walked into them, gave him a rib-squeezing hug, and said, "Hello, Papa."

He held her tightly, breathing in her physical scent as well as the dark psychic scent he'd missed so keenly during the last few days.

For a moment, that dark scent became swift and penetrating. But when she leaned back to look at him, her sapphire eyes told him nothing. He shivered with apprehension.

Jaenelle kissed his cheek. "I'm going to unpack. Mephis needs to talk." She turned to Mephis, who was still leaning wearily against the wall. "Thank you, Mephis. I had a grand time, and I'm sorry I caused you so much trouble."

Mephis gave her a warm hug. "It was a unique experience. Next time I'll be a little more prepared."

Jaenelle laughed. "You'd take me back to Amdarh?"

"Wouldn't dare let you go alone," Mephis grumped.

As soon as she was gone, Saetan slid an arm around Mephis's shoulders. "Come to my study. You could use a glass of yarbarah."

"I could use a year's sleep," Mephis grumbled.

Saetan led his eldest son to the leather couch and warmed a glass of yarbarah for him. Sitting on a footstool, Saetan rested Mephis's right foot on his thigh, removed the shoe and sock, and began a soothing foot massage. After a few silent minutes, Mephis roused enough to remember the yarbarah and take a sip.

Continuing his massage, Saetan said quietly, "So tell me."

"Where do you want me to start?"

Good question. "Do any of those packages contain clothes?" He couldn't keep the wistful note out of his voice.

Mephis's eyes gleamed wickedly. "One. She bought you a sweater." Then he yelped.

"Sorry," Saetan muttered, gently rubbing the just-squeezed toes while the mutter turned into a snarl. "I don't wear sweaters. I also don't wear nightshirts." He flinched as the words released more memories. Carefully setting Mephis's right foot down, he stripped off the left shoe and sock and began massaging that foot.

"It was difficult, wasn't it?" Mephis asked softly.

"It was difficult. But the debt's been paid." Saetan worked silently for another minute. "Why a sweater?"

Mephis sipped the yarbarah, letting the question hang. "She said you needed to slouch more, both physically and mentally."

Saetan's eyebrow snapped up.

"She said you'd never sprawl on the couch and take a nap if you were always dressed so formally."

Oh, Mother Night. "I'm not sure I know how to sprawl."

"Well, I heartily suggest you learn." Mephis sent the empty glass skimming through the air until it slid neatly onto a nearby table.

"You've got a mean streak in your nature, Mephis," Saetan growled. "What's in the damn packages?"

"Mostly books."

Saetan remembered not to squeeze the toes. "Books? Perhaps my old wits have gone begging, but I was under the impression we have a very large room full of books. Several, in fact. They're called libraries."

"Apparently not these kinds of books."

Saetan's stomach was full of butterflies. "What kind?"

"How should I know?" Mephis grumbled. "I didn't *see* most of them. I just paid for them. However . . ."

Saetan groaned.

". . . at every bookseller's shop—and we went to every one in Amdarh—the waif would ask for books about Tigrelan or Sceval or Pandar or Centauran, and when the booksellers showed her legends and myths about those places that were written by Dhemlan authors, she would politely—she was always polite, by the way—tell them she wasn't interested in books of legends unless they came directly from those people. Naturally the booksellers, and the crowd of customers that gathered during these discussions, would explain that those Territories were inaccessible places no one traded with. She would thank them for their help, and they, wanting to stay in her good graces and have continued access to my bank account, would say, 'Who is to say what is real and what is not? Who has seen these places?' And she would say, 'I have,' and pick up the books she'd already purchased and be out the door before the bookseller and customers could pick their jaws up from the floor."

Saetan groaned again.

"Want to hear about the music?"

Saetan released Mephis's foot and braced his head in his hands. "What about the music?"

"Dhemlan music stores don't have Scelt folk music or Pandar pipe music or . . ."

"Enough, Mephis." Saetan moaned. "They're all going to be on my doorstep wanting to know what kind of trade agreements might be possible with those Territories, aren't they?"

Mephis sighed, content. "I'm surprised we beat them here."

Saetan glared at his eldest son. "Did *anything* go as expected?"

"We had a delightful time at the theater. At least I'll be able to go back *there* without being snarled at." Mephis leaned forward. "One other thing. About music." He clasped his hands and hesitated. "Have you ever heard Jaenelle sing?"

Saetan probed his memory and finally shook his head. "She's got a lovely speaking voice so I just assumed. . . . Don't tell me she's tone-deaf or sings off-key."

"No." There was a strange expression in Mephis's eyes. "She doesn't sing off-key. She . . . When you hear her, you'll understand."

"Please, Mephis, no more surprises tonight."

Mephis sighed. "She sings witchsongs . . . in the Old Tongue."

Saetan raised his head. "Authentic witchsongs?"

Mephis's eyes were teary bright. "Not like I've ever heard them sung before, but yes, authentic witchsongs."

"But how—" Pointless to ask how Jaenelle knew what she knew. "I think it's time I went up to see our wayward child."

Mephis rose stiffly. He yawned and stretched. "If you find out what all that stuff is that I paid for, I'd like to know."

Saetan rubbed his temples and sighed.

"I bought you something. Did Mephis warn you?"

"He mentioned something," Saetan replied cautiously.

Her sapphire eyes twinkled as she solemnly handed him the box.

Saetan opened it and held up the sweater. Soft, thick, black with deep pockets. He stripped off his jacket and shrugged into the sweater.

"Thank you, witch-child." He vanished the box and sank gracefully to the floor, finally stretching out his legs and propping himself up on one elbow. "Sufficiently slouched?"

Jaenelle laughed and plopped down beside him. "Quite sufficient."

"What else did you get?"

She didn't quite look him in the eye. "I bought some books."

Saetan eyed the piles of neatly stacked books that formed a large half-circle around her. "So I see." Reading the nearest spines, he recognized most of the Craft books. Copies were either in the family library or in his own private library. Same with the books on history, art, and music. They were the beginning of a young witch's library.

"I know the family has most of these, but I wanted copies of my own. It's hard to make notes in someone else's book."

Saetan experienced a hitch in his breathing. Notes. Handwritten guides that would help explain those breathtaking leaps she made when she was creating a spell. And he wouldn't have access to them. He gave himself a mental shake. *Fool. Just borrow the damn book.*

It hit him then, a bittersweet sadness. She would want a collection of her own to take with her when she was ready to establish her own household. So few years to savor before the Hall was empty again.

He pushed those thoughts aside and turned to the other stacks, the fiction. These were more interesting since a perusal of her choices would tell him a lot about Jaenelle's tastes and immediate interests. Trying to find a common thread was too bewildering, so he simply filed away the information. He considered himself an eclectic reader. He had no idea how to describe her. Some books struck him as being too young for her, some too gritty. Some he passed over with little interest, others reminded him of how long it had been since he'd browsed through a bookseller's shop for his own amusement. Lots of books about animals.

"Quite a collection," he finally said, placing the last book carefully on its stack. "What are those?" He pointed to the three books half-hidden under brown paper.

Blushing, Jaenelle mumbled, "Just books."

Saetan raised an eyebrow and waited.

With a resigned sigh, Jaenelle reached under the brown paper and thrust a book at him.

Odd. Sylvia had reacted much the same way when he'd called unexpectedly one evening and found her reading the same book. She hadn't heard him come in, and when she finally did glance up and notice him, she immediately stuffed the book behind a pillow and gave him the strong impression it would take an army to pull her away from her book-hiding pillow and nothing less would make her surrender it.

"It's a romantic novel," Jaenelle said in a small voice as he called in his half-moon glasses and started idly flipping the pages. "A couple of women in a bookseller's shop kept talking about it."

Romance. Passion. Sex.

He suppressed—barely—the urge to leap to his feet and twirl her around the room. A sign of emotional healing? Please, sweet Darkness, please let it be a sign of healing.

"You think it's silly." Her tone was defensive.

"Romance is never silly, witch-child. Well, sometimes it's silly, but not *silly.*" He flipped more pages. "Besides, I used to read things like this. They were an important part of my education."

Jaenelle gaped at him. "Really?"

"Mmm. Of course, they were a bit more—" He scanned a page. He carefully closed the book. "Then again, maybe not." He removed his glasses and vanished them before they steamed up.

Jaenelle nervously fluffed her hair. "Papa, if I have any questions about things, would you be willing to answer them?"

"Of course, witch-child. I'll give you whatever help you want in Craft or your other subjects."

"Nooo. I meant . . ." She glanced at the book in front of him.

Hell's fire, Mother Night, and may the Darkness be merciful. The whole prospect filled him with delight and dread. Delight because he might be able to help her paint a different emotional canvas that would, he hoped, balance the wounds the rape had caused. Dread because, no matter how knowledgeable he was about any subject, Jaenelle always viewed things from an angle totally outside his experience.

Menzar's thoughts, Menzar's imaginings flooded his mind again.

Saetan closed his eyes, fought to stop the images.

"He hurt you."

His body reacted to the midnight, sepulchral voice, to the instant chill in the room. "I was the one performing the execution, Lady. He's the one who is very, very dead."

The room got colder. The silence was more than silence.

"Did he suffer?" she asked too softly.

Mist. Darkness streaked with lightning. The edge of the abyss was very close and the ground was swiftly crumbling beneath his feet.

"Yes, he suffered."

She considered his answer. "Not enough," she finally said, getting to her feet.

Numbed, Saetan stared at the hand stretched toward him. Not enough? What had her Chaillot relatives done to her that she had no regrets about killing? Even he regretted taking a life.

"Come with me, Saetan." She watched him with her ancient, haunted eyes, waiting for him to turn away from her.

Never. He grasped her hand, letting her pull him to his feet. He would never turn away from her.

But he couldn't deny the shiver down his spine as he followed her to the music room that was on the same floor as their suites. He couldn't deny the instinctive wariness when he saw that the only light in the room came from two freestanding candelabras on either side of the piano. Candles, not candle-lights. Light that danced with every current of air, making the room look alien, sensual, and forbidding. The candles lit the piano keys and the music stand. The rest of the room belonged to the night.

Jaenelle called in a brown-paper package, opened it, and leafed through the music. "I found a lot of this tucked into back bins without any kind of preservation spell on them to protect them." She shook her head, annoyed, then handed him a sheet of music. "Can you play this?"

Saetan sat on the piano bench and opened the music. The paper was yellowed and fragile, the notation faded. Straining to see it in the flickering candlelight, he silently went through the piece, his fingers barely touching the keys. "I think I can get through it well enough."

Jaenelle stood behind one candelabra, becoming part of the shadows.

He played the introduction and stopped. Strange music. Unfamiliar and yet . . . He began again.

Her voice rose, a molten sound. It soared, dove, spiraled around the notes he was playing and his soul soared, dove, spiraled with her voice. A Song of Sorrow, Death, and Healing. In the Old Tongue. A song of grieving . . . for both victims of an execution. Strange music. Soul-searing, heart-tearing, ancient, ancient music.

Witchsong. No, more than that. The songs of Witch.

He didn't know when he stopped playing, when his shaking hands could no longer find the keys, when the tears blinded him. He was caught in that voice as it lanced the memory of the execution and left a clean-bleeding wound—and then healed that.

Mephis, you were right.

"Saetan?"

Saetan blinked away the tears and took a shuddering breath. "I'm sorry, witch-child. I . . . I wasn't prepared."

Jaenelle opened her arms.

He stumbled around the piano, aching for her clean, loving embrace. Menzar was a fresh scar on his soul, one that would be with him forever, like so many others, but he no longer feared to hold her, no longer doubted the kind of love he felt for her.

He stroked her hair for a long time before gathering his courage to ask, "How did you know about this music?"

She pressed her face deeper into his shoulder. Finally she whispered, "It's part of what I am."

He felt the beginning of an inward retreat, a protective distancing between himself and her.

No, my Queen. You say "It's part of what I am" with conviction, but your retreat screams your doubt of acceptance. That I will not permit.

He gently rapped her nose. "Do you know what else you are?"

"What?"

"A very tired little witch."

She started to laugh and had to stifle a yawn. "Since daylight is so draining for Mephis, we did most of our wandering after sunset, but I didn't want to waste the daytime sleeping, so . . ." She yawned again.

"You *did* get some sleep, didn't you?"

"Mephis made me take naps," she grumbled. "He said it was the only way he'd get any rest. I didn't think demons needed to rest."

It was better not to answer that.

She was half-asleep by the time he guided her to her room. As he removed her shoes and socks, she assured him she was still awake enough to get ready for bed by herself and he didn't need to fuss. She was sound asleep before he reached her bedroom door.

He, on the other hand, was wide-awake and restless.

Letting himself out one of the Hall's back doors, Saetan wandered across the carefully trimmed lawn, down a short flight of wide stone steps, and followed the paths into the wilder gardens. Leaves whispered in the light breeze. A rabbit hopped across the path a body length in front of him, watchful but not terribly concerned.

"You should be more wary, fluffball," Saetan said softly. "You or some other member of your family has been eating Mrs. Beale's young beans. If you cross her path, you're going to end up the main dish one of these nights."

The rabbit swiveled its ears before disappearing under a fire bush.

Saetan brushed his fingers against the orange-red leaves. The fire bush was full of swollen buds almost ready to bloom. Soon it would be covered with yellow flowers, like flames rising above hot embers.

He took a deep breath and let it out in a sigh. There was still a desk full of paperwork waiting for him.

Comfortably protected from the cool summer night, his hands warm in the sweater's deep pockets, Saetan strolled back to the Hall. Just as he was climbing the stone steps below the lawn, he stopped, listened.

Beyond the wild gardens was the north woods.

He shook his head and resumed walking. "Damn dog."

CHAPTER FIVE

1 / Kaeleer

Luthvian studied her reflection. The new dress hugged her trim figure but still didn't look deliberately provocative. Maybe letting her hair flow down her back looked too youthful. Maybe she should have done something about that white streak that made her look older.

Well, she *was* youthful, a little over 2,200 years old. And that white streak had been there since she was a small child, a reminder of her father's fists. Besides, Saetan would know if she tried to conceal it, and she certainly wasn't dressing up for *him*. She just wanted that daughter of his to recognize the caliber of witch who had agreed to train her.

With a last nervous glance at her dress, Luthvian went downstairs.

He was punctual, as usual.

Roxie pulled the door open at the first knock.

Luthvian wasn't sure if Roxie's alacrity was curiosity about the daughter or her desire to prove to the other girls that she had the skill to flirt with a dark-Jeweled Warlord Prince. Either way, it saved Luthvian from opening the door herself.

The daughter was a very satisfying surprise. She hadn't realized Saetan had adopted his little darling, but there wasn't a drop of Hayllian blood in the girl—and there was certainly none of his. Immature and lacking in social skills, Luthvian decided as she watched the brief greetings at the door. So what had possessed Saetan to give the girl his protection and care?

Then the girl turned toward Luthvian and smiled shyly, but the smile didn't reach those sapphire eyes. And there was no shyness in those eyes. They were filled with wariness and suppressed anger.

"Lady Luthvian," Saetan said as he approached her, "this is my daughter, Jaenelle Angelline."

"Sister," Jaenelle said, extending both hands in formal greeting.

Luthvian didn't like this assumption of equality, but she'd straighten that out privately, away from Saetan's protective presence. For now she returned the greeting and turned to Saetan. "Make yourself comfortable, High Lord." She tipped her chin toward the parlor.

"Perhaps you'd like a cup of tea, High Lord?" Roxie said, brushing against Saetan as she passed.

This wasn't the time or place to correct the ninny's ideas about Guardians, especially *this* Guardian, but it did surprise her when Saetan thanked Roxie for the offer and retreated into the parlor.

"You know," Roxie said, eyeing Jaenelle and smiling too brightly, "no one would ever believe you're the High Lord's daughter."

"Get the tea, Roxie," Luthvian snapped.

The girl flounced down the hall to the kitchen.

Jaenelle stared at the empty hallway. "Look beneath the skin," she whispered in a midnight voice.

Luthvian shivered. Even then she might have dismissed that sudden change in Jaenelle's voice as girlish theatrics if Saetan hadn't appeared at the parlor door, silently questioning and very tense.

Jaenelle smiled at him and shrugged.

Luthvian led her new pupil to her own workroom since Saetan had insisted the lessons be private. Maybe later, if the girl could catch up, she could do some of the lessons with the rest of the students.

"I understand we're to start with the very basics," Luthvian said, firmly closing the door.

"Yes," Jaenelle replied ruefully, fluffing her shoulder-length hair. She wrinkled her nose and smiled. "Papa has managed to teach me a few things, but I still have trouble with basic Craft."

Was the girl simpleminded or just totally lacking in ability?

Luthvian glanced at Jaenelle's neck, trying to detect a recent healing or a faint shadow of a bruise. If the girl was just fresh fodder, why bother training her at all? No, that made no sense, not if *he* was going to instruct

Jaenelle in the Hourglass's Craft. Something was missing, something she didn't understand yet.

"Let's start with moving an object." Luthvian placed a red wooden ball on her empty worktable. "Point your finger at the ball."

Jaenelle groaned but obeyed.

Luthvian ignored the groan. Apparently Jaenelle was as much of a ninny as the rest of her students. "Imagine a stiff, thin thread coming out of your fingertip and attaching itself to the ball." Luthvian waited a moment. "Now imagine your strength running through the thread until it just touches the ball. Now imagine reeling in the thread so that the ball moves toward you."

The ball didn't move. The worktable, however, did. And the built-in cupboards that filled the workroom's back wall tried to.

"Stop!" Luthvian shouted.

Jaenelle stopped. She sighed.

Luthvian stared. If it had just been the worktable, she might have dismissed it as an attempt to show off. But the cupboards?

Luthvian called in four wooden blocks and four more wooden balls. Placing them on the worktable, she said, "Why don't you work by yourself for a minute. Concentrate on *lightly* making the connection between yourself and the object you're trying to move. I need to look in on the other students, then I'll be back."

Jaenelle obediently turned her attention to the blocks and balls.

Luthvian left the workroom in a hurry, her hands and teeth clenched. There was only one person she wanted to look in on, and he'd damn well better have some answers.

She felt the chill in the front hallway before she heard the giggle.

"Roxie!" she snapped as she caught the doorway to stop her forward momentum. "You have spells to finish."

Roxie waved her hand airily. "Oh, I've just got one or two left."

"Then do them."

Roxie pouted and looked at Saetan for support.

There was no expression on his face. Worse, there was no expression in his eyes. Hell's fire! He was ready to rip out that lash-batting ninny's throat and she didn't even realize it!

Luthvian dragged Roxie out of the parlor and down the hall, finally shoving her toward the student workroom.

Roxie stamped her foot. "You can't treat me like this! My father's an important Warlord in Doun and my mother's—"

Luthvian squeezed Roxie's arm, and hissed, "Listen, you little fool. You're playing with someone you can't even begin to understand."

"He likes me."

"He wants to kill you."

Roxie looked stunned for a moment. Then a calculating look came into her eyes. "You're jealous."

It took all of her self-control not to slap the ninny hard enough to make her spin. "Go to the workroom and *stay* there." She waited until Roxie slammed the workroom door before returning to the parlor.

Pacing restlessly, Saetan was swearing under his breath as he raked his fingers through his hair. His anger didn't surprise her, but the effort he was making to keep it from being felt beyond this room did.

"I'm surprised you didn't give Roxie a real taste of your temper," Luthvian said, staying close to the door. "Why didn't you?"

"I have my reasons," he snarled.

"Reasons, High Lord? Or just one?"

Saetan snapped to a halt and looked past her. "Is the lesson over already?" he asked uneasily.

"She's practicing by herself." Luthvian hated talking to him when he was angry, so she decided to be blunt. "Why are you bothering to teach her the Hourglass's ways when she's still untrained?"

"I never said she was untrained," Saetan replied, starting to pace again. "I said she needed help with basic Craft."

"Until a witch has the basics, she can't do much else."

"Don't bet on it."

Saetan kept pacing, but it wasn't out of anger. Luthvian watched him and decided she didn't like seeing the High Lord nervous. She didn't like it at all. "What haven't you told me?"

"Everything. I wanted you to meet her first."

"She's got a lot of raw power for someone who doesn't wear Jewels."

"She wears Jewels. Believe me, Luthvian, Jaenelle wears Jewels."

"Then what—"

A loud whoop sent them hurrying to her workroom.

Saetan pushed the door open and froze. Luthvian started to push past him but ended up clinging to his arm for support.

The table was slowly revolving clockwise and also rotating as if it were on a spit. There were now a dozen wooden boxes, some flush to the table's top, others floating above it, and all of them were spinning slowly. Seven brightly colored wooden balls were performing an intricate dance around the boxes. And every single object was maintaining its position to that revolving, rotating table.

With a lot of effort, Luthvian thought she might be able to control something that intricate, but it should have taken years to acquire that kind of skill. You just didn't start with one ball you couldn't move and end up with this in a matter of minutes.

Saetan let out a groaning laugh.

"I think I'm getting the hang of this thread-to-object stuff," Jaenelle said as she glanced over her shoulder and grinned at them. Then she yelped as everything began to wobble and fall.

Luthvian extended her hand at the same moment Saetan extended his. She froze the smaller objects in place. He caught the table.

"Damn and blast!" Jaenelle plopped on air like a puppet with cut strings and glowered at the table, boxes, and balls.

Laughing, Saetan righted the table. "Never mind, witch-child. If you could do it perfectly on the first try, you wouldn't have much fun practicing, would you?"

"That's true," Jaenelle said with bouncing enthusiasm.

Luthvian vanished the boxes and balls, trying not to laugh at Saetan's immediate dismay. What did he think the girl would do? Try to manipulate an entire roomful of furniture?

Apparently so, because they were involved in a friendly argument about which room Jaenelle could use for practice.

"Definitely not the reception rooms," Saetan said. He sounded like a man who was desperately trying to believe the bog beneath his feet was firm ground. "There are empty rooms in the Hall and there's plenty of old furniture in the attics. Start with that. Please?"

Saetan saying please?

Jaenelle gave him a look of exasperated amusement. "All right. But only so you won't get into trouble with Beale and Helene."

Saetan let out a heartfelt sigh.

Jaenelle laughed and turned to Luthvian. "Thank you, Luthvian."

"You're welcome," Luthvian said weakly. Were all the lessons going to be like this? She wasn't sure how she felt about that. "We'll have your next lesson in two days," she added as they left the workroom.

Jaenelle wandered down the hall and studied the paintings. Was she really interested in the art or did she simply understand the adult need for private conversation after dealing with her?

"Can you survive it?" Saetan asked quietly.

Luthvian leaned toward him. "Is it always like this?"

"Oh, no," Saetan said dryly. "She was on her best behavior today. It's usually much worse."

Luthvian stifled a laugh. It was fun seeing him thrown off stride. He seemed so accessible, so . . .

The laughter died. He wasn't accessible. He was the High Lord, the Prince of the Darkness. And he had no heart.

Roxie came out of the student workroom. Luthvian wasn't sure what the girl had done to her dress, but there was a lot more cleavage showing than there'd been a short while ago.

Roxie looked at Saetan and licked her upper lip.

Although he was trying to hide it, Luthvian felt his revulsion and the beginning of hot anger. A moment later, those feelings were swept away by a bone-chilling cold that couldn't possibly come from a male.

Not even him.

"Leave him alone," Jaenelle said, her eyes fixed on Roxie.

There was something too feral, too predatory about the way Jaenelle approached Roxie. And that cold was rising from depths Luthvian didn't even want to imagine.

"We have to go," Saetan said quickly, grabbing Jaenelle's arm as she began to glide past him.

Jaenelle bared her teeth and snarled at him. It wasn't a sound that could possibly come from a human throat.

Saetan froze.

Luthvian watched them, too frightened to move or speak. She had no idea what was passing between them, but she kept hoping he was strong enough to contain Jaenelle's anger—and knew with dreadful certainty that he wasn't. He wore the Black Jewels, and he didn't outrank his daughter. May the Darkness be merciful!

The cold was gone as suddenly as it appeared.

Saetan released Jaenelle's arm and watched her until the front door closed behind her. Then he sagged against the wall.

As a Healer, Luthvian knew she should help him, but she couldn't make her legs move. That's when it finally struck her that the girls hadn't reacted to the cold or the danger, that the buzzing voices were speculating on the outward drama without any understanding at all.

"She's rather spoiled," Roxie said, giving Saetan her best pout.

He glared at her so malevolently she shrank back into the workroom, stepping on the other girls who were crowded around the doorway.

"Finish your spells," Luthvian said. "I'll check them in a minute." She closed the workroom door and rested her head against it.

"I'm sorry," Saetan said. He sounded exhausted.

"You shielded the girls, didn't you?"

Saetan gave her a tired smile. "I tried to shield you, too, but she rose past me too fast."

"Better that you didn't." Luthvian pushed away from the door and smoothed her gown. "But you were right. It was better having the first lesson and knowing what it will be like to teach her before coming to terms with what she is."

She saw his golden eyes change.

"And what do you think she is, Luthvian?" he asked too softly.

Look beneath the skin.

She looked him in the eye. "Your daughter."

Saetan strolled along the edge of the wide dirt road. Jaenelle was a little ways ahead of him and didn't seem to be in any hurry, so he didn't feel a pressing need to catch up with her. Besides, it was better to let her calm down before asking her what he needed to ask, and, since she was a Queen, the land would soothe her faster than he could.

In that, she was like every other Queen he'd ever known. No matter what other talents they had, the Queens were the ones most drawn to the land, the ones who most needed that contact with the earth. Even the ones who spent most of their time residing in larger cities had a garden where their feet could touch the living earth, quietly listening to all the land had to tell them.

So he strolled, relishing the ability once again to walk down a road on a summer morning and see the sun-kissed land. To his right was Doun's fenced-in common pastures, where all the villagers' cattle and horses grazed. To his left, just past the stone wall that surrounded Luthvian's lawn and gardens, was meadowland dotted with wildflowers. In the distance were stands of pine and spruce. Beyond them rose the mountains that ringed Ebon Rih.

Jaenelle stepped off the road and stopped, her back to all that was civilized, her sapphire eyes fixed on the wild. He approached her slowly, reluctant to disturb her meditation.

Nothing had happened at Luthvian's that could explain the intensity of Jaenelle's anger. Nothing had prepared him for that confrontation when she had turned on him, because part of her anger had been at him, and he still didn't know what he'd done to cause it.

She turned toward him, outwardly calm but still ready to fight.

Fight with a Queen when there's no other choice. Good, sound advice from the Steward of the first court he'd ever served in.

"What did you think of Luthvian?" Saetan asked as he offered Jaenelle his right arm.

Jaenelle studied him for a moment before linking arms with him. "She knows Craft." She wrinkled her nose and smiled. "I rather like her, even if she was a bit prickly today."

"Witch-child, Luthvian's always a bit prickly," Saetan said dryly.

"Ah. Especially with you?"

"We have a past." He waited for the inevitable questions, and became slightly uncomfortable when Jaenelle didn't ask any. Maybe past affairs weren't of interest to her. Or maybe she already had all the answers she required. "Why were you so angry with Roxie?"

"You're not a whore," Jaenelle snapped, pulling away from him.

Suddenly it seemed much darker, but when he looked up, the sky was just as blue as it had been a moment before and the clouds were still puffy and white. No, the storm gathering around him was standing a few feet away with her hands clenched and her feet spread in a fighting stance—and tears in her haunted eyes.

"No one said I was a whore," Saetan said quietly.

The tears spilled down Jaenelle's cheeks. "How could you let that bitch do that to you?" she screamed at him.

"Do what?" he snapped, failing to keep his frustration in check.

"How could you let her look at you like . . . force you . . ."

"FORCE ME? How in the name of Hell do you think that child could force me to do anything?"

"There are ways!"

"What ways? No one was ever stupid enough to try to force me even before I made the Offering, let alone since I began wearing the Black."

Jaenelle faltered.

"Listen to me, witch-child. Roxie is a young woman who's recently had her first sexual experience. Right now she thinks she owns the world and every male who looks at her will want to be her lover. In my younger years, I was a consort in a number of courts. I understand the game older, experienced men are expected to play. We're *supposed* to let girls practice on us because we have no interest in warming their beds. By our approval or disapproval, we help them understand how a man thinks and feels." He raked his fingers through his hair. "Although, I'll grant you, Roxie's a bit of a cunt."

Jaenelle scrubbed the tears from her face. "Then you didn't mind?"

Saetan sighed. "The truth? While listening to her giggling crudities, I was giving myself immense pleasure imagining what it would be like to hear her bones snapping."

"Oh."

"Come here, witch-child." He wrapped his arms around her, holding her tight while he rested his cheek on her head. "Who were you really angry for, Jaenelle? Who were you trying to protect?"

"I don't know. I sort of remember someone who had to submit to women like Roxie. It hurt him, and he hated it. It's not even a memory. More like a feeling because I can't recall who or where or why I would have known someone like that."

Which explained why she hadn't asked about Daemon. He was too entwined with the trauma that had cost her two years of her life, a trauma she'd locked away somewhere inside her. And all her memories of Daemon were locked away with it.

Saetan asked himself, again, if he shouldn't tell her what had happened. But he could only tell her a small part of it. He couldn't tell her who had raped her because he still didn't know. And he couldn't tell her what had happened between her and Daemon while they were in the abyss.

And the truth was he was afraid to tell her anything at all.

"Let's go home, witch-child," he whispered into her hair. "Let's go home and explore the attics."

Jaenelle laughed shakily. "How will we explain this to Helene?"

Saetan groaned. "I'm supposed to own the Hall, you know. Besides, it's very large and has a lot of rooms. If we're lucky, it'll take her a while to figure it out."

Jaenelle stepped back. "Race you home," she said, and vanished.

Saetan hesitated. He took a long look at the meadow with its wild-flowers and the mountains in the distance.

He would give it a little while longer before he began searching for Daemon Sadi.

2 / Kaeleer

Greer crept behind the row of junipers that bordered one side of the lawn behind SaDiablo Hall. The sun was almost up. If he didn't get to the south tower before the gardeners began scurrying about, he'd have to hide in the woods again. He might be demon-dead now, but he'd spent his life in cities. The rustling quiet and blanket dark of a country night unnerved him, and despite not being able to sense another presence, he couldn't shake the feeling he was being watched. And then there was that damned howling that seemed to sing the night awake.

He couldn't believe someone like the High Lord didn't have guard spells around the Hall. How else could a place this size be protected? But the Dark Priestess had assured him that Saetan had always been too lax and arrogant to consider such things. Besides, the south tower had always been Hekatah's domain, and with each of her many renovations, she'd added secret stairways and false walls so that there were entire rooms tucked away that her own spells still kept carefully hidden. One of those rooms would keep him sheltered and shielded.

Provided he could reach it.

Slipping his hands into his coat pockets, Greer left the junipers' protection and walked purposefully toward the south tower. That was one of the rules of a good assassin: act as if you belong. If he was seen, he hoped he'd be dismissed as a tradesman or, better yet, a guest.

When he finally reached the door in the south tower, he began walking slowly to the left, his left hand feeling the stones for the catch that would open the secret entrance. Unfortunately, it had been so long,

Hekatah couldn't remember exactly how far the entrance was from the door, especially since she'd made sure the alterations at the Kaeleer Hall didn't match the ones she'd made in Terreille.

Just when he thought he'd have to return to the door and start over, he found the chipped stone that held the hidden latch. A moment later, he was inside the tower, climbing a narrow stone stairway.

Shortly after that, he discovered just how far the Dark Priestess had misled him—or had misled herself.

There were no luxuriously furnished apartments in the south tower, no ornate beds, no elegant daybeds, no rugs, no drapes, no tables, no chairs. Room after room was empty and swept clean.

Greer put his left hand over the black silk scarf around his throat and pushed down the panic.

Swept clean and empty. Just like the secret staircase, which should have been thick with dust and cobwebs. Which meant it wasn't as much of a secret as Hekatah thought.

He tried to tell himself it didn't matter since he was already dead, but he'd been in the Dark Realm long enough to have heard stories about what happened to demons who crossed the High Lord, and he didn't want to find out firsthand how much truth there was in those stories.

He returned to the chamber that had once belonged to Hekatah and began a systematic search for the hidden rooms.

They, too, were empty and clean. Either her spells had broken down over time or someone else had broken them.

There had to be somewhere he could hide! The sun was too high now, and even with the quantity of fresh blood he'd been consuming, the daylight weakened him, drained him. If all the rooms had been found . . .

At last he found a hidden room within a hidden room. More of a cubbyhole, really. Greer couldn't imagine what it had been used for, but it was disgustingly grimy and cobwebbed, and therefore safe.

With his back pressed into a corner, Greer wrapped his arms around his knees and began to wait.

3 / Kaeleer

Andulvar rapped sharply on the study door and walked in before getting a response. Swinging toward the back of the room, he stopped as Saetan quickly—and rather guiltily—hid the book he'd been reading.

Hell's fire, Andulvar thought as he settled into the chair facing the desk, when was the last time Saetan looked that relaxed? There he was, the High Lord of Hell, with his feet on the desk, wearing house slippers and a black sweater. Seeing him like that, Andulvar regretted that the days were long past when they could have gone to a tavern and wrangled over a couple of pitchers of ale.

Amused by Saetan's discomfort, Andulvar said, "Beale told me you were in here—taking care of correspondence, I believe he said."

"Ah, yes, the worthy Beale."

"Not many houses can claim a Red-Jeweled Warlord for a butler."

"Not many would want to," Saetan muttered, dropping his feet to the floor. "Yarbarah?"

"Please." Andulvar waited until Saetan poured and warmed the blood wine. "Since you're not doing correspondence, what are you doing? Besides hiding from your intimidating staff?"

"Reading," Saetan replied a bit stiffly.

Always the patient hunter, Andulvar waited. And waited. "Reading what?" he finally asked. His eyes narrowed. Was Saetan blushing?

"A novel." Saetan cleared his throat. "A rather ... actually, a very erotic novel."

"Reminiscing?" Andulvar asked blandly.

Saetan growled. "Trying to anticipate. Adolescent girls ask the most terrifying questions."

"Better you than me."

"Coward."

"No argument there," Andulvar said, refusing to rise to the bait. Then he paused. "How are things going?"

"Why ask me?" Saetan propped his feet on the corner of the desk.

"You're the High Lord."

Saetan put a hand over his heart and sighed dramatically. "Ah, someone who remembers." He sipped the yarbarah. "Actually, if you want to know how things are going, you should ask Beale or Helene or Mrs. Beale. They're the triangle who run the Hall."

"A Blood triangle always has a fourth side."

"Yes, and whenever something comes up that requires 'Authority,' they prop me up, dust me off, and plunk me in the great hall to deal with it." Saetan's warm smile lit his golden eyes. "My chief functions are to be the Lady's loyal guardian and, since Beale would never deign to have his attire ruined by hysterics, to be a shoulder to cry on when Jaenelle throws her tutors off their stride—which seems to be averaging out to three or four times a week."

"The waif's doing all right then."

Saetan's smile vanished, replaced by a bleak, haunted expression. "No, she's not doing all right. Damn it, Andulvar, I'd hoped . . . She's trying so very, very hard. She's still Jaenelle. Still inquisitive and gentle and kind." He sighed. "But she's unable to respond to the overtures of friendship from the staff. Oh, I know." He waved a hand, dismissing an unspoken protest. "The relationship of servants to the Lady of the house is what it is. But it's not just them. Between that business with Menzar and the friction that exists between her and the rest of Luthvian's students, she's become timid. She avoids people whenever she can. Sylvia hasn't been able to coax her into another shopping trip, and that Lady has tried. She and her son, Beron, called a few days ago. Jaenelle managed to talk with them for about five minutes before bolting from the room.

"She has no friends, Andulvar. No one to laugh with, no one to do silly girl things with. She hasn't made the Offering yet, and she's already too aware of the gulf between herself and the rest of the Blood." Saetan slumped in his chair. "If only there was some way to get her to resume her life again."

"Why don't you invite that little ice harpy from Glacia to visit?" Andulvar said.

"Do you think she would be brave enough to come to the Hall?"

Andulvar snorted. "Considering the letter she wrote you, if you let that one through the door, she'll probably be stepping on your toes."

Saetan smiled wistfully. "I hope so, Andulvar. I do hope so."

Regretting that the easy mood would change, Andulvar drained his glass and set it carefully on the desk. "It's time you told me why you wanted me to come back to the Hall."

★ ★ ★

"Tarl was the one who suggested you might be able to help," Saetan said as he and Andulvar made their way to one of the walled gardens.

"I'm a hunter and a warrior, not a gardener, SaDiablo," Andulvar said gruffly. "How am I supposed to help him?"

"A large dog has staked out a territory in the north woods. I first heard it the night Sylvia told me there was something wrong in Halaway. It's killed a couple of young deer, but outside of that, the foresters haven't been able to find a trace of it. A few nights ago, it helped itself to a couple of chickens."

"Your foresters should be able to handle it."

Saetan opened the wooden gate that led into the low-walled garden. "Tarl found something else this morning." He nodded to the head gardener, who was standing near the back flower bed.

Tarl brushed his fingers against the brim of his cap and left.

Saetan pointed to the soft earth between two young plants. "That."

Andulvar stared at the clear, deep paw print for a long time before kneeling down and placing his hand beside it. "Damn, it's big."

Saetan knelt beside Andulvar. "That's what I thought, but this is your expertise. What really bothers me is it seems so deliberate, so carefully placed, as if it's a message or a signal of some kind."

"And who's supposed to be getting this message?" Andulvar rumbled. "Who would be expected to come in here and see it?"

"Since Lord Menzar's abrupt departure, Mephis has quietly checked everyone who serves the Hall, inside staff and out. He didn't find anything that would make me believe they can't be trusted."

Andulvar frowned thoughtfully at the print. "Could be a lover's signal for a secret tryst in the garden."

"Trust me, Andulvar," Saetan said dryly, "there are simpler and more effective ways of setting up a romantic adventure than this." He pointed to the paw print. "Besides, short of removing the dog's foot, how would anyone find the brute, bring it here, and convince it to leave one print in this exact spot?"

"I'm going to look around," Andulvar said abruptly.

While Andulvar studied the rest of the walled gardens in the waning daylight, Saetan studied the print. He'd managed to push aside the nagging worry until Andulvar had arrived, almost hoping the Eyrien would look at the print and shrug it off with an easy explanation. Now Andulvar was worried, and Saetan didn't like it. *Was* someone trying to set up a meeting? Or just lure someone away from the Hall?

Snarling softly, Saetan brushed dirt across the print until there was no trace of it. He got to his feet, brushed the dirt from his knees, glanced at the flower bed, and froze.

The paw print was as deep and as clear as it had been a minute ago.

"Andulvar!" Saetan dropped to his knees and smoothed dirt across the print again.

Andulvar rushed in, the air from his wings stirring the young plants, and knelt beside Saetan.

They watched in silence while the dirt rolled away from the print.

Andulvar swore viciously. "It's been spelled."

"Yes," Saetan said too softly. He used the equivalent strength of a White Jewel to obliterate the print again. When it came back just as quickly, he went to the Yellow, the next level of descent. Then he tried Tiger Eye, Rose, and Summer-sky. Finally, at the strength of the Purple Dusk Jewel, the print was barely discernible.

With a vicious swipe of his hand, Saetan used the strength of his Birthright Red to eliminate the print.

It didn't return.

"Someone wanted to be very sure this print wasn't carelessly erased," Saetan said, wiping his hand on the grass.

Andulvar rubbed his fist against his chin. "Keep the waif from wandering around by herself, even in these gardens. Prothvar and I aren't much help in the daylight, but we'll keep watch at night."

"You think someone's foolish enough to penetrate the Hall?"

"Looks like someone already has. That's not what's bothering me." Andulvar pointed to the now-smooth dirt. "That's not a dog, SaDiablo. It's a wolf. It's hard to believe a wolf would choose to get this close to humans, but even if it's being controlled by someone, what's the point of bringing it here?"

"Bait," Saetan said, immediately sending out a psychic call to Jaenelle. Her distracted acknowledgment reassured him that she was sufficiently engrossed in her studies to remain indoors.

"Bait for what?"

Instead of answering, Saetan made a sweeping probe of the Hall and the surrounding land. There was that muzziness in the south tower, the fading effects of the shielding spells Helene and Beale had broken as they cleared out the tower and uncovered Hekatah's secret rooms. There was also that odd ripple in the north woods.

Saetan probed a little longer and then stopped. Getting into the Hall had never been difficult. Getting out was another matter.

"Bait for what, SaDiablo?" Andulvar asked again.

"For a young girl who's lonely and loves animals."

4 / Kaeleer

Greer huddled in a corner of the secret cubbyhole, whimpering as that dark mind rolled through the very stones, probing, searching.

He struggled to keep his mind carefully blank as the surge of dark power washed over him. He couldn't safely bolt before sunset, but if he were caught here, how would he explain his presence? Having lost one little darling, Greer doubted any explanation would appease the High Lord right now.

When the psychic probe faded, Greer stretched out his legs and sighed. As much as he feared the High Lord, he didn't relish going back to Hekatah without any information. She would insist he try again.

It would have to be tonight. He would find the girl's room, look her over, and return to Hell. If Hekatah wanted to get any closer and risk coming face-to-face with Saetan, she could do it herself.

5 / Kaeleer

Saetan headed for his suite, hoping a little rest would bring inspiration. Earlier that evening, he'd tried to convince Jaenelle to contact some of her friends. He'd failed miserably and, in the process, had learned a lot about an adolescent witch's emotional volatility.

Wondering if he could enlist Sylvia as an ally in future emotional battles and still puzzling over the wolf print in the garden, he felt the warning signs a moment too late.

A psychic tidal wave of fear and rage crashed against his mind and sent him reeling into the wall. He clutched his head as knife-edged pain stabbed at his temples, and tasted blood as his teeth cut his lip.

Moaning at the merciless throbbing in his head, he sank to the floor and instinctively tried to strengthen his inner barriers against another mind-tearing assault.

When no other psychic wave crashed against his inner barriers, Saetan raised his head and probed cautiously. He stared at the door across the hall from where he huddled. "Witch-child?"

An agonized scream came from behind Jaenelle's door.

Saetan pushed himself to his feet, stumbled across the hall, and plunged into a room consumed by the most violent psychic storm he'd ever encountered. Except for a strong, swirling wind which bent the plants and twisted the curtains, the physical room appeared untouched, but it felt like it was filled with strands of spun glass that snapped as he passed through it, cutting the mind instead of the body.

Head down and shoulders hunched, Saetan gritted his teeth and forced himself, step by mind-slicing step, toward the bed, where Jaenelle thrashed and screamed.

When he touched her arm, she flung herself away from him.

Barely able to think, Saetan threw himself on top of her and wrapped his arms and legs around her. They rolled on the bed, tangled in the sheets she had shredded with her nails, while she fought and screamed. When she couldn't free her arms and legs, she half twisted in his arms, her teeth snapping a breath away from his throat.

"Jaenelle!" Saetan roared in her ear. "Jaenelle! It's Saetan!"

"Noooooo!"

Drawing on the reserved power in the Black Jewels, Saetan rolled once more, pinning Jaenelle between the bed and his body. He opened his inner barriers and sent out the message that she was safe, that he was with her, knowing if she struck him now, she'd destroy him.

Jaenelle brushed against his vulnerable mind and stopped moving.

Shaking, Saetan rested his cheek against her head. "I'm with you, witch-child," he whispered. "You're safe."

"Not safe," Jaenelle moaned. "Never safe."

Saetan clamped his teeth together, sickened by the images that suddenly flowed into his mind. He saw them all as she had once seen them. Marjane, hanging from the tree. Myrol and Rebecca, handless. Dannie and Dannie's leg. And Rose.

Tears rolled down his face as he held Jaenelle and made those agonizing memories his own. Now he finally understood what she'd endured as a child, what had been done to her, why she had never feared Hell or its citizens. As the memories flowed from her mind to his, he could see the building, the rooms, the garden, the tree.

And he remembered Char coming to him, troubled by a bridge and the maimed children who were traveling over it to the *cildru dyathe*'s island. A bridge Jaenelle had built once between Hell and . . . Briarwood.

The moment he thought the name, he felt Jaenelle's eyes open.

Suddenly there was impenetrable, swirling mist. It parted abruptly, and he looked down into the abyss. Every instinct urged him to flee, to get away from the cold rage and madness spiraling up from the depths.

But woven into the madness and rage were gentleness and magic, too. So he waited at the edge of the abyss for whatever would happen. He wouldn't run from his Queen.

The mist closed in again. He couldn't see her, but he felt her when Jaenelle rose from the abyss. And he shuddered as her sepulchral, midnight whisper rang through his mind.

★Briarwood is the pretty poison. There is no cure for Briarwood.★

Then she spiraled back down, and his mind was his own again.

Jaenelle stirred against him. "Saetan?" She sounded so young, so frail, so uncertain.

Saetan kissed her cheek. "I'm here, witch-child," he said hoarsely, cradling her to his chest. He gingerly probed the room, and quickly discovered using Craft wasn't going to be possible until the psychic storm completely faded.

"What . . ." Jaenelle said groggily.

"You were having a nightmare. Do you remember?"

A long silence. "No. What was it about?"

Saetan hesitated . . . and said nothing.

A boot scuffed on the balcony outside the open glass door. Someone hurried down the stairs.

Saetan's head snapped up. Since probing for the intruder's identity was useless, he frantically tore at the sheets tangled around his legs and sprang toward the balcony door. "PROTHVAR!" He tried to create a ball of witch-light to spotlight the garden, but Jaenelle's psychic storm absorbed his power, and the flash of light he managed left him night-blind.

On the far side of the garden, something snarled viciously. A man screamed. There was a brief, furious struggle, a blinding sizzle as the strength of two Jewels was unleashed and absorbed, the sound of odd-gaited footsteps, another snarl, and then a door slamming.

And then silence.

The bedroom door burst open. Saetan pivoted, his teeth bared, as Andulvar sprang into the room, an Eyrien war blade in his hand.

"Stay with her," Saetan snapped. He ran down the balcony stairs, reaching for the spells that would seal the Hall and prevent anyone from leaving. Then he swore. That tidal wave of power had shattered all of his spells—which meant the intruder could find a way out before they could hunt him down. And once he got away far enough from the effects of the storm, he could catch the Winds and just disappear.

"But where were you hiding that I didn't feel your presence before?" Saetan snarled, grinding his teeth in frustration as Prothvar landed beside him in the garden.

The Eyrien Warlord held out a torn black silk scarf. "I found this near the south tower."

Saetan stared at the scarf Greer had worn the first time he came to the Hall. His golden eyes glittered as he turned toward the south tower. "I've been too complacent about Hekatah's games and Hekatah's pets. But this pet has made one mistake too many."

"Hekatah!" Cursing, Prothvar dropped the scarf and wiped his hand on his trousers. Then he smiled. "I don't think her pet left as intact as he came. There are also wolf prints near the south tower."

Wolf. Saetan stared at the south tower. A wolf and Greer. Bait and an abductor? But that snarl, that clash of Jewels.

A movement on the balcony caught his eye.

Jaenelle looked down at them. Andulvar's arm was around her shoulders, tucking her close to his left side. His right hand still held the large, wicked-looking war blade.

"Papa, what's wrong?" Jaenelle called.

With a nod to Saetan, Prothvar vanished the scarf and slipped into the shadows to stand guard.

Saetan slowly crossed the garden and climbed the stairs, frustrated that the lingering effects of the witch storm made it impossible for him to use Craft to keep anyone else from reaching her rooms.

Andulvar stepped back as Jaenelle flung herself into Saetan's arms. He kissed her head, and the three of them went into her bedroom.

"What happened?" Jaenelle said, shivering as she watched Andulvar close the balcony doors and physically lock them.

That she had to ask indicated too much about her state of mind. Saetan hesitated. "It was nothing, witch-child," he finally said, holding her close. "An unexplained noise." But was it something she had seen or felt that had triggered those memories?

Andulvar and Saetan exchanged a look. The Eyrien Warlord Prince looked pointedly at the bed, then at the balcony doors.

Saetan nodded slightly. "Witch-child, your bed's a bit . . . rumpled. Since it's so late, rather than waking a maid to change it, why don't you stay in my room tonight?"

Jaenelle's head snapped up. There was shock, wariness, and fear in her eyes. "I could make up the bed."

"I'd rather you didn't."

Saetan felt her reach for his mind and waited. Unless she deliberately picked his thoughts, he could keep the reason for his concern from her but not the feeling of concern.

Jaenelle withdrew from him and nodded.

Relieved that she was still willing to trust him, Saetan led her to his suite across the hall and tucked her into his bed. After Andulvar left to check the south tower, he poured and warmed a glass of yarbarah, and settled into a chair nearby. A long time later, Jaenelle's breathing evened out, and he knew she was asleep.

A wolf, he thought as he watched over her. A friend or an enemy?

Saetan closed his eyes and rubbed his temples. The headache was subsiding, but the past hour had left him exhausted. Still, he kept seeing that print in the garden, a spelled message someone was supposed to understand.

But that snarl, *that clash of Jewels.*

Saetan snapped upright in the chair and stared at Jaenelle.

Not all the dreamers who had shaped this Witch had been human.

It fit. If it was true, it all fit.

Maybe, since Jaenelle hadn't gone to see her old friends, they were starting to come to her.

6 / Hell

Hekatah screamed at Greer, "What do you mean she's alive?"

"Just what I said," Greer replied as he inspected his torn arm. "The girl he's keeping at the Hall is that pale bitch granddaughter of Alexandra Angelline."

"But you destroyed her!"

"Apparently she survived."

Hekatah paced the small, dirty, sparsely furnished room. It couldn't be true. It just couldn't. She glanced at Greer, who was slumped in a chair. "You said it was dark, difficult to see. You never got into the room itself. It couldn't be the same girl. He told you she walked among the *cildru dyathe*."

"He called her Jaenelle," Greer said, examining his foot.

Hekatah's eyes widened. "He lied about it." Her face turned ugly with rage and hate. "That gutter son of a whore *lied about it*!"

Then she remembered that terrifying presence on the *cildru dyathe's* island. If the girl was really alive, she could still be shaped into the puppet Queen whom Hekatah needed to rule the Realms.

Hekatah ran her fingers over a scarred table. "Even if she survived physically, she's of little use to me if she has no power."

Cradling his torn arm, Greer took the bait. "She still has power. There was a fierce witch storm filling that room. It began before the High Lord entered. The Darkness only knows how he survived it."

Hekatah frowned. "What was he doing in her room at that hour?"

Greer shrugged. "It sounded like they were rolling around on the bed, and it wasn't a friendly tussle."

Hekatah stared at Greer but didn't see him. She saw Saetan, hot-blooded and hungry, easing his appetites—*all* his appetites—with that young, dark-blooded witch who should have belonged to her. A Guardian was still capable of that kind of pleasure. A Guardian . . . who valued honor. Oh, he could try to ignore the scandal and condemnation, but by the time she was done, she'd create such a firestorm around him even his most loyal servants would hate him.

But it had to be done delicately so that, unlike that fool Menzar, Saetan wouldn't be able to trace it back to her.

Hekatah studied Greer. The torn muscle in his forearm could be hidden by a coat, but that foot. . . . Whether it was snapped off and replaced with something artificial or left on and laced into a high boot, the dragging walk would be obvious—as were the maimed hands. A pity such a useful servant was so deformed and, therefore, so conspicuous. But he'd be able to perform this one last assignment. In fact, his deformities would work in her favor.

Hekatah allowed herself a brief smile before putting on her saddest expression. She sank to her knees beside Greer's chair. "Poor darling," she cooed, stroking his cheek with her fingertips, "I've let that bastard's schemes distract me from more important concerns."

"What concerns, Priestess?" Greer asked cautiously.

"Why, you, darling, and those ferocious wounds his beast inflicted on you." She wiped at her eyes as if they could still hold tears. "You know there's no way to heal these wounds now, don't you, darling?"

Greer looked away.

Hekatah leaned forward and kissed his cheek. "But don't worry. I have a plan that will pay Saetan back for everything."

"You wanted to see me, High Lord?"

Saetan's eyes glittered. He leaned against the blackwood desk in his private study in the Dark Realm and smiled at the Dea al Mon Harpy. "Titian, my dear," he crooned in a voice like soft thunder, "I have an assignment for you that I think will be very much to your liking."

CHAPTER SIX

1 / Kaeleer

Saetan, along with the rest of the family, lingered at the dinner table, reluctant to have the meal and the camaraderie end.

At least some good had come from that unpleasant night last week. Jaenelle's nightmare had lanced the festering wound of those suppressed memories, easing a little of her emotional pain. He knew that soul wound wasn't healed, but for the first time since she'd returned from the abyss, she was more like the child they remembered than the haunted young woman she'd become.

"I think Beale would like to clear the table," Jaenelle said quietly, glancing at the butler standing at the dining room door.

"Then why don't we have coffee in the drawing room," Saetan suggested, pushing his chair back.

When Jaenelle walked toward the door, followed by Mephis, Andulvar, and Prothvar, he lingered a moment longer. It was so good to hear her laugh, so good to—

A movement at the window caught his attention. Immediately probing for the intruder, he took a step back when strangely scented, feral emotions pushed against his mind, challenging him, daring him to touch.

Anger. Frustration. Fear. And then . . .

The howl stopped conversations midword as Andulvar and Prothvar spun around, their hunting knives drawn. Saetan barely noticed them, too intent on Jaenelle's reaction.

She closed her eyes, took a deep breath, tipped her head back, and howled. It wasn't an exact imitation of the wolf's howl. It was eerier somehow because it turned into witchsong. A wild song.

And he realized, with a shivering sense of wonder, that she and the wolf had sung this song before, that they knew how to blend those two voices to create something alien and beautiful.

The wolf stopped howling. Jaenelle finished the song and smiled.

A large gray shape leaped through the window, passing through the glass. The wolf landed in the dining room, snarling at them.

With a welcoming cry, Jaenelle rushed past Andulvar and Prothvar, dropped to her knees, and threw her arms around the wolf's neck.

In that moment, Saetan caught the psychic scent he was searching for. The wolf was one of the legendary kindred. A Prince, but not, thank the Darkness, a Warlord Prince. He also caught a glimpse of the gold chain and the Purple Dusk Jewel hidden in the wolf's fur.

Still snarling, the wolf pressed against Jaenelle, urging her toward the window while it kept its body between her and the Eyriens.

Pushed off-balance, Jaenelle's arms tightened around the wolf's neck. "Smoke, you're being rude," she said in that quiet, firm Queen voice that no male in his right mind would defy.

Smoke gave her a quick lick and changed his snarl to a deep growl.

"What bad male?" Jaenelle scanned each concerned male face and shook her head. "Well, it wasn't one of them. This is my pack."

The growling stopped. There was intelligence and new interest in the wolf's eyes as he studied each man, then waved the tip of his tail once as a reluctant greeting.

Another brief pause. Jaenelle blushed. "No, none of them are my mate. I'm not old enough for a mate," she added hurriedly as Smoke gave them all a look of blatant disapproval. "This is Saetan, the High Lord. He's my sire. My brother, Prince Mephis, is the High Lord's pup. And this is my uncle, Prince Andulvar, and my cousin, Lord Prothvar. And that's Lord Beale. Everyone, this is Prince Smoke."

As he greeted his kindred Brother, Saetan wondered which had startled the others more: kindred suddenly appearing, Jaenelle's conversing with a wolf, or the family labels she'd given them.

There was an awkward pause after the introductions. Andulvar and Prothvar glanced at him, then sheathed their knives, keeping their movements slow and deliberate. Mephis remained still but ready to respond, and Beale, hovering in the doorway, was silently awaiting instructions. Smoke looked uneasy, and there was a bruised, uncertain look in Jaenelle's eyes.

He had to do something quickly. But what did one say to a wolf? More important, what could he do to make Jaenelle's furry friend feel comfortable enough and welcome enough to want to stay? Well, what did one say to any guest?

"May I offer you some refreshments, Prince Smoke?" Said out loud, the name combined with a Blood title sounded silly to him even if it was an apt description of the wolf's coloring. Then again, maybe human names sounded just as silly to a wolf. Saetan raised an eyebrow at Beale and wondered how his stoic Warlord butler was going to react to a four-footed guest.

It was quickly apparent that any friend of Jaenelle's, whether he walked on two legs or four, would be treated as an honored guest.

Beale stepped forward, made his most formal bow, and addressed his inquiries to Jaenelle. "There is the beef roast from dinner, if Prince Smoke doesn't object to the meat being cooked."

Jaenelle looked amused, but her voice was steady and dignified. "Thank you, Beale. That would be quite acceptable."

"A bowl of cool water as well?"

Jaenelle just nodded.

"We'll be more comfortable in the drawing room," Saetan said. He slowly approached Jaenelle, offering a hand to help her to her feet.

Smoke tensed at his approach but didn't challenge him or back away. The wolf didn't trust humans, didn't want him close enough to touch Jaenelle, but was at a loss of how to stop it without incurring his Lady's disapproval.

He's not so different from the rest of us, Saetan thought as he escorted Jaenelle to the family drawing room.

Without conscious thought, the men waited for Jaenelle to choose a seat before settling into chairs and couches far enough away from her so the wolf wouldn't be upset and close enough not to miss anything. Saetan sat opposite her chair, aware that Smoke's attention was focused on him and had been since the introductions were made.

He felt grateful for the distraction Beale provided moments later when the butler appeared with a silver serving tray holding coffee for Jaenelle, yarbarah for the rest of them, and bowls of meat and water for Smoke. Beale set the bowls of meat and water in front of Smoke, placed the tray on a table in front of Jaenelle, and, when no one indicated a further requirement, reluctantly left the room.

Smoke sniffed at the meat and water but remained seated by Jaenelle's chair, pressed against her knees. Saetan added the hefty dose of cream and sugar that Jaenelle liked in her coffee, then poured and warmed yarbarah, passing the glasses to the others before warming one for himself.

"Is Prince Smoke alone?" he asked Jaenelle. Until he could find out how kindred communicated with humans, he had no choice but to direct his questions to her.

Jaenelle watched Smoke studying the bowls and didn't answer.

Saetan stiffened when he realized the wolf was doing exactly what he would have done in unfamiliar and possibly hostile territory—using Craft to probe the meat and drink, looking for something that shouldn't be there. Looking for poison. And he also realized who had taught the wolf to look for poisons—which made him wonder why she'd needed to teach that lesson in the first place.

"Well?" Jaenelle said quietly.

Smoke shifted his feet and made a sound that expressed uncertainty.

Jaenelle gave him an approving pat. "Those are herbs. Humans use them to alter the flavor of meat and vegetables." Then she laughed. "I don't know why we want to change the taste of meat. We just do."

Smoke selected a hunk of beef.

Jaenelle gave Saetan an amused smile, but there was sadness in her eyes and a touch of anxiety. "Smoke's pack is still in their home territory. He came alone because . . . because he wanted to see me, wanted to know if I'd come and visit his pack like I used to."

He missed you, witch-child. They all miss you. Saetan swirled the yarbarah in his glass. He understood her anxiety. Smoke was here instead of protecting his mate and young. That Jaenelle had taught them about poisons made it obvious that the kindred wolves faced dangers beyond natural ones. It would require some adjustments, but if Smoke was willing . . . "How much territory does a pack need?"

Jaenelle shrugged. "It depends. A fair amount. Why?"

"The family owns a considerable amount of land in Dhemlan, including the north woods. Even with the hunting rights I've granted the families in Halaway, there's plenty of game. Would that be sufficient territory for a pack?"

Jaenelle stared at him. "You want a wolf pack in the north woods?"

"If Smoke and his family would like to live there, why not?" Besides, the benefits certainly wouldn't be one-sided. He'd provide territory and protection for the wolf pack, and they'd provide companionship and protection for Jaenelle.

The silence that followed wasn't really silence but a conversation the rest of them couldn't hear. Jaenelle's expression was carefully neutral. Smoke's, as he studied each man in the room, was unreadable.

Finally Jaenelle looked at Saetan. "Humans don't like wolf-kind."

Saetan steepled his fingers and forced himself to breathe evenly. Jaenelle had rarely mentioned kindred. He knew she had visited the dream-weaving spiders in Arachna and once, when he'd first met her, she had mentioned unicorns. But Smoke's presence and the ease with which she and the wolf communicated spoke of a long-established relationship. What other kindred might know the sound of her voice, her dark psychic scent? What others might be willing to risk contact with humans in order to be with her again? Compared to what might be out there in those mist-enclosed Territories, what was a wolf?

The girl and the wolf waited for his answer.

"I rule this Territory," he said quietly. "And, as I said, the Hall and its land are personal property. If the humans don't want our kindred Brothers and Sisters as neighbors, then the humans can leave."

He wasn't sure if he was trying to reach out with his mind or if Smoke was trying to reach toward him, but he caught the edge of those alien, feral thoughts. Not thoughts, really, more like emotions filtered through a different lens but still readable. Surprise, followed by swift understanding and approval. Smoke, at least, knew exactly why the offer was being made.

Unfortunately, Jaenelle, reaching for her coffee, caught some of it, too. "What bad male?" she asked, frowning.

Smoke suddenly decided the meat was interesting.

From Jaenelle's annoyed expression, Saetan deduced the wolf had turned evasive. Since it wasn't a topic he wanted her to pursue, he decided to satisfy his own curiosity, aware of the effort Andulvar, Prothvar, and Mephis were making to sit quietly and not begin a barrage of questions. The kindred had always been elusive and timid about contact with humans, even before they had closed their borders. Now there was a wolf, kindred and wild, sitting in his drawing room.

"Prince Smoke is kindred?" Saetan asked, his tone more confirmation than question.

"Of course," Jaenelle said, surprised.

"And you can communicate with him?"

"Of course."

He felt the wave of frustration coming from the others and clenched his teeth. *Remember who you're talking to.* "How?"

Jaenelle looked puzzled. "Distaff to spear. The same way I communicate with you." She fluffed her hair. "You can't hear him?"

Saetan and the other men shook their heads.

Jaenelle looked at Smoke. "Can you hear them?"

Smoke looked at the human males and whuffed softly.

Jaenelle became indignant. "What do you mean I didn't train them well? I didn't train them at all!"

Smoke's expression as he turned back to the meat was smug.

Jaenelle muttered something uncomplimentary about male thought processes, then said tartly, "Does the beef at least meet with your approval?" She gave Saetan a brittle smile. "Smoke says the beef is much better than the squawky white birds." Her expression changed from annoyed to dismayed. "Squawky white birds? Chickens? You ate Mrs. Beale's chickens?"

Smoke whined apologetically.

Saetan leaned back in his chair. Oh, it was so satisfying to see her thrown off stride. "I'm sure Mrs. Beale was delighted to feed a guest— even if she wasn't aware of it," he added dryly, remembering too well his cook's reaction when she learned about the missing hens.

Jaenelle pressed her hands into her lap. "Yes. Well." She nibbled her lower lip. "Communicating with kindred isn't difficult."

"Really?" Saetan replied mildly, amused by the abrupt return to the original topic of conversation.

"You just . . ." Jaenelle paused and finally shrugged. "Shuck the human trappings and take one step to the side."

It wasn't the most enlightening set of instructions he'd ever heard, but having seen beneath her mask of human flesh, the phrase "shuck the human trappings" gave him some uncomfortable things to wonder about.

Was it more comfortable, more natural for her to reach for kindred minds? Or did she see kindred and human as equal puzzles?

Alien and Other. Blood and more than Blood. Witch.

"What?" he asked, suddenly realizing they were all watching him.

"Do you want to try it?" Jaenelle asked gently.

Her haunted sapphire eyes, dark with their ancient wisdom, told him she knew exactly what troubled him. She didn't dismiss his concerns, which was sufficient acknowledgment that he had a reason to be concerned. And no reason at all.

Saetan smiled. "Yes, I'd like to try it."

Jaenelle touched the minds of the four men just outside the first inner barrier and showed them how to reach a mind that wasn't human.

It was simple, really. Rather like walking down a narrow, hedged-in lane, sidestepping through a gap in the hedge, and discovering that there was another well-worn path on the other side. Human trappings were nothing more than a narrow view of communication. He—and Andulvar, Prothvar, and Mephis, and maybe Smoke as well—would always be aware of the hedge and would have to travel through a gap. For Jaenelle, it was just one wide avenue.

Human. Smoke sounded pleased.

Filled with wonder, Saetan smiled. *Wolf.*

Smoke's thoughts were fascinating. Happiness because Jaenelle was glad to see him. Relief that the humans accepted him. Anticipation of bringing his pack to a safe place—clouded by darker images of kindred being hunted, and the need to understand these humans in order to protect themselves. Curiosity about how humans marked their territory since he hadn't smelled any scent markers in this stone place. And a yearning to water a few trees himself.

"I think we should go for a walk," Jaenelle said, standing quickly.

The human males stepped through the gaps in the mental hedge, their thoughts once more their own.

"After your walk, there's no reason Smoke has to return to the woods tonight," Saetan said casually, ignoring the sharp look Jaenelle gave him. "If your room's too warm, he could always bed down on the balcony or in your garden."

I will keep the bad male away from the Lady.

Apparently Smoke was accustomed to sliding through the mental hedge. Saetan also noticed the wolf sent the thought on a spear thread, male to male, so that Jaenelle couldn't pick it up.

Thank you, Saetan replied. "Finished tomorrow's studies?"

Jaenelle wrinkled her nose at him and bid them all good night, Smoke eagerly trotting beside her as they headed for an outside door.

Saetan turned to the others.

Andulvar whistled softly. "Sweet Darkness, SaDiablo. Kindred."

"Kindred," Saetan agreed, smiling.

Andulvar and Mephis returned the smile.

Prothvar drew his hunting knife from its sheath and studied the blade. "I'll go with him to bring the pack home."

Images of hunters and traps pushed away the smiles.

"Yes," Saetan said too quietly, "do that."

2 / Terreille

Seething that her afternoon's intended amusement was now spoiled, Dorothea SaDiablo gave the young Warlord who was her current toy-boy a final, throat-swabbing kiss before dismissing him. Her eyes narrowed at the hasty way he fixed his clothes and left her sitting room. Well, she would take care of that little discipline problem tonight.

Rising gracefully from the ornate gold-and-cream daybed, she swished her hips provocatively as she walked to a table and poured a glass of wine. She drained half the glass before turning to face her son—and caught him pressing a fist into his lower back, trying to ease the chronic ache. She turned away, knowing her face reflected the revulsion she felt now every time she looked at him.

"What do you want, Kartane?"

"Did you find out anything?" he asked hesitantly.

"There's nothing to find out," Dorothea replied sharply, setting the glass down before it broke in her hand. "There's nothing wrong with you." Which was a lie. Anyone who looked at him knew it was a lie.

"There must be some reason why—"

"There is nothing wrong with you." Or, more truthfully, nothing she could do about it. But there was no need to tell him that.

"There has to be something," Kartane persisted. "Some spell—"

"Where?" Dorothea said angrily, turning to face him. "Show me where. There is nothing, I tell you, *nothing.*"

"Mother—"

Dorothea slapped him hard across the face. "Don't call me that."

Kartane stiffened and said nothing else.

Dorothea took a deep breath and ran her hands along her hips, smoothing the gown. Then she looked at him, not bothering to hide her disgust. "I'll continue to look into the matter. However, I have other appointments right now."

Kartane bowed, accepting the dismissal.

As soon as she was alone, Dorothea reached for the wine and swore when she saw how badly her hand was shaking.

Kartane's "illness" was getting worse, and there wasn't a damn thing she could do. The best Healers in Hayll couldn't find a physical reason for his body's deterioration because there wasn't one. But she'd pushed the Healers until a few months ago, when Kartane's screams had woken her and she'd learned about the dreams.

It always came back to that girl. Greer's death, Kartane's illness, Daemon's breaking the Ring of Obedience, Hekatah's obsession.

It always came back to that girl.

So she had gone to Chaillot secretly and had discovered that all the males who had been associated with a place called Briarwood were suffering in similar ways. One man screamed at least once a day that his hands were being cut off, despite being able to see them, move them. Two others babbled about a leg.

Furious, she had gone to Briarwood, which had been abandoned by then, to search for the tangled web of dreams and visions that she was sure had ensnared them all.

Her efforts had failed. The only thing she had been able to draw from Briarwood's wood and stone was ghostly, taunting laughter. No, not quite the only thing. After she had been there an hour, fear had thickened the air—fear and a sense of expectant waiting. She could have pried a little more, pushed a little harder. If she had, she was sure she would have found a strand that would have led her into the web. She was also sure she wouldn't have found a way out again.

It always came back to that girl.

She had returned home, dismissed the Healers, and begun insisting there was nothing wrong with him whenever Kartane pushed for her help.

She would keep on insisting, not only because there was nothing she could do, but because it would serve another purpose. Once Kartane felt certain he would get no help from her, he would look elsewhere. He would look for the one person he had always run to as a child whenever he needed help.

And sooner or later, he would find Daemon Sadi for her.

3 / Kaeleer

Saetan stormed through the corridors, heading for the garden room that opened onto a terrace at the back of the Hall.

Three days since Jaenelle, Prothvar, and Smoke had left to bring Smoke's pack to the Hall! Three gut-twisting, worried days full of thoughts of hunters and poison and how young she must have been when she'd first met the kindred, had first started teaching them to avoid man-made traps without a thought of what might happen to her if she'd been caught in one of those traps—or the other kinds of traps a Blood male might set for a young witch.

But she had been caught in "that kind of trap," hadn't she? He hadn't kept her safe from that one.

Now, finally, she was home. Had been home since just before dawn and *still* remained in the gardens bordering the north woods, *still* hadn't come up to the Hall to let him know she was all right.

Saetan flung open the glass doors, strode out onto the terrace, and sucked the late afternoon air through his clenched teeth. Teetering at the edge of the flagstones, he tasted that held breath and shuddered.

The air was saturated with Jaenelle's feelings. Anguish, grief, rage. And a hint of the abyss.

Saetan stepped back from the terrace edge, his anger bleached by the primal storm building at the border of the north woods. It had gone wrong. Somehow, it had gone very wrong.

As anxiety replaced anger, as he wavered between waiting for her to come to him and going out to find her, he finally caught the quality of the silence, the dangerous silence.

Step by careful step, he retreated to the glass doors.

She was home. That's what mattered. Andulvar and Mephis would be rising with the dusk. Prothvar would rise, too, meet them in the study and tell them what happened.

There was no reason to intrude on her precarious self-control.

Because he didn't want to find out what would happen if the silence shattered.

Prothvar moved as if he'd endured a three-day beating.

Perhaps he had, Saetan thought as he watched the demon-dead Warlord warm a glass of yarbarah.

Prothvar lifted the glass to drink, but didn't. "They're dead."

Mephis made a sound of protest and dismay. Andulvar angrily demanded an explanation.

Saetan, remembering the dangerous silence that had filled the air, barely heard them. If he'd asked her about the wolf print earlier, if Smoke hadn't had to wait so long to reach her . . .

"All of them?" His voice broke, hushing Andulvar and Mephis.

Prothvar shook his head wearily. "Lady Ash and two pups survived. That's all that was left of a strong pack when the hunters were through harvesting pelts."

"They can't be the only kindred wolves left."

"No, Jaenelle said there are others. And we did find two young wolves from another pack. Two young, terrified Warlords."

"Mother Night," Saetan whispered, sinking into a chair.

Andulvar snapped his wings open and shut. "Why didn't you gather them up and get out of there?"

Prothvar spun to face his grandfather. "Don't you think I tried? Don't you—" He closed his eyes and shuddered. "Two of the dead ones had made the change to demons. They had been skinned and their feet had been cut off, but they still—"

"Enough!" Saetan shouted.

Silence. Brittle, brittle silence. Time enough to hear the details. Time enough to add another nightmare to the list.

Moving as if he would shatter, Saetan led Prothvar to a chair.

They let him talk, let him exorcise the past three days. Saetan rubbed Prothvar's neck and shoulders, giving voiceless comfort. Andulvar knelt beside the chair and held his grandson's hand. Mephis kept the glass of yarbarah filled. And Prothvar talked, grieving because the kindred were innocent in a way the human Blood were not.

Someone else needed that kind of comfort. Someone else needed their strength. But she was still in the garden with the kindred and, like the kindred, was not yet able to accept what they offered.

"Is that all?" Saetan asked when Prothvar finally stopped talking.

"No, High Lord." Prothvar swallowed, choked. "Jaenelle disappeared for several hours before we left. She wouldn't tell me where she'd been or why she'd gone. When I pushed, she said, 'If they want pelts, they'll have pelts.'"

Saetan squeezed Prothvar's shoulders, not sure if he was giving comfort or taking it. "I understand."

Andulvar pulled Prothvar to his feet. "Come on, boyo. You need clean air beneath your wings."

When the Eyriens were gone, Mephis said, "You understand what the waif meant?"

Saetan stared at nothing. "Do you have commitments this evening?"

"No."

"Find some."

Mephis hesitated, then bowed. "As you wish, High Lord."

Silence. Brittle, brittle silence.

Oh, he understood exactly what she'd meant. Beware the golden spider who spins a tangled web. The Black Widow's web. Arachna's web. Beware the fair-haired Lady when she glides through the abyss clothed in spilled blood.

If the hunters never returned, nothing would happen. But they would return. Whoever they were, wherever they'd come from, they would return, and one kindred wolf would die and awaken the tangled web.

The hunters would still get their harvest, would still do the killing and the cutting and the skinning. Only one, confused and frightened, would leave with the bounty, and once he'd returned to wherever he'd come from, then, and only then, would the web release him and show him that the pelts he'd harvested didn't belong to wolf-kind.

4 / Kaeleer

Lord Jorval rubbed his hands gleefully. It was almost too good to be true. A scandal of this magnitude could topple anyone, even someone so firmly entrenched as the High Lord.

Remembering his new responsibilities, Jorval altered his expression to one more suitable to a member of the Dark Council.

This was a very serious charge, and the stranger with the maimed hands had admitted that he had no evidence except what he'd seen. After what the High Lord had done to the man's hands before dismissing him from service, it was understandable why he refused to stand before the Dark Council and testify against the High Lord in person. Still, something should be done about the girl.

A strong young Queen, the stranger had said. A Queen who could, with proper guidance, be a great asset to the Realm. All that glorious potential was being twisted by the High Lord's perversions, being forced to submit to . . .

Jorval jerked his thoughts away from those kinds of images.

The girl needed someone who could advise her and channel that power in the right direction. She needed someone she could depend on. And since she wasn't *that* young, maybe she needed more than that from her legal guardian. She might even expect, *want,* that kind of behavior . . .

But getting the girl away from Saetan would require a delicate touch. And the stranger had warned him about moving too quickly. A Dhemlan Queen could officially protest the High Lord's treatment of the girl, but Jorval didn't know any of them except by name or reputation. No, somehow the Dark Council itself had to be pressured into calling the High Lord to account.

And they could, couldn't they? After all, the Dark Council had granted the High Lord guardianship, and no one had forgotten what he'd done to gain that guardianship. It wouldn't be unusual for the Council to express concern about the girl's welfare.

A few words here. A hesitant question there. Strenuous protests that it was only a foul, unsubstantiated rumor. By the time it finally reached Dhemlan and the High Lord, no one would have any idea where the rumor started. Then they would see if even Saetan could withstand the rage of all the Queens in Kaeleer.

And he, Lord Jorval of Goth, the capital of Little Terreille, would be ready to assume his new and greater responsibilities.

5 / Kaeleer

The pushing turned into a shove. "Wake up, SaDiablo."

Saetan tried to pull the covers over his bare shoulder and pushed his head deeper into the pillows. "Go away."

A fist punched his shoulder.

Snarling, he braced himself on one elbow as Andulvar tossed a pair of trousers and a dressing robe onto the bed.

"Hurry," Andulvar said. "Before it's gone."

Before what was gone?

Rubbing his eyes, Saetan wondered if he might be allowed to splash some water on his face to wake up, but he had the distinct impression that if he didn't dress quickly, Andulvar would drag him through the corridors wearing nothing but his skin.

"The sun's up," Saetan muttered as he pulled on his clothes. "You should have retired by now."

"You were the one who pointed out that Jaenelle's presence has altered the Hall so that demons aren't affected by daylight as long as we stay inside," Andulvar said as he led Saetan through the corridors.

"That's the last time I tell you anything," Saetan growled.

When they reached a second floor room at the front of the Hall, Andulvar cautiously parted the drapes. "Stop grumbling and look."

Giving his eyes a final rub, Saetan braced one hand against the window frame and peered through the opening in the drapes.

Early morning. Clear, sunny. The gravel drive was partially raked. The landing web was swept. But the work looked interrupted, as if something had caused the outdoor staff to withdraw. They were still outside, and he picked up their excitement despite their shields. It was as if they were trying, almost hopefully, to go undetected.

Frowning, Saetan looked toward the left and saw a white stallion grazing on the front lawn, its hindquarters facing the windows. Not plain white, Saetan decided. Cream, with a milk-white mane and tail.

"Where did he come from?" Saetan looked inquiringly at Andulvar.

Andulvar snorted softly. "Probably from Sceval."

"What?" Saetan looked outside again at the same moment the stallion raised his head and turned toward the Hall. "Mother Night," he whispered, clutching the drapes. "Mother Night."

The ivory horn rose from the majestic head. Around the horn's base, glinting in the morning sun, was a gold ring. Attached to the ring was an Opal Jewel.

"That's a Warlord Prince having breakfast on your front lawn," Andulvar said in a neutral voice.

Saetan stared at his friend in disbelief. True, Andulvar had seen the stallion first and had time to take in the wonder of it, but was he really so jaded that the wonder could pass so quickly? There was a *unicorn* on the front lawn! A . . . kindred Warlord Prince.

Saetan braced himself against the wall. "Hell's fire, Mother Night, and may the Darkness be merciful."

"Think the waif knows about him?" Andulvar asked.

The question was answered by a wild, joyous whoop as Jaenelle sprinted across the gravel drive and slid to a stop a foot away from that magnificent, deadly horn.

The stallion arched his neck, raised his tail like a white silk banner, and danced around Jaenelle for a minute. Then he lowered his head and nuzzled her palms.

Saetan watched them, hoping nothing would disturb the lovely picture of a girl and unicorn meeting on a clear summer morning.

The picture shattered when Smoke streaked across the lawn.

The stallion knocked Jaenelle aside, laid his ears back, lowered that deadly horn, and began pawing the ground. Smoke skidded to a stop and bared his teeth in challenge.

Jaenelle grabbed a handful of the unicorn's mane and thrust out her other hand to stop Smoke. Whatever she said made the animals hesitate.

Finally, Smoke took a cautious step forward. The unicorn did the same. Muzzle touched muzzle.

Looking amused but exasperated, Jaenelle mounted the unicorn—and then scrambled to keep her seat when he took off at a gallop.

He stopped abruptly and looked back at her.

Jaenelle fluffed her hair and said something.

The stallion shook his head.

She became more emphatic.

The stallion shook his head and stamped one foot.

Finally, looking annoyed and embarrassed, she wrapped her hands in the long white mane and settled herself on his back.

The stallion walked away from the Hall, staying on the grass next to the drive. When they turned back toward the Hall, he changed to an easy canter. When they started the second loop, Smoke joined them.

"Come on," Saetan said.

He and Andulvar hurried to the great hall. Most of the house staff were pressed against the windows of the drawing rooms on either side of the hall, and Beale was peering through a crack in the front door.

"Open the door, Beale."

Startled by Saetan's voice, Beale jerked away from the door.

Pretending he didn't see Beale struggling to assume a proper stoic expression, Saetan swung the door open and stepped out while Andulvar stayed in the shadowy doorway.

She looked beautiful with her wind-tossed golden hair and her face lit from within by happiness. She belonged on a unicorn's back with a wolf beside her. He felt a pang of regret that she was cantering over a clipped lawn instead of in a wild glade. It was as if, by bringing her here, he had somehow clipped her wings—and he wondered if it were true. Then she saw him, and the stallion turned toward the door.

Reminding himself that he wore the darker Jewel, Saetan tried to relax—and couldn't. A Blood Prince, even a wolf, would accept his relationship with Jaenelle simply because he, a Warlord Prince, claimed her. Another Warlord Prince would challenge that claim, especially if it might interfere with his own, until the Lady acknowledged it.

As he went down the steps to meet them, Saetan felt the challenge being issued from the other side of the mental hedge, a demand that he acknowledge the stallion's prior claim. He silently met the challenge, opening himself just enough for the other Warlord Prince to feel his strength. But he didn't deny the unicorn's claim to Jaenelle.

Interested, the stallion pricked his ears.

"Papa, this is Prince Kaetien," Jaenelle said as she stroked the stallion's neck. "He was the first friend I made in Kaeleer."

Oh, yes. A *very* prior claim. And not one to be taken lightly. In the Old

Tongue, "kaetien" meant "white fire," and he didn't doubt for a moment that the name fit this four-footed Brother.

"Kaetien," Jaenelle said, "this is the High Lord, my sire."

Kaetien backed away from Saetan, his ears tight to his head.

"No, no," Jaenelle said hurriedly. "He's not *that* one. He's my *adopted* sire. He was the friend who was teaching me Craft, and now I'm living with him here."

The stallion snorted, relaxed.

Watching them, Saetan kept his feelings carefully hidden. He wouldn't push—yet—but sometime soon he and Kaetien were going to have a little talk about Jaenelle's sire.

Kaetien pawed the gravel as two young grooms slowly approached. The older of the two brushed his fingers against his cap brim. "Do you think the Prince would like some feed and a little grooming?"

Jaenelle hesitated, then smiled as she continued to stroke Kaetien's neck. "I should have my breakfast now," she said quietly. She tried to finger-comb her hair and made a face. "And I could use some grooming myself."

Kaetien tossed his head in what could be interpreted as agreement.

Jaenelle dismounted and ran up the steps. Then she spun around, her hands on her hips and fire in her eyes. "I did not fall off! I just wasn't balanced."

Kaetien looked at her and snorted.

"My legs are not weak, there's nothing wrong with my seat, and I'll thank you to keep your nose in your own feed bag! *I do so eat!*" She looked at Saetan. "Don't I?" She narrowed her eyes. "Don't I?"

Since silence was his safest choice, Saetan didn't reply.

Jaenelle narrowed her eyes a little more and snarled, "Males."

Satisfied, Kaetien followed the grooms to the stables.

Muttering under her breath, Jaenelle stomped past Andulvar and Beale and headed for the breakfast room.

With a cheerful whuff, Smoke continued his morning rounds.

"He deliberately baited her," Andulvar said from the doorway.

"It would seem so," Saetan agreed, chuckling. They headed for the breakfast room—slowly. "But isn't it comforting to know that some of our Brothers have developed a wonderful knack for badgering her."

"That particular Brother probably knows how much ground he can cover in a flat-out gallop."

Saetan smiled. "I imagine they both know."

★　★　★

She was sitting at the breakfast table, shredding a piece of toast.

Saetan cautiously took a seat on the opposite side of the table, poured a cup of tea, and felt grateful toast was the only thing she seemed interested in shredding.

"Thanks for backing me up," she said tartly.

"You wouldn't want me to lie to another Warlord Prince, would you?"

Jaenelle glared at him. "I'd forgotten how bossy Kaetien can be."

"He can't help it," he said soothingly. "It's part of what he is."

"Not all unicorns are bossy."

"I was thinking of Warlord Princes."

She looked startled. Then she smiled. "You should know." She reached for another piece of toast and began shredding it, her mood suddenly pensive. "Papa? Do you really think they'd come?"

His hand stuttered but he got the cup to his lips. "Your human friends?" he asked calmly.

She nodded.

He reached across the table and covered her restless hands with his. "There's only one way to find out, witch-child. Write the invitations, and I'll see that they're delivered."

Jaenelle wiped her hands on her napkin. "I'm going to see how Kaetien's doing."

Saetan picked at his breakfast steak for a while, drank another cup of tea, and finally gave up. He needed to talk to someone, needed to share the apprehension and excitement fizzing in his stomach. He'd tell Cassandra, of course, but their communication was always formal now and he didn't want to be formal. He wanted to yip and chase his tail. Sylvia? She liked Jaenelle and would welcome the news—all the news—but it was too early to drop in on her.

That left him with one choice.

Saetan grinned.

Andulvar would be comfortably settled in by now. A punch in the shoulder would do him good.

6 / Hell

Titian cleaned her knife with a scrap from the black coat while the other Harpies hacked up the meat and tossed the pieces to the pack of Hounds waiting in a half circle around the body.

The body twitched and still feebly struggled, but the bastard could no longer scream for help and the muted sounds he made filled her with satisfaction. A demon couldn't feel pain the way the living did, but pain was a cumulative thing, and he hadn't been dead long enough for his nerves to forget the sensation.

A Harpy tossed a large chunk of thigh toward the pack. The pack leader snatched it in midair and backed away with his prize, snarling. The rest of the pack re-formed the half circle and waited their turn. The Hound bitches watched their pups gnaw at fingers and toes.

Demons weren't usually the Hell Hounds' meat. There was better prey for these large, black-furred, red-eyed hunters, prey as native to this cold, forever-twilight Realm as the Hounds themselves. But this demon's flesh was saturated with too much fresh blood—blood Titian knew hadn't come from voluntary offerings.

It had taken a while to hunt him down. He hadn't strayed far from Hekatah since the High Lord had made his request. Until tonight.

There were no Gates in Hekatah's territory, and the closest two were now fiercely guarded. One was beside the Hall, a place Hekatah no longer dared approach, and the other was in the Harpies' territory, Titian's territory. Not a place for the unwary, no matter how arrogant. That meant Hekatah and her minions had to travel a long distance on the Winds to reach another Gate, or they had to take risks.

Tonight, Greer took a risk and paid for it.

If he'd had time to use his Jewels, it might have turned out differently, but he'd been allowed to reach the Dark Altar and go through the Gate unchallenged, so he had no reason to expect they'd be waiting for his return. Once he'd left the Sanctuary, the Harpy attacks had come so fast and so fierce all he could do was shield himself and try to escape. Even so, a number of Harpies burned themselves out and vanished to become a whisper in the Darkness. Titian didn't grieve for them. Their twilight existence had dissolved in fierce joy.

In the end it was one frightened mind against so many enraged ones probing for weakness, while Titian's trained Hounds constantly lunged at the body, forcing Greer to use more and more of the reserved strength in his Jewels to keep them away. The Harpies broke through his inner barriers at the same moment Titian's arrow drove through his body and pinned it to a tree.

As the Harpies pulled the body away from the tree and began carving up the meat, Titian picked through Greer's mind as delicately as if she were picking the meat from a cracked nut. She saw the children he'd feasted on. She saw the narrow bed, the blood on the sheets, the familiar young face that had been bruised by his maimed hands. She saw Surreal's horn-handled dagger driving into his heart, slicing his throat. She saw him smiling at her when his own knife had slit *her* throat centuries ago. And she saw where he'd been tonight.

Titian sheathed the knife and checked the blade of the small ax propped beside her.

She regretted not bringing him down before he reached Little Terreille. If Greer's assessment of Lord Jorval was correct, the whispers would begin soon.

A Guardian wasn't a natural being in a living Realm. There would always be whispering and wondering—especially when that Guardian was also the High Lord of Hell. And she could guess well enough how the Kaeleer Queens were going to react to the rumors.

She would visit her kinswomen, tell them what she wanted from them if the opportunity presented itself. That would help.

Titian picked up her ax. The Harpies moved aside for their Queen.

The limbs were gone. The torso was empty. The eyes still held a glimmer of intelligence, a glimmer of Self. Not much, but enough.

With three precise strokes, Titian split Greer's skull. Using the blade, she opened one of the splits until it was wide enough for her fingers. Then she tore the bone away.

She looked into Greer's eyes. Still enough there.

Whistling for the pack leader, she walked away, smiling, while the Hound began feasting on the brain.

7 / Kaeleer

Saetan brushed his hair for the third time because it gave him something to do. Like buffing his long, black-tinted nails twice. Like changing his jacket and then changing back to the first one.

He stopped himself from reaching for the hairbrush again, straightened his already straight jacket, and sighed.

Would the children come?

He hadn't requested a reply to the invitation because he had wanted to give the children as much time as possible to gather their courage or wear down their elders' arguments—and because he was afraid of what rejection dribbling in day after day might do to Jaenelle.

As he had promised, he or other members of the family had delivered all the invitations. Some had been left at the child's residence. Most had been left at message stones, the piles of rocks just inside a Territory's border where travelers or traders could leave a message requesting a meeting. He had no idea how messages left in those places reached the intended person, and he doubted those children would be here this afternoon. He didn't know what to expect from the children in the accessible Territories. He only hoped Andulvar was right and that little witch from Glacia would be here, stepping on his toes.

Taking a deep breath that still came out as a sigh, Saetan left his suite to join the rest of the family and Cassandra in the great hall.

Everyone was there except Jaenelle and Sylvia. Halaway's Queen had been delighted when he'd told her about the party and had used her considerable enthusiasm to browbeat Jaenelle into a shopping trip for a new outfit. They didn't come back with a dress, but he'd had to admit, grudgingly, that the soft, full, sapphire pants and long, flowing jacket were very feminine-looking, even if the skimpy gold-and-silver top worn beneath the jacket. . . . As a man, he approved of the top; as a father, it made him grind his teeth.

As soon as she saw him, Cassandra took his arm and led him away from the other men. "Do you think it's wise for everyone to be out here?" she asked quietly. "Won't it be too intimidating?"

"And whom would you ask to leave?" Saetan replied, knowing full well he was one of the people she thought should be absent.

After receiving his note, Cassandra had arrived to help with the preparations, but she'd acted too forcedly cheerful, as if she were really preparing for the moment when Jaenelle would face an empty drawing room. Sylvia, on the other hand, had thrown herself into the preparations and had bristled at anyone who dared to express a doubt.

A wise man would have locked himself in his study and stayed there.

Only a fool would have left two witches alone when they were constantly circling and spitting at each other like angry cats.

When Cassandra didn't answer his question, Saetan took his place in the great hall. Andulvar was one step behind him on his left. Mephis and Prothvar were on Andulvar's left and a little to the side so that they weren't part of the official greetings. Cassandra stood on Saetan's right, one step behind. By rights she should have stood beside him, Black with Black, and he was only too aware of why she was using an option of Protocol to distance herself from him.

Saetan turned toward the sound of feet racing down the staircase in the informal drawing room.

Sylvia burst into the great hall, looking a little too lovely with her golden eyes shining and her cheeks flushed. "The wolf pups hid Jaenelle's shoes and it took a while to find them," she said breathlessly. "She's on her way down, but I didn't want to be late."

Saetan smiled at her. "You're not—"

A clock struck three times.

Cassandra made a quiet, unhappy sound and stepped away from him.

For the first time since he'd told her about the party, Sylvia's eyes filled with concern.

They all stood in the great hall, silently waiting, while Beale stood woodenly by the front door and the footmen who would take the outer garments stared straight ahead.

The minutes ticked past.

Sylvia rubbed her forehead and sighed. "I'd better go up—"

"We don't need any more of *your* kind of help," Cassandra said coldly as she brushed past Sylvia. "You set her up for this."

Sylvia grabbed Cassandra's arm and spun her around. "Maybe I was too enthusiastic, but you did everything but say outright that she would never have a friend for the rest of her life!"

"Ladies," Saetan warned, stepping toward them.

"What could you possibly know about wearing the Black?" Cassandra snapped. "I *lived* with that isolation—"

"La—"

BOOM!

"Hell's fire," Andulvar muttered.

BOOM!

Beale leaped to open the front door while it was still intact.

She swept into the great hall, stopping where the sunlight coming from the lead glass window above the double doors produced a natural spotlight. Tall and slim, she wore severely tailored, dark blue trousers, a loose jacket, and heeled boots. Her white-blond hair rose in spiky peaks above her head like sculptured ice. Darkened eyebrows and lashes framed ice-blue eyes.

"Sisters," she said, giving Sylvia and Cassandra a perfunctory nod that couldn't quite be called insolent. Then her eyes raked over Saetan from head to toe.

Saetan held his breath. Even if Lord Morton hadn't slunk in behind her, he would have bet this was Karla, the young Glacian Queen.

"Well," Karla said, "you're not bad-looking for a corpse."

Before he could reply, Jaenelle's serene but amused voice said, "You're only half-right, darling. He's not a corpse."

Karla whirled toward the informal drawing room, where Jaenelle leaned against the doorway, her fingers hooked in the jacket thrown over one shoulder.

Karla let out a screech that raised the hairs on Saetan's neck.

"You've got tits!" Karla pulled open the blue jacket, revealing a silver, just as skimpy top. "So do I, if you call these lovely little bee stings tits." Smiling the wickedest smile Saetan had ever seen, she turned back to him. "What do you think?"

He didn't stop to think. "Are you asking if I think they're lovely or if I think they're bee strings?"

Karla closed the jacket, crossed her arms, and narrowed those ice-blue eyes. "Sassy, isn't he?"

"Well, he *is* a Warlord Prince," Jaenelle replied.

Ice-blue eyes met sapphire eyes. Both girls smiled.

Karla shrugged. "Oh, all right. I'll be a polite guest." She stepped up to Saetan, and that wicked smile bloomed. "Kiss kiss."

He refused to give her the satisfaction of seeing him wince.

Karla turned away from him and headed for Jaenelle. "*You've* got some explaining to do. I had to figure out all those damn spells by myself." She swept Jaenelle into the drawing room and closed the door.

Saetan stared at his shoe. "Damn it, she *did* step on my toes," he muttered before realizing Morton had come close enough to hear him.

"H-High Lord."

"Lord Morton, I have only one thing to say to you."

"Sir?" Morton tried to suppress a shiver.

Saetan tried to suppress a rueful smile and couldn't. "You have my heartfelt sympathy."

Morton melted with relief. "Thank you, sir. I could use it."

"Help yourself to the refreshments in there," Saetan said, making a slight gesture toward the closed door. "And if they start making plans to knock down any walls, let me know."

BANG!

For one panicked moment, Saetan thought the caution had been made too late. Then he realized someone was, more or less, knocking on the front door.

If Karla was ice, this one was fire, with her dark red hair flowing down her back, her green eyes flashing, and a swirling gown that looked like an autumn woods in motion. She headed for Saetan but veered when Jaenelle and Karla poked their heads out of the drawing room. Grinning, she held up a cloth bundle. "I wasn't sure if we would end up in the stables or digging in the garden, so I brought some real clothes."

Saetan stifled a growl. Didn't *any* of them like to dress up?

The girls disappeared into the drawing room—and closed the door.

The youth who'd come in with the fire witch was tall, good-looking, and a couple of years older. He had curly brown hair and blue eyes. Smiling, he extended one hand in informal greeting.

With his stomach sinking toward his heels, Saetan clasped the offered hand. There were a lot of ways he could describe those blue eyes. They all meant trouble.

"You must be the High Lord," the young Warlord said with a smile. "I'm Khardeen, from the isle of Scelt." He jerked his thumb toward the drawing room. "That's Morghann."

The drawing room door opened. Jaenelle approached them hesitantly. Then she held out both hands in formal greeting. "Hello, Khary."

Khary looked at the offered hands and turned back to Saetan. "Did Jaenelle ever tell you about her adventure with my uncle's stone—"

"Khary," Jaenelle gasped, glancing nervously at Saetan.

"Hmm?" Khary smiled at her. "Did you know that a proper hug can toss a thought right out of a man's head? It's a well-known fact. I'm surprised you hadn't heard of it."

Jaenelle had been balanced on the balls of her feet, ready to bolt. Now her heels came down and her eyes narrowed. "Really."

Watching the two of them, Saetan decided the prudent thing was to stand still and keep his mouth shut.

Seconds passed. When Jaenelle didn't move, Khardeen turned back to him. "You see, my—"

Jaenelle moved.

"You don't have to hug *all* the air out of me," Khary said as he carefully wrapped his arms around her.

"Now what were you going to say?" Jaenelle asked ominously.

"About what?" Khary replied sweetly.

Laughing, Jaenelle threw her arms around his neck. "I'm glad you came, Khardeen. I've missed you."

Khary gently untangled himself. "We'll have plenty of time to catch up on things. Right now you'd better get back to your sisters or I'll get the sharp side of Morghann's tongue for the rest of the day."

"Compared to Karla, Morghann's tongue doesn't have a sharp side."

"All the more reason then."

With another nervous glance at Saetan, Jaenelle bolted for the drawing room. She had just reached it when someone knocked on the door. It almost sounded polite.

They must have appeared on the landing web within seconds of each other and approached the door en masse because he knew this group didn't come from the same Territories. And since they spared him no more than an uneasy glance before focusing on Jaenelle, he was forced to deduce who they were by the names on the invitations.

The satyrs from Pandar were Zylona and Jonah. The small, pixie-faced darling with the dusky hair and iridescent wings who was perched on Jonah's shoulder was Katrine from Philan, one of the Paw Islands. The black-haired, gray-eyed youth who strongly reminded Saetan of the young wolves now living in the north woods was Aaron from Dharo. Sabrina, a hazel-eyed brunette, was also from Dharo. The two tawny-skinned, dark-striped youngsters were Grezande and Elan from Tigrelan.

The last of the group—a petite witch with a lusciously rounded figure, soft brown eyes, and dark brown hair—hugged Jaenelle, shyly approached him, and introduced herself as Kalush from Nharkhava.

There was a sweetness about her that made Saetan want to cuddle her.

Instead, he slid his hands beneath her offered ones in formal greeting, and said, "I'm honored to meet you, Lady Kalush."

"High Lord." She had a husky voice that would do wonderfully bad things to young men's libidos. He pitied her father.

Beale, looking slightly dazed, started to close the door when it was yanked out of his grasp.

Saetan pushed Kalush toward Andulvar and tensed.

The centaurs walked in.

The young witch, Astar, headed for the girls. The Warlord Prince continued down the great hall until he was standing in front of Saetan.

"High Lord." The greeting sounded more like a challenge.

"Prince Sceron."

Sceron was a few years older than the others, old enough to have begun filling out the massive shoulders and the powerfully built upper body. The rest of him would have done any stallion proud.

There was an unasked question in Sceron's eyes, and an anger in him that seemed ready to blaze into rage.

Jaenelle stepped into that frozen silence, balled her hand into a fist, and drove it into Sceron's upper arm.

Sceron grabbed her and lifted her until they were eye to eye.

"That's for not saying hello," Jaenelle said.

Sceron studied her face and finally smiled. "You are well?"

"I was better before you rumpled me."

Laughing, Sceron put her down.

Someone gasped.

Saetan felt a shiver run up his spine and looked toward the door.

Because he hadn't expected them to come, he hadn't thought about how the others would react to their presence. But they had come. The Children of the Wood. The Dea al Mon.

They both had the slender, sinewy build that was as inherent to their race as the delicately pointed ears. Both wore their silver hair long and unbound. Both had the large, forest-blue eyes, although the girl's had a touch more gray.

The girl, Gabrielle, stopped just inside the door. The boy—oh, no, it would be extremely foolish to think of Chaosti as a boy—came forward slowly, silently.

Saetan fought the instincts that always came to the fore at the appearance of an unknown Warlord Prince. Because they hadn't approached him, Elan and Aaron hadn't pricked those instincts. Sceron had just managed to scratch the surface. But this one, calmly staring at him with those large eyes, made all the aggressiveness and territoriality that was part of a Warlord Prine boil to the surface.

Saetan felt himself rising to the killing edge, and knew Chaosti was also rising, but instinct was driving him too hard to hold it back.

"Chaosti," Jaenelle said in her midnight voice.

Chaosti slowly turned to face her.

"He's my father, Chaosti," Jaenelle said. "By my choice."

After a long moment, Chaosti placed a hand over his heart. "By your choice, cousin," he replied in a deceptively quiet tenor voice.

Jaenelle led the girls into the informal drawing room and closed the door.

The males let out a collective sigh of relief.

Chaosti turned to face Saetan. "She's been away so long and has been deeply missed. Titian said you weren't to blame, but—"

"But I'm the High Lord," Saetan said with a trace of bitterness.

"No," Chaosti replied, smiling coolly, "you are not Dea al Mon."

Saetan felt his body relax. "Why do you call her 'cousin'?"

"Gabrielle and I belong to the same clan. Grandmammy Teele is the matriarch. She also adopted Jaenelle." Chaosti's smile turned feral. "So you are kin of my kin—which makes you Titian's kin as well."

Saetan wheezed.

Khardeen approached them. "If we want anything to eat, I think we're going to have to fight for it," he said to Chaosti.

"I'll accept any challenge a male wants to make," Chaosti snapped.

"The girls are between us and the food."

Chaosti sighed. "Challenging another male would be easier."

"Safer, too."

"Gentlemen," Beale said. "Refreshments are also being served in the formal drawing room."

"Have you ever heard that red-haired witches have hot tempers?" Khardeen asked as he and Chaosti followed the other males into the formal drawing room.

"There are no red-haired witches among the Dea al Mon," Chaosti replied, "and they *all* have hot tempers."

"Ah. Well, then."

The door closed behind them.

Saetan jumped when a hand squeezed his shoulder.

"You all right?" Andulvar asked quietly.

"Am I still standing up?"

"You're vertical."

"Thank the Darkness." Saetan looked around. He and Andulvar were the only ones left in the great hall. "Let's hide in my study."

"Agreed."

They drank two glasses of yarbarah and finally relaxed when an hour had passed without any shrieks, bangs, or booms.

"Mother Night." Saetan wearily stripped off his jacket and slumped in one of the comfortable, oversized chairs.

"By my count," Andulvar said as he refilled the glasses, "including the waif, you've got ten adolescent witches in one room—Queens every one of them, and two besides Jaenelle who are natural Black Widows."

"Karla and Gabrielle. I noticed." Saetan closed his eyes.

"In the other room, you have seven young males, four of whom are Warlord Princes."

"I noticed that, too. It makes a very interesting First Circle, don't you think?"

Andulvar muttered in Eyrien. Saetan chose not to translate it.

"Where do you think the others went?" Andulvar asked.

"If Mephis and Prothvar have any sense at all, they're hiding somewhere. Sylvia is no doubt passing out nutcakes and sandwiches. Cassandra?" Saetan shrugged. "I don't thinks she was prepared for this."

"Were you?"

"Shit." When someone tapped on the study door, Saetan thought about sitting up straighter, then decided not to bother. "Come."

A smiling Khardeen entered and placed sixteen sealed envelopes on the blackwood table. "I told Jaenelle I'd drop these off to you. We're going out to meet the wolves and the unicorn."

"Finished devouring the kitchen already?" Saetan asked as he picked up one of the envelopes.

"At least until dinner."

"Plant your feet, Warlord," Saetan said, stopping Khardeen's hasty retreat. He broke the formal seal, called in his half-moon glasses, and read the message. Then he stared at Khary. "This is from Lady Duana."

"Mmm," Khary said, rocking on his heels. "Morghann's grandmother."

"The Queen of Scelt is Morghann's grandmother?"

Khary stuffed his hands into his pockets. "Mmm."

Saetan placed his glasses carefully on the table. "Let's skip the hunt and just tree the prey. Do all these letters say the same thing?"

"What's that, High Lord?" Khary asked innocently.

"All of these letters give permission for an extended visit?"

"So I gathered."

"Define 'extended visit.' "

"Not long. Just the rest of the summer."

Saetan couldn't speak. Wasn't sure what he'd say if he could.

"Everything is being taken care of," Khary said soothingly. "Lord Beale and Lady Helene are taking care of the room assignments right now, so there's nothing for you to worry about."

"Noth—" Saetan's voice cracked.

"And it *is* a reasonable compromise, High Lord. You get to spend time with her and we get to spend time with her. Besides, the Hall is the only place big enough for all of us. And, as my uncle pointed out, having all of us in one place would surely drive a man to drink, and that being the case, he'd rather it be you than him."

Saetan made a weak gesture of dismissal and waited until the door was safely closed before bracing his head in his hands. "Mother Night."

CHAPTER SEVEN

1 / Kaeleer

Saetan steepled his fingers and stared at Sylvia. "I beg your pardon?"
"You have to talk to Tersa," Sylvia said again.

Damn her. Why was she being so insistent?

With difficulty, he leashed his temper. It wasn't Sylvia's fault. She had no way of knowing how he and Tersa were connected.

"Would you like some wine?" he finally asked, his deep voice betraying too much of his heart.

Sylvia eyed the decanter on the corner of his desk. "If that's brandy, why don't you pour yourself a glass and hand me the decanter."

Saetan filled two brandy snifters and floated one to her.

Sylvia took a generous swallow and choked a little.

"That's not exactly the way to drink good brandy," he said dryly, but he slugged back a good portion of his own glass, despite the headache he knew it would give him. "All right. Tell me about Tersa."

Sylvia leaned forward, her arms braced on the chair, both hands cupped around the snifter. "I'm not a child, Saetan. I understand that some people slip into the Twisted Kingdom and some people are shoved—and a very brave few make a deliberate choice. And I know most Black Widows who become lost in the Twisted Kingdom aren't harmful to others. In their own way, they're extraordinarily wise."

"But?"

Sylvia pressed her lips together. "Mikal, my youngest son, spends quite a bit of time with her. He thinks she's wonderful." She finished the brandy and held out her glass for a refill. "Lately she's been calling him Daemon."

Her voice was so low, so husky he had to strain to hear her. He wished, bitterly, that he hadn't heard.

"Mikal shrugs it off," Sylvia continued after taking another large swallow of brandy. "He says anyone stuffed that full of interesting things to say could easily get confused about everyday things, and she'd probably known a boy named Daemon and used to tell him the same kind of interesting stuff."

She never got the chance. He was already lost, to both of us, by the time he was Mikal's age. "But?"

"The last couple of times Mikal's gone to see her, she keeps telling him to be careful." Sylvia closed her eyes and frowned in concentration. "She says the bridge is very fragile, and she'll keep sending the sticks." She opened her eyes and poured herself another brandy. "Sometimes she just holds Mikal and cries. She keeps sticks she's collected from every yard in the village in a big basket in her kitchen and panics if anyone goes near them. But she can't, or won't, tell Mikal or me why the sticks are important. I've had every bridge around Halaway checked and they're all sound, even the smallest footbridge. I thought maybe she'd tell you."

Would she tell him? Would she let him broach the one subject she refused to discuss with him? When he went to see her, one hour each week, Tersa talked about her garden; she told him what she'd had for dinner; she showed him a piece of needlepoint she was working on; she talked about Jaenelle. But she wouldn't talk about their son.

"I'll try," he said quietly.

Sylvia put her empty glass on the desk and stood up, swaying.

Saetan went around the desk, cupped his hand under her elbow, and led her to the door. "You should go home and take a nap."

"I never take naps."

"After that much brandy, I doubt you'll have a choice."

"My metabolism will burn it up fast enough." Sylvia hiccuped.

"Uh-huh. Did you realize you called me Saetan?"

She turned so fast she fell against him. He liked the feel of her. It disturbed him that he liked the feel of her.

"I'm sorry, High Lord. I'm sorry."

"Are you?" he asked softly. "I'm not sure I am."

Sylvia stared at him. She hesitated. She said nothing.

He let her go.

★   ★   ★

"You're going out?"

Jaenelle leaned against the wall opposite his bedroom door, her finger tucked between the pages of a Craft book to hold her place.

Amused, Saetan raised an eyebrow. It was usually the parent who insisted on knowing his offspring's whereabouts, not the other way around. "I'm going to see Tersa."

"Why? This isn't your usual evening to see her."

He caught the slight edge in her voice, the subtle warning. "Am I that predictable?" he asked, smiling.

Jaenelle didn't smile back.

Before her own catastrophic plunge into the abyss or wherever she'd spent those two years, Jaenelle had gone into the Twisted Kingdom and had led Tersa back to the blurred boundary that separated madness and sanity. That was as far as Tersa could go—or was willing to go.

Jaenelle had helped her regain a little of the real world. Now that they were living near each other, Jaenelle continued to help Tersa fill in the pieces that made up the physical world. Small things. Simple things. Trees and flowers. The feel of loam between strong fingers. The pleasure of a bowl of soup and a thick slice of fresh-baked bread.

"Sylvia came to see me this afternoon," he said slowly, trying to understand the chill emanating from Jaenelle. "She thinks Tersa's upset about something, so I wanted to look in on her."

Jaenelle's sapphire eyes were as deep and still as a bottomless lake. "Don't push where you're not welcome, High Lord," Witch said.

He wondered if she knew how much her eyes revealed. "You'd prefer I not see her?" he asked respectfully.

Her eyes changed. "See her if you like," his daughter replied. "But don't invade her privacy."

"There's no wine." Tersa opened and closed cupboards, looking more and more confused. "The woman didn't buy the wine. She always buys a bottle of wine on fourth-day so it will be here for you. She didn't buy the wine, and tomorrow I was going to draw a picture of my garden and show it to you, but third-day's gone and I don't know where I put it."

Saetan sat at the pine kitchen table, his body saturated with sorrow until it felt too heavy to move. He'd joked about being predictable. He hadn't realized that his predictability was one of Tersa's touchstones, a means by which she separated the days. Jaenelle had known and had let him come to learn the lesson for himself.

With his hands braced on the table, he pushed himself up from the chair. Every movement was an effort, but he reached Tersa, who was still opening cupboards and muttering, seated her at the table, put a kettle on the stove, and, after a little exploring in the cupboards, made them both a cup of chamomile tea.

As he put the cup in front of her, he brushed the tangled black hair away from her face. He couldn't remember a time when Tersa's hair didn't look as if she'd washed it and let it dry in the wind, as if her fingers were the only comb it had ever known. He suspected it wasn't madness but intensity that made her indifferent. And he wondered if that wasn't one of the reasons, when he'd finally agreed to that contract with the Hayllian Hourglass to sire a child, that he'd chosen Tersa, who was already broken, already teetering on the edge of madness. He'd spent over an hour brushing her hair that first night. He'd brushed her hair every night of the week he'd bedded her, enjoying the feel of it between his fingers, the gentle pull of the brush.

Now, sitting across from her, his hands around the mug, he said, "I came early, Tersa. You didn't lose third-day. This is second-day."

Tersa frowned. "Second-day? You don't come on second-day."

"I wanted to talk to you. I didn't want to wait until fourth-day. I'll come back on fourth-day to see your drawing."

Some of the confusion left her gold eyes. She sipped her tea.

The pine table was empty except for a small azure vase holding three red roses.

Tersa gently touched the petals. "The boy picked these for me."

"Which boy is that?" Saetan said quietly.

"Mikal. Sylvia's boy. He comes to visit. Did she tell you?"

"I thought you might mean Daemon."

Tersa snorted. "Daemon's not a boy now. Besides, he's far away." Her eyes became clouded, farseeing. "And the island has no flowers."

"But you call Mikal Daemon."

Tersa shrugged. "Sometimes it's nice to pretend that I'm telling him stories. Jaenelle says it's all right to pretend."

A cold finger whispered down his spine. "You've told Jaenelle about Daemon?"

"Of course not," Tersa said irritably. "She's not ready to know about him. All the threads are not yet in place."

"What threads—"

"The lover is the father's mirror. The brother stands between. The mirror spins, spins, spins. Blood. So much blood. He clings to the island of maybe. The bridge will have to rise from the sea. The threads are not yet in place."

"Tersa, where is Daemon?"

Tersa blinked, drew a shuddering breath. She stared at him, frowning. "The boy's name is Mikal."

He wanted to shout at her, *Where's my son? Why hasn't he gone to the Keep or come through one of the Gates? What's he waiting for?* Useless to shout at her. She couldn't translate what she'd seen any better than she had. One thing he did understand. All the threads were not yet in place. Until they were, all he could do was wait.

"What are the sticks for, Tersa?"

"Sticks?" Tersa looked at the basket of sticks in the corner of the kitchen. "They have no purpose." She shrugged. "Kindling?"

She withdrew from him, exhausted by the effort of keeping the stones of reality and madness from grinding her soul.

"Is there anything I can do for you?" he asked, preparing to leave.

Tersa hesitated. "It would anger you."

Right now, he didn't feel capable of that strong an emotion. "It won't anger me. I promise."

"Would you . . . Would you hold me for a minute?"

It rocked him. He, who had always craved physical affection, had never thought to offer her an embrace.

He closed his arms around her. She wrapped her arms around his back and rested her head on his shoulder.

"I don't miss the rutting, but it feels good to be held by a man."

Saetan gently kissed her tangled hair. "Why didn't you mention it before? I didn't know you wanted to be held."

"Now you do."

2 / Kaeleer

The Dark Council whispered.

At first it was only a thoughtful look, a troubled frown. The High Lord had done many things in his long life—look what he'd done to the Council itself in order to become the girl's guardian—but it was hard to believe he was capable of *that*. He had always insisted that the strength of a Territory, the strength of the Realm, depended on the strength of its witches, especially its Queens. To think he would do such things with a vulnerable girl, a dark young Queen . . .

Oh, yes, they had inquired about the girl before now, but the High Lord had always responded tersely. The girl was ill. She could have no visitors. She was being privately tutored.

Where had the girl been during the past two years? What had she been subjected to? Was Jorval sure?

No, Lord Jorval insisted, he was not sure. It was only a spurious rumor made by a dismissed servant. There was no reason to suspect it wasn't just as the High Lord had said. The girl probably *was* ill, an invalid of some kind, perhaps too emotionally or physically fragile for the stimulation of visitors.

The High Lord had made no mention of the girl being ill until the Council requested to see her the first time.

Jorval stroked his dark beard with a thin hand and shook his head. There was no evidence. Only the word of a man who couldn't be found.

Murmurs, speculations, whisssspers.

3 / The Twisted Kingdom

He clung to the sharp grass on the crumbling island of *maybe* and watched the sticks float toward him. They were evenly spaced like the boards of a rope bridge strung across the endless sea. But the footing would be precarious at best, and there were no ropes to hang on to. If he tried to use them, he would sink beneath the vast sea of blood.

He was going to sink anyway. The island continued to crumble. Eventually there wouldn't be enough left to hold him.

He was tired. He was willing to let it suck him down.

The sticks broke formation, swirled and re-formed, swirled and re-formed over and over again into rough letters.

You are my instrument.

Words lie. Blood doesn't.

Butchering whore.

He tried to scramble away from that side of the island, but the other side kept crumbling, crumbling. There was only enough room now for him to lie there, helpless.

Something moved beneath the sea of blood, disturbing the sticks and their endless words. The sticks swirled around his small island, bumped against the crumbling edges of *maybe*, and piled up against each other to form a fragile, protective wall.

He leaned over the edge and watched the face float upward, sapphire eyes staring at nothing, golden hair spread out like a fan.

The lips moved. *Daemon*.

He reached down and gently lifted the face out of the sea of blood. Not a head, just a face, as smooth and lifeless as a mask.

The lips moved again. The word sounded like the sigh of the night wind, like a caress. *Daemon*.

The face dissolved, oozed through his fingers.

Sobbing, he tried to hold it, tried to re-form it into that beloved face. The harder he tried, the quicker it slipped through his fingers until there was nothing left.

Shadows in the bloody sea. A woman's face, full of compassion and understanding, surrounded by a mass of tangled black hair.

Wait, she said. *Wait. The threads are not yet in place.*

She vanished in the ripples.

Finally, there was an easy thing to do, a thing without pain, without fear.

Making himself as comfortable as possible, he settled down to wait.

4 / Kaeleer

Saetan wondered if there was something wrong with the bookcases behind his desk or if there was something wrong with his butler, because Beale had been staring at the same spot for almost a minute.

"High Lord," Beale said stiffly, still staring at the bookcases.

"Beale," Saetan replied cautiously.

"There's a Warlord to see you."

Saetan carefully set his glasses on top of the papers covering his desk, and folded his hands to keep them from shaking. "Is he cringing?"

Beale's lips twitched. "No, High Lord."

Saetan sagged in his chair. "Thank the Darkness. At least he's not here because of something the girls have done."

"I don't believe the Ladies are involved, High Lord."

"Then send him in."

The Warlord who entered the study was a head taller than Saetan, twice as wide, and solid muscle. His hands were big enough to engulf a man's skull and strong enough to crush one. He looked like a rough man who would wrench what he wanted from the land or from other people. But beneath that massive body and roaring voice was a heart filled with simple joy and a soul too sensitive to bear harsh treatment.

He was Dujae. Five hundred years ago, he had been the finest artist in Kaeleer. Now he was a demon.

Saetan knew it was hypocritical to be angry with Dujae for coming here since Mephis, Andulvar, and Prothvar were all frequently in residence at the Hall since Jaenelle had returned with him, and they all had contact with the children. Even so, keeping the Dark Realm separated from the living Realms had always been a knife-edged dance, and he was uncomfortably aware that, even when living, he'd straddled that line. Now with all the children spending the summer at the Hall and the Dark Council pressuring him for an interview with Jaenelle, having demons coming into Kaeleer for an audience with him was beyond tolerance.

"Twice a month I hold an audience in Hell for any who wish to come before me," he said coldly. "You've no business here, Lord Dujae."

Dujae stared at the floor, his long, thick fingers pulling at the brim of the shabby blue cap he held in his hands. "I know, High Lord. Forgive me. I should not have come here, but I could not wait."

Saetan could, and did.

Dujae crushed the cap in his hands. When he finally looked up, there was only despair in his eyes. "I am so tired, High Lord. There is nothing left to paint, no one to teach, to share with. No purpose, no joy. There is nothing. Please, High Lord."

Saetan closed his eyes, his anger forgotten. It happened sometimes. Hell was a cold, cruel, blasted Realm, but it had its measure of kindness. It was a place where the Blood could make peace with their lives, a suspended time to take care of unfinished business. Some did nothing with that last gift, enduring weeks or years or centuries of tedium before finally fading into the Darkness. Others embraced that time to nurture talents they'd ignored while living or chosen to forsake in order to follow another road. Others, cut off before they were finished, continued as they had lived. Dujae had died in his prime, suddenly, unexpectedly. When he realized he could still paint, he had accepted being demon-dead with a joyous heart.

Now he was asking Saetan to release him from the dead flesh, to consume the last of his psychic strength and let him become a whisper in the Darkness.

It happened sometimes. Not often, thankfully, but sometimes the desire to continue faded before the psychic strength. When that happened, a demon came to him and asked for a swift release. And because he was the High Lord, he honored those requests.

Saetan opened his eyes and blinked hard to clear his vision. "Dujae, are you sure?"

"I'm—"

Karla exploded into the room. "That overbearing, overdressed, overscented sewer rat says my drawing is deficient!" Her eyes filled with tears as she flung a sketch pad onto Saetan's desk.

He vanished his glasses before the sketch pad landed on them.

"He's a grubby-minded prick," Karla wailed. "This isn't my life's work, this isn't my road. This is supposed to be fun!"

Saetan surged out of his chair. There had been so many tutors coming and going in the past three weeks he couldn't remember this particular ass's name, but if the man could reduce Karla to tears, he was probably shredding Kalush and Morghann, to say nothing of Jaenelle.

Dujae reached for the sketch pad.

"No!" Karla dove for the pad, too upset to remember she could vanish it before Dujae's hand closed around it.

Her forehead hit Dujae's arm. She stumbled backward into Saetan. He wrapped his arms around her and ground his teeth, hating the anguish pouring out of her.

Dujae studied the sketch. He shook his head slowly. "This is terrible," he rumbled, flipping the pages back to earlier sketches. "Obscene," he roared. He shook the sketch pad at Karla. "You call him sewer rat? You are too kind, Lady. He's a—"

"Dujae," Saetan warned, first to prevent Dujae from possibly teaching Karla a pithy phrase she didn't already know and second because he'd felt Karla perk up.

Dujae looked at Saetan and took a deep breath. "He is not a good instructor," he finished lamely.

Karla sniffed. "You don't think my drawings are good either."

Dujae flipped to the last sketch. "What is this?" he demanded, stabbing the paper with his finger.

Karla pulled her shoulders back and narrowed her eyes.

Saetan stifled a groan and held on tighter.

"It's a vase," she said coolly.

"Vase. Bah!" Dujae ripped the page from the pad, crumpled it, and threw it over his shoulder. He pointed at Karla.

Did Dujae realize just how close his finger was to Karla's teeth?

"You are a Queen, yes?" Dujae continued to roar. "You do this for fun when you are finished with the hard lessons of your Craft, yes? You do this because Ladies must learn many things to be good Queens, yes? You do not make polite, itsy-bitsy drawings." He scrunched up his shoulders, scrunched up his face, tucked his wrist under his chin, and made tiny scratching motions. "Bah!" He pulled Karla out of Saetan's arms, spun her around, engulfed her hand in his own, and began making large, circular motions. "There is fire in your heart, yes? That fire needs charcoal and a large pad to express itself. Then when you want to draw a vase, you draw a vase."

"B-but—" Karla stammered, watching her hand sweep round and round.

"That vase you try to draw, that is someone else's vase. Use it as a model. Models are good. Then you draw YOUR VASE, the one that reveals the fire, the one that says I am a witch, I am a Queen, I am—" Dujae finally hesitated.

"Karla," she said meekly.

"KARLA!" Dujae roared.

"What's going on?" Jaenelle asked from the doorway. Gabrielle stood beside her.

Saetan settled on the corner of his desk and crossed his arms, resigned to whatever the little darlings were about to do.

Seeing the other girls, Dujae released Karla and stepped back.

"Do we have any charcoal?" Karla asked, wiping her eyes.

"We have some, but Lord Stuffy says charcoal is messy and not the proper medium for Ladies," Gabrielle said tartly.

Saetan stared at Gabrielle and wondered what sort of idiot he'd hired as an art instructor.

Then he felt the blood rush out of his head. He gripped the desk, willing himself not to faint. He'd never fainted. This would be a very bad time to start.

With the other girls around them, he hadn't recognized the triangle of power. Karla, Gabrielle, Jaenelle. Three strong Queens who were also natural Black Widows.

May the Darkness be merciful, he thought. *That trio could tear apart anything or anyone—or build anything they wanted.*

"High Lord?"

Saetan blinked. He took a deep breath. His lungs still worked, sort of. Finally sure he wasn't going to keel over, he looked around. Dujae was the only one left in the room.

Dujae twisted his cap. "I did not mean to interfere."

"Too late now," Saetan muttered.

Three blond heads appeared at the study door.

"Hey," Karla said. "We've got the charcoal and large sketch pads. Aren't you coming?"

Dujae continued to twist his cap. "I cannot, Ladies."

"Why not?" Jaenelle asked as the three of them entered the study.

Dujae looked beseechingly at Saetan, who refused to look at anything but the point of his shoe.

"I—I am Dujae, Lady."

Jaenelle looked pleased. "You painted *Descent into Hell.*"

Dujae's eyes widened.

"Why can't you give us drawing lessons?" Gabrielle said.

"I am a demon."

Silence.

Karla cocked a hip and crossed her arms. "What, there's some rule that says drawing has to be taught in the daytime? Besides, the sun's up now and you're here."

"That's because the Hall retains enough dark power so that sunlight doesn't bother the demon-dead when they're inside," Jaenelle said.

"So that's not a problem," Karla said.

"And if you don't want to be here during the daylight hours, candle-lights or balls of witchlight would make a room bright enough to work in," Gabrielle said.

Dujae looked helplessly at Saetan. Saetan studied his other shoe.

"Is your ego so puffed up that it's beneath you to teach a few little witches how to draw?" Karla asked with sweet malevolence.

"Puffed up? No, no, Ladies, I would be honored but—"

"But?" Jaenelle asked softly in her midnight voice.

Dujae shuddered. Saetan shivered.

"I am a demon."

Silence.

Finally Karla snorted. "If you don't want to teach us, just say so, but stop using a paltry excuse to weasel out of it."

They left, closing the study door behind them.

Dujae twisted his cap.

Saetan stared at his shoe. "Dujae," he said quietly, "it takes a strong but sensitive personality to deal with these young Ladies, not to mention tal-ent. If you decide to become their art instructor, I can either provide you with wages which, I admit, aren't much use in the Dark Realm, or you can add whatever you want for your own projects to the list of supplies you'll provide me for them. However, if you decide to decline"—he looked Dujae in the eye—"*you* can go out there and try to explain it to them."

There was panic in Dujae's eyes. There was also only one door out of the study.

"But, High Lord, I am a demon."

"Didn't impress them, did it?"

Dujae sagged. "No." Then he shrugged and smiled. "It has been a long time since I have done portraits, and they have interesting faces, yes? And too much fire to be wasted on polite, itsy-bitsy drawings."

Saetan waited half an hour before strolling into the great hall. Staying well in the background, he watched the coven.

The girls were sitting on the floor in a circle, busily sketching a still life of vase, apple, and trinket box. Dujae squatted next to Kalush, explaining something in a rumbling murmur before turning to Morghann, who had a stick of charcoal poised above her sketch pad.

Jaenelle put down her pad, wiped her fingers on the towel she was sharing with Karla, and approached him, smiling, nothing more than a delightful, delighted woman-child enjoying a creative endeavor.

Saetan slipped an arm around her waist. "The truth, witch-child," he said quietly. "Was the other one really a bad instructor?"

Jaenelle ran her finger down the gold chain that held his Birthright Red Jewel. "He wasn't right for us, any of us, and—"

He wouldn't let her duck her head, wouldn't let her hide the eyes he was learning to read so well, that told him so much. "And?"

"He was afraid of me," she whispered. "Not just me," she quickly amended. "He didn't like being around Queens. Even Kalush made him uneasy. So he was always saying things like 'ladies' do this and 'ladies' don't do that. Hell's fire, Saetan, we aren't 'ladies,' we don't want to be 'ladies.' We're witches."

He wrapped his arms around her. "Why didn't you tell me?" He seemed to be asking that a lot lately.

Jaenelle shrugged. "We hadn't gotten around to telling you that the music instructor and the dancing instructor already bolted this week."

Saetan let out a chuckling sigh. "Well, lessons and summertime are probably a bad combination anyway." He kissed her hair. "Dujae came here because he wanted to be released."

"Not really. He just needed something to spark his interest again."

Saetan watched Dujae move around the circle, gesturing, rumbling encouragement, frowning as he studied Karla's sketch before saying something that made her laugh. There was no despair in Dujae's eyes now, no hint of the pain that had driven him to seek out the High Lord.

"We aren't puppet masters, witch-child," Saetan murmured. "We're very powerful, but we must be careful about pulling strings to make other people dance."

"Depends on why the strings are being pulled, don't you think?" She looked at him with those ancient sapphire eyes and smiled. "Besides, we just overrode a silly excuse. If it was his time, he would have gone."

She returned to her spot on the floor, Karla on her right, Gabrielle on her left.

He returned to his study and warmed a glass of yarbarah.

Puppet masters. Manipulators. Hekatah and her schemes. Jaenelle and her sensitivity to other hearts. Such a fine, fragile line, with intent the only difference.

He picked up the latest letter from the Dark Council. There was something beneath the terse words that disturbed him, but it was too vague for him to define. He couldn't put them off much longer. A few more weeks at most. What then?

Such a fine, fragile line.

What then?

5 / Kaeleer

Jaenelle picked up a small vial and tapped three amethyst-colored granules into the large glass bowl on the worktable. "Why are members of the Dark Council coming here?"

Saetan eyed the thick, bubbling liquid that covered the bottom third of the bowl and sincerely hoped the stuff wasn't a new tonic. "Since my legal guardianship was granted by the Council, they want to look in on us to see how we live."

"If they're members of the Council, they're also Jeweled Blood. They should know how we live." Jaenelle picked up a vial of red powder and held it up to the light.

Saetan crossed his arms and leaned against the wall. He wouldn't, couldn't tell her about the latest "request" from the Council. Their strident insistence had made it easy to read between the lines. They weren't just coming to look in on a guardian and his ward. They were coming to pass judgment on him.

"I'm not going to have to wear a dress, am I?" Jaenelle growled as she dipped her little finger into the vial of red powder. Using her nail as a scoop, she tapped the powder into the bowl.

Saetan bit his tongue before the lie could slip out. "No. They said they wanted to see a normal afternoon."

Jaenelle looked at him over her shoulder. "Have we ever had a normal afternoon?"

"No," Saetan said mournfully. "We have typical afternoons, but I don't think anyone would consider them normal."

Her silvery, velvet-coated laugh filled the room. "Poor Papa. Well, since I don't have to dress up and simper, I'll try not to offend their delicate sensibilities." She handed him a vial of black powder. "Put a pinch of that in the bowl and stand back."

The butterflies in his stomach were having a grand time. "What happens then?"

Jaenelle laced her fingers. "Well, if I mixed the powders in the right proportions to the spell, it'll create an impressive illusion."

Saetan looked from his nervously smiling daughter to the bowl on the table to the vial in his hand. "And if you didn't mix them in the right proportions?"

"It'll blow up the table."

An hour later, as he lay in a deep, hot bath, soaking the soreness out of his muscles, he had to give her full marks for her fast reflexes and the strength of her protective shields. Except for knocking them both to the floor, the explosion hadn't damaged anything in the room—except the glass bowl and the table. And he had to admit that the shape that had started rising out of the bowl had been impressive.

Two days from now, the Dark Council would come to the Hall. He would show them courtesy and endure their presence because, in the end, it didn't matter what they thought. No one was going to take her away from him. If the Council had to learn that lesson twice, so be it.

He doubted it would come to that. Remembering the awe-filled moment between the shape starting to rise from the mist and the table exploding, he let out a moan that turned into a chuckle. The Dark Council wanted to spend a typical afternoon with Jaenelle?

The poor fools would never survive it.

CHAPTER EIGHT

1 / Kaeleer

It started going wrong the moment the two members of the Dark Council walked through the front door, looked around, and shivered.

SaDiablo Hall was a dark-gray structure that rose above the land and cast a long shadow. He'd built it to be imposing, but hadn't planned on having a stony-faced, Red-Jeweled butler frightening his guests before they even crossed the threshold. As for the chill in the air . . . Helene had let him know, with stiff courtesy, what she thought of the Council coming to poke and pry into her domain, and all of the servants had spent the day scurrying away from the kitchen and Mrs. Beale.

Dark-Jeweled houses always had Blood servants, but when *all* the witches in a household decided to express their displeasure, the phrase "cold comfort" took on a whole new meaning.

"Good afternoon," Saetan said, coming forward to greet the two men.

The elder of the two bowed. "We appreciate your taking the time to see us, High Lord. I'm Lord Magstrom. This is Lord Friall."

Saetan liked Lord Magstrom. A man in his twilight years, he had a kind face framed by a cloud of white hair and blue eyes that probably twinkled most of the time. Those eyes were serious now but not condemning. Lord Magstrom, at least, would make his decision based on his own integrity and honor.

Lord Friall, on the other hand, had already decided. Weedy-looking for all the hair cream and finery, he kept glancing around with distaste and dabbing his lips with a scented, lace-edged handkerchief.

Saetan led them to the formal drawing room to the right of the great hall. It was a large room, but the furniture was arranged so that tall, painted screens could be placed across its width to divide it. The screens were in place, making this section appear cozy. The plastered walls were painted ivory. All the pictures were serene watercolors. The furniture was dark but not heavy and comfortably arranged over subtly patterned Dharo carpets. There was a bouquet of fresh flowers on a table near the windows. Saetan watched Lord Magstrom tactfully look over the room and knew the man was as pleased with the tasteful decorations as he was.

"It's a delightful room, High Lord," Lord Magstrom said as he accepted a seat. "Do you use it often?"

Saetan shoved his hands into his sweater pockets. "No," he said after a slight but noticeable hesitation. "We don't have many formal guests." He turned toward a movement in the doorway. "Ah, Beale."

The butler stood in the doorway, empty-handed.

Saetan raised an eyebrow. "Refreshments for our guests?"

"They'll be ready momentarily, High Lord." Beale bowed and retreated, leaving the door open.

Saetan was tempted to close the door but decided against it. No point forcing Beale to demean himself by listening at the keyhole.

"Have we come at an awkward time?" Lord Friall asked, looking pointedly at Saetan's casual attire while he continued to pat his lips with the scented handkerchief.

Perfume won't help what's troubling you, Lord Friall, Saetan thought coldly. *My psychic scent permeates the very stones of the Hall.* Saetan glanced down at the white cotton shirt unbuttoned low enough so that the Black Jewel around his neck wasn't completely hidden, the black cotton trousers that were already rumpled, and the sweater. "I gather you were expecting a more formal meeting. However, since I had understood that the Council wanted some indication of our usual living arrangements, those two expectations are incompatible."

"Surely—" Friall began, but he was cut off by Beale bringing in the refreshment tray.

Saetan studied the tray. It was sparse by Mrs. Beale's usual standards. There were plenty of sandwiches but none of the nutcakes or spiced tarts. "I don't suppose Mrs. Beale would—"

Beale set the tray on a table with an almost-inaudible thump.

"No," Saetan said dryly, "I don't suppose she would." He poured the coffee and offered the sandwiches while he tried to ignore the twinkle in Lord Magstrom's eyes. Settling into a corner of the couch where he could keep an eye on the door, he smiled at Lord Friall and wondered if his clenched teeth would survive the afternoon. "You were saying?"

"Surely—"

The front door slammed.

Catching the psychic scent and the emotional undercurrents, Saetan whistled a sharp command and resigned himself to disaster.

A moment later, Karla stuck her head around the corner. "Kiss kiss," she said, doing her best to look innocent.

Having already dealt with several of the coven's spells that had gone awry, Karla trying to look innocent scared him silly. But, if he was lucky, he might never have to know what she'd been up to.

Karla pointed toward the ceiling. "I'm late for my art lesson."

Saetan groaned softly and massaged his temple. Had he remembered to tell Dujae not to come today? "Please ask Jaenelle to come down. These gentlemen would like to see her."

Karla's ice-blue eyes swept over Magstrom and Friall. "Why?" She jerked her chin toward Lord Magstrom. "The grandfather looks harmless enough, but why would she want to talk to a fribble?"

Friall sputtered.

Lord Magstrom raised his cup to hide his smile.

Saetan was sure half his teeth were going to shatter. "Now."

"Oh, all right. Kiss kiss," Karla said, and was gone.

"Lady Karla is a friend of your ward?" Lord Magstrom asked mildly.

"Yes." Saetan's lips twitched. "She and Jaenelle's other friends are staying with us for the summer—if I survive it."

Lord Magstrom blinked.

"She's a little bitch," Friall sputtered, dabbing his lips with his handkerchief. "Hardly a suitable companion for your ward."

"Karla's a Queen and a natural Black Widow," Saetan said coldly, "as well as a Healer. She's an exuberant—but formidable—young lady. Like my daughter."

He caught Lord Magstrom's arrested look. Hadn't the Council checked the register at the Keep? As soon as Jaenelle had returned to them, he and Geoffrey had prepared the listing for her. They had agreed not to include the Territory—or Realm—where she had been born, or anything else that could lead someone back to her Chaillot relatives, but they *had* included that the Black was her Birthright Jewel. Didn't the Council know who, and what, they were dealing with? Or had the Tribunal chosen not to tell these men?

Lord Magstrom accepted another cup of coffee. "Your . . . daughter . . . is a Black Widow Queen? And a Healer as well?"

"Yes," Saetan replied. "Didn't the Council mention it?"

Lord Magstrom looked troubled. "No, they didn't. Perhaps—"

A woman let out a screech that made all three men jump. As Lord Magstrom dabbed at the spilled coffee and murmured apologies, a young wolf leaped into the drawing room. Friall let out a screech of his own and leaped behind his chair. Veering away from the screeching human, the wolf bounded behind the couch, came around the other side, and finally pressed himself against Saetan's legs, his head and one paw in Saetan's lap and a pleading expression in his eyes.

Saetan reminded himself that, compared to most days, they were having a quiet afternoon. He rubbed the young wolf's head and sighed. "Now what have you done?"

"I'll tell you what he's done." A red-faced woman filled the drawing room doorway.

Friall whimpered.

The wolf whined.

Lord Magstrom stared.

Mother Night, Mother Night, Mother Night. "Ah, Mrs. Beale," Saetan said calmly while he pressed a damp palm into the wolf's fur.

Mrs. Beale wasn't fat. She was just . . . *large*. And she didn't need to use Craft to lift a fifty-pound sack of flour with one hand.

Mrs. Beale pointed a finger at the wolf. "That walking muff just ate the chickens I was preparing for tonight's dinner."

Saetan looked down at the wolf. "Bad muff," he said mildly.

The wolf whined, but the tip of his tail dusted the floor.

Saetan sighed and turned his attention back to the huffing woman. "If there's no time to prepare more of our own, perhaps you could send someone to the butcher's in Halaway?"

Mrs. Beale huffed even more and said in a voice that rattled the windows, "Those chickens had been marinating in my special plum wine sauce since last night."

"Must have been tasty," Saetan murmured.

The wolf licked his chops and whuffed softly.

Mrs. Beale growled.

"What about a different meat?" Saetan said quickly. "I'm sure our young friend could find a couple of rabbits."

"Rabbits?" Mrs. Beale waved her hand, slicing the air in several directions. "I'm to fill *rabbits* with my nut and rice stuffing?"

"No, of course not. How foolish of me. A stew perhaps? I noticed last week that Jaenelle and Karla had second helpings of your stew."

"Noticed myself that that serving dish had come back empty," Mrs. Beale muttered. She pointed at the wolf. "Two rabbits. And not scrawny ones either." She turned on her heel and stomped away.

Lord Magstrom sighed gustily.

Lord Friall stumbled into his chair.

Saetan wondered if he had any bone left in his legs. This was turning into a typical afternoon after all. He scratched the wolf behind the ears. "You understand?" He held up two fingers. "Two plump bunnies for Mrs. Beale. Tarl says there are plenty of them fattening themselves up in the vegetable garden." He gave the wolf a last scratch. "Off with you."

After nuzzling Saetan's hand, the wolf trotted out the door.

"You let a woman like that work here when there are children in the house?" Friall sputtered. "And you keep a wolf for a pet?"

"Mrs. Beale is an excellent cook," Saetan replied mildly. *Besides,* he added silently, *who would have the balls to dismiss her?* "And the wolf isn't a pet. He's kindred. Several of them live with us. Another sandwich, Lord Magstrom?"

Looking a bit dazed, Lord Magstrom took another sandwich, stared at it for a moment, then set it on his plate.

"What's going on?" Jaenelle asked. Smiling politely at Magstrom and Friall, she settled next to Saetan on the couch.

"We're having bunny stew for dinner instead of chicken."

"Ah. That explains Mrs. Beale." Her lips twitched. "I suppose I should explain human territoriality to the wolves to avoid further misunderstandings."

"At least Mrs. Beale's territory," Saetan said, smiling at his fair-haired daughter, aware that the way Jaenelle sat so close to him was open to misinterpretation.

"Is that your usual way of dressing, Lady Angelline?" Lord Friall asked, once more dabbing his lips with his handkerchief.

Jaenelle looked at the baggy overalls she had acquired from one the gardeners and the white silk shirt Saetan had unknowingly donated to her wardrobe. She lifted one loose braid and studied the feathers, small bells, and seashells attached to the strips of leather woven into her hair. Then her eyes swept over Friall. "Sometimes," she said coolly. "Do you always dress like that?"

"Of course," Friall said proudly.

"Why?"

Friall stared at her.

Remember their delicate sensibilities, witch-child.

Screw their delicate sensibilities.

Saetan flinched. Her mood had shifted.

He dropped one arm around her shoulders. "Lord Magstrom would like to ask you a few questions." Hopefully the older Warlord felt the emotional currents in the room and would tread carefully.

"Before the interrogation begins, may I ask you something?"

Lord Magstrom fiddled with his cup. "This isn't an interrogation, Lady," he said gently.

"Really?" she said in her midnight voice.

Magstrom shivered. His hand shook as he set his cup on the table.

Hoping to divert her, Saetan groaned theatrically. "What do you want to ask?"

Her sapphire eyes studied him. Concern faded to exasperated amusement. "It isn't that bad."

"That's what you said the last time."

Jaenelle gave him her best unsure-but-game smile. "Dujae wants to know if we can have a wall."

He tried not to panic. "A wall? Dujae wants one of my walls?"

"Yes."

Saetan pressed his fingertips against his temple. Something was clogging his throat. He wasn't sure if it was a shriek or a laugh. "Why does Dujae want a wall?"

"We're going to paint it." She pondered this for a moment. "Well, I guess saying we're going to paint it isn't quite accurate. We're going to draw on it. Dujae says we need to think more expansively and the only way to do that is to have an expansive canvas to work on and the only thing big enough is a wall."

Uh-huh. "I see." Saetan looked around the tastefully decorated room and sighed. "There are lots of empty rooms here. Why don't you pick one in the same wing as the rumpus room."

Jaenelle frowned. "We don't have a rumpus room."

Saetan tweaked one of her braids. "You wouldn't say that if you'd ever been in the room under it while you were all doing . . . whatever."

Jaenelle gave him a look of amused tolerance. "Thank you, Papa." She bussed his cheek and bounded off the couch.

Saetan grabbed the back of her overalls and pulled her down beside him. "Dujae can wait a bit. Lord Magstrom has a few questions."

The cold fire was back in her eyes, but she settled against him on the couch, her hands demurely in her lap, and gave the two men a look of polite impatience.

Saetan nodded at Lord Magstrom.

His hands loosely clasped on the arms of the chair, Lord Magstrom smiled at Jaenelle. "Is art a favorite study of yours, Lady Angelline?" he asked politely. "I have a granddaughter about your age who enjoys 'mucking about with colors,' as she puts it."

At the mention of a granddaughter, Jaenelle looked at Lord Magstrom with interest. "I enjoy drawing, but not as much as music," she said after a moment's thought. "Much more than mathematics." She wrinkled her nose. "But then, anything's better than mathematics."

"Arnora holds mathematics in the same high regard," Lord Magstrom said seriously, but his blue eyes twinkled.

Jaenelle's lips twitched. "Does she? A sensible witch."

"What other subjects do you enjoy?"

"Learning about plants and gardening and healing and weaponry and equitation is fun . . . and languages. And dancing. Dancing's wonderful, don't you think? And of course there's Craft, but that's not really a lesson, is it?"

"Not really a lesson?" Lord Magstrom looked startled. He accepted another cup of coffee. "With so much studying, you don't have much time to socialize," he said slowly.

Jaenelle frowned and looked at Saetan.

"I believe Lord Magstrom is referring to dances and other public gatherings," he said carefully.

Her frown deepened. "Why do we need to go out for dancing? We've got enough people here who play instruments and we dance whenever we want to. Besides, I promised Morghann I'd spend a few days in Scelt with her when they have the harvest dances, and Kalush's family invited me to go to the theater with them, and Gabrielle—"

"Dujae," Friall said tightly. "Dujae is teaching you to draw?"

Saetan squeezed Jaenelle's shoulder but she shrugged away from him.

"Yes, Dujae is teaching me to draw," Jaenelle said, the chill back in her voice.

"Dujae is dead."

"For centuries now."

Friall dabbed at his lips. "You study drawing with a demon?"

"Just because he's a demon doesn't make him less of an artist."

"But he's a *demon*."

Jaenelle shrugged dismissively. "So are Char and Titian and a number of my other friends. Who I call a friend is no business of yours, Lord Friall."

"No business," Friall sputtered. "It most certainly *is* the Council's business. It was a show of faith that the Council allowed something like the High Lord to keep a young girl in the first place—"

"*Something* like the High Lord?"

"—and to soil a young girl's sensibilities by forcing her to consort with demons—"

"He never forces me. *No one* forces me."

"—and submit to his own lustful attentions—"

The room exploded.

There was no time to think, no time to protect himself from the spiraling fury rising out the abyss.

Drawing everything he could from his Black Jewels, Saetan threw himself on Jaenelle as she lunged for Friall. Wild, vicious sounds erupted from her as she fought to break free and reach the Warlord, who stared at her in shock while windows shattered, paintings crashed to the floor, plaster cracked as psychic lightning scored the walls, and the furniture was ripped to pieces.

Hanging on grimly, Saetan let the room go, using his strength to shield the other men, using himself as a buffer between Jaenelle's rage and flesh. She wasn't trying to hurt him. That was the terrifying irony. She was simply trying to get past the barriers he was placing between her and Friall. He opened his mind, intending to press against her inner barriers and force her to feel a little of the pain he was enduring. But there were no barriers. There was only the abyss and a long, mind-shattering fall.

*Please, witch-child. *Please!**

She came at him with frightening speed, cocooned him in black mist, and then brought him up to the depth of the Red Jewel before she turned and glided back down into the comfortable sanctuary of the abyss.

Silence.

Stillness.

His head throbbed mercilessly. His tongue hurt. His mouth was full of blood. He felt too brittle to move. But his mind was intact.

She loved him. She wouldn't deliberately hurt him. She loved him.

Pulling that thought around his bruised mind and battered body like a warm cloak, Saetan surrendered to oblivion.

Lord Magstrom woke to a none-too-gentle slap. Blinking to clear his vision, he focused on the dark wings and stern face.

"Drink this," the Eyrien snapped, shoving a glass into Magstrom's hands. He stepped back, fists braced on his hips. "Your companion is finally coming around. He's lucky to be here at all."

Magstrom gratefully sipped his drink and looked around. Except for the chairs he and Friall were sitting in, the room was empty. The painted screens that divided the room were gone. The furniture on the other side was tumbled but intact. If not for the black streaks on the ivory walls that looked like lightning gone to ground, he might have thought they'd been moved to a different room, that it had been a hallucination of some kind.

He'd heard of Andulvar Yaslana, the Demon Prince. He knew it was a measure of his own terror that he found shivering comfort in having an Ebon-gray-Jeweled demon standing over him. "The High Lord?" he asked.

Andulvar stared at him. "He almost shattered the Black trying to keep you safe. He's exhausted, but he'll recover with a few days of rest." Then he snorted. "Besides, it'll give the waif an excuse to dose him with one of her restorative tonics, and that, thank the Darkness, should keep her from thinking too much about what happened."

"What did happen?"

Andulvar nodded at Friall. Beale was still waving smelling salts under Friall's nose, but the butler's expression strongly suggested he'd rather toss the intruder onto the drive and be done with it. "He pissed her off. Not a smart thing to do."

"Then she's unstable? Dangerous?"

Andulvar slowly spread his dark wings. He looked huge. And there was no concern in his gold eyes, only an unspoken threat.

"Simply by being Blood, we're all dangerous, Lord Magstrom," Andulvar growled softly. "She belongs to the family, and we belong to her. Never forget that." He folded his wings and crouched beside Magstrom's chair. "But in truth, Saetan's the only thing that stands between you and her. Don't forget that either."

An hour later, Magstrom and Friall's coach rolled down the well-kept drive, then onto the road that ran through Halaway.

It was dusk on a late summer afternoon. Wildflowers painted meadows with bright colors. Trees stretched their branches high above the road, creating cool tunnels. It was beautiful land, lovingly tended, shadowed for thousands of years by SaDiablo Hall and the man who ruled there.

Shadowed and protected.

Magstrom shivered. He was a Warlord who wore Summer-sky Jewels. He acted as the caretaker of the village where he'd been born and where he'd contentedly spent his life. Until he'd been asked to serve on the Dark Council, his dealings with those who wore darker Jewels had been diplomatic and, fortunately, seldom. The Blood in Goth, Little Terreille's capital, were interested in court intrigue, not in a village that looked across a river into the wooded land of Dea al Mon.

But now a curtain had been drawn back, just a little, and he had seen dark power, truly dark power.

Saetan's the only thing that stands between you and her.

The girl had to stay with the High Lord, Magstrom thought as the coach rolled through Halaway to the landing web where they would catch the Winds and go home. For all their sakes, she had to stay.

Saetan woke slowly as someone settled on the end of his bed. Grunting, he propped himself up on one elbow and stroked the candle-light on the bedside table just enough to dimly light the room.

Jaenelle sat cross-legged on his bed, her eyes haunted, her face pinched and pale. She handed him a glass. "Drink this. It'll help soothe your nerves."

He took a sip and then another. It tasted of moonlight, summer heat, and cool water. "This is wonderful, witch-child. You should have a glass yourself."

"I've had two." She tried to smile but couldn't quite manage it. She fluffed her hair and bit her lower lip. "Saetan, I don't like what happened today. I don't like what . . . almost happened today."

He drained the glass, set it on the bedside table, and reached for her hand. "I'm glad. Killing should never be easy, witch-child. It should leave a scar on your soul. Sometimes it's necessary. Sometimes there's no choice if we're trying to defend what we cherish. But if there's an alternative, take it."

"They'd come here to condemn you, to hurt you. They had no right."

"I've been insulted by fools before. I survived."

Even in the dim light he saw her eyes change.

"Just because he was using words instead of a knife, you can't dismiss it, Saetan. He hurt you."

"Of course he hurt me," Saetan snapped. "Being accused of—" He closed his eyes and squeezed her hand. "I don't tolerate fools, Jaenelle, but I also don't kill them for being fools. I simply keep them out of my life." He sat up and took her other hand. "I am your sword and your shield, Lady. You don't have to kill."

Witch studied him with her ancient, haunted sapphire eyes. "You'll take the scars on your soul so that mine remains unmarked?"

"Everything has a price," he said gently. "Those kinds of scars are part of being a Warlord Prince. You're at a crossroads, witch-child. You can use your power to heal or to harm. It's your choice."

"One or the other?"

He kissed her hand. "Not always. As I said, sometimes destruction is necessary. But I think you're more suited to healing. It's the road I'd choose for you."

Jaenelle fluffed her hair. "Well, I do like making healing brews."

"I noticed," he said dryly.

She laughed, but the amusement quickly faded. "What will the Dark Council do?"

He leaned back on his pillows. "There's nothing they can do. I won't let them take you away from your family and friends."

She kissed his cheek. The last thing she said before she left his bedroom was, "And I won't let them put more scars on your soul."

2 / Kaeleer

He had expected it, even prepared for it. It still hurt.

Jaenelle stood silently in the petitioner's circle, her fingers demurely laced in front of her, her eyes fixed on the seal carved into the front of the blackwood bench where the Tribunal sat. She wore a dress she had borrowed from one of her friends, and her hair was pulled back in a tight, neat braid.

Knowing the Council watched his every move, Saetan stared at nothing, waiting for the Tribunal to begin their vicious little game.

Because he had anticipated the Council's decision, he'd allowed no one but Andulvar to come with them. Andulvar could take care of himself. He would take care of Jaenelle. The moment the Tribunal announced the Council's verdict, the moment Jaenelle protested and turned to him for help . . .

Everything has a price.

Over 50,000 years ago, he'd been instrumental in creating the Dark Council. Now he'd destroy it. One word from her, and it would be done.

The First Tribune began to speak.

Saetan didn't listen. He scanned the faces of the Council. Some of the witches looked more troubled than angry. But most of their eyes glittered like feral, slithery things gathered for the kill. He knew some of them. Others were new, replacements for the fools who had challenged him once before in this room. As he watched them watching him, his regret at his decision to destroy them trickled away. They had no right to take his daughter away from him.

"—and so it's the careful opinion of this Council that appointing a new guardian would be in your best interest."

Tensed, Saetan waited for Jaenelle to turn to him. He'd gone deep into the Black before they'd reached the Council chambers. There were dark Jewels here that might hold out long enough to try to attack, but the Black unleashed would shatter every mind caught in the explosion of psychic energy. Andulvar was strong enough to ride out the psychic storm. Jaenelle would be held safe, protected in the eye of the storm.

Saetan took a deep breath.

Jaenelle looked at the First Tribune. "Very well," she said quietly, clearly. "When the sun next rises, you may appoint a new guardian—unless you reconsider your decision before then."

Saetan stared at her. No. No! She was the daughter of his soul, his Queen. She couldn't, wouldn't walk away from him.

She did.

She didn't look at him when she turned and walked down the center of the chamber to the doors at the far end. When she reached the doors, she sidestepped away from Andulvar's outstretched hand.

The doors closed.

Voices murmured. Colors swirled. Bodies moved past him.

He couldn't move. He'd thought he was too old for illusions, too heart-bruised to hope, too hardened to dream. He'd been wrong. Now he swallowed the bitterness of hope, choked on the ashes of dreams.

She didn't want him.

He wanted to die, wanted, desperately, that final death before pain and grief overwhelmed him.

"Let's get out of here, SaDiablo."

Andulvar led him away from the smug faces and the glittering eyes.

Tonight, before the sun rose again, he would find a way to die.

He'd forgotten the children would be waiting for him.

"Where's Jaenelle?" Karla asked, trying to look past him and Andulvar as they entered the family drawing room.

He wanted to slink away to his suite, where he could lick his wounds in private and decide how to accomplish the end.

He would lose them, too. They'd have no reason to visit, no reason to talk with him once Jaenelle was gone.

Tears pricked his eyes. Grief squeezed his throat.

"Uncle Saetan?" Gabrielle asked, searching his face.

Saetan cringed.

"What happened?" Morghann demanded. "Where's Jaenelle?"

Andulvar finally answered. "The Dark Council is going to choose another guardian. Jaenelle's not coming back."

"WHAT?" they yelled in unison.

Their voices pummeled him, questioning, demanding. He was going to lose all of these children who had crept into his heart over the past few weeks, whom he'd foolishly allowed himself to love.

Karla raised her hand. The room was instantly silent. Gabrielle moved forward until the two girls stood shoulder to shoulder.

"The Council appointed another guardian," Karla said, spacing out the words as she narrowed her eyes.

"Yes," Saetan whispered. His legs were going to buckle. He had to get away from them before his legs buckled.

"They must be mad," Gabrielle said. "What did Jaenelle say?"

Saetan forced himself to focus on Karla and Gabrielle. It would be the last time he would ever see them. But he couldn't answer them, couldn't get the damning words out.

Andulvar guided Saetan to a couch and pushed him down. "She said they could appoint a new guardian in the morning."

"Were those her exact words?" Gabrielle asked sharply.

"What difference does it make?" Andulvar snarled. "She made the decision to walk away from—"

"Damn your wings, you son of a whoring bitch," Karla screamed at him. "*What did she say?*"

"Stop it!" Saetan shouted. He couldn't stand having them argue, having the last hour with them tainted by anger. "She said—" His voice cracked. He clamped his hands between his knees, but it didn't stop them from shaking. "She said when the sun next rose they could appoint another guardian unless they reconsidered their decision by then."

The mood in the room changed to a little uneasiness blended with strong approval and calm acceptance. Puzzled, Saetan watched them.

Karla plopped down on the couch beside him and wrapped her arms around one of his. "In that case, we'll all stay right here and wait with you."

"Thank you, but I'd rather be alone." Saetan tried to rise, but Chaosti's stare unnerved him so badly he couldn't find his legs.

"No, you wouldn't," Gabrielle said, squeezing past Andulvar so that she could settle on the other side of him.

"I want to be alone right now," Saetan said, trying, but failing, to get that soft thunder into his voice.

Chaosti, Khary, and Aaron formed a wall in front of him, flanked by the other young males. Morghann and the rest of the coven circled the couch, trapping him.

"We're not going to let you do something stupid, Uncle Saetan," Karla said gently. Her wicked smile bloomed. "At least wait until the sun next rises. You're not going to want to miss it."

Saetan stared at her. She knew what he intended to do. Defeated, he closed his eyes. Today, tomorrow, what difference did it make? But not while they were still here. He wouldn't do that to them.

Satisfied, Karla and Gabrielle snuggled close to him while the other girls drifted toward the other couches.

Khary rubbed his hands together. "Why don't I see if Mrs. Beale is willing to brew up some tea?"

"Sandwiches would be good, too," Aaron said enthusiastically. "And some spiced tarts, if we didn't finish them. I'll go with you."

SaDiablo? Andulvar said on an Ebon-gray spear thread.

Saetan kept his eyes closed. *I won't do anything stupid.*

Andulvar hesitated. *I'll tell Mephis and Prothvar.*

No reason to answer. No answer to give. Because of him, Jaenelle would be lost to all of them. Would her new guardian welcome the wolves and the unicorns? Would he welcome the Dea al Mon and Tigre, the centaurs and satyrs? Or would she be forced to sneak an hour with them now and then, as she had done as a child?

As the hours passed and the children dozed in chairs or on the floor around him, he let it all go. He'd savor this time with them, savor the weight and warmth of Karla's and Gabrielle's heads nestled on his shoulders. Time enough to deal with the pain . . . after the sun rose.

"Wake up, SaDiablo."

Saetan sensed Andulvar's urgency but didn't want to respond, didn't want to tear the veil of sleep where he'd found a little comfort.

"Damn it, Saetan," Andulvar hissed, "*wake up.*"

Reluctantly, Saetan opened his eyes. At first he felt grateful that Andulvar stood in front of him, blocking his view of the windows and the traitorous morning. Then he realized the candle-lights were lit, and necessary, and there was a flicker of fear in the Eyrien's eyes.

Andulvar stepped aside.

Saetan rubbed his eyes. Sometime during the night Karla and

Gabrielle had slumped from his shoulders and were now using his thighs for pillows. He couldn't feel his legs.

He finally looked at the windows.

It was dark.

Why was Andulvar shoving him awake in the middle of the night?

Saetan glanced at the clock on the mantle and froze. Eight o'clock.

"Mrs. Beale wants to know if she should serve breakfast," Andulvar said, his voice strained.

The boys began to stir.

"Breakfast?" Khary said, stifling a yawn as he ran his fingers through his curly brown hair. "Breakfast sounds grand."

"But," Saetan stammered. The clock was wrong. It had to be wrong. "But it's still dark."

Chaosti, the Child of the Wood, the Dea al Mon Warlord Prince, gave him a fierce, satisfied smile. "Yes, it is."

A duet of giggles followed Chaosti's words as Karla and Gabrielle pushed themselves upright.

Saetan's heart pounded. The room spun slowly. He'd thought the Council's eyes had held a feral glitter, but that had been tame compared to these children who smiled at him, waiting.

"Black as midnight," Gabrielle said with sweet venom.

"Caught on the edge of midnight," Karla added. She rested her forearm on his shoulder and leaned toward him. "How long do you think it's going to take the Council to reconsider their decision, High Lord? A day? Maybe two?" She shrugged and rose. "Let's find breakfast."

With Andulvar in the lead, the children drifted out of the family drawing room, chatting and unconcerned.

Watching them, Saetan remembered something Titian had told him years before. *They know what she is.* He saw Khardeen, Aaron, and Chaosti exchange a look before Khary and Aaron followed the others. Chaosti stayed by the window, waiting.

Another triangle of power, Saetan thought as he approached the window. Almost as strong and just as deadly. May the Darkness help whoever stood in their way. "You knew," he said quietly as he stared out the window at the moonless, starless, unbroken night. "You knew."

"Of course," Chaosti said, smiling. "Didn't you?"

"No."

Chaosti's smile faded. "Then we owe you an apology, High Lord. We thought you were worried about what was going to happen. We didn't realize you didn't understand."

"How did you know?"

"She warned them when she set the terms. 'When the sun next rises.' " Chaosti shrugged. "Obviously the sun wasn't going to rise."

Saetan closed his eyes. He was the Black-Jeweled High Lord of Hell, the Prince of the Darkness. He wasn't sure that was a sufficient match for these children. "You're not afraid of her, are you?"

Chaosti looked startled. "Afraid of Jaenelle? Why should I be? She's my friend, my Sister, and my cousin. And she's the Queen." He tipped his head. "Are you?"

"Sometimes. Sometimes I'm very afraid of what she might do."

"Being afraid of what she might do isn't the same as being afraid of Jaenelle." Chaosti hesitated, then added, "She loves you, High Lord. You are her father, by her choice. Did you really think she'd let you go unless that's what you wanted?"

Saetan waited until Chaosti joined the others before answering.

Yes. May the Darkness help him, yes. He'd let his feelings tangle up his intellect. He'd been prepared to destroy the Council in order to keep her. He should have remembered what she'd said about not letting the Council put more scars on his soul.

She had stopped the Council, and she had stopped him.

It shamed him that he hadn't understood what Karla, Gabrielle, Chaosti, and the others had known as soon as they heard the phrasing she'd used. Loving her as he did, living with her while she stretched daily toward the Queen she'd become, he should have known.

Feeling better, he headed for the breakfast room.

There was just one thing that still troubled him, still produced a nagging twinge between his shoulder blades.

How in the name of Hell had Jaenelle done it?

3 / Hell

Hekatah stared out the window at the sere landscape. Like the other Realms, Hell followed the seasons, but even in summer, it was still a cold, forever-twilight land.

It had gone wrong again. Somehow, it had gone wrong.

She'd counted on the Council's being able to separate Saetan and Jaenelle. She hadn't foreseen the girl resisting in such a spectacular, frightening way.

The girl. So much power waiting to be tapped. There had to be a way to reach her, had to be some kind of bait with which to entice her.

As the thought took shape, Hekatah began to smile.

Love. A young man's ardor pitted against a father's affection. For all her power, the girl was a soft-hearted idiot. Torn between her own desires and another's needs—needs she could safely accommodate since she'd already been opened—she'd comply. Wouldn't she? If the male was skilled and attractive? After a while, with the help of an addictive aphrodisiac, she'd need the mounting far more than she'd need a father. Rejection would be all the discipline required if she balked at something her beloved wanted. All that dark, lovely power offered to a cock and balls who would, of course, be controlled by Hekatah.

Hekatah nibbled on her thumbnail.

This game required patience. If she was frightened of sexual overtures and repelled all advances . . . No need to worry about that. Saetan would never tolerate it, would never permit her to become frigid. He strongly believed in sexual pleasure—as strongly as he believed in fidelity. The latter had been a nuisance. The former guaranteed his little darling would be ripe for the picking in a year or two.

Smiling, Hekatah turned away from the window.

At least that gutter son of a whore was good for something.

4 / Kaeleer

Saetan handed Lord Magstrom a glass of brandy before settling into the chair behind his blackwood desk. It was barely afternoon, but after three "days" of unyielding night, he doubted many men were going to quibble about when they tossed back the first glass.

Saetan steepled his fingers. At least the fools in the Council had the sense to send Lord Magstrom. He wouldn't have granted an audience to anyone else. But he didn't like the Warlord's haggard appearance, and he hoped the elderly man would fully recover from the strain of the past three days. He'd spent most of his long life living between sunset and sunrise, and even he found this unnatural darkness a strain on his nerves. "You wanted to see me, Lord Magstrom?"

Lord Magstrom's hand shook as he sipped the brandy. "The Council is very upset. They don't like being held hostage this way, but they've asked me to put a proposal before you."

"I'm not the one you have to negotiate with, Warlord. Jaenelle set the terms, not me."

Lord Magstrom looked shocked. "We assumed—"

"You assumed wrong. Even I don't have the power to do this."

Lord Magstrom closed his eyes. His breathing was too rapid, too shallow. "Do you know where she is?"

"I think she's at Ebon Askavi."

"Why would she go there?"

"It's her home."

"Mother Night," Magstrom whispered. "Mother Night." He drained the glass of brandy. "Do you think we'll be able to see her?"

"I don't know." No point telling Magstrom that he'd already tried to see Jaenelle and, for the first time in his life, had been politely but firmly refused entrance to the Keep.

"Would she talk to us?"

"I don't know."

"Would—Would you talk to her?"

Saetan stared at Magstrom, momentarily shocked before fiery cold rage washed through him. "Why should I?" he said too softly.

"For the sake of the Realm."

"You *bastard*!" Saetan's nails scored the blackwood desk. "You try to take my daughter away from me and you expect *me* to smooth it over? Did you learn nothing from your last visit? No. You just chose to tear apart the life she's starting to build again with no thought to what it might do to her. You try to tear out my heart, and then when you discover there are penalties for playing your vicious little games, you want me to fix it. You dismissed me as her guardian. If you want to end this, *you* go up to Ebon

Askavi and *you* face what's waiting for you there. And in case you don't yet realize who you're dealing with, I'll tell you. Witch is waiting for you, Magstrom. Witch in all her dark glory. And the Lady isn't pleased."

Magstrom moaned and collapsed in the chair.

"Damn." Saetan took a deep breath and leashed his temper as he filled another glass with two fingers of brandy, called in a small vial from his stock of healing powders, and tapped in the proper dosage. Cradling Magstrom's head, he said, "Drink this. It'll help."

When Magstrom was once more aware and breathing easier, Saetan returned to his own chair. Bracing his head in his hands, he stared at the nail marks on the desk. "I'll take her the Council's proposal exactly as it's given to me, and I'll bring back her answer exactly as it's given to me. I'll do nothing more."

"After what you said, why would you do that?"

"You wouldn't understand," Saetan snapped.

Magstrom was silent for a moment. "I think I need to understand."

Saetan ran his fingers through his thick black hair and closed his golden eyes. He took a deep breath. If their positions were reversed, wouldn't he want an answer? "I stand at the window and worry about the sparrows and the finches and all the other creatures of the day, all the innocents who can't comprehend why the daylight doesn't come. I cradle a flower in my hand, hoping it will survive, and feel the land grow colder with each passing hour. I'm not going for the Council or even the Blood. I'm going to plead for the sparrows and the trees." He opened his eyes. "Now do you understand?"

"Yes, High Lord, I do." Lord Magstrom smiled. "How fortunate that the Council agreed to let me negotiate the terms of the proposal. If you and I can reach an agreement, perhaps it will be acceptable to the Lady as well."

Saetan tried, but he couldn't return the smile. They'd never seen Jaenelle's sapphire eyes change, never seen her turn from child to Queen, never seen Witch. "Perhaps."

He'd felt grateful when Draca granted him entrance to the Keep. He didn't feel quite so grateful about it when Jaenelle pounced on him the moment he entered her workroom.

"Do you understand this?" she demanded, thrusting a Craft book into his hands and pointing to a paragraph.

His insides churning, he called in his half-moon glasses, positioned them carefully on his nose, and obediently read the paragraph. "It seems simple enough," he said after a moment.

Jaenelle plopped on air, spraddle-legged. "I knew it," she muttered, crossing her arms. "I knew it was written in male."

Saetan vanished his glasses. "I beg your pardon?"

"It's gibberish. Geoffrey understands it but can't explain it so that it makes sense, and you understand it. Therefore, it's written in male—only comprehensible to a mind attached to a cock and balls."

"Considering his age, I don't think Geoffrey's balls are the problem, witch-child," Saetan said dryly.

Jaenelle snarled.

Stay here, a part of him whispered. *Stay with her in this place, in this way. They don't love you, never cared about you unless they wanted something from you. Don't ask her. Let it go. Stay.*

Saetan closed the book and held it tight to his chest. "Jaenelle, we have to talk."

Jaenelle fluffed her hair and eyed the closed book.

"We have to talk," he insisted.

"About what?"

That she'd pretend not to know pricked his temper. "Kaeleer, for a start. You have to break the spell or the web or whatever you did."

"When it ends is the Council's choice."

He ignored the warning in her voice. "The Council asked me—"

"You're here on behalf of the *Council?*"

Between one breath and the next, he watched a disgruntled young witch change into a sleek, predatory Queen. Even her clothes changed as she furiously paced the length of her workroom. By the time she finally stopped in front of him, her face was a cold, beautiful mask, her eyes held the depth of the abyss, her nails were painted a red so dark it was almost black, and her hair was a golden cloud caught up at the sides by silver combs. Her gown seemed to be made of smoke and cobwebs, and a Black Jewel hung above her breasts.

She'd gotten one of her Black Jewels set, he thought as his heart pounded. When had she done *that?*

He looked into her ancient eyes, silently challenging.

"Damn you, Saetan," she said with no emotion, no heat.

"I live for your pleasure, Lady. Do with me what you will. But release Kaeleer from midnight. The innocent don't deserve to suffer."

"And whom do you call innocent?" she asked in her midnight voice.

"The sparrows, the trees, the land," he answered quietly. "What have they done to deserve having the sun taken away?"

He saw the hurt in her eyes before she yanked the book out of his hands and turned away.

"Don't be daft, Saetan. I would never hurt the land."

Never hurt the land. Never hurt the land. Never never never.

Saetan watched the air currents in the room. They were pretty. Reds, violets, indigos. It didn't matter that air currents didn't have color. Didn't even matter if he was hallucinating. They were pretty.

"Is there a chair in this room?" He wondered if she heard him. He wondered if he said the words out loud.

Jaenelle's voice made the colors dance. "Didn't you get *any* rest?"

A chair hugged him, warm against his back. A thick shawl wrapped around his shoulders, a throw covered his legs. A healing brew spiked with brandy thawed his tight muscles. Warm, gentle hands smoothed back his hair, caressed his face. And a voice, full of summer winds and midnight, said his name over and over.

He needn't fear her. There was nothing to fear. He needed to take these things in stride and not become distraught over the magnitude of her spells. After all, she was still wearing her Birthright Jewels, still cutting her Craft baby teeth. When she made the Offering . . .

He whimpered. She shushed him.

Cocooned in the warmth, he found his footing again. "The sun's been rising for the sparrows and the trees hasn't it, witch-child?"

"Of course," she said, settling on the arm of the chair.

"In fact, it's been rising for everything but the Blood."

"Yeesss."

"All the Blood?"

Jaenelle fluffed her hair and snarled. "I couldn't get the species separated so I had to lump them all together. But I did send messages to the kindred so they'd know it was temporary," she added hurriedly. "At least, I hope it's temporary."

Saetan snapped upright in the chair. "You did this without knowing for sure you could undo it?"

Jaenelle frowned at him. "Of course I can undo it. *Whether* I undo it depends on the Council."

"Ah." He needed to sleep for a week—as soon as he saw the sun rise. "The Council asked me to tell you that they've reconsidered."

"Oh." Jaenelle shifted on the chair arm. The layers of her gown split, revealing her entire leg.

She had nice legs, his fair-haired daughter. Strong and lean. He'd strangle the first boy who tried to slip his hand beneath her skirt and stroke that silky inner thigh.

"Would you help me translate that paragraph?" Jaenelle asked.

"Don't you have something to do first?"

"No. It has to be done at the proper hour, Saetan," she added as his eyebrow started to rise.

"Then we might as well fill the time."

They were still struggling with that paragraph two hours later. He was almost willing to agree that there were some things that couldn't be translated between genders, but he kept trying to explain it anyway because it filled him with perverse delight.

Despite her strength and intuition, there were still, thank the Darkness, a few things his fair-haired Lady couldn't do.

PART III

CHAPTER NINE

1 / Terreille

He had been in the salt mines of Pruul for five years.
Now it was time to die.

In order to reach the fierce, clean death he'd promised himself, he had to get beyond Zuultah's ability to pull him down with the Ring of Obedience. It wouldn't be difficult. Thinking him cowed, the guards didn't pay much attention to him anymore, and Zuultah had gotten lax in her use of the Ring. By the time they remembered what they never should have forgotten about him, it would be far too late.

Lucivar yanked the pick out of the guard's belly and drove it into the man's brain, sending just enough Ebon-gray power through the metal to finish the kill by shattering the guard's mind and Jewels.

Baring his teeth in a feral smile, he snapped the chains that had held him for the past five years. Then he called in his Ebon-gray Jewels and the wide leather belt that held his hunting knife and his Eyrien war blade. A lot of foolish Queens over the centuries had tried to force him to surrender those weapons. He'd endured the punishment and the pain and had never admitted they were always within reach—at least until he used them.

Unsheathing the war blade, he ran toward the mine's entrance.

The first two guards died before they realized he was there.

The next two blew apart when he struck with the Ebon-gray.

The rest were entangled by frantic slaves trying to get out of the way of an enraged Warlord Prince.

Fighting his way clear of the tangled bodies, he reached the mine entrance and ran across the slave compound, mentally preparing himself for a blind leap into the Darkness, hoping that, like an arrow released from a bow, he'd fly straight and true to the closest Wind and freedom.

Nerve-searing agony from the Ring of Obedience shredded his concentration at the same moment a crossbow bolt went through his thigh, breaking his stride. Howling with rage, he unleashed a wide band of power through his Ebon-gray ring, ripping the pursuing guards apart, body and mind. Another blast of pain from the Ring tore through him. He pivoted on his good leg, braced himself, and aimed a surge of power at Zuultah's house.

The house exploded. Stones smashed into surrounding buildings.

The pain from the Ring stopped abruptly. Lucivar probed swiftly and swore. The bitch was alive. Stunned and hurt, but still alive. He hesitated, wanting that kill. A weak strike at his inner barriers pulled his attention back to the surviving guards. They ran toward him, trying to braid their Jewels' strength in order to overwhelm him.

Fools. He could tear them apart piece by piece, and would have for the joy of paying pain back with pain, but by now someone would have sent out a call for help and if Zuultah came to enough to use the Ring of Obedience . . .

Battle lust sang in his veins, numbing physical pain. Maybe it would be better to die fighting, to turn the Arava Desert into a sea of blood. The closest Wind was a long, blind leap away. But, Hell's fire, if Jaenelle could do it when she was seven, then he could do it now.

Blood. So much blood.

Bitterness centered him, decided him.

Unleashing one more blast of power from the Ebon-gray, he gathered himself and leaped into the Darkness.

Bracing himself against the well, Lucivar filled the dipper again with sweet, cool water and drank slowly, savoring every swallow. Filling the dipper a last time, he limped to the nearby remains of a stone wall and settled himself as comfortably as possible.

That blind leap into the Darkness had cost him. Zuultah had roused enough to send another bolt through the Ring of Obedience just as he'd launched himself into the Darkness, and he'd drained half the strength in his Ebon-gray Jewels making the desperate reach for the Winds.

He sipped the water and stubbornly ignored what his body screamed at him. Hunger. Pain. A desperate need to sleep.

A hunting party from Pruul was three, maybe four hours behind him. He could have lost them, but it would have taken time he didn't have. A message relayed from mind to mind would reach Prythian, Askavi's High Priestess, faster than he could travel right now, and he didn't want to be caught by Eyrien warriors before he reached the Khaldharon Run.

And, if at all possible, there was a debt he wanted to call in.

Lucivar secured the dipper to the well and emptied the bucket. Satisfied that everything was as he'd found it, he faced south and sent out a summons on an Ebon-gray thread, pushing for his maximum range.

Sadi!

He waited a minute, then turned to face southeast.

Sadi!

After another restless minute, he turned east.

Sadi!

A flicker. Faint, different somehow, but still familiar.

Lucivar sighed like a satisfied lover. It was a fitting place for the Sadist to go to ground—in more ways than one. Plenty of broken, tumbled rock among those ruins. Some of them should be large enough to use as a makeshift altar. Oh, yes, a very fitting place.

Smiling, he caught the Red Wind and headed east.

Except for stories about Andulvar Yaslana, Lucivar had never had much interest in history. But Daemon had once insisted that SaDiablo Hall in Terreille had been intact until about 1,600 years ago, that something had happened—not an attack, but something—that had broken the preservation spells that had held for more than 50,000 years and had begun the building's decay.

Treading carefully through the broken ruins, Lucivar thought Daemon might have been right. There was a deep emptiness about the place, as if its energy had been deliberately bled out. The stones felt dead. No, not dead. Starved. Every time he touched one as he made his way toward an inner courtyard, it felt as if the stone was trying to suck his strength into itself.

He followed the smell of woodsmoke, shaking off his uneasiness. He hadn't come here to ponder phantoms. He'd be one soon enough.

Baring his teeth in a feral smile, he unsheathed the war blade and stepped into the courtyard, staying back from the circle of firelight.

"Hello, Bastard."

Daemon slowly looked up from the fire and just as slowly pinpointed the sound. When he finally did, his smile was gentle and weary.

"Hello, Prick. Have you come to kill me?" Daemon's voice sounded rusty, as if he hadn't spoken for a long time.

Concern warred with anger until it became another flavor of anger. And the difference in Daemon's psychic scent bothered him. "Yes."

Nodding, Daemon stood up and removed his torn jacket.

Lucivar's eyes narrowed as Daemon unbuttoned the remaining buttons on his shirt, pulled the shirt aside to expose his chest, and stepped around the fire to stand where the light best favored the attacker. It felt wrong. Everything felt wrong. Daemon knew enough about basic survival and living off the land—Hell's fire, *he* had seen to that—to have kept himself in better condition than this. Lucivar studied the dirty, ragged clothes, Daemon's halfstarved body shivering in the firelight, the calm, almost hopeful look in those bruised, exhausted eyes, and ground his teeth. The only other person he'd ever met who was that indifferent to her physical well-being was Tersa.

Maybe Daemon's voice wasn't rusty from disuse but hoarse from screaming himself awake at night.

"You're caught in it, aren't you?" Lucivar asked quietly. "You're tangled up in the Twisted Kingdom."

Daemon trembled. "Lucivar, please. You promised you'd kill me."

Lucivar's eyes glittered. "Do you feel her under you, Daemon? Do you feel that young flesh bruising under your hands? Do you feel her blood on your thighs while you drive into her, tearing her apart?" He stepped forward. "Do you?"

Daemon cringed. "I didn't . . ." He raised a shaking hand, twisting his fingers in the thick tangle of hair. "There's so much blood. It never goes away. The words never go away. Lucivar, please."

Making sure he had Daemon's attention, Lucivar stepped back and sheathed the war blade. "Killing you would be a kindness you don't deserve. You owe her every drop of pain that can be wrung out of you for the rest of your life and, Daemon, I wish you a very long life."

Daemon wiped his face with his sleeve, leaving a dirt smear across his cheek. "Maybe the next time we meet you can—"

"I'm dying," Lucivar snapped. "There won't be a next time."

There was a flicker of understanding in Daemon's eyes.

Something clogged Lucivar's throat. Tears pricked his eyes. There would be no reconciliation, no understanding, no forgiveness. Just a bitterness that would last beyond the flesh.

Lucivar limped out of the courtyard as fast as he could, using Craft to support his wounded leg. As he picked his way through the broken stones toward the remains of the landing web, he heard a cry so full of anguish the stones seemed to shudder. He stumbled to the web, gasping and tear-blind, unwilling to turn back, unwilling to leave.

But just before he caught the Gray Wind that would take him to Askavi and the final run, he looked at the ruins of the Hall and whispered, "Good-bye, Daemon."

Lucivar stood on the canyon rim at the halfway point in the Khaldharon Run, waiting for the sun to rise enough to light the canyon far below him.

Craft was the only thing keeping him on his feet now, the only thing that would let him use the greasy, tattered mess his wings had become after the slime mold had devoured them.

Intent on watching the sun rise, he also watched the small, dark shapes flying toward him—Eyrien warriors coming for the kill.

He looked down the Khaldharon Run, judging shadows and visibility. Not good. Foolish to throw himself into that dangerous intermingling of wind and the darker Winds when he couldn't distinguish the jagged canyon walls from the shadows, couldn't judge the curves that would create sudden wind shifts, when his wings barely functioned. At best it would be a suicide run.

Which was exactly why he was there.

The small, dark shapes flying toward him got larger, closer.

To the south of him, the sunlight touched the rock formation called the Sleeping Dragons. One faced north, the other south. The Khaldharon Run ended there and the mystery began, because no one who had entered one of those yawning, cavernous mouths had ever returned.

Several miles south of the Sleeping Dragons, the sun kissed the Black Mountain, Ebon Askavi, where Witch, his young, dreamed-of Queen would have lived if she'd never met Daemon Sadi.

The Eyrien warriors were close enough now for him to hear their threats and curses.

Smiling, he unfurled his wings, raised his fist, and let out an Eyrien war cry that silenced everything.

Then he dove into the Khaldharon Run.

It was as exhilarating, and as bad, as he'd thought it would be.

Even with Craft, his tattered wings didn't provide the balance he needed. Before he could compensate, the wind that howled through the canyon smashed him into the side wall, breaking his ribs and his right shoulder. Screaming defiance, he twisted away from the rock, pouring the strength of the Ebon-gray into his body as he plunged back into the center of the wild mingling of forces.

Just as the other Eyriens dove into the Run, he caught the Red thread and began the headlong race toward the Sleeping Dragons.

Instead of cutting in and out of the looping, twisting Winds within his range of strength to make a run as close to the canyon center as possible, he held to the Red, following it through narrow cuts of rock, pulling his wings tight to arrow through weatherworn holes that scraped his skin off as he passed through them.

His right foot hung awkwardly from the ripped ankle. The outer half of his left wing hung useless; the frame snapped when a gust of wind shoved him against a rock. The muscles in his back were torn from forcing his wings to do what they could no longer do. A deep, slicing belly wound pushed his guts out below the wide leather belt.

He shook his head, trying to clear blood out of his eyes, and let out a triumphant roar as he gauged his entry between the sharp stones that looked like petrified teeth.

A final gust of wind pushed him down as he shot through the Dragon's mouth. A "tooth" opened his left leg from hip to knee.

He drove into swirling mist, determined to reach the other side before he emptied the Jewels and his strength gave out.

Movement caught his eye. A startled face. Wings.

"Lucivar!"

He pushed to his limit, aware of the pursuers gaining on him.

"LUCIVAR!"

The other mouth had to be . . . There! But . . .

Two tunnels. The left one held lightened twilight. The right one was filled with a soft dawn.

Darkness would hide him better. He swung toward the twilight.

A rush of wings on his left. A hand grabbing at him.

He kicked, twisted away, and drove for the right-hand tunnel.

"LUU-CI-VAARRR!"

Past the teeth and out, driving upward past the canyon rim toward the morning sky, pumping useless wings out of stubborn pride.

And there was Askavi, looking as he imagined it might have looked a long time ago. The muddy trickle he'd flown over was now a deep, clear river. Barren rock was softened by spring wildflowers. Beyond the Run, sunlight glinted off small lakes and twisting streams.

Pain flooded his senses. Blood mixed with tears.

Askavi. Home. Finally home.

He pumped his wings a last time, arched his body in a slow, painfully graceful backward curve, folded his wings, and plummeted toward the deep, clear water below.

2 / The Twisted Kingdom

The wind tried to rip him off the tiny island that was his only resting place in this endless, unforgiving sea. Waves smashed down on him, soaking him in blood. So much blood.

You are my instrument.

Words lie. Blood doesn't.

The words circled him, mental sharks closing in to tear out another piece of his soul.

Gasping, he choked on a mouthful of bloody foam as he dug his fingers into rock that suddenly softened. He screamed as the rock beneath his hands turned into pulpy, violet-black bruises.

Butchering whore.

Nooooo!

I loved her! he screamed. *I *love* her! I never meant her harm.*

You are my instrument.

Words lie. Blood doesn't.

Butchering whore.

The words leaped playfully over the island, slicing him deeper and deeper with each pass.

Pain deepening anguish deepening agony deepening pain until there was no pain at all.

Or, perhaps, no one left to feel it.

3 / Terreille

Surreal stared at the dirty, trembling wreck that had once been the most dangerous, beautiful man in the Realm. Before he could shy away, she pulled him into the flat, threw every physical bolt on the door, and then Gray-locked it for good measure. After a moment's thought, she put a Gray shield on all the windows to lessen the chance of a severed artery or a five-story uncontrolled dive.

Then she took a good look at him and wondered if a severed artery would be such a bad thing. He'd been mad the last time she'd seen him. Now he looked as if he'd been sliced open and scooped out as well.

"Daemon?" She walked toward him, slowly.

He shook, unable to control it. His bruised-looking eyes, empty of everything but pain, filled with tears. "He's dead."

Surreal sat on the couch and tugged on his arm until he sat beside her. "Who's dead?" Who would matter enough to produce this reaction?

"Lucivar. Lucivar's *dead!*" He buried his head in her lap and wept like a heartsick child.

Surreal patted Daemon's greasy, tangled hair, unable to think of one consoling thing to say. Lucivar had been important to Daemon. His death mattered to Daemon. But even thinking of expressing sympathy made her want to gag. As far as she was concerned, Lucivar was also responsible for some of the soul wounds that had pushed Daemon over the edge, and now the bastard's death might be the fatal slice.

When the sobs diminished to quiet sniffles, she called in a handkerchief and stuffed it into his hand. She'd do a lot of things for Sadi, but she'd be damned if she'd blow his nose for him.

Finally cried out, he sat next to her, saying nothing. She sat quietly and stared at the windows.

This backwater street was safe enough. She'd returned several times since Daemon's last visit, staying longer and longer each time. It felt comfortable here. She and Wyman, the Warlord Daemon had healed, had developed a casual friendship that kept loneliness at bay. Here, with some-one looking after him, maybe Daemon could heal a little.

"Daemon? Would you stay here with me for a while?" Watching him, she couldn't tell what he was thinking, even *if* he was thinking.

Eventually, he said, "If you want."

She thought she saw a faint flicker of understanding. "You promise to stay?" she pressed. "You promise not to leave without telling me?"

The flicker died. "There's nowhere else to go."

4 / Kaeleer

A light breeze. Sunlight warming his hand. Birdsong. Firm comfort under him. Soft cotton over him.

Lucivar slowly opened his eyes and stared at the white ceiling and the smooth, exposed beams. Where . . . ?

Out of habit, he immediately looked for ways out of the room. Two windows covered by white curtains embroidered with morning glories. A door on the wall opposite the bed he was lying on.

Then he noticed the rest of the room. The pine bedside table and dresser. The piece of driftwood turned into a lamp. A cabinet, its top bare except for a simple brass stand for holding music crystals. An open work-basket stuffed with skeins of yarn and floss. A large, worn, forest-green chair and matching hassock. A needlework frame covered with white material. An overstuffed bookcase. Braided, earth-tone rugs. Two framed charcoal sketches—head views of a unicorn and a wolf.

Lucivar's lip curled automatically when he caught the feminine psychic scent that saturated the walls and wood. Then he frowned. For some reason, that psychic scent didn't repulse him.

He looked around the room again, confused. This was Hell?

A door opened in the room beyond. He heard a woman's voice say, "All right, go look, but don't wake him."

He closed his eyes. The door opened. Nails clicked on the wood floor. Something snuffled his shoulder. He kept his muscles relaxed, feigning sleep while his senses strained to identify the thing.

Fur against his bare skin. A cold, wet nose sniffing his ear.

Then a snort that made him twitch, followed by satisfied silence.

Giving in to curiosity and the warrior's need to identify an enemy, Lucivar opened his eyes and returned the wolf's intent gaze for a moment before it let out a pleased whuff and trotted out the door.

He barely had time to gather his wits when the woman pushed the door fully open and leaned against the doorway. "So you've finally decided to rejoin the living."

She sounded amused, but if the rest of her was anything to go by, the hoarseness in her voice was caused by strain, fatigue, and overuse. Painfully thin. The way the trousers and shirt hung on her, she'd probably dropped the weight far too fast to be healthy. The long, loose braid of gold hair looked as dull as her skin, and there were dark smudges under those beautiful, ancient sapphire eyes.

Lucivar blinked. Swallowed hard. Finally remembered to breathe. "Cat?" he whispered. He raised his hand in a mute plea.

She raised one eyebrow and walked toward him. "I know you said you would find me when I was seventeen, but I had no idea you would do it in such a dramatic fashion."

The moment she touched his hand, he pulled her down on top of him and wrapped his arms around her squirming body, laughing and crying, ignoring her muffled protests as he said, "Cat, Cat, Cat, OOWWW!"

Jaenelle scrambled off the bed and out of reach, breathing hard.

Lucivar rubbed his shoulder. "You bit me." He didn't mind the bite—well, yes, he did—but he didn't like her pulling away from him.

"I *told* you I couldn't breathe."

"Do we need to?" he asked, still rubbing his shoulder.

Judging by the look in her eyes, if she were actually feline, she'd be puffed to twice her size.

"I don't know, Lucivar," she said in a voice that could scorch a desert. "I could always remove your lungs and we'd find out firsthand if breathing is optional."

The tiny doubt that she might not be kidding was sufficient to make him swallow the flippant remark he was about to make. Besides, he had enough confusing things to think about, not to mention doing something about the urgent, basic message his body was now sending. Hell's fire, he'd never imagined being dead would feel so much like being alive.

He rolled onto his side, wondering if his muscles were always going to feel so limp—weren't there *any* advantages to being a demon?—and thrust his legs out from under the covers.

"Lucivar," Jaenelle said in a midnight voice.

He gave her a measuring look and decided to ignore the dangerous glitter in her eyes. He levered himself upright, pulled the sheet across his lap, and grinned weakly. "I've always been proud of my accuracy and aim, Cat, but even I can't water the flowers from here."

Thankfully, he didn't understand anything she said after the first Eyrien curse she flung at him.

She slung his arm over her shoulders, wrapped her arm around his waist, and pulled him to his feet. "Just take it slow. I've got most of your weight."

"The males who serve here should be doing this, not you," Lucivar snarled as they shuffled to the door, not sure if he was more embarrassed about being naked or needing her support.

"There aren't any. Hey!"

He almost overbalanced both of them reaching for the door, but he needed to tighten his hand around something. His darling Cat was here alone, unprotected, with no one but a wolf for company? Taking care of his . . . "You're a young woman," he said through clenched teeth.

"I'm a fully qualified Healer." She tugged at his waist. It didn't do any good. "You were easier to take care of before you woke up."

He snarled at her.

"Lucivar," Jaenelle said in that voice Healers used on irascible patients and idiots, "you've been in a healing sleep for the past three weeks. Taking that into consideration as well as what it took to put you back together, I think I've seen every inch of you more than once. Now, are you going to dribble on the floor like an untrained puppy or are we going to get to where you wanted to go?"

A fierce desire to get well enough to stand on his own two feet so that he could strangle her got him to the bathroom. Pride made him snarl her out the door. Stubbornness kept him upright long enough to do what was necessary, tie a bath towel around his waist, and reach the bathroom door.

By then his energy and useful emotions were tapped out, so he didn't protest when Jaenelle helped him walk to a stool near a large pine table in the cabin's main room. She moved behind him, her hands firm and gentle as they explored his back. He kept his eyes fixed on the outside door, not ready yet to ask about the healing. Then he felt one of his wings slowly unfurl, guided by those same gentle hands.

The wing closed. The other stretched out. As she came around to the front, he turned his head and stared at a wing that was healthy and whole. Stunned, he bit his lip and blinked back tears.

Jaenelle glanced at his face, then returned her attention to the wing. "You were lucky," she said quietly. "In another week there wouldn't have been enough healthy tissue left to rebuild them."

Rebuild them? Considering the damage the slime mold and the salt mines had done, even the best Eyrien Healers would have cut off the wings. How could she rebuild them?

Mother Night, he was tired, but there were too many things here that didn't fit his expectations. He desperately needed to understand and didn't know where to begin.

Then Jaenelle bent over to look at the lower part of the wing and the jewelry around her neck swung out of her shirt. Later he'd ask why Witch was wearing a Sapphire Jewel. Right now, all his attention was caught by the hourglass pendant that hung above the Jewel.

The hourglass was the Black Widows' symbol, both a declaration and a warning about the witch who wore it. An apprentice wore a pendant with the gold dust sealed in the top half of the glass. A journeymaid's pendant had the gold dust evenly divided between top and bottom. A fully trained Black Widow wore an hourglass with all the gold dust in the bottom chamber.

"When did you become a fully trained Black Widow?"

The air around him cooled. "Does it bother you that I am?"

Obviously it bothered some people. "No, just curious."

She gave him a quick smile of apology and continued her inspection. The air returned to normal. "Last year."

"And you became a qualified Healer?"

She carefully folded the wing and started checking his right shoulder. "Last year."

Lucivar whistled. "Busy year."

Jaenelle laughed. "Papa says he's thrilled he survived it."

He could almost hear the blade against the whetstone as his temper rose to the killing edge. She had a father, a family, and yet lived without human companionship, not even a servant. Exiled here because of the

Hourglass? Or because she was Witch? Once he was fit again, this father of hers would have a few things to adjust to—like the Warlord Prince who now served her.

"Lucivar." Jaenelle's voice seemed as far away as the hand squeezing his taut shoulder. "Lucivar, what's wrong?"

Time moved slowly at the killing edge, measured by the beat of a war drum heart. The world became filled with individual, razor-sharp details. A blade would flow through muscle, humble bone. And the mouth would fill with the living wine as teeth sank into a throat.

"*Lucivar.*"

Lucivar blinked. Felt the tension in Jaenelle's fingers as she gripped his shoulders. He backed from the edge, step by mental step, while the wildness in him howled to run free. Senses dulled by the salt mines of Pruul were reborn. The land called him, seducing him with scents and sounds. She seduced him, too. Not for sex, but for another kind of bond, in its own way just as powerful. He wanted to rub against her so that her physical scent was on his skin. He wanted to rub against her so that *his* physical scent on *her* warned others that a powerful male had some claim to her, was claimed by her. He wanted . . .

He turned his head, catching her finger between his teeth, exerting enough force to display dominance without actually hurting her. Her hand relaxed in submission, embracing the wild darkness within him. And because she *could* embrace it, he surrendered everything.

A minute later, completely returned to the mundane world, he noticed the open outer door and the three wolves standing on the covered porch, studying him with sharp interest.

Jaenelle, now inspecting his collarbone and chest muscles, glanced at the wolves and shook her head. "No, he can't come out and play."

Making disappointed-sounding whuffs, the wolves went back outside.

He studied the land framed by the open door. "I never thought Hell would look like this," he said softly.

"Hell doesn't." She slapped his hand when he tried to stop her from probing his hip and thigh.

Forcefully reminding himself that he shouldn't smack a Healer, he gritted his teeth and tried again to find some answers. "I didn't know that demon-dead children grew up or that demons could be healed."

She gave him a penetrating look before examining his other leg. Heat and power flowed from her hands. "*Cildru dyathe* don't and demons can't. But I'm not *cildru dyathe* and you're not a demon—although you did your damnedest to become one," she added tartly. She pulled up a straight-backed chair, sat down facing him, and took his hands in hers. "Lucivar, you're not dead. This isn't the Dark Realm."

He'd been so sure. "Then . . . where are we?"

"We're in Askavi. In Kaeleer." She watched him anxiously.

"The Shadow Realm?" Lucivar whistled softly. Two tunnels. One a lightening twilight, the other a soft dawn. The Dark Realm and the Shadow. He grinned at her. "Since we're not dead, can we go exploring?"

He watched, intrigued, as she tried to force her answering grin into a sober, professional expression.

"When you're fully healed," she said sternly, then spoiled it with a silvery, velvet-coated laugh. "Oh, Lucivar, the dragons who live on the Fyreborn Islands are going to love you. You not only have wings, you're big enough to wave whomp."

"Wave what?"

Her eyes widened and her teeth caught her lower lip. "Umm. Never mind," she said too brightly, bouncing off her chair.

He caught the back of her shirt. After a brief tussle that left him breathing hard and left her looking more than a little rumpled, she was once again slumped in the chair.

"Why are you living here, Cat?"

"What's wrong with it?" she said defensively. "It's a good place."

Lucivar narrowed his eyes. "I didn't say it wasn't."

She leaned forward, studying his face. "You're not one of those males who gets hysterical about every little thing, are you?"

He leaned forward, forearms braced on thighs, and smiled his lazy, arrogant smile. "I never get hysterical."

"Uh-huh."

The smile showed a hint of teeth. "Why, Cat?"

"Wolves can be real tattletales, did you know that?" She looked at him hopefully. When he didn't say anything, she fluffed her hair and sighed. "You see, there are times when I need to get away from everyone and just be with the land, and I used to come and camp out here for a few days, but during one of those trips it rained and I was sleeping on the wet ground and got chilled and the wolves went running off to tell Papa and he said he appreciated my need to spend some time with the land but he saw no reason why I couldn't have the option of some shelter and I said that a lean-to would probably be a reasonable idea so he had this cabin built." She paused and gave him an apprehensive smile. "Papa and I have rather different definitions of 'lean-to.' "

Looking at the large stone hearth and the solid walls and ceiling, and then at the woman-child sitting in front of him with her hands pressed between her knees, Lucivar reluctantly let go of the knot of anger he'd felt for this unknown father of hers. "Frankly, Cat, I like your papa's definition better."

She scowled at him.

Black Widow and Healer she might be, but she was also almost grown, with enough of the endearing awkwardness of the young to still remind him of a kitten trying to pounce on a large, hoppy bug.

"So you don't live here all the time?" he asked carefully.

Jaenelle shook her head. "The family has several residences in Dhemlan. Most of the time I live at the family seat." She gave him a look he couldn't read. "My father is the Warlord Prince of Dhemlan—among other things."

A man of wealth and position then. Probably not the sort who'd want a half-breed bastard as a companion for his daughter. Well, he'd deal with that when the time came.

"Lucivar." She fixed her eyes on the open door and chewed her lip.

He sympathized with her. This was sometimes the hardest part of the healing, telling the patient honestly what could—and could not—be mended. "The wings are just decorative, aren't they?"

"No!" She took a deep breath. "The injuries were severe. All of them, not just the wings. I've done the healing, but what happens now depends, in large part, on you. I estimate it will take another three months for your back and wings to heal completely." She chewed her lip. "But, Lucivar, there's no margin for error in this. I had to pull everything you had to give for this healing. If you reinjure *anything*, the damage may be permanent."

He reached for her hand, caressed her fingers with his thumb. "And if I do it your way?" He watched her carefully. There were no false promises in those sapphire eyes.

"If you do it my way, three months from now we'll make the Run."

He lowered his head. Not because he didn't want her to see the tears, but because he needed a private moment to savor the hope.

When he had himself under control again, he smiled at her.

She smiled back, understanding. "Would you like a cup of tea?" When he nodded, she bounced out of the chair and went through the door to the right of the stone hearth.

"Any chance of persuading my Healer to add a bit of food to that?"

Jaenelle's head popped out of the kitchen doorway. "How does a large slice of fresh bread soaked in beef broth sound?"

About as edible as the table leg. "Do I have any choices?"

"No."

"Sounds wonderful."

She returned a few minutes later, helped him shift from the stool to a straight-backed chair that supported his back, then placed a large mug on the pine table. "It's a healing brew."

His lip curled in a silent snarl. Every healing brew he'd ever had forced down his throat had always tasted like brambles and piss, and he'd reached the opinion that Healers made them that way as a penalty for being hurt or ill.

"You don't get anything else until you drink it," Jaenelle added with a distasteful lack of sympathy.

Lucivar lifted the cup and sniffed cautiously. It smelled . . . different. He took a sip, held it in his mouth for a moment, then closed his eyes and swallowed. And wondered how she'd distilled into a healing brew the solid strength of the Askavi mountains, the trees and grasses and flowers that fleshed out the earth beneath, the rivers that flowed through the land.

"This is wonderful," he murmured.

"I'm pleased you approve."

"Really, it is," he insisted, responding to the laughter in her voice. "These things usually taste awful, and this tastes good."

Her laughter turned to puzzlement. "They're supposed to taste good, Lucivar. Otherwise, no one would want to drink them."

Not being able to argue with that, he said nothing, content to sip the brew. He was even content enough to feel a mild tolerance for the bowl of broth-soaked bread that Jaenelle placed in front of him, a tolerance that sharpened considerably when he noticed the slivers of beef sprinkled over the bread.

Then he noticed she was going to eat the same thing.

"I'm not the only one you drained to the limit in order to do this healing, am I, Cat?" he said quietly, unable to completely mask the anger underneath. How dare she risk herself this way, when there was no one to look after her?

Her cheeks colored faintly. She fiddled with her spoon, poked at the bread, and finally shrugged. "It was worth it."

He stabbed at the bread as another thought occurred to him. He'd let that wait for a moment. He tasted the bread and broth. "Not only do you make a good healing brew, you're also a decent cook."

She smacked the bread with her spoon, sending up a small geyser of broth. Wiping up the mess, she let out a hurt sniff and glared at him. "Mrs. Beale made this. I can't cook."

Lucivar took another mouthful and shrugged. "Cooking isn't that difficult." Then he looked up and wondered if a grown man had ever been beaten to death with a soup spoon.

"You can cook?" she asked ominously. Then she huffed. "Why do so many males know how to cook?"

He bit his tongue to keep from saying, "self-preservation." He ate a couple more spoonfuls of bread and broth. "I'll teach you to cook—on one condition."

"What condition?"

In the moment before he answered, he sensed a brittle fragility within her, but he could only respond as the Warlord Prince he was. "The bed's big enough for both of us," he said quietly, aware of how quickly she paled. "If you're not comfortable with that, fine. But if someone's going to sleep in front of the hearth, it's going to be me."

He saw the flash of temper, quickly reined in.

"You need the bed," she said through gritted teeth. "The healing isn't done yet."

"Since there's no one else here to look after you, I, as a Warlord Prince, have the duty and the privilege of overseeing your care." He was invoking ancient customs long ignored in Terreille, but he knew by her frustrated snarl that they still applied in Kaeleer.

"All right," she said, hiding her shaking hands in her lap. "We'll share the bed."

"And the blankets," he added.

The hostile look combined with the suppressed smile told him she wasn't sure what to think about him. That was all right. He wasn't sure, either.

"I suppose you want a pillow, too."

He smiled that lazy, arrogant smile. "Of course. And I promise not to kick you if you snore."

With her command of the Eyrien language, the girl could have made a Master of a hunting camp blush.

It hit him later, when he was comfortably settled on his belly in the bed, his wings open and gently supported, and Jaenelle and the wolves were out doing walkies—a silly word that struck him as an accurate description of the intricate, furry dance three wolves would perform around her while taking a late afternoon stroll.

He had made the Khaldharon Run intending to die and, instead, not only had survived but had found the living myth, his dreamed-of Queen.

Even as he smiled, the tears began, hot and bitter.

He was alive. And Jaenelle was alive. But Daemon . . .

He didn't know what had happened at Cassandra's Altar, or how that sheet had gotten drenched with Jaenelle's blood, or what Daemon had done, but he was beginning to understand what it had cost.

Pressing his face into the pillow to muffle the sobs, squeezing his eyes shut to deny the images his mind conjured, he saw Daemon. In Pruul that night, exhausted but determined. In the ruins of SaDiablo Hall in Terreille, burned out by the nightmare of madness and ready to die. He heard again Daemon's frightened, enraged denial. Heard again that anguished cry rising from the broken stones.

If he hadn't been so chained by bitterness that night, if he'd left with Daemon, they would have found a way through the Gates. Together, they would have. And they would have found her and had these years with her, watching her grow up, participating in the experiences that would transform a child into a woman, a Queen.

He would still do that. He would be with her during the final years of that transformation and would know the joy of serving her.

But Daemon . . .

Lucivar bit the pillow, muffling his own scream of anguish.

But Daemon . . .

CHAPTER TEN

1 / Kaeleer

Lucivar stood at the edge of the woods, not quite ready to step across the line that divided forest shadow from sun-drenched meadow. The day was warm enough to appreciate shade. Besides, Jaenelle was away on some kind of obligatory trip so there was no reason to hurry back.

Smoke trotted up, chose a tree, lifted a leg, and looked expectantly at Lucivar.

"I marked territory a ways back," Lucivar said.

Smoke's snort was a clear indication of what wolves thought about a human's ability to mark territory properly.

Amused, Lucivar waited until Smoke trotted off before stepping into the sunlight and spreading his wings to let them dry fully. The spring-fed pool Jaenelle had shown him wasn't quite warm enough yet, but he'd enjoyed the brisk dip.

He fanned his wings slowly, savoring the movement. He was halfway through the healing. If everything continued to go well, next week he would test his wings in flight. It was hard to be patient, but, at the end of the day, when he felt the good, quiet ache in his muscles, he knew Jaenelle was setting the right pace for the healing.

Folding his wings, Lucivar set off for the cabin at an easy pace.

Lulled by earlier physical activity and the day's warmth, it took him a moment to realize something wasn't right about the way the two young wolves raced toward him. Jaenelle had taught him how to communicate with the kindred, and he'd been flattered when she'd told him they were highly selective about which humans they would speak to. But now, bracing himself as the wolves ran toward him, he wondered how much their opinion of him depended upon her presence.

A minute later he was engulfed in fur, fighting for balance while the wolf behind him wrapped its forelegs around his waist and pushed him forward and the one in front of him placed its paws on his shoulders and leaned hard against him, earnestly licking his face and whimpering for reassurance.

Their thoughts banged against his mind, too upset to be coherent.

The Lady had returned. The bad thing was going to happen. They were afraid. Smoke guarding, waiting for Lucivar. Lucivar come now. He was human. He would help the Lady.

Lucivar got untangled enough to start walking quickly toward the cabin. They didn't say she was hurt, so she wasn't wounded. But something bad was going to happen. Something that made them afraid to enter the cabin and be with her.

He remembered how uneasy Smoke had been when Jaenelle told them she was leaving for a few days.

Something bad. Something a human would make better.

He sincerely hoped they were right.

He opened the cabin door and understood why the wolves were afraid.

She sat in the rocking chair in front of the hearth, just staring.

The psychic pain in the room staggered him. The psychic shield around her felt deceptively passive, as easy to brush aside as a cobweb. Beneath the passivity, however, lay something that, if unleashed, would extract a brutal price.

Pulling his wings in tight, Lucivar carefully circled around the shield until he stood in front of her.

The Black Jewel around her neck glowed with deadly fire.

He shook, not sure if he was afraid for himself or for her. He closed his eyes and made rash promises to the Darkness to keep from being sick on the spot.

Having lived in Terreille most of his life, he recognized someone who had been tortured. He didn't think she'd been physically harmed, but there were subtle kinds of abuse that were just as destructive. Certainly, her body had paid a terrible price over the past four days. The weight she'd put on had been consumed along with the muscle she'd built up by working with him. Her skin was stretched too tight over her face and looked fragile enough to tear. Her eyes . . .

He couldn't stand what he saw in those eyes.

She sat there, quietly bleeding to death from a soul wound, and he didn't know how to help her, didn't know if there was anything he *could* do that would help her.

"Cat?" he called softly. "Cat?"

He felt her revulsion when she finally looked at him, saw the emotions writhing and twisting in those haunted, bottomless eyes.

She blinked. Sank her teeth into her lower lip hard enough to draw blood. Blinked again. "Lucivar." Neither a question nor a statement, but an identification painfully drawn up from some deep well inside her. "Lucivar." Tears filled her eyes. "Lucivar?" A plea for comfort.

"Drop the shield, Cat." He watched her struggle to understand him. Sweet Darkness, she was so young. "Drop the shield. Let me in."

The shield dissolved. So did she. But she was in his arms before the first heart-tearing sob began. He settled them in the rocking chair and held her tight, murmuring soothing nothings, trying to rub warmth into icy limbs.

When the sobs eased to sniffles, he rubbed his cheek against her hair. "Cat, I think I should take you to your father's house."

"No!" She pushed at him, struggling to get free.

Her nails could have opened him to the bone. The venom in her snake tooth could have killed him twice over. One surge of the Black Jewels could have blown apart his inner barriers and left him a drooling husk.

Instead, she struggled futilely against a stronger body. That told him more about her temperament than anything else she might have done— and also explained why this had happened in the first place. Her temper had probably slipped once and the result had scared the shit out of her. Now she didn't trust herself to display *any* anger—even in self-defense. Well, he *could* do something about *that*.

"Cat—"

"No." She gave one more push. Then, too weak to fight anymore, she collapsed against him.

"Why?" He could think of one reason she was afraid to go home.

The words spilled out of her. "I know I look bad. I know. That's why I can't go home now. If Papa saw me, he'd be upset. He'd want to know what happened, and I can't tell him that, Lucivar. I can't. He'd be so angry, and he'd have another fight with the Dark Council and they'd just cause more trouble for him."

To Lucivar's way of thinking, having her father explode in a murderous rage over what had been done to her would be all to the good. Unfortunately, Jaenelle didn't share his way of thinking. She'd rather endure something that devastated her than cause trouble between her beloved papa and the Dark Council. That might suit her and the Dark Council and her papa, but it didn't suit him.

"That's not good enough, Cat," he said, keeping his voice low. "Either you tell me what happened, or I bundle you up and take you to your father right now."

Jaenelle sniffed. "You don't know where he is."

"Oh, I'm sure if I create enough of a fuss, someone will be happy to tell me where to find the Warlord Prince of Dhemlan."

Jaenelle studied his face. "You're a prick, Lucivar."

He smiled that lazy, arrogant smile. "I told you that the first time we met." He waited a minute, hoping he wouldn't have to prod her and knowing he would. "Which is it going to be, Cat?"

She squirmed. He could understand that. If someone had cornered him the way he'd cornered her, he'd squirm, too. He sensed she wanted physical distance between them before explaining, but he figured he'd hear something closer to the truth if she remained captured on his lap.

Finally giving up, she fluffed her hair and sighed. "When I was twelve, I was hurt very badly—"

Was that how they had explained the rape to her? Being hurt?

"—and Papa became my legal guardian." She seemed to have a hard time breathing, and her voice thinned until, even sitting that close, he had to strain to hear her. "I woke up—came back to my body—two years later. I . . . was different when I came back, but Papa helped me rebuild my life piece by piece. He found teachers for me and encouraged my old friends to visit and he u-understood me." Her voice turned bitter. "But the Dark Council didn't think Papa was a suitable guardian and they tried to take me away from him and the rest of the family, so I stopped them and they had to let me stay with Papa."

Stopped them. Lucivar turned over the possibilities of how she could have stopped them. Apparently, she hadn't done quite enough.

"To placate the Council, I agreed to spend one week each season socializing with the aristo families in Little Terreille."

"Which doesn't explain why you came back in this condition," Lucivar said quietly. He rubbed her arm, trying to warm her up. He was sweating. She still shivered.

"It's like living in Terreille again," she whispered. The haunted look filled her eyes. "No, worse than that. It's like living in—" She paused, puzzled.

"Even aristos in Little Terreille have to eat," he said gently.

Her eyes glazed over. Her voice sounded hollow. "Can't trust the food. Never trust the food. Even if you test it, you can't always sense the badness until it's too late. Can't sleep. Mustn't sleep. But they get to you anyway. Lies are true, and truth is punished. Bad girl. Sick-mind girl to make up such lies."

An icy fist pressed into Lucivar's lower back as he wondered what nightmare in the inner landscape she was wandering through right now.

Capturing her chin between his thumb and finger, Lucivar turned her head, forcing her to look at him. "You're not a bad girl, you're not sick, and you don't lie," he said firmly.

She blinked. Confusion filled her eyes. "What?"

Would she understand if he told her what she'd said? He doubted it. "So the food is lousy and you don't sleep well. That still doesn't explain why you came back in this shape. What did they do to you, Cat?"

"Nothing," she whispered, closing her eyes. Her throat worked convulsively. "It's just that boys expect to be kissed and—"

"They expect *what*?" Lucivar snarled.

"—I'm f-f-frigid and—"

"Frigid!" Lucivar roared, ignoring her frightened squeak. "You're seventeen years old. Those strutting little sons of whoring bitches shouldn't be trying *anything* with you that would even bring up the question of whether or not you're 'frigid.' And where in the name of Hell were the chaperons?"

He rocked furiously, petting her hair with one hand while his other arm tightened protectively around her. Her yip of pain when he accidentally pinched her arm snapped him out of a red haze. He muttered an apology, resettled her in his lap, and began rocking at a more soothing tempo. After a couple of minutes, he shook his head.

"Frigid," he said with a snort of disgust. "Well, Cat, if objecting to having someone slobber on you or grope and squeeze you is their definition of frigid, then I'm frigid, too. They have no right to use you, no matter what they say. Any man who tells you otherwise deserves a knife between the ribs." He gave her a considering look, then shook his head. "You'd probably find it hard to gut a man. That's all right. I don't."

Jaenelle stared at him, wide-eyed.

He wrapped his hand around the back of her neck and massaged gently. "Listen to me, Cat, because I'll only say this once. You're the finest Lady I've ever met and the dearest friend I've ever had. Besides that, I love you like a brother, and any bastard who hurts my little sister is going to answer to me."

"Y-you can't," she whispered. "The agreement—"

"I'm not part of that damn agreement." He gave her a little shake, wondering how he could get that frail, bruised look out of her eyes. Then he squelched a grin. He'd do what he'd do with any feline he wanted to spark—rub her the wrong way. "Besides, Lady," he said in a courteous snarl, "you broke a solemn promise to me, and breaking a promise to a Warlord Prince is a serious offense."

Her eyes flashed fire. He could almost feel her back arch and the non-existent fur stand on end. Maybe he wouldn't have to dig that hard to bring a little of her temper to the surface.

"I never did!"

"Yes, you did. I distinctly remember teaching you what to do—"

"They weren't standing behind me!"

Lucivar narrowed his eyes. "You don't have any human male friends?"

"Of course I do!"

"And not one of them has ever taken you behind the barn and taught you what to do with your knee?"

Her fingernails suddenly required her attention.

"That's what I thought," Lucivar said dryly. "So I'll give you a choice. If one of those fine, rutting aristo males does something you don't like, you can give him a hard knee in the balls or I can start with his feet and end with his neck and break every bone in between."

"You couldn't."

"It's not that difficult. I've done it before."

He waited a minute, then tapped her chin. She closed her mouth.

Then she seemed to shrink into herself. "But, Lucivar," she said weakly, "what if it's my fault that he's aroused and needs relief?"

He snorted, amused. "You didn't actually fall for that, did you?"

Her eyes narrowed to slits.

"I don't know how things are in Kaeleer, but it used to be, in Terreille, that a young man could register at a Red Moon house and not only get his 'relief' but also learn how to do more than a thirty-second poke and hump."

She made a choking sound that might have been a suppressed laugh.

"And if they can't afford a Red Moon house, they can get their own 'relief' easily enough."

"How?"

Lucivar suppressed a grin. Sometimes catching her interest was as easy as rolling a ball of yarn in front of a kitten. "I'm not sure an older brother is the right person to explain that," he said primly.

She studied him. "You don't like sex, do you?"

"Not my experience of it, no." He traced her fingers, needing to be honest. "But I've always thought that if I cared about a woman, it would be wonderful to give her that kind of pleasure." He shook himself and set her on her feet. "Enough of this. You need to eat and get your strength back. There's beef soup and a loaf of fresh bread."

Jaenelle paled. "It won't stay down. It never does after . . ."

"Try."

When they sat down to eat, she managed three spoonfuls of soup and one mouthful of bread before she bolted into the bathroom.

His own appetite gone, Lucivar cleared the table. He was pouring the soup back into the pan when Smoke slunk into the kitchen.

Lucivar?

Lucivar lifted his bowl of soup. "You want some of this?"

Smoke ignored the offer. *Bad dreams come now. Hurt the Lady. She not talk to us, not see us, not want males near. Not eat, not sleep, walk walk walk, snarl at us. Bad dreams now, Lucivar.*

Do the bad dreams always come after one of these visits? Lucivar asked, narrowing his thoughts to a spear thread.

Smoke bared his teeth in a silent snarl. *Always.*

Lucivar's stomach clenched. So it didn't end once she got away from Little Terreille. *How long?* The kindred had a fluid sense of time, but Smoke, at least, understood basic divisions of day and night.

Smoke cocked his head. *Night, day, night, day . . . maybe night.*

So she'd spend tonight and the next two days trying to outrun the nightmares hovering at the edge of her vision by depleting an already exhausted body that she would mercilessly flog until it collapsed under the strain of no food, no water, no rest. What kind of dreams could drive a young woman to such masochistic cruelty?

He found out that night.

The change in her breathing snapped him out of a light sleep. Propping himself up on one arm, he reached for her shoulder.

Can't wake when bad dreams come. Standing at the foot of the bed, Smoke's eyes caught the moonlight.

Why?

Not see us. Not know us. All dreams.

Lucivar swore under his breath. If every sound, every touch got sucked into the dreamscape . . .

Jaenelle's body arched like a tightly strung bow.

He studied the clenched, straining muscles and swore again. She'd be hurting sore in the morning.

The tension went out of her body. She collapsed against the mattress, twitching, moaning, sweat-soaked.

He had to wake her up. If it took throwing her into a cold shower or walking her around the meadow for the rest of the night, he was going to wake her up.

He reached out again . . . and she began to talk.

Every word was a physical blow as the memories poured out.

His head bowed, his body flinching, he listened as she talked about and to Marjane, Myrol and Rebecca, Dannie, and, especially, Rose. He listened to the horrors a child had witnessed and endured in a place called Briarwood. He listened to the names of the men who had hurt her, hurt them all. And he suffered with her as she relived the rape that had torn her apart physically and had shattered her mind, the rape that had made her desperately try to sever the link between body and spirit.

As she plunged once again into an abyss beyond reach, she took a deep, ragged breath, murmured a name, and was still.

He watched her for several minutes until he felt reasonably sure she was just sleeping deeply. Then he went into the bathroom and was quietly, but thoroughly, sick.

He rinsed out his mouth, padded into the kitchen, and poured a generous dose of whiskey. Naked, he stepped onto the porch and let the night air dry the sweat from his skin while he sipped his drink.

Smoke came out of the cabin, standing so close his fur tickled Lucivar's bare leg. The two young wolves remained huddled at the far end of the porch.

She never remembers, does she? Lucivar asked Smoke.

No. The Darkness is kind.

Maybe she just wasn't ready to face those memories. He certainly wasn't going to push her. But he had the uneasy feeling that the day would come when someone or something would force that door open and she would have to face her past. Until then, there were some things he would hold in silence—and he hoped she would forgive him.

He'd heard pain when she'd talked about the men who had hurt her. He'd heard pain when she'd talked about the man who had raped her.

But the only time she'd mentioned Daemon, his name had sounded like a promise, like a caress.

Blinking back tears and leashing his guilt, Lucivar finished the whiskey and turned to go back inside.

2 / Kaeleer

Lucivar settled on the tree stump that marked the usual halfway point for walkies. Summer was over. The healing was complete. Two days ago, he had successfully made the Khaldharon Run. Yesterday, he and Jaenelle had gone to the Fyreborn Islands to play with the small dragons who lived there. He would have happily spent today being lazy, but something had pushed Jaenelle out of the cabin the moment they'd returned this morning, and the way she shied away from his questions told him it had to do with him.

Well, if you couldn't entice the kitten with a ball of yarn, you certainly could provoke her with a fast dunk in a tub of cold water.

"You could have warned me, Cat."

Jaenelle bristled. "I *told* you to watch your angle when you whomped that wave." Her eyes flicked to his right side. She chewed her lower lip. "Lucivar, that bruise looks awfully nasty. Are you sure—"

"I wasn't talking about the wave," Lucivar said through his teeth. "I was talking about the pickleberries."

"Oh." Jaenelle sat down near the tree stump. She gave him a slanty-eyed look. "Well, I did think the name was sufficient warning so that a person wouldn't just sink his teeth into one."

"I was thirsty. You said they were juicy."

"They are," Jaenelle pointed out so reasonably that he wanted to belt her. She wrapped her arms around her knees. "The dragons were extremely impressed by the sounds you made. They wondered if you were demonstrating territorial claims or a mating challenge."

Lucivar shuddered at the memory of biting into that aptly named fruit. Juicy, yes. When he'd bitten into it, the juice had flooded his mouth with golden sweetness for a moment before the tartness made his teeth curl and his throat close. He'd stomped and howled so much he could understand why the dragons thought he'd been showing them examples of Eyrien display. To add to the insult, the dragons had chomped on pickleberries throughout that whole damn performance while Jaenelle had nibbled daintily and watched with wide-eyed apprehension.

The little traitor. She was sitting close enough to reach, the trusting little fool. No weapons. He wanted his bare hands on her. Strangling would be too quick, too permanent. Pulling her across his lap and whacking her ass until his hand got hot . . .

She shifted her hips, putting her just out of reach.

Lucivar bared his teeth in a smile, acknowledging the movement.

Shifting a little farther, she began to pluck grass. "I gave Mrs. Beale a pickleberry once," she said in a small voice.

Lucivar stared at the meadow. Over the past three months, he'd heard plenty of stories about the cook who worked for Jaenelle's family. "Did you tell her what it's called?"

"No." A small, pleased smile curved Jaenelle's lips.

He clenched his teeth. "What happened?"

"Well, Papa asked me if I had any idea why those sounds were coming from the kitchen and I said I did have some idea and he said 'I see,' stuffed me into one of our private Coaches, and told Khary to take me to Morghann's house since Scelt was on the other side of the Realm."

Struggling to keep a straight face, Lucivar clamped his right hand over his left wrist hard enough to hurt. It helped.

"The next morning, Mrs. Beale cornered Papa in his study and told him that I'd given her a sample of a new kind of fruit and, having thought about it, she'd decided that it would enhance the flavor of a number of common dishes and she'd appreciate having some. Then she set a wicker basket on Papa's desk and Papa had to tell her that he didn't know where the fruit came from and Mrs. Beale pointed out that, obviously, I did, and Papa just as politely pointed out that I was not at home at the moment and Mrs. Beale suggested that he and her wicker basket go find me and bring back the desired fruit. So he did and we did and because the Fyreborn Islands are a closed Territory, Mrs. Beale is envied by other cooks for her ability to produce this unique taste in the food she prepares."

Lucivar rubbed his head vigorously, then smoothed back his shoulder-length black hair. "Does Mrs. Beale outrank your father?"

"Not by a long shot," Jaenelle said tartly, and then added plaintively, "It's just that she's rather . . . *large.*"

"I'd like to meet Mrs. Beale. I think I'm in love." He looked at Jaenelle's horrified expression, fell off the stump, and laughed himself silly. He laughed even harder when she poked him, and said worriedly, "You were joking, weren't you, Lucivar? Lucivar?"

With a whoop, he yanked her down on top of him and wrapped his arms around her tight enough to hold her and loose enough not to panic her. "You should have been Eyrien," he said once his laughter had settled to a quiet simmer. "You've got the brass for it."

Then he smoothed her hair away from her face. "What is it, Cat?" he asked quietly. "What am I going to find so bitter to swallow that you wanted to give me this burst of sweetness first?"

Jaenelle traced his collarbone. "You're healed now."

He could almost taste her reluctance. "So?"

She rolled away from him and leaped to her feet, a movement so graceful nothing tame could have made it.

He rose more slowly, snapped his wings open to clear away the dust and bits of grass, settled on the tree stump again, and waited.

"Even after the war between Terreille and Kaeleer, people came through the Gates," Jaenelle said quietly, her eyes fixed on the horizon. "Mostly those who'd been born in the wrong place and were seeking 'home.' And there's always been some trading between Terreille and Little Terreille.

"A couple of years ago, the Dark Council decided to allow more open contact with Terreille, and aristo Blood began pouring in to see the

Shadow Realm. The number of lower-ranking Blood wanting to immigrate to Kaeleer should have warned the Council about what courts are like in Terreille, but Little Terreille opened its arms to embrace the kinship ties. However, Kaeleer is not Terreille. Blood Law and Protocol can be . . . understood differently.

"Too many Terreilleans refused to understand that what they could get away with in Terreille isn't tolerated in Kaeleer, and they died.

"A year ago, in Dharo, three Terreillean males raped a young witch for sport. Raped her until her mind was so broken there was no one left to sing back to the body. She was my age."

Lucivar concentrated on his clenched hands, forcing them to open. "Did they catch the bastards who did it?"

Jaenelle smiled grimly. "The Dharo males executed those men. Then they banished the rest of the Terreilleans in Dharo, sending them back to Little Terreille. Within six months, the fatality rate for Terreilleans in most Territories was over ninety percent. Even in Little Terreille it was over half. Since the slaughter strained good feelings between the Realms, the Dark Council passed some rules of immigration. Now, a Terreillean who wants to immigrate has to serve a Kaeleer witch to her satisfaction for a specified time. Non-Jeweled Blood have to serve for eighteen months. The lighter Jewels have to serve three years, the darker Jewels five. Queens and Warlord Princes of any rank have to serve five years."

Lucivar felt sick. His body shook. He felt detached sympathy for it. *To her satisfaction.* That meant the bitch could do anything to him and he would have to allow it if he wanted to stay in Kaeleer.

He tried to laugh. It sounded panicked.

She knelt beside him and petted him anxiously. "Lucivar, it won't be so bad. Truly. The Queens. . . . Serving in Kaeleer isn't like serving in Terreille. I know all of the Territory Queens. I'll help you find someone who suits you, someone you'll enjoy serving."

"Why can't I serve you?" He spread his hands over her shoulders, needing her to be his anchor as he fought against hurt and panic. "You like me—at least some of the time. And we work well together."

"Oh, Lucivar," Jaenelle said gently, cupping his face in her hands. "I always like you. Even when you're being a pain in the ass. But you should have the experience of serving in a Kaeleer court."

"You'll be setting up your court in a year or two."

"I'm not going to have a court. I don't want to have that kind of power over someone else's life. Besides, you don't want to serve me. You don't know about me, don't understand—"

He lost patience. "What? That you're Witch?"

She looked shocked.

He rubbed her shoulders, and said dryly, "Wearing the Black at your age makes it rather obvious, Cat. Anyway, I've known who, and what, you were since I met you." He tried to smile. "The night we met, I'd asked the Darkness for a strong Queen I'd be proud to serve, and there you were. Of course, you were a bit younger than I'd imagined, but I wasn't going to be picky about it. Cat, please. I've waited a lifetime to serve you. I'll do anything you want. Please don't send me away."

Jaenelle closed her eyes and rested her head against his chest. "It's not that easy, Lucivar. Even if you can accept what I am—"

"I *do* accept what you are."

"There are other reasons why you might not be willing to serve me."

Something inside him settled. He understood the custom of passing tests or challenges in order to earn a privilege. Whether she realized it or not, she was offering him a chance. "How many?"

She looked at him blankly.

"How many reasons? Set a number, now. If I can accept them, then I can choose to serve you. That's fair."

She gave him a strange look. "And will you be honest with yourself as well as with me about whether you can really accept them?"

"Yes."

She pulled away from him, sitting just out of reach. After several minutes of tense silence, she said, "Three."

Three. Not a dozen or so to natter about. Just three. Which meant he had to take them seriously. "All right. When?"

Jaenelle flowed to her feet. "Now. Pack a bag and plan to stay overnight." She headed for the cabin at a swift pace.

Lucivar followed her but didn't try to catch up. Three tests would determine the next five years of his life.

She'd be fair. Whether she liked the end result or not, she'd be fair. And so would he.

As he approached the cabin, the wolves ran out to greet him, offering furry comfort to the adopted member of their pack.

Lucivar buried his hands in their fur. If he had to serve someone else, would he ever see them again?

He would be honest. He wouldn't abuse her trust in him.

But he was going to win.

3 / Kaeleer

Lucivar's heart pounded against his chest. He had never been inside the Keep, not even an outside courtyard. A half-breed bastard wasn't worthy of entering this place. If he'd learned nothing else in the Eyrien hunting camps, he'd learned that, no matter what Jewels he wore or how skilled he was with weapons, his birth made him unworthy to lick the boots of the ones who lived in Ebon Askavi, the Black Mountain.

Now he was here, walking beside Jaenelle through massive rooms with vaulted ceilings, through open courtyards and gardens, through a labyrinth of wide corridors—and the prickle between his shoulder blades told him that something had been watching him since he entered the Keep. Something that flitted inside the stone, hid inside shadows, created shadows where shadows shouldn't exist. Not malevolent—at least, not yet. But the stories about what guarded the Keep were the fireside tales that frightened young boys sleepless.

Lucivar twitched his shoulders and followed his Lady.

By the time they reached the upper levels that appeared to be more inhabited, Lucivar began wistfully eyeing the benches and chairs that lined the corridors and promising himself a drink of water from the next indoor fountain or decorative waterfall they came to.

Jaenelle had said nothing since they'd stepped off the landing web in the outer courtyard. Her silence was supportive but not comforting. He understood that. Ebon Askavi was Witch's home. If he served her, he had to come to terms with the place without leaning on her.

She reached an intersection of corridors, glanced left, and smiled. "Hello, Draca. This is Lucivar Yaslana. Lucivar, this is Draca, the Keep's Seneschal."

Draca's psychic scent, filled with great age and old, dark power, unnerved him as much as the reptilian cast of her features. He bowed respectfully, but was too nervous to speak a proper greeting.

Her unblinking eyes stared at him. He caught a whiff of emotion that unraveled his nerves even more. For some reason, he amused her.

"Sso, you have finally come," Draca said. When Lucivar didn't answer, she turned to Jaenelle. "He iss sshy?"

"Hardly that," Jaenelle said dryly, looking amused. "But a bit overwhelmed, I think. I gave him the long tour of the Keep."

"And he iss sstill sstanding?" Draca sounded approving.

Lucivar would have appreciated her approval more if his legs weren't shaking so badly.

"We have guestss. Sscholarss. You will wissh to dine privately?"

"Yes, thank you," Jaenelle said.

Draca stepped aside, moving with careful, ancient grace. "I will let you continue your journey." She stared at Lucivar again. "Welcome, Prince Yasslana."

Jaenelle led him down another maze of corridors. "There's someone else I want you to meet. By then, Draca will have a guest room ready for you, one with a whirl-bath. It'll be good for those tight leg muscles." She studied his face. "Did she intimidate you?"

He'd promised honesty. "Yes."

Jaenelle shook her head, baffled. "Everyone says that. I don't understand. She's a marvelous person when you get to know her."

He glanced at the Black Jewel hanging above the V neckline of her slim, black tunic-sweater and decided against trying to explain it.

After another flight of stairs and several twists and turns, Jaenelle finally stopped in front of a door. He sincerely hoped their destination was behind it. A door stood open at the end of the corridor. Voices drifted out of the room, enthusiastic and hot, but not angry. Must be the scholars.

Ignoring the voices, Jaenelle opened the door, and they stepped into part of the Keep's library. A large blackwood table filled one side of the room. At the other end were comfortable chairs and small tables. The back wall was a series of large arches. Beyond them, stacks of reference books stretched out of sight. The arch on the far right was fitted with a wooden door.

"The rest of the library is general reference, Craft, folklore, and history," Jaenelle said. "Things anyone can come and use. These rooms contain the older reference material, the more esoteric Craft texts, and the Blood registers, and can only be used with Geoffrey's permission."

"Geoffrey?"

"Yes?" said a quiet baritone voice.

He was the palest man Lucivar had ever seen. Skin like polished marble combined with black hair, black eyes, black clothes, and deep red lips that looked inviting in an unnerving sort of way. But there was something strange about his psychic scent, something inexplicably different. Almost as if the man weren't . . .

Guardian.

The word slammed into Lucivar, freezing his lungs.

Guardian. One of the living dead.

Jaenelle made the introductions. Then she smiled at Geoffrey. "Why don't you get acquainted? There's something I want to look up."

Geoffrey looked pained. "At least tell me the name of the volume before you leave. The last time I couldn't tell your father where you 'looked something up,' he treated me to some eloquent phrases that would have made me blush if I was still capable of doing it."

Jaenelle patted Geoffrey's shoulder and kissed his cheek. "I'll bring the book out and even mark the page for you."

"So kind of you."

Laughing, Jaenelle disappeared into the stacks.

Geoffrey turned to Lucivar. "So. You've finally come."

Why did they make him feel like he'd kept them waiting?

Geoffrey lifted a decanter. "Would you like some yarbarah? Or some other refreshment?"

With some effort, Lucivar found his voice. "Yarbarah's fine."

"Have you ever drunk yarbarah?" Geoffrey asked drolly.

"It's drunk during some Eyrien ceremonies." Of course, the cup used for those ceremonies held a mouthful of the blood wine. Geoffrey, he noted apprehensively, was filling and warming two wineglasses.

"It's lamb," Geoffrey said, handing a glass to Lucivar and settling into a chair beside the table.

Lucivar gratefully sank into a chair opposite Geoffrey and sipped the yarbarah. There was more blood in the mixture than was used in the ceremonies, the wine more full-bodied.

"How do you like it?" Geoffrey's black eyes sparkled.

"It's . . ." Lucivar struggled to find something mild to say.

"Different," Geoffrey suggested. "It's an acquired taste, and here we drink it for other reasons than ceremonial."

Guardian. Was the blood mixed with the wine ever human? Lucivar took another swallow and decided he wasn't curious enough to ask.

"Why have you never come to the Keep, Lucivar?"

Lucivar set the glass down carefully. "I was under the impression a half-breed bastard wouldn't be welcome here."

"I see," Geoffrey said mildly. "Except for those who care for the Keep, who has the right to decide who is welcome and who is not?"

Lucivar forced himself to meet Geoffrey's eyes. "I'm a half-breed bastard," he said again, as if that should explain everything.

"Half-breed." Geoffrey sounded as if he were turning the word over and over. "The way you say it, it sounds insulting. Perhaps dual bloodline would be a more accurate way to think of it." He leaned back, cradling the wineglass in both hands. "Has it ever occurred to you that, without that other bloodline, you wouldn't be the man you are? That you wouldn't have the intelligence and strength you have?" He waved his glass at Lucivar's Ebon-gray Jewel. "That you never would have worn those? For all that you are Eyrien, Lucivar, you are also your father's son."

Lucivar froze. "You know my father?" he asked in a choked voice.

"We've been friends for many years."

It was there, in front of him. All he had to do was ask.

It took him two tries to get the word out. "Who?"

"The Prince of the Darkness," Geoffrey said gently. "The High Lord of Hell. It's Saetan's bloodline that runs through your veins."

Lucivar closed his eyes. No wonder his paternity had never been registered. Who would have believed a woman who claimed to be seeded by the High Lord? And if anyone *had* believed her, imagine the panic that would have caused. Saetan still walked the Realms. Mother Night!

Had Daemon ever learned who had sired them? He would have been pleased with *this* paternal bloodline.

The thought lanced through him. He locked it away.

At least there was one thing he was still sure of. Maybe. He looked at Geoffrey, afraid of either answer. "I'm still a bastard."

Geoffrey sighed. "I'm reluctant to pull the rest of the ground out from under you but, no, you're not. He formally registered you the day after you were born. Here, at the Keep."

He wasn't a bastard. They . . . "Daemon?" Had he said it out loud?

"Registered as well."

Mother Night. They weren't bastards. He scrambled, clawing for solid ground that kept turning into quicksand under him. "Doesn't make any difference since no one else knew."

"Have you ever been encouraged to play stud, Lucivar?"

Encouraged, pressured, imprisoned, punished, drugged, beaten, forced. They'd been able to use him, but they'd never been able to breed him. He'd never known if the reason was physical or if, somehow, his own rage had kept him sterile. He'd wondered sometimes why they'd wanted his seed so badly. Knowing who had sired him and the potential strength of any offspring he might produce . . . Yes, they'd overlook a great deal to have him sire offspring for specific covens, specific aristo houses with failing bloodlines.

He gulped the yarbarah. Cold, it tasted thick. Shaking and choking, he wondered if his stomach was going to stay down.

A small water glass and another decanter appeared. "Here," Geoffrey said as he quickly filled the glass and shoved it into Lucivar's hand. "I believe whiskey is the proper drink for this kind of shock."

The whiskey cleansed his mouth and burned all the way down. He held out the glass for a refill.

By the time he drained his fourth glass, he was still shaking, but he also felt fuzzy and numb. He liked fuzzy and numb.

"What did you do to Lucivar?" Jaenelle asked, dropping the book on the table. "I thought I was the only one who made him look like that."

"Fuzzy and numb," Lucivar murmured, resting his head against her.

"So I see," Jaenelle replied, petting him.

A soft warmth surrounded him. That felt nice, too.

"Come on, Lucivar," Jaenelle said. "Let's tuck you into a bed."

He didn't want her to think four paltry glasses of whiskey could put him under the table, so he stood up.

The last things he clearly remembered seeing before the room began moving in unpredictable ways were Geoffrey's gentle smile and the understanding in Jaenelle's eyes.

4 / Kaeleer

Jaenelle was gone before he woke the next morning, leaving him to deal with a throbbing head and the emotional upheaval on his own. When he'd found out she'd left him at the Keep, he'd come close to hating her, silently accusing her of being cold, cruel, and unfeeling.

He spent the two days she was gone exploring the Keep and the mountain called Ebon Askavi. He returned for meals because he was expected to, spoke only when required, and retreated to his room each evening. The wolves offered silent company. He petted and brushed them and, finally, asked the question that had bothered him.

Yes, Smoke told him reluctantly, Lucivar had cried. Heart pain. Caught-in-a-trap pain. The Lady had petted and petted, sung and sung.

It had been more than a dream, then.

In one of the dreamscapes Black Widows spun so well, Jaenelle had met the boy he had been and had drawn the poison from the soul wound. He had wept for the boy, for the things he hadn't been allowed to do, for the things he hadn't been allowed to be. But he didn't weep for the man he'd become. "Ah, Lucivar," she'd said regretfully as they'd walked through the dreamscape. "I can heal the scars on your body, but I can't heal the scars of the soul. Not yours, not mine. You have to learn to live with them. You have to choose to live beyond them."

He couldn't remember anything else in the dream. Perhaps he wasn't meant to. But because of it, he didn't weep for the man he'd become.

Lucivar and Jaenelle stood on the wall of one of the Keep's outer courtyards, looking out over the valley.

Jaenelle pointed to the village below them. "Riada is the largest village in Ebon Rih. Agio is at the northern end of the valley. Doun is at the southern end. There are also several landen villages and a number of independent farmsteads, Blood and landen." She brushed stray hairs from her face. "Outside of Doun, there's a large stone house. The property's surrounded by a stone wall. You can't miss it."

He waited. "Is that where we're going?" he finally asked.

"I'm going back to the cabin. You're going to that house."

"Why?"

She kept her eyes fixed on the valley. "Your mother lives there."

A large, three-story, stone house. A low stone wall separating two acres of tended land from the wildflowers and grasses. Vegetable garden, herb garden, flower gardens, rock garden. In one corner, a stand of trees that whispered, "forest."

A solid place that should have welcomed. A place that gave no comfort. Conflicting emotions too familiar, even after all this time.

Sweet Darkness, don't let it be her.

Of course, it was her. And he wondered why she had abandoned him when he was so young he couldn't remember her and then tolerated his visits as a youth without ever once hinting that she was his mother.

He pushed the kitchen door wide open but remained outside. Until he crossed the threshold, she wouldn't realize he was there. How many times had he suggested that she extend her territorial shield a few feet beyond the stone walls she lived in so she'd have some warning of an intruder? One time less than she'd rejected the suggestion.

Her back was to the door as she fussed with something on the counter. He recognized her anyway by that distinctive white streak in her black hair and the stiff, angry way she always moved.

He stepped into the kitchen. "Hello, Luthvian."

She whirled around, a long-bladed kitchen knife in her hand. He knew it wasn't personal. She'd caught the psychic scent of a grown male and had reached automatically for a knife.

She stared at him, her gold eyes growing wider and wider, filming with tears. "Lucivar," she whispered. She took a step toward him. Then another. She made a funny little sound between a laugh and a sob. "She did it. She actually did it." She reached for him.

Lucivar flicked a glance at the knife and didn't move toward her.

Confusion swiftly changed to anger and changed back again. He saw the moment she realized she was pointing a knife at him.

Shaking her head, Luthvian dropped the knife on the kitchen table.

Lucivar stepped farther into the kitchen.

Her tear-bright eyes roamed over him, not like a Healer studying her Sister's Craft but like a woman who truly cared. She pressed one trembling hand against her mouth and reached for him with the other.

Hopeful, heart full, he linked his hand with hers.

And she changed. As she always did, had done since the first time the youth she'd tolerated like a stray-turned-sometimes-pet showed up on her doorstep wearing the traditional dress of an Eyrien warrior, and he'd learned, painfully, that the Black Widow Healer he'd thought of as a friend didn't feel the same way about him after she could no longer call him "boy" and believe it.

Now, as she backed away from him, her eyes filled with wary distrust, he realized for the first time how young she was. Age and maturity became slippery things for the long-lived races. There was rapid growth followed by long plateaus. The white streak in her hair, her Craft skills, her temper and attitude had all helped him believe she was a mature woman granting him her company, a woman centuries older than he. And she was centuries older—and had been just old enough to breed and successfully carry a child to term.

"Why do you despise Eyrien males so much?" he asked quietly.

"My father was one."

Sadly, she didn't have to explain it any better than that.

Then he saw her do what she'd done a hundred times before—subtly shift the way her eyes focused. It was as if she created a sight shield that vanished his wings and left him without the one physical attribute that separated Eyriens from Dhemlans and Hayllians.

Swallowing his anger and a small lump of fear, he pulled out a kitchen chair and straddled it. "Even if I'd lost my wings, I'd still be an Eyrien warrior."

Moving restlessly around the kitchen, Luthvian picked up the knife and shoved it back in the knife rack. "If you'd grown up someplace where males learned how to be decent men instead of brutes—" She wiped her hands on her hips. "But you grew up in the hunting camps like the rest of them. Yes, even without your wings, you'd still be an Eyrien warrior. It's too late for you to be anything else."

He heard the bitterness, the sorrow. He heard the things that were unsaid. "If you felt that strongly, why didn't you do something?" He kept his voice neutral. His heart was being bruised to pulp.

She looked at him, emotions flashing through her eyes. Resignation. Anxiety. Fear. She pulled a chair close to his and sat down. "I had to, Lucivar," she said, pleading. "Giving you to Prythian was a mistake, but at the time I thought it was the only way to hide you from—"

him.

She touched his hand and then pulled away as if burned. "I wanted to keep you safe. She promised you would be safe," she added bitterly. Then her voice turned eager. "But you're here now, and we can be together." She waved her hand, silencing him before he could speak. "Oh, I know about the immigration rule, but I've been here long enough to count as a Kaeleer witch. The work wouldn't be hard, and you'd have plenty of time to be out on the land. I know you like that." She smiled too brightly. "You wouldn't even have to live in the house. We could build a small cabin nearby so that you would have privacy."

Privacy for what? he wondered coldly as the inside kitchen door opened. He felt walls and chains closing in on him.

"What do you want, Roxie?" Luthvian snapped.

Roxie stared at him, her lips turning up in a pouty smile. "Who are you?" she asked, eyeing him hungrily.

"None of your business," Luthvian said tightly. "Get back to your lessons. *Now.*"

Roxie smiled at him, her finger tracing the V neckline of her dress. It made his blood burn, but not the way she imagined.

Lucivar's hands curled into fists. He'd smashed that look off a lot of faces over the centuries. There was battle-fire in the voice he kept low and controlled. "Get the slut out of here before I break her neck."

Roxie's eyes widened in shock.

Luthvian surged out of her chair, tossed Roxie out of the kitchen, and slammed the door.

Fine tremors ran through him. "Well, now I know why I need privacy. It would be an extra selling point for your school, wouldn't it? Your students would have the use of a strong Warlord Prince. You could assure fretful parents that their daughters would have a safe Virgin Night. I wouldn't dare provide anything else since the witch I serve has to be served *to her satisfaction.*"

"It wouldn't be like that," Luthvian insisted, gripping the back of a chair. "You'd get something out of it, too. Hell's fire, Lucivar, you're a Warlord Prince. You need sexual relief on a regular basis just to keep your temper in check."

"I've never needed it before," he snarled, "and I don't need it now. I can keep my temper in check just fine—when I choose to."

"Then you don't choose to very often!"

"No, I don't. Especially when I'm being forced into a bed."

Luthvian smashed the chair against the table. She bared her teeth. "Forced to. Oh, yes, it's such an onerous task to give a little pleasure, isn't it? Forced to! You sound like—"

your father.

He'd tolerated her temper before, withstood her tantrums before. He'd tried to be understanding. He was trying hard now. What he couldn't understand was why a man like the High Lord had ever wanted to mount and breed such a troubled young woman.

"Tell me about my father, Luthvian."

Desperation and a keening rage flooded the kitchen. "It's past. It's done. He's not part of our lives."

"Tell me."

"He didn't want us! *He didn't love us!* He threatened to slit your throat in the cradle if I didn't do what he wanted." The length of the table stood between them. She stood there, shaking, hugging herself.

So young. So troubled. And he couldn't help her. They would destroy each other inside of a week if he tried to stay here with her.

She gave him a wavering smile. "We can be together. You can stay—"

"I'm already in service." He hadn't meant for it to come out so harshly, but it was kinder than saying he would never serve her.

Vulnerability crystallized into rejection, rejection froze into rage. "Jaenelle," Luthvian said, her voice dangerously empty. "She has a gift for wrapping males around her little finger." She braced her hands on the table. "You want to know about your father? Go ask precious Jaenelle. She knows him better than I ever did."

Lucivar snapped to his feet, knocking the chair over. "No."

Luthvian smiled with pleased malice. "Be careful how you play with your sire's toys, little Prince. He just might snip your balls off. Not that it would matter."

Never taking his eyes off her, Lucivar righted the chair and backed away to the outer kitchen door. Years of training kept him surefooted as he crossed the threshold. One more step. Two.

The door slammed in his face.

A moment later, he heard dishes smashing on the floor.

She knows him better than I ever did.

It was late afternoon by the time he reached the cabin. He was dirty, hungry, and shaking from physical and emotional fatigue.

He approached slowly but couldn't bring himself to step onto the porch where Jaenelle sat reading.

She closed the book and looked at him.

Wise eyes. Ancient eyes. Haunting and haunted eyes.

He forced the words out. "I want to meet my father. Now."

She studied him. When she finally answered, her gentle compassion inflicted pain he had no defense against. "Are you sure, Lucivar?"

No, he wasn't sure! "Yes, I'm sure."

Jaenelle remained seated. "Then there's something you need to understand before we go."

He heard the warning underneath the gentleness and compassion.

"Lucivar, your father is also my adopted father."

Frozen, he stared at her, finally understanding. He could accept them both or walk away from both, but he wouldn't be allowed to serve her and battle with a man who already had a claim on her love.

She'd been right when she'd said there were reasons he might not be able or willing to serve her. The Keep he could handle. He could deal with Luthvian as well. But the High Lord?

There was only one way to find out.

"Let's go," he said.

5 / Kaeleer

Jaenelle stepped off the landing web. "This is the family seat."

Lucivar reluctantly stepped off the web. A few months ago, he'd walked through the ruins of SaDiablo Hall in Terreille. Ruins didn't prepare a man for this dark-gray mountain of a building. Hell's fire, an entire court could live in the place and not get in each other's way.

Then the significance of her living at the Hall finally hit him, and he turned and stared at her as if he'd never seen her before.

All of those amusing stories she had told him about her loving, beleaguered papa—she had been talking about Saetan. The Prince of the Darkness. The High Lord of Hell. The man who had built the cabin for her, who had helped her rebuild her life. He couldn't reconcile the conflicting images of the man any better than he could reconcile the Hall with the manor house he'd imagined.

And he would never reconcile anything by just standing there.

"Come on, Cat. Let's knock on the door."

The door opened before they reached the top step. The large man standing in the doorway had the stoic, unflappable expression of an upper servant, but he also wore a Red Jewel.

"Hello, Beale," Jaenelle said as she breezed through the door.

Beale's lips turned up in the tiniest hint of a smile. "Lady."

The smile disappeared when Lucivar walked in. "Prince," Beale said, bowing the exact, polite distance.

The lazy, arrogant smile came automatically. "Lord Beale." He put enough bite in his voice to warn the other man not to tangle with him, but not enough to issue a challenge. He'd never challenged a servant in his life. On the other hand, he'd never met a Red-Jeweled Warlord who was a butler by profession.

Ignoring the subtle, stiff-legged displays of dominance, Jaenelle called in the luggage and dumped it on the floor. "Beale? Would you ask Helene to prepare a suite in the family wing for Prince Yaslana?"

"It would be my pleasure, Lady."

Jaenelle pointed toward the back of the great hall. "Papa?"

"In his study."

Lucivar followed Jaenelle to the last right-hand door, trying, unsuccessfully, to think of another reason besides amusement for the sudden gleam in Beale's eyes.

Jaenelle tapped on the door and went in before anyone answered. Lucivar followed close on her heels and then stumbled as the man standing in front of the blackwood desk turned around.

Daemon.

While they stared at each other, both too startled to respond, Lucivar took in the details that denied the gut reaction.

The dark psychic scent was similar, yet subtly different. The man before him was an inch or two shorter than Daemon and more slender in build, but moved with the same feline grace. The thick black hair was silvered at the temples. His face—lined by laughter as well as by the weight of burdens—belonged to a man at the end of his prime or a little beyond. But that face. Masculine. Handsome. The warmer, rougher model for Daemon's cold, polished beauty. And the final touch—the long, black-tinted nails and the Black-Jeweled ring.

Saetan crossed his arms, leaned back against the desk, and said mildly, "Witch-child, I'm going to throttle you."

Instinctively, Lucivar bared his teeth and stepped forward to protect his Queen.

Jaenelle's aggrieved, adolescent wail stopped him cold.

"That's the sixth time in two weeks and I've barely been home!"

Anger flooded Lucivar. How dare the High Lord threaten her!

Except his darling Cat didn't seem the least bit intimidated and Saetan seemed to be fighting hard to keep a straight face.

"Sixth time?" Saetan said, his deep voice still mild but laced with an undercurrent of amusement.

"Twice from Prothvar, twice from Uncle Andulvar—"

All the blood drained out of Lucivar's head. *Uncle Andulvar?*

"—once from Mephis, and now you."

Saetan's lips twitched. "Prothvar always wants to throttle you so that's no surprise, and you do have a knack for provoking Andulvar, but what did you do to annoy Mephis?"

Jaenelle stuffed her hands in her trouser pockets. "I don't know," she grumped. "He said he couldn't discuss it while I was in the room."

Saetan's rich, warm laugh filled the room. When his laughter and Jaenelle's temper were both at a simmer, he looked knowingly at Lucivar. "And I suppose Lucivar has never threatened to throttle you, so he wouldn't understand the impulse to express the desire even when there was no intention of ever carrying it out."

"Oh, no," Jaenelle replied. "He just threatens to wallop me."

Saetan stiffened. "I beg your pardon?" he asked softly, coldly.

Lucivar shifted back into a fighting stance.

Startled, Jaenelle looked at both of them. "You're going to argue about the *word* when you mean the same thing?"

"Stay out of this, Cat," Lucivar snarled, watching his adversary.

Snarling back, she threw a punch at him with enough temper behind it that it could have broken his jaw if he hadn't dodged it.

The tussle that followed was just turning into fun when Saetan roared, "Enough!" He glared at them until they separated, then he rubbed his temples and growled, "How in the name of Hell did the two of you manage to live together and survive?"

Eyeing Jaenelle warily, Lucivar grinned. "She's harder to pin now."

"Don't rub it in," Jaenelle muttered.

Saetan sighed. "You might have warned me, witch-child."

Jaenelle laced her fingers together. "Well, there really wasn't any way for Lucivar to be prepared, so I figured if you both were unprepared, you'd start out on even ground."

They stared at her.

She gave them her best unsure-but-game smile.

"Witch-child, go terrify someone else for a while."

After Jaenelle slipped out of the room, they studied one another.

"You look a lot better than the last time I saw you," Saetan said, breaking the silence, "but you still look ready to keel over." He pushed away from the desk. "Care for some brandy?"

Turning toward the less formal side of the room, Lucivar settled into a chair designed to accommodate Eyrien wings and accepted the glass of brandy. "And when was the last time you saw me?"

Saetan sat on the couch and crossed his legs. He toyed with the brandy glass. "Shortly after Prothvar brought you to the cabin. If he hadn't been standing guard duty at the Sleeping Dragons, if he hadn't managed to reach you before—" He stroked the rim of the glass with a fingertip. "I don't think you realize how severe the injuries were. The internal damage, the broken bones . . . your wings."

Lucivar sipped his brandy. No, he hadn't realized. He'd known it was bad, but once he was in the Khaldharon Run, he'd stopped caring what happened physically. If what Saetan said was true . . .

"So you let a seventeen-year-old Healer take it on alone," he said, struggling to keep a tight rein on his rising anger. "You let her do that much healing, knowing what it would do to her, and left her without so much as a helper or servant to look after *her*."

Saetan's eyes filled with anger that was just as tightly leashed. "*I* was there to take care of her. I was there all the time she put you back together. I was there to coax her to eat when she could. I was there to watch the web during the resting times so she could get a little sleep. And when you finally started rising from the healing sleep, I held her and fed her spoonfuls of honeyed tea while she wept from exhaustion and pain because her throat was so raw from singing the healing web. I left the day before you woke because you had enough to deal with without having to come to terms with me. How dare you assume—" Saetan clamped his teeth together.

Dangerous, shaky ground. There might be a great many things he could no longer afford to assume.

Lucivar refilled his glass. "Since there was so much damage, wouldn't it have been better to split the healing between two Healers?" He kept his voice carefully neutral. "Luthvian's a temperamental bitch most of the time, but she's a good Healer."

Saetan hesitated. "She offered. I wouldn't let her because your wings were involved."

"She would have removed them." A small lump of fear settled in Lucivar's stomach.

"Jaenelle was sure she could rebuild them, but it would require a systemic healing—one Healer singing the web because everything had to be pulled into it. There could be no diversions, no hesitations, no lack of commitment to the whole. Doing it Luthvian's way, the two of them could have healed everything but your wings. Jaenelle's way was all or nothing—either you came out of it whole or you didn't survive."

Lucivar could see them—two strong-willed women standing on either side of a bed that held his mangled body. "You decided."

Saetan drained his glass and refilled it. "I decided."

"Why? You threatened to slit my throat in the cradle. Why fight for me now?"

"Because you're my son. But I would have slit your throat." Saetan's voice was strained. "May the Darkness help me, if she'd cut off your wings, I would have."

Cut off your wings. Lucivar felt sick. "Why did you breed her?"

Saetan set the glass down and raked his fingers through his hair. "I didn't mean to. When I agreed to see her through her Virgin Night, I honestly didn't think I was still fertile, and she swore that she'd been drinking the brew to prevent pregnancy, swore it wasn't her fertile time. And she never told me she was Eyrien." He looked up, his eyes filled with pain. "I didn't know. Lucivar, I swear by all I am, until I saw the wings, I didn't know. But you're Eyrien in your soul. Altering your physical appearance would have changed nothing."

Lucivar drained his glass and wondered if he dared ask. This meeting was bruising Saetan as badly as it was bruising him—if not worse. But he had come here to ask so that he could make an honest decision. "Couldn't you have been there sometimes? Even in secret?"

"If you have some objection to my not being part of your life, take it up with your mother. That was her choice, not mine." Saetan closed his eyes. His fingers tightened around his glass. "For reasons I've never been able to explain rationally to myself, I agreed to try to breed with a Black Widow in order to bring a strong, dark bloodline back into the long-lived races. Dorothea was the Hayllian Hourglass's choice but not mine." He hesitated. "Have you ever met Tersa?"

"Yes."

"An extraordinarily gifted witch. Dorothea would never have become the force she is in Terreille if Tersa had survived her Virgin Night. Tersa was my choice. And Tersa became pregnant."

With Daemon. Had Daemon ever known, ever guessed?

"A couple of weeks later, she asked me to see a friend through her Virgin Night, a young Black Widow with strong potential who, if I refused, would end up broken and shattered. I was still capable of performing the service, and I wouldn't have refused Tersa anything within reason. *Everyone* was willing to accommodate Tersa at that point. No one wanted her to become distressed enough to miscarry since there would be no second chances.

"A few weeks after I saw Luthvian through her Virgin Night, she told me she was pregnant with my child. There was an empty house on the estate, about a mile from the Hall. I insisted she and Tersa live there instead of with Dorothea's court. Tersa wasn't much older than Luthvian, but she understood a great deal more, especially about Guardians. She was content with the companionship I offered. Luthvian was more high-strung and had discovered the pleasure of the bed. She craved sex. For a while, I could still provide the kind of intimacy she wanted. By the time I couldn't, she had lost interest. But after she healed from the birthing, the hunger returned. By then, I could satisfy her in other ways but not the way she craved.

"Between the fights about raising you in Dhemlan, as she wanted, or raising you in Askavi, where I believed you needed to be, and my sexual inability, our relationship became strained to the point that, when she was spoon-fed half-truths about Guardians, she chose to believe them.

"Dorothea timed her schemes well. With Prythian's help, I lost both of you. Within a day, I lost both of you."

Not Luthvian. Daemon.

A sigh shuddered out of Saetan. "Lucivar, for what it's worth, I've never regretted your existence. I've regretted the pain you've endured, but not you. And I'm very glad you survived."

Unable to think of anything to say, Lucivar nodded.

Saetan hesitated. "Would you tell me something, if you can?"

Lucivar knew what Saetan was going to ask. He wasn't sure what he thought about the man who had sired him, but for this moment at least, he could look beyond the titles and the power and see a man asking about one of his children.

He closed his eyes, and said, "He's in the Twisted Kingdom."

Saetan lay on the couch in his study, desperately glad to be alone.

Everything has a price.

He just hadn't expected the price to be so high.

Regrets were useless. And guilt was useless. A Warlord Prince's first duty was to his Queen. But Daemon . . .

Shards of memories floated through him, pricking his heart.

Tersa ripely pregnant, holding his hand against her belly.

Luthvian's constant circle of anger and sexual hunger.

Daemon sitting in his lap while he read a bedtime story.

Lucivar fluttering around the room, laughing gleefully while just staying out of his reach.

Jaenelle turning his study upside down the first time he tried to show her how to use Craft to retrieve her shoes.

Tersa's madness. Luthvian's fury.

Lucivar lying on the bed in the cabin, his body torn apart.

Daemon, lying on Cassandra's Altar, his mind so terribly fragile.

Jaenelle rising out of the abyss after two heartbreaking years.

Fragments. Like Daemon's mind.

Which explained why, during the careful searches he had made over the past two years, he hadn't been able to find this son who was like a mirror. He'd been looking in the wrong place.

A regret slipped in, as useless as any other.

He might be able to find Daemon, but the one person who could have brought Daemon out of the Twisted Kingdom without question was Jaenelle. And Jaenelle was the one person who couldn't know what he intended to do.

CHAPTER ELEVEN

1 / Kaeleer

Waiting for dinner, Saetan's stomach tightened another notch.

Jaenelle had been home for a week, helping Lucivar adjust to the family—and helping the family adjust to Lucivar—when a pointed letter from the Dark Council arrived, reminding her that she had not finished her visit to Little Terreille.

He still didn't understand Lucivar's cryptic remark, "Knees or bones, Cat," but Jaenelle had stomped out of the Hall spitting Eyrien curses, and Lucivar had seemed grimly pleased.

That had been three days ago.

She had returned abruptly that afternoon, snarled at Beale, "Tell Lucivar I used my knee," and had locked herself in her room.

Disturbed, Beale had informed him of her return and the comment meant for Lucivar, and had added that the Lady seemed unwell.

Jaenelle always seemed unwell after a visit to Little Terreille. He'd never been able to pry the reason for that out of her. Nothing she said about the activities she'd participated in explained the strained, haunted look in her eyes, the weight loss, the restless nights afterward, or the inability to eat.

The only person besides Beale who saw Jaenelle after she returned was Karla. And Karla, teary-eyed and distressed, had picked a fight with the one person she could count on to give her a battle—Lucivar.

After enduring a vicious harangue about males, Lucivar had hauled her out to the lawn, handed her one of the Eyrien sticks, and let her try to whack him. He'd pushed and taunted her until her muscles and emotions finally gave out. He'd offered no explanation, and the fury in his eyes had warned all of them not to ask.

The dining room door opened. Andulvar, Prothvar, and Mephis joined him, the concern in their eyes needing no words.

Karla arrived a minute later, moving stiffly. Lucivar came in behind her, threw an arm around her shoulders—which, amazingly, produced no temperamental explosion—and helped her into a chair.

Beale appeared, looking as strained as Saetan felt, and said, "The Lady says she will be unable to join you for dinner."

Lucivar pulled out the chair on Saetan's right. "Tell the Lady she's joining us for dinner. She can come down on her own two feet or over my shoulder. Her choice."

Beale's eyes widened.

A low growl of displeasure came, unexpectedly, from Mephis.

The room smelled dangerous.

Wanting to avoid the confrontation building up between the men in the family, Saetan nodded to Beale, silently backing Lucivar.

Beale hastily retreated.

Lucivar just leaned against the chair and waited.

Jaenelle appeared a few minutes later, her face drained of color except for the dark smudges underneath her eyes.

Smiling that lazy, arrogant smile, Lucivar pulled out the chair beside his and waited.

Jaenelle swallowed hard. "I—I'm sorry. I can't."

She moved fast. Lucivar moved faster.

In stunned silence, they watched him drag her to her place at the table and dump her in the chair. She immediately shot upward, smacking into the fist he calmly held above her head. Dazed, she didn't protest when he pushed her chair up to the table and sat down beside her.

Saetan sat down, torn between his concern for Jaenelle and his desire to treat Lucivar to the same kind of affection.

Andulvar, Prothvar, and Mephis took their seats, bristling. If Lucivar noticed the anger being directed at him, he ignored it.

The arrogance of not acknowledging the displeasure of males of equal or darker rank galled Saetan, but he held his tongue and his temper. There would be time to unleash both later.

"You're going to eat," Lucivar said calmly.

Jaenelle stared at the place setting in front of her. "I can't."

"Cat, if we have to dump the soup on the floor so that you can puke into the tureen, then that's what we'll do. But you're going to eat."

Jaenelle snarled at him.

A pale, shaky footman brought the soup.

Lucivar put a ladle full into her bowl and filled his own halfway. He picked up his spoon and waited.

Her snarl grew louder as she reluctantly picked up her spoon.

After a narrow-eyed, considering look at Lucivar, Karla asked a question about a Craft lesson she was working on.

Mephis responded, and the discussion covered the first course.

Jaenelle ate one spoonful of soup.

Andulvar shifted in his seat, rustling his wings.

Saetan flicked a glance at Andulvar, warning him to keep still. He'd caught the scent of feminine anger. He'd caught Lucivar's tightly focused awareness of Jaenelle and her rising temper—a temper Lucivar was able to provoke with frightening ease.

With each dish offered in the second course, Lucivar selected food for her, pricked at her, scraped away her self-control.

"Liver?" Lucivar asked.

"Only if it's yours," she snapped, her eyes glittering queerly.

Lucivar smiled slightly.

By the end of the second course, Jaenelle was an explosion waiting for a spark, and Saetan couldn't understand the point of taunting her.

Until the meat course.

Lucivar slipped a small piece of prime rib onto her plate and then stacked two large pieces on his own.

Jaenelle stared at the tender, pink-centered meat for a long moment. Then she picked up her knife and fork and began to eat with single-minded intensity. When the meat was gone, she turned to her right and looked at Karla's plate.

Karla's face paled to a ghastly white.

When Jaenelle turned to her left and Saetan got a good look at her eyes, he realized that Lucivar had turned the meal into a violent, brilliantly choreographed dance designed to bring the predatory side of Witch to the surface.

Finally her attention fixed on Lucivar's plate. Snarling softly, she licked her lips and raised her fork.

Keeping his movements slow and deliberate, Lucivar transferred the second piece of prime rib from his plate to hers.

She stabbed the meat with her fork and bared her teeth at him.

Lucivar withdrew his utensils and hands and calmly resumed his meal while Jaenelle devoured the meat.

By the time they reached the fruit and cheese course, Jaenelle's attention was entirely focused on Lucivar and his offerings of food. When he held up the last grape, she stared at it for a moment, then wrinkled her nose and sat back with a contented sigh.

And the woman-child Saetan knew and loved returned.

For the first time since the meal began, Lucivar looked at the other men sitting at the table, and Saetan felt keen sympathy for this son with the battle-weary look in his golden eyes.

After the coffee was served, Lucivar took a deep breath and turned to Jaenelle. "By the way, you owe me a piece of jewelry."

"What jewelry?" Jaenelle asked, baffled.

"Kaeleer's equivalent to the Ring of Obedience."

She choked on her coffee.

Lucivar thumped her back until she gave him a teary-eyed glare. He smiled at her. "Will you tell them, or shall I?"

Jaenelle looked at the men who made up her family. She hunched her shoulders, and said in a small voice, "In order to fill the immigration requirement, Lucivar's going to serve me for the next five years."

This time Saetan choked.

"And?" Lucivar prodded.

"I'll come up with something," Jaenelle said testily. "Although why you want to wear one of those Rings is beyond me."

"I did a little checking while you were gone. Males have to wear a Restraining Ring as part of the immigration requirements."

Jaenelle let out an exasperated snort. "Lucivar, who's going to be foolish enough to ask you to prove you're wearing one?"

"That Ring is physical proof that I serve you, and I want it."

Jaenelle gave Saetan one fleeting, pleading look—which he ignored. "All right. I'll come up with something," she growled, pushing her chair back. "Karla and I are going to take a walk."

Karla, gathering her wits faster than the men could, moaned to her feet and shuffled after Jaenelle.

Andulvar, Prothvar, and Mephis swiftly found excuses to leave.

After the brandy and yarbarah were brought to the table, Saetan dismissed the footmen, grimly amused by their strained eagerness to return to the servants' hall. His staff didn't gossip to outsiders—Beale and Helene saw to that—but only a fool would think they didn't talk among themselves. Lucivar's arrival had caused quite a stir. Lucivar in service to their Lady . . .

If tonight was a sample of what to expect, it was going to be an interesting—and long—five years.

"You play an intriguing game," Saetan said quietly as he warmed a glass of yarbarah. "And a dangerous one."

Lucivar shrugged. "Not so dangerous, as long as I don't push her past surface temper."

Saetan studied Lucivar's carefully neutral expression. "But do you understand who, and what, lies beneath that surface temper?"

Lucivar smiled tiredly. "I know who she is." He sipped his brandy. "You don't approve of my serving her, do you?"

Saetan rolled his glass between his hands. "You've been able to do more in three months to improve her physical and emotional health than I've been able to do in two years. That galls a little."

"You laid a stronger foundation than you realize." Lucivar grinned. "Besides, a father's supposed to be strong, supportive, and protective. Older brothers, on the other hand, are naturally a pain in the ass and are inclined to be overprotective bullies."

Saetan smiled. "You're an overprotective bully?"

"So I'm told frequently and with great vigor."

Saetan's smiled faded. "Be careful, Lucivar. She has some deep emotional scars you're not aware of."

"I know about the rape—and about Briarwood. When she's pushed too hard, she talks in her sleep." Lucivar refilled his glass and met Saetan's cool stare. "I slept with her. I didn't mount her."

Slept with her. Saetan kept a tight rein on his temper while he sifted through the implications of that statement and weighed it against the amount of physical contact Jaenelle allowed Lucivar without retreating into that chilling emotional blankness that always scared the rest of them. "She didn't object?" he asked carefully.

Lucivar snorted. "Of course she objected. What woman wouldn't after being hurt that badly? But she objected more to having her patient sleeping in front of the hearth, and I objected just as strongly to having the Healer who saved my life sleeping in front of the hearth. So we reached an agreement. I didn't complain about the way she hogged the pillows, tangled the covers, sprawled over more than her share of the bed, made those cute little noises that we don't call snoring no matter what it sounds like, and growled at everything and everyone until she had her first cup of coffee. And she didn't complain about the way I hogged the pillows, tangled the covers, sprawled over more than my share of the bed, made funny noises that woke her up and stopped the minute she was awake, and tended to be overly cheerful in the morning. And we both agreed that neither of us wanted the other for sex."

Which, for Jaenelle, would have made the difference.

"Do you pay much attention to who immigrates to Kaeleer?" Lucivar asked suddenly.

"Not much," Saetan replied cautiously.

Lucivar studied his brandy. "You wouldn't know if a Hayllian named Greer came in, would you?"

The question chilled him. "Greer is dead."

Lucivar fixed his eyes on the dining room wall. "Being the High Lord of Hell, you could arrange a meeting, couldn't you?"

Why was Lucivar straining to breathe evenly?

"Greer is *dead,* not just a citizen of the Dark Realm."

Lucivar's jaw tightened. "Damn."

Saetan clenched his teeth. Sweet Darkness, how was Lucivar involved with Greer? "Why are you so interested in him?"

Lucivar's hands curled into tight fists. "He was the bastard who raped Jaenelle."

Saetan's temper exploded. The dining room windows shattered. Zigzag cracks raced across the ceiling. Swearing viciously, he rechanneled the power to strike the drive out front, turning the gravel into powder.

Greer. Another link between Hekatah and Dorothea.

Saetan sank his nails into the table, tearing through the wood again and again, an unsatisfying exercise since he wanted *flesh* beneath his nails.

The training was too deeply ingrained in him. Damn the Darkness, it was too deeply ingrained. He couldn't kill a witch in cold blood. And if he was going to break the code of honor he'd lived by all his life, he should have done it more than five years ago when it might have made a difference, might have saved Jaenelle. Not now, when she already bore the scars. Not now, when it wouldn't change anything.

Hands clamped on his wrists. Tightened. Tightened some more.

"High Lord."

He should have torn that bastard apart the first time Greer asked about Jaenelle. Should have shredded his mind. What was *wrong* with him? Had he become too tame, too docile? What was he doing, trying to appease those puny fools in the Dark Council when they were doing something that hurt his daughter, his Queen?

"High Lord."

And who was this fool who dared lay hands on the Prince of the Darkness, the High Lord of Hell? No more. *No more.*

"*Father.*"

Saetan gulped air, fought to clear his head. Lucivar. Lucivar was pinning his arms to the table.

Someone pounded on the door. "Saetan! Lucivar!"

Jaenelle. Sweet Darkness, not Jaenelle. He couldn't see her now.

"SAETAN!"

"Please," he whispered. "Don't let her—"

The door shattered.

"Get out, Cat," Lucivar snapped.

"What—"

"OUT!"

Andulvar's voice. "Go upstairs, waif. We'll take care of this."

Voices arguing, fading.

"Yarbarah?" Lucivar asked after a long, tense silence.

Saetan shuddered, shook his head. Until he was settled, if he tasted blood, he would want it hot from the vein. "Brandy."

Lucivar pressed a glass into his hand.

Saetan gulped the brandy. "You should have gotten out of here."

Lucivar raised his glass with an unsteady hand and offered a wobbly grin. "I've had some experience tangling with the Black. All in all, you're not too bad. Daemon always scared the shit out of me when he turned savage." He drained his glass and refilled both of them. "I hope you didn't redecorate in here recently. You're going to have to do it again, but it doesn't look like the room's going to fall in on us."

"The girls didn't like the wallpaper anyway." Ten good reasons to hold his temper. Ten good reasons to unleash it. And always, always, for Blood males like him, the fine line he had to walk to hold on to the balance between two conflicting instincts. "The Harpies executed Greer," he said abruptly. "They have a distinct sensibility when it comes to that sort of thing."

Lucivar nodded.

Steady. He would need to be steady for the days ahead. "Lucivar, see if you can persuade Jaenelle to show you Sceval. You should meet Kaetien and the other unicorns."

Lucivar regarded him steadily. "Why?"

"I have some business I want to take care of. I'll need to stay at the Keep in Terreille for a few days, and I'd prefer it if Jaenelle wasn't around to ask questions or wonder where I was."

Lucivar considered this for a minute. "Do you think you can do it?"

Saetan sighed wearily. "I won't know until I try."

2 / Terreille

Saetan carefully secured his Black-Jeweled ring to the center of the large tangled web. It had taken two days of searching through Geoffrey's Hourglass archives to find the answer. It had taken two more to construct the web. He'd given himself two nerve-fraying days more to rest and slowly gather his strength.

Draca had said nothing when he'd asked for a guest room and workroom at the Terreille Keep, but the workroom had been supplied with a frame large enough to hold the tangled web. Geoffrey had said nothing about the requested books, but he had added a couple of books Saetan wouldn't have thought of.

Saetan took a deep breath. It was time.

Normally a Black Widow needed physical contact to guide someone out of the Twisted Kingdom. But sometimes blood-ties could cross boundaries otherwise impossible to cross, and no one had a stronger tie to Daemon than he did. The tie of father to son; more, the bond of that night at Cassandra's Altar.

And the Blood shall sing to the Blood.

Pricking his finger, Saetan placed a drop of blood on the four anchor threads that held the web to its wooden frame. The blood flowed down the top threads, and up the bottom threads. Just as the drops reached his ring, Saetan lightly touched the Black Jewel, smearing it with blood.

The web glowed. Saetan sang the spell that opened the dreamscape that would lead him to the one he sought.

A tortured landscape, full of blood and shattered crystal chalices.

Taking another deep breath, Saetan focused his eyes on the Black-Jeweled ring and began the inward journey into madness.

Daemon.

He raised his head.

The words circled, waiting for him. The edges of the tiny island crumbled a little more.

Daemon.

He knew that voice. *You are my instrument.*

Daemon!

He looked up. Flattened himself against the pulpy ground.

A hand hovered over him, reached for him. A light-brown hand with long, black-tinted nails. A wrist appeared. Part of a forearm. Straining to reach him.

He knew that voice. He knew that hand. He hated them.

Daemon, reach for me. I can show you the road back.

Words lie. Blood doesn't.

The hand shook with the effort to reach him.

Daemon, let me help you. Please.

Inches separated them. All he had to do was raise his hand and he could leave this island.

His fingers twitched.

Daemon, trust me. I can help you.

Blood. So much blood. A sea of it. He would drown in it. Because he'd trusted that voice once and he'd done something . . . he'd done . . .

LIAR! he screamed. *I'll never trust you!*

Daemon. An anguished plea.

NEVER!

The hand began to fade.

Fear swamped him. He didn't want to be alone in this sea of blood with the words circling, waiting to slice into him again and again. He wanted to grab the hand and hold tight, wanted whatever lies might ease this pain for a little while.

But he owed someone this pain because he'd done something . . .

Butchering whore.

That voice, that hand had tricked him into hurting someone. But, sweet Darkness, how he wanted to trust, wanted to hold on.

Daemon. A whisper of sound.

The hand faded, withdrew.

He waited.

The words circled and circled. The island crumbled a little more.

He waited. The hand didn't return.

He pressed himself against the pulpy ground and wept in relief.

Saetan sank to his knees. The threads of the tangled web were blackened, crumbling. He caught his ring as it fell from the center of the web and slipped it on his finger.

So close. A hand span at most. A moment of trust. That's all it would have taken to begin the journey out of that pain and madness.

That's all it would have taken.

Stretching out on the cold stone floor, Saetan pillowed his head on his arms and wept bitterly.

3 / Kaeleer

Saetan looked at Lucivar and shook his head.

"Well," Lucivar said, his voice tight, "you tried." After a minute he added, "You're wanted in the kitchen."

"In the kitchen? Why?" Saetan asked as Lucivar herded him toward Mrs. Beale's undisputed territory.

Lucivar smiled and dropped a friendly hand on Saetan's shoulder. The gesture filled him with foreboding. "How was your trip?"

"Traveling with Cat is an experience."

"Do I really want to know about this?"

"No," Lucivar said cheerfully, "but you're going to anyway."

Jaenelle sat cross-legged on the kitchen floor. A brown-and-white

Sceltie puppy tumbled about in front of her. Her lap was full of a large, white . . . kitten?

"Hello, Papa," Jaenelle said meekly.

Papa High Lord, said the puppy. When Saetan didn't answer, the puppy looked at Jaenelle. *Papa High Lord?*

"Kindred." Saetan cleared his throat. His voice went back to a deep baritone. "The Scelties are kindred?"

"Not all of them," Jaenelle said defensively.

"About the same ratio of Blood to landen as other species," Lucivar said, grinning. "You're taking this a lot better than Khardeen did. He sat down in the middle of the road and became hysterical. We had to drag him over to the side before he got run over by a cart."

A muffled chuckle-snort came from the direction of the worktable where Mrs. Beale was busily chopping up some meat.

"And with that one little explanation, the humans suddenly realized why some of the Scelties matured so late and had a longer life span," Lucivar added with annoying cheerfulness. "After Ladvarian made it clear that Cat belonged to him—"

Mine! said the puppy.

The kitten lifted a large, white, furry paw and squashed the puppy.

Ours! said the puppy, wriggling out from beneath the paw.

"—we fixed a strong sedative for the Warlord who had just discovered that his bitch was also a Priestess."

"Mother Night." Saetan switched to a Red spear thread. *Why does a male Sceltie have a name with an Eyrien feminine ending?*

That's what he said his name is. Who am I to argue? "After that," Lucivar continued, "Khary dragged us to Tuathal to see Lady Duana, who had a few pointed things to say about not being told there were kindred in her Territory."

Yes, he was sure the Queen of Scelt would have had quite a few things to say—and would have a few more to say to *him*.

Jaenelle hid her face in the kitten's fur.

Lucivar, damn his soul, seemed to be enjoying this now that he could dump it into someone else's lap.

Since Jaenelle wasn't jumping into the conversation, Lucivar continued the tale. "In the invigorating discussion that followed, it came out that there are also two breeds of horses who are kindred."

Saetan swayed. Lucivar propped him up.

The Scelts were noted horsemen. Khary's and Morghann's families especially were passionate about horses.

"Imagine how surprised people were when they discovered their horses could talk back to them," Lucivar said.

Saetan knelt beside Jaenelle. At least if he fainted now he wouldn't fall so far. "And our feline Brother?"

Jaenelle's fingers tightened in the kitten's fur. Her eyes held a dark, dangerous look. "Kaelas is Arcerian. He's an orphan. His mother was killed by hunters."

Kaelas. In the Old Tongue, the word meant "white death." It usually referred to a kind of snowstorm that came with little warning—swift, violent, and deadly.

Saetan switched to a spear thread again. *I suppose no one named him, either.*

Nope, Lucivar replied.

Saetan didn't like the sober caution in Lucivar's tone. He reached out to pet the kitten.

Kaelas took a swipe at him.

"Hey!" Jaenelle said sharply. "Don't swat the High Lord."

Kaelas snarled, displaying an impressive set of baby teeth. The claws weren't anything to shrug off either.

"Here you are, sweeties," Mrs. Beale cooed, setting two bowls on the kitchen floor. "Some meat and warm milk."

Saetan eyed his cook. This was the same woman who always cornered him whenever the wolf pups chased the bunnies through her garden? Then he looked at the bowl of chopped meat and frowned. "Isn't that the cold roast you were going to serve for lunch?"

Mrs. Beale glared at him. Lucivar prudently stepped behind him.

Abandoning the kitchen to Mrs. Beale and her charges, Saetan headed for his suite. Lucivar went with him.

"The puppy's cute," Saetan said. If that was the best he could do, he definitely needed to rest.

"Don't let puppy cute fool you," Lucivar said quietly. "He's a Warlord, and there's a shrewd intelligence inside that furry little head. Combine that with a large Warlord Prince predator and you've got a partnership that needs to be handled with care."

Saetan stopped at the door of his suite. "Lucivar, just how big do Arcerian cats get?"

Lucivar grinned. "Let's just say you ought to start putting strengthening spells on the furniture now."

"Mother Night," Saetan muttered, stumbling to his bed. The paperwork on his desk could wait. He didn't need to look for trouble.

He'd just started to doze off when he felt eyes staring at him. Rolling over, Saetan blinked at Ladvarian and Kaelas. Someone—he snorted—had already taught Ladvarian to air walk. True, the puppy wobbled, but he was, after all, a puppy.

Groaning, Saetan rolled back over, hoping they would go away.

Two bodies landed on the bed.

Well, he didn't have to worry about rolling over on the Sceltie. He wasn't going to roll anywhere with Kaelas pressed against his back—except, perhaps, onto the floor.

And where was Jaenelle?

The Lady, he was told, was taking a bath. They wanted a nap. Since Papa High Lord was taking a nap, they would stay with him.

With grim determination, Saetan closed his eyes.

He didn't need to look for trouble. It had just pounced on him.

CHAPTER TWELVE

1 / Kaeleer

Carrying a glass globe and a small glass bowl, both cobalt blue, Tersa walked a few feet into her backyard, her bare feet sinking into ankle-deep snow. The full moon played hide-and-seek among the clouds, much as the vision had eluded her throughout the day. She had lived within visions for so many centuries, she understood that this one needed to be given a physical shape before revealing itself.

Letting her body be the dreamscape's instrument, she used Craft to sail the globe and bowl through the air. When they reached the center of the lawn, they settled quietly into the snow.

She took a step toward them, then looked down. Her nightgown brushed the snow, disturbing it. That wouldn't do. Pulling it off, she tossed it near the cottage's back door and walked toward the globe and bowl. She stopped. Yes. This was the right place to begin.

One long stride to keep the snow pristine between her shuffled footsteps from the cottage and the footsteps that would guide the vision. Placing one foot carefully in front of the other, heel to toe, she waited. There was something else, something more.

Using Craft to sharpen a fingernail, she cut the instep of each foot deep enough for the blood to run freely. Then she walked the vision's pattern. When it brought her back to her first footstep, she leaped to reach the snow disturbed by shuffled footsteps.

As she turned to see the pattern, the journeymaid Black Widow who was staying with her for a few weeks called out, "Tersa? What are you doing outside at this time of night?"

Snarling, Tersa whirled back to face the young witch.

The journeymaid studied her face for a moment. Fetching the discarded nightgown, she tore it into strips, wrapped Tersa's feet to absorb the blood, then moved aside.

Urgency pushed Tersa up the stairs to her bedroom. Opening the curtains, she looked down at the yard and the lines she had drawn in the snow with her blood.

Two sides of a triangle, strong and connected. The father and the brother. The third side, the father's mirror, was separated from the other two and the middle was worn away. If it broke fully, that side would never be strong enough again to complete the triangle.

Moonlight and shadows filled the yard. The cobalt globe and bowl that rested in the center of the triangle became sapphire eyes.

"Yes," Tersa whispered. "The threads are now in place. It's time."

Receiving Jaenelle's silent permission, Saetan entered her sitting room. He glanced at the dark bedroom where Kaelas and Ladvarian were awake and anxious. Which meant Lucivar would be appearing soon. In the five months since he'd begun serving her, Lucivar had become extraordinarily sensitive to Jaenelle's moods.

Saetan sat down on the hassock in front of the overstuffed chair where Jaenelle was curled up. "Bad dream?" he asked. She'd had quite a few restless nights and bad dreams in the past few weeks.

"A dream," she agreed. She hesitated for a moment. "I was standing in front of a cloudy crystal door. I couldn't see what was behind it, wasn't sure I *wanted* to see. But someone kept trying to hand me a gold key, and I knew that if I took it, the door would open and then I would *have* to know what was hidden behind it."

"Did you take the key?" He kept his voice soft and soothing while his heart began to pound in his chest.

"I woke up before I touched it." She smiled wearily.

This was the first time she remembered one of those dreams upon waking. He had a good idea what memories were hidden behind that crystal door. Which meant they needed to talk about her past soon. But not tonight. "Would you like a brew to help you sleep?"

"No, thank you. I'll be all right."

He kissed her forehead and left the room.

Lucivar waited for him in the corridor. "Problem?" Lucivar asked.

"Perhaps." Saetan took a deep breath, let it out slowly. "Let's go down to the study. There's something we need to discuss."

2 / Kaeleer

"Cat!" Lucivar rushed into the great hall. He didn't know what had set her off, but after talking with Saetan last night, he wasn't about to let her go anywhere by herself.

Fortunately, Beale was equally reluctant to let the Lady rush out the door without telling someone her destination.

Caught between them, Jaenelle unleashed her frustration with enough force to make all the windows rattle. "Damn you both! I have to *go*."

"Fine." Lucivar approached her slowly, holding his hands up in a placating gesture. "I'm going with you. Where are we going?"

Jaenelle raked her fingers through her hair. "Halaway. Sylvia just sent a message. Something's wrong with Tersa."

Lucivar exchanged a look with Beale. The butler nodded. Saetan and Mephis would be back at any moment from their meeting with Lady Zhara, the Queen of Amdarh, Dhemlan's capital—and Beale would remain in the great hall until they arrived.

"Let me go!" Jaenelle wailed.

Thank the Darkness, it didn't occur to her to use force against them. She could easily eliminate what amounted to token resistance.

"In a minute," Lucivar said, swallowing hard when her eyes turned stormy. "You can't go out in your socks. There's snow on the ground."

Jaenelle swore. Lucivar called in her winter boots and handed them to her while a breathless footman brought her winter coat and the belted, wool cape with wing slits that served as a coat for him.

A minute later, they were flying toward Tersa's cottage.

The journeymaid Black Widow who was staying with Tersa flung the door open as soon as they landed. "In the bedroom," she said in a worried voice. "Lady Sylvia is with her."

Jaenelle raced up to the bedroom with Lucivar right behind her.

Seeing them, Sylvia sagged against the dresser, the relief in her face overshadowed by stark concern. Lucivar put his arm around her, uneasy about the way she clung to him.

Jaenelle circled the bed to face Tersa, who was frantically packing a small trunk. Scattered among the clothing strewn on the bed were books, candles, and a few things Lucivar recognized as tools only a Black Widow would own.

"Tersa," Jaenelle said in a quiet, commanding voice.

Tersa shook her head. "I have to find him. It's time now."

"Who do you have to find?"

"The boy. My son. Daemon."

Lucivar's heart clogged his throat as he watched Jaenelle pale.

"Daemon." Jaenelle shuddered. "The gold key."

"I have to find him." Tersa's voice rang with frustration and fear. "If the pain doesn't end soon, it will destroy him."

Jaenelle gave no sign of having heard or understood the words. "Daemon," she whispered. "How could I have forgotten Daemon?"

"I must go back to Terreille. I must find him."

"No," Jaenelle said in her midnight voice. "*I'll* find him."

Tersa stopped her restless movements. "Yes," she said slowly, as if trying hard to remember something. "He would trust you. He would follow you out of the Twisted Kingdom."

Jaenelle closed her eyes.

Still holding Sylvia, Lucivar braced himself against the wall. Hell's fire, why was the room slowly spinning?

When Jaenelle opened her eyes, Lucivar stared, unable to look away. He'd never seen her eyes look like that. He hoped he'd never again see her eyes look like that. Jaenelle swept out of the room.

Leaving Sylvia to manage on her own, Lucivar raced after Jaenelle, who was striding toward the landing web at the edge of the village.

"Cat, the Hall's in the other direction."

When she didn't answer him, he tried to grab her arm. The shield around her was so cold it burned his hand.

She passed the landing web and kept walking. He fell into step beside her, not sure what to say—not sure what he *dared* say.

"Stubborn, snarly male," she muttered as tears filled her eyes. "I *told* you the chalice needed time to heal. I *told* you to go someplace safe.

Why didn't you listen to me? Couldn't you obey just *once*?" She stopped walking.

Lucivar watched her grief slowly transform into rage as she turned in the direction of the Hall.

"Saetan," she said in a malevolent whisper. "You were there that night. You . . ."

Lucivar didn't try to keep up with her when she ran back to the Hall. Instead, he sent a warning to Beale on a Red spear thread. Beale, in turn, informed him that the High Lord had just arrived.

He hoped his father was prepared for this fight.

3 / Kaeleer

He felt her coming.

Too nervous to sit, Saetan leaned against the front of his blackwood desk, his hands locked on the surface in a vise grip.

He'd had two years to prepare for this, had spent countless hours trying to find the right phrases to explain the brutality that had almost destroyed her. But, somehow, he had never found the right time to tell her. Even after last night, when he realized the memories were trying to surface, he had delayed talking to her.

Now the time had come. And he still wasn't prepared.

He'd arrived home to find Beale fretting in the great hall, waiting to convey Lucivar's warning: "She remembers Daemon—and she's furious."

He felt her enter the Hall and hoped he could now find a way to help her face those memories in the daylight instead of in her dreams.

His study door blew off the hinges and shattered when it hit the opposite wall. Dark power ripped through the room, breaking the tables and tearing the couch and chairs apart.

Fear hammered at him. But he also noted that she didn't harm the irreplaceable paintings and sculpture.

Then she stepped into the room, and nothing could have prepared him for the cold rage focused directly at him.

"Damn you." Her midnight voice sounded calm. It sounded deadly.

She meant it. If the malevolence and loathing in her eyes was any indication of the depth of her rage, then he was truly damned.

"You heartless bastard."

His mind chattered frantically. He couldn't make a sound. He desperately hoped that her feelings for him would balance her fury—and knew they wouldn't, not with Daemon added to the balance.

She walked toward him, flexing her fingers, drawing part of his attention to the dagger-sharp nails he now had reason to fear.

"You used him. He was a friend, and *you used him.*"

Saetan gritted his teeth. "There was no choice."

"There *was* a choice." She slashed open the chair in front of his desk. "THERE WAS A CHOICE!"

His rising temper pushed the fear aside. "To lose you," he said roughly. "To stand back and let your body die and lose *you*. I didn't consider that a choice, Lady. Neither did Daemon."

"You wouldn't have lost me if the body had died. I would have eventually put the crystal chalice back together and—"

"You're Witch, and Witch doesn't become *cildru dyathe*. We *would* have lost you. Every part of you. He knew that."

That stopped her for a moment.

"I gave him all the strength I had. He went too deep into the abyss trying to reach you. When I tried to draw him back up, he fought me and the link between us snapped."

"He shattered his crystal chalice," Jaenelle said in a hollow voice. "He shattered his mind. I put it back together, but it was so terribly fragile. When he rose out of the abyss, anything could have damaged him. A harsh word would have been enough at that point."

"I know," Saetan said cautiously. "I felt him."

The cold rage filled her eyes again. "But you left him there, didn't you, Saetan?" she said too softly. "Briarwood's uncles had arrived at the Altar, and you left a defenseless man to face them."

"He was supposed to go through the Gate," Saetan replied hotly. "I don't know why he didn't."

"Of course you know." Her voice became a sepulchral croon. "We both know. If a timing spell wasn't put on the candles to snuff them out and close the Gate, then someone had to stay behind to close it. Naturally it was the Warlord Prince who was expected to stay."

"He may have had other reasons to stay," Saetan said carefully.

"Perhaps," she replied with equal care. "But that doesn't explain why he's in the Twisted Kingdom, does it, High Lord?" She took a step closer to him. "That doesn't explain why you left him there."

"I didn't know he was in the Twisted Kingdom until—" Saetan clamped his teeth to hold the words back.

"Until Lucivar came to Kaeleer," Jaenelle finished for him. She waved a hand dismissively before he could speak. "Lucivar was in the salt mines of Pruul. I know there was nothing he could do. But you."

Saetan spaced out the words. "Getting you back was the first requirement. I gave my strength to that task. Daemon would have understood that, would have demanded it."

"I came back two years ago, and there's nothing draining your strength now." Pain and betrayal filled her eyes. "But you didn't even try to reach him, did you?"

"Yes, I tried! DAMN YOU, I TRIED!" He sagged against the desk. "Stop acting like a petty little bitch. He may be your friend, but he's also my *son*. Do you really think I wouldn't try to help him?" The bitter failure filled him again. "I was so close, witch-child. So close. But he was just out of reach. And he didn't trust me. If he would have tried a little, I would have had him. I could have shown him the way out of the Twisted Kingdom. But he didn't trust me."

The silence stretched.

"I'm going to get him back," Jaenelle said quietly.

Saetan straightened up. "You can't go back to Terreille."

"Don't tell me what I can or can't do," Jaenelle snarled.

"Listen to me, Jaenelle," he said urgently. "You can't go back to Terreille. As soon as she realized you were there, Dorothea would do everything she could to contain you or destroy you. And you're still not of age. Your Chaillot relatives could try to regain custody."

"I'll take that chance. I'm not leaving him to suffer." She turned to leave the room.

Saetan took a deep breath and let it out slowly. "Since I'm his father, I can reach him without needing physical contact."

"But he doesn't trust you."

"I can help you, Jaenelle."

She turned back to look at him, and he saw a stranger.

"I don't want your help, High Lord," she said quietly.

Then she walked away from him, and he knew she was doing a great deal more than simply walking out of a room.

Everything has a price.

Lucivar found her in the gardens a couple of hours later, sitting on a stone bench with her hands pressed between her knees hard enough to bruise. Straddling the bench, he sat as close as he could without touching her. "Cat?" he said softly, afraid that even sound would shatter her. "Talk to me. Please."

"I—" She shuddered.

"You remember."

"I remember." She let out a laugh full of knife-sharp edges. "I remember all of it. Marjane, Dannie, Rose. Briarwood. Greer. All of it." She glanced at him. "You've known about Briarwood. And Greer."

Lucivar brushed a lock of hair away from his face. Maybe he should get it cut short, the way Eyrien warriors usually wore it. "Sometimes when you have bad dreams you talk in your sleep."

"So you've both known. And said nothing."

"What could we have said, Cat?" Lucivar asked slowly. "If we had forced someone else to remember something that emotionally scarring, you would have thrown a fit—as well as a few pieces of furniture."

Jaenelle's lips curved in a ghost of a smile. "True." Her smile faded. "Do you know the worst thing about it? I forgot him. Daemon was a friend, and I forgot him. That Winsol, before I was . . . he gave me a silver bracelet. I don't know what happened to it. I had a picture of him. I don't know what happened to that either. And then he gave everything he had to help me, and when it was done, everyone walked away from him as if he didn't matter."

"If you had remembered the rape when you first came back, would you have stayed? Or would you have fled from your body again?"

"I don't know."

"Then if forgetting Daemon was the price that had to be paid in order to keep those memories at bay until you were strong enough to face them . . . He would say it was a fair price."

"It's very easy to make statements about what Daemon would say since he's not here to deny them, isn't it?" Tears filled her eyes.

"You're forgetting something, little witch," Lucivar said sharply. "He's my brother, and he's a Warlord Prince. I've known him longer and far better than you."

Jaenelle shifted on the bench. "I don't blame you for what happened to him. The High Lord—"

"If you're going to demand that the High Lord shoulder the blame for Daemon being in the Twisted Kingdom, then you're going to have to shovel some of that blame onto me as well."

She twisted around to face him, her eyes chilly.

Lucivar took a deep breath. "He came to get me out of Pruul. He wanted me to go with him. And I refused to go because I thought he had killed you, that he was the one who had raped you."

"*Daemon?*"

Lucivar swore viciously. "Sometimes you can be incredibly naive. You have no idea what Daemon is capable of doing when he goes cold."

"You really believed that?"

He braced his head in his hands. "There was so much blood, so much pain. I couldn't get past the grief to think clearly enough to doubt what I'd been told. And when I accused him, he didn't deny it."

Jaenelle looked thoughtful. "He seduced me. Well, seduced Witch. When we were in the abyss."

"He what?" Lucivar asked with deadly calm.

"Don't get snarly," Jaenelle snapped. "It was a trick to make me heal the body. He didn't really want me. Her. He didn't . . ." Her voice trailed away. She waited a minute before continuing. "He said he'd been waiting for Witch all his life. That he'd been born to be her lover. But then he didn't want to be her lover."

"Hell's fire, Cat," Lucivar exploded. "You were a twelve-year-old who had recently been raped. What did you expect him to do?"

"I wasn't twelve in the abyss."

Lucivar narrowed his eyes, wondering what she meant by that.

"He lied to me," she said in a small voice.

"No, he didn't. He meant exactly what he said. If you had been eighteen and had offered him the Consort's ring, you would have found that out quick enough." Lucivar stared at the blurry garden. He cleared his throat. "Saetan loves you, Cat. And you love him. He did what he had to do to save his Queen. He did what any Warlord Prince would do. If you can't forgive him, how will you ever be able to forgive me?"

"Oh, Lucivar." Sobbing, Jaenelle threw her arms around him.

Lucivar held her, petted her, took aching comfort from the way she held him tight. His silent tears wet her hair. His tears were for her, whose soul wounds had been reopened; for himself, because he may have lost something precious so soon after it was found; for Saetan, who may have lost even more; and for Daemon. Most of all, for Daemon.

It was almost twilight when Jaenelle gently pulled away from him. "There's someone I need to talk to. I'll be back later."

Worried, Lucivar studied her slumped shoulders and pale face. "Where—" Caution warred with instinct. He floundered.

Jaenelle's lips held a shadow of an understanding smile. "I'm not going anywhere dangerous. I'll still be in Kaeleer. And no, Prince Yaslana, this isn't risky. I'm just going to see a friend."

He let her go, unable to do anything else.

Saetan stared at nothing, holding the pain at bay, holding the memories at bay. If he released his hold and they flooded in . . . he wasn't sure he would survive them, wasn't sure he would even try.

"Saetan?" Jaenelle hovered near the open study doorway.

"Lady." Protocol. The courtesies given and granted when a Warlord Prince addressed a Queen of equal or darker rank. He'd lost the privilege of addressing her any other way, of being anything more.

When she entered the room, he walked around the desk. He couldn't sit while she was standing, and he couldn't offer her a seat since the rest of the furniture in his study had been destroyed and he hadn't allowed Beale to clear up the mess.

Jaenelle approached hesitantly, her lower lip caught between her teeth, her hands twining restlessly. She didn't look at him.

"I talked to Lorn." Her voice quivered. She blinked rapidly. "He agreed with you that I shouldn't go to Terreille—except the Keep. We decided that I would create a shadow of myself that can interact with people so that I can search for Daemon while my body remains safe at the Keep. I'll only be able to search three days out of every month because of the physical drain the shadow will place on me, but I know someone I think will help me look for him."

"You must do what you think best," he said carefully.

She looked at him, her beautiful, ancient, haunted eyes full of tears. "S-Saetan?"

Still so young for all her strength and wisdom.

He opened his arms, opened his heart.

She clung to him, trembling violently.

She was the most painful, most glorious dance of his life.

"Saetan, I—"

He pressed a finger against her lips. "No, witch-child," he said with gentle regret. "Forgiveness doesn't work that way. You may want to forgive me, but you can't do it yet. Forgiving someone can take weeks, months, years. Sometimes it takes a lifetime. Until Daemon is whole again, all we can do is try to be kind to one another, and understanding, and take each day as it comes." He held her close, savoring the feeling, not knowing when, or if, he'd ever hold her like this again. "Come along, witch-child. It's almost dawn. You need to rest now."

He led her to her bedroom but didn't enter. Safe in his own room, he felt the loneliness already pressing down on him.

He curled up on his bed, unable to stop the tears he'd held back throughout the long, terrible night. It would take time. Weeks, months, maybe years. He knew it would take time.

But, please, sweet Darkness, please don't let it take a lifetime.

4 / Terreille

Surreal walked down the neglected street toward the market square, hoping her icy expression would offset her vulnerable physical state. She shouldn't have used that witch's brew to suppress last month's moontime, but the Hayllian guards Kartane SaDiablo had sent after her had been breathing down her neck then and she hadn't felt safe enough to risk being defenseless during the days when her body couldn't tolerate the use of her power beyond basic Craft.

Damn all Blood males to the bowels of Hell. When a witch's body made her vulnerable for a few days, it also made every Blood male a potential enemy. And right now she had enough enemies to worry about.

Well, she'd pick up a few things at the market and then hole up in her rooms with a couple of thick novels and wait it out.

Stifled, frightened cries came from the alley up ahead.

Calling in a long-bladed knife, Surreal slipped to the edge of the alley and peeked around the corner.

Four large, surly, Hayllian men. And one girl who was barely more than a child. Two of the men stood back, watching, as one of their comrades held the girl and the other's hands yanked her clothes aside.

Damn, damn, damn. It was a trap. There was no other reason for Hayllians to be in this part of the Realm, especially in this part of a dying city. She should just slip back to her rooms. If she was careful, they might not find her. There would be other Hayllians waiting around the places where she might purchase a ticket for a Web Coach, so that was out. And riding the Winds without the protection of a Coach might not be suicidal right now, but it would feel damn close.

But there was that girl. If she didn't intervene, that child was going to end up under those four brutes. Even if someone "rescued" her afterward, she'd be passed from man to man until the constant use or the brutality of one of them killed her.

Taking a deep breath, Surreal rushed into the alley.

An upward slash opened one man from armpit to collarbone. She swung her arm, just missing the girl's face, and managed to get in a shallow slash across the other's chest while she tried to pull the girl away.

Then the other two men joined the fight.

Diving under a fist that would have pulped one side of her head, Surreal rolled, sprang up, took two running steps and, because no one tried to stop her from going deeper into the alley, spun around.

A dead end behind her, and the Hayllians blocking the only way out.

Surreal looked at the girl, wanting to express her regret.

Smiling greedily as one of the unwounded men dropped a small bag of coins into her hands, the girl pulled her clothes together and hurried out of the alley.

Mercenary little bitch.

Surreal tried hard to remember the other girls she'd helped over the past five years, but remembering them didn't diminish the overwhelming sense of betrayal. Well, she'd come full circle. She'd come up from living in stinking alleys. Now she'd die in one, because she wasn't about to let

Kartane SaDiablo truss her up and hand her over as a present to the High Priestess of Hayll.

The men stepped forward, smiling viciously.

"Let her go."

The quiet, eerie, midnight voice came from behind her.

Surreal watched the men, watched surprise, uneasiness, and fear harden into a look that always meant pain for a woman.

"Let her go," the voice said again.

"Go to Hell," the largest Hayllian said, stepping forward.

A mist rose up behind the men, forming a wall across the alley.

"Just slit the bitch's throat and be done with it," the man with the shoulder wound said.

"Can't have any fun and games with the half-breed, so the other will have to learn some manners," the largest man said.

Thick mist suddenly filled the alley. Eyes, like burning red gems, appeared, and something let out a wet-sounding snarl.

Surreal screamed breathlessly as a hand clamped on her left arm.

"Come with me," said that terrifyingly familiar midnight voice.

The mist swirled, too thick to see the person guiding her through it as easily as if it were clear water.

More snarls. Then high-pitched, desperate screams.

"W-what—" Surreal stammered.

"Hell Hounds."

To the right of her, something hit the ground with a wet plop.

Surreal tried hard to swallow, tried hard not to breathe.

The next step took them out of the mist and back to the welcome sight of the neglected street.

"Are you staying around here?" the voice asked.

Surreal finally looked at her companion and felt a stab of disappointment immediately followed by a sense of relief. The woman was her height, and the body in the form-fitting black jumpsuit, though slender, definitely didn't belong to the child she remembered. But the long hair was golden, and the eyes were hidden behind dark glasses.

Surreal tried to pull away. "I'm grateful you got my ass out of that alley, but my mother told me not to tell strangers where I live."

"We're not strangers, and I'm sure that's not all Titian told you."

Surreal tried again to pull away. The hand on her arm clamped down harder. Finally realizing she still held a weapon in her other hand, Surreal swung the knife, bringing it down hard on the woman's wrist.

The knife went through as if there was nothing there and vanished.

"What are you?" Surreal gasped.

"An illusion that's called a shadow."

"Who are you?"

"Briarwood is the pretty poison. There is no cure for Briarwood." The woman smiled coldly. "Does that answer your question?"

Surreal studied the woman, trying to find some trace of the child she remembered. After a minute, she said, "You really are Jaenelle, aren't you? Or some part of her?"

Jaenelle smiled, but there was no humor in it. "I really am." A pause. Then, "We need to talk, Surreal. Privately."

Oh, yes, they needed to talk. "I have to go to the market first."

The hand with the dagger-sharp, black-tinted nails tightened for a moment before releasing her. "All right."

Surreal hesitated. Snarls and crunching noises came out of the mist behind them. "Don't you have to finish the kill?"

"I don't think that'll be a problem," Jaenelle said dryly. "Piles of Hound shit aren't much of a threat to anyone."

Surreal paled.

Jaenelle's lips tightened. "I apologize," she said after a minute. "We all have facets to our personalities. This has brought out the nastier ones in mine. No one will enter the alley and nothing will leave. The Harpies will arrive soon and take care of things."

Surreal led the way to the market square, where she bought folded breads filled with chicken and vegetables from one vendor, small beef pies from another, and fresh fruit from a third.

"I'll make you a healing brew," Jaenelle said when they finally returned to Surreal's rooms.

Still wondering why Jaenelle had sought her out, Surreal nodded before retreating into the bathroom to get cleaned up. When she returned, there was a covered plate on the small kitchen table and a steaming cup filled with a witch's brew.

Settling into a chair, Surreal sipped the brew and felt the pain in her abdomen gradually dull. "How did you find me?" she asked.

For the first time, there was amusement in Jaenelle's smile. "Well, sugar, since you're the only Gray Jewel in the entire Realm of Terreille, you're not that hard to find."

"I didn't know someone could be traced that way."

"Whoever is hunting you can't use that method. It requires wearing a Jewel equal or darker than yours."

"Why did you find me?" Surreal asked quietly.

"I need your help. I want to find Daemon."

Surreal stared at the cup. "Whatever he did at Cassandra's Altar that night was done to help you. Hasn't he suffered enough?"

"Too much."

There was sorrow and regret in Jaenelle's voice. The eyes would have told her more. "Do you have to wear those damn dark glasses?" Surreal asked sharply.

Jaenelle hesitated. "You might find my eyes disturbing."

"I'll take the chance."

Jaenelle raised the glasses.

Those eyes belonged to someone who had experienced the most twisted nightmares of the soul and had survived.

Surreal swallowed hard. "I see what you mean."

Jaenelle replaced the glasses. "I can bring him out of the Twisted Kingdom, but I need to make the link through his body."

If only Jaenelle had come a few months ago.

"I don't know where he is," Surreal said.

"But you can look for him. I can stay in this form only three days out of the month. He's running out of time, Surreal. If he isn't shown the road back soon, there won't be anything left of him."

Surreal closed her eyes. *Shit.*

Jaenelle poured the rest of the brew into Surreal's cup. "Even a Gray-Jeweled witch's moontime shouldn't give her this much pain."

Surreal shifted. Winced. "I suppressed last month's time." She wrapped her hands around the cup. "Daemon lived with me for a little while. Until a few months ago."

"What happened a few months ago?"

"Kartane SaDiablo happened," Surreal said viciously. Then she smiled. "Your spell or web or whatever it was you spun around Briarwood's uncles did a good job on him. You wouldn't even recognize the bastard." She paused. "Robert Benedict is dead, by the way."

"How unfortunate," Jaenelle murmured, her voice dripping venom. "And dear Dr. Carvay?"

"Alive, more or less. Not for much longer from what I've heard."

"Tell me about Kartane . . . and Daemon."

"Last spring, Daemon showed up at the flat where I was living. Our paths have crossed a few times since—" Surreal faltered.

"Since the night at Cassandra's Altar."

"Yes. He's like Tersa used to be. Show up, stay a couple of days, and vanish again. This time he stayed. Then Kartane showed up." Surreal drained her cup. "Apparently he's been hunting for Daemon for some time, but, unlike Dorothea, he seems to have a better idea of where to look. He started demanding that Daemon help him get free of this terrible spell someone had put on him. As if he'd never done anything to deserve it. When it became apparent that Daemon was lost in the Twisted Kingdom and, therefore, useless, Kartane looked at me—and noticed my ears. At the same moment he realized I was Titian's child—and his—Daemon exploded and threw him out.

"I guess he figured that bringing Sadi to Dorothea wouldn't buy him enough help, but bringing Dorothea his only possible offspring would be a solid bargaining chip. And a female offspring who could continue the bloodline would provide strong incentive—even if she was a half-breed.

"Daemon insisted that we leave immediately because Kartane would return after dark with guards. And he did.

"Before Daemon and I caught the Wind and headed out, we had agreed on a city in another Territory. He was right behind me, riding close. And then he wasn't there anymore. I haven't seen him since."

"And you've been running since then."

"Yeah." She felt so tired. She wanted to lose herself in a book, in sleep. Too much of a risk now. The rest of the Hayllian guards would start wondering about those four men, would start looking soon.

"Eat your food, Surreal."

Surreal bit into the folded bread and finally wondered why she hadn't tested that brew—and wondered why she didn't care.

Jaenelle checked the bedroom, then studied the worn sofa in the living area. "Do you want to tuck up in bed or curl up here?"

"Can't," Surreal mumbled, annoyed because she was going to cry.

"Yes, you can." Taking comforters and pillows from the bedroom,

Jaenelle turned the sofa into an inviting nest. "I can stay two more days. No one will disturb you while I'm here."

"I'll help you search," Surreal said, snuggling into the sofa.

"I know." Jaenelle smiled dryly. "You're Titian's daughter. You wouldn't do anything else."

"Don't know if I like being that predictable," Surreal grumbled.

Jaenelle made another cup of the healing brew, gave Surreal first choice of two new novels, and settled into a chair.

Surreal drank her brew, read the first page of the novel twice, and gave up. Looking at Jaenelle, questions buzzed inside her head.

She didn't want to hear the answers to any of them.

For now, it was enough that, once they found Daemon, Jaenelle would bring him out of the Twisted Kingdom.

For now, it was enough to feel safe.

PART IV

CHAPTER THIRTEEN

1 / Kaeleer

"Spring is the season of romance," Hekatah said, watching her companion. "And she's eighteen now. Old enough to enjoy a husband."

"True." Lord Jorval traced little circles on the scarred table. "But selecting the *right* husband is important."

"All he needs to be is young, handsome, and virile—and capable of obeying orders," Hekatah snapped. "The husband will merely be the sexual bait that will lure her away from that monster. Or do you want to live under the High Lord's thumb, once his 'daughter' sets up her court and begins her reign?"

Jorval looked stubborn. "A husband could be much more than sexual bait. A mature man could guide his Queen wife, help her to make the right decisions, keep unhealthy influences away from her."

Frustrated to the point of screaming, Hekatah sat back and curled her hands around the wooden arms of the chair so that she wouldn't reach across the table and rip half that fool's face off.

Hell's fire, she missed Greer. He had understood subtlety. He had understood the sensible precaution of using intermediaries whenever possible to avoid being in the direct line of fire. As a member of the Dark Council, Jorval was extremely useful in keeping the Council's dislike and distrust of Saetan quietly simmering. But he lusted for Jaenelle Angelline and entertained fantasies of nightly bouts of masterful sex which made the pale bitch pliant and submissive to his every whim, in and out of the bed. Which was fine, but the fool couldn't seem to see past the sweaty sheets to consider what might be waiting to have a little chat with him.

She was fairly sure that Saetan would grit his teeth and endure an unwelcome male his Queen was besotted with. He was too well trained and too committed to the old ways of the Blood to do otherwise. But the Eyrien half-breed. . . . *He* wouldn't think twice about tearing his Lady out of her lover's arms—or tearing off her lover's arms—and keeping her isolated until she was clearheaded again.

And she doubted either of them could be convinced that Jaenelle was panting and moaning for someone who looked like Lord Jorval.

"He must be young," Hekatah insisted. "A pretty boy with enough experience between the sheets to be convincing, and charming enough for her family to believe, however doubtfully, that she's wildly in love."

Jorval sulked.

Tightening her hold on her temper a little more, Hekatah altered her voice to sound hesitant. "There are reasons for caution, Jorval. Perhaps you remember a colleague of mine." She curled her hands until they looked like twisted claws.

Jorval abandoned his sulk. "I remember him. He was most helpful. I'd hoped he would return." When Hekatah said nothing, he took an unsteady breath. "What happened to him?"

"The High Lord happened to him," Hekatah replied. "He made the mistake of drawing attention to himself. No one has seen him since."

"I see."

Yes, finally, he *was* beginning to see.

Hekatah leaned forward and stroked Jorval's hand. "Sometimes the duties and responsibilities of power require sacrifices, Lord Jorval." When he didn't protest, she hid a triumphant smile. "Now, if you were to arrange a marriage for Jaenelle Angelline with the son of a man you felt comfortable working with—a handsome, controllable son—"

"How would that help me?" Jorval demanded.

Hekatah stifled her irritation. "The father would advise the son on the policies and changes that should be implemented in Kaeleer—changes that, at Jaenelle's insistence, would be accepted. A great many decisions are made during pillow talk, as I'm sure you know."

"And how would that help me?" Jorval demanded again.

"Just as the son follows the advice of the father, so the father follows the advice of his friend—who just happens to be the only source for the tonic that keeps the Lady so hungry for the son's attentions that she'll agree to anything."

"Ah." Jorval stroked his chin. "Aahhh."

"And if, for some reason, the High Lord or some other member of the family"—the flicker of fear in Jorval's eyes told her he'd already had a close brush with Lucivar Yaslana's temper—"should react badly, well, finding another hot, handsome boy would be easy enough, but finding strong, intelligent men to guide the Realm . . ." Hekatah spread her hands and shrugged.

Jorval considered her words for several minutes. Hekatah waited patiently. As much as he might want the hot sexual fantasy, Jorval wanted power—or the illusion of power—much more.

"Lady Angelline will be coming to Little Terreille in two weeks. And I do have a . . . friend . . . with a suitable offspring. However, getting Lady Angelline to agree to the marriage . . ."

Hekatah called in a small bottle and set it on the table. "Lady Angelline is well-known for her compassion and her healing abilities. If, by some terrible accident, a child were injured, I'm sure she could be prevailed upon to do the healing. If the injuries were life-threatening, the power expended for a full healing would leave her physically and mentally exhausted. Then, if someone she trusted were to offer her a relaxing glass of wine, she would probably be too tired to test it. The wedding would, regrettably, have to be a small, quiet affair that would take place shortly afterward. Between the fatigue and this brew mixed with the wine, she would be compliant enough to say what she was told to say and sign what she was told to sign.

"The young couple would stay at the wedding feast for a short time before retreating to their room to consummate the marriage."

Jorval's nostrils flared. "I see."

Hekatah called in a second bottle. "The proper dose of this aphrodisiac, slipped into her wine during the wedding toast, will make her hungry for her new husband."

Jorval licked his lips.

"The next morning, the second dose must be given. This is very important because her hunger must be strong enough to override the High Lord's desire for an interview with her husband. By the time she's ready to release the boy from his conjugal duties, the High Lord won't be able to deny or object to the attachment without looking like a tyrant or a jealous fool." Hekatah paused, not pleased with the way Jorval was eyeing those bottles. "And the wise man guiding this affair will never be suspected—unless he calls attention to himself."

With visible effort, Jorval put his fantasies aside. He carefully vanished the bottles. "I'll be in touch."

"There's no need," Hekatah said a little too quickly. "Knowing I could help is enough. I'll let you know where, and when, to pick up the next supply of the aphrodisiac."

Jorval bowed and left.

Hekatah sat back, exhausted. Jorval was ignorant of, or chose to ignore, the common courtesies. He'd brought no refreshment and had offered none. Probably thought he was too important. And he was, damn him. Right now he was too important to her plans for her to insist on the amenities. However, once the little bitch was sufficiently cut off from Saetan, she would be able to eliminate Jorval.

Two weeks. That would give her enough time to complete the rest of her plan and set the trap that would, with luck, get rid of a half-breed Eyrien Warlord Prince as well.

2 / Kaeleer

Something felt wrong.

Lucivar set the armload of wood into the box by the kitchen hearth.

Very wrong.

Straightening up, he made a sweeping psychic probe of the area, using Luthvian's house as the center point.

Nothing. But the feeling didn't go away.

Preoccupied with the nagging uneasiness, he didn't move when Roxie entered the kitchen, didn't really notice the light in her eyes or the way her walk changed as she came toward him.

He'd spent the past two days doing chores for Luthvian while dodging Roxie's amorous advances. Two days was about all he and Luthvian could manage together, and they only managed that because she was busy with her students most of the day, and he left right after dinner to spend the night in a mountain clearing.

"You're so strong," Roxie said, running her hands over his chest.

Not again. Not again.

Normally he wouldn't have allowed a woman to touch him like that.

Normally he would have considered that tone of voice an invitation to an intimate introduction to his fist.

So why was he afraid? Why were his nerves buzzing?

Sever it this time. Break the link for good. No. Can't. Won't be able to reach him if . . .

Roxie's arms wound around Lucivar's neck. She rubbed her breasts against his chest. "I haven't had a Warlord Prince yet."

Where was the fear coming from?

You can't have this body. This body is promised to him.

Roxie pressed against him. She playfully nipped his neck. He set his hands on her hips, holding her still while he concentrated on finding the source of that wasp-angry buzzing.

No. Not again.

It was coming from the Ring of Honor Jaenelle had given him. The buzzing, the fear, the cold rage building under the fear. Those weren't his feelings washing through him, but hers.

Hell's fire, Mother Night, and may the Darkness be merciful. Hers.

"I see you've changed your tune," Luthvian said tartly as she entered the kitchen.

Cold, cold rage. If it wasn't banked quickly . . .

"I have to go," Lucivar said absently. He felt the pull of arms around his neck and automatically shoved the body away from him.

Luthvian started swearing.

Ignoring her, he turned toward the door and wondered for a moment why Roxie was lying in a heap on the kitchen floor.

"You have to service me!" Roxie shouted, pushing herself into a sitting position. "You got me aroused. You have to service me."

Spinning around, Lucivar snapped a leg off a kitchen chair and tossed it into Roxie's lap. "Use that." He headed out the door.

I won't allow this. I will not submit to this.

"Lucivar!"

Snarling, he tried to shake off Luthvian's hand. "I have to go. Cat's in trouble."

Luthvian's hand tightened. "You're sure, aren't you? You sense her well enough that you're sure."

"Yes!" He didn't want to hit her. He didn't want to hurt her. But if she didn't let him go . . .

The hand on his arm trembled. "You'll send word to me? You'll let me know if . . . if she needs help?"

Lucivar gave Luthvian a hard, steady look. She might be jealous of the way the men in the family were drawn to Jaenelle, but she cared. He kissed her cheek roughly. "I'll send word."

Luthvian stepped back. "You spent all those years training to be a warrior, so go make yourself useful."

No.

Lucivar sped along the Ebon-gray Web, squeezing out all the speed he could, knowing it was already too late.

I won't let you.

Whatever happened, he'd take care of her afterward. Sweet Darkness, please let there be an afterward. He pushed harder.

No feelings from the Ring. No buzzing. Nothing at all except . . .

Noooooo!

. . . the rage. Mother Night, the rage!

Lucivar thrust his way through the sick-faced crowd, homing in on the spot where Jaenelle's unleashed power was concentrated. A middle-aged Warlord stood on one side of the hallway, babbling at a grim-looking Mephis. The aftertaste of power swirled behind a door on the opposite side.

Lucivar swung toward the door.

"Lucivar, no!"

Ignoring Mephis's command, Lucivar snapped the Gray lock his demon-dead elder brother had placed on the door.

"Lucivar, don't go in there!"

Lucivar threw the door open, stepped inside the room, and froze.

In front of him, a finger lay on the carpet, its gold ring partially melted into the flesh, the Jewel shattered to a fine powder.

It was the largest—and the only identifiable piece—of what must have been a full-grown man. The rest was splattered all over the room.

The buzzing in his head warned him to take a normal breath before he passed out. If he took a normal breath while standing in this room, he'd heave for a week.

But there was something wrong about the room, and he wasn't leaving until he figured it out.

When he did, Lucivar's temper rose to the killing edge.

One male body. One demolished bed. The rest of the furniture, although ruined by bone fragments and blood, was untouched.

Lucivar backed out of the room and turned toward the man who had been babbling at Mephis. "What did you do to her?" he asked too calmly.

"To *her*?" The Warlord pointed a shaking hand toward the room. "Look what that bitch did to my son. She's mad. Mad! She—"

Roaring an Eyrien war cry, Lucivar slammed the Warlord against the wall. "WHAT DID YOU DO TO HER?"

The Warlord squealed. No one tried to help him.

"Lucivar." Mephis held up a handful of papers. "It appears Jaenelle got married this afternoon to Lord—"

Lucivar snarled. "She wouldn't marry willingly without the family present." He bared his teeth at the Warlord. "Would she?"

"T-they were in l-love," the Warlord stammered. "A whirlwind r-romance. She didn't want you to know until it was done."

"Someone didn't," Lucivar agreed. Smiling, he called in the Eyrien war blade and held it up where the Warlord could see it. "Do you want your face?" he asked mildly.

"Lucivar," Mephis warned.

"Stay out of this, Mephis," Lucivar snapped, his barely restrained fury freezing everyone in the hallway.

Think. She'd been afraid, and very little frightened Jaenelle. She'd been afraid, but also angry enough to consider breaking the link between spirit and body, determined enough to abandon the husk rather than submit. Think. If this was Terreille . . .

"What did you give her?" When the Warlord didn't answer, Lucivar set the edge of the war blade against the man's cheek. The skin sliced cleanly. The blood ran.

"A m-mild brew. To calm her down. She was afraid. Afraid of all of them. Especially y-you."

A stupid thing to say to a man holding a weapon large enough and sharp enough to cut through bone.

They had drugged her. Something strong enough to scramble her wits while still leaving her capable of signing the marriage contract. That still didn't explain that room.

"Afterward," Lucivar crooned. "What did you give her to prepare her for the marriage bed?" When the Warlord just stared at him, he shifted the war blade, cut a little deeper this time. "Where are the bottles?"

Panting, the Warlord waved a hand toward a nearby door.

Mephis went into the room, then returned with two small bottles.

Lucivar vanished the war blade, took one bottle, and flicked the top off. Probed the drops in the bottom. If he'd been given a drink with this in it, he wouldn't have touched it. Under normal circumstances, Jaenelle wouldn't have either.

He vanished that bottle, took the other one that was still half filled with a dark powder, and swore viciously. He knew—how well he knew!—what a large dose of *safframate* would do to someone of his build and weight. He could imagine the agony it would produce in Jaenelle.

He held up the bottle. "You gave her this? Then you're responsible for what's in that room."

The Warlord shook his head violently. "It's harmless. Harmless! Added to a glass of wine, it's just a variety of the Night of Fire brew. Always use a Night of Fire brew on the wedding night."

Lucivar bared his teeth in a smile. "Since it's harmless, you won't mind drinking the other dose. Mephis, get him a glass of wine."

Sweat popped out on the Warlord's forehead.

Mephis disappeared for a minute, then returned with the wine.

After pouring almost all of the dark powder into the wine, Lucivar handed the bottle to Mephis and took the wineglass. His other hand closed around the Warlord's throat. "Now, you can drink this, or I can tear your throat out. Your choice."

"W-want a hearing before the Dark Council," the Warlord whimpered.

"That's certainly within your rights," Mephis agreed quietly. He looked at Lucivar. "Are you going to tear his throat out or shall I?"

Lucivar laughed maliciously. "Wouldn't do him much good to go to the Council then, would it?" His fingers dug into the Warlord's throat.

"D-drink."

"I knew you'd be reasonable," Lucivar crooned. He loosened his hold enough to let the Warlord swallow the wine.

"Now." He threw the Warlord into the room where Mephis had found the bottles. "In order to give the Dark Council an accurate accounting, I think you should enjoy the same experience you intended for Lady Angelline." After sealing the room with an Ebon-gray shield and adding a timing spell, he turned to a man hovering nearby. "The shield will vanish in twenty-four hours."

This time he didn't have to shove his way through the crowd. They pressed against the walls to let him pass.

Mephis caught up with him before he got out of the manor house. Probing the area, he walked into the nearest empty room—someone's study. He found it grimly appropriate, even if it wasn't Saetan's.

Mephis locked the door. "That was quite a show you put on."

"The show's just started." Lucivar prowled the room. "I didn't see you trying to stop me."

"We can't afford to be publicly divided. Besides, there wasn't any point in trying to stop you. You outrank me, and I doubt you'd let brotherly feelings get in your way."

"You got that right."

Mephis swore. "Do you realize the trouble we're going to have with the Dark Council over this? We're not above the Law, Lucivar."

Lucivar stopped in front of Mephis. "You play by your rules, and I'll play be mine."

"She signed a marriage contract."

"Not willingly."

"You don't know that. And twenty witnesses say otherwise."

"I wear her Ring. I can *feel* her, Mephis." Lucivar's voice shook. "She was ready to break the link rather than submit to being mounted."

Mephis said nothing for a full minute. "Jaenelle has problems with physical intimacy. You know that."

Lucivar slammed his fist into the door. "Damn you! Are you so blind or have your balls dried up so much you'll submit to anything rather than have someone bleat about the SaDiablo family misusing their power? Well, I'm not blind and there's nothing wrong with my balls. She's my Queen—mine!—and rules or not, Laws or not, Dark Council or not, if someone makes her suffer, I will pay them back in kind."

They stared at each other, Lucivar breathing hard, Mephis unmoving.

Finally, Mephis slumped against the door. "We can't go through this again, Lucivar. We can't go through the fear of losing her again."

"Where is she?"

"Father took her to the Keep—with strict orders for the rest of the family to stay away."

Lucivar pushed Mephis aside. "Well, we all know how well I follow orders, don't we?"

3 / Kaeleer

Saetan looked like a man who had barely survived a battlefield.

Which wasn't far from the truth, Lucivar thought as he quietly closed the door of Jaenelle's sitting room at the Keep.

"My instructions were explicit, Lucivar."

The voice had no strength. The face looked gray and strained.

Lucivar pointed casually to the Birthright Red Jewels Saetan wore. "You're not going to be able to toss me out wearing those."

Saetan didn't call in the Black.

Lucivar guessed, correctly, that getting Jaenelle to the Keep in her present physical and emotional condition had drained the Black.

Saetan limped to a chair, swearing softly. He tried to lift a decanter of yarbarah from the side table. His hand shook violently.

Crossing the room, Lucivar took the decanter, filled a glass, and warmed the blood wine. "Do you need fresh blood?" he asked quietly.

Saetan stared at him coldly.

Even after all these centuries, Luthvian's accusations were still deep wounds barely scabbed over. Guardians needed fresh blood from time to time to maintain their strength. At first, Lucivar had tried to understand Saetan's anger at being offered blood hot from the vein, tried not to feel insulted that the High Lord would accept that gift from anyone but him. Now he felt annoyed that someone else's words still hung between them. He wasn't a child. If the son willingly offered the gift, why couldn't the father graciously accept it?

Saetan looked away. "Thank you, but no."

Lucivar pressed the wineglass into Saetan's hand. "Drink this."

"I want you away from here, Lucivar."

Lucivar poured a large glass of brandy for himself, booted a footstool over to Saetan's chair, and sat down. "When I walk away from here, I'm taking her with me."

"You can't," Saetan snapped. "She's . . ." He raked his fingers through his hair. "I don't think she's sane."

"Not surprising since they dosed her with *safframate*."

Saetan glared at him. "Don't be an ass. *Safframate* doesn't do that to a person."

"How would you know? You've never been dosed with it." Lucivar struggled to keep the bitterness out of his voice. This wasn't the time to worry old hurts.

"I've used *safframate*."

Lucivar narrowed his eyes and studied his father. "Explain."

Saetan drained his glass. "*Safframate* is a sexual stimulant that's used to prolong stamina, prolong one's ability to give pleasure. The seeds are the size of a snapdragon seed. You add one or two crushed seeds to a glass of wine."

"One or two seeds." Lucivar snorted. "High Lord, in Terreille they crush it into a powder and use it by the spoonful."

"That's madness! If you gave someone that much—" Saetan stared at the closed door that led into Jaenelle's bedroom.

"Exactly," Lucivar said softly. "Pleasure very quickly becomes pain. The body becomes so stimulated, so sensitive that contact with anything hurts. The sex drive obliterates everything else, but that much *safframate* also blocks the ability to achieve orgasm so there's no relief, just driving need and sensitivity that's constantly increased by the stimulation."

"Mother Night," Saetan whispered, slumping in his chair.

"But if, for whatever reason, a person doesn't submit to being used until the drug wears off . . . well, the encounter can turn violent."

Saetan blinked back tears. "You were used like that, weren't you?"

"Yes. But not often. Most witches didn't think riding my cock was worth having my temper in the bed with it. And most of the ones who tried didn't walk away intact if they walked away at all. I had my own definition of violent passion."

"And Daemon?"

"He had his own way of dealing with it." Lucivar shuddered. "They didn't call him the Sadist for nothing."

Saetan reached for the yarbarah. His hand still shook, but not as badly as before. "What do you suggest we do for Jaenelle?"

"She doesn't deserve to endure this alone, and she'll never agree to sex for whatever small relief it might give her. So that leaves violence." Lucivar drained his brandy glass. "I'm taking her into Askavi. I'll keep us away from the villages. That way, if anything goes wrong, no one else will get caught in the backlash."

Saetan lowered his glass. "What about you?"

"I promised myself I'd take care of her. That's what I'm going to do."

Not giving himself any more time to think, Lucivar set his glass on the table and crossed the room. He paused at the door, not sure how to approach a witch strong enough to tear his mind apart with a thought. Then he shrugged and opened the door, trusting instinct.

The bedroom felt heavy with the growing psychic storm. He stepped into the room and braced himself.

Jaenelle paced frantically, her hands gripping her upper arms tight enough to bruise. She glanced at him and bared her teeth. Her eyes held revulsion and no recognition. "Get out."

Relief swept through him. Every second she resisted the desire to attack a male increased his chances of surviving the next few days.

"Pack a bag," Lucivar said. "Casual clothes. A warm jacket for evenings. Walking boots."

"I'm not going anywhere," Jaenelle snarled.

"We're going hunting."

"No. Get out."

Lucivar braced his hands on his hips. "You can pack a bag or not, but we're going hunting. Now."

"I don't want to go anywhere with you."

He heard the desperation and fear in her voice. Desperation because she didn't want to leave the safety of this room. Fear because he was pushing her and, cornered, she might strike back and hurt him.

It gave him hope.

"You can leave this room on your own two feet or over my shoulder. Your choice, Cat."

She grabbed a pillow and shredded it, swearing viciously in several languages. When his only response was to step toward her, she scrambled away from him, putting the bed between them.

He wondered if she saw the irony of it.

"You're running out of time, Cat," he said softly.

She grabbed another pillow and threw it at him. "Bastard!"

"Prick," he corrected. He started around the bed.

She ran for the dressing room door.

He got there ahead of her, his spread wings making him look huge. She backed away from him.

Saetan stepped into the bedroom. "Go with him, witch-child."

Trapped between father and brother, she stood there, shaking.

"We'll get away from everyone," Lucivar coaxed. "Just the two of us. Lots of fresh air and open ground."

The thoughts flashed through her eyes, over her face. Open ground. Room to maneuver. Room to run. Open ground, where she wouldn't be trapped in a room with all this maleness pulling at her, choking her.

"You won't touch me." Not a question or a demand. A plea.

"I won't touch you," Lucivar promised.

Jaenelle's shoulders slumped. "All right. I'll pack."

He folded his wings and stepped aside so that she could slip into the dressing room. The defeat in her voice made him want to weep.

Saetan joined him. "Be careful, Lucivar," he said quietly.

Lucivar nodded. He already felt tired. "It'll be better in the open, out on the land."

"Experience?"

"Yeah. We'll stop at the cabin first to pick up the sleeping bags and other gear. Ask Smoke to join us. I think she'll be able to tolerate him. And if anything goes wrong, he can send word."

Saetan didn't need to ask what could go wrong. They both knew what a Black-Jeweled Black Widow Queen could do to a man.

Saetan ran his hands over Lucivar's shoulders. He kissed his son's cheek. "May the Darkness embrace you," he said hoarsely, turning away. Lucivar pulled Saetan into a hard hug.

"Be careful, Lucivar. I don't want anything to happen to you now that you're finally here. And I *don't* want you with me in Hell."

Lucivar leaned back and smiled his lazy, arrogant smile. "I promise to stay out of trouble, Father."

Saetan snorted. "You mean it as much now as you did when you were little," he said dryly.

"Maybe even less."

Left alone while Jaenelle finished packing, Lucivar wondered if he was doing the right thing. He already mourned the game they would hunt, the animals who would die so savagely. If the four-legged bloodletting wasn't enough, she would turn on him. He expected her to. When she did, Saetan wouldn't find his son waiting for him in the Dark Realm. There wouldn't be anything left of him to wait.

4 / Kaeleer

"The Dark Council is quite distressed over the whole matter." Lord Magstrom shifted uneasily in his chair.

Saetan held his temper through sheer force of will. The man sitting on the other side of his blackwood desk had done nothing to deserve his rage. "The Council isn't alone in its distress."

"Yes, of course. But for Lady Angelline to . . ." Magstrom faltered.

"Among the Blood, rape is punishable by execution. At least it is in the rest of Kaeleer," Saetan said too softly.

"It's punishable by execution in Little Terreille as well," Magstrom replied stiffly.

"Then the little bastard got what he deserved."

"But . . . they were newly married," Magstrom protested.

"Even if that were true, which I doubt despite the damn signatures, a marriage contract doesn't excuse rape. Drugging a woman so that she's incapable of refusing doesn't mean she's agreed to anything. I'd say Jaenelle expressed her refusal quite eloquently, wouldn't you?" Saetan steepled his fingers and leaned back in his chair. "I've analyzed the two 'harmless substances' Jaenelle was given. Being a Black Widow, I have the training to reproduce them. If you choose to insist they had nothing to do with Jaenelle's behavior, why don't I make up another batch? We can test them on your granddaughter. She's Jaenelle's age."

Clutching the arms of the chair, Lord Magstrom said nothing.

Saetan rounded the desk and poured two glasses of brandy. Handing one to Lord Magstrom, he rested his hip on the corner of his desk. "Relax. I wouldn't do that to a child. Besides," he added quietly, "I may lose two of my children within the next few days. I wouldn't wish that on another man."

"Two?"

Saetan looked away from the concern and sympathy in Magstrom's eyes. "The first brew they gave Jaenelle inhibits will. She would have said what she'd been told to say, done what she'd been told to do. Unfortunately, that particular brew also has the side effect of magnifying emotional distress. A large dose of *safframate* and a forced sexual encounter were just the kind of stimulants that would have pushed her to the killing edge. And she'll remain on the killing edge until the drugs totally wear off."

Magstrom sipped his brandy. "Will she recover?"

"I don't know. If the Darkness is merciful, she will." Saetan clenched his teeth. "Lucivar took her to Askavi to spend some time with the land, away from people."

"Does he know about these violent tendencies?"

"He knows."

Magstrom hesitated. "You don't expect him to return, do you?"

"No. Neither does he. And I don't know what that will do to her."

"I like him," Magstrom said. "He has a rough kind of charm."

"Yes, he does." Saetan drained his glass, fighting not to give in to grief before there was a need to. He tightened his control. "No matter what the outcome, Jaenelle will no longer visit Little Terreille without a full escort of my choosing."

Magstrom pushed himself out of the chair and carefully set his glass on the desk. "I think that's for the best. I hope Prince Yaslana will be among them."

Saetan held on until Lord Magstrom left the Hall. Then he threw the brandy glasses against the wall. It didn't make him feel better. The broken glass reminded him too much of a shattered crystal chalice and two sons who had paid dearly because he was their father.

He sank to his knees. He'd already wept for one son. He wouldn't grieve for the other. Not yet. He wouldn't grieve for that foolish, arrogant Eyrien prick, that charming, temperamental pain in the ass.

Ah, Lucivar.

5 / Kaeleer

"Damn it, Cat, I told you to wait." Lucivar threw an Ebon-gray shield across the game trail, half-wincing in anticipation of her running into it face first.

She stopped inches away from the shield and spun around, her glazed eyes searching for a spot in the thick undergrowth that she could push her way through.

"Stay away from me," she panted.

Lucivar held up the waterskin. "You ripped up your arm on the thorns back there. Let me pour some water over the cuts to clean them."

Looking down at her bare arm, she seemed surprised at the blood flowing freely from half a dozen deep scratches.

Lucivar gritted his teeth and waited. She'd stripped down to a sleeveless undershirt that offered her skin no protection in rough country, but right now sharp pain didn't hurt as much as the constant rub of cloth against oversensitive skin.

"Come on, Cat," he coaxed. "Just stick your arm out so that I can pour some water over it."

She cautiously held out her arm, her body angled away from him. Stepping only as close as necessary, he poured water over the scratches, washing away the blood and, he hoped, most of the dirt.

"Have a sip of water," he said, offering the waterskin. If he could coax her into taking a drink, maybe he could coax her into standing still for five minutes—something she hadn't done since he'd brought them to this part of Ebon Rih.

"Stay away from me." Her voice came out low and harsh. Desperate.

He shifted slightly, still offering the water.

"*Stay away from me.*" She whirled and ran through the Ebon-gray shield as if it weren't there.

He took a long drink and sighed. He would get her through this, somehow. But after the past two days of unrelenting movement, he wasn't sure how much more either of them could take.

Lucivar leaned against a tree, finding a little comfort in the rhythmic *whack whack whack* coming from the clearing. At least destroying the abandoned shack with a sledgehammer gave Jaenelle an outlet for sexual rage and burning energy. Even more important, it was an outlet that would keep her in one place for a little while.

Hell's fire, he was tired. The Masters of the Eyrien hunting camps couldn't match Jaenelle's ability to set a grueling pace. Even Smoke, with that tireless, ground-eating trot, was struggling. Of course, unlike one drug-driven witch, wolves liked to do things like eat and sleep, two items now high on Lucivar's list of sensual pleasures.

He called in his sleeping bag, unrolled it, and used Craft to fix it in the air high enough so that his wings wouldn't drag the ground. Pushing the top of the sleeping bag against the tree trunk, he sat down with a groan he didn't try to stifle.

Lucivar?

Lucivar looked around until he spotted Smoke peering at him from behind a tree. "It's all right. The Lady's tearing up a shack."

Smoke whined and hid behind the tree.

He puzzled over the wolf's distress, then hastily sent a mental picture of the broken-down structure.

Cabin made by stupid humans. Smoke sneezed.

Lucivar smothered a laugh. He couldn't argue with Smoke's conclusion. The wolf's reference points for a "proper human den" included the Hall, the cottages in Halaway, the family's other country houses, and Jaenelle's cabin. So it made sense that Smoke would see the shack as a den made by an inept human.

As knowledge of the kindred's reemergence spread, the human Blood had divided into two camps arguing over the intelligence and Craft abilities of the nonhuman Blood. It had amused and dismayed the few humans who had the opportunity to work with the wild kindred to discover that they had similar prejudices about humans. Humans were divided into two groups: their humans and other humans. Their humans were the Lady's humans—intelligent, well trained, and willing to learn the ways of others without insisting their way was best. The other humans were dangerous, stupid, cruel, and—as far as the feline Blood were concerned—prey. Both the Arcerian cats and the kindred tigers had a "word" for humans that roughly translated as "stupid meat."

Lucivar had argued once that since humans were dangerous and could hunt with weapons as well as Craft, they shouldn't be considered stupid. Smoke had pointed out that the tusked wild pigs were dangerous, too. They were still stupid.

Reassured that the Lady wasn't attacking anything with four feet, Smoke disappeared for a moment, returning with a dead rabbit. *Eat.*

"Have you eaten?" When Smoke didn't answer, Lucivar called in the food pack and large flask Draca had given him before he and Jaenelle left the Keep. He'd almost refused the food, thinking there would be plenty of fresh meat, thinking there would be time to build a fire and cook it. "You keep the rabbit," he said, digging into the pack. "I don't like raw meat."

Smoke cocked his head. *Fire?*

Lucivar shook his head, refusing to think about fires and sleep. He pulled a beef sandwich out of the pack and held it up.

Lucivar eat. Smoke settled down to his rabbit dinner.

Lucivar sipped from the flask of whiskey and slowly ate his sandwich, his attention partly focused on the sound of breaking wood.

This trip hadn't gone as he'd expected. He'd brought Jaenelle out here so that she could release the savage, drug-induced needs on nonhuman prey. He'd come with her to give her the target that would enrage, and satisfy, the bloodlust the most—a human male.

She'd refused to hunt, refused to buy herself a little relief at the cost of another living creature. Including him.

But she'd had no mercy for her own body. She had treated it like an enemy worthy of nothing but her contempt, an enemy that had betrayed her by leaving her vulnerable to someone's sadistic game.

Lucivar?

Lucivar shook his head, automatically probing for the source of Smoke's anxiety. A few birds chattering. A squirrel scrambling through the branches overhead. The usual wood sounds. *Only* the usual sounds.

His heart pounded as he and Smoke ran to the little clearing.

The shack was now a pile of broken timbers. A few feet away, Jaenelle sat on the ground, spraddle-legged, her hands still gripping the sledge-hammer's handle while the head rested between her feet.

Approaching cautiously, Lucivar squatted beside her. "Cat?"

Tears flowed down her face. Blood dribbled down her chin from the bite in her lower lip. She gulped air and shuddered. "I'm so tired, Lucivar. But it grabs me and . . ."

Her muscles tightened until her body shook from the tension. Her back arched. The cords in her neck stood out. She sucked air through clenched teeth. The sledgehammer's handle snapped in her hands.

Lucivar waited, not daring to touch her while her muscles were tight enough to snap. It didn't last more than a couple of minutes. It felt like hours. When it finally passed, her body sagged and she began crying so hard he thought it would tear him apart.

She didn't fight him when he put his arms around her, so he held her, rocked her, and let her cry herself out.

He felt the sexual tension rising as soon as she stopped crying, but he held on. If he was reading the intensity correctly, she was over the worst of it now.

After several minutes, she relaxed enough to rest her head on his shoulder. "Lucivar?"

"Mmm?"

"I'm hungry."

His heart sang. "Then I'll feed you."

Fire?

Jaenelle's head snapped up. She stared at the wolf standing at the edge of the clearing. "Why does he want to build a fire?"

"Damned if I know why he wants one. But if we did build one, I could make some laced coffee."

Jaenelle pondered this for a while. "You make good laced coffee."

Taking that for a "yes," Lucivar led Jaenelle to the other side of the clearing while Smoke started searching the debris for pieces of wood big enough to use for fuel.

Lucivar called in the food pack, flask, and sleeping bag he'd left by the creek. Jaenelle wandered from one side of the clearing to the other, nibbling the sandwich he'd given her. He kept an eye on her as he built the fire, called in the rest of their gear, and made camp. She seemed restless but not uncontrollably driven, which was good since they were losing the light and the day's warmth.

By the time he had the whisky-laced coffee ready, Jaenelle was tucked in her sleeping bag, shivering, eagerly reaching for the cup he handed her. He didn't suggest that she put on another layer of clothes. As long as she focused on the fire being the source of warmth, she'd be reluctant to wander away from it until morning.

He was rummaging through the food pack, looking for something else he could offer her to eat, when he heard a delicate snore.

After more than two days of unrelenting movement, Jaenelle slept.

Lucivar closed her sleeping bag and added a warming spell to keep her comfortable as the temperature dropped throughout the night. He pulled the coffeepot away from the heat and added more wood to the fire. Then he pulled off his boots and settled into his sleeping bag.

He should put a protective shield around the camp. He doubted a four-footed predator would want what was left in the food pack enough to challenge the combined scents of human and wolf, but they were on the northern border of Ebon Rih and uncomfortably close to Jhinka territory. The last thing Jaenelle needed right now was being jolted awake by a Jhinka hunting party's surprise attack.

Lucivar was sound asleep before he finished the thought.

6 / Hell

Resigned to the intrusion, Saetan settled back in one of the chairs by the fire and poured two glasses of yarbarah. He'd decided to spend some time in his private study beneath the Hall because he hadn't wanted to deal with any more frightened, clamoring minds—not after the past twenty-four hours. But Black-Jeweled Warlord Prince or not, High Lord or not, a man didn't refuse a Dea al Mon Queen when she asked for an audience—especially when she was also a demon-dead Harpy.

"What can I do for you, Titian?" he asked politely, handing her a glass of the warmed blood wine.

Titian accepted the glass and sipped delicately, her large blue eyes never looking away from his gold ones. "You've made the citizens of Hell very nervous. This is the first time, in all the centuries you've been the High Lord, that you've purged the Dark Realm."

"I rule Hell. I can do as I please here," Saetan said mildly. Even a fool could have heard the warning under the mild tone.

Titian hooked her long, fine, silver hair behind her pointed ear and chose to ignore the warning. "Do as you please or do what you must? It didn't escape the notice of the observant that the Dark Priestess's followers were the only ones consumed in this purge."

"Really?" He sounded politely interested. In truth, he felt relieved the connection had been made. Not only would the rest of the demon-dead relax once they realized his choice of who had been hurried to the final death was based on a specific allegiance, anyone Hekatah approached in the future would think long and hard about the cost of such allegiance. "Since you've no personal concern, why are you here?"

"You missed a few. I thought you should know."

Saetan quickly masked his distaste and dismay. Titian always saw too much. "You'll give me the names." It wasn't a question.

Titian smiled. "There's no need. The Harpies took care of them for you." She hesitated for a moment. "What about the Dark Priestess?"

Clenching his teeth, Saetan stared at the fire. "I couldn't find her. Hekatah's very good at playing least-in-sight."

"If you had, would you have hurried her return to the Darkness? Would you have sent her to the final death?"

Saetan flung his glass into the fireplace and instantly regretted it as the fire sizzled and the smell of hot blood filled the room.

He'd been asking himself that question since he'd made the decision to eliminate all the support Hekatah had among the demon-dead. If he had found her, could he have coldly drained her strength until she faded into the Darkness? Or would he have hesitated, as he'd done so many times before, because centuries of dislike and distrust couldn't erase the simple fact that she'd given him two of his sons. Three if he counted . . . but he didn't, couldn't count that child, just as he'd never allowed himself to consider who had held the knife.

He jerked when Titian brushed her hand over his.

"Here." She handed him another glass of warmed yarbarah. Sitting back, she traced the rim of her own glass with one finger. "You don't like killing women, do you?"

Saetan gulped the blood wine. "No, I don't."

"I thought so. You were much cleaner, much kinder with them than you were with the males."

"Perhaps by your standards." By his own standards, he'd been more than sufficiently brutal. He shrugged. "We are our mothers' sons."

"A reasonable assumption." She sounded solemn. She looked amused.

Saetan twitched his shoulders, unable to shake the feeling that she'd just dropped a noose over his head. "It's a pet theory of mine about why there's no male rank equal to a Queen."

"Because males are their mothers' sons?"

"Because, long ago, only females were Blood."

Titian curled up in her chair. "How intriguing."

Saetan studied her warily. Titian had the same look Jaenelle always had when she'd successfully cornered him and was quite willing to wait until he finished squirming and told her what she wanted to know.

"It's just something Andulvar and I used to argue about on long winter nights," he grumbled, refilling their glasses.

"It may not be winter but, in Hell, the nights are always long."

"You know the story about the dragons who first ruled the Realms?"

Titian shrugged, indicating that it didn't matter if she knew or not. She'd settled in to hear a story.

Saetan raised his glass in a salute and smiled grudgingly. Jeweled males might be trained as defenders of their territories, but no male could beat a Queen when it came to tactical strategy.

"Long ago," he began, "when the Realms were young, there lived a race of dragons. Powerful, brilliant, and magical, they ruled all the lands and all the creatures in them. But after hundreds of generations, there came a day when they realized their race would be no more, and rather than have their knowledge and their gifts die with them, they chose to give them to the other creatures so that they could continue the Craft and care for the Realms.

"One by one, the dragons sought their lairs and embraced the forever night, becoming part of the Darkness. When only the Queen and her Prince, Lorn, were left, the Queen bid her Consort farewell. As she flew through the Realms, her scales sprinkled down, and whatever creature her scales touched, whether it walked on two legs or four or danced in the air on wings, whatever creature a scale touched became blood of her blood—still part of the race it came from, but also Other, remade to become caretaker and ruler. When the last scale fell from her, she vanished. Some stories say her body was transformed into some other shape, though it still contained a dragon's soul. Others say her body faded and she returned to the Darkness."

Saetan swirled the yarbarah in his glass. "I've read all the old stories—some from the original text. What's always intrigued me is that, no matter what race the story came from, the Queen is never named. In all the stories, Lorn is mentioned by name, repeatedly, but not her. The omission seems deliberate. I've always wondered why."

"And the Prince of Dragons?" Titian asked. "What happened to him?"

"According to the legends, Lorn still exists, and he contains all the knowledge of the Blood."

Titian looked thoughtful. "When Jaenelle turned fifteen and Draca said that Lorn had decided Jaenelle would live with you at the Hall, I had thought she was just saying that to block Cassandra's objections."

"No, she meant it. He and Jaenelle have been friends for years. He gifted her with her Jewels."

Titian opened and closed her mouth without making a sound.

Her stunned expression pleased him.

"Have you seen him?"

"No," Saetan replied sourly. "*I've* not been granted an audience."

"Oh, dear," Titian said with no sympathy whatsoever. "What does the legend have to do with the Blood once being all female, and why didn't we keep it that way?"

"You would have liked that, wouldn't you?"

She smiled.

"All right, my theory is this. Since the Queen's scales gifted the Craft to other races, and since like calls to like, it seems reasonable that only the females were able to absorb the magic. They became bonded to the land, drawn by their own body rhythms to the ebb and flow of the natural world. They became the Blood."

"Which would have lasted one generation," Titian pointed out.

"Not all men are stupid." When she looked doubtful, Saetan let out an exasperated sigh. The only thing more pointless than arguing with a Harpy about the value of males was trying to teach a rock to sing. He would have better luck with the rock. "For theory's sake, let's say we're talking about the Dea al Mon."

"Ah." Titian settled back, content. "*Our* males *are* intelligent."

"I'm sure they're relieved you think so," Saetan said dryly. "So, upon discovering that some of the women in their Territory suddenly had magical powers and skills . . ."

"The best young warriors would offer themselves as mates and protectors," Titian said promptly.

Saetan raised an eyebrow. Since landens, the non-Blood of each race, tended to be so wary of the Blood and their Craft, that wasn't quite the way he'd always pictured it, but he found it interesting that a Dea al Mon witch would make that assumption. He'd have to ask Chaosti and Gabrielle at some point. "And from those unions, children were born. The girls, because of gender, received the full gift."

"But the boys were half-Blood with little or no Craft." Titian held out her glass. Saetan refilled it.

"Witches don't bear many children," Saetan continued after refilling his own glass. "Depending on the ratio of sons to daughters, it could have taken several more generations before males bred true. Through all that time, the power would have been in the distaff gender, each generation learning from the one before and becoming stronger. The first Queens probably appeared long before the first Warlord, let alone a male stronger than that. By then, the idea that males served and protected females would have been ingrained. In the end, what you have is the Blood society where Warlords are equal in status to witches, Princes are equal to Priestesses and Healers, and Black Widows only have to defer to Warlord Princes and Queens. And Warlord Princes, who are considered a law unto themselves, are a step above the other castes and a step—a long step—beneath the Queens."

"When caste is added to each individual's social rank and Jewel rank, it makes an intriguing dance." Titian set her glass on the table. "An interesting theory, High Lord."

"An interesting diversion, Lady Titian. Why did you do it? Why did you offer me your company tonight?"

Titian smoothed her forest-green tunic. "You are kin of my kin. It seemed . . . fitting . . . to offer you comfort tonight since Jaenelle could not. Good night, High Lord."

Long after she'd gone, Saetan sat quietly, watching the logs in the fireplace break and settle. He roused himself enough to pour and warm one last glass of yarbarah, content now with the solitude and silence.

He didn't dispute her theory of why males came to serve, but it wasn't his. It wasn't just the magic that had drawn the males. It was the inner radiance housed within those female bodies, a luminescence that some men had craved as much as they might have craved a light they could see glowing in a window when they were standing out in the cold. They had craved that light as much as they had craved being sheathed in the sweet darkness of a woman's body, if not more.

Males had become Blood because they'd been drawn to both.

And, as he knew all too well, they still were.

7 / Kaeleer

Lucivar lay on his back in the young grass, his hands behind his head, his wings spread to dry after the quick dip in the spring-fed pool. Jaenelle was still splashing around in the cold water, washing the sweat and dirt out of her long hair.

He closed his eyes and groaned contentedly as the sun slowly warmed and loosened tight muscles.

Yesterday, he'd awakened just before dawn to find Jaenelle busily rummaging through the food pack. They'd managed a hasty meal before the physical tension produced by the drugs forced her to move.

It wasn't the unrelenting drive of the previous days, and as the day wore on, physical tension gave way to emotional storms. Anger would flood her suddenly, then turn to tears. He gave her space while she raged and swore. He held her while she cried. When the storm passed, she'd be fine for a little while. They would walk at an easy pace, stopping to pick wild berries or rest near a stream. Then the cycle would start over, each time with a little less intensity.

This morning, he and Smoke had brought down a small deer. He'd kept enough meat to fill the small, cold-spelled food box he'd brought with him and had sent Smoke back to the Keep with the rest. If Saetan wasn't at the Keep, Smoke would go on to the Hall to let the High Lord know that the worst had passed and they would spend a few more days in Askavi before coming home. ·

Home. He'd lived in Kaeleer for a year now, and the way witches treated males in the Shadow Realm still bewildered him sometimes.

One day he'd walked in on a discussion Chaosti, Aaron, and Khardeen were having about how the Ring of Honor worn by males in a Queen's First Circle differed from the Restraining Ring Terreillean males were required to wear until they proved themselves trustworthy. He told them about the Ring of Obedience that was used in Terreille.

They didn't believe him. Oh, intellectually they understood what he said, but they had never known the saturating, day-to-day fear Terreillean males lived with, so they didn't, *couldn't*, believe him.

Wondering if the boys simply weren't old enough to have firsthand experience in the ways a witch kept her males leashed, he had asked Sylvia, Halaway's Queen, how a Queen controlled a male who didn't want to serve in her court.

She'd gaped at him a moment before blurting out, "Who'd want one?"

A few months ago, while in Nharkhava running an errand for the High Lord, he'd been invited to tea by three elderly Ladies who had praised his physique with such good-natured delight that he couldn't feel insulted. Feeling comfortable with them, he had asked if they'd heard anything about the Warlord Prince who had recently killed a Queen.

They reluctantly admitted that the story was true. A Queen who had acquired a taste for cruelty had been unable to form a court because she couldn't convince twelve males to serve her willingly. So she decided to *force* males into service by using that Ring of Obedience device. She had collected eleven lighter-Jeweled Warlords and was looking for the twelfth male when the Warlord Prince confronted her. *He* was looking for a younger cousin who had disappeared the month before. When she tried to force him to submit, he killed her.

What happened to the Warlord Prince?

It took them a moment to understand the question.

Nothing happened to the Warlord Prince. After all, he did exactly what he was supposed to do. Granted, they all wished he had simply restrained that horrible woman and handed her over to Nharkhava's Queen for punishment, but one has to expect this sort of thing when a Warlord Prince is provoked enough to rise to the killing edge.

Lucivar had spent the rest of that day in a tavern, unsure if he felt amused or terrified by the Ladies' attitude. He thought about the beatings, the whippings, the times he'd screamed in agony when pain was sent through the Ring of Obedience. He thought of what he'd done to earn that pain. He sat in that tavern and laughed until he cried when he finally realized he would never be able to reconcile the differences between Terreille and Kaeleer.

In Kaeleer, service was an intricate dance, the lead constantly changing between the genders. Witches nurtured and protected male strength and pride. Males, in turn, protected and respected the gentler, but somehow deeper, feminine strength.

Males weren't slaves or pets or tools to be used without regard to feelings. They were valuable, and valued, partners.

That, Lucivar had decided that day, was the leash the Queens used in Kaeleer—control so gentle and sweet a man had no reason to fight against it and every reason to fiercely protect it.

Loyalty, on both sides. Respect, on both sides. Honor, on both sides. Pride, on both sides.

This was the place he now proudly called home.

"Lucivar."

Lucivar shot to his feet, cursing silently. Considering the tension he felt in her, he was lucky she hadn't taken off without him.

"Something's wrong," she said in her midnight voice.

He immediately probed the area. "Where? I don't sense anything."

"Not right here. To the east."

The only thing east of them was a landen village under the protection of Agio, the Blood village at the northern end of Ebon Rih.

"There's something wrong there, but it's elusive," Jaenelle said, her eyes narrowed as she stared eastward. "And it feels *twisted* somehow, like a snare filled with poison bait. But it slips away from me every time I try to focus on it." She snarled, frustrated. "Maybe the drugs are messing up my ability to sense things."

He thought about the Queen who had ensnared eleven young men before being killed. "Or maybe you're just the wrong gender for the bait." Keeping his inner barriers tightly shielded, he sent a delicate psychic probe eastward. A minute later, swearing viciously, he snapped the link and clung to Jaenelle, letting her clean, dark strength wash away the foulness he'd brushed against.

He pressed his forehead against hers. "It's bad, Cat. A lot of desperation and pain surrounded by . . ." He searched for some way to describe what he'd felt.

Carrion.

Shuddering, he wondered why the word came to mind.

He could fly over the village and take a quick look. If the landens were fighting off a Jhinka raiding party, he was strong enough to give them whatever help they needed. If it was one of those spring fevers that sometimes ran through a village, it would be better to know that before sending a message to Agio since the Healers would be needed.

His main concern was finding a safe—

"Don't even think it, Lucivar," Jaenelle warned softly. "I'm going with you."

Lucivar eyed her, trying to judge just how far he could push her this time. "You know, the Ring of Honor you had made for me won't stop me the way the Restraining Ring would have."

She muttered an Eyrien curse that was quite explicit.

He smiled grimly. That pretty much answered the question of how far he could push. He looked toward the east. "All right, you're going with me. But we'll do this my way, Cat."

Jaenelle nodded. "You're the one with fighting experience. But . . ." She pressed her right palm against the Ebon-gray Jewel resting on his chest. "Spread your wings."

As he opened his wings to their full span, he felt a hot-cold tingle from the Ring of Honor.

She stepped back, satisfied. "This shield is braided into the protective shield already contained in the Ring. You could drain your Jewels to the breaking point, and it will still hold around you. It's fixed about a foot out from your body and will mesh with mine so we can stay tight without endangering each other. But make sure you keep clear of anything else you don't want to damage."

Having made regular circuits to all the villages in Ebon Rih, Lucivar knew the landen village and surrounding land fairly well. Plenty of low hills and woodland within striking distance of the village—perfect hiding places for a Jhinka raiding party.

The Jhinka were a fierce, winged people made up of patriarchal clans loosely joined together by a dozen tribal chiefs. Like the Eyriens, they were native to Askavi, but they were smaller and had a fraction of the life span of the long-lived Eyriens. The two races had hated each other for as long as either of them could remember.

While Eyriens had the advantage of Craft, the Jhinka had the advantage of numbers. Once drained of his psychic power and the reserves in the Jewels, an Eyrien warrior was as vulnerable as any other man when fighting against overwhelming odds. So, accepting the slaughter required to bring down an enemy, the Jhinka had always been willing to meet an Eyrien in battle.

With two exceptions. One walked among the dead, the other among the living. Both wore Ebon-gray Jewels.

"All right," Lucivar said. "We'll run on this White radial thread until we're past the village, then drop from the Winds and come in fast from the other side. If this is a Jhinka raid, I'll handle it. If it's something else . . ."

She just looked at him.

He cleared his throat. "Come on, Cat. Let's give whoever is messing with our valley a reason to regret it."

8 / Kaeleer

Dropping from the White Wind, Lucivar and Jaenelle glided toward the peaceful-looking village still a mile away.

You said we'd go in fast, Jaenelle said on a psychic thread.

I also said we'd do this my way, Lucivar replied sharply.

There's pain and need down there, Lucivar.

There was also the foulness that now eluded him. It was still there. Had to be. That he could no longer sense it, would never have sensed it if he'd simply come to check on the village, made him uneasy. He would have stumbled into whatever trap was waiting down there.

He felt the predator wake in her at the same moment she began a hawk-dive, dropping toward the village at full speed. Swearing, he folded his wings and dove after her just as hundreds of Jhinka appeared out of nowhere, screeching their battle cries as they tried to surround him and pull him down.

Using Craft to enhance his speed, Lucivar drove through the Jhinka swarm, relishing the screams when they hit his protective shield. Roaring an Eyrien war cry, he unleashed the power in his Ebon-gray Jewels in short, controlled bursts.

Jhinka bodies exploded into a bloody mist full of severed limbs.

He burst through the bottom of the swarm, coming out of his dive a wing-length from the ground. *Cat!*

Come down the main street, but hurry. The tunnel won't hold for long. Avoid the side streets. They're . . . fouled. There's a shielded building at the other end of the village.

Flying low, Lucivar swung toward the main street, hit the village boundary at top speed, and swore every curse he knew as his shield brushed against the psychic witch storm engulfing the deceptively peaceful-looking village. The shield sizzled like drops of cold water flicked into a hot pan. All the ensnaring psychic threads flared as if they were physical threads made out of lightning.

Pushing hard, he flew through the already contracting tunnel Jaenelle had created as she passed through the witch storm and finally caught up with her a block away from the shielded building. A fast psychic probe showed him the parameters of the domed, oval-shaped shield that protected a two-story stone building and ten yards of ground all around it.

Four men ran toward the edge of the shield, waving their arms and shouting, "Go back! Get away from here!"

Behind the men, thousands of Jhinka rose from the low hills beyond the village, filling the sky until they blotted out the sun.

Jaenelle passed through the building's shield as easily as if it were a thin layer of water. Distracted by the men and the approaching Jhinka, Lucivar felt like he was passing through a wall of warm taffy.

As soon as they were inside the building's shield, Lucivar landed next to the four men. The protective shield Jaenelle had created for him contracted to a skintight sheath, produced a mild tingle in the Ring of Honor, then vanished completely.

"How many wounded?" Jaenelle snapped.

Lord Randahl, the Agio Warlord who was Lady Erika's Master of the Guard, replied reluctantly, "Last count, about three hundred, Lady."

"How many Healers?"

"The village had two physicians and a wisewoman who could do a bit of herb healing. All dead."

Knowing better than to interrupt when Jaenelle focused on healing, Lucivar waited until she ran into the building before snapping out his own demands. "Who's holding the shield?"

"Adler is," Randahl said, jerking a thumb toward a young, haggard-faced Warlord.

Lucivar glanced toward the low hills. The Jhinka would descend on them at any moment. "Can you push your shield out another inch or two all around?" he asked Adler. "I'll put an Ebon-gray shield behind it. Then you can drop your shield and rest."

The young Warlord nodded wearily and closed his eyes.

Seconds after Lucivar put up his shield, the Jhinka attacked. They slammed against the invisible barrier, their bodies piling up five and six deep as they clawed at the shield. Some of the Jhinka, pressed between the shield and the rest of the swarm, were smothered or crushed by the mass of writhing bodies. Dead, hate-filled eyes stared at the five men below.

"Hell's fire," Randahl muttered. "Even during the worst attacks, they didn't come in like *this*."

Lucivar studied the middle-aged Warlord for a moment before returning his attention to the Jhinka. *Maybe they hadn't trapped what they'd wanted until now.*

He could feel the pressure of all those bodies piling up on the shield, could feel the Ebon-gray Jewels release drop after drop of his reserve strength. While all the Jewels provided a reservoir for the psychic power, the darker the Jewel, the deeper the reservoir. As the second darkest Jewel, the

Ebon-gray provided a cache of power deep enough that, if he didn't need to use them for anything beyond maintaining the shield against physical attacks, he could hold the Jhinka off for a week before he felt the strain. Someone would come looking for them before that. All he needed to do was wait.

But there was that witch storm to consider. He felt certain someone had created this trap especially for him. He'd have to check with Randahl, but he suspected the first Jhinka attack hadn't given them time to get in supplies. And Jaenelle needed other Healers to assist with the wounded. The Darkness knew she had the psychic reserves to do all the healing, but her body wouldn't hold up under that kind of demand, especially after the drugs and the physical strain of the past few days.

Besides, no one had ever accused him of having a passive temper.

Lucivar vanished his Ebon-gray ring and called in his Birthright Red. The Ebon-gray around his neck would feed the shield. The Red . . .

"Tell your men to stay tight to the building," Lucivar said quietly to Randahl. "It's time to even up the odds a bit."

Smiling his lazy, arrogant smile, he raised his right hand and triggered the spell he'd spent years perfecting. Seven thin psychic "wires" shot out of the Red Jewel in his ring. Keeping his arm straight, he made leisurely sweeps back and forth, always careful that he didn't stray too close to the building. Back and forth. Up and down.

Jhinka blood ran down the shield. Jhinka bodies slithered and slid as the ones who could see the danger tried to push themselves out of the pile before that sweeping arm returned.

Satisfied with the panicked scramble on that side of the shield, he walked around the building, his hand always aimed at the shield.

And the Jhinka died.

He was starting a third circuit when the Jhinka who were still trying to pile onto the shield finally caught the panic of the ones trying to get away from it. Chittering and screeching, they rose off the shield and headed for the low hills.

Lucivar drew the psychic "wires" back into his ring, ended the spell, and slowly lowered his arm.

Randahl, Adler, and the two Warlords Lucivar hadn't been introduced to yet stared, sick-faced, at the blood running down the shield, at the pieces of bodies sliding to the ground.

"Mother Night," Randahl whispered. "Mother Night."

They wouldn't look at him. Or rather, whenever their glances brushed in his direction, he saw the worried speculation that they might have something locked inside with them that was far more dangerous and deadly than the enemy waiting outside.

Which was true.

"I'm going to check on the Lady," Lucivar said abruptly.

Being a Master of the Guard, Randahl would try to act normally once he had a few minutes to steady himself. If nothing else, the man would fall back on the Protocol for dealing with a Warlord Prince. But the others . . .

Everything has a price.

Lucivar approached the front of the building and gave himself a moment to steady his own feelings. If other Blood couldn't deal with a Warlord Prince on the killing edge, wounded landens most certainly couldn't. And right now, hysteria could trigger a vicious desire for bloodletting. A male coming away from the killing edge needed someone, preferably female, to help him stabilize. That was one of the many slender threads that bound the Blood. The witches, during their vulnerable times, needed that aggressive male strength, and the males needed, sometimes desperately, the shelter and comfort they found in a woman's gentle strength.

He needed Jaenelle.

Lucivar smiled bitterly as he entered the building. Right now, everyone needed Jaenelle. He hoped—sweet Darkness, how he hoped!—being near her would be enough.

The community hall held various-sized rooms where the villagers could gather for dances or meetings. At least, he assumed that's what it was for. He'd never had much contact with landens. As he scanned the largest room, aching for Jaenelle's familiar presence, he felt the pain and fear of the wounded landens sitting against the walls or lying on the floor. The pain he could handle. The fear, which spiked in the ones who noticed him, undermined his shaky self-control.

Lucivar started to turn away when he noticed the young man lying on a narrow mattress near the door. Under normal circumstances, he might have assumed the man was another landen, but he'd seen too many men in similar circumstances not to recognize a weak psychic scent.

Dropping to one knee, Lucivar carefully lifted the side of the doubled-over sheet that covered the body from neck to feet. His eyes shifted from the wounds to the still, pain-tight face and back again. He swore silently. The gut wounds were bad. Men had died from less. They weren't beyond Jaenelle's healing skill, but he wondered if she could rebuild the parts that were no longer there.

Lowering the sheet, Lucivar left the room, his curses becoming louder and more vicious as he searched for some empty room where he could try to leash a temper spiraling out of control.

Randahl hadn't said any of his men had been wounded. And why was the boy—no, man; anyone with those kinds of battle wounds didn't deserve to be called a boy—kept apart from the others, tucked against a shadowed wall where he might easily go unnoticed?

Catching the warmth of a feminine psychic scent, Lucivar threw open a door and stepped inside the kitchen before he realized, too late, the woman trying to pump water one-handed wasn't Jaenelle.

She spun around when the door crashed against the wall, throwing her left arm up as if to stop an attacker.

Lucivar hated her. Hated her for not being Jaenelle. Hated her for the fear in her eyes that was pushing him toward blind rage. Hated her for being young and pretty. And most of all, hated her because he knew that, at any second now, she would bolt and he would be on her, hurting her, even killing her before he could stop himself.

Then she swallowed hard, and said in a quiet, quivering voice, "I'm trying to boil some water to make teas for the wounded, but the pump's stiff and I can't work it with one hand. Would you help me?"

A knot of tension eased inside him. Here, at least, was a landen female who knew how to deal with Blood males. Asking for help was always the easiest way to redirect one of them toward service.

As Lucivar came forward, she stepped aside, trembling. His temper started to climb again until he noticed the bandaged right arm she held over her stomach, her hand tucked between her dress and apron.

Not fear then, but fatigue and blood loss.

He placed a chair close enough for her to supervise, but far enough away so that he wouldn't keep brushing against her. "Sit down."

Once she was seated, he pumped water and set the filled pots on the wood-burning stove. He noticed the bags of herbs laid out on the wooden table next to the double sink and looked at her curiously. "Lord Randahl said the wisewoman died along with your two physicians."

Her eyes filled with tears as she nodded. "My grandmother. She said I had the gift and was teaching me."

Lucivar leaned against the table, puzzled. Landen minds were too weak to give off a psychic scent, but hers did. "Where did you learn how to handle Blood males?"

Her eyes widened with anxiety. "I wasn't trying to control you!"

"I said handle, not control. There's a difference."

"I—I just did what the Lady said to do."

The tension inside him loosened another notch. "What's your name?"

"Mari." She hesitated. "You're Prince Yaslana, aren't you?"

"Does that bother you?" Lucivar asked in a colorless voice. To his surprise, Mari smiled shyly.

"Oh, no. The Lady said we could trust you."

The words warmed him like a lover's caress. But, having caught the slight emphasis in her tone, he wondered whom the landens in the village couldn't trust. His gold eyes narrowed as he studied her. "You have some Blood in your background, don't you?"

Mari paled a little and wouldn't look at him. "My great-grandmother was half-Blood. S-some people say I'm a throwback to her."

"From my point of view, that's no bad thing." Her naked relief was too much for him, so he began inspecting the bags of herbs. She'd be too quick to think she was the cause of his anger, so he fiddled with the bags until he had his feelings leashed again.

In his experience, half-Blood children were seldom welcomed or accepted by either society. The Blood didn't want them because they didn't have enough power to expend on all the basic things the Blood used Craft for and, therefore, could never be more than base servants. The landens didn't want them because they had too much power, and that kind of ability, untrained and free of any moral code, had produced more than its share of petty tyrants who had used magic and fear to rule a village that wouldn't accept them otherwise.

The water reached a boil.

"Sit down," Lucivar snapped when Mari started to rise. "You can tell me from there what you want blended. Besides," he added with a smile to take the sting out of the snap, "I've blended simple healing brews for a harder taskmistress than you."

Looking properly sympathetic and murmuring agreement that the

Lady could be a bit snarly about mixing up healing brews, Mari pointed out the herbs she intended to use and told him the blends she wanted.

"Do you see much of the Lady?" Lucivar asked as he pulled the pots off the stove and set them on stone trivets arranged at one end of the table. Despite Jaenelle's continued refusal to set up a formal court, her opinions were heeded throughout most of Kaeleer.

"She comes by for an afternoon every couple of weeks. She and Gran and I talk about healing Craft while her friends teach Khevin."

"Who's—" He bit off the question. He'd thought the young man's psychic scent was so weak because of the seriousness of the wounds. But it was strong for a half-Blood. "Which friends are teaching him?"

"Lord Khardeen and Prince Aaron."

Khary and Aaron were good choices if you were going to teach basic Craft to a half-Blood youth. Which didn't excuse Jaenelle from not asking *him* to participate. Lucivar carefully lowered the herb-filled gauze pouches into the pots of water. "They're both strongly grounded in basic Craft." Then, feeling spiteful, he added, "Unlike the Lady, who still can't manage to call in her own shoes."

Mari's prim sniff caught him by surprise. "I don't see why you all make such a fuss about it. If I had a friend who could do all those wonderful bits of magic, *I* wouldn't begrudge fetching her shoes."

Annoyed, Lucivar grumbled under his breath as he rattled through the cupboards searching for the cups. Damn woman certainly *was* a throwback. If nothing else, she had a witch's disposition.

He shut up when he saw how pale Mari had become. A little ashamed, he ladled out a cup of one of the healing brews and stood over her while she drank it.

"I saw Khevin when I came in," Lucivar said quietly. "I saw the wounds. Why didn't Khary and Aaron teach him how to shield?"

Mari looked up, surprised. "They did. Khevin's the one who shielded the community hall when the Jhinka started to attack."

"I think you'd better explain that," Lucivar said slowly, feeling as if she'd just punched the air out of him. A strong half-Blood might have enough power to create a personal shield for a few minutes, but he shouldn't have been able to create and hold a shield large enough to protect a building. Of course, Jaenelle had uncanny instincts when it came to recognizing strength that had been blocked in some way.

Mari, looking puzzled, confirmed that. "Khevin met the Lady one day when she came to visit Gran and me. She just looked at him for a long minute and then said he was too strong not to be properly trained in the Craft. When she came the next time, she brought Lord Khardeen and Prince Aaron. Creating a shield was the first thing they taught him."

Mari's hand started to tremble. The cup tipped.

Lucivar used Craft to steady the cup so that the hot liquid wouldn't spill on her.

"They were the first friends Khevin's ever had." Her eyes pleaded with him to understand. Then she blushed and looked down. "Male friends, I mean. They didn't laugh at him or call him names like some of the young Warlords from Agio do."

"What about the older Warlords?" Lucivar asked, careful to keep the anger out of his voice.

Mari shrugged. "They seemed embarrassed if they saw him when they came to check on the village. They didn't want to know he existed. They didn't want to see me around either," she added bitterly. "But with Lord Khardeen and Prince Aaron. . . . When the lesson was over, they would stay a little while to have a glass of ale and just talk. They told him about the Blood's code of honor and the rules Blood males are supposed to live by. Sometimes it made me wonder if the Blood in Agio had ever heard of those rules."

If they hadn't, they were going to. "The shield," he prompted.

"All of a sudden, the sky was filled with Jhinka screaming like they do. Khevin told me to come to the community hall. We . . . the Lady says that sometimes a link is formed when people like us are . . . close."

Lucivar glanced at her left hand. No marriage ring. Lovers then. At least Khevin had known, and given, that pleasure.

"I was at this end of the village, delivering some of Gran's herb medicines. The adults wouldn't listen to me, so I just grabbed a little girl who was playing outside and yelled at the other children to come with me. I—I think I *made* some of them come with me.

"When we got to the community building, Khevin had a shield around it. He was sweating. It looked like it was hurting him."

Lucivar was sure that it had.

"He said he'd tried to send a message to Agio on a psychic thread, but he wasn't sure anyone would hear it. Then he told me someone had to stay inside the shield in order to reach through it to bring another person in. He brought me through just as one of the Jhinka flew at us. The Jhinka hit the shield so hard it knocked him out. Khevin got his ax—he'd been chopping wood when the attack started. He went through the shield and k-killed the Jhinka. By then all the men in the village were in the streets, fighting. Khevin stayed outside to protect the children while I pulled them through the shield.

"By then the Jhinka were all around us. A lot of the women who tried to reach the building didn't make it, or were badly wounded by the time I pulled them through the shield. Gran . . . Gran was almost within reach when one of the Jhinka swooped down and . . . He laughed. He looked at me and he laughed while he killed her."

Lucivar refilled the cup and put a warming spell on the pots while Mari groped in her apron pocket for a handkerchief.

She sipped the herbal tea, saying nothing for a minute. "Khevin couldn't keep fighting and hold the shield, too. Even I could see that. He had a-arrows in his legs. He couldn't move very fast. They caught him before he could go through the shield and did that to him. Then Lord Randahl and the others came and started fighting.

"Two of the Warlords were shielding the wounded, leading them here, while the other two kept killing and killing.

"Khevin's shield started to fail. I was afraid the Warlords would put up another one that I couldn't get through, and Khevin would be left outside. As I reached out and grabbed him, a Jhinka saw me and slashed my arm. I pulled Khevin through just before the Warlords slipped inside and put up another shield."

Mari sipped her tea. "Lord Adler started swearing because they couldn't break through the witch storm around the village to send a message to Agio. But Lord Randahl just kept looking at Khevin.

"Then he and Lord Adler picked Khevin up l-like he was finally worth something. They took the mattress and sheets from the caretaker's bed and did what they could to make him comfortable." Mari stared at the cup, tears running down her face. "That's it."

Lucivar took the empty cup, wanting to offer her some comfort but not sure if she could accept it from a Warlord Prince. Maybe from someone like Aaron, who was the same age, but from him?

"Mari?"

Relief washed through him when Jaenelle walked into the kitchen.

"Let's see your arm," Jaenelle said, gently loosening the bandage and ignoring Mari's stammered pleas to take care of Khevin. "First your arm. I need you whole so you can help me with the others. We're going to need some mild—ah, you've already prepared some."

While Jaenelle healed the deep knife wound that had opened Mari's arm from elbow to wrist, Lucivar ladled out cups of the healing teas and put a warming spell on each cup. After a bit of cupboard hunting, he found two large metal serving trays. Full, they'd be too heavy for Mari—especially since Jaenelle had just warned her that the kind of fast healing she was going to have to do wasn't going to hold up under strain—but the young Warlords out there could do the heavy hauling and lifting now that he was maintaining the shield.

Jaenelle solved the problem by putting a float spell on both trays so that they hovered waist high. Mari didn't need to lift, just steer.

With Lucivar and Mari guiding the trays, the three of them went to the large room. Jaenelle ignored the clamor that began as soon as the villagers saw her and went to the shadowed wall where Khevin lay.

Mari hesitated, biting her lip, obviously torn between her desire to go to her lover and her duties as assistant Healer. Lucivar gave her shoulder a quick, encouraging squeeze before he joined Jaenelle. He didn't know what help he could give her, but he'd do whatever he could.

As Jaenelle started to lift the sheet, Khevin's eyes opened. With effort, he grabbed her hand.

She stared at the young man, her eyes blank. It was as if she had gone so deep within herself that the windows of the soul could no longer reveal the person who lived within.

"Do you fear me?" she asked in a midnight whisper.

"No, Lady." Khevin licked his dry lips. "But it's a Warlord's privilege to protect his people. Take care of them first."

Lucivar tried to reach her with a psychic thread, but Jaenelle had shut him out. *Please, Cat. Let him have his pride.*

She reached under the sheet. Khevin moaned a wordless protest.

"I'll do as you ask because you asked," she said, "but I'm going to tie in some of the threads from the healing web I've built *now* so that you'll stay with me." She smoothed the sheet and rested one long-nailed finger at the base of his throat. "And I warn you, Khevin, you had better stay with me."

Khevin smiled at her and closed his eyes.

Cupping her elbow, Lucivar led Jaenelle into the hallway. "Since they won't be needed for the shield, I'll send the younger Warlords in to help with the fetching and carrying."

"Adler, yes. Not the other two."

The ice in her voice chilled him. He'd never heard any Queen condemn a man so thoroughly.

"Very well," he said respectfully. "I can—"

"Keep this place safe, Yaslana."

He felt the quiver, swiftly leashed, and locked his emotions up tight. Hell's fire, even if the drugs were out of her system enough for her to do the healings, her emotions weren't stable. And she knew it.

"Cat . . ."

"I'll hold. You don't have to watch your back because of that."

He grinned. "Actually, it's when you're hissing and spitting that you're the most useful when it comes to guarding my back."

Her sapphire eyes warmed a little. "I'll remind you of that."

Lucivar headed for the outside door. He'd have to keep an eye on her to make sure she drank some water and had a bite to eat every couple of hours. He'd slip a word to Mari. It was always easier to get Jaenelle to eat if someone else was eating, too.

As he turned back, he felt the impact of bodies against the shield and heard the warning shouts from the Warlords outside.

He'd talk to Mari later. The Jhinka had returned.

9 / Kaeleer

Lucivar leaned against the covered well and gratefully took the mug of coffee Randahl handed to him. It tasted rough and muddy. He didn't care. At that moment, he would have drunk piss as long as it was hot.

The Jhinka had attacked throughout the night—sometimes small parties striking the shield and then fleeing, sometimes a couple hundred battering at the shield while he sliced them apart. There had been no sleep, no rest. Just the steadily increasing fatigue and physical drain of channeling the power stored in the Jewels as well as the steady drain of that power—a more rapid drain than he had anticipated. Randahl and the other Warlords had exhausted their reserves by the time he and Jaenelle had arrived yesterday, so he was now their only protection and most of their fighting ability.

Because the shield hadn't extended more than a couple of inches below the ground, he'd discovered, almost too late, that the Jhinka had been using the piles of bodies for cover while they dug under the shield. So now the shield went down five feet before turning inward and running underground until it reached the building's foundation.

While they were fighting the Jhinka who'd gotten under the south side of the shield, Lucivar had responded to instinct and raced to the north side of the building, reaching the corner just as one of the Jhinka ran toward the well. The earthenware jar the Jhinka carried had contained enough concentrated poison to destroy their only water supply. So the well now had a separate shield around it.

As soon as the attack on the well had been thwarted and the shield extended, the witch storm had re-formed over the building. No longer spread out to cover the whole village and hide the destruction, it had become a tight mass of tangled psychic threads, an invisible cloud full of psychic lightning that sizzled every time it brushed the shield.

The extra shielding and the constant reinforcement against another's Craft were doing what the Jhinka alone couldn't do—draining him to the breaking point. It would take another day. Maybe two. After that, weak spots would appear in the shield—spots the witch storm could penetrate to entangle already exhausted minds, spots the Jhinka could break through to attack already exhausted bodies.

He'd briefly toyed with the idea of insisting that Jaenelle return to the Keep for help. He'd dismissed the idea just as quickly. Until the healings were done, nothing and no one would convince her to leave. If he admitted the shield might fail, more than likely she would throw a Black shield around the building, straining a body already overtaxed by the large healing web she'd created to strengthen all the wounded until she could get to them. Totally focused on the healing, she wouldn't give a second thought to driving her body beyond its limits. And he already knew what she would say if he argued with her about the damage she was doing to herself: everything has a price.

So he'd held his tongue and his temper, determined to hold out until someone from Agio or the Keep came looking for them.

Now, in the chill, early dawn, he couldn't find enough energy to produce any body heat, so he wrapped his cold hands around the warm mug.

Randahl sipped his coffee in silence, his back turned toward the village.

He was a fair-skinned Rihlander with faded blue eyes and thinning, cinnamon hair. His body had a middle-years thickness but the muscles were still solid, and he had more stamina than the three younger Warlords put together.

"The women who can are helping out in the kitchen," Randahl said after a few minutes. "They were pleased to get the venison and other supplies you brought with you. They're using most of the meat to make broth for the seriously wounded, but they said they'd make a stew with the rest. You should have seen the sour looks they gave Mari when she insisted that we get the first bowls. Hell's fire, they even whined about giving us this sludge to drink, and me standing right there." He shook his head in disgust. "Damn landens. It's gotten to the point where the little ones run, screaming, whenever we walk into a village. They go around making signs against evil behind our backs, but they squeal loud enough when they need help."

Lucivar sipped his quickly cooling coffee. "If you feel that way about landens, why did you come to help when the Jhinka attacked?"

"Not for *them*. To protect the land. Won't have that Jhinka filth in Ebon Rih. We came to protect the land—and to get those two out." Randahl's shoulders sagged. "Hell's fire, Yaslana. Who would have thought the boy could build a shield like that?"

"No one in Agio, obviously." Before Randahl could snap a reply, Lucivar continued harshly, "If Mari and Khevin matter to you, why didn't you let them live in Agio instead of leaving them here to be sneered at and slighted?"

Randahl's face flushed a dull red. "And what would an Ebon-gray Warlord Prince know about being sneered at or slighted?"

Lucivar didn't know whether he made the decision because he no longer cared what people knew about him or because he wasn't sure he and Randahl would survive. "I grew up in Terreille, not Kaeleer. I was too young to remember my father when I was taken from him, so I grew up being told, and believing, that I was a half-breed bastard, unwanted and unclaimed. You don't know what it's like to be a bastard in an Eyrien hunting camp. Sneered at?" Lucivar laughed bitterly. "The favorite taunt was 'your father was a Jhinka.' Do you have any idea what that means to an Eyrien? That you were sired by a male from a hated race and that your mother must have accepted the mount willingly since she carried you full term and birthed you? Oh, I think I know how someone like Khevin feels."

Randahl cleared his throat. "It shames me to say it, but it wasn't any easier for him in Agio. Lady Erika tried to make a place for him in her court.

Felt she owed it to him because her ex-Consort had sired the boy. But he wasn't happy, and Mari and her grandmother were here. So he came back."

And had endured ostracism from the landens and taunts from the young Blood males—which explained why the two Warlords now using Craft to move the Jhinka bodies away from the shield were being kept as far away from Jaenelle as possible.

Lucivar finally answered the question he saw in Randahl's eyes. "Two of Lady Angelline's friends were training Khevin."

Randahl rubbed the back of his neck. "Should have thought to ask her ourselves. She has a way about her."

Lucivar smiled wearily. "That she does." And she might also have some idea of where the young couple might relocate. If they survived.

For a moment, he allowed himself to believe they would survive.

Then the Jhinka returned.

10 / Kaeleer

Randahl shaded his eyes against the late afternoon sun and studied the low hills that were black with waiting Jhinka. "They must have called up all the clans from all the tribes," he said hoarsely. Then he sagged against the back of the community hall. "Mother Night, Yaslana, there must be five thousand of them out there."

"More like six." Lucivar widened his stance. It was the only way his tired, trembling legs would keep him upright.

Six thousand more than the hundreds he'd already killed during the past few days and that witch storm still raging around them, feeding on the shield to maintain its strength and draining him in the process. Six thousand more and no way to catch the Winds because that storm made it impossible to detect those psychic roadways.

They could shield and they could fight, but they couldn't send out a call for help and they couldn't escape. The food had run out yesterday. The well dried up that morning. And there were still six thousand Jhinka waiting for the sun to sink a little farther behind the low western hills before they attacked.

"We're not going to make it, are we?" Randahl said.

"No," Lucivar replied softly. "We're not going to make it."

In the past three days, he'd drained both Ebon-gray Jewels as well as his Red ring. The Red Jewel around his neck was now the only power reserve they had, and that wasn't going to hold much beyond the first attack. Randahl and the other three had exhausted their Jewels before he and Jaenelle had arrived. There hadn't been enough food or rest to bring any of them back up to strength.

No, the males weren't going to make it. But Jaenelle had to. She was too valuable a Queen to lose in a trap that, he was convinced, had been set to destroy him.

Satisfied that he'd lined up every argument that Protocol gave him to make this demand, Lucivar said, "Ask the Lady to join me here."

No fool, Randahl understood why the request was being made now.

Alone for a moment, Lucivar rolled his neck and stretched his shoulders, trying to ease the tense, tired muscles.

It is easier to kill than to heal. It is easier to destroy than to preserve. It is easier to tear down than to build. Those who feed on destructive emotions and ambitions and deny the responsibilities that are the price of wielding power can bring down everything you care for and would protect. Be on guard, always.

Saetan's words. Saetan's warning to the young Warlords and Warlord Princes who gathered at the Hall.

But Saetan had never mentioned the last part of that warning: sometimes it was kinder to destroy.

He wasn't strong enough to give Jaenelle a swift, clean death. But even at full strength, Randahl and the other Warlords wore lighter-rank Jewels, and landens had no inner defense against the Blood. Once Jaenelle and Mari were away from here, once the Jhinka started their final attack, he would make a fast descent, pull up every drop of power he had left, and unleash that force. The landens would die instantly, their minds burned away. Randahl and the others might survive for a few seconds longer, but not long enough for the Jhinka to reach them.

And the Jhinka . . . they, too, would die. Some of them. A lot of them. But not all of them. He would be left, alone, when the survivors tore him apart. He would make sure of it. He'd fought Jhinka in Terreille. He'd seen what they did to captives. When it came to cruelty, they were an ingenious people. But then, so were many of the Blood.

Lucivar turned as movement caught his eye.

Jaenelle stood a few feet away, her eyes fixed on the Jhinka.

She wore nothing but the Black Jewel around her neck.

He could understand why. Even her underclothes wouldn't have fit. All the muscle, all the feminine curves she'd gained over the past year were gone. Having no other source of fuel, her body had consumed itself in its struggle to be the receptacle for the power within. Bones pressed against pale, damp, blood-streaked skin. He could count her ribs, could see her hipbones move as she shifted her feet. Her golden hair was dark and stiff with the blood that must have been on her hands when she ran her fingers through it.

Despite that, or perhaps because of it, her face was strangely compelling. Her youth had been consumed in the healing fire, leaving her with a timeless, ageless beauty that suited her ancient, haunted sapphire eyes. It looked like an exquisite mask that would never again be touched by living concerns.

Then the mask shattered. Her grief and rage flooded through him, sending him careening against the building.

Lucivar grabbed the corner and hung on with a desperation rapidly being consumed by overwhelming fear.

The world spun with sick speed, spun in tighter and tighter spirals, dragging at his mind, threatening to tear him away from any sane anchor. Faster and faster. Deeper and deeper.

Spirals. Saetan had told him something about spirals, but he couldn't see, couldn't breathe, couldn't think.

His shield broke, its energy sucked down into the spiral. The witch storm got pulled in, too, its psychic threads snapping as it tried to remain anchored around the building.

Faster and faster, deeper and deeper, and then the dark power rose out of the abyss, roaring past him with a speed that froze his mind.

Lucivar jerked away from the building and staggered toward Jaenelle. Down. He had to get her down on the ground, had to—

Pop.

Pop pop.

Pop pop pop pop pop.

"MOTHER NIGHT!" Adler screamed, pointing toward the hills.

Lucivar wrenched a muscle in his neck as he snapped his head toward the sound of Jhinka bodies exploding.

Another surge of dark power flashed through what was left of the witch storm's psychic threads. They flared, blackened, disappeared.

He thought he heard a faint scream.

Pop pop pop.

Pop pop.

Pop.

It took her thirty seconds to destroy six thousand Jhinka.

She didn't look at anyone. She just turned around and started walking slowly, stiffly toward the other end of the village.

Lucivar tried to tell her to wait for him, but his voice wouldn't work. He tried to get to his feet, not sure how he'd ended up on his knees, but his legs felt like jelly.

He finally remembered what Saetan had told him about spirals.

He didn't fear her but, Hell's fire, he wanted to know what had set her off so that he had some idea of how to deal with her.

Hands pulled at his arm.

Randahl, looking gray-skinned and sick, helped him get to his feet.

They were both panting from the effort it took to reach the building and brace themselves against the stone wall.

Randahl rubbed his eyes. His mouth trembled. "The boy died," he said hoarsely. "She'd just finished healing the last landen. Hell's fire, Yaslana, she healed all three hundred of them. Three hundred in three days. She was swaying on her feet. Mari was telling her she had to sit down, had to rest. She shook her head and stumbled over to where Khevin was lying, and . . . and he just smiled at her and died. Gone. Completely gone. Not even a whisper of him left."

Lucivar closed his eyes. He'd think about the dead later. There were still things that needed to be done for the living. "Are you strong enough to send a message to Agio?"

Randahl shook his head. "None of us are strong enough to ride the Winds right now, but we're overdue by a day, so someone ought to be out on the roads searching for us."

"When your people arrive, I want Mari escorted to the Hall."

"We can look after her," Randahl replied sharply.

But would Mari want to be looked after by the Blood in Agio?

"Escort her to the Hall," Lucivar said. "She needs time to grieve, and she needs a place where her heart can start to heal. There are some at the Hall who can help her with that."

Randahl looked unhappy. "You think the Dhemlan Blood will be kinder to her than we were?"

Lucivar shrugged. "I wasn't thinking of the Dhemlan Blood. I was thinking of the kindred."

Having gotten Randahl's agreement, Lucivar stopped inside the community hall long enough to see Mari and tell her she would be going to the Hall. She clung to him for a few minutes, crying fiercely.

He held her, giving what comfort he could.

When two of the landen women, casting defiant looks at the rest, offered to look after Mari, he let her go, sincerely hoping he'd never have to deal with landens again.

He found Jaenelle a few steps outside the village boundary, curled up into a tight ball, making desperate little sounds.

He dropped to his knees and cradled her in his arms.

"I didn't want to kill," she wailed. "That's not what the Craft is for. That's not what *my* Craft is for."

"I know, Cat," Lucivar murmured. "I know."

"I could have put a shield around them, holding them in until we got help from Agio. That's what I meant to do, but the rage just boiled out of me when Khevin . . . I could feel their minds, could feel them wanting to hurt. I couldn't stop the anger. I couldn't *stop* it."

"It's the drugs, Cat. The damn things can scramble your emotions for a long time, especially in a situation like this."

"I don't like killing. I'd rather be hurt than hurt someone else."

He didn't argue with her. He was too exhausted and her emotions were too raw. Nor did he point out that she'd reacted to a friend's pain and death. What she couldn't, or wouldn't, do for her own sake she would do for someone she cared for.

"Lucivar?" Jaenelle said plaintively. "I want a bath."

That was just one of the things he wanted. "Let's go home, Cat."

11 / Terreille

Dorothea SaDiablo sank into a chair and stared at her unexpected guest. "Here? You want to stay *here*?" Had the bitch looked into a mirror lately? How was she supposed to explain a desiccated walking corpse that looked like it had just crawled out of an old grave?

"Not here in your precious court," Hekatah replied, her fleshless lips curling in a snarl. "And I'm not asking for your permission. I'm *telling* you that I'm staying in Hayll and require accommodations."

Telling. Always telling. Always reminding her that she never would have become the High Priestess of Hayll without Hekatah's guidance and subtle backing, without Hekatah pointing out the rivals who had too much potential and would thwart her dream of being a High Priestess who was so strong even the Queens yielded to her.

Well, she *was* the High Priestess of Hayll, and after centuries of twisting and savaging males who, in turn, did their own share of savaging, there were no dark-Jeweled Queens left in Terreille. There were no Queens, no Black Widows, no other Priestesses equal to her Red Jewel. In some of the smaller, more stubborn Territories, there were no Jeweled Blood at all. Within another five years, she would succeed where Hekatah had failed—she would be *the* High Priestess of Terreille, feared and revered by the entire Realm.

And when that day came, she would have something very special planned for her mentor and adviser.

Dorothea settled back in her chair and suppressed a smile. Still, the bag of bones might have a use. Sadi was still out there somewhere, playing his elusive, teasing game. Although she hadn't felt his presence in quite some time, every time she opened a door, she expected to find him on the other side waiting for her. But if a Red-Jeweled Black Widow High Priestess was staying at the country lodge she kept for more vigorous and imaginative evenings, and if he happened to become aware of a witch living there quietly . . . well, her psychic scent permeated the place and he might not take the time to distinguish between the scent of the place and the occupant's psychic scent. It would be a shame to lose the building, but she really didn't think there would be anything left of it by the time he was done.

Of course, there wouldn't be anything left of Hekatah, either.

Dorothea tucked a loose strand of black hair back into the simple coil around her head. "I realize you weren't asking my permission, Sister," she purred. "When have you ever *asked* me for anything?"

"Remember who you speak to," Hekatah hissed.

"I never forget," Dorothea replied sweetly. "I have a lodge in the country, about an hour's carriage ride from Draega. I use it for discreet entertaining. You're welcome to stay there as long as you please. The staff is very well-trained, so I do ask that you not make a meal out of them. I'll supply you with plenty of young feasts." Frowning at a fingernail, she called in a nail file and smoothed an edge, studied the result, and smoothed again. Finally satisfied, she vanished the nail file and smiled at Hekatah. "Of course, if my accommodations aren't to your liking, you can always return to Hell."

Greedy, ungrateful bitch.

Hekatah opaqued another mirror. Even that little bit of Craft was almost too much.

This wasn't the way she'd planned to return to Hayll, hidden away like some doddering, drooling relative dispatched to some out-of-the-way property with no one but hard-faced servants for company.

Of course, once some of her strength returned . . .

Hekatah shook her head. The amusements would have to come later.

She considered ringing for a servant to come and put another log on the fire, then dismissed the idea and added the wood herself. Curling up into an old, stuffed chair, she stared at the wood being embraced and consumed by the flames.

Consumed just like all her pretty plans.

First the fiasco with the girl. If that was the best Jorval could do, she was going to have to rethink his usefulness.

Then the Eyrien managed to escape her trap and destroy all those lovely Jhinka that she'd cultivated so carefully. And the backlash of power that had come through her witch storm had done *this* to her.

And last, but far from least, was that gutter son of a whore's purge of the Dark Realm. There was no safe haven in Hell now, and no one, *no one* to serve her.

So, for now, she had to accept Dorothea's sneering hospitality, had to accept handouts instead of the tribute that was her due.

No matter. Unlike Dorothea, who was too busy trying to grab power and gobble up Territories, she had taken a good long look at the two living Realms.

Let Dorothea have the crumbling ruins of Terreille.

She was going to have Kaeleer.

CHAPTER FOURTEEN

1 / Kaeleer

Saetan braced his hand against the stone wall, momentarily unbalanced by the double blast of anger that shook the Keep.

"Mother Night," he muttered. "*Now* what are they squabbling about?" Mentally reaching out to Lucivar, he met a psychic wall of fury.

He ran.

As he neared the corridor that led to Jaenelle's suite of rooms, he slowed to a walk, pressing one hand against his side and swearing silently because he didn't have enough breath to roar. Wouldn't have mattered anyway, he thought sourly. Whatever was provoking his children's tempers certainly wasn't affecting their lungs.

"Get out of my way, Lucivar!"

"When the sun shines in Hell!"

"Damn your wings, you've no right to interfere."

"I serve you. That gives me the right to challenge anything and anyone that threatens your well-being. And that includes you!"

"If you serve me, then obey me. GET OUT OF MY WAY!"

"The First Law is not obedience—"

"Don't you dare start quoting Blood Laws to me."

"—and even if it was, I still wouldn't stand here and let you do this. It's suicidal!"

Saetan rounded the corner, shot up the short flight of stairs, and stumbled on the top step.

In the dimly lit corridor, Lucivar looked like something out of the night-tales landens told their children: dark, spread wings blending into the darkness beyond, teeth bared, gold eyes blazing with battle-fire. Even the blood dripping from the shallow knife slash in his left upper arm made him look more like something other than a living man.

In contrast, Jaenelle looked painfully real. The short black nightgown revealed too much of the body sacrificed to the power that had burned within her while she'd done the healing in the landen village a week ago. If cared for, the flesh wouldn't suffer that way, not even when it was the instrument of the Black Jewels.

Seeing the results of her careless attitude toward her body, seeing the hand that held the Eyrien hunting knife shake because she was too weak to hold a blade that, a month ago, she had handled easily, he gave in to the anger rising within him. "Lady," he said sharply.

Jaenelle spun to face him, weaving a little as she struggled to stay on her feet. Her eyes blazed with battle-fire, too.

"Daemon's been found."

Saetan crossed his arms, leaned against the wall, and ignored the challenge in her voice. "So you intend to channel your strength through an already weakened body, create the shadow you've been using to search Terreille, send it to wherever his body is, travel through the Twisted Kingdom until you find him, and then lead him back."

"Yes," she said too softly. "That's exactly what I'm going to do."

Lucivar slammed the side of his fist against the wall. "It's too much. You haven't even begun to recover from the healings you did. Let this friend of yours keep him for a couple of weeks."

"You can't 'keep' someone who's lost in the Twisted Kingdom," Jaenelle snapped. "They don't see or live in the tangible world the way everyone else does. If something spooks him and he slips away from her, it could be weeks, even months before she finds him again. By then it may be too late. *He's running out of time.*"

"So have her bring him to the Keep in Terreille," Lucivar argued. "We can hold him there until you're strong enough to do the healing."

"He's insane, not broken. He still wears the Black. If someone tried to 'hold' you, what sort of memories would that stir up?"

"She's right, Lucivar," Saetan said calmly. "If he thinks this friend is leading him into a trap, no matter what her real intentions, what little trust he has in her will shatter, and that will be the last time she finds him. At least, while there's anything worth finding."

Lucivar thumped the wall with his fist. He kept thumping the wall while he swore, long and low. Finally, he rubbed the side of his hand against the other palm. "Then I'll go back to Terreille and get him."

"Why should he trust you?" Jaenelle said bitterly.

Pain flared in Lucivar's eyes.

Saetan felt Jaenelle's inner barriers open just a crack. He didn't stop to think. At the moment when she was torn between anger at and distress for Lucivar, he swept in and out of that crack, tasting the emotional undercurrents.

So their little witch thought she could force them to yield. Thought she had an emotional weapon they wouldn't challenge.

She was right. She did.

But now, so did he.

"Let her go, Lucivar," Saetan crooned, his voice a purring, soft thunder. Still leaning against the wall with his arms crossed, he tilted his upper body in a mocking bow. "The Lady has us by the balls, and she knows it."

He felt bitterly pleased to see the wariness in Jaenelle's eyes.

She looked quickly at both of them. "You're not going to stop me?"

"No, we're not going to stop you." Saetan smiled malevolently. "Unless, of course, you don't agree to pay the price for our submission. If you refuse, the only way you'll walk out of here is by destroying both of us."

Such a neat trap. Such sweet bait.

He confused her, had finally managed to unnerve her. She was about to find out how neatly he could spin her into a web.

"What's your price?" Jaenelle asked reluctantly.

One casual, flicking glance took in everything from her head to her feet. "Your body."

She dropped the knife.

It probably would have cut off a couple of toes if Lucivar hadn't vanished it in midair.

"Your body, my Lady," Saetan crooned. "The body you treat with such contempt. Since you obviously don't want it, I'll take it in trust for the one who already has a claim to it."

Jaenelle stared at him, her eyes wide and blank. "You want me to leave this body? L-like I did before?"

"Leave?" His voice sounded silky and dangerous. "No, you don't have to leave. I'm sure the claimant would be perfectly willing to give you a permanent loan. But it would be a loan, you understand, and you would be expected to give the body the same kind of care you'd give any object lent to you by a friend."

She studied him for a long time. "And if I don't take care of it? What will you do?"

Saetan pushed away from the wall.

Jaenelle flinched, but her eyes never left his.

"Nothing," he said too softly. "I won't fight with you. I won't use physical strength or Craft to force you. I'll do nothing except keep a record of the transgressions. I'll never ask you for an explanation, and I'll never explain for you. *You* can try to justify abusing part of what Daemon paid for with dear coin."

Jaenelle's face turned dead-white. Saetan caught her as she swayed and held her against his chest.

"Heartless bastard," she whispered.

"Perhaps," he replied. "So what is your answer, Lady?"

Jaenelle! You promised!

Jaenelle jumped out of his arms, back-pedaled to try to keep her balance, and ended up with her back smacking against the wall.

Saetan studied Jaenelle's guilty expression and began to feel maliciously cheerful. Noting that Lucivar had come up on her blind side, he turned his attention toward the annoyed, half-grown Sceltie and the silent, but equally annoyed, Arcerian kitten who now weighed as much as Lucivar and still had five more years to grow.

"What did the Lady promise?" he asked Ladvarian.

You promised to eat and sleep and read books and take easy walkies until you healed, Ladvarian said accusingly, staring at Jaenelle.

"I am," Jaenelle stammered. "I did."

You've been playing with Lucivar.

Lucivar stepped away from the wall so that they could see his left arm. "She was playing rough, too."

Ladvarian and Kaelas snarled at Jaenelle.

"This is different," Jaenelle snapped. "This is important. And I wasn't playing with Lucivar. I was fighting with him."

"Yes," Lucivar agreed mournfully. "And all because I thought she should be resting instead of pushing herself until she collapsed."

Ladvarian and Kaelas snarled louder.

⋆For shame, Lady,⋆ Saetan said, using a Black thread to keep the conversation private. ⋆Breaking a promise to your little Brothers. Care to agree to my terms now, or shall we all snarl a bit longer?⋆

Her venomous look was not only an answer but a good indication of how often she lost these kinds of "discussions" once Ladvarian and, therefore, Kaelas made up their furry little minds about something.

"My Brothers." Saetan tipped his head courteously toward Ladvarian and Kaelas. "The Lady would never break a promise without good reason. Despite the risks to her own well-being, she has pledged herself to a delicate task, one that cannot be delayed. Since this promise was made before the one she made to you, we must yield to the Lady's wishes. As she said, this is important."

⋆What's more important than the Lady?⋆ Ladvarian demanded.

Saetan didn't answer.

Jaenelle squirmed. "My . . . mate . . . is trapped in the Twisted Kingdom. If I don't show him the way out, he'll be destroyed."

⋆Mate?⋆ Ladvarian's ears perked up. His white-tipped tail waved once, twice. He looked at Saetan. ⋆Jaenelle has a mate?⋆

Interesting that the Sceltie looked to him for confirmation. Something to keep in mind in the future.

"Yes," Saetan said. "Jaenelle has a mate."

"She won't have if she's delayed much longer," Jaenelle warned.

They all politely stepped aside and watched her painfully slow journey down the corridor.

Saetan had no doubt that she would use Craft to float her body as soon as she was out of their sight, which would put more strain on her physically but would also speed her journey to the Dark Altar that stood within Ebon Askavi. And except for being carried, that was the only way she was going to reach the Gate that would take her to the Keep in Terreille.

After Ladvarian and Kaelas had trotted off to tell Draca about the Lady's mate, Saetan turned to Lucivar. "Come into the healing workroom. I'll take care of that arm."

Lucivar shrugged. "It's not bleeding anymore."

"Boyo, I know the Eyrien drill as well as you do. Wounds are cleansed and healed." ⋆And I want to talk to you in a shielded room away from furry ears.⋆

"Do you think she'll make it?" Lucivar asked a few minutes later as he watched Saetan clean the shallow knife wound.

"She has the strength, the knowledge, and the desire. She'll bring him out of the Twisted Kingdom."

It wasn't what Lucivar meant, and they both knew it.

"Why didn't you stop her? Why are you letting her risk herself?"

Saetan bent his head, avoiding Lucivar's eyes. "Because she loves him. Because he really *is* her mate."

Lucivar was silent for a minute. Then he sighed. "He always said he'd been born to be Witch's lover. Looks like he was right."

2 / Terreille

Surreal watched Daemon prowl the center of the overgrown maze and wondered how much longer she would be able to keep him here.

He didn't trust her. She couldn't trust him.

She'd found him about a mile from the ruins of SaDiablo Hall, weeping silently as he watched a house burn to the ground. She didn't ask about the burning house, or about the twenty freshly butchered Hayllian guards, or why he kept whispering Tersa's name over and over.

She'd taken his hand, caught the Winds, and brought him here. Whoever had owned this estate had either abandoned it by choice or had been forced out or killed when Dhemlan Terreille had finally caved in to Hayll's domination. Now Hayllian guards used the manor house as a barracks for the troops who were teaching the Dhemlan people about the penalties of disobedience.

Daemon had watched passively while she'd used illusion spells to fill in the gaps in the hedges that would lead to the center of the maze. He'd said nothing when she created a double Gray shield around their hiding place.

His passive obedience had melted away when she called in the small web Jaenelle had given her and placed four drops of blood in its center to awaken it, turning it into a signal and a beacon.

He'd started prowling after that, started smiling that cold, familiar, brutal smile while she waited. And waited. And waited.

"Why don't you call your friends, Little Assassin?" Daemon said as he glided past the place where she sat with her knees up and her back against the hedge. "Don't you want to earn your pay?"

"There's no pay, Daemon. We're waiting for a friend."

"Of course we are," he said too softly as he made another circuit around the center of the maze. Then he stopped and looked at her, his gold eyes filled with a glazed, cold fire. "She liked you. She asked me to help you. Do you remember that?"

"Who, Daemon?" Surreal asked quietly.

"Tersa." His voice broke. "They burned the house Tersa had lived in with her little boy. She had a son, did you know that?"

Hell's fire, Mother Night, and may the Darkness be merciful. "No, I didn't know that."

Daemon nodded. "But that bitch Dorothea took him from her, and she went far, far away. And then that bitch put a Ring of Obedience on the little boy and trained him to be a pleasure slave. Took him into her bed and . . ." Daemon shuddered. "You're blood of her blood."

Surreal scrambled to her feet. "Daemon. I'm not like Dorothea. I don't acknowledge her as kin."

Daemon bared his teeth. "Liar," he snarled. He took a step toward her, his right thumb flicking the ragged ring-finger nail. "Silky, court-trained liar." Another step. "Butchering whore."

As he raised his right hand, Surreal saw a tiny, glistening drop fall from the needlelike nail under the regular nail.

She dove to his left, calling in her stiletto as she fell.

He was on her before she hit the ground.

She screamed when he broke her right wrist. She screamed again when he clamped his left hand over both of her wrists, grinding bones.

"*Daemon,*" she said, breathless and panicked as his right hand closed around her throat.

"Daemon."

Surreal gulped back a sob of relief at the sound of that familiar midnight voice.

Hope and horror filled Daemon's eyes as he slowly raised his head. "Please," he whispered. "I never meant. . . . *Please.*" He threw his head back, let out a heart-shattering cry, and collapsed.

Using Craft, Surreal rolled him off her and sat up, cradling her broken wrist. Dizzy and nauseous, she closed her eyes as she felt Jaenelle approach. "I realize arriving a few seconds sooner would have made a less dramatic entrance, but I would've appreciated it more."

"Let me see your wrist."

Surreal looked up and gasped. "Hell's fire, what happened to you?"

During the other times when Jaenelle's "shadow" had joined Surreal to search for Daemon, it had been impossible to guess she wasn't a living woman unless you tried to touch her. No one would mistake this transparent, wasted creature for something that walked the living Realms. But the sapphire eyes were still filled with their ancient fire, and the Black Jewels still glowed with untapped strength.

Jaenelle shook her head and wrapped her hands around Surreal's wrist. A flash of numbing cold was followed by a steadily growing warmth. Surreal felt the bones shift and set.

Jaenelle's transparent hands pulsed, fading and returning again and again. For a moment, she faded completely, her Black Jewels suspended as if waiting for her return.

When she reappeared, her eyes were filled with pain and she panted as if she couldn't draw a full breath.

"Collapsing," Jaenelle gasped. "Not now. Not *yet*." Her transparent body convulsed. "Surreal, I can't finish the healing. The bones are set, but . . ." A tooled, leather wristband hovered in the air. Jaenelle slipped it over Surreal's wrist and snapped it shut. "That will help support it until it heals."

Surreal's left forefinger traced the stag head set in a circle of flowering vines—the same stag that was a symbol for Titian's kin, the Dea al Mon.

Before she could ask Jaenelle about the wristband, something heavy hit the ground nearby. A man cursed softly.

"Mother Night, the guards heard us." Using her left arm for leverage, Surreal got to her feet. "Let's get him out of here and—"

"I can't leave here, Surreal," Jaenelle said quietly. "I have to do what I came here to do . . . while I still can."

The Black Jewels flared, and Surreal felt a shivering, liquid darkness flow into the maze.

Jaenelle tried to smile. "They won't find their way through the maze. Not *this* maze, anyway." Then she looked sadly at Daemon's gaunt, bruised body and gently brushed the long, dirty, tangled black hair off his forehead. "Ah, Daemon. I had gotten used to thinking of my body as a weapon that was used against me. I'd forgotten that it's also a gift. If it's not too late, I'll do better. I promise."

Jaenelle placed her transparent hands on either side of Daemon's head. She closed her eyes. The Black Jewel glowed.

Listening to the Hayllian guards thrashing around somewhere in the maze, Surreal sank to the ground and settled down to wait.

Daemon.

The island slowly sank into the sea of blood. He curled up in the center of the pulpy ground while the word sharks circled, waiting for him.

Daemon.

Hadn't they all been waiting for the end of this torment? Hadn't they all been waiting for the debt to be paid in full? Now she was calling him, calling for his complete surrender.

Move your ass, Sadi!

He rolled to his hands and knees and stared at the golden-maned, sapphire-eyed woman who stood on a blood-drenched shore that hadn't existed a minute ago. A tiny spiral horn rose from the center of her forehead. Her long gown looked as if it were made from black cobwebs and didn't quite hide her delicate hooves.

The pleasure of seeing her made him giddy. Her mood made him cautious. He carefully sat back on his heels. *You're annoyed with me.*

Let me put it this way, Jaenelle replied sweetly. *If you go under and I have to pull you out, I'm going to be pissed.*

Daemon shook his head slowly and tsked. *Such language.*

With precise enunciation, she spoke a phrase in the Old Tongue.

His jaw dropped. He choked on a laugh.

That, Prince Sadi, is language.

You are my instrument.

Words lie. Blood doesn't.

Butchering whore.

He swayed, steadied himself, rose carefully to his feet. *Have you come to call in the debt, Lady?*

He didn't understand the sorrow in her eyes.

I'm here because of a debt, she said, her voice filled with pain. She slowly raised her hands.

Between the shore and the sinking island, the sea churned, churned, churned. Waves lifted and froze into waist-high walls. Between them, the sea solidified, becoming a bridge made of blood.

Come, Daemon.

His hands lightly brushed the crests of the red, frozen waves. He stepped onto the bridge.

The word sharks circled, tore off chunks of the island, tried to slice away the bridge beneath his feet.

You are my instrument.

Jaenelle called in a bow, nocked an arrow, and took aim. The arrow sang through the air. The word shark thrashed as it withered and sank.

Words lie. Blood doesn't.

Another arrow sang a death song.

Butchering who—

The island and the last word shark sank together.

Jaenelle vanished the bow, turned away from the sea, and walked into the twisted, shattered-crystal landscape.

Her voice reached him, faint and fading. ⋆Come, Daemon.⋆

Daemon rushed across the bridge, hit the shore running, and then swore in frustration as he searched for some sign of where she'd gone.

He caught her psychic scent before he noticed the glittering trail. It was like a ribbon of star-sprinkled night sky that led him through the twisted landscape to where she perched on a rock far above him.

She looked down at him, smiling with exasperated amusement. ⋆Stubborn, snarly male.⋆

⋆Stubbornness is a much-maligned quality,⋆ he panted as he climbed toward her.

Her silvery, velvet-coated laugh filled the land.

Then he finally got a good look at her. He sank to his knees. ⋆I owe you a debt, Lady.⋆

She shook her head. ⋆The debt is mine, not yours.⋆

⋆I failed you,⋆ he said bitterly, looking at her wasted body.

⋆No, Daemon,⋆ Jaenelle replied softly. ⋆I failed *you*. You asked me to heal the crystal chalice and return to the living world. And I did. But I don't think I ever forgave my body for being the instrument that was used to try to destroy me, and I became its cruelest torturer. For that I'm sorry because you treasured that part of me.⋆

⋆No, I treasured *all* of you. I love you, Witch. I always will. You're everything I'd dreamed you would be.⋆

She smiled at him. ⋆And I—⋆ She shuddered, pressed her hand against her chest. ⋆Come. There's little time left.⋆

She fled through the rocks, out of sight before he could move.

He hurried after her, following the glittering trail, gasping as he felt a crushing weight descend on him.

Daemon. Her voice came back to him, faint and pain-filled. *If the body is going to survive, I can't stay any longer.*

He fought against the weight. *Jaenelle!*

You have to take this in slow stages. Rest there now. Rest, Daemon. I'll mark the trail for you. Please follow it. I'll be waiting for you at the end.

JAENELLE!

A wordless whisper. His name spoken like a caress. Then silence.

Time meant nothing as he lay there, curled in a ball, fighting to hang on to the glittering trail that led upward while everything beneath him pulled at him, trying to drag him back down.

He held on fiercely to the memory of her voice, to her promise that she would be waiting.

Later—much later—the pulling eased, the crushing weight lessened.

The glittering trail, the star-sprinkled ribbon still led upward.

Daemon climbed.

Surreal watched the sky lighten and listened to the guards shouting and cursing as the maze sizzled from the explosions of power against power. Throughout the long night, the guards had pounded their way toward the center of the maze as Jaenelle's shields broke piece by piece. If the screams were any indication, it had cost the guards dearly to break as much of her shields as they had.

There was some satisfaction in that, but Surreal also knew what the surviving guards would do to whomever they found in the maze.

"Surreal? What's happening?"

For a moment, Surreal couldn't say anything. Jaenelle's eyes looked dead-dull, the inner fire burned to ash. Her Black Jewels looked as if she'd drained most of the reserve power in them.

Surreal knelt beside Daemon. Except for the rise and fall of his chest, he hadn't stirred since he collapsed. "The guards are breaking through the shield," she said, trying to sound calm. "I don't think we have much time left."

Jaenelle nodded. "Then you and Daemon have to leave. The Green Wind runs over the edge of the garden. Can you reach it?"

Surreal hesitated. "With all the power that's been unleashed in this area, I'm not sure."

"Let me see your Gray ring."

She held out her right hand.

Jaenelle brushed her Black ring against Surreal's Gray.

Surreal felt a psychic thread shoot out of the rings as they made contact, felt the Green Web pull at her.

"There," Jaenelle gasped. "As soon as you launch yourself, the thread will reel you into the Green Web. Take the beacon web with you. Destroy it completely as soon as you can."

Daemon stirred, moaned softly.

"What about you?" Surreal asked.

Jaenelle shook her head. "It doesn't matter. I won't be coming back. I'll hold the guards long enough to give you a head start."

Jaenelle opened Daemon's tattered shirt. Taking Surreal's right hand, she pricked the middle finger and pressed it against Daemon's chest while she murmured words in a language Surreal didn't know.

"This binding spell will keep him with you until he's out of the Twisted Kingdom." Jaenelle faded, came back. "One last thing."

Surreal took the gold coin that hovered in the air. On one side was an elaborate S. On the other side were the words "Dhemlan Kaeleer."

"That's a mark of safe passage," Jaenelle said, straining to get the words out. "If you ever come to Kaeleer, show it to whomever you first meet and tell them you're expected at the Hall in Dhemlan. It guarantees you a safe escort."

Surreal vanished the coin and the small beacon web.

Daemon rolled onto his side and opened his eyes.

Jaenelle floated backward until she faded into the hedge. *Go quickly, Surreal. May the Darkness embrace you.*

Swearing quietly, Surreal tugged Daemon to his feet. He stared at her with simpleminded bewilderment. She pulled his left arm over her shoulders and winced as she tightened her right arm around his waist.

Taking a deep breath, she let the psychic thread reel them through the Darkness until she caught the Green Wind and headed north.

The hiding place was ready and waiting.

Before the night when she'd drunkenly broken the warm friendship that had existed between them, Daemon had told her about two people:

Lord Marcus, the man of business who took care of Daemon's very discreet investments, and Manny.

Shortly after Jaenelle had contacted her, she'd gone to see Lord Marcus about finding a hiding place and had discovered that one already existed—a small island that was owned by "a reclusive invalid Warlord" who lived with a handful of servants.

Daemon owned the island. Everyone who lived there had been physically or emotionally maimed by Dorothea SaDiablo. It was a sheltered place where they could rebuild some semblance of a life.

She hadn't dared go to the island while she was still hunting for Daemon because she'd been afraid of leading Kartane SaDiablo there. Now she and Daemon could both drop out of sight, and the fictitious invalid Warlord and his newly acquired companion would become a reality.

But first there was one fast stop to make, one question to ask. She hoped beyond words that Manny would say "yes."

Surreal . . .

Surreal tried to strengthen the distaff thread. *Jaenelle?*

Surreal . . . g . . . Keep . . . o . . .

Surreal tightened the leash on her emotions as the distaff thread snapped. She'd do her best to keep Daemon safe.

Because she owed him. Because what was left of Jaenelle cared.

Not allowing herself to think about what was happening in the center of the maze, Surreal flew on.

3 / Kaeleer

Ladvarian's frantic barking and Lucivar's shouted "Father!" snapped Saetan out of his worried brooding. Propelling himself out of a chair in Jaenelle's sitting room at the Keep, he rushed to the door leading into her bedroom, then clung to the frame, paralyzed for a moment by the sight of the ravaged body Lucivar held in his arms.

"Mother Night," he muttered as he grabbed Kaelas by the scruff of the neck and pulled the snarling young cat off the bed. Throwing back the bedcovers, he placed a warming spell on the sheets. "Put her down."

Lucivar hesitated.

"Put her down," he snapped, unnerved by the tears in Lucivar's eyes.

As soon as Lucivar gently laid Jaenelle on the bed, Saetan knelt beside her. Laying one hand lightly against her chest, he used a delicate psychic tendril to sense and catalog the injuries.

Lungs collapsing, arteries and veins collapsing, heart erratic and weak. The rest of the inner organs on the verge of failing. Bones as fragile as eggshells.

Jaenelle, Saetan called. Sweet Darkness, had she severed the link between body and spirit? *Witch-child!*

Saetan? Jaenelle's voice sounded faint and far away. *I made a mess of it, didn't I?*

He fought to remain calm. She had the knowledge and the Craft to perform the healing. If he could keep her connected with her body, they might have a chance to save her. *You could say that.*

Did Ladvarian bring the healing web from the Keep in Terreille?

"Ladvarian!" He instantly regretted shouting because the Sceltie just cowered and whined, too upset to remember how to speak to him. *Stay calm, SaDiablo. Temper is destructive in any healing room, but it could be fatal in this one.* "The Lady is asking about the healing web," he said quietly. "Did you bring it?"

Kaelas planted his front paws on either side of the small dog's body and gave his friend an encouraging lick.

After another nudge from Kaelas, Ladvarian said, *Web?* He stood up, still safely sheltered by the cat's body. *Web. I brought the web.*

A small wooden frame appeared between Ladvarian and the bed.

To Saetan's eye, the healing web attached to the frame looked too simple to help a body as damaged as Jaenelle's. Then he noticed the single thread of spidersilk that went from the web to the Black-Jeweled ring attached to the frame's base.

Three drops of blood on the ring will waken the healing web, Jaenelle said.

Saetan looked at Lucivar, who stood near the bed as if waiting for a fatal blow. He hesitated—and swore silently because he still felt the sting of old accusations even though he wasn't asking for himself. "She needs three drops of blood on the ring. I don't dare give her mine. I'm not sure what a Guardian's blood will do to her."

Rage flashed in Lucivar's eyes, and Saetan knew his son had understood why he'd hesitated to ask.

"Damn you to the bowels of Hell," Lucivar said as he pulled a small knife out of the sheath in his boot. "You *didn't* take my blood when I was a child, so stop apologizing for something you didn't do." He jabbed a finger and let three drops of blood fall on the Black-Jeweled ring.

Saetan held his breath until the web started glowing.

Lucivar sheathed the knife. "I'm going to fetch Luthvian."

Saetan nodded. Not that Lucivar had waited for his agreement before stepping through the glass door that led to Jaenelle's private garden and launching himself skyward.

Jaenelle's body twitched. Through the psychic tendril, Saetan could feel the Craft in the web washing through her, stabilizing her. He glanced at the web and tried to block out any feelings of despair. One-third of the threads were already darkened, used up.

I didn't expect it to be this bad, Jaenelle said apologetically.

Luthvian will be here soon.

Good. With her help, I can transfer the power my body can't hold now into the web to use for the healing.

He felt her fade. *Jaenelle!*

I found him, Saetan. I marked a trail for him to follow. And I . . . I told Surreal to take him to the Keep, but I'm not sure she heard me.

Don't think about it now, witch-child. Concentrate on healing.

She drifted into a light sleep.

By the time Luthvian arrived at the Keep, two-thirds of Jaenelle's simple healing web was used up, and he wondered if there would be enough time to create another one before the last thread darkened.

He couldn't stay and watch. As soon as Luthvian regained enough of her composure to begin, he retreated to the sitting room, taking Ladvarian and Kaelas with him. He didn't ask where Lucivar was. He simply felt grateful that they wouldn't rub against each other's fraying tempers for a little while.

He paced until his leg ached. He embraced the physical discomfort like a sweet lover. Far better to focus on that than the heart-bruises that might be waiting for him.

Because he wasn't sure if he could stand another bedside vigil.

Because he didn't know if she'd succeeded enough to make her suffering worth it.

4 / The Twisted Kingdom

He learned as he climbed.

She had left small resting places next to the glittering trail: violets nestled against a boulder; sweet, clean water trickling down stone to a quiet pool that soothed the spirit; a patch of thick, green grass large enough to stretch out on; a plump, brown bunny watching him while it stuffed its face with clover; a cheerful fire that melted the first layer of ice around his heart.

At first, he'd tried to ignore the resting places. He learned he could pass one, maybe two, while he fought against the weight that made each step more difficult. If he tried to pass a third, he found the trail blocked. Instinct always warned him that if he stepped off the glittering trail to go around the obstruction, he might never find his way back. So he'd backtrack and rest until he absorbed the weight and found it comfortable to go on.

He slowly realized the weight had a name: body. This confused him for a while. Didn't he already have a body? He walked, he breathed, he heard, he saw. He felt tired. He felt pain. This other body felt different, heavy, solid. He wasn't sure he liked absorbing its essence into himself—or, perhaps, having it absorb him.

But the body was part of the same delicate web as the violets, the water, the sky, and the fire—reminders of a place beyond the shattered landscape—so he resigned himself to becoming reacquainted with it.

After a while, each resting place held an intangible gift, too: a Craft puzzle piece, one small aspect of a spell. Gradually the pieces began to make a whole and he learned the basics of the Black Widows' Craft, learned how to build simple webs, learned how to be what he was.

So he rested and treasured her little gifts and puzzles.

And he climbed to where she had promised to be waiting.

PART V

CHAPTER FIFTEEN

1 / Kaeleer

"The first part of our plan is coming along nicely," Hekatah said. "Little Terreille is, at last, justly represented in the Dark Council."

Lord Jorval smiled tightly. Since slightly more than half of the Council members now came from Little Terreille, he could agree that the Territory that had always felt wary of the rest of the Shadow Realm was, at last, "justly" represented. "With all the injuries and illnesses that have caused members to resign in the past two years, the Blood in Little Terreille were the only ones willing to accept such a heavy responsibility for the good of the Realm." He sighed, but his eyes glittered with malicious approval. "We've been accused of favoritism because so many voices come from the same Territory, but when the other men and women who were judged worthy of the task refused to accept, what were we to do? The Council seats must be filled."

"So they must," Hekatah agreed. "And since so many of those new members, who owe their current rise in status to your supporting their appointment to the Council, wouldn't want to find themselves distressed because they didn't heed your wisdom when it came time to vote, it's time to implement the second part of our plan."

"And that is?" Jorval wished she would take off that deep-hooded cloak. It wasn't as if he hadn't seen her before. And why had she chosen to meet in a seedy little inn in Goth's slums?

"To broaden Little Terreille's influence in the Shadow Realm. You're going to have to convince the Council to be more lenient in their immigration requirements. There are plenty of Blood aristos here already. You need to let in the lesser Blood—workers, craftsmen, farmers, hearth-witches, servants, lighter-Jeweled warriors. Stop deciding who can come in by whether or not they can pay the bribes."

"If the Terreillean Queens and the aristo males want servants, let them use the landens," Jorval said in a sulky voice. The bribes, as she well knew, had become an important source of income for a number of Blood aristos in Goth, Little Terreille's capital.

"Landens are demon fodder," Hekatah snapped. "Landens have no magic. Landens have no Craft. Landens are about as useful as Jhin—" She paused. She tugged her hood forward. "Accept Terreillean landens for immigration, too. Promise them privileges and a settlement after service. But bring in the lesser Terreillean Blood as well."

Jorval spread his hands. "And what are we supposed to do with all these immigrants? At the twice-yearly immigration fairs, the other Territories altogether only take a couple dozen people, if that. The courts in Little Terreille are already swelled and there are complaints about the Terreillean aristos always whining about serving in the lower Circles and not having land to rule like they expected. And none of the ones already here have fulfilled their immigration requirement."

"They will have land to rule. They'll establish small, new territories on behalf of the Queens they're serving. That will increase the influence the Queens in Little Terreille have in Kaeleer as well as providing them with an additional source of income. Some of that land is obscenely rich in precious metals and precious gems. In a few years, Little Terreille's Queens will be the strongest force in the Realm, and the other Territories will have to submit to their dominance."

"What land?" Jorval said, failing to hide his exasperation.

"The unclaimed land, of course," Hekatah replied sharply. She called in a map of Kaeleer, unrolled it, and used Craft to keep it flat. One bony finger brushed against large areas of the map.

"That's not unclaimed land," Jorval protested. "Those are closed Territories. The so-called kindred Territories."

"*Exactly*, Lord Jorval," Hekatah said, tapping the map. "The *so-called kindred* Territories."

Jorval looked at the map and sat up straighter. "But the kindred are supposed to be Blood. Aren't they?"

"Are they?" Hekatah countered with venomous sweetness.

"What about the human Territories, like Dharo and Nharkhava and Scelt? Their Queens might file a protest on the kindred's behalf."

"They can't. Their lands aren't being interfered with. By Blood Law, Territory Queens *can't* interfere outside their own borders."

"The High Lord . . ."

Hekatah waved a hand dismissively. "He has always lived by a strict code of honor. He'll viciously defend his own Territory, but he won't step one toe outside of it. If anything, he'll stand *against* those other Territories if they step outside the Law."

Jorval rubbed his lower lip. "So the Queens of Little Terreille would eventually rule all of Kaeleer."

"And those Queens would be consolidated under one wise, experienced individual who would be able to guide them properly."

Jorval preened.

"Not you, idiot," Hekatah hissed. "A male can't rule a Territory."

"The High Lord does!"

The silence went on so long Jorval began to sweat.

"Don't forget who he is or what he is, Lord Jorval. Don't forget about his particular code of honor. You're the wrong gender. If *you* tried to stand against him, he would tear you apart. *I* will rule Kaeleer." Her voice sweetened. "You will be my Steward, and as my trusted right hand and most valued adviser, you will be so influential there won't be a woman in the Realm who would dare refuse you."

Heat filled Jorval's groin as he thought of Jaenelle Angelline.

The map rolled up with a snap, startling him.

"I think we've postponed the amenities long enough, don't you?" Hekatah pushed back the cloak's hood.

Jorval let out a faint scream. Leaping up, he knocked over his chair, then tripped over it when he turned to get away from the table.

As Hekatah slowly walked around the table, Jorval scrambled to his feet. He kept backing away until he ended up pressed against the wall.

"Just a sip," Hekatah said as she unbuttoned his shirt. "Just a taste. And maybe next time you'll remember to provide refreshments."

Jorval felt his bowels turn to water.

She'd changed in the last two years. Before, she'd looked like an attractive woman past her prime. Now she looked like someone had squeezed all the juice out of her flesh. And the liberally applied perfume didn't mask the smell of decay.

"There's one other very important reason why *I'm* going to rule Kaeleer," Hekatah murmured as her lips brushed his throat. "Something you shouldn't forget."

"Yes, P-Priestess?" Jorval clenched his hands.

"With me ruling, the Realm of Terreille will support our efforts."

"It will?" Jorval said faintly, trying to take shallow breaths.

"I guarantee it," Hekatah replied just before her teeth sank into his throat.

2 / Kaeleer

The new two-wheeled buggy rolled smartly down the middle of the wide dirt road that ran northeast out of the village of Maghre.

Saetan tried—again—to tell Daffodil that he should keep the buggy on the right-hand side of the road. And Daffodil replied—again—that if he did that, Yaslana and Sundancer wouldn't be able to trot alongside. He would move over if another wagon came down the road. He knew how to pull a buggy. The High Lord worried too much.

Sitting beside him, Jaenelle glanced at his clenched hands and smiled with sympathetic amusement. "Being the passenger when you're used to having control isn't an easy adjustment to make. Khary thinks kindred-drawn conveyances should have a set of reins attached to the front of the buggy to give the passenger something to hold on to, just to feel more se-cure."

"Sedatives would be more helpful," Saetan growled. He forced his hands open and pressed them firmly on his thighs, ignoring Lucivar's low chuckle and trying hard not to resent the reins attached to the headstall Sundancer wore.

Much to the humans' chagrin, the kindred had insisted that reins be kept as part of the riding equipment because humans needed something to hold on to when kindred ran and jumped. Fortunately, after the initial shock three years ago when the Scelt people had learned how many Blood races inhabited their island, the humans there had enthusiastically embraced their kindred Brothers and Sisters.

"Aren't we stopping at Morghann and Khary's house?" Jaenelle asked, clapping a hand on top of her head to keep the wide-brimmed straw hat from blowing away.

"They wanted to show us something and said they'd meet us," Lucivar replied. "Sundancer and I will go on ahead and see if they're waiting." He and the Warlord Prince stallion took off cross-country.

Daffodil made a wistful sound but kept trotting down the road. A few minutes later, he turned off the main road and trotted smartly down a long, tree-lined drive.

Jaenelle's eyes lit up. "We're going to see Duana's country house? Oh, it's such a lovely place. Khary mentioned that someone had taken a lease on it and was fixing it up a bit."

Saetan breathed a sigh of relief. Trust Khary to know just how much to say to pique her interest and still not give it away.

It had taken her six months to heal after she went into the Twisted Kingdom to save Daemon two years ago. She had remained at the Keep for the first two months, too ill to be moved. After he and Lucivar brought her back to the Hall, it had taken her another four months to get her physical strength back. During that time, her friends had once again taken up residence at the Hall, resigning from the courts they were serving in so that they could be with her. She had welcomed the coven's presence but had shied away from the boys seeing her—the first show of feminine vanity she had ever displayed.

Bewildered by her refusal to see them, they had settled in to care from a distance and had channeled their energy into looking after the coven. During that time, under his watchful but blind eye, some friendships had bloomed into love: Morghann and Khardeen, Gabrielle and Chaosti, Grezande and Elan, Kalush and Aaron. He'd watched the girls and had wondered if Jaenelle's eyes would ever shine like that for a man. Even if that man was Daemon Sadi.

When Daemon and Surreal didn't show up at the Terreille Keep, he had tried to locate them. After a few weeks, he stopped because there were indications that he wasn't the only one looking for them, and he had decided that failure was preferable to leading an enemy to a vulnerable man. Besides, Surreal was Titian's daughter. Wherever she had chosen to go to ground, she had hidden her tracks well.

And there was another reason he didn't want to stir things up. Hekatah had never returned to the Dark Realm. He suspected she was well hidden in Hayll. As long as she stayed there, she and Dorothea could rot together, but she would also latch on to any sign of his renewed interest in Terreille and hunt down the cause.

"Lucivar and Sundancer made better time than we did," Jaenelle noted as they pulled up in front of the well-proportioned sandstone manor house.

Daffodil snorted.

"No," Saetan said sternly as he helped Jaenelle out of the buggy. "Buggies *do not* go over fences."

"Especially when the human riding in it doesn't know he's responsible for getting his half over," Jaenelle murmured. She shook out the folds of her sapphire skirt and straightened the matching jacket, too busy to look him in the eye.

Which was just as well.

Jaenelle looked up at the manor house and sighed. "I hope the new tenants will give this place the love it deserves. Oh, I know Duana's busy and prefers living in her country house near Tuathal, but this land needs to be sung awake. The gardens here could be so lovely."

Acknowledging Lucivar's pleased smile, Saetan pulled a flat, rectangular box out of his pocket and handed it to Jaenelle. "Happy birthday, witch-child. From the whole family."

Jaenelle accepted the box but didn't open it. "If it's from the whole family, shouldn't I wait until we're back home to open it?"

Saetan shook his head. "We agreed you should open that here."

Jaenelle opened the box and frowned at the large brass key.

Letting out an exasperated growl, Lucivar turned her around until she was facing the front of the house. "It fits the front door."

Jaenelle's eyes widened. "Mine?" She looked at the front door, then at the key, then back to the front door. "Mine?"

"Well, the family purchased a ten-year lease on the house and land," Saetan replied, smiling. "Duana said that, short of tearing the house down, you could do whatever you wanted with the place."

Jaenelle gave both of them a choke-hold hug and raced to the door. It flew open before she reached it.

"SURPRISE!"

Smiling at her stunned expression, Saetan pushed her into the house at the same time Khary and Morghann pulled her forward into the crowd.

His throat tightened as he watched Jaenelle being passed from friend to friend for a birthday hug. Astar and Sceron, from Centauran. Zylona and Jonah, from Pandar. Grezande and Elan, from Tigrelan. Little Katrine, from Philan. Gabrielle and Chaosti, from Dea al Mon. Karla and Morton, from Glacia. Morghann and Khary, from Scelt. Sabrina and Aaron, from Dharo. Kalush, from Nharkhava. Ladvarian and Kaelas. Had the Shadow Realm ever seen a gathering such as this?

The years when the coven and the male circle had gathered at the Hall had passed so swiftly, and the youngsters were no longer children to be cared for, but adults to be met on equal ground. All the boys had made the Offering to the Darkness, and all of them wore dark Jewels. If the strong friendship between Khary, Aaron, and Chaosti survived the demands of young adulthood and serving in different courts, they would be a formidable, influential triangle of strength in the coming years. And the girls were almost ready to make the Offering. When they did . . . ah, the power!

And then there was Jaenelle. What would become of the lovely, gifted daughter of his soul when she made the Offering?

He tried to shake off his mood before she felt it. But today was a bittersweet day for him, which was why the family had celebrated her birthday—together, privately—a couple of days ago.

A roll of thunder silenced the chatter.

"There now," Karla said with a wicked smile. "Let Uncle Saetan give Jaenelle the grand tour while we finish setting out the food. This might be the only chance we'll get to play in the kitchen."

The girls scampered off to the back of the house.

"I think we'd better help them," Khary said, leading the young men, who hustled off to save the house and edibles.

Lucivar promised to be back, muttering something about unhitching Daffodil before the horse tried to do it himself.

"Duana said that any furniture you don't want to use can be tucked in the attics," Saetan said after he and Jaenelle explored downstairs.

Jaenelle nodded absently as they headed upstairs. "I've seen some grand pieces that would be perfect for this place. There was a—" Open-mouthed, she stood in the bedroom doorway and stared at the canopied bed, dresser, tables, and chests.

"The horde downstairs bought this for you. I gather you had admired something similar often enough that they figured you would like it."

Jaenelle stepped into the room and ran her hand over the dresser's silky maple wood. "It's wonderful. All of it's wonderful. But, why?"

Saetan swallowed hard. "You're twenty years old today."

Jaenelle raised her right hand and fluffed her hair. "I know that."

"My legal guardianship ends today."

They stared at each other for a long moment.

"What does that mean?" she asked quietly.

"Exactly that. My *legal* guardianship ends today." He saw her relax as she assimilated the distinction. "You're a young woman now, witch-child, and should have a place of your own. You've always loved Scelt. We thought it would be helpful to have a home base on this side of the Realm as well as the other." When she still didn't say anything, his heart started pounding. "The Hall will always be your home. We'll always be your family—as long as you want us."

"As long as I want you." Her eyes changed.

It took everything he had in him not to sink to his knees and beg Witch to forgive him.

Jaenelle turned away from him, hugging herself as if she were cold. "I said some cruel things that day."

Saetan took a deep breath. "I did use him. He was my instrument. And even knowing what I know, if I had the choice to make again, I would do it again. A Warlord Prince is expendable. A good Queen is not. And, in truth, if we had done nothing and you hadn't survived, I don't think Daemon would have either. I know I wouldn't have."

Jaenelle opened her arms.

He stepped into them and held her tight. "I don't think you've ever realized how strong, how necessary the bond is between Warlord Princes and Queens. We need you to stay whole. That's why we serve. That's why *all* Blood males serve."

"But it's always seemed so unfair that a Queen can lay claim to a man and control every aspect of his life if she chooses to without him having any say in the matter."

Saetan laughed. "Who says a man has no choice? Haven't you ever noticed how many men who are invited to serve in a court decline the privilege? No, perhaps you haven't. You've had too many other things occupying your time, and that sort of thing is done very quietly." He paused and shook his head, smiling. "Let me tell you an open secret, my darling little witch. You *don't* choose us. *We* choose *you.*"

Jaenelle thought about this and growled, "Lucivar's never going to give that damn Ring back, is he?"

Saetan chuckled softly. "You could try to get it back, but I don't think you'd win." He rubbed his cheek against her hair. "I think he'll serve you for the rest of his life, regardless of whether or not he's actually with you."

"Like you and Uncle Andulvar, with Cassandra."

He closed his eyes. "No, not like me and Andulvar."

She pulled back far enough to study his face. "I see. A bond as strong as family."

"Stronger."

Jaenelle hugged him and sighed. "Maybe we should find Lucivar a wife. That way he would have someone else to pester besides me."

Saetan choked. "How unkind of you to dump Lucivar on some unsuspecting Sister."

"But it would keep him busy."

"Consider for a moment the possible consequence of that busyness."

She did. "A houseful of little Lucivars," she said faintly.

They both groaned.

"All right," Jaenelle grumbled. "I'll think of something else."

"You two get lost up here?"

They jumped. Lucivar smiled at them from the doorway.

"Papa was just explaining that I'm stuck with you forever."

"And it only took you three years to figure that out." Lucivar's arrogant smile widened. "You don't deserve the warning, but while you've been up here busily, but futilely, rearranging my life, Ladvarian's been downstairs busily rearranging yours. The exact quote was 'We can raise and train the puppies here.'"

"Who's we?" Jaenelle squeaked. "What puppies? *Whose* puppies?"

Lucivar stepped aside as Jaenelle flew out of the room, muttering.

Saetan found the doorway blocked by a strong, well-muscled arm.

"You wouldn't have helped her do something that silly, would you?" Lucivar asked.

Saetan leaned against the doorway and shook his head. "If the right woman comes into your life, you won't let her go. I'm the last man who would tell you to compromise. Marry someone you can love and accept as she is, Lucivar. Marry someone who will love and accept you. Don't settle for less."

Lucivar lowered his arm. "Do you think the right man will come into Cat's life?"

"He'll come. If the Darkness is kind, he'll come."

3 / The Twisted Kingdom

He stood at the edge of the resting place for a long time, studying the details, absorbing the message and the warning. Unlike the other resting places she'd provided for him, this one disturbed him.

It was an altar, a slab of black stone laid over two others. At its center was a crystal chalice that once had been shattered. Even from where he stood, his eyes could trace every fracture line, could see where the pieces had been carefully fitted back together. There were sharp-edged chips around the rim where small pieces had been lost, chips that could cut a man badly. Inside the chalice, lightning and black mist performed a slow, swirling dance. Fitted around the chalice's stem was a gold ring with a faceted ruby. A man's ring.

A Consort's ring.

He finally stepped closer.

If he read the message correctly, she had healed but was soul-scarred and not completely whole. By claiming the Consort's ring, he would have the privilege of savoring what the chalice held, but the sharp edges could wound any man who tried.

However, a careful man . . .

Yes, he decided as he studied the sharp-edged chips, a careful man who knew those edges existed and was willing to risk the wounds would be able to drink from that cup.

Satisfied, he returned to the trail and continued climbing.

4 / Kaeleer

Saetan fell out of bed in his haste to find out why Lucivar was roaring so early in the morning.

A part of his mind insisted that he couldn't go charging out of the room wearing nothing but his skin, so he grabbed the trousers he'd dropped over a chair when the birthday party finally wound down but didn't stop to put them on. He wrenched his arm when he tried to open the door that had swollen from last night's rain. Swearing, he gripped the doorknob and, using Craft, tore the door off its hinges.

By then the hallway was stuffed with bodies in various stages of dress. He tried to push past Karla and got a sharp elbow in the belly.

"What in the name of Hell is going on here?" he yelled.

No one bothered to answer him because, at that moment, Lucivar stepped out of Jaenelle's bedroom and roared, "CAT!"

Apparently Lucivar didn't have any inhibitions about standing stark naked in front of a group of young men and women. Of course, a man in his prime with that kind of build had no reason to feel inhibited.

And no one in their right mind would tease a man who vibrated with such intense fury.

"Where are Ladvarian and Kaelas?" Lucivar demanded.

"More to the point," Saetan said, pulling on his trousers, "where's Jaenelle?" He looked pointedly at the Ring of Honor that circled Lucivar's organ. "You can feel her through that, can't you?"

Lucivar quivered with the effort to stay in control. "I can feel her, but I can't *find* her." His fist hammered down on a small table and split it in half. "Damn her, I'm going to whack her ass for this!"

"Who are you to dare say that?" Chaosti snarled, pushing to the front of the group, his Gray Jewel glowing with his gathering power.

Lucivar bared his teeth. "I'm the Warlord Prince who serves her, the warrior sworn to protect her. *But I can't protect her if I don't know where she is.* Her moon's blood started last night. Do I need to remind you how vulnerable a witch is during those days? Now she's upset—I can feel that much—and her only protection is two half-trained males *because she didn't tell me where she was going.*"

"That's enough," Saetan said sharply. "Leash the anger. NOW!" While he waited, he called in his shoes and stuffed his feet into them. Then he froze Chaosti and Lucivar with a look.

When no one moved, he stepped away from the group and pressed his back against the wall for support. He took a few deep breaths to calm his own temper, closed his eyes, and descended to the Black.

While it was true that witches couldn't channel Jeweled strength during their moon time without pain, that wouldn't stop Jaenelle.

Using himself as a center point, he cautiously pushed his Black-Jeweled strength outward in ever-widening circles, looking for some sense of her that would at least give him an idea of where she was. The circles widened farther and farther, beyond the village of Maghre, beyond the isle of Scelt, until . . .

Kaetien!

He felt fear and horror braiding with anger growing into rage.

Black rage. Spiraling rage. Cold rage.

He started to pull back to escape the psychic storm that was about to explode over Sceval. He strengthened his inner barriers, knowing that it wouldn't help much. Her rage would flood in under his barriers, where he had no protection from it. He just hoped he had enough time to warn the others.

KAETIEN!

As she unleashed the strength of her Black Jewels, Jaenelle's anguished scream filled his head and paralyzed him. A rush of dark power smashed against him, tossing him around like a tidal wave tosses driftwood, at the same time a psychic shield snapped up around Sceval.

Then, nothing.

He floated just beyond that shield, scared but oddly comforted—like being safely indoors while a violent storm raged outside.

He must have gotten caught between the conflicting uses of Black power when Jaenelle put up the shield to contain the storm. Clever little witch. And all that psychic lightning had a terrifying kind of beauty. He wouldn't mind just floating here for a while, but he had the nagging feeling there was something he should do.

High Lord.

Damn troublesome voice. How was he supposed to think when . . .

Father.

Father. Father. Hell's fire, Lucivar!

Up. He had to go up, out of the Black. Had to get his head clear enough to tell Lucivar . . . Which way was up?

Someone grabbed him and dragged him out of the abyss. He sputtered and snarled. Did him as much good as a puppy snarling when it was picked up by the scruff.

The next thing he knew, something was pressed against his lips and blood was filling his mouth.

"Swallow it or I'll knock your damn teeth down your throat."

Ah, yes. Lucivar. Both of him.

His eyes finally focused. He pushed Lucivar's wrist away from his mouth. "Enough." He tried to get to his feet, which wasn't easy with Lucivar holding him down on one side and Chaosti holding him down on the other. "Is everyone all right?"

Karla bent over him. "*We're* fine. *You're* the one who fainted."

"I didn't faint. I got caught . . ." He started struggling. "Let me up. If the storm's over, we have to get to Sceval."

"Cat's there?" Lucivar asked, hauling him to his feet.

"Yes." Remembering Jaenelle's anguished scream, Saetan shuddered. "You and I have to get there as soon as possible."

Karla poked a sharp-nailed finger into his bare chest. "*We* have to get there as soon as possible."

Before he could argue, they'd all disappeared into their rooms.

"If we move, we can get there ahead of the rest of them," Lucivar said quietly as they entered Saetan's bedroom. He called in his own clothes and hurriedly dressed. "Are you strong enough for this?"

Saetan pulled on a shirt. "I'm ready. Let's go."

"Are you strong enough for this?"

Saetan brushed past Lucivar without answering. How could a man answer that question when he didn't know what was waiting for him?

"Mother Night," Saetan whispered. "Mother Night."

He and Lucivar stood on a flat-topped hill that was one of Sceval's official landing places, the gently rolling land spread out below them. Large meadows provided good grazing. Stands of trees provided shade on summer afternoons. Creeks veined the land with clean water.

He had stood on this hill a handful of times in the past five years, looking down on the unicorns while the stallions kept careful watch over the grazing mares and the foals playing tag.

Now he looked down on a slaughter.

Turning to the north, Lucivar shook his head and swore softly. "This wasn't a few bastards who had come for a horn to take home as a hunting trophy, this was a war."

Saetan blinked away tears. Of all the Blood, of all the kindred races, the unicorns had always been his favorite. They had been the stars in the Darkness, the living examples of power and strength blended with gentleness and beauty. "When the others arrive, we'll split up to look for survivors."

The unicorns attacked at the same moment the coven and the male circle appeared on the hill.

"Shield!" Saetan and Lucivar shouted. They threw Black and Ebongray shields around the whole group while the other males formed a protective circle around the coven.

The eight unicorn stallions veered off before they hit the shields headon, but the power they were channeling through their horns and hooves created blinding-bright sparks as they scraped across the invisible barriers.

"Wait!" Saetan shouted, the thunder in his voice barely competing with the stallions' screams and trumpeted challenges. "We're friends! We're here to help you!"

★You are not friends,★ said an older stallion with a broken horn. ★You are humans!★

"We're friends," Saetan insisted.

★YOU ARE NOT FRIENDS!★ the unicorns screamed. ★YOU ARE HUMANS!★

Sceron took a step forward. "The Centauran people have never fought with our unicorn Brothers and Sisters. We do not wish to fight now."

★You come to kill. First you call us Brothers and then you come to kill. No more. NO MORE. This time, we kill!★

Karla stuck her head over Saetan's shoulder. "Damn your hooves and horns, we're *Healers*. Let us take care of the injured!"

The unicorns hesitated for a moment, then shook their heads and charged the shields again.

"I don't recognize any of them," Lucivar said, "and they're too bloodcrazed to listen."

Saetan watched the stallions charge the shields over and over again. He sympathized with their rage, fully understood their hatred. But he couldn't walk away until they were calm enough to listen because more would die if they weren't cared for soon.

And because Jaenelle was among those bodies, somewhere.

Then the unicorns stopped attacking. They circled the group, snorting and pawing the ground, their horns lowered for another charge.

"Thank the Darkness," Khary muttered as a young stallion slowly climbed up the hill, favoring his left foreleg.

Relieved, the girls began murmuring about healing teams.

Watching the young stallion approach, Saetan wished he could share their confidence, but out of all of Kaetien's offspring, Mistral had always been the most wary of humans—and the most dangerous. Necessary traits for a young male who everyone anticipated would be the next Warlord Prince of Sceval, but damned uncomfortable for the man on the receiving end of that distrust.

"Mistral." Saetan stepped forward, raising his empty hands. "You've known all of us since you were a foal. Let us help."

I have known you, Mistral said reluctantly.

That sounds ominous, Lucivar said on an Ebon-gray spear thread.

If this goes wrong, get everyone else out of here, Saetan replied. *I'll hold the shield.*

We still have to find Cat.

Get them out, Yaslana.

Yes, High Lord.

Saetan took another step forward. "Mistral, I swear to you by the Jewels that I wear and by my love for the Lady that we mean no harm."

Whatever Mistral thought about a human male laying claim to the Lady was lost when Ladvarian's light tenor pounded into their heads.

High Lord? High Lord! We have some little ones shielded, but they're scared and won't listen. They keep running into the shield. Jaenelle is crying and won't listen either. High Lord?

Saetan held his breath. Which would prove stronger—Mistral's loyalty to his own kind or his love for and belief in Jaenelle?

Mistral looked toward the north. After a long moment, he snorted. *The little Brother believes in you. We will trust. For now.*

Desperately wanting to sit down and not daring to show any sign of weakness, Saetan cautiously lowered the Black shield.

A moment later, Lucivar dropped the Ebon-gray.

They divided into groups. Khary and Morghann went to help Ladvarian and Kaelas with the foals. Lucivar and Karla headed north from the landing place with Karla as primary Healer, Lucivar as secondary, and the rest of their team scouting for the wounded and providing assistance. Saetan, Gabrielle, and their team headed south.

It hurt to look at the mares' hacked-up bodies. It hurt even worse to see a young colt lying dead over his dam, his forelegs sliced off. There were some he could save. There were many more where all he could do was take away the pain to ease the journey back to the Darkness.

Hours passed as he searched for the foals that might be hidden under their dams. He found yearlings hidden in shallow dips in the land, dips that held a power unlike any he'd ever felt before. He didn't trespass into those places. The young unicorns watched him with terrified eyes as he carefully circled around them looking for wounds. It came to him slowly as he stepped around torn human bodies that any of the unicorns who had reached these places had, at worst, minor cuts or scratches.

He continued to work, ignoring the headache the sun gave him, ignoring the aching muscles and growing fatigue.

His emotions numbed as a defense against the slaughter.

But they weren't numb enough when he found Jaenelle and Kaetien.

"There, my fine Lady," Lucivar said, running one hand down the mare's neck. "It'll feel sore for a few days, but it will heal well."

The mare's colt snorted and pawed the ground until Lucivar gave them a few carrot chunks and a sugar lump.

When the mare and her colt moved off, he helped himself to a long drink of water and half of a cheese sandwich while he waited for the next unicorn to gather the courage to be touched by a human.

May the Darkness bless Khary's equine-loving heart. After a rapid look at the carnage, Khary and Aaron had gone back to Maghre. They'd returned with Daffodil and Sundancer pulling carts loaded with healing supplies, food for the humans, changes of clothes, blankets, and Khary's "bribes"—carrots and sugar lumps.

Seeing Daffodil and Sundancer working confidently with the humans had acted as a balm on the unicorns' fear. The words "I serve the Lady" had produced an even stronger response. On the strength of those words, most of the unicorns had let him touch them and heal what he could.

Taking the last bite of his sandwich, he watched a yearling colt cautiously approach him, its skin twitching as the flies buzzed around the shoulder wound protected by a fading shield.

Lucivar spread his arms, showing empty hands. "I serve—"

The yearling bolted as Sceron's war cry shattered the uneasy truce and Kaelas roared in challenge.

Calling in his Eyrien war blade, Lucivar launched himself skyward.

As he sped toward the man running for the landing place, he coldly ticked off each little scene as it flashed under him: Morghann, Kalush, and Ladvarian herding the foals into the trees; Kaelas pulling a man down and tearing him open; Astar pivoting on her hindquarters as she nocked an arrow in a Centauran bow; Morton shielding Karla and the unicorn she was healing; Khary, Aaron, and Sceron protecting each others' backs as they unleashed the strength of their Jewels in short, controlled bursts that ripped the invading humans apart.

Focusing on his chosen prey, Lucivar unleashed a burst of Ebon-gray power just as the man reached the bottom of the hill.

The man fell, both legs neatly broken, his Yellow Jewel drained.

Lucivar landed at the same moment the old stallion with the broken horn charged the downed man. *Wait!* he yelled as he threw a tight Red shield over the man.

The stallion screamed in rage and pivoted to face Lucivar.

Wait, Lucivar said again. *First I want answers. *Then* you can pound him.*

The stallion snorted but stopped pawing the ground.

Keeping a watchful eye on the stallion, Lucivar dropped the shield. Applying a foot to a shoulder, he rolled the man over onto his back. "This is a closed Territory," he said harshly. "Why are you here?"

"I don't have to answer to the likes of you."

Brave words for a man with two broken legs. Stupid, but brave.

Using the Eyrien war blade, Lucivar pointed to the man's right knee and looked at the stallion. "Once. Right there."

The stallion reared and happily obliged.

"Shall we try this again?" Lucivar asked mildly once the man stopped screaming. "The other knee or a hand next? Your choice."

"You've no right to do this. When this is reported—"

Lucivar laughed. "Reported to whom? And for what? You're an invader waging war on the rightful inhabitants of this island. Who's going to care what happens to you?"

"The Dark Council, that's who." Sweat beaded the man's forehead as Lucivar fingered the war blade. "You've no claim to this land."

"Neither do you," Lucivar said coldly.

"We've a claim, you bat-winged bastard. My Queen and five others were given this island as their new territory. We came here first to settle the territory boundaries and take care of any problems."

"Like the race that's ruled this land for thousands of years? Yes, I can see how that might be a problem."

"No one rules here. This is unclaimed land."

"This is the unicorns' Territory," Lucivar said fiercely.

"I hurt," the man whined. "I need a Healer."

"They're all busy. Let's get back to something more interesting. The Dark Council has no right to hand out land, and they have no right to replace an established race who already has a claim."

"Show me the signed land grant. My Queen has one, properly signed and sealed."

Lucivar gritted his teeth. "The unicorns rule here."

The man rolled his head back and forth. "Animals have no rights to the land. Only human claims are considered legitimate. Anything that lives here now lives by the Queens' sufferance."

"They're kindred," Lucivar said, his voice roughened by feelings he didn't want to name. "They're Blood."

"Animals. Just animals. Get rid of the rogues, the rest might be useful." The man whimpered. "Hurt. Need a Healer."

Lucivar took a step back. Took another. Oh, yes. Wouldn't the Terreillean bitch-Queens just love to ride around on unicorns? It wouldn't bother them in the least that the animals' spirits would have to be broken before they could do it. Wouldn't bother them at all.

Three glorious years of living in Kaeleer couldn't cleanse the 1,700 years he'd lived in Terreille. He tried very hard to put the past aside, but there were nights when he woke up shaking. He could control his mind for the most part, but his body still remembered all too well what a Ring of Obedience felt like and what it could do.

Swallowing hard, Lucivar licked his dry lips and looked at the old stallion. "Start with the arms and legs. It'll take longer for him to die that way."

Vanishing his war blade, he turned and walked away, ignoring the sound of hooves smashing bone, ignoring the screams.

★   ★   ★

Saetan stumbled over a severed arm and finally admitted he had to stop. Jaenelle's blood-tonic allowed him to tolerate, and enjoy, some daylight, but he still needed to rest during the hours when the sun was strongest. As the morning gave way to afternoon, he'd worked in the shade as much as possible, but that hadn't been enough to counteract the drain strong sunlight caused in a Guardian's body, and he couldn't take the strain of doing so much healing for so many hours.

He had to stop.

Except he couldn't until he found Jaenelle.

He'd tried everything he could think of to locate her. Nothing had worked. All Ladvarian could tell him was she was here and she was crying, but neither Ladvarian nor Kaelas could give him the barest direction of where to search. When he finally got Mistral to understand his concern, the stallion said, "Her grief will not let us find her."

Saetan rubbed his eyes and hoped his fatigue-fogged brain kept working long enough to get him to the camp Chaosti and Elan had set up. He was too tired, too drained. He was starting to see things.

Like the unicorn Queen standing in front of him, who looked like she was made of moonlight and mist, with dark eyes as old as the land.

It took him a minute to realize he could see through her.

"You're—"

Gone, said the caressing, feminine voice. *Gone long and long ago. And never gone. Come, High Lord. My Sister needs her sire now.*

Saetan followed her until they reached a circle of low, evenly spaced stones. In the center, a great stone horn rose up from the land. An old, deep power filled the circle.

"I can't go there," Saetan said. "This is a sacred place."

An honored place, she replied. *They are nearby. She grieves for what she could not save. You must make her see what she did save.*

The mare stepped into the circle. As she approached the great stone horn, she faded until she disappeared, but he still had the feeling that dark eyes as old as the land watched him.

The air shimmered on his right. A veil he hadn't known was there vanished. He walked toward the spot. And he found them.

The bastards had butchered Kaetien. They had cut off his legs, his tail, his genitals. They had sliced open his belly.

They had cut off his horn.

They had cut off his head.

But Kaetien's dark eyes still held a fiery intelligence.

Saetan's stomach rolled.

Kaetien was demon-dead in that mutilated body.

Jaenelle sat next to the stallion, leaning against the open belly. Tears trickled from her staring eyes. Her white-knuckled hands were wrapped around Kaetien's horn.

Saetan sank to his knees beside her. "Witch-child?" he whispered.

Recognition came slowly. "Papa? P-Papa?" She threw herself into his arms. The quiet tears became hysterical weeping. Kaetien's horn scraped his back as she clung to him.

"Oh, witch-child." While he and the others had been searching for survivors, she'd been sitting there all day, locked in her pain.

"May the Darkness be merciful," said a voice behind him.

Saetan looked over his shoulder, feeling every muscle as he turned his head. Lucivar. Living strength that could do what he could not.

Lucivar stared at Kaetien's head and shook himself.

Saetan listened to the swift conversations taking place on spear threads, but he was too tired to make sense out of them.

Lucivar dropped to one knee, took a handful of Jaenelle's blood-matted hair, and gently pulled her head away from Saetan's shoulder. "Come on, Cat. You'll feel better once you've had a sip of this." He pressed a large silver flask against her mouth.

She choked and sputtered when the liquid went down her throat.

"This time swallow it," Lucivar said. "This stuff does less harm to your stomach than it does to your lungs."

"This stuff will melt your teeth," Jaenelle wheezed.

"What did you give her?" Saetan demanded when she suddenly sagged in his arms.

"A healthy dose of Khary's home brew. Hey!"

Saetan found himself braced against Lucivar's chest. He concentrated on breathing for a minute. "Lucivar. You asked if I was strong enough for this. I'm not."

A strong, warm hand stroked his head. "Hang on. Sundancer's coming. We'll get you to the camp. The girls will take care of Cat. A few minutes more and you can rest."

Rest. Yes, he needed rest. The headache that was threatening to tear his skull apart was gaining in intensity with every breath.

Someone took Jaenelle out of his arms. Someone half carried him to where Sundancer waited. Strong hands kept him on the stallion's back.

The next thing he knew, he was sitting in the camp wrapped in blankets with Karla kneeling beside him, urging him to drink the witch's brew she'd made for him.

After drinking a second cup, he submitted to being pushed, plumped, and rearranged in a sleeping bag. He snarled a bit at being fussed over until Karla tartly asked how he expected them to get Jaenelle to rest when he was setting such a bad example?

Not having an answer for that, he surrendered to the brew-dulled headache and slept.

Lucivar sipped laced coffee and watched Gabrielle and Morghann lead Jaenelle to a sleeping bag. She stopped, ignoring their coaxing to lie down and rest. Her eyes lost their dull, half-dazed look as her attention focused on Mistral hovering at the edge of the camp, still favoring his wounded left foreleg.

Lucivar felt very thankful that the cold, dangerous fire in her eyes wasn't directed at him.

"Why hasn't that leg been tended?" Jaenelle asked in her midnight voice as she stared at the young stallion.

Mistral snorted and fidgeted. He obviously didn't want to admit he hadn't allowed anyone to touch him.

Lucivar didn't blame him.

"You know how males get," Gabrielle said soothingly. " 'I'm fine, I'm fine, tend the others first.' We were just about to take care of him when you and Uncle Saetan came in."

"I see," Jaenelle said softly, her eyes still pinning Mistral to the ground. "I thought, perhaps, because they were human, you were insulting my Sisters by refusing to let them heal you."

"Nonsense," Morghann said. "Now, come on, set a good example."

Once they got her tucked in, they descended on Mistral.

It would be all right, Lucivar thought dully. It had to be all right. The unicorns and the other kindred wouldn't lose all their trust in humans and retreat again behind the veils of power that had closed them off from the rest of Kaeleer. Cat would see to that. And Saetan . . .

Hell's fire. Until today, he hadn't given much thought to the differences between a Guardian and the living. At the Hall, those differences seemed so subtle.

He hadn't realized strong sun would cause so much pain, hadn't fully appreciated how many years the High Lord had walked the Realms. Oh, he *knew* how old Saetan was, but today was the first time his father had seemed *old*.

Of course, the rest of them were feeling pretty beaten physically and emotionally, so it wasn't much of a yardstick to measure by.

Khary squatted beside him and splashed some of the home brew into the already heavily laced coffee. "There's something bothering our four-footed Brothers," he said quietly. "Something more than that." He waved a hand at the still, white bodies lying within sight.

The unicorns hadn't cared what happened to the human bodies—except to insist that the intruders not remain in their land—but they had been vehement about not moving the dead unicorns. The Lady would sing them to the land, they had said.

Whatever that meant.

But as the wounded mares and foals had been led to this side of the landing hill, the surviving stallions had become more and more upset.

"Ladvarian might know," Lucivar said, sipping his coffee. He sent out a quiet summons. A few minutes later, the Sceltie trotted wearily into the camp.

Moonshadow's missing, Ladvarian said when Lucivar asked him. *Starcloud was getting old. Moonshadow was going to be the next Queen. She wears an Opal Jewel. One of the mares said she saw humans throw ropes and nets around Moonshadow, but she didn't see where they went.*

Lucivar closed his eyes. From what he could tell, all of the Blood males who had invaded Sceval had worn lighter Jewels, but enough of them with spelled nets and ropes could control an Opal-Jeweled Queen. Were the spelled nets preventing her from calling to the others, or had she been taken off the island altogether?

"I'll be back before twilight," he said, handing the cup to Khary.

"Watch your back," Khary said softly. "Just in case."

Lucivar flew north. As he flew, he kept sending the same message: He served the Lady. The Lady was at a camp near the landing hill. Healers were with the Lady.

He saw a few small herds of unicorns, who ran for the trees as best they could as soon as they sensed him.

He saw a lot of still, white bodies.

He saw even more exploded human corpses, and thanked the Darkness that Jaenelle had somehow kept her rage confined to this island.

And he wondered about the pockets of power he kept sensing as he flew over woods and clearings. Some were faint; others much stronger. He was turning away from an especially strong one that was in the trees to his left when something grabbed him. Something angry and desperate.

Using his Birthright Red, he broke the contact, but it took effort.

You serve the Lady, said a harsh male voice.

Lucivar hovered, breathing hard. *I serve the Lady,* he agreed cautiously. *Do you need help?*

She needs help.

Landing, he allowed the power to guide him through the trees until he reached its source. In a hollow, a mare lay tangled in nets and ropes, breathing hard and sweating.

"Ah, sweetheart," Lucivar said softly.

While most of the unicorns were some shade of white, there were a few rare dappled grays. This mare was a pale pewter with a white mane and tail. An Opal Jewel hung from a silver ring around her horn.

She was not only a Queen, she was also a Black Widow. The only combination that was rarer was the Queen/Black Widow/Healer. He'd never heard of a witch like that when he'd lived in Terreille. In Kaeleer, there were only three—Karla, Gabrielle, and Jaenelle.

Standing very still, Lucivar slowly spread his dark, membranous wings. He'd heard enough disparaging remarks about "human bats" in his life to recognize the advantage his wings might give him now. Wings, like hooves and fur, were usually part of the kindred's domain.

"Lady Moonshadow," he said, keeping his voice low and soothing, "I am Prince Lucivar Yaslana. I serve the Lady. I'd like to help you."

She didn't reply, but the panic in her eyes gradually receded.

He walked toward her, gritting his teeth as the male power surrounding her swelled, then ebbed.

"Easy, sweetheart," he said, crouching beside her. "Easy."

Her panic spiked when his hand touched her withers.

Lucivar swore silently as he cut the nets and ropes. They'd tried to break her, tried to shatter her inner web. The only difference between what the Terreillean bastards had tried to do to her and what they usually did to human witches was physical rape. Maybe that's why they hadn't succeeded before Jaenelle had unleashed the Black. They hadn't been able to use their best weapon.

"There now," Lucivar said as he tossed the last of the ropes away. "Come on, sweetheart. On your feet. Easy now."

Step by step, he coaxed her out of the trees and into the clearing. Her fear increased with every step she took away from that power-filled hollow. He needed to get her to the camp before her fear finished what those bastards had started. A radial line from the Rose Wind was close enough to catch, and he could certainly guide and shield her for the short trip, but how to convince her to trust him that much?

"Mistral's going to be very glad to see you," he said casually.

Mistral? Her head swung around. He dodged the horn before it impaled him. *He is well?*

"He's at the camp with the Lady. If we ride the Rose Wind, we'll get there before twilight."

Pain and sorrow filled her thoughts. *The lost ones must be sung to the land at twilight.*

Lucivar suppressed a shiver. Suddenly he very much wanted to be back in the camp. "Shall we go, Lady?"

Everyone had returned to the camp, physically weary and heartsore. Everyone except Lucivar.

As he drank the restorative brew Karla had made for him, Saetan tried not to worry. Lucivar could take care of himself; he was a strong, fit, well-trained warrior; he knew his limitations, especially after extending himself so much today; he wouldn't do anything foolish like try to take on a gang of Blood-Jeweled males alone just because he was pissed about the kindred deaths.

And tomorrow the sun would rise in the west.

"He's fine," Jaenelle said quietly as she settled next to him on one of the logs the boys had dragged from somewhere to provide seats around the fire. Tucking the spell-warmed blanket around herself, she smiled rue-fully. "The Ring's *supposed* to let me monitor *his* spikes of temper. I hadn't realized I'd messed up somewhere when I created it until Karla, Morghann, Grezande, *and* Gabrielle bitched about my setting a bad prece-dent since all the boyos want a Ring that works like that." Her voice took on a hint of whine. "I always thought it was just extraordinary intuition that he always showed up whenever I felt grumpy. *He* certainly never hinted it was anything more than that."

"He's not an idiot, witch-child," Saetan replied, sipping his brew to hide his smile.

"That's debatable. But why did he have to go and tell the others?"

He understood why the Queens were annoyed. The foundation of any official court was twelve males and a Queen. Through the Ring of Honor, a Queen could monitor every nuance of a male's life. But because the Queens respected the privacy of the males who served them and because no woman in her right mind would want to keep track of the emotional currents of that many men, they usually adjusted their monitoring to block out everything but things like fear, rage, and pain—the kinds of feelings that indicated the wearer needed help.

Each man, however, only had to keep track of one Queen.

He'd have to talk to Lucivar about the self-imposed limits of that kind of monitoring. He'd be interested in where his son drew the line.

"Speaking of the pain in the ass who's not an idiot," Jaenelle said, pointing to the two figures walking slowly toward the camp.

Mistral bugled wildly. *Moonshadow! Moonshadow!*

He took off at a gallop. At least, he tried to.

As Mistral leaped forward, Gabrielle jumped up from her seat on the other log, reached out, closed her hand as if she'd grabbed something, and jerked her hand up.

Mistral hung in the air, his legs flailing.

Gabrielle's arm shook from the effort of holding that much weight suspended, even if she was using Craft. Watching her, Saetan decided he and Chaosti needed to have a chat very soon. A witch who could pull a trick like that after an exhausting day of healing was a Lady who needed careful handling.

"If you gallop on that leg, I'll knock you silly," Gabrielle said.

It's Moonshadow!

"I don't care if it's the Queen of the unicorns or your mate," Gabrielle replied hotly. "You're not galloping on that leg!"

"Actually," Jaenelle said with a dry smile, "she's both."

"Well, Hell's fire." Gabrielle set Mistral down but didn't let go.

"Gabrielle," Chaosti said in that coaxing tone of voice Saetan labeled male-soothing-female-temper. "She's his mate. He's been worried. I wouldn't want to wait if it were you. Let him go."

Gabrielle glared at Chaosti.

"He'll walk," Chaosti said. "Won't you, Mistral?"

Mistral wasn't about to turn down allies, even if they did have only two legs. *I'll walk.*

Reluctantly, Gabrielle released him.

Mistral plodded toward Moonshadow, his head down like a small boy who's been scolded and hasn't yet gotten away from the scolder's watchful eyes.

"Now see what you did," Khary said. "You made his horn wilt."

"I'll bet your horn wilts too when you're scolded," Karla said with a wicked smile.

Before Khary could reply, Jaenelle set her cup down and said quietly, "It's time."

Everyone became subdued as she walked into the trees.

"Do you know what's supposed to happen?" Lucivar asked Saetan when he reached the camp and sat down next to his father.

Saetan shook his head. Like everyone else in the camp, he couldn't take his eyes off the mare. "Mother Night, she's beautiful."

"She's also a Black Widow Queen," Lucivar said dryly, watching Mistral escort his Lady. "Well, if someone's going to get kicked for fussing, better him than me."

Saetan laughed softly. "By the way, your sister has something she wants to discuss with you." When he didn't get a response, he looked at his son. "Lucivar?"

Lucivar's mouth hung open, his eyes fixed on the trees to Saetan's left—the trees Jaenelle had walked into a few minutes before.

He turned . . . and forgot how to breathe.

She wore a long, flowing dress made of delicate black spidersilk. Strands of cobwebs dripped from the tight sleeves. Beginning just above her breasts, the dress became an open web framing her chest and shoulders. Black Jewel chips sparkled with dark fire at the end of each thread.

Black-Jeweled rings decorated both hands. Around her neck was a Black Jewel centered in a web made of delicate gold and silver strands.

It was a gown made for Jaenelle the Witch. Erotic. Romantic. Terrifying. He could feel the latent power in every thread of that gown. And he knew then who had created it: the Arachnians. The Weavers of Dreams.

Saying nothing, Jaenelle picked up Kaetien's horn and glided toward open ground, the gown's small train flowing out behind her.

Saetan wanted to remind her that it was her moon time, that she shouldn't be channeling her power through her body right now. But he remembered that, behind the human mask, Witch had a tiny spiral horn in the center of her forehead, so he said nothing.

She spent several minutes walking around, looking at the ground as if she wanted a particular site.

Finally satisfied, she faced the north. Raising Kaetien's horn to the sky, she sang one keening note. She lowered her hands, pointed the horn at the ground, and sang another note. Then she swept her arms upward and began to sing in the Old Tongue.

Witchsong.

Saetan felt it in his bones, felt it in his blood.

A ghostly web of power formed under her bare feet and swiftly spread across the land. Spread and spread and spread.

Her song changed, became a dirge filled with sorrow and celebration. Her voice became the wind, the water, the grass, the trees. Circling. Spiraling.

The still, white bodies of the dead unicorns began to glow. Mesmerized, Saetan wondered if, viewed from above, the glowing bodies would look like stars that had come to rest on sacred ground.

Perhaps they were. Perhaps they had.

The song changed again until it became a blend of the other two. Ending and beginning. From the land and back to the land.

The unicorn bodies melted into the earth.

Kindred didn't come to the Dark Realm. Now he knew why. Just as he knew why humans would never easily settle in kindred Territories without the kindred's welcome. Just as he knew what had created those pockets of power he'd avoided so carefully.

Kindred never left their Territories, they became part of it. What strength was left in each of them became bound with the land.

The ghostly web of power faded.

Jaenelle's voice and the last of the daylight faded.

No one moved. No one spoke.

Coming back to himself, Saetan realized Lucivar's arm was around his shoulders.

"Damn," Lucivar whispered, brushing away tears.

"The living myth," Saetan whispered. "Dreams made flesh." His throat tightened. He closed his eyes.

He felt Lucivar leave him and reach for something.

Opening his eyes, he watched Lucivar support Jaenelle into the camp. Her face was tight with pain and exhaustion, but there was peace in her sapphire eyes.

The coven gathered around her and led her into the trees.

Talking quietly, the boys stirred the pots of stew, sliced bread and cheese, gathered bowls and plates for the evening meal.

Beyond the firelight, the unicorns settled down for the night.

Khary and Aaron took bowls of stew and water out to where Ladvarian and Kaelas were keeping watch over the foals.

When the girls returned, Jaenelle was dressed in trousers and a long, heavy sweater. She gave Lucivar a halfhearted snarl when he wrapped her in a spell-warmed blanket and settled her on the log next to Saetan, but she didn't grumble about the food he brought.

They all talked quietly as they ate. Small talk and gentle teasing. Nothing about what they'd done today or what still waited for them tomorrow. Despite their best efforts, they'd covered a very small part of Sceval, and only Jaenelle knew how many unicorns lived there.

Only Jaenelle knew how many had been sung back to the land.

"Saetan?" Jaenelle said, resting her head against his shoulder.

He kissed her forehead. "Witch-child?" She didn't respond for so long he thought she'd dozed off.

"When does the Dark Council next meet?"

5 / Kaeleer

Lord Magstrom tried to keep his mind on the petitioner standing in the circle, but she had the same complaints as the seven petitioners before her, and he doubted the twenty petitioners after her would have anything different to say to the Dark Council.

He had thought that, when he became Third Tribune, his opinions might carry a little more weight. He had hoped his position would help quell the continued, whispered insinuations about the SaDiablo family.

That none of the Territory Queens outside of Little Terreille believed there was any truth in those whispers should have told the Council something. That the Dark Council's judgments had been respected and trusted by all of the Blood races for all the years the High Lord and Andulvar Yaslana had served in the Council should have told them even more—especially since it was no longer true.

Lord Jorval was First Tribune now, and it was disturbing how easily he shaped other Council members' opinions.

And now this.

"How can I settle the territory granted to me when my men are being slaughtered before they even set up camp?" the Queen petitioner demanded. "The Council has to do something!"

"The wilderness is always dangerous, Lady," Lord Jorval said smoothly. "You were warned to take extra precautions."

"Precautions!" The Queen quivered in outrage. "You said these beasts, these so-called kindred had a bit of magic."

"They do."

"That wasn't just a bit of magic they were using. That was Craft!"

"No, no. Only the human races are Blood, and only the Blood has the power to use Craft." Lord Jorval looked soulfully at the Council members seated on either side of the large chamber. "But, perhaps, since we know so little about them, we were not fully aware of the extent of this animal magic. It may be that the only way our Terreillean Brothers and Sisters will be able to secure the land granted to them is if the Kaeleer Queens they're serving are willing to send in their own warriors to clear out these infestations."

And every Queen who sent assistance would expect a higher percentage of the profit from the conquered land, Magstrom thought sourly. He was about to antagonize the rest of the Council—again—by reminding the members that the Dark Council had been formed to act as arbitrators to prevent wars, not to provoke them. Before he could speak, a midnight voice filled the Council chamber.

"Infestations?" Jaenelle Angelline strode toward the Tribunal's bench and stopped just outside the petitioner's circle, flanked by the High Lord and Lucivar Yaslana. "Those infestations you speak of, Lord Jorval, are kindred. They are Blood. They have every right to defend themselves and their land against an invading force."

"We're not invading!" the petitioning Queen snapped. "We went in to settle the unclaimed land that was granted to us by the Dark Council."

"It's not unclaimed," Jaenelle snarled. "It's kindred Territories."

"Ladies." Lord Jorval had to raise his voice to be heard over the muttering of Council members and petitioners. "Ladies!" When the Council and the petitioners subsided, Lord Jorval smiled at Jaenelle. "Lady Angelline, while it's always a pleasure to see you, I must ask that you not disrupt a Council meeting. If there is something you wish to bring before the Council, you must wait until the petitioners who have already requested an audience have been heard."

"If all the petitioners have the same complaint, I can save the Council a great deal of time," Jaenelle replied coldly. "Kindred Territories are not unclaimed land. The Blood have ruled there for thousands of years. The Blood still rule there."

"While it pains me to disagree," Lord Jorval said gently, "there are no Blood in these 'kindred territories.' The Council has studied this matter most diligently and has reached the conclusion that, while these animals may be thought of as 'magical cousins,' they are not Blood. One must be human to be Blood. And this Council was formed to deal with the Blood's concerns, the Blood's rights."

"Then what are the centaurs? What are the satyrs? Half-human with half rights?"

No one answered.

"I see," Jaenelle said too softly.

Lord Magstrom's mouth felt parched. His tongue felt shriveled. Did no one else remember what had happened the last time Jaenelle Angelline had stood before the Council?

"Once the Blood are established in these Territories, they will look after the kindred. Any disagreements can then be brought to the Council by the human representatives for those Territories."

"You're saying that the kindred require a human representative before they're entitled to any consideration or any rights?"

"Precisely," Lord Jorval said, smiling.

"In that case, *I* am the kindred's human representative."

Lord Magstrom suddenly felt as if a trap had been sprung. Lord Jorval was still smiling, still looked benign, but Magstrom had worked with him enough to recognize the subtle, underlying cruelty in the man.

"Unfortunately, that isn't possible," Lord Jorval said. "This Lady's claim may be under dispute"—he nodded at the petitioning Queen—"but you have no claim whatsoever. You don't rule these Territories. Your rights are not being infringed upon. And since neither you nor yours are affected by this, you have no justifiable complaint. I must ask you now to leave the Council chambers."

Lord Magstrom shuddered at the blankness in Jaenelle's eyes. He sighed with relief when she walked out of the Council chamber, followed by the High Lord and Prince Yaslana.

"Now, Lady," Lord Jorval said with a weary smile, "let's see what we can do about your *rightful* petition."

"Bastards," Lucivar snarled as they walked toward the landing web.

Saetan slipped an arm around Jaenelle's shoulders. Lucivar's open anger didn't worry him. Jaenelle's silent withdrawal did.

"Don't fret about it, Cat," Lucivar continued. "We'll find a way around those bastards and keep the kindred protected."

"I'm not sure there *is* a legitimate way around the Council's decision," Saetan said carefully.

"And you've never stepped outside the Law? You've never overruled a bad decision by using strength and temper?"

Saetan clenched his teeth. In trying to explain why the family had difficulties with the Dark Council, someone must have told Lucivar why the Council made him Jaenelle's guardian. "No, I'm not saying that."

"Are you saying kindred aren't important enough to fight for because they're animals?"

Saetan stopped walking. Jaenelle drifted a little farther down the flagstone walk, away from them.

"No, I'm not saying that, either," Saetan replied, struggling to keep his voice down. "We have to find an answer that fits the Council's new rules or this will escalate into a war that tears the Realm apart."

"So we sacrifice the nonhuman Blood to save Kaeleer?" Smiling bitterly, Lucivar opened his wings. "What am I, High Lord? By the Council's reckoning of who is human and who is not, what am I?"

Saetan took a step back. It could have been Andulvar standing there. It *had* been Andulvar standing there all those years ago. *When honor and the Law no longer stand on the same side of the line, how do we choose, SaDiablo?*

Saetan rubbed his hands over his face. *Ah, Hekatah, you spin your schemes well. Just like the last time.* "We'll find a legitimate way to protect the kindred and their land."

"You said there wasn't a legitimate way."

"Yes, there is," Jaenelle said softly as she joined them. She leaned against Saetan. "Yes, there is."

Alarmed by how pale she looked, Saetan held her against him, stroking her hair as he probed gently. Nothing physically wrong except the fatigue brought on by overwork and the emotional stress of tallying the kindred deaths. "Witch-child?"

Jaenelle shuddered. "I never wanted this. But it's the only way to help them."

"What's the only way, witch-child?" Saetan crooned.

Trembling, she stepped away from him. The haunted look in her eyes would stay with him forever.

"I'm going to make the Offering to the Darkness and set up my court."

CHAPTER SIXTEEN

1 / Kaeleer

Banard sat in the private showroom at the back of his shop, sipping tea while he waited for the Lady.

He was a gifted craftsman, an artist who worked with precious metals, precious and semiprecious stones, and the Blood Jewels. A Blood male who wore no Jewel himself, he handled them with a delicacy and respect that made him a favorite with the Jeweled Blood in Amdarh. He always said, "I handle a Jewel as if I were handling someone's heart," and he meant it.

Among his clients were the Queen of Amdarh and her Consort, Prince Mephis SaDiablo, Prince Lucivar Yaslana, the High Lord and, his favorite, Lady Jaenelle Angelline.

Which was why he was sitting here long after the shops had closed for the day. As he'd told his wife, when the Lady asked for a favor, why, that was almost like serving her, wasn't it?

He nearly spilled his tea when he looked up from his musings and saw the shadowy figure standing in the doorway of the private showroom. His shop had strong guard spells and protection spells—gifts from his darker-Jeweled clients. No one should have been able to get this far without triggering the alarms.

"My apologies, Banard," said the feminine, midnight voice. "I didn't mean to startle you."

"Not at all, Lady," Banard lied as he increased the illumination of the candle-lights around the velvet-covered display table. "My mind was wandering." He turned to smile at her, but when he saw what she held in her hands, he broke out in a cold sweat.

"There's something I'd like you to make for me, if you can," Jaenelle said, stepping into the small room.

Banard gulped. She had changed since he'd last seen her a few months ago. It was more than the Widow's weeds she was wearing. It was as if the fire that had always burned within her was now closer to the surface, illuminating and shadowing. He could feel the dark power swirling around her—brutal strength offset by a worrisome fragility.

"This is what I'd like you to make," Jaenelle said.

A piece of paper appeared on the display table.

Banard studied the sketch for several minutes, wondering what he could say, wondering how to refuse gracefully, wondering why she, of all people, would have the thing she held in her hands.

As if understanding his silence and reluctance, Jaenelle caressed the spiraled horn. "His name was Kaetien," she said softly. "He was the Warlord Prince of the unicorns. He was butchered a few days ago, along with hundreds of his people, when humans came in to claim Sceval as their territory." Tears filled her eyes. "I've known him since I was a little girl. He was the first friend I made in Kaeleer, and one of the best. He gifted me with his horn. For remembrance. As a reminder."

Banard studied the sketch again. "If I may make one or two suggestions, Lady?"

"That's why I came to you," Jaenelle said with a trembling smile.

Using a thin, charcoal pencil, Banard altered the sketch. At the end of an hour of fine-tuning, they were both satisfied.

Alone again, Banard made another cup of tea and sat for a while, studying the sketch and staring at the horn he couldn't yet bring himself to touch.

What she wanted made would be a fitting tribute for a beloved friend. And it would be an appropriate tool for such a Queen.

2 / Kaeleer

Saetan paced the length of the sitting room Draca had reserved for them at the Keep. Reserved? Confined them to was closer to the truth.

Lucivar abandoned his chair and stretched his back and shoulders. "Why is it that your pacing isn't supposed to annoy me, but when I start pacing I get chucked into the garden?" he asked dryly.

"Because I'm older and I outrank you," Saetan snarled. He pivoted and paced to the other side of the room.

From sunset to sunrise. That's how long it took to make the Offering to the Darkness. It didn't matter if a person came away from the Offering wearing a White Jewel or a Black, that's how long it took. From sunset to sunrise.

Jaenelle had been gone three full days.

He had remained calm when the first dawn had passed into late morning because he could still remember how shaky he'd felt after making the Offering, how he'd remained in the altar room of the Sanctuary for hours while he adjusted to the feel of the Black Jewels.

But when the sun began to set again, he'd gone to the Dark Altar in the Keep to find out what had happened to her. Draca had forbidden him entrance, sharply reminding him of the consequences of interrupting an Offering. So he'd returned to the sitting room to wait.

When midnight came and went, he'd tried to reach the Dark Altar again and had found all the corridors blocked by a shield even the Black couldn't penetrate. Desperate, he'd sent an urgent message to Cassandra, hoping she would be able to break through Draca's resistance. But Cassandra hadn't responded, and he'd cursed this evidence of her further withdrawal.

She was tired. He understood that. He came from a long-lived race and had already gone several lifetimes beyond the norm. Cassandra had lived hundreds, had watched the people she'd come from decline, fade, and finally be absorbed into younger, emerging races. When she had ruled, she had been respected, revered.

But Jaenelle was loved.

So Cassandra hadn't responded. Tersa had.

"Something's wrong," Saetan snarled as he passed the couch and low table Tersa hunched over while she arranged puzzle pieces into shapes that had meaning only for her. "It doesn't take this long."

Tersa poked a puzzle piece into place and pushed her tangled black hair away from her face. "It takes as long as it takes."

"An Offering is made between sunset and sunrise."

Tersa tilted her head, considering. "That was true for the Prince of the Darkness. But for the Queen?" She shrugged.

Cold whispered up Saetan's spine. What would Jaenelle be like when she was the Queen of the Darkness?

He crouched opposite Tersa, the table between them. She paid no more attention to him than she did to Lucivar's silent approach.

"Tersa," Saetan said quietly, trying to catch her attention. "Do you know something, see something?"

Tersa's eyes glazed. "A voice in the Darkness. A howling, full of joy and pain, rage and celebration. The time is coming when the debts will be paid." Her eyes cleared. "Leash your fear, High Lord," she said with some asperity. "It will do her more harm now than anything else. Leash it, or lose her."

Saetan's hand closed over her wrist. "I'm not afraid *of* her, I'm afraid *for* her."

Tersa shook her head. "She will be too tired to sense the difference. She will only sense the fear. Choose, High Lord, and live with what you choose." She looked at the closed door. "She is coming."

Saetan tried to rise too quickly and winced. He'd overworked his bad leg again. Tugging down the sleeves of his tunic jacket and smoothing back his hair, he wished, futilely, that he'd bathed and changed into fresh clothes. He also wished, futilely, that his heart would stop pounding so hard.

Then the door opened and Jaenelle stood on the threshold.

In the seconds before rational thought fled, his mind registered her hesitation, her uncertainty. It also registered the amount of jewelry she was wearing.

Lorn had gifted her with thirteen uncut Black Jewels. An uncut Jewel was large enough to be made into a pendant and a ring, as well as providing smaller chips that could be used for a variety of purposes. If he was estimating correctly, she'd taken the equivalent of six of those thirteen Jewels in with her when she made the Offering. Six Black Jewels that, somehow, had been transformed into more than Black.

Into Ebony.

No wonder it had taken her so long to make the descent to her full strength. He couldn't begin to estimate the power at her disposal now. Since the day he'd met her, he'd known it would come to this. She was traveling roads now the rest of them couldn't even imagine.

What would it do to her?

His choice.

The thought shocked him with its clarity. It freed him to act.

Stepping forward, he offered his right hand.

Wild-shy, Jaenelle slipped into the room, hesitated a moment, then placed her hand in his.

He pulled her into arms, burying his face against her neck. "I've been worried sick about you," he growled softly.

Jaenelle stroked his back. "Why?" She sounded genuinely puzzled. "You've made the Offering. You know—"

"It doesn't usually take three days!"

"Three days!" She jerked back, stumbling into Lucivar, who had come up behind her. "Three *days*?"

"Do we have to observe Protocol from now on?" Lucivar asked.

"Don't be daft," Jaenelle snapped.

Grinning, Lucivar immediately wrapped his left arm around her, pinning her arms to her sides and holding her tight against his chest. "In that case, I propose dunking her in the nearest fountain."

"You can't do that!" Jaenelle sputtered, squirming.

"Why not?" Lucivar sounded mildly curious.

The reason she gave was inventive but anatomically impossible.

Since laughing wouldn't be diplomatic, even if it was prompted by the relief that wearing Ebony Jewels hadn't changed her, Saetan clenched his teeth and stayed silent.

Tersa, however, finally stirred herself and joined them. Shaking her head, she gave Jaenelle a poke in the shoulder. "There's no use wailing about it. You've taken up the responsibilities of a Queen now, and part of your duties is taking care of the males who belong to you."

"Fine," Jaenelle snarled. "When do I get to pound him?"

Tersa tsked. "They're males. They're allowed to fuss and pet." Then she smiled and patted Jaenelle's cheek. "Warlord Princes especially need physical contact with their Queen."

"Oh," Jaenelle said sourly. "Well, that's just fine then."

Tersa stretched out on the couch.

"All right, grumpy little cat, you have a choice," Lucivar said.

"Not one of your choices," Jaenelle groaned, sagging against him.

"Does either of those choices include food and sleep?" Saetan asked.

"And a bath?" Jaenelle added, wrinkling her nose.

"One does," Lucivar said, releasing her.

"Then I don't want to know what the other one is." Jaenelle rubbed her back. "Your belt buckle bites."

"So do you."

Saetan rubbed his temples. "Enough, children."

Amazingly, they both stopped. Gold and sapphire eyes studied him for a moment before they left the room, arms about each other's waists.

"You did well, Saetan," Tersa said quietly.

Picking up a blanket draped over a chair, Saetan tucked it around Tersa and smoothed back her hair. "I had help," he replied, then laughed softly when she batted at his hand. "Males are allowed to fuss and pet, remember?"

"I'm not a Queen."

Saetan watched her until she fell asleep. "No, but you are a very gifted, very extraordinary Lady."

3 / Kaeleer

Telling himself he wasn't nervous, despite the pounding heart and sweaty palms, Saetan entered the large stone chamber that Draca had indicated was the place where the invited guests were to wait until they were summoned to the Dark Throne. Except for the blackwood pillars that contained the candle-lights and a few long tables against the walls that held assorted beverages, the room was bare of furniture.

Which was just as well since threading their way through seating designed for humans would have made the kindred more tense than they already were, and some species—like the small dragons from the Fyreborn Islands—needed a generous amount of space. Saetan noticed, with growing uneasiness, that *all* the kindred, not just the ones who had had little or no contact with people, weren't mingling with the human Blood, even though most of the humans present were friends—or had been before the slaughters. That they were in this closed, confined space at all said a great deal for their devotion to Jaenelle.

That was one worry. Ebon Rih was the Keep's Territory in Kaeleer— Jaenelle's Territory now. Ruling Ebon Rih wouldn't help the kindred or keep the human invaders out of their Territories. Traditionally, the Queen of Ebon Askavi had considerable influence in all the Realms, but would that influence and the innate caution within the Blood not to antagonize a mature dark power be enough? Would any of the fools in Kaeleer's Dark Council even recognize who they were challenging?

Another worry was who was going to make up Jaenelle's court. He'd always assumed that the coven and Jaenelle's male friends would form the First Circle. It wasn't unprecedented for Queens to serve in a stronger

Queen's court since District Queens served Province Queens who, in their turn, served the Territory Queen. That was the web of power that kept a Territory united.

But Queens who ruled a Territory didn't serve in other courts. They were the final law of their land and yielded to no one.

In the past week, while Jaenelle rested after making the Offering, her coven, Queens all, had also made the Offering. And every one of them had been chosen as the new Queen of their respective Territories, the former Queens stepping aside and accepting positions in the newly formed courts.

The boys, too, had come to power. Chaosti was now the Warlord Prince of Dea al Mon and Gabrielle's Consort. Khardeen, Morghann's Consort, was the ruling Warlord of Maghre, his home village. After accepting Kalush's Consort ring, Aaron had become the Warlord Prince of Tajrana, the capital of Nharkhava. Sceron and Elan were the Warlord Princes of Centauran and Tigrelan, serving in the First Circles of Astar's and Grezande's courts. Jonah now served as First Escort for his sister, Zylona, and Morton served as First Escort for his cousin Karla.

As feminine voices drifted down the corridor behind him, Saetan headed for the table where Lucivar, Aaron, Khary, and Chaosti were gathered. Geoffrey and Andulvar nodded in greeting but didn't break away from their conversation with Mephis and Prothvar. Sceron, Elan, Morton, and Jonah were talking to a diminutive Warlord Prince Saetan hadn't seen before. Little Katrine's First Escort or Consort?

"The tailor did an excellent job," Saetan told Lucivar, accepting the glass of warmed yarbarah.

"Uh-huh." The reply sounded sour, but after a moment Lucivar shook his head and laughed. He put his hand over his heart. "I represent a challenge worthy of good Lord Aldric who, as he happily informed me while he was sticking pins everywhere, had never designed formal attire that had to accommodate wings."

"Well, now that he has your measurements—" Saetan began.

"Oh, no." Lucivar shook his head, wearing an expression Saetan recognized all too well from his own dealings with good Lord Aldric. " 'Each fabric has a character of its own, Prince Yaslana,' " Lucivar said, mimicking the tailor's mournful voice. " 'We must learn how each one will flow around these marvelous additions to your physique.' "

Khary, Aaron, and Chaosti coughed in unison.

"Maybe he just wants to stroke your wings," Karla said as she joined them. She slid her hand over Saetan's shoulder and leaned against his back, her sharp chin digging into his other shoulder. "They *are* impressive. Is it true that the length of your"—her ice-blue eyes flicked to Lucivar's groin—"is in direct proportion to your wings?"

Lucivar made a very crude sexual gesture.

"Touchy, isn't he? But not touchable? Ah, well. Kiss kiss."

"Stuff yourself, Karla," Lucivar said, baring his teeth in a smile.

Karla laughed. "It's so good to be back among the surly. A few days ago I said 'kiss kiss' and everyone tried to." She shuddered dramatically, then ruffled Saetan's hair, cheerfully ignoring the accompanying snarl. "You know what, Uncle Saetan?"

"What?" Saetan replied warily, sipping his yarbarah.

Karla's wicked smile bloomed. "Since you're the Warlord Prince of Dhemlan and rule that Territory, and I'm the Queen of Glacia and rule *that* Territory, now whenever Dhemlan has to deal with Glacia, you get to deal with me."

Saetan choked.

"Appalling thought, isn't it, that you're going to have to deal with all the things you taught me."

"Mother Night," Saetan gasped as Karla plucked the glass out of his hand and thumped his back.

"What'd you do to Uncle Saetan?" Morghann asked, accepting a glass of wine from Khary.

"Just reminded him that we're now the Queens he has to deal with."

"How unfair, Karla," Kalush said, joining them. "You should have eased into it instead of springing it on him."

"How?" Karla frowned. "Besides, he knew it already. Didn't you?"

Saetan retrieved his glass and drained it to avoid answering. After all the hours he, Geoffrey, Andulvar, and Mephis had spent chewing over the implications of having this particular group of Queens coming into power at this time, none of them had thought of the obvious—that he was going to have to deal with them as Territory Queens.

A gong sounded throughout the Keep. Once. Twice. Thrice. Then, after a pause, a fourth time.

Four times for the four sides of a Blood triangle, the fourth side being what was held within the other three. Like the three males—Steward, Master of the Guard, and Consort—who formed a strong, intimate triangle around a Queen.

At the back of the room, huge double doors opened outward, revealing a dark emptiness.

Paying no attention to the hesitant stirring around him, Saetan set his glass aside, smoothed his hair, and straightened his new clothes. Since Protocol dictated that processions went from light Jewels to dark, first all the males and then the females, he would be at the end of the male line.

So he didn't realize no one had moved and that everyone was looking at him until Lucivar poked him.

"Protocol dictates—" he began.

"Screw Protocol," Karla replied succinctly. "*You* go first."

When everyone nodded agreement, he slowly walked toward the double doors. Lucivar and Andulvar fell into step on either side of him. Mephis, Geoffrey, and Prothvar followed them.

"What's in there?" Lucivar asked quietly.

"I don't know," Saetan replied. "I've never been in this part of the Keep before." He glanced back at Geoffrey, who shook his head.

They reached the doors and stopped. The lights from the room behind them revealed the first handful of wide, descending steps.

We'll all break our necks trying to go down without lights.

The thought was barely completed when little sparkles embedded in the dark stone began to glow, growing brighter and brighter.

Like swirls of stars, Saetan thought, his breath catching. Like the poem Geoffrey quoted to him years ago, about the great dragons who had created the Blood. *They spiral down into ebony, catching the stars with their tails.*

Ebony had once been the poetic term for the Darkness.

Saetan froze, his foot suspended over the first step.

Was it still?

"Something wrong?" Lucivar whispered.

Saetan shook his head and slowly descended, grateful for the solid Eyrien strength on either side of him.

When he reached the bottom step, a second set of double doors swung inward. The midnight-black chamber slowly lightened, the dark giving way to the dawn. The light gradually spread from their end of the chamber to the other. But he noticed, as he moved forward, that it didn't illuminate the ceiling. At thrice his height, the light gave way to twilight, which, in its turn, yielded once again to the dark.

The back wall began to lighten from either side. Filling the wall, as high as the light reached, was a highly detailed bas-relief. A dreamscape, a nightscape, shapes rising up from and dissolving into others. Kindred shapes. Human shapes. Blending. Entwined. Fierce and beautiful. Ugly and gentle.

The light finally reached the center of the back wall and the Dark Throne. Three wide steps ran around the dais on three sides. On the dais itself was a simple blackwood chair with a high, carved back. Its simplicity said that the power that ruled here had no need for ornamentation or ostentation—especially when it was protected on the right-hand side by a huge dragon head coming out of the stone.

"Mother Night," Andulvar said in a hushed voice. "She created a sculpture of Lorn's head."

"Hell's fire," Lucivar whispered. "Where'd she find so many uncut Jewels to make the scales?"

Trembling, Saetan shook his head, unable to speak. Maybe Andulvar couldn't see the darkness beyond the lit bas-relief from where he stood, a darkness that suggested another large chamber beyond this one. Maybe he couldn't see the iridescent fire in the dragon's scales. Maybe he'd forgotten the sound of that ancient, powerful voice. Maybe . . .

Eyelids slowly opened. Midnight eyes pinned them where they stood.

Geoffrey clutched Saetan's arm, his fingers digging in hard enough to hurt. "Mother Night, Saetan," Geoffrey said, his breathing ragged. "The Keep is his lair. He's been here all the time."

He hadn't expected Lorn to be so big. If the body was in proportion to the head . . .

Dragon scales. The Jewels were dragon scales somehow transformed into hard, translucent stones. Had there been dragons who matched the specific colors of the Jewels or had they all been that iridescent silver-gold, changing color to match the strength of the recipient?

Saetan gingerly touched the Black Jewel around his neck. His Birthright Red and the Black had been uncut Jewels. Were there two missing scales somewhere along the great body that must lie in the next chamber that would have matched his uncut Jewels?

Then he finally understood why there had been a hint of maleness in the uncut Jewels Jaenelle had been gifted with.

Lorn. The great Prince of the Dragons. The Guardian of the Keep.

Needing to get his mind focused on something other than the power that ancient body must contain, Saetan turned to Geoffrey. "His Queen. What was the name of his Queen?"

"Draca," said a sibilant voice behind them.

They turned and stared at the Keep's Seneschal.

Her lips curled in a tiny smile. "Her name wass Draca."

Looking into her eyes, Saetan wondered what subtle spell had been lifted that allowed him to see what he should have guessed long before. Her age, her strength, the uneasiness so many felt in her presence. Which made him think of something else. "Does Jaenelle know?"

Draca made a sound that might have been a laugh. "Sshe hass alwayss known, High Lord."

Saetan grimaced, then gave in as gracefully as he could. Even if he'd thought to ask, he doubted he'd have gotten an answer. Jaenelle was very good at keeping her own counsel.

"Are they relatives of yours?" Lucivar asked, indicating the Fyreborn dragons who were staring at Lorn.

"You are all relativess," Draca replied, looking pointedly at Lucivar's Ebon-gray Jewel. "We created the Blood. All the Blood. Therefore, you are all dragonss under the sskin."

Saetan glanced at the kindred who were edging closer. "You, of course, would know." He saw amusement in Draca's eyes.

"It iss not I who ssayss sso, High Lord. *Jaenelle* ssayss sso." Draca looked past them to the Dark Throne.

As one, they turned.

Dressed in that cobwebby black gown and wearing Ebony Jewels, Jaenelle sat serenely in the blackwood chair. Her long golden hair was brushed away from the face that finally revealed its unique beauty.

"The time has come for me to take up my duties as the Queen of Ebon Askavi," Jaenelle said. Her voice wasn't loud, but it carried throughout the chamber. "The time has come for me to choose my court."

A breathless tension filled the chamber.

Saetan concentrated on breathing slowly, steadily. For days he'd been telling himself that court service was for the young and vigorous, that he'd never intended to serve formally, that the unspoken service he performed was enough, that he had experienced serving in the Dark Court at Ebon Askavi when he'd been Cassandra's Consort.

Except he hadn't, because, in a way he couldn't put into words, it hadn't really been the Dark Court. Not like this one.

And he suddenly understood why Cassandra had withdrawn from them.

This was the court he had waited to serve in. *This* was the court he'd always craved. He wanted to serve the daughter of his soul, who had finally come into her dark, glorious power.

Witch. The living myth. Dreams made flesh.

This had been *his* dream.

And Lucivar's, he realized, seeing the fire in his son's eyes. Yes, Lucivar would have craved a Queen who could meet his strength.

Jaenelle's voice pulled him back. "Prince Chaosti, will you serve in the First Circle?"

Gracefully, Chaosti knelt on one knee, a fisted hand over his heart. "I will serve."

Saetan frowned. How was Chaosti going to serve in Jaenelle's First Circle when he'd already accepted service in Gabrielle's First Circle?

"Prince Kaelas, will you serve in the First Circle?"

I will serve.

He became more and more puzzled as Jaenelle called out name after name. Mephis, Prothvar, Aaron, Khardeen, Sceron, Jonah, Morton, Elan. Ladvarian, Mistral, Smoke, Sundancer.

And then he, Andulvar, and Lucivar were the only males left standing, and everything in him waited for her next words.

"Lady Karla, will you serve in the First Circle?"

"I will serve."

Shock ripped through Saetan, quickly followed by pain so intense he didn't think it would be possible to survive it. She hadn't forgiven him. At least, not enough.

"Lady Moonshadow, will you serve in the First Circle?"

I will serve.

He swallowed hard. He couldn't react, *wouldn't* let the others see the hurt. But if she was going to allow Mephis and Prothvar to serve, why not Andulvar? Why not Lucivar, who already served her?

He barely heard the other names being called out. Gabrielle,

Morghann, Kalush, Grezande, Sabrina, Zylona, Katrine, Astar, Ash. On and on until all the witches had accepted a place in the court.

Draca and Geoffrey couldn't formally serve because they served the Keep itself. If there was comfort knowing that, it was a bitter brew.

He could feel Lucivar trembling beside him.

After a moment's silence, Jaenelle rose and walked down the three steps. Her eyes narrowed as she looked at him. He felt her exasperation as she lightly brushed against the first of his inner barriers.

She pushed up her left sleeve and made a small cut in her wrist.

Blood welled and ran.

"Prince Lucivar Yaslana, will you serve as First Escort and Warlord Prince of Ebon Rih?"

Lucivar stared at her for a heartbeat or two, then slowly approached her. "I will serve." He sank to his knees, held her left hand with his right, and placed his mouth over the wound.

Absolute surrender. Lifetime surrender. By accepting her blood, Lucivar surrendered every aspect of his being for all time. She would rule him, body and soul, mind and Jewels.

It wasn't long—it was a lifetime—before Lucivar lifted his mouth, rose, and stepped to one side, looking dazed.

Not surprising, Saetan thought. From where he stood, he could smell the heat, the strength that flowed in her veins.

"Prince Andulvar Yaslana, will you serve as Master of the Guard?"

"I will serve," Andulvar said, approaching her and sinking to his knees to accept the lifeblood.

When Andulvar stepped aside, Jaenelle looked at Saetan. "Prince Saetan Daemon SaDiablo, will you serve as Steward of the Dark Court?"

Saetan approached slowly, searching her eyes for some clue that would tell him which answer she truly wanted. Since he couldn't ask the question aloud, he reached hesitantly for her mind. *Are you sure?*

Of course I'm sure, she replied tartly. *There are times, Saetan, when you're an idiot. The only reason I waited was so that the three of you would know what you were getting into before you agreed.*

In that case . . . He sank to his knees. "I will serve."

Just before his mouth closed over the wound, just before his tongue had the first taste of her blood at its mature strength, Jaenelle added, *Besides, who else is going to be willing to referee squabbles?*

Giving her a sharp look, he took the blood. Night sky, deep earth, the song of the tides, the nurturing darkness of a woman's body. And fire. He tasted all of it, savored it as it washed through him, burned through him, branded him as hers.

He lifted his mouth and brushed a finger over the wound, using healing Craft to seal it and stop the flow of blood. *It needs to be healed properly.*

Soon. She withdrew her hand and returned to the Dark Throne.

No, he decided as he got to his feet and heard everyone else rising, this wasn't a good time for a display of male stubbornness. Besides, the ceremony would be over shortly.

Notice anything odd about this court? Lucivar asked him as tension filled the chamber again.

Surprised by the question, Saetan looked at all the solemn, determined faces. *Odd? No. They're the same . . .*

It finally struck him. He'd thought of it, discussed it, and then had been so hurt when Jaenelle passed over him that he had failed to see it. The coven had joined the First Circle, and they shouldn't have because they were Territory Queens . . .

Karla stepped forward. "My Queen. May I speak?"

"You may speak, my Sister," Jaenelle replied solemnly.

. . . and Territory Queens served no one.

Contained fire lit Karla's ice-blue eyes as she said triumphantly, "Glacia yields to Ebon Askavi!"

Saetan choked on his heart. Mother Night! Karla was making Jaenelle the ruling power of the Territory *she* was supposed to rule.

Gabrielle stepped forward. "Dea al Mon yields to Ebon Askavi!"

"Scelt yields to Ebon Askavi!" Morghann shouted.

"Nharkhava!" "Dharo!" "Tigrelan!" "Centauran!"

Sceval! *Arceria!* *The Fyreborn Islands!*

Someone nudged his back, breaking his stunned silence. "Dhemlan yields to Ebon Askavi!"

He jumped when Andulvar roared, "Askavi yields to Ebon Askavi!"

The shouted names of the Territories that now stood in the shadow of Ebon Askavi finally stopped echoing through the chamber. Then a small voice drifted into their minds.

Arachna yields to the Lady of the Black Mountain.

"Mother Night," Saetan whispered, and wondered if the Weavers of Dreams were spinning their tangled webs across the chamber's ceiling.

"I accept," Jaenelle said quietly.

Lucivar briefly squeezed Saetan's shoulder in amused sympathy. "Should I wish the Steward of this court my congratulations or condolences?" he said quietly.

"Mother Night." Saetan staggered back a step. Hands grabbed his arms, keeping him upright.

Lucivar laughed softly as he slipped around Saetan. He climbed the steps to the Throne and extended his right hand. Jaenelle rose and placed her left hand over his right. A wide aisle opened up as the new court stepped aside to allow the First Escort to lead his Queen from the chamber.

Starting to follow, Saetan felt something hold him back. Waving Andulvar and the others on, he felt his throat tighten as the kindred shyly blended in with the humans, once more offering their trust.

The chamber emptied, Draca and Geoffrey being the last to leave.

No longer having an excuse, Saetan turned toward Lorn. As they stared at one another, he felt gentle sadness pressing down on him, a sadness all the more terrible because it was cloaked in understanding. He knew then why Lorn had remained apart. He had experienced that kind of sadness, too, when petitioners had stood before him, terrified of the Prince of the Darkness, the High Lord of Hell. He knew how it felt to crave affection and companionship and have it denied because of what he was.

Fingering his Black Jewel, he said, "Thank you."

★You have made good usse of my gift. You have sserved well.★

Saetan thought of all he'd done in his life. All the mistakes, the regrets. All the blood spilled. "Have I?" he asked quietly, more to himself than Lorn.

★You have honored the Darknesss. You have resspected the wayss of the Blood. You have alwayss undersstood what the Blood were meant to be—caretakerss and guardianss. You have ussed teeth and clawss when teeth and clawss were needed. You have protected your young. The Darknesss hass ssung to you, and you have followed roadss few but the Dragonss have walked. You have undersstood the Blood'ss heart, the Blood'ss ssoul. You have sserved well.★

Saetan took a deep breath. His throat felt too tight to make an answer. "Thank you," he said hoarsely.

There was a long pause. *Ass sshe iss the daughter of your ssoul, you are the sson of mine.*

Saetan clutched the Jewel around his neck. Did Lorn have any idea what those words meant to him?

It didn't matter. What mattered was it formed a bond between them, a bridge he could cross. He would finally be able to talk to the keeper of all the Blood's Craft knowledge. Maybe he'd even find out how Jae—

"If I'm the daughter of Saetan's soul and he's the son of yours, does that make you my grandfather?" Jaenelle asked, joining them.

No, Lorn replied promptly.

"Why not?"

Hot, dusty-dry air hit them with enough force to push them back a couple of steps.

"I suppose that's an answer," Jaenelle grumped. She shook her arms to untangle all the cobwebby strands. "Although I don't see why you're getting all snorty about one little granddaughter."

"And the wide assortment of grandnieces and nephews that come with her," Saetan muttered under his breath.

Jaenelle gave him a sharp look and her wrists a last shake. "Well, at least you've finally met. You should've invited him sooner," she added, giving Lorn an I-told-you-so look.

He wass not ready. He wass too young.

Saetan would have protested but Jaenelle beat him to it.

"I was much younger when you invited me," Jaenelle said.

Saetan pressed an arm against his stomach and tried very hard to keep his expression neutral. But the emotional flavor of baffled male he was picking up from Lorn was making it very difficult.

I did not invite you, Jaenelle, Lorn said slowly.

"Yes, you did. Sort of. Well, not as blatantly as Saetan did—"

Saetan clamped his teeth together and made a funny, fizzy noise.

"—but I heard you, so I answered." She smiled at both of them.

Being smiled at like that was a good reason for a man to panic.

Before he had time to, Jaenelle rapidly headed for the stairs, muttering something about having to be there for the toast, and Lucivar had a very strong hand clamped on his shoulder.

"If great-grandpapa is finished with you," Lucivar said with a feral smile, "I'd like you to come upstairs and lean hard on Karla because,

Queen of Glacia or not, if she makes one more of those smart-ass remarks about wingspans, I'm going to drop her into a deep mountain lake."

"Lucivar, this is a dignified occasion," Saetan said at the same time Lorn said, ★I am not your great-grandpapa.★

"No, you're not," Lucivar agreed. "But since no one was quite sure how many generations separate them from you—and it's different for each race or species—it was decided to condense all the generations into one 'great.' As for this being a dignified occasion, it was. As for the party that's waiting for Saetan to make the opening toast, I suspect it's going to be a lot of things and none of them are going to be remotely close to dignified." Lucivar looked at them and let out a pitying sigh. "You're both old enough to know better. And you've both known Jaenelle long enough to know better."

Saetan found himself being steered toward the doors at the other end of the chamber.

"Come on, be a good papa and let great-grandpapa dragon get some rest before all the little dragons pile on top of him."

Reaching the stairs, Saetan thought that the inner doors to the chamber closed just a little too quickly.

★We will talk,★ Lorn said softly. ★There iss much to talk about.★

Yes, there was, Saetan thought as he entered the upper chamber, accepted a glass of yarbarah, and looked at the animated, laughing faces that now ruled Kaeleer.

He wondered what Lorn thought about the many-strand web Jaenelle had woven over Kaeleer, the web that had called so many races out of the mist they'd hidden in for thousands of years.

And he wondered what the Dark Council was going to think.

4 / Kaeleer

Lord Magstrom rubbed his forehead and wished, violently, that this session of the Dark Council would end soon. Lord Jorval, the First Tribune, had been making soothing noises and deftly evading making firm promises since the first petitioner had stepped into the circle. They all wanted the same thing: assurance that the males sent into the kindred lands that had been granted as human territories wouldn't be slaughtered by these "Hell-spawned animals."

The Council couldn't give such assurances.

The stories told by the few survivors who returned from those first attempts to secure the land had roused a great anger in the people of Little Terreille and demands for retaliation. The piles of mutilated corpses—some partially eaten—that clogged the main street of Goth a few days later when all the males who had gone into kindred lands were mysteriously returned had chilled that anger into furious impotence.

Everyone wanted something done to make these unclaimed lands safe for human occupation. No one wanted to face what was already living in those "unclaimed" lands.

"I assure you, Lady," Lord Jorval said to the strident petitioner, "we're doing everything possible to rectify the situation."

"When I came here, I was promised land to rule and males who knew how to serve properly," the Terreillean Queen replied angrily.

Lord Magstrom wondered if anyone else had noticed that the majority of Kaeleer-born males, even with the enticement of serving in the First or Second Circle of a Terreillean Queen's court, resigned with bitter animosity after a few weeks of service. Terreillean males pleaded to serve Kaeleer-born Queens, willing to serve in the Thirteenth Circle as a menial servant if that's all that was available. Over the past three years, he'd had a few tearfully beg him to approach minor Queens outside of Little Terreille and see if there was any way they could serve in a Territory like Dharo or Nharkhava. They would do anything, they'd told him. Anything.

For some of the younger ones he thought might be acceptable to those Territory Queens, he'd written respectful letters pointing out the men's skills and their pledged willingness to adapt to the ways of the Shadow Realm. Some had been accepted into service. At each turn of the season, he received brief letters from each of those young men, and all of them expressed their relief and delight in their new life.

But the pleas were getting more desperate as more and more Terreilleans flooded into Little Terreille. And with every plea, with every story he heard about Terreille, he worried more and more about his youngest granddaughter. Even in his small village incidents had already occurred, and it was no longer wise for a woman to travel after dusk without a strong escort. Was that how it had begun in Terreille, with fear and distrust spiraling deeper and deeper until there was no way to stop it?

"Your request has been noted," Lord Jorval said, making a gesture that indicated dismissal. "Will the next—"

The doors at the end of the chamber blew open with a force that sent them crashing into the walls.

Jaenelle Angelline glided into the Council chamber, once again standing outside the petitioner's circle, once again flanked by the High Lord and Prince Lucivar Yaslana. Along the edges of her black, cobwebby gown's low neckline were dozens of Black Jewel chips glittering with dark fire. Around her neck was a Black—Black?—Jewel set in a necklace that looked like a spider's web made of delicate gold and silver strands. In her hands . . .

Lord Magstrom's hands shook.

She held a scepter. The lower half was made of gold and silver and had two Black-looking Jewels inset above the hand-hold. The upper half of the scepter was a spiraled horn.

Fingers pointed at the horn. Murmurs filled the chamber.

"Lady Angelline, I must protest your interrupting—" Jorval began.

"I have something to say to this Council," Jaenelle said coldly, her voice carrying over the others. "It will not take long."

The murmurs grew louder, more forceful.

"Why is *she* allowed to have a unicorn's horn?" the dismissed Terreillean Queen shouted. "*I* wasn't allowed to have one as compensation for my men being killed."

There was no expression on the High Lord's face as he looked at the Terreillean Queen. Lucivar, however, didn't try to hide his loathing.

"*Silence.*" Jaenelle didn't raise her voice, but the undisguised malevolence in it hushed everyone. She looked at the Terreillean Queen and spoke five words.

Lord Magstrom knew enough of the Old Tongue to recognize the language but not enough to understand. Something about remembering?

Jaenelle caressed the horn, stroking it from base to tip and back down. "His name was Kaetien," she said in her midnight voice. "This horn was a gift, freely given."

"Lady Angelline," Jorval said, pounding on the Tribunal's bench as he tried to regain order.

From the seats closest to the Tribunal's bench, Lord Magstrom heard harsh voices talking about *some* people who thought they could ignore the authority of the *Council*.

Jaenelle swung the scepter in an arc, holding it for a moment when the horn pointed at the floor before swinging it up until it pointed at the chamber ceiling.

A cold wind whipped through the chamber. Thunder shook the building. Lightning came down from the ceiling and entered the unicorn's horn.

Dark power filled the chamber. Unyielding, unforgiving power.

When the thunder finally stopped, when the wind finally died, the shaking members of the Dark Council climbed back into their seats.

Jaenelle Angelline stood calmly, quietly, the scepter once again held in both hands. The unicorn's horn was unmarked, but Magstrom could see the flashes of lightning now held within those Black-but-not-Black Jewels, could feel the power waiting to be unleashed.

"Hear me," Jaenelle said, "because I will say this only once. I have made the Offering to the Darkness. I am now the Queen of Ebon Askavi." She pointed the scepter at the Tribunal's bench.

Lord Magstrom shook. The horn was pointing straight at him. He held his breath, waiting for the strike. Instead, a rolled parchment tied with a blood-red ribbon appeared in front of him.

"That is a list of the Territories that yielded to Ebon Askavi. They now stand in the shadow of the Keep. They are mine. Anyone who tries to settle in my Territory without my consent will be dealt with. Anyone who harms any of my people will be executed. There will be no excuses and no exceptions. I will say it simply so that the members of this Council and the intruders who thought to take land they had no right to claim can never say they misunderstood." Jaenelle's lips curled into a snarl. "STAY OUT OF MY TERRITORY!"

The words rang through the chamber, echoing and reechoing.

Her sapphire eyes, eyes that didn't look quite human, held the Tribunal for a long moment. Then she turned and glided out of the Council chamber, followed by the High Lord and Prince Yaslana.

Magstrom's hands shook so hard it took him four tries to untie the blood-red ribbon. He unrolled the parchment, ignoring the fact that he should have given it to Jorval as First Tribune.

Name after name after name after name. Some he'd heard of as stories his grandmother used to tell him. Some he'd heard of as "unclaimed land." Some he'd never heard of at all.

Name after name after name.

At the bottom of the parchment, above Jaenelle's signature and black-wax seal, was a map of Kaeleer, the Territories that now stood in the shadow of the Keep shaded in.

Except for Little Terreille and the island that had been granted to the Dark Council centuries ago, the Shadow Realm now belonged to Jaenelle Angelline.

Magstrom looked at the graceful, calligraphic signature. She had stood before the Council twice as a maid, and twice they had ignored the warnings of what she would become. Now they had to deal with a Queen who would not tolerate mistakes.

He shuddered and looked at the seal. In the center was a mountain. Overlaying the mountain was a unicorn's horn. Around the edge of the seal were five words in the Old Tongue.

A small piece of folded paper suddenly appeared on top of the seal. Magstrom grabbed it at the same moment Jorval pulled the parchment out of his hands. While Jorval and the Second Tribune read the list to the rest of the Council, their voices quivering more and more as they realized what it meant, Magstrom unfolded the paper, keeping it hidden.

A masculine hand had written the same five words that were on the seal. Below them was the translation.

For remembrance. As a reminder.

Magstrom looked up.

The High Lord stood just outside the open chamber doors.

Magstrom nodded slightly and vanished the paper, relieved no one had noticed that Saetan had remained behind to give him that message.

He would take the warning to heart and send a message home tonight. His two older granddaughters had made happy marriages outside of Little Terreille. He'd tell Arnora, his youngest granddaughter, to go to one of her sisters' homes immediately. Once she was there, surely there would be some way of persuading the new Queen of Dharo or Nharkhava to permit her to stay.

Half-listening to the Council's indignant, frightened babbling, Magstrom felt a flicker of hope for Arnora's future. He didn't know the new Queens, but he knew someone who did.

After all the whispers, after all the stories, he thought it was fitting irony that the one person he could go to who would sympathize with his concerns and assist him was the High Lord of Hell.

5 / Kaeleer

"I never wanted to rule," Jaenelle said as she and Saetan strolled through the Keep's moonlit gardens. "I never wanted power over anyone's life but my own."

Saetan slipped an arm around her waist. "I know. That's why you're the perfect Queen to rule Kaeleer." When she looked puzzled, he laughed softly. "You're the one person who can weave all the separate strands into a unified web while still encouraging every strand to remain distinct. If you promise not to snarl at me, I'll tell you a secret."

"What? Okay, okay. I promise not to snarl."

"You've been ruling Kaeleer unofficially for years now, and you're probably the only person who hasn't realized it."

Jaenelle snarled, then muttered, "Sorry."

Saetan laughed. "Forgiven. But knowing that should be some comfort. I doubt there's going to be much difference between the official Dark Court and the unofficial one that was formed the first summer the coven and the boyos descended on the Hall and made it a second home."

Jaenelle brushed her hair away from her face. "Well, if that's true, then you *really* were an idiot not to have realized you would become the Steward since you've been the unofficial Steward for at least as long as I've been the unofficial Queen."

Since there was no good way to respond to that, he didn't.

"Saetan . . ." Jaenelle nibbled her lower lip. "You don't think they'll start acting differently now, do you? It's never made a difference before, but . . . the coven and the boyos aren't going to start acting subservient, are they?"

Saetan raised an eyebrow. "I'm surprised any of you know the word, let alone what it means." He hugged her. "I wouldn't worry about it. I think Lucivar's about as subservient as he's going to get."

Jaenelle leaned against him and groaned. Then she perked up a bit. "Well, that's one good thing about forming the court. At least I found something for him to do that'll keep him from being underfoot and badgering me all the time."

Saetan started to reply, then thought better of it. She was entitled to a few illusions—especially since they wouldn't last long.

Jaenelle yawned. "I'm going in. I'm telling the bedtime story tonight." She kissed his cheek. "Good night, Papa."

"Good night, witch-child." He waited until she'd gone inside before heading for the far end of the garden.

"The waif turned in early?" Andulvar asked, falling into step.

"She's doing the bedtime story and howl-along," Saetan replied.

"She'll be a good Queen, SaDiablo."

"The best we've ever had." They walked in silence for a couple of minutes. "The bitch has gone to ground again?"

Andulvar nodded. "Plenty of indications that she's got her hooks firmly into the Dark Council, but no sign of her. Hekatah was always good at staying out of the nastiness once she got it started. It still surprises me that she managed to get herself killed in the last war between the Realms." He rubbed the back of his neck and sighed. "It must be biting Hekatah's ass that the waif's got the kind of power over a Realm that she's always wanted."

"Yes, it must be. So stay sharp, all right?"

"We should warn all the boyos before they return to their own Territories so they know what to look for in case she tries to come in from another direction."

"Agreed. But if the Darkness is kind, we'll have some time for these youngsters to get some ground under their feet before we have to deal with another of Hekatah's schemes."

"If the Darkness is kind." Andulvar cleared his throat. "I know why you've wanted to wait, and I know who you've been waiting for, but, Saetan, Jaenelle's a grown woman and she's the Queen now. The triangle should be complete. She should have a Consort."

Saetan rested his arms on the top of the garden's stone wall. A soft, night wind sang through the pines beyond the garden. "She already has a Consort," he said quietly, firmly. "As First Escort, Lucivar can stand in for most of a Consort's duties and be the third side of the triangle until . . ." His voice faded.

"If ever, SaDiablo," Andulvar said with gentle roughness. "Until someone wears the Consort's ring, every ambitious buck in the Realm—and not a few of them being straight from Terreille—is going to be trying to slip into her bed for the power and prestige he'll gain by being her Consort. She needs a good man, Saetan, not a memory. She needs a strong, flesh-and-blood man who'll warm her bed at night because he cares about *her*."

Saetan stared at the land beyond the garden. "She has a Consort."

"Does she?" When Saetan didn't answer, Andulvar patted his shoulder and walked away.

Saetan stayed there a long time, listening to the night wind's song. "She has a Consort," he whispered. "Doesn't she?"

The night wind didn't answer.

6 / The Twisted Kingdom

He climbed.

The land wasn't as twisted here or as steep, but the mist-wisps that filled the hollows sometimes covered the trail, leaving him with the unsettling feeling that nothing existed below his knees.

As time passed, he realized the place felt familiar, that he had explored these roads before when he had been strong and whole. He had entered the borderland that separated sanity from the Twisted Kingdom.

The air held a dew-fresh softness. The light was gentle, like early morning. Somewhere nearby, birds chirped and twittered the day awake, and in the distance was the sound of heavy surf.

His crystal chalice was almost intact. During the long climb, the fragments had fit into place, one by one. There were a few slivers, a few memories missing. One in particular. He couldn't remember what he had done the night Jaenelle had been brought to Cassandra's Altar.

As he passed between two large stones that stood like sentinels, one on either side of the trail, the mist rose up around him.

Ahead of him were the water, the birds, the smell of rich earth, the warmth of the sun—and her promise that she would be waiting for him.

Ahead of him was sanity.

But there was also knowledge there, pain there. He could feel it.

Daemon.

A familiar voice, but not the one he longed to hear. He sorted through his memories until he could attach a name to the voice.

Manny. Talking to someone about toast and eggs.

Daemon.

He knew that voice, too. Surreal.

A part of him ached for ordinary conversation, for simple things like toast and eggs. A part of him was very afraid.

He took a step backward . . . and felt a door gently close behind him.

The stone sentinels had become a high, solid wall.

He leaned against it, trembling.

No way back.

Daemon.

Gathering up his shredded courage, he walked toward the voices, toward the promise.

Walked out of the Twisted Kingdom.

QUEEN
OF THE
DARKNESS

—◡—

BOOK III

PART 1

CHAPTER ONE

1 / Terreille

Dorothea SaDiablo, the High Priestess of the Territory called Hayll, slowly climbed the stairs to the large wooden platform. It was a bright morning in early autumn, and Draega, Hayll's capital, was far enough south that the days were still warm. The heavy black cloak that shrouded Dorothea's body made her sweat. Under the deep hood, her hair was damp and her neck itched. No matter. In a few minutes, she could shed the cloak.

When she reached the platform, she saw the lumpy canvas that stretched across the front, closest to the waiting crowd, and automatically began taking shallow breaths through her mouth. Foolish. She'd used every spell she knew to keep what was beneath that canvas a secret until the proper time. Forcing herself to breathe naturally, she walked across the platform, stopping a few feet behind the canvas.

Watching her, with wariness and resentment, were the Queens of all the Territories in the Realm of Terreille. She had demanded that each Territory Queen bring her two strongest Province Queens and any Warlord Princes who served her. She knew that many of the Queens, especially those from the far-western Territories, had come expecting a trap of some kind.

Well, the bitches were right. But if she presented the bait in the right way, they would throw themselves into the trap without a second thought.

Dorothea raised her arms. The crowd's rippling murmurs faded to silence. Using Craft to enhance her voice so that everyone would hear her, she began the next move in a deadly game of power.

"My Sisters and Brothers, I called you here to warn you about a terrible discovery I made recently, something that threatens every one of the Blood in the entire Realm of Terreille.

"In the past, I've done some unspeakably cruel things. I have been responsible for the destruction of Queens and some of the best males in the Realm. I have bred fear into the Blood in order to be the controlling power in Terreille. Me. A High Priestess who knows better than anyone that a Priestess can't be a substitute for a Queen, no matter how skilled or how strong she is in her Craft.

"I will shoulder the sorrow and burden of those acts for the rest of my life. But I tell you this now: I HAVE BEEN USED! A few weeks ago, while using my skills as a Black Widow to spin a tangled web of dreams and visions, I inadvertently ripped through a mental shroud that had surrounded me for all the centuries I've been the High Priestess of Hayll. I fought my way through that mental fogging and finally saw what my tangled webs had been trying to tell me for so very long.

"There is someone who wants to dominate Terreille. There is someone who wants to subjugate all the Blood in this Realm. But it isn't me. I've been the instrument of a monstrous, malevolent being who wants to crush us and consume us, who plays with us the same way a cat plays with a mouse before it strikes the killing blow. That monster has a name—a name that has been feared for thousands upon thousands of years, and with good reason. Our destroyer is the Prince of the Darkness, the High Lord of Hell."

Uneasy murmurs rose from the crowd.

"You doubt me?" Dorothea shouted. She tore off the cloak and tossed it aside. Her wispy, white hair, which had been thick and black a few weeks ago, fell around her shoulders. Her sagging, deeply lined face twisted, and tears filled her gold eyes as the murmurs changed to shocked exclamations. "Look what happened to me when I fought to free myself from his insidious spells. *Look at me.* This is the price I paid, so that you would be aware of the danger."

Dorothea pressed a hand against her chest, gasping for breath.

Her Steward stepped forward and gently grasped her arm to support her. "You must stop, Priestess. This is too much for you to endure."

"No," Dorothea gasped, still using Craft to enhance her voice. "I must tell them everything while I can. I may not have another chance. Once he realizes I know about him . . ."

The crowd grew silent.

Lowering her hand, Dorothea stood as straight as she could, ignoring the ache in her spine. "I was not the High Lord's only instrument. There are those among you who have had the misfortune to have had Daemon Sadi or Lucivar Yaslana serving in your courts. May the Darkness forgive me, I sent those monsters into fragile Territories, and because of them, Queens have died. Sometimes whole courts were torn apart. I, like Prythian, Askavi's High Priestess, thought we were sending them into service in other courts by our own choice, in the hope that they could be controlled. But we were manipulated into sending them to those Territories *because they are the High Lord's sons*! They are that bestial creature's seeds, and they have grown up to be his tools of destruction. The control Prythian and I thought we had over them was nothing but an illusion, a blind to conceal their true purpose.

"Both of them disappeared several years ago. Most of us hoped they had died. Not so. I've learned from some brave Brothers and Sisters who are now living in the Kaeleer Territory called Little Terreille that both Yaslana and Sadi are in the Shadow Realm, where the High Lord has been living under the guise of being the Warlord Prince of Dhemlan. The viper's children have returned to the nest.

"There's more. The High Lord has an unhealthy influence over most of the Territory Queens in Kaeleer, as well as absolute control over a young woman who is the strongest witch in all the Realms. With her strength behind him, he will overwhelm us—unless we strike first. We have no choice, my Brothers and Sisters. If we don't crush the High Lord and everyone in his service, the cruelty I have done as his instrument will seem like a child's game in comparison."

Dorothea paused for a moment. "Many of you have friends or loved ones who have fled to Kaeleer in order to escape the violence that has been strangling Terreille. Look at what has happened to many of those who have run straight into the High Lord's seductive embrace."

Using Craft, she whipped away the canvas covering the front of the platform. Then she clamped her hand over her mouth to keep from gagging as the flies rose from the mutilated corpses.

Screams filled the air. A piercing shriek of grief and rage rose above the other voices. Then another, and another, as the people nearest the platform recognized what was left of a face or recognized a distinctive piece of jewelry.

Using Craft again, Dorothea gently drew the canvas over the bodies. She waited several minutes for the screams to fade to muffled sobs.

"Know this," she said. "I will use every bit of Craft I have learned, every drop of strength that I have in me to defeat this monster. But if I stand alone, I will surely be defeated. If we stand and fight together, we have a chance to rid ourselves of the High Lord and those who serve him. Many of us won't survive this fight, but our children—" Her voice broke. It took her a moment to continue. "But our children will know the freedom we paid so dearly to give them."

Turning around, she stumbled. Her Steward and Master of the Guard supported her across the platform and down the steps. Tears and a fierce pride filled their eyes as they gently settled her into her open carriage for the short ride back to her mansion. When they tried to go with her, she shook her head.

"Your duties are here," she said weakly.

"But, Priestess—" the Master of the Guard started to protest.

"Please," Dorothea said. "Your strength will serve me better if you remain here." Calling in a folded piece of paper, she handed it to her Steward. "If these Queens ask to see me, arrange for an audience this afternoon." She saw the protest in his eyes, but he said nothing.

Her coachman clucked softly to his horses.

Dorothea leaned back against the seat and closed her eyes to hide her glee. *Well, you son of a whoring bitch, I've made the first move. And now there's nothing you can do that can't be used against you.*

2 / Terreille

Alexandra Angelline shivered despite the morning sun's warmth as she waited for Philip Alexander to return from his examination of the torn bodies lying on the wooden platform. She put a warming spell on the heavy wool shawl, knowing it was useless. No outer source of heat was going to thaw the cold inside her.

It's too soon, she thought desperately. *Wilhelmina had gone through the Gate yesterday morning. She* can't *be among . . .*

Vania and Nyselle, the two Province Queens she'd brought with her, had already returned to the inn, along with their escorts. They hadn't offered to wait with her. A few years ago—a few *weeks* ago—they would have. They had still believed in her then, despite the problems in her family.

But a few weeks ago, someone had sent cryptic messages to the thirty strongest witches in Chaillot—excluding herself and her daughter, Leland—inviting them to take a tour of Briarwood and promising to solve the riddle of what had happened to the young girls in their families who had been admitted to the hospital and then disappeared without a trace. Briarwood, which had been built to heal emotionally disturbed children, had been closed for several years now, ever since that mysterious illness started consuming dozens of men from the aristo families in Beldon Mor, Chaillot's capital—an illness that had seemed linked to that place.

The witches had arrived on the specified night, and they had learned the secrets and the horrors of Briarwood. Their guide, a demon-dead girl named Rose, showed no mercy as she introduced them to the ghosts. One Priestess found her cousin, who had disappeared when they were children, bricked up inside a wall. A Province Queen recognized what was left of a friend's daughter.

They saw the gaming rooms. They saw the cubicles that contained the narrow beds. They saw the vegetable garden and the girl with one leg.

Numbed by what they saw, they followed Rose, who smiled at them and told them in precise detail how and why each child had died. She told them about the other demon-dead children who had gone to the Dark Realm to live with the rest of the *cildru dyathe*. She recited the list of Briarwood's "uncles," the men who had supported and used that twisted carnal playground. And she recited a list of broken witches from aristo families who had been "cured" of their emotional instability—and stripped of their inner power—and then returned home.

One of the men Rose had named was Robert Benedict, Leland's former husband and an important member of the male council—a council already decimated by that mysterious illness.

When a Healer in the group had asked about the illness, Rose had smiled again, and said, "Briarwood is the pretty poison. There is no cure for Briarwood."

Alexandra clutched her shawl and kept shivering.

The rage that had swept through Chaillot had torn it apart. Beldon Mor became a battleground. The members of the male council who had not yet died from the illness were viciously executed. After several men from aristo families died of poison, many others fled to inns or one of their clubs because they were terrified to eat or drink anything that might have passed through the hands of the women in their families.

And after the first wave of rage had passed, the witches had turned their fury on her. They didn't blame her for Briarwood, since it had been built before she had become Queen of Chaillot, but they *did* blame her, bitterly, for her blindness. She had been so intent on keeping Hayll's influence out of Chaillot and trying to retain some power in the face of the male council that she hadn't seen the danger that already existed. They said it was like arguing with a man about groping your breast when he already had his cock sheathed between your legs.

They blamed her because Robert Benedict had lived in her house for all those years and had bedded her daughter. If she couldn't recognize the danger when it sat across from her day after day, how could she protect her people against any other kind of threat?

They blamed her for Robert Benedict and for all the young witches who had died or were broken in Briarwood.

She blamed herself for what happened to Jaenelle, her younger granddaughter. She had allowed that strange, difficult child to be locked away in that place. She hadn't known Briarwood's secrets, but if she hadn't dismissed Jaenelle's fanciful stories, if she had accepted them as a child's plea for attention instead of an annoying social problem, Jaenelle never would have been sent to Briarwood. And if she hadn't dismissed the girl's hatred for Dr. Carvay, would she have learned the truth sooner?

She didn't know. And it was too late to find the answers.

Now she had another family problem. Eleven years ago, Wilhelmina Benedict, Robert's daughter by his first marriage, had run away after claiming that Robert had made a sexual advance. Philip Alexander, Robert's bastard half brother, had found his niece, but he had refused to say where she was. At the time, Alexandra had been furious with him for keeping Wilhelmina's location a secret from her. Lately, she had wondered if Philip had had some inkling about what lay beneath Briarwood's solicitous veneer, especially when it had been his vehemence that had been the final push to close the place.

A couple of days ago, she had received a letter from Wilhelmina, informing her that the girl was going to Kaeleer, the Shadow Realm. No— Wilhelmina was twenty-seven now, no longer a girl. That didn't matter. She was still family. Still her granddaughter.

Alexandra shook her head to break the pattern of her thoughts and noticed Philip walking toward her. Holding her breath, she searched his gray eyes.

"She's not among them," Philip said quietly.

Alexandra released her breath in a sigh. "Thank the Darkness." But she understood what hadn't been said: *not yet.*

Philip offered his arm. She accepted, grateful for the support. He was a good man, the opposite of his half brother. She had been pleased when he and Leland had decided to handfast, and had been even more pleased when they chose to marry after the handfast year was done.

Alexandra looked back at the platform where Dorothea SaDiablo had made her horrifying speech. "Do you believe her?" she asked softly.

Philip guided her through clusters of people who were still too shocked to do more than huddle together while they gathered the courage to look at the mutilated bodies. "I don't know. If even half of what she said is true . . . if Sadi . . ." He choked.

She still had nightmares about Daemon Sadi. So did Philip, for different reasons. Sadi had threatened her when Jaenelle had been put in Briarwood for the last time, had given her a taste of the grave. When he unleashed his dark power in order to break the Ring of Obedience, he had destroyed half the Jeweled Blood in Beldon Mor. Caught in that explosive unleashing, Philip's strength had been broken back to the Green Jewel that was his birthright.

"We can get a Coach this evening," Philip said. "If we buy passage on one that rides the darker Winds, we'll be home by tomorrow."

"Not yet. I'd like you to talk to Dorothea's Steward. See if you can set up an audience for me."

"You're a Queen," Philip snapped. "You shouldn't have to beg an audience from a Priestess, no matter who—"

"Philip." She squeezed his arm. "I'm thankful for your loyalty, but right now we *are* beggars. I can't afford any more assumptions. I'm not convinced that Dorothea isn't the monster she's always appeared to be, but I *am* convinced that the High Lord *is* a greater threat." She shuddered. "We have to go to Kaeleer to find Wilhelmina. We can't afford to go there without having as much knowledge of the enemy as we can gain, no matter what the source."

"All right," Philip said. "What about Vania and Nyselle? Will they go with us?"

"They'll stay or go as they choose. They certainly won't care what I do." She sighed. "Who would have thought, even a month ago, that I would have to entertain the idea of Dorothea being an ally?"

3 / Terreille

Kartane SaDiablo wandered through the formal gardens, trying hard to ignore the speculative or pitying glances of the few people who hadn't retreated indoors.

He had waited until Dorothea's carriage was out of sight before walking away from the platform. The mutilated bodies that had been left for grisly inspection didn't bother him. Hell's fire, Dorothea had done that much—or worse—to people when she was feeling playful. But no one seemed to remember that. Or, perhaps, most of the fools here had never witnessed one of the High Priestess's moods.

But the Steward and the Master of the Guard . . . Ball-withered idiots. They had actually had *tears* in their eyes when they helped her into the carriage. How could they believe she'd been under a spell for all these centuries, that she hadn't reveled in her victims' pain?

Oh, she had certainly sounded sincere and remorseful. He didn't believe it for a moment. Any man who had ever had to pleasure Dorothea in a bed wouldn't have believed it. Daemon wouldn't have, that's for sure.

Daemon. The High Lord's son. That explained a great deal about his "cousin." All those years, when Daemon had been raised as a bastard in Dorothea's court, had she known? She must have. Which meant that the High Lord of Hell would have no love for the High Priestess of Hayll.

Which circled back to his own concerns.

The mysterious illness that had started almost thirteen years ago was consuming him. All the other men who had enjoyed Briarwood's secret little playground were already in the grave. Because he was Hayllian, one of the long-lived races, and because he had never gone back to Chaillot, he was the only one left. And he could feel that he was running out of time.

After the connection between the illness and Briarwood had been revealed a few weeks ago, he had started thinking—when his mind wasn't so consumed in nightmares that he *could* think—and he always came to the same conclusion: the only Healers who might be powerful enough to cure this illness before it destroyed him, and the only ones who would be ignorant of the cause, were in Kaeleer. They would probably be serving in the courts of the Territory Queens, who, if Dorothea hadn't been lying about *that,* were under the High Lord's control. Which meant he had to find something that would buy the High Lord's assistance. Thanks to Dorothea's little speech, he now had information he thought the Prince of the Darkness would find very interesting.

Pleased with his decision, Kartane smiled. He would spend a few more days sniffing out information and then pay a little visit to the Shadow Realm.

4 / Terreille

Alexandra Angelline gingerly settled into a chair, relieved that Dorothea had chosen a private receiving room instead of a formal audience room. This meeting was going to be difficult enough without enduring a court full of sneering Hayllians.

But being alone with Dorothea also had disadvantages. She'd heard that Hayll's High Priestess had been a handsome woman. Oh, the ghost of that loveliness was still there, but there was a definite stoop to Dorothea's shoulders, a twistiness to her spine. Age spots dotted the backs of her brown hands, and the face and hair . . .

It happens to all of us, eventually, Alexandra thought as she watched Dorothea pour tea into delicate cups. But what would it feel like to go to bed one night a woman in her prime and wake the next morning as a crone?

"I'm . . . grateful . . . you granted me an audience," Alexandra said, trying not to choke on the words.

Dorothea's lips curled in a slight smile as she handed Alexandra a cup of tea. "I'm surprised you asked for one." The smile faded. "We haven't seen eye to eye in the past. And considering what happened to your family, you have good reason to hate me." She hesitated, took a sip of tea, and continued softly, "It wasn't my idea to send Sadi to Chaillot, but I can't remember who suggested it or why I agreed. There's a veil over those memories that I still can't pierce."

Alexandra lifted her cup toward her lips, but put it down again without drinking. "You think the High Lord arranged it?"

"Yes, I do. Sadi is a beautiful, vicious weapon, and his father knows how to use him well. And they did achieve their goal."

"What goal?" Alexandra said angrily. "Sadi tore my family apart and killed my younger granddaughter. What was achieved by *that*?"

Dorothea sat back, took a sip of tea, and said quietly, "You forget, Sister. The girl's body was never found."

Something about the expectant way Dorothea was looking at her made Alexandra shiver. "That doesn't mean anything. He's a very discreet gravedigger." She put the cup and saucer on the table, the tea untouched. "I didn't come here to talk about the past. Just how dangerous is the High Lord?"

"Daemon Sadi is his father's son. Does that answer your question?"

Alexandra tried but couldn't suppress a shudder. "And you really think he wants to destroy the Blood in Terreille?"

"I'm sure of it." Dorothea touched her white hair. "I paid a heavy price to be sure of it."

"My other granddaughter, Wilhelmina Benedict, recently went to Kaeleer," Alexandra said softly.

Dorothea stiffened. "How recently?"

"She went through the Gate yesterday."

"Mother Night," Dorothea said, collapsing in her chair. "I'm so sorry, Alexandra. So very, very sorry."

"Prince Philip Alexander and I intend to go to Kaeleer as soon as that 'service fair' is over and visitors are permitted again. Hopefully, we'll be able to find her and convince whatever Queen she's signed a contract with to release her."

"She's in far more danger than that," Dorothea said worriedly.

"There's no reason for her to draw anyone's attention," Alexandra said, fear making her voice sharp. "There's no reason for her to accept a contract outside of Little Terreille."

"There are two reasons: the High Lord and the witch he controls. If you don't find her quickly, Wilhelmina will end up in his dark embrace, and there will be no hope for her then."

Despite the warm room, a chill ran down Alexandra's spine.

Dorothea just looked at her for a long moment. "I told you—Sadi and the High Lord achieved their goal. No one hunts very long for a corpse when the living need care. And your granddaughter's body was never found."

Alexandra stared at Dorothea. "You think *Jaenelle* is this powerful witch under the High Lord's control? *Jaenelle?*" She laughed bitterly. "Hell's fire, Dorothea, Jaenelle couldn't even do *basic* Craft."

"If you know how to read between the lines of some of the . . . less available . . . records of the Blood's history, you'll find that there have been a few women—very few, thank the Darkness—who had enormous reservoirs of power that they were unable to tap by themselves. They required an . . . emotional . . . bond with someone who had the skill to channel the power in order to use it. But they didn't always have the choice about *how* it was used." Dorothea paused. "The gossip that has recently filtered in from Little Terreille about the High Lord's pet describes her as 'eccentric,' 'somewhat emotionally disturbed.' Does that sound familiar?"

Alexandra couldn't catch her breath. There wasn't enough air in the room. Why wasn't there enough air?

"If you'll take it, I'll give you whatever help I can." Dorothea looked at her sadly. "You can't ignore this, Alexandra. No matter what you want to think or what you want to believe, you can't ignore the fact that the High Lord's pet witch, the witch Daemon Sadi helped him acquire, goes by the name Jaenelle Angelline."

5 / Terreille

Dorothea pulled aside the dark, heavy curtains and stared out at the night-shrouded garden. She felt drained, physically and emotionally. Oh, how she had wanted to dig her nails in and scratch out the pathetically hopeful look in the eyes of the males in her First Circle. They wanted to grasp at any excuse for her behavior over the past centuries. They wanted to believe that a *male* had made her cruel, a *male* had manipulated her and controlled her thoughts, a *male* had been behind her rise to power and the viciousness afterward that had made it possible to soften and harvest most of the other Territories in Terreille.

They didn't want to give her any credit at all. They wanted her to be a victim so that they wouldn't feel ashamed of serving her, so that they could pretend they served out of a sense of honor instead of avarice and fear.

Well, once Kaeleer fell, she would make a few changes in her court. Maybe she would even arrange for the fools to die in battle, choking on their bloody honor.

"You did well today, Sister," said a harsh but still girlish voice. "I couldn't have done better myself."

Dorothea didn't turn around. Looking at Hekatah, the demon-dead Dark Priestess and self-proclaimed High Priestess of Hell, always turned her stomach. "They were your words, not mine, so it's not surprising that you're pleased."

"You still need me," Hekatah snarled as she shuffled to a chair near the fire. "Don't forget that."

"I never forget that," Dorothea replied softly, keeping her eyes focused on the garden.

It had been Hekatah who had seen her potential when she was a young witch still learning a Priestess's duties as well as the Black Widows' Craft. It had been Hekatah who had nurtured her ambitions and dreams of power, who had pointed out the possible rivals who could interfere with those dreams. And it had been Hekatah who had helped eliminate those rivals. The Dark Priestess had been there, every step of the way, guiding, advising.

She couldn't remember just when she realized that Hekatah needed her just as much as she needed Hekatah. That need made them despise each other, but they were bound together by the common dream of ruling an entire Realm.

"Do you really think, after all we've done to gain control of Terreille, those Queens will believe it was all the High Lord's fault?"

"If you cast the persuasion spells correctly, there's no reason they won't believe it," Hekatah said with sweet venom.

"There's nothing wrong with my Craft skills, Priestess," Dorothea replied with equal venom, turning to face the other woman.

"Your skills didn't help you elude the spell Sadi wrapped around you, did they?"

"No more than your skills protected you or have helped you reverse the damage."

Hekatah hissed angrily, and Dorothea turned back to the window, feeling a brief satisfaction at the well-aimed barb.

Seven years ago, Hekatah had tried to gain control of Jaenelle Angelline and eliminate Lucivar Yaslana. Something had gone wrong with her scheme, and the backlash of that confrontation had stripped away her ability to pass as one of the living, had made her look like a decaying, desiccated corpse. For the first couple of years, she had insisted that all she needed was to consume large quantities of fresh blood in order to restore her body. But the demon-dead were, in a sense, spirits that still had too much psychic power to return to the Darkness and were now housed in dead flesh. While the power lasted and could be renewed, the body could be maintained by consuming blood. But nothing was going to restore Hekatah's looks. The juice had been wrung out of her dead flesh, and the past seven years had been a slow decay of a body that had died 50,000 years ago.

"They'll believe the High Lord has been responsible for all the perversion in Terreille," Hekatah said, coming up behind Dorothea close enough for her reflection to be visible in the window's night-darkened glass. "They *want* to believe it. He's a myth, a terrifying story that has been whispered for thousands of years. And anyone who has doubts about *him* will have no doubts at all about Yaslana and Sadi. The thought of the three of them coming together and having the use of a strong witch as their tool will be enough to unite Terreille against Kaeleer. In the end, it doesn't matter *why* they join the fight, only that they fight."

"We've gained one reluctant ally this afternoon—Alexandra Angelline, the Queen of Chaillot." Dorothea's lips curled in a vicious smile. "She was shocked to discover that her younger granddaughter has been under the High Lord's thumb for all these years, thanks to Daemon Sadi."

Hekatah frowned. "She's a fool, but she isn't stupid. If she convinces Jaenelle to help her maintain control of Chaillot . . ."

Dorothea shook her head. "She doesn't believe Jaenelle has any power. I could see it in her eyes. I spun her a little story about women who are reservoirs of raw power—she didn't believe that either. She can accept that Sadi and the High Lord might have wanted Jaenelle for their own twisted reasons, but she'll continue to believe what she *wants* to believe about Jaenelle Angelline. Once she gets to Little Terreille, Lord Jorval will be waiting to offer his assistance. *He'll* never mention that Jaenelle is the Queen of Ebon Askavi. And I doubt Alexandra will believe anything *anyone* at the Hall tells her."

Hekatah laughed gleefully.

"And I imagine that once she actually meets Prince Saetan Daemon SaDiablo, the High Lord of Hell, she'll be more than happy to send along any information she thinks will be useful to us."

"And if he discovers her deceit . . ." Hekatah shrugged. "Well, we would have had to get rid of her after the war anyway."

Dorothea stared at their reflections in the glass. They had been lovely women once. Now Hekatah looked like a corpse that the worms had been feasting on, and she . . .

Sadi had created some kind of spell to age and twist her body, but he hadn't done anything to diminish her sexual appetite. The Blood called him the Sadist, but she hadn't really appreciated the depths of his cruelty. He had known her appetites—how could he not since he'd had to satisfy them when he was young? He had also known the humiliation she would feel when she saw revulsion in the eyes of the males she rode instead of that exciting combination of lust and fear. Now, after her tearful confession, she wouldn't even be able to indulge in that much.

"You've informed your pet Queens that they'll have to abstain from their more—imaginative—pleasures for the time being?" Hekatah asked.

"I've told them," Dorothea replied irritably. "Whether they *will* restrain themselves is difficult to say."

"Any who indulge will have to be eliminated."

"And how do we explain *that*?"

Hekatah made an impatient sound. "Obviously they, too, have been under the High Lord's spell. Your gallant struggle to free yourself from his power also freed a number of your Sisters, but, unfortunately, not all of them. All it will take is one or two of them being killed for the others to understand the message and behave properly."

"And after we've won?"

"After we've won, we can do whatever we damn well please. We'll rule the Realms, Dorothea. Not just Terreille, but *all* of them—Terreille, Kaeleer, and Hell."

Wanting to savor that possibility, Dorothea didn't say anything for several minutes. Then finally, reluctantly, she asked, "Do you really think that fear of the High Lord will be enough to start a war? Do you really think this will work?"

What was left of Hekatah's lips pulled back in a terrible smile. "It worked the last time."

6 / Kaeleer

The Queen of Arachna settled next to the shoulder of the weary, golden-haired woman who leaned against a flat-sided boulder.

Is bad? the large golden spider asked in her soft voice.

Jaenelle Angelline brushed her hair away from her face and sighed. Her haunted sapphire eyes narrowed a little against the early-morning sunlight as she once again studied the delicate strands of the tangled web that she'd woven during the night. "Yes, it's bad. A war is coming. A war between the Realms."

Can stop?

Jaenelle shook her head slowly. "No. No one can stop it."

The spider shifted uneasily. The air around the woman tasted of sadness—and a growing, cold rage. *The two-legs have fought before. Is more bad this time?*

"You may look."

Accepting the formal invitation, the Arachnian Queen opened her mind to the dreams and visions in the large tangled web Jaenelle had spun between a boulder and a nearby tree.

So much death. So much pain and sorrow. And a creeping taint that soiled the ones remaining.

Pulling back from the dreams and visions, she studied the web itself and noticed two odd things. One was the delicate silver ring set with an Ebony Jewel that had been placed in the center of the web. A Jewel chip was rarely woven into a tangled web because the magic that shaped those webs was powerful—and dangerous—enough, and this particular Jewel belonged to Jaenelle, who was Witch, the living myth, dreams made flesh. The other odd thing was the triangle. Many threads were connected to that ring, but overlying them were three threads that formed a triangle around it.

Intrigued, the spider continued to study the web. She had seen that triangle before. Strength, passion, courage. Loyalty, honor, love. She could almost taste the male tang in those threads.

"If Kaeleer accepts Terreille's challenge and goes to war," Jaenelle said softly, "it will destroy the Blood in both Realms. All the Blood. Even the kindred."

Some will live. It is always so.

"Not this time. Oh, there will be some who will physically survive the war, but . . ." Jaenelle's voice broke. She took a deep breath. "All of my Sisters, all of my friends will be gone. All of the Queens will be gone. All of the Warlord Princes."

All?

"There will be no Queens left to heal the land, no Queens left to hold the Blood together. The slaughter will continue until there's no one left to slaughter. The witches will be as barren as the land. The gift of power that had been given to us so long ago will be the final weapon that destroys us. If Kaeleer goes to war with Terreille."

Must fight, the spider said. *Must stop creeping taint.*

Jaenelle smiled bitterly. "War won't stop it. I know who nurtured the seeds, and if eliminating Dorothea and Hekatah would stop this from coming, I'd destroy them right now. But it wouldn't stop anything, not anymore. It would only delay it, and that would be worse. This is the right place and the right time to cleanse that taint out of the Blood."

You speak paths that go no place, the spider scolded. *You say can't fight but must fight. You confused? Maybe you read web wrong.*

Jaenelle turned her head toward the spider, a dryly amused look on her face. "And where did I learn to weave a tangled web? If I'm not reading it right, maybe I wasn't taught correctly."

The spider used Craft to make a harsh, buzzing sound that indicated severe disapproval. *Not fault of teaching spider if little spider pay more attention to catching fly than doing lesson.*

Jaenelle's silvery, velvet-coated laugh filled the air. "I never once tried to catch a fly. And I *did* pay attention to the teaching spider. After all, she *was* the Dream Weavers' Queen at the time."

The Arachnian Queen resettled herself, somewhat mollified.

Jaenelle's humor faded as she turned her sapphire eyes back to the web. "Terreille will go to war."

Then Kaeleer will war.

"This web shows two paths," Jaenelle said very quietly.

No, the spider replied firmly. *One web, one vision. That is the way.*

"Two paths," Jaenelle insisted. "Following the second path, Kaeleer doesn't go to war with Terreille, and the Queens and Warlord Princes survive to heal and protect the Shadow Realm."

★Then who war with Terreille?★

Jaenelle hesitated. "The Queen of the Darkness."

★But *you* are Queen!★

Jaenelle exhaled sharply. "A war that cleanses the Realms, calls in the debts, takes back the gift of power that was given. There's a way. There *must* be a way, but the web can't show me yet because of that." Her finger pointed to the triangle. "That's not the Queen's triangle." Her finger traced the left side of the triangle. "That thread is the High Lord." She traced the bottom thread. "And that thread is Lucivar." Her finger hesitated at the triangle's right side. "But that thread isn't Andulvar. It should be, since he's the Master of the Guard, but it's someone else. Someone who isn't here yet, someone who can guide me to the answers I need to walk that other path."

★The thread not tell you its name?★

"It says the mirror is coming. What kind of answer is—" Tensing, Jaenelle scrambled to her knees. "Daemon," she whispered. "*Daemon.*"

The spider shifted uneasily. Witch had flavored the air with intense pleasure when she had whispered that name—but underneath the pleasure there was a little taste of fear.

"I have to go," Jaenelle said hurriedly as she leaped to her feet. "I still need to stop at a couple of kindred Territories before I return to the Hall." She hesitated, glanced at the spider. "With your permission, I'd like to keep this one for a while."

★Your webs be welcome among the Weavers of Dreams.★

Raising her hand, Jaenelle used Craft to put a protective shield on the tangled web's threads. She looked back at the spider. "May the Darkness embrace you, Sister."

★And you, Sister Queen,★ the spider replied formally.

The Arachnian Queen waited until Jaenelle caught one of the Winds, those psychic pathways through the Darkness, before she used Craft to float gently toward the tangled web.

One web, one vision. That was the way. But when Witch spun a web . . .

Using instinct and all of her training, the spider cautiously brushed a leg against a small thread that floated loose from the Ebony ring. The tangled web showed her the second path.

The spider quickly backed away. ★No!★ she called, sending out her psychic communication thread as far as it would reach. *No! *Not* a second path. *Not* an answer! You not walk this path!*

No answer. Not even a flicker from Witch's powerful mind to indicate that she had heard.

You not walk this path, the spider said again sadly, seeing clearly where that path would end.

Perhaps not. Witch could weave a tangled web better than any other Black Widow, but even Witch couldn't always sense all the flavors in the threads.

The Arachnian Queen turned back to the web and felt a mild tug. Walking on air, she followed the tug to a thread near the tree-anchored side of the web. Cautiously, she brushed a leg against the thread.

Dog. The brown-and-white dog she had seen in the first web she had spun after the cold season had passed. She had asked Witch to bring the dog, Ladvarian, to the Weavers' island. She had wanted to see this Warlord—and she had wanted him to see her.

She plucked the Ladvarian thread and felt its vibration run through the web. Many of the threads connected to the Ebony ring—the kindred threads—began to shine brightly. The human threads shone, too, but not so bright, not so sure. She must remember that. And that triangle . . .

With her leg still resting on the Ladvarian thread, the spider let her mind sail to the secret cave, the sacred cave in the center of the island. There the Arachnian Queens had gone time after time to listen to dreams—and to weave, thread by thread, the very special webs that bound dreams to flesh, that were the first tangible step in creating Witch.

Small webs. Larger webs. Sometimes only one race, only one kind of dreamer, had dreamed Witch into being. Other times the dreamers had come from different places with different needs that somehow had fit together to become one dream.

When that dream's time in the flesh was done and it no longer walked the Realms, the Arachnian Queen would respectfully cut the anchor threads that held the web to the cave walls, roll the spidersilk into a ball, deposit it in a niche, and then use Craft to coax crystals to grow over the opening. There were many closed niches, more than the human Blood realized. But then, the kindred had always been far more faithful dreamers.

There was one web in the cave that had been started long, long ago. Generation after generation after generation, the Arachnian Queens had brushed one of the anchor threads of that web, had listened to the dreams, and then had added more strands. So many dreamers in this web, so many dreams that had fit together to become one. Twenty-five years ago, by human reckoning, that dream had finally become flesh.

In the center of that special web was a triangle. Three strong dreamers. Three threads that had been reinforced so many times they were now thick and very powerful.

And each Queen, as she consumed the freely offered flesh of the one who had come before her, had been told the same thing: Remember this web. Know this web. Know every thread.

The spider pulled her mind back to the new web.

Dreams made flesh. A spirit nurtured in the Darkness, shaped by dreams. And a tangled web, equally nurtured and hidden in a cave full of ancient power, that guided that spirit to the right kind of flesh.

There had been times, when the spider had seen terrible things in her webs of dreams and visions, when she had wondered if that particular spirit had, in fact, found the right flesh; had wondered if, perhaps, some of the threads had been too old. No, there had been a reason why this one had been shaped into this flesh. The pain and the wounds had not been the fault of the dreaming—or the dreamers.

The spider drew silk out of her body and carefully attached it to the Ladvarian thread.

So. Witch would choose the second path, blind to the fact that, while she would save Kaeleer and those she loved, she would also destroy Kaeleer's Heart.

There *had* to be a way to save Kaeleer's Heart.

Spinning out an anchor thread between the tree trunk and a sturdy branch, the Arachnian Queen began to weave her own tangled web.

CHAPTER TWO

1 / Kaeleer

Lucivar Yaslana flipped the list back to the first page of neatly written names and stepped away from the table, faintly amused by the men who were caught between wanting to review the lists at that table and *not* wanting to get too close to *him*.

That was one advantage he had over the other males who were drifting from table to table to check the service fair lists. No one jostled him or complained about how long it took him to scan the names, because no one wanted to tangle with a Warlord Prince who wore Ebon-gray Jewels, was an Eyrien warrior bred and trained, and had a vicious temper and a reputation for unleashing that temper—and his fists—without a second thought. When added to his belonging to one of the strongest families in the Realm and also serving in the Dark Court at Ebon Askavi, it was little wonder that other men quickly yielded.

But even all of that didn't help him feel comfortable while he was at the service fair in Goth, Little Terreille's capital. No matter what they called it, this fair had too much of the flavor of the slave auctions still held in the Realm of Terreille.

Slowly making his way to the door, Lucivar took a deep breath and then wished he hadn't. The large room was overcrowded, and even with the windows open, the air stank of sweat and fatigue—and the fear and desperation that seemed to rise up from the hundreds of names on those lists.

As soon as he was outside the building, Lucivar spread his dark, membranous wings to their full span. He wasn't sure if it was out of defiance for all the times that natural movement had earned him the cut of a lash or just that he wanted to feel the sun and wind on them for a moment after being inside for several hours—or if it was simply a way to remind himself that he was now the buyer, not the merchandise.

Folding his wings, he set off for the far corner of the fairground that was reserved for the Eyrien "camp."

He'd noted several Eyrien names that were of interest to him, but not the one name—the Hayllian name—that was the main reason he'd spent the past several hours searching through those damn lists. But he'd been searching the lists for Daemon's name for the past five years, ever since the idiots in the Dark Council had decided this twice-yearly "service fair" was the way to funnel the hundreds of people who were fleeing from Terreille and trying to find a fingerhold in Kaeleer. And he thought, as he did every time, about why Daemon's name wasn't there. And he rejected, as he did every time, all the reasons except one: he wasn't looking for the right name.

But that wasn't likely. No matter what name Daemon Sadi used to get to Kaeleer, once at the fair he would use his own name. There were too many people here who would recognize him, and since the penalty for lying about the Jewels one wore was immediate expulsion from the Realm—either back to Terreille or to the final death—changing his name while admitting that he wore the Black Jewels would only make him look like a fool because he was the *only* male besides the High Lord who had worn the Black in the entire history of the Blood. The Darkness knew Daemon was many things, but he wasn't a fool.

Pushing aside his own stab of disappointment, Lucivar wondered how he was going to explain this to Ladvarian. The Sceltie Warlord had been so insistent about Lucivar checking the lists carefully this time, had seemed so certain. Most people would think it odd to feel apprehensive about disappointing a dog that just reached his knees, but when that dog's best friend was eight hundred pounds of feline temper, a smart man didn't dismiss canine feelings.

Lucivar put those thoughts aside as he reached the Eyrien "camp": a large corral of barren, beaten earth, a poorly made wooden barracks, a water pump, and a large trough. Not so different from the slave pens in Terreille. Oh, there were better accommodations on the fairground for those who still had the gold or silver marks to pay for them, with hot water and beds that were more than a sleeping bag on the ground. But for most, it was like this: a struggle to look presentable after days spent waiting, wondering, hoping. Even here, among a race where arrogance was as natural as breathing, he could pick up the scents of exhaustion brought on by too little food, too little sleep, and nerves frayed to the breaking point. He could almost taste the desperation.

Opening the gate, Lucivar stepped inside. Most of the women were near the barracks. Most of the men were in small groups, nearer the gate. Some glanced at him and ignored him. A few stiffened in recognition and looked away, dismissing him in the same way they had dismissed the bastard boy he'd believed himself to be.

But a few of the males moved toward him, every line of their bodies issuing a challenge.

Lucivar gave them a slow, arrogant smile that blatantly accepted the challenge, then turned his back on them and headed for the Warlord whose concentration was focused on the two boys moving through a sparring exercise with the sticks.

One of the boys noticed him and forgot about his sparring partner. The other boy pounced on the advantage and gave the first one a hard poke in the belly.

"Hell's fire, boy," the Warlord said with so much irritation it made Lucivar grin. "You're lucky all you've got is a sore belly and not a dent in that thick head of yours. You dropped your guard."

"But—" the boy said as he started to raise his hand and point.

The Warlord tensed but didn't turn. "If you start worrying about the man who hasn't reached you yet, the one you're already fighting is going to kill you." Then he turned slowly and his eyes widened.

Lucivar's grin sharpened. "You're getting soft, Hallevar. You used to give me the bruised belly and then a smack for getting it."

"Do you drop your guard in a fight?" Hallevar growled.

Lucivar just laughed.

"Then what are you bitching for? Stand still, boy, and let's take a look at you."

The youngsters' mouths were hanging open at Hallevar's disrespect for a Warlord Prince. The males who had noticed him and had decided to talk—or fight—had formed a semicircle on his right. But he stood still while Hallevar's eyes traveled over his body; he said nothing in response to the older man's small grunts of approval, and he bit back a laugh at Hallevar's glaring disapproval of the thick, black, shoulder-length hair.

His hair was a break from tradition, since Eyrien warriors wore their hair short to deprive an enemy of a handhold. But after escaping from the salt mines of Pruul eight years ago and ending up in Kaeleer instead of dead, he had shrugged off quite a few traditions—and by doing so, had found others that were even older.

"Well," Hallevar finally growled, "you filled out well enough, and while your face is nowhere near as pretty as that sadistic bastard you call a brother, it'll fool the Ladies long enough if you can keep that temper of yours on a tight leash." He rubbed the back of his neck. "But this is the last day of the fair. You haven't left yourself much time to draw anyone's attention."

"Neither have you," Lucivar replied, "and putting those pups through their paces isn't going to show anyone what you can do."

"Who wants gristle when they can have fresh meat?" Hallevar muttered, looking away.

"Don't start digging your grave," Lucivar snapped, not pleased with how relieved he felt when anger fired Hallevar's eyes. "You're a seasoned warrior and an experienced arms master with enough years left in you to train another generation or two. This is just another kind of battlefield, so pick up your weapon and show some balls."

Hallevar smiled reluctantly.

Needing some balance, Lucivar turned toward the other men. Out of the corner of his eye, he noticed some of the women coming over. And he noticed that some were bringing young children with them.

He clamped down on the emotions that started churning too close to the surface. He had to choose carefully. There were those who could adjust to the way the Blood lived in Kaeleer and would make a good life for themselves here. And there were those who would die swiftly and violently because they couldn't, or wouldn't, adjust. He had made a few bad choices during the first couple of fairs, had offered a trust that he shouldn't have offered. Because of it, he carried the guilt for the shattered lives of two witches who had been raped and brutally beaten—and he carried the memory of the sick rage he'd felt when he'd executed the Eyrien males who had been responsible. After that, he'd found a way to confirm his choices. He hadn't always trusted his own judgment, but he never doubted Jaenelle's.

"Lucivar."

Lucivar honed his attention to the Sapphire-Jeweled Warlord Prince who had moved to the front of the group. "Falonar."

"It's *Prince* Falonar," Falonar snarled.

Lucivar bared his teeth in a feral smile. "I thought we were being informal, since I'm sure an aristo male like you wouldn't forget something like basic courtesy."

"Why should I offer you basic courtesy?"

"Because I'm the one wearing the Ebon-gray," Lucivar replied too softly as he shifted his weight just enough to let the other man see the challenge and make the choice.

"Stop it, both of you," Hallevar snarled. "We're all on shaky ground in this place. We don't need it yanked out from under us because you two keep wanting to prove whose cock is bigger. I thumped both of you when you were snot-nosed brats, and I can still do it."

Lucivar felt the tension slide away and took a step back. Hallevar knew as well as he did that he could snap the older man in half with his hands or his mind, but Hallevar had been one of the few who had seen the potential warrior and hadn't cared about his bloodlines—or the lack of them.

"That's better," Hallevar said to Lucivar with an approving nod. "And you, Falonar. You've had a couple of offers, which is more than most of us can say. Maybe you'd better consider them."

Falonar's face tightened. He took a deep breath and let it out. "I guess I should. It doesn't look like the bastard's going to show."

"What bastard is that?" Lucivar asked mildly. More of the women and some of the men who had refused to acknowledge him had wandered over.

It was a young Warlord who answered. "The Warlord Prince of Ebon Rih. We'd heard . . ."

"You heard . . . ?" Lucivar prodded when the Warlord didn't finish, noticing the way the man shifted a bit closer to the witch who was holding an adorable little girl in her arms. Lucivar's gold eyes narrowed as he opened his psychic senses a little more. A little Queen. His gaze shifted to the boy who had a two-fisted grip on the woman's skirt. There was strength there, potential there. He felt something inside him shift, sharpen. "What did you hear?"

The Warlord swallowed hard. "We heard he's a hard bastard, but he's fair if you serve him well. And he doesn't . . ."

It was the fear in the woman's eyes and the way her brown skin paled that honed Lucivar's temper. "And he doesn't plow a woman unless she invites him?" he said too softly.

He felt a flash of female anger nearby. Before he could locate the source, he remembered the children who probably already carried too many scars. "You heard right. He doesn't."

Falonar shifted, bringing Lucivar's attention—and his temper—back to someone who could handle it. Then he gave Hallevar a sharp look, and a couple of other men that he'd known before centuries of slavery had taken him away from the Eyrien courts and hunting camps.

"Is that what you've been waiting for?" It took effort, but he kept his voice neutral.

"Wouldn't you?" Hallevar replied. "It may not be the Territory that we knew in Terreille, but they call it Askavi here, too, and maybe it won't feel so . . . strange."

Lucivar clenched his teeth. The afternoon was fleeing. He had to make some choices, and he had to make them *now*. He turned back to Falonar. "Are you going to choke every time you have to take an order from me?"

Falonar stiffened. "Why should I take any orders from *you*?"

"Because I *am* the Warlord Prince of Ebon Rih."

Shock. Tense stillness. Some of the men—a good number of the men who had wandered over—looked at him in disgust and walked away.

Falonar narrowed his eyes. "You already have a contract?"

"A longstanding one. Think carefully, Prince Falonar. If serving under me is going to be a bone in your throat, you'd better take one of those other offers, because if you break the rules that I set, I'll tear you apart. And you—and everyone else who was waiting—had better think about what Ebon Rih is."

"It's the Keep's Territory," Hallevar said. "Same as the Black Valley in Terreille. We know that."

Lucivar nodded, his eyes never leaving Falonar's. "There's one big differ-ence." He paused and then added, "I serve in the Dark Court at Ebon Askavi."

Several people gasped. Falonar's eyes widened. Then he looked at the Ebon-gray Jewel that hung from the gold chain around Lucivar's neck, but it was a considering look, not an insulting one. "There's really a Queen there?" he asked slowly.

"Oh, yes," Lucivar replied softly. "There's a Queen there. You should also know this: I present her with my choices about who serves me in Ebon Rih, but the final decision is hers. If she says 'no,' you're gone." He looked at the tense, silent people watching him. "There's not much time left to make a decision. I'll wait by the gate. Anyone who's interested can talk to me there."

He walked to the gate, aware of the eyes that watched him. He kept his back to them and looked at the corrals set up as waiting areas for other races. He observed everything and saw nothing.

It shouldn't matter anymore. He had a place here, a family here, a Queen he loved and felt honored to serve. He was respected for his intelligence, his skill as a warrior, and the Jewels he wore. And he was liked and loved for himself.

But he had spent 1,700 years believing he was a half-breed bastard, and the insults and the blows he'd received as a boy in the hunting camps had helped shape the formidable temper he'd inherited from his father. The courts he'd served in as a slave after that had put the final vicious edge on it.

It shouldn't matter anymore. It *didn't* matter anymore. He wouldn't allow it to hurt him. But he also knew that if Hallevar decided to go back to Terreille or accept whatever crumbs were offered in another court instead of signing a contract with him, it would be a long time before the Warlord Prince of Ebon Rih returned to the service fair.

"Prince Yaslana."

Lucivar almost smiled at the reluctance in Falonar's voice, but he kept his face carefully neutral as he turned to face the other man. "The bone's choking you already?" The careful wariness he saw in Falonar's eyes surprised him.

"We never liked each other, for a lot of reasons. We don't have to like each other now in order to work together. We've fought together against the Jhinka. You know what I can do."

"We were green fighters then, both taking orders from someone else," Lucivar said carefully. "This is different."

Falonar nodded solemnly. "This is different. But for the chance to serve in Ebon Rih, I'm willing to set aside the past. Are you?"

They had been rivals, competitors, two young Warlord Princes struggling to prove their dominance. Falonar had gone on to serve in the High Priestess of Askavi's First Circle. He had gone to slavery.

"Can you follow orders?" Lucivar asked. It wasn't an unreasonable question. Warlord Princes were a law unto themselves. Unless they gave their hearts as well as their bodies, following orders wasn't easy for any of them. Even then, it wasn't easy.

"I can follow orders," Falonar said, and then added under his breath, "When I can stomach them."

"And you're willing to follow the rules I've set, even if it means losing some of the privileges you may have come to expect?"

Falonar narrowed his gold eyes. "I suppose you don't break any rules anymore?"

The question surprised a laugh out of Lucivar. "Oh, I still break some. And I get my ass kicked for it."

Falonar opened his mouth, then closed it again.

"The Steward and the Master of the Guard," Lucivar said dryly, answering the unspoken question.

"Those Jewels would give you some leverage," Falonar said, tipping his head to indicate Lucivar's Ebon-gray Jewel.

"Not with those two."

Falonar looked startled, then thoughtful. "How long have you been here?"

"Eight years."

"Then you've already served out your contract."

Lucivar gave Falonar a sharp-edged smile. "Plant your ambitions somewhere else, Prince. Mine's a lifetime contract."

Falonar tensed. "I thought Warlord Princes were required to serve five years in a court."

Lucivar nodded and clamped down on the pleasure that jumped through him when he saw Hallevar coming toward him. "That's what's required." He smiled wickedly. "It only took the Lady three years to realize that wasn't what I agreed to."

Falonar hesitated. "What's she like?"

"Wonderful. Beautiful. Terrifying." Lucivar gave Falonar an assessing look. "Are you coming to Ebon Rih?"

"I'm coming to Ebon Rih." Falonar nodded to Hallevar and stepped aside for the older man.

"I'd like to come with you," Hallevar said abruptly.

"But?" Lucivar said.

Hallevar looked over his shoulder at the two boys who were hovering out of earshot. He turned back to Lucivar. "I said they were mine."

"Are they?"

Hallevar's eyes filled with heat. "If they'd been mine, I would have acknowledged them, whether or not the mothers denied paternity. A child isn't considered a bastard if a sire is listed, even if the man doesn't get a chance to be a father."

The words stung. Prythian, the High Priestess of Askavi in Terreille, and Dorothea SaDiablo had spun their lies in order to separate him from Luthvian, his mother, and they had altered his birth documents because they hadn't wanted anyone to know who his father really was. It had stunned him to learn that the hard feelings he carried inside him because of that deceit were nothing compared to Saetan's rage.

"One has a mother who's a whore in a Red Moon house," Hallevar said. "Stands to reason she wouldn't know whose seed she carried. The other woman was the known lover of an aristo Warlord. The witch he'd married was barren, and everyone knew he made sure his mistress didn't invite another man to her bed. He wanted the child, would have acknowledged the child. But when it was born, she named a dozen men in the court that she claimed might have been the sire. She did it on purpose, and because she wanted revenge on the father, she condemned the child."

Lucivar just nodded, fighting the anger that burned in him.

"This is a new place, Lucivar," Hallevar pleaded. "A new chance. You know what it's like. You should understand better than anyone. They're not strong like you. Neither of them will wear dark Jewels. But they're good boys, and they'll carry their weight. And they are full-blooded Eyriens," he added.

"So they don't carry the stigma of being half-breeds?" Lucivar asked with deadly control.

"I never used that word with you," Hallevar said quietly.

"No, you didn't. But it's an easy enough word to say without thinking. So I'll give you fair warning, Lord Hallevar. It's a word you would do well to forget, because there's nothing I could do to save you if you said it within my father's hearing."

Hallevar stared at him. "Your father is here? You know him?"

"I know him. And believe me, you haven't seen temper until you've been on the receiving end of my father's rage."

"I'll remember. What about the boys?"

"No lies, Hallevar. I'll take them for themselves, subject to the Queen's approval just like any other male."

Hallevar smiled, obviously relieved. "I'll tell them to fetch our things." A curt wave of his hand had the two boys racing toward the barracks. Without looking at Lucivar, he asked, "Is he proud of you?"

"When he doesn't want to throttle me or kick my ass."

Hallevar tried to swallow a laugh and ended up wheezing. "I'd like to meet him."

"You will," Lucivar promised dryly.

Whether it was seeing the first ones being accepted or needing a little time to gather their courage, others approached him.

There was the young Warlord, Endar, and his wife, Dorian, their son, Alanar, and their little Queen daughter, Orian.

The woman was frightened, the man tense. But the little girl gave him a sweet smile and leaned away from her mother, her arms reaching for him.

Lucivar took her, settled her on his hip, and grinned. "Don't get any ideas, bright-eyes. I'm taken," he told her as he tickled gently and made her giggle. When he gave the girl back to her mother, Dorian stared at him as if he'd grown another head.

Next came Nurian, a Healer who hadn't completed her training yet, and her younger sister, Jillian, who was on the cusp of changing from girl to woman.

There was Kohlvar, a weapons maker. And there were Rothvar and Zaranar, two warriors Lucivar remembered from the hunting camps.

One thought nagged at him as he talked with them. Why were they here? Kohlvar had been a young man, by the standard of the long-lived races, when Lucivar was first sent away from Askavi. Even then, when Kohlvar was just past his journeymanship, he'd been known for the strength and the balance of the weapons he made. He should have made a good living in Terreille, and he could have stayed away from court intrigue if he'd chosen to. Rothvar and Zaranar were seasoned warriors, the kind who could have found a position in most of the courts in Askavi or accepted any independent work they chose.

And why would an aristo Warlord Prince like Falonar leave Terreille?

The wariness inside him grew. Were things far worse in Terreille than anyone here suspected, or were these men here for another reason?

Lucivar pushed those thoughts aside. He hadn't sensed anything in the people who had approached him that would make him decide against them, so he would let the questions rest for now. And he would let Jaenelle pass judgment.

By the time the last man left to fetch his things from the barracks, Lucivar had agreed to take twenty males and a dozen females.

How many of these people would survive the full term of their contracts? he wondered as they hurried toward him with the meager belongings they had been allowed to bring with them. There were other dangers in Kaeleer beyond the ones they expected. And there were the demon-dead. Considering where he was taking them, they would quickly have to come to terms with having the demon-dead walk among them.

He took a deep breath and let it out slowly. "Ready?"

It amused him, but didn't surprise him, when Falonar looked over the group and answered him as if he'd already accepted the man as his second-in-command.

"We're ready."

2 / Kaeleer

Daemon Sadi crossed his legs at the knee, steepled his fingers, and rested his long, black-tinted nails against his chin. "What about the Queens in the other Territories?" he asked in his deep, cultured voice.

Lord Jorval smiled wearily. "As I've explained before, Prince Sadi, the Queens outside of Little Terreille are not eager to accept their Terreillean Brothers and Sisters into their courts, and even the immigrants who do get contracts are made to feel less than welcome."

"Did you inquire?" Daemon's gold eyes glazed slightly. A stranger or slight acquaintance might have thought he looked tired or bored, but that sleepy look would have terrified anyone who really knew him.

"I inquired," Jorval said a bit sharply. "The Queens didn't reply."

Daemon glanced at the four sheets of paper spread out on the desk in front of him. In the past two days, he and Jorval had sat in this room six times. Those sheets of paper, listing the four Queens who were interested in obtaining his services, had been offered to him at the first meeting. They had been the only ones offered.

Jorval folded his hands and sighed. "You must understand. A Warlord Prince is considered a dangerous asset, even when he wears a lighter Jewel and is serving among his own people. A man with your strength and reputation . . ." He shrugged. "I realize your expectations might be different. The Darkness knows, there are so many who have an unrealistic idea of life in Kaeleer. But I can assure you, Prince, that having four Queens who are willing to accept the challenge of having you serve in their courts for the next five years is unusual—and not an opportunity that should be brushed aside."

Daemon didn't give any indication that the warning had been felt as much as a physical jab would have been. No, he couldn't brush aside the narrow choices if he wanted to stay in Kaeleer. But he wasn't sure he could stomach any of those women long enough to do what he had originally come here to do. And he couldn't help wondering how large a gift Jorval would receive from whichever Queen he chose.

Suddenly it was too much: the lack of sleep, the pressure to make an unpalatable choice, the nerves that were strained because of what he had planned to do—and the questions that had arisen from the gossip he had sifted through as he walked around the service fair.

"I'll consider them and let you know," Daemon said, moving toward the door with the graceful speed that tended to make people think of a feline predator.

"Prince Sadi," Jorval called sharply.

Daemon stopped at the door and turned.

"The last bell will ring in less than an hour. If you haven't made a choice by then, you will no longer have a choice. You will have to accept whatever offer is made or leave Kaeleer."

"I'm aware of that, Lord Jorval," Daemon said too softly.

He left the building, slipped his hands into his trouser pockets, and began walking aimlessly.

He despised Lord Jorval. There was something about the man's psychic scent, something tainted. And there were too many things hidden behind the dark, flat eyes. From the moment he'd met Jorval, he'd had to fight against the instinctive desire to rise to the killing edge and tuck the thin Warlord into a deep, secret grave.

Why had Lord Magstrom handed him over to Jorval? He had talked to the elderly man briefly when he arrived in Goth late on the third day of the fair and had been cautiously willing to trust the man's judgment. When he had expressed his desire to serve in a court outside of Little Terreille, Magstrom's blue eyes had twinkled with amusement.

The Queens outside of Little Terreille are very selective in their choices, Magstrom had said. *But they do have an advantage for a man like you—they know how to handle dark-Jeweled males.*

Magstrom had promised to make some inquiries, and they had arranged to meet early the following morning. But when Daemon arrived for the meeting, it was Lord Jorval who was waiting for him with the names of four Queens who wanted to control his life for the next five years.

Questionable food smells that he caught in passing sharpened an already keen temper by reminding him that he'd eaten almost nothing in the past two days. The clash of strong perfumes mingled with equally strong body odors helped him remember why he hadn't eaten.

More than that, the inability to sleep and the lack of appetite were due to the questions that had no answers. At least, not here.

It had taken him five years after walking out of the Twisted Kingdom to come to Kaeleer. There had been no hurry. Jaenelle had not been waiting for him as she had promised when she had marked the trail to lead him out of madness. He *still* didn't know what had really happened when he had tried to bring Jaenelle out of the abyss in order to save her body. His memories of that night, thirteen years ago, were still jumbled, still had pieces missing. He had a vague memory of someone telling him that Jaenelle had died—that the High Lord had tricked another male into being the instrument that had destroyed an extraordinary child.

So when Jaenelle *hadn't* been on the island where Surreal and Manny had kept him safe and hidden, and when Surreal had told him about the shadow Jaenelle had created in order to bring him out of the Twisted Kingdom . . .

He had spent the past five years believing that he had killed the child who was his Queen; had spent the past five years believing that she had used the last of her strength to bring him out of madness so that he would call in the debt owed to her; had spent the past five years honing his Craft skills and allowing his mind to heal as much as it could for only one reason: to come to Kaeleer and destroy the man who had used him as the instrument—his father, the High Lord of Hell.

But now that he was here . . .

Gossip and speculation about the witches in the Shadow Realm flowed through this place, currents of thoughts easily plucked from the air. The currents that had unnerved him as he'd walked around the fair yesterday were the speculations about a strange, terrifying witch that could see a man's soul in a glance. According to the gossip, anyone who signed a contract outside of Little Terreille was brought before this witch, and anyone found wanting didn't live to see another sunrise.

He might have dismissed that gossip except that it finally occurred to him that, perhaps, Jaenelle *had* been waiting for him, but not in Terreille. He'd let grief cloud his thinking, locking away all but the best memories of the few months he had known her. So he'd forgotten about the ties she already had to Kaeleer.

If she really *was* in the Shadow Realm, he'd already lost five years he could have spent with her. He wasn't going to spend the next five in some other court, yearning from a distance.

If, that is, she really *was* alive.

A change in the psychic scents around him pulled him from his thoughts. He looked around and swore under his breath.

He was at the far end of the fairgrounds. Judging by the sky, he'd have to run in order to get back to the administrators' building and make a choice before the bell ending the last day of the fair rang. Even then, he might not have a choice if Jorval wasn't waiting for him.

As he turned to go back, he noticed one of the red banners that indicated a station where court contracts were filled out. There were a few Eyriens standing to one side, and a line of them waiting their turn. But it was the Eyrien warrior watching the proceedings that froze Daemon where he stood.

The man wore a leather vest and the black, skintight trousers favored by Eyrien warriors. His black hair fell to his shoulders, which was unusual for an Eyrien male. But it was the way he stood, the way he moved that felt so painfully familiar.

A wild joy filled Daemon, even as his heart clogged his throat and tears stung his gold eyes. *Lucivar.*

Of course, it couldn't be. Lucivar had died eight years ago, escaping from the salt mines of Pruul.

Then the man turned. For a moment, Daemon thought he saw the same fierce joy in Lucivar's eyes before it was lost in blazing fury.

Seeing the fury and remembering that the unfinished business between them could only end in blood being spilled, Daemon retreated behind the cold mask he'd lived behind for most of his life and started to walk away.

He'd only gone a few steps before a hand clamped on his right arm and spun him around.

"How long have you been here?" Lucivar demanded.

Daemon tried to shake off the hand, but Lucivar's fingers dug in hard enough to leave bruises. "Two days," Daemon replied with chilly courtesy. He felt the mask slip and knew he needed to get away from here before his emotions spilled over. Right now, he wasn't sure if he would meet Lucivar's anger with tears or rage.

"Have you signed a contract?" Lucivar shook him. "Have you?"

"No, and there's little time left to do it. If you'll excuse me."

Lucivar snarled, tightened his grip, and almost yanked Daemon off his feet. "You weren't on the lists," he muttered as he pulled Daemon toward the table under the red banner. "I checked. You weren't on any of the damn lists."

"I apologize for the incon—"

"Shut up, Daemon."

Daemon clenched his teeth and lengthened his stride to match his brother's. He didn't know what kind of game Lucivar was playing, but he'd be damned if he'd go into it being dragged like a reluctant puppy.

"Look, Prick," Daemon said, trying to balance Lucivar's volatile temper with reason, "I have to—"

"You're signing a contract with the Warlord Prince of Ebon Rih."

Daemon let out an exasperated huff. "Don't you think you should discuss it with him beforehand?"

Lucivar gave him a knife-edged look. "I don't usually discuss things with myself, Bastard. Plant your feet."

Daemon felt the ground roll unexpectedly and decided it was good advice. "Have long have you been in Kaeleer?" he asked, feeling weak.

"Eight years." Lucivar hissed as an older Eyrien Warlord signed the contract and stepped away from the table. "Hell's fire. Why is that little maggot taking so long to write a line of information?" He took a step toward the table. Then he turned back, and said too softly, "Don't try to walk away. If you do, I'll break your legs in so many places you won't even be able to crawl."

Daemon didn't bother to respond. Lucivar didn't make idle threats, and in a physical fight, Daemon knew he couldn't beat his Eyrien half brother. Besides, the ground under his feet kept shifting in unexpected ways that threatened his balance.

The Warlord Prince of Ebon Rih. Lucivar was the Warlord Prince of the territory that belonged to Ebon Askavi, the Black Mountain that was also called the Keep—that was also the Sanctuary of Witch.

That didn't necessarily mean anything. The land existed whether a Warlord Prince watched over it or not—or a Queen ruled there or not.

But Lucivar being alive here nourished the hope in Daemon that he had been wrong about Jaenelle's death as well. Had she sent Lucivar to the service fair to look for him? Had one of Lord Magstrom's inquiries reached her after all? Was she . . .

Daemon shook his head. Too many questions—and this wasn't the time or place to get answers. But, oh, how he began to hope.

As Lucivar approached the table, someone called, "Prince Yaslana. Here are two more for the contract."

Turning toward the voice, Daemon felt the ground shift a little more. Two men, a Sapphire-Jeweled Warlord and a Red-Jeweled Warlord Prince, were pulling two women toward the table. A brown-haired man with a black eye patch and a pronounced limp angrily followed them.

The frightened woman had dark hair, fair skin, and blue eyes. It had been thirteen years since he'd seen Wilhelmina Benedict, Jaenelle's half sister. She had grown into a beautiful woman, but was still filled with the brittle fear she'd had as an adolescent. Her eyes widened when she saw him, but she said nothing.

The snarling woman with the long black hair, light golden-brown skin, delicately pointed ears, and blazing gold-green eyes was Surreal. She had left the island four months ago, giving no explanation except there was something she had to do.

At first, he didn't know the limping man. When he saw the flash of recognition in the man's blue eye, he felt a stab of pain under his heart. Andrew, the stable lad who had helped him escape the Hayllian guards after Jaenelle had been taken back to Briarwood.

"Lord Khardeen. Prince Aaron," Lucivar said, formally greeting the Sapphire-Jeweled Warlord and the Red-Jeweled Warlord Prince.

"Prince Yaslana, these Ladies should be part of the contract," Prince Aaron said respectfully.

Lucivar gave both women a look that could have flayed flesh from bone. Then he looked at Khardeen and Aaron. "Accepted."

Wilhelmina trembled visibly, but Surreal hooked her hair behind her pointed ears and narrowed her eyes at Lucivar. "Look, sugar—"

"Surreal," Daemon said quietly. He shook his head. The last thing any of them needed was Surreal and Lucivar tangling with each other.

Surreal hissed. When she tried to shake off Prince Aaron's hand, the man let her go, then shifted to block any attempt she might make to leave. Eyeing Lucivar with intense dislike, she moved until she stood beside Daemon. "Is that your brother?" she asked in a low voice. "The one who's supposed to be dead?"

Daemon nodded.

She watched Lucivar for a minute. "*Is* he dead?"

For the first time since he'd arrived in Kaeleer, Daemon smiled. "The demon-dead can't tolerate daylight—at least according to the stories—so I would say Lucivar is very much alive."

"Well, can't you reason with him? I have a mark of safe passage and a three-month visitor's pass. I didn't come here to sign a contract for court service, and the day I jump when that son of a bitch snaps his fingers is the day the sun is going to shine in Hell."

"Don't make any bets on it," Daemon muttered, watching Lucivar study the member of the Dark Council who was filling out the contract.

Before Surreal could reply, Wilhelmina sidled over to them. "Prince Sadi," she said in a voice that trembled on the edge of panic. "Lady."

"Lady Benedict," Daemon replied formally while Surreal nodded in acknowledgment.

Wilhelmina glanced fearfully at Lucivar, who was now talking to the older Eyrien Warlord. "He's scary," she whispered.

Surreal smiled maliciously and raised her voice. "When a man wears his pants that tight, they tend to pinch his balls, and that tends to pinch his temper."

Aaron, who was standing near them, coughed violently, trying to muffle his laughter.

Seeing Lucivar break off his conversation and head toward them, Daemon sighed and wished he knew a spell that would make Surreal lose her voice for the next few hours.

Lucivar stopped an arm's length away, ignoring the way Wilhelmina shrank away from him, focusing his attention on Surreal. He smiled the lazy, arrogant smile that was usually the only warning before a fight.

Surreal lowered her right hand so that her arm hung at her side.

Recognizing that as *her* warning signal, Daemon slipped his hands out of his trouser pockets and shifted slightly, prepared to stop her before she was foolish enough to pull a knife on Lucivar.

"You're Titian's daughter, aren't you?" Lucivar asked.

"What do you care?" Surreal snarled.

Lucivar studied her for a moment. Then he shook his head and muttered, "You're going to be a pain in the ass."

"Then maybe you should let me go," Surreal said with sweet venom.

Lucivar laughed, low and nasty. "If you think I'm going to explain to the Harpy Queen why her daughter's in another court when I was standing here, then you'd better think again, little witch."

Surreal bared her teeth. "My mother is *not* a Harpy. And I'm not a little witch. And I'm not signing any damn contract that gives you control over me."

"Think again," Lucivar said.

Daemon's hand clamped on Surreal's right forearm. Aaron clamped down on her left arm.

The bell indicating the end of the service fair rang three times.

Surreal swore furiously. Lucivar just smiled.

Then a man's voice, rising in protest, made them all turn their attention toward the table.

Daemon caught sight of the fussily dressed man who was busily straightening papers and ignoring the young Eyrien Warlord.

Snarling, Lucivar strode to the table, slipped through the line of confused, upset Eyriens, and stopped beside the man who was still pretending not to notice any of them.

"Is there a problem, Lord Friall?" Lucivar asked mildly.

Friall shook back the lace at his wrists and continued to gather up his papers. "The bell ending the fair has rung. If these people are still available when you arrive tomorrow for claiming day, you can sign them to a contract under the first-offer rule."

Daemon tensed. Lord Jorval had explained the first-offer rule of the service fair several times. During the fair, immigrants had the right to refuse an offer to serve in a court, or wait to see if another offer was made from a different court, or try to negotiate for a better position. But the day after the service fair was a claiming day. There was only one choice. Immigrants could accept whatever was offered by the first court to fill out a claim for them—and Jorval had implied that any position offered at a claiming was usually a demeaning one—or they could return to Terreille and attempt to come back for the next fair. He had spent two million gold marks in bribes in order to get on the immigration list for this service fair. He had the means to do it again if he dared risk going back to Terreille. But most had spent everything they had for this one chance at a hopefully better life. They would sign a contract for the privilege of crawling if that was the only way to stay in Kaeleer.

"Now, Lord Friall," Lucivar said, still sounding mild, "you know as well as I do that a person has to be accepted before the final bell, but there's an hour afterward for the contracts to be filled out and signed."

"If you want to sign the contract for the ones already listed, you can take them with you now. The others will have to wait until tomorrow," Friall insisted.

Lucivar raised his right hand and scratched his chin.

The rest happened so fast, Daemon didn't even see the move. One moment, Lucivar was scratching his chin. The next, his Eyrien war blade was delicately resting on Friall's left wrist.

"Now," Lucivar said pleasantly, "you can finish filling out that contract or I can cut off your left hand. Your choice."

"Shit," Surreal muttered as she moved closer to Daemon.

"You can't do this," Friall whimpered.

Lucivar's hand didn't seem to move, but a thin line of blood began to flow from Friall's wrist.

"I'll inform the Council," Friall wailed. "You'll be in trouble."

"Maybe," Lucivar replied. "But you'll still be without a left hand. If you're lucky, that's all you'll lose. If you're not . . ."

A hurried movement made Daemon glance to the left. Lord Magstrom, the Dark Council member he had first talked with, stopped at the other end of the table.

"May I be of some assistance, Prince Yaslana?" the elderly man asked breathlessly.

Lucivar looked up, and Magstrom froze. The color drained from his face.

"Mother Night," Aaron muttered. "He's risen to the killing edge."

Daemon didn't move. Neither did anyone else. A Warlord Prince who had risen to the killing edge was violent and uncontrollable. He wore the Black, the only Jewel darker than Lucivar's Ebon-gray, but any effort he made to try to contain his brother would only snap whatever self-control Lucivar still had. At the very least, Friall would die. At the worst, there would be a slaughter.

"Lord Friall says the contracts can't be filled out after the last bell," Lucivar said with deceptive mildness.

"I'm sure he misunderstood," Magstrom replied quickly. "There's an hour's leniency after the last bell in order to fill out the papers." When Lucivar said nothing, he took a careful breath. "Lord Friall seems to be indisposed. With your permission, I will finish filling out the contracts."

By this time, the white lace around Friall's left wrist was a wet, bright red. Snot ran from the man's nose as he wept silently.

At Lucivar's slight nod, Magstrom pulled the papers away from the small pool of blood on the table and picked up the pen lying next to them. Retreating to the other end of the table, Magstrom sat down.

Lucivar raised his left hand and pointed at Daemon. "He's first."

Magstrom filled out the top of the contract and then looked at Daemon expectantly. Beads of sweat dotted his forehead.

Move, damn you, move. For a tense moment, Daemon's body refused to obey. When his legs finally started working, he had the chilling sensation that he was walking on thin, cracked ice where one false step could lead to disaster.

"Daemon Sadi," Magstrom said quietly, writing the name in neat script. "From Hayll, isn't that right?"

"Yes," Daemon replied. To his own ears, his voice sounded hoarse, hollow. If Magstrom noticed, the man gave no indication.

"When we met, I recall that you said you wore a dark Jewel, but I don't remember which one."

When he'd met with Magstrom, he'd said the Red was his Birthright Jewel, but he had evaded mentioning his Jewel of rank. There could be no evading now. "The Black."

Magstrom looked up, his eyes wide with shock. Then he quickly filled in the space on the paper. "And you brought two servants?"

"Manny is a White-Jeweled witch. Jazen is a Purple Dusk Warlord."

Magstrom wrote down the information, then turned the contract around. "Just sign here and then put your initials in the spaces for the other two signatures to indicate that you accept responsibility for your servants." As Daemon bent down to sign the contract, he whispered, "This court would have been my choice for you. You belong here."

Saying nothing, Daemon stepped away from the table to make room for Surreal. He glanced once at Lucivar, whose glazed gold eyes just stared at him.

"Name?" Magstrom asked.

"Surreal."

When she didn't say anything else, Magstrom said gently, "While they are not often used in Kaeleer, it is customary to formally record a family name."

Surreal stared at him. Then she smiled maliciously. "SaDiablo."

Magstrom gasped. Khardeen and Aaron gaped at her for a moment before turning away from the table.

Daemon closed his eyes and didn't listen to the rest of her answers. Since she was Kartane SaDiablo's bastard daughter, she had probably intended it as a slap against his mother, Dorothea. There was no reason for her to know that the name had meaning in Kaeleer.

"Hell's fire, Mother Night, and may the Darkness be merciful," two voices said in unison.

Daemon opened his eyes. Aaron and Khardeen stood in front of him, watching Surreal move away from the table.

Aaron looked at him. "Is that really her family name?"

Daemon hesitated. He didn't know what kind of stigma being a bastard carried in Kaeleer, and he owed Surreal too much to reveal a potentially vulnerable spot. "The man who sired her goes by that name," he replied cautiously.

"What do you think we should do?" Aaron asked Khardeen.

"Sell tickets," Khardeen replied promptly. "And then find a safe place to watch the explosion."

Their amusement at Surreal's expense made Daemon's temper flash. "Is this going to be a problem?"

"You could say that," Khardeen said gleefully. Then he settled his face into a serious expression. "You see, what Lady Surreal hasn't realized yet is that by formally declaring herself as part of the SaDiablo family, she's just acquired Lucivar as a cousin."

"And if you think Lucivar has a dominating personality with other males, you should see him with the women in the family," Aaron added.

And with Jaenelle?

The question went unspoken because he didn't want to see a blank expression on their faces when they heard the name—and because he wasn't sure what he would do if he saw recognition. It would be better to ask Lucivar that question—in private. And the questions he now had about women and family . . . Those, too, would be asked later.

"And we're not even going to try to imagine what's going to happen when she tangles with the males on the Dea al Mon side of her family," Khardeen said.

"Why should they be involved at all?" Daemon asked.

"Because she's Titian's daughter, finally come home," Aaron said. Then he grinned. "Lady Surreal is about to find out that she now has male relatives from both her bloodlines who are going to make her life their business—and several of those males are Warlord Princes."

Mother Night! "She's never going to tolerate that," Daemon said.

"Well, she's not going to have a lot of choice," Khardeen replied.

"The Blood are matriarchal. Isn't that true in Kaeleer?"

"Of course," Aaron said cheerfully. "But males do have rights and privileges, and we take full advantage of them." He studied Daemon for a moment. "Why don't you try to keep her calm while we keep an eye on Lucivar. If nobody pushes him, he should be able to keep his temper leashed."

"Do you know him that well?" Daemon asked.

He saw the knowledge in their eyes that they had kept carefully masked until now. They knew he was Lucivar's brother. And they knew . . .

"We all serve in the same court, Prince Sadi," Aaron said quietly. "We all serve in the Lady's First Circle."

Then they walked away from him.

They might as well have shouted it from the rooftops. *She's alive!*

Joy and trepidation warred inside him, causing his heart to pound too hard, his blood to whip through his veins too fast. *She's alive!*

But what did she think of him? What did she *feel* for him?

No answers. Not here. Not yet.

With exaggerated care, Daemon walked over to Surreal. The moment he stopped moving, he swayed like a willow in a heavy wind.

Surreal wrapped her arms around his left arm and planted her feet. "What's wrong?" she asked quietly, urgently. "Are you ill?"

She, better than anyone, would be able to guess exactly what was wrong, but he wasn't about to admit it. Not now. "I've had almost no sleep and very little food in the past few days," he said.

She narrowed her eyes but accepted the truth that was also a lie. "I can understand that. This place makes my skin crawl."

Daemon tapped into the reservoir of power stored in his Black Jewel. It rushed through his body, and for the first time since he'd seen Lucivar, he felt steady.

Surreal sensed the change in him. She loosened her grip, but still kept one arm companionably linked with his. "Why do you think the old Warlord doing the contracts looked so shocked when I said my family name was SaDiablo? Is that bitch Dorothea that well-known here?"

"I don't know," Daemon said carefully. "But I have heard that the name of the Warlord Prince of Dhemlan is S. D. SaDiablo." This wasn't the time to tell her that the Warlord Prince of Dhemlan was also the High Lord of Hell—and his and Lucivar's father.

"Shit," Surreal muttered. Then she shrugged. "Well, I'm not likely to meet him, and if someone asks, I can just say that we *might* be distantly related. Very distantly."

Remembering Khardeen's and Aaron's comments, Daemon made a sound that might have been a whimper.

"You sure you're all right?" Surreal asked, studying him.

"I'm fine." Just fine. More than fine. He would believe it, insist on it, until it was true. "Do me a favor. Ask Khardeen or Aaron if we're going to be traveling in the Web Coaches, and then contact Manny so that she and Jazen can meet us there."

She didn't ask why he didn't do it himself, and he was grateful.

Finally, the last Eyrien had signed the contract and moved away from the table. Lucivar, who hadn't moved or said anything since Lord Magstrom started filling out the contracts, called in a clean cloth, wiped the blood off his war blade, vanished both, and walked around the table to sign the contracts.

Holding his bleeding wrist against his chest, Friall wiped his nose on his clean sleeve and said in a sulky voice, "You have to make copies. He can't take the contracts until you make copies."

Lucivar slowly straightened up and turned toward Friall.

A male voice swore softly.

Giving Friall a sharp glance, Magstrom said hurriedly, "I'll give Prince Yaslana blank contracts. The Steward of the Court can make the copies and return them to the Dark Council for the clerks to record." When Friall seemed about to protest, and surely get himself killed, Magstrom added, "I've seen Lord Jorval do this a number of times. He explained that the Stewards could be trusted to make an accurate copy, and it was the only way to expedite getting the immigrants settled in their new homes."

Calling in a thin leather case, Lucivar slipped the contracts inside and then vanished it. He nodded politely at Magstrom, turned to face the waiting immigrants, and snarled, "Let's go."

Daemon turned smoothly as Lucivar approached him and matched the Eyrien's stride.

They had walked like this before, side by side. Not often, because the Terreillean Blood, who were afraid of them individually, were terrified of them when they were together. Even the Ring of Obedience hadn't been enough to stop the destruction they had caused in Terreillean courts.

As they headed for the Coaches that were designed to ride the Winds, Daemon wondered how long they could put off the unfinished business between them.

It was almost full dark by the time they reached the two large, Ebon-gray shielded Coaches at the far end of the landing area.

Lucivar dropped the Ebon-gray shields, opened the door of the first Coach, looked at Daemon, and said, "Get in."

Daemon glanced around. "My servants aren't here yet."

"I'll look for them. Get in."

Looking at Lucivar's still-glazed eyes, and picking up a strained urgency in his brother's psychic scent, Daemon obeyed.

Surreal, Wilhelmina, and Andrew quickly came in behind him, followed by several Eyriens. A minute later, Daemon breathed a sigh of relief as Jazen helped Manny up the steps into the Coach. A couple more Eyriens came in, and then an Ebon-gray shield snapped up around the Coach, effectively locking everyone but Daemon inside, since he was the only one who wore a Jewel darker than Lucivar's.

A Web Coach this size could usually accommodate thirty people, but Eyriens required more room because of their wings. Noticing the lack of seats, Daemon wondered if the Coach was usually used for conveying something other than humans, or if Lucivar, intending to bring Eyriens, had had the usual seats removed. The only thing that could be used for seats were a few sturdy wooden boxes pushed up against the walls, with cushions on top of them and an open front for storage.

After studying the people packed against the walls in order to leave a narrow aisle in the center, Daemon turned his attention to the Coach. At the front was a door that led to the driver's compartment. Maybe one other person could sit with the driver, giving the rest a little breathing room. Moving carefully, Daemon made his way to the short, narrow corridor at the back of the Coach. On the left was a small private room that held a narrow desk and a straight chair, an easy chair and hassock, and a single bed. The room on the right held a sink and toilet.

Daemon was about to step back into the main compartment when he heard Lucivar's voice just outside the Coach's open door.

"I don't give a damn what that sniveling little maggot says," Lucivar snarled.

"Lord Friall's conduct is not in question here," said a voice Daemon recognized as Lord Jorval's. "This will be brought before the Dark Council, and I can assure you we will not be intimidated into ignoring your vicious conduct."

"You have a problem with me, you can take it up with the Steward, the Master of the Guard, or my Queen."

"Your Queen fears you," Jorval sneered. "Everyone knows that. She can't control you properly, and the Steward and Master of the Guard certainly aren't going to demand any restraints on your temper since it suits their purpose so well."

Lucivar's voice lowered to a malevolent hiss. "Just remember, Lord Jorval, that while you and Friall are whining to the Council, I'm going to make the Territory Queens aware that there are some members of the Council who blatantly ignore their own rules about the service fair."

"That is an outright lie!"

"Then Friall is incompetent and shouldn't be given the task."

"Friall is one of the finest members of the Council!"

"In that case, was he just pissed because he'd expected to get his percentage of the bribes at the table and didn't realize you'd already pocketed them?"

"How dare you!" A long pause followed. "Perhaps Lord Friall was partly responsible for this unfortunate incident, but the Council will stand firm about this other matter."

"And what matter is that?" Lucivar crooned.

"We cannot allow you to have in your service a male who wears Jewels darker than yours."

"The Queens in Little Terreille do it all the time."

"They're Queens. They know how to control males."

"So do I."

"The Council forbids it."

"The Council can go to the bowels of Hell."

Lucivar suddenly filled the Coach's doorway.

"You can't do this!" Jorval yelled from behind him.

Lucivar turned and gave Jorval a lazy, arrogant smile. "I'm an Ebon-gray Warlord Prince. I can do anything I damn well want to." He shut the door in Jorval's face, then glanced at the driver's compartment at the front of the Coach, sending an order on a psychic thread. The Coach immediately lifted.

When Daemon took a step to reenter the main compartment, Lucivar shifted in front of him, effectively blocking the mouth of the corridor. Accepting the unspoken order, Daemon slipped his hands into his trouser pockets and leaned against the wall.

When he felt sure that Lucivar was through giving his silent instructions to whoever was driving the Coaches, he used an Ebon-gray spear thread to ask, ★Will this get you into trouble?★

★No,★ Lucivar replied. He looked over the immigrants. Every one of them quickly looked away in order to avoid meeting his eyes.

★Won't this Council send a demand for some kind of discipline?★

★They'll send it. The Steward will read it, probably show it to the Master of the Guard, and then they'll ignore it.★

Daemon realized his breathing was too quick, too shallow, but he couldn't change it as he forced himself to ask the next question. ★Will they show it to your Queen?★

★No,★ Lucivar said slowly. ★They won't mention this to the Queen if they can avoid it. And if they can't, they'll try to minimize it without lying outright.★

★Why?★

Because the Dark Council has pushed her before, and the results scared the shit out of everyone. Lucivar shifted. "We're away from Goth," he said, raising his voice slightly. "Make yourselves as comfortable as you can. It'll be a couple of hours before we get to where we're going."

"Aren't we going to Ebon Rih?" someone asked.

"Not yet." Lucivar stepped into the small corridor, forcing Daemon to move back. He slid the door to the private compartment open, said, "Inside," and went through the doorway sideways to accommodate his wings.

Daemon followed reluctantly and slid the door closed.

Lucivar stood at one end of the room. Daemon remained at the door.

Lucivar took a deep breath, let it out slowly. "I'm sorry I lashed out at you. I wasn't angry with *you*. I—Damn it, Daemon, I checked every list I could think of, and I must have missed your name. If it wasn't for blind luck, you would've ended up in another court, and there might have been no way to get you out of that contract."

Daemon felt one layer of tension ease. He forced his lips to curve in a smile. "Well, luck favored us this time." Then he looked, really looked, at Lucivar, and the smile became genuine. "You're alive."

Lucivar returned the smile. "And you're sane."

Daemon felt a tremor run through his body and tightened his self-control. Tears stung his eyes. "Lucivar," he whispered.

He didn't know which of them moved first. One moment they were standing as far away from each other as they could in the small room, the next they were in each other's arms, holding on as if their lives depended on it.

"Lucivar," Daemon whispered again, pressing his face against his brother's neck. "I thought you were dead."

"Hell's fire, Daemon," Lucivar said softly, hoarsely, "we couldn't find you. We didn't know what happened to you. We looked. I swear, we did look for you."

"It's all right," Daemon stroked Lucivar's head. "It's all right."

Lucivar's arms tightened around him so hard his ribs ached.

Daemon's hand fisted in Lucivar's hair. "Lucivar . . . I know there are things that need to be settled between us. But can we put them aside, just for a little while?"

"We can put them aside," Lucivar said quietly.

Daemon stepped back. Using his thumbs, he gently wiped the tears from Lucivar's face. "We'd better join the others." He turned and reached for the door.

Standing behind him, Lucivar's left hand gripped Daemon's left arm. Daemon placed his right hand over it for a moment. As his fingers slid away from Lucivar's, he looked down, and the significance of what he'd seen but hadn't really *seen* finally hit him.

"Daemon," Lucivar said urgently. "There's one thing I need to tell you. I think you may already know, but you need to hear it."

She's alive! Another tremor went through Daemon's body. "No," he said. "Not now." He slid the door open and stumbled into the corridor. Barely keeping his balance, he went into the bathroom and Black-locked the door. His body shook violently. His stomach twisted viciously. Leaning over the sink, he fought the need to be sick.

Too late.

If he had tried to find her five years ago, when he'd first returned from the Twisted Kingdom, maybe it would have been different. If he had searched for the High Lord and at least tried to find out what had really happened that night at Cassandra's Altar . . .

Too late.

He could hold on. He *would* hold on. His mind was far more fragile than he allowed anyone to realize. Oh, it was intact. He had lost a few memories, a few small shards of the crystal chalice, but he was whole, and he was sane. But the healing would never be complete because he had lost the one person he needed to complete it. It hadn't mattered when he had only wanted to stay in one piece long enough to destroy the High Lord. It didn't really matter now. He could survive long enough to see her, just once.

There was nothing else he could do. If it had been any other man, he would have used everything he was and everything he knew in order to be her lover. If it had been any other man. But not Lucivar. He wouldn't become his brother's rival.

So he couldn't let Lucivar tell him what he desperately needed to hear. Not because he didn't want to know for sure that Jaenelle was alive, but because he wasn't ready to be told about the gold wedding ring on Lucivar's left hand.

3 / Kaeleer

Surreal pushed the last of the cushioned boxes together to form a bench against one wall. "Sit down, Manny," she said to the older woman.

"Wouldn't be right," Manny said. "A servant shouldn't be sitting."

Surreal gave her a slashing look. "Don't be an ass. You're a 'servant' because that's the only way Sadi could bring you with him."

Manny tightened her lips in disapproval. "No need for you to be using that kind of language, especially with children around. Besides, I was a servant for a good many years. It was an honest living and nothing I'm ashamed of."

Unlike me? Surreal wondered. She had never denied that she had been a very successful whore for centuries before she quit thirteen years ago, no longer able to stomach the bedroom games. That night at Cassandra's Altar had left its mark on all of them.

Manny's feelings about women who worked in Red Moon houses were ambivalent. What would she think if she knew about Surreal's other profession? How comfortable would the older woman have been if she had known that Surreal had been—and still was—a very successful assassin?

Didn't matter. They had become friends during the two years when Daemon had been rising out of the Twisted Kingdom, but after he regained his sanity, Manny had made a mental shift, treating both of them to the domestic affection that existed between a special servant and an aristo child. Daemon hadn't noticed anything odd about this behavior; maybe Manny had always treated him like that. But it had annoyed Surreal, who had grown up hard and fast on the streets. It had also given her a lot of practice in dealing with Manny's set opinions.

"Look," she said very softly. "Lady Benedict's servant doesn't look like he can stand up for two hours without being in pain. If you sit down, you can badger him into sitting."

A few minutes later, Manny, Andrew, Wilhelmina Benedict, and Surreal were sitting on the makeshift bench.

Surreal glanced at the remaining space on her right. Where in the name of Hell was Sadi? He wasn't as mentally stable as he pretended to be, and seeing Lucivar must have been a shock. But what had the *Eyrien* thought about seeing his half brother again? After Jaenelle disappeared thirteen years ago, Daemon had gone to Pruul, intending to get Lucivar out of the salt mines. For some reason, Lucivar had refused to go with him. She had always suspected, because of what Daemon wouldn't say, that there had been a vicious collision of tempers and that a rift had formed between them. And she had always suspected that the reason for that rift had begun, like so many other things, at Cassandra's Altar.

The driver's compartment door slid open. Lord Khardeen stepped out and glanced at the Eyriens, who tensed at his appearance. Saying nothing, he walked to the end of the makeshift bench and sat down beside Surreal.

Directly across from them was the woman with the two young children. They had the brown skin, gold eyes, and black hair that was typical of the three long-lived races, but the little girl's hair had a slight, natural curl. Surreal wondered if the girl's hair indicated that one of the parent's bloodlines wasn't pure Eyrien, if those curls had betrayed a secret, and if that was the reason these people had left their home Territory.

The older boy stayed close to his mother, but the little girl smiled at Khardeen and took a couple of steps toward him.

"Woofer," she said happily, holding out a worn stuffed animal.

Khardeen leaned forward and smiled. "That he is. What's his name?"

"Woofer." She gave the toy a squeezing hug. "Mine."

"Right you are."

Watching Khardeen apprehensively, the woman reached for the little girl. "Orian, don't bother the Warlord."

"She's no bother," Khardeen said pleasantly.

The woman pulled the girl close to her and tried to smile. "She likes animals. My husband's mother made her a girl doll before we left, but Orian wanted to bring this one."

And where was your own mother while that bitch was giving you a verbal knife? Surreal wondered as she watched shadows gather in the woman's eyes and picked up a flicker of shame in the psychic scent. Well, that answered which side of the girl's heritage was in question.

The Warlord who had protested when Friall refused to finish the contract turned away from his conversation with a couple of Eyrien males, glanced sharply at Khardeen, and then moved protectively closer to the woman and children.

Khardeen leaned back, returning that sharp glance with a mild look.

Sitting next to him, with his arm brushing hers, Surreal felt his tension—and anger?—but he gave no outward sign of it. When he looked at her, his expression was solemn, but his blue eyes held amusement.

"I wonder how the little Queen's mother will react when she sees the 'woofers' her daughter's going to be hugging," he said softly.

"Will they bite her?" Surreal asked.

"The girl? No. The mother?" Khardeen shrugged.

Hearing the warning underneath the amusement, Surreal shivered. Then Daemon approached them, and she took a sharp breath.

He moved carefully, like a man who had received a fatal wound and was quietly bleeding to death.

Khardeen stood up and gestured toward the vacated seat. "Why don't you sit down? I've got a couple of things to see to."

As soon as Daemon sat down, he wrapped his arms around himself.

She'd seen that protective gesture before, when he had been pushing too hard at his Craft studies, when dreams had haunted his sleep.

Khardeen gave her a questioning look. She shook her head. She appreciated his concern, but there was nothing anyone could do for Daemon just then except let him retreat until he felt strong enough to face the world again.

A minute later, Lucivar came out of the private room, his expression carefully blank.

For the rest of the journey, Daemon sat beside her with his eyes closed and Lucivar stood near the back of the Coach, talking quietly to the Eyrien males who cautiously approached him.

For the rest of the journey, she wondered what had happened in that private room. And she worried.

4 / Kaeleer

Lord Jorval cowered in the chair and watched the Dark Priestess storm around the outer room of the suite he'd rented for this meeting.

Red Moon houses hadn't existed in Kaeleer until four years ago—and *still* didn't exist anywhere outside of Little Terreille. But certain influential Council members, himself included, had argued that the stronger immigrating males, who had little chance of having a Kaeleer-born woman for a lover, needed some way to relieve their sexual tension. The Queens in Little Terreille had yielded to the argument with no more than a token protest since they quickly recognized the usefulness of such places. Now a visit to a Red Moon house became a way of rewarding males for good behavior in the Queens' courts. They could take their frustrations and aggressions out on women who couldn't refuse them, who couldn't demand courtesy and obedience. And no one noticed—or cared, if they did—that all the women in those houses were immigrants who had been claimed the day after a service fair.

And some Kaeleer males, himself included, had discovered the pleasure that could be had from a cringing woman's obedience.

He'd chosen this Red Moon house, on the edge of the slums that had sprung up near the fairground, because the proprietors wouldn't ask any questions. The two men who owned the place didn't care if a woman was damaged physically or mentally, as long as they were suitably compensated. And they wouldn't care about the youth who was now bound and gagged in the other room—the offering he had brought in the hopes it would lessen the Dark Priestess's rage.

Hekatah threw off the cloak that had shrouded her face and body.

Jorval swallowed hard. He had become violently ill once at the sight of her decaying, demon-dead body. Her punishment for his lack of control had given him nightmares for months.

There were times when he desperately wished he'd never met her or become entangled in her schemes. But she had been behind his rise to power in the Dark Council, and he had discovered that she owned him before he even realized he had agreed to serve her.

"There were four Queens suitable for our purpose," Hekatah snarled. "*Four*. And you still couldn't manage to get him tucked away until we found a way to use him."

"I tried, Priestess," Jorval said, his voice quivering. "I blocked the inquiries Sadi made about serving outside of Little Terreille. Those were the only names I offered him."

"Then why isn't he with one of them?"

"He walked out of the last meeting," Jorval cried. " I didn't know he had signed another contract until Friall told me."

"He signed another contract," Hekatah crooned. *"With his brother!"*

Jorval's chest jerked with the effort to breathe. "I tried to stop it! I tried . . ." His voice trailed off as Hekatah slowly approached him.

"You didn't handle him well," she said, her girlish voice becoming dangerously gentle. "Because of that, he's now connected with the court we wanted unaware of his presence in Kaeleer, and we have no way of using that Black-Jeweled strength for our own purposes."

Jorval tried to get up. Fear clogged his throat when he realized she was using Craft to keep him pinned to the chair.

She settled gracefully in his lap and wrapped one arm around his neck. As her long nails brushed against his cheek, he wondered if he was going to lose an eye. Maybe that would be best. Blind, he wouldn't be able to see her. On second thought, no. She wore darker Jewels than he did. She could force his mind open and leave an image that was a hundred times worse than her actual appearance.

He whimpered as his stomach rolled ominously.

"Just as there are rewards for success, there are penalties for failure," Hekatah said as she stroked his face.

Knowing what was required, he whispered, "Yes, Priestess."

"And you did fail me, didn't you, darling?"

"Y-Yes, Priestess."

What was left of her lips curved in a smile. Using Craft, she called in a stoppered crystal bottle and a small silver cup. They floated in the air while she removed the stopper and poured the dark, thick liquid into the cup. She closed the bottle and vanished it, then held the cup up to Jorval's lips.

"I brought you a fresh offering," he said weakly.

"I saw him. Such a pretty boy, full of the hot sweet wine." She pressed the cup against his lower lip. "I'll get to him shortly."

Having no choice, Jorval opened his mouth. The liquid slid over his tongue like a long warm slug. He gagged on it, but managed to swallow.

"Is it poison?" he asked.

Hekatah vanished the cup and leaned back, her eyes widening in surprise. "Do you really think I would poison a man who's loyal to me? And you are loyal to me, aren't you, darling?" She shook her head sadly. "No, darling, this is just a little aphrodisiac brew."

"S-*Safframate?*" He would have preferred poison.

"Just enough to make the evening interesting," Hekatah replied.

He sat there, helpless, while she caressed skin that began to quiver at the slightest touch. Groaning, he wrapped his arms around her, no longer noticing the smell of decay, no longer caring about who or what she was, no longer caring about anything except using the female body that was sitting on his lap.

When he tried to thrust his tongue into her mouth, she pulled back with a satisfied laugh.

"Now, darling," she said while she caressed him, "you're going to bring one of those whores up here."

The lust-fog cleared a little. "Up here?"

"We still have to take care of your punishment," Hekatah said gently, viciously. "Get one that has golden hair and blue eyes."

The lust became fierce, almost painful. "Like Jaenelle Angelline."

"Exactly. Think of this as a little rehearsal for the day when that pale bitch has to submit to me." She kissed his temple, licked the throbbing pulse. "Will it excite you if I sip a little blood while you're locked inside her?"

Jorval stared at her, wildly aroused and terrified.

"I'll drink from her, too. By then you won't care if you're mounting a corpse, but I won't do that to you, darling. This is just a rehearsal, after all, for the night when you'll have Jaenelle under you."

"Yes," Jorval whispered. "Yes."

"Yes," Hekatah echoed, satisfied. She stood up and slowly walked to the bedroom door. "Don't worry about the whore telling anyone about our little game. I'll fog the bitch's mind so that she'll never be certain about anything except that she was well used."

Rising, Jorval moved unsteadily to the outer door, painfully aware that Hekatah watched him.

"The pretty boy will be the appetizer and the dessert," Hekatah said. "Fear gives blood such a delightfully piquant taste, and by the end of the evening, he'll be fully ripened. So don't spend too much time making your choice, darling. An appetizer doesn't take long to consume, and if I become impatient, we may have to adjust your punishment. And you wouldn't want that, would you?"

He waited until the bedroom door closed behind her before whispering, "No, I wouldn't want that."

5 / Kaeleer

A warm hand gently squeezed his shoulder.

"Daemon," Lucivar said quietly. "Come on, old son. We've arrived."

Daemon reluctantly opened his eyes. He wanted to withdraw from the world, wanted to sink into the abyss and just disappear. Soon, he promised himself. Soon. "I'm all right, Prick," he said wearily. It was a lie, and they both knew it.

Getting stiffly to his feet, Daemon rolled his shoulders. His muscles hummed with tension while a violent headache gathered behind his eyes. "Where are we?"

Saying nothing, Lucivar guided him out of the Coach.

Surreal stood just outside the Coach's door, staring up at the massive, gray stone building. "Hell's fire, Mother Night, and may the Darkness be merciful. What is this place?"

Prince Aaron grinned at her. "SaDiablo Hall."

"Oh, shit."

The ground spun under Daemon's feet. He flung out an arm. Lucivar grabbed him, steadied him. "I can't," he whispered. "Lucivar, I can't."

"Yes, you can." Holding his arm, Lucivar led him to the double front doors. "It'll be easier than you think. Besides, Ladvarian's been waiting to meet you."

Daemon didn't have the energy to wonder, much less care, why this Ladvarian wanted to meet him, not when the next step might bring him face-to-face with the High Lord again—or Jaenelle.

Lucivar pushed the doors open. Daemon followed him into the great hall, the rest of the immigrants crowding behind him. They'd only gone a few steps when Lucivar stopped suddenly and swore under his breath.

Daemon glanced around, trying to understand the flash of wariness he'd picked up from Lucivar. At the far end of the hall, a maid knelt under one of the crystal chandeliers, wiping the floor. A few feet away from them stood a large Red-Jeweled Warlord dressed in a butler's uniform. His expression was more icy than stoic.

Eyeing the butler, Lucivar said cautiously, "Beale."

"Prince Yaslana," Beale replied with stiff formality.

Lucivar winced. "What—"

Someone giggled. They all looked up.

High overhead, a naked Eyrien boy, barely more than a toddler, balanced precariously on the nearest chandelier.

Lucivar glanced at Beale, sighed, and took a couple of steps forward. "What are you doing up there, boyo?"

"Flyin'," the toddler said.

"Take a guess," the maid growled as she dropped her cloth into a bucket and got to her feet.

"Slipped past your keepers, did you?" Lucivar muttered.

The toddler giggled again and then made a very rude noise.

"Come down, Daemonar," Lucivar said sternly.

"No!"

Tears stung Daemon's eyes as he stared at the boy. He swallowed hard to get his heart out of his throat.

Lucivar took another step forward and slowly spread his dark, membranous wings. "If you don't come down, I'll come up and get you."

Daemonar spread his little wings. "No!"

Lucivar shot into the air. As he passed the chandelier, he made a grab for Daemonar, who ducked and dove. The boy flew like a drunken bumblebee trying to elude a hawk, but he managed to stay out of reach.

"Boy's got some good moves," Hallevar said approvingly, moving to the front of the crowd.

Surreal glanced at the older Eyrien Warlord. "He seems to be getting the better of Yaslana."

Hallevar snorted as Lucivar swept past Daemonar and tickled his foot, making the boy squeal and dodge. "He could have caught him on the first pass. The young one will have to concede the battle, but it'll stay in his mind that he put up a good fight. No, Lucivar understands how to train an Eyrien warrior."

Daemon barely heard them. Hell's fire! Couldn't Lucivar see the boy was getting tired? Was he going to push until the baby fell to the floor?

As the toddler headed toward him, he stepped forward, reached up, and grabbed one chubby leg.

Daemonar shrieked and furiously flapped his little wings.

Pulling down gently, Daemon wrapped his other arm around Daemonar, drawing the boy against his chest.

A small fist smacked his chin. The other small hand grabbed a handful of his hair and yanked, making his eyes water. An indignant shriek lanced his ear and made his head vibrate.

Lucivar landed and rubbed the back of his hand against his mouth. It didn't quite erase the smile. Hooking his left arm around the boy's middle, he carefully pried open the small hand. "Let go of your Uncle Daemon. We want him to like you." He stepped back quickly, then he tethered the boy's feet with one hand and growled, "That's not a good place to kick your father."

Daemonar made a rude noise and grinned.

Lucivar looked at the squirming boy and said ruefully, "At the time, you seemed like a good idea."

"Yeah!" Then Daemonar noticed the woman holding the little girl. "Baby!" he shouted, squirming to get loose. "Mine!"

"Mother Night," Lucivar muttered, turning to block Daemonar's view.

Two wet, disheveled women entered the hall. One of them held up a large towel. "We'll take him, Prince Yaslana."

"Thank the Darkness." With a little effort, Lucivar and the two women got Daemonar bundled up in the towel and out of the great hall.

Watching them, Daemon's heart ached. The boy looked like Lucivar. He wasn't sure if he felt regretful or relieved that there was no hint of sapphire in the child's gold eyes, no lightening of the black hair and brown skin, no trace of the mother's exotic beauty.

Lucivar returned quickly.

"Once the guests are settled in their rooms, dinner will be served in the formal dining room," Beale said.

"Thank you, Beale," Lucivar replied a bit meekly.

"Are there any arrangements the household should be aware of?"

Lucivar made a "come-here" gesture to the young Warlord who had remained protectively close to the woman with the two young children. "This is Lord Endar, Lady Dorian's husband."

Endar stiffened under Beale's scrutiny.

Prince Aaron wrapped a hand around Surreal's arm and pulled her forward. "I'll escort Lady SaDiablo and Lady Benedict to their rooms."

"Lady SaDiablo?" Beale said, startled.

Aaron grinned.

Surreal hissed.

"I'm sure the High Lord will be pleased to welcome the Lady," Beale said, a suspicious twinkle in his eyes.

Before Surreal could stop him, Aaron brushed her hair back, revealing a delicately pointed ear. "So will Prince Chaosti."

Beale's lips twitched. Then he resumed his stoic demeanor and turned to the immigrants. "Those of you who are here as servants will follow Holt," he said, indicating the waiting footman. "The rest of you will follow me."

As soon as all the Eyriens except Prince Falonar had left the great hall, along with Manny, Jazen, and Andrew, Surreal turned to Lucivar. "Shouldn't you have told him to let the children stay with their parents? I doubt they're going to feel easy, being in a strange place."

Prince Aaron vigorously cleared his throat.

Lord Khardeen tipped his head back and studied the ceiling.

Lucivar just stared at her for a moment before saying slowly, "If you want to tell Beale or Helene how to run this place, you go right ahead and try. Just let me get out of the line of fire before you do."

"Come on, Lady Surreal," Aaron said. "Let's get you settled in before you start bringing the place down around us."

Lucivar waited until Aaron and Khardeen had escorted Surreal and Wilhelmina out of the hall before turning to Falonar. "What?"

Falonar squared his shoulders. "Why did you single out Endar?"

"As long as the household knows that Endar is Dorian's husband, no one will challenge his being in her bed. And believe me, there are males here who won't hesitate to tear him apart if they aren't made aware that he's in her bed by her choice." He took a deep breath, let it out slowly. "I'll explain the rules tomorrow. For tonight, just tell the men to keep their distance from all the women." He paused, and then added, "You'd better get settled in. We'll be here for a few days."

After Falonar left, Lucivar turned to Daemon. "Come on. Let's finish this so we can both get some food and rest."

Daemon followed Lucivar up the staircase in the informal receiving room and through the labyrinth of corridors. After a couple of minutes of silence, he said, "You named him Daemonar."

"It was the closest I could come and still keep the name Eyrien," Lucivar said quietly, his voice a little thick.

"I'm flattered."

Lucivar snorted. "Well, you would have been when he was an infant. Once he got his feet under him, he turned into a little beast." He raked a hand through his shoulder-length hair. "And it is *not* all my fault. I didn't do this by myself. But nobody seems to remember that."

"I can't imagine why," Daemon said dryly, watching Lucivar swell with indignation.

"When he does something adorable, he's his mother's son. When he does something clever, he's the High Lord's grandson. But when he acts like a rotten little beast, he's *my* son." Lucivar rubbed his chest. "Sometimes I swear he does things just to see if my heart will stop."

"Like tonight?"

Lucivar waved his hand dismissively. "No, that was just . . . just . . . shit. What can I tell you? He's a little beast."

They turned a corner and almost ran into a lovely Eyrien woman. She wore a long, practical nightgown and clutched a thick book.

"Your son," she said, spacing out the words, "is not a beast."

"Never mind that," Lucivar said, narrowing his eyes. "Marian, why aren't you in bed? You should be resting today."

Marian let out her breath in an exasperated huff. "I dozed for most of the morning. I played with Daemonar for a little while this afternoon, and then we both took a nap. I just got up to borrow a book. I'm going to get tucked back in before Beale brings up a cup of hot chocolate and a plate of biscuits."

Lucivar's eyes narrowed a little. "Didn't you eat today?"

Daemon stared at Lucivar in amazement. Even an idiot—or an Eyrien male—should be able to tell that this woman was silently sputtering.

"Uncle Andulvar checked on me to make sure I had eaten a good breakfast. Prothvar brought me a midmorning snack. I ate lunch with Daemonar. Sure that I must be starving, Mephis brought me a midafternoon snack. And your father already inquired about what I ate for dinner. I've been fussed over enough today."

"I'm not fussing," Lucivar growled—and then added under his breath, "I haven't had a chance to fuss."

Marian looked pointedly at Daemon. "Shouldn't you be looking after your guests?"

"He's not a guest. He's my brother."

Smiling warmly, Marian held out her hand. "You must be Daemon. Oh, I'm so glad you've finally come. Now I have another brother."

Brother? Taking her hand, Daemon gave Lucivar a quizzical look.

Running a possessive hand down Marian's waist-length hair, Lucivar said warmly, "Marian does me the honor of being my wife."

And Daemonar's mother. The floor dropped out from under Daemon and then came up again fast and hard.

Marian squeezed his hand, her eyes filled with concern. Lucivar's gaze was sharper.

Emotions collided in him, banging against his fragile sanity. Unable to offer them any reassurances, he took a step back and began, again, the exhausting effort of regaining control of his feelings.

Perhaps sensing that he needed time, Lucivar tugged at the book Marian held, trying to see the title.

She clutched it harder and stepped away from him.

"Is that a sniffle book?" Lucivar asked suspiciously.

Marian opened and closed her wings with a snap. "A what?"

"You know. One of those books that women like to read and get all weepy over. The last time you read one of those, you got upset when I came in to find out what was wrong. You threw the book at me."

Marian's sputtering was no longer silent. "I didn't get upset because of the *book*. You came storming into the room with weapons drawn and you scared me."

"You were crying. I thought you were hurt. Look, I just want to know ahead of time if you're going to get weepy over it."

"When Jaenelle read it, I'll bet you didn't barge in on her when she got weepy."

Lucivar eyed the book as if it had just grown fangs. "Oh. *That* book." He curled an arm protectively over his belly. "Actually, I did barge in on her. Her aim was better than yours."

Marian's growl turned into a laugh. "Poor Lucivar. You try so hard to protect the women in the family, and we don't show our appreciation, do we?"

Lucivar grinned. "Well, if there are any interesting love scenes in that story, mark the pages and you can appreciate me in a few days."

Marian glanced at Daemon and blushed.

Lucivar gently kissed her, then stepped aside to let her pass. "Get into bed now."

"I'll see you tomorrow, Daemon," Marian said a little shyly.

"Good night, Lady Marian," Daemon said. It was all he could manage.

They watched her until she went into her and Lucivar's suite, then Lucivar reached out. Daemon stiffened, rejecting the touch.

Dropping his hand, Lucivar said, "The High Lord's suite is just down this corridor. He'll want to see you."

Daemon couldn't move. "I thought you married Jaenelle."

"Why would you think I married Jaenelle?"

The surprise in Lucivar's voice woke Daemon's temper. "You were here," he snarled. "Why wouldn't you want to marry her?"

Lucivar didn't say anything for a long minute. Then, quietly, "That was always your dream, Daemon. Not mine." Turning, he walked down the corridor. "Come on."

Daemon followed slowly. When Lucivar stopped and knocked on a door, he kept walking, drawn to the strong, dark, feminine psychic scent coming from a room on the opposite side of the corridor.

"Daemon?"

Lucivar's voice faded, muted by a powerful tide of emotions.

Daemon opened a door and walked into a sitting room. One wall had built-in bookshelves above a row of closed, waist-high wooden cabinets. A couch, two triangular side tables, and two chairs formed a bracket of furniture around a long, low table. A pair of sinuous, patinaed lamps sat on the side tables. Next to one chair was a large basket full of skeins of wool and silk and a partially completed piece of needlework. A desk sat in front of the glass doors that led out to the balcony. A tiered stand filled with plants occupied one corner.

The psychic scent washed over him, through him. Oh, he remembered that dark scent. But there was something different about it now, something delicately, deliciously musky.

His body tightened, then swelled with male interest before his mind understood the significance of that difference. Then he noticed the sapphire slippers near one chair. A woman's slippers.

Against all reason, despite all desire, even when he had thought that Lucivar had married her, he hadn't fully absorbed the fact that she was no longer the child he had known. She had grown up.

The walls of the room faded to gray, then darkened and began to close in, forming a tunnel around him.

"Daemon."

He remembered that deep voice, too. He had heard it amused. He had heard it full of rage and fierce power. He had heard it hoarse and exhausted. He had heard it plead with him to reach up, to accept the help and strength being offered.

Turning slowly, he stared at Saetan. The Prince of the Darkness. The High Lord of Hell. His father.

Saetan extended his hand, with its slender fingers and long, black-tinted nails. "Daemon . . . Jaenelle is alive," he said softly.

The room shrank. The tunnel kept closing. The hand waited for him, offering strength, safety, comfort—all the things he'd rejected when he'd been in the Twisted Kingdom.

"Daemon."

He took a step forward. He raised his hand, with its slender fingers and long, black-tinted nails. This time, he feared his own fragility. This time, he would accept the promises Saetan offered.

He took another step, reaching for the hand that mirrored his own.

Just before his fingers touched Saetan's, the room disappeared.

"Keep your head down, boyo. Breathe, slow and easy. That's right."

Calm strength and warmth flowed from the hand that stroked his head, his neck, his spine.

The effort made him queasy, but after a moment Daemon got his brain and body working together enough to open his eyes. He stared at the carpet between his feet—earth-brown, with swirls of young green and burnt red. Obviously the carpet couldn't decide if it was representing spring or autumn.

"Do you want some brandy or a basin?" Lucivar asked.

Why would he want a basin?

His stomach jumped. He swallowed carefully. "Brandy," he said, gritting his teeth and hoping it wasn't the wrong choice.

When Lucivar returned, Daemon got a generously filled snifter shoved into his hand and a basin shoved between his feet.

The hand rubbing Daemon's spine stopped moving. "Lucivar," Saetan said, his voice equally amused and annoyed.

"Helene won't be pleased with him if he pukes on the carpet."

Daemon didn't know the word Saetan used, but it sounded nasty. It was petty, but he felt childishly pleased that his father had taken his side.

"Go to Hell," he said, sitting up enough to take a sip of brandy.

"I'm not the one whose nose was heading for the floor a minute ago," Lucivar growled, rustling his wings.

"Children," Saetan warned.

Since his stomach didn't immediately reject the brandy, Daemon took another sip—and finally edged around the questions that needed answers. "She's really alive?"

"She's really alive," Saetan replied gently.

"She's lived here since . . ." He couldn't bring himself to say it.

"Yes."

Daemon turned his head, needing to see the answer in Saetan's eyes as well as hear it. "And she healed?"

"Yes."

But he saw the flicker of hesitation in those gold eyes.

Taking another sip of brandy, he slowly realized that, while Jaenelle's dark psychic scent filled the room, it wasn't recent. "Where is she?"

"She's making her autumn tour of the kindred Territories," Saetan said. "We try not to interrupt her during that time, but I could—"

"No." Daemon closed his eyes. He needed some time to regain his balance before he met her again. "It can wait." It had already waited for thirteen years. A few more days wouldn't matter.

Saetan hesitated, then glanced at Lucivar, who nodded. "There is something you need to think about before she returns." He called in a small jeweler's box, then pushed the lid open with his thumb.

Daemon stared at the faceted ruby in the gold ring. A Consort's ring. He'd seen that ring in the Twisted Kingdom, circling the stem of a crystal chalice that had been shattered and carefully pieced together. Jaenelle's chalice. Jaenelle's promise.

"That's not for you to offer," Daemon said. He gripped the brandy snifter to keep from reaching for the ring.

"I'm not the one who's offering it, Prince. As the Steward of the Dark Court, it was given into my keeping."

Daemon carefully licked his lips. "Has it ever been worn?" Jaenelle was twenty-five now. There was no reason to think—to hope—it had never circled another man's finger.

Saetan's eyes held a mixture of relief and sadness. "No." He shut the box and held it out.

Daemon's hand closed over it convulsively.

"Come on, boyo," Saetan said as he handed the brandy snifter to Lucivar and helped Daemon stand up. "I'll show you to your room. Beale will bring a tray up in a few minutes. Try to eat and get some sleep. We'll talk again in the morning."

★   ★   ★

Opening the glass door, Daemon stepped out onto the balcony. The silk robe was too thin and couldn't stop the night air from leaching the warmth he'd gained from a long bath, but he needed to be outside for a moment, needed to listen to the water singing over stone in the natural-looking fountain at the center of the garden below. There were only a couple of rooms surrounding the garden that showed a soft glow of light. Guest rooms? Or did Aaron and Khardeen occupy those rooms?

Saetan had said no man had worn the Consort's ring, but . . .

Daemon took a deep breath, let it out slowly. She was a Queen, and a Queen was entitled to any pleasure the males in her court could provide.

And he was here now.

Shivering, he went into his room, secured the glass door, and drew the curtains. He slipped out of the robe, got into bed, then pulled the covers up over his naked body. Shifting to his side, he stared for several minutes at the jeweler's box he'd set on the bedside table.

He was here now. The choice was his now.

He took the Consort's ring out of the box and slipped it on the ring finger of his left hand.

6 / Kaeleer

As Surreal placed the last of her toiletries in the bathroom cabinet, she paused, listening. Yes, someone had entered her bedroom. Had the maid returned for another polite verbal struggle? She'd *told* the woman she didn't need help unpacking—and had wondered about the maid's muttered comment. *No question about it, you're a SaDiablo.*

So maybe she'd been a little hasty. After all, she didn't want to have to launder her own clothes for however long she would be there.

Moving toward the bathroom door, Surreal sent a cautious psychic probe into the bedroom. Her lips curled into a snarl. Not the maid back for another round, but a *male* making himself comfortable in her room. Then she paused. The psychic scent was definitely male—but there was something about it that was just a little off.

Calling in her favorite stiletto, she used Craft to place a sight shield around it. With her arms down and her right hand curled loosely around the hilt, no one would suspect she had a weapon ready—unless they knew she was an assassin. More than likely, it was a male who had heard of her former profession and figured she'd be delighted to accommodate him—like those balless pricks at the service fair who kept pushing her to sign a contract to serve in an "aristo" Red Moon house.

Well, if this male was expecting a jolly, she would just inform him that she would have to talk to the Steward first about compensation. Unless it *was* the Steward. Did he really expect her to buy her way out of a contract she hadn't wanted to sign in the first place?

With her temper simmering, Surreal strode into the bedroom—and stopped short, not sure if she wanted to yell or laugh.

A large gray dog had his head buried in her open trunk. The tip of his tail wagged like a brisk metronome as he sniffed her clothes.

"Find anything interesting?" Surreal asked.

The dog leaped away from the trunk, heading for the door. Then he stopped, a nervous quiver running through his body as his brown eyes stared at her. His tail gave a couple of hopeful *tock-tocks* before it curled between his legs.

Surreal vanished the stiletto. Keeping one eye on the dog, she checked the trunk. If he'd done anything disgusting on her clothes . . . Seeing that he hadn't done more than sniff, she relaxed and turned to face him.

"You're big," she said pleasantly. "Are you allowed inside?"

"Rrrf."

"You're right. Considering the size of this place, that was a silly question." She held out her hand in a loose fist.

Accepting the invitation, he eagerly sniffed her hand, sniffed her feet, sniffed her knees, sniffed . . .

"Get your nose out of my crotch," Surreal growled.

He took two steps back and sneezed.

"Well, that's your opinion."

His mouth opened in a doggy grin. "Rrrf."

Laughing, Surreal put her clothes away in the tall wardrobe and mirrored dresser. After hanging the last piece, she closed the trunk.

Seeing that he had her attention again, the dog sat down and offered a paw.

Well, he seemed friendly.

After shaking his paw, she ran her hands through his fur, scratched behind his ears, and rubbed his head until his eyes started to blissfully close. "You're a pretty boy, aren't you? A big furry boy."

He gave her chin two enthusiastic, if sloppy, kisses.

Surreal straightened up and stretched. "I have to go now, boyo. Somewhere in this place is my dinner, and I intend to find it."

"Rrrf." The dog bounded to the door, his tail wagging.

She eyed him. "Well, I suppose you *would* know where to find the food. Just let me get ready, then we'll go hunting the elusive dinner."

"*Rrrf.*"

Hell's fire, Surreal thought as she washed her hands and brushed her hair. She must be more tired than she realized if she was imagining tonal qualities in the dog's sounds that made it seem like he was really answering her. And she would have sworn that last "Rrrf" was full of amusement. Just as she would have sworn that someone kept trying to reach her on a psychic communication thread and that *she* was the one who kept fumbling the link.

The dog's mood had changed by the time she came back. When she opened the bedroom door, he gave her a sad look, then slunk into the corridor.

Prince Aaron leaned against the opposite wall.

He was a handsome man with black hair, gray eyes, and a height and build women would find appealing. Standing next to Sadi he would come in a poor second—well, so would any other man—but she didn't think he'd ever lacked invitations to the bed.

Maybe that explained the wariness under the arrogant confidence.

"Since you don't know your way around yet, I stopped by to escort you and Lady Benedict to the dining room," Aaron said, looking like he was fighting hard not to smile. "But I see you already have an escort."

The dog's ears pricked up. The tail went *tock-tock*.

The corridor filled with annoying male undercurrents. Surreal briefly considered giving one of them a hard smack just to break up whatever was going on, but losing her escorts would mean trying to find the dining room on her own.

Fortunately, Wilhelmina Benedict chose that moment to leave her room, which was next to Surreal's. After Aaron explained about being their escort, he offered each woman an arm, and the three of them, with the dog trailing close behind, began the long walk through the Hall.

"The servants must be exhausted by the end of the day," Surreal said as they turned into another corridor.

"Not really," Aaron replied. "The staff works on a rotation and are assigned to a wing of the Hall. That way everyone gets to work in the family wing and the wings where the court resides when it's here."

"You mean I'm going to have the same argument with *another* maid?" Surreal almost wailed.

Aaron shot her an amused look. "You mean you drew your own bath?"

"I didn't bother to bathe," Surreal snapped. "Sit upwind."

Smart-ass.

He didn't have to say it out loud. His expression was sufficient.

Surreal glanced back at her furry escort. Well, animals should be a safe subject for small talk. "He is allowed inside, isn't he?"

"Oh, yes," Aaron said. "Although, I was surprised to see him. The pack tends to stay in the north woods when there are strangers here."

"The pack? What kind of dog is he?"

"He's not a dog. He's a wolf. And he's kindred."

Wilhelmina jumped and gave the wolf a frightened look. "But . . . aren't wolves wild animals?"

"He's also a Warlord," Aaron said, ignoring Wilhelmina's question.

Surreal felt a little queasy. She'd heard about the kindred, who supposedly had some kind of small animal magic. But calling him a Warlord . . . "You mean he's Blood?"

"Of course."

"Why is he in the Hall?"

"Well, offhand, I'd say he was looking for a friend."

Hell's fire, Mother Night, and may the Darkness be merciful, Surreal thought. What did *that* mean? "I guess he's not really wild then. If he's in the house, he must be tame."

Aaron gave her a feral smile. "If by 'tame' you mean he doesn't pee on the carpets, then he's tame. But then, by that standard, so am I."

Surreal clamped her teeth together. Screw small talk. In this place, it turned into verbal quicksand.

She echoed Wilhelmina's sigh of relief when they reached a stairway. Hopefully the dining room wasn't too far away and she could put some distance between herself and her escort. Escorts. Whatever.

Shit.

Maybe Khardeen would be in the dining room. He was a Warlord, which made him an equal caste, and her Gray Jewels outranked his Sapphire, which gave her an advantage. Right now, she wanted an advantage because she had the strong impression that, of her two escorts, the one with the more impressive set of teeth was really the less dangerous one.

Surreal stared at the closed wooden door and wished she'd done this before eating. The thick beef and vegetable stew had been delicious, as had been the bread, cheese, and slightly tart apples, and she'd consumed them with enthusiasm. Now, her tightened stomach was packing that food into a hard ball.

Snarling quietly, she raised her fist to knock on the door. Hell's fire, this was just a required meeting with the Steward of the court . . . who now had the authority to control her life . . . who was also the Warlord Prince of Dhemlan . . . who was also the High Lord of Hell . . . whose name was Saetan Daemon SaDiablo.

"Rrrf?"

Surreal looked over her shoulder. The wolf cocked his head.

"I think you'd better stay out here," she said, giving the door one hard rap. When a deep voice said, "Come," she slipped inside the room, closing the door before the wolf could follow her.

The room was a reversed L. The long side contained a comfortable sitting area with tables, chairs, and a black leather couch. The walls held a variety of pictures, ranging from dramatic oil paintings to whimsical charcoal sketches. Intrigued by those choices, she turned toward the alcove.

Dark-red velvet covered the side walls. The back wall contained floor-to-ceiling bookshelves. A blackwood desk filled the center of the space. Two candle-lights lit its surface and the man sitting behind it.

At first glance, she thought Daemon was playing some kind of trick on her. Then she looked closer.

His face was similar to Daemon's, but handsome rather than beautiful. He was definitely older, and his thick black hair was heavily silvered at the temples. He wore half-moon glasses, which made him look like a benevolent clerk. But the elegant hands had long, black-tinted nails like Daemon's. On his left hand, he wore a Steward's ring. On his right, a Black-Jeweled ring.

"Why don't you sit down," he said as he continued making notes on the paper in front of him. "This will take a minute."

Surreal sidled over to the chair in front of the desk and gingerly sat down. His voice had the same deep timbre as Daemon's, had the same ability to reach a woman's bones and make her itchy. At least the sensual heat that poured out of Daemon even when he kept it tightly leashed was muted in the High Lord. Maybe that was just age.

Then he tucked the pen in its holder, laid the glasses on the desk, leaned back in his chair, and steepled his fingers, resting them against his chin.

Her breath clogged in her throat. She'd seen Daemon sit exactly that way whenever a conversation was "formal." Hell's fire, what *was* the connection between Sadi and the High Lord?

"So," he said quietly. "You're Surreal. Titian's daughter."

A shiver went through her. "You knew my mother?"

He smiled dryly. "I still do. And since I am kin to her kin, she considers me a tolerable friend, despite my being male."

The words that had been rankling inside her all through the journey here burst out. "My mother is *not* a Harpy."

Saetan gave her a considering look. "A Harpy is a witch who died violently by a male's hand. I'd say that describes Titian, wouldn't you? Besides," he added, "being the Harpy Queen is hardly an insult."

"Oh." Surreal hooked her hair behind her ears. He made it sound so matter-of-fact, and there was no mistaking the respect in his voice.

"Would you like to see her?" Saetan asked.

"But . . . if she's demon-dead . . ."

"A meeting could be arranged here at the Hall. I could ask her if she would be willing."

"Since you're the High Lord, I'm surprised you wouldn't just order her to come," Surreal said a bit tartly.

Saetan chuckled. "Darling, I may be the High Lord, but I'm also male. I'm not about to give an order to a Black Widow Queen without a very good reason."

Surreal narrowed her eyes. "I can't picture you as submissive."

"I'm not submissive, but I do serve. You would be wise not to confuse those two things when dealing with the males in this court."

Oh, wonderful.

"Especially since you've formally declared yourself part of this family," Saetan added.

Mother Night. "Look," Surreal said, leaning forward. "I didn't know anyone was using that name here." *And I certainly didn't expect to meet them.*

"All things considered, you have as much right to that name as Kartane SaDiablo," he said cryptically. "And since you *did* list it, you're stuck with the results."

"Which are?" Surreal asked suspiciously.

Saetan smiled. "The short version is, as the patriarch of this family, I am now responsible for you and you are answerable to me."

"When the sun shines in Hell," Surreal shot back.

"Be careful what conditions you set, little witch," he said softly. "Jaenelle has an uncanny—and sometimes disturbing—way of meeting someone's terms."

Surreal swallowed hard. "She really is in Kaeleer?"

Saetan held up the mark of safe passage that had been sitting on his desk. "Isn't that why you came?"

She nodded. "I wanted to find out what happened to her."

"Why don't you save those questions for Jaenelle. She'll be home in a few days."

"She lives *here*?"

"This isn't her only home, but, yes, she lives here."

"Does Daemon know?" she asked. "He wasn't at dinner."

"He knows," Saetan said gently. "He's feeling a bit unsettled."

"That's an understatement," she muttered. Then she thought of something else, something that had nagged at her curiosity for thirteen years. If there was anyone in the Realms who would know the answer, she figured it was the High Lord. "Have you ever heard of the High Priest of the Hourglass?"

His smile had a sharp edge. "I *am* the High Priest."

"Oh, shit."

His laughter was warm and full-bodied. "You're willing to snarl at me as the High Lord, the Steward, and the family patriarch, but knowing I'm the Priest knocks your feet out from under you?"

Surreal glared at him. Put that way, it *did* sound silly. But it was disconcerting to find out that the dangerous male she'd caught a whiff of that night at Cassandra's Altar was the same amused man sitting on the other side of the desk. "Then you can tell Daemon what happened that night. You can tell him what he doesn't remember."

Saetan shook his head. "No, I can't. I can confirm what happened while we were linked, and I can tell him what happened after. But there's only one person who can tell him what took place in the abyss."

Surreal sighed. "I'm almost afraid of what he'll find out."

"I wouldn't be too concerned. When Jaenelle formally set up her court, the Consort's ring was set aside for him, by her decree. So whatever happened between them couldn't have been that distressing. At least for her," he added solemnly. Rising, he came around the desk. "I still have to meet with several of the Eyriens tonight as well as get the reports from Aaron, Khardeen, and Lucivar. If you need any help understanding the Blood here, please come and talk to me."

Accepting dismissal, Surreal rose and glanced at the door. "There is one other thing."

Saetan studied the closed door. "I see you've met Lord Graysfang."

Surreal choked back a laugh.

"I know. Their names sound as strange to us as ours do to them. Although they may have more reason to think so. When kindred young are born, a Black Widow makes that mental sidestep into the dreams and visions. Sometimes she sees nothing. Sometimes she names one of the young according to the visions."

"Well," Surreal said, smiling, "he is gray, and he does have fangs. Aaron said he was in the Hall because he's looking for a friend."

Saetan gave her an odd look. "I'd say that's accurate. The kindred dogs and horses relate well to the human Blood since they've lived among them for so long, although, until eight years ago, in secret. The rest of the kindred tend to stay away from most humans. But whenever they come across a human who is compatible with them, they try to form a bond, to better understand us."

"Why me?" Surreal asked, intrigued.

"The Queens here have strong courts, and the males in the First Circle are entitled to the first share of their time and attention. A youngster like Graysfang has to wait for his turn and then has to share that time with other young males in the same position. But you're a Gray-Jeweled witch who does not, as yet, have any other male claims."

"Except the males in the family," Surreal said sourly.

"Except the males in the family," Saetan agreed. "On both sides."

She sputtered.

"But that claim isn't quite the same thing. You're not a Queen, whose courts are set up by a different Protocol. So if you accept Graysfang before the other males realize you're here, he will hold the dominant position over any male except your mate, even if the other male wears darker Jewels. Since he's not old enough to make the Offering to the Darkness and still wears his Birthright Purple Dusk Jewel, the odds of a darker-Jeweled male becoming interested in you are rather high."

"Which still doesn't explain why he's interested in me in the first place."

Saetan reached out slowly. His left index finger hooked the gold chain around her neck and drew it out of her shirt until her Gray Jewel hung between them.

At first, she thought the caress accompanying that movement was a subtle kind of seduction. Then she realized that, for him, it wasn't meant to be seductive at all. It was simply a gesture that was as natural to him as breathing.

Which wasn't doing *her* breathing a whole lot of good.

"Consider this," he said. "He may not have been given that name because he's gray and has fangs but because he is Gray's fang."

"Mother Night," Surreal said, looking down at her Jewel.

He lowered her Jewel until it rested above her breasts. "The decision about him is yours, and I'll support any decision you make. But think carefully, Surreal. A Black Widow's visions should not be dismissed in haste."

Nodding, she savored the feel of his hand on her lower back as he guided her to the door. When he reached for the doorknob, she put her hand on the door to keep it shut. "What's your connection with Daemon?"

"He and Lucivar are my sons."

That figured.

"Daemon inherited your looks," she said.

"He also inherited my temper."

Hearing the warning in his voice, she noticed, at the back of his golden eyes, the same wariness she had seen in Aaron's. Hell's fire, she was going to have to find someone to talk to soon who could explain the male-female rules in Kaeleer. Being wary of her as an assassin was one thing. Being wary of her as a woman . . . She didn't like it. Not coming from him. She didn't like it at all.

"I'd like to meet my mother," she said abruptly.

Saetan nodded. "The court's coming in this evening, and I can't leave until the Queen approves the new arrivals, but I'll see that a message gets to Titian."

"Thank you." *Damn it, stop delaying. Get out of here.* She bolted from the room as soon as he opened the door.

As Graysfang anxiously trotted beside her, she kept feeling that odd psychic brush against her inner barriers.

She would have gotten lost twice without him, although she noticed there were footmen in all the major corridors. Each man rose from his chair, glanced at Graysfang, smiled at her, and said nothing. So she followed the wolf until, with a sigh, she was safely in her room.

When he left her a minute later to take care of his own nightly business, she quickly undressed and pulled on a pair of long-sleeved pajamas. She still preferred silky nightgowns most of the time, but there were times—like tonight—when she wanted to wear something that looked and felt asexual.

Dumping her soiled clothes into a basket in the bathroom, she hurried through her nighttime ritual, slipped into bed, and turned off the candle-light on the bedside table.

Someone had put a light warming spell on the sheets. Probably the maid. Silently thanking the woman, Surreal snuggled under the covers.

She was just starting to doze off when a shape passed through the glass door. She tensed, waiting, until a body landed lightly on the bed, circled three times, then settled next to her with a content sigh.

Twisting her upper body slightly, she looked at Graysfang. Feeling that odd psychic brush again, she followed it, too tired to think about what she was doing and more concerned with whether or not she was going to end up with fleas in the morning.

No fleas, said a sleepy male voice on a psychic thread. *Kindred know spells for fleas and other itchies.*

With a yelp, Surreal shot into a sitting position.

Graysfang leaped up, his teeth bared and hackles raised. *Where is the danger?* he demanded. *I smell no danger.*

"You can talk!"

Slowly, Graysfang's hackles smoothed. He covered his teeth. ★I am kindred. We do not always *want* to talk to humans, but we can talk.★

Mother Night, Mother Night, Mother Night.

Wagging his tail, he leaned forward and licked her cheek. ★You heard me!★ he said happily. ★You are not even trained yet and you can hear kindred!★ He raised his head and howled.

Surreal grabbed his muzzle. "Hush. You'll wake everyone."

★Ladvarian will be pleased.★

"Great. I'm delighted." *Who in the name of Hell is Ladvarian?* "Let's just go to sleep now, all right?" And since she didn't know how she had made this link in the first place, how was she going to sever it so that her thoughts were private again?

She felt a gentle mental push, then that odd brush again.

"Rrrf."

"Thank you," Surreal said weakly. *In the morning,* she thought as she snuggled back under the covers and felt Graysfang settle himself against her back. *She'd think about this in the morn . . .*

CHAPTER THREE

1 / Kaeleer

Daemon carefully adjusted the cuffs of his shirt and jacket. He felt steadier that morning, but not rested. His sleep had been broken by vague dreams and flashes of memory, by the knowledge that nothing but a door separated his bedroom from Jaenelle's, and by an aroused, restless body that knew quite fiercely what it wanted.

Slipping his hands into his trouser pockets made him aware of the Consort's ring on his left hand. As if he hadn't been aware of it from the moment he'd woken up. It wasn't just the unfamiliar feel of a ring on that hand; it was the duties and responsibilities that came with that ring that made him uneasy. Oh, his body would perform its duties eagerly enough. At least, he thought it would. And that was the point, wasn't it? He really didn't know how he would respond when he met Jaenelle again. And he didn't know how she would respond to him.

Finally aware that Jazen, his valet, was still dawdling through the morning tasks, Daemon studied the man.

"Did you get settled in all right last night?" Daemon asked.

Jazen made an effort to smile but didn't look at him. "The servants' quarters here are very generous."

"And the servants?"

"They're . . . polite."

Daemon felt the beginning chill of temper and reined it in, hard. Jazen had already endured enough. If he had to shake the Hall down to its foundation, he'd make sure the man's life wasn't made more difficult by servants who had no understanding of the brutality men faced in the Terreillean Territories under Dorothea's control.

"I'm not sure what's going to be required of me today."

Jazen nodded. "The other personal servants indicated that dress would be relaxed today since the First Circle will be assessing the new arrivals. Those who sit at the High Lord's table do dress for dinner. Not formal dress," he added when Daemon raised one eyebrow. "But I gathered the Ladies are usually casual in their attire during the day."

Daemon turned that bit of information over and over as he made his way through the corridors toward the dining room. Based on his experience in Terreillean courts, casual attire meant practical dresses made of fabrics only slightly less sumptuous than those worn to dinner.

Then he turned a corner and noticed the fair-skinned, red-haired witch coming toward him. She wore threadbare, dark-brown trousers and a long, baggy, heather-green sweater that was decoratively patched. There was approval in the fast assessment her green eyes made over his body but no active interest. "Prince," she said politely as she passed him.

"Lady," he replied with equal politeness, wondering how such a stickler as he suspected Beale to be would allow a servant to dress like that. When he caught a whiff of her psychic scent, he spun around and stared at her until she turned the corner and disappeared.

A Queen. That woman was a *Queen.*

His stomach growled, which finally got him walking again.

A Queen. Well, if *that* was the Ladies' idea of casual attire, he wholeheartedly approved of the High Lord's insistence on dressing for dinner—a sentiment he strongly suspected he should keep to himself.

He had almost reached the dining room when he met up with Saetan.

"Prince Sadi, there's something I need to discuss with you," Saetan said quietly, but his expression was grim.

Saetan using the formal title caused a chill down Daemon's spine.

"Then shall we get it over with?" Daemon replied as he followed Saetan to the High Lord's official study. He felt one layer of tension ease when Saetan leaned against the front of the blackwood desk instead of sitting behind it.

"Are you aware that your valet is fully shaved?" Saetan asked softly, ominously.

"I'm aware of it," Daemon replied with equal softness.

"There are very few of our laws that, when broken, justify that punishment. All of them are sexual."

"Jazen didn't do anything except be at the wrong place at the wrong time," Daemon snarled. "Dorothea did that to him to entertain her coven."

"Are you sure of that?"

"I was there, High Lord. There wasn't a damn thing I could do for him except slip past the drugs they'd given him to keep him aware and knock him out. His family took care of him for a while, but many of them are in personal service. Once the word got out—and Dorothea always made sure that it did—Jazen would have been considered tainted because, *of course,* it wouldn't have happened to him if he hadn't deserved it. If he had stayed with his family, they would have lost their positions as well. He's a good man, and a loyal one. He deserved far better than what happened to him."

"I see," Saetan said quietly. He straightened up. "I'll explain the situation to Beale. He'll take care of it."

"How much will you have to tell him?" Daemon asked warily.

"Nothing more than that the maiming was unjustified."

Daemon smiled bitterly. "Do you really think that will change the other servants' opinion of him? That they'll believe it?"

"No, all it will do is suspend judgment until the Lady returns." Saetan looked solemn. "But you have to understand, Prince. If Jaenelle turns against him, there's nothing you or I or anyone else can do or say that will make any difference. In Kaeleer, once you step outside of Little Terreille, Witch *is* the law. Her decisions are final."

Daemon considered this, then nodded. "I'll accept the Lady's judgment." As he followed Saetan to the dining room, he kept hoping that the woman Jaenelle had become wasn't too different from the child he remembered—and had loved.

2 / Kaeleer

Lord Jorval's heart pounded as he returned to the room where the sandy-haired man with worried gray eyes waited. He sat down behind the desk and clasped his hands together to hide the tremors of excitement.

"Have you already found out where my niece has gone?" Philip Alexander asked.

"I have," Jorval replied solemnly, "When you explained the family connections, I had a suspicion of where to look."

Philip gripped the arms of the chair hard enough to snap wood. "Did she sign a contract with a court in Little Terreille?"

"Unfortunately, no," Jorval said, struggling to put just the right amount of sympathy in his voice. "You must understand, Prince Alexander. We had no way of knowing who she was. A couple of Council members remembered her saying that she was trying to find her sister, but they had assumed the sister had immigrated earlier—and in a sense, that is true. But the Dark Council was never provided with a record of where Jaenelle Angelline came from before the High Lord acquired guardianship over her. There was no reason for them to link the two women, and by the time they began to wonder about the significance of her inquiries, it was too late."

"What do you mean, 'too late'?" Philip snapped.

"She was . . . persuaded . . . to sign a contract with the Warlord Prince of Ebon Rih—and *he* is Lucivar Yaslana."

Satisfaction warmed Jorval as he watched Philip's face pale. "I see you've heard of him. So you can appreciate the danger your niece is in. And it's not just Yaslana, although he's bad enough." He paused, giving Philip time to swallow the hook as well as the bait.

"She's trapped with all three of them, isn't she? She's trapped with Yaslana, Sadi, and the High Lord—just like Jaenelle."

"Yes." Jorval sighed. "To the best of our knowledge, Yaslana took her to SaDiablo Hall in Dhemlan. How long she'll remain there . . ." He spread his hands in a helpless gesture. "You may have some chance of slipping her away from the Hall, but once he takes her into the mountains that ring Ebon Rih, it's unlikely you'll ever get her back—at least while there's enough left of her to be worth the risk."

Philip sagged in the chair.

Jorval just waited. Finally, he said, "There is nothing the Dark Council can do officially to help you at this time. However, *unofficially*, we will do everything in our power to restore Jaenelle Angelline and Wilhelmina Benedict to their rightful family."

Philip got to his feet like a man who had taken a savage beating. "Thank you, Lord Jorval. I will convey this information to my Queen."

"May the Darkness guide and protect you, Prince Alexander."

Jorval waited a full minute after Philip left before he leaned back in his chair and sighed, well satisfied by their meeting. Thank the Darkness that Philip was a Prince. He would worry and brood, but, unlike a Warlord Prince, he *would* go back to Alexandra Angelline and abide by her decision. And how fortunate that Philip hadn't thought to ask if Yaslana served a Queen—or who she was. Of course, he would have lied if he'd been asked, but how interesting that Philip hadn't considered, even for a moment, that Jaenelle might be a Queen powerful enough to control the males in the SaDiablo family.

As for Alexandra Angelline . . . She would be useful in distracting the High Lord and dividing loyalties in the court at Ebon Askavi—as long as she didn't realize the *real* importance of getting Jaenelle away from the Dark Court.

3 / Kaeleer

Daemon wandered through the Hall's first floor rooms, distractedly noting each room's function, his mind too full of impressions he'd received during breakfast. When he came to a door that led to one of the open courtyards, he went outside and paced, hoping that the fresh air and greenery would help clear his head.

He'd expected to find the dining room full of people. After all, the Eyriens would want to eat before going on to whatever plans Lucivar had for them. And he'd expected Khardeen and Aaron to be there and knew they would notice, and understand the significance of, the Consort's ring. He'd been prepared for that. But he *hadn't* been prepared for the *other* males who made up the First Circle.

There was Sceron, the Red-Jeweled Warlord Prince of Centauran. The dark-haired centaur had stood near the dining table, eating a vegetable omelet while talking with Morton, a blond-haired, blue-eyed Warlord from Glacia. Then there was the Green-Jeweled Warlord, Jonah, a satyr whose dark pelt covered him from his waist to his cloven hooves but didn't quite cover the parts of him that were blatantly male. There was Elan, a Red-Jeweled Warlord Prince from Tigrelan, who had tawny, dark-striped skin and whose hands ended with sheathed claws. Watching Elan,

Daemon would have bet the man had more in common with the dark-striped cat he'd glimpsed from a window than just physical markings.

And then there was Chaosti, the Gray-Jeweled Warlord Prince of the Dea al Mon, with his long silver-blond hair, delicately pointed ears, and slightly too large forest-blue eyes. Every territorial instinct in Daemon had come roaring to the surface at the sight of Chaosti—perhaps because Chaosti was the kind of man who could be a formidable rival no matter what Jewels he wore or perhaps because Daemon saw a little too much of himself in the other man. Only Saetan's presence had kept a sharp-edged greeting from turning into an open confrontation. That meeting had left him edgy, and far too aware of his own inner fragility.

Next came the older, Gray-Jeweled Warlord Prince who had introduced himself as Mephis, his older brother. The room had tilted a bit when Daemon realized that, as Saetan's eldest son, Mephis had been demon-dead for more than 50,000 years. He might have recovered his balance if Prince Andulvar Yaslana and Lord Prothvar Yaslana hadn't walked in at that moment, and the collective shock of the Eyrien males who realized who they must be—and then realized *what* they must be—hadn't hit him like a runaway wagon. After one raking look at the fearful Eyriens and a murmured comment to the High Lord, the demon-dead Warlord Prince and his grandson had left the room.

By that point, Daemon had sincerely wished for brandy instead of coffee—a wish that must have been apparent. The stuff Khardeen had poured into his coffee from a silver flask hadn't been brandy, but it had successfully furred his nerves enough for him to be able to eat.

Still too jangled to enjoy the meal, he'd just finished his modest breakfast when Surreal stormed in, muttering something about it taking more time than expected "to get us brushed." She had looked shocked when she saw Chaosti, who was the only person she had seen who came from the same race as her mother, but the moment he'd moved toward her, she had bared her teeth and announced that the next male who approached her before breakfast was going to get brushed with the edge of a knife.

She, at least, had enjoyed a quiet, and undisturbed, breakfast.

He was just about to leave the room when a tall, slender witch with spiky, white-blond hair walked in, took one look at him, and said loudly enough to be heard in every corner of the Hall, "Hell's fire, *he's a Black Widow!*"

That he was a natural Black Widow—and, besides Saetan, the *only* male Black Widow—was something he'd been able to successfully hide for all the centuries since his body had reached sexual maturity, just as he'd been able to hide the snake tooth and venom sack beneath the ring-finger nail of his right hand. Whatever he had done instinctively to suppress other Black Widows' ability to detect him had failed him now, when there was nothing he could do about such a public betrayal.

The tension in the room had faded when Saetan replied mildly, "Well, Karla, he *is* my son, and he *is* the Consort."

The witch's surprise had changed to sharp speculation. "Oh," she said. "In that case . . ." A slow, wicked smile bloomed. "Kiss kiss."

Brushing past Lucivar, he had escaped from the dining room and had spent the past hour wandering through the Hall, trying to get his churning thoughts and emotions under control.

"Are you lost?"

Daemon glanced over to where Lucivar leaned against a doorway. "I'm not lost," he snapped. Then he stopped pacing and sighed. "But I am very confused."

"Of course you are. You're male." Grinning at Daemon's snarl, Lucivar stepped into the courtyard. "So if one of the darlings in the coven offers to explain things to you, don't take her up on it. She'll sincerely be trying to help, but by the time she's done 'unconfusing' you, you'll be banging your head against a wall and whimpering."

"Why?"

"Because for every five rules you'd learned in Terreille about a male's proper behavior in a court, the Kaeleer Blood know only one of them—and they interpret it very differently."

Daemon shrugged "Obedience is obedience."

"No, it's not. For Blood males, the First Law is to honor, cherish, and protect. The second is to serve. The third is to obey."

"And if obedience interferes with the first two laws?"

"Toss it out the window."

Daemon blinked. "You actually get away with that?"

Lucivar scratched the back of his head and looked thoughtful. "It's not so much a question of getting away with it. For Warlord Princes, it's almost a requirement of court service. However, if you ignore an order from the Steward or the Master of the Guard, you'd better be sure you can justify your action and be willing to accept the consequences if they won't accept it, which is rare. I got into more trouble with the High Lord as my father than as the Steward."

Father. Steward. The ties of family and court.

"Why are you here, Prick?" Daemon asked warily. "Why aren't you at the practice field observing the warriors you selected?"

"I was looking for you because you *didn't* show up at the practice field." Lucivar shifted slightly, balancing his weight.

Not yet, Daemon thought. *Not now.* "And because we have unfinished business," he said slowly.

"And because we have unfinished business." Lucivar took a deep breath, let it out slowly. "I accused you of killing Jaenelle. I accused you of viler things than that. I was wrong, and it cost you your sanity and eight years of your life."

Daemon looked away from the regret and sadness in Lucivar's eyes. "It wasn't your fault," he said softly. "I was already fragile."

"I know. I sensed that—and I used it as a weapon."

Remembering the fight they'd had that night in Pruul, Daemon closed his eyes. Lucivar's fury hadn't hurt him as much as his own fear that the accusations might possibly be true. If he'd been sure of what had happened at Cassandra's Altar, the fight would have ended differently. Lucivar wouldn't have spent more years in the salt mines of Pruul, and he wouldn't have spent eight years in the Twisted Kingdom.

Daemon opened his eyes and looked at his brother, finally understanding that Lucivar wasn't offering to meet him on a killing field for something *he* had done, but as reparation for whatever pain he'd suffered in the Twisted Kingdom. Oh, Lucivar would fight, and fight hard because he had a wife and a young son to consider, but he wouldn't hesitate if Daemon demanded it, even knowing what the outcome would be when Ebon-gray faced Black.

He also knew why Lucivar was forcing the issue. His brother didn't want the wife and child weighed in the balance, didn't want Daemon to have enough time to develop feelings for them before making this decision. Following the old ways of the Blood, if he forgave this debt now, he couldn't demand reparation later. Otherwise, they would always be wary of each other, always feel the need to guard their backs while waiting for the unexpected strike.

And, in a way, hadn't the debt already been paid? His years in the Twisted Kingdom balanced against Lucivar's years in the salt mines of

Pruul. His grief when he believed Lucivar was dead balanced against Lucivar's grief over Jaenelle's supposed death by Daemon's hand. And if their positions had been reversed, would he have believed any differently or acted any differently?

"Is that the only unfinished business between us?" Daemon asked.

Lucivar nodded cautiously.

"Then let it go, Prick. I've already grieved for the loss of my brother once. I don't want to do it again."

They studied each other for a minute, weighing the things that went beyond words. Finally, Lucivar relaxed. His smile was lazy, arrogant, and so irritatingly familiar that Daemon smiled in return.

"In that case, Bastard, you're late for practice," Lucivar said, gesturing Daemon toward a door.

"Kiss my ass," Daemon growled, falling into step.

"Not a good suggestion, old son. I have a tendency to bite, remember?" Smiling, Lucivar massaged his upper arm. "So does Marian. She tends to get feisty when she's riled."

Seeing the warmth and pleasure in Lucivar's eyes, Daemon ruthlessly suppressed a surge of envy.

Finally reaching an outside door, they headed for the Eyriens gathered at the far end of the expansive lawn.

"By the way," Lucivar said, "while you were brooding—"

"I wasn't brooding," Daemon snarled.

"—you missed the fun this morning."

Daemon clenched his teeth. He wouldn't ask. Wouldn't. "What fun?"

"See the embarrassed-looking wolf standing by himself?"

Daemon looked at the gray-furred animal watching a group of women going through some kind of exercise with Eyrien sticks. "Yes."

"Graysfang wants to be Surreal's friend. He's young and he doesn't have much experience with humans, especially the females. Apparently, in an effort to strengthen that friendship and improve his understanding of females, he joined Surreal while she was taking a shower. Since her head was under the water at the moment, she didn't realize he was there until he stuck his nose where he shouldn't have."

"That would have improved his understanding of females," Daemon said dryly.

"Exactly. Then, when he whined that he had soap in his fur, she dragged him all the way into the shower and washed him. So now he smells like flowers."

Daemon bit his lip. "There's an easy remedy for that."

Lucivar cleared his throat. "Well, there usually would be, but as soon as they got outside, she threatened to smack him if he got dirty."

"Everything has a price," Daemon said in a choked voice. Noticing the woman Surreal was talking to, he gave Lucivar a sharp nudge. "Should Marian be doing something that strenuous during her moon time?"

Lucivar hissed. "Don't you start." He stopped walking and studied the women through narrowed eyes. "I told her she could do one round of the warmup drill. She'll sneak a little more in under the guise of demonstrating the moves, but after that she'll be content to rest."

Daemon looked at the women and then at Lucivar. "You told your wife how much she could do?"

"Of course I didn't tell my wife," Lucivar said indignantly. "Do I look like a fool? The Warlord Prince of Ebon Rih told a witch who lives in his territory."

"Ah. That's different."

"Damn right it is. If I told my wife, she would have tried to dent my head with a stick."

Daemon laughed as they continued toward the Eyrien warriors. "Now I *am* sorry I missed it."

Lucivar focused his attention on Falonar and Rothvar, who had just stepped into the practice circle, while Daemon watched Surreal and Marian go through a couple of moves.

"Who is she?" Daemon asked when the spiky-haired witch joined the other women.

Lucivar glanced at the women, then turned his attention back to the Eyrien warriors. "That's Karla, the Queen of Glacia. She's a Black Widow Queen and a Healer. One of three who have a triple gift."

A triple gift and a big mouth, Daemon thought darkly.

"You're excused from the practice today, but I'll expect you to be on time tomorrow," Lucivar said.

Daemon sputtered. "I am *not* going to drill with sticks against Eyrien warriors."

Lucivar snorted and looked at Daemon's feet. "I've got some boots that will fit you until you can get your own made."

"I'm not doing this."

"Until the official transfer is made, I own the contract you signed, old son. You've got no choice."

Daemon swore quietly, viciously.

Lucivar started to step away from him to speak to Falonar.

"Give me one good reason why I should put myself through this," Daemon demanded through clenched teeth.

Lucivar turned back to him. "Do you understand how good I am with the Eyrien sticks?" he asked quietly.

"I've seen you."

"Jaenelle can put me in the dirt." Lucivar grinned when Daemon's jaw dropped. "Not often, I grant you, but she's done it."

Daemon thought about that little nugget of information while Lucivar talked with the Eyrien males. He thought hard. When Lucivar returned, giving him a questioning look, he stripped off his jacket, rolled up his shirtsleeves, and growled, "Where are the damn boots?"

4 / Kaeleer

Pulling her shawl more tightly around her, Alexandra Angelline wrapped her arms around her waist as she stared out the streaked inn window that overlooked the service fairgrounds. The rain that had started falling an hour earlier was more of a drizzle that only managed to smear the dirt that covered everything rather than a downpour that would wash it away.

This is Kaeleer? she thought bleakly. *This is the Shadow Realm that so many were so desperate to reach?* Oh, it was probably unfair to judge an entire Realm by ground that had been scraped bare by the hundreds of people who had waited there, hoping to be chosen for a service contract. But she knew that, no matter what else she saw, this is what she would always picture whenever someone mentioned Kaeleer.

She felt someone approach, but didn't turn when her daughter, Leland, joined her at the window.

"Why would Wilhelmina have wanted to come to this place?" Leland murmured. "I'll be glad when we can leave here."

"You don't have to stay, Leland. Especially now that Vania and Nyselle have so graciously insisted on accompanying me."

"They didn't come with us out of loyalty," Leland said quietly but bitterly. "They just wanted a chance to see the Shadow Realm and knew they might not get in any other way."

Alexandra clenched her teeth while the truth of Leland's remark gnawed at her. Vania and Nyselle, the two Province Queens who grudgingly had accompanied her to Hayll, had become sickening in their solicitousness as soon as she announced she was going to Kaeleer to look for Wilhelmina. So they and their Consorts had come with her, along with Philip and Leland and a five-man escort. Four of the escorts had come with her from Chaillot. The other one, chosen by Dorothea SaDiablo, had been "borrowed" from one of Dorothea's pet Queens in another Territory. The man made her skin crawl, but Dorothea had assured her that he would be able to slip Wilhelmina away from her "captors" and deliver her to another loyal group of males already in position in Kaeleer.

It pains me to say it, Dorothea had said, *but if you can free only one of your granddaughters from the High Lord's control, it must be Jaenelle. She is the danger to Terreille.*

Alexandra didn't believe for a moment that Jaenelle was anything more than a stalking-horse being used to hide whoever—or whatever— was the *real* threat to Terreille. But, sweet Darkness, she hoped she wouldn't have to make a choice between Wilhelmina and Jaenelle—because she knew in her heart which child would be left behind.

"Besides," Leland added softly, "I need to stay. She was always such a strange child, but Jaenelle was . . . is . . . my daughter. To think she's been under that monster's control all this time . . ." Leland shuddered. "There's no telling what he's done to her."

And no way to tell what had been done to her in Briarwood. Had she really been mentally fragile or had that place made her so? No, she decided firmly. Jaenelle's stays at Briarwood might have weakened an already fragile stability, but the child's eccentricities had been the reason why she had decided to send the girl to Briarwood in the first place.

"What are we going to do?" Leland asked quietly.

Alexandra looked over her shoulder at the other people restlessly waiting for her decision. Philip, whose self-control had broken several times while he'd given her Lord Jorval's information, would go with her, not only because he had married Leland, but also because he genuinely cared for Wilhelmina and Jaenelle. Vania and Nyselle would go in order to see more of Kaeleer than this dirty piece of barren ground. The Consorts and escorts would follow the Queens out of duty. Would curiosity and duty be enough against something like the High Lord?

It didn't matter. She would take whatever help she could get.

As she turned back to the window, she said, "Prince Alexander, please arrange passage on a Coach as soon as possible. We're going to SaDiablo Hall."

5 / Kaeleer

Certain that he had more muscle aches than muscles, Daemon slowly made his way to the great hall where, Beale had informed him, the High Lord was waiting.

Never again. Never never never. He should have remembered what "I'll start you off easy" meant, should have remembered that other kinds of exercise didn't prepare the body for Eyrien weapons drills. Oh, if he wanted to be fair—and he had no intention of being fair in the foreseeable future—Lucivar *had* started him with the basic warmup drills. But even moving at the practice pace, when you had Lucivar as a working partner, you *worked*.

Then he opened a door at the far end of the great hall and forgot about his aching muscles when he saw Saetan brush the hair away from the face of an attractive Dhemlan witch. There was tenderness in that action, and affection as well. Wondering if he was reading things correctly, he moved forward as quietly as possible.

The witch noticed him first. Looking flustered, she took a long step back and watched him tensely. But it was the flash of anger he picked up from his father that made him wary.

Then Saetan turned, saw him, and relaxed for a moment before hurrying toward him.

"What happened to you?" Saetan demanded. "Are you hurt?"

"Lucivar happened to me," Daemon replied through gritted teeth.

"Why were you and Lucivar tangling?" Saetan asked in a deceptively neutral voice that had a strong undertone of parental disapproval.

"We weren't tangling, we were drilling. But I'm delighted that someone besides me has trouble understanding the distinction."

The witch turned away from them and started making funny noises. When she turned back, her gold eyes were bright with laughter. "I'm sorry," she said, not sounding the least bit sorry. "Having been on the receiving end of Lucivar's instruction, I understand how you feel."

"Why were you doing weapons drills with Lucivar?" Saetan asked.

"Because I'm an idiot." Daemon raised his hand to brush the hair off his forehead. His arm froze halfway through the motion, stuck. He slowly lowered his arm, grateful it would go back down. "I really want to be there the next time Jaenelle puts him in the dirt."

"Who doesn't?" the witch murmured.

Saetan let out an exasperated sigh. "Sylvia, this is Daemon Sadi. Daemon, this is Lady Sylvia, the Queen of Halaway."

Sylvia's eyes widened. "This is the *boy?*"

Daemon bristled until Saetan gave him a sharp mental jab.

" 'Boy' is a relative term," Saetan said.

"I'm sure it is," Sylvia replied, trying to school her face into an appropriate expression.

Saetan just looked at her.

"Well," Sylvia said too brightly, "I'll just go say hello to the coven and let the two of you sort this out."

"Are you going to lend me that book?" Saetan asked, his lips curving in a knowing, malicious smile.

"What book is that, High Lord?" Sylvia asked, attempting to look innocent while blushing furiously.

"The one you won't admit to reading."

"Oh, I don't think it would interest you," Sylvia mumbled.

"Considering your reaction every time I've mentioned it, I think I would find it very interesting reading."

"You could buy your own copy."

"I would prefer to borrow yours."

Sylvia glared at him. "I'll lend it to you on the condition that *you* admit to the *coven* that you're reading it."

Saetan said nothing. A faint blush colored his cheeks.

Satisfied, Sylvia smiled warmly at Daemon. "Welcome to Kaeleer, Prince Sadi."

"Thank you, Lady," Daemon replied courteously. "Meeting you has been highly instructive."

Saetan hissed. Sylvia didn't waste any time removing herself from their company.

As soon as she left, Saetan raked his fingers through his hair, then inspected the empty hand. "I understand perfectly why her father's hair fell out," he growled. "Mine just keeps getting grayer, for which, I suppose, I should be thankful."

"She's a friend?" Daemon asked blandly.

"Yes, she's a friend," Saetan snapped, putting too much emphasis on the last word. He gave Daemon a sour look. "Come on, puppy. You'd better sit down before you fall down."

Daemon obediently followed his father into the official study, amused by and intensely curious about the edgy, defensive tone in Saetan's voice.

By the time he'd gotten his rebelling muscles to yield enough to let him sit down, Andulvar Yaslana had joined him and Saetan.

"You didn't do too badly for a novice," Andulvar said.

"As soon as I can move again, I'm going to flatten his head," Daemon growled.

Saetan and Andulvar exchanged an amused look.

"Ah," Saetan said, "the centuries may pass, but the sentiment remains the same."

"You said much the same thing the first time you and Lucivar pounded on each other," Andulvar said.

Daemon studied the two men through narrowed eyes.

"The two of you were only a couple of years older than Daemonar," Saetan said. "You found a long pole that was the right diameter for a child's hand, cut it in half, and then Lucivar set out to show you the drills he'd been practicing."

"He's always had a natural talent for weapons," Andulvar said, "but at that age, he wasn't good at explaining the drills."

"So," Saetan said, "he got in a couple of good whacks, and you, by luck or temper, got in a couple of whacks yourself. At which point, the two of you tossed aside the sticks and started using your fists. Manny put an end to it by dumping a bucket of cold water over both of you."

Daemon had to make a conscious effort not to squirm. "Are you going to do this every time?" he growled at Saetan.

"Do what?" Saetan asked blandly.

"Trot out embarrassing stories from my childhood."

Saetan just smiled.

"Come on, puppy," Andulvar said. "You need a hot bath, a rubdown, and something to eat. The morning's still young, and you've got the rest of the day ahead of you."

Daemon's snarl turned into a yelp when Andulvar grabbed the back of his shirt and hauled him to his feet.

"One moment," Saetan said quietly.

Sensing the change in mood, Daemon turned to face Saetan squarely. "You sent for me."

Saetan studied Daemon for a minute. "I've received a request. Whether you want to honor it is totally your choice. If you decide you're not ready, or don't want to at all, I'll try to explain."

Daemon felt ice rush through his veins, but he resisted the urge to give in to the cold rage. He had a lot to learn about the give-and-take between males and females in Kaeleer. He shouldn't assume that a request made here meant the same thing as a request made in Terreille.

"What's the request?"

Saetan said gently, "Your mother would like to see you."

6 / Kaeleer

Sipping a cup of herbal tea, Karla wandered around the inner garden, hoping the sound of the fountain would soothe her. She looked up once, apprehensively, at the second floor windows on the south side of the courtyard. Was Sadi up there right now, watching her from behind the sheer curtains?

Hell's fire, I shouldn't have blurted out that he is a Black Widow. She'd realized that the moment she saw the cold fury in his eyes. But she'd been disturbed by the tangled web she'd woven a couple of days ago and so preoccupied with trying to understand the cryptic images she'd seen . . . Well, seeing Daemon Sadi certainly explained a lot of those images. She'd seen the High Lord looking into a mirror, but the reflection wasn't him. She'd seen truths protected by lies. She'd seen a Black-Jeweled Black Widow who became an enemy in order to remain a friend. And she'd seen death held back by a ring. Her death.

Troubled by her inability to interpret the vision of the High Lord, she had begun to wonder if she'd misread the tangled web somehow. Now there were no more doubts.

She drained the cup and sighed. There was one more thing she'd better get straightened out before Jaenelle returned—for all their sakes.

Daemon reached for the black jacket he had laid on his bed, then paused when he heard the tapping again, a little louder this time. Someone was outside the glass balcony door of his sitting room.

Leaving the jacket, he went into the sitting room, pulled aside the curtain, and stared at the spiky-haired witch standing on the balcony. His first impulse was to release the curtain and ignore her. He didn't want her physical presence or her psychic scent in his rooms. He didn't want anyone wondering why he was entertaining another woman before he'd had a chance to be formally accepted by the Queen.

He didn't give a damn that she was a Territory Queen. But the fact that she was in the First Circle of Jaenelle's court *did* matter.

Reluctantly, he opened the door and stepped back to let her enter.

"I have an appointment in a few minutes," he said coldly.

"I came to apologize," Karla said. "It won't take long. I'm not very good at them, so I tend to keep them short."

Daemon slipped his hands into his trouser pockets and waited.

Karla took a deep breath. "I shouldn't have announced your belonging to the Hourglass so publicly. The First Circle would have been told in any case, but I shouldn't have blurted it out like that. I was thinking about something else that had been puzzling me, and when I saw you . . ." She shrugged.

"How did you know? No one in Terreille realized what I am."

Her lips curved. "Well, I doubt any of them has spent the past ten years annoying Uncle Saetan. Those of us who have would notice the similarities in your psychic scents and reach the correct conclusion."

Daemon blinked. "*Uncle* Saetan?"

Her lips finished curving into that wicked smile. "He adopted Jaenelle, and the rest of us adopted him. We came to stay for a summer and never quite went home again. You can imagine how thrilled he was to discover he'd acquired ten adolescent witches instead of just one—and the boyos, too, of course."

"Of course," Daemon said, fighting not to smile. "Some surprise."

"Mmm. That first summer, when we all piled in on him, the coven became very adept at brewing soothing tonics. It was so distressing to hear him whimper."

Daemon choked on a laugh. Then his amusement faded. She was clever, this Queen with the ice-blue eyes and spiky white-blond hair. She must realize how much he wanted to hear stories of Jaenelle's youth.

Karla studied him. "If it would make you feel better, you can threaten to throttle me."

He was speechless for a moment. "I beg your pardon?"

"In this court, it's the acceptable way for a male to express annoyance with a witch."

"Threatening to throttle a woman is considered acceptable?" Daemon asked, sure that he had misunderstood something.

"As long as he says it calmly so you know he doesn't mean it."

A male who could remain calm in this place must have an amazing amount of self-control, Daemon thought. He rubbed his forehead and began to understand Lucivar's warning about having one of the coven explain things to him.

"Having Lucivar threaten you doesn't bother you?" Daemon asked. Since Lucivar usually sounded calm when he threatened someone, only a fool wouldn't take him seriously.

Karla twitched her shoulders. "Oh. Well. *Lucivar*. He rarely says anything if he's annoyed with you. He just picks you up and tosses you into the nearest body of water." She paused. "Although to be fair—"

"Who wants to be fair?" Daemon growled.

"Spent the morning with him, didn't you?" Karla said knowingly. "If it's a watering trough or a fountain, he dunks you rather than tosses you so that you don't get hurt. However, that's Lucivar. We strongly discourage other males from acquiring that particular habit."

"If you didn't, you'd be wet most of the time," Daemon muttered.

Before Karla could respond to that comment, Morghann, the Queen of Scelt—the red-haired Queen he'd seen earlier that morning—and Gabrielle, the Queen of the Dea al Mon, gave the balcony door a token tap before walking in.

"The coven's rooms all face this inner garden, so it's quicker to use the balcony doors rather than walking all the way around inside," Morghann said at the same time Karla said, "Where's Surreal?"

Gabrielle hooked her silver-blond hair behind her pointed ears and grinned. "Chaosti claimed her on the pretense of giving her a tour of the Hall. She was still snarling about having to apologize to Graysfang for sounding like she meant it when she threatened to smack him."

"I was explaining some of the rules to Daemon," Karla said.

"I really do have an appointment," Daemon muttered, then said, "Come in,"—loudly—when someone knocked on the sitting room door.

Saetan walked in, took one look at the three women, and stopped.

"Kiss kiss," Karla said.

"We were going to explain the rules to Daemon," Morghann said.

"May the Darkness have mercy on Daemon," Saetan said dryly.

"I'll get my jacket," Daemon said, not about to ignore a chance to retreat. Pride kept him from bolting into his bedroom. Common sense made him linger far longer than necessary, so that when he finally walked back into his sitting room, Saetan was the only one waiting for him.

"Have they gone off to plague someone else?" Daemon asked sourly as they left his suite and started walking through the corridors.

Saetan chuckled. "For the moment."

Daemon hesitated. "Maybe you'd better explain those rules to me."

"I'll give you a book of court Protocol to review."

"No, I meant the rules that are peculiar to this court. Like—"

"I don't want to know," Saetan said quietly but firmly.

"You have to know. You're the Steward."

"Exactly. And if this court has some rules that I have been blissfully ignorant of for the five years that I've been the Steward, I do not want to know about them now."

"But—" Daemon said. The implacable look in Saetan's eyes stopped him. "That's a prissy attitude for you to take."

"From where you're standing, I suppose it is. From where I'm standing, it makes a world of sense. You're younger. Deal with it."

Before he could make a comment he might regret, a small brown-and-white dog raced up to them and stopped a few feet away, his tail wagging in effusive greeting.

He's here! Jaenelle's mate is finally here!

Daemon felt as if the wind had been knocked out of him, not only because he had heard the dog but because he'd seen the Red Jewel hidden in the white ruff.

"Daemon, this is Lord Ladvarian," Saetan said. "Ladvarian, this—"

A Black-Jeweled Warlord Prince, Ladvarian said as he danced around in front of them. *He's a Black-Jeweled Warlord Prince. I have to tell Kaelas.* The dog dashed down the corridor and disappeared.

"Mother Night," Saetan said under his breath. "Come on. Let's get out of here before you meet anyone else. You've already had a sufficient amount of education for your first day in the court."

"He's kindred," Daemon said weakly as he followed Saetan. "When Lucivar said someone named Ladvarian would be pleased to see me, I thought . . . Unless he meant someone else?"

"No, that's Ladvarian. He would have gone to the service fair to look for you himself, but kindred aren't well received in Little Terreille, and I wasn't willing to risk him. His ability to explain kindred behavior to humans and human behavior to the kindred makes him unique. And his influence on Prince Kaelas is not to be taken lightly."

"Who's Kaelas?"

Saetan gave him an odd look. "Let's save Kaelas for another day."

Daemon studied the well-kept cottage and neat yard. "I'd always wanted Tersa to live in a place like this."

"She's comfortable here," Saetan said, opening the front door. "A journeymaid Black Widow lives with her as a companion. And then there's Mikal," he added as they followed the sound of voices to the kitchen.

Daemon stepped into the kitchen, gave the boy sitting at the kitchen table a quick glance, and then focused on Tersa, who was muttering to herself as she busily arranged an assortment of food.

Her black hair was as tangled as he remembered it, but the dark-green dress was clean and looked warm.

The boy hastily swallowed a mouthful of nutcake before saying in a suspicious voice, "Who's he?"

Tersa looked up. Joy brightened her gold eyes and made her smile radiant. "It's the boy," she said as she rushed into Daemon's arms.

"Hello, sweetheart," Daemon said, feeling swamped by the pleasure of seeing her again.

"*He's* not a *boy*," the boy said.

"Mikal," Saetan said sternly.

Leaning away from Daemon, Tersa looked at Mikal, then back at Daemon. "He is a large boy," she said firmly. She pulled Daemon toward the table. "Sit down. Sit. There is food. You should eat."

Daemon sat across from the boy, who openly regarded him as an unwelcome rival. "Shouldn't you be in school?"

Mikal rolled his eyes. "It's not a school day."

"But you did finish the chores your mother assigned to you *before* you came here," Saetan said mildly, accepting the glass of red wine Tersa offered him while his eyes never left Mikal.

Mikal squirmed under that knowing stare, and finally muttered, "Most of them."

"In that case, after we've eaten, I'll escort you home and you can finish them," Saetan said.

"But I have to help Tersa weed the garden," Mikal protested.

"The weeds will still be there," Tersa said serenely. She looked at the two "boys," frowned at the glasses of milk she held, then put both of them in front of Mikal. She patted Daemon's shoulder. "He is old enough for wine."

"Thank the Darkness," Daemon said under his breath.

The meal was eaten with little conversation. Saetan inquired about Mikal's schoolwork and got the expected evasive answers. Tersa tried to make mundane comments about the cottage and garden, but each time the remarks became more disjointed.

Daemon clenched his teeth. He wanted to tell her to stop trying. It hurt to watch her struggling so hard to walk the borderland of sanity for his sake, and seeing the concern and resentment in Mikal's eyes as her control continued to crumble stabbed at him.

Saetan set his wineglass on the table and rose. "Come on, puppy," he said to Mikal. "I'll take you home now."

Mikal quickly grabbed a nutcake. "I haven't finished eating."

"Take it with you."

When they left, with Mikal still loudly protesting, Daemon looked at Tersa. "It's good to see you again," he said softly.

Sorrow filled her eyes. "I don't know how to be your mother."

He reached for her hand. "Then just be Tersa. That was always more than enough." He felt her absorb the acceptance, felt the tension drain from her body.

Finally, she smiled. "You are well?"

He returned the smile and lied. "Yes, I'm well."

Her hand tightened on his. Her eyes lost focus, became distant and farseeing. "No," she said quietly, "you're not. But you will be." Then she stood up. "Come. I'll show you my garden."

7 / Kaeleer

Saetan shifted to a sitting position on the couch in his study. He didn't need to use a psychic probe to know who was on the other side of the door. The scent of her fear was sufficient. "Come."

Wilhelmina Benedict entered the room, each step a hesitation.

Watching her, Saetan tightened the reins on his temper. It wasn't her fault. She had been barely more than a child herself thirteen years ago. There was nothing she could have done.

But if Jaenelle hadn't stayed in Chaillot in order to protect Wilhelmina, that last, terrible night at Briarwood wouldn't have happened. She would have left the family that hadn't understood or cherished what she was. She would have come to Kaeleer, would have come to *him*—and would have escaped the violent rape that had left her with so many deep emotional scars.

It wasn't fair to hold Wilhelmina in any way responsible for what had happened to Jaenelle, but he still resented her presence in his home and her reappearance in her sister's life.

"What can I do for you, Lady Benedict?" He tried, but he couldn't keep the edge out of his voice.

"I don't know what to do." Her voice was barely audible.

"About what?"

"All the other people who signed the contract have something to do, even if it's just making a list of their skills. But I—"

She wrung her hands so hard Saetan winced in sympathy for the delicate bones.

"He hates me," Wilhelmina said, her voice rising in desperation. "Everyone here hates me, and I don't know why."

Saetan pointed at the other end of the couch. "Sit down." As he waited for her to obey, he wondered how such a frightened, emotionally brittle woman had managed to make the journey through one of the Gates between the Realms and then tried to acquire a contract at the service fair. When she was seated, he said, "Hate is too strong a word. No one here hates you."

"Yaslana does." She pressed her fists into her lap. "So do you."

"I don't hate you, Wilhelmina," he said quietly. "But I do resent your presence."

"Why?"

Faced with her hurt and bewilderment, he was tempted to blunt the truth, but decided to give her the courtesy of honesty. "Because you're the reason Jaenelle didn't leave Chaillot soon enough."

Her swift change from frightened to fierce startled him, and he realized it shouldn't have. He should have looked for the common ground between her and Jaenelle instead of letting the past cloud his judgment.

"You know where to find her, don't you? *Don't you?*"

She looked like she was about to shake the answer out of him. Intrigued by the change in her, he wondered if she would actually try.

"Not at the moment," he said mildly. "But she'll be home soon."

"Home?" Her fierceness changed back to bewilderment and then thoughtfulness as she looked around the study. "Home?"

"I'm her adopted father." When she didn't react to that, he added, "Lucivar is her brother."

She jumped as if he'd jabbed her with a pin. Her blue eyes were filled with something close to horror as she stared at him. "Brother?"

"Brother. If it's any comfort to you, while you're both related to the same woman, you're not related to each other."

Her relief was so blatant he almost laughed.

"Does she like him?" Wilhelmina asked in a small voice.

He couldn't help it. He did laugh. "Most of the time." Then he studied her. "Is that why you came to Kaeleer? To find Jaenelle?"

She nodded. "Everyone else said she had died, that Prince Sadi had killed her, but I knew it wasn't true. He never would have hurt Jaenelle. I thought she had gone to live with one of her secret friends or with her teacher." She looked at him as if she were trying to measure what she saw against something she knew. "It was you, wasn't it? She came to *you* for lessons."

"Yes." He waited. "What made you think of Kaeleer?"

"She told me. After." Wilhelmina brushed a finger against her Sapphire

Jewel. "When Prince Sadi unleashed his Black Jewels to escape the Hayllians who had come for him, I heard Jaenelle yelling 'ride it, ride it.' So I did. When it was over, I was wearing a Sapphire Jewel. Everyone was upset about that because they thought I had somehow made the Offering to the Darkness. But it wasn't my Jewel. It was Jaenelle's. I couldn't actually use it, but it protected me. Sometimes, when I was scared or didn't know what to do, it always gave the same answer: Kaeleer. I left home because Bobby—" She pressed her lips together and took a couple of deep breaths. "I left home. As soon as I was twenty, I made the Offering. I got this Jewel. The other one disappeared."

"And you've spent these past years trying to find a way here?"

She hesitated. "I wasn't ready for a long time. Then, one day, I started wondering if I would *ever* be ready. So I came anyway."

Which meant this woman had more courage than was readily apparent.

"Tell me something, Wilhelmina," Saetan said gently. "If, thirteen years ago, Jaenelle had decided to leave Chaillot and had asked you to go with her, would you have?"

It took her a long time to answer. Finally, reluctantly, she said, "I don't know." She looked around the room, sadness in her eyes. "Jaenelle belongs here. I don't."

"You're Jaenelle's sister and a Sapphire-Jeweled witch. Don't judge too quickly." *And I, too, will try not to judge too quickly.* "Besides, you would have had a different opinion of this place if you'd been here while ten adolescent witches were in residence," he added in a deliberately mournful voice.

Her eyes widened. "You mean the Queens who are here?"

"Yes."

"Oh, dear."

"That's one way of putting it."

She ducked her head as she stifled a laugh. When she dared to look at him again, he could tell she was thinking hard, reassessing the Hall and the people who resided here.

"I still don't have anything to do," she said hesitantly.

The almost-hopeful expectation in her eyes made him realize she had taken a long step toward accepting him as the family patriarch—and expecting him to fulfill the duties of that position.

"Lucivar didn't say *anything*?" he asked, fully aware that the only reason Lucivar had brought her there was to keep her away from anyone who might try to use her relationship to Jaenelle.

For the first time, a bit of temper flashed in her eyes. "He told me to try not to faint because it will upset the males if I do."

Saetan sighed. "Coming from Lucivar, that was almost tactful. He's right. Blunt, but right. Males react strongly to feminine distress."

Wilhelmina frowned. "Is that why that large striped cat keeps following me?"

Saetan looked at the study door. A quick question on a psychic spear thread gave him the answer. "His name is Dejaal. He's Prince Jaal's son. He's appointed himself your protector until you feel comfortable with the other males at the Hall."

"He's kindred? I had heard stories—"

"The Blood in Little Terreille don't have much use for the kindred, and the kindred have even less use for the Blood in Little Terreille," Saetan said, and then added silently, *Except when they're hungry.*

Rising, he offered a hand to Wilhelmina and led her to the door. He called in a grooming brush and gave it to her. "If you want to do something that will help all of us right now, take Dejaal out to one of the gardens and brush him. Once you get used to him, perhaps it will be easier for you to be around the rest of us."

"If it's supposed to make me feel easier, maybe I should brush Lucivar instead," she said with just a hint of tartness.

Saetan burst out laughing. "Darling, if you want to get along with Lucivar, just show him that bit of steel in your backbone. Since he's lived with Jaenelle for the past eight years, he'll recognize it for what it is."

8 / Kaeleer

"Are you sure this is the path back to the Hall?" Daemon asked as he ducked under a low-hanging branch.

We left the path, Ladvarian said. *We have to cross the creek, and the path has no bridge.*

"I don't need a bridge to cross the creek."

Ladvarian looked at Daemon's shoes. *You would get wet.*

"I'd survive," Daemon muttered.

When he left Tersa's cottage, he'd found Ladvarian waiting to escort him back to the Hall. At first, he'd wondered if this was a subtle kind of insult, implying that he couldn't find his way back by himself. Then, when Ladvarian offered to show him a footpath that ran between Halaway and the Hall, he'd wondered if he was being set up for an ambush. Finally he realized the dog just wanted to spend a little time getting to know the male whose duties made him an important part of the Queen's life.

What he didn't like was the growing impression that he was being labeled as a human who needed to be coddled.

He stopped walking. "Look, this has got to stop. I may not be an Eyrien warrior, but I'm perfectly capable of walking a couple of miles without collapsing, I can get across a creek without getting wet if I choose to, and I don't need a short furball treating me like I can't survive if I'm not inside a house full of servants. Do you understand?"

Ladvarian wagged his tail. *Yes. You want to be treated like a Kaeleer male.*

Daemon rocked back on his heels and studied the Sceltie. "Is that what I said?"

Yes. Ladvarian headed off at an abrupt angle. *This way.*

A minute later, they arrived at the creek. Ladvarian trotted up to the bank and leaped. By rights, he should have landed in the middle of the creek, but he kept sailing over it, and when he landed, he was standing a foot above the ground, a doggy grin on his face.

Daemon looked at the creek, looked at the Sceltie, and then air walked over the creek to the other bank.

Did Jaenelle teach you that?

Remembering the afternoon when Jaenelle had shown him how to walk on air, Daemon's chest tightened. "Yes," he said softly, "she did."

She taught me, too. Ladvarian sounded pleased.

As soon as they walked through another stand of trees, Daemon saw the road. The drive, he amended. Once the north road out of Halaway crossed the bridge, it became the drive up to the Hall, and the land spread out before him was the family estate.

He headed for the drive, then spun around when Ladvarian growled, half-expecting an attack despite the dog's display of friendship.

But Ladvarian was facing the way they'd come. The bridge was out of sight because of the roll of the land, but the wind was coming from that direction.

"What is it?" Daemon asked, opening his first inner barrier enough to sense the area around them.

Humans are coming. Three carriages. I've warned the other males, but we have to get back now. Ladvarian started trotting in a direct line toward the Hall, forcing Daemon into a fast walk to keep up.

"What's wrong with humans coming to the Hall?"

Ladvarian's psychic scent became hostile. *They feel wrong.*

The sudden fierceness was a sharp reminder that the small male trotting beside him was also a Red-Jeweled Warlord, and if Lucivar had overseen some of Ladvarian's training, the Sceltie was a far more effective fighter than anyone might suspect.

Nighthawk will take you to the Hall. He runs faster.

Before Daemon could wonder about that cryptic remark, he heard the hoofbeats pounding toward him.

Under other circumstances, once he saw the black horse, he would have declined the offer—not only because riding a stallion bareback wasn't a healthy idea, but because, for just a moment, the wind and the horse's movement had lifted its forelock and he'd seen the Gray Jewel hidden underneath. Despite the difference in their species, he recognized the aggressive psychic scent of another Warlord Prince. But when he didn't move after the horse pulled up, Ladvarian nipped his calf.

Go, Daemon. Now.

He barely had time to mount and grab a fistful of the long mane before Nighthawk took off at a flat-out gallop cross-country. Wondering how Ladvarian was going to keep up with them at that pace, he glanced back and saw the dog balanced on the horse's rump.

When the horse angled toward the last, long, straight section of the drive, Daemon tugged on the mane, and shouted, "Ease up," worried that Nighthawk would slip on the gravel at that speed.

He felt a slight lift, and then heard . . . nothing. No pounding hooves, no scattering gravel. Looking over Nighthawk's left shoulder, he saw those driving legs racing on air straight for the front door.

They were close enough to see the details of the dragon's head doorknocker before Nighthawk sat back on his haunches and finally came to a stop a hand span away from the steps.

Daemon dismounted and walked up the steps, not sure if his legs were trembling from muscle tension or frayed nerves. When he reached the door and looked back, there was no sign of Nighthawk, but he could sense the stallion's presence nearby.

"Hell's fire," he muttered as a footman opened the door.

Ladvarian rushed in ahead of him and disappeared.

Daemon entered more slowly, feeling the press of male hostility. Besides the footman, the only visible person in the great hall was Beale, the butler, but he doubted they were the only ones present.

"It seems we're about to have company," Daemon said as he smoothed back his hair and straightened his black jacket.

"So it would seem," Beale replied blandly. "If you would remain here, Prince Yaslana and the High Lord will be arriving shortly."

Daemon looked around, then stepped into the formal receiving room just far enough not to be seen by whoever walked through the door.

Observing the move, Beale shifted position, putting himself directly in Daemon's line of sight.

Lucivar, Daemon said, using an Ebon-gray spear thread.

I'm coming in through the servants' door at the back of the hall.

If any of them manage to slip past us, is there any way for them to reach the living quarters?

The only way to the upper floors from that part of the Hall is by using the staircase in the informal receiving room. Don't worry about it. Kaelas is there. Nothing's going to get up those stairs. And the High Lord is coming down from that direction.

Daemon heard the carriages pull up in front of the Hall, saw Beale nod to the footman when someone banged on the door.

Footsteps. Rustling clothes. Then a woman's voice.

"I demand to see Wilhelmina Benedict."

Cold rage slipped through him so fast he was riding the killing edge before he realized he'd taken the first step toward it. He hadn't heard her voice in thirteen years, but he recognized it.

"Lady Benedict is not available," Beale said in a bland voice.

"Don't tell me that. I'm the Queen of Chaillot and I—"

Daemon stepped out of the receiving room. "Good afternoon, Alexandra," he said too calmly. "Such a pleasure to see you again."

"You." Alexandra stared at him, her eyes wide and fearful. Then the anger came. "You arranged for that 'tour' of Briarwood, didn't you?"

"All things considered, it was the least I could do." He took a step toward her. "I told you I would wash the streets of Beldon Mor with blood if you betrayed me."

"You also said you would put me in my grave."

"I decided that letting you live was a more thorough punishment."

"You bastard! You—" Alexandra started shivering. All of her entourage started shivering.

The intense, burning cold hit him a moment later, stunning him enough that he slipped away from the killing edge.

A moment after that, Saetan stepped into the great hall.

Is that what I look like when I go cold? Daemon wondered, unable to look away from glazed, sleepy eyes and the malevolently gentle smile.

"Lady Angelline." Saetan's voice rolled through the Hall like soft thunder. "I always knew we would meet someday to settle the debt, but I never thought you would be foolish enough to come here."

Alexandra clenched her hands but couldn't stop shaking. "I came to take my granddaughters home. Let them go, and we'll leave."

"Lady Benedict will be informed that you're here. If she wants to see you, a meeting will be arranged—fully chaperoned, of course."

"You dare imply that *I* present some kind of danger?"

"I know you do. The only question is, how much of a danger."

Alexandra's voice rose. "You have no right—"

"I rule here," Saetan snarled. "You're the one who has no rights, Lady. None at all. Except those I grant you. And I grant you little."

"I want to see my granddaughters. *Both* of them."

Something savage flickered at the back of Saetan's eyes. He looked at Leland and Philip, then turned his attention back to Alexandra. His voice dropped into a singsong croon. "I had two long, terrible years in which to come up with the perfect execution for the three of you. It will take you two long, terrible years to die, and every minute of it will be filled with more pain than you can imagine. However, in this case, I must have my Queen's consent before I begin." He turned away from them. "Beale, prepare some rooms for our guests. They'll be staying with us for a while."

As he walked past Daemon toward his study, their eyes met.

Daemon looked at Leland, who was clinging to Philip and crying softly; at the other Queens and their males, who were cowering in a tight group; and, finally, at Alexandra, who stared at him with terrified eyes and whose skin was bleached of any color.

Turning on his heel, he headed for the study and noticed Lucivar standing quietly at the back of the hall.

If you go in there, be careful, Bastard, Lucivar said.

Nodding, Daemon walked into the study.

Saetan stood by the desk, carefully pouring a glass of brandy. He looked up, poured a second glass, and extended it toward Daemon.

Daemon accepted the glass and took a healthy swallow, hoping it would thaw him a little.

"Another male's rage shouldn't throw you so much it knocks you away from the killing edge," Saetan said quietly.

"I'd never felt anything quite like that before."

"And if you feel it again, will it throw you again?"

Daemon looked at the man standing an arm's length away from him and understood it was the Steward of the Dark Court and not his father who was asking the question. "No, it won't."

Moving carefully, as if he were too aware that any sudden movement might unleash the violence still raging inside him, Saetan leaned against his blackwood desk.

Keeping his own movements equally controlled, Daemon poured himself another brandy. "Do you think the Queen will give her consent?"

"No. Since her relatives inflicted harm on her and not someone else, she'll oppose the execution. But I'll still make the request."

Daemon gently swirled the brandy in his glass. "If, for some reason, she doesn't oppose it, may I watch?"

Saetan's smile was sweet and vicious. "My darling Prince, if Jaenelle actually gives her consent, you can do more than watch."

9 / Kaeleer

Lord Magstrom sighed as he laid his stack of files on the large table already filled with stacks of files. He sighed again when his elbow jostled a corner stack and the top bulging file spilled on the floor. Going down on one knee, he began collecting the papers.

Thank the Darkness claiming day had ended and the autumn service fair was officially over. Perhaps he should decline to work the service fair next spring. The grueling hours were taxing for a man his age, but it was the heartbreaking hope and desperation on the immigrants' faces that wrung him dry. How could he look at a woman no older than his youngest granddaughter and not want to help her find a place to live where the fear lurking at the back of her eyes would be replaced by happiness? How could he talk to a courteous, well-spoken man who had been horrifically scarred by repeated attempts to "teach him obedience" and not want to send him to some quiet village where he could regain his self-respect and not have to wonder what was going to happen to him every time the Lady who ruled there looked in his direction?

There weren't places like that in Little Terreille. Not anymore. But it was the Queens in this Territory that continued to offer contracts and stuff their courts with immigrants. The other Queens in Kaeleer, in the Territories that answered to the Queen of Ebon Askavi, were more cautious and far more selective. So he did his best to find the immigrants who had a skill or a dream or *something* that might buy them a contract outside of Little Terreille, and he brought those people to the attention of the males in Jaenelle Angelline's First Circle when they came to the service fair. As for the others, he filled out the contracts and wished them luck and good life—and wondered if their new life in Little Terreille would really be any different than the life they had tried to escape.

And he tried not to think at all about the ones who hadn't been fortunate enough to receive *some* kind of contract and were sent back to Terreille.

Magstrom shook his head as he shuffled the papers into some kind of order. Such sloppy work, stuffing the immigration entry lists into the same file as the service lists and the lists of those who were returning to Terreille. How could the clerks be expected to—

His hand tightened on a sheet of paper. The Hayllian entry list. But *he* had been in charge of the Hayllian list—until the end of the third day, when Jorval had decided to oversee that particular list. There had been twenty names on the list he'd given Jorval. Now there were only twelve. Had someone recopied the list and only put down the names of the people who had been accepted into service? No, because Daemon Sadi's name wasn't there.

Magstrom quickly shuffled through the papers for the Hayllian list of people returning to Terreille which the guards would use to make sure no one tried to slip away and go into hiding. Four names listed. Since Sadi was now in Dhemlan, that left three people unaccounted for who had been on the entry list he had given to Jorval.

When he heard footsteps approaching, he stuffed the papers back into the file, grunted softly as he stood up, and hurriedly placed the file on a stack where it wouldn't just spill back onto the floor.

The footsteps stopped at the door, then continued on.

Magstrom listened for a moment, then used Craft to probe the area. No one there. But a shiver of uneasiness rippled down his back.

Pushed by that uneasiness, he left the building and hurried to the inn where he had been staying during the service fair. As soon as he reached his room, he began to pack.

By rights, he should have sought out other Council members and mentioned the disparities in the Hayllian lists. Maybe it was a simple clerical error—too many names, too much work rushed through. But who would "forget" to put a Warlord Prince like Daemon Sadi on the list? Unless the omission had been deliberate. And if that were the case, who knew how many other lists had similar disparities, how many Terreilleans who had come to Kaeleer were now unaccounted for?

And who knew what might happen to the evidence of those disparities if he told the wrong Council members about it?

If he rode the White Wind, which would be the least demanding, he could still be at the Nharkhava border by dawn. Because one of his granddaughters lived there, Kalush, the Queen of Nharkhava, had granted him a special dispensation that allowed him to visit her Territory without having to go through the formalities every time. And if, once he reached the border landing web, he requested an escort to his granddaughter's house . . . The guards might think it an odd request, but they wouldn't refuse to assist an elderly man. After he had a little sleep, he would compose a letter to the High Lord, explaining about the disparities in the lists.

Maybe it *was* only a clerical error. But if it was, in fact, the first glimpse of trouble, at least Saetan would have some warning—and would also know where to look for the source.

Jorval looked at the sheet of paper lying under the table and the papers hastily stuffed back into the bulging file.

So. The old fool had gotten curious. How unfortunate.

Magstrom might have been a thorn in the Dark Council's side for a good many years now, but he'd had his uses—especially since he was the only Council member who could request an audience with the High Lord and actually be granted one.

But it would seem that Magstrom's usefulness was coming to an end. And he wasn't about to forget that if it hadn't been for Magstrom's interference yesterday afternoon, the Dark Priestess would have had her Black-Jeweled weapon safely tucked away somewhere where he could be useful.

He was tempted to send someone to take care of Magstrom that night, but the timing might lead certain people—like the High Lord—to look into the service fair a little too closely.

He could wait. Magstrom couldn't have seen *that* much. And if anything was questioned, it was easy enough to dismiss a clerk or two for negligence and offer profuse apologies.

But when the time did come . . .

10 / Kaeleer

Alexandra huddled in the chair in front of the blackwood desk.

The High Lord requests your presence.

Requests? *Demands* was more like it. But the study had been empty when that large, stone-faced butler had opened the door for her and, after fifteen minutes, she was still waiting. Not that she was in any hurry to face the High Lord again.

She strengthened the warming spell she'd put on her shawl and then grimaced at the futility of seeking a little warmth in this place. It wasn't so much the *place*—which was actually quite beautiful if you could get past the oppressive, dark feel of it—it was the *people* who produced a bone-deep chill.

She didn't think it was out of courtesy that she and her entourage had been given dinner in a small dining room located near the guest rooms. He wouldn't have cared that she was too physically and emotionally exhausted to cope with meeting whoever else lived there. He wouldn't have cared that she wouldn't have been able to choke down a mouthful of food if she had to sit at a table with Daemon Sadi.

No, she and her people had dined alone because he hadn't wanted her presence at his table.

And now, when she wanted to do nothing more than retire to her room and get whatever sleep she could after an exhausting day, *he* had requested her presence—and then didn't even have the courtesy to be there when she arrived.

She should leave. She was a Queen, and the insult of keeping her waiting had gone on long enough. If the High Lord wanted to see her, let him come to her.

As she stood up, the door opened and his dark psychic scent flooded the room. She sank back into the chair. It took all her self-control not to cower as he walked past her and settled into the chair behind the blackwood desk.

"When a male asks to speak with a Queen, he doesn't keep her waiting," Alexandra said, trying to keep her voice from quivering.

"And you, being such a stickler about courtesy, have never kept anyone waiting?" Saetan asked mildly after a long pause.

The queer, burning glitter that filled his eyes scared her, but she sensed this was the only chance she would have. If she backed down now, he would never concede anything.

She filled her voice with the cool disdain she used whenever an aristo male needed to be put in his place. "What a Queen does is beside the point."

"Since a Queen can do anything she damn well pleases, no matter how cruel the act, no matter how much harm she causes."

"Don't twist my words," she snapped, forgetting everything else about him except that he was male and shouldn't be allowed to treat a Queen this way.

"My apologies, Lady. Since you twist so much yourself, I'll do my best not to add to it."

She gave herself a moment to think. "You're deliberately trying to provoke me. Why? So you can justify executing me?"

"Oh, I already have all the justification I need for an execution," Saetan said mildly. "No, it's simpler than that. Your being terrified of me gets us nowhere. If you're angry, you'll at least talk."

"In that case, I want my granddaughters returned to me."

"You have no right to either of them."

"I have every right!"

"You're forgetting something very basic, Alexandra. Wilhelmina is twenty-seven. Jaenelle is twenty-five. The age of majority is twenty. You have no say in their lives anymore."

"Then neither do you. *They* should decide to stay or leave."

"They've already decided. And I do have far more say in their lives than you. Wilhelmina signed a contract with the Warlord Prince of Ebon Rih. He, in turn, serves in the Dark Court. I'm the Steward. So court hierarchy gives me the right to make some decisions about her life."

"What about Jaenelle? Does she serve in this Dark Court, too?"

Saetan gave her an odd look. "You really don't understand, do you? Jaenelle doesn't serve, Alexandra. Jaenelle is the Queen."

For a moment, the conviction in his voice almost convinced her.

No. *No.* If Jaenelle were really a Queen, she would have *known.* Like would have recognized like. Oh, there *might* actually be a Queen who ruled this court, but it wasn't, *couldn't be,* Jaenelle.

But his declaration gave her a weapon. "If Jaenelle is the Queen, you have no right to control her life."

"Neither do you."

Alexandra clamped her hands around the arms of the chair and gritted her teeth. "The age of majority acknowledges certain conditions that have to be met. If a child is deemed incapable in some way, her family maintains its right to take care of her mental and physical well being and make decisions on her behalf."

"And who decides if the child is incapable? The family that gets to maintain control of her? How very convenient. And don't forget, you're talking about a Queen who outranks you."

"I forget nothing. And don't you try to take the moral high ground with me—as if you had any concept of what morality means."

Saetan's eyes iced over. "Very well, then. Let's take a look at *your* concept of morality. Tell me, Alexandra. How did you justify it when it was obvious Jaenelle was being starved? How did you justify the rope burns from her being tied down, the bruises from the beatings? Did you just shrug it all off as the discipline needed to control a recalcitrant child?"

"You lie!" Alexandra shouted. "I never saw any evidence of that."

"You just tossed her into Briarwood and didn't bother to see her again until you decided to let her out?"

"Of course I saw her!" Alexandra paused. An ache spread through her chest as she remembered the distant, almost accusing way Jaenelle would look at them sometimes when she and Leland went to visit. The wariness and suspicion in her eyes, directed at them. She remembered how much it had hurt, and how Leland wept silently on the way home, when Dr. Carvay had told them that Jaenelle was too emotionally unstable to have any visitors. And she remembered the times she had felt relieved that Jaenelle was safely tucked away so others wouldn't have firsthand knowledge of the girl's fanciful tales. "I saw her whenever she was emotionally stable enough to have visitors."

Saetan snarled softly.

"You sit there and judge me, but you don't know what it was like trying to deal with a child who—"

"Jaenelle was seven when I met her."

For a moment, Alexandra couldn't breathe. Seven. She could imagine that voice wrapping itself around a child, spinning out lies. "So when she told her stories about unicorns and dragons, you encouraged her."

"I believed her, yes."

"Why?"

His smile was terrible. "Because they exist."

She shook her head, struck mute by the collision of too many thoughts, too many feelings.

"What would it take to convince you, Alexandra? Being impaled on a unicorn's horn? Would you still insist he was a fanciful tale?"

"You could trick anyone into believing anything you choose."

His eyes got that glazed, sleepy look. "I see." He stood up. "I don't give a damn what you think of me. I don't give a damn what you think about anything. But if I sense one flicker of distress from Wilhelmina or Jaenelle because of you, I'll bring everything I am down on you." He looked at her with those cold, cold eyes. "I don't know why Jaenelle ended up with you. I don't know why the Darkness would place such an extraordinary spirit in the care of someone like you. You didn't deserve her. You don't deserve even to know her."

He walked out of the room.

Alexandra sat there for a long time.

Tricks and lies. He'd said Jaenelle had been seven, but how old had she really been when the High Lord first started whispering his sweetly poisoned lies into a child's ear. Perhaps he had even created illusions of unicorns and dragons that looked real enough to be convincing. Maybe the uneasy way Jaenelle had sometimes made her feel had really been an aftertaste of him and not the child herself.

She couldn't deny that horrors had been done at Briarwood. But had those men done those things by choice or had an unseen puppet master been pulling the strings? She had experienced Daemon Sadi's cruelty. Wasn't it likely that his father had refined his taste for it? Had all that pain and suffering been caused in order to make one particular child so vulnerable she became emotionally dependent on these men?

Dorothea had been right. The High Lord was a monster. Sitting there, Alexandra was certain of only one thing: she would do whatever she had to in order to get Wilhelmina and Jaenelle away from him.

He felt Daemon's hands slide up his shoulder blades, then settle on his shoulders a moment before those strong, slender fingers began kneading tight muscles.

"Did you tell her Jaenelle is Witch?" Daemon asked softly.

Saetan took a sip of yarbarah, the blood wine, then closed his eyes to better savor the feel of tension and anger draining away as Daemon coaxed his muscles to relax. "No," he finally said. "I told her Jaenelle was the Queen, which should have been enough, but . . ."

"It wouldn't have mattered," Daemon said. "That last night, at the Winsol party, when I finally understood what Briarwood really was, I had intended to tell Alexandra about Jaenelle. I'd convinced myself that she would help me get Jaenelle away from Chaillot."

"But you didn't tell her."

Daemon's hands paused, then started working on another group of knotted muscles. "I overheard her tell another woman that Witch was only a symbol for the Blood, but if the living myth did appear, she hoped someone would have the courage to strangle it in its cradle."

A bolt of anger flashed through Saetan, but he couldn't tell if it was his or Daemon's. "Mother Night, how I hate that woman."

"Philip and Leland aren't exactly innocent."

"No, they're not, but they only follow Alexandra's lead both as their Queen and the family matriarch. She accused me of spinning lies to ensnare Jaenelle, but how many lies did *they* tell by cloaking them in the conviction of truth?" He made a sound that might have been a bitter laugh. "I can tell you how many. I've had years to observe the emotional scars their words left on her."

"And what happens when she finds out they're here?"

"We'll deal with that when it comes."

Daemon leaned closer, brushed his lips against Saetan's neck. "I can create a grave no one will ever find."

The kiss followed by that statement jolted Saetan enough to remember that this son still needed careful handling. He might indulge in imaginary gravedigging to channel some of his anger, but, just then, Daemon wouldn't hesitate to do it.

He jolted again when he felt the feather-light brush of dark, feminine power across the deepest edge of his inner barriers.

"Saetan?" Daemon said too softly.

Wolf song filled the night.

"No," Saetan replied gently but firmly as he stepped away far enough to turn and face Daemon. "It's too late for that."

"Why?"

"Because that chorus of welcome means Jaenelle is back." When Daemon paled, Saetan ran a hand down his son's arm. "Come to my study and have a drink with me. We'll bring Lucivar with us since he's probably fussed over Marian enough by now to annoy her."

"What about Jaenelle?"

Saetan smiled. "Boyo, after one of these trips, greeting males, no matter who they are, comes in a poor third on her list of priorities—the first being a very long, hot bath and the second being an enormous meal. Since we can't compete with those, we might as well sit back and relax while we wait for her to get around to us."

11 / Kaeleer

Surreal stormed through the corridors. Each time she came to an intersection, a silent, solemn-faced footman pointed in the right direction. Probably the first one had warned the others after she'd snarled at him, "Where's the High Lord's study?"

It struck her as a little odd that none of the servants had seemed startled by her roaring through the corridors wearing nothing but a night-gown. Well, considering that the witches had to deal with the males who lived in this place, it probably wasn't unusual.

When she finally reached the staircase that led down to the informal receiving room, she hitched her nightgown up to her knees to keep from tripping on the hem, raced down the stairs and into the great hall, and swore because the marble floor was cold against her bare feet. In lieu of a knock, she walloped the study door once and then stomped up to the blackwood desk where Saetan sat watching her, a glass of brandy raised halfway to his lips.

Daemon and Lucivar, comfortably slouched in two chairs in front of the desk, just stared at her.

Now that she was there, she wasn't quite as willing to address the High Lord directly, so she half turned toward Daemon and Lucivar and tossed out the question, "Don't I have the right to decide if I want a male in my bed?"

The air behind the desk instantly chilled, but Lucivar said blandly, "Graysfang?" and the air returned to normal.

The smirk in Lucivar's voice had her turning toward him fully. "I don't know about you, but I'm not used to sleeping with a wolf."

"What's wrong with Graysfang staying with you?" Daemon asked.

The soothing tone he was putting into his voice only infuriated her. "He farts," she snapped, then waved her hand dismissively. "Well, so do the rest of you."

Someone made a choking sound. She *thought* it was Daemon.

"Do you resent his being there because he's a wolf or because he's interfering with another kind of male warming your bed?" Lucivar asked.

Maybe it hadn't been meant as a slur that she used to be a whore, but she took it as such because then she could vent her temper on him. "Well, sugar, from where I'm standing, there's not much to choose between you. He takes up more than his share of the bed, he snores, and he gives slobbery kisses. But if I had to choose, I'd pick him. At least *he* can lick his *own* balls!"

A glass hit the desk with an ominous *thunk*.

Surreal closed her eyes and bit her lip.

Shit. She'd been so focused on being mad at Lucivar, she'd forgotten about the High Lord.

Before she could turn, Saetan had a firm grip on her arm and was pulling her toward the door.

"If you don't want Graysfang in your room at night, tell him," Saetan said, sounding like he had something stuck in his throat. "If he persists . . . Well, Lady, he wears a Purple Dusk Jewel and you wear a Gray. A shield around your room should take care of the problem."

"I *did* shield the room," Surreal protested. "And I still woke up and found him there. He sounded pleased that I'd shielded the room against the 'strange males,' but when he realized he couldn't get in, he had somebody named Kaelas help him through the shield."

Saetan's hand froze over the doorknob. He straightened up slowly. "Kaelas helped him through the shield," he said, spacing out the words.

She nodded cautiously.

Saetan swiftly opened the door. "In that case, Lady, I strongly suggest you and Graysfang get this settled between you."

The next thing she knew, she was standing in the great hall, staring at a firmly closed door.

"You said you'd help," she muttered. "You said I could come to you if I needed anything."

When the door opened again, she half-expected the High Lord to call her back. Instead, Daemon and Lucivar got shoved into the hall and the door was slammed shut behind them.

They stared at the door for a moment, then looked at her.

"Congratulations," Lucivar said. "You've been here a little over twenty-four hours and you've already gotten tossed out of his study. Even I was here three days before he tossed me out the first time."

"Why don't you go sit on a spear," Surreal growled.

Lucivar shook his head and tsked. Daemon seemed to be straining a lot of muscles to keep from laughing.

"So why did he toss the two of you out?" Surreal asked.

"For privacy. You'll notice there are very strong shields around that room now, including an aural one." Lucivar looked at the closed study door. "Having witnessed this behavior a number of times, the males in the First Circle have come to the conclusion that he's either sitting there laughing himself silly or he's indulging in a fit of hysterics, and either way, he doesn't want us to know."

"He *said* he would help me," Surreal snarled.

Lucivar's eyes were bright with laughter. "I'm sure he'd intended to explain a few things to Graysfang—right up until you mentioned Kaelas."

"That name keeps coming up," Daemon said. "Just who is Kaelas?"

Lucivar eyed Daemon thoughtfully, then directed the answer to Surreal. "Kaelas is an Arcerian Warlord Prince who wears a Red Jewel. But because of some quirk in his talent or his training, he can get through any kind of shield—including a Black."

"Mother Night," Daemon muttered.

"He's also eight hundred pounds of feline muscle and temper." Lucivar smiled grimly. "We all try not to upset Kaelas."

"Shit," Surreal said weakly.

"Come on," Lucivar said. "We'll escort you to your room."

Walking between two strong males suddenly sounded like a good idea.

After a couple of minutes, Surreal said, "At least, being that big, he'll be easy enough to spot."

Lucivar hesitated. "The Arcerian Blood always use sight shields when they hunt. It makes them very effective predators."

"Oh." Being friends with a wolf was sounding better and better by the minute.

When they reached her room, she said good night and went inside.

Graysfang was standing exactly where she'd left him. Well, she *had* told him to "Stay right there," and he had taken her at her word.

Looking at the sadness in those brown eyes, she sighed.

Puppy love. It was a term whores used to describe clumsy, eager young males during their first few weeks of sexual experience. For a short time, they would try to please so they wouldn't be refused the bed. But after the novelty wore off, they would address those same women with a hardness in their eyes and a sneer in their voices.

"Tomorrow we're going to have to come to an agreement about a few things," Surreal told Graysfang.

His tail went *tock-tock,* just once.

Giving in, she climbed into bed and patted the covers beside her. He jumped up on the bed and lay down, watching her cautiously. She ruffled his fur, turned off the light, and found herself smiling. She had ended up in a place where, when someone spoke of puppy love, they were talking about a real puppy.

12 / Kaeleer

Too edgy to sleep and too restless to find distraction in a book, Daemon wandered through the dimly lit corridors of the Hall.

You're running, he thought, bitterly aware of the doubts and fears that had come swarming up when he had neared his suite of rooms—and had sensed Jaenelle's presence in the adjoining suite.

For most of his 1,700 years, he had believed, without question, that he'd been born to be Witch's lover. Thirteen years ago, faced with a twelve-year-old girl, that conviction hadn't been shaken. His heart had been committed; it was just the physical union that would have been delayed a few more years. But a brutal rape and the years he'd been lost in madness separated them now, and he wasn't sure he could stand to face her and see only a sense of obligation or, worse, pity in her eyes.

He needed to find a place that would help him regain his balance.

Daemon paused, then smiled reluctantly as he realized that he hadn't been running so much as searching. Somewhere on the grounds of the estate, there would be a place dedicated to performing the Blood's formal rituals for the sacred days in each season, but he doubted Saetan would build a home that didn't also contain a place for informal, private meditations.

He closed his eyes and opened his inner senses. A moment later, he was moving again, heading back toward the part of the Hall that contained the family living quarters.

He would have missed the entrance completely if he hadn't caught a glimpse of his reflection in the door's glass.

Stepping outside, he looked down at the sunken garden. Raised flower beds bordered all four sides except where the stone steps led down into the garden. Two statues dominated the space. A few feet in front of them were a raised stone slab and a wooden seat. Carefully positioned candlelights illuminated the statues and the steps.

The statues pulled at him. He went down the steps, hesitated a moment, then stepped onto the grass.

Power filled the air, making it almost too rich to breathe. As he filled his lungs with it, he felt his body absorb the strength and peace contained within this garden. On the stone slab were half a dozen candles in tinted glass containers. Choosing one at random, he used Craft to create a little tongue of witchfire and light it. A hint of lavender reached him before he walked over to the fountain that contained the female statue.

The back of the fountain was a curved wall of rough stone curtained by water that spilled into a stone-enclosed pool. The woman rose halfway out of the pool, her face lifted toward the sky. Her eyes were closed, and there was a slight smile on her lips. Her hands were raised as if she were just about to wipe the water from her hair. Everything about her embodied serene strength and a celebration of life.

He didn't recognize the mature body, but he recognized that face. And he wondered if the sculptor had continued his exquisite detail beneath the hips that rose out of the water, wondered what his fingers would find if he slid his hand past her belly.

Because he wondered, he turned to the other statue—the male.

The beast.

His visceral response to the crouched, blatantly male body that was a blend of human and animal was a gut-deep sense of recognition. It was as if someone had stripped him of his skin to reveal what really lay beneath.

Massive shoulders supported a feline head that had its teeth bared in a snarl of rage. One paw/hand was braced on the ground near the head of a small sleeping woman. The other was raised, the claws unsheathed.

Someone like Alexandra would look at this creature and assume it was about to crush and tear the female, that the only way to control that physical strength and rage would be to keep it chained. Someone like Alexandra would never look beyond that assumption to notice the small details. Like the sleeping woman's hand reaching out, her fingertips just brushing the paw/hand near her head. Like the way the crouching body sheltered her. Like the way the glittering, green stone eyes stared at whoever approached, and the fact that the snarling rage came from the desire, the *need*, to protect.

Daemon took a deep breath, let it out slowly—and then tensed. He hadn't heard any footsteps, but he didn't have to turn around to know who now stood at the foot of the stairs. "What do you think of him?" he asked quietly.

"He's beautiful," Jaenelle replied in her midnight voice.

Daemon slowly turned to face her.

She wore a long black dress. The front lacing ended just below her breasts, revealing enough fair skin to make a man's mouth water. Her golden hair flowed over her shoulders and down her back. Her ancient sapphire eyes didn't look as haunted as he remembered, but he had the painful suspicion that he was the reason for the sadness he saw in them.

As the silence between them lengthened, he couldn't move toward her any more than he could move away.

"Daemon . . ."

"Do you understand what he represents?" he asked quickly, tipping his head just enough to indicate the statue.

Jaenelle's lips curved into just a hint of a dry smile. "Oh, yes, Prince, I understand what he represents."

Daemon swallowed hard. "Then don't insult me by offering regrets. A male is expendable. A Queen is not—especially when she is Witch."

She made an odd sound. "Saetan said almost the same thing once."

"And he was right."

"Well, being a Warlord Prince made from the same mold, you would think that, wouldn't you?" She started to smile. Then her eyes narrowed. Her attention sharpened.

Daemon had the distinct impression there was something about him that didn't please her. When her intense focus ended a moment later, he realized that she had made some decision about him, just as she had done the first time he'd met her. And now, like then, he didn't know what she had decided.

The Consort's ring was a heavy weight on his finger, but, because of it, he could ask for one thing he desperately needed.

"May I hold you for a minute?"

He tried to tell himself that her hesitation came from surprise and not wariness, but he didn't believe it. That didn't stop him from closing his arms around her when she walked up to him. That didn't stop the tears from stinging his eyes when her arms cautiously circled his waist and she rested her head on his shoulder.

"You're taller than I remember," he said, brushing his cheek against her hair.

"I should hope so."

Her voice sounded a bit tart, but he could hear the smile in it.

Oh, how his hands wanted to caress and explore, but he was afraid she would pull away from him, so he kept them still. She was alive, and he was with her. That's all that mattered.

He could have stayed that way for the rest of the night, just holding her, feeling the easy rise and fall of her breathing, but after a few minutes she drew away from him.

"Come on, Daemon," she said, holding out her hand. "You need to get some rest, and my orders were to herd you back to your room so that you'd get some sleep before daylight."

His temper sharpened instantly. "Who would dare give *you* orders?" he snarled.

She gave him a look full of exasperated amusement. "Guess."

He almost said "Saetan," and then thought about it. "Lucivar," he said grimly.

"Lucivar," Jaenelle agreed as she took his hand and pulled him toward the stairs. "And trust me, boyo, having Lucivar haul you out of bed because you weren't on the practice field when he told you to be is not an experience you want to have."

"What's he going to do? Pour a bucket of water over me?" Daemon said as they reached the corridor and headed toward their suites.

"No, because soaking the bed would get Helene mad at him. But he wouldn't hesitate to shove you under a cold shower."

"He hasn't—"

She just looked at him.

His opinion was blunt and explicit. "Why do you put up with that?"

"He's bigger than me," she grumbled.

"Someone should remind him that he serves you."

Jaenelle laughed so hard she staggered into him. "He reminds me of that himself whenever it suits him. And when it doesn't, I end up dealing with my big brother. Either way, most of the time it's easier just to go along with him."

They had reached the door to Jaenelle's suite. He reluctantly let go of her hand.

"He hasn't changed at all, has he?" Daemon said, feeling a stab of anxiety as he remembered how volatile Lucivar had always been in a court.

When he looked at Jaenelle, there was an odd light in her eyes. "No," she said in her midnight voice, "he hasn't changed at all. But then, he, too, understands what that statue represents."

CHAPTER FOUR

1 / Kaeleer

"Tell me again why I had to miss breakfast," Daemon said, breathing heavily as he wiped his sweaty face and neck with a towel.

"Because no one wants to dance around in it if you miss a block and get hit in the belly," Lucivar replied, sipping his coffee while he watched Palanar and Tamnar go through a warmup routine with the sticks. "And we're getting an earlier start this morning because I want the males finished before the women get here for their first lesson."

Daemon took a sip of Lucivar's coffee, then handed the mug back. "You're really going to teach the women how to use the sticks?"

"By the time I'm done with them, they'll be able to handle sticks, bow, and knife."

A sharp command by Hallevar had the youths stepping back and then going through a move again slowly.

"I'll bet the warriors weren't pleased when you told them," Daemon said, watching the moves.

"They bitched about it. Most of the women didn't look happy about it either. I don't expect them to become warriors, but they'll be able to defend themselves long enough for a warrior to reach them."

Daemon eyed Lucivar thoughtfully. "Is that why you taught Marian?"

Lucivar nodded. "She kept resisting because Eyrien females traditionally didn't touch a warrior's weapons. I told her if a male hurt her because she was too stubborn to learn how to defend herself, I'd beat the shit out of her. And she told me if I ever raised a hand to her, she'd gut me. I figured we were making progress."

Daemon laughed. The laughter backed up into his lungs when he saw Jaenelle striding over the lawn, heading toward them. His senses sharpened to a razor's edge, the heat of desire washed through him, and the smell of other males became a declaration of rivalry.

"Rein it in, old son," Lucivar murmured, glancing over his shoulder and then at Daemon.

Palanar and Tamnar finished their routine, and Hallevar and Kohlvar stepped into the practice circle.

Palanar shifted his mouth into a sneer. "Here comes a chirpy, trying to grow some balls."

Daemon whipped around, his eyes filmed with the red haze of fury.

Hallevar pivoted and smacked Palanar on the buttocks with his stick hard enough to make the boy jump.

"That's my sister, boyo," Lucivar said too quietly.

Palanar looked sick. Someone else muttered a vicious curse.

"Now, I'm going to forget you said that," Lucivar continued just as quietly, "as long as I never hear it again. But if I do, there will come a morning when you step into the practice circle, and I'll be waiting for you."

"Y-yes, sir," Palanar stammered. "I'm sorry, sir."

Hallevar cuffed the boy on the back of the head. "Go get something to eat," he growled. "Maybe with some food in you, you'll use more of your head than just your mouth."

Palanar slunk away, Tamnar trailing behind him.

Hallevar eyed the distance between them and Jaenelle, figured she was close enough to have heard, and swore softly. "I taught him better than that."

Lucivar rolled a shoulder. "He's old enough to want his cock admired. That makes him stupid." He looked at the older Warlord. "He can't afford to be stupid. What the Queens in this court may be willing to overlook from a youngster, the males in the court won't—at least, not a second time."

"I'll blister his ears to make sure he gets the message," Hallevar promised. "Might as well blister Tamnar's while I'm at it." He went back to the circle and began the warmup routine with Kohlvar.

Daemon turned toward Jaenelle, Palanar already forgotten. When he saw the feral look in her eyes, his smile died before it formed.

Lucivar simply raised his left arm.

With one wild-shy glance at him and a murmured greeting he could barely hear, Jaenelle ducked under Lucivar's arm.

Lucivar lowered his arm, and the hand that settled at her waist tucked her tight against his side. Her right arm rested against his back, her hand curled over his bare shoulder.

They stand that way often, Daemon thought as he fought to rein in his jealousy—and the hurt—because she had barely spared him a glance.

But he suspected that Lucivar was better prepared to deal with the feral look in her eyes than he was. That hurt, too.

"Do you want the introductions now?" Lucivar asked quietly.

Jaenelle shook her head. "I want to warm up first."

"When you're ready, I'll go a round with you."

She glanced at Lucivar's bare chest. "I would have thought you'd already done your workout."

"I've gone through two of them. Haven't worked up a sweat yet."

"Ah."

Lucivar paused. "Your sister's here."

"I know." She flicked a glance at the empty women's practice circle. "I'm surprised you haven't dragged her out here."

"She's got another thirty minutes to arrive on her own before she gets dragged." Lucivar grinned wickedly. "I promise I'll go easy."

"Uh-huh."

That, Daemon thought sourly, he would like to see.

"We also have company," Lucivar said.

Her eyes iced over. "I know," she said in her midnight voice.

Daemon took a step toward her. He didn't know what he could say or do, but he was certain he—or someone—had to shift the mood she was in.

Lucivar . . . he began.

Just keep things soft and easy, Bastard, Lucivar replied. *The workout will take the edge off her.*

Daemon took another step toward her. Her expression changed to something close to panic—and he realized that, last night when she had let him hold her, the Queen had been doing her duty for one of the males in her First Circle, but the *woman* didn't want to get anywhere near him.

As she darted away from Lucivar—and him—she almost ran into Jazen, who was carrying a tray containing a pot of fresh coffee and clean mugs.

"Who are you?" Jaenelle said a little too softly.

Jazen stared into her eyes, frozen. "Jazen," he finally said. "Prince Sadi's valet."

Her eyes changed from ice to curiosity. "Is it interesting work?"

"It would be more interesting if he wore something besides a black suit and a white shirt all the time," Jazen muttered.

Lucivar choked back a laugh. Daemon felt the blood rush into his face and wasn't sure if it was from temper or embarrassment. Jazen looked horrified.

Then Jaenelle's silvery, velvet-coated laugh rang out. "Well, we'll do our best to rumple him up for you." As she walked past Jazen, she brushed her left hand over his shoulder. "Welcome to Kaeleer, Warlord."

Daemon waited until she had reached the women's practice circle before turning to his valet. "Should I apologize for being boring in my taste in clothes? And why in the name of Hell are you out here doing a footman's work?"

"Beale asked me to bring this tray out." Jazen gulped. "I don't know why I said that other."

"You said what you've been thinking," Lucivar said, amused. "Don't worry about it. By the time we're done with him, you'll have to work hard to keep him looking pristine."

Daemon snarled at his brother, then glared at Jazen.

"I'll take that," said Holt, one of the footmen who had carried out the other trays.

Jazen glanced at Daemon, handed the tray to Holt, and made as quick a retreat as possible without actually running.

"Looks like breakfast is being served out here," Lucivar said as he eyed the various dishes that were being set out on the table.

Daemon took a deep breath and watched Jaenelle go through the warmup movements. "I should talk to her, explain about Jazen before she passes judgment."

Lucivar gave him an odd look. "Old son, she just did. She welcomed him to Kaeleer. That's all anyone needs to know."

"This way," Marian said, making a friendly "come on" gesture to Wilhelmina Benedict while she eyed Surreal's loose-sleeved tunic and trousers. "What are you wearing under the tunic?"

Surreal worked to keep her voice warm. Marian didn't seem the type to be interested in a former whore's underwear. "Why?"

"Lucivar will insist that you strip down for the lesson."

"Strip?" Wilhelmina said. "In front of those men?"

"You don't want your movements restricted by your clothing," Marian said kindly. "And you'll want to put on something dry afterward."

"I take it I'm going to be sweating," Surreal said. She glanced at Wilhelmina and wondered if that kind of exercise was a good idea. The young woman looked as pale as water and scared enough to break.

"I don't think he'll work the beginners that hard, but you . . ." Marian's gold eyes flicked to Surreal's pointed ears. "You're Dea al Mon. He may push you harder, just to find out what you can already do."

"Lucky me," Surrel muttered as they headed across the lawn toward the other women who were already gathered at the practice circle.

Marian smiled. "My first weapon was the skillet."

"Sounds dangerous," Surreal said, returning the smile.

"I'd been working for Lucivar as his housekeeper for about four months. My moon's blood had started that morning, and I wasn't feeling well. Looking back, I realize that he must have gone through the other moontimes with his teeth clenched to keep from saying anything. But that morning, he started fussing at me to take it easy, and I took it as a criticism that I couldn't do my job. I threw a pot at him. Well, not really *at* him. I didn't want to *hit* him, I just felt mad enough that I needed to throw something. It hit the wall about two feet away from where he was standing.

"He looked at the pot for a minute, then picked it up and went outside. I could hear him throwing it, and thought he was doing that instead of using his fists on me the way some Eyrien males would have.

"He came back inside, muttering, took one of the skillets, and went back out. A few minutes later, he dragged me outside. He said a pot didn't have the right balance, but a skillet would work if it was thrown properly. I spent two months practicing slinging a skillet before he declared me proficient enough to suit him." Marian grinned at the memory.

"What does he consider proficient?" Surreal asked.

Marian didn't look amused now. "Being able to break bone nine out of ten times."

Surreal just gaped at her for a moment, and then started thinking hard.

She was a damn good assassin. Just how much, under Lucivar's training, could those skills be honed?

When they reached the practice circle, Wilhelmina hung back. Surreal pushed her way to the front. When an Eyrien warrior snarled at her for elbowing him in the ribs, she snarled back, pleased that he was the one to give ground.

She looked around, saw Daemon, and felt her breathing hitch. He looked calm enough, standing there with a mug of coffee in one hand, but his face had that set look that she'd seen when they were in the Coach on the way here. It wasn't as bad as it had been then, but it wasn't good.

Then Lucivar started talking, and she put her concern for Daemon aside for the time being.

"There are reasons why Eyrien males are the warriors," Lucivar said, his eyes skimming over the women as he paced slowly down the line and back again. "We're bigger, stronger, and we have the temperament for killing. You have other strengths and other skills. Most of the time, that works out well. But that's no reason for you to be unable to defend yourselves. And before you give me any shit about not being able to handle a weapon, I'll remind you that most of you don't have any trouble using kitchen knives, and some of them are as big as a hunting knife. They just look different. And some of you will want to wiggle out of this training by telling me that, no matter how much she knows, a woman can't hold her own against a male. Right?" Looking at the other practice circle, he roared, "CAT! Get over here!"

Wondering why he'd want a feline, Surreal looked toward the circle. Her breath came out in a hiss as the woman talking to Karla, Morghann, and Gabrielle turned around. "Jaenelle," she whispered.

She focused on Daemon again. He didn't look shocked to see Jaenelle. Maybe they'd already had a chance to talk. Maybe . . . No, it was probably way too early to think about *those* maybes.

The other women strode toward the practice circle. Jaenelle came more slowly, her eyes fixed on Lucivar while she whipped the stick around her waist with enough force to sting the air.

Lucivar sidestepped to the middle of the circle, always watching her. "Come play with me, Cat," he said, giving her an arrogant smile.

She snarled at him and began to circle.

"Hallevar," Lucivar said as he circled with her. "Call the time."

Surreal felt Falonar tense beside her.

"What's time?" she asked, nudging him when he didn't answer.

"Ten minutes," Falonar replied grimly. "He'll beat her into the ground long before that."

Surreal slashed a look at Daemon and started to sweat. If that happened, what would Sadi do? Easy answer. The hard question was, what could any of them do to stop him from tearing Lucivar apart?

The first clash of the sticks had her heart jumping into her throat. After that she wasn't aware of anything except Jaenelle and Lucivar moving gracefully through a savage dance.

Seconds passed into minutes.

"Mother Night," Falonar whispered. "She's making him work for it."

Lucivar's chest glistened with sweat. Surreal could hear his deep, harsh breathing. Her own sweat chilled her skin when she saw the wild look in Jaenelle's eyes.

She didn't know how much time had passed when, after half a dozen lightning-fast moves, Jaenelle lost her balance for a split second. Lucivar danced back just long enough to let her get her feet solidly under her before attacking again.

"He could have put her on the ground right then and ended it," Falonar said softly.

"He wants to work her, not get her mad enough to really go after him," Chaosti replied just as softly, stepping up behind Surreal.

Finally, Hallevar yelled, "TIME!"

Lucivar and Jaenelle circled, thrust, clashed.

"DAMN YOU BOTH, I SAID TIME!"

They broke apart, backed away.

Hallevar strode into the circle and took the stick away from Lucivar. He looked at Jaenelle, hesitated, then backed off when Lucivar shook his head.

"Come on, Cat," Lucivar gasped as he moved toward her. "We've got to walk to cool down."

Her head snapped up. She braced her feet in a fighting stance.

Lucivar held up his hands and kept moving forward.

The wild look in her eyes faded. "Water."

"Walk first," he said, taking the stick away from her.

"Prick," she snarled halfheartedly, but she walked with him.

"If you don't give me a hard time about it, you can even have break-fast." Lucivar handed the stick to Falonar as he and Jaenelle walked past. He took a couple of towels from Aaron, draped one over Jaenelle's neck, and began to rub himself down with the other.

Looking around, Surreal noticed that Khardeen was also in the crowd, watching and alert. And she noticed, with a sigh of relief, that Saetan was talking quietly with Daemon.

Turning back to Falonar, she brushed her fingers against the stick. "Do you think I'll ever get half that good with one of these?" She half-expected some dismissive comment, but when he didn't answer, she looked up to see him studying her seriously.

"If you can become half as proficient with this as she is, you'll be able to take down any male except an Eyrien warrior," Falonar said slowly. "And you'll be able to take down half of them as well." Then he looked at Marian. "Are you all right, Lady?"

Marian let out a shuddering breath. "I'm fine, thank you, Prince Falonar. It's just . . . sometimes when they're so intense . . ."

Falonar bowed just enough to show respect, then left them to talk with Hallevar.

"Are you really all right?" Surreal asked, drawing Marian a little ways away from the crowd.

Marian's smile was a trifle strained. "Lucivar's always tense after he's been at the service fair, and he's been worried about Daemon."

Looking back, Surreal saw Daemon walking toward the Hall with the High Lord. Well, that was one worry out of the way for the moment.

She also noticed the way Jaenelle kept glancing at Daemon while Lu-civar piled food on a plate. She smiled.

"Usually I can help him relieve the tension," Marian continued.

Her self-conscious expression told Surreal exactly how Marian helped relieve the tension. The woman had guts to get into a bed with a man like Lucivar when his temper was already on the edge.

"Since that wasn't an option this time . . ."

No, Surreal thought as Marian gave her a speculative look. If Lucivar had never suggested an alternative to intercourse, *she* certainly wasn't going to supply the information.

After a moment, Marian shrugged. "Usually when Jaenelle is his spar-ring partner, they just keep working through the moves until he's sweated out the tension. But this morning . . . Jaenelle's relatives showing up like this has put her on edge, too."

"Yeah, seeing her family again isn't a reason to cheer."

Marian stiffened. "Her *family* lives here."

"Yes," Surreal said after a minute, "I guess they do."

2 / Kaeleer

Wilhelmina walked silently beside Lucivar as he escorted her to her room. She wished he would put his arm around her. Maybe then she would stop shivering. Maybe then she wouldn't feel so afraid.

That was funny. A few hours ago, she'd been terrified of him, especially after she'd seen him and Jaenelle attacking each other with the sticks.

Afterward, she'd tried to slip back to the Hall before anyone noticed because she'd been sure her heart would just burst if any of those Eyrien warriors snarled at her when she couldn't do the exercises properly. But Lucivar had noticed her slinking away. He'd grabbed the back of her tunic and hauled her into the practice circle.

And he'd been kind. While other Eyriens instructed the other women, and Marian and some of the coven had demonstrated the moves, he had worked with her and the girl, Jillian. Never in a hurry, never impatient, his hands firm but gentle when he repositioned her body, his voice always calm and encouraging.

She hadn't expected that from him. And she hadn't expected him to stay with her when she went to meet Alexandra, Leland, and Philip.

She should have said "no" when the High Lord told her they were here and wanted to talk to her. But she'd felt an obligation to see them, since they'd come all this way.

They'd been angry when Lucivar refused to let the Province Queens and the escorts into the room and refused to leave himself. Oh, he'd gone out onto the balcony, but no one was going to forget his presence.

She could tell they had been as insulted as she had been relieved, but they *had* been glad to see her. They'd all hugged her and complimented her on how pretty she'd become and how worried they had been about her and how much they'd missed her . . .

And then Alexandra told her not to worry. They would find a way to break the contract and get her out of this place and away from these people. She'd tried to explain that she intended to honor the contract, that the High Lord and Prince Yaslana weren't the monsters Alexandra was trying to make them out to be.

They didn't listen, just as they hadn't listened years ago when her father, Robert Benedict, had tried to force himself on her after Jaenelle disappeared—a few months after he had come down with the illness that had finally killed him. She had run away because she'd been afraid that, one day, no one would hear her screams or, if they did, would ignore them because she was turning into a "difficult" child, just like Jaenelle.

They didn't listen. Because they were so sure they were right, so sure that they knew what was best. Even Philip. He kept telling her that it would be all right now, that Robert was dead so it would be all right. But it wouldn't be, *couldn't be,* all right because they thought of her as being "damaged" somehow—she could see that in their eyes—and anything she thought or felt or wanted would be colored by that conviction. And because she cared for Philip and knew he would be hurt by it, she couldn't tell them why she *really* wanted to stay there.

Her fear that they might actually be able to take her away after she'd struggled so hard to get to Kaeleer had escalated to the point where she had leaped up from the couch, and yelled, "No! I don't want to!"

Lucivar was in the room and hurrying her away from them before anyone else could move.

But she couldn't stop shaking, and the fear was eating her alive.

Lucivar's hand came down on her shoulder, stopping her. A moment later, he called in a flask. He vanished the cap, gripped the back of her head with one hand, and held the flask up to her lips.

"If you keep shaking like that, you're going to rip something," he said, sounding annoyed. "Take a sip of this. It'll settle your nerves."

"I don't want a sedative," Wilhelmina said, trying to pull away as desperation swelled inside her. "There's nothing wrong with me."

"Nothing except you've gone way past scared, and that's not good for you." Lucivar paused, studying her. "It's not a sedative, Wilhelmina," he said quietly. "It's Khary's home brew. It's got a kick to it that will mellow you out—and it'll also keep you from breaking apart. Now, hold your nose and swallow."

She didn't hold her nose. She *did* swallow the sip he gave her.

Golden.

It flowed over her tongue like ripe plums and summer heat, pooled in her stomach for a moment, and then flowed into her limbs.

When he offered her another swallow, she took it. That glorious heat melted her fear and produced a sensuous warmth inside her. If she had another sip, she might even feel brave—fiercely, wonderfully brave.

But Lucivar wasn't offering another sip. She wasn't aware that he'd released her, but he had the cap in one hand now and the flask in the other, and he was going to take away that delicious heat.

She snatched the flask and ran down the corridor, whipped around a corner, and guzzled as much as she could before he caught up to her and took it away.

She leaned against the wall and smiled at him. She felt enormously pleased when he took a couple of steps back and watched her warily.

Lucivar sniffed the flask, took a small sip, and said, "Shit."

"That would be a rude thing to do in the corridor."

He swore softly while he capped the flask and vanished it, but it sounded more like laughter. "Come on, little witch. Let's get you settled somewhere while you can still walk."

She walked toward him to prove that she could, but the floor suddenly got lumpy, and she tripped and fell against him.

"I am very brave," she told him, leaning against his chest.

"You are very drunk."

"Mmmm not." Then she remembered the important thing she had to do. The most important thing. "I want to see my sister." She smacked her hand as hard as she could against the surface she was leaning on to emphasize her point. She looked at her stinging hand. "It hurts."

"We'll have matching bruises," Lucivar said dryly.

"Okay."

Muttering, he steered her through the corridors.

She felt so wonderful, she wanted to sing, but all the songs she knew seemed so . . . polite. "Do you know any naughty songs?"

"Mother Night," he muttered.

"Don't know that one. How does it go?"

"This way," he said, steering her around a corner.

She got away from him and ran down the corridor, flapping her arms. "I can flyyyyy."

When he caught her again, he wrapped one arm around her waist, knocked once on the door in front of them, and hauled her inside.

"Cat!"

Tears filled Wilhelmina's eyes when Jaenelle walked out of the adjoining room. The warm smile of greeting was all she needed to see.

Slipping out of Lucivar's grip, she stumbled a couple of steps and hugged Jaenelle.

"I've missed you," Wilhelmina said, laughing while tears ran down her face. "I've missed you so much. I'm sorry I wasn't braver. You were my little sister, and I should have looked after you. But you were the one who always looked after me." She leaned back, holding Jaenelle's shoulders for balance. "You're so pretty."

"And you're drunk." Those sapphire eyes stared at Lucivar. "What did you do to her?"

"Her nerves were so strained after meeting your relatives, I was afraid she'd break. So I asked Khary for the strongest brew he had in a flask because I figured she wouldn't take more than a sip." Lucivar winced. "She guzzled half the flask—and it wasn't one of his home brews, it was the concoction you created."

Jaenelle's eyes widened. "You let her drink a 'gravedigger'?"

"No no no," Wilhelmina said, shaking her head. "You shouldn't ever drink a gravedigger until he's had a bath." She smiled placidly when Jaenelle and Lucivar just stared at her.

"Mother Night," Lucivar muttered.

"Do you know that song?" Wilhelmina asked Jaenelle.

"What did you have for breakfast?" Jaenelle demanded.

"Water. I was too nervous to eat. But I'm not nervous anymore. I am very brave and fierce."

Lucivar wrapped one hand around her arm. "Why don't you sit on the couch now?"

She headed straight across the room—more or less. When he started to lead her around the table, she dug in her heels.

"I can go through the table," she announced proudly. "I studied my Craft. I want to show Jaenelle that I can do that now."

"You want to do something really challenging?" Lucivar asked. "Then let's walk *around* the table. Right now, that will be impressive."

"Okay."

Getting around the table *was* sufficiently challenging, especially since Lucivar kept getting his feet in the way. When she finally reached the couch, she plopped down next to Jaenelle. "I brushed Dejaal, and now he likes me. If I brushed Lucivar, do you think he'd like me, too?"

"He'd promise to like you if you stopped stepping on him," Lucivar growled softly while he pulled off her shoes.

"It's Marian's job to brush Lucivar," Jaenelle said solemnly.

"Okay."

"Why don't I have some coffee and toast sent up?" Lucivar said.

Wilhelmina watched Lucivar until he left the room. "I used to think he was scary. But he's just big."

"Uh-huh. Why don't you lie down for a little while?" Jaenelle said.

Wilhelmina obeyed. When Jaenelle finished tucking a blanket around her, she said, "Everyone said you had died, but when they talked to me, they said we had 'lost' you. But I always knew you weren't lost because you told me where to find you. How could you be lost when you knew where you were?"

She looked into Jaenelle's sapphire eyes. The mind behind those eyes was so vast. But she wasn't afraid of that anymore. "You always knew where you were. Didn't you?"

"Yes," Jaenelle replied softly. "I always knew."

3 / Kaeleer

Alexandra paused, took a deep breath, and opened the door without knocking.

The golden-haired woman grinding herbs with a mortar and pestle didn't turn around, didn't indicate in any way that she knew someone was there. A large bowl floated above the worktable, heated by three tongues of witchfire. A spoon lazily stirred the bowl's contents.

Alexandra waited. After a minute, she said in a tight voice, "Could you stop fiddling with that for a minute and say 'hello' to your grandmother? After all, it's been thirteen years since I've seen you."

"A minute or so won't make any difference to a greeting that's waited for thirteen years," Jaenelle replied, pouring the finely ground herbs into the bowl's bubbling contents. "But it *will* make a difference to this tonic developing the right potency." She half turned, gave Alexandra one slashing glance, then focused her attention on the brew.

Alexandra clenched her teeth, remembering why she had found this granddaughter so different to deal with. Even as a small child, Jaenelle had displayed these gestures of superiority, implying that *she* had no reason to show respect for her elders or yield to a Queen.

Why? For the first time, Alexandra wondered. She'd always assumed, along with everyone else, that those displays were attempts to compensate for not wearing the Jewels, for being less than the other witches in the family. But, perhaps, they had been a result of someone—like the High Lord—whispering sweet lies into a child's ear until the girl truly believed she was superior.

She shook her head. It was hard to believe that the child who had been unable to do the simplest Craft lessons could grow up to become some terrible, powerful threat to the Realm of Terreille as Dorothea claimed. If that were *true,* where was the power? Even now, when she was trying to sense Jaenelle's strength, it felt . . . muted . . . just as it always had. Distant, which was the way a Blood female who didn't have enough psychic strength to wear a Jewel felt.

That meant Jaenelle *was* just a pawn in an elaborate game. The High Lord—or, perhaps, the mysterious Queen who ruled this court—wanted a figurehead to hide behind.

"What are you making?" Alexandra asked.

"A tonic for a young boy who's ill," Jaenelle replied, adding a dark liquid to the brew.

"Shouldn't a Healer be doing that?" *Hell's fire,* are *they really letting her make tonics for people?*

"I *am* a Healer," Jaenelle replied tartly. "I'm also a Black Widow and a Queen."

Of course you are. With effort, Alexandra bit back the words. She would remain calm; would forge a bond, somehow, with her younger granddaughter; would remember that Jaenelle had already endured some terrible experiences.

Then Jaenelle finished making the tonic and turned around.

Staring into those sapphire eyes, Alexandra forgot about remaining calm or forging a bond. Staggered by the . . . *something* . . . that looked at her out of those eyes, she groped for an explanation that would fit.

When she found it, she wanted to weep.

Jaenelle was insane. Totally, completely insane. And that monster who ruled here indulged that insanity for his own reasons. He let Jaenelle think she was Healer and a Black Widow and a Queen. He would probably let her give that tonic to a sick little boy, regardless of what the stuff would actually do to a child.

"Why are you here, Alexandra?"

Alexandra shivered at the sound of that midnight voice, then gave herself a mental shake. The child had always indulged in theatrics. "I came to take you and Wilhelmina home."

"Why? For the past thirteen years, you thought I was dead. Since that was far more convenient for you than having me alive, why didn't you just continue to pretend I was dead?"

"We weren't pretending," Alexandra said hotly. Jaenelle's words hurt, mostly because they were true. It *had* been easier mourning a dead child than dealing with the difficult girl. But she would never admit *that*. "We thought you *were* dead, that Sadi had killed you."

"Daemon would never have hurt me."

But you would—and did. That was the message underneath the cold, flat reply.

"Leland is your mother. I'm your grandmother. We're your *family*, Jaenelle."

Jaenelle shook her head slowly. "This body can trace its bloodline to you. That makes us related. It doesn't make us family." She moved toward the door. When she was just about to pass Alexandra, she stopped. "You apprenticed with an Hourglass coven for a little while, didn't you? Before you had to make the choice between becoming a Black Widow and becoming Chaillot's Queen."

Alexandra nodded, wondering where this was leading.

"You learned enough to make the simplest tangled webs, the kind that would absorb a focused intent and draw that object to you. Isn't that true?" When she nodded again, Jaenelle's eyes filled with sadness and understanding. "How many times did you sit before one of those webs dreaming that something would help you keep Chaillot safe from Hayll's encroachment?"

Alexandra couldn't speak, could barely breathe.

"Has it ever occurred to you that that may be the answer to the riddle? Saetan was also an intense dreamer. The difference is that when the dream appeared, he recognized it." Jaenelle opened the door. "Go home, Alexandra. There's nothing—and no one—for you here."

"Wilhelmina," Alexandra whispered.

"She'll fulfill the eighteen months of her contract. After that, she can do as she pleases." There was something awful and ironic about Jaenelle's smile. "The Queen commands it."

Alexandra took a deep breath. "I want to see this Queen."

"No, you don't," Jaenelle replied too softly. "You don't want to stand before the Dark Throne." She paused. "Now, if you'll excuse me, I have to finish this tonic. It's simmered long enough."

Dismissed. As casually as that, she was being dismissed.

Alexandra left the workroom, relieved to be away from Jaenelle. She found one of the inner gardens and settled on a bench. Maybe the sun would take away the chill that had seeped into her bones. Maybe then she could believe she was shaking from cold and not because Jaenelle had mentioned something she had never told anyone.

Her paternal grandmother had been a natural Black Widow. That's what had drawn Alexandra to the Hourglass in the first place. But by then, the aristo Blood in Chaillot were already starting to whisper about Black Widows being "unnatural" women, and the other Queens and the Warlord Princes would *never* have chosen a Queen who was also a witch of the Hourglass covens.

So she left her apprenticeship and, a few years later when her maternal grandmother stepped down, became the Queen of Chaillot. But during her first few years as Queen, she *had* secretly woven those simple tangled webs. She *had* dreamed that something or someone would appear in her life that would help her fight against Hayll's undermining of Chaillot society. At the time, she had thought it would be a Consort—a strong male who would support and help her. But no man like that had ever appeared in her life.

Then, when her Black Widow grandmother had been dying, Alexandra had been given what she came to think of as the riddle. *What you dream for will come, but if you're not careful, you'll be blind until it's too late.*

So she had waited. She had watched. The dream hadn't come. And she would not, *could not,* believe that a disturbed, eccentric child had been the answer to the riddle.

4 / Kaeleer

As he stared out the window, he reached inside his shirt and fingered the slim glass vial that hung from a chain around his neck. The High Priestess of Hayll had assured him that she and the Dark Priestess had woven the strongest spells they knew to keep him undetected. So far, they had worked No one sensed he was anything more than another escort Alexandra Angelline had brought with her. He was just a bland man, almost invisible. That suited him perfectly.

It had sounded so easy when he'd been given the assignment. Find the target, drug her so that she would be complacent, and then slip her out of the Hall to the men who would be waiting just beyond the boundaries of the estate. When he'd seen the size of the place, he'd thought it would be even easier.

But, despite its size, the Hall was crawling with aggressive males, from the lowest male servant right up to the High Lord. And the bitches *never* seemed to be alone. He'd lingered in corridors for hours without so much as a sniff of either one of them.

He shuddered as he remembered his one glimpse of the golden-haired bitch. He'd been told, repeatedly, that she was his primary target, but he had no intention of getting anywhere near *her* because something about her spooked him, and he wasn't sure the spells would hold up under that sapphire stare. So he would snatch the other one, the sister. But he would have to do it soon. He could only dodge just so long around so many bristling, suspicious males.

Maybe he would escort Wilhelmina Benedict all the way back to Hayll. Once he got her out, what difference did it make if he was found to be missing?

And it would make no difference to him if Alexandra was left behind to explain her granddaughter's disappearance—or was the one who ended up paying whatever price the High Lord chose to extract.

5 / Terreille

The rage twisted inside Dorothea like a choking vine. The brief report dangled from one hand.

"You're distressed, Sister," Hekatah said as she shuffled into the room and took a seat.

"Kartane was gone to Kaeleer." She couldn't draw a deep enough breath to give her voice any strength.

"Gone to see if any of their Healers can cure him?" Hekatah thought about that for a moment. "But why now? He could have gone anytime in the last few years."

"Perhaps because he thinks he has something to barter now that would be worth more than gold marks."

Hekatah hissed, immediately understanding. "How much does he know?"

"He was at my 'confession' the other day, but that's not much to tell someone."

"It's enough to put Saetan on his guard," Hekatah said ominously. "It's enough to make him start asking questions."

"Then perhaps something should be arranged before Kartane has a chance to talk to anyone outside of Little Terreille," Dorothea said softly, almost absently. She could think of a number of interesting "arrangements" that could be made for a son who wanted to woo her enemy.

Hekatah stood up and paced around the room for a minute. "No. Let's see if we can use Kartane as bait to lure a specific Healer to Little Terreille."

Dorothea snorted. "Do you really think Jaenelle Angelline is going to help *Kartane*?"

"I'll go to Little Terreille tonight and speak to Lord Jorval. He'll know how to phrase a discreet request." When Hekatah reached the door, she paused. "When your little Warlord comes home, perhaps you should give him a lesson in loyalty."

Dorothea waited until Hekatah left before going over to the fire. She dropped the report into it, watched the flames devour the paper.

When the war they were going to start was over, she would build a bonfire and watch the flames devour that desiccated walking corpse. And while she watched Hekatah burn, she would give her son that lesson in loyalty.

6 / Kaeleer

"I need a favor," Karla said abruptly after ten minutes of small talk and discussion about the Eyriens whom Lucivar had brought in.

Jaenelle glanced up from the piece of needlepoint she was working on, her eyes filled with wary amusement. "All right."

"I want a Ring of Honor like you gave the boyos in the First Circle."

"Darling, they wear the Ring of Honor on their cocks. You may be ballsy, but you don't have one of *those*."

"The kindred males don't wear them there. You had small Rings made that attach to the chain holding their Jewels."

"So you want a Ring of Honor," Jaenelle said, still sounding amused, still adding stitches to the needlepoint design.

Karla nodded solemnly. "For everyone in the coven."

Jaenelle looked up, no longer amused.

Karla met that look, recognizing by the subtle change in the sapphire eyes that she was no longer talking to Jaenelle, her friend and Sister. She was talking to Witch, the Queen of Ebon Askavi. *Her* Queen.

"You have a reason," Jaenelle said in her midnight voice. It wasn't a question.

"Yes." How much would she need to say to convince Jaenelle? And how much of what she'd seen in the tangled web could be left unsaid?

A few minutes passed in silence.

Jaenelle resumed her stitching. "If it's going to be worn on a finger, it should look decorative enough so that it's real purpose isn't obvious," she said quietly. "I assume you're mostly interested in the Ring because of the protection spells I added to it."

"Yes," Karla said quietly. The protection spells, the Ebony shields Jaenelle added to the Rings, were the reason she wanted one.

"Do you want the Rings linked just between the coven or linked to the boyos as well?"

Karla hesitated. A typical Ring of Honor allowed a Queen to monitor the emotions of the males in her First Circle. Because of a quirk in the way Jaenelle had made the first Ring of Honor—the one Lucivar *still* wore—the First Circle males in the Dark Court had the same means of gauging the Queen's mood. Did she, or any of the coven, really want to deal with males who were even more attuned to feminine moods than the boyos already were? Was a little emotional distance worth not having a means of sending a warning that couldn't, in any way, be blocked? "They should be linked with the First Circle males."

"I'll get the Rings made as soon as possible," Jaenelle said quietly.

"Thank you, Lady," Karla replied, acknowledging the Queen rather than the friend.

Another silence filled the room.

"Anything else?" Jaenelle finally asked.

Karla took a deep breath, let it out slowly. "I don't like your relatives."

"*Nobody* here likes my relatives," Jaenelle replied, but there was a sharp edge underneath the amusement—and sorrow. Then she added very quietly, "Saetan formally requested my consent for their executions."

"Did you give it?" Karla asked neutrally. She already knew the answer. She had been in the same position five years ago when she became Queen of Glacia. She had exiled her uncle, Lord Hobart, instead of executing him, even though she strongly suspected he had been behind the death of her parents and Morton's.

Jaenelle, if pushed, would choose the same.

"If it's any consolation, I do like your sister," Karla said when Jaenelle didn't answer the question. "She'll adjust to living in Kaeleer just fine if she can stop being scared long enough to catch her breath."

Jaenelle looked a little pained. "Lucivar got her drunk. She offered to brush him."

"Oh, Mother Night." When the laughter finally fizzled out, Karla groaned her way off the couch, said good night to Jaenelle, and headed for her own suite.

In the privacy of her bedroom, she indulged in a few grunts and moans as she got ready for bed. No matter how much she exercised when she was home, it always took her a few days to adjust to the workouts Lucivar put her through. But she wasn't about to miss a chance to get a little extra training from him. Especially now.

Later, as she was drifting off to sleep, it occurred to her that Jaenelle, who was a strong and very gifted Black Widow, might have had her own reasons for agreeing to the favor.

7 / Kaeleer

With exaggerated care, Daemon tied the robe's belt. The hot bath had warmed and loosened his tight, tired muscles. A large quantity of brandy would blur the mental sharp edges. Neither of those things would ease a bruised, bleeding heart.

Jaenelle didn't want him. That was becoming painfully clear.

When she had come looking for him last night, he had thought she had been pleased to see him, had hoped that they could begin again. But today she had shied away from him whenever he tried to approach her, using Lucivar or Chaosti or the whole coven as a buffer. It had forced him to realize that she had given him the title of Consort out of some sense of obligation, but she didn't want *him*.

How long, he wondered as he walked into his bedroom, could he stand watching her interact with the other males in her court while he was being shut out of her life? How long could his sanity hold together when, day after day, he was close enough to touch her but wasn't allowed to? How long . . .

Seeing the mound in the dim light, he thought someone had come in and dumped a white fur cover over his bed without smoothing it out.

Then a head lifted off his pillows and muscles rippled under the white fur as the huge cat shifted position.

The front paws, dangling over the side of the bed, flexed, displaying impressive claws. Gray eyes stared at him as if daring him to do more than breathe.

Even if he hadn't seen the Red Jewel lying against the white fur, Daemon would have had no doubts about who was sprawled on his bed.

We all try not to upset Kaelas, Lucivar had said.

Hell's fire, Mother Night, and may the Darkness be merciful.

With his heart pounding in his throat, Daemon cautiously backed toward the door. Saetan's suite was right across from his. He could . . .

Something large thumped against the other side of the door just as his hand touched the knob.

Kaelas curled his lips in a silent snarl.

There was only one escape open to him.

Never taking his eyes off Kaelas, Daemon sidled over to the door that separated his bedroom from Jaenelle's. He opened the door only as much as necessary, slipped into her bedroom, Black-locked the door, and added a Black shield. If what Lucivar had said about Kaelas being able to get through any shield was true, the lock and shield were useless, but they made him feel a little better.

As he backed farther into Jaenelle's room, he began to shake. It wasn't because of Kaelas, exactly. Any man with a healthy survival instinct would be cautiously afraid of a cat that size—especially when that cat was also a Red-Jeweled Warlord Prince. But he knew that, before he had shattered his mind the first time that night at Cassandra's Altar, he wouldn't have felt this kind of overwhelming fear. He would have had enough confidence in himself to match that feline arrogance even while being prudent enough to yield. Now . . .

"Daemon?"

He twisted around, suddenly finding it impossible to breathe.

Jaenelle stood in the doorway that led to the rest of her suite, dressed in sapphire-blue pajamas.

Seeing her, he lost his balance in too many ways.

She ran to him, wrapped her arms around his waist to keep him from falling. "What's wrong? Are you ill?"

"I—" He was sweating from the effort to take a deep enough breath.

"Can you walk far enough to sit on the bed?"

Unable to speak, he nodded.

"Sit down," Jaenelle said. "Put your head between your knees."

When he obeyed, his robe parted. He leaned over farther, hoping, since she was crouched in front of him, that he wasn't revealing anything she didn't want to see.

"Can you tell me what's wrong?" Jaenelle asked as her fingers brushed through his hair.

You don't love me. "On my bed," he gasped.

Jaenelle swiveled to look at the door adjoining their rooms. Her eyes narrowed. "What's Kaelas doing in your room?"

"Sleeping. On my bed."

"It's your room. Why didn't you tell him to get off?"

Why? Because he didn't want to die tonight.

But she sounded so baffled, he raised his head to look at her. She was serious. She wouldn't think twice about hauling eight hundred pounds of snarling feline off a bed.

Jaenelle stood up. "I'll get him—"

Daemon grabbed her hand. "No. It's all right. I'll find another bed. A couch. Hell's fire, I'll sleep on the floor."

Those ancient eyes studied him. Something odd flickered at the back of them for a moment. "Do you want to sleep here tonight?" she asked quietly.

Yes. No. He didn't want to come to her as a frightened, needy male. But he also wouldn't refuse the only invitation to her bed he might ever receive. "Please."

She pulled the covers back as far as she could with him still sitting on the bed. "Get in."

"I—" His face heated.

"I gather you wear the same thing to bed as every other male here," Jaenelle said dryly.

Which meant "nothing."

She moved to the other side of the room, her back politely turned.

Daemon quickly slipped out of the robe and slipped into the massive bed. No wonder she had offered to let him stay there. The bed was so big she would never notice another occupant.

A minute later, she got into bed, keeping well to her side of it. As she turned off the candle-light, she murmured, "Good night, Daemon."

He lay in the dark a long time listening to her breathe, certain that, like him, she wasn't asleep.

Eventually, the warm bed, the murmur of the fountain in the garden below, and the scent of whatever soap or perfume she used lulled him into a deep sleep.

The quiet, almost furtive sounds roused him.

Daemon opened his eyes.

Darkness. Swirling mist.

Propping himself up on one elbow, he looked around and saw her standing next to the altar. The golden mane that wasn't quite hair and wasn't quite fur. The delicately pointed ears. The thin stripe of fur that ran down her spine to the fawn tail that flicked over her buttocks. The human legs that ended in hooves. The hands that had sheathed claws.

Witch. The living myth. Dreams made flesh.

He was back in the misty place, deep in the abyss. The place where . . .

He rose slowly. Moving carefully so that he wouldn't startle her, he walked around the altar until he was standing across from her.

On the altar was a crystal chalice laced with hairline cracks. As he silently watched, she picked up a sliver of crystal and slipped it into place.

Something shifted inside him. Looking more intently at the chalice, he realized it was his own shattered mind.

He noticed three other tiny fragments. As he reached for one, she slapped his hand.

"Do you have any idea how much searching I had to do to find these?" she snarled at him.

She turned the chalice, slipped another tiny sliver into place.

The mist swirled, danced, spun.

Falling, falling, falling into the abyss. His mind shattering. Waking up in the misty place. Seeing Jaenelle as Witch for the first time as she pieced his crystal chalice back together.

Another sliver slipped into place.

A narrow bed with straps to bind hands and feet—the bed from Briarwood. A sumptuous bed with silk sheets. A seductive trap made of love and lies and truth— a trap to save a child. The Sadist whispering that she would take the bait because he, in all his male sexual glory, was the bait.

The last sliver was slipped into place.

Re-forming the psychic link with Saetan after he had persuaded Jaenelle to ascend to the level of the Red Jewels. The two of them forcing her to heal her own torn, bleeding body. Jaenelle's panic when the males from Briarwood started fighting the defenses Surreal had created in the corridors leading to the Altar. Cassandra opening the Gate between the Realms and taking Jaenelle away.

His crystal chalice glowed, heated as Witch's dark power covered all the cracks and sealed them.

Now that the gaps were filled in, the memories re-formed, and, finally, he knew *exactly* what had happened at Cassandra's Altar thirteen years ago. Finally, he knew *exactly* what he had done—and not done.

He took a deep breath, let it out slowly.

She glanced at him, nerves warring with the sharp, feral intelligence that filled her ancient eyes. "The missing pieces made weak spots that kept the chalice fragile. You should be fine now."

"Thank you."

"I don't want your gratitude," she snapped.

Studying her, Daemon opened his inner barriers just enough to taste her emotions. The hurt inside her surprised him.

"What *do* you want?" he asked quietly.

She nervously caressed the stem of the chalice. He wondered if she realized he could feel those caresses. And he wondered if she had any idea what those caresses were doing to him. He started to move around the altar, his fingers lightly brushing the stone.

"Nothing," she said in a small voice as she shifted a half step away from him. Then she added, "You lied to me. You didn't want Witch."

The fire of anger washed through him, waking the part of him the Blood in Terreille had called the Sadist. When the anger cooled, another kind of fire took its place.

His voice shifted into a sexual purr. "I love you. And I've waited a lifetime to be your lover. But you were too young, Lady."

She raised her head, her body stiff with dignity. "I wasn't too young here, in the abyss."

Slowly, he continued moving around the altar. "Your body had been violated. Your mind had shattered. But even if that hadn't been the case, you were still too young—even here in the abyss."

He came up behind her. His fingers lightly brushed her hips, her waist. Moving upward, he spread his hands across her ribs, his fingers just brushing the undersides of her breasts. He moved closer, smiling with savage pleasure as the fawn tail's nervous flicking teased and aroused him.

He kissed the spot where her neck and shoulder joined. The first kiss was light and chaste. With the second kiss, he used his teeth to hold her still while the tip of his tongue caressed and tasted her skin.

He could feel her heart pounding, feel each breathy pant.

Leaving a trail of soft kisses up her neck, he finally whispered in her ear, "You're not too young anymore."

She let out a breathless squeak when he gently rubbed himself against her.

Suddenly his hands were empty, and he was alone.

Hungry desire roared through him. He turned in a slow circle, searching, probing—the predator seeking his prey.

The last thing he was fully aware of was the mist thickening and swirling up around him until there was nothing else.

★　　★　　★

He struggled to get past the thick fog of sleep when something grabbed his arm and dragged him out of bed. Groggy, he tried to wake up enough to wonder why he was being pushed and prodded across the room.

He didn't have any trouble waking up after Lucivar shoved him into the shower cubicle and turned on the cold water full blast.

Daemon clawed at the dial until he managed to shut off the water. Bracing one hand against the wall, he tried to convince his cold-tightened muscles to let go of his lungs long enough for him to take a breath. Then he glared at Lucivar.

"Jaenelle woke up in a similar mood," Lucivar said mildly. "Must have been an interesting night."

"Nothing happened," Daemon growled as he swiped his hair back.

"Nothing physical," Lucivar said. "But I've danced with the Sadist enough times to recognize him when I see him."

Daemon just waited.

Lucivar's lips curled into that lazy, arrogant smile. "Welcome to Kaeleer, brother," he said softly. "It's good to have you back." He paused at the bathroom door. "I'll bring you a cup of coffee. That and a hot shower ought to wake you up enough."

"Enough for what?" Daemon asked warily.

Lucivar's smile turned wicked. "You're late for practice, old son. But, all things considered, I'll give you another fifteen minutes to get to the field before I come looking for you again."

"And if you have to come looking again?" Daemon asked too softly.

"Trust me. If I have to come looking for you again, you're not going to like it."

He already didn't like it. But he sipped the coffee Lucivar brought him while the hot water pounded his neck and back—and the Sadist began planning the quiet, gentle seduction of Jaenelle Angelline.

CHAPTER FIVE

1 / Kaeleer

Alexandra walked through the corridors, Philip beside her. She would have preferred Leland's company rather than an unavailable male, but the way Philip had quickly offered to accompany her meant he wanted to discuss something with her in private without making it obvious.

Irritated by his presence, she snapped, "We've been here for over a week and nothing's happened. How long does that 'escort' expect us to be able to remain guests?"

Philip didn't have to point out that Osvald, the escort Dorothea had provided, hadn't been able to get close to either Wilhelmina or Jaenelle without having to deal with at least one male chaperon, let alone get close enough to slip the women away from the Hall. He also didn't have to point out that they would be "guests" until the High Lord—or the *real* Queen who ruled this court—decided otherwise.

"Lucivar came to see me this morning," Philip said abruptly.

Hearing the tightness in his voice, Alexandra glanced at him, then took a closer look at the flush darkening Philip's face. Was that anger or embarrassment? "And?"

"He strongly suggested that you tighten your hold on Vania's leash before she gets hurt. It seems she's too aggressive in her efforts to coax a Kaeleer male into her bed. He said if she's that itchy for a male, she should invite her Consort, since that's why he's here."

Personally, Alexandra thought Vania acted like a slut. But Vania was also generous about sharing the use of her males with visiting Queens—a generosity Alexandra never refused whenever she visited that Province. She had kept no steady lover in her own court for more than twenty-five years—ever since she had asked Philip to see Leland through her Virgin Night. It wouldn't have been fair to any of them if she had asked him to warm her bed after that when he really wanted to be her daughter's lover, and the other men she had considered since then had been far more interested in the power they might wield as her Consort than in giving her pleasure.

But remembering Vania's generosity—and the fact that no male currently warmed *her* bed, either—made Alexandra defensive. "She wouldn't have to be 'aggressive' if this court remembered to provide visiting Queens with the basic amenities."

"I mentioned that," Philip said through gritted teeth. "And was told that there are no males in this court whose service requirements include that duty."

"I find that hard to believe. Not every Queen who comes here would necessarily have a Consort at that moment or have brought him. There must be *some* arrangement—" She stopped, shaken by the depth of the insult. "It's because we're from Terreille, isn't it?"

"Yes," Philip said flatly. "He said there are a few males in the Second and Third Circles who would normally be willing to accommodate a guest of the court if asked, but because Terreillean Queens don't know how to enjoy a male without mistreating him, no Kaeleer male would willingly offer himself." He hesitated. "He also said there are no pleasure slaves in Kaeleer."

That verbal slap hurt as much as a blow because it was a reminder that, for a few months, Daemon Sadi had been a pleasure slave in her court.

"I see," she said tightly.

"Despite his anger over the situation, Lucivar actually seemed concerned," Philip said, sounding baffled. "Mostly because Vania's fixed her efforts on Prince Aaron."

"Aaron *is* a very handsome man, and—"

"He's married."

There wasn't much she could say to that, not when she could feel waves of anxiety rolling off of Philip. Vania's marked attention toward a married man would be a sharp reminder of his own vulnerability.

While more and more aristo marriage contracts in Terreille were being made for social or political reasons, most Blood males still cherished the idea of marriage because it was the one relationship where the genders met on common ground as partners. Or as close to being partners as was possible—or reasonable. It also meant that male fidelity was a marriage requirement, and any man who looked beyond his wife's bed could swiftly find himself without home or family, could even lose his children.

"There's another reason to curb Vania," Philip said. "If the males here get any more riled . . ."

"I know," Alexandra replied sharply. They would never get Wilhelmina and Jaenelle away from the Hall if the males became more hostile than they already were. "I know," she said again, softening her voice. "I'll talk to her."

"Soon?"

She disliked herself for thinking less of him because of the anxiety in his voice.

"Yes, Philip," she said gently, "I'll talk to her soon."

2 / Kaeleer

An interesting gathering, Daemon thought as he slipped his hands into his trouser pockets and wondered what it meant when the Steward of the Court summoned the Master of the Guard, the Consort, and the First Escort to his study in order to "discuss something."

He'd spent the past couple of days studying the book of Protocol Saetan had given him and had been surprised by the differences between these rules and the ones he had been taught in Terreille. *This* Protocol, while reinforcing the matriarchal nature of the Blood, gave males some rights and privileges that helped balance the power. Which explained the refreshing lack of fear and subservience in these males. They understood the boundaries that defined acceptable male behavior, and within those boundaries, they stood on solid ground, never having to wonder what would happen to them if they were no longer in a particular Lady's favor.

He'd also been surprised by the section of Protocol that involved First Circle males since he'd never even seen the vaguest mention of it in Terreille.

There was a phrase that summed up a male's surrender into formal service: Your will is my life. It gave the Queen the right to do anything she pleased with a male, including kill him. That wasn't new, and, in Terreille, it was a serious risk. What *was* different was the tacit agreement on the Queen's part that, by accepting the male, she was also accepting his right to have a say in her decisions and *her* life. If a Queen gave an order and the majority of males in her First Circle opposed it, she could yield to their decision or dismiss them from her court. *But she couldn't hurt them for opposing her.*

If the males in Terreille had known about that part of Protocol, they might have been able to keep the behavior of Dorothea's pet Queens in check, might have been able to keep the younger strong witches safe and whole, might have found a way to fight the threats of slavery and castration that had made most of the males too afraid to challenge the witches in power.

But something—or someone—must have purged the sections about male power from the books of Protocol in Terreille so long ago that no one had remembered they existed.

No wonder Terreilleans found living in Kaeleer such a shock. And now it finally made sense why immigrants from Terreille were required to serve in a court. They would need that time to absorb the new rules and understand how those rules applied to day-to-day living.

Which made him even more curious to observe the formal give-and-take between a Queen and the male triangle.

Assuming, of course, the Queen was going to show up.

"Did anyone tell Cat she's supposed to be here?" Lucivar asked, echoing Daemon's thought.

Saetan gave Lucivar a bland look. "I told her. However, Lord Ladvarian had already cornered her to discuss a couple of things. I expect she'll be along as soon as she can talk herself around whatever he and Kaelas have in mind." That bland look was then aimed at Daemon.

Daemon met that look with one equally bland while his heart rate kicked up to a gallop—because he had the distinct feeling that whatever Ladvarian and Kaelas wanted to discuss with Jaenelle had to do with him.

He was trying to think of a reasonable excuse to drag Lucivar into the great hall for a minute to ask him why the kindred were so interested in the Consort when Jaenelle rushed into the room.

"Sorry I'm—" She checked when she saw them, and her rush suddenly became cautious. "Is this family or court?" she asked warily.

"Court," Saetan replied.

Fascinated, Daemon watched the subtle shift from woman to Queen.

"And what is the court's pleasure?" Jaenelle asked quietly.

No hint of a sneer or sarcasm in her voice, Daemon decided as he recognized one of the ritual openings for discussion.

"I received a message from Lord Jorval," Saetan said with equal calm, although his eyes seemed a little too carefully blank. "A person from a prestigious aristo family has come to Kaeleer seeking the assistance of a Healer for an illness that has baffled all the Healers in Terreille. Since you're known to be the best Healer in the Realm, he urgently requests that you come to Goth to offer your opinion."

Lucivar snarled quietly but viciously. A small, but sharp, hand gesture from Andulvar silenced him.

"Jorval also says that, while he's been assured that the illness is not contagious, it does seem to afflict only males. And since he doesn't want any harm to come to the males of your court—"

This time Andulvar snorted.

"—he has offered to provide you with an escort while you're in Little Terreille."

"NO!" Lucivar exploded into movement, pacing furiously. "You are *not* going into Little Terreille to do a healing without a full escort of your own males. Not again. Never again. If this person wants to see you so badly, why doesn't he come here?"

"I can think of a few reasons," Jaenelle said with dry amusement as she watched Lucivar.

Daemon's blood sang when her eyes met his for a moment. Then it chilled when he glanced at Saetan and saw something flicker at the back of those golden eyes. What was the High Lord trying to hide behind that deliberately blank gaze—and what would happen if the leash holding it back snapped?

"Did Jorval mention where this person is from? Or anything else that might be useful?" Jaenelle asked, turning back to Saetan while Lucivar paced and swore.

"Only that the short-lived races seem most affected," Saetan said.

Jaenelle's lips softened in a hint of a dreamy smile that was malevolent enough to make Daemon shiver. "The races from the western part of Terreille?" she asked in her midnight voice.

"He didn't say, Lady."

Jaenelle nodded thoughtfully. "I'll think about it."

"There's nothing to think about," Lucivar snarled. "You're not going. You may not remember much of what happened seven years ago, *but I do.* We're not going through that again, especially you."

Daemon studied Lucivar. Behind the fury was fear bordering on panic. He suppressed a sigh, not happy that his first official act as the Consort might be opposing his Queen. But anything that spooked Lucivar so badly wasn't something Daemon was going to easily agree to.

Then he noticed Jaenelle's face as she turned toward Lucivar—and wondered how any man would dare oppose Witch now that she had reached maturity and had come into her full power.

Lucivar froze in midstride as those sapphire eyes fixed on him. His body trembled, but he met her gaze, and his voice was steady as he said quietly, "The only way you're going into Little Terreille is by going through me."

Then he walked out of the study.

Jaenelle's shoulders slumped for a moment, then straightened again as she turned to face Daemon. "Please go with him."

"Why?" Daemon asked too softly.

The Queen stare melted a little into exasperation. "Because you're strong enough to hold him back, and I don't want him getting the boyos riled about something I haven't even decided to do yet."

It was the first thing she had asked of him, and he wasn't sure he could do it. "What happened seven years ago?"

Her face went death pale, and it took her a moment to answer. "Why don't you ask Lucivar? As he said, he remembers it better than I do."

He waited a few heartbeats. Then, "How long do you need?"

Now she looked at Saetan. "Would an hour be convenient?"

"It would be our pleasure to reconvene in an hour," Saetan said.

"All right," Daemon said. "I can hold him for an hour."

Nodding to acknowledge that she heard him, she hurried out of the room.

Daemon stared at the closed door, fully aware that Andulvar and Saetan were waiting for some indication of what he was going to do. "I am going to ask him," he said quietly. "And if I don't like the answer, she's going to have to go through me, too." He would sacrifice any chance of being her lover if that's what it took to protect her.

"You're not going to like the answer," Saetan said, "but I wouldn't worry about having to take a stand. If Jaenelle decides she's going into Little Terreille, she's going to have to go through the whole First Circle to do it. Since it isn't likely that she'll fight the court that hard over this particular healing, it's only respectful to allow the Lady the time to reach that conclusion on her own."

"In that case, if you'll excuse me, I'd better see what I can do about restraining Lucivar's temper."

3 / Kaeleer

Lucivar is unhappy, Ladvarian said as he watched Jaenelle stare at the waterfall and tiered pools she had built in this inner garden several years ago.

"I want to think, Warlord," Jaenelle said quietly. "Alone."

The Sceltie shifted his feet, thought a moment, then stood firm. *He's snarly and upset and he won't talk to any of us.* This particular smell of anger and fear on Lucivar only happened when Jaenelle or Marian did something to upset the Eyrien. Since Marian hadn't done anything unusual—he'd already checked—that meant Jaenelle had done something. Or was going to do something.

His lips pulled back in a silent snarl. *Jaenelle.*

As she turned to face him, he saw the large blackwood hourglass resting on her hand. Saying nothing, she turned it over, set it on the stone lip of the lowest pool, and walked to the other end of the garden.

Ladvarian growled softly at the hourglass.

The kindred had trouble understanding the way humans carved up a day into these little chunks called hours and minutes. They had understood easily enough that sometimes human females wanted to be left alone, but, for a while, they had come back too soon and had gotten snarled at. So the High Lord and the Lady had made these hourglasses because they were easy to understand. If the sand was all at the bottom, the female was ready to play again. If it wasn't, the kindred would go away without disturbing her.

Jaenelle had two sets of hourglasses. Each set had an hourglass sized for one hour, a half hour, and a quarter hour. Jaenelle used the set made of light-colored wood as a request for private time and could be interrupted if necessary. Witch, the Queen, used the set made from blackwood, and those hourglasses were a silent command.

Ladvarian trotted out of the garden, accepting the dismissal.

He wouldn't challenge his Queen, but he had learned that, if nipped sharply enough, Lucivar would lash out. And then Ladvarian and the other males would find out what the Lady was planning to do.

4 / Kaeleer

Using Craft, any of the Jeweled Blood would be able to send an ax cleanly through a chunk of wood. Lucivar, Daemon decided as he watched the ax come down and split the wood in half, wasn't using anything but muscle and temper.

And that, more than anything else he'd observed since arriving in Kaeleer, told him how different serving in a court was here. In Terreille, Lucivar would have picked a fight with another strong male, and the resulting violence would have triggered a vicious brawl that could tear a court apart. Here he was venting his temper by chopping wood that would warm the Hall in the winter days ahead.

"She send you out here to keep me hobbled?" Lucivar snarled as he swung the ax again.

"What happened seven years ago, Lucivar?" Daemon asked quietly. "Why are you so against Jaenelle doing a healing in Little Terreille?"

"You're not going to talk me around this, Bastard."

"I'm not interested in talking you around this. I just want to know why I'm about to draw the line that puts me on the opposing side of my Queen's wishes."

The ax came down just hard enough to set the blade into the chopping block.

Lucivar called in a towel and wiped the sweat off his face. "Seven years ago she had been in Little Terreille, making one of those visits that had been a concession to the Dark Council. A child had been badly injured, and she was asked to do the healing. Whoever set it up did it well. The injury was extensive enough that the healing would have left her physically and mentally exhausted but not enough that she might have called in other Healers than the ones in Little Terreille. Because if she'd called Gabrielle or Karla for help, a male escort would have come with them.

"When the healing was done, someone gave her food or drink that was drugged, and she was too tired to detect it. It made her complacent enough to do what she was told—and she was told to sign a marriage contract."

The cold slipped through Daemon's veins, sweet and deadly. *You weren't here. You can't think of it as a betrayal since you weren't here.* It didn't matter. A Consort could be nothing more than a physical accommodation. But a husband . . . "Then where is he?" he asked too softly.

Lucivar twisted the towel. "He didn't survive the consummation."

"You took care of that? Thank you."

"He was dead when I got there." Lucivar closed his eyes and swallowed hard. "Hell's fire, Daemon, she splattered him all over the room." He opened his eyes. The bleakness in them made Daemon shiver. "They gave her a large dose of *safframate* on top of the other drug."

Daemon's body went completely numb for a moment. He knew all too well what *safframate* could do to a person. "You took care of her?" Meaning, *you gave her the sex she needed?* There was no room in him now to feel jealousy or betrayal, just the desperate hope that Lucivar had done what was needed.

Lucivar looked away. "I took her hunting in Askavi."

Daemon just stared at his brother, letting the magnitude of those words ripen. "You went out with her as *bait?*"

"What was I supposed to do?" Lucivar snapped. "Let her stay locked up in Ebon Askavi suffering? Bloodletting relieves the pain of *safframate* as well as sex does." He paused to take a deep breath and regain control. "It wasn't easy, but we survived it."

And that, Daemon realized, was all Lucivar intended to say about a period of time that must have been a nightmare for him.

"She's only been back to Little Terreille a couple of times since then, and then only with a full, armed escort that included me," Lucivar said. "She hasn't been back at all since she formally set up her court."

"I see," Daemon said quietly. "It's almost time to hear her decision. Do you want to get cleaned up?"

"What for?" Lucivar asked with a grim smile. "Once I hear it, I'll probably be back out here anyway."

5 / Kaeleer

"May I help you?"

Osvald, the escort, clenched his teeth, then made an effort to smile as he turned to face the footman. Hell's fire, wasn't there *one* male in this whole damn place who wasn't spoiling for a fight? "I seem to have gotten turned around, so I thought I'd admire the pictures in this part of the Hall."

"I would be happy to show you the way back to your room," Holt said with frigid courtesy.

In Terreille, he could have had the footman whipped for no better reason than sufficient lack of subservience. In Terreille, servants wouldn't wear their Jewels so blatantly that it forced their social superiors to acknowledge that strength. It galled him that he, who was favored by the High Priestess of Hayll, had to acknowledge that a *footman* was also an Opal-Jeweled Warlord.

"This way," Holt said just as Wilhelmina stepped out of her room.

Osvald swore silently. If Holt had shown up a few minutes later, he could have had the bitch and gotten out of this place.

Then the large striped cat stepped out of the room and immediately fixed those unblinking eyes on him, making him glad of Holt's presence. When the cat's lips began to lift into a snarl, he didn't need any more urging. He offered Wilhelmina a polite greeting—and felt intensely relieved when she returned it so automatically it sounded like casual familiarity, the kind of automatic response the other bitches in this place only gave to males they knew fairly well. With every other male, there was that slight pause that practically screamed "stranger."

That could work to his advantage, he thought as he followed Holt back to the wing where Alexandra and her entourage had been quartered. It wouldn't seem odd for an escort to deliver a message from one Lady to another—especially if it was assumed he'd been working for that family for a number of years.

Yes, that could work very well.

6 / Kaeleer

When they work in tandem, they're dangerous, Andulvar said to Saetan, using an Ebon-gray communication thread.

Looking at Lucivar and Daemon, Saetan understood the distinction Andulvar was making. All Warlord Princes were dangerous, but when two men with complementary strengths became a team . . . *So were we at their age,* he replied dryly. *We still are.*

If it ever came down to a fight, I wouldn't want to go up against those two, Andulvar said thoughtfully.

Any amusement Saetan felt fled with that statement. His heart wanted to shout, *They'll never be enemies. They're my children, my sons.* But another part of him—the part that had to assess the potential danger of another strong male—couldn't be sure. He *had* been sure when it had been Lucivar alone. But Daemon . . .

Lucivar had endured a brutal childhood, but in some ways, it had been a clean brutality. He hadn't gotten entangled in a court until he was a youth. But Daemon had been raised in Dorothea's court, and he had taken the twisted lessons taught there into himself, had made them a part of himself, and then used them as a weapon.

While he might fight individuals, Lucivar had been able to embrace loyalty to family and court. Saetan strongly suspected that Daemon's loyalty would always be superficial, that the only loyalty the rest of them could count on was his commitment to Jaenelle. Which meant Daemon was capable of doing *anything* in the name of that loyalty. Which meant this son had to be handled very, very carefully.

It didn't help that Jaenelle was acting like a rabbit to Daemon's fox. With any other man, Saetan might have found this chase amusing. He knew the boyos certainly did, and he understood why they were delighted by her reaction to Daemon. But he didn't think Daemon found it the least bit amusing, and he wondered what would happen when his son's temper finally snapped—and who would suffer because of it.

When Jaenelle entered the study, Saetan put aside the problem that hadn't arrived yet in order to deal with the one already at the door.

"High Lord," Jaenelle said formally.

"Lady," Saetan replied, equally formal.

She took a deep breath and turned to Lucivar. "Prince Yaslana, as First

Escort, I want you to arrange for accommodations somewhere along the border of Little Terreille for myself and a limited escort. Not an inn. A private house or a guard station. Somewhere that ensures discretion. It can be in whichever Territory you choose. You can decide the time of the meeting—although not within the next three days."

He wasn't standing close enough to her to catch the scent, but he could tell by the sudden blaze in Daemon's eyes and the sharpness in Lucivar's that her moon's blood had started. He wanted to sigh. Hell's fire, how was he supposed to channel Daemon's instinctive aggression while fighting to control his own? Witches were vulnerable during the first three days of their moontimes because they couldn't wear their Jewels or do more than basic Craft without causing themselves physical pain. And when it was his Queen who was vulnerable, a Warlord Prince's temper rode the killing edge during those days.

"You don't have to tell anyone about the arrangements you've made," Jaenelle continued. "Although, out of courtesy, you should inform the Steward, the Master of the Guard, and the Consort. The Steward will contact Lord Jorval to confirm the meeting place in Little Terreille."

"What's the point of setting up a secure place if you're going to go to Little Terreille?" Lucivar asked, but Saetan noticed he was keeping his tone carefully respectful.

"Because I'm going to go to Little Terreille without *going* to Little Terreille. That will satisfy the court's concerns about my well-being and still allow me to meet with this person."

Lucivar narrowed his eyes, considering. "You could just refuse."

"I have my own reasons for doing this," Jaenelle replied in her midnight voice.

And that, Saetan knew, would decide the matter for Lucivar.

Except Lucivar was still studying her. "If I agree to this, do we get to fuss for the next three days without getting snarled at?"

That's all it took to change the Queen back into a stuttering, snarling younger sister. "Who is 'we'?" she asked ominously.

"The family."

Saetan wondered if anyone else had noticed that the look Daemon gave his brother should have left Lucivar bleeding. And he wondered if Lucivar even realized that, whether he had included or excluded Daemon under the term "family," it wasn't sitting well with the Queen's Consort.

"Papa!" Jaenelle said, whirling around to face him.

"Witch-child?" he replied mildly, but he could feel beads of sweat forming on his forehead as Daemon's face shifted into a cold, unreadable mask.

She stared at him for a moment, then whirled back to Lucivar. "Within reason," she snapped. "And I get to decide what's reasonable."

When Lucivar just grinned at her, she stomped out of the study. The grin faded when he looked at Andulvar. "Since you're the Master of the Guard, she should have asked you to make the arrangements."

Andulvar shrugged. "My ego's not bruised, puppy. She's too good a Queen not to understand the needs of the males who serve her. Right now, you need to make the arrangements more than I do." His smile had sharp edges. "But if you don't inform me of your arrangements, I *will* be insulted."

"If you have time now, we could take a look at a map," Lucivar said.

"You're learning, puppy," Andulvar said as he draped an arm over Lucivar's shoulders and led him out of the study. "You're learning."

When Daemon made no move to leave, Saetan leaned against the blackwood desk. "Something on your mind, Prince?"

"I don't give a damn what familial ties you and Lucivar claim to have with her, I am *not* her brother," Daemon said too quietly.

"No one said you were. The fact that I'm her adopted father and you happen to be my son is irrelevant. You've never thought of her as a sister, and she's never thought of you as a brother. That hasn't changed."

The chill in Daemon's eyes thawed to bleakness. "She may not think of me as a brother, but she also doesn't want me to be anything else."

Saetan snapped to attention. "That isn't true."

Daemon's soft laugh held bitterness and grief. "It usually takes me less than an hour to seduce a woman when I'm trying. And usually not more than two when I'm not. I can't even get close enough to talk to her most of the time."

Daemon's acknowledged ability to seduce chilled Saetan. Because the people telling the tales didn't know they were talking about his son, he'd heard enough stories about the Sadist to feel uneasy. Those bedroom skills, like the man who wielded them, were a double-edged sword.

If Daemon felt driven enough to use those skills prematurely . . .

Saetan crossed his arms to hide the slight tremor in his hands. "The boyos find this little chase between you and Jaenelle amusing."

"Do they?" Daemon asked too softly.

"And, I confess, so do I." *Or would, if I could be certain you weren't going to go for my throat before I finish this.*

Daemon's gold eyes held a bored, sleepy look Saetan knew too well—because there had been times when he had looked into a mirror and seen it in his own eyes.

"Do you?" Daemon asked.

"A couple of days ago, Jaenelle asked for my opinion about the dress she was wearing for dinner."

"I remember it. It's a lovely gown."

"I'm delighted that you appreciated it." Saetan paused. "Can you also appreciate that, in the thirteen years she's lived here, Jaenelle has never been concerned enough about clothes to ask for my opinion about something she was wearing. And can you appreciate that she wasn't asking for my opinion as her Steward or her father but as a man. And I admit that, considering the way that dress fit her, my opinion of it as a father would have differed considerably from my opinion as a man."

Daemon almost smiled.

"She sees you as a man, Daemon. A *man,* not a male friend. For the first time in her life, she's trying to deal with her own lust. So she's running."

"She's not the only one trying to deal with it," Daemon muttered, but the sleepy look had changed to sharp interest. "I *am* her Consort. She could just—"

Saetan shook his head. "Do you really think Jaenelle would demand that from you?"

"No." Daemon raked his fingers through his hair. "What can I do?"

"You don't need to do anything more than you're already doing." Saetan thought for a moment. "Do you know how to make a brew to ease moontime discomfort?"

"I know how to make a few of them."

Saetan smiled. "In that case, I suggest that the Consort prepare one for his Lady. I don't think even Jaenelle would disagree about that falling into the category of 'reasonable fussing.'"

7 / Kaeleer

Surreal paused in the dining room doorway and swore under her breath. The only people in the room were Alexandra and her entourage.

Hell's fire. Why couldn't Jaenelle have left well enough alone? The meals had certainly been more relaxed and the conversation more interesting when Alexandra and her people had been taking their meals separately. When she had pointed that out to Saetan, he had informed her it had been Jaenelle's idea to have Alexandra and the others join the rest of them for meals, in the hope that they might acquire some understanding about Kaeleer.

The intention might have been good, Surreal thought crossly as she strode to the table, but the reality was a miserable failure. Not one of them, from Alexandra right down to the least-ranking escort, wanted to understand *anything* about the Blood in Kaeleer. And the midday meals were the worst since Saetan didn't preside over them.

As she reached the table, the two Province Queens, Vania and Nyselle, gave her looks that mingled smug superiority with disgust. She might have taken it personally if she hadn't known that they looked at *all* the witches there in exactly the same way—including the Queens who far outranked them.

Then Vania looked at the doorway, and her expression changed to predatory delight.

Glancing over, Surreal saw Aaron pause in the doorway—and decided that a man who had been told the date of his execution looked pretty much the same way. Figuring that he didn't need another woman staring at him, she turned her attention to the table.

The first point of interest was the way this group had split. Alexandra, Philip, and Leland were sitting at one end of the table. Nyselle was sitting at the other end, her Consort and the escorts ranged around her. Vania's Consort sat on his Lady's left, looking unhappy. The chair on Vania's right was empty, as were the ones across from her.

The second point of interest was the serving dishes on the table. Breakfast and the midday meal were usually set out on the huge sideboard so that everyone could fill a plate and take a seat as they pleased. Dinner was the only meal that had a set starting time, and was the only meal where the footmen served the food. *This* midday meal had been set out family-style, as if only a small number of people were expected.

That was fine, Surreal thought as she began filling her plate from the closest serving dishes. That was just *fine*—as long as everyone else was going hungry to avoid eating with the guests. But if she found out that another midday meal was being quietly served elsewhere, she was going to have a few things to say to *someone* about not being told.

"May I sit with you?" Aaron asked quietly as he joined her.

She was about to make a tart reply about there being plenty of chairs when she saw the hunted look in his eyes.

As if her noticing him had given him some kind of permission, he shifted closer to her. Close enough for her to feel the way his muscles quivered with the strain of keeping strong emotions tightly leashed.

"Why don't you sit over here, Aaron?" Vania said, giving him a coy smile while she patted the chair on her right.

Well, that more than explained the hunted look.

During the time Surreal had been at the Hall, she'd observed that the males—from the most menial male servant right up to the High Lord—had some very particular ideas about what was considered acceptable physical distance, and the cold courtesy they could all turn on a woman was usually an effective determent when that distance wasn't respected. The males in the First Circle not only tolerated being approached and touched by all of the witches in the First Circle, they welcomed that friendly intimacy. But they didn't welcome it from anyone else.

He considers me one of them, she realized, feeling a jolt of pleasure at the acceptance. *He considers me safe.* Because of that, her "Of course," in reply to his question was as soothing as she could make it. Which, for some reason, distressed him.

I was a good whore, she thought as she picked up the serving fork and the carving knife from the platter holding the roasted turkey. *A damned good whore. So why is it that, all of a sudden, males are impossible to figure out?*

"Would—"

Surreal turned her head to look at Aaron, the carving knife poised over the turkey. "You weren't going to suggest that I don't know how to handle a knife, were you, sugar?"

Aaron's eyes widened. "I would never be so foolish as to suggest that a Dea al Mon witch didn't know how to handle a knife," he said, sounding suspiciously meek. "I was going to ask if you would mind cutting a slice for me."

"Of course you were," she replied tartly. She felt something in him relax and swore silently about perverse male behavior. Then again, she mused as she cut the turkey breast, maybe the males were just so used to that blend of tart and sweet in a witch's personality, they could relax around it. It could be an acquired taste, like pickleberries.

The thought made her chuckle.

After placing the serving fork and carving knife back on the platter, she settled down to eat. There wasn't much conversation, which suited her just fine—especially since all of Vania's remarks were aimed at Aaron and his replies had become curt to the point of rudeness.

Hoping to break, or at least change, the tension that was getting thicker by the minute, Surreal looked up, intending to ask Alexandra when she and her party were going to leave. But she didn't say anything because she found herself looking straight at Vania. There was a nasty kind of anger in the woman's eyes directed right at Aaron.

After toying with her food for a minute, Vania pushed her plate away and smiled coyly. "I declare, I'm just too tired to eat right now. Aaron was so stimulating this morning."

It took Surreal a moment too long to understand that remark.

With a howl of rage, Aaron lunged across the table, grabbed Vania by the hair, and yanked her forward. His left hand closed on the carving knife and swung it toward her throat.

Surreal grabbed Aaron's left wrist with both hands and pulled back as hard as she could. He gave her a couple of inches before his muscles bunched and his arm surged forward.

The knife's point jabbed Vania's neck. She screamed as blood began flowing from the wound.

Surreal poured the power of her Gray Jewels into her hands to give her added strength, but there was some kind of tight shield around Aaron that just absorbed the power.

All right. Muscle against muscle. She could hold him off for the few seconds needed for the other men at the table to help her.

Except no one moved.

Then she got a glimpse of Aaron's face and knew none of the other people in the room were going to approach a Warlord Prince who looked that cold and merciless.

She fought harder, used every bit of leverage she could find. She didn't give a damn if Vania got her throat slit, but she didn't want Aaron to get into trouble because the bitch had pushed him too far.

Surreal? Graysfang said anxiously.

Help me!

The wolf must have been nearby because he was in the dining room seconds after she called.

*Surreal . . . *

Don't just stand there. Do something!

Aaron is First Circle, Graysfang whined. *I can't bite Aaron.*

Then find someone who can!

Graysfang rushed out of the room.

If she could have, she would have used Craft to vanish the knife, but Aaron had extended that damned shield to include the weapon. She couldn't get the knife, couldn't even break his wrist to stop him.

Her grip on his wrist slipped for an instant—long enough for the knife to slice Vania's neck again.

Then Chaosti was there, his hands clamped on Aaron's right wrist. Lucivar's hands closed over hers, adding more force and strength.

Aaron fought against them mindlessly, intent only on the kill.

"Damn it, Aaron," Lucivar snarled. "Don't force me to break your wrist."

Good luck, Surreal thought sourly as Lucivar's hands tightened on hers. She just hoped he remembered her hands were in the way before he started breaking bones.

Aaron seemed far past the ability to hear them, but he reacted when an icy midnight voice said, "Prince Aaron, *attend.*"

Aaron began shivering uncontrollably. Lucivar quickly took the carving knife away from him and vanished it. Chaosti pried Aaron's right hand open, releasing Vania's hair.

Vania kept screaming—had been screaming, Surreal realized, since the first jab.

"*SILENCE.*"

Ice instantly coated all the glasses on the table. Vania glanced in Jaenelle's direction and stopped screaming.

"Prince Aaron," Jaenelle said too calmly. "*Attend.*"

Flinching, Aaron slowly straightened up. Chaosti and Lucivar released him and stepped aside.

Deathly pale, Aaron walked over to where Jaenelle stood and sank to his knees.

"Wait for me in the High Lord's study," Jaenelle said.

With effort, Aaron got to his feet and left the dining room.

Surreal looked at those frozen sapphire eyes, felt the lightest brush of immense, barely controlled rage, and started to shake. Her legs gave out. She sat on the table.

Jaenelle slowly approached the table and turned her eyes on Lucivar. "You knew about this."

Lucivar took several shallow breaths before answering. "I knew."

"And you did nothing."

He swallowed hard. "I had hoped it would be taken care of quietly."

Jaenelle just stared at him. Then, "I'll see you in the High Lord's study in thirty minutes, Prince Yaslana."

"Yes, Lady."

Those sapphire eyes pinned Chaosti next. "And you after him."

"It will be my pleasure, Lady," Chaosti replied, his voice husky.

Oh, I doubt that very much, Surreal thought, still shaking.

Then Jaenelle looked at Vania—and the cold began to burn.

"If you ever again cause one of my males any physical, mental, or emotional distress, I will hang you by your heels and skin you alive."

No one spoke, no one moved until Jaenelle walked out of the room.

Could she do that? Surreal wondered. She didn't realize she had spoken out loud until Lucivar made a sound that was a cross between a laugh and a whimper.

"In the mood she's in right now? Not only could she do it, she wouldn't bother using a knife."

Surreal looked at her own hands, thought about it for a moment, and then wondered if anyone would be upset if she threw up on the floor.

"Surreal?" Lucivar's hand shook as he lifted her head up.

He's scared shitless. Hell's fire, Mother Night, and may the Darkness be merciful.

"Surreal? Are you injured?"

The sharp concern in Lucivar's voice made her focus her attention. "Hurt? No, I don't think—"

"There's blood on your face and neck."

"Oh." Her gorge rose. "I must have gotten splashed when . . ." Keeping her mouth shut seemed like a very good idea right now.

Lucivar looked over his shoulder. "Falonar?"

"Prince Yaslana," Falonar replied quietly.

"Your sole duty this afternoon is to take care of Lady Surreal."

"It will be my pleasure."

"Lady Vania needs a Healer," one of the escorts said frantically.

"Well, shit," Surreal said, suddenly feeling a bit drunk, "they really are alive. They can talk and they can move. The way they were sitting on their thumbs a few minutes ago, I'd doubted it. I really had."

"Shut up, bitch," an escort yelled.

Lucivar, Chaosti, and Falonar snarled at the man.

"I suggest you ask Lord Beale to send for the Healer in Halaway," Lucivar said coldly.

"Surely the Hall keeps a Healer," Alexandra said, sounding outraged.

"There's Lady Gabrielle and Lady Karla," Lucivar replied. "If I were you, I wouldn't ask either of them right now."

"You could always ask Jaenelle," Surreal said with a venomous smile.

Frightened silence met that statement.

With Vania supported by two of the escorts, Alexandra and her entourage quickly left the room. Lucivar and Chaosti gave Falonar a hard look before leaving.

Falonar approached Surreal cautiously. "This must have been . . . distressing . . . for you." He looked like he was about to bite down on a toad. "Do you need smelling salts or something?"

Surreal narrowed her eyes. "Sugar, I'm an assassin. I've done worse than this at a dinner table."

"I wasn't talking about . . ." He looked at the blood-splashed table.

"Oh." At least he was smart enough to realize it wasn't *Aaron* who had scared her.

He paused, then added, "I meant no insult."

"None taken," she replied. It was her turn to pause. "On any other day, I'd be willing to find out what the rules are for inviting a man to have a sweaty afternoon of sex, just to get my mind off this for a few hours. But I don't think sex of any kind would be a good idea today."

Surprise and interest flickered in Falonar's eyes, and his voice held regret. "No, I don't think it would be a good idea . . . today."

"So why don't we go through another practice round with the sticks? I'd like to get out of this building for a while."

Falonar nodded thoughtfully. "You can handle a knife?"

Surreal smiled. "I can handle a knife." She glanced at his groin. "I can also handle spears quite well."

He actually blushed a little. "A bow?"

Still smiling, she shook her head.

"A new skill requires concentration."

"So do some old skills . . . if you want to do them right."

His blush deepened while his interest sharpened.

Surreal stood up. "Let's go concentrate on a new skill."

"And discuss the possibility of practicing old skills?"

"Oh, definitely."

In charity with each other, they hurried to escape the growing fury that filled the Hall.

8 / Kaeleer

Daemon paused outside Jaenelle's sitting room. He took a deep breath, straightened his shoulders, and knocked on the door.

No answer.

She was there. He could feel the fury swirling in the room. And he could feel the cold.

He knocked again, then went into the room, ignoring the fact that he hadn't been invited.

Jaenelle prowled the sitting room, her arms wrapped around her middle. She glared at him, and snarled, "Go away, Daemon."

She should have been resting today, Daemon thought as his temper sharpened. Probably had been before that scene in the dining room.

"Since I'm the only male in the First Circle who isn't the recipient of your displeasure, I thought I'd check and see if you needed anything. Why is that, by the way?" Despite his efforts to keep his tone mild, his voice had an edge to it. Rationally, he knew he should be grateful to have escaped the verbal lashing the others had received. Instead, he resented the exclusion—until he got the full thrust of that frozen sapphire stare.

"Did you know you should have reported Vania's stalking of Aaron?" Jaenelle asked too quietly.

"No, I didn't. Even if I had known, I wouldn't have reported it."

"Why in the name of Hell not?" Jaenelle shouted.

Heat. Daemon felt his legs weaken as relief washed through him. Thank the Darkness, this was no longer cold rage but hot anger. He could work around hot anger. "Because she *was* stalking him. Aaron wasn't casting any lures or making any unspoken invitations. She was trying to push him into her bed because she wanted the conquest. She didn't give a damn what it would do to him."

"Exactly."

She still didn't understand. Daemon raked his fingers through his hair. "Hell's fire, woman, the man has a wife and an infant daughter. If he had said anything, would Kalush really believe he was innocent?"

"Of course she would!" Jaenelle shouted. "But if he didn't feel he could tell Kalush, he could have told me or Karla or Gabrielle."

"How would that have helped?" Daemon shouted back. "You would have told Kalush, and he'd still be under suspicion for something he didn't do, didn't even *want* to do."

"Why do you keep harping about suspicion? This—"

"I am not harping."

"—has nothing to do with suspicion."

"Then why are you so furious with him?" Daemon roared.

"BECAUSE HE GOT HURT AND HE SHOULDN'T HAVE!" Jaenelle's eyes suddenly filled with tears. "I'm mad at him because he got hurt. Don't you think I know how ecstatic and terrified he's been since Kalush got pregnant? How much she and Arianna mean to him? How vulnerable he feels about another woman showing interest in him?" She swiped at a tear that rolled down her face. "But you all hid it so well, we weren't picking up anything but the edginess the boyos have felt since those . . . people . . . came to the Hall. If we'd known, the coven would have done something before now."

Hearing something underneath the words, Daemon narrowed his gold eyes. "What else?"

Jaenelle hesitated. "Alexandra is my grandmother."

He advanced on her so fast, she took a quick step back and tripped on the train of her gown. Catching her by the arms, he pulled her up against him. "You are *not* going to wallow in guilt, Jaenelle," he said fiercely. "Do you hear me? You're not going to do it. She's your *grandmother*. A grown woman. As an adult, she's responsible for her own actions. As a Queen, she's responsible for controlling her own court. If anyone should share the blame with Vania, it's Alexandra. She was warned about this and did nothing." When she started to argue, he gave her enough of a shake to make her bare her teeth and snarl at him. "If you want to shoulder guilt and blame because they're here, then Wilhelmina is equally guilty and equally to blame."

Oh, the protective fierceness in those eyes.

Daemon ran his hands soothingly up and down her arms. "If one granddaughter shouldn't be blamed for Vania's actions or Alexandra's lack of action, how can you, in all fairness, blame the other?"

"Because I'm the Queen, and a Queen not only controls her court, she protects it."

Daemon snarled in frustration and muttered a few uncomplimentary things about female stubbornness.

"It's not stubbornness when you're right," Jaenelle snapped.

He couldn't win this fight if that was the stand she was going to take, so he tried to shift them to different ground. "All right. We should have reported it." Or taken care of it themselves better than they had.

She stared at him suspiciously. "Why are you agreeing with me all of a sudden?"

Daemon raised one eyebrow. "I would think you would prefer having males agree with you," he said mildly. "Should I keep arguing?"

"When any of you gives up this quickly, it's only because another of you has gotten into position to continue the argument from another angle."

"You make the First Circle sound like a hunting pack," Daemon said, trying hard to suppress a chuckle.

"I think they learned that tactic from the wolves," Jaenelle replied sourly.

Daemon began massaging her neck and shoulders.

She closed her eyes. "Did you know you and Lucivar were the only living human males in the First Circle that Vania didn't try to bed?"

"She wouldn't have dared try with me," Daemon said too softly.

"And she was smart not to try with Lucivar. When someone puts him in that position, he has a tendency to hit first and discuss after."

"Sounds like a successful deterrent."

"Mmm. Oh, right there."

Daemon obligingly focused on a knot of tight muscle. As he caressed and massaged, he subtly coaxed her to lean against him until her arms were around his waist and her head rested on his shoulder. "Lucivar's very hurt over your being so angry with him," he said quietly. "All the boyos are."

"I know." She sighed. "I'm too tired to think of a task for each of them. I guess I'll have to stub my toe."

"I beg your pardon?" His hands stopped caressing for a moment.

"I'll stub my toe, and then I'll let them all fuss and fetch and carry, and they'll know I'm not angry with them anymore."

"They'll actually believe a stubbed toe is a serious injury?"

Jaenelle snorted softly. "Of course not. It's more like a ritual."

"I see. The Queen can't apologize for the discipline but has to give a clear signal that it's done."

"Exactly. If it had been just one of them, I would have asked his assistance with something that I could just as easily do myself, and he would have understood. With so many, I'll have to let them fuss." Her voice took on a bit of a growl. "They'll plump pillows and tuck blankets around me that I don't want. They'll make me take naps."

"So it's not just forgiveness, but a little revenge thrown in."

"The revenge isn't so little. Usually, one of the coven will sneak a book in so I can read during my 'naps.' Once, when Papa came in to check on me, I stuffed the book under a pillow, but not quite well enough. He didn't say anything. When Khary and Aaron came in, he even poked the book farther under the pillow to hide it better. Then Saetan had the balls to say I looked flush so that they could fuss even more."

Daemon paused for a moment, sorting through the distinction she made between "Papa" and "Saetan." "Sweetheart," he said carefully, "if Saetan has balls, then so does Papa."

"It sounds disrespectful somehow to say that about Papa."

"I see," Daemon said in a tone of voice that indicated he didn't see at all.

"Papa," Jaenelle explained, "is charming and intelligent, a well-rounded companion."

Thinking of Saetan and Sylvia, Daemon said dryly, "I don't think Saetan is the companion who's well-rounded."

A long pause. Then, "You would call Sylvia's figure well-rounded?"

Daemon bit his tongue. Was she asking about Sylvia because she had picked up a stray thought of his or through an obvious connection of topics? And how in the name of Hell was a Consort supposed to safely answer that? "Her figure is more well-rounded than his," he hedged—and then threw Saetan into the verbal pit without a qualm. "They do seem fond of each other, even if Sylvia *won't* lend him that book."

When Jaenelle raised her head, there was nothing cold about the gleam in her eyes. "What book?"

"You mentioned *what?*"

Daemon rubbed the back of his neck as he warily studied his father. He had felt some obligation, male to male, to give Saetan fair warning—and now sincerely wished he hadn't.

Saetan stared at him. "Whatever possessed you to tell her about it in the first place?"

Oh, no. He was not going to repeat anything that had led up to that comment. "Jaenelle's in a much better mood now."

"I'm sure she is." Saetan rubbed his hands over his face. "What's she doing now?"

"Resting," Daemon said. "I'm going to talk to Beale about having a tray brought to her sitting room. We'll have dinner there and then play cards for a while."

The way Saetan's eyes suddenly glittered made him nervous.

"You're going to play cards with Jaenelle?" Saetan asked.

"Yes," Daemon replied cautiously.

"In that case, Prince, I'd say you've more than made up for mentioning that book."

9 / Kaeleer

Osvald lingered in the corridor.

At first, he'd thought Vania's greedy lust was going to spoil all their plans. But after the pale bitch-Queen had ripped into the males of the court because of it, they'd all gone off to lick their emotional wounds and hadn't been seen for the rest of the day.

Jaenelle's fury would have been a gift that had fallen into his hands if

Wilhelmina Benedict had been in her room. But she wasn't, and he had no idea where to look for her. If she was with the other bitches, he couldn't approach her. He didn't want any of them taking special notice of him before he was ready to disappear.

Soon, he thought as he returned to his own room. Soon.

10 / Kaeleer

And they call me *the Sadist,* Daemon thought as he eyed the game board and cards—and did his best not to snarl in frustration.

"You almost won that round," Jaenelle offered, trying not to look too gleeful as she tallied up the scores.

Daemon bared his teeth in a poor imitation of a smile. "My deal?"

Nodding, Jaenelle busily turned the paper over, drew a line down the middle, and wrote their names at the top.

Daemon picked up the cards and began shuffling the deck.

Hell's fire, he shouldn't be having *this* much trouble with a card game. It was just a variation of the game "cradle" that Jaenelle had played as a child. All right, it was *twenty-six* variations of "cradle." He still shouldn't be having this much trouble winning a round. But there was something a little *off* about this game, something that defied rational thinking. *Male* thinking.

A game board with colored stones and bone discs with symbols etched on one side. A hand of cards. And the convoluted interaction between them. He could picture the coven sitting around on a stormy winter afternoon, putting this game together piece by piece, building one variation off another, adding bits from other games distinct to their own cultures, until they had created something that was pure torture for the male brain. He particularly despised the wild card game because the player in control of the board when the wild card turned up could call for a different variation—which could turn a good hand and game plan into garbage.

There had to be a way to turn that to his advantage. Had to . . .

Continuing to shuffle the cards, Daemon studied the game board carefully, studied the stones and the bone discs. Thought about how each piece *could* interact with the other pieces—and the cards.

Yes, that would work. That would work quite well.

"Which variation do you want to play?" Jaenelle asked as she placed the stones and discs in their starting positions.

Daemon gave her the smile that used to terrify the Queens in Terreille. "Variation twenty-seven."

Jaenelle just frowned at him. "Daemon, there is no variation twenty-seven."

He dealt the cards and purred, "There is now."

11 / Kaeleer

She was so young, Surreal thought as she studied her mother. *I had thought of her as being so big, so strong. But she's smaller than me . . . and she was so young when she died.*

Titian tucked her feet up on the window seat and wrapped her arms around her knees. "It's good you've come to Kaeleer."

Surreal stared out the window. But the night-darkened glass didn't show her anything but her own reflection—and that made her think of the questions that had gone unanswered for too long. "Why didn't we come here before?" she asked quietly. "Why didn't you go home after you got away from Kartane?" She hesitated. "Was it because of me?"

"*No,*" Titian said sharply. "I chose to keep you, Surreal. I had to fight against my body's instinctive rejection of a child conceived by force, and *I chose you.*" Now Titian hesitated. "There were other reasons not to go home then. If I had, your life would have been easier, but . . ."

"But what?" Surreal snapped. "If you had gone home, you wouldn't have had to whore for food and shelter. If you had gotten out of Terreille, you wouldn't have died so damn young. What reason is good enough to balance those things?"

"I loved my father," Titian said softly. "And I loved my brothers. Rape is punishable by execution, Surreal. If I had gone home as soon as I escaped from Kartane, my father and brothers would have gone to Hayll to kill him."

Surreal stared at her. "How in the name of Hell did they expect to get past all of Dorothea's guards in order to get to Kartane?"

"They would have died," Titian said simply. "And I didn't want my father and brothers to die. Can you understand that?"

"Not really, since I've spent most of my life preparing for the day when I can kill Kartane. Now, if it had been your mother . . ." Surreal tried to smile and couldn't. "What do you think your father would have said about your choice?"

Titian's smile was rueful. "I *know* what he said. He was in the Dark Realm for a little while before he returned to the Darkness. But he lived the full span of his years, Surreal, and my brothers raised children who never would have been born." She paused. "And if I had chosen differently, you wouldn't have been in Chaillot thirteen years ago, and we would have lost the greatest Queen the Blood has ever known."

"And if you hadn't ended up in Terreille, under Kartane, you would have been a Queen and a Black Widow."

"I still *am* a Queen and a Black Widow," Titian snapped. "When Kartane broke me, he severed me from the strength that would have been mine, but he couldn't take away what I am."

"I'm sorry," Surreal said, not sure how to express regret without giving insult.

"Don't shoulder regrets, little witch," Titian said gently as she got to her feet. "And don't shoulder the burden of anyone's actions but your own." She held out her hand. "Come on. You'll need your wits about you if you're sparring with Lucivar tomorrow."

Surreal rose wearily and followed Titian. Between that scene with Vania at midday, the extra workout with Falonar, and coping with the aftermath of Jaenelle's fury, she was more than ready to crawl into bed. She had hugged more distressed males that day than she had in her entire life. Which reminded her of something else. "How *do* I deal with the male relatives I've suddenly acquired?"

"You set your boundaries," Titian replied as they reached the corridor near Surreal's room. "You decide what you're willing to let them do for you and what you have to do for yourself. Then you tell them—gently. This is Kaeleer, Surreal. You have to handle the males—" Titian froze. Her nostrils flared.

"Titian?" Surreal asked, startled by the awful expression on her mother's face. "What's wrong?"

"Where's the High Lord?" Titian snarled. Not waiting for an answer, she ran for the nearest staircase.

Surreal raced after her, catching up to her when Titian jerked to a halt in front of a door.

Titian banged the door once with her fist, then flung it open. "High Lord!"

A muffled sound came from the adjoining room.

Titian flung that door open and rushed into the room. Surreal rushed in behind her, then stopped abruptly.

Saetan froze in the act of reaching for the dressing robe that was on his bed. He slowly straightened up and turned to face them.

Surreal couldn't stop herself from giving him one quick, professional—and approving—glance.

Titian didn't seem to notice that she had walked in on a naked, and now irritated, man.

"There's a tainted male in the Hall," Titian said abruptly.

Saetan stared at her for a moment. Then he grabbed the robe, said tersely, "Where?" and was out the door, with Titian at his heels, before Surreal could gather her wits.

By the time she caught up to them, Titian was questing back and forth in the corridor like a hound searching for a scent while Saetan prowled more slowly. Neither of them paid any attention to her arrival.

"It was here," Titian said as she searched. "It was *here*."

"Can you still sense it?" Saetan asked too quietly.

Titian's shoulders tensed. "No. But it *was* here."

"I'm not doubting you, Lady."

"But you sense nothing."

"No. Which only means that whoever created the spells designed to hide him knew exactly who and what to hide him from."

"Hekatah did this," Titian said.

Saetan nodded. "Or Dorothea. Or both. Whoever he is, they made sure he would blend in so there would be no reason to give him a closer look. The only thing they couldn't anticipate was a Harpy catching a trace of his true psychic scent. But why was he lingering here?" He turned to study the doors. "Surreal's room. And Wilhelmina's room."

Surprised by her own discomfort, Surreal cleared her throat. "It could just be a man who hasn't heard that I retired from the Red Moon houses."

Saetan gave her a long, assessing look, then turned to Titian, who shook her head. "I agree," he said cryptically. He knocked sharply on Wilhelmina's door. When he got no answer, he went in. He came out a minute later. "She's in the garden with Dejaal. He'll stay with her."

It took Surreal a moment to connect the name with the young tiger she had frequently seen with Wilhelmina.

"Graysfang is on his way," Saetan said, giving Surreal a hard look. "He's not to leave your side tonight."

It took her another moment to fit the pieces together. She bristled. "Wait just a minute, High Lord. I can take care of myself."

"He's a Warlord," Saetan snapped. "He defends and protects."

"He wears Purple Dusk to my Gray. You can't assume that this other male wears a lighter Jewel than he does."

"I'm assuming nothing. *He defends and protects.*"

Furious, Surreal strode up to Saetan and grabbed two fistfuls of his robe. "He's not fodder," she snarled. "It's not right for him to die when I'm perfectly capable of defending myself."

Dry amusement slowly filled Saetan's eyes. "You will not wound his pride by telling him he isn't capable of protecting you. However, since the Queens share your opinion, it *is* considered acceptable for you to provide the protective shields for both of you and to guard his back."

"Oh." Releasing him, Surreal tried to smooth the wrinkles in his robe that her fists had made. When she noticed Saetan's amusement growing, she gave up and stepped back.

"Will you station guards tonight?" Titian asked.

Saetan thought for a moment, then shook his head. "No. Nothing that obvious tonight. The Ladies in the court will be protected. The rest we'll deal with in the morning." He looked at Surreal. "I'd like you to stay in your room tonight, or the inner garden your room overlooks. No one will be coming at you or Wilhelmina from that direction."

All of Surreal's instincts sharpened as she considered all the ways an assassin could gain access. "Are all these rooms occupied?" she asked thoughtfully. Slip into an empty room, slip through the garden, enter the victim's room through the glass doors that opened onto the garden . . .

"A couple of the guest rooms are empty," Saetan said, "but no one will be coming at you through the garden. Kaelas will be there."

Daemon took one look at Saetan and Titian, stepped into the corridor, and closed Jaenelle's sitting room door. "Lady Titian," he said respectfully, masking his surprise at seeing her. He knew she was demon-dead, but he hadn't expected to see her at the Hall—and he didn't like her tense stance any more than he liked Saetan's controlled neutrality.

"As Steward of the Court, I'm formally requesting that you remain with the Queen tonight," Saetan said quietly. "*All night.*"

Daemon tensed. This evening was the first time since Jaenelle had finished healing his mind that she'd been willing to spend time with him, and he'd hoped playing a few hands of cards would remind her that he was a friend, which was the first step toward her accepting him as her lover. But if he told her he was going to spend the night in her bed, she'd start running from him again. Didn't Saetan understand that?

Yes, he realized as he studied that controlled neutrality, Saetan understood. But the Steward of the Court, while sympathizing with the Consort's hesitation and feelings, felt compelled to dismiss them.

"I'm making this request to all the Consorts and First Escorts," Saetan added.

Daemon nodded as he considered that bit of information. A formal request like that, in this court, was equal to a call to battle. Every Warlord Prince at the Hall would be riding the killing edge that night. "Will Lucivar be with Marian?"

"No," Saetan said, "Prothvar will stay with Marian and Daemonar. Lucivar will . . . tour . . . the Hall tonight."

"Where will Kaelas be?" Daemon asked. Suddenly that feline strength and temper were a comfort.

"Kaelas will be in the garden. It will give him more flexibility."

"Then I'll wish you a good night—and good hunting," Daemon added too softly. "High Lord. Lady."

"Is there a problem?" Jaenelle asked when he returned to the sitting room.

Daemon hesitated but couldn't think of any other way to say it. "The Steward has formally requested that I remain with you tonight."

The flicker of panic in her eyes hurt him, but it was the knife-edged way she focused on the sitting room door that made him wary—especially when that focus shifted to him.

"Is that request being made of all the Consorts and First Escorts?" Witch asked in her midnight voice.

"Yes, Lady, it is."

A long silence. Then Jaenelle wrinkled her nose. "A *formal* request seems a bit much just to get the boyos off the couches tonight."

Daemon suppressed a sigh of relief. She was willing to pretend that that's all the request meant. Most likely, she just wanted a few more hours before admitting that Alexandra or one of her entourage had done something serious that would have to be dealt with.

"Would you like to play another round?" he asked, taking his seat.

She narrowed her eyes. "Whose deal is it?"

He smiled at her. "Mine."

"Why didn't you tell him about the tainted male?" Titian asked.

"I can't count on Daemon's control right now," Saetan replied after a long pause. "A Warlord Prince who's focused on being accepted as a Consort has an extremely volatile temper."

After a moment, Titian shook her head. "Even if everyone else didn't sense the spells Dorothea and Hekatah created, I don't understand why Jaenelle didn't notice them."

"Nor do I. But as I said, Dorothea and Hekatah knew exactly who they had to hide him from," Saetan replied, feeling his heartbeat thicken until he could feel each thump like a blow.

"Even so, Jaenelle always takes a careful look at the people who intend to stay in Kaeleer."

"But she would have no reason to look that closely at someone who *wasn't* intending to stay, especially if emotional and personal issues were being used as a blind to hide a different purpose."

Titian frowned. "Who else is staying at the Hall?"

"Jaenelle's Chaillot relatives and their companions." He saw his own hatred reflected in Titian's face.

"And you haven't done anything about them?"

"My formal request for execution was denied," Saetan replied, doing his best not to respond to the accusation in her voice. "I'll choke on it, but I'll abide by it. Besides, there will be another time and another place to settle those debts," he added softly.

Titian nodded. "If I slip into their rooms, maybe I can sense something. Then we could quietly take care of the tainted male tonight."

Saetan snarled in frustration. "Except for that bitch Vania, no one has *done* anything yet that justifies an execution." He shook his head. "We've made sure nothing will happen tonight. After breakfast, I'll talk to Jaenelle about getting those . . . *people* . . . out of the Hall and out of Kaeleer."

"I suppose that's best." They walked in silence for a while. "Are *all* of Jaenelle's relatives here?"

"Except for Robert Benedict. He died a few years ago—and was in the Dark Realm for a very brief time."

Titian stopped walking. Saetan turned to face her. She lifted her hand and pressed it lightly against his face.

"And, during that time, did he have a private conversation with the High Lord of Hell?" she asked with malevolent sweetness.

"Yes," Saetan replied too softly, "he did."

CHAPTER SIX

1 / Kaeleer

Daemon's nerves were raw when he and Jaenelle walked into the dining room the next morning, and the speculative looks from the other males in the First Circle didn't help. The fact that it was Jaenelle's moontime and he couldn't have done more than warm the bed didn't matter. He knew what was expected of a Consort, and he knew the other men were aware that he wasn't fulfilling those duties.

He tried to push those thoughts aside. There were reasons to be alert that day.

Lucivar stood near the sideboard, sipping a mug of coffee, while Khardeen and Aaron filled their plates. Leland and Philip, the only members of Alexandra's entourage who were present, were eating breakfast at one end of the table. Surreal and Karla were at the other end.

A greedy look filled Jaenelle's eyes when she focused on the mug in Lucivar's hand. "Are you going to share that?"

Lucivar bared his teeth in a smile. "No."

She gave him a frigid look but kissed his cheek anyway.

Daemon could have cheerfully killed Lucivar for being given that kiss. It was a grumpy, habitual kiss, but still a kiss—which was more than *he'd* gotten that morning. Since killing Lucivar wasn't an option—at that moment, anyway—he watched Jaenelle select two slices of pear and a spoonful of scrambled eggs.

As she turned away from the sideboard, Lucivar reached over, jabbed a fork into a hunk of steak, and dumped it on her plate. "You need the meat today. Eat it."

She snarled at him. Lucivar just sipped his coffee.

"Long night?" Daemon quietly asked Lucivar.

"I've had longer," Lucivar replied with a smile that turned sharp as he flicked a glance at Philip and Leland, then raised his voice just enough to carry. "What about you, old son? You look like you put in a long night yourself."

"It was interesting," Daemon said cautiously. He wasn't about to admit that he and Jaenelle had played cards until, bleary-eyed, they had fallen into bed for a few hours of restless, broken sleep.

Jaenelle snorted. "There's something a bit sneaky about the positions in variation twenty-seven that give a male so much of an advantage, but I haven't worked it out . . . yet."

Daemon noticed Philip's white-lipped anger—and he noticed the way Khardeen and Aaron snapped to attention.

"You know twenty-seven variations?" Khardeen asked slowly.

Daemon said nothing.

"Yes, he does," Jaenelle grumbled. "And that variation is brilliant. Sneaky, but brilliant." She studied the platter of steaks, selected two more pieces, and headed for the table.

Before Daemon could reach for a plate, Khardeen was holding one arm and Aaron had the other, and they were hustling him out of the dining room.

"We'll get breakfast later," Khary said as he and Aaron led Daemon to the nearest empty room. "First, we need to have a little talk."

"It's not what you think," Daemon said. "It's really nothing."

"Nothing?" Aaron sputtered, while Khary said, "If you've figured out a new variation of 'cradle' that gives a man the advantage, it's your duty as a Brother of the First Circle to share it with the rest of us before the coven figures out how to beat it."

He just stared at them, not sure he had heard them correctly.

Aaron smiled. "Well, what did you *think* Consorts do at night?"

Daemon burst out laughing.

2 / Kaeleer

Osvald knocked on Wilhelmina's door, then stepped back and firmly gripped the carved wooden box with both hands.

It hadn't taken much persuasion to convince Alexandra to keep most of her people in their rooms. It had taken more to convince her to send Leland and Philip down to breakfast in order to give the appearance that everyone else was merely late. With so many absent, no one would be sure exactly who was missing until he was long gone from the Hall.

Assuming, of course, that the spells Dorothea and the Dark Priestess had prepared to cut a "door" in the High Lord's defensive shields actually worked.

No. He wouldn't doubt. The spells that had kept him from being detected were proof enough that Dorothea and the Dark Priestess knew how to deal with the bastard who ruled this place. He would escape with the lesser of the two prizes, true, but that lesser prize, sufficiently squeezed, might be enough bait to in turn capture Jaenelle Angelline.

Everything was in place. The three men Dorothea had arranged to help him were waiting at the bridge. There *was* a Dark Altar beside the Hall, but she had warned him that the detection spells around that Altar would immediately alert the High Lord, and he would never get the Gate open in time to escape. So he would take Wilhelmina to Goth, where Lord Jorval would help him reach another of the Gates.

By this evening, he would be back in Terreille with his prize, and Alexandra and the fools who were with her would still be explaining Wilhelmina's disappearance to the High Lord . . . or dying.

Smiling, Osvald knocked on Wilhelmina's door again. A moment later, impatient, he knocked harder. She was in there. He'd made sure of it this time. What was taking her so long to open a damn door?

It was tempting to use one of the simple compulsion spells Dorothea had prepared for him, but he only had two of them and didn't want to waste one for this. Still, every minute's delay increased the chance of someone noticing him.

He was just about to give in and trigger one of the compulsion spells when the door finally opened. "Good morning, Lady Wilhelmina." Smiling, he lifted the box just enough to draw it to her attention. "Lady Alexandra asked me to bring this to you."

"What is it?" Wilhelmina asked, sounding anything but eager.

"A token of her regard for you—and a gesture of goodwill. She's planning to leave soon and has felt distressed that her concern for you may have been misunderstood. She hopes that, by accepting this little memento, you'll be able to remember her fondly in the days to come."

Wilhelmina still looked wary. "Why didn't she bring it herself?"

Osvald looked at her sadly. "She feared you might refuse the gift and didn't want to face that rejection in person."

"Oh," Wilhelmina said quietly, her wariness slowly changing to sympathy. "I hold no ill feelings toward her."

He held the box out, both to entice and to keep his face as far away from it as possible. When she opened the lid, a drugged mist would burst out of the box. Startled, she would gasp and inhale enough of the highly potent drug to make her sufficiently compliant so that he could get her away from the room and this corridor before forcing the second, liquid dose down her throat.

Inside the room, something thumped to the floor.

That damned striped cat.

Osvald triggered the first compulsion spell and shaped the command. *Step into the corridor and close the door. Step into the corridor and close the door. Step into . . .*

He smiled when, looking slightly confused, Wilhelmina obeyed.

"I was told to report your reaction to the gift," he said, sounding apologetic about putting her to the extra bother.

She stayed close to the door, her hand still gripping the knob.

Cursing silently, he triggered the second compulsion spell. *Step close to the box and raise the lid. Step close to the box . . .*

Moving as if her muscles fought against the effort, Wilhelmina stepped close to the box and slowly lifted the lid.

3 / Kaeleer

With Graysfang beside her, Surreal wandered around one of the inner gardens. The cryptic remarks Jaenelle and Karla had made at breakfast about a new variation intrigued and worried her.

There were plenty of sexual variations that gave the male an advantage, so she didn't think they were talking about *that* . . . unfortunately. Daemon was getting burned by his own sexual energy, and the strain of trying to keep it leashed sufficiently in order not to scare Jaenelle was starting to show. She wasn't sure how much longer he could endure the easy affection Jaenelle gave to the other males in the First Circle before he lashed out. Maybe she should talk to the High Lord . . .

Graysfang snarled. Before she could ask what was wrong, he took off, heading straight for the wall. As he approached, he leaped and climbed air as if he were climbing a steep hill, scrambled over the roof, and was gone.

"Graysfang!" Surreal shouted.

Dejaal is being attacked, he replied. *I'm going to help him.*

Surreal swore viciously as she ran for the nearest door.

"Surreal!"

She spun around.

Falonar strode toward her from the other side of the garden. "Lucivar sent me to find you since you didn't show up for—"

"Can you get me over this roof?" Surreal said with enough fury in her voice to make him check his stride. "Graysfang said Dejaal is under attack, and the son of a bitch took off without me!"

In the two strides it took him to reach her, he made the shift from cautious male to warrior. "Hold on to me," he ordered.

Surreal hesitated a moment, trying to decide what she could hold on to without impeding his wings. She hooked one arm around his neck and snugged the fingers of her other hand under his wide leather belt.

It wasn't until she felt his wings pumping that she wondered if he could carry an extra person's weight. "I'm going to learn to do that air walking so I won't have to be carted around," she growled.

"I don't mind carrying you," Falonar snapped, setting her none too gently on the roof.

Surreal clenched her teeth. One male at a time. And it was the furry gray one who had first dibs on her temper. "Do you see him?" she asked as she scanned the courtyard below.

"No. He could have—"

A blast of Jeweled power came from the next courtyard, followed by a woman's scream.

Falonar launched them off the roof with enough force that Surreal wrapped her legs around one of his to give herself another way to hold on. She gritted her teeth as her body, with appalling timing, expressed its approval of the hard male thigh riding between her legs. Which did nothing for her temper.

"If he gets hurt because he didn't wait for me, I'm going to smack him so hard he'll have to lift his tail to see the world," she snarled.

"Wait here," Falonar said as he looked down into the courtyard.

"Do you like having balls?" Surreal snapped, twisting to look around. But she pulled her fingers out from under his belt so that he wouldn't worry that she'd meant the threat.

She caught her breath and swore. The young tiger, Dejaal, was lying in the courtyard, not moving. A footman writhed in agony. Graysfang was dashing back and forth, not actively engaging in an attack but still holding the attention of the man who had a firm grip on Wilhelmina, who was struggling ineffectively.

She swore again when she recognized the man. Osvald. One of Alexandra's escorts. Mother Night.

"Can you keep your balance?" Falonar asked a moment before he let go and stepped away from her.

At least he asked, Surreal thought as she used Craft to prevent a fast slide off the roof.

Graysfang dashed in low, as if he were trying to hamstring Osvald.

Surreal saw the flash of Osvald's Opal Jewel. She threw a Gray shield around Graysfang, fast enough to prevent him from receiving a killing blast of power but not in time to keep him from being knocked over by the clash of Gray and Opal strength.

Seeing the wolf go down, Wilhelmina screamed and clawed at the hand clamped around her arm. Osvald swung around and hit her with enough force to send her to the ground, stunned. Then he turned to make another attack on Graysfang, who had gotten shakily to his feet.

"Tell the wolf to back off," Falonar said as he called in his Eyrien longbow and nocked an arrow.

Surreal quickly obeyed—and felt relief when Graysfang responded. As kindred howls and roars alerted everyone in the Hall, she could sense the flood of furious male strength coming toward them from all directions. And she sensed the cold feminine power coming in its wake.

Falonar took aim.

"Put it through the bastard," Surreal whispered.

"We don't know what's going on down there," Falonar replied.

Don't we? Surreal thought viciously. *What more do you need to see?*

As Osvald turned back toward Wilhelmina, Falonar loosed the arrow, sending it through the man's left knee.

Osvald went down, screaming.

Grabbing Surreal's left arm, Falonar dropped them off the roof—a jump barely slowed by his spread wings.

"Guard the woman," Falonar said as he ran toward Osvald, the Eyrien bow now replaced by a bladed stick.

"I can—"

"*Do as you're told.*"

No time to argue. Calling in her meanest knife, Surreal ran toward Wilhelmina. She saw Osvald grasp Wilhelmina's ankle with his left hand and cursed his cleverness. Maybe someone else would know how to do it, but as long as he had physical contact with Wilhelmina, she couldn't throw a protective shield around the young woman. Then she saw sunlight flash on the short knife in his right hand—and knew by the mixture of rage and triumph on his face that the poison on that knife would be quick and lethal.

Another flash in the sunlight. As Osvald's hand arced down to drive the knife into Wilhelmina's leg, Falonar sliced through the wristbones as easily as if they were soft butter, then turned the blade of his stick in order to catch the severed hand and the knife it still held and flip it away from Wilhelmina.

The bladed stick flashed down again, severing the hand that grasped Wilhelmina's ankle.

A moment later, Surreal reached Wilhelmina—and Lucivar and most of the First Circle males poured into the courtyard. So did Karla and Gabrielle.

So did Alexandra and her entourage.

It didn't turn out quite like you'd planned, did it? Surreal thought as she watched Alexandra scan the courtyard and turn sickly pale. Vanishing her knife, she placed one hand on Wilhelmina's back, the other hand on Graysfang as soon as he wobbled up to her, and created a Gray shield around the three of them. It probably wasn't necessary, but there was no reason to take chances. She looked at Falonar, who had positioned himself so that, the next time, the bladed stick would come down on the bastard's neck. She put a shield around him, too. She felt his surprise and pleasure when her shield settled around him—and wondered why he was afraid.

Gabrielle rushed over to help the footman while Karla, without actually touching Osvald, used healing Craft to seal the severed blood vessels.

"What's going on here?" Alexandra demanded, the sharp edge in her voice sounding more frightened than angry. "Why are you attacking one of my escorts?"

"Did you send him?" Lucivar asked, an odd note in his voice.

"I sent him to bring a gift to Wilhelmina," Alexandra said.

There was something queer and bitter about Lucivar's laugh. "And the bastard delivered it, didn't he?"

"When I went to deliver the gift, Lady Wilhelmina wasn't feeling well," Osvald whimpered. "I offered to walk with her so that she could get some fresh air. Then that *creature* attacked us."

Lucivar looked at Osvald, then at Falonar. "If that bastard says anything else, cut his tongue out."

Falonar looked shocked, but nodded.

"How dare you?" Alexandra said. "You're so quick to make demands to *me* about controlling my court, yet you allow this—"

"Shut up," Lucivar snapped. "Things are bad enough right now. Don't make it worse."

Surreal gave Lucivar a sharp look. What was going on here?

Shivering, Graysfang moved closer to her. *Queen's rage is bad, Surreal. Males fear Queen's rage. Even Kaelas.*

Following the wolf's gaze, Surreal saw the huge white cat standing on the roof next to a tiger. That was Kaelas? *Mother Night!*

Who's the tiger? she asked.

That is Jaal. He is Dejaal's sire.

Surreal swallowed hard. The tiger was dwarfed by Kaelas, but he was still twice as large as the young tiger lying in the courtyard. *Dejaal is dead, isn't he?*

He has returned to the Darkness, Graysfang said sadly.

How were they going to explain this to Jaenelle?

As if the thought had conjured the woman, Jaenelle walked into the courtyard, flanked by Daemon and Saetan.

Surreal might have taken some comfort in their presence if the High Lord's face hadn't turned gray at the sight of Dejaal's body.

Alexandra started to speak, but before she could make a sound, her hands flew up to her throat and her eyes became wide and terrified.

Surreal wasn't sure which one of the males had acted, but she would have bet it was Daemon who had created the phantom hand that was now choking Alexandra into silence.

Everyone moved out of the way as Jaenelle walked over and knelt beside Dejaal. The hand that caressed the fur was gentle and loving, but the eyes that finally looked up and focused on Wilhelmina . . .

What Surreal saw in those sapphire eyes went so far beyond cold rage there were no words for it.

Yes, there were, she realized as Graysfang whimpered softly. *This* was what the wolf had meant by Queen's rage.

Hell's fire, Mother Night, and may the Darkness be merciful.

She said the only thing she could think of, the only thing that, she hoped, would release her from those eyes. "She's alive."

Jaenelle looked at Karla, who bowed formally before walking over to examine Wilhelmina.

"You said the right thing," Karla whispered to Surreal as she examined Wilhelmina. Then she swore and added, "Whatever else you do, follow Protocol to the letter." Taking a deep breath, she stood up and faced Jaenelle. "Wilhelmina has some bruises from the struggle—and she's been heavily drugged."

"Can you counteract it?" Jaenelle asked too calmly.

"I need more time to determine the exact nature of the drug that was used," Karla answered quietly. "But I'm sensing nothing that will cause permanent harm. My recommendation is closely supervised isolation and rest. With your permission, I'll take her to her room now and look after her."

"Thank you, Sister."

Responding to Karla's slight gesture, her cousin, Morton, picked up Wilhelmina and followed Karla out of the courtyard.

Surreal remained crouched beside Graysfang, unwilling to make a movement that would draw those sapphire eyes back in her direction.

"What about me?" Osvald whimpered.

Falonar glanced at Lucivar, silently asking if he should carry out his order and cut out the man's tongue. Lucivar shook his head, the barest of movements.

Jaenelle crossed the courtyard, looked down at Osvald, and smiled. "I'm going to take care of you personally."

Lucivar leaped forward. "Lady, with respect, Dejaal was our Brother, and it's the males' right—"

Jaenelle silenced him by simply raising her hand. For a moment, she just stood there, but Surreal felt the flick of power that burst from her as a quickly expanding psychic probe—and realized that no one wearing a Jewel lighter than the Gray would have sensed anything at all.

"There are three men waiting by the bridge that leads to Halaway," Jaenelle said. A terrible glitter filled her eyes as she looked at Osvald. "Three strangers. I don't care what you do with them."

Osvald floated to an upright position. When Jaenelle turned and walked out of the courtyard, he floated after her, protesting his innocence.

"Kalush and Morghann are coming," Gabrielle said, her eyes filling with tears. "We'll stay with Dejaal until . . ."

Pointing at Alexandra, Lucivar looked at Falonar. "You and Surreal escort these . . . people . . . to their rooms." He paused. "If *any* of them give you any trouble, kill them."

"My pleasure," Surreal said. Falonar just nodded.

Lucivar left the courtyard, followed by the other Warlord Princes in the First Circle. When Daemon turned to follow them, Saetan said, "No. You stay with me."

Quickly rounding up her prisoners, Surreal hurried them—and Falonar and Graysfang—out of the courtyard. She didn't know what the High Lord had in mind, but she'd rather not be around while they discussed it.

Daemon stepped aside as Morghann and Kalush rushed into the courtyard.

"Let's get out of here," Saetan said, his voice rough with suppressed grief—and something that might have been fear.

It was that fear—and his concern for the man—that made Daemon follow his father. But even those things weren't sufficient for him to swallow his own anger.

As they slowly headed away from the courtyard, Daemon said, "I may not have Lucivar's talent with weapons, but I can deal with an enemy quite effectively."

Saetan stopped walking. "Remember who you're talking to, Prince. If anyone can appreciate how effective you are as a predator, it's me."

"Then why did you stop me?"

"Lucivar doesn't need your help to handle whoever is waiting at the bridge for that bastard—especially not with the males who went with him. But I *do* need you. Right now, I need every drop of strength and every grain of skill you've got in order to handle Jaenelle. Hell's fire, Daemon. Don't you realize what happened here?"

With enormous effort, Daemon held on to his temper. "Alexandra played the bitch and arranged to have her own granddaughter abducted."

Saetan slowly shook his head. "Alexandra was working with Dorothea and Hekatah in order to abduct her own granddaughter."

Daemon absorbed the impact of the words—and realized what might happen once Jaenelle learned *that*. "Mother Night."

"And may the Darkness be merciful," Saetan added. "We have an enraged Queen who, by now, has gone so deep into the abyss we have no chance of reaching her that way—and no way at all to deflect whatever she might unleash in her present emotional state."

"What can I do?" Daemon asked, knowing with dread certainty where the conversation was leading.

"It's what *we* can do as Steward and Consort, what Protocol gives us the *right* to do in situations like this."

"Protocol didn't take into account dealing with a Queen who's twice as strong as a Black-Jeweled Warlord Prince!"

Saetan's hand shook a little as he smoothed his hair back. "More like six times our combined strength."

"What?" Daemon said weakly. He braced a hand against the wall.

"There's no real way to measure Jaenelle's strength. But considering the number of Birthright Black Jewels that were transformed into Ebony when she made the Offering to the Darkness, my best guess is that, at her full strength, she's six times more powerful than our full strength combined."

"Mother Night." Daemon concentrated on breathing for a minute. "Just when were you going to mention this to me? Or weren't you?"

Saetan winced. "I wanted you to be . . . comfortable . . . with each other before I told you. But now—"

A blast of power shook the Hall, tossing them to the floor.

Daemon felt as if he were desperately holding on to a crumbling bank inches from a raging flood that would not only sweep him away but crush him in the process.

He felt Saetan grab him, dig in, hold on.

That rush of power vanished as quickly as it had struck—and that scared him more than the blast. For Jaenelle to unleash and reabsorb that much power that quickly . . .

"Jaenelle," Daemon said, springing to his feet. He sent out a psychic probe, a quick, casting search for her, and brushed against a spot in the Hall that was burning cold. Despite his pulling back quickly, the lancing pain almost drove him to his knees. And that drove him forward.

"Daemon, no!" Saetan said, struggling to get to his feet.

Daemon ran through the corridors. He didn't need to search anymore. The corridors got colder and colder the closer he got to the room where she had unleashed that power.

"Daemon!"

He heard Saetan running to catch up to him, but by then he'd reached the door to the room. Using Craft, he opened the door, then stepped into the room.

The cold had a jagged edge that was physically painful, but he barely noticed it because, as he looked around, he couldn't quite understand what he was seeing. It wasn't until he realized that the odd red speckles on the windows were frozen drops of blood that his mind identified the rest . . .

"Daemon."

. . . and he understood what Lucivar had been telling him about Jaenelle's forced marriage. *She splattered him all over the room.*

"*Daemon.*"

He heard the plea in Saetan's voice, but couldn't respond to it. A peculiar numbness had settled over his emotions . . . and without being able to feel, he could think.

He knew why Saetan hadn't wanted him to see this room. By the very nature of his duties, a Consort couldn't be inhibited when dealing with his Queen. A Consort knowingly and willingly made himself physically vulnerable to her in ways no other male in the court had to. A Consort who feared his Queen couldn't function in the bed.

But he'd seen this side of her before. Oh, it had been only a faint glimpse, but he'd known that this was another facet of Witch.

And this was the side of her that would be drawn to the surface by intense arousal as well as intense rage. Could he live with that? Could he lead the sexual dance once he brought out this side of her?

The heat of the sexual hunger inside him, the driving need to mate with Witch that suddenly engulfed him, burned away the emotional numbness. And left in its place a chilling approval of what he saw.

He stepped out of the room and closed the door.

"Daemon," Saetan said softly, watching him.

Daemon smiled. "It's a pity about the wallpaper. It was a lovely design."

4 / Kaeleer

"Well," Surreal said as she pushed her hair away from her face, "I don't think any of the 'guests' are going to be eager to leave their rooms right now, do you?"

"No," Falonar replied, sounding a bit queasy, "I don't."

"Yeah." Surreal leaned against the wall and closed her eyes. "Shit."

"Were you hurt by . . . *that*?" Falonar asked, meaning the blast of power that had shaken the Hall. He briefly touched her shoulder before stepping back.

Surreal shook her head. *Hurt? No. Scared shitless? Oh, yes.*

But the people who lived with Jaenelle *didn't* live in constant fear. In fact, thinking about how Karla and Lucivar had acted in the courtyard, she would have called their behavior cautious rather than fearful—and that caution wasn't usually in evidence either.

Putting those thoughts aside for the moment, she scowled at Falonar and decided to tackle something easier—like the arrogant way he had been tossing out orders after they reached the courtyard. "I could have handled that bastard."

Falonar looked insulted. "It's a male's right to defend and protect."

Surreal bared her teeth. "I've heard that song before, and—"

"Then you should heed that song, Lady—and respect it."

"Why? Because poor little me isn't capable of handling myself in a fight?" she said with venom-laced sweetness.

"Because you're deadlier," he snarled. He paced a few steps away from her, swore, paced back. "*That's* why males defend, Lady Surreal. Because you females are deadlier when you're roused—and you're merciless when you're riding the killing edge. At least if I go down first in a fight, I don't have to deal with you afterward."

Not sure if she'd just been complimented or insulted, Surreal said nothing. She was about to concede that he *might* have a point when he growled at her, "You've picked a lousy time to play the bitch. It's going to be hard enough facing Yaslana without having to dance with you right now."

Now that *was* an insult. "Since you feel like that, sugar, I'll just get out of your way." She pushed away from the wall.

Falonar reached out, touched her arm. "Surreal . . . You were right. I should have killed that bastard. Now I'll have to accept the consequences for that error." He hesitated, and added quietly, "He could have killed you or Lady Benedict with that poisoned knife."

She shrugged. "You couldn't have known about the knife, and he didn't kill either one of us, so—"

"What difference does that make?" Falonar said harshly. "My error gave him the chance."

Surreal studied him. "You think you're going to be punished?"

"That's a certainty. The only question is how severe it will be."

"Well, I have a few things to say about that. When Lucivar gets around to discussing this—"

"There is no discussion," Falonar snapped. "He's the Warlord Prince of Ebon Rih. I serve him. He'll do as he pleases." He looked away. "I'd rather be tied to the whipping posts than be sent back to Terreille."

"There's no reason for you to be punished at all!"

Falonar smiled grimly. "That's the way it is, Lady Surreal."

We'll just see about that, Surreal thought.

5 / Kaeleer

Daemon watched Saetan pour a large brandy. "Can you drink that?" he asked, keeping his voice mildly curious.

"It gives me vicious headaches," Saetan replied, pouring a second glass for Daemon. "But I doubt it's going to make the one I've already got any worse, so . . ." He raised his glass in a salute, then swallowed half the brandy. "Dejaal was Prince Jaal's son."

Mentioning the tiger Warlord Prince seemed an abrupt change of subject. "Lucivar found the men?"

"And got the information we wanted before they were executed."

Daemon studied his father. Something wasn't quite right here. Since he didn't know what questions to ask, he voiced his own concern. "Jaenelle isn't here, is she?"

Saetan shook his head. "She's gone to Ebon Askavi—and has asked to be left alone for the time being."

"Are you going to abide by her wishes?" Daemon asked carefully.

Saetan's look was steady and far too knowing. "*We* are going to abide by her wishes. If she needs to remain cold in order to make the decisions that have to be made, forcing her to feel before she's ready would be cruel."

Daemon nodded. He didn't like it, but he could accept it. His thoughts went back to the three men who had been waiting to help Osvald abduct Wilhelmina. "Those men served Hekatah and Dorothea?"

"They worked for them."

He felt Saetan retreat, so he pressed. "Lucivar executed the men?" It wouldn't have been Lucivar's first kill, so *that* couldn't be bothering Saetan. Was there something different about a formal execution?

"The other males in the First Circle withdrew their right to collect any part of the debt that was owed them for the death of a Brother," Saetan said.

"What does that mean?" Daemon asked slowly.

Saetan hesitated, then finished the brandy before replying. "It means they gave those men to Jaal . . . and to Kaelas."

6 / Kaeleer

Fuming silently, Surreal glared at the four men in the High Lord's study. She had snarled her way into this little discussion, only to be bluntly told that they would tolerate her presence as long as she didn't interfere. Her opinion wasn't requested or required.

If it had been any other men, she would have given them her opinion of *that,* probably delivered on the end of her stiletto. But Lucivar looked like he'd been pushed hard enough and wouldn't hesitate to throw her out—*through* the door. And Saetan and Andulvar Yaslana weren't the kind of men who would allow anyone to step on their authority as Steward and Master of the Guard.

What really bit her was that Falonar hadn't looked at her once since she'd managed to win enough of the argument to stay in the room. She would have thought that he'd be grateful to have someone speak in his defense. But he . . .

Well, that was fine. That was *just fine*. She didn't need to be there, wasting her time on a thick-skinned, hardheaded male who didn't want her there in the first place.

She looked at Lucivar at that moment, saw the sharp amusement in his gold eyes, and knew that, now, if she tried to leave, she would be ordered to stay. So instead of cursing herself for her own stubbornness, she cursed Lucivar instead. And seeing his amusement deepen, realized he knew it— the prick.

Saetan leaned against his blackwood desk and crossed his arms. "Prince Falonar, please explain your actions this morning."

His voice sounded polite, only mildly curious. Surreal wondered if that was a bad sign.

Falonar responded. In Surreal's opinion, the dry recitation of actions fell far short of an explanation, but the other men didn't seem to notice that.

When Falonar finished speaking, Saetan looked at Andulvar and Lucivar, then back at Falonar. "You erred on the side of caution," Saetan said quietly. "That's understandable—and, in a Warlord Prince, also unacceptable. You can't afford the luxury of caution."

Falonar swallowed hard. "Yes, sir."

"You do understand that discipline is required?"

"Yes, sir."

Saetan nodded, appearing satisfied. He looked at Lucivar. "This is your decision."

Falonar turned to face Lucivar.

Lucivar studied him for a moment. "Five days of extra guard duty, beginning tomorrow."

Instead of looking relieved, Falonar looked as if he'd been slapped.

"Anything else we need to discuss?" Saetan asked.

Lucivar looked at her, then at Saetan, who, after a pause, dipped his head in the barest of nods.

Lucivar opened the study door and waited.

After bowing to Saetan and Andulvar, Falonar walked out. Since it seemed the proper thing to do, Surreal also bowed to the two men, then followed Falonar out of the study so fast she stepped on his heels.

Swearing, he lengthened his stride, finally stopping when he reached the center of the great hall.

Surreal caught up to him. "Well, that wasn't—" The dislike and anger in his face as he watched Lucivar approach them stopped her.

"Five days of extra guard duty is an insult," Falonar said.

Surreal grabbed two fistfuls of her long tunic to keep from belting him. Fool. Idiot. He should be grateful it wasn't worse.

"It's not an insult," Lucivar replied mildly. "It's fair. You made a mistake, Falonar. Some reparation has to be made for it. You acted, but you also hamstrung yourself by being too cautious."

"I realize what my caution could have cost."

"Yes, you do. Which is why the discipline is fair." Lucivar's mouth curved in a lazy, arrogant smile. "Don't worry about it. You'll stand extra guard duty plenty more times before you've been here a year. I certainly did."

Falonar stared at him. "You?"

The smile sharpened. "Hard to believe that I would err on the side of caution, isn't it? But I wanted to stay in Kaeleer, and I wanted to serve my Queen, so I kept my temper leashed as much as possible—for me. And ended up in that study, facing those two, more times than I care to count." Lucivar paused. "This is Kaeleer. Here, a Warlord Prince's temper is considered an asset to a court."

Falonar took a moment to digest this. Then, courteously, "Extra guard duty doesn't seem like much when a witch could have died."

"Well, there is another part to your . . . discipline," Lucivar said. He tipped his head toward Surreal. "You get to cope with her until sunrise. Since she looks like she's going to break her teeth unless she gets to yell at a male, it might as well be you." The smile got even sharper. "Of course, you could always offer to warm her bed and see if that buys you any leniency."

Falonar choked. Surreal made a sound like a teakettle ready to boil over.

"You consider spending a night with me a form of *discipline*?" Surreal shouted. "You prick. You . . . *I* would call it a reward!"

Lucivar shrugged. "Please yourself. Just keep in mind that, if you both decide to extend this 'discipline' past tonight, you have to have formal permission from the Steward of the Court. He agreed to overlook that formality until sunrise, but not after that. And this is an area where it isn't wise to push Saetan's temper."

After he left them, Surreal and Falonar eyed each other.

"It would seem that I didn't keep my . . . interest . . . in being with you as . . . restrained . . . as I had thought since Lucivar noticed it," Falonar said.

Or the High Lord did, Surreal thought. As family patriarch and sexual chaperon, she didn't think much got past that man.

"So," Falonar said warily. "Are you going to yell at me?"

Surreal smiled at him. "Well, sugar, I may not yell *at* you. With the right incentive, I may just yell."

CHAPTER SEVEN

1 / Kaeleer

Lord Jorval settled into a chair in Kartane SaDiablo's sitting room. "Your meeting with the Healer has been delayed."

"Why?" Kartane said sharply. "I had thought it was all arranged."

"It was," Jorval soothed. "But there was an . . . incident . . . at the Healer's residence, so it will be a few more days before she can meet with you."

"You could insist," Kartane said. "Perhaps she doesn't realize how important I—"

"It would do no good to insist," Jorval interrupted. "When she comes here, you want her attention on you, not on some domestic trivia."

"Then I suppose I have no choice but to wait."

Jorval rose. "No choice at all."

An incident has occurred that requires postponing . . .

An incident, Jorval thought as he walked back to his own home. That was how the High Lord had so carefully, so courteously phrased it. Since the men who had been in Halaway to assist the escort had suddenly disappeared, and there was no word from or sign of the escort, he had a good idea what sort of "incident" was delaying Jaenelle Angelline's trip to Little Terreille.

Which meant he had to inform the Dark Priestess that, in all probability, Alexandra was no longer a useful tool.

Hekatah wouldn't be pleased about that, would probably come to Little Terreille in a foul temper—which she would take out on him.

But, perhaps, he could redirect that temper. Perhaps now would be a good time to take care of that other little problem.

Reaching his home, he rushed into his study and penned a quick note to Lord Magstrom.

2 / Kaeleer

"Where is my escort?" Alexandra demanded as soon as she took a seat in the High Lord's study. After being confined for two days, she felt relieved to be out of her room, but she felt no relief at being in *this* room—or being with *him*.

Saetan leaned back in his chair and steepled his fingers, resting the long, black-tinted nails against his chin. His gold eyes looked sleepy—just as they had when he'd first seen her.

Conscious of the chill in the room, she pulled her shawl more tightly around herself.

"It's interesting that Osvald is the first person you ask about," Saetan said too mildly.

"Who *should* I have asked about?" Alexandra snapped, fear making her voice sharp.

"Your granddaughter, Wilhelmina. She is recovering from the drugs that bastard gave her. There will be no permanent damage."

"Of course there's no damage. He only gave her a mild sedative."

"What he gave her was a great deal more than a *mild* sedative, Lady," Saetan replied, his own voice turning sharp.

Alexandra hesitated. He was lying. Of course he was lying.

Saetan looked at her, curious. "I keep wondering what sort of payment Dorothea and Hekatah offered you that was worth your granddaughter's life."

She shot out of the chair. "You're insulting!"

"Am I?" he replied, his voice returning to that infuriating—and frightening—mildness.

"I wasn't selling Wilhelmina to Dorothea, I was just trying to get her away from *you*!"

A queer look came over his face. "Yes, that always seems sufficient justification, doesn't it? Just get the child away from me and be damned to what happens to the child. A lifetime of pain, of humiliation and torture, is certainly better than being with me."

Alexandra settled back in the chair and watched him. He had turned inward, following some private thought—and she didn't think he was talking about Wilhelmina anymore.

"What did you think was going to happen to Wilhelmina?" he asked.

"Osvald was going to get her out of Kaeleer, and then we would take her home."

As Saetan studied her, a deep sadness filled his eyes. "Not a payment then," he said softly, "but a bargaining chip."

"What are you talking about?"

"How were you planning to get Wilhelmina out of Hayll?"

Alexandra stared at him. "She wasn't going to Hayll."

"Yes, she was. Those were the orders, Alexandra. Wilhelmina would have been Dorothea's 'guest' for as long as you were willing to make concessions. How many concessions could you have made to Hayll before your people choked on them and refused to accept you as their Queen any longer? What could you have bargained with then to keep her safe?"

"No," Alexandra said. "*No*. Dorothea agreed to help me because—" Because Dorothea was preparing to go to war with this man and had wanted Jaenelle's alleged dark power away from his control. But she couldn't let him know that. "Wilhelmina wasn't a bargaining chip." But wouldn't Jaenelle have become exactly that? A bargaining chip in the game of war? That was different. Jaenelle was obviously already permanently warped by the High Lord's attentions, and if *Jaenelle* had ended up as Dorothea's "guest" . . .

With brutal honesty, Alexandra knew that she would never have made any concessions to Hayll to ensure Jaenelle's well-being. She would have told her court about a family sacrifice made for the good of her people. And in truth, she wouldn't have felt more than a twinge of guilt over that sacrifice. Always such a difficult child, always . . .

"Wilhelmina wasn't a bargaining chip," she said again lamely.

Saetan snorted softly. "Think what you choose."

That casual dismissal, as if it no longer mattered, disturbed her. "What happened to Osvald? Were his wounds at least treated?"

Something queer filled Saetan's eyes. "He was executed. So were the three men who had been waiting for him."

Alexandra stared at him. "What right do you have—"

"He tried to abduct one member of the court and killed another. Did you really expect us to just sit back and swallow that?"

"He wasn't abducting her!" Alexandra shouted. "He was helping her leave this place. That animal attacked him. He had to defend himself."

"He was taking her against her will. That's abduction."

"He was carrying out the wishes of her family."

"She's a grown woman," Saetan snarled. "You have no right to make decisions on her behalf."

"She's mentally fragile. She doesn't have the ability to make—"

"Is that how you deal with anyone who doesn't agree with you?" Saetan's voice rose to a roar. "You declare them mentally incompetent so you can justify locking them away in a place that revels in violating and torturing them?"

"*How dare you!*"

"Knowing what I know about Briarwood, I dare a great deal."

The air whooshed out of her lungs. His eyes were filled with the hatred he no longer bothered to mask.

With effort, she gathered her strength and sat up straight to face him. "I am a Queen—"

"You're a naive, snotty little bitch," Saetan replied in a singsong croon that made the words feel like a violent—and violating—caress. "Live a long life, Alexandra. Live a long life and burn yourself out at the end of it so that you return straight to the Darkness. If you don't, if you end up making the transition to demon-dead, I'll be waiting for you."

It took her a moment to understand him. The High Lord *of Hell*.

"Robert Benedict made the transition," Saetan crooned, "and he paid his part of the debt that is owed to me for what was done to the daughter of my soul."

"I owe you nothing." Alexandra tried to sound firm, but she couldn't stop her voice from shaking.

Saetan smiled a gentle, terrible smile.

She had to get out of there, had to get away from him. "Since this is supposed to be a court, I think it's time I talked to this mysterious Queen of yours. The *real Queen*. In fact, I demand to talk to her."

He went absolutely still. "It seems she wants to talk to you, too," he said in an odd voice. "You've been summoned to Ebon Askavi to stand before the Dark Throne."

3 / Kaeleer

With her heart pounding in her throat, Alexandra followed the High Lord down the dark stone stairs. The huge double doors at the bottom of the stairs swung open silently, revealing intense darkness.

She had protested when she had learned that Leland, Philip, and the rest of her entourage had also been summoned to the Keep. Not that it had made any difference. No one had made the slightest indication that they had even heard her protests, let alone might comply with them.

She had also protested when Daemon and Lucivar had joined the High Lord as "escorts." Now she felt pathetically grateful for the male strength that was guarding her. She had found the Hall frightening, but compared to the Keep, the Hall was just a pleasant manor house.

As Saetan walked forward, torches began to light until only the back of the room was still too dark to see at all.

Another torch lit. She stared at the huge dragon head coming out of the back wall. Its silver-gold scales gleamed. Its eyes were as dark as midnight. On a dais beside the head was a simple blackwood chair. The woman who sat in it was still too much in shadow for Alexandra to make out more than the shape.

So this was the Queen of Ebon Askavi.

The light in the room shifted somehow, softly illuminating the unicorn's horn that was part of the scepter the woman held in her hands.

As Alexandra stared at the rings on those hands, a shiver of fear ran down her spine. At first glance, she would have said the rings held pieces of a Black Jewel, but the Jewels in those rings felt darker than the Black. Which was impossible—wasn't it?

The light continued to grow, and as it grew, the power in the room swelled. The woman's face was still in shadow, but now Alexandra could make out the black gown and another Black-but-not-Black Jewel that was set in a necklace that looked like a spiderweb of gold and silver threads.

The light grew. Alexandra looked up and found herself staring into Jaenelle's frozen sapphire eyes.

Long seconds passed before those eyes shifted to look at Leland and Philip, Vania and Nyselle, and the Consorts and escorts who had come with them.

Released from that frozen stare, Alexandra pressed a hand to her stomach, desperately trying not to double over. In this formal setting, she finally understood what Jaenelle had said at their first meeting at the Hall. *The difference is that when the dream appeared, he recognized it.*

The dark power that flowed from Jaenelle could have kept Chaillot free of Dorothea's influence. But how could she have been expected to recognize *this* in a difficult, eccentric *child*?

. . . he recognized it.

She dared a quick glance at Daemon. He had recognized it, too. Had recognized it and . . .

But wasn't that what Dorothea had said? The Sadist and the High Lord had recognized the potential of all that dark power and had set out to seduce and shape it. It was clear now why Dorothea had wanted control of Jaenelle, but that didn't alter the possible truth of what she had said about Daemon and the High Lord.

The thoughts kept spinning, twisting—until those sapphire eyes pinned her again.

"You conspired with Dorothea SaDiablo and Hekatah SaDiablo, who are known enemies, with the intent of handing over to them a member of my court, my sister." The voice, while quiet, filled the immense room. "In attempting to carry out that plan, you killed another member of my court, a young Warlord Prince."

Leland stirred, shrugging off Philip's attempt to restrain her. "It was just an animal."

Something vicious and terrible filled Jaenelle's face. "He was Blood . . . and he was a Brother. His life was worth as much as yours."

"I didn't kill him," Alexandra said, her voice muted.

Underneath the ice in those sapphire eyes was deadly rage bordering on madness. "You didn't strike the killing blow," Jaenelle agreed. "Because of that, I have decided not to execute you."

Alexandra would have fallen if Philip hadn't reached out to steady her. *Execute her?*

"However," Jaenelle continued, "everything has a price, and a price will be paid for Dejaal's life."

Desperation began to well up in Alexandra. "There is no law against murder."

"No, there isn't," Jaenelle replied too softly. "But a Queen can demand a price for the life that was lost."

Vania or Nyselle whimpered. She wasn't sure which one.

"You are no longer welcome in Kaeleer. You will never again be welcome in Kaeleer. If any of you return for any reason, you will be executed. There will be no reprieve."

"Can she do that?" Nyselle whispered.

Jaenelle's eyes flicked to the Province Queens before returning to Alexandra. "I am the Queen. My will is the law."

And no one, Alexandra realized, *no one* would defy that will.

"You will be taken to Cassandra's Altar and sent back through that Gate to Terreille," Jaenelle said. "High Lord, you will see to the arrangements."

"It will be my pleasure, Lady," Saetan replied solemnly.

"You're dismissed." The scepter swung until the unicorn's horn pointed right at Alexandra's breast. "Except you."

Leland made a wordless protest, but didn't argue when Philip, looking pale and sick, took her arm and led her from the room. The other members of the entourage hurried after them, followed more slowly by Saetan, Daemon, and Lucivar.

When the double doors had closed and they were the only people left in the room, Jaenelle lowered the scepter. "You should have gone when I first told you to. Now . . ."

It took Alexandra a minute to speak. "And now?"

Jaenelle didn't answer.

Alexandra swayed, then took a half step to catch her balance as the room began to spiral and everything went dark.

What in the name of Hell just happened? Alexandra wondered as she caught her balance. Then she looked around.

She stood alone in the center of a large stone circle. The floor was perfectly smooth. Surrounding the circle was a solid wall of sharp, jagged rock that soared high above her head. Beyond that wall . . .

She felt the enormous pressure pushing against those walls, as if something was trying to break in and crush this space.

Where . . . ?

We're deep in the abyss, said a midnight voice.

Alexandra turned toward Jaenelle's voice—and stared at the creature who now stood a few feet away. Stared at the slender, naked human body;

at the human legs that ended in delicate hooves; at the human hands that had unsheathed claws instead of fingernails; at the delicately pointed ears; at the gold mane that wasn't quite hair and wasn't quite fur; at the tiny spiral horn in the middle of its forehead; at the frozen sapphire eyes.

What are you? Alexandra whispered.

I am dreams made flesh, the other answered. *I am Witch.*

Jaenelle's voice. Jaenelle's strange eyes. But . . .

Alexandra backed away. No. *No.* *You're what's inside . . .*

She couldn't say it. Revulsion choked her. This is what her daughter Leland had birthed? *This?*

What did you do with my granddaughter? Alexandra demanded.

I did nothing to her.

You must have! What did you do? Devour the spirit in order to use the flesh?

If you mean the husk you call Jaenelle, that flesh was always mine. I was born within that skin.

Never! Never! You couldn't have come from Leland.

Why? Witch asked.

Because you're monstrous.

A painful silence. Then Witch said coldly, *I am what I am.*

And whatever that is, it didn't come from my daughter. It didn't come from me.

Your dreams—

NO! THERE IS NO PART OF ME IN YOU!

Another long silence. Beyond the wall of rocks, it sounded like a fierce storm was gathering.

Have you anything else to say? Witch asked quietly.

I will never have anything to say to you, Alexandra replied.

Very well.

The rock walls vanished. The power in the abyss rushed in to fill the empty space—and tried to fill the vessel inside that space.

Alexandra felt that rushing flood of power start to crush her, then felt another source of dark power balance and control that flood, to keep her mind from shattering. Something inside her snapped and, for a fleeting second, she felt intense pain and agonizing grief.

And then she felt nothing at all.

* * *

Alexandra woke slowly. She was lying in a bed, covered up and comfortably warm, but it only took a moment for her to realize something was wrong. Her head had an odd stuffed-with-wool feeling, and her body ached as if she had a fever.

She opened her eyes, saw Saetan sitting in a chair near the bed, and said hoarsely, "I don't want you."

"I don't want you either," he replied dryly as he reached for a mug sitting on the bedside table. "Here. This will help clear your head."

With a grunt, she propped herself up on one elbow—and saw her Opal Jewels, the pendant and ring, lying on the table. They were empty, completely drained of the reservoir of stored power.

Instinctively, desperately, she turned inward, reaching for the depth of her Opal strength. She couldn't even reach the depth of the White. She was sealed off from the abyss, and her mind felt as if it had been encased in stone.

"You still have basic Craft," Saetan said quietly.

Alexandra stared at him in horror. "Basic Craft?"

"Yes."

She continued to stare as she remembered that crushing flood of power and the fleeting moment of pain. "She broke me," Alexandra whispered. "That bitch *broke me*."

"Take care what you say about my Queen," Saetan snarled.

"What are you going to do?" she snapped. "Rip my tongue out?"

He didn't have to answer. She saw it in his eyes.

"Drink this," he said too quietly as he handed her the mug.

Not daring to do otherwise, she drank the brew and handed the mug back to him.

"I'm not even a witch anymore," she said as tears filled her eyes.

"A witch is still a witch, even if she's broken and can no longer wear the Jewels. A Queen is still a Queen."

Alexandra laughed bitterly. "Oh, that's so easy to say, isn't it? What kind of Queen can I be? Do you really think I can hold a court around me?"

"Other Queens have. Psychic strength is only one factor that attracts strong males and entices them to serve. You don't need that kind of strength if you have the use of theirs."

"And do you think I can hold on to a strong-enough court to remain the Queen of Chaillot?"

"No," Saetan replied quietly after a long pause. "But that has nothing to do with your ability to wear Jewels."

She choked on the insult, not daring to do anything else. "Do you realize what's going to happen to Chaillot now?"

"Your people will, in all probability, choose another Queen."

"There *isn't* another Queen strong enough to be accepted as the Territory Queen. That's why—"—*I still rule.* No, she couldn't say that to him.

She pushed herself into a sitting position, then waited for her head to clear. That odd, muffled feeling would go away eventually, but the sense of loss *never* would. The bitch who had masqueraded as her granddaughter had done this to her. "She's monstrous," she muttered.

"She is the living myth, dreams made flesh," Saetan said coldly.

"Well, she wasn't *my* dream," Alexandra snapped. "How that repulsive, distorted creature could be *anyone's* dream—"

"Don't cross that line again, Alexandra," Saetan warned.

Hearing the edge in his voice, she hunched to make herself smaller. She could grit her teeth and hold her tongue because she had no choice, but she couldn't stop thinking about that creature. It had lived in her house. She shuddered. *Every year at Winsol, we dance for the glory of Witch. Every year, we celebrate* that.

She didn't realize she had spoken out loud until the room turned to ice. "I want to go home," she said in a small voice. "Can you arrange that?"

"It would be my pleasure," Saetan crooned.

4 / Kaeleer

Daemon stared with intense dislike at the blackwood hourglass floating outside Jaenelle's door. When he'd noticed it the first time he'd tried to check on Jaenelle, Ladvarian, the Sceltie Warlord, had explained what it meant. So he had accepted Ladvarian's offer to act as guide and had done a little exploring of the Keep. Returning an hour later, he'd discovered that the hourglass had been turned, the sand trickling into the base to mark another hour of solitude. This was the third time the sand had almost run out, and *this* time he was going to be waiting at the door when the last grain of sand dropped.

"You are impatient?" asked a sibilant voice.

Daemon turned toward Draca, the Keep's Seneschal. When they had first arrived at the Keep, Lucivar had given him a cryptic warning: *Draca is a dragon in human form.* The moment he'd seen the Seneschal, he'd understood what Lucivar meant. Her looks, combined with the feel of great age and old, deep power, had fascinated him.

"I'm worried," he replied, meeting the dark eyes that stared right through him. "She shouldn't be alone right now."

"Yet you sstand outsside the door."

Daemon gave the floating hourglass a killing look.

Draca made a sound that might have been muted laughter. "Are you alwayss sso obedient?"

"Almost never," Daemon muttered—and then remembered who he was talking to.

But Draca nodded, as if pleased to have something confirmed. "It iss wisse for maless to know when to yield and obey. But the Conssort iss permitted to bend many ruless."

Daemon considered the words carefully. It was hard to catch inflections in that sibilant voice, but he thought he understood her. "You know more of the finer points of Protocol than I do," he said, watching her closely. "I appreciate the instruction."

Her face didn't alter, but he would have sworn she smiled at him. As she turned away, she added, "The glasss iss almosst empty."

His hand was on the doorknob, quietly turning it as the last grains of sand trickled into the hourglass's base. As he opened the door, he saw the hourglass turning to declare another hour of solitude. He slipped quickly into the room and closed the door behind him.

Jaenelle stood by a window, looking out at the night, still dressed in the black gown. As a man, that gown appealed to him in every way a woman's garment could, and he hoped she didn't just wear it for formal occasions.

He stepped away from those thoughts. Not only were they useless tonight, they teased his body into wanting to respond to her in a way that wouldn't be acceptable.

"Are they gone?" Jaenelle asked quietly, still staring out the window.

Daemon studied her, trying to decide if it was meant as small talk or if she had withdrawn so deep within herself she really didn't know.

"They're gone." He moved toward her slowly, cautiously, until he was only a few feet away and at an angle where he could see her profile.

"It was the appropriate punishment," Jaenelle said as another tear rolled down her face. "It's the appropriate punishment when one Queen violates another's court to do harm."

"You could have asked one of us to do it," Daemon said quietly.

Jaenelle shook her head. "I'm the Queen. It was mine to do."

Not if you're going to eat your heart out because of it.

"There's a traditional way to break one of the Blood, to strip away the power without doing any other harm. It's quick and clean." She hesitated. "I took her deep into the abyss."

"You took her to the misty place?"

"No," Jaenelle said too sharply, too quickly. "That's a special place. I didn't want it tainted—" She bit her lip.

He didn't want to examine the relief he felt at knowing Alexandra hadn't fouled the misty place with her presence.

As he continued to study her, it struck him with the force of a blow: she hadn't withdrawn so far into herself because she grieved over having to break another witch; she had withdrawn in order to deal with some kind of personal pain.

"Sweetheart," he said quietly, "what's wrong? Please tell me. Let me help."

When she turned to look at him, he didn't see a grown woman or a Queen or Witch. He saw a child in agony.

"Leland . . . Leland cared, I think, but I never expected much from her. Philip cared, but there was nothing he could really do. Alexandra was the m-mother in the family. She was the one who had the strength. She was the one we all wanted to please. And I could never please her, could never be . . . I loved all of them—Leland and Alexandra and Philip and Wil-helmina." Jaenelle's breathing hitched on a suppressed sob. "I loved *her*— and she s-said I was m-monstrous."

Daemon just stared at her, the sudden rage that engulfed him making it impossible to speak for a moment. "The bitch said *what?*"

Startled by the venom in his voice, she gave him a clear-eyed look before she crumbled again. "She said I was monstrous."

He could almost see all the deep childhood scars reopening, bleeding. This was the final rejection, the final pain. The child had defied that rejection, had tried to justify the sparse love given only with conditions placed on it. The child had tried to justify being sent to that horror, Briarwood. But the child was no longer a child, and the agony of having to face a bitter truth was ripping her apart.

He also realized that, faced with this emotional battering, she was now clinging to the one solid wall of her childhood: Saetan's love and acceptance.

Well, he could give her another wall to cling to. He opened his arms enough to invite but not enough to demand. "Come here," he said softly. "Come to me."

It broke his heart the way she crept toward him without looking at him, the way her body was braced for rejection.

His arms closed around her, comforting and protecting.

"She was a good Queen, wasn't she?" Jaenelle asked in a pleading voice a few minutes later.

Daemon felt a stab of pain. At another time, the lie would have been easy enough to say, but not tonight. Knowing he was going to rip away her last justification for Alexandra's behavior, he gave her the truth as gently as he could. "Compared to the other Queens in Terreille, she was a good Queen. Compared to any of the Queens I've met since I've been in Kaeleer . . . No, sweetheart, she was not a good Queen."

Pain flowed with the tears as Jaenelle finally gave up the people she had once tried to love.

He held her, saying nothing. Just held her while he let all of his love surround her.

The door opened quietly. Ladvarian walked in, followed by Kaelas.

Daemon watched them, and wondered if they had decided on their own to defy the command for solitude or if they had equated his presence with permission to enter.

After a minute, the tip of Ladvarian's tail waved once. *We will come back later.*

They left as quietly as they had come.

CHAPTER EIGHT

1 / Kaeleer

Lord Magstrom nervously wandered around the room where the records from the service fair were stored. He'd only been home a couple of days and was still catching up on the official business of his own village. But Lord Jorval had urgently requested him to return to Little Terreille's capital to discuss something of the "utmost importance."

He'd spent several days with his eldest granddaughter and her husband—days that had been filled with excitement and apprehension instead of the rest he so badly needed. His granddaughter was pregnant with her first child, and, though delighted, she was also quite ill. So he'd spent most of his time reassuring her husband that his granddaughter wouldn't divorce a man she loved just because she couldn't keep her breakfast down for a few weeks.

He shouldn't have said "a few weeks." The younger man had looked ready to faint when he'd said that.

He *had* written a hurried letter to the High Lord about the discrepancies he had found in the service fair records but then had hesitated over sending it, wondering if his own exhaustion had made something sinister out of what was really just sloppy clerical work.

No matter. As soon as he was home again, he would write a more thoughtful, carefully worded letter, one that expressed concern rather than alarm.

He had just reached this decision when the door swung open and Lord Jorval entered the room.

"I'm glad you came, Magstrom," Jorval said a little breathlessly. "I wasn't sure who else I could trust. But anyone who's worked with you knows you couldn't be involved in *this*."

"And just what is 'this'?" Magstrom asked cautiously.

Jorval went to the shelves holding the records and pulled out a thick folder.

Magstrom's stomach tightened. It was the Hayllian folder—the same one he had examined before his hasty departure from Goth.

Jorval's hands trembled as he leafed through the papers, then put several on the large table. "Look. There are discrepancies in these lists." Hurrying to the shelves, he pulled out several folders and dumped them on the table. "And not only in the Hayllian lists. At first I thought it was a clerical error, but . . ." Taking a sheet of paper from one of the folders, he pointed. "Do you remember this man? He was most unsuitable to immigrate to Kaeleer. *Most* unsuitable."

"I remember him," Magstrom said faintly. A brute of a man whose psychic scent had made his skin crawl. "He was accepted into a court?"

"Yes," Jorval said grimly. "This one."

Magstrom squinted at the scrawled writing. The Queen's name and the territory she ruled were almost illegible. The only thing he could definitely make out was that the territory was in Little Terreille. "Who is this . . . Hektek?"

"I don't know. There is no Queen named Hektek who rules so much as a village in Little Terreille. But thirty Terreilleans were accepted into this alleged court. *Thirty*."

"Then where are these people going?"

Jorval hesitated. "I think someone is secretly creating an army right under our noses, using the service fair to cover the tracks."

Magstrom swallowed hard. "Do you know who?" he asked, halfexpecting Jorval to accuse the High Lord—which was ridiculous.

"I think so," Jorval replied, an odd glitter appearing in his eyes. "If what I suspect is true, the Territory Queens in Kaeleer must be warned immediately. That's why I asked you to come. I'm to meet someone tonight who claims to have information about the people missing from the lists. I wanted another member of the Council to come with me as a witness to confirm what was said. I wanted you because, if we *are* in danger, the High Lord will listen to you."

That decided Magstrom. "Since there may be some risk in revealing this information, we shouldn't keep this person waiting."

"No," Joryal replied, sounding queer, "we shouldn't."

They found an available horse-drawn cab almost as soon as they left the building. A heavy silence filled the cab until, a few minutes later, it pulled up.

Magstrom stepped out, looked around, and felt a jagged-edged fear. They were at the edge of Goth's slums, not a place for the unwary—or for an older man at any time.

"I know," Jorval said hurriedly as he took Magstrom's arm and began leading him through narrow, dirty streets. "It seems an unlikely meeting place, but I think that's why it was chosen. Even if someone recognized us, they would think they were mistaken."

Breathing heavily, Magstrom struggled to keep up with Jorval. He could feel eyes watching them from shadowed doorways—and he could sense the flickers of power coming from the ones who watched. There were many reasons why a dark-Jeweled male could end up in a place like this.

Finally, they slipped into the back door of a large building and silently climbed the stairs. At a second floor door, Jorval fumbled with a key, then stepped aside to allow Magstrom to enter the suite.

The furnishings in the sitting room were secondhand and shabby. The room itself looked as if even minimal cleaning hadn't been done in a long time. And it stank of decay.

"Something wrong?" Jorval asked in an oddly gleeful voice.

Magstrom moved toward the narrow windows. A little air might help relieve the smell. "I think a mouse or a rat must have died behind the walls, so—"

Jorval made a queer sound—a sharp, high-pitched giggle—at the same time the bedroom door opened and a hooded figure stepped into the sitting room.

Magstrom turned—and couldn't say a word.

Knucklebones peeked out of the split skin as brown hands pushed the hood back.

Magstrom stared at the hate-filled gold eyes in the ravaged, decaying face. She took a step toward him. He took a step back. Then he took another . . . and another . . . until there was nowhere to go.

Jorval smiled at him. "I thought it was time you met the Dark Priestess."

2 / Kaeleer

"Is something wrong?" Daemon asked Saetan. He glanced at Lucivar, who was intently studying their father.

Saetan finally looked up from the sheet of paper lying in the middle of his desk. "I received a letter from Lord Jorval, informing me that Lord Magstrom was brutally killed last night."

Daemon let his breath out slowly while Lucivar swore. "I met Magstrom briefly at the service fair. He seemed to be a decent man."

"He was," Saetan replied. "And he was the only member of the Dark Council Jaenelle was willing to deal with."

"How did he die?" Lucivar asked bluntly.

Saetan hesitated. "He was found in an alleyway in the Goth slums. The body was so torn up that speculation is running wild that Magstrom was killed by kindred."

Daemon said, "Why would they suspect the kindred?" at the same time Lucivar snarled, "It was a full death?"

"Yes, it was a full death," Saetan said grimly, answering Lucivar's question first. "So there's not even a chance of Magstrom being a ghost in the Dark Realm long enough to tell someone what really happened to him. There are feral dog packs, and they *can* be a danger, but a Craft shield would have protected Magstrom from them. Only a pack of kindred, or one who wore darker Jewels than Magstrom, could have drained his psychic power to finish the kill."

"Is that likely?" Daemon asked.

"If an unknown human wanders into one of the kindred Territories, it's almost a given. But in Goth? No."

"So he was mutilated in order to hide the real death wounds."

"So it would seem."

"Does Jorval want to postpone the healing?" Lucivar asked.

Saetan shook his head. "The meeting is still set for late this afternoon. Is everything ready?"

Lucivar nodded. "We'll be leaving within the hour."

"The place you're taking Jaenelle to is secure?" Saetan asked.

"It's a guardhouse in Dea al Mon," Lucivar said. "Chaosti will come with us, and the Dea al Mon guards will supply the added physical protection. Cat said she has a few errands to run in Amdarh, so we'll go directly there afterward, and probably stay for a day or two. Chaosti will return here and report."

With effort, Daemon caged the jealousy that was chewing him up inside. There was no reason for Lucivar to think twice about making plans to spend a couple of days with Jaenelle, despite the Eyriens still waiting to be settled in Askavi before winter set in, despite his having a wife and child. Jaenelle was not only his sister but his Queen. There was no question that he would go with her whenever or wherever she needed him.

Putting those thoughts aside, Daemon concentrated on the timetable. He hadn't really been aware of the journey from Goth to the Hall, but it had to have taken a couple of hours at the least. Going to this secret location in Dea al Mon would probably take even more time. If Lucivar was planning to leave within the hour to reach the guardhouse, he was planning to arrive so that there would be just enough time for Jaenelle to rest and eat a late midday meal before doing whatever she was going to do. Just enough time . . .

The Sadist in him woke up. He looked at Saetan and saw his own suspicions reflected in his father's eyes. "When was the body found?" he asked too softly.

Lucivar jerked to attention, then swore viciously.

Saetan returned his stare for a moment. "If Jorval had been informed immediately, there would have been just enough time to pen a hasty note and send it here by courier."

"*Was* it hastily written?"

"No, I wouldn't say so."

Which meant Jorval had known about Magstrom's death before the body had been found. And Jorval was the one who had made these arrangements for Jaenelle to come to Little Terreille.

As soon as he and Lucivar were away from Saetan's study, Daemon settled one hand on Lucivar's shoulder, his long, black-tinted nails providing just enough bite to ensure that he had his brother's undivided attention. "You will do anything you have to in order to keep her safe and take care of her, won't you?"

"I'll keep her safe, Bastard. You can count on that." Then Lucivar smiled that lazy, arrogant smile. "But you're the one who's going to take care of her. You've got less than an hour to get packed, old son. Bring enough to get you through a couple of days in Amdarh as well."

Daemon stared at Lucivar, then stepped back and slipped his hands into his trouser pockets. "She's not comfortable with me, Prick." Not even to Lucivar would he admit how Jaenelle had practically fled her own rooms in order to get away from him after he had spent the night with her. "My being there would only distress her."

"You're her Consort," Lucivar said sharply. "Stand your ground."

"But . . ."

"She isn't going to pay attention to either of us before this meeting, and I'll be with you when you go to Amdarh. While she's swearing about tripping over me, she isn't going to have time to feel nervous about being around *you*." Lucivar rode over another, more feeble protest. "I want you at that guardhouse, Daemon."

He finally understood. Lucivar didn't want him there because he was the Consort, but because he was the Sadist.

Daemon nodded. "I'll be ready to leave when you are."

3 / Kaeleer

Seeing the contained grief in Jaenelle's eyes, Lucivar didn't need to ask if she'd been told about Lord Magstrom's death. He almost asked if she wanted to postpone the meeting, but didn't bother. There was something else in her eyes that told him she would see this meeting through, for her own reasons.

He eyed the large flat case that stood near her traveling bag. She had several cases like that of different sizes that contained the wooden frames she used to weave her various webs.

"You're expecting to weave a healing web that size?" he asked.

"It's not for a healing web; it's for the shadow."

He eyed the case again. A "shadow" was an elaborate illusion that could fool the eye into believing a person was really there. Jaenelle could create one that was so realistic, the only difference between it and her real body was that, while the shadow could pick up or touch anything, it couldn't *be* touched. She had made that kind of shadow eight years ago, when she had begun her search for Daemon to bring him out of the Twisted Kingdom, and he still clearly remembered the kind of physical toll it had taken.

"Do you feel well enough to channel that much power through your body to make the shadow capable of doing an extensive healing?"

"There won't be much healing required," Jaenelle replied calmly.

That wasn't the impression he or Saetan had gotten from Jorval's urgent letters, but he knew better than to say anything. Serving Jaenelle in the past few years had taught him when to yield.

She vanished the case and traveling bag, then picked up a hooded, full-length black cape. "Shall we go?"

4 / Kaeleer

Kartane SaDiablo restlessly paced the sitting room of his suite.

The bitch was late. If he'd been home, the bitch wouldn't have dared keep Dorothea's son waiting. Hell's fire, he'd almost be glad to get back to Hayll.

Working himself up to insulted outrage, he almost missed the quiet knock on the door. He pulled himself together. He needed this bitch, who, Jorval assured him, was the best Healer in Kaeleer. If he was uncivil, nothing and no one could stop her from walking out the door again.

He walked over to the windows and looked out. There was no reason for her to know he had been waiting anxiously, no reason to give her even that little bit of power over him. "Come in," he said when the knock sounded again.

He didn't hear the door open, but when he turned around, a figure shrouded in a hooded black cape stood inside the room.

At first he thought it was that witch Dorothea called the Dark Priestess, but there was something slimy about the Dark Priestess's psychic scent and this one's scent . . .

Kartane frowned. He couldn't detect a psychic scent at all. "You're the Healer?" he asked doubtfully.

"Yes."

Kartane shivered at the sound of that midnight voice. Trying to ignore his uneasiness, he reached up to unbutton his shirt. "I suppose you want to examine me."

"That won't be necessary. I know what's wrong with you."

His fingers froze around the button. "You've seen this before?"

"No."

"But you know what it is?"

"Yes."

Annoyed by the terse answers, he tossed aside any effort at civility. "Then what in the name of Hell is it?"

"It's called Briarwood," replied the midnight voice.

The blood drained out of Kartane's head, leaving him dizzy.

"Briarwood is the pretty poison," the voice continued as fair-skinned hands reached up and pushed the hood back. "There is no cure for Briarwood."

Kartane stared at her. The last time he'd seen her, thirteen years ago, she had been more like a drugged puppet than a child—a plaything locked in one of Briarwood's cubicles, waiting to be used. But he'd never forgotten those sapphire eyes, or the terror he'd felt after he'd tried to touch her mind.

"You." The word came out as nothing more than exhaled breath. "I thought Greer destroyed you."

"He tried."

It hit him then. He pointed an accusing finger at her. "You did this to me. *You* did this!"

"I created the tangled web, yes. As far as what's happened to you, Kartane, you did this to yourself."

"No!"

"Yes. To each is given what he gave. That was the only command I spun into the web."

"Since you did this, you can damn well undo it!"

She shook her head. "Many of the children who were the threads of that tangled web have returned to the Darkness. They're out of reach, even for me, and there's no way to undo the web without them."

"You lie," Kartane shouted. "If I hand you enough gold, you'd find a way fast enough."

"There is no cure for Briarwood. But there *is* an end to this, if that's any consolation. To each is given what he gave."

"WHAT DOES THAT MEAN?"

"Every blow, every wound, every rape, every moment of fear that you ever inflicted on another is coming back to you. You're taking back what you gave, Kartane. When you've taken it all back, the debt will be paid, and the web will release you as it did the other males who amused themselves in Briarwood."

"They're all dead, you stupid bitch! I'm the last one left. No one survived this web of yours."

"The web only set the terms. If none of the others survived . . . How many of the children who were sent to Briarwood survived any of you?"

"Since you didn't come here to heal me, why *did* you bother to come? Just to gloat?"

"No. I came to stand as witness for those who are gone."

Kartane studied her, then shook his head. "You can end this."

"I've already told you, I can't."

"You can end this. You can stop this pain. And you're damn well going to!"

With a howl of rage, Kartane rushed her—and went right through her. He hit the door, unable to stop himself.

When he turned around, there was no one else in the room.

5 / Kaeleer

Daemon approached Jaenelle cautiously, reluctant to disturb her solitude and not sure what to think about the odd blend of sadness and satisfaction on her face. The solitude was an illusion, of course. When she had left her room in the guardhouse and gone out to sit near the creek, Lucivar, Chaosti, and half a dozen Dea al Mon guards had followed her, swiftly disappearing into the woods. He couldn't see any of them, but he knew they were nearby, watching and listening.

"Here," he said quietly, handing her a mug. "It's just herbal tea. Nothing fancy." When she thanked him, he slipped his hands into his trouser pockets, feeling self-conscious. "Is everything all right?"

Jaenelle hesitated. "I did what I went to do." She took a sip of the tea, peered into the cup, then looked at him. "What's in this?"

"A little of this and that."

"Uh-huh."

If that doubtful tone had come from any other woman, he would have felt insulted. But the concentration—and hint of frustration—in her eyes as she took another sip indicated that her doubt was caused by his dismissive "nothing fancy" rather than the brew itself.

She eyed him speculatively. "I don't suppose you would be willing to exchange the recipe for this brew for one of mine?"

Since she liked it that much, it was tempting to refuse so that he would be the only one who could make it for her, but he quickly realized that the time spent with her over a table full of herbs would serve him far better.

Daemon smiled. "I know a couple of brews you might find interesting."

Jaenelle returned the smile, then drained the mug and stood up. "I'd like to head out to Amdarh soon," she said as they walked back to the guardhouse. "That way, we can get settled in tonight."

Despite Lucivar's and Chaosti's firm warnings, Daemon had to bite his tongue to keep from suggesting that she eat something first. They had told him her resistance against any attempt to get some food into her would be in direct proportion to her mood when she returned from this meeting. He'd only needed one glance at her face when she came out of her room to know any suggestion would have been pointless.

"I think you'll like Amdarh," Jaenelle said. "It's a beautiful—" She stopped walking, then sniffed the air. "Is that stew?"

"I believe it is," Daemon replied mildly. "Lucivar and Chaosti made it. It should be just about done."

"They made wildwood stew?"

"I believe that's what it's called."

Jaenelle eyed him. "I suppose you're hungry."

Even if he had never picked up a cue before in his life, he couldn't have missed that one. "Actually, I am. Do you think we could wait until after dinner before heading to Amdarh?"

Jaenelle turned her head away from him, but not enough that he couldn't see her lick her lips. "It wouldn't take that long to have a bowl of stew. Or two," she added as she hurried toward the guardhouse.

Daemon lengthened his stride to keep up, and wondered how much of a tussle the males were going to have in order to get their fair share.

6 / Kaeleer

Kartane burst into Jorval's dining room. "Is that bitch alive?" he demanded.

Jorval hurried toward him while a man Kartane had never seen before sat at the table and just stared.

"Lord Kartane," Jorval said anxiously. "If I'd known the healing would be done so soon, we would have waited din—"

"Damn you, just answer the question! Is she alive?"

"Lady Angelline? Yes, of course she's alive. Why do you ask? Didn't she arrive?"

"She arrived," Kartane snarled.

"I don't understand," Jorval said, almost wailing. "She's the best Healer in the Realm. If she—"

"SHE'S THE ONE WHO DID THIS TO ME!"

Jorval's shocked look was quickly replaced by a sly one. "I see. Please, come and join us. I can see you've had a distressing afternoon. Perhaps some food and company will help."

"Nothing will help until that bitch is made to heel," Kartane snapped, accepting a chair at the table and a quickly filled glass of wine. He glared at the other man, who continued to stare at him.

"Lord Kartane," Jorval said smoothly, "may I present Lord Hobart? He, too, has reasons to want to see Jaenelle Angelline subdued."

"Not just Jaenelle Angelline," Hobart growled.

"Oh?" Kartane said, pushing his anger aside as his interest in Hobart sharpened.

"Lord Hobart had controlled the Territory of Glacia for several years," Jorval said. "When his niece became the Territory Queen—"

"The ungrateful bitch EXILED me!" Hobart shouted.

"And you want to regain control," Kartane said, starting to lose interest. Then Jorval added, "Lady Karla is a close friend of Jaenelle's."

Kartane randomly selected food from the dishes offered as he nibbled on that bit of information. There was nothing he would have liked better right then than to hurt a close friend of the bitch. "I may be able to help. My mother is the High Priestess of Hayll."

Not only didn't Hobart look sufficiently impressed, he looked distinctly uneasy. He cleared his throat. "It's a generous offer, Lord Kartane. A very generous offer, but . . ."

"But you're already receiving some assistance from the Dark Priestess," Kartane guessed. When Hobart paled, he crossed two fingers and held them up. "Perhaps you're not aware that my mother and the Dark Priestess are like that."

Hobart swallowed hard. Jorval merely drank his wine and watched them out of dark eyes filled with sly glee.

"I see," Hobart finally said. "In that case, your help is most welcome."

CHAPTER NINE

1 / Kaeleer

Andulvar settled into a chair in front of Saetan's blackwood desk. "Karla says you've been in here sulking for the past two hours, ever since you got a message from Lady Zhara."

Saetan gave his longtime friend his iciest stare. "I. Am. Not. Sulking."

"All right." Andulvar waited. "Then what *are* you doing?"

Saetan leaned back in his chair. "Answer me this: if I were to run away from home, is there anywhere in any of the Realms I could go and not be found?"

Andulvar scratched his chin. "Well, if you wanted to hide from the Dhemlan Queens or the coven, there are quite a few places you could go to ground. If you wanted to hide from your male offspring, there are a few places in the Dark Realm that would take even Mephis a while to think of. But if *Jaenelle* was looking for you . . ."

"Which is precisely why I'm still sitting here." Saetan rubbed his forehead and sighed. "Zhara has summoned me to Amdarh to take care of a problem for her."

Andulvar frowned. "Lucivar's in Amdarh, isn't he? If Zhara needs help from a male stronger than the ones who serve in her court, why didn't she ask him?"

Saetan narrowed his golden eyes and let the words fall like precisely dropped stones. "Lucivar is in Amdarh with Jaenelle."

The silence thickened into a solid curtain.

"Ah," Andulvar finally said. "Well, Daemon—"

"Is in Amdarh with Lucivar and Jaenelle."

"Mother Night," Andulvar muttered, then added warily, "What did Zhara say?"

Saetan picked up the message and read in a funereal voice, " 'Your children are having a wonderful time. Come and get them.' "

2 / Kaeleer

Daemon braced his head in his hands and closed his eyes.

"Mother Night," Lucivar said, enunciating very carefully.

"I've never been this drunk," Daemon moaned quietly. .

Lucivar stared at him with bloodshot eyes. "Sure you have."

"Maybe a couple of times in the stupid phase of my youth, but not since I've worn the Black. My body burns it up too fast to get drunk."

"Not this time," Lucivar said, then added after a long, possibly thoughtful, pause, "I've been this drunk."

"Really? When?"

"Last time I went on a crawl with Jaenelle. Big mistake. Should have remembered it. Would have, too, if I'd been sober when I *did* remember it."

After a minute's painful effort, Daemon gave up trying to decipher that comment and found something else to think about. "I've never been thrown out of a city before."

"Sure you have," Lucivar said in a hearty voice that made them both whimper.

Daemon shook his head and realized his error a bit too late. Even when he managed to stop, the room continued moving back and forth, and what was left of his brain sloshed noisily inside his skull. He swallowed carefully. "I've been thrown out of courts and wasn't allowed back into the city because that was the Queen's territory, but that's different."

"Iz all right," Lucivar said. "In a few weeks, Zhara will welcome you with open arms."

"She didn't seem like a foolish woman. Why would she do that?"

"Because we provide a restraining influence on Jaenelle."

"We do?"

They just stared at each other until the dining room door opened.

Daemon braced himself, absolutely certain that hearing the door slam would kill him.

"Mother Night," Surreal said, choking back laughter. "They're pathetic."

"Aren't they?" There was no laughter in Saetan's reply.

The soft footsteps approaching the table made the room vibrate.

"Please don't yell," Daemon whimpered.

"I wouldn't dream of yelling," Saetan replied in a voice that, nonetheless, rattled Daemon's bones. "There would be no point in yelling. You'd both be on the floor, insensible, after the first word. So I'll save the lecture until you're sober enough to listen to it, because I intend to deliver it with considerable volume. The only question I want answered right now is what in the name of Hell did you two pour down your throats to get in this condition?"

"Gravediggers," Lucivar mumbled.

"How many?" Saetan asked ominously.

Lucivar took a couple of careful breaths. "Not sure. Things got a bit blurry after the seventh one."

"After the—" Long pause. "Are either of you capable of walking to your rooms?"

"Sure," Lucivar said. It took him a couple of tries, but he got to his feet.

Not to be outdone, Daemon stood up, too—and regretted it.

"You take Lucivar," Saetan said to Surreal. "He isn't listing quite as much."

"That's because I didn't finish the drinks." Lucivar pointed at Daemon, tipped, and almost flattened Surreal against the table. "That's why *you're* so drunk. I *told* you not to finish them."

Daemon tried to make a rude noise and ended up spitting on Saetan.

Without further comment, he was hauled out of the room and up a terrifyingly steep set of stairs. Once he reached his bed, he tried to lie down, but was hauled upright and undressed while his father's ire made the room pulse.

"Do you need a basin?" Saetan asked with no sympathy whatsoever.

"No," Daemon replied meekly.

Finally, he was allowed to lie down. The last thing he was aware of was Saetan's hand brushing his hair back in a gentle caress.

Surreal closed the door of Lucivar's room at the same moment Saetan stepped out of Daemon's room.

"I appreciate your assistance," Saetan said when they met at the top of the stairs.

Surreal grinned. "I wouldn't have missed this for anything."

They started down the stairs together. "You got Lucivar settled?"

"He snarled a lot and kept telling me to keep my hands off him since he's a married man. He didn't want to get undressed, but I pointed out that, since he was married, he should know better than to try to get into a bed wearing boots in that condition. While we wrestled with the boots, we pondered how that little fish got wedged under the laces."

Saetan stopped at the foot of the stairs. "How *did* it get under the laces?"

"He has no idea. So I gave the fish a proper burial at sea, so to speak, managed to convince Lucivar that stripping to the waist was not improper since I'm family, and let what was left of him fall into bed." Surreal looked around. "Say, aren't you going to tuck Jaenelle in?"

"At this moment," Saetan said dryly, "Jaenelle is in the kitchen, tucking into a very large breakfast."

"Oh, dear," Surreal said, then started to laugh.

3 / Kaeleer

Karla removed the ring from the jeweler's box and slipped it on the second finger of her right hand. It was a simple ring of yellow and white gold, with a small oval sapphire. A tasteful design, but nothing that would really catch the eye, yet feminine enough that no one would wonder about a woman wearing it. An everyday ring rather than flash and glitter. "It's perfect."

"I had asked Banard to have that one done first," Jaenelle said, "but he'd gotten all the rings for the coven done since the designs are simple." She paused, then added, "I also ordered rings made for Surreal and Wilhelmina. They'll be ready next week."

Karla nodded as she studied the ring. "How do I activate the shield inside it?"

"You would deliberately activate it through your Gray Jewel. Otherwise, it's keyed in the same way the boyos' Rings of Honor are and will respond to fear, rage, and pain caused by a serious wound. It's set for fairly intense emotions because, when it activates, everyone else within range who wears a Ring that's connected to this one is going to act as if it was a call to battle. Which it is."

"How much range does it have?" Karla asked. "If it gets activated, would Morton sense it even if he's not in the same city?"

Jaenelle gave her an odd look. "Karla, if something wakes the shield in that ring, not only will you have Morton pounding on your door, you're going to have Sceron, Jonah, Kaelas, Mistral, and Khary showing up on your doorstep—along with our Sisters in that part of the Realm."

"Mother Night!" Karla frowned at the ring. "But ... I know the boyos have used this shield on occasion and it didn't make the rest of them go berserk."

"I wouldn't count on their responding to a signal picked up from a ring worn by a Queen in the same way they respond to a signal from another Brother in the court," Jaenelle said dryly. "Besides, at this point, the males are all attuned to each other. They can tell when to remain on alert but to wait for another signal and when to drop everything and head for the person in trouble with all possible speed."

"And you don't think they'll wait?"

"Not a chance."

Karla sighed. That was a little more male attention than she'd anticipated, and she was glad of the warning.

"I'll link it to your Gray Jewel now," Jaenelle said, holding out her right hand.

"Won't the boyos pick that up?" Karla asked, placing her right hand in Jaenelle's.

"Yes, and it will take them under two minutes to figure out that someone in the coven is wearing a ring they can connect with now."

Well, there's safety in numbers, Karla thought. *With all of us wearing a ring like this—*

"And it will take them about another minute to figure out the distinctive feel of this particular ring and recognize it as you."

"Hell's fire."

Jaenelle's smile was sympathetic but amused. "Wait until Lucivar shows up the first time. It's an experience."

"I'm sure it is," Karla mumbled.

A moment later, she felt a flash of cold followed by heat. The ring throbbed against her finger. The sensations faded, but she could sense the deep reservoir of power waiting just out of reach.

"The other thing to be aware of is that, when the shield wakes, the only people who will be able to reach you if you physically need help are the rest of the First Circle," Jaenelle said.

Karla nodded. "In that case, I'd better always wear it. It wouldn't do to have someone else slip it on and have that kind of protection."

"No one else can wear this ring. It was made for you. If anyone else tried to activate the shield, the results would be . . . unpleasant."

"I see." She didn't ask Jaenelle to define "unpleasant."

Jaenelle studied Karla for a moment. "Wear it well, Sister."

"Thank you. I will."

"I'd better see that the rest of the coven gets their rings." Jaenelle picked up the bag that held the other ring boxes, then hesitated. "Do you really have to leave tomorrow?" she asked a little plaintively.

"Duty calls," Karla said with a smile. She waited until Jaenelle left the room before adding, "And Uncle Saetan made it quite clear that no excuse for staying would be considered acceptable."

All the Queens were returning to their home Territories. So were the First Circle males. Lucivar was taking his family and the other Eyriens to Ebon Rih. Surreal and Wilhelmina would go with him as well. Andulvar and Prothvar were already on their way to Askavi, and Mephis had left for his town house in Amdarh.

She understood why Saetan was clearing the Hall. They all did. By tomorrow afternoon, all the friends Jaenelle had used as buffers would be gone. Her only human companions would be the High Lord, who, Karla was sure, was going to make himself scarce, and Daemon. The Consort would have a clear field in which to woo his Lady.

"May the Darkness help us," Karla muttered as she strode to the door and threw it open. Then she stood in the doorway and stared.

Lucivar, Aaron, Chaosti, Khardeen, and Morton smiled at her.

"Well, well, well," Lucivar crooned. "Look who we found."

Trying to return the smile, Karla said weakly, "Kiss kiss," and sincerely hoped it wouldn't take Jaenelle long to activate the other rings.

CHAPTER TEN

1 / Kaeleer

After spending two weeks in Ebon Rih, Surreal returned to the Hall, took one look at Daemon, and went hunting for Jaenelle.

She finally tracked Jaenelle down—actually, Graysfang tracked down Ladvarian, who was with Jaenelle—in a part of the Hall so far away from the family's living quarters that it practically guaranteed no one would think to look there.

Jaenelle stepped out of a room and noticed Surreal striding down the corridor. Her face lit up with pleasure. "Surreal! I didn't expect you back so—"

Surreal grabbed Jaenelle's arm and hauled the younger woman back into the room. "This is girl talk," she growled at Graysfang and Ladvarian. "Go water some bushes." Then she slammed the door on two startled, furry faces.

"Surreal," Jaenelle said, shaking free of the hard grip, "did something happen in—"

"What in the name of Hell are you doing?" Surreal shouted.

Jaenelle looked wary and baffled. "I was reading."

"I'm not talking about what you were doing five minutes ago. I'm talking about Daemon. Why are you doing this to him?"

Jaenelle flinched and said defensively, "I'm not doing anything to him."

"That's exactly the point. Damn it, Jaenelle, he's your *Consort*. Why *aren't* you using him?"

In the flick of a moment, she saw a defensive young woman change into an angry Queen.

"He's been used enough, don't you think?" Jaenelle said quietly in her midnight voice. "And I am *not* going to be the next in a long list of women who have forced him into physical intimacy."

"But—" Surreal took a mental step back. She hadn't expected this to be the reason for Jaenelle's resistance—and she was sure Daemon had no idea this was why he was getting locked out of the bedroom. *Ah, sugar,* she thought sadly. *You made all the wrong moves for all the right reasons.* "That was different. He was a pleasure slave then, not a Consort."

"*Is* there that much difference, Surreal?"

Remember who you're talking to. Remember what she must have seen in Briarwood—and what sort of conclusions a twelve-year-old girl who knew about that side of sex would come to about the time Daemon had spent as a pleasure slave.

"The boys who are Consorts don't seem to mind performing their duties, Quite the opposite, in fact."

"They've never been pleasure slaves. They've never been forced. All right, yes, sometimes a Consort is asked to give more than he feels like giving at that moment, but when a man accepts the Consort's ring, he goes into that kind of service willingly and by his own choice."

"Daemon made that choice," Surreal pointed out quietly. "Not because he wants the status of being the Consort and is willing to put up with the duties that go along with it, but because he wants to be your lover." She studied Jaenelle. "You do care about him, don't you?"

"I love him."

Surreal heard such a deep river of feelings in those simple words.

"Besides," Jaenelle said, shifting back into a nervous young woman, "I'm not sure he really does want to do . . . *that.* He hasn't even tried to kiss me," she added sadly.

Surreal hooked her hair behind her pointed ears. Damn, damn, damn. How had the ground gotten so boggy so fast? "If I understand the rules a Consort is supposed to play by, isn't the Queen supposed to initiate the first kiss so that the Consort knows his attentions will be welcome?"

"Yes," Jaenelle said reluctantly.

"But you haven't kissed him either?"

Jaenelle snarled in frustration and started pacing. "I'm not twelve anymore."

Surreal braced her hands on her hips. "Sugar, from where I'm standing, that's all to the good."

Jaenelle threw up her hands and shouted, "Don't you understand? I don't know how to do any of this!"

Surreal just stared. "You've never been kissed? Family kisses and friendly kisses don't count," she quickly amended.

A disgusted look filled Jaenelle's face. "Teeth, tongues, and drool."

"Wolves and dogs don't count either."

Jaenelle let out a huff of laughter, and said dryly, "I wasn't referring to the kindred."

Shit. "Haven't you received even *one* kiss you liked?"

Jaenelle hesitated. "Well, Daemon kissed me once."

"Well, there you—"

"When I was twelve."

Surreal bristled automatically at the thought of a grown man kissing a child, then took a moment to consider the man. There were kisses and there were *kisses*. And Daemon would know exactly how to kiss a young girl without crossing the line—especially when that girl had been Jaenelle. "He kissed you when you were twelve," she said carefully.

Jaenelle shrugged and looked uncomfortable. "It was at Winsol, just before . . . everything happened. He had given me a silver bracelet, and I thought a kiss was a more grown-up way of saying thank you."

"Okay," Surreal said, nodding. "So you kissed him, and then he kissed you."

"Yes."

"And he didn't drool on you?"

Jaenelle's lips twitched. "No, he didn't drool."

"So why can't you kiss him now?"

"Because I'm not twelve anymore!" Jaenelle shouted.

"What's that got to do with it?" Surreal shouted back.

"I don't want him to laugh at me!"

"I doubt laughing would be his first response. As a matter of fact, I don't think it would even occur to him." Surreal paused. *Hell's fire, this is as bad as talking to an adolescent girl.*

She let that thought sink in and settle. If she put age aside and only considered experience, *wasn't* she talking to an adolescent girl? There had to be some key she could turn, some way to make it seem like Daemon desperately needed help. If he needed help, Jaenelle would . . .

"You know, sugar, Daemon is as nervous as you are."

"Why would Daemon be nervous?" Jaenelle asked warily. "He *knows* how to kiss, and he's—"

"A virgin."

Jaenelle's mouth fell open. "But . . . But he's—"

"A virgin. Granted, he may know a bit about kissing, but there's a whole lot he only knows in theory."

"But . . . Surreal, he *can't* be."

"Trust me, he is."

"Oh."

"So you can see why he'd be nervous," Surreal said, feeling a little nervous herself. If Daemon ever found out about this little chat, she could end up the main ingredient in a carnivore's stew. "Frankly, sugar, if push comes to shove, all you have to do is lie there. But if *he's* nervous about his ability to perform well . . ." Cocking her elbow, Surreal stiffened her hand and fingers, then let them droop.

Jaenelle studied the drooping hand long enough for Surreal to start to sweat before saying, "Oh." Her eyes widened. "Oooh." Then she shook her head. "No, that wouldn't happen to Daemon."

That naive assurance of Daemon's ability was touching. Scary, but touching. And not something she was going to introduce to reality.

"Let's sit down," Surreal said, heading for a couch. "Thirty minutes ought to be enough, but we might as well be comfortable."

"Enough for what?" Jaenelle said, settling on the other end of the couch.

"I'm going to explain the basics of kissing." There was a slight edge to Surreal's smile. "You would agree that I know a few things about kissing?"

"All right," Jaenelle replied cautiously.

"And you never thought to ask me about it in the month that I've been in Kaeleer?" And *that* rankled.

"I thought about it," Jaenelle muttered. "It didn't seem polite."

Oh, Mother Night. Well, *that* would explain the glazed look she sometimes noticed in the High Lord's eyes. How many nights had he sat in his study totally flummoxed by dealing with a Queen this powerful who still worried about being polite?

"I thank you for your concern, but, since we're family, I wouldn't have been offended by a little girl talk."

There was speculation in Jaenelle's eyes. Surreal could almost see the questions piling up.

"For today, let's just stick to basic kissing."

"Should I take notes?" Jaenelle asked earnestly.

"No," Surreal replied slowly, "but I think you should try some hands-on practice as soon as possible."

Surreal quietly closed the door and hurried down the corridor. She wasn't sure that look of intense concentration that had been on Jaenelle's face boded well for the man on the receiving end of that attention, but she'd done her best. Any further instructions would have to come from Daemon—and good luck to him. For a woman who had grown up around some of the most sensual males Surreal had ever met, Jaenelle was appallingly dense about sex. Maybe it had taken Daemon's arrival to wake her up sexually, but you would think she would have picked up *some* clues.

How in the name of Hell did two inexperienced lovers ever figure out how to do anything? Surreal wondered. Which made her think about how many things could go wrong once Daemon and Jaenelle got past kissing.

Which made her think that, maybe, she should tell the High Lord about this little chat. Maybe she should. Just in case.

She turned a corner and almost ran into the very last person she wanted to see right now.

"What's wrong?" Daemon asked.

"Wrong?" Surreal said, taking a step back. "Why should anything be wrong?"

"You look pale."

Oh, shit. "Um." Maybe she should tell *him* about that little chat, just to give him a little warning. *Daemon, Jaenelle and I had a little talk about sex. I think you'll enjoy the results.*

Maybe not.

"Surreal?" Daemon said, an edge coming into his voice.

Surreal took a deep breath. "Act nervous. It will help."

Then she was past him, running through the corridors. A few minutes later, breathless, she burst into Saetan's study.

Saetan froze, his pen poised above the papers on his desk. "Surreal," he said cautiously.

She sat down in the chair in front of his desk and smiled a bit desperately. "Hi. I thought I would keep you company for a while."

"Why?"

"Do I need a reason?"

Apparently that question meant something different to him because he carefully put the pen back in its holder, set his half-moon glasses on the desk, leaned back in his chair, and stared at the study door before fixing that stare on her.

"If you're intending to watch me do paperwork, would you like to move that chair behind the desk?" he asked mildly.

That would put him between her and any irate male—namely Daemon—who might come through the door. "What a marvelous idea," Surreal said. She picked up the chair and brought it around the desk.

Before she could sit down, Saetan picked the chair up again and moved it closer to the bookcases that filled the back of the alcove. "Sit down," he said as he walked his fingers over the titles on one shelf. Selecting a book, he handed it to her. "This is a history of the Dea al Mon. You should learn a bit more about your mother's people. And it will be a reasonable excuse for why you're sitting there should anyone come in and wonder about it." He paused. Waited. "*Are* you expecting anyone?"

"No, I'm not expecting anyone."

"I see. In that case, I'll do a bit more paperwork while you catch your breath. Then we'll have a little chat."

Surreal gave him a weak smile. "It seems to be my day for little chats."

Fortunately, his response to that was muttered softly enough that she could pretend she didn't hear it.

2 / Kaeleer

Daemon stared at the empty corridor, shook his head, then kept walking. He'd spent the day walking, first on the grounds of the estate and now along the corridors of the Hall.

In the month that he'd been in Kaeleer, he'd come to love the place. Loved the feel of it, the sprawling mass of it, the furnishings in it.

And he was going to have to leave it.

He'd come to that conclusion after another long, sleepless night. Oh, the boyos had tried to help with their stories about pursuing their Ladies, but it was becoming painfully clear that there was no hope for him. Maybe if he wasn't wearing the Consort's ring, wasn't reminded every minute of the relationship it implied, he could accept being just a friend or—may the Darkness help him—another older brother. Maybe he could get past desire that had become painful and just . . .

Just what? Watch Jaenelle accept another man one day? Pretend he could quench the fire raging inside him?

A month wasn't long, was no time at all in the courtship dance. But he had already waited so long for Witch to appear. Then, when she'd offered him the Consort's ring, he had hoped . . .

He would talk to Saetan, give back the ring, see if there was a remote court somewhere in the Realm where he could serve out the required time in order to remain in Kaeleer. He would . . .

A door opened. Jaenelle stepped into the corridor. Her face turned pale at the sight of him.

He stopped walking. He might have to give up everything else, but he wouldn't give up loving her.

"Um. Daemon," Jaenelle said in an odd voice. "Do you have a minute?"

"Of course." It cost him, but he gave her a warm, reassuring smile and followed her into the room.

Standing out of reach, she stared at the floor, looking uneasy and intense—as if she was trying to find the right way to break bad news.

She's going to ask me to return the Consort's ring. As soon as that thought formed, Daemon ruthlessly buried any ideas about noble sacrifices. He wasn't going to give up that easily. And he wasn't going to return the Consort's ring without a fight.

"How hard can it be?" Jaenelle muttered.

Daemon just waited.

Letting out a big sigh, Jaenelle walked up to him, braced her hands on his shoulders, rose up on her toes a little, mashed her lips against his, then scampered back out of reach and eyed him warily.

Daemon wasn't sure what to say about this unexpected move. As a kiss, it left a lot to be desired. As a kiss from Jaenelle . . .

It took effort not to lick his lips.

"Are you nervous?" Jaenelle asked, still eyeing him warily.

He was going to have a little chat with Surreal about the uselessness of cryptic advice. But at least he had some idea what the right answer should be.

"Actually, I'm terrified that I may say or do something stupid and you won't want to kiss me again."

Maybe that was too much of the right answer. Now she looked worried. Then she threw up her hands in a gesture of exasperated helplessness.

"I don't know what I'm doing," she almost wailed. And then added under her breath, "Surreal should have let me take notes."

Daemon clamped his tongue between his teeth. Yes, he really needed to have a little chat with Surreal.

Jaenelle began pacing. "It always sounds so easy in love stories."

"Kissing isn't difficult," Daemon said carefully.

She glared at him as she paced past him. "Lucivar said the same thing about cooking," she growled. "The wolves didn't even wait for it to come out of the oven before they were digging the hole to bury it."

That sounded like an interesting story. He'd have a little chat with Lucivar, too.

"Kissing isn't difficult," Daemon said firmly. "You just kissed me."

"Not very well," she grumbled.

Knowing better than to answer that, Daemon studied her. Frustration. Embarrassment. And an emotion that knocked the wind out of him—longing. "Why did you ask Surreal about kissing?"

"*She told you that?*"

"No, I guessed." And between overhearing Jaenelle's remark about taking notes and receiving Surreal's succinct instructions, it wasn't difficult to reach the correct conclusion.

Jaenelle grumbled and snarled a few comments in a language he thankfully didn't understand. Then, "I wanted to impress you, and I didn't want you to laugh."

"Laughing isn't what comes to mind at the moment," Daemon said dryly. He raked his fingers through his hair. "Sweetheart, if it's any comfort, I want to impress you, too."

"You do?" She sounded astonished.

He started to wonder what had happened in the past thirteen years that would make her so stunned by that idea—but he already knew. She had told him the first time he'd ended up in the misty place, when he'd tried to bring Witch back to heal her wounded body. When it came to physical pleasure, the males wanted to indulge themselves in the body without having to deal with the one who lived inside it. And Jaenelle, with the horrors of Briarwood in her past, would never yield that way.

"Yes, I do," he said.

She pondered this. "Kaelas is annoyed with you."

It seemed like an abrupt shift in topic—and not a welcome one. "Why?" he asked cautiously.

"Because I haven't been sleeping well lately and I keep kicking him. He's decided it's your fault."

Oh, wonderful. "I haven't been sleeping well either."

She turned away, looking distressed.

Enough, Daemon thought. It was more his fault than hers that they had struggled through the past month. Saetan had told him she'd never had a lover, and yet he'd expected an open-armed welcome to her bed. He had acted as if she were an experienced woman who would take advantage of his availability.

That had been his biggest mistake. Jaenelle didn't have it in her to take advantage of anyone who served in her court. Well, she had made the first stumbling move. Now it was his turn.

He loosened the choke-hold control on his sexuality just enough to produce a subtle feel in the air, without it being strong enough for her to recognize it.

"Come here," he said quietly.

Looking baffled, she obeyed.

Setting his hands lightly on her waist, he drew her close to him. "Kiss me again. Like this." He brushed his lips against hers, softly, delicately. "And this." He kissed the corner of her mouth. "And this." He kissed her throat.

She imitated each move—until she kissed his throat. When the tip of her tongue licked his skin, he tilted her head up, lightly fastened his mouth on hers, and kissed her in earnest. Kissed her with all the hunger that had been building inside him during the past month, during a lifetime. Kissed her while his hands roamed over her back and hips and delicately explored her breasts. Kissed her until she moaned. Kissed her until she opened for him and let his tongue dance with hers. Kissed her until her hands slid up his back and clamped on his shoulders. Kissed her until the moan turned into a hungry snarl and he felt her nails prick his skin through the shirt and jacket.

And then realized he had taken them farther than he had meant to right now. Returning his hands to her waist, he eased back to the light, easy kisses.

Sensing his withdrawal, she snarled again—and there was anger as well as hunger in the sound. "You don't want me?" she asked in her midnight voice.

He nudged her hips toward him just enough to prove his answer. "Yes, I want you." He gave in for one more moment, fastened his mouth on her neck and sucked hard enough to leave a love bite. Tearing his mouth away, he gave her little butterfly kisses from jaw to temple. "But this is just playtime, just an appetizer."

"Playtime?" Witch said suspiciously.

"Mmm," he replied, licking the spot on her forehead where the tiny spiral horn would be if they were in the abyss. "This isn't the right place for more than playtime."

"Why?"

"Because I'd like my first time to be in a bed."

Her anger vanished instantly. "Oh. Yes, that would be more comfortable," Jaenelle said.

Will you invite me to your bed tonight? He knew better than to ask so bluntly, but he also knew he *had* to ask. "May I come to you tonight?" Feeling her tense, he quickly pressed a finger against her lips. "No words. Just a kiss will be answer enough."

Her answer was everything he had hoped it would be.

3 / Kaeleer

Daemon braced his hands on the dresser and closed his eyes.

Breathe, damn you, he thought fiercely. *Just breathe.*

How in the name of Hell did men *do* this the first time? Maybe, for a youth, the thrill was enough to push him past the doubts. Maybe it was easier the first time when the woman wasn't quite so special—or when the next hour wouldn't determine whether the woman you desperately wanted would have you.

He knew dozens upon dozens of ways to kiss, to caress, to arouse a woman and make her crave having him in her bed.

He couldn't remember a single one.

Daemon straightened up, retied the belt on the robe he wore over silk pajama bottoms . . . and swore with heartfelt intensity.

He should have just followed where those kisses had been leading them this afternoon, should have given in to the hunger he had awakened in Jaenelle, should have acted instead of stepping back and giving himself the past several hours to think himself into a panic.

But, wanting more than sex for his own sake as well as hers, he *had* stepped back—and now sincerely hoped that when he walked into her bedroom . . .

He smiled at the bitter irony of it, that the one thing he had never done with a woman, the one thing he had never wanted to do and now wanted more than anything, was the one thing he might not be *able* to do.

What got him moving was the concern that if he delayed much longer, Jaenelle might perceive it as a kind of rejection.

When he tapped on the door between their bedrooms, he took the muffled sound for an invitation and went in.

The only light in the room came from the fire burning in the hearth and scented candles grouped here and there throughout the room. The covers of the huge bed were turned down. Covered dishes, two glasses, and a bottle of sparkling wine filled a table near the hearth.

Jaenelle stood in the middle of the room, twisting her laced fingers. The edge of what looked like a sheer nightgown made of black spidersilk peeked beneath the hem of a thick, shabby robe—one he imagined she wore on rainy evenings when she snuggled up in her room to read. She looked like a lost waif rather than a sex-hungry woman.

She studied him a moment. "You look like I feel."

"Sick and terrified?" He winced, wished he hadn't said that.

She nodded. "I thought . . . some food . . ." She glanced at the covered dishes and turned pale. Then she glanced at the bed and turned paler. "What are we going to do?" she whispered.

He hadn't done either of them any favors by giving them time to think. "Basics," he said. "We'll start with something extremely simple." He took a step forward and opened his arms. "A hug."

She considered this a moment. "That sounds easy enough," she said, and stepped into his embrace.

He closed his eyes and held her lightly. Just held her. Breathed in the scent of her.

After a while, his fingers flexed. There was a comforting appeal to the texture of her shabby robe, to the way her hair brushed against his hand.

His arms tightened, drew her closer as his hand stroked up and down her back, just for the simple pleasure of it.

She sighed. The tension in her muscles eased a bit, and she rested against him more fully.

He wasn't thinking of seduction when his hands began to wander over her—or when her hands hesitantly stroked him.

He wasn't thinking of seduction when his body delighted in how different the silky skin of her neck felt under his mouth compared to the robe beneath his hands.

He wasn't thinking of sex when he opened his robe and then hers so that only that film of spidersilk separated skin from skin. Or when even the spidersilk no longer separated them.

He wasn't thinking of sex when his mouth settled over hers and he sent them both sliding into dark, hot desire.

And by the time he found himself in bed, listening to her purr with pleasure while he moved inside her, he wasn't able to think at all.

4 / Terreille

Dorothea held up a letter. "It seems Kartane has become acquainted with Lord Jorval and Lord Hobart."

Hekatah's lips curved in an awful grin. "Such useful males. One gathers Kartane got no satisfaction from the High Lord."

"It appears not," Dorothea replied, striving to sound indifferent while the fury of Kartane's betrayal singed her blood. "He suggests that Lord Hobart would welcome any assistance Hayll can provide to wrest Glacia away from the bitch-Queen niece. He will remain in Little Terreille to act as a liaison."

"It sounds as if your son finally understands to whom he owes his loyalty."

Dorothea crushed the letter. "He's not my son. Not anymore. He's just a tool like any other."

5 / Kaeleer

Lucivar walked to the far end of the low-walled garden that bordered one side of his home. Marian was reading a bedtime story to Daemonar, and the wolves had gathered in the room to listen, too, so he knew whatever Prothvar wanted to tell him wouldn't be overheard.

Two weeks ago, Saetan had sent Surreal back to Ebon Rih with a terse—and oddly harried—note, bluntly telling him to stay away from the Hall. The only reason he had obeyed was because Saetan had signed it as the Steward of the Court. After two weeks of silence, Andulvar, as Master of the Guard, had sent Prothvar to the Hall to request more information from the Steward. Now Prothvar was here, wanting to see him away from anyone. "Problem?" Lucivar asked quietly.

Prothvar's teeth gleamed as his mouth curved in a feral smile. "Not as long as you stay away from the Hall. I gathered it's rather uncomfortable living there right now if you wear Jewels darker than the Red."

"Mother Night," Lucivar muttered, rubbing the back of his neck. What in the name of Hell had happened? "Maybe the High Lord should send Daemon here for a while."

"Oh, I don't think it would be wise to try to shift Daemon away from the Hall."

Lucivar just stared at Prothvar for a moment. Then he grinned. "Well, it's about time."

"For both of them."

"So why does Saetan have his back up?"

"Because, despite Daemon's efforts to shield the bedroom, the . . . um . . . revelry tends to leak through the shields and makes the darker-Jeweled residents itchy. And neither of them wants to broach the subject with Jaenelle to ask *her* to create the shields since she's happily oblivious to anything but her Consort at the moment—and Saetan, not to mention Daemon, wants to keep it that way."

"Well," Lucivar said blandly, "if Saetan needs a respite from the frolic going on in the Hall, he could always spend an evening—or two—with Sylvia."

"Now, Lucivar," Prothvar scolded, "you know they're just friends."

"Of course they are." Noticing the moon, Lucivar did a quick mental tally, then gave Prothvar a sharp look. "Has anyone talked to Daemon about drinking a contraceptive brew?"

"That was taken care of. I had the impression that Daemon would welcome a child in the future, but, right now, he wants to enjoy his Lady's bed."

"In that case, Saetan should have a few days' reprieve fairly soon." Lucivar glanced back at the lights shining from the windows of his home and thought about enjoying his own Lady's bed as soon as Daemonar was asleep. But he asked politely, "Do you want to come in? I have some yarbarah."

"Thanks, but no," Prothvar replied. "I still have to report to Andulvar." He said good night, spread his dark wings, and vaulted into the night sky.

As Lucivar walked back to his home, a lone wolf howled. He grinned. Since the sound was coming from the direction of Falonar's eyrie, he didn't have to ask where Surreal was spending the night.

So Surreal was snuggled up with Falonar, Jaenelle was snuggled up with Daemon, and Marian . . .

When he entered the eyrie, she was standing in the kitchen doorway. She smiled in that quiet way that always excited his body and thrilled his heart.

"I was going to make some tea," she said. "It's cold tonight."

He returned the smile, then gave her a long, very thorough kiss. "I have a better way to warm you up."

6 / Kaeleer

The Arachnian Queen floated in the air in front of her tangled web of dreams and visions—the web she had linked to the web Witch had spun. The cold season was almost upon them. It was time for the Dream Weavers to settle into the caves and burrows, but she needed to see this web once more . . . just to be sure.

She studied Witch's tangled web first.

One small thread was dark, dark, dark. The first death.

There would be more. Many more.

Then she studied her own tangled web.

But not until the warming earth season. Even humans tended to remain in their lairs during the cold season.

So then. She could settle into her own lair in the sacred cave where she would rest and dream the soft dreams. When the seasons turned again, she would speak to the brown dog, Ladvarian. He was the link between kindred and human Blood. The kindred obeyed him and humans listened to him. And she needed him for what had to be done.

Because when the earth warmed next time, she would need all her strength and skill—and all the strength and skill the brown dog would gather for her—in order to save Kaeleer's Heart.

PART II

CHAPTER ELEVEN

1 / Kaeleer

After tucking the note in the center drawer, Morton locked his desk and frowned. It troubled him that the Sanctuary Priestess hinted at deep concerns but said nothing to the point—especially since that Sanctuary contained a Dark Altar, one of the thirteen Gates that linked the Realms of Terreille, Kaeleer, and Hell.

There had been several troubled—and troubling—messages from the Priestess over the winter months. Supplies missing. Voices late at night. Indications that the Gate had been opened without the Priestess's knowledge or consent.

Of course, the woman had reached an age where insignificant memories might slip away without being noticed. There were reasonable explanations for all the concerns. The supplies might have simply gotten used up but weren't replaced. The young Priestess-in-training might have taken a lover and the late-night voices were an assignation. The Gates . . .

That was the item that troubled him—and troubled Karla, too. Were some Terreilleans using the Gate in Glacia to slip into Kaeleer instead of enduring the service fairs? There had always been a few who, by luck or some instinct, had managed to light the black candles in the right order and speak the right spell to open a Gate between the Realms. It was even said in stories that the power contained in those ancient places would sometimes recognize a spirit's need to go home and open the Gate into the right Realm whether the person knew the spell or not. More likely, that person had found the key in some old Craft text. But the other made a better story for the telling during the long winter nights.

So he would go to that little village near the Arcerian border and talk to the Priestess.

Morton checked his pockets to make sure he had a clean handkerchief and a few silver marks so that he could buy a bit of dinner and a round at the tavern. Last, he used the lightest touch of Craft to make sure his Opal Jewel was linked to the Ring of Honor around his organ.

He smiled. Ever since Jaenelle had given the coven similar Rings, the males in the First Circle, by unspoken consensus, had begun wearing theirs all the time. That extra way of being able to decipher feminine moods had annoyed the witches as much as it had pleased the males.

Morton paused at his door, then shook his head. There was no reason to bother Karla. He would go to the village, talk to the Priestess, and then report to his cousin.

Besides, he thought as he left the mansion that was the Queen's residence, Karla's moontime was giving her more discomfort than usual this month. And she'd had minor illnesses on and off all winter—sniffles, a "weather ache" in her joints, light touches of flu. The two Healers who served in Karla's court couldn't find anything wrong that would account for this sudden vulnerability. They had suggested that, perhaps, she had been working too hard and was just worn down. She had dismissed that, saying caustically that she, too, was a Healer, and a Gray-Jeweled one at that. If something was wrong, wouldn't she know it?

Of course she would. But ruling a Territory that had people who still supported Lord Hobart and his ideas of how Blood society *should* be, Karla might ignore a great deal in order to appear invulnerable. But if it was a more serious illness, she would tell *him,* wouldn't she? She wouldn't use Craft to hide an illness from other Healers instead of getting help, would she?

Knowing the answer to *that,* Morton swore. Well, Jaenelle was making her spring tour of the Territories and would be in Scelt in a couple of days. He would send a message to her through Khardeen, formally requesting her services as a Healer on Karla's behalf.

Having made that decision, he caught one of the Winds and rode that psychic path through the Darkness to the Priestess's village.

2 / Kaeleer

Despite his kitten's grumble-growl impatience, Kaelas kept to an easy trot. After all, the kitten was only half his size and had half the stride. Even at this easy pace, KaeAskavi had to run every few steps in order to keep up with him.

This journey pleased him because he had never known his own sire. That had not been the Arcerian way. A small coven of Arcerian witches might den near each other for protection and for the different Craft skills each one knew. But the males had been on the outside, viewed as a threat once the kittens were born.

It was true that the Arcerian males who weren't kindred had been known to kill their own kittens, and being kindred didn't eliminate feline instinct or behavior. But the kindred males had resented this exclusion—especially the Warlord Princes. They were allowed to leave meat near their mates' dens, and they could watch their kittens from a distance, but they had never been allowed to play with them or even be the ones to teach them about hunting and Craft.

Having been raised by the Lady and having lived among her human kin, he had resented the exclusion even more. Other kindred males weren't excluded. And human males certainly weren't. They were allowed to play with their kittens and groom them and teach them.

So he had brought his mate to the Hall shortly after Lucivar's kitten had been born. She had recognized another predator, even if he did have wings and only two legs. She had watched Lucivar handle his young one. She had watched the High Lord. And she had observed the human she-cat's—and the Lady's—approval of having the human kitten handled by these full-grown males.

Because of that visit, and because she had felt honored that the Lady had done the naming of her kitten—a name that, in the Old Tongue, meant White Mountain—his mate had warily allowed him into the den soon after KaeAskavi had been born.

So his kitten was learning the Arcerian way of hunting, and the human ways that Lucivar had quietly taught *him*. That much exposure to humans had whetted KaeAskavi's curiosity about humans—which brought them to the reason for this journey.

While on a solitary prowl, KaeAskavi had wandered too close to a human village in Glacia and had met a human she-kitten. Instead of being afraid of a large predator, she had been delighted with him, and they became friends. After many secret meetings throughout the summer and early winter, the she-cats, both human and feline, had found out about the friendship—and neither had been pleased.

So KaeAskavi had turned to him, wanting his approval of the friendship to this young human female.

In a way that his mate never would, Kaelas could understand his kitten's fascination with the human she-kitten. KaeAskavi was a Warlord Prince, and Warlord Princes found it harder to do without female companionship. It would be many many seasons before KaeAskavi or the little female would look for a mate. If the she-kitten was a suitable friend, why not let them have each other for companions?

Not that he particularly liked humans. He had never forgotten the hunters who had killed his own dam. But some humans were capable of being more than just meat. The ones who belonged to the Lady, for instance. And the Lady's mate. Despite having only two legs and small fangs, there was much that was feline in that one, and he approved.

So he would look at this little female, and, if he thought she could be accepted by the kindred, he would ask the Lady to look at her, too. The Lady would know if this was a proper friend for his kitten.

Suddenly, the wind shifted so that it was coming from the village, still a mile away.

Kaelas froze. Blood and death scented the air.

Della! KaeAskavi lunged forward.

With one swipe, Kaelas bowled the kitten over.

When blood and death are in the air, you do not run toward it, Kaelas said sternly.

Della's village!

Using Craft, Kaelas probed the area around them. The season humans called spring had already come to other lands, but here winter still had fangs—and deep snow.

Make a den. Stay hidden, Kaelas ordered.

KaeAskavi snarled, but immediately rolled to a submissive posture when Kaelas stepped toward him.

I can fight, KaeAskavi said defiantly.

You will hide until I call you. Kaelas waited a moment. *What does the kitten's den look like?*

From KaeAskavi's mind, he received an image of a small human den, open ground, and then a thick stand of trees where KaeAskavi had waited for his friend.

Stay here, Kaelas said. *Make the den.*

Kaelas didn't wait to see if KaeAskavi would obey him. Wrapping himself in a sight shield and air walking so that he left no prints in the snow, he headed for the village, his full, ground-eating stride covering the distance within minutes.

The air near the village smelled of fear and desperation as well as blood and death. His sharp ears picked up the sounds of fighting, the clash of human weapons.

He cautiously used Craft to probe the village and bared his fangs in a silent snarl as he detected a Green-Jeweled Warlord Prince. Something about that one's scent . . .

Reaching a spot in the trees that looked directly on the back of the she-kitten's den, he heard a female scream and a male's roar. Then a window opened. A young human female climbed out the window and jumped into the snow. But when she tried to rise, she fell again, lame.

Kaelas burst out of the trees, charging toward the spot where the she-kitten lay at the same time an Eyrien Warlord came around the corner of the house. Spotting the she-kitten, the Eyrien raised his bloody weapon and moved forward for the kill.

The human male sensed no danger until eight hundred pounds of hatred slammed into him.

Kaelas bit off the arm that held the weapon while his claws tore open the belly. One blast of psychic power burned out the human's mind, finishing the kill.

He paused to bite some clean snow. Like its psychic scent, there was something about this human that tasted like bad meat.

He shook his head, then turned toward the girl, who was staring at the dead male. *Little one,* he growled.

She pushed herself up and looked around desperately. "KaeAskavi?"

Kaelas, he said. With the same gentleness he used with his own kitten, he seized her by the middle and loped off with her, heading for the shelter of the trees.

She made no sound. She didn't struggle. He approved of her courage. And now she was an orphan, as he had once been.

Choosing a spot where the snow had drifted deep, he set the girl down on air, quickly dug a small den, set the girl inside it, then covered up most of the entrance. *Stay,* he ordered.

She curled up in a small, shivering ball.

He loped back to the human den and passed through the wall next to the window the girl had come from. The room smelled of her—and other things, bad things.

The door leading into the rest of the den was open. He could see a bloody female arm. Sensing no life, he didn't bother to go over and sniff her to be sure.

He wished Ladvarian was there with him. Despite living almost all of his life among humans, he didn't understand them as well as the dog did. The dog would have known what the little female needed most.

He thought for a moment. She would need human fur. Using Craft, he opened the drawers and wardrobe, and vanished everything inside them.

What else would Ladvarian bring? Looking around the room, he vanished the puffy bedcovering that smelled of feathers. The kitten could be wrapped in that and kept warm. The urgent need to leave this place pushed at him, but he thought for a moment more.

Kindred had little use for things, but . . .

He saw it, lying next to the bed. At first, he felt blind hatred, but when he went over to sniff the white toy cat, he realized it had been made from fluffy cloth and not Arcerian fur as he'd first thought. It smelled strongly of the she-kitten—and, fainter, the she-cat's smell was there, too. And there was a psychic smell on it, a smell he associated with the Lady. The High Lord had called it love.

Vanishing the toy, he moved cautiously toward the open door. The dead female had a knife still clutched in one hand. She had fought a stronger male in order to save her kitten—as his own dam had fought against the hunters so that he could escape.

He thought, looking at her, that if she could know her kitten was safe and protected, she wouldn't mind the little female being among the Arcerian cats now.

Passing through the back wall of the house, he stopped near the dead Eyrien male. Using Craft, he passed the remains through the first few inches of snow, then pushed them down deep. The snow was stained with blood and gore, but he didn't think anyone would be looking for this one right away. And until they dug up the body, they wouldn't know that the human hadn't been killed by one of his own kind.

Hurrying back to the trees, Kaelas summoned KaeAskavi. *Come quickly . . . and silently.*

Reaching the makeshift den, he dug out the entrance. Calling in the puffy bedcovering, he laid it on the snow, using two spells he had learned from the Lady—a warming spell on the inside and a spell to keep the covering dry on the outside. Lifting out the she-kitten, he awkwardly wrapped her in the covering.

She just stared.

Feeling uneasy, he sniffed her carefully. She wasn't dead, but he knew those staring, unseeing eyes weren't good.

Sensing KaeAskavi's approach, he lifted his head. He could detect the faint shadowing of the lighter-Jeweled sight shield, and softly growled approval.

Della! KaeAskavi sniffed the bundled female.

Take the she-kitten to my mate, Kaelas said. *Use the Winds as soon as you reach a thread you can ride. The little one needs help quickly.*

My dam will not accept a human kitten in her den, KaeAskavi protested.

Tell her the human she-cat fought against hunters to save the kitten—and died.

KaeAskavi stood perfectly still for a moment, then said sadly, *I will tell her.* Carefully gripping the covering with his teeth, he trotted off with the she-kitten.

Kaelas waited, keeping track of them through a psychic thread. When he felt KaeAskavi catch the Wind that would take the young cat closest to the home den, he turned back to the village.

3 / Kaeleer

The Green-Jeweled Eyrien Warlord Prince looked upon the carnage with satisfaction. This Gate was now secured for the Dark Priestess's use. She had already selected the sixty pale-skinned, fair-haired people who would replace the ones he and his men had just slaughtered—people she had acquired at the last couple of service fairs. As long as the village looked inhabited and the people appeared to be going about their usual business, he doubted anyone would give any of them a second look. And if a visitor *should* know the village well enough to realize that the people were all strangers, what was one more corpse?

He turned as the Warlord who was his second-in-command approached. "Did that old bitch Priestess send the message?"

The Warlord nodded. "Sent to Lord Morton, the Glacian Queen's cousin and First Escort."

"And he usually responds to those messages?"

"Yes. And he usually comes alone."

"Then we'd better figure on having company soon. Assign five men with longbows to take up a position behind the landing web."

The Warlord studied the carnage. "If Morton sees this, he might just catch the Winds again and go back to report."

"Then I'll just have to make sure I provide a strong enough lure to get him off the landing web but still within easy range of the bowmen," the Warlord Prince said. "The old Priestess is dead?"

"Yes, Prince."

He heard a faint, pain-filled cry. "And the young Priestess?"

The Warlord smiled viciously. "She's getting the appropriate reward for betraying her own people."

4 / Kaeleer

Daemon followed Khardeen into the house. "It was kind of you to invite me to dinner."

"Kindness has nothing to do with it," Khary replied. "There's no sense having you rattle around by yourself while you're waiting for Jaenelle."

He'd accompanied her for much of the Spring visit to the Kaeleer Territories, but when it came time to visit the kindred, she had gently but firmly suggested that he go on to Scelt, where she would meet him. They would spend a few days here before visiting the rest of the Territories on this side of the Realm. "Well, you didn't have to give up an afternoon to show me around Maghre. I could have wandered about the village by myself."

"That wasn't kindness either," Khary said after requesting coffee and cakes. He settled into a comfortable chair by the fire. "It got me out of the house. As for dinner, it'll be a pleasure talking to someone who isn't going to snarl at me because of a queasy stomach."

"Is Morghann feeling all right otherwise?" Daemon asked, taking the other chair.

"Oh, she's doing fine for a dark-Jeweled witch in the early stages of pregnancy. Or so Maeve tells me often enough." Khary's smile was a bit rueful.

"But a Territory Queen who's suddenly restricted to basic Craft while she carries a babe is not a Lady with a smooth temper."

"Since you both had to stop drinking the contraceptive brew for this to happen, you're not entirely to blame," Daemon said with a smile.

"Ah, but I'm not the one who loses my breakfast. That seems to make a difference. And there are other—frustrations—for her at the moment. You didn't hear the tussle this morning? I'm surprised since your house is barely a half mile from ours. I was sure all of Maghre heard her shouting this morning."

"At you?"

"No, thank the Darkness. At Sundancer." After thanking the maid who brought the tray, Khary poured the coffee. "Morghann wanted to go riding this morning. Maeve, who's the Healer in Maghre, had said it was fine. *Jaenelle* had said it was fine as long as Morghann felt well enough."

"But?" Daemon said, the coffee cup halfway to his lips.

"Sundancer didn't think it was fine. He said that since mares in foal weren't ridden, he didn't think a human mare in foal should ride."

"Oh, dear," Daemon said—and then laughed. "No wonder you wanted to get out of the house."

The door opened. Morghann scowled at the tray, then at Khary. But she smiled at Daemon.

Setting his cup down, he rose to give her a kiss. In the months since he'd come to Kaeleer, he'd learned the value of these little gestures of affection—and he'd learned to take pleasure in them.

Khary, he noticed with some amusement and a good dollop of sympathy, had also risen but had wisely not tried to approach his wife.

A maid appeared at the door. "Would you be wanting a cup of that herbal tea Maeve made up for you, Lady Morghann?"

"I suppose," Morghann growled.

Giving Khary a quick glance, Daemon put on his best smile. "Darling," he said to Morghann, "I'm so glad you joined us."

"Why?" Morghann said darkly as she took a seat.

"Because Jaenelle's birthday is in a couple of months, and I wanted your advice about a gift."

As they discussed ideas, Morghann became involved enough not to notice she was drinking a Healer's tea instead of coffee. She even nibbled a little piece of nutcake—which meant the men could have some without having the tray dumped over their heads.

At the end of an hour, Morghann rose. "I have some correspondence to take care of. I'll see you at dinner?"

"I look forward to it," Daemon replied.

She kissed his cheek—and then gave Khary a more generous kiss.

Khary waited a minute after the door had closed behind her. He lifted his coffee cup in a salute. "That was very well done, Prince Sadi. My thanks."

Daemon lifted his cup in response. "It was my pleasure, Lord Khardeen."

5 / Kaeleer

Morton took a couple of steps away from the landing web and froze, unable to take his eyes off the bodies lying in the snow.

What in the name of Hell had happened?

He felt a mild hum from his Ring of Honor, almost like a question. That snapped him out of his shock enough to create an Opal shield. He almost activated the shield in the Ring, then hesitated. That would summon the other boyos—and alarm Karla. He didn't want to do either of those things. Not yet.

He tried probing the area, but didn't pick up anything that would lead him to believe he was in danger. But he *did* sense the presence of several living people.

His first reaction was to rush forward to help the survivors. Then his training kicked in. Whatever had happened here was more than he could handle alone. And now that he'd been here for a minute, something more than the slaughter felt *wrong* about this place.

He took a step back, intending to catch the Winds, head for the nearest village, and bring back help.

As he took another step back, an Eyrien came around the corner of a building and saw him.

"Lord Morton?" the Eyrien called.

Morton didn't recognize the Green-Jeweled Warlord Prince. He tensed, ready to catch the Winds and run.

"Lord Morton!" The Eyrien raised a hand and hurried toward him. "Thank the Darkness, you got Yaslana's message!"

That name was enough to catapult Morton a few feet toward the Eyrien. "What happened here?"

"We're not sure," the Eyrien answered, stopping a few feet away. "Yaslana found tracks heading away from the Dark Altar. He took some of the men and followed them." He looked over Morton's shoulder, his face stamped with concern. "Didn't you bring any Healers?"

"No, I—"

It happened too fast. A blast of the Eyrien's Green-Jeweled power shattered his Opal shield at the same moment three arrows pierced his body. The Ebony shield in Jaenelle's Ring of Honor snapped up around him. Two more arrows hit the shield and turned to dust.

He used Craft to remain standing and cursed himself for a thrice-times fool for not activating the shield in the first place. But there was nothing they could do to him now, not even stop him from walking or crawling back to the landing web and riding the Winds away from there. And the wounds, while painful, weren't that serious. He had an arrow in each leg and one in the left shoulder, but it was high enough . . .

He felt a deadly cold filling his limbs and knew what it had to be. Poison on the arrow tips. But how virulent a poison?

He saw the answer in the Eyrien's cruel smile.

He fell to his knees. No time to give all the warnings he needed to give. No time. So he focused on sending a warning to the person who had always mattered the most to him.

As the body's death closed in on him, he gathered his strength and sent one word. *KARLA!*

6 / Kaeleer

Karla sat at her dressing table, one hand braced on the table, the other pressed against her abdomen. The cramps didn't usually last this long, and they weren't usually this painful.

"Here you are," Ulka said sympathetically, setting a steaming mug on the dressing table. "This moontime brew will make you feel different in no time."

"Thanks, Ulka," Karla murmured. She had accepted Ulka into her Third Circle for the same reason she had accepted other witches from Glacia's aristo families—to placate them after she had exiled her uncle, Hobart. And while she didn't personally like Ulka, she had to admit the woman had been a solicitous companion this winter, fussing a little too much over the minor illnesses but having a good instinct of when to gossip and when to stay quiet.

As soon as the brew cooled enough, Karla took a large swallow. Making a disgusted face, she set the mug down. The brew had an odd, rancid taste. Hell's fire, had some of the herbs gotten moldy or gone bad somehow? Then again, a lot of things hadn't tasted quite right to her all winter. Or maybe she'd just gotten spoiled by the delicious-tasting brews Jaenelle made. It didn't matter how it tasted. It wasn't going to ease the pain if it sat in the cup.

As she reached for the mug again, she looked in the mirror. A chill ran through her when she saw the watchful anticipation in Ulka's eyes. "You poisoned it, didn't you?" Karla said flatly.

"Yes," Ulka said, sounding smug and pleased.

Karla felt her body sluggishly gathering itself to fight off the poison. Because she was a Black Widow, she had a stronger tolerance for poisons than other people would have, but even a Black Widow could succumb to a poison her body couldn't recognize or tolerate.

As she stared at the other woman's reflection, she finally knew. All the minor illnesses, all the foods that had tasted a little off. And Ulka always there, being so helpful, acting so concerned. "You've slipped mild poisons into a lot of things this winter."

"Yes."

Poisons which had weakened her body but never made her ill enough to become suspicious—despite having been warned of her own death in the tangled web she'd created last fall. Oh, she'd been careful. She knew too much about poisons not to be. The fact that she hadn't been able to detect the poisons meant that whatever plants had been used weren't native to Glacia. She would have recognized one of *those* instantly, no matter how it was disguised.

With effort, Karla got to her feet. One moment her legs were full of fiery spikes, the next they were numb. She flooded her body with her Gray strength, accepting the pain her own power caused during her moontime in order to fight the poison.

As one staggering wave of pain ripped through her, she felt the Ebony shield in the ring Jaenelle had given her surround her.

"Why?" Karla asked. How could she have misjudged this bitch so badly? What had she missed?

Ulka pouted. "I thought I would be an important Lady in your court. I should have been in your First Circle, not the *Third*."

"A witch who would poison her Queen isn't suitable to serve in the First Circle," Karla said dryly. "It's a question of loyalty."

"I *was* loyal," Ulka snapped. "But being loyal to you didn't get me anywhere. And then I got a better offer. Once you're gone and Lord Hobart controls Glacia again, I *will* be an important Lady."

"All you'll be is some man's whore," Karla said flatly.

Ulka's face became ugly. "And you'll be dead! And don't think they won't finish the kill to make sure they're rid of *all* of you!"

The ring Jaenelle had given her produced a sharp, warning tingle seconds before Morton's warning cry filled her mind.

KARLA!

Morton? Morton!

Nothing. An emptiness where someone had been for as long as she could remember.

Another kind of cold filled Karla—a cold that fed her body, gave her strength. "You killed Morton," she said too quietly.

"*I* didn't," Ulka replied. "But he's dead by now."

The bladed Eyrien stick Lucivar had given her was in her hands and whistling through the air before Ulka had time to realize the danger. The blades, honed to a killing edge, swept through Ulka's leg bones as easily as they swept through the woman's wool dress.

Blood gushed. Ulka fell, screaming.

Karla staggered, braced herself. She couldn't use her body this way and fight the poison long enough for . . .

For what? With Morton dead, who would be able to reach her fast enough? No matter. She would fight to live for as long as she could. And she had more power at her disposal than her enemies had imagined since she didn't have to use her Gray Jewels to shield herself.

Looking down at Ulka, Karla raised the bladed stick. "Well, bitch, I may not be able to finish the kill, but I can make damn sure you're of no use to anyone when you become demon-dead."

She cut off Ulka's hands, then her head. The last stroke tore through the belly and severed the spine.

Karla staggered back a few steps, away from the growing pool of blood. Sinking to the floor, she carefully stretched out, her right arm wrapped around her belly, her left hand clamped around the bladed stick.

She had seen her own death in her tangled web, and she'd done what she could to change that part of the vision. But if she had to die now, she would accept it.

Dark power washed over her, warming icy limbs. She felt a tendril of power wrap around her and recognized a healing thread helping her fight against the poison.

Cradled by Jaenelle's strength, she turned inward to concentrate on the battlefield her body had become.

7 / Kaeleer

Daemon snarled in frustration when he felt the tingling coming from Jaenelle's Ring of Honor. He hadn't yet learned how to interpret all the information that could be absorbed from the Ring. He recognized this particular sensation as a call for help, but had no idea where the call was coming from. "Do you—" he said, turning toward Khardeen.

The intense blankness in Khary's eyes, the sense of focused listening, stopped him from saying anything more.

"Morton," Khary said quietly. "And *Karla*." He lunged for the door.

Daemon grabbed him. "No. You're needed here."

"That's not the way it works," Khary said sharply. "When one of us needs help—"

"You all take the bait?" Daemon asked just as sharply. "You have a pregnant Queen who can't defend herself without risking a miscarriage. Your place is here. I'll take care of Karla—and Morton." He studied Khary. "Who else will have heard that call for help?"

"Everyone in the First Circle who lives in the western part of Kaeleer. The Ring has more of a range than if we were trying to reach someone on our own, but the alert wouldn't be felt beyond that. However, every male who felt that call for help will relay a warning through a communication thread to the First Circle within *his* range."

"Then relay this message to the First Circle as fast as you can: 'Stay put. Stand guard.' " Daemon paused. "And locate Jaenelle."

"Yes," Khary said grimly. "The Queens need to be protected. Especially her."

Satisfied, Daemon rushed out of the house and swore. He couldn't reach any of the Winds from here.

He started to run down the drive, then turned toward the sound of pounding hooves. Sundancer slid to a stop beside him.

I heard the call, Sundancer said. *You must ride the Winds?*

"Yes."

I can run faster. Mount.

Grabbing a fistful of Sundancer's mane, he swung up on the Warlord Prince's bare back.

It was a short but harrowing ride. The stallion chose the fastest route to reach the nearest Winds without regard for what lay in his path, and Daemon's legs were shaking when he slid off Sundancer's back. Before he could say anything, the stallion pivoted and was gone.

Fight well! Sundancer said as he raced back to Khary and Morghann's house.

"You can count on it," Daemon replied too softly. Catching the Black Wind, he headed for Glacia.

8 / Kaeleer

Kaelas made an effortless leap to the roof of a human den in time to see Morton fall. He snarled silently, the desire to attack warring with the instinct for caution. Slipping down to the depth of his Red Jewel, where he couldn't be detected by the winged males who were there, he opened his mind and carefully let a psychic tendril drift toward Morton.

The first thing he sensed was the Lady's shield. That wasn't a problem. The Lady had made a Ring of Honor for the kindred males, too. So he had the same protection and, more important right now, he had the means to safely slip past that shield.

The moment he did, he knew Morton's body was dead, but he could still sense Morton, very faintly, inside it. Morton was a Brother in the Lady's court, and the Brothers looked after each other. That was important. So he would get his Brother away from the enemy and then decide what to do next.

Looking in the opposite direction, he saw the Sanctuary that held the Dark Altar. Near it was a large, old tree that wouldn't wake again. The pale humans would have cut it down and burned it in their fires. They wouldn't need it now.

Using Craft, he opened the Sanctuary door, letting it swing as if it hadn't been latched properly.

Leaping from the roof, he circled around the backs of the human dens, air walking so that he would leave no tracks. Just because the sight shield made him invisible was no reason to be careless. Playing "stalk and pounce" with Lucivar had taught him that.

Thinking of Lucivar, he remembered something else: never show your full strength to an enemy until it was needed.

His Birthright Jewel was the Opal. Morton's Jewel of rank was the Opal. Yes, *that* might confuse the winged males.

Baring his teeth in what might have been a feline smile, Kaelas unleashed a burst of Opal strength at the dead tree. It exploded. Flaming branches soared through the air in all directions. Another burst of power shattered windows in the dens near the Sanctuary. Another burst of power sent enough snow into the air to form a small blizzard. The last controlled burst of power slammed the Sanctuary door.

The Green-Jeweled Eyrien Warlord Prince had spun around at the first blast, his face twisted with fury. Other males were shouting. When the Sanctuary door slammed, the Eyrien started running, shouting orders.

"What about that bastard?" one of the other men called out.

The Warlord Prince hesitated for a moment. "Leave him. He's not going anywhere. We'll finish the kill after we take care of our new guests."

Kaelas moved forward in stalk position, using all of his senses to keep track of the winged humans. Then, a burst of speed brought him to Morton.

One sniff of the body had him backing away, confused. Morton smelled like poisoned meat. He did not want to set his teeth in poisoned meat. But he had to get Morton away from the winged males.

Moving forward again, he brushed against the Lady's shield, felt it recognize itself in the Ring of Honor he wore and let him in. He put a snug Opal shield around Morton's left arm. When he took that arm between his teeth, the Opal shield was between him and the poisoned meat. Satisfied, he used Craft to float Morton on the air, expanded his sight shield to cover both of them, then raced for the trees.

When he was among the trees, he slowed slightly, but didn't stop until he reached the hiding den KaeAskavi had dug. Releasing Morton's arm, he studied the den. The human would fit easily enough without the pointed sticks—the arrows—poking out. But the Healer would need the stick part to remove the arrow. Wouldn't she?

After a little thought, he used Craft to shear the shafts in half. He tucked Morton into the den and placed the sheared-off shafts next to him. Then he paused again.

He had never seen human Blood become demon-dead. He didn't know how long it would take for Morton to wake and reclaim the dead flesh. But he *did* know that when Morton woke and found himself in a strange place, he would wonder if the enemy had put him there.

Kaelas pressed a forepaw into the snow near Morton's head, leaving a deep imprint, then put a shield over the print, so that it couldn't be brushed away carelessly. Morton would see the print and understand.

Pleased that he had worked out the complicated thinking required to deal with humans, he covered up the den, leaving a small airhole. A dead human didn't need air, but the freshness would show Morton the easiest place to dig free.

Now to take care of the bad winged males.

After sending out a summons for the dark-Jeweled Arcerian Warlords and Warlord Princes to join him, Kaelas headed back to the village.

9 / Kaeleer

Ignoring the official landing web, Daemon dropped from the Winds as close as he could get to Karla's home. The moment he appeared on a street, he wrapped a Black sight shield, psychic shield, and protective shield around himself. He ran a couple of blocks, turned a corner, and stopped.

The street was full of struggling, fighting men. Blasts of Jeweled power made the air smell like lightning. Those who had already drained their Jewels, or had never worn them, were fighting with mundane weapons. He spotted some women, fighting desperately but ineffectively.

So familiar. He didn't need the whiff of rot present in some of the psychic scents to recognize Dorothea's hand in this. He'd seen it too many times in Terreille. Those whose ambition far outstripped their ability would sell their own people for Hayll's "assistance." The fighting would eliminate the strongest males and females, the ones best able to oppose Dorothea, and the ones who were left . . .

This time he didn't have to be subtle. This time he didn't have to dance around the agony Dorothea would inflict on him if she suspected his interference. But being subtle had become ingrained in him. Besides, a silent predator was the most feared.

Smiling a cold, cruel smile, Daemon slipped his hands into his trouser pockets and glided between clumps of fighters—invisible, undetectable— and left devastation in his wake.

He entered Karla's mansion. The fighting must have started here and spread into the street. He stepped over corpses, homed in on the psychic scents that had a flavor he associated with Dorothea, and killed those fighters so swiftly, so cleanly their opponents froze for a moment, stunned and confused.

A Warlord Prince wearing the badge of the Master of the Guard was fighting off other males near the staircase, using the last of his Jeweled strength to shield himself against three men who were still fresh.

Three flicks of Black power. Three men fell.

As he started up the stairs, Daemon saw the sharp hunter's look in the other Warlord Prince's eyes, saw the moment the man guessed something dangerous was climbing the stairs.

A White-Jeweled Warlord rushed at the Warlord Prince, forcing him to turn toward the enemy who was attacking.

Daemon climbed the stairs. Even exhausted, the Warlord Prince would have no trouble with the Warlord, and it would keep him occupied a little while longer.

No need to hunt for Karla's room. The Ring of Honor led him unerringly, the throbbing against his organ irritating him enough to hone a temper that had already risen to the killing edge.

The door stood open. He saw a hacked-up woman lying on a blood-soaked carpet. He saw five men sending blast after blast of power against the shield surrounding another woman. Karla.

He didn't know who the men were—and didn't care. Reaching up from the depth of the Black, he slipped under the men's inner barriers and unleashed iced rage, turning their brains into gray dust and consuming their psychic strength, finishing the kill.

He was across the room before they fell. Kneeling beside Karla, he dropped the sight shield and reached out cautiously.

The shield around her held a feral, deadly hunger.

Not sure how to get through the shield, and wondering what he might unleash if he did it incorrectly, Daemon took a deep breath and brought his hand a little closer.

A flick of power against his palm. A tasting. An acceptance.

His hand passed, unharmed, through the shield.

"Karla," he said as his hand closed on her arm. "*Karla.*" Her rasping effort to breathe told him she was still alive. But if she'd gone so deep into a healing sleep that she couldn't hear him . . .

"Kiss kiss," Karla rasped.

Relief washed through him. He leaned over her so that she could see him without trying to move her head. "Kiss kiss."

"Poisoned," she said. "Can't identify. Bad."

Pushing her robe aside, Daemon laid his left hand on her chest and sent out a careful psychic probe. His knowledge of healing Craft was limited, but he knew about poisons. And he recognized at least part of this one.

"Get your hand . . . off my . . . tit," Karla said.

"Don't be bitchy," Daemon replied mildly, probing a little more. Her body was fighting it far better than he would have thought possible, but she wouldn't survive without more help than he could give her. He hesitated. "Karla . . ."

"About . . . three hours left. Body . . . can't fight more . . ."

Riding the Black Winds, it had taken him almost two hours to get there from Scelt. Pandar and Centauran were closer, but he didn't know Jonah or Sceron as well as he knew Khardeen, and he didn't know if the satyr or centaur Healers could deal with this poison.

Besides, Jaenelle would most likely head for Scelt. And that decided him.

"I'm getting you out of here," he said as he started to lift her. Then he realized her hand was still clamped around the bladed stick. "Sweetheart, let go of the stick."

"Have to clean . . . the blades. Can't . . . put a weapon away . . . without cleaning the blades. Lucivar . . . would skin me."

Daemon almost gave her his succinct opinion about that, but glancing over his shoulder at the hacked-up woman, he swallowed any criticism he might have had about Lucivar's training methods. "I'll clean the blades. And I promise I'll never tell Lucivar you didn't do it yourself."

Karla's lips curved in the barest of smiles. "You'd be likable if . . . you weren't so *male*."

"My Queen likes me that way," Daemon said dryly. He vanished the bladed stick, carefully lifted Karla, and turned.

Her Master of the Guard blocked the doorway. "What are you doing with my Queen?"

"Taking her away from here," Daemon answered quietly. "She's been poisoned. She needs help."

"We have Healers."

"Would you trust them?" Daemon saw the moment's hesitation. "I have no quarrel with you, Prince. Don't force me to go through you."

The other man studied him, focused on the Black-Jeweled Ring. "You're Lady Angelline's Consort."

"Yes."

The man stepped aside. As Daemon passed him, he said quietly, "Please take care of her."

"I will." Daemon paused. "Have you seen Morton?"

The Master of the Guard shook his head.

There was no time to think about Morton or what might have happened to him. "If you see him, tell him I'm taking Karla to Scelt. Don't tell anyone *but* Morton."

The man nodded. "Come this way. There's a Craft-powered carriage out back. It'll get you to the Winds faster."

The Master of the Guard drove the carriage while Daemon held Karla, using those precious minutes to wrap Black shields around her to protect her during the ride on the Winds. They stopped a few feet from where he had landed.

"May the Darkness embrace you, Prince," the man said.

"And you." Wrapping his arms around Karla, Daemon caught the Black Wind and rode hard toward Scelt.

He stopped once, halfway there, to send a message to Khary. *I'm on my way back with Karla. She's been poisoned. We'll need a Healer and a Black Widow. The best you have.*

Jaenelle's on her way here, Khary replied.

That was all he needed to know. He caught the Black Wind again and continued the journey, knowing the sand in the hourglass was trickling away far too fast.

10 / Kaeleer

Sight shielded, Kaelas and twenty Arcerian males crouched on the roofs of the human dens, watching the bad winged males move around the village. Some of the dens had lights now that night had closed around them, and he could smell food cooking.

Meat? one of the Arcerian Warlords asked.

No, Kaelas replied. He felt a ripple of anger run through the other males. *The meat tastes bad.*

We have come for the hunt but will have no meat to bring back to the home dens? another male asked irritably.

We promised the Lady we wouldn't hunt human meat, a younger male said tentatively.

These males killed a male who belonged to the Lady, Kaelas said firmly. *They killed the pale humans who belonged to Lady Karla.*

Another ripple of anger, this time directed at the bad winged males. Arcerians didn't have much use for humans, but they liked Lady Karla and adored the Lady. For them, they would hunt and return to the dens without meat.

The wind shifted slightly, brought a different scent.

We will take the animals that belonged to the pale humans, Kaelas said. *The humans do not need them now. It will be payment for work.* He was pleased that he remembered that peculiar human idea. If the Lady snarled at him for taking animals from a human village, he could use those words.

Payment for work? a couple of males echoed. Then one of them asked, *This is a human thing?*

Yes. We kill these bad males, then we can take good meat back to the dens.

Satisfied, the Arcerians settled down to study their prey.

Kaelas watched the winged males for a minute. *We must hunt fast . . . and silent.*

Fast kills, the others agreed.

Kaelas watched the Green-Jeweled Warlord Prince walk to a den near the Sanctuary. *But not for that one.*

11 / Kaeleer

Jaenelle was waiting for him by the time Daemon reached Khary and Morghann's house.

"She's bleeding too much for this just to be moon's blood," he said abruptly as he rushed into the guest room, followed by Morghann, Khary, and Maeve, the village Healer. "And there's not much time left."

Jaenelle placed a hand on Karla's chest, her eyes focusing on something only she could see. "There's enough," she said too calmly.

Morghann laid a padding of towels on the bed.

Daemon gave her a cold stare as he laid Karla on the bed. Was the woman more worried about her precious linens than about a friend who had been poisoned?

"It'll disturb her less to change a towel than to change the linens," Morghann said quietly, her eyes clearly telling him she knew what he'd been thinking—and had been hurt by it.

There was no time for an apology. Morghann and Maeve stripped off the bloody nightgown and robe, and quickly wiped the blood off Karla's skin. Jaenelle paid no attention to the physical ministrations, remaining focused on the healing.

Daemon was about to tell her what he knew about the poison when he looked down at his blood-soaked sleeve. Memories of being soaked in Jaenelle's blood rushed at him. He ripped off the jacket, then the shirt. Khary took them and handed him a wet cloth.

As he scrubbed the blood off his skin, Jaenelle said, "There were two poisons used. I don't know one of them."

Handing the cloth back to Khary, Daemon moved to the bed. "One of them comes from a plant that only grows in southern Hayll."

Jaenelle looked up, her eyes blank and iced. "Do you know an antidote?" she asked with an odd calm that scared him.

"Yes. But the herbs I have are several years old. I don't know if they'll still be potent enough."

"I can make them potent enough. Make the antidote, Daemon."

"What about the other poison?" he asked as he started clearing a work space on the bedside table.

"It's witchblood."

A chill went through him. Witchblood only grew where a witch had been violently killed—or where she had been buried. Used as a poison, it was virulent and deadly—and usually undetectable.

"You can detect it?" Daemon asked cautiously.

"I can recognize witchblood in any of its forms," Jaenelle replied in her midnight voice.

Another memory rushed at him. Jaenelle staring at the bed of witchblood she had planted in an alcove on the Angelline estate. *Did you know that if you sing to them correctly, they'll tell you the names of the ones who have gone?*

Even dried into a poison, did the plants tell Witch the names of the ones who were gone?

Locking away the memories, along with his heart, Daemon concentrated on making the antidote.

"Maeve," Jaenelle said, "get some basic plasters ready. We'll have to draw out some of the poison. Morghann, I want you to leave the room. Don't come back for any reason until I tell you."

"But—"

Jaenelle just looked at her.

Morghann hurried out of the room.

"May I stay?" Khary asked quietly. "You three will be involved in the healing. You'll need a free pair of hands to fetch things."

"This won't be easy, Lord Khardeen," Jaenelle said.

Khary paled a little. "She's my Sister, too."

Jaenelle nodded her consent, then leaned over the bed and said so softly Daemon was sure he was the only one close enough to hear, "Arms or legs, Karla?"

The answer, if she got one, was private—Sister to Sister. But it began a healing so gruesome he desperately hoped he would never witness anything like it again.

12 / Kaeleer

Kaelas listened to the sounds coming from the room and snarled silently. The Green-Jeweled Eyrien Warlord Prince was mating with the pale female, the young Priestess. Her cries disturbed him. They were not like the sounds the Lady made with Daemon. There was fear and pain in *these* sounds.

He almost slipped through the Green shield the male had placed around the room, almost decided to repay Morton's death with a fast kill instead of the kind of death that was owed when the female cried, "But I helped you. *I helped you!*"

Remembering KaeAskavi's she-kitten, who was now an orphan, and all the other pale humans that had belonged to Lady Karla and were now dead, Kaelas took a step back. The female had fouled her own den, had brought in poisoned meat. She deserved this winged male for a mate.

Careful not to disturb the Green shield and alert the male, he placed a Red shield around the room, caging the humans. He added a Red psychic shield so that when the male noticed he was trapped, he wouldn't be able to warn the other winged males.

Slipping out of the building, Kaelas paused, listened. There were more winged males than cats, but that didn't matter. The Green-Jeweled Warlord Prince was the only one of the winged males who wore one of the dark Jewels, and he was already caged. Among the cats here, Kaelas was the only one who wore a Red Jewel, but the shields from the Opal, Green, and Sapphire Jewels the others wore would protect them while they attacked with teeth and claws.

Now, Kaelas said.

Silent, invisible, the cats spread out and went hunting.

CHAPTER TWELVE

1 / Kaeleer

Lucivar and Falonar stood back at a prudent distance and watched the women at archery practice. Hallevar stood a few feet behind the women, giving instructions that could be heard in the still morning air as clearly as the smack of sticks coming from the arms practice field.

The weather had turned overnight, bringing the warm promise of spring. It wouldn't last, but while it did, Lucivar intended to have the women on the practice field for a couple of hours every morning. This was the first day they were actually aiming an arrow at a target. Watching them would have been amusing if he hadn't felt so edgy.

A day and a half had passed since Daemon's order to "stay put and stand guard" had been relayed through the First Circle—an order which, a couple of hours later, had been reinforced by Jaenelle. The only other message he had received had been equally brief: Karla had been poisoned and Morton was missing.

He would have disregarded the order if Daemon hadn't been with Jaenelle, but he knew that if anyone could protect the Queen better than he could, it was the Sadist.

So he'd stayed . . . and watched . . . and waited.

Falonar huffed out a breath as a spattering of arrows made a pathetic attempt to reach the targets. "Do you really think they can do this?" he asked doubtfully.

Lucivar snorted. "During your first six months in the hunting camps, you couldn't hit anything smaller than the side of a mountain."

Falonar just looked at him. "But I didn't whine about taking up time that could be used to air out the bedding. What's the point of pretending they can use a—*shit*." That when a woman with a bow fully drawn started to turn toward Hallevar as he added instructions. Hallevar leaped forward and shoved her so that the arrow skittered along the grass instead of into the woman next to her.

Lucivar and Falonar both winced at the language Hallevar used to explain that little error.

"Do you see?" Falonar demanded.

"Hallevar didn't learn to leap like that because this was the first time someone had done something so stupid," Lucivar replied. He paused, then added, "What's really biting your ass about this?"

Falonar scuffed a boot over the ground. "If we aren't the warriors and protectors, we don't have much to offer—until a woman is looking for a stud. And that's not easy to stomach."

"Can you cook?" Lucivar asked mildly.

Falonar glared at him. "Of course I can cook. Any Eyrien who's been in the hunting camps knows how to do rough-and-ready cooking."

Lucivar nodded. "Then relax. Just because a woman knows how to catch her own dinner doesn't mean she's going to grow balls any more than you're going to grow tits just because you know how to cook it." He watched Surreal put an arrow into the outer ring of the target and smiled. "Do you want to go over and tell *her* you don't think she's capable of handling a bow?"

"Not while she's got a weapon in her hand," Falonar muttered.

They jumped when one of the women let out a loud yelp.

Lucivar relaxed when he noticed the way Hallevar was rubbing one hand over his mouth and the woman was surreptitiously rubbing her forearm against her right breast.

"Five minutes of free practice," Hallevar called before hurrying toward the other two men.

"What happened?" Falonar demanded.

"Damnedest thing," Hallevar said, breaking into a wide grin. "Didn't think to warn them about it 'cause . . . well, Hell's fire, I've never *had* to consider it before. How was I supposed to know you could catch a tit with a bowstring?"

"Catch a—" Falonar looked at the women—who had all turned to glare at the men. He looked at the ground and cleared his throat—several times. "Bet it stings."

Lucivar felt his jaw muscles cramp with the effort to keep from laughing. "Yes, I'm sure it does. I didn't think to warn Marian when I taught her, and I'd already worked with Jaenelle. But Marian's got . . . a bit more chest."

Falonar choked.

Hallevar just nodded solemnly. "That's a fine, respectful way to phrase it—especially when there's a handful of women out there who might just get mad enough to actually hit something if you phrased it any other way."

"Precisely," Lucivar said dryly. "Work them through one more quiver and—"

He was running toward the arms practice field before the first panicked scream could be drowned out by furious shouts. He leaped up on the low stone wall that separated the two fields. Ice formed around his heart when he saw Kaelas give a Green-Jeweled Eyrien Warlord Prince a casual swat that opened up the back of one thigh. The ice became a painful cage when he saw Rothvar and Zaranar running toward the stranger with weapons drawn.

NO! he shouted on a spear thread. *I'll gut any man who raises a weapon!*

They skidded to a stop, their shock at his order rivaling their fury. But they, and the other men on the practice field, obeyed.

"Help me!" the stranger yelled as he swung his war blade at Kaelas, trying to keep the cat in front of him while he limped backward toward the other men. "Damn you all to the bowels of Hell, *help me!*"

Lucivar turned, looked back at the women. *Marian, take all the women up to our eyrie. Close the shutters.*

Lucivar, what—

Do it!

He strode toward the loose circle of men, Falonar and Hallevar right behind him. A gut-sick satisfaction filled him as he watched how easily Kaelas dodged the stranger's attempts to counterattack—and he wondered what the other men would say if they knew *he* had been the one who had taught the cat how to move with and against human weapons.

As soon as the Eyrien shifted into a fighting stance, Kaelas charged. The speed and the sheer weight behind the charge knocked the man back several feet. The claws ripped open the Eyrien's shoulders and followed through down the arms, leaving them useless. The cat leaped away and began lazily circling a man barely able to get to his feet.

Falonar looked behind them and cursed softly, viciously. Turning and opening his wings to hide the practice field, he snarled, "Go back with the other women."

"Don't give me any of that—oh, shit," Surreal said as she dodged Falonar and got a good look at the man and cat.

Kaelas continued the light, almost playful swats, inflicting surface wounds that would slowly bleed out his prey. He continued until the Eyrien stranger spread his torn wings and tried to fly. The cat leaped with the man, then landed lightly. The man, with his back ripped open, fell heavily.

"Mother Night," Surreal whispered, "he's *playing* with that man."

"He's playing," Lucivar said grimly as nerves twisted his belly, "but it's not a game. This is an Arcerian execution."

Surreal understood before Falonar did. Lucivar saw her face tighten—and he saw her eyes fill with cool professional interest.

"Yaslana," Falonar warned.

Lucivar sensed the growing tension in the other men and knew it wouldn't be long before one of them disobeyed his order and joined the "fight." He started to move closer.

Kaelas must have sensed it, too, because the playfulness ended. The Eyrien stranger screamed as the claws ripped his chest open, ripped his thighs to the bone.

"Kaelas," Lucivar said firmly, "that's—" He felt the crackle of Red-Jeweled power as the paw lashed out again. The object flew at him so fast, he instinctively caught it before it slammed into his chest. For a second or two, Lucivar stared at the head that had been severed at the base of the neck. Then he dropped it.

"Mother Night," Surreal said softly.

The Eyrien's right hand, with its Green-Jeweled ring, sailed through the air and plopped on the ground next to the head.

With a full-throated snarl of rage, Kaelas gutted the man, then defecated in the open belly before moving away from the corpse. Finally, he looked at Lucivar. *That one is still inside . . . for the High Lord.*

Lucivar tried to swallow. Kaelas had deliberately not finished the kill. *Why?*

He killed Morton, Kaelas replied, making the effort to use a communication thread that could be heard by all the humans present. *And he killed the pale humans that belonged to Lady Karla.*

Fury washed through Lucivar, a cleansing fire. *Where?* An image appeared in his mind, oddly focused but clear enough for him to identify the place. *My thanks, Brother,* he said, using a spear thread directed specifically at the cat.

Kaelas leaped, caught the Winds, and disappeared.

"I've done a lot of things as an assassin," Surreal said, hooking her hair behind her ears, "but I've never shit on the body. Is that some kind of feline quirk?"

"It's the way Arcerians show contempt for an enemy," Lucivar said. He looked at Falonar, who seemed to be fighting not to be sick. A quick glance was enough to confirm that most of the men were doing the same, despite their experience on battlefields. "I don't recognize him. Do you?"

Falonar shook his head.

"I do," Rothvar said heavily as he approached them. "When he found out I was immigrating to Kaeleer, he offered me a place in his company. Said he wasn't going to have to lick any bitch's boots, that he'd be ruling a fine piece of land before a year was out. I never liked him, so I said no. But . . ." He glanced at the head, then away. "I heard . . . thought I heard . . . Did the cat speak true?"

"He wouldn't lie." Lucivar took a deep breath. "Falonar, select four men to go with us." Looking around, he realized Surreal was no longer with them.

Falonar turned, too, and swore. "Damn it, she's probably off someplace puking her guts—"

Surreal leaped over the low stone wall and trotted toward them, a large, dented metal bucket in one hand. When they just looked at her, she huffed and said tartly to Lucivar, "Were you planning to tuck that thing under your arm to take it to the High Lord?"

Lucivar smiled reluctantly. "Thanks, Surreal." He hesitated. His hands were already bloody, but he still hesitated.

She didn't. With another huff, she dumped the head and hand into the bucket, then covered the bucket with a piece of dark cloth.

The men winced. She snarled at them.

Seeing the wariness in Falonar's eyes, Lucivar said, "You have your orders, Prince."

Falonar and Rothvar left with more speed than discretion.

"Tell me he hasn't done as much on a battlefield," Surreal said with a hint of bitterness. "I suppose everything would have been just fine if I'd clung to his arm and begged for smelling salts."

"Don't condemn him out of hand," Lucivar said quietly. "He isn't used to a woman like you."

Surreal turned on him. "And what kind of woman is that?"

"A Dea al Mon witch."

Her smile came slowly, but it was genuine. "I suppose I should have been more tactful." She waved a hand at the bucket, then hesitated. "I'd like to go with you."

"No. I want you to stay here with the other women."

Her eyes frosted. "Why?"

Abruptly impatient, he snarled, "Because you wear the Gray, and I trust you." He waited until he knew she understood. "My eyrie has Ebon-gray shields, but Marian can key them. Don't let anyone in that she doesn't know—for any reason. I'll be back as soon as I can."

Surreal nodded. "All right. But you be careful. If you get hurt, I'll smack you."

Lucivar waited until she was out of earshot before he waved Hallevar over to him. "Send Palanar to my mother's house. He's to escort Lady Luthvian to my eyrie without delay."

Hallevar shifted uneasily. "She'll take a strip out of the boy."

"Tell her it's an order from the Warlord Prince of Ebon Rih," Lucivar said. "Then I want you to keep an eye open around here. If you see anything, hear anything, sense anything you don't like, you send one of the boys to the Keep and the other to the Hall for help. The wolf pack will also keep watch. If you see anyone who doesn't live right here, whether you knew them well in Terreille or not, treat them as an enemy. Understand?"

Nodding, Hallevar went off to attend his duties.

A short time later, Lucivar and five of his men were flying toward the Keep.

2 / Kaeleer

Lucivar set the metal bucket on the opposite end of the worktable and watched Saetan pour fresh blood into a bowl of simmering liquid. "I thought you would be at the Hall, waiting for the reports to come in."

"Draca sent for me," Saetan replied, lightly stirring the bowl's contents. "What brings you here?"

"Morton is dead."

Saetan's hand hesitated a moment, then resumed stirring. "I know."

Lucivar tensed, then said cautiously, "He's in the Dark Realm?"

"No, he's here. That's why Draca sent for me. He came to report."

Lucivar paced restlessly. "Good. I'll talk to him before—"

"No."

The implacable tone in Saetan's voice stopped him—for a moment. "I don't care if he's demon-dead now."

"He does." Saetan's voice gentled. "He doesn't want to see you, Lucivar. Not any of you."

"Why in the name of Hell not?" Lucivar shouted.

Saetan snarled. "Do you think it's easy making the transition? Do you think anything will be the same for him? He's *dead*, Lucivar. He's a young man who will never do a great many things now, who is no longer who and what he used to be. There are reasons why the dead remain, for the most part, among the dead."

Lucivar resumed his pacing. "It's not like the First Circle isn't used to being around the demon-dead."

"You didn't know them when they walked among the living," Saetan said softly. "There were no ties with them that needed to be cut. Yes, the ties *do* need to be cut," he said, overriding Lucivar's protest. "The living have to move on—and so do the dead. If you can't respect that, at least respect the fact that he needs time to adjust before he has to deal with the rest of you."

Lucivar swore softly. "How bad . . . ?"

Saetan set the spoon down and moved to the other end of the table. "The wounds aren't visible when he's dressed. In fact, they wouldn't have been fatal if the arrows hadn't been poisoned."

"Poisoned," Lucivar said flatly as he stared down at the bucket.

"There's not much Morton could tell you, and without more information, even what he knows doesn't help us much."

Lucivar pointed at the bucket. "You may find your answers in there."

Saetan lifted the dark cloth, looked inside the bucket, then let the cloth drop.

"Kaelas," Lucivar said, answering the unspoken question.

"I see," Saetan said quietly. "You're returning to Ebon Rih?"

Lucivar shook his head. "I'm taking a few men to the Dark Altar in Glacia to look around, see if there are any answers there."

"Our Queen's order was quite direct," Saetan said mildly.

"I'll risk her anger."

Saetan nodded. "Then, as Steward of the Court, I formally request that you go to the Dark Altar in Glacia to determine what happened."

"I don't need to hide behind your title," Lucivar snapped.

Saetan smiled dryly. "I'm doing this as much for Jaenelle as for you. This way, she can gracefully back away from having to confront you about disobeying a direct order."

"Oh. In that case . . ."

"Get going, boyo. Report to me at the Hall. And Prince Yaslana," Saetan added when Lucivar reached the door, "remember Glacia isn't your territory. You're not the law there."

"Yes, sir, I'll remember. We just witness and report."

3 / Kaeleer

Seeing the guarded look in Marian's eyes and the way Luthvian managed to convey silently her disapproval of her son's choice of a wife, Surreal wondered how pissed off Lucivar would be if they took his mother into the garden and used her for target practice.

"How did you manage to bake anything this morning?" Nurian, the journeymaid Healer, asked as she accepted a nutcake from the plate Marian was passing around. "And how do you get anything else done after these morning workouts?"

"Oh," Marian said with a shy smile, "I'm used to it by now, and—"

"You're a Healer," Luthvian interrupted, giving Nurian a cool stare. "*Your* finding it difficult to practice a demanding Craft after these workouts is understandable. But they're hardly an excuse for neglecting one's duties when you're talking about *hearth Craft.* After all—"

"If you'll excuse us," Surreal said, hauling Luthvian to her feet. "There's something Lady Luthvian and I need to discuss."

"Let go of me," Luthvian snarled as Surreal dragged her out of the room. "You don't treat a Black Widow Healer like she was—"

"A hearth-witch?" Surreal said with venomous sweetness as she shoved Luthvian into the garden.

"Exactly," Luthvian replied darkly. "But I don't suppose a *whore*—"

"Shut up, bitch," Surreal said too quietly.

Luthvian sucked in air. "You forget your place!"

"No, sugar, that's exactly what I'm not forgetting. You may belong to a higher caste, but my Jewels outrank yours. I figure that evens things out—at least within the family. You don't like me, and that suits me just fine because I don't like you either."

"Crossing a Black Widow isn't wise," Luthvian said softly.

"Crossing an assassin isn't wise either." Surreal smiled when Luthvian's eyes widened. "So let's make this simple. If you make one more disparaging remark about Marian, I'm going to bang your face against the wall until some sense gets knocked into you."

"What do you think Lucivar would say about *that*?" Luthvian's voice sounded certain, but there was doubt in her eyes.

"Oh," Surreal replied, "I don't think Lucivar would say anything to *me*." Watching the verbal thrust hit the mark, she felt a brief moment of pity for Luthvian. The woman drove people away, and then seemed bewildered to find herself alone.

"He could have done better," Luthvian grumbled. "He didn't have to settle for a Purple Dusk hearth-witch."

Surreal studied Luthvian. "This doesn't have anything to do with Lucivar, does it? You're embarrassed because *your* son married a *hearth-witch*. Marian is just a gentle, caring woman who loves him and whose presence makes him happy. If he had married a Black Widow Healer and was miserable, well, that would have been all right because he had married a woman worthy of a Warlord Prince. Right?" *Besides,* she added silently, *the High Lord approves of his son's choice.* Which, she suspected, was the major reason Luthvian never would. "Remember what I said, Luthvian." She started to walk away.

"Just because the High Lord tolerates your using the SaDiablo name doesn't change what you were—and still are," Luthvian said nastily.

Surreal looked over her shoulder. "No," she said, "it doesn't. You would do well to remember that, too."

4 / Kaeleer

Lucivar felt the tingle of residual power the moment he stepped off the landing web. While the other Eyriens stared at the dead bodies and muttered uneasily, he kept his eyes on the pressed-down snow a few feet in front of him. He moved toward it, then skirted around it.

"What?" Falonar asked as he avoided the spot, too.

"Morton died there," Lucivar said quietly.

"He's not the only one who died," Rothvar said grimly, looking at the savaged Eyrien corpses.

"No, he's not the only one," Lucivar replied. *But he's the one I watched grow from a decent youth into a fine man.* "Rothvar, you and Endar—"

If he hadn't spent the past eight years living around kindred, he never would have picked up that particular psychic scent—and wouldn't have known the Arcerian cats were there until it was far too late.

He scanned the village roofs with a seemingly casual eye while he quietly sank to the depth of his Ebon-gray Jewel and probed the area. Eight Arcerians. Two of them Warlord Princes. All of them wearing darker Jewels.

"Keep your hands away from your weapons," Lucivar said, keeping his voice low and even. "We've got company." Moving slowly, he unbelted the short wool cape and opened it to expose his chest and the Ebon-gray Jewel that hung from the chain around his neck. He held his arms out, away from his weapons. "I am Lucivar Yaslana," he said in a loud voice. "I belong to the Lady. And these males belong to me."

I'm not sensing anything, Falonar said on a Sapphire spear thread.

Kindred don't usually announce their presence, Lucivar said dryly. *Especially the Arcerians.*

Mother Night! Falonar looked at the savaged Eyrien bodies. *Those cats are still here? How many?*

Eight of them. Let's hope they decide we're friends, or this is going to turn into a mess.

Lucivar waited until his arms began to ache. Finally there was a wary psychic touch. *You are Kaelas's Brother,* said a growling voice.

And he is my Brother, Lucivar replied. He lowered his arms.

Why are you here? the cat demanded.

To stand witness for the Lady.

A long pause. ★Kaelas told us to guard this place so that no more bad meat comes through the Gate.★

Lucivar hoped the cats watching him thought the shiver was due to the cold and not the reference to Eyriens being "bad meat." ★Kaelas is wise.★

★You look and then go.★ That wasn't a question.

Lucivar turned toward his men. He raised his voice to make sure the nearest Arcerian cat would hear the orders. "Raise basic shields."

Five men gave him blank looks followed by swift comprehension. Protective shields snapped up around them.

★*Will* these shields protect us?★ Falonar asked Lucivar, using a Sapphire thread so that the other men couldn't hear him.

★No,★ Lucivar replied shortly. "Weapons to hand." He called in his Eyrien war blade, then nodded when the others followed his example. "Kohlvar, you and Endar keep watch at the landing web. Rothvar and Zaranar, take the left side of the village. Falonar, with me." ★And if one of the Arcerians actually shows himself, give him the same courtesy you would give any other warrior,★ he added on a general spear thread.

They moved slowly, carefully, fully aware that the cats watched every movement, every gesture.

"How did those cats manage to kill this many Eyriens without anyone sounding an alarm?" Falonar asked quietly when they had checked half the houses on their side of the village. It was obvious that a number of the men hadn't suspected a thing before the attack.

"When an Arcerian is hunting, you don't usually know he's there until he kills you," Lucivar replied absently as he quickly checked through another house. There was evidence of at least minimal fighting in all the houses, but that had been Glacian against Eyrien. "That makes them very efficient."

When they reached the living quarters in the Sanctuary, they both stared at the young Priestess—or what was left of her.

"Hell's fire," Falonar said, disgust filling his voice as he backed away from the door. "Well, I guess gang rape *is* a kind of slow execution. But why keep just this one? And why beat her to death when they'd probably already done enough to kill her?"

"Because the other women fought, while this one expected a different kind of reward," Lucivar replied. When Falonar stared at him with horror-filled eyes, he laughed, a low, nasty sound. "You spent enough time in the Terreillean courts to know how to get dirty, Prince Falonar. *Some-one* had to help that Green-Jeweled bastard go through the Gate to get back to Terreille—or at least keep the old Priestess from realizing the Gate was being used without her knowledge or consent. As for the beating . . . I guess when the bastard realized he was trapped in here, he needed to take it out on someone."

"The cat didn't kill him slow enough," Falonar muttered, turning away from the room. "Not nearly slow enough."

I imagine the High Lord will know how to extract the final payment for the debt, Lucivar thought, but he didn't tell Falonar *that.*

As they left the Sanctuary, Zaranar made a "come here" gesture.

"Rothvar's at the back door," Zaranar said uneasily. "I think you should handle this. All we've done is keep an eye on the doors," he added quickly.

Before Lucivar could move, Kohlvar sent an urgent message. *Prince, there's a Glacian at the landing web who says he's Lady Karla's Master of the Guard. He's got forty guards with him.*

Tell him to stay put, Lucivar replied sharply as he and Falonar headed for the back of the house. *I'll talk to him in a few minutes.*

Before he reached the back door, he could hear the nervous snarls coming from inside the house. Rothvar stepped aside. Lucivar started to go in, then stopped abruptly.

The Arcerian Warlord was almost full-grown, so there wasn't much room in the small kitchen for a cat his size to pace. On the table was an odd assortment of food. On the floor was a goat, neatly killed.

When Lucivar took a step toward the goat, the cat pounced on it and snarled.

Mine, the cat said.

"All right," Lucivar replied mildly.

The cat seemed puzzled by his easy agreement. *Payment for work.*

Interesting, Lucivar thought. Was this a kindred testing of a human idea? "Since you're guarding this place instead of hunting, it's fair that you be paid with meat."

Relaxing a little, the cat looked at the table. So did Lucivar. There wasn't anything on it he thought a cat would want to eat. "Is that also pay-ment for work?"

Human food. The cat made it sound more like a hopeful question.

"Yes, it is."

A she-kitten would like this food?

Lucivar rubbed his chin. "I don't know."

The cat growled, but the sound was filled with discouragement. *We burned some meat for her, but she would not eat.* He wrinkled his lips to indicate what he thought of ruining good meat by cooking it. *I promised to bring human food.*

A chill whispered down Lucivar's spine. "A child survived this place?"

Yes. The she-kitten. KaeAskavi's friend. The cat studied him, then asked hesitantly, *You will help?*

Lucivar blinked away tears that would only confuse the cat. "Yes, I will help."

5 / Kaeleer

"Did we do the right thing?" Daemon asked as he and Lucivar air walked above the deep snow toward the place that was designated as an official landing web. They weren't making that effort just to avoid floundering in waist-high snow; tracks might have shown an enemy where the Arcerian dens were located.

"What else could we do?" Lucivar replied wearily. "The girl has lost her mother, her village, everyone she knew. KaeAskavi's the only friend she has left. There are pockets of fighting going on throughout Glacia, so placing her in another village . . . There's no guarantee she would survive the next time a place is attacked. Marian and I would take her to live with us, but . . ."

Daemon shook his head. "You were right about that. She wouldn't be able to handle being around Eyriens right now." Which was why Lucivar had insisted that Daemon come with him to Arceria in the first place.

"And we can't take her anywhere else," Lucivar added grimly. "Not until we know if this attack was part of Hobart's attempt to regain control of Glacia or if it's something more. You said the girl was physically all right."

"She sprained an ankle, but the Arcerian Healers have the Craft to take care of injured limbs. Other than that, she was . . . unharmed." He couldn't say the word "rape." He would never forget the fear that had jolted through him when he had crawled into that den and seen Della—fair-haired, blue-eyed, ten-year-old Della. She didn't look anything like Jaenelle, except in coloring, but that had been enough to cause the memories of what had happened in Chaillot thirteen years ago to come rushing back at him. His hands had trembled as he'd cautiously examined her for injuries, as he had used a delicate psychic probe to answer that particular question. His hands had also trembled because she had been gripping a stuffed toy cat in one hand and a fistful of KaeAskavi's fur in the other—which meant the cat had been literally breathing down his neck. It was the way she had held on to KaeAskavi that had forced him to leave her there. She needed to feel safe in order to heal—and snuggling up to four hundred pounds of muscle and fur obviously made her feel very safe.

Lucivar rested a hand on Daemon's shoulder. "A few weeks among the Arcerians won't hurt her. At least this way she can be 'mothered' without feeling like she's letting someone take her mother's place."

Daemon nodded. "Are you going back to Ebon Rih?" He had been planning to go to the Keep since Jaenelle was on her way there with Karla and Morghann.

Lucivar shook his head. "The High Lord asked me to report to him at the Hall. This side trip has delayed that report for a couple of days, so I'd better get my ass there before he decides to take a piece out of it."

"Then I'll go with you."

When they reached the place where they could catch the Winds, Lucivar hesitated. "How is Karla? I didn't get to see her before they left for the Keep."

Daemon stared at the unbroken snow. "She'll live. Jaenelle thinks she can heal the legs enough for Karla to walk again."

"Jaenelle *thinks* she can?" Lucivar paled. "Mother Night, Daemon, if *Jaenelle* isn't sure, what was done—"

"Don't ask," Daemon said too sharply. He made an effort to soften his voice. "Don't ask. I . . . don't want to talk about it." But this was Lucivar who was asking, so he tried. "There's no antidote for witchblood. The poison had to be drawn into some part of the body in order to save the internal organs and then drawn out. It . . . killed a lot of the muscle, and that muscle had to be . . ." His gorge rose as he thought of the withered limbs that had been healthy legs.

"Let it go," Lucivar said gently. "Let it go."

They both took a couple of unsteady breaths before Daemon said,

"The sooner we make our reports, the sooner we can go home." For him, home wasn't a place, it was a person—and right then, he needed to know that Jaenelle was safe.

6 / Terreille

"Kartane sent a report." Dorothea carefully selected a piece of sugared fruit, took a bite, and chewed slowly just to make Hekatah wait.

"And?" Hekatah finally asked. "Has the Gate in Glacia been secured for our use? Is the village ready for our handpicked immigrants?"

Dorothea selected another piece of fruit. This time she gave it a couple of delicate licks before answering. "The villagers were eliminated. So were the Eyriens."

"*What? How?*"

"The messenger who met with Kartane couldn't find out what happened to the Eyriens, only that they had killed the villagers and had, in turn, been killed." She paused. "Lord Hobart's dead as well."

Hekatah stood perfectly still. "And the bitch-Queen, Karla? Was that, at least, successful?"

Dorothea shrugged. "She disappeared during the fighting. But since Ulka died rather . . . dramatically . . . one would assume she consumed the poison."

"Then that's the end of her," Hekatah said with a little smile of satisfaction. "Even if someone manages to figure out an antidote for the Hayllian poison in time, the witchblood will finish things."

"Our plans for Glacia are also finished. Or hasn't that occurred to you?"

Hekatah waved that away. "Considering what we *have* achieved, that's a minor inconvenience."

Dorothea dropped the fruit back into the bowl. "We've achieved *nothing!*"

"You're becoming inflexible, Dorothea," Hekatah said with venomous sweetness. "You're starting to act as old as you look."

Dorothea's blood pounded in her temples, and she wanted—oh, how she wanted—to unleash just a little of the feelings that had been growing more virulent. She hated Hekatah, but she also needed the bitch. So she sat back and inflicted a wound that would hurt much deeper than any physical blow. "At least I still have all my hair. That bald patch is starting to ooze, dearest."

Hekatah automatically lifted a hand to cover the spot. With effort, she lowered it before it reached her head.

The impotent hatred in Hekatah's dull gold eyes scared Dorothea a little but also produced a sense of vicious satisfaction.

"We can make do with sneaking through the other Gates," Hekatah said. "We have something better now."

"And what is that?" Dorothea asked politely.

"The excuse we needed to start the war." Hekatah's smile was pure malevolence.

"I see," Dorothea said, returning the smile.

"The immigrants we had picked to replace the villagers will go to Glacia—just as they would have if Hobart had given us that village as payment for our assistance. We'll also add a few immigrants from other Terreillean Territories. The escorts will be males who don't know where the original village was located. Only the Coach drivers will be told where to drop off the happy families—and that won't be anywhere near a settled area, so there won't be any chance of detection. The escorts will, of course, be dismayed to see no sign of a village waiting for inhabitants." A dreamy look filled Hekatah's eyes. "The company of Eyrien warriors who will be waiting for them will take care of things. The slaughter will be . . . horrible. But there will be a couple of survivors who will manage to escape. They'll live long enough to get back to Little Terreille and tell a few people about how Terreilleans are being butchered in Kaeleer. And they'll live long enough to say that two men had been giving the orders—a Hayllian and an Eyrien."

"No one in Terreille will think it's anyone but Sadi and Yaslana," Dorothea said gleefully. "They'll think the High Lord ordered the attack and sent his sons to oversee it."

"Exactly."

"Which will prove that all my warnings were justified. And once people start wondering why there has been no word from friends or loved ones . . ." Dorothea sank back in her chair with a sigh of pleasure. Then she straightened up reluctantly. "We still have to find a way to contain Jaenelle Angelline."

"Oh, with the proper incentive, she'll willingly place herself in our hands."

Dorothea snorted. "What kind of incentive would make her do that?"

"Using someone she loves as bait."

7 / Kaeleer

Chilled to the bone, Saetan listened to Lucivar's and Daemon's reports. He would have liked to believe Lord Hobart had hired a company of Eyriens to help him seize control of Glacia, would have liked to believe Morton's death and the attack on Karla were strictly a Glacian concern. But he'd had other reports in the past twenty-four hours. Two District Queens in Dharo had been killed, along with their escorts. A mob of landens had attacked a kindred wolf pack that had recently formed around a young Queen. While the males were dealing with that threat, some Blood had outflanked them, killed the Queen, and vanished, leaving the landens behind to be slaughtered by the enraged males. In Scelt, a Warlord Prince, a youth still not quite old enough to make the Offering to the Darkness, had been found behind the tavern in his home village. His throat had been slit.

Even more troubling, Kalush had been attacked while walking through a park in Tajrana, her own capital city. The only reason neither she nor her infant daughter had been harmed was because her attackers couldn't break through the protective shield around her—the Ebony shield that was in the ring Jaenelle had given her—and because Aaron, alerted by the link through the Ring of Honor he wore, had arrived riding the killing edge and had destroyed the attackers with a savagery that bordered on insanity.

It didn't take any effort to see the pattern, especially since he recognized it. Fifty thousand years slipped away as if they had never existed. It might have been Andulvar and Mephis sitting there, voicing their concerns about swift, seemingly random attacks to a man who had insisted that, as a Guardian, he could no longer interfere with the affairs of the living. He was still a Guardian, but he was too entangled in the affairs of the living to obey the rules Guardians abided by.

They were going to war.

He wondered if Daemon and Lucivar realized it yet.

And he wondered how many loved ones he would have to assist through the transition to becoming demon-dead this time—and how many would disappear without a trace. Like Andulvar's son, Ravenar. Like his own son, his second son, Peyton.

"Father?" Daemon said quietly.

He realized they were both watching him intently, but it was Daemon he focused on. The son who was a mirror, who was his true heir. The son he understood the best—and the least.

Before he could start to tell them about the other attacks, Beale knocked on the study door and walked in.

"Forgive the intrusion, High Lord," Beale said, "but there's a Warlord here to see you. He has a letter."

"Then take the letter. I don't want to be disturbed at the moment."

"I suggested that, High Lord. He said he needs to deliver it in person."

Saetan waited a moment. "Very well."

Lucivar sprang out of his chair and positioned himself so that he would flank anyone standing near the desk. Daemon rose and resettled himself on a corner of the desk.

The intense warrior and the indolent male. Saetan imagined they had played these roles before—and played them well. With Lucivar's temper so close to the surface, the attention would be on him—but the death blow would come from Daemon.

The Warlord who entered the study was pale, nervous, and sweating. He paled even more when he saw Lucivar and Daemon.

Saetan walked around the desk. "You have a letter for me?"

The Warlord swallowed hard. "Yes, sir." He extended an envelope, the ink a little smeared from his hands.

Saetan probed the envelope. Found nothing. No trace of a spell. No trace of poison. He took it and looked at the Warlord.

"I found that in the guest room desk this morning," the man said hurriedly. "I didn't know it was there."

Saetan looked at the envelope. There was nothing on it except his name. "So you found it this morning. Is that significant?"

"I hope not. I mean—" The man took a deep breath, made an effort to steady himself. "Lord Magstrom is—was—my wife's grandfather. He came to visit us last fall, just before . . . Well, before. He seemed disturbed about something, but we weren't paying much attention. My wife . . . We had just found out for sure that she was pregnant. She'd had a miscarriage the year before, and we were concerned that it might happen again. The Healer says she has to be careful."

Why was the man pleading with him? "Is your wife well?"

"Yes, thank you, she is, but she's had to be careful. Grandfather Magstrom didn't mention the letter. At least, I don't remember him mentioning it, and then, after he . . . was killed . . ." The man's hands trembled. "I hope it wasn't something urgent. As soon as I found it, I knew I had to come right away. I hope it wasn't urgent."

"I'm sure it's not," Saetan replied gently. "I expect it's just the usual information Lord Magstrom sent me after a service fair—a confirmation more than anything else."

The man's relief was visible.

Saetan glanced at the Warlord's Yellow Jewel. "May I offer you the use of a Coach to take you home?"

"Oh, I don't want to put you through any bother."

"It's no bother—and with a driver who can ride the darker Winds, you'll be home in time to have dinner with your Lady."

The Warlord hesitated a moment longer. "Thank you. I—don't like to be away from her too long." He looked a little sheepish. "She says I fuss."

Saetan smiled. "You're going to become a father. You're entitled to fuss." He led the man out of the study, gave Beale instructions about the Coach, and returned to Daemon and Lucivar. Using the letter opener on his desk, he carefully slit the envelope. He called in his half-moon glasses, opened the letter, and began to read.

"You got reports from Magstrom about the service fair?" Lucivar asked, accepting the glass of brandy Daemon poured for him.

"No." And the more he read, the less he liked receiving this one. As he read the letter a second time, he barely listened to Daemon's and Lucivar's conversation—until Daemon said something that caught his attention. "What did you say?"

"I said Lord Magstrom had indicated that he was going to send letters to some of the Queens outside of Little Terreille," Daemon repeated, swirling the brandy in his glass. "But after Jorval took over handling my immigration, I was told that the Queens outside of Little Terreille wouldn't consider a Black-Jeweled Warlord Prince."

Lucivar snorted. "Jorval probably arranged for the letters not to be sent. Hell's fire, Daemon, you've met the other Territory Queens. They're the coven. If a letter had reached any one of them, she would have had her Steward at the service fair to sign the contract as fast as he could travel."

"Read this," Saetan said, handing the letter to Daemon.

"I don't understand," Daemon said when he'd read half the letter. "Aren't the lists supposed to indicate every immigrant at the service fair?"

"Yes, they are," Lucivar said grimly, reading over Daemon's shoulder. "And you weren't on any of them." He looked at Saetan. "I did mention that at the time."

"Yes, you did," Saetan replied, "but, since Daemon *did* end up in the Dark Court, I failed to appreciate the significance of that remark."

Daemon handed the letter back to Saetan. "There must have been a list somewhere. Otherwise, how would the Queens in Little Terreille have known I was available?"

Saetan kept his voice mild. "What Queens were those?"

"There were four Queens in Little Terreille who were willing to have me," Daemon said slowly. "Jorval insisted they were the only ones."

"So, if you hadn't met Lucivar by chance . . ."

Daemon froze. "I would have signed a contract with one of them."

Swearing quietly, Lucivar started to pace.

Saetan just nodded. "You would have signed a contract with one of Jorval's handpicked Queens, and you would have ended up tucked away somewhere in Little Terreille—with no one else aware that you *were* there."

"What would have been the point of that?" Daemon said irritably.

"In Little Terreille they use the Ring of Obedience on immigrating males," Lucivar snapped. "*That's* the point. It would have been Terreille all over again."

"Not necessarily," Saetan said, still keeping his voice mild. "If Daemon was well treated, was handled with care—which I'm sure was part of the agreement—he would have had no reason *not* to use the strength of his Jewels against an enemy who was threatening the Queen he served. And after the first unleashing of the Black, there would have been no turning back. The lines would have been drawn."

Daemon stared at him.

"What does it matter?" Lucivar said, looking at the two of them uneasily. "Daemon's with us."

"Yes," Saetan said softly, "he is. But where are the other men whose names disappeared from those lists?"

8 / Kaeleer

The golden spider studied the two tangled webs of dreams and visions. More deaths. Many deaths.

It was time.

Remember this web. Remember every strand, every thread.

Throughout the cold season, she had been pulled away from her own dreaming, compelled to study the web that had shaped this living myth, the Queen who was Witch. And she had realized it would not be enough, because living inside the flesh had changed this dream. It was *more* now. And, somehow, she needed to add that "more" to the web. Without it, Kaeleer's Heart would be gone for too many seasons—and would not be quite the same when the dream returned.

She continued to study the webs.

The brown dog, Ladvarian, was the key. He would be able to bring her the "more" she needed.

Yes. It was time.

She returned to the chamber within the sacred caves, and began to weave the web for dreams that were already made flesh.

CHAPTER THIRTEEN

1 / Kaeleer

The First Circle of the Dark Court gathered at the Keep.

At least, the humans in the First Circle had gathered, Saetan amended as he listened to Khardeen's grim report about the attacks that had taken place in Scelt during the past three weeks. There had been attacks *everywhere* in the last three weeks. Maybe that was why the kindred hadn't answered Jaenelle's summons to come to the Keep. Maybe the kindred Queens and Warlord Princes didn't dare withdraw their strength away from their own lands. Or maybe it was the beginning of a rift between humans and kindred. Maybe they were withdrawing from what they considered a human conflict in order to save themselves.

But he would have thought Ladvarian, at the very least, would have come so that he could explain things to the rest of the kindred. *He* would have realized the conflict wouldn't be confined to humans. Hell's fire, kindred had *already* been attacked.

But Ladvarian wasn't there—and it worried him.

Two other things worried him: the flickers of grief and resignation he was picking up from Andulvar, Prothvar, and Mephis—who had all fought, and died, in the last war between Terreille and Kaeleer—and the fact that Jaenelle had been sitting there for the past two hours with such blankness in her eyes he started to wonder if she hadn't created a simple shadow to fill a space at the table.

"Just defending against these attacks isn't going to save our lands or our people," Aaron said. "There are Terreillean armies gathering against us.

If the enemy who's already *in* Kaeleer gains control of a Gate and opens it for those armies . . . We need to do something *now*."

"Yes, you do need to do something," Jaenelle said in a hollow voice. "You need to retreat."

Protests from all sides rose up in a wave of sound.

"You need to retreat," Jaenelle repeated. "And you will send all of the Queens and Warlord Princes in your Territories to the Keep."

Stunned silence met that statement.

"But, Jaenelle," Morghann said after a moment, "the Warlord Princes are needed to lead the fighting. And asking Queens to leave their lands while their people are under attack . . ."

"They won't be needed if the people retreat."

"Just how far are we supposed to retreat?" Gabrielle snapped.

"As far as necessary."

Aaron shook his head. "We need to gather our warriors into armies to fight against the Terreilleans and—"

"Kaeleer *will not* go to war with Terreille," Jaenelle said in her midnight voice.

Chaosti sprang up from his seat. "We're already at war!"

"No, we are not."

"So we're at war with Little Terreille, since that's where these attackers have been hiding," Lucivar growled. "It's the same thing."

Jaenelle's eyes turned to ice. "We're not at war with anyone."

"Cat, you're not thinking—"

"Remember to whom you speak."

Lucivar looked into her eyes and paled. Finally, reluctantly, he said, "My apologies, Lady."

Jaenelle rose. "If there's time to retreat before the attack, do it. If not, keep the fighting to a minimum. *Defend* for as long as it takes to retreat, but don't attack. And get the Queens and Warlord Princes to the Keep. There will be no exceptions, and I'll accept no excuses."

A long silence filled the room after Jaenelle left.

"She's not thinking clearly," Kalush said reluctantly.

"She's been acting strange since the first attack," Gabrielle snapped, then looked apologetically at Karla.

"It's all right," Karla said slowly, with obvious effort. "She *has* been acting strange. I've wondered if healing me affected her somehow."

"What's affected her is her aversion to killing," Lucivar snarled. "But she's usually clear-sighted enough to be able to see the obvious. We're at war. Dancing around the word isn't going to change the fact."

"You would defy your Queen?" Daemon asked mildly, almost lazily.

Lucivar's instant, razor-edged tension startled all of them.

What's happening between them? Saetan wondered as Daemon and Lucivar just stared at each other. Seeing the sleepy look in Daemon's eyes, he felt ice wrap around his spine.

"I don't think the Lady understands the repercussions of her order," Lucivar said carefully.

"Oh," Daemon purred, "I think she understands them quite well. You just don't agree with her. That's not sufficient reason to disobey her."

"Considering what you've done in other courts, you're not exactly a model of obedience," Lucivar said with a little heat.

"That's irrelevant. We're talking about you and this court. And I'm telling you, Yaslana, that you will not distress her with defiance or disobedience. If you do . . ." Daemon merely smiled.

Lucivar shuddered.

After Daemon glided out of the room, Saetan asked, "Is he bluffing?" He became uneasy when Lucivar just stared at the table. "Lucivar?"

"The Sadist doesn't bluff," Lucivar said roughly. "He doesn't need to." He strode out of the room.

"It would seem there's nothing more to discuss," Saetan said, rising from the table. A flick of a glance brought Andulvar, Prothvar, and Mephis to their feet.

Letting the other men precede him, he had almost shut the door when he heard Aaron say, "What do we really know about Daemon Sadi?"

He closed the door silently. When he turned toward the other men, he saw the same question in Andulvar's eyes—and he was no longer sure he had an answer.

2 / Kaeleer

"What do we really know about Daemon Sadi?" Aaron said.

Karla let the murmurs of opinion and conversation become a wash of sound as she sank deeper into her own thoughts.

What did they really know about Daemon Sadi?

He was a Black-Jeweled Warlord Prince and a natural Black Widow— an explosively dangerous, beautiful-looking man.

He was the High Lord's mirror, but not a perfect reflection.

He was a man who, for most of his life, had been chained in one way or another to Dorothea SaDiablo, Kaeleer's enemy.

He was a man who understood women. Unable to stand the pity in the servants' eyes when they had helped her into the bath the first few days after the healing, she had insisted that she didn't need help. Using Craft, she was able to undress and get herself into the tub but wasn't able to wash herself well enough, especially because the reaction to the poisons was causing her skin to slough off at a grotesque rate. One evening, Daemon had shown up to assist her. She had snapped at him, had told him to go away. His answer, spoken in such a pleasant voice it had taken her a few seconds to comprehend the words, was so creatively obscene she was in the tub being gently, but thoroughly, washed before she could think again. His touch hadn't been impersonal, nor had it been sexual, but by the time he'd started massaging her scalp, she'd been awash in sensual pleasure like she'd never experienced before.

So she understood why the others were worried. A woman could easily become addicted to that touch, would be willing to do a great many things in order to prevent it from being withdrawn. And Jaenelle *had* been acting strange since the first attack. But she didn't think it had anything to do with Daemon.

There was one other thing she knew about Daemon Sadi, something she had seen in the tangled web that had warned her about her own death: he was the friend who would become an enemy in order to remain a friend.

3 / Kaeleer

"What is it about Daemon that scares the shit out of Lucivar?" Andulvar asked as soon as the four men entered a small sitting room in the Keep.

"I don't know," Saetan replied, avoiding their stares by warming a glass of yarbarah over a tongue of witchfire.

He *didn't* know. Lucivar had always evaded talking about the times he and Daemon had tangled when they'd come together in Terreillean courts. Lucivar had said once that if he had a choice of going up against the Sadist or the High Lord, he would choose the High Lord because he would have some chance of winning.

What was it about that smile of Daemon's that could shake Lucivar so badly? What was it about the Sadist that could make a man as aggressive as Lucivar back down? And what might Daemon's presence in the Keep mean to the rest of them?

"High Lord!" Prothvar jerked Saetan's hand away from the tongue of witchfire just before the yarbarah began to boil.

Saetan put the glass down. The yarbarah wouldn't be drinkable.

"SaDiablo," Andulvar said quietly, "should we be watching our backs?"

It didn't occur to him to offer a reassuring lie. "I don't know."

4 / Kaeleer

Ladvarian wearily trotted toward Halaway, responding to a gentle but insistent summons. Every so often, he snarled to vent his frustration and growing anger.

How could a place as big as the Hall not have what he needed? Oh, he'd found plenty of things that were *almost* right but nothing that *was* right. That accounted for his frustration. The anger . . .

The kindred had waited so long for this living myth to come. *This* one. This special one. And now it was going to be spoiled by humans.

No. It *wouldn't* be spoiled. The kindred were gathering. As soon as the Weaver of Dreams told them what to do, they would act.

When he reached the neat cottage in Halaway, he went to the back door and barked once, politely.

Tersa opened an upstairs window. "Come inside, little Brother."

Using Craft, he floated upward to the window and went in. Most of the kindred referred to Tersa as "the Strange One." They meant no disrespect. They recognized that she was a Black Widow who wandered roads most of the Blood would never see. She was special. She had that in common with the Lady.

Even knowing all that didn't prevent his hackles from rising when he stepped into the room.

A low, narrow bed—*exactly* the kind he had searched for at the Hall.

He approached it cautiously and opened his inner and outer senses. It had no smells. There should be human smells as well as a residual psychic scent from the humans who had made the bed, mattress, and bedcovers.

"It has all been cleansed," Tersa said calmly. "There are no psychic scents to interfere with the weaving of dreams."

The weaving of dreams? Ladvarian said cautiously.

"That trunk will provide storage and can be used as a bedside table as well. Remember to bring clothing for warm weather as well as clothing for the spring. Favorite things. Clothes that will be strong with her scent, even if they've been cleaned."

Ladvarian backed away. *Why should I bring clothing?*

Tersa smiled and said gently, "Because Witch does not have fur." Her eyes looked into an inner distance, became unfocused and farseeing. "It is almost time for the debts to be paid. Those who survive will serve, but few will survive. The howling . . . Full of joy and pain, rage and celebration. She is coming." Her eyes focused on him again. "And the kindred will anchor the dream in flesh."

Yes, Lady, Ladvarian said respectfully.

Tersa picked up a cobalt-blue bowl from a nearby dresser. Using Craft, she rested the bowl on the air. "When you next see the Weaver of Dreams, tell her this is how to get the 'more' she needs."

Ladvarian shifted his weight restlessly from one paw to the other. The Arachnian Queen had not mentioned Tersa. Why did Tersa know so much about the Arachnian Queen?

Tersa dipped one finger into the bowl. As she raised her hand, a drop of water clung to her finger. Instead of falling, the drop began to expand, like a little bubble of blown glass, a pearl of water. Using her thumbnail, Tersa jabbed a finger on her other hand. A drop of blood welled up on the finger. "And the Blood shall sing to the Blood."

Ladvarian felt the power flowing into that drop of blood.

"Let blood be memory's river." Turning her hand, she brushed the drop of blood against the drop of water. The blood flowed through the water bubble until it was contained inside it.

After placing a protective shield around it, Tersa tucked the water bubble into a small padded box and extended it toward Ladvarian. "Look."

He opened his mind, sent out a tentative psychic probe.

Images, memories flowed past him. Memories of a young girl leading an exhausted woman out of the Twisted Kingdom. Memories of Jaenelle, older, promising to find Daemon. Memories of conversations, laughter, delight in the world. Tersa's memories.

"You will tell the Weaver?" Tersa asked.

Ladvarian vanished the box. *I will tell her.*

"One other thing, little Brother. Don't refuse Lorn's gift. The Weaver will need that, too."

5 / Kaeleer

Leaving the door open, Daemon walked into Jaenelle's workroom. She had been spending hours there every day since she'd brought Karla to the Keep to continue the healing, but he didn't think her distraction or the controlled frenzy of her activities had anything to do with Karla. In fact, he was certain he was the only one who had been allowed a glimpse of that frenzy. Something was eating at her, and after the little scene in the meeting room, he was determined to find out what.

"Jaenelle, we need to talk."

She glanced up from the mound of books that filled one table. "I don't have time to talk now, Daemon," she said dismissively.

With a flick of a thought, he slammed the door so hard all the objects in the room jumped—including her.

"Make time," he said too softly. When she started to protest, he cut her off. "I'll do anything for you. *Anything.* But before I pit myself against the rest of the First Circle, I want to know why."

"Kaeleer cannot go to war with Terreille." Her voice trembled.

"Why?"

Hot, angry tears filled her eyes. "Because if we go to war, every person who was in that room will die."

"You don't know that," he snapped.

The tears spilled over, slicing his heart. "Yes, I do."

Daemon rocked back on his heels. She was a very strong, very gifted Black Widow. If she'd seen their deaths in a tangled web of dreams and visions, there was no room for doubt. *That* explained her resistance.

He took a deep breath to steady himself. "Sweetheart . . . sometimes killing is necessary. Sometimes it's the only path to take in order to save what is good."

"I know that." Jaenelle slammed a book on the table. "I've spent the past three weeks searching for an answer. No, I've spent longer than that, but time is running out. I can feel it."

"Jaenelle," he said carefully, "you have the strength . . ." The look in her eyes was almost hateful, but he pushed on. "A portion of your strength would eliminate a Terreillean army."

"And while I was eliminating that one, six more would be killing the Kaeleer Blood in other Territories. Even if I do destroy them, one army at a time, it won't make any difference."

"You wouldn't be the only one fighting," Daemon insisted, bracing one hand on the table to lean toward her. "Hell's fire, woman, look at the strength of the males in this Realm. Look at the Jewels. The Blacks. The Ebon-grays. The Grays. We have the dominant strength."

"Kaeleer had the dominant strength in the last war, too," Jaenelle replied quietly. "And Kaeleer won—barely, but Kaeleer won. But all those males died. And it didn't make any difference. The taint that fed that war is still in the Blood, even stronger now."

"Hekatah and Dorothea can be destroyed."

Jaenelle moved around the table in order to pace. "It wouldn't do any good at this point. Even if they're destroyed, even if Kaeleer wins the initial war, the Shadow Realm won't win. The taint's too widespread now. Terreille will keep sending armies. Will keep sending them and sending them, and the fighting will go on and on, in Terreille as well as in Kaeleer, until the Blood can't remember who they are or that they were supposed to be the caretakers of the Realms."

"We're at war, Jaenelle," Daemon said earnestly. "It doesn't matter if it's been formally declared or not. We *are* at war."

"No."

"You have the strength to make the difference. If you unleash—"

"I can't."

"You can."

"*I can't.*"

"WHY NOT?"

She turned on him. "BECAUSE, DAMN YOU, I'M TOO STRONG! If I unleash my strength, it will destroy the Blood. *All* the Blood. In Terreille. In Kaeleer. In Hell."

Daemon's legs turned to water. Weakly, he pushed aside some books so that he could sit on the table. *You had said she was six times stronger than our combined strength. Oh, Father, you were so wrong. Six times? Six hundred times? Six thousand times?*

Enough power to wipe the Blood out of existence.

With her arms wrapped around herself, Jaenelle paced. "The Keep is the Sanctuary. It wouldn't be affected. But how many could it hold? A few thousand at most? Who chooses, Daemon? What if the wrong choices are made and the taint is still there, hidden because someone is so damn sure she's right?"

She was thinking of Alexandra. Would anyone have considered Alexandra tainted? Misguided, certainly, but unless they were obviously twisted, the Queens would definitely be among the chosen. And what about someone like Vania? Not tainted the way Jaenelle was talking about, but the kind of woman who could sour the males around her and eventually ruin a land. Exactly the kind of woman Dorothea cultivated.

"The Blood are the Blood," Jaenelle continued. "Two feet, four feet, it doesn't matter. The Blood are the Blood. The gift of Craft came from one source, and it binds all of us."

So not even the kindred could be spared. No wonder this had been ripping her apart.

"Does Kaeleer win?" Daemon asked quietly.

A full minute passed before Jaenelle answered. "Yes. But the price for winning will be all the Kaeleer Queens and all the Warlord Princes."

Daemon thought about the decent people he had met since he'd come to Kaeleer. He thought about the kindred. He thought about the children. Most of all, he thought about Daemonar, Lucivar's son. If, for some reason, they didn't destroy Dorothea and Hekatah, and those two got their hands on Daemonar . . . "Do it," he said. "Unleash your strength. Destroy the Blood."

Jaenelle's mouth fell open. She stared at him.

"Do it," he repeated. "If that's the only way to get rid of the taint Dorothea and Hekatah have spread in the Blood, then, by the Darkness, Jaenelle, show some mercy for those you love and do it."

She began pacing again. "There has to be a way to separate Blood from Blood. There *has* to be."

A memory teased him, but he couldn't catch hold of it while her frenzied movement seemed to put everything in motion. "Stand still," he snapped.

She came to an abrupt halt and huffed.

He raised a hand, commanding silence. The memory continued to tease, but he caught the tail of it. "I think there's a way."

Her eyes widened but she obeyed the command for silence.

"A few centuries ago, there was a Queen called the Gray Lady. When a village she was staying in was about to be attacked by Hayllian warriors, she found a way to separate the villagers from the Hayllians so that when she unleashed her strength, the villagers were spared."

"How did she do it?" Jaenelle asked very quietly.

"I don't know." He hesitated—and wondered why he hesitated. "A man I knew was with her at the time. A few years before his death, he sent a message to me that he had made a written account of the 'adventure' and had left it for me in a safe place. She was a good Queen, the last Queen to hold Dorothea at bay. He wanted her remembered."

Jaenelle leaped at him, grabbed him. "Then you *do* know how she did it!"

"No, I *don't* know. I never picked up the written account. I decided to leave it where it was, out of Dorothea's reach."

"Do you think you could find it?" Jaenelle asked anxiously.

"That shouldn't be difficult," Daemon replied dryly as he wrapped his arms around her, suddenly needing to touch her. "He left it with the Keep's librarian."

"I retrieved it from the Terreillean Keep the first time you came to Ebon Askavi with Jaenelle," Geoffrey said as he handed Daemon a carefully wrapped parcel. "I wondered at the time why you didn't ask for it. What made you think of it now?"

The question sounded innocently curious, but there wasn't anything innocent about it.

Looking straight into Geoffrey's black eyes, Daemon smiled. "I just remembered it."

He didn't unwrap it, didn't look at it. He probed it just enough to make sure there weren't any spells hidden in it that would be triggered if someone besides him handled it. Then he gave it to Jaenelle and spent the next several hours denying access to the Queen to just about every member of the First Circle. That had caused hard feelings but was easy enough.

No one but the Steward, the Master of the Guard, and the Consort were permitted free access to the Queen's chambers. Lucivar had taken one look at him and had retreated. Stalling Saetan and Andulvar had been much more difficult, and he sensed it wouldn't take many more polite confrontations to erode their trust in him. Considering Jaenelle's behavior lately, he could appreciate their concern. It still hurt.

When he finally returned to her, he found her in her sitting room, her arms wrapped around herself, staring bleakly out the window.

"It didn't help?" he asked softly, resting a hand lightly on her shoulder.

"Actually, it did. I found the answer. I can't do the same thing they did, but I can use it as the foundation for what I need to do."

She turned and kissed him with a desperation that frightened him, but he gave her what she needed. For hours, he gave her what she needed.

When she was finally content just to lie wrapped in his arms, she said, "I love you." And fell asleep.

Despite being physically and emotionally exhausted, Daemon lay awake a long time—and wondered why "I love you" sounded so much like "good-bye."

6 / Kaeleer

"The Lady changed her mind," Saetan said formally to the Territory Queens who made up the coven. "You and the males in the First Circle are to remain at the Keep, but the other Queens in your Territories may stay where they are."

"Why are *we* required to stay?" Chaosti demanded. "Our people are *dying*. We should be home, preparing to fight."

"Why did she change her mind?" Morghann asked. "What did she say when you asked her?"

Saetan hesitated. "The instructions were relayed by the Consort."

He felt their flickers of anger and their growing suspicion about Daemon. Worse, he had those same feelings.

"The Queen commands," he said, knowing how inadequate that sounded when they were all receiving reports of fighting in their homelands.

"That's fine, High Lord," Aaron said coolly. "The Queen commands.

But, obviously, no one has informed the kindred of that fact. None of *them* who are members of the First Circle have to stay at the Keep."

They all looked at each other as that realization sank in. But it was Karla who finally asked, "Where *are* the kindred?"

Saetan watched the drops of rain trickle down the window.

When Jaenelle had given the order for all the Queens to come to the Keep, he hadn't protested for one reason: Sylvia. He had wanted her in the Keep where she would be safe.

But now that Jaenelle had changed her mind—or had had it changed for her—he would issue his own orders as the Warlord Prince of Dhemlan and summon all the Dhemlan Queens to the Hall. It was a risk. The Hall didn't have the defenses the Keep had. *No place* had the defenses the Keep had. But it had been designed to withstand attack, and its defenses were better than anywhere else the Queens might be forced to retreat if the fighting escalated. And it was big enough that the Queens could bring their families with them, bring their children.

He wanted her safe. And her boys, too, Mikal and Beron.

Sassy, opinionated, lovely Sylvia. Mother Night, he loved her.

Even after he realized that the potency of Jaenelle's tonic after she had made the Offering to the Darkness had brought back the hunger of a man—and the ability to satisfy it—he might have resisted becoming Sylvia's lover, might have found the strength to remain just a friend if he hadn't sensed the hurt in her that her last Consort had inflicted. She had shut herself away from sexual pleasure, hadn't been intrigued enough by any man to try again—until she had become friends with him.

They weren't acknowledged lovers. At his insistence, they maintained the illusion in public of being just friends. Oh, his reasons had been very logical, very considerate. He knew Luthvian would be enraged if he openly became another woman's lover, and he hadn't wanted her to take her anger out on the rest of the family—or on Sylvia. And he hadn't wanted people backing away from her because she had chosen a Guardian for a lover.

At first, she had gone along with him, mostly because she was rediscovering the pleasures of the bed, and had been able to accept that he was a lover in the bedroom and a friend outside of it. But gradually, over the past year, she had become more and more unhappy with the secrecy, had wanted an acknowledged relationship.

He had expected her to leave him. Instead, one night during the Winsol celebrations a few months ago, she had asked him to marry her. And, may the Darkness help him, he had wanted to say yes. Had wanted to share a bed with her, a *life* with her.

But he didn't say yes. Not because of Luthvian or because he was a Guardian, but because of a vague uneasiness that had warned him to take care, to wait. So he had smiled and said, "Ask me next Winsol."

He had understood why, for a few weeks after that, there were no invitations to her bed. He had understood why she was always "busy" when he stopped at her home to spend a little time with the boys.

He had missed the friend far more than he'd missed the lover, but he *had* missed those hours in her bed.

Then, just a few days before the attack in Glacia, they had gone to Amdarh for a couple of days to spend time together away from everyone else, to try to rebuild their relationship. And they had made love, but he had known as soon as he touched her that, despite wanting him, she was trying to keep her distance from him emotionally, that she was trying to protect herself from being hurt again. Even when she was caught up in her climax, he had known.

Now, staring at the rain, he almost wished he had said "yes" at Winsol, almost wished he had asked her to stand with him before a Priestess when they had arrived in Amdarh. And he wished he could make love with her one more time to erase the unhappiness that had been in the bed with them that last time.

But the conviction had been growing in him for days now that there wouldn't be another chance.

There were things he should have said that night in Amdarh. He'd never really told her how much she meant to him, how much he loved her. He should have. Now he could give her nothing but words, but at least he could give her that much.

Turning away from the window, he sat at the desk and began to write.

CHAPTER FOURTEEN

1 / Kaeleer

"I need a favor," Jaenelle said as she moved stiffly to her worktable and picked up two small glass jars.

"You have only to ask," Titian replied. *She's been channeling too much power without giving her body time to recover. What is she planning that demands so much?*

"A discreet favor."

"Understood."

"I need blood from two people who have been tainted by Dorothea or Hekatah. Preferably one of each."

Titian thought for a very brief moment. "Lord Jorval lives in the capital of Little Terreille, does he not?"

Jaenelle swallowed. Even that seemed to take effort. "Yes, Jorval is in Goth. And so, at the moment, is Kartane SaDiablo."

"Ah." Looking at the exhausted woman, Titian remembered the child Jaenelle had been. And she remembered other things. "Will it matter if neither of them sees the next sunrise?"

A deadly cold filled Jaenelle's sapphire eyes. "No."

Titian smiled. "In that case, with your permission, I'll take Surreal with me. It's time to pay some debts."

2 / Kaeleer

In the enormous chamber where the Dark Throne resided, Ladvarian trembled as he looked at Lorn. It wasn't that he was afraid of Lorn—at least, not usually. It was just that Lorn was the Prince of the Dragons, the legendary race who had created the Blood. Lorn was very, *very* old, and very wise, and very *big*. Ladvarian was smaller than one of Lorn's midnight eyes. Just then, that made him feel *very* small.

And then there was Draca, the Keep's Seneschal, who had been Lorn's mate and the Dragon Queen before she had sacrificed her true form in order to give other creatures the Craft.

Sacrifices. No, he would *not* think about sacrifices. There was not going to be a sacrifice. The kindred would not allow it.

But being summoned here by Lorn and Draca when the Arachnian Queen was so close to finishing that special web of dreams . . . It frightened him. If they forbade the kindred from doing this . . . The kindred would do it anyway, whatever the cost.

Little Brother, Lorn said in his deep, quiet, thundering voice.

Prince Lorn. Ladvarian was trembling enough for them to see it.

I have a gift for you, little Brother. Give thiss to the Weaver of Dreamss.

A flat, beautifully carved box appeared in the air before Ladvarian. When it opened, he saw a simply designed pendant made of white and yellow gold and an equally simple ring. But it was the Jewel in those pieces that made his hackles rise and his ears flatten tight to his head.

It had no color, and yet it wasn't colorless. Restless, it shimmered, hungry to complete its transformation. It tugged at him, seeking a bond with his mind.

He took a step back. As he looked up at Lorn, angry and confused enough to issue a challenge that would have been foolish as well as futile, he realized Lorn's scales had that same translucent shimmer. Knowledge crashed in on him. He took another step back and whined.

Do not fear, little Brother. It iss a gift. The Weaver will need it for her web.

Gathering his courage, Ladvarian approached the box. *I have never seen a Jewel like this.*

And you never will again, Lorn replied gently. *There will never be another one like it.*

Still cautious, Ladvarian said, *It has no rank. It does not know what it is.*

It doess not yet know what it iss, Lorn agreed. *But it doess have a name: Twilight'ss Dawn.*

*   *   *

When Ladvarian was on his way back to Arachna with the box, Draca and Lorn stared at each other.

"You rissk much giving him a Jewel like that," Draca said.

★There iss reasson to rissk much,★ Lorn replied. ★Witch hass almosst completed her web?★

"Yess." For the first time since she had met Jaenelle, she felt the weight of her years.

★We cannot heal the taint, Draca,★ Lorn said softly. ★Sshe can.★

"I know. When I gave the gift of magic, I gave it freely, knowing I could never alter what wass done with it." Draca hesitated. "If sshe doess thiss, sshe will be desstroyed."

★Sshe iss Kaeleer'ss Heart. Sshe musst not be desstroyed.★ Lorn paused and added softly, ★The kindred have alwayss been sstrong dreamerss.★

"Will they be sstrong enough?"

The question neither could answer hung between them.

3 / Kaeleer

A stealthy movement and the sudden glow of a small ball of witchlight woke Jorval from an uneasy sleep. "Priestess?"

A hand grabbed his hair, yanked his head up. "No," said the silver-haired woman as her knife cut his throat. "I am vengeance."

4 / Kaeleer

"Enough," Daemon said, leading Jaenelle into her sitting room. "You need to rest."

"The web's almost complete. I need to—"

"*Rest.* If you make an error because you're too exhausted to think clearly, this will all be for nothing."

Making a weak attempt to snarl, she collapsed into a chair.

Daemon wanted to rage at her but knew it wouldn't do any good. She had dropped weight she couldn't afford to lose at a frightening speed. Putting obstacles in her path would only force her to waste energy she couldn't spare, so he took the other path.

"You told me a few minutes ago that you still needed a couple of things to complete the web."

"Those things will take time," she protested.

He bent down and kissed her softly, persuasively. When he felt her yield, he murmured against her lips, "We'll have a quiet dinner. Then we'll play a couple of hands of 'cradle.' I'll even let you win."

Her huff of laughter provoked another hunger. His kiss deepened as his hand caressed her breast.

"I think I am hungry," Jaenelle said breathlessly when he finally gave her a chance to speak.

After they had thoroughly satisfied one hunger, they finally sat down to dinner.

5 / Hell

Pain woke him.

Kartane opened his eyes. Two fading balls of witchlight provided enough light for him to clearly see that he was outside. Then he realized he was upside down. *Someone had tied him upside down.*

Something rustled the bushes nearby.

Turning his head a little, he stared at an odd pile of brown clothing, neatly folded.

Suddenly, his heart pounded. Suddenly, it was hard to breathe.

The surrounding shadows shifted just enough for him to see that the odd pile wasn't clothing, it was brown skin.

As he drew in a breath to scream, glowing red eyes appeared in the darkness around him.

Even with her head under the water, Surreal heard Kartane scream.

She popped up out of the water, then immediately lowered herself to her neck. The pool, fed by a hot spring, was delightfully warm, but the air was cool enough to bite.

She heard snarls, a howl, a terrified shriek.

The air wasn't the only thing around there that had a bite.

"So this is Hell," she said, looking around. It was too dark to see much, but the area around the pool had a kind of stark beauty.

"This is Hell," Titian replied, a blissful smile on her face. She straightened up and gave Surreal a searching look. "Has the debt been paid to your satisfaction, Surreal?"

The snarls and shrieks stopped for a moment, then started again.

"Yes," Surreal said, leaning back with a sigh, "I'm satisfied."

6 / Kaeleer

"Sometimes the heart reveals more than panes of glass can."

Saetan turned away from the window, tensed, took a step forward, stopped. "Tersa, why are you at the Keep?"

Smiling, Tersa walked across the room and held out a thick envelope. "I came to give you this."

Even before he took the envelope, he knew who it was from. Sylvia always added a drop of lavender oil to her wax seal.

Laying one hand on his shoulder, Tersa kissed him on the lips—a lingering kiss that surprised him. Worried him.

She stepped back. "That was the other part of the message." She was almost at the door before he gathered his wits.

"Tersa, this can't be the only reason you traveled to the Keep."

"No?" she said, looking puzzled. Then, "No, it wasn't."

He waited. She said nothing.

"Darling," he prodded gently, "why are you here?"

Her eyes cleared, and he felt certain that, for the first time in all the centuries he had known her, he was seeing a glimpse of Tersa as she had been before she was broken. She was formidable—and a bit dazzling.

"I'm needed here," she said quietly, then walked out of the room.

He stood there for several minutes, staring at the envelope in his hands. "Show some balls, SaDiablo," he finally muttered as he carefully opened the envelope. "No matter what the letter says, it isn't the end of the world."

It was a long letter. He read it twice before he tucked it away.

He hadn't been able to give Sylvia more than words, but apparently, thankfully, that had been enough.

7 / Terreille

Dorothea prowled around the room. "Armies are gathering all over Terreille, the Territories in the Shadow Realm have been attacked for weeks now by the people we had hidden in Little Terreille, and Kaeleer *still* hasn't formally declared war."

"That's because Jaenelle Angelline doesn't have the backbone to go along with her power," Hekatah said as she carefully arranged her full-length cape. "She's just a mouse scurrying around in her hidey-hole while the cats gather for the feast."

"Even a mouse will bite," Dorothea snapped.

"This mouse won't bite," Hekatah replied calmly. "She's too emotionally squeamish to take the step that would begin a full-scale slaughter."

Dorothea wasn't as sure of that as Hekatah seemed to be, but Jaenelle's sparing Alexandra's life after the abduction failed certainly seemed to indicate a lack of the proper temperament. *She* certainly wouldn't have spared the bitch. That lack in Jaenelle was in their favor, but . . . "You seem to be forgetting that the High Lord has fangs and isn't the least bit squeamish about using them."

"I forget nothing where Saetan is concerned," Hekatah snarled. "His honor hobbles him, just as it always has, and his own emotional failings will muzzle him. With the right persuasion, he'll tuck his tail between his legs and submit to whatever we require of him."

She hoped that rotting sack of bones was right. They *had* to eliminate Saetan, Lucivar, and Daemon. When those three were gone, the Terreillean armies would be able to destroy the Kaeleer Queens and Warlord Princes. Entire armies would be slaughtered in the process, but they *would* win the war. And then she would rule the Realms—after she hurried the Dark Priestess to a well-deserved, and permanent, rest.

Pleased by that thought, Dorothea stopped prowling long enough to notice that Hekatah was preparing to go out. "Where are you going?"

Hekatah smiled malevolently. "To Kaeleer. It's time to collect the first part of the bait that will give us control of Jaenelle Angelline."

8 / Kaeleer

Finally admitted to Jaenelle's sitting room, Andulvar studied her and thought of several things he'd like to do to Daemon Sadi. Damn it, the man was her Consort and should have been taking care of her. She was far too thin, and the skin under her eyes was faintly bruised from exhaustion. And there was a queer, almost desperate glitter in her eyes.

"Prince Yaslana," Jaenelle said quietly.

So. It was going to be formal.

"Lady," Andulvar replied stiffly. "Since I'm obviously not here as your uncle, am I here as your Master of the Guard?" When she flinched, he regretted the harshness of his words. She didn't look like she could endure too many more emotional blows.

"I—There's something I need to tell you. And I need your help."

He did his best to soften his tone. "Because I'm your Master of the Guard?"

She shook her head. "Because you're the Demon Prince. After Saetan, you have the most authority in Hell. The demon-dead will listen to you—and follow you."

He went to her and hugged her gently, afraid that if he held on to her the way he wanted to she would shatter. "What is it, waif?"

She eased back just enough to look him in the eyes. "I've found a way to get rid of Dorothea and Hekatah and the taint they've left in the Blood. But the rest of the Blood will be at risk unless the demon-dead are willing to help me."

Thirty minutes later, Andulvar closed the sitting room door, took a couple of steps, then sagged against the wall.

Mother Night.

He didn't doubt the plan would work. Jaenelle wouldn't have said she could do it if she had any doubts. But . . . *Mother Night.*

He had fought in the last war between Terreille and Kaeleer. That war had devastated both Realms, and millions had died. And it had made no difference. They were standing on the edge of that same cliff, fighting against a greed and ambition that would simply go to ground again if it wasn't finally, completely eliminated.

Like Mephis and Prothvar, he had known it would be futile to fight another war in the same way. Like them, he had looked around the table when the First Circle argued for a formal declaration of war and had wondered how many would still be among the living when it was over.

Jaenelle hadn't wondered. She had *known* none of them would survive. Hell's fire, no wonder she had been doing anything she could to keep them in the one place where they would be safe.

And now she had a *plan* that . . . Mother Night.

Even after she had told him, there was something about it that hadn't felt quite *right*—as if she had glossed over something. Saetan would have known what it was, but Saetan . . .

She *was* right about that. The coven and the boyos would need Saetan's wisdom and experience to mend the wounds already inflicted on Kaeleer. So he couldn't tell his friend what Jaenelle intended to do, couldn't take the chance that Saetan might choose to throw his strength in with the rest of them instead of staying behind. He couldn't do that because, after everything was over, the High Lord would be needed by the living.

Ladvarian waited in the shadows until he was sure Andulvar was really gone. Then he slipped into Jaenelle's sitting room.

She was staring out the window. He wanted to tell her it would be all right, even though he wasn't sure it would be. Yes, he was. It *would* be all right. The kindred would not doubt. The kindred would be strong. But he couldn't tell her that because this was a time for fangs and claws. This was a time for killing. And they weren't sure she would be able to kill if they told her what was going to happen afterward.

But there was something else he *had* to tell her.

Jaenelle?

There was as much sadness as pleasure in her eyes when she turned and saw him. "What is it, little Brother?"

I have a message for you—from the Weaver of Dreams.

She went absolutely still, and he was afraid Witch might look right into him and see what he wanted to hide.

"What is the message?"

She said the triangle must stay together in order to survive. The mirror can keep the others safe, but only if they're together. He hesitated when she just stared at him. *Who is the mirror?*

"Daemon," she replied absently. "He's his father's mirror."

She seemed lost for a moment, long enough to make him nervous. *Do you understand the message?*

"No," she said, looking very pale. "But I'm sure I will."

9 / Kaeleer

Luthvian heard her bedroom door open, but she continued stuffing clothes into a travel bag and didn't turn around. Damn Eyrien pup, coming up to her room without permission. And damn Lucivar for insisting that she come to the Keep and insisting that she have an escort. She didn't need an escort—especially not Palanar, who was barely old enough to wipe his own nose.

As she started to turn around to tell him just that, a caped figure rushed at her. Instantly, instinctively, she threw up a Red shield. A blast of Red power struck her at the same moment, preventing the shield from forming, and the figure was on her. They tumbled to the floor.

Luthvian didn't realize she'd been knifed until the enemy yanked the blade out of her body.

Being a Healer, she knew it was bad—a killing wound.

Furious, knowing she didn't have long, she ripped the hood off her enemy and then stared for a moment, frozen. "You."

Hekatah rammed the knife into Luthvian's belly. "Bitch," she hissed. "I could have made something of you. Now I'll just turn you into carrion."

Luthvian tried to fight, tried to scratch and claw, but her arms felt too heavy to lift. She couldn't do anything even when Hekatah's teeth sank into her throat and her blood fed the vile bitch.

Nothing to be done for the body, but the Self . . .

Gathering her strength and her rage, she channeled it into her inner barriers.

Hekatah pounded against them as she fed, pounded and pounded, trying to blast them open to finish the kill. But Luthvian hung on, letting rage form the bridge between life and death as she poured her strength into her inner barriers. Poured and poured until there was nothing left. Nothing.

At some point, the pounding stopped, and Luthvian felt a grim satisfaction that the bitch hadn't been able to break through.

Far, far away, she felt Hekatah roll off her. Somewhere in the vague, misty distance she saw sharp nails descending toward her face.

The hand stopped before the nails touched her eyes.

"No," Hekatah said. "If you manage to make the transition to demon-dead, I want you to see what I do to your boy."

Movement. The bedroom door closed. Silence.

Luthvian felt herself fading. With effort, she flexed her fingers—just a little.

Her rage had burned through the transition without her being aware of it, without Hekatah being able to sense it. She was demon-dead, but she didn't have the strength to hold on. Her Self would soon become a whisper in the Darkness. Perhaps, someday, when it had rested and regained some strength, the Self would leave the Darkness and return to the living Realms. Perhaps.

How many times had Lucivar told her to set up warning shields around the house? And every time he'd tried, she had dismissed it with a sneer. But she'd been secretly pleased that he had tried.

It had been a test, but she had been the only one who had known that. Every time he had mentioned the shields again after she had dismissed the idea, every time he had endured her sharp tongue while he helped her in some way had been a test to prove that he cared about her.

Oh, there were times when, seeing the tightness in his face and the coolness in his eyes, she had told herself it would be the last time, the last test. The next time he mentioned the shields, she would do what he wanted so that he would know she cared about him, too.

Then the next time would come and she would want, would *need,* just one more test. One more. And one more. Always one more.

Now there would be no more tests, but her son, her fine Eyrien War-lord Prince, would never know she had loved him.

All she would have needed was an hour as one of the demon-dead. An hour to tell him. She couldn't even leave him a message. Nothing.

No. Wait. Maybe she *could* say the most important thing, the thing that had been chewing at her ever since Surreal had lashed out at her.

She gathered everything that was left of her strength, shaped it into a bubble to hold one thought, then pushed it upward, upward, upward until it rested just outside her inner barriers.

Lucivar would find it. She knew he would.

No anchor. Nothing to hold on to. Filled with regrets tempered by one bubble of acknowledged love, she faded away and returned to the Darkness.

10 / Kaeleer

Palanar knocked reluctantly on the kitchen door. He supposed being asked to escort Lady Luthvian to the Keep was an honor, but she had made it very clear that she didn't like Eyrien males. So he wasn't really sure if this was Hallevar's way of showing confidence in him or a subtle punishment for something he'd done.

He opened the door and cautiously poked his head into the kitchen. "Lady Luthvian?"

She was there, standing near the table, staring at him. Then she smiled and said, "No balls, little warrior?"

Stung, he stepped into the kitchen. "Are you ready?" he asked, striving to put the same arrogance into his voice that Falonar or Lucivar would have had.

She looked at the traveling bag next to her, then at him.

Since when did Luthvian expect a male to carry anything? The last time he'd tried, she'd almost dented his head. Hallevar had been right when he'd said, "Best resign yourself to the fact that a female can change her mind faster than you can fart."

He took a couple of steps toward her, then stopped again.

"What's wrong?" she asked suspiciously.

She stank. That's what was wrong. Really *stank*. But he wasn't about to say *that*. Then he noticed she looked a little . . . strange.

"What's wrong?" she asked again, taking a step toward him.

He took two steps back.

Her face shifted, wavered. For a moment, he thought he saw someone else. Someone he didn't know—and didn't *want* to know.

And he remembered something else Hallevar had told him: sometimes running was the smartest thing an inexperienced warrior could do.

He ran for the door.

He didn't reach it. Power blasted through his inner barriers. Needles stabbed into his mind, grew hooks and dug deeper, tore out little bits of his Self. His body vibrated from the fierce tug-of-war as he tried to get out the door while she drew him back into the room.

Helpless, he felt himself turn around—and saw the witch who held him captive. He screamed.

"You will go exactly where I tell you to go," she said. "Say exactly what I tell you to say."

"N-n-no."

Gold eyes glittered in her decayed face, and pain seared him.

"It's a small task, puppy. And when it's done, I'll set you free."

She held out a small crystal. It floated through the air. His left hand reached out and took it.

She told him exactly where to go, exactly what to say, exactly what to do with the spell in the crystal. Then he was turned around again, like a marionette with knotted strings. He walked out the door.

A warrior would not do this, no matter the price. A warrior would not do this.

He tried to bring his right hand up to reach his knife. He could cut his throat, cut his wrists, do *something* to get away from her.

His hand closed on the hilt.

Dying won't save you, little warrior, the witch said. *I am the Dark Priestess. You can't escape me that way.*

His hand dropped to his side, empty.

Now go!

Palanar spread his wings and flew as fast as he could to do what a warrior would not do.

It wasn't the wind in his face that made him weep.

11 / Kaeleer

Lucivar landed at his eyrie, and shouted, "Marian!" Where in the name of Hell was the woman? he thought as he strode toward the door. She should have arrived at the Keep hours ago.

He walked through the door, saw the neat pile of traveling bags. His heart stopped for a moment. By the time he felt it beat again, he had risen to the killing edge. *"Marian!"*

The eyrie was a big place, but it didn't take him long to give it a thorough search. Marian and Daemonar weren't there. But she had packed, so what had prevented her from leaving? Maybe Daemonar was ill? Had she taken him over to Nurian's eyrie to have the Healer look at him?

As the Warlord Prince of Ebon Rih, his eyrie was set a little apart from the other eyries nestled in the mountain, but it was only a couple of minutes before he landed in front of Nurian's home. Before his feet touched the ground, he knew they weren't there.

"Lucivar!"

Lucivar turned as Hallevar hurried up to him. He noticed Falonar and Kohlvar as they walked out of the communal eyrie that was as close as Eyriens came to having inns and taverns. Both men, hearing the agitation in Hallevar's voice, moved toward him.

"Have you seen that pup, Palanar?" Hallevar asked.

Before Lucivar could respond, Falonar jumped in. "Didn't you send him to escort Lady Luthvian to the Keep?"

"I did," Hallevar said grimly. "And told him to get his ass right back here." He looked at Lucivar. "I wondered if he might be dawdling at the Keep to dodge some chores."

"Palanar didn't arrive at the Keep. Neither did Luthvian. Neither did Marian and Daemonar," Lucivar added too quietly.

The other men stiffened.

"I sent him first thing this morning," Hallevar said.

"Any sign of trouble at your eyrie?" Falonar asked sharply.

"No," Lucivar said. "The bags were packed and set near the door." He swore softly, viciously. "Where in the name of Hell did she go?"

"She went to Lady Luthvian's," said a young female voice.

They all turned and stared at Jillian, Nurian's young sister.

She hunched her shoulders and looked ready to bolt back into the eyrie.

Hallevar pointed a finger at the ground a few feet away from him. "Here, little warrior," he said sternly.

Scared now, Jillian crept to the spot, glanced at the large warriors surrounding her, then stared at her feet.

"Make your report," Hallevar said in that tone that, although encouraging, had made every young male who had trained under him snap to attention.

It had the same effect on Jillian. She stood upright and focused on Hallevar. "I was doing my stamina run this morning." She waited until she got Hallevar's approving nod. "And I thought I would take the path to Prince Yaslana's eyrie because I thought, well, maybe Lady Marian would want a little help with Daemonar, that I could look after him for a bit so she could get some of her chores done. It wasn't like I was shirking the rest of my workout or anything, 'cause looking after Daemonar *is* work."

Despite being worried, Lucivar's lips twitched as he fought not to smile.

"I was almost there when I saw Marian standing at the door talking to Palanar. He looked . . . sick. He was sweating hard, and . . . I don't know. I've never seen anyone look like that. And then Marian jerked like someone had hit her, but Palanar didn't touch her. He said, 'Bring the boy.' She went inside and came back out with Daemonar. Daemonar took one look at Palanar and started howling. You know, that sound Daemonar makes when he doesn't like something?"

Lucivar nodded. He felt a cold sweat forming on his skin.

"Palanar grabbed one of Marian's arms. He kept saying, 'I'm sorry, I'm sorry.' "

"Did he see you?" Lucivar asked too quietly.

Jillian shook her head. "But Marian did. She looked right at me, and her face had the same sick look that Palanar's did, and she said, 'Luthvian's.' Then they left." Having finished her report, her confidence faded as she looked up at the grim-faced men.

"You didn't report this to anyone?" Lucivar asked.

Pale now, Jillian shook her head again. "I—Nurian wasn't home when I got back, and . . . I didn't know I was supposed to report," she finished in a barely audible voice.

And would have been reluctant to go to one of the warriors and be casually dismissed because she was female. A few months of living in Kaeleer weren't enough to overcome survival tactics that had been learned from the time she had gotten out of the cradle.

"When a warrior sees something strange, he—or she—should report to—her—superiors," Hallevar said in a firm but gentle voice. "That's one of the ways a young warrior gains experience."

"Yes, sir," Jillian whispered.

"That was a fine first report, Jillian," Lucivar said. "Now go back to your chores."

Jillian's shoulders went back. Her eyes shown with pleasure. "Yes, sir."

None of them spoke until the girl had gone back inside.

"Sounds like a compulsion spell," Falonar said quietly.

"Yes," Lucivar replied grimly, "it does. Falonar, keep an eye on things here."

"You're going to Luthvian's?" Hallevar asked quickly as Lucivar stepped away from them. "Then I'm going with you."

"No, you're not," Falonar said. "Kohlvar, you bring everyone up close to the eyries. Hallevar, you have the most influence with the youngsters. Keep a tight leash on them."

"And where will you be?" Lucivar asked too softly.

Falonar squared off to face him. "*I'm* going with you."

They found Palanar on the ground outside the kitchen door.

"I'll look after him," Falonar said. "You go on."

Calling in his Eyrien war blade, Lucivar kicked open the kitchen door and lunged into the room. The stink inside gagged him, reminded him too strongly of carrion.

That thought catapulted him through the other downstairs rooms. Finding them empty, he surged up the stairs. He kicked the bedroom door open—and saw Luthvian. He probed the room swiftly to make sure no one was waiting for the moment when he dropped his guard, then he knelt beside the body.

At first he thought she was still alive. The wounds he could see were bad, but there would have been more blood if she had bled out. When he brushed her hair away from her neck, he saw why there wasn't a lot of blood.

He rested a hand on her head. All right. The body was dead, but she was strong enough to make the transition to demon-dead. If there was any sign that she was still there, fresh blood would strengthen her.

He probed cautiously so that he wouldn't punch through her inner barriers and inadvertently finish the kill.

Just outside her inner barriers was an odd little bubble of power. He paused, considered. The bubble had a feeling of emotional warmth that made him suspect. It wasn't the sort of feelings he associated with Luthvian. But there was nothing he could detect that made him believe he would be in danger, so he brushed a psychic tendril against it, lightly.

Lucivar . . . I was wrong about Marian. You chose well. I wish you both happy.

Tears stung his eyes. He brushed against the inner barriers. They opened with no resistance. He searched for her, searched for the least little flicker of her spirit. Nothing.

Luthvian had returned to the Darkness.

One tear spilled over. "Hell's fire, Luthvian," he said in a broken voice. "Why did you have to wait until you were dead to tell me that? Why—"

"Lucivar!"

He shot to his feet, responding to the grief and anger in Falonar's voice. He paused at the door, looked back. "May the Darkness embrace you, Mother."

Falonar was waiting for him in the kitchen.

"Palanar?" Lucivar asked.

Falonar shook his head. He didn't need to ask about Luthvian. "I saw that." He pointed to a folded sheet of paper on the table.

Lucivar stared at the paper that had his name on it. He didn't recognize the handwriting and felt an instinctive revulsion against touching it. Using Craft, he unfolded the paper, read it, and stormed out the door.

"Lucivar!" Falonar shouted, running after him. "Where are you going?"

"Get back to the eyries," Lucivar said as he strapped the fighting gauntlets over his forearms. "You're in charge now, Prince Falonar."

"Where are you going?"

Lucivar rose to the killing edge, felt the sweet, cold rage wash through him. "I'm going to get my wife and son away from those bitches."

12 / Kaeleer

The attack started the moment Falonar returned to the eyries. His Sapphire shield snapped up around him a second before an arrow would have gone through his back. He called in his longbow, nocked an arrow, added a bit of Sapphire power to the head, and let it fly.

He took a moment to probe the area and assess the enemy. Then he swore viciously. There was a full company of Eyrien warriors out there. None of them wore a Jewel darker than the Green, so his Sapphire Jewels would balance the odds a little, but his own warriors were far outnumbered. Every man would go down fighting, but that wasn't going to save the women and children.

"The communal eyrie!" Hallevar shouted as he herded women and children in that direction. "Move! Move!"

Smart move, Falonar thought approvingly as he let another arrow fly. It was big enough to hold all of them and give his warriors one concentrated battleground instead of scattered ones.

His shield deflected a dozen more arrows. Having risen to the killing edge, he embraced the cold rage and fought with a mind cleansed of emotions. *His* arrows found their targets.

Someone screamed. Looking to his left, he saw Nurian struggling with an Eyrien Warlord. He started to turn, but before he could draw his bow, another warrior rushed at him with a bladed stick. Vanishing the bow and arrow, he called in his own bladed stick and met the attack. As he danced back and looked for an opening, Nurian screamed again.

Screw honor. This was war. When his adversary came at him again, he met the blow with a dirty, nasty maneuver he'd recently learned from Lucivar that dispatched the enemy with a vengeance.

Even as he turned, expecting to be too late to save the Healer, he heard Jillian shout, "Down, Nurian!"

Hearing Jillian changed Nurian from helpless woman to apprentice warrior. She kicked viciously at the Warlord's groin at the same time she threw herself backward. The kick didn't land solidly, but it was enough to startle the man into letting go of her, and the unexpected move threw him off-balance. As he tried to right himself, an arrow whizzed through the air and buried itself in his chest.

Jillian was already nocking another arrow and taking aim while Nurian scrambled to her feet and ran, hunched over to stay out of the line of fire.

He threw a Sapphire shield in front of Jillian just in time to stop the arrows that would have gone right through her. "Retreat!" he shouted, ready to foam at the mouth when Jillian calmly sent another arrow flying. "Damn you, warrior, *retreat!*"

That startled her, but it was Nurian's shout that made her run.

Ready to cover their retreat, Falonar glanced back—and swore every vicious curse he knew. Nurian was now standing braced to fight with nothing but an Eyrien stick. Not even a *bladed* stick. What in the name of Hell did the woman think she could do with that? Did she think a warrior was going to come at her barehanded? Fool. *Idiot.*

He backed toward her, always watching for the next attack. "Retreat," he snarled at her—and then noticed that Jillian, instead of running all the way to the communal eyrie, had stopped halfway there to take up a rear-guard position. "Disobey me again and I'll personally whip the skin off your backs. *Both of you.* Now *retreat!*"

They responded the same way any Eyrien warrior would have—they ignored the threat and held their positions. So *he* retreated, forcing them back with him. *That* they were willing to do. Lucivar must have been out of his mind to think a *woman* would obey a sensible order. Which made Falonar extremely grateful that Surreal wasn't there. The Darkness only knew how he could have held *her* back in this fight.

When they got close enough to the communal eyrie, Hallevar grabbed Jillian and Kohlvar practically threw Nurian through the door-way. Falonar was the last one in. As soon as he crossed the threshold, he filled the doorway with a Sapphire shield so that they would be protected but still have a good view. Some of the men had taken up positions at the shielded downstairs' windows. Others had gone to the upper rooms. The women and children were all huddled in the main community room.

Hallevar joined him at the door. "You think they're regrouping?"

"I don't know."

Behind them, he heard Tamnar say a bit resentfully, "Well, *little warrior,* looks like you made your first kill."

He and Hallevar both turned and blasted the same message at Tamnar. ⋆SHUT UP!⋆

The boy flinched, looked shocked at the harsh reprimand, then slunk over to the window Kohlvar guarded.

Jillian stared at them, her normally brown skin an unhealthy gray. "I killed him?"

Before Falonar could phrase a cautious reply, Hallevar snorted. "You just scratched him enough to let Nurian get away."

Some of the tension drained out of the girl. "Oh. That's . . . Oh."

"You take a backup position over there," Hallevar said, pointing to a far corner of the room.

"Okay," Jillian said, sounding a little dazed.

Falonar turned back to look out the doorway. "She put that arrow right through the bastard's heart," he said, keeping his voice quiet.

"No reason for her to know that right now," Hallevar replied just as quietly. "Let her believe she just nicked him. We can't afford to have her freeze up if it comes down to that."

"If it comes down to that," Falonar said softly as he settled in to wait.

13 / Kaeleer

Saetan prowled the corridors of the Keep, too restless to stay in one place, too edgy to tolerate being around anyone.

Lucivar should have been back *hours* ago. He knew Lucivar had slipped out of the Keep late that morning to find out what was delaying Marian's and Daemonar's arrival, but the afternoon was waning, and there was no sign of any of them.

He doubted anyone else had noticed. The coven and the boyos were gathered in one of the large sitting rooms, just as they had gathered every day since Jaenelle had ordered them to remain at the Keep. So they wouldn't realize Lucivar was gone. And Jaenelle and Daemon . . . Well, they weren't likely to have noticed either.

Surreal had noticed Lucivar's absence, but she'd shrugged it off, saying he was probably with Prothvar and Mephis. Which made him realize that he hadn't seen either of *them* lately.

Somehow he had to find a way to make Jaenelle listen to him, had to find out why she was keeping such a stranglehold on all of them. Whether they acknowledged it or not, they were at war. The Queens and males in the First Circle weren't going to tolerate staying there indefinitely while their people were fighting. *Something* had to change. *Someone* had to act.

14 / Kaeleer

Falonar accepted the mug of ale Kohlvar handed to him.

"Makes no sense," Kohlvar said, shaking his head. "No direct attacks anymore, no efforts at a siege, just a few arrows now and then to make sure we know they're still out there."

"They've got us pinned down," Falonar replied. "We're outnumbered, and they know it."

"But what's the sense of pinning us down?"

We can't go anywhere, Falonar thought. *We can't* report *anything.*

"What's the sense?" Kohlvar repeated.

"I don't know. But I expect we'll find out sooner or later."

The answer came at twilight. One Warlord openly approached the communal eyrie, his hands held away from his sides, away from his weapons.

"I have a message," he shouted, holding up a white envelope.

"Put it on the ground," Falonar shouted back.

The Warlord shrugged, set the envelope on the ground, then placed a small rock over it to keep it from blowing away. He walked back the way he had come.

A few minutes later, Falonar watched the Eyrien company take flight.

He waited another hour before he used Craft to bring the envelope to the doorway. Still standing on the other side of the Sapphire shield, he created a ball of witchlight to illuminate the writing, the name of the recipient.

Dread shivered through him. It was the same handwriting as the note that had been left for Lucivar. But this one was addressed to the High Lord.

He called Kohlvar, Rothvar, Zaranar, and Hallevar over. "I'm going to take that to the Keep and give my report."

"Could be a trap," Hallevar said. "They could be waiting for you to make a move."

Yes, he was sure it *was* a trap—but not for him.

"I don't think they're going to bother us anymore, but maintain a watch. Stay sharp. Don't let *anyone* in, no matter who they are. I'll stay at the Keep until morning. If I come back before that . . . do your best to kill me."

They understood him. If he came back before that, they should assume he was being controlled and respond accordingly.

"May the Darkness protect you," Hallevar said.

Falonar passed through the Sapphire shield. Taking the envelope, he launched himself skyward and headed for the Keep.

15 / Kaeleer

Saetan stared at the sheet of paper. Too many feelings crowded him, so he pushed them all aside.

> *I have your son.*
> *Hekatah*

Which also meant she had Marian and Daemonar, since that was the only bait she could have used to provoke Lucivar into going to Hayll.

Now Lucivar was being used as the bait for *him*.

He understood the game. Hekatah and Dorothea would be willing to trade: him for Lucivar, Marian, and Daemonar.

Of course, they wouldn't let Lucivar go, *couldn't* let him go. As soon as he got Marian and Daemonar safely out of reach, he'd turn on Hekatah and Dorothea with all the destructive power that was in him.

So this was a false bargain right from the beginning.

He could go to Hayll and destroy Dorothea and Hekatah. Two Red-Jeweled Priestesses were no match for a Black-Jeweled Warlord Prince. He could go there, throw a Black shield around Lucivar, Marian, and Daemonar to keep them safe, then unleash his strength—and kill every living thing for miles around him.

But it wouldn't stop the war. Not now. Maybe it never would have. And it was the war that had to be stopped, not just the two witches who had started it.

So he would play their game . . . because it would finally give him the weapon he needed.

Everything has a price.

He removed the Black-Jeweled pendant and set it on the desk. He removed the Steward's ring from his left hand—the ring that contained the same Ebony shield Jaenelle had put into the Rings of Honor.

Even if Daemon was influencing Jaenelle, even if he *was* the reason she was resisting a formal declaration of war, even *he* couldn't stop her reacting. Not to this.

Don't think. Be an instrument.

By walking into the trap Dorothea and Hekatah had set for him, he was going to unleash the one thing he *knew* would bring out the explosive, savage side of Jaenelle—his own pain.

Of course, he would never be the same after those two bitches were done with him. He would never . . .

He opened the desk drawer, caressed the lavender-scented envelope. "Sometimes duty walks a road where the heart can't follow. I'm sorry, Sylvia. It would have been an honor to be your husband. I'm sorry."

He closed the drawer, picked up his cape, and quietly left the Keep.

16 / Kaeleer

Daemon glided through the Keep's corridors. He'd spent the past several hours making three months' worth of tonics for Karla, according to the instructions Jaenelle had given him. When he'd questioned her, reminding her that healing tonics that had blood in them would lose their potency over that amount of time, she had told him she had calculated that so the potency would taper off the way it needed to. And when he'd ask why . . .

Well, it was to be expected that she would be drained by unleashing the amount of power needed to stop Dorothea and Hekatah *completely*. The fact that it would take her three months to recover worried him. And now that she was so close to finishing . . . whatever it was . . . he was also worried that the boyos might finally slip the leash and throw themselves into battle.

They were feeling too hostile toward him just then to listen to anything he might say, but he hoped Saetan would still be reasonable. He was fairly sure he could say enough for the High Lord to understand that Jaenelle's evasion had a purpose, that all they needed was a few more days. A few more days and the threat to Kaeleer would end, the threat Dorothea and Hekatah had always been to the Blood would end.

He knocked on Saetan's door, then went in cautiously when it was Surreal who said, "Come in."

She was standing behind the small desk. Falonar stood beside her, looking tired and angry. Surreal didn't look tired, and she was a long way past angry. "Look at this," she said.

Even from where he stood, he could see the pendant and the Steward's ring. Slipping his hands into his trouser pockets, he walked around the desk, silently acknowledging the emotional cut when she deliberately moved away from him. He read the message and felt a claw-sharp chill rip down his back.

"*Now* are you finally going to do something?" Surreal asked, slamming her hands on the desk. "They're not killing strangers anymore. You can't keep your distance anymore. *Those bitches have your father and brother.*"

It cost him dearly, but he managed to get that bored tone in his voice. "Lucivar and Saetan chose to take the risk when they disobeyed orders. It doesn't change anything." *Couldn't* change anything. Not if Jaenelle was going to save Kaeleer.

"They've also got Marian and Daemonar."

Of course they did. He felt concerned about Marian, but not really worried. If Marian were raped or harmed in any way, not even a Ring of Obedience would stop Lucivar from starting a full-scale slaughter. So he wasn't really worried about Marian, but just the thought of Daemonar in those bitches' hands for even an hour . . . "There's bound to be some kind of ransom demand," he said dismissively. "We'll see what we can accommodate."

"Accommodate?" Surreal said. "*Accommodate?* Don't you know what Dorothea and Hekatah will do to them?"

Of course he knew, far better than she did.

Surreal's voice filled with venom. "Are you at least going to tell Jaenelle?"

"Yes, I suppose the Lady will have to be told about this inconvenience." He walked out of the room while Surreal was still sputtering curses.

He wished she had cried. He wished she had shouted, screamed, raged, swore, wept bitterly. He didn't know what to do with this still woman he had cradled on his lap for the past hour.

He had told her as gently as he could. She had said nothing. Just put her head on his shoulder and turned inward, going down so deep into the abyss he couldn't even feel her.

So he held her. Sometimes his hands stroked, caressed—not to arouse her but to relax her. He *could* have drawn her back with sex, but it would have violated the trust she had in him, and *that* he wouldn't do. When his hand had rested on her chest, it was to reassure himself that her heart was still beating. Each warm breath against his throat was an unspoken promise that she would return to him.

Finally, after almost two hours had passed, she stirred. "What do you think will happen now?" she asked as if there had been no time at all between the question and his news.

"Even riding the Black Winds, it would have taken Saetan a couple of hours or more to get to Hayll. We don't know when he left—"

"But he would have gotten there by now."

"Yes." He paused, thought it through again. "Lucivar and Saetan aren't the prize. They're the bait. And bait becomes less valuable if it's damaged. So I think they're safe enough for the moment."

"Dorothea and Hekatah expect me to surrender Kaeleer in order to get Lucivar and Papa back, don't they?" When he didn't answer, Jaenelle raised her head and studied him. "No. That would never do, would it? In order to hold on to Kaeleer, they have to be able to control me, use my strength to rule."

"Yes. Lucivar and Saetan are the bait. You're the prize." Daemon brushed her hair away from her face. "How close are you to finishing your . . . spell?" He knew it was far more than that, but it was as good a word as any.

"A few more hours." She stirred a little more. "I should get back to it."

His hold on her tightened. "Not yet. Sit with me a little while longer. Please."

She relaxed against him. "We'll get them back, Daemon."

Father. Brother. He closed his eyes and pressed his cheek against her head, needing the warmth and contact. "Yes," he murmured, "we'll get them back."

17 / Kaeleer

Ladvarian studied the chamber that would be Witch's home for a while. An old carpet that he had brought from the Hall covered the stone floor. He had also taken a couple of lamps that used candle-lights and lots of scented candles. The narrow bed Tersa had given him was in the center of the chamber. The trunk was beside it and held a few changes of clothes, a couple of the books Jaenelle liked to read when she needed to snuggle up and rest for a day, her favorite music crystals, and some grooming things.

He had brought no pictures because three walls and the ceiling of the chamber were covered with layers of healing webs. The back of the chamber was filled with the tangled web of dreams and visions that had shaped the living myth, dreams made flesh, Witch.

Is it ready? he respectfully asked the large golden spider who was the Weaver of Dreams.

Web is ready, the Arachnian Queen replied, delicately brushing a leg against one of the drops of blood sealed in shielded water bubbles. *I add memories now. But . . . Need human memories.*

Ladvarian bristled. *She was *our* dream more than theirs.*

*But theirs, too. Need kindred *and* human memories for this Witch.*

Ladvarian's heart sank. It had been easy with the kindred. He had told them what was required and that it was for the Lady. That's all the kindred had needed to know. But humans would want to know why, why, why. They would take time to persuade—and time was something he didn't have.

The Strange One will help you, the spider said.

*But the Lady knows packs of humans, whole *herds* of humans. How—*

The First Circle have strong memories. They will be enough. Ask the Gray Black Widow. For a human, she is a good weaver.

She meant Karla. Yes. If he could persuade Karla . . .

Wait for the right time to ask. After Witch has gone to her own web. The humans will listen better then.

I'll go to the Keep now and wait. Ladvarian looked around one more time. There was nothing left to do. The chamber was ready. The tangled web was ready. The kindred who belonged to the Lady's court were gathered on the Arachnians' island to give their strength to the Weaver's web when the time came.

One more thing, the spider said. *Gray dog. You know this dog?*

An image appeared in Ladvarian's mind. *That's Graysfang. He's a wolf.*

Send him to me. There is something he must learn.

18 / Terreille

It was a war camp, not the sort of place he would have looked for Hekatah or Dorothea. Around the wide perimeter, metal stakes had been driven into the ground every few yards. Embedded in the stakes were two crystals, one on each side, spelled so that anything going between them would break their contact with the crystal in the next stake and would alert the guards. The camp itself had clusters of tents for the guards, a few small wooden cabins built close together near the camp's center, and two wooden huts that had heavily barred windows and layers of guard spells around them. In front of the cabins were six thick wooden stakes that had heavy chains attached to them. For prisoners. For bait.

As soon as he walked past the perimeter stakes, they knew he was coming. On the journey there, he had thought again about what he was going to do. He could kill Hekatah and Dorothea. He could unleash the strength of his Black Jewels, destroy everyone in the camp, and take Lucivar, Marian, and Daemonar home. But it wouldn't stop the war. Terreille needed to be confronted with a power that would terrify the people sufficiently that they wouldn't *dare* fight against it. So it always came back to provoking Jaenelle enough for her to unleash her Ebony power and give the Terreilleans a reason to stay in their own Realm.

As he walked toward the center of the camp, guards followed him. No one approached him or tried to touch him.

Round candle-lights set on top of tall metal poles lit the bloodstained bare ground at the exact center of the camp. Lucivar was chained to the last stake. The lash wounds on his chest and thighs had scabbed over and didn't appear to be deep enough to cause him serious harm. There were bruises on his face, but those, too, would cause no permanent damage.

Saetan stopped at the edge of the light. He hadn't seen Hekatah in ten years—hardly more than a breath of time for someone who had lived as long as he had. And he had known her for most of those years. Even so, despite Dorothea standing beside her, she had withered so much, *decayed* so much, he wasn't really sure it was her until she spoke.

"Saetan."

"Hekatah." He walked to the center of the bare ground.

"You've come to bargain?" Hekatah asked politely.

He nodded. "A life for a life."

She smiled. "For *lives*. We'll throw the bitch and the babe into the bargain. We don't really have any use for them."

Did she think he didn't know they would never give up Daemonar? They had been striving for centuries to get a child out of Lucivar or Daemon that they could control and breed in order to bring back a darker bloodline.

"My life for theirs," he said. *Everything has a price.*

"NO!" Lucivar shouted, struggling against the spelled chains. *"Kill them!"*

Ignoring Lucivar, he focused on Hekatah. "Do we have a bargain?"

"For a chance to see the High Lord humbled?" Hekatah said sweetly. "Oh, yes, we have a bargain. As soon as you're restrained, I'll set the others free. I swear it on my word of honor."

They ordered him to strip—and he did.

Removing his Black-Jeweled ring, he tossed it on the ground. He had put a tight shield around it so that no one could actually touch it. If he needed to call it back to him, he didn't want their foulness absorbed by the gold.

As two guards chained him to the center post, Hekatah slipped a Ring of Obedience over his organ.

"You look well for someone your age," she said, stepping back to give his naked body a thorough inspection.

He smiled gently. "Unfortunately, darling, I can't say the same about you."

Viciousness twisted Hekatah's face. "It's time you learned a lesson, *High Lord*." She raised her hand at the same time Dorothea, with a look of perverted glee, raised hers.

Lucivar had once tried to explain to the boyos why a Ring of Obedience could force a powerful male to submit, so Saetan thought he was ready for it.

Nothing could have prepared him for the pain that filled his cock and balls before it spread through his body. His nerves were on fire, while agony settled between his legs. He couldn't fight it, could barely think.

His sons had endured this, had *fought* against Dorothea's control knowing that *this* was waiting after every act of defiance. For centuries, they had endured this. How could a man not become twisted by this? How . . .

He screamed—and kept on screaming until his body just shut down.

19 / Kaeleer

Surreal paced back and forth in Karla's sitting room, growing angrier by the minute. She wasn't sure why she'd chosen to vent her frustrations to Karla. Maybe it was because Karla had seemed so damned indifferent to everything that had been happening.

All right, that wasn't fair. The woman was grieving for her cousin, Morton, not to mention that she was slowly recovering from a vicious poisoning. Even so . . .

"The bastard sounded like it was an inconvenience that would interfere with his manicure," Surreal raged at Karla. " 'We'll see what we can accommodate.' Hell's fire, it's his father and brother!"

"You don't know what he intends to do," Karla said blandly.

The blandness pushed Surreal's temper up another notch. "He doesn't plan to do anything!"

"How do you know?"

Surreal sputtered, swore, paced. "It's as if he and Jaenelle *want* us to lose this war."

For the first time, temper heated Karla's voice. "Don't be an ass."

"Now, look, sugar—"

"No, *you* look," Karla snapped. "It's about time all of you looked and thought and remembered a few things. The boyos' instincts are pushing them toward battle. They can't change that any more than they can change being male. And the coven is made up of Queens whose instincts are urging them to protect their people."

"Which is exactly what they should be doing!" Surreal shouted. "And you don't seem to have that problem," she added nastily. Then she glanced at Karla's covered legs and regretted the words.

"When Jaenelle was fifteen," Karla said, "the Dark Council tried to say that Uncle Saetan was unfit to be her legal guardian. They decided to appoint someone else. And she said they could 'when the sun next rises.' Do you know what happened?"

Finally standing still, Surreal shook her head.

"The sun didn't rise for three days," Karla said mildly. "It didn't rise until the Council rescinded their decision."

Surreal sank to the floor. "Mother Night," she whispered.

"Jaenelle didn't want a court, didn't want to rule. The only reason she became the Queen of Ebon Askavi was to stop the Terreilleans who were coming into the kindred Territories and slaughtering the kindred. Do you really think a woman who would do those things has spent the past three weeks wringing her hands and hoping this will all go away? I don't. She needs us here for a reason—and she'll tell us when it's time to tell us." Karla paused. "And I'll tell you one other thing, just between us: sometimes a friend must become an enemy in order to remain a friend."

Karla was talking about Daemon. Surreal thought for a moment, then shook her head. "The way he's been acting—"

"Daemon Sadi is totally committed to Witch. Whatever he does, he does for her."

"You don't know that."

"Don't I?" Karla said too softly.

Black Widow. The words bloomed in Surreal's mind until there wasn't room for anything else. Black Widow. Maybe Karla *wasn't* indifferent to what was happening. Maybe she had *seen* something in a tangled web. "Are you sure about Sadi?"

"No," Karla replied. "But I'm willing to consider the possibility that what he says in public may be very different from what he does in private."

Surreal raked her fingers through her hair. "Well, Hell's fire, if Daemon and Jaenelle *were* planning something, they could at least tell the court."

"I was poisoned by a member of my court," Karla said quietly. "And let's not forget Jaenelle's grandmother, because I'm sure Jaenelle hasn't. So tell me, Surreal, if you were trying to find a way to totally destroy those two bitches, who would *you* trust?"

"She could have trusted the High Lord."

"And where is he right now?" Karla asked.

Surreal didn't say anything, since they both knew the answer.

20 / Terreille

"I think it's time to let Jaenelle know you're here," Hekatah said, circling behind Saetan. "I think we should send a little gift."

He felt her grab the little finger of his left hand. He felt the knife cut through skin and bone. And he felt rage when she dropped to her knees and clamped her mouth over the wound to drink his blood. A Guardian's blood.

Gathering his strength, he sent a blast of heat down his arm, psychic fire that cauterized the wound.

Hekatah jerked away from him, screaming.

While he had the chance, he used a little healing Craft to cleanse the wound and seal up the flesh enough to keep infection at bay.

Hekatah kept screaming. Dorothea rushed out of her cabin. Guards came running from every direction.

Finally the screaming stopped. He heard Hekatah scrabble for something on the ground, then slowly get to her feet. As she circled around him, he saw what the blast of power had done. Since her mouth had been clamped on the wound, the psychic fire had kept going after it cauterized the blood vessels. It had melted part of her jaw, grotesquely reshaping her face.

In one hand, she held his little finger. In the other, she held the knife. "You're going to pay for that," she said in a slurred voice.

"No," Dorothea said, stepping forward. "You said yourself that we have to keep the damage to a minimum until Jaenelle is contained."

Hekatah turned toward Dorothea. Saetan felt sure the sick revulsion on Dorothea's face would drive Hekatah past any ability to think rationally.

"Until Jaenelle is contained," Hekatah said with effort. "But . . . that doesn't mean . . . he can't pay." Turning toward him, she raised her hand.

For the second time, the agony from the Ring of Obedience ripped through him. That was devastating enough. Hearing Lucivar's pain-filled, but still enraged, war cry as Hekatah also punished the son for the deeds of the father produced an agony in him that cut far deeper.

21 / Kaeleer

Daemon wished Surreal hadn't been around when Geoffrey brought the small, ornately carved box that had been delivered to the Keep in Terreille. He *had* suggested that, since the verbal message had said it was a "gift" for Jaenelle, Surreal's presence wasn't required. She had countered by saying she was family and had just as much right to know what was going on as he or Jaenelle did. Which, unfortunately, was true.

"Do you want me to open it?" he asked Jaenelle when she had just stood there staring at the box for several minutes.

"No," she said too calmly. Using Craft, she flipped the lid off the box.

The three of them stared at the little finger nestled in a bed of silk— a little finger with a long, black-tinted nail.

"Well, sugar, I'd say that message is to the point," Surreal said as she stared at Jaenelle. "How many more pieces do you need to get back *before you do something?* We're running out of time!"

"Yes," Jaenelle said. "It's time."

She's in shock, Daemon thought. Then he looked at her eyes—and couldn't suppress the shudder. They were sapphire ice. But behind the ice was a Queen who had been pushed far beyond even the cold rage males were capable of unleashing. Because he was looking for it, because he could descend far enough into the abyss to feel it, he sensed that Hekatah's little gift had fully awakened the feral side, the *deadly* side of Witch. She was no longer a young woman who had received her father's finger as a demand for her surrender; she was a predator studying the bait laid out by an enemy.

Dorothea and Hekatah had seen the young woman. They had no idea who they were *really* dealing with.

"Come with me," Jaenelle said, lightly touching his arm before she walked out of the room.

Even through his shirt and jacket, her hand felt so cold it burned.

Careful to keep his eyes and expression bland, he looked at Surreal— and felt a little dismayed by the fury that looked back at him. That was when he realized that, despite being chilled to the bone, the room was still warm.

Jaenelle had given no outward warning of the rage just underneath the surface, no indication of power being gathered for a strike. Nothing.

He glanced at the finger again, felt his stomach clench. Then he walked out of the room.

Damn them both, Surreal thought as she stared at the finger in the box. Oh, there had been a little flicker of dismay in Sadi's face when he first saw it, but that had disappeared quickly enough. And from Jaenelle? Nothing. Hell's fire! She had shown more temper and concern when Aaron had been cornered by Vania! At least then there had been that freezing, terrifying rage. But the woman gets *a piece of her father* sent to her and . . . nothing. Not a damn thing. No reaction at all.

Well, fine. If that's the way those two wanted to play the game, that was just fine. *She* wore a Gray Jewel and *she* was a skilled assassin. There was no reason she couldn't slip into Terreille and get Lucivar and the High Lord—and Marian and Daemonar—away from those two bitches.

Surreal bit her lower lip. Well, getting *all* of them out in one piece *might* be a problem.

All right, so she'd think about it a little, work up some kind of plan. At least *she* was going to do something!

And maybe, while she was thinking, she would mention this little incident to Karla to see if the Black Widow still thought there was more going on than *nothing*.

By the time Daemon reached her workroom, the ice in Jaenelle's eyes had shattered into razor-edged shards, and he saw something in them that terrified him: cold, undiluted hatred.

"What do you expect will happen now?" Jaenelle asked too calmly.

Daemon slipped his hands into his trouser pockets to hide the trembling. He quietly cleared his throat. "I doubt anything more will happen until the messenger returns to Hayll and reports the delivery of the box. It's almost midmorning now. They aren't going to expect you to be capable of making any decisions immediately. So we've got a few hours. Maybe a little more than that."

Jaenelle paced slowly. She seemed to be arguing with herself. Finally she sighed—as if she'd lost the argument—and looked at him. "The Weaver of Dreams sent me a message. She said the triangle must remain together in order to survive, that the other two sides weren't strong enough without the strength of the mirror—and the mirror would keep them *all* safe."

"The mirror?" Daemon asked cautiously.

"You are your father's mirror, Daemon. You're one side of the triangle."

The memory flashed in his mind of Tersa, years ago, tracing a triangle in the palm of his hand, over and over, while she had explained the mystery of the Blood's four-sided triangle.

"Father, brother, lover," he murmured. Three sides. And the fourth side was the triangle's center, the one who ruled all three.

"Exactly," Jaenelle replied.

"You want me to go to Hayll."

"Yes."

He nodded slowly, suddenly feeling like he was on a very thin, shaky footbridge, and one false step would send him plummeting into a chasm he would never escape. "If I walked in to try another exchange of prisoners, that would buy a few more hours."

"I never said anything about you handing yourself over to them," Jaenelle snapped. Her face had been pale since she'd seen Saetan's finger. Now it got paler. "Daemon, I need seventy-two hours."

"Sev—But everything is ready. All you would need to do is gather your strength and unleash it."

"I need seventy-two hours."

He stared at her, slowly coming to terms with what she was telling him. In a controlled dive into the abyss, he could descend to the level of his Black Jewels in a few minutes and gather his full strength. It was going to take her *seventy-two hours* to do the same thing.

Hell's fire, Mother Night, and may the Darkness be merciful.

But there was no way for him to . . .

He saw the knowledge in her eyes—and fought against the shame it produced in him. He should have known he couldn't hide the Sadist from Witch. And he finally understood what she was asking of him.

Unable to meet her eyes anymore, he turned away and began his own slow prowl around the room.

It was just a game. A dirty, vicious game—the kind the Sadist had always played so well. As he gave that part of himself free rein, the plan took shape as easily as breathing.

But . . . Everything has a price. If he was going to lose the companionship of almost everyone he had ever cared about, the reward would have to justify the cost.

"I can do this," he crooned, slowly circling around her. "I can keep Dorothea and Hekatah off-balance enough to keep the others safe and also prevent those *Ladies* from giving the orders to send the Terreillean armies into Kaeleer. I can buy you seventy-two hours, Jaenelle. But it's going to cost me because I'm going to do things I may never be forgiven for, so I want something in return."

He could taste her slight bafflement before she said, "All right."

"I don't want to wear the Consort's ring anymore."

A slash of pain, quickly stifled. "All right."

"I want a wedding ring in its place."

A flash of joy, immediately followed by sorrow. She smiled at him at the same time her eyes filled with tears. "It would be wonderful."

She meant that. So why the sorrow, why the anguish? He would have to deal with that when he got back.

His temper was already getting edgy, dangerous. "I'll take that as a 'yes.' There are things I'll need that I can't create well enough for this game."

"Just tell me what you need, Daemon."

He didn't want to do this. Didn't want to go back to that kind of life, not even for seventy-two hours. He was going to mutilate the life he'd begun to build here, and the coven, the boyos, they would never—

"Do you trust me?" he snapped.

"Yes."

No hesitation, no doubts.

He finally stopped moving and faced her. "Do you know how desperately I love you?"

Her voice shook when she answered, "As much as I love you?"

He held her, held on to her as his lifeline, his anchor. It would be all right. As long as he had *her,* it would be all right.

Finally, reluctantly, he eased back. "Come on, we've got a lot of work to do."

"That's the last of it," Jaenelle said several hours later. She carefully packed the box that held all the spelled items she had created for him. "Almost the last of it."

Daemon sipped the coffee he had brewed strong enough to bite. Physically, he was tired. Mentally, he was reeling. As Jaenelle created each of the spells he had asked for, he'd had to learn how to use them—which meant she'd explained the process to him as she created one, then had him practice with it while she created the ones he would take with him. She'd reviewed his efforts, given more instructions on how to hone the effect—and never once asked him what he intended to do, for which he was grateful. Of course, he didn't know exactly what *she* was going to do either. There were some things one Black Widow did not ask another.

Jaenelle held up a vial about the size of her index finger that was filled with dark powder. "This is a stimulant. A strong one. One dose will keep you on your feet for about six hours. You can mix it with any kind of liquid—" She eyed the coffee. "—but if you mix it with something brewed like *that* it's going to have more kick."

"That's one dose?" Daemon asked. Then he bit his tongue to keep from laughing and wished he could have a picture of the look on her face.

"There are enough doses in here for the next three days and then some," she said dryly.

"Well, I'd better find out what it does." Daemon held out the mug of coffee.

She opened the vial, tapped it lightly over the mug. The sprinkle of powder dissolved instantly.

He took a sip. A little nutty, just a little sharp. Actually quite—

He wheezed. His body suddenly had a kind of battlefield alertness, a fierce need to *move*. His mind was no longer hazed by mental fatigue. After the first few explosive seconds, he felt himself settle down, but there remained that bright reservoir of energy.

He drained the mug, waited a few seconds. No physical changes, just the feeling that the reservoir got delightfully bigger.

Jaenelle carefully packed the vial into the box. "Everything has a price, Daemon," she said firmly.

That sobered him. "It's addictive?"

The look she gave him could have cut a man in half. "No, it is not. *I* use this sometimes—which you will *not* mention to any of the family. They'd throw three kinds of fits if they knew. This will keep you going, even if you don't get any food or sleep, but if you don't renew the dose every six hours, your feet are going to go out from under you and you'd better be prepared to sleep for a day."

"In other words, if I miss a dose, I'm not going to be able to flog myself awake again no matter what's going on around me."

She nodded.

"All right, I'll remember."

She held up another vial, this one full of a dark liquid. "This is a tonic for Saetan. I figured he's going to be weakened physically, so I made it strong. It's going to have a kick like a team of draft horses. Add it to an equal amount of liquid—wine or fresh blood."

"If I use the stimulant, can I use my blood for that tonic?"

"Yes," Jaenelle said, almost managing to keep her lips from twitching. "But if you *do* use your blood, make sure you pour it down his throat before you tell him what it is because it'll kick like *two* teams of draft horses—and he will not be happy with you for the first couple of minutes."

"Fair enough." He just hoped Saetan would be in good enough condition that he could howl about being dosed.

Jaenelle took a deep breath, let it out slowly. "That's it then."

Daemon set the mug down on the worktable. "I want to supervise making up the food pack. It won't take long. Will you wait for me?"

Her smile didn't reach her haunted sapphire eyes. "I'll wait."

"Prince Ssadi."

Daemon hesitated, turned toward the voice. "Draca."

She held out one hand, closed in a loose fist. Obediently, he put his hand under hers. When she opened her hand, colored bangles poured into his—the kind of bangles women sewed on dresses to catch the light.

Baffled, he looked at the bangles, then at her.

"When the time iss right, give thesse to Ssaetan. He will undersstand."

She knows, Daemon thought. *She knows, but . . .* No, Draca wouldn't say anything to the coven or the boyos. The Seneschal of Ebon Askavi would keep her own council for her own reasons.

As she walked away, he slipped the bangles into his jacket pocket.

Surreal jumped when the door to her room flew open.

"What in the name of Hell do you think you're doing?" Daemon demanded, slamming the door.

"What does it look like I'm doing?" Surreal snapped. Silently, she swore. A few more minutes and she would have been able to slip away undetected.

"It *looks* like you're about to ruin several hours of careful planning," Daemon snapped back.

That stopped her. "What planning?" she asked suspiciously.

He swore with a creative vileness that surprised her. "What do you think I've been doing since we got that *gift* this morning? And what did you think *you'd* be able to do, going in alone?"

"I've been an assassin for a lot of years, Sadi. I could have—"

"One-on-one kills," he snarled. "That's not going to get you very far in an armed camp. And if you unleash the Gray to get rid of the guards, you can be sure the four people you're going in for will be dead by the time you reach them."

"You don't know—"

"I do know," Daemon shouted. "I grew up under that bitch's control. I *do* know."

Her anger couldn't match his, especially when he'd been able to put his finger on every doubt she had about succeeding. "You have a better idea?"

"Yes, Surreal, I have a better idea," Daemon replied coldly.

Surreal licked her lips, took a careful breath. "I could help, create a diversion or something. Hell's fire, Daemon, those people are my family, too, the first family I've ever had. They mean something to me. Let me help."

Something queer filled his eyes as he stared at her. "Yes," he said in a silky croon, "I think you could be very helpful." His voice shifted, became irritated and efficient as he looked over the supplies piled on her bed. "At least you had the good sense to realize you would need to bring your own food and water since you won't be able to trust consuming anything that might be there." He headed for the door. "I'll need a couple more hours. Then we'll go."

"But—" The look he gave her had her backing down. "A couple of hours," she agreed.

It wasn't until he was gone that she began to wonder just what it was she had agreed to do.

Little fool, Daemon thought as he stormed back to Jaenelle's workroom. *Idiot.* If the kitchen staff hadn't mentioned that Surreal had requested a similar food pack, he wouldn't have known she was planning to go to Hayll, wouldn't have been prepared to deal with her presence. Oh, he could use her help in this game. It hadn't taken him more than a minute to recognize how many ways she could help. But, damn it, if she'd gone in and gotten everyone riled before he arrived . . . He had to buy Jaenelle seventy-two hours. A straight, clean fight would have gotten the others out, but it wouldn't have done *that.*

So he would play out his game—and Surreal would have a chance to dance with the Sadist.

He walked into the workroom and snarled at Jaenelle, "I'll need a couple more items."

Her eyes widened when he told her what he wanted, but she didn't say anything except, "I think I'd better give you a Ring that has a shield *no one* can get through."

Since he figured both Lucivar and Surreal would want to tear his heart out in a few hours' time, he thought that was an excellent idea.

The three of them stood outside the room that held the Dark Altar at the Keep.

Jaenelle hugged Surreal. "May the Darkness embrace you, Sister."

"We'll get them back," Surreal said, returning the hug. "Count on it." Glancing at Daemon, she went into the Altar's room and quietly closed the door.

Daemon just looked at Jaenelle, his heart too full to say anything. Besides, words seemed so inadequate at the moment. He brushed a thumb across her cheek, kissed her gently. Then he took a deep breath. "The game begins at midnight."

"And at midnight, seventy-two hours later, you're going to be riding the Winds back to the Keep in Terreille. No stops, no delays." She paused, waited for him to nod agreement, then added, "Don't ride any Wind darker than the Red. The others will be unstable."

It took effort to keep his jaw from dropping. A strong witch storm could create a disturbance on *part* of the psychic roadways through the Darkness, could even throw someone off the Web to be lost in the Darkness, but "unstable" sounded much, much worse.

"All right," he finally said. "We'll stay on the Red."

"Daemon," Jaenelle said softly, "I want you to promise me something."

"Anything."

Her eyes filled with tears. It took her a moment to regain control. "Thirteen years ago, you gave everything you had in order to help me."

"And I'll give you everything again," he replied just as softly.

She shook her head fiercely. "No. No more sacrifices, Daemon. Not from you. That's what I want you to promise me." She swallowed hard. "The Keep is going to be the only safe place. I want your promise that, at the appointed hour, you'll be on your way there. No matter who you have to walk away from, no matter who you have to leave behind, *you must get to the Keep before dawn.* Promise me, Daemon." She gripped his arm hard enough to hurt. "I have to know you'll be safe. Promise me."

Gently, he removed her hand, then raised it to place a kiss in her palm—and smiled. "I'm not going to do anything that will make me late for my own wedding."

Pain flashed in her eyes, making him wonder if she really *wanted* to marry him. No. He wouldn't begin to doubt, couldn't *afford* to doubt. "I'll come back to you," he said. "I swear it."

She gave him a brief, fierce kiss. "See that you do."

She looked pale and exhausted. There were dark smudges under her eyes. She had never looked more beautiful to him.

"I'll see you in a few days."

"Good-bye, Daemon. I love you."

As he approached the Dark Altar that was a Gate between the Realms, he didn't find Jaenelle's last words reassuring.

22 / Kaeleer

Karla eased herself into a chair in Jaenelle's sitting room. She could use Craft to float herself from place to place, and could even stand on her own now for a little while with the help of two canes. But channeling power through her body left her quickly exhausted, and standing made her legs ache. Still, the daily cup of Jaenelle's tonic *was* working. But she had an uneasy feeling she would need her strength for something else very soon.

It was the first time since Jaenelle had refused to allow Kaeleer to go to war that Karla had seen her. But even now, when *Jaenelle* had summoned her and Gabrielle, the Queen of Ebon Askavi was keeping her back to them, just staring out the window.

"I need the two of you to keep the boyos leashed for another few days," Jaenelle said quietly. "It won't be easy, but it's necessary."

"Why?" Gabrielle demanded. "Hell's fire, Jaenelle, we need to gather into armies and *fight*. Scattered the way we are now, we're barely holding our own and we aren't even fighting the armies that are bound to come in from Terreille, just the Terreilleans who were already in Kaeleer. The *bastards.* It's time to go to war. We *have* to go to war. It's not just the people who are dying. The *land* is being destroyed, too."

"The Queens can heal the land," Jaenelle replied, still not looking at them. "That is the Queens' special gift. And not as many of our people have died as you seem to think."

"No," Gabrielle said bitterly, "they're just dying of shame because they've been ordered to abandon their land."

"They can survive a little shame."

Karla laid a hand on Gabrielle's arm. Trying to keep her voice reasonable, she said, "I don't think there's any choice now, Jaenelle. If we don't stop retreating and start attacking, we aren't going to have a place to take a stand when the Terreillean armies *do* get here."

"They won't receive orders to enter Kaeleer for a few more days. By then, it won't make any difference."

"Because we'll be forced to surrender," Gabrielle snapped.

Karla's hand tightened on Gabrielle's arm. She didn't have much strength, but the gesture was enough to leash the other Queen's temper—at least for the moment.

"Is Kaeleer finally going to war with Terreille?" she asked.

"No," Jaenelle said. "Kaeleer will not go to war with Terreille."

It was the slight inflection that made ice run through Karla's body. The way Gabrielle's arm tensed under her hand, she knew the other woman had heard it, too.

"Then who *is* going to war with Terreille?"

Jaenelle turned around.

Gabrielle sucked in her breath.

For the first time, they were seeing the dream beneath the flesh.

Karla stared at the pointed ears that had come from the Dea al Mon, the hands with sheathed claws that had come from the Tigre, the hooves peeking out from beneath the black gown that could have come from the centaurs or the horses or the unicorns. Most of all, she stared at the tiny spiral horn.

The living myth. Dreams made flesh. But, oh, had any of them really thought about who the dreamers had been?

No wonder the kindred love her. No wonder we've all loved her.

Karla quietly cleared her throat to ask the question she suddenly hoped wouldn't be answered. "Who *is* going to war with Terreille?"

"I am," Witch said.

CHAPTER FIFTEEN

1 / Terreille

Half-blinded by the pain inflicted on him during the past two days, Saetan watched Hekatah approach and give him a long, slow study. Whenever the whim had struck either of them, she and Dorothea had used the Ring of Obedience on him, but more carefully now, stopping just before the moment when he would have fainted from the pain. Worse, for him, they had left him chained to the post through the daylight hours. Already weakened by pain, the afternoon sun had drained his psychic strength and stabbed at his eyes, producing a headache so violent even the pain from the Ring couldn't engulf it.

Bit by bit, pain had chewed away all the revitalizing effects Jaenelle's tonics had produced in him, changing his body back to where it had been when he'd first met her—closer to the demon-dead than to the living.

If he could have made a fast transition from Guardian to demon-dead, he might have considered it—the kind of transition Andulvar and Prothvar had made on the battlefield all those long centuries ago. They had both been so deep in battle fury, they hadn't even realized they had received deathblows. If he could have done it that way, he might have. It would be easy enough to slit a vein and bleed himself out, and there would be less pain. But he would be more vulnerable, and without a supply of fresh blood, the sunlight would weaken him to the point that, when Jaenelle finally came, he would be a liability to her instead of finding some way to fight with her.

When Jaenelle finally came. *If* Jaenelle ever came. She should have reacted by now, should have been there by now—if she was coming at all.

"I think it's time to send Jaenelle another little gift," Hekatah said, her girlish voice now slurred by the misshapen jaw. "Another finger?" She used the same tone another woman might use when trying to decide the merits of serving one dish over another at dinner. "Perhaps a toe this time. No, too insignificant. An eye? Too disfiguring. We don't want her to start thinking you've become too repulsive to rescue." Her eyes focused on his balls—and she smiled. "It's dead meat now, but it will still be useful for *this* anyway."

He didn't react. Wouldn't allow himself to react. It *was* dead meat now—the last part revitalized, the first part to die. He wouldn't react. And he wouldn't think of Sylvia. Not now. Not ever again.

With their eyes locked on each other, Hekatah stepped closer, closer. One of her hands stroked him, caressed him, closed around him to hold him for the knife.

An enraged shriek tore through the normal nighttime sounds.

Hekatah jumped back and whirled toward the sound.

Surreal came flying into the camp as if she'd been tossed by a huge hand. Her feet hit the ground first, but she couldn't stop the forward momentum. She tucked and rolled, coming up on her knees facing the darkness beyond the area illuminated by candle-lights.

"YOU COLD-BLOODED, HEARTLESS BASTARD!" Surreal screamed. "YOU GUTLESS SON OF A WHORING BITCH!"

Dorothea burst out of her cabin, shouting, "Guards! *Guards!*"

The guards rushed in from three sides of the camp. No one came out of the darkness facing them.

"GUARDS!" Dorothea shouted again.

From out of that darkness, a deep, amused voice said, "They aren't going to answer you, darling. They've been permanently detained."

Daemon Sadi stepped out of the darkness, stopping at the edge of the light. His black hair was a little wind-mussed. His hands were casually tucked in his trouser pockets. His black jacket was open, revealing the white silk shirt that was unbuttoned to the waist. The Black Jewel around his neck glittered with power. His golden eyes glittered, too.

Seeing that queer glitter in Daemon's eyes, Saetan shivered. Something was wrong here. *Very* wrong.

Hekatah turned halfway, resting the knife against Saetan's belly. "Take one more step and I'll gut him—and kill the Eyrien, too."

"Go ahead," Daemon said pleasantly as he walked into the camp. "It'll save me the trouble of arranging a couple of careful accidents, which I would have had to have done soon anyway since the Steward and the First Escort were becoming . . . troublesome. So, you kill them, I destroy you—and then I return to Kaeleer to console the grieving Queen. Yes, that will work out quite nicely. You'll be blamed for their deaths, and Jaenelle will never look at me and wonder why I'm the only male left whom she can depend on."

"You're forgetting about the Master of the Guard," Hekatah said.

Daemon smiled a gentle, brutal smile. "No, I haven't. I didn't forget about Prothvar or Mephis either. They're no longer a concern."

For a moment, Saetan thought Hekatah *had* gutted him. But while the wound wasn't physical, the pain *was*. "No," he said. "No. You couldn't have."

Daemon laughed. "Couldn't I? Then where are they, old man?"

Because he had wondered the same thing, Saetan couldn't answer that. But he still found himself denying it. "You couldn't have. *They're your family.*"

"My family," Daemon said thoughtfully. "How convenient that they decided to become 'family' after I became the Consort to the strongest Queen in the history of the Blood."

"That's not true," Saetan said, straining forward despite the knife Hekatah still held against his belly. It was mad to be arguing about this, but all his instincts shouted at him that it had to be *now*, that there might not be another chance to alter that look in Daemon's eyes.

"Isn't it?" Daemon said bitterly. "Then where were they 1,700 years ago when I was a child? Where were *you*? Where were *any* of you during all the years between then and now? Don't talk to me about *family*, High Lord."

Saetan sagged against the post. Mother Night, every worry he'd had about Daemon's loyalty was coming true.

"How very touching," Hekatah sneered. "Do you expect us to believe that? You're your father's son."

Daemon's gold eyes fastened on Hekatah. "I think it's more accurate to say I'm the man my father *might* have been if he'd had the balls for it."

"Don't listen to him," Dorothea said suddenly. "It's a trick, a trap. He's *lying.*"

"It seems to be his day for it," Surreal muttered bitterly.

Giving Surreal a brief, dismissive glance, Daemon shifted his attention to Dorothea. "Hello, darling. You look like a hag. It suits you."

Dorothea hissed.

"I brought you a present," Daemon said, glancing at Surreal again.

Dorothea looked at Surreal's pointed ears and sneered. "I've heard of her. She's nothing but a whore."

"Yes," Daemon agreed mildly, "she's a first-class slut who will spread her legs for anything that will pay her. She's also your granddaughter. Kartane's child. The only one he'll ever sire. The only continuation of *your* bloodline."

"No slut is *my* granddaughter," Dorothea snarled.

Daemon raised one eyebrow. "Really, darling, I thought that would be the convincing argument. The only difference between you is she's under a male most of the time while you're on top of him. But your legs are spread just as wide." He paused. "Well, there is *one* other difference. Since she was getting paid for it, *she* had to acquire some skill in bed."

Dorothea shook with rage. "Guards! Seize him!"

Twenty men surged forward, then dropped in their tracks.

Daemon just smiled. "Perhaps I should kill the rest of them now to eliminate further annoyances."

Hekatah carefully lowered the knife. "Why are you here, Sadi?"

"Your little schemes are interfering with my plans, and that annoys me."

"Terreille is going to war with Kaeleer. That's hardly a 'little scheme.' "

"Well, that all depends on whether you have the power to win, doesn't it?" Daemon crooned. "However, I'm not interested in ruling a Realm that's been devastated by a war, so I decided it was time we had a little talk."

Dorothea jumped forward. "Don't listen to him!"

"How can *you* rule a Realm?" Hekatah asked, ignoring Dorothea.

Daemon's smile became colder, crueler. "I control the witch who has the strength to kill every living thing in the Realm of Terreille."

"NO!" Saetan shouted. "You *do not* control the Queen."

When Daemon's eyes fixed on him, he started to shiver again.

"Don't I?" Daemon purred. "Haven't you wondered why she didn't respond to the 'gift,' High Lord? Oh, she was greatly distressed. Hasn't done anything but weep since your finger arrived. But she isn't here—and she isn't going to be because she values having my cock inside her more than she values you. Any of you." For the first time, Daemon glanced at Lucivar.

Saetan shook his head. "No. You can't do this, Daemon."

"Don't tell me what I can do. You had your chance, old man, and you didn't have the balls to take it. Now it's *my* turn, and I intend to rule."

"That's just another lie," Dorothea snapped. "You've never been interested in ruling."

Daemon turned searing, cold anger on her. "What would *you* know about what I wanted, bitch? You never offered me a chance to rule *anything*. You just wanted to use my strength without ever offering anything in return."

"I did offer you something!"

"What? *You?* You had your use of me, Dorothea. How could you imagine enduring more of that would be any kind of reward?"

"You *bastard*! You—" She took a step toward him, her hand raised like a claw.

A blow from a phantom hand knocked her off her feet. She fell on top of Surreal, who swore viciously and pushed her off.

Tearing his eyes away from Daemon, Saetan looked at Hekatah—and realized she was shaking, but it wasn't from anger.

"What is it you want, Sadi?" Hekatah said, unable to keep her voice steady.

A long, chilling moment passed before Daemon turned his attention back to her. "I came to negotiate on my Queen's behalf."

"I told you," Dorothea muttered—but she didn't try to get up.

"And what will you tell your Queen?" Hekatah asked.

"That I arrived too late to save any of them. I'm sure I can prod her into a suitably violent reaction."

"She'll destroy more than us if she unleashes that kind of power."

Daemon's smile was a satisfied one. "Exactly. She'll destroy everything. And once all of you are gone . . . Well, there *will* have to be a few more battles in Kaeleer to eliminate the more troublesome males in the court. But after that, I think things will settle down quite nicely." He turned and started to walk away.

He'll never get her to destroy everyone in Terreille, Saetan thought, closing his eyes against the sick feelings churning in his stomach. *He'll never twist her that* much. *Not Jaenelle.*

"Wait," Hekatah said.

Saetan opened his eyes.

Daemon was almost at the edge of the light. Turning, he raised one eyebrow in inquiry.

"Was that the only reason you came here?" Hekatah asked.

Daemon glanced at Lucivar again and smiled. "No. I thought I would settle a few debts while I was here."

Hekatah returned the smile. "Then, perhaps, Prince, we do have something to talk about. But not right now. Why don't you indulge yourself while I—while Dorothea and I think about how we might settle this amicably between us."

"I'm sure I can find something amusing to do to pass the time," Daemon said. He walked out of the light, disappeared into the darkness.

Hekatah looked at Saetan. It wasn't possible for him to keep his feelings hidden right now, to keep his face blank.

Dorothea got to her feet and pointed at Surreal. "Secure that bitch," she snapped at a couple of guards. Then she turned to Hekatah. "You can't really believe Sadi."

"The High Lord does," Hekatah said quietly. "And *that's* very interesting." She hissed when Dorothea started to protest. "We'll discuss this in private."

She walked to her cabin with Dorothea reluctantly following.

After chaining Surreal to the post on Saetan's left, the guards gathered up the dead men, and, with uneasy glances at the surrounding darkness, finally returned to their duties.

"Your son's a cold-blooded bastard," Surreal said quietly.

Saetan thought about the look in Daemon's eyes. He thought about the man he should have known well—and didn't know at all. Closing his eyes, he rested his head against the post, and said, "I only have one son now—and he's Eyrien."

"Hello, Prick."

Lucivar turned his head, watched Daemon glide out of the darkness and circle around to stand directly in front of him.

He had watched that initial game closely, waiting for some sign from

Daemon that it was time to attack. The spelled chains couldn't have held him by themselves, and, unlike Saetan, the pain from the Ring of Obedience didn't debilitate him for long—at least, it didn't drain him the way it seemed to drain the High Lord. No, what had made him hold back and wait was the threat to Marian and Daemonar. There was always a guard inside the far hut that was being used as one of the prisons, and that guard had orders to kill his wife and son if he broke free. So he had waited, especially after Saetan had surrendered to those two bitches, because he had realized that Saetan had known there wouldn't be an exchange, had walked in expecting to become a prisoner, and had had a reason for doing it.

So when he saw Daemon, he figured the game was about to begin. But now, seeing that bored, sleepy, *terrifying* look . . . He'd danced with the Sadist enough times in the past to know that look meant they were all in serious trouble.

"Hello, Bastard," he said carefully.

Daemon stepped closer. His fingertips drifted up Lucivar's arm, over the shoulder, traced the collarbone.

"What's the game?" Lucivar asked quietly. Then he shivered as Daemon's fingers drifted up his neck, along his jaw.

"It's simple enough," Daemon crooned, brushing a finger over Lucivar's lower lip. "You're going to die, and I'm going to rule." He met Lucivar's eyes and smiled. "Do you know what it's like in the Twisted Kingdom, Prick? Do you have any idea? I spent eight years in that torment because of you."

"You forgave the debt," Lucivar snarled softly. "I gave you the chance to settle it, and you chose to forgive it."

Daemon's hand gently settled on Lucivar's neck. He leaned forward until his lips almost brushed Lucivar's. "Did you really think I would forgive you?"

From the far hut, they both heard a child's outraged howl.

Daemon stepped back. Smiled. Slipped his hands into his trouser pockets. "You're going to pay for those years, Prick," Daemon said softly. "You're going to pay dearly."

Lucivar's heart pounded in his throat as Daemon glided toward the hut that held Marian and Daemonar. "Bastard? Bastard, wait. *I'm* the one who owes the debt. You can't . . . Daemon? *Daemon!*"

Daemon walked into the hut. A moment later, the guard hurried out.

"DAEMON!"

A few minutes after that, Lucivar heard his son scream.

Dorothea's hands closed into fists. "I'm telling you, it's a trick of some kind. I *know* Sadi."

"Do you?" Hekatah snapped.

I think it's more accurate to say I'm the man my father might *have been if he'd had the balls for it.*

Yes, she had been able to sense the ruthlessness, the ambition, the cruel sexuality in Daemon Sadi. It frightened her a little. It excited her even more.

"He's never been interested in using his strength to acquire power. He fought against every attempt I made to bring him around."

"That's because you handled him wrong," Hekatah snarled. "If you had doted on Sadi the way you had doted on that excuse for a son—"

"You used to think it was amusing that I was playing bedroom games with the High Lord's boy. You said it would make a man out of him."

And it had. It had honed Sadi's cruelty, his taste for perverse pleasure. She had sensed that, too. Just as she had sensed that it wouldn't be easy to get around his deep hatred for Dorothea. Well, she wouldn't let that interfere with her *own* ambitions. Besides, Dorothea was becoming difficult, unreliable. She would have had to eliminate the bitch after the war was won anyway.

"I tell you, he's up to something," Dorothea insisted. "And you're just letting him wander around the camp to do who knows what."

"What am I supposed to do?" Hekatah snapped. "Without any leverage, we can't go up against the Black and expect to win."

"We've *got* leverage," Dorothea said through clenched teeth.

Hekatah let out a nasty laugh. "What leverage? If he really *has* destroyed Andulvar, Prothvar, and Mephis, he's not going to squirm because Saetan's guts are spilling out on the ground."

"You picked the wrong man, the wrong threat," Dorothea said irritably, waving a hand. "He may not give a damn about Saetan, but he's always buckled when Lucivar was threatened. Lucivar's been the one chain we could count on to hold Sadi. If you threatened—" She paused, sniffed, looked toward the door, and said uneasily, "What's that smell?"

★　★　★

"What's that smell?" Surreal muttered. It was well past midnight. Were the guards roasting some meat for tomorrow's meals? Possibly, but she couldn't imagine anyone wanting to eat anything that smelled that vile. "Do you smell it?" She turned her head to look at Saetan—and didn't like what she saw. Not one little bit. Since Daemon walked out of the camp the first time, the High Lord had just been staring straight ahead. Just staring. "Uncle Saetan?"

He turned his head, slowly. His eyes focused on her—too slowly.

Checking to make sure there weren't any guards around at the moment, she leaned toward him as much as she could. "Uncle Saetan, this isn't exactly the time to start taking mental side trips. We've got to think of a way to get out of here."

"I'm sorry you're here, Surreal," he said in a worn-out voice. "Truly, I am sorry."

Me, too. "Lucivar's got the physical strength, and I can handle myself in a fight, but you've got the experience to come up with a plan that can use that strength to our best advantage."

He just looked at her. The smile that finally curved his lips was gently bitter. "Sweetheart . . . I've gotten very old in the past two days."

She could see that, and it scared her. Without him, she wasn't sure they *could* get out of there.

Hearing a door open, she immediately straightened up and looked away from him.

"Hell's fire," Dorothea said irritably, "what's that smell?" She stepped between the posts that held Saetan and Surreal.

Surreal clenched her teeth. She wore a Gray Jewel; Dorothea wore a Red. It would be easy enough to slip under Dorothea's inner barriers and weave a death spell—something nasty so that, when it triggered, the screams and confusion might give them a chance to get away.

She began a careful descent so that no one would notice it, but before she reached the depth of her Gray Jewel, another door opened.

The vile smell intensified, making her gag.

Daemon Sadi strolled out of the prison hut, his hands in his trouser pockets. He kept moving until he reached the center of the lighted area. He didn't look at them. His glittering eyes were focused intently on Lucivar, who stared back at him.

No one dared move.

Finally, Daemon looked toward the prison hut and said pleasantly, "Marian, darling, come out and show your foolish husband the price for my years in the Twisted Kingdom."

Two naked . . . *things* . . . floated out of the hut into the light. An hour ago, they had been a woman and a small boy. Now . . .

Surreal began panting in an effort to keep her stomach down. Mother Night, Mother Night, Mother Night.

Marian's fingers and feet were gone. So was the long, lovely hair. Daemonar's eyes were gone, as well as his hands and feet. Their wings were so crisped, the slight movement of floating made pieces break off. And their skin . . .

Smiling that cold, cruel smile, the Sadist released his hold on Marian and Daemonar. The little boy hit the ground with a *thump* and began screaming. Marian landed on the stumps of her feet and fell. When she landed, her skin split, and . . .

Not blood, Surreal realized as she stared with numb, sick fascination. Cooking juices oozed out from those splits in the skin.

The Sadist hadn't just burned them, he had *cooked* them—and they were still alive. Not even demon-dead, *alive*.

"Lucivar," Marian whispered hoarsely as she tried to crawl toward her husband. "Lucivar."

Lucivar screamed, but the scream of pain changed to an Eyrien war cry. Chains snapped as he exploded away from the post, charging right at Daemon. When he had covered half the distance, a hard psychic blow knocked him off his feet, sent him rolling back toward the post. He surged to his feet, rushed at Daemon again—and was struck down again. And again. And again.

When he couldn't get to his feet, he crawled toward Daemon, his teeth bared, his eyes filled with hate.

Sadi reached down, grabbed Daemonar's arm, and twisted it off the way another man would twist off a drumstick.

That got Lucivar to his feet. When he charged this time, he slammed into a Black shield and went to his knees.

Daemon just watched him and smiled.

He tried to break through the shield, tried to smash his way through it, claw his way through it, battered himself against it—and finally just braced himself against it, crying.

"Daemon," he pleaded. "Daemon . . . show a little mercy."

"You want mercy?" Daemon replied gently. With predatory speed, he stepped on Daemonar's head.

The skull smashed like an eggshell.

Daemon walked over to Marian, who was still whispering, still trying to crawl. Even over Lucivar's anguished howls, the rest of them could hear the bones snap when Daemon stepped on her neck.

Using Daemonar's arm as a pointer, Sadi gestured elegantly at the two bodies, all the while watching Lucivar and smiling. "They're both still strong enough to make the transition to demon-dead," he said pleasantly. "It's doubtful the brat is going to remember much of anything, but your wife's last thoughts of you . . . How kindly will she remember you, Prick, knowing you were the cause of this?"

"Finish it," Lucivar begged. "Let them go."

"Everything has a price, Prick. Pay the price, and I'll let them go."

"What do you want from me," Lucivar said in a broken voice. "Just tell me what you want from me."

Daemon's smile turned colder, meaner. "Prove you can be a good boy. Crawl back to the post."

Lucivar crawled.

Two of the guards who had been standing beyond the lighted area, watching, approached Lucivar and helped him to his feet while two others replaced the broken chains.

They were very gentle with him when they secured him to the post.

Lucivar looked at Daemon with grief-dulled eyes. "Satisfied?"

"Yes," Daemon said too softly. "I'm satisfied."

Surreal felt a flick of dark power, then another. She reached out to Marian, almost terrified that her psychic touch would get an answer. But there was nothing, *no one,* left.

That was when she finally realized she was crying, *had* been crying.

Dropping Daemonar's arm, Sadi used a handkerchief to meticulously wipe the grease from his hand. Then, walking over to Surreal, he used the same handkerchief to wipe the tears from her face.

She almost puked on him.

"Don't waste your tears on *them,* little witch," Daemon said quietly. "*You're* next."

She watched him walk away, disappear once more into the darkness. *I may be next, you cold-hearted bastard, but I won't go down without a fight. I can't win against you, but I swear by all that I am that I won't go down without a fight.*

Saetan closed his eyes, unable to bear the sight of the still figures lying a few feet away from him.

I knew he was dangerous, but I didn't know he had this in him. I helped him, encouraged him. Oh, witch-child, what kind of monster did I allow into your bed, into your heart?

As soon as they returned to Hekatah's cabin, Dorothea fell into the nearest chair. She had done some cruel, vicious things in her life, but this . . .

She shuddered.

Hekatah braced her hands on the table. "Do you still think he'll buckle if we threaten Lucivar?" she asked in a shaky voice.

"No," Dorothea replied in a voice just as shaky. "I don't know what he'll do anymore." For centuries, the Blood in Terreille had called him the Sadist. Now she finally understood why.

2 / Kaeleer

Karla watched Tersa build strange creations with brown wooden building blocks. She was grateful for the older woman's presence, and knew Gabrielle felt the same way.

Jaenelle had disappeared shortly after she had talked to them. They, in turn, had talked to the rest of the coven, only telling them that the boyos needed to be held back for a few more days. They hadn't told the others about Witch's intention of going to war with Terreille—alone. They had understood the unspoken command when Jaenelle had finally shown them the dream that lived beneath the human skin.

So the coven, unhappy but united, had rounded up the boyos before any of them could slip the leash. It hadn't been easy, and the males' hostility toward what they considered a betrayal had been vicious enough to make Karla wonder if any of the marriages in the First Circle would survive. Some of those marriages *might* have been destroyed right there and then if Tersa hadn't come along and scolded the boyos for their lack of courtesy. Since the males weren't willing to attack *her*, they had given in.

Almost twenty-four hours of enforced togetherness hadn't made things any easier, but it was the only way to ensure the males' continued presence. Even by the Keep's standards, the sitting room the coven had chosen as a place of confinement was a large room with several clusters of furniture and lots of pacing room—and it wasn't big enough. The coven mostly kept to the chairs and couches to avoid being snarled at by a pacing male. And when the boyos weren't pacing, they were huddled together, muttering.

"How many days are we going to have to do this?" Karla muttered to herself.

"As many as it takes," Tersa replied quietly. She studied her newest creation for a minute, then knocked it down.

The wooden blocks clattered on the long table in front of the couch, but no one jumped this time, having gotten used to the noise. No one even paid much attention to Tersa's odd creations. The boyos, in an attempt to prove they *could* be courteous, had admired and inquired about the first few . . . structures . . . but when Tersa's replies became more and more confusing, they finally backed off and left her alone.

In fact, Karla would have bet they weren't paying attention to much of anything going on in the room—until Ladvarian came in and trotted over to her.

The Sceltie looked unbearably weary, and there was a deep sadness in his brown eyes—and just a bit of an accusation.

Karla? Ladvarian said.

"Little Brother," Karla replied.

Two bowls appeared on the small table next to Karla's chair. One was filled with . . .

Karla carefully picked one up, studied it.

. . . bubbles of water that had protective shields around them to form a kind of skin. The other bowl had one red bubble.

I need a drop of blood from each of you, Ladvarian said.

"Why?" Karla asked as she studied the bubble. It was a brilliant little piece of Craft.

For Jaenelle.

Hearing that, Chaosti jumped in. "If Jaenelle wants something from us right now, she can ask us herself."

"*Chaosti,*" Gabrielle hissed.

Chaosti snarled at her.

Ladvarian cringed at the anger in the room, but his eyes never left Karla.

"Why?" Karla asked.

"Why why why," Tersa said irritably as she knocked over the building blocks. "Humans can't even give a little gift without asking why why why. It is for your Queen. What more do you need to know?" Then, as if the outburst had never happened, she began arranging blocks again.

Karla shivered as she stared at Ladvarian. There were two ways to interpret "for Jaenelle." Either the dog was just the courier and was bringing these drops of blood to Jaenelle because *she* needed them for something . . . or Ladvarian wanted them *for Jaenelle.* But how to ask the right questions and get something more than an evasive answer. Because she was certain Ladvarian would become evasive if she pushed too hard.

"I'm not sure I can give you a drop of blood, little Brother," Karla said carefully. "My blood is still a bit tainted from the poison."

"That will have no effect on this," Tersa said absently as she used Craft to hold blocks in the air. "But what is in your *heart* . . . Yes, that *will* affect a great deal."

"Why?" Karla asked—and then winced when Tersa just looked at her. She turned her attention back to Ladvarian. "So, that's all we have to do? Just put a drop of blood into each bubble?"

★When you give the blood, you must think about Jaenelle. *Good* thoughts,★ he added in a growl as he glanced at the other males.

Karla shook her head. "I don't understand. Why—"

"Because the Blood will sing to the Blood," Tersa answered quietly. "Because blood is the memory's river."

Exasperated, Karla looked at Tersa, but it was the structure that caught her eye first.

A spiral. A glistening black spiral.

Then the brown wooden blocks crashed down on the table.

★Karla,★ Gabrielle said softly.

★I saw it.★ She looked at Tersa, who looked back at her with frighteningly clear-sighted eyes. *She knows. Mother Night, whatever is going to happen . . . Tersa knows. And so does Ladvarian.*

And knowing that much, there was no longer any need to ask "why."

Glancing at Ladvarian for permission, Karla sent out the most delicate psychic tendril she could create and lightly touched the red bubble.

Ladvarian, as a puppy, being taught by Jaenelle to air walk. Being brushed and petted. Being taught . . .

She backed away. Those memories were private, the best he had to give.

She swallowed hard—and tasted tears. "What Jaenelle is trying to do . . . Is it dangerous?"

★Yes,★ Ladvarian answered.

"Have other kindred given this gift?"

★All the kindred who know her.★

And I'll bet none of them asked why why why. Karla looked at the rest of the First Circle. No trace of anger. Not anymore. They would think about Jaenelle's actions over the past few weeks and reach the right conclusion.

"All right, little Brother," Karla said. Before she could use her thumbnail to prick a finger, Gabrielle touched her shoulder.

"I think . . ." Gabrielle hesitated, took a deep breath. "I think this should be done as ritual."

So that it would be as powerful as they could make it. "Yes, you're right." Karla set the clear bubble back into the bowl.

"I'll get what we need," Gabrielle said.

"I'll go with you," Morghann said.

As Gabrielle and Morghann walked past the males, Chaosti and Khary reached out, each one giving his wife a gentle touch of apology before stepping aside.

With a weary sigh, Ladvarian moved out of the way and lay down.

Tersa stood up.

"Tersa?" Karla said. "Aren't you going to give the gift?"

Those clear-sighted eyes looked into her. Then Tersa smiled, said, "I already have," and left the room.

That was enough to tell Karla who had shown the kindred how to create those brilliant little pieces of Craft.

Watching the males shift places and take up their usual protective stance, Karla's eyes filled with tears, and she wished, futilely, that Morton could have been standing among them.

We'll be all right, she thought when she saw Aaron wrap his arms around Kalush. *The harsh words will be forgiven, and we'll be all right.*

But would Jaenelle?

3 / Terreille

"It's your turn, little bitch," Daemon said as he unfastened the chains from the post.

Surreal stared at him. It was after midnight—was, in fact, almost twenty-four hours since he had killed Marian and Daemonar. The day had been quiet enough. Sadi had prowled around the camp, making everyone nervous, and Dorothea and Hekatah had played least-in-sight.

"What are you going to do with the bitch?" Dorothea said, approaching the posts.

Until now.

Daemon looked at Dorothea and smiled. "Well, darling, I'm going to use her to give you what you've always wanted."

"Meaning what?" Dorothea asked uneasily.

"Meaning," Daemon purred, "that I'm going to break your slut of a granddaughter. And then I'm going to mount her until she's seeded with my child. She's ripe for it. It'll catch. And I'll make sure she has all the incentive she needs not to try to abort it. Your bloodline and me, Dorothea. Exactly what you've wanted from me. And all you'll have to overlook is the fact that the result might have pointed ears."

Laughing, he dragged Surreal into the same hut that had held Marian and Daemonar.

She waited until he had turned to close the door before she called in her stiletto and launched herself at him. He spun around, raised an arm to block the knife. She twisted, bringing the knife in under his arm, intending to drive it between his ribs up to the hilt. Instead, the knife hit a shield, slid right past him, and went into the door.

Before she could yank the knife out of the wood, Daemon grabbed her, shoved her back to the center of the small room. Screaming, she launched herself at him again. He caught her hands and roughly pushed her back until her knees hit the edge of the narrow bed. She went down with him on top of her.

He rolled off immediately, sprang to his feet. "That's enough."

She leaped off the bed and hurled every curse she knew at the top of her lungs before she lunged at him again.

He pushed her away and swore viciously. "Damn it, Surreal, *that's enough.*"

"If you think I'm going to spread my legs for you, you'd better think again, *Sadist*."

"Shut up, Surreal," Daemon said quietly but intensely.

She felt the shields go up around the hut. Not just a Black protective shield but a Black aural shield as well. Which meant no one could hear what was happening inside.

He took a deep breath, raked his fingers through his hair. "Well," he said dryly, "that little performance ought to convince the bitches that something is happening in here."

She had been gathering herself to spring at him again, intending to go for his balls this time. But that tone and those words sounded so . . . *Daemon* . . . that she paused. And remembered Karla's warning about a friend who becomes an enemy in order to remain a friend.

He eyed her, then approached warily. "Let's see your wrists."

She held out her hands, watching him—and saw the fury in his eyes when he snapped off the manacles and looked at the raw skin underneath.

Surreal huffed. "Damn it, Sadi, what kind of game are you playing?"

"A vicious one," he replied, calling in a leather box. He looked through it, pulled out a jar, and handed it to her. "Put that on your wrists."

She opened the jar, sniffed. A Healer's ointment. While she applied it to her wrists, he called in another box. There were several balls of clay sitting in nests of paper. Two of the nests were empty.

"Do you still have the food pack you brought?"

"Yes. I haven't had a chance to eat any of it," she added tartly.

"Then eat something now," he said, still looking through the box. "I'd give you some from mine, but I gave most of it to Marian."

A chill went down Surreal's spine. There was a funny buzzing in her head. "To Marian?"

"Do you remember the shack we stopped at when we got to Hayll?"

"Yes." Of course she remembered it. It was a couple of miles away from the camp. That was where Daemon had changed into the Sadist. One minute he had been carefully explaining about the sentries and the perimeter stakes that would alert the guards, and the next thing she knew, she was tied up and he was purring threats about how she should have stayed under Falonar and stayed out of his way. He had scared her, badly. And the fact that he had made her furious now. "You could have told me, you son of a bitch."

He looked up. "Would you have been as convincing?"

She bristled, insulted. "You're damn right I would have been."

"Well, we're going to have a chance to find out. You said you wanted to help, Surreal. That you were willing to be a diversion."

She *had* said that, but she'd thought she would have known *when* she was being a diversion. "So?"

"So now you will be." He approached her, held up a small gold hoop. "Listen carefully. This will produce the illusion that you're broken." He slipped the hoop through one of the links of the necklace that held her Gray Jewel. "No one will be able to detect that you're still wearing the Gray unless you use it. If you *do* need to use it, then don't hesitate. I'll figure out some way to deal with things here."

"The High Lord will know I'm not broken."

Daemon shook his head as he turned back to search for something else in the box. "You'd have to wear Jewels darker than the Black to be able to detect that spell."

Darker than the *Black*? Sadi couldn't make a spell like that. Which meant . . .

Mother Night.

"This"—Daemon held up a tiny crystal vial before attaching it to the necklace—"will convince anyone who thinks to check that you're not only fertile but you're now pregnant. A Healer would be able to tell within twenty-four hours," he added, answering her unspoken question.

Lifting the necklace, Surreal studied the vial. "You asked Jaenelle to create an illusion that I was pregnant with your child?"

She saw his face tighten.

Yes, he had asked Jaenelle. And it had hurt him to ask.

Looking to change the subject, she pointed to the balls of clay. "What are those?"

"The raw spells to create shadows."

Shadows. Illusions that could be made to fool someone into believing the person in front of them was real.

"Marian and Daemonar," she said weakly, staring at the two empty nests of paper.

"Yes," he replied sharply.

She hissed at him. "You didn't trust me, a *whore,* to put on a good show, but you figured *Lucivar* would be convin—" Her voice trailed away. "He doesn't know, does he?"

"No," Daemon said quietly, "he doesn't know."

Her legs weakened so abruptly, she sat on the floor. "Hell's fire, Mother Night, and may the Darkness be merciful."

"I know." Daemon hesitated. "I'm buying time, Surreal. I have got to buy enough time and still get everyone out of here. In order to make Dorothea and Hekatah believe Marian and Daemonar were dead, Lucivar had to believe it."

"Mother Night." Surreal rested her forehead on her knees. "What's worth paying a price like this?"

"My Queen needs the time in order to save Kaeleer."

"Oh, shit, Sadi." She looked up at him. "Tell me something. Even though you knew it was an illusion, how did you keep your stomach down afterward?"

He swallowed hard. "I didn't."

"You're mad," she muttered as she climbed to her feet.

"I serve," he said sharply.

Sometimes, for a male, it amounted to the same thing.

"All right," she said as she hooked her hair behind her pointed ears. "What do you need me to do?"

He hesitated, then started to hedge. "It's dangerous."

"Daemon," she said patiently, "what do you need?" When he still didn't answer, she took a guess. "You want me to wander around the camp whimpering and looking like a woman who's been raped out of her mind and is now terrified of what will happen to her if she miscarries the child that was produced from that rape. Right?"

"Yes," he said faintly.

"And then what?"

"Marian and Daemonar are at that shack. Slip out of camp tomorrow night, pick them up, and then go to the Keep. Don't stop, don't go anywhere else. Get to the Keep. You'll have to ride the Red Wind. The darker ones are unstable."

"Un—Never mind, I don't want to know about that." She thought everything through carefully. Yes, she could play this out. A woman that broken would spend a lot of time hiding, so letting people get glimpses of her throughout the day would be enough—and would hide the fact that she had disappeared.

Daemon reached for one of the balls of clay.

"What's that for?" Surreal asked.

"You would have fought for as long as you could," Daemon said, not looking at her. "You would look like you'd fought. After I create the illusion, you can carry this and—"

"No." Surreal shrugged out of her jacket and started unbuttoning her shirt. "You can't play all of this out with illusions. Not if you want to convince Dorothea and Hekatah long enough to buy the time Jaenelle needs."

His eyes turned hard yellow. "I'll give up a great deal for this, Surreal, but I'm *not* going to break my vow of fidelity."

"I know," she replied quietly. "That's not what I meant."

"Then what *did* you mean?" Daemon snapped.

She took a deep breath to steady herself. "You have to make the bruises real."

4 / Kaeleer

Calling in the bowl, Ladvarian placed it carefully on the chamber floor and watched the Arachnian Queen delicately touch the little bubbles now filled with blood and memories.

Is good, the spider said with approval. *Good memories. Strong memories. As strong as kindred.*

Ladvarian looked at the bowl that sat in front of the huge tangled web. There were still a lot of the kindred's gifts left in the bowl. It wasn't a fast thing the Weaver was doing.

You must rest, the spider said as she selected a bubble from the humans' offerings and floated up to a thread in the web. *All kindred must rest. Must be strong when the time comes to anchor the dream to flesh.*

Will you have enough time to add all the memories? Ladvarian asked respectfully.

The Weaver of Dreams didn't reply for a long time. Then, *Enough. Just enough.*

5 / Terreille

The whimpering wasn't all feigned.

But, Hell's fire, Surreal thought as she wandered aimlessly around the camp, she hadn't expected to have to goad Daemon quite *that* much before he finally got down to business. And she'd understood that the anger behind his teeth and hands was because he'd had to touch a woman besides Jaenelle in a few intimate places. But, shit, he didn't have to bite her breast quite *that* hard.

On the other hand, he had chosen his marks very carefully. Judging by the look in people's eyes when they saw her, the bruises were impressive, but none of them impeded movement or would freeze a muscle if she had to fight.

The hardest part had been seeing the hatred in Saetan's eyes. She'd wanted to tell him. Oh, how she'd wanted to say something, anything, to get that look out of his eyes. And she might have if Daemon hadn't chosen that moment to glide by and make a devastatingly cutting remark. After that, throughout the rest of the morning, she had avoided the High Lord—and she hadn't dared get anywhere near Lucivar.

But she had made sure that Dorothea had seen her. She'd felt the bitch trying to probe her to find out if she was really broken and really pregnant. Apparently the illusion spells had held up because Dorothea gently suggested that she lie down for a while and rest. The bitch was almost drooling over the idea of being able to get her hands on *any* child sired by Sadi.

She'd go back and hide for a little while, wait until sunset, then put in an appearance so that Hekatah could sniff around her. Then all she had to do was slip past the sentries and the perimeter markers, pick up Marian and Daemonar, and get them home. That was all she . . . *Shit.*

She hadn't been paying attention to exactly where she was going—and now found herself staring right into Lucivar's eyes.

He had spent the morning watching her whenever she appeared. It was a good act, but it was just a little off. Not that anyone else would have noticed. Oh, he was sure Dorothea and Hekatah and plenty of the guards had seen broken witches, but he doubted any of them had ever paid any attention to those women after the breaking. He, on the other hand, had taken care of a few of them in a number of courts. He hadn't been able to stop the breaking, but he'd taken care of them afterward. And they all had one thing in common: the first day or two after they were broken, they were cold. They huddled up in shawls and blankets, stayed close to any source of heat that was available to them.

But there was Surreal, wandering through the camp, wearing nothing over a shirt that seemed torn in all the right places to display some impressive bruises. And that made him think about a lot of things.

"You should put on a jacket, sweetheart," he said gently.

"Jacket?" Surreal said feebly while her hands tried to cover some of the rips in the shirt.

"A jacket. You're cold."

"Oh. No I'm—"

"*Cold.*"

She shivered then, but it wasn't from cold, it was from nerves.

"You don't have to carry that bastard's child," Lucivar said quietly. "You can abort it. A broken witch still has that much power. And once you're barren, there's no reason for anyone to look in your direction."

"I can't," Surreal said fearfully. "I can't. He would be so mad at me and . . . " She looked at the spot where Marian and Daemonar had died.

He wondered if he was wrong, if her mind really *was* so torn apart she didn't quite feel the cold yet. If *that* was true, then he understood the fear in her voice now. She was afraid the Sadist would do the same thing to her that he had done to Marian and Daemonar.

But what he saw in her eyes when she looked at him again wasn't fear, it was hot frustration.

The blood in his veins, which had felt so sluggish since he had crawled back to the post two nights ago, raged through him once again.

"Surreal . . ." He saw Daemon appear on the other side of the circle of bare ground a moment before she did.

With an almost-convincing cry, Surreal ran off.

Lucivar stared at Daemon. From across the distance, Daemon returned the stare.

"You bastard," Lucivar whispered. Daemon wouldn't have heard the words, but it didn't matter. Sadi would know what had been said.

Daemon walked away.

Lucivar leaned his head back against the post and closed his eyes.

If Surreal wasn't broken, if this was all a game, then Marian and Daemonar . . .

He should have remembered that about the Sadist. He, better than anyone else there, knew how vicious Daemon could be, but the Sadist had *never* harmed an innocent, had never hurt a child.

He had been waiting for the signal, but the game had begun before Daemon had walked into the camp. Still, he had played his part well—and would continue to do so.

Because understanding and forgiving were two very different things.

6 / Terreille

Drifting in a pain-hazed doze, Saetan felt the cup against his lips. The first swallow he took out of reflex, the second out of greed. As the taste of fresh blood filled his mouth, the Black power in it flowed through him, offering strength.

Hold on, a deep voice whispered in his mind. *You have to hold on. Please.*

He heard the weariness in that voice. He heard a son's plea to a father, and he responded. Being the man he was, he couldn't do otherwise. So he pushed his way through the haze of pain.

When he opened his eyes, all he saw was waning daylight, and he wondered if he'd just dreamed the plea he'd heard in Daemon's voice.

But he could still taste the dark, rich, fresh blood.

Closing his eyes again, he let his mind drift.

He was standing in an enormous cavern somewhere in the heart of Ebon Askavi. Etched in the floor was a huge web lined with silver. In the center where all the tether lines met was an iridescent Jewel the size of his hand, a Jewel that blended the colors of all the other Jewels. At the end of each tether line was an iridescent Jewel chip the size of his thumbnail.

He had been in this place once before, on the night when he had linked with Daemon in order to draw Jaenelle back to her body.

But there was something else in the cavern now.

Stretching across that silver web on the floor were three massive, connected tan-

gled webs that rose from about a foot from the floor to almost twice his height. In the center of each web was an Ebony Jewel.

Witch stood in front of those webs, wearing that black spidersilk gown, holding the scepter that held two Ebony Jewels and the spiral horn Kaetien had gifted her with when he'd been killed five years ago.

Behind the webs were dozens of demon-dead. One of them approached the webs, smiled, then faded. At the moment the person faded, a little star the same color as the person's Jewel bloomed on the middle web.

Puzzled, he moved to get a better look at the tangled webs.

The first one repulsed him. The threads looked swollen, moldy, tainted. At the end of every single tether line of that web was an Ebony Jewel chip.

The middle one was beautiful, filled with thousands of those little colored stars and a sprinkling of Black and Ebony Jewel chips.

The last one was a simple web, perfect in its symmetry, made of gray, ebon-gray, and black threads. It, too, had Black and Ebony Jewel chips that had been carefully placed on the threads to form a spiral.

He glanced at Witch, but she was focused on the task, so he shifted again to watch.

He saw Char, the leader of the cildru dyathe, approach the webs. The boy grinned at him, waved a jaunty good-bye, and faded to become another bright star.

Titian approached him, kissed his cheek. "I'm proud to have known you, High Lord." She walked over to the webs and faded.

As he watched her, something nagged at him. Something about the structure of those webs. But before he could figure it out, Dujae, the artist who had given the coven drawing lessons, approached him.

"Thank you, High Lord," the huge man said. "Thank you for allowing me to know the Ladies. All the portraits I have done of them are at the Hall in Kaeleer now. My gift to you."

"Thank you, Dujae," he replied, puzzled.

As Dujae walked away, Prothvar stepped up. "It's a different kind of battlefield, but it's a good way to fight. Take care of the waif, Uncle Saetan." Prothvar hugged him.

Cassandra came next. Cassandra, whom he hadn't seen since the first party when they had all met the coven and the boyos.

She smiled at him, a sad smile, then pressed her hand against his cheek. "I wish I had been a better friend. May the Darkness embrace you, Saetan." She kissed him. When she faded, a glorious Black star began to shine in the middle web.

"Mephis," he said when his eldest son approached. "Mephis, what—"

Mephis smiled and hugged him. "I was proud to have you for a father, and honored to know you as a man. I'm not sure I ever told you that. I wanted you to know. Good-bye, Father. I love you."

"And I love you, Mephis," he said, holding on hard as he felt grief swell inside him.

When Mephis faded into the web, the only one left of the demon-dead was Andulvar.

"Andulvar, what's going on?"

"And the Blood will sing to the Blood," Andulvar replied. "Like to like." He looked at the webs. "She found a way to identify those who have been tainted from those who still honor the ways of the Blood. But she needed help to keep those who followed the old ways from being swept away with the rest when she unleashes. That's what the demon-dead will do—our strength will anchor the living. We'll burn out in the doing, but as Prothvar said, it's a good way to fight."

Andulvar smiled at him. "Take care of yourself, SaDiablo. And take care of those pups of yours. Both of them. Just remember that your mirror truly is your mirror. You only have to look to see the truth." Andulvar hugged him. "No man could have asked for a better friend or a better Brother. Hold on. Fight. You have the hardest burden, but your sons will help you."

Andulvar walked to the webs. He spread his dark wings, raised his arms . . . and faded.

As he blinked back tears, Jaenelle walked over to him. He wrapped his arms around her. "Witch-child . . ."

She shook her head, kissed him, and smiled. But her eyes were filled with tears.

"Thank you for being my father. It was glorious, Saetan." Then she leaned close and whispered in his ear, "Take care of Daemon. Please. He'll need you."

She didn't fade into the web, she just disappeared.

Wiping the tears with the back of his hand, he approached the webs and studied them carefully.

The first web, the moldy web, were the Blood tainted by Dorothea and Hekatah. The second web, with all its Jewel stars, were the Blood who still honored the old ways. The third web, with its spiral, was Witch.

As he continued to study the webs, he began to shake his head, slowly at first, *then faster and faster. "No, no, no, witch-child," he muttered. "You can't connect them like this. If you unleash your full strength . . ."*

It would blast through the large Ebony Jewel in the center of the first web, travel through all the strands, sweep up all the minds that resonated with those strands, then hit all the Ebony chips, meeting a smaller portion of itself in a devastating collision of power that would destroy anyone caught in it. Then it would continue on to the next web, barely diminished.

The middle web, with all those thousands of beads of power, would provide tremendous resistance as her strength swept through it. The demon-dead, providing a shield and anchor for the living, would absorb some of her power as it flooded over them, but not all of those thousands of beads of power would be enough. That unleashed strength would continue on to the third web and . . .

The power would flow through that perfect symmetry, burn out the web, and shatter every Jewel chip as it came blasting back through the spiral. And once the last Jewel chip shattered, the only thing left to reabsorb the rest of the power would be . . .

"NO, witch-child," he shouted, turning round and round, searching for her. "No! A backlash like that will rip you apart! Jaenelle!"

He turned back to the webs. Maybe, if he could link himself to Witch's web somehow, draw every drop of reserve power out of his Birthright Red Jewels and his Black . . . Maybe he could shield her enough to keep her safe when the rest of that explosion of power came screaming back at her.

He took a step forward . . .

. . . and everything faded.

Saetan opened his eyes. Deep twilight. Almost night.

A dream? Just a dream? No. He had been a Black Widow too long not to know the difference between a dream and a vision. But it was fading. He couldn't *quite* remember, and there was something about that vision that was desperately important for him to remember.

That was when he noticed Daemon standing a few feet in front of him, watching him with frightening intensity.

Just remember that your mirror truly is your mirror. You only have to look to see the truth.

Andulvar's words. Andulvar's warning.

So, with eyes blinded by tears, he looked at his mirror, his namesake, his true heir. And saw.

Still watching him, Daemon reached into his jacket pocket. His hand came out as a loose fist. He opened his fingers, tipped his hand.

Little colored bangles, the kind women sewed on dresses to catch the light, spilled to the ground.

Saetan stared at them. They chilled him, but he couldn't say why.

And when he looked up again at Daemon . . . He could almost hear the unspoken plea to think, to know, to remember. But his mind was still too full of the other vision that had turned elusive.

Daemon walked away.

Saetan closed his eyes. Bangles and webs. If he could find the connection, he would also find the answers.

7 / Terreille

Surreal swore silently as she stared at the perimeter stakes. There had to be a trick to getting past them. Hell's fire, Daemon had gotten them into the camp without anyone realizing it, but she'd still been too stunned by his shift into the Sadist to pay much attention. And he'd gotten Marian and Daemonar *out* without anyone realizing it.

Could it be as simple as jumping over them so the contact between the crystals wasn't broken? No, she would have remembered *that*.

"What are you doing out here?" a voice demanded.

Shit.

She turned to face the sentry who was moving toward her. She was too far away from the camp for anyone to believe she was just a broken witch wandering around. But she had to try to convince this bastard. Or kill him quietly. If she ended up in a fight and used her Gray Jewels, Daemon would know she'd run into trouble and alter the rest of his plans. And *that* would allow those bitches to realize they'd been tricked and *really* start the war.

"The hut's lost," she said, waving her hand in a vague gesture.

He came closer, his eyes full of suspicion and doubt. "Answer me, bitch. Why are you out here?"

"The *hut's* lost," she repeated, doing her best to imitate the way Tersa's mind tended to meander. She pointed. "It should be near that fuzzy post, but it wandered off."

The sentry looked in that direction. "That's a *tree,* you stupid bitch. Now—" He stopped, raked her body with his eyes, then smiled. Looking around to make sure no one else was nearby, he reached for her.

She took a step back, placed a protective hand over her abdomen, and shook her head. "Can't touch another male. He'll get mad at me if I touch another male."

The sentry gave her an evil grin. "Well, he's not going to know, is he?"

Surreal hesitated. That would certainly get her close enough to ram a knife between his ribs, but it would also take time she didn't have. The Gray Jewels then, and a fast kill—and may the Darkness help Sadi with whatever was going to happen in the camp afterward.

Down, Surreal!

She felt hind legs brush against her back as she dove.

A moment later, the sentry lay dead, his throat torn out.

A sight shield faded, revealing the blood-splashed wolf.

"Graysfang?" Surreal whispered. She touched the Jewel beneath her shirt. Gray's fang. The High Lord had been right.

Skirting the dead sentry, she reached for the wolf.

Wait, Graysfang said.

That's when she saw the small golden bump between his ears. The bump lifted, floated to the nearest perimeter stake, and uncurled its legs.

Surreal stared at the small gold spider as it busily spun a simple tangled web between two of the stakes. When it was done, it picked its way to the center of the web.

The sentry vanished. There was no trace of blood on the ground.

They will not find him now, Graysfang said. *They can only see what the web lets them see.* He gently closed his teeth around Surreal's arm and started tugging her.

"What about the spider?"

She will stay to guard the web. Hurry, Surreal.

She shook her arm free of his teeth. It would be easier to keep up with him if she wasn't hunched over. Switching to a communication thread, she asked, *What are you doing here? How did you get through the perimeter stakes?*

Humans are foolish. The meat trail is unguarded. Too many legs moving on the trail. The humans got tired of baring their fangs when it was only meat.

Meat trail? Oh, *game* trail. ★How did you know about the trail? How did you find me?★

★The Weaver of Dreams told me to learn the two-legged cat's scent and follow his tracks. He is a good hunter,★ Graysfang added with approval. ★There is much feline in him. Kaelas says so.★

Sadi, with the predatory grace even the kindred recognized. Graysfang had followed Sadi. ★Who's this Weaver?★ She got a quick image of a large golden spider—and stumbled.

Damn fool of an idiot wolf. It was bad enough that he had gone to Arachna and brought a *small* spider back with him. But to deal with the *Queen* . . .

★She asked me, Surreal,★ Graysfang said meekly when she snarled at him. ★It's a bad thing to refuse the Weaver.★

Surreal gritted her teeth and picked up the pace. ★We'll talk about it later.★

As soon as she saw the game trail, she recognized the place. This was where Daemon had brought them through the camp's perimeter. ★I couldn't have found this place again by myself.★

★You have a small snout,★ the wolf said kindly. ★You cannot smell tracks.★

Surreal looked at Graysfang—at Gray's fang—and smiled.

"Let's go," she whispered. "Do you know the way to the shack?"

★I know.★

An hour later, she, Marian, Daemonar, and Graysfang were riding the Red Wind to the Keep.

8 / Terreille

"I think it's time we had a little talk," Hekatah said, trying to smile coyly at Daemon.

"Really?"

Oh, the arrogance, the surliness, the *meanness* in that voice. If his father had been even half the man the son was . . .

"It takes so long for a Realm to recover from a war, it would be foolish to go through with it if it can be avoided," she said, reaching up to caress his face as she wove a seduction spell around him.

He stepped back. "Don't ever touch me without my permission," he snarled softly. "Not even Jaenelle is allowed to touch me without my permission."

"And she submits?"

He smiled that cold, brutal smile. "She submits to a great many things—and begs for more."

Hekatah looked into his glazed eyes and shivered with excitement. The air was filled with the earthy tang of sex. She had him. He just didn't know it yet. "A partnership would serve us both well."

"But you already have a partner, Hekatah—one I will not deal with in any way."

She waved a hand dismissively. "She can be taken care of easily enough." She paused. "Darling Dorothea hasn't been sleeping well. I think I'll give her a little cup of something that will help."

He stared at her with those glazed eyes, a man aroused to the point of being frightening—and terribly exciting.

"In that case . . ." Daemon's hands cupped her face. His lips brushed against hers.

She was disappointed by the gentleness—until he *really* kissed her. Mean, dominating, unforgiving, demanding, painfully exciting.

But she was demon-dead. Her body *couldn't* respond that way, couldn't . . .

She drowned in that kiss, staggered by sensations her body hadn't felt in centuries.

He finally raised his head.

She stared at him. "How . . . It isn't possible."

"I think we've just proved that's a lie," Daemon crooned. "I punish women who lie to me."

"Do you?" Hekatah whispered, swaying. She couldn't look away from the cruel pleasure in his eyes. "I'll take care of Dorothea."

He kissed her again. This time she felt the mockery in the gentleness. There was nothing gentle about him. Nothing.

"I'll take care of Dorothea," she said again. "And then we'll be partners."

"And I promise you, darling," Daemon purred, "you're going to get everything you deserve."

9 / Terreille

Dorothea woke up late in the morning and groaned at the pain in her belly. It felt like a year's worth of moontime cramps had settled in her gut. She couldn't get sick now. *Couldn't.* Maybe a cup of herbal tea or some broth. Hell's fire, she was cold. Why was she so damn cold?

Shivering, she dragged herself out of bed—and fell.

After the shock came fear as she remembered the brew Hekatah had made for her last night. To help her sleep. What had she been thinking of not to test something that came from Hekatah's hand?

She hadn't been thinking. Hadn't . . .

That bitch. That walking piece of carrion must have used a compulsion spell on her to get her to drink it—and then to forget that she'd been *ordered* to drink it.

Her muscles constricted, twisted.

Not sick. Poisoned.

She needed help. She needed . . .

Her cabin door opened and closed.

Gasping from the effort, she rolled onto her side and stared at Daemon Sadi.

"Daemon," she whimpered, trying to hold out a hand toward him. "Daemon . . . help . . ."

He just stood there, studying her. Then he smiled. "Looks like witchblood was part of last night's little brew," he said pleasantly.

She couldn't draw a full breath. "You did this. *You* did this."

"You were becoming a problem, darling. It's nothing personal."

She felt the pain of the insult even through the physical pain. "Hekatah . . ."

"Yes," Daemon purred, "Hekatah. Now, don't worry, darling. I've put an aural and a protective shield around your cabin, so you'll be quite undisturbed for the rest of the day."

He walked out of the cabin.

She tried to crawl to the door, tried to scream for help. Couldn't do either.

It didn't take long for her world to become nothing but pain.

★　　★　　★

Daemon closed the door of the prison hut he'd been using whenever he needed to stay somewhere for a little while. Reaching into his jacket pocket, he withdrew the Jewels he'd gone to Dorothea's cabin to retrieve—Saetan's Black ring; Lucivar's pendant, ring, and Ring of Honor. He knew her well, knew exactly where to probe for a hiding place. It hadn't taken him more than a minute to slip around her guard spells and lift the Jewels while he stood there and talked to her.

He studied the Jewels and sighed with relief. Both men had put strong shields around the jewelry before handing them over to those bitches, so there was no way the pieces could have been tampered with or tainted. Still . . .

Setting the Jewels into the washbasin, he poured water over them, added some astringent herbs for cleansing, then let them soak.

This would be the last day, the last night. He could endure it that much longer. *Had* to endure it.

He closed his eyes. *Soon, sweetheart. A few more hours and I'll be on my way home, on my way back to you. And then we'll be married.*

Picturing Jaenelle slipping the plain gold wedding ring onto his finger, he smiled.

And then he remembered the seduction spell Hekatah had woven around him. Oh, he'd been aware of it, could have easily broken it—but he had let his body respond to it while he touched Hekatah. Kissed Hekatah. Hated Hekatah.

Just a game. A nasty, vicious game.

He barely made it to the chamber pot before he was quietly, but thoroughly, sick.

10 / Terreille

"It's your turn, Prick."

Because he was looking for it, because he knew *what* to look for, Lucivar saw the sick desperation in Daemon's eyes.

So he remained passive while Daemon unchained him and led him into the other prison hut, the one closest to them. And he stayed impassive while Daemon feverishly rumpled the small bed.

Then he let out an anguished Eyrien war cry that startled Daemon badly enough to fall onto the bed.

"Hell's fire, Prick," Daemon muttered as he stood up.

"Convincing enough?" Lucivar asked mildly.

Daemon froze.

All the masks dropped away. Lucivar saw a man physically and emotionally exhausted, a man barely able to stay on his feet.

"Why?" he asked quietly.

"I had to buy Jaenelle some time. I needed your hate to do it."

That simple. That painful. Daemon would regret it, deeply regret it, but he wouldn't hesitate to rip out his brother's heart if that's what Jaenelle needed from him. Which was exactly what he had done.

"You're here with Jaenelle's consent," Lucivar said, wanting the confirmation.

"I'm here at her command."

"To play out this game."

"To play out this game," Daemon agreed quietly.

Lucivar nodded, let out a bitter laugh. "Well, Bastard, you've played a good game." He paused, then said coldly, "Where are Marian and Daemonar?"

Daemon's hand shook a little as he raked his fingers through his hair. "Since Surreal didn't have to blast anyone with the Gray to get away from here, I have to assume she safely reached the hiding place where I had left them. They're all at the Keep by now."

Lucivar let that sink in, allowed himself a moment's relief and joy. "So now what happens?"

"Now I create a shadow of you, and you head for the Keep. Stay on the Red Wind. The darker ones are unstable."

Shadows. Daemon never could have created shadows that convincing. Not by himself. And Jaenelle . . . Jaenelle, having grown up around Andulvar and Prothvar, would have expected an Eyrien warrior to be able to accept the pain of the battlefield, no matter what that battlefield looked like.

"What do you need?" Lucivar asked.

Daemon hesitated. "Some hair, skin, and blood."

"Then let's play the game through."

They worked together in silence. The only sound Lucivar made during that time was a sigh of relief when Daemon slipped the Ring of Honor over his cock and used it to remove the Ring of Obedience in a way that wouldn't be detected.

Putting on the Ebon-gray Jewels Daemon had returned to him, he watched the final steps to the spell that would create a shadow of himself. And shuddered when he saw the tormented, anguished creature whose lips were pulled back in a rictus grin.

"Hell's fire, Bastard," Lucivar said, feeling queasy. "What was it you did to me that I would have ended up looking like *that*?"

"I don't know," Daemon replied wearily. "But I'm sure Hekatah can imagine something." He hesitated, swallowed hard. "Look, Prick, for once in your life, just do as you're told. Get to the Keep. Everyone who matters the most to you is waiting for you there."

"Not everyone," Lucivar said softly.

"I'll get the High Lord out." Daemon waited.

Lucivar knew what Daemon was waiting for, what he hoped for. He wanted to be told that Saetan wasn't the only one left who mattered.

Lucivar said nothing.

Daemon looked away, and said wearily, "Let's go. There's one more game to play."

11 / Terreille

Saetan stared at the bangles lying on the ground. Why had Daemon made such a point of them? And why did they chill him so much?

He hissed in frustration, then jolted at the sibilant sound.

"You wish to undersstand thiss?" Draca had asked.

Bangles floating in a tank of water. Draca holding an egg-shaped stone attached to a thin silk cord. "A sspiral."

The stone moving in a circular motion, spiraling, spiraling, until all the water was in motion, all the bangles caught.

"A whirlpool," Geoffrey had said.

"No," Draca had replied. "A maelsstrom.... Sshe will almosst alwayss sspiral.... You cannot alter her nature.... But the maelsstrom.... Sshield her, Ssaetan. Sshield her with your sstrength and your love and perhapss it will never happen."

"And if it does?" he had asked.

"It will be the end of the Blood."

End of the Blood.

End of . . .

Those bangles weren't a message from Daemon, they were a warning from *Draca*. Jaenelle was spiraling down to her full strength to unleash the maelstrom. The end of the Blood. Was that why she had insisted that the First Circle remain at the Keep? Because it would be the only place that could withstand that devastating power? No. Jaenelle didn't like to kill. She wouldn't destroy all the Blood if she could . . .

Damn it. *Damn it,* he needed to draw that vision back. Needed to see those webs again in order to remember that one important thing that was eluding him. Deliberately eluding him. A veil had been drawn across that vision to keep him from remembering that one thing until it was too late.

But if she *was* going to unleash the maelstrom, what in the name of Hell was Daemon doing *here*?

Stalling. Buying time. Keeping Dorothea and Hekatah distracted. Playing games to . . . Marian and Daemonar. Then Surreal. He'd heard Lucivar cry out a couple of hours ago, but there had been no sign of him since then. Which only left . . .

A shadow fell across the bangles.

He looked up into Daemon's glazed eyes.

"It's time to dance," Daemon crooned.

He might have said something, but he could smell Hekatah nearby. So he let Daemon lead him into the prison hut, said nothing while he was tied to the bed.

When Daemon stretched out beside him, he whispered, "When does the game end?"

Daemon tensed, swallowed hard. "In a couple more hours," he said, keeping his voice low. "At midnight." He laid a hand gently on Saetan's chest. "Nothing's going to happen. Just—"

They both heard someone brush against the door, both knew who was listening.

Saetan shook his head. Everything has a price. "Make it convincing, Daemon," he whispered.

He saw the sick resignation and the apology in Daemon's eyes before his son kissed him.

And he learned why the Blood called Daemon the Sadist.

Saetan lay on his side, staring at the wall.

Daemon had actually done very little. *Very* little. But he'd managed to

convince that bitch who had hovered outside the door that a son was rap-
ing his own father without actually doing anything that would prevent either of them from being able to look the other in the eye. A rather
impressive display of skill.

And very brief. He'd been concerned about that, but when Daemon
walked out of the hut, he'd heard a murmured comment and Hekatah's
delighted, abrasive laugh.

So, while Daemon continued to prowl and keep the camp on edge,
he'd had time to rest, to gather his strength, to think.

The game ended at midnight. What was the significance of midnight?
Well, it was called the witching hour, that moment suspended between
one day and the next. And it would be seventy-two hours from the time
Daemon appeared in the camp.

Saetan jerked upright. Seventy-two hours.

*Confined to a sitting room in the Keep, he had paced. "From sunset to sun-
rise. That's how long an Offering takes. For the White, for the Black, that's how
long it takes."*

*"For the Prince of the Darkness," Tersa had said as she pushed around the
pieces of a puzzle. "But for the Queen?"*

When Jaenelle had made the Offering to the Darkness, it had taken
her three days. *Seventy-two hours.*

"Mother Night," he whispered, shifting into a sitting position.

The door opened. Daemon rushed in and dropped a bundle of clothing on the bed.

Before Saetan could say anything, one of Daemon's hands was
clamped behind his head and the other was holding a cup to his lips,
pouring warm liquid down his throat. He had no choice but to swallow
or choke. He swallowed. A moment later, he wished he had choked.

"Hell's fire, what did you just give me?" he gasped as he bent over and
pressed his forehead to his knees.

"A tonic," Daemon said, vigorously rubbing Saetan's back.

"Stop that," Saetan snapped. He turned his head just enough to glare
at Daemon. "*Whose* tonic?"

"Jaenelle's—with my blood added."

Saetan swore softly, viciously, with great sincerity.

Daemon winced and muttered, "She said it would kick like two teams
of draft horses."

"Only someone who's never had to drink one of these little tonics would describe it that mildly."

Daemon went down on his knees in front of Saetan and busily undid the chains. "I couldn't search for your clothes, so I brought you these. They should fit well enough."

Saetan gritted his teeth as Daemon massaged his legs and feet. "Where did you get them?"

"Off a guard. He won't be needing them."

"Damn things probably have lice."

"Deal with it," Daemon growled. Taking a ball of clay out of his jacket pocket, he rolled it into a stubby cylinder, then carefully forced the Ring of Obedience to open enough to slide off Saetan's organ. It clamped down on the clay with the same viciousness it had clamped down on flesh.

Setting the cylinder on the bed, Daemon glanced at Saetan's organ and sucked in a breath.

"It doesn't matter," Saetan said quietly. "I'm a Guardian. I'm past that part of my life."

"But—" Daemon pressed his lips together. "Get these on." After helping Saetan into the trousers, he knelt again to deal with the socks and boots. "It's almost midnight. We'll be cutting it close since we've got to cover a bit of ground in order to reach the nearest strand of the Winds. But in a few more hours, we'll be at the Keep. We'll be home."

The desperate eagerness in Daemon's eyes tore the veil off the vision.

Two webs. One moldy, tainted. The other beautiful, full of shining beads of power.

She had found a way to separate those who lived by the ways of the Blood from those who had been perverted by Hekatah and Dorothea.

But the third web . . .

She was a Queen, and a Queen wouldn't ask for what she herself wouldn't give. And perhaps it was also the only selfish thing she'd ever done. By sacrificing herself, she wouldn't have to carry the burden of all the lives she was about to destroy. But . . .

He doesn't know. You didn't tell him. He came here expecting you to be waiting for him when he got back. Oh, witch-child.

Which is why she had asked him to take care of Daemon, why she had known he would need to.

Maybe it wasn't too late. Maybe there was still a way to stop it, to stop her.

"Let's go," he said abruptly.

Daemon put a sight shield over both of them, and they slipped away from the camp.

By the time they reached the place where they could catch the Winds, a cold, sharp wind had begun to blow.

Saetan stopped, drew a breath through his mouth, tasted the air.

"It's just the wind," Daemon said.

"No," Saetan replied grimly, "it's not. Let's go."

12 / Terreille

Two hours later, Hekatah burst into Dorothea's cabin, waving a stubby clay cylinder. "We've been tricked. They're all gone. That thing in the prison hut isn't Lucivar, it's some kind of illusion. And Saetan . . ." She hurled the cylinder across the room. "That bastard Sadi *lied* to us."

Lying on the floor where she'd been all day, Dorothea stared at Hekatah. As her bowels released more bloody flux, she started to laugh.

13 / Kaeleer

A storm had been gathering all night—thunder, lightning, wind. Now, as dawn approached, the wind had turned fierce, sounding almost as if it had a voice.

"Come," Tersa said, helping Karla over to a couch. "You must lie down now. Morghann, come over here and lie on the floor."

"What's going on?" Khardeen asked as Morghann obediently lay down on the floor near the couch. He retrieved a pillow and slipped it under his wife's head.

"It would be better for all of you to sit on the floor. Even the Keep will feel this storm."

The First Circle glanced at each other uneasily and obeyed.

"What is it?" Karla asked when Tersa placed an arm protectively over her and rested the other hand on Morghann's shoulder.

"The day has come for the debts to be called in and for the Blood to answer for what they've become."

"I don't understand," Karla said. "What does the storm mean?"

Lightning flashed. The wind howled.

Tersa closed her eyes—and smiled. "She is coming."

14 / Terreille

He'd cut it too close. He hadn't expected the ride on the Winds to be that rough or that Saetan's physical endurance would give out so fast—or his own. They'd had to drop from the Red Wind to the Sapphire and finally, on the last part of the journey, down to the Green.

They couldn't land at the Keep itself. Some kind of shields had come down all around the place. So he'd homed in on Lucivar's Ebon-gray Jewel—and the one small place in the shields that Lucivar was using his Jewels to keep open—and dropped them from the Winds as close as he could. It hadn't been close enough, not for two exhausted men trying to scramble up a steep mountain path.

Now, with the gate in sight and Lucivar's mental urging to hurry, Daemon half carried Saetan up the slope, fighting a fierce, howling wind for every step.

Almost there. Almost. Almost.

The sky was getting lighter. The sun would lift above the horizon at any moment.

Hurry. Hurry.

"Saetan! SAE-TANNNN!"

Daemon looked behind them. Hekatah was scrambling up the slope. The bitch must have ridden the Red Wind all the way in order to get there right behind them.

Not wasting his breath to swear, he picked up the pace as best as could, dragging Saetan with him.

"Sadi!" Hekatah screamed. "You lying bastard!"

"MOVE!" Lucivar shouted. He was using Craft to hold the gate open, straining physically and mentally to keep it from closing and locking them out.

Closer. Almost there. Almost.

Daemon grabbed the bars of the gate, used the strength in his Black Jewel to hold it open. "Get him inside," he said, shoving Saetan at Lucivar. Then he turned and waited.

Hekatah came up the slope, stopped a few feet away. "You lying bastard."

Daemon smiled. "I didn't lie, darling. I told you you were going to get everything you deserved." He let go of the gate. It slammed shut, and the last shield came down over it.

As he turned and ran across the open courtyard, he heard Hekatah screaming. And he heard a wild howling, a sound full of joy and pain, rage and celebration.

He crossed the threshold into the safety of the Keep a moment before Jaenelle unleashed the maelstrom.

You musst wake, said a deep, sibilant voice. *You *musst* wake.*

Daemon opened his eyes. It took him a moment to understand why everything looked a little . . . *strange* . . . and readjust. It took him another moment to confirm that he was still distantly linked to his body—and that his body was lying on the cold stone floor of the Keep where he and Lucivar and Saetan had fallen when Jaenelle unleashed her full strength.

You are the triangle who helped sshape the web of dreamss. Now you musst hold the dream. There iss not much time.

Groaning, he sat up and looked around. And was instantly wide-awake. *Mother Night, where are we?*

He reached over Saetan's prone body and shook Lucivar.

Hell's fire, Bastard, Lucivar said. He raised his head. *Shit.*

Both of them reached for Saetan, shook him awake.

Father, wake up. We're in trouble, Daemon said.

Now what? Saetan growled. He raised himself up on his elbows. His eyes widened. *Mother Night.*

And may the Darkness be merciful, Lucivar added. *Where are we?*

Somewhere in the abyss. I think.

Climbing carefully to their feet, they looked around.

They were standing on the edge of a deep, wide chasm. Stretching across the chasm was an Opal web. Below them were webs the colors of the darker Jewels. Above them were webs the colors of the lighter Jewels.

What are we doing here? Lucivar asked.

We're the triangle who helped shape the dream, Daemon said. *We're supposed to hold the dream.*

Don't go cryptic on me, Bastard, Lucivar growled.

Daemon snarled at him.

Saetan raised his hand. They both fell silent.

Who told you that? Saetan asked.

A sibilant voice. Daemon paused. *It sounded like Draca, but it was male.*

Saetan nodded. *Lorn.* He looked around again.

Far, far, far above them, lightning flashed.

Why did Jaenelle ask you to come to Hayll, Daemon? Saetan asked.

She said that the triangle had to remain together in order to survive. That the mirror had the strength to keep the other two safe.

She saw that in a tangled web?

No. The Weaver of Dreams told her.

Lucivar began to swear.

Saetan's look was sharp, penetrating, thoughtful.

The lightning flashed a little closer.

Father, brother, lover, Saetan said softly.

Daemon nodded, remembering the triangle Tersa had traced on his palm. *The father came first. The brother stands between.* When they both looked at him, he shifted uneasily. *Something Tersa said once.*

Warnings from Tersa, the Arachnian Queen, and Draca, Saetan said. *A man might ignore one at his own peril, but all three?* He shook his head slowly. *I think not.*

The lightning flashed a little closer.

That's all well and good, Lucivar growled, *but I would prefer a straightforward order.*

Thesse webss are the besst magic I can give you, Lorn said irritably. *Usse them to hold the dream. If sshe breakss through all of them, sshe will return to the Darknesss. You will losse her.*

Lucivar puffed out a breath. *That's clear enough. So where—* He looked up as the lightning flashed again. *What's that?*

They all looked up, waited for the next flash—and saw the small dark speck plummeting toward the webs.

Jaenelle, Daemon whispered.

She'll rip right through them, Saetan said. *We'll have to use our own strength to try to slow her speed.*

All right, Lucivar said. *How do we go?*

Saetan looked at Daemon, then at Lucivar. *Father, brother, lover.* He didn't wait for an answer. He exploded upward, racing to intercept Witch before she hit the White web.

Lucivar watched for a moment, then turned to the webs, his eyes narrowed. *If she hits them in the center, she'll break through them. So we'll roll her.* He clamped a hand on Daemon's shoulder, pointed with the other hand. *Not so close to the edge that you'll risk hitting the chasm walls, but away from the center. Then twist and roll while you're using your own strength as a brake.*

Daemon looked at the webs. *What will that do?*

For one thing, the countermovement should slow the speed. And if she gets wrapped in the webs—

We'll form a cocoon of power.

Lucivar nodded. *I'll go up to the Rose. I don't know how much strength Saetan has left. If he's still able to hold her, I can add my strength to his. If not . . . *

Where should I be? Daemon asked, willing to defer to Lucivar's ability and fighting experience.

The Green. I should be able to hold her that far. Lucivar hesitated. *Good luck, Bastard.*

And you, Prick.

Lucivar soared upward.

A moment later, Daemon heard Saetan's roar of defiance as the White web shattered. In the flash, he could see two small figures falling, falling.

He floated down to the Green web.

The Yellow web shattered. Then the Tiger Eye.

He heard Lucivar's war cry.

As the Rose web shattered, he saw a twirl of color as Lucivar rolled, fighting against the speed of the fall.

They hit the Summer-sky. Holding on to Witch's legs, Lucivar rolled the other way, catching most of the web before they crashed through.

The Purple Dusk. The Opal.

Daemon met him halfway between the Opal and the Green.

Let go, Prick, before you shatter the Ebon-gray.

With a cry that was part defiant, part pain, and part fear, Lucivar let go.

Rage filled Daemon. Love drove him. He and Witch hit the Green web. He rolled, but he didn't have Lucivar's skill. They broke through close to the middle of the web. He kept rolling so that when they hit the

Sapphire, they were close to the edge. He rolled the other way, wrapping her in the web's power.

They broke through the Sapphire, but they weren't falling as fast now. He had a little more time to brace, to plan, to pour the strength of his Black Jewels into fighting the fall.

They hit the Red, rolled, clung for a second before falling to the Gray. Only half the Gray strands broke immediately. He strained back as hard as he could. When the other half broke, he rolled them *upward* while the web swung them down toward the Ebon-gray. He pulled against the swing, slowing it, slowing it.

When the other side of the Gray broke, they sailed down to the Ebon-gray. The web sagged when they landed, then stretched, then stretched a little more before the strands began to break.

His Black Jewels were almost drained, but he held on, held on, held on as they floated onto the Black web.

And nothing happened.

Shaking, shivering, Daemon stared at the Black web, not quite daring to believe.

It took him a minute to get his hands to unlock from their grip. When he was finally able to let go, he floated cautiously above the web. Near her shoulder, he noticed two small broken strands. Very carefully, he smoothed the Black strands over the other colors that cocooned her.

He could barely see her, only just enough to make out the tiny spiral horn. But that was enough.

We did it, he whispered as his eyes filled. *We did it.*

Yess, Lorn said very quietly. *You have done well.*

Daemon looked up, looked around. When he looked back at Witch, she faded.

Everything faded.

15 / Terreille

Saetan opened his eyes, tried to move, and found himself trapped by two warm bodies curled up around him. His sons.

Oh, witch-child. I hope it was worth the price.

He tried to move again, growled when he couldn't, and finally jabbed Lucivar with an elbow.

Lucivar just growled back and cuddled closer.

He shoved at Lucivar again because he couldn't, even in this small way, push Daemon aside. Not now.

Lucivar's growl turned into a snarl, but he finally stirred. And that woke Daemon.

"I'm delighted you find me such a comfortable pillow," Saetan said dryly, "but a man my age prefers not to sleep on a cold stone floor."

"Neither does a man *my* age," Lucivar grumbled, getting to his feet. He rolled his shoulders, stretched his back.

Daemon sat up with a groan.

Watching him, Saetan saw the light fill Daemon's eyes, the joy, the eagerness. It broke his heart.

He accepted Daemon's help in getting to his feet—and noted Lucivar's coolness toward his brother. That would change. Would *have* to change. But Lucivar wouldn't be approachable until he'd seen Marian and Daemonar, so there was no point in sparking that Eyrien temper. Besides, he was too damn tired to take on Lucivar right now.

As he walked to the doors, they fell into step on either side of him.

Twilight. The whole day had passed.

They walked across the open courtyard. Lucivar opened the gate.

A gust of wind made something flutter, catching Saetan's attention. A scrap of cloth from a woman's gown. Hekatah's gown.

He didn't mention it.

"I don't have the strength right now," he said quietly. "Would you two . . ."

Lucivar looked toward the south, Daemon toward the north. After a minute, their faces had the same grim, deliberately calm expression.

"There are a few Blood," Daemon said slowly. "Not many."

"The same," Lucivar said.

A few. Only a few. Sweet Darkness, let them get a different answer in Kaeleer. "Let's go home."

He felt the difference as soon as they walked through the Gate between the Realms. When they walked out of the Altar Room, Daemon and Lucivar both looked in the direction that would lead them to the First Circle—and the others.

He turned in the opposite direction, not quite ready to deal with what was going to come. "Come with me." Reluctantly, they obeyed.

He led them to a low-walled terrace that overlooked Riada, the closest Blood village.

Daemon looked down at the village. Lucivar looked in the direction of the Eyrien community.

Daemon sighed with relief. "I don't know how many people had lived there yesterday, but there are still a lot of Blood there."

"Falonar!" Lucivar cried. He looked at them and grinned. "The whole community. They're all right. Badly shaken up, but all right."

"Thank the Darkness," Saetan whispered. The tears came, as much from pride as grief. Prothvar had said it was a different kind of battlefield but a good one to fight on. He'd been right. It *was* a worthy battlefield. Instead of seeing more friends join the demon-dead, they had gone knowing those friends would live. Char, Dujae, Morton, Titian, Cassandra, Prothvar, Mephis, Andulvar. He would miss them. Mother Night, how he would miss them. "And the Blood shall sing to the Blood. You sang the song well, my friends. You sang it well."

He would have to tell Lucivar and Daemon—and Surreal—about this, too. But not yet. Not now.

He dreaded it, but he knew he couldn't hold either of them back much longer. "Come on, puppies. I'm sure the coven's going to have a few things to say about this."

It was worse than he'd expected.

The coven and the boyos fell all over Lucivar, who had his arms wrapped around Marian and Daemonar. Daemon they greeted with cool reserve. Except Karla, who had said, "Kiss kiss," and then *had* kissed him. And Surreal, who had given Daemon a cool stare, and said, "You look like shit, Sadi." He would have lashed out at her for that if Daemon hadn't commented dryly that her compliments were as effusive as ever—and if she hadn't grinned at the remark.

And Tersa, who had held her son's face between her hands and looked into his eyes. "It will be all right, Daemon," she had said gently. "Trust one who sees. It *will* be all right."

Saetan wasn't sure Daemon noticed the coolness, wasn't sure he even noticed who had greeted him and who hadn't. His eyes kept scanning the room for someone who wasn't there—someone who wasn't going to be there.

He was trying to think of a reasonable excuse to get Daemon away from the others when Geoffrey appeared at the door. "Your presence is requested at the Dark Throne. Draca would like to see you."

As they filed out of the room, Saetan stepped in beside Lucivar. "Stay close to your brother," he said quietly.

"I think it would be better—"

"Don't think, Prince, just follow orders."

Lucivar gave him a measuring look, then moved ahead to catch up with Daemon.

Surreal tucked her arm through his. "Lucivar's pissed?"

"That's one way of putting it," Saetan replied dryly.

"If you think it will help, I could give him a good kick in the balls. Although I have a feeling that when Marian realizes what he's pissed about, she'll do a better job than either of us can."

Saetan let out a groaning chuckle. "Now *that* will be interesting." Then he sobered. "Daemon played the same game with you."

"Yes, he did. But sometimes the best way to fool an enemy is to convince a friend."

"Your mother said almost the same thing to me once—after she punched me."

"Really?" Surreal smiled. "It must run in the family."

He decided it was better not to ask her to clarify that.

Baffled, Daemon waited for whatever announcement Draca was going to make. Not that it mattered. He would have to slip away to Amdarh in the next few days, talk to that jeweler, Banard, about designing a wedding ring for Jaenelle. He'd gotten her some earrings there for Winsol and had liked what he'd seen of the man's work.

Her birthday would be coming up soon. Would she mind having a wedding on her birthday? Well, maybe *he* would. He didn't really want to share the celebration of their wedding day with anything else. But they could have it soon after that. She would still be tired, still be recovering from this spell, but they could find a quiet place for the honeymoon. It didn't matter where.

Where was she? Maybe she was already in her room, recovering.

Maybe that's what Draca was going to tell them—that Jaenelle had prevented the war, that Kaeleer was safe. As soon as this announcement was over, he'd slip up to her room and snuggle in next to her. Well, he'd take a bath first. He wasn't exactly smelling his best at the moment.

Where *was* she?

Then he looked at Lorn and felt a flicker of uneasiness.

No. They had saved her. The triangle *had* saved her. She'd expended so much of herself, had risen so far out of herself she'd been plummeting back down, but they had stopped the fall. They *had* stopped the fall.

Lucivar came up beside him, close enough to brush shoulders with him. Saetan stepped up on his other side with Surreal close by.

Draca picked something up from the Throne's seat, hesitated, then turned to face them.

Daemon froze.

She was holding Jaenelle's scepter. But the metal was all twisted, and the two Ebony Jewels were shattered. Not just drained. *Shattered.* So was the spiral horn.

"The Queen of Ebon Asskavi iss gone," Draca said quietly. "The Dark Court no longer existss."

Someone began screaming. A scream full of panic, rage, denial, pain.

It wasn't until Lucivar and Saetan grabbed him and held him back that he realized the person who was screaming was himself.

16 / Kaeleer

"What was the point of it?" Gabrielle demanded angrily while the tears fell unheeded. "What was the point of offering the memories if they weren't going to do any good?"

Surreal raked her fingers through her hair and decided smacking someone probably wasn't going to help much. Well, it would make *her* feel better. Thank the Darkness she and Uncle Saetan had been able to heavily sedate Daemon. He couldn't have tolerated any of this right now.

She would have liked to have found out more about this memory thing, but she was more intrigued by the fact that Tersa seemed too calm and undisturbed—and also a little angry. It would take someone mucking up something very important to make Tersa angry.

"Yes, Tersa," Karla said testily, "what *was* the point?"

"Blood is the memory's river. And the Blood shall sing to the Blood," Tersa replied.

Gabrielle said something succinct and obscene.

"Shut up, Gabrielle," Surreal snapped.

Tersa was sitting on the long table in front of the couch, next to a pile of wooden building blocks. Surreal crouched down beside her. "What were the memories for?" she asked quietly.

Tersa brushed her tangled hair away from her face. "To feed the web of dreams. It was no longer complete. It had lived, it had grown."

"But she's gone!" Morghann wailed.

"The Queen is gone," Tersa said with some heat. "Is that all she was to you?"

"No," Karla said. "She was Jaenelle. That was enough."

"Exactly," Tersa said. "It is still enough."

Surreal jolted, hardly daring to hope. She touched Tersa's hand, waited until she was sure she had the woman's attention. "The Queen is gone, but Jaenelle isn't?"

Tersa hesitated. "It's too soon to know. But the triangle kept the dream from returning to the Darkness, and now the kindred are fighting to hold the dream to the flesh."

That brought protests from Gabrielle and Karla.

"Wait a minute," Gabrielle said, glancing at Karla, who nodded. "If Jaenelle is hurt and needs a Healer, she should have *us*."

"No," Tersa said, her anger breaking free. "She should *not* have you. *You* could not look at what was done to that flesh and believe it could still live. But the kindred do not doubt. *The kindred will not believe anything else.* That is why, if it can be done, they are the ones who can do it." She jumped up and ran out of the room.

Surreal waited a moment, then followed. She didn't find Tersa, but she found Graysfang hovering nearby, whining anxiously.

She studied the wolf. Kindred do not doubt. They would sink in and fight for that dream with fangs and claws and never give it up. Well, she would never have a snout that could smell tracks, but she could damn well learn how to be as stubborn as a wolf. She would sink her teeth into the belief that Jaenelle was simply recovering somewhere private after performing an extremely difficult spell. She would sink in and hold on to that.

For Jaenelle's sake.

For Daemon's sake.

And for her own sake, because she wanted her friend to come back.

CHAPTER SIXTEEN

1 / Kaeleer

Daemon walked down the steps that led to the garden in the Hall, the garden that had two statues.

When he woke up from the sedative Surreal and Saetan had given him, he had asked to leave the Keep. They had gone with him. So had Tersa.

Lucivar hadn't.

That had been a week ago.

He wasn't sure what he'd done during the days since. They had simply passed. And at night . . .

· At night, he crept from his own bed into Jaenelle's because it was the only place he could sleep. Her scent was there, and in the dark, he could almost believe that she was simply away for a little while, that he would wake one morning and find her cuddled up next to him.

He stared at the statue of the male, with its paw/hand curved protectively above the sleeping woman. Part human, part beast. Savagery protecting beauty. But now he saw something else in its eyes: the anguish, the price that sometimes had to be paid.

He turned away from it, walked over to the other statue, stared at the woman's face—that familiar, beloved face—for a long, long time.

The tears came—again. The pain was always there.

"Tersa keeps telling me that it will be all right, to trust one who sees," he told the statue. "Surreal keeps telling me not to give up, that the kindred will be able to bring you back. And I want to believe that. I *need* to believe that. But when I ask Tersa about you directly, she hesitates, says it's too soon to know, says the kindred are fighting to hold the dream to the flesh. *Fighting* to hold the dream to the flesh." He laughed bitterly. "They're not fighting to hold the dream to flesh, Jaenelle. They're fighting to put enough of you together again for there to be something *for the dream to come back to.* And you knew what would happen, didn't you? When you decided to do this, *you knew.*"

He paced, circled, came back to the statue.

"I did it for you," he said quietly. "I bought the time, I played the game. For you." His breathing hitched, came out in a sob. "I knew I would have to do some things that wouldn't be forgiven. I *knew* it when you asked me to go to Hayll, but I did it anyway. F-for you. Because I was going to come back to you, and the rest of it wouldn't matter. B-because I was coming back to *you.* But you sent me there knowing you wouldn't be here when I got back, knowing . . ." He sank to his knees. "You said no sacrifices. You made me promise I wouldn't make any sacrifices. But what do you call this, Jaenelle? *What do you call this?* When I got back, we were going to get *m-married.* . . . And you left me. Damn you, Jaenelle, I did this for you, *and you left me.* You left me."

He collapsed on the grass near the statue, sobbing.

Lucivar rested a fist against the stone wall and bowed his head.

Mother Night. Daemon had gone into that game expecting to come back for his own wedding. *Mother Night.*

He was here because Marian had ripped into him that morning, giving him the full thrust of the temper that lived beneath her quiet nature. She'd told him that, yes, he'd been hurt, but he'd been hurt *to save them.* She'd asked him if he would have preferred losing a wife or son in truth in order for his feelings to be spared. And she'd told him that the man she had married would have the courage to forgive.

That had brought him here.

But now . . .

When they'd both been slaves in Terreille, he and Daemon had played games before, had used each other, had hurt each other. Sometimes they'd done it to relieve their own pain, sometimes it had been for a better reason. But they'd always been able to look past those games and forgive the hurt *because there had been no one else.* They'd fought with each other, but they'd also fought *for* each other.

He had other people now, a wider circle to love. A wife, a son. Maybe that had made the difference. He didn't *need* Daemon. But, Hell's fire, Daemon needed *him* right now.

But it was more than that. Thirteen years ago, he had wrongfully accused Daemon of killing Jaenelle. That had been the first hard shove that had ended with Daemon spending eight years in the Twisted Kingdom, lost in madness. And Daemon had forgiven him because, he'd said, he'd already grieved for a brother once and didn't want to do it again.

Daemon had believed a painful lie for thirteen years. *He'd* believed one for a couple of days. Marian had been right to rip into him.

So he would do what he could to mend things, for his own sake as well as for Daemon's. Because, during those long centuries of slavery when they'd had no one but each other, their anger had sometimes flared to moments of hate, but underneath there had always been love.

Pushing away from the wall, Lucivar walked down the steps, knelt in the grass beside Daemon. He touched his brother's shoulder.

Daemon looked at him out of a face devastated by grief before lunging into the open arms.

"I want her back," Daemon cried. "Oh, Lucivar, *I want her back.*"

Lucivar held on tight as his own tears fell. "I know, old son. I know."

2 / Kaeleer

"You're *leaving*?" Lucivar leaped to his feet and stared at Saetan. "What do you mean, 'leaving'? To go where?" Pacing behind the two chairs in front of the blackwood desk, he pointed an accusing finger at his father. "You are *not* going to the Dark Realm. *There's no one left there.* And you are *not* going to be alone."

"Lucivar," Saetan said quietly. "Lucivar, please listen."

"When the sun shines in Hell."

Prick, Daemon said on an Ebon-gray spear thread.

And why in the name of Hell are you just sitting there? Lucivar demanded. *He's your father, too.*

Daemon bit back exasperation. *Let him talk, Prick. If we don't like what we hear, then we'll do something about it.* "You're leaving because of Sylvia?" he asked Saetan.

Lucivar froze, swore softly, then settled back into the chair.

"That's part of it," Saetan said. "A Guardian isn't meant to be among the living. Not that way." He hesitated, then added, "If I stay . . . I *can't* stay and be a friend and encourage her to . . . She deserves to be with someone who can give her more than I can now."

"You could come to Ebon Rih and live with us," Lucivar said.

"Thank you, Lucivar, but no. I've . . ." Saetan took a deep breath. "I've been offered a position at the Keep as assistant historian/librarian. Geoffrey says he's starting to feel his years, and it's my fault that he's had more work now than he's ever had because I'm the one who introduced the coven to the Keep's library, and it's time I started making myself useful."

"The Keep is only a mountain away from our eyrie," Lucivar said.

"You *will not* bring Daemonar to the library."

Lucivar gave Saetan a sharp smile. "Did you bring me there when I was his age?"

"Once," Saetan said dryly. "And Geoffrey *still* reminds me of that little adventure on occasion." He glanced at Daemon. "I'll come and visit both of you, just to find out how much trouble you're causing."

Daemon felt a tension ease. He wanted to see his father, but not at Ebon Askavi. He would never again set foot in the Keep.

"The family owns three counties in Dhemlan," Saetan said. "I've divided them between you. Daemon, I'm giving you the Hall and all the land and tithes that go with it. Lucivar, you'll have the land that's near the Askavi border. The other property you'll own together."

"I don't need land," Lucivar protested.

"You're still the Warlord Prince of Ebon Rih because the people *want* you to be the Warlord Prince of Ebon Rih. But Daemonar may not want to rule—or you may have other sons or daughters who want a different kind of life. You'll be the caretaker of that land because the SaDiablo family *has been* the caretaker of that land for thousands of years. Is that understood?"

"Yes, sir," Lucivar said quietly.

"And you?" Saetan said, pointedly looking at Daemon.

"Yes, sir," he replied just as quietly. Well, that explained why Saetan had insisted on spending the past two months teaching him the family business. He'd thought it was just a way to keep him occupied and too busy to think too much.

He'd welcomed the work, especially when he realized that Saetan had shouldered the burden of helping Geoffrey with a far more difficult task. He and Lucivar had been told the results, but he knew he couldn't have tolerated accumulating the information.

Over forty percent of the Blood in Terreille were gone. Completely gone. Another thirty percent had been broken back to basic Craft. The Blood who were left in Terreille were reeling from the devastation—and the sudden freedom.

He hadn't asked what had happened to Alexandra, Leland, and Philip—and Saetan hadn't offered the information. Or if he had, it had only been to Wilhelmina.

The numbers were about the same in Little Terreille as they were for the Realm of Terreille. But the rest of Kaeleer was mostly untouched—except for Glacia. Karla was struggling to reunite her people and re-form her court. The taint Dorothea and Hekatah had spread in the Blood might have been destroyed, but the scars remained.

Everything has a price.

"What about Jaenelle's house in Maghre?" Lucivar asked.

Daemon shook his head. "Let Wilhelmina have it. She's decided to settle in Scelt, and—"

"The house was leased for Jaenelle," Saetan said firmly. "It remains for Jaenelle. If you have no objections to Wilhelmina living there until she finds a place of her own, so be it."

Daemon backed down. He loved that house, too, but he wasn't sure he could ever live there again. And he wasn't really sure if Saetan truly believed Jaenelle *was* coming back or if his father just wasn't willing to do anything that would acknowledge that she *wasn't*. After all, it had been two months now with no news of any kind, just Tersa's continued—and useless—assurance that it would be all right. "Is that it?"

He read the message in Saetan's eyes. "I'll be with you in a minute," he said to Lucivar when his brother rose and looked at him.

When they were alone, Saetan said carefully, "I know how you feel about Ebon Askavi now."

Daemon rushed in. "I truly hope you will come to visit, Father, because I'll never set foot in the Keep again."

Saetan said gently, "You have to go one more time. Draca wants to see you."

3 / Kaeleer

"There iss ssomething I want to sshow you." Draca unlocked a door and stepped aside.

Daemon walked into a huge room that was a portrait gallery. Dozens upon dozens of paintings hung on the walls.

At first, he saw only one. The last one.

Unable to look at it, he turned his back to it and began to study the rest of them in order. Some were very, very old, but all of them had been exquisitely done. As he slowly walked around the room, he realized the portraits spanned the species who made up the Blood—and they were all female.

When he reached the last one, he studied Jaenelle's portrait for a long time, then looked at the signature. Dujae. Of course.

He turned and looked at Draca.

"They were all dreamss made flessh, Prince," Draca said gently. "Some only had one kind of dreamer, otherss were a bridge. Thesse were Witch."

"But—" Daemon looked at the portraits again. "I don't see Cassandra's portrait here."

"Sshe wass a Black-Jeweled witch, the Queen of Ebon Asskavi. But sshe wass not Witch. Sshe wass not dreamss made flessh."

He shook his head. "Witch wears the Black. She's always a Black-Jeweled Queen."

"No. That iss not alwayss the dream, Daemon. There have been quiet dreamss and sstrong dreamss. There have been Queenss and ssongmak-erss." She paused, waited. "Your dream wass to be Conssort to the Queen of Ebon Asskavi. Iss that not true?"

Daemon's heart began to pound. "I thought they were the same. I thought Witch and the Queen of Ebon Askavi were the same."

"And if they are not?"

Tears stung his eyes. "If they hadn't been the same, if I'd had to choose between the Queen and Jaenelle . . . I never would have set foot in this place. Excuse me, Draca. I—"

He started to rush past her, but he saw her hand move as if to hold him back. He could have avoided her easily, but, being who she was, he couldn't be that disrespectful.

Her ancient hand moved slowly, came to rest on his arm.

"The Queen of Ebon Asskavi iss gone," she said very quietly. "But sshe who iss Kaeleer'ss Heart, sshe who iss Witch, sstill livess."

4 / Kaeleer

"You'll take the income I've provided for you," Saetan snarled as he and Surreal walked through one of the Hall's gardens. He'd thought this would be a simple task, something to occupy a bit of time while he waited for Daemon to return from the Keep.

Surreal snarled back. "I don't need a damn income from you."

He stopped and turned on her. "Are you or are you not family?"

She stepped up to him until they were toe to toe. "Yes, I'm family, but—"

"Then take the damn income!" he shouted.

"Why?" she shouted back.

"Because I love you!" he roared. "And I want to give you that much."

She swore at him.

Hell's fire, why were his children all so *stubborn*?

He leashed his temper. "It's a gift, Surreal. Please take it."

She hooked her hair behind her ears. "If you're going to put it *that* way . . ."

A wolf raised its voice in an odd series of yips and howls.

"That's not Graysfang," Surreal said.

Saetan tensed. "No. It's one of the pack from the north woods."

Worry filled her eyes. "One of them has come back? Why does it sound like that?"

"The Tigre use drums to signal messages—just for fun things, a dance, an impromptu gathering," Saetan replied absently. "The wolves became intrigued by it and developed a few particular howls of their own."

The same series of yips and howls came again.

"Graysfang could have mentioned that," Surreal grumbled. "What's that one mean?"

"It means there's a message that should be heeded."

The wolf raised its voice again in a different song. Then another wolf joined in. And another. And another.

Listening, he started to cry—and laugh. There was only one reason the wolves raised their voices in quite that way.

Surreal gripped his arm. "Uncle Saetan, what is it?"

"It's a song of celebration. Jaenelle has come back."

5. / Kaeleer

It was early autumn, almost a year since he'd first come to Kaeleer.

Daemon carefully landed the small Coach in the meadow and stepped out. At the edge of the meadow, Ladvarian waited for him.

For weeks, he had raged and pleaded, begged and sworn. It hadn't done any good. Draca had insisted that she didn't know exactly where the kindred had hidden Jaenelle. She had also insisted that the healing was still very delicate and a strong presence—and difficult emotions—could easily interfere. Finally, exasperated, she had suggested that he make himself useful.

So he'd thrown himself into work. And every evening he had written a letter to Jaenelle, telling her about his day, pouring out his love. Two or three times a week, he went to the Keep and annoyed Draca.

Now, finally, the message had come. The kindred had done all they could. The healing wasn't complete, but the rest would take time, and she should be in a warm human den now.

So he'd been told where to bring the Coach that would take Jaenelle back to the Hall.

He crossed the meadow, stopped a few feet in front of Ladvarian. The Sceltie looked too thin, but there was joy—and wariness—in the brown eyes.

"Ladvarian," Daemon said quietly, respectfully.

Daemon. Ladvarian shifted uneasily. *Human males . . . Some human males pay too much attention to the outside.*

He understood the warning, heard the fear. And now he understood why they hadn't let him come sooner—they'd been afraid he wouldn't be able to stand what he saw. They were still afraid.

"It doesn't matter, Ladvarian," he said gently. "It doesn't matter."

The Sceltie studied him. *She is very fragile.*

"I know." Draca had drummed that into him before she'd let him come.

She sleeps a lot.

He smiled dryly. "I've hardly slept at all."

Satisfied, Ladvarian turned. *This way. Be careful. There are many guard webs.*

Looking around, he saw the tangled webs that could ensnare a person's mind and draw him into peculiar dreams—or hideous nightmares.

He walked carefully.

They walked for several minutes before they came to a path that led to a sheltered cove. A large tent was set up well back from the waterline. The colored fabric would keep out most of the sun but seemed loosely woven enough to let in air.

Closer to the water were several poorly made sand castles. Watching Kaelas trying to pack sand with one of those huge paws made him smile.

The front flaps of the tent were pulled back, revealing the woman sleeping inside. She wore a long skirt of swirling colors. The amethyst-colored shirt was unbuttoned and had slid to her sides, displaying her from the waist up.

Daemon took one look at her and bolted away from the tent.

He stopped a few yards away and just tried to draw a normal breath while his stomach twisted wildly.

The kindred had done their very best. They had given months of focused, single-minded devotion to produce this much healing. He never *ever* wanted to know what she had looked like when they had brought her here.

He felt Ladvarian come up behind him. Since the Sceltie *had* seen what she had looked like, the dog probably couldn't understand his reaction. "Ladvarian . . ."

She rose from the healing webs too soon, Ladvarian said in a voice that was bitter and accusing. *Because of you.*

Daemon turned slowly, his heart bleeding from the verbal wound.

*We *tried* to tell her you weren't hurt. We *tried* to tell her that she had to stay down in the healing webs longer. We *tried* to tell her that the Stra— that Tersa would tell you that she was coming back, that the High Lord would take care of his pup. But she kept saying that you were hurting and that she had promised. She stayed in the webs long enough for her insides to heal and then she rose. But when she saw . . .*

Daemon closed his eyes. No. Sweet Darkness, *no.* She would have been in pain, would have suffered. And she wouldn't have if she'd stayed down in the healing webs.

"Tersa did tell me," he said in a broken voice. "Over and over again. But . . . all I knew for certain was that Jaenelle had promised to marry me and then had left me, and . . ." He couldn't go on.

Maybe we could have told you, Ladvarian said reluctantly after a long silence. *We didn't think humans would believe that she could heal—at least, wouldn't believe enough. But, maybe, if we had told you about all the webs, you *could* have believed.*

Not likely. No matter how much he would have *wanted* to believe, the doubts would have crept in—and might have destroyed everything he wanted to save. "Tersa told me it would be all right. I didn't listen."

More silence. Then, *It is hard to listen when your paw is caught in a trap.*

That understanding, that much forgiveness, hurt. He looked at the Sceltie, needing to see the truth. "Ladvarian . . . did I cripple her?"

No, Ladvarian said gently. *She *will* heal, Prince. She is healing more and more every day. It will just take longer.*

Daemon walked back to the tent, stepped inside.

This time, he only saw Jaenelle.

She's all there, Ladvarian said anxiously.

Nodding, Daemon slipped off his shoes and jacket, then carefully stretched out beside her, propped on one elbow so that he could look at her. He reached out, tentatively brushed his fingers over her short golden hair, almost afraid to touch even that much. She was so fragile. So terribly, terribly fragile. But alive.

We had to crop her fur.

Considering the condition she must have been in, it was a practical solution to grooming problems the kindred must have faced.

His fingers brushed over her cheek. Her face, although horribly thin, was the same.

Then he noticed the Jewel resting on her chest. At first, he thought it was a Purple Dusk. Then, in its depths, he saw glints of Rose, Summersky, and Opal. Green, Sapphire, and Red. Gray and Ebon-gray. And just a hint of Black.

It's called Twilight's Dawn, Ladvarian said. *There's no other Jewel like it.* Then the Sceltie retreated, leaving him alone with her.

He watched her while she slept. Just watched her. After a while, he found the courage to let his fingers explore a little.

Ladvarian was right. She was all there, but she was barely more than a thin sheath of skin over organs and bones.

As one finger delicately traced her nipple, he stopped, thought about the open shirt, then looked at the beach where Ladvarian stood near Kaelas, watching him. *She didn't know I was coming, did she?*

No, Ladvarian replied.

He didn't have to ask why. If he hadn't been able to accept what he saw, the kindred would never have told her he had come—and Ladvarian would have taken her somewhere else, to *someone* else to heal over the winter months.

He knew *his* answer to that. He loved her, and all he wanted was to be with her. But, despite what Ladvarian had said . . . *because* of what Ladvarian had said . . . he was no longer sure she would want *him*.

Then she stirred a little, and he knew he wasn't going anywhere unless she sent him away.

Carefully bracing himself so that he wouldn't hurt her, he leaned over and brushed his lips against hers.

He raised his head. Her haunted sapphire eyes stared at him.

"Daemon?" There was so much uncertainty in her voice.

"Hello, sweetheart," he said, his voice husky with the effort not to cry. "I've missed you."

Her hand moved slowly, with effort, until it rested against his face. Her lips curved into a smile. "Daemon."

This time, when she said his name, it sounded like a promise, like a lovely caress.